Christmas
1988

To Mother
        Frances
        Grandma

with LOVE

From   Terry
        Cynthia
        Paul & Justin

THE
TENANTS
OF TIME

ALSO BY THOMAS FLANAGAN

The Year of the French

THE TENANTS OF TIME

THOMAS FLANAGAN

A William Abrahams Book

E. P. DUTTON　▪　NEW YORK

Published in the United States by E. P. Dutton,
a division of NAL Penguin Inc.,
2 Park Avenue, New York, N.Y. 10016.

Published simultaneously in Canada
by Fitzhenry and Whiteside, Limited, Toronto.

Library of Congress Cataloging-in-Publication Data
Flanagan, Thomas, 1923–
The tenants of time.
"A William Abrahams book"—Verso t.p.
I. Title.
PS3556.L3445T4   1988   813'.54   87-13632
ISBN: 0-525-24606-1

COBE

Designed by Nancy Etheredge

3 5 7 9 10 8 6 4 2

A list of principal characters will be found beginning on page 821.

Part One

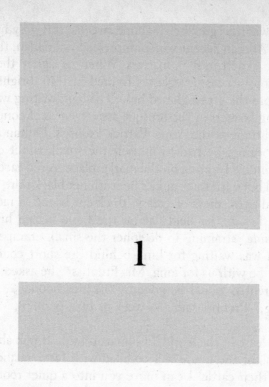

1

[Patrick Prentiss]

Long after the Fenian rising in Kilpeder in 1867, after both Robert Delaney and Ned Nolan were dead, after Ardmor had settled in Italy, at a time when only Hugh MacMahon was alive who knew one part of the story, and old Lionel Forrester who knew another part, a stranger to Kilpeder found himself given over, at first without realising it, to fitting the pieces together. By the time that he knew he might never finish, and so put the pieces back into the box of the past, he had come to believe that what happened in Kilpeder between the rising of 1867 and the fall of Parnell in 1891 had a shape, a design, a theme which worked itself out in the variations of a dozen lives. But there was nothing that he could do with his knowledge. He had fallen in love with the past, a profitless love.

On a June night in 1904 Patrick Prentiss came for the first time to Kilpeder and booked a room at the Arms. He was a quietly dressed man in his middle twenties, grey herringbone tweeds, soft grey hat, a topcoat across his arm. And an accent which impressed Gilmartin, the proprietor of the Arms, an expert in such matters. When he signed the register, he took from a morocco case eyeglasses framed in thin, bright gold which caught light from the green-globed bulb. His handwriting was unlike the scrawls of strong-farmers or the brusque assertiveness of commercial travellers, the usual trade at the Arms. Patrick Prentiss. Dublin and London.

In the morning, he had to himself the small, sunlit dining room, wide, curved window fronting on the marketplace. A red-faced young girl, slender-waisted but with thick ankles beneath her black skirt, brought him porridge, boiled eggs, slices of greasy, thick-cut bacon, a rack of toast, a pot of tea. As he ate, he held flat on the table before him a copy of *Muirhead's Guide,* straining to decipher the small, cramped type.

Gilmartin was waiting for him, behind the short counter of black oak. "Will you be with us for long, Mr. Prentiss?" he asked, expecting to be told that Prentiss would be gone by the afternoon.

"Not long," Prentiss said. "A week or two, perhaps. Will that be a problem?"

"Not the least in the world," Gilmartin said. "Look about you. But on Thursday night the house will be filled with farmers and auctioneers bellowing like their cattle. I can move you into a quiet room in the rear of the house, with a view of mountains. It has been complimented by priests and by solicitors."

Prentiss looked about him. Musty, frayed red carpeting, with a scattering of heavy chairs, their black leather cracked. On the walls, glassencased, hung trout and perch, skins iridescent, eyes wide and staring. A large photograph, sepia-coloured, of a hunt assembled: riders, horses, hounds. An oil painting, garish, of distant mountains, the hills purple and slate-grey, cerulean sky, puffs of cottony cloud.

"Those are the mountains," Gilmartin said. "The Derrynasaggarts. Are you a stranger to this part of the country?"

"I have heard of the Derrynasaggarts," Prentiss said. "Beyond them is Kerry."

"And the fabled Lakes of Killarney. In summer, I have travellers here on the way to the lakes from England and from Germany. Germans have told me that they do not have the like of them there. Entire books have been written about them."

Prentiss, because he had read several of those books, had no wish to visit them, paths worn thin by generations of guides and vacationers, jaunting cars with picnic baskets, boatmen with well-thumbed versions of sentimental legends. It was Kilpeder, this somnolent market town, which had drawn him, and the wild hills which ringed it.

He walked to the open door, and stood looking out into the market square. Not a soul was yet abroad, and the shops were closed. He faced a handsome stone market house with the proportions of an earlier century, blocks of grey, dressed stone, a pediment. Stretching away from it, in either direction, shops, public houses, one shop larger by far than all the others: its name, D. Tully and Son, worked upon a red-painted board in gilded, intricate scroll. On Prentiss's side of the square, at the near end, stood gates to an estate, stone birds with outstretched wings perched upon the posts. Facing the gates, at an angle, a trim, single-spired Protestant church, its oak doors shut. To his right, rows of shops ran down towards a constabulary barracks, and beyond the barracks, labourers' cottages straggled along the Macroom road towards the heavy spires and needless, ornamental buttresses of the Catholic church. A man emerged from one of the cottages, and walked slowly, heavy-footed, towards the square. At the distance, his shapeless jacket had the colour of rain.

"I have a letter to the schoolmaster," Prentiss said.

"Ah," Gilmartin said. "Nothing simpler." He joined Prentiss at the door. "Christy Mannion. The school is down the road there, in Chapel Street, beyond the church, and the master's house beside it."

"Not Mannion," Prentiss said. "Hugh MacMahon."

Gilmartin smiled. "The schoolmaster that was. He is long out of it. Hughie lives now far out from the town, on the Killetin road. You will need a horse or a trap for that, and I have none myself. The livery stable can sort that out for you easily enough, and set you upon your road."

Now, from the barracks, a constable stepped out into watery sunlight, his tunic unbuttoned.

"He was my own master," Gilmartin said. "A decent old party. A learned man. Christy Mannion is only trotting along after him, a young one from Dublin who has everything by rote. Today's teaching is all examinations and certificates. A learned man. He has been in correspondence with scholars."

The constable raised a hand to the labourer, in easy salutation, and the man touched a hand to his cap.

"More peaceful here," Prentiss said, "than it was in 'sixty-seven."

Surprised, Gilmartin stared at him, and then grinned again, a glint of gold. "Our hour of glory, by God. The battle of Clonbrony. There was talk a few years ago of a statue in the square, but nothing could be agreed as to the design, or what the words should say. Tis better so, the look that some of the statues have in towns that could be named."

They stood a moment in windless air, and then Gilmartin said, "Hugh MacMahon was there, did you know that? One of the Fenians of

Clonbrony. There are few enough of them now, save for some fellows who had tagged along."

"I did know that," Prentiss said. "That is why I have a letter to him."

Gilmartin stood idly in the doorway, arms akimbo, and watched Prentiss walk towards the livery stable, across the square. From within came the sounds of the three skivvies about their tasks, scratches of brooms upon carpeting. Constable MacGann joined him, a beefy man, red-faced, clear blue eyes beneath tall helmet.

"Now there," Gilmartin said, head jerking, "is a well-spoken young fellow from Dublin and London who has travelled here for the purpose of calling in on Hugh MacMahon. I thought at first he had business at the Castle."

"Small wonder," MacGann said. "Master MacMahon's name is known to the scholars and professors of the world." Gilmartin disliked his Ulster accent, thorns and brambles.

"Because of Clonbrony Wood," Gilmartin said. "Or so he says."

" 'Attend you gallant Irishmen,' " MacGann half said, half sang. "Would you not think all that over and done with and given a respectful funeral."

"So it was thought some years ago," Gilmartin said. "And then Ned Nolan decided to pay us a visit."

"A distressful country," MacGann said, "when you cannot even sort out the heroes from the rogues."

"Ah, well," Gilmartin said, lazy and malicious in the sun's first warmth, "tis no business of mine, thanks be to God."

Prentiss, for his first visit to the man who had not yet become his friend, rode out from Kilpeder in a horse and trap, holding in his mind the liveryman's complicated directions to Killetin. He rode down past Tully's shop and the barracks where once, long before, young men had rushed forward into a hail of rifle fire, square, sturdy bricks and narrow windows; past the Catholic church, its doors open for early Mass, within blue-caped statues, a gilded tabernacle unglinting in sacerdotal shadow; past the schoolhouse where the man who was to be his friend had once drilled the young of Kilpeder, stick in hand; past cottages, swaybacked, their thatch uneven and soot-sullied; and out at last upon the emptiness of the post road to Macroom. At a cross three miles beyond the town, marked, as promised, by a small wayside shrine to the Virgin, he swung to the left, towards hills.

Morning sunlight brightened new corn and hay, green-leafed fields of potato, dense-grassed pasturelands, cattle in the fields, black and brown-dappled, distant houses, whitewashed, thatched. The ditches to his either hand were hedged, bramble-flowered. A chattering of birds, and one whose cry he could not recognize, a long note and then two short ones. His ears strained for other sounds, but heard none save hoof-fall upon close-packed earth, the creak of wheels.

Prentiss's right hand held the reins, loosely, and his left one rested, by chance, upon his copy of *Muirhead,* squat, blue-covered, a voluminous guide for visitors to the island, smothering them with electroplated facts, sketches, local history, maps. For Prentiss, the book offered melancholy confirmation of the inadequacies of language. "Smaller roads," *Muirhead* might have said, had it descended to minutiae, "lead northwards towards such villages as Killetin," without holding birdsong in mind, flowering hedges.

Some months before, in London, in his rooms in Pump Court, and almost a year after he was first tempted to write about the Fenian rising, when the package of books which included the *Muirhead* had arrived from Blackwell's, he had settled himself at once in his chair beside the fire to read the entry for Kilpeder. "A typical market town of West Cork," he had read, "situated on the Macroom-Killarney road, with little to interest the visitor save Ardmor Castle, its grounds and ornamental gardens, seat of the Earls of Ardmor." Prentiss, Irish by birth, by a Dublin childhood, by family holidays near Lough Corrib, had understood the weary tone, had almost sympathised, had almost imagined Kilpeder, constructing it from memories of country towns he knew, Longford and Mullingar. And yet *Muirhead,* if Prentiss was right, understood nothing, its language the accurate lies of all guidebooks.

"History," *Muirhead* announced, employing with confidence a word which had become for Prentiss a tangle of shadows. "Kilpeder and the lands about it, stretching westwards to the Derrynasaggarts, lay originally within the possession of the Gaelic clan of O'Donovan. Its central portion passed later to the powerful Norman family of Barry, who built upon the banks of the Sullane an imposing fortress and keep. It changed hands several times between these two families during the tumultuous Desmond and Tyrone rebellions of the Tudor period. In 1584, Sir Tadg O'Donovan was hanged, from a tree in what is now the demesne, by Lord Deputy Perrot. What is said to be that tree, although with doubtful accuracy, is shown to the curious. The original castle was besieged and destroyed in 1599 by Hugh O'Neill, the rebellious and outlawed Earl of Tyrone. In the seventeenth century, the lands of Kilpeder passed to the Forresters, a Dorset family, later raised to the peerage."

Poor tree of doubtful accuracy, Prentiss had thought beside his London fire, the traffic of Fleet Street faint in his ears. He imagined a night scene, the light of torches, a half dozen men-at-arms shoving and hauling Tadg O'Donovan to an oak tree, upon one of whose branches a noose of hemp has been flung in haste. His hair is a mat, and an untended beard falls upon his chest. He screams with anger and fear, and jerks his head backward towards his surrendered fortress. He wears a soiled doublet, buff breeches. He is barefoot. The knighthood which once he accepted as reward and promise of fealty to the English queen forgotten now, shrivelled by treason. Perrot, Lord Deputy, mounted, sits idly, other tasks upon his mind. O'Donovan shouts out words, a jumble of Gaelic and English. Perrot does not attend them. O'Donovan twists, contorted, upon the tree of doubtful accuracy, buff breeches fouled. And that tree is noted in a guidebook and shown to the curious.

But perhaps, Prentiss thought now, riding through flat pastureland towards foothills, he himself had no better knowledge than *Muirhead* of how the past had been, his own version compounded from Scott and Hugo, his readings in Tudor history, for which Ireland was a sullen western fen, a bog sucking down horsemen and reputations, kernes and gallowglasses shaggy-bearded, treacherous, and ignorant. At New College, Oxford's cloistered serenities, living within England's unshattered past, its stones weathering into honey, unblackened by flame, he had read with shamed fascination in the scarred and fragmentary history of his own people, to the sympathetic amusement of his tutor. Tea and buttered scones at half-five, beyond the window a comely cloister, herb-scented, and between them, tutor and scholar, pieces of what passed as history, sullied, charred at the edges. Now this fascination had carried him to West Cork, towards the house of a retired schoolmaster.

MacMahon had seen him from the window, horse and trap upon the winding, hedged road, and was waiting for him at the small, fussy, needless gate, beside the kind of garden to which retirement devotes its hours. Wild dog rose stretched along the low wall of rough fieldstone. A thin man, tall and erect, high forehead, shock of thinned white hair, fierce clipped moustache, behind thick spectacles, wide eyes the colour of hazelnuts.

"You are welcome, Mr. Prentiss," he said, and held out an arm to help him down. "You are as young a man as I had expected. I do not know why I expected that, to tell you the truth." Accent of West Cork thick upon his speech, thicker than Gilmartin's, worldly innkeeper, quick, musical speech. A face strangely unlined for a man of his years. How old?

Prentiss thought. In 'sixty-seven, he would have been in his early twenties, young for a schoolmaster, but already married. "A young man of studious and respectable appearance," the *Cork Examiner* had written, "with the eager face of the enthusiast. He was neatly dressed, in marked contrast to many of his confederates." Today he was dressed in salt-and-pepper tweed, shirt unironed but snowy white, pale blue tie.

The cottage was as neat as MacMahon himself. They stood briefly in the small hall, with its whitewashed walls, wide floorboards painted red, and then MacMahon opened for them the door to the parlour. Across the rear wall, boards, stained brown, had been hammered into place from floor to ceiling, and the wall was a forest of books. They strained the shelving. Facing them, a formal bookcase of mahogany, between the windows. Two chairs beside the blackened fireplace, deep-cushioned, rump-sprung, the upholstery frayed and faded. Sunlight filled the room.

While MacMahon made tea, Prentiss walked the wall of books, placed without order or design—history, African travel, theology, a score of texts in Latin caught his eye, Livy, Sallust, a few in French, the poems of Lamartine, a novel by Hugo. He had not expected this—a schoolmaster in West Cork, a life of teaching sums to the sons of farmers and shopkeepers, the geography of the world, Magna Carta, and the battle of Waterloo.

Twin-framed by windows, meadows spread on either side of heavy mahogany, deep-grassed. Cattle, far-off dots of brown, lay within shade. As though the books, the room itself, had been wafted here, a gift of magic.

MacMahon fussed with tea things: Delft willow-patterned, thin precise slices of bread. A jar held preserve, sweet, cloying odour of hedges. "The case between the window is from the old house, in Kilpeder. It was one of Mary's great prides; there was a sideboard that went with it, and a kind of cabinet that stood upon claws. But there was no room ever for all the books. They used stand in great piles in the bedroom, without rhyme or reason. She used say that I would one day myself become a book. She would wake up one morning and find it beside her in the bed."

"You have a great appetite for them," said Prentiss.

"Appetite," MacMahon said, testing the word. Precisely, with white, brown-flecked hands, he poured the tea. "You have the right of it, I think. For years, I thought that I was gathering up knowledge and wisdom in great double handfuls, but in the end, tis but an appetite, like any other."

"One that I share with you," Prentiss said, and let the words hang in the air until he had received his cup, had tasted it. "Excellent," he said, remembering, with a shudder, his breakfast.

"The trick of it lies in the brewing," MacMahon said. "Bob Delaney swore by the cheapest of teas. They were sold to the poor, he used say, and they will not stand for inferior stuff. Tis their only pleasure. And Bob, you know," he said, stirring his own, "would have known of such matters, the years of his boyhood that he spent behind Tully's counter, measuring it out of the bins into little sacks."

"You were friends, were you not?" Prentiss said. "Yourself and Robert Delaney."

MacMahon smiled at him, tentative, gentle smile behind the fierce moustache.

"As I wrote back to you when I had read your fine letter, Mr. Prentiss, it would be an honour to tell you whatever I know. Years and years ago, you would see bits and pieces about Clonbrony in the papers, but they were all rubbish. I never even saved them. Tis different with yourself, a graduate of Oxford University, who has written learned essays for the great reviews of London and Edinburgh."

"Twice," Prentiss said. "I hadn't meant to deceive you."

"Even so," MacMahon said. "Tis a knack I have never mastered. I tell you, Mr. Prentiss, with that appetite you spoke of, there are great gobs of fact that have stuck in my mind. There is little that has happened in West Cork since the days of the ancient Fomorians that it isn't stuck away somewhere. But if ever I try to write out a bit of it, I make a terrible hames of it. Tis an art, surely, and it may be that only those who have been to university have its mystery in their keeping."

"I doubt that," Prentiss said. "And so would those writers over there on your shelves."

"Ach, those fellows," MacMahon said, as though speaking of dubious drinking companions. "But Clonbrony Wood, now. I wouldn't think it worth your efforts."

"Do you recall it to mind often?"

"Indeed I do not. I am an old man now, and Clonbrony Wood was a few hours of it, a long time ago. Tis far different things that come unbidden to my mind, without rhyme or reason. I recall it clearly enough, mind you, you will be relieved to know, and the months that led up to it, and the months that led away. But it was not my life, my true life, nor any part of it. My true life was with Mary, and with our boys. All the years before the boys set forth to seek their fortunes, and before Mary died. My life was the house in Chapel Street, and the schoolhouse beside it. What I best remember is the parlour there in Chapel Street, and the piano that was a ransom of six months' salary. It is the music of life that you remember at the end of things, Mr. Prentiss, and not the gunfire of a bitter afternoon."

"Yes, of course," Prentiss said, attracted but disconcerted by this abrupt intensity. "I did not mean—"

"Mind you," MacMahon said, and the muscles of his speech relaxed, as though in apology, "it is a matter to which I have given thought, as you can see. Tis strange that there is the self that I think I am, a schoolmaster at the end of his time, but with a zest for old things, and for poetry written in a language understood now by but a handful. But I was in Clonbrony Wood right enough, and carried my weapon and fired it off. I was lodged afterwards in Cork Gaol, and stood in the assizes. I rarely travel now so far distant as Cork, but when I did, I used sometimes to stand before the gaol, or the courthouse, and try to repeople them in my imagination, as they had been in 'sixty-seven. The trials were a great sensation, as you can imagine. State trials, they were."

"I know," Prentiss said. "I have read them."

Less convincing even than MacMahon's efforts to repeople the public buildings of Cork, words upon pages turning brown, paraphrases by a court stenographer, speeches which may well have been impassioned, withering, now flattened out. All save one man's, and his responses had been too terse to admit paraphrase.

"Double lines of Constabulary," MacMahon said, "with rifles at the ready, and each day a batch of us were marched in, our hands manacled behind our backs. Not the Clonbrony men alone, mind you. Fenians from Skibbereen and Tralee and Tipperary. And mounted cavalry and dragoons, foot soldiers. And beyond them a great crowd of the curious."

"Was the crowd for you?" Prentiss asked.

MacMahon laughed, an unexpected, mirthful yelp. "They were for excitement. Cork City people are mad for excitement. Every shawlie and corner boy from the Coal Quay. I mind one old shawlie shouted out to Paddy Ennis, 'Tis well for you, could you not find permanent employment?' Paddy rounded to take a swing at her, forgetting his manacles and his ankle chains, and stumbled into the fellow beside him. Paddy Ennis from Knockmany, his brother was for years parish priest in Listowel."

"A long time ago," Prentiss said gently, "but you remember it well enough."

"Yes," MacMahon said, nodding, "I have forgotten none of it. How could I forget it?"

Uncertain for a moment, Prentiss moved to place his cup upon the low table, but MacMahon took it from him.

"How could I forget it?" MacMahon said again. "There was nothing like it, ever, in the rest of my life. It was like that for the most of us. Not for all. Not for Bob Delaney, of course."

"Nor for Edward Nolan," Prentiss said.

Quickly, MacMahon raised his eyes from the table. "No," he said. "Nor for Ned."

"But he was your friend as well, was he not?" Prentiss said. "Yourself and Delaney and—"

MacMahon shook his head. "Vincent Tully," he said. "Bob and Vincent and myself were the great pals. The Three Musketeers. And Mary. We took the oath together, the three of us, in Cork City, before ever Ned came back to Kilpeder to take command of us. Well do I mind that day in Cork City, and the three of us taking the oath from the Centre. You understand how it all was organised, do you not, Mr. Prentiss, Head Centres and Centres and all the rest of it?" He laughed again. "By God, the three of us thought we had been initiated into the most sacred of life's mysteries. The Irish Republican Brotherhood."

"I understand a bit of it," Prentiss said, "but not as much as I will need to know."

"For that you must look elsewhere," MacMahon said dryly, "for there my knowledge begins and ends. I can tell you who was the Centre for Cork; he has been dead for years. Twas Joseph Tumulty of Cork City, a ship's chandler in a prosperous way of trade, and he gave us the oath in the office of his shop, with windows that looked out upon the Lee. In later years he used boast about it. By then he was the very image of respectability, with a house in Montenotte. A terrible old bore he had become, if the truth be told, but in 'sixty-five, when he gave us the oath, he was a man of great determination."

"It is all shadows and fragments," Prentiss said. "Who were the Head Centres, and where the power was, and who drew up the plans and made the decisions. That is why I wanted to write about one local action, about Clonbrony. It is Clonbrony, after all, that is best remembered, in the songs and all the rest of it."

"Ah well," MacMahon said. "And why not? Tis all long past. There should be more of that, if you will take the judgement of an uneducated man. Tis my own great love, history. But there are times, do you know, when I will sit in this chair on a winter's evening, with a good fire, and a jug of heated spirits, and my Macaulay open on my lap, and I will ask myself how in God's name does he know what he tells us he knows. There will be little notes at the foot of each page, like brambles in a field, but they fail to persuade me." MacMahon folded his arms across tweed, and smiled with mischief.

At that moment, Prentiss resolved a resemblance which had been nagging him. It was to Oliver Richards, his tutor, who did not at all resemble MacMahon in appearance, although both had wide brown eyes, spectacles-shielded. A portly man, fussy, prematurely old, his hands darting constantly to tobacco jar, decanter, papers scattered across the table. To prove his point, he would jump from low-slung chair, bounce on small, neat feet to his shelves of books, talking steadily as his fingers sought out titles. He had written nothing, ever, that Prentiss could discover. Nor any resemblance in background, for Richards was a Wiltshire clergyman's son who had become a fellow at twenty-seven, and whose life since then had been the university.

"I have a friend," Prentiss said, "who shares your doubts. He wonders if history should be written at all."

"Ach," MacMahon said, dismay in his voice, "I did not say that at all. Without history, we would be scant better than the barefooted heathen of Africa. Tis my great love," he said again, and his eyes drifted towards the wall of books.

But for Prentiss, MacMahon himself was history, not the grand history of Gibbon and Macaulay, ordered paragraphs and apposite quotations marching across centuries, sweeping up men, kings, ideas, armies, but a fragment of the past, a man grown old with the extent of his life thickening upon his memories of a few weeks of insurrection.

"It ended there for me," MacMahon said. "But not for Ned Nolan nor Bob Delaney, and least of all did it end there for poor Vincent. Ach, sure I held to the oath for years afterwards, and if anyone asked was I still a Fenian, I would say yes, that I was, but at last, in later years, I knew as much of their mischief as any man reading the *Cork Examiner*. There was so much else that came afterwards, the Land War and the boycotting and Home Rule and Parnell. But I stood aside from it all, although I watched with pride as Bob went forward from strength to strength, a member of Parliament and one of Parnell's faithful band, as they were called. And you would now and again hear of Ned, or see his name. But I stood clear of it all, or as clear as a man could in those times. Tis all past now."

"Ned Nolan," Prentiss said, noticing that he spoke the name with a slight awkwardness. "He was different from the rest of you, was he not?"

MacMahon looked at him directly, and before speaking settled his eyeglasses on the bridge of his nose. "Different?" he said. "Well, now, he could not have been all that different from myself, do you know. We were first cousins, his father and my mother were brother and sister. When he came to Kilpeder, he lodged with Mary and myself in Chapel Street, and he was there with us until the arms raid. A great difficulty that was for me at the trial. Counsellor Bourke had his work cut out for him in the matter of *Regina versus MacMahon.*"

"But there is a world of difference, Mr. MacMahon, if I may say so, between a man like yourself and the sort of man that Nolan became."

"Became?" MacMahon said. "I wonder, Mr. Prentiss, what sort of man would you become, if you spent seven years in Portland Prison. There was once a drawing of it, in the *Illustrated London News.* The exterior only was displayed, a grey, terrible place of stone, with beyond it rocks and a bleak strand. The words beneath said that it was reserved for the most hardened of England's criminals."

"I know," Prentiss said. "I have read accounts of how the Fenian convicts fared. It is difficult to accept. Of course, from the English point of view, that is what he was. An English criminal."

"From his point of view," MacMahon said, "he was not English. As for hardening, twas a great school for hardening. He came out as hard as their stones. Tis a monstrous crime what is done to men in such places. What was done in the streets of Kilpeder and in Clonbrony Wood was done in the open air, beneath the skies, where it could be judged by God and by men alike."

"He was different, then," Prentiss said, "before Portland? You see, for everyone with whom I have talked about Clonbrony, that is the sticking point. It is the one action of the Rising that everyone has heard about—a gallant action, it could be called; you were all astonishingly brave, you know, when the odds are weighed. And there at the centre of it all is Ned Nolan, and what he became, and how he ended."

After a pause, without having answered, MacMahon stood up, and walked to one of the windows. When he turned, he was smiling.

"A few years back," he said, "there was a great rush of patriotic statues in Munster. They were most of them the work of an ornamental stonemason named Bracken, from Templemore, beyond in Tipperary. A great devotee of hurling and of the revival of the native language and the native garb and all the rest of it, and in the meanwhile, making tons out of statues of Saint Brigit for churches and of rebel pikemen for market squares. Nothing would do but that Kilpeder should have its 'sixty-seven memorial, to overbalance the old obelisk which declared our slavish devotion to the Earls of Ardmor. But what sort of memorial, in God's name? All Ireland knew the doleful tale of dark Clonbrony Wood, and our battle against the might of England. But did all Ireland know that Bob Delaney, the second-in-command at Clonbrony, was living out his last years, a broken man, with no friends save myself and a stableman, and a few farmers who remembered what he had done for them in the old days, and would trust him with the drawing up of a will?"

Reminiscent, MacMahon's smile broadened to a kind of chortle, and for a moment it seemed to Prentiss that it was directed at him, as he sat attentive, puzzled not by MacMahon's words but by his tone.

From a corner cupboard, MacMahon took out a bottle, cut-glass tumblers, talking, with his back to Prentiss.

"At the latter end, Bob was drinking a bit more than he should, and who to blame him, with each afternoon spent, as though oath-bound, in the law office which few now visited. I know for a fact that he kept his bottle there, he took it out for me often enough, when I walked down from the schoolhouse to ask him home for tea. More than he should, but never too much. The hand was always steady, and he dressed always as he had done in the days of his great progress, a well-cut suit, and smooth clean linen. But certain I am that he drank alone, which is good for no man. There he used sit of a winter's afternoon, as the sunlight faded, with all that was lodged in his mind for the remembering."

MacMahon left the room, to fill a water jug, and from the short distance, Prentiss could hear the creak of the pump, MacMahon's mirthful laugh as, doubtless, he rehearsed phrases to himself. Living alone, Prentiss thought, and with a love of words, he would polish his stories, perhaps, with no auditors, speaking them aloud. When he returned, he placed glasses and stoneware jug among the teacups, and carefully measured whiskey.

"There now," he said, "and a drop of water to christen it. At any event, at the height of the 'sixty-seven memorial discussions, he walked into Conefry's, as he very seldom did. Conefry was a bitter anti-Parnellite in those days, although he has mellowed of late. Live and let live—the publican's bible. 'I have been giving thought,' he said, 'to our great issue of the moment.' Twas into the snug he had gone, and had called up a large brandy for himself. 'And it seems to me a matter easily resolved. What is required is a plain plinth, absolutely plain and chaste, that being the great strength of Mr. Bracken's art.' Which it was not; he was notorious for curlicues and dabs of chiselled shamrocks. 'And atop it, a statue of Vincent Tully. Of all the men of Clonbrony, it was Vincent had the looks; he had the cut of a hero.' Which, by the by, was far indeed from the case. Poor Vincent was as pleasant a companion as ever lived, and irresistible to the ladies, but he had not the look of a hero. 'And Tully and Son would stand behind the expense,' he added."

He lifted his glass to Prentiss, but absently, mind upon his tale.

"Bob had a bitter tongue, and most especially in those latter years. I can well imagine the silence he left behind him in the snug, and then off with him to Chapel Street, to tell me about it. The two of us knowing whose name it was that would never appear at all upon the memorial.

[15]

In the end, it was never built. Tis better so. The song is his memorial."

The water-softened whiskey was pungent upon Prentiss's tongue, its taste that of the mild morning. The anecdote, he suspected, had had its point, but for the moment it escaped him. He saw MacMahon as a savourer of such stories, rounded and gnomic.

"But Nolan," he said, persisting. "You respected him, as he was then. You all followed him."

"We trusted him," MacMahon said. "And were we not right to trust him? He led us out upon the appointed day and hour, when in fifty towns across the length and breadth of Ireland, the leaders quailed. But for all of the month that he was with us, sleeping beneath my roof, and having his meals with us, I never felt that I knew him. Bob was his great friend, and that was the queer thing. Before that, and for years past, it had been Bob and Vincent and myself. But then it was Bob and himself. I have never seen two men take so to one another."

"They were determined men," Prentiss said. "To judge by their later lives."

MacMahon held his tumbler in his two hands. He looked down into his whiskey, then looked up at Prentiss and smiled. "They were that, Mr. Prentiss. Great strength of character."

They talked until well past noon, when MacMahon promised Prentiss wryly that he would be there every day, and would welcome a chat. They had by then had three whiskeys each, and Prentiss had refused a fourth. He felt a bit light-headed in the summer sun, but MacMahon was as steady as at the first, a cool, open, well-mannered man, as he seemed to Prentiss, the good manners of a provincial at ease in his province. Sunlight now gilded the books, falling upon buckram and leather, upon sun-faded lettering. A tutor bidding good afternoon to a favored student, MacMahon walked with him to the garden gate.

"Five years I have been living up here," he said, "and not once have I tired of it."

"Neighbors must be thin upon the ground," Prentiss said.

"They are," MacMahon said. "But there are people down the road named Nagle. Their house is hidden by the bend, but I can walk there in less than an hour. I was master to the father, and to the lads after him."

"You must have given letters and sums to half of Kilpeder," Prentiss said. "That must be a great satisfaction to you."

"The latest in a line," MacMahon said. "There has never been a time when there was not a schoolmaster here. In the other time there were hedge masters, poets one or two of them were. Before the famine, the country beyond here, stretching away to the border, was Gaelic-speaking, and you will still hear it spoken. With all your interest in guns and drums and drums and guns, Mr. Prentiss, do you know that this part of Munster was once famous for poetry?"

No, Prentiss said that he did not, his tone flat, perhaps, because MacMahon, after looking at him for a moment, said mildly, "It was. Come take a look." And he held the gate.

Together, they crossed the road to an open field, and passed through the wicket of the low fence. Prentiss, in driving there, had not been aware of moving towards higher ground, but he saw now that the pasture in which they stood was an eminence, commanding, in the direction which they faced, a view across ascending fields to the near foothills. Beyond, the mountains glistened at noon, sunlight falling flat upon stone.

"Beyond there," MacMahon said, and Prentiss turned his head towards the other, distant mountains, the Derrynasaggarts.

"A populous land," MacMahon said. "Before your time, before mine. Before the famine. West Cork suffered badly in those years, you know that of course. Skibbereen, Skull, Crosshaven, the towns along the coast; there were dreadful times in them. It was never quite that bad here, but it was bad enough. Tis a queer thing about the famine, the way it is never spoken of now. And twas the same almost from the first. I mind that I was a child in the years that came after, but the country people would speak only of the bad times that had been in it, would speak quickly of it, and then move on to something else. But it swept through those vales we are looking at, and across those hills. And it took half the people away with it, into famine graves or across the Atlantic."

Prentiss saw fields, stone-enclosed, the intense green of summer, cattle, cottages. Along a distant boreen, a man walked slowly, paused.

"Twas my great pleasure," MacMahon said, "to find what could be found of the life that was lived in those places. There were lovely poems written, and some of the country people had them to heart. I have them copied down in a thick ledger book, and notes upon the men that made them. Tis all gone now."

Prentiss, looking out upon grey rock, green grasses, tried, without success, to see with the eyes of MacMahon's imagination. MacMahon's history was invisible, had left no scar upon the land. Somewhere, perhaps, hidden by foothills, there might be a cluster of empty cabins, roofless, nettles upon mounds of fallen stones.

"The famine did for the people," MacMahon said, "but by then, the poetry was a trickle. Do you know what did for the poetry, Mr. Prentiss? Twas us, twas the schoolmasters of Kilpeder and of the other towns, with our letters and sums. We gave them English, and we scourged the Gaelic out of them. Today, in those townlands, you will find lads ashamed of their grandparents who have not the English, or who use it poorly. And there was I, preserving the poetry as a curiosity. Like the olden explorers, who used bring home to London a Red Indian chieftain or two, in feather headdress and painted face."

"It is a language I know nothing of, I fear," Prentiss said. "Not a word."

"Ah well," MacMahon said. "You may be missing little, when all is said and done. Tis no proper part of your subject. The lads who were out in 'sixty-seven were all of them English-speakers. The Gaels, out there in the hills, lived in a different world from ours. Wild creatures we thought them, when they came into the town, and twas not their speech alone. The men had all of them a wild mountainy look, and the women as shy as hares."

But Prentiss had a troubled sense, faint, nagging, that it might indeed be a part of his subject, and one of which he would never have knowledge.

"From here," MacMahon said, "you can almost see Clonbrony Wood, the great object of your scholarship." The word *scholarship* moved faintly within the inverted commas of what Prentiss was coming to recognise as MacMahon's irony, helpful, amused, a tutor's irony.

A hand upon his shoulder, MacMahon turned him towards the south. The farms were larger, and the landscape moved more gently, smoothing towards the river.

"Just there," MacMahon said. "There is your Clonbrony. Twas thicker then, and twice again as large. The Ardmor estate has been selling off the timber."

A shadow upon fields of light green.

"We can see Castle Ardmor from here as well, can we not?"

"We can, of course," MacMahon said.

Kilpeder was a cluster of roofs. Beyond it, the Ardmor demesne was a crusted jewel—gardens, lake, the house itself, upon a low hill, facing water.

"Of the original castle," *Muirhead* had told him, "nothing remains save the ivied ruins of the keep. The present castle, built in 1720 after a design by Richard Cassels, is a handsome edifice in the Palladian manner, its magnificent façade of exceptionally tall yet well-proportioned windows commanding a matchless prospect of the tumultuous Derrynasaggart hills. The celebrated gardens, too, were reputedly laid out after a formal design by Cassels, but these were transformed and greatly extended, in the romantic mode, by the third earl. The grounds contain an artificial lake and waterfall, fed by the Sullane, sheds and dairies thatched after the ornamental Swiss manner, a grotto and a herbal labyrinth, and a herd of red deer. The composition, however, is neither random nor busy, so spacious is the demesne, and the effect is most pleasing. Ardmor Castle is closed to the public, but the grounds may be visited by arrangement with the estate agent."

"Up to the very walls of the demesne," MacMahon said, and Prentiss looked towards him, puzzled.

"It has all been sold off, nibbled away, save for the home farms, and a handful of farms that are out on long leases. And the new act will do for those, I should not wonder. The lands of the Ardmors lie now behind their walls. But tis lovely, is it not, with the lake winking, and the windows catching the sun."

"Lovely indeed," Prentiss said, but it was too far off for him to say anything more. His sense of such grand houses had been shaped upon a softer island of low hills and rolling meadows. Beside Castle Ardmor sprawled Kilpeder's low huddle of streets, broken by spires at either end. And beyond, fields moved upwards towards the hill upon which he now stood with MacMahon. And beyond that hill, in the near distance, the first rises of those hills which *Muirhead* had rightly called "tumultuous." Between hills and jewelled demesne there seemed no proper links of feeling or terrain.

"Mind you," MacMahon said, "in Fenian days, in the days of the Rising, twas far different. The Ardmors then were the lords of the walk, themselves and the lesser landlords. They owned the earth, so it seemed to us then, and all that grew upon it or flew above it. We had grown up to that, and our parents and grandparents before us. It was a different world."

"But the Fenians changed nothing," Prentiss said. "Some barracks and coast-guard stations captured for a few hours, a few crossroads scuffles. And after that, trials and prisons in England."

MacMahon laughed. "Indeed we changed nothing. It was the Land War brought the changes, the Land War and Parnell and the boycotting. But tis never easy to say where things begin. By God, Mr. Prentiss, we had them frightened for a few weeks, all the same. The landlords of Kerry packing up their families and their silver plate and riding into Killarney for safety. You never know."

"But it all must look very much now as it did then," said Patrick Prentiss, of Dublin and Clongowes Woods, Oxford and London, a year in Paris, half envious, although for the moment only, of a life lived out beneath the one sky, the shadows of early evening falling always upon the same hills, corners of barns and shops, upon the dust of familiar roads, generations of hawthorn.

"Indeed it does," MacMahon said, and added, dryly, "from this distance."

"Kilpeder itself," *Muirhead,* who maintained austere standards in this regard, had told Prentiss, "is a typical market town of the southwest, with little to interest the summer visitor. The eighteenth-century market house, at once graceful and functional, is mentioned in 'The Lament for Art O'Leary,' a poem in the Gaelic language which commemorates a local tragedy of 1773. Supposedly the work of Ellen O'Leary, Art's widow, it is almost certainly the product of the rogue poet Owen Ruagh Mac-Carthy, who briefly kept a hedge school in the town. The large and assertive Roman Catholic church was built, with many Gothic Revival embellishments, after a plan by Pugin. In 1867, there was a skirmish in Kilpeder between Crown forces and Fenian rebels, and recent years saw severe political and agrarian disturbances. It has since returned to its somnolent condition. Travellers from Cork or Mallow may wish to avail themselves of the inconvenient but picturesque road which passes into Kerry over the wild Derrynasaggarts, and thence along the lovely little Flesk River into the lake district of Killarney."

"Beyond there," MacMahon said, pointing away from the demesne, "in the village of Turrisk, there is a famine grave. You might wish one day to visit it. It might give you an historical perspective, if those are the proper words."

"Yes," Prentiss said, and in flickering thought considered how *Muirhead* might accommodate this information. The phrase itself, although thin and chill, lacked resonance for him.

But MacMahon could see a sunken field, around it a low railing of rusted iron, the grass rank and unscythed. Perhaps it all began there, MacMahon thought, in the famine grave. How many there, two hundred, three? Four hundred, surely, in Skibbereen's mass grave, on the height above the river. Unvisited, without a marker, a buried shame.

Prentiss had pushed his reading glasses to his forehead. Now he took them off and folded the earpieces, the sun catching them for a moment, semaphores flashing towards mountains, grave, demesne, the low, spired town. MacMahon, who had already decided that he liked him, smiled. A courteous young man, on embassy from the great world of books and scholarship, the libraries of Oxford and London bulging with books. I have become a crumb of history, he thought with contentment.

They arranged that they would meet each day, here, or on occasion for dinner in the Kilpeder Arms, and as they walked towards the road, towards Prentiss's trap, Prentiss thanked him again.

But MacMahon, a hand resting upon the opened gate, erect, without schoolmaster's stoop, shook his head.

"You know right enough, Mr. Prentiss, that it is more pleasure than chore when an old man is bid remember. What is a bother is that I remember too much, things that would be of no interest to you at all. Of no value."

"I do not know what is of value to me," Prentiss said, moving suddenly to a tone which MacMahon had not heard from him before. "Neither in history nor in much else."

"Like the rest of us," MacMahon said, and sought to match the tone.

They shook hands, formally, two historians met in conclave, upon open fields shadowed by mountains.

Unexpected, Prentiss thought, as the trap rolled him jauntily along, back to Kilpeder. What had he expected, riding down from Dublin to Mallow on the Cork train, past fields and villages, herds drowsing beneath early leafed trees, on distant hills the silhouettes of ruined keeps, separated from them by movement, green plush, stained wood, a dirt-streaked window? A rural schoolmaster, mind and imagination lightly freighted with Christian Brothers half history, patriotic catchphrases, boasts about the days when he had carried a gun for Ireland. Not MacMahon surely, hazel eyes alert and ironical behind thick glasses, unspoken meanings trembling upon the light webs of his pleasantries. He saw MacMahon now, provisionally, against the wall of his books, noontime sunlight upon the books. Across the geography of MacMahon's life, of which he now knew that he knew nothing, he rode back to the shops of Kilpeder, the market square, to the barracks where, in the dawn hours of a March morning gone now for almost forty years, a few score of young fellows, frieze-coated, armed with plundered rifles, had approached along a silent street thick with unfamiliar snow, to the falcon-guarded gates of a demesne within which, deep-buried beyond beech and heavy oak, lay waiting for him a part of what he did not yet know. The wheels of his trap clicked like a clock as they rolled across space.

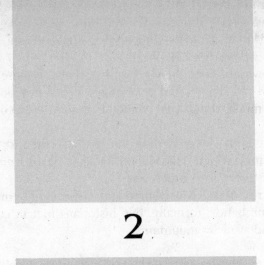

2

[Hugh MacMahon]

If I knew where to begin, perhaps I would myself be a learned historian, like young Mr. Prentiss, whose trap I stood by the gate watching, until at last it rolled out of sight, leaving me alone and lonely within my world. And yet I cannot help but believe, despite logic and history, that for me it began upon that winter evening at the end of the January of 1867, when, at teatime, Ned Nolan came first to the door of our house in Chapel Street.

Light was already drained away from the street, so short a day do we have of it in Munster's winters, and behind him, the two spires of Saint Jarlath's down the road were growing dim against the sky. He was a dark lad, with nothing about him save his height and heavy-boned frame to suggest our kinship, and yet I knew at once who he was. To be sure, we had been expecting him for weeks, and strangers came seldom to Kilpeder, and almost never to my house, save for the yearly visit from one of the inspectors of schools. I see him now in memory, a long face beneath the soft dark hat, long of jaw and with cheekbones high and raw as those of a Red Indian, with the eyes sunk deep, eyes dark as his hat, and a long, thin lip. He was holding his case by its grip, immense and bulging, made of some soft material. "I am your cousin Ned Nolan," he said, "I am back from America," and in welcome I seized his arm with my two hands and drew him into the house. The street behind him was deserted.

But I doubt if that vivid memory is fully truthful, for how could I so clearly have seen his eyes, in the gloaming, and with them shaded by the wide brim of his hat? In truth, it was only when I had led him to the front room, and he had taken off the hat to pay his respects to Mary, that I had a clear view of him. And Mary was to remember nothing dramatic about him at all, but rather saw a tall, gawky young fellow in clothes of an American cut, with tan square-toed boots, travel-stained, as the expression has it, in need of a wash and famished for a meal. There you have a difference between Mary and myself, and Mary's clear head is the one to trust.

And Mary it was who carried him off into the scullery and set him to work with water, soap, and towel, while she busied herself in the kitchen, preparing the tea. She was still at that task when he came back into the front room, and by then I had brought out bottle and tumblers that he might wet the dust of his journey.

"Is it from Cork that you have come to us, Ned?" I asked him.

"From Dublin," he said, shaking his head. "First London, and then Manchester, and then the Liverpool boat to Dublin. But I was in Cork City the last two nights."

"A fine city," I said, "with the wide Lee and the cathedral and all the river traffic." But what was Cork to a fellow who had lived in New York and travelled the States this way and that? He had lived the most of his life in New York, yet there was but the faintest of Yankee twang to his speech, which had the dip and cadence of my own.

"You have been expected here," I said, "and you are most welcome. You would not be more welcome in your own home."

"It is my home," he said. "Kilpeder is my home. I have no other." At the door he had said to me, "I am back from America." As though he had but gone there the year before to try his luck, and then drifted back. But it might well be true, I reflected, if he had been three full years in the Federal army, as was said, and his father dying in the midst of it.

"We know of your poor father passing away," I said. "I am sorry for your trouble. My own uncle, and I can scarce remember him at all. I was a little fellow like yourself when you and he set sail. But my mother spoke often of him, of course, and many others as well."

"Yes," he said.

"There was a lovely account of him and of the funeral in the *Nation*. I have it saved. A procession in New York, with O'Mahony and Doheny and the others in attendance, and three flags, the tricolour and the American and the sunburst. One of the stalwarts of 'forty-eight, O'Mahony said of him at the graveside, or some such phrase, one of the faithful and the true."

"I know that," Ned said. "Twas written up in the Irish papers of New York as well, and a bundle was sent to me."

"Of course," I said, although for a moment puzzled. "You were away in the war."

"That was it," he said. "Away in the war."

"But that was very hard of them," I said. "That they would not give you leave. Sure, O'Mahony was in their army as well, was he not?"

"A colonel," Ned said, "in command of a regiment. He was guarding Rebel prisoners up the Hudson, an hour's ride from New York on the cars. I was far distant, in Tennessee."

Tennessee. It was one of those words upon which our imagination of America was formed, Shenandoah, Susquehanna, Indian words savouring of pine forest, mountain streams, prairies stretching limitless towards huge orange suns. And for the past few years, stained with the smoke of cannon, engravings in the London journals of cavalry in riverbed combat, sabres swinging wide and deadly, breastworks and great batteries of artillery stretching out to the horizon, infantry on the move across broken earth, past dead-branched trees. Banners and bayonets and the rich, bacony smell of Indian names.

"When we were taken back to New York," he said, "at the war's end, I went first of all to his grave. Twas said in one of the papers that a subscription was being taken up for a gravestone, but there was only the mound of grassy earth, and a card fixed to a metal post, and the year and place of his birth and death. There was a wreath upon the mound, of vine leaves dyed black, with a green ribbon tied to it."

"Ah well," I said, and handed him a tumbler of whiskey. "His friends would be subscribing their dollars for a different purpose, if you take my meaning. He would have approved."

"He would indeed," Ned said, and for the first time he smiled, so that I saw him for what he was—not a black-coated stranger against an evening sky, but a fellow no older than myself, and awkward within a land that was strange to him, for all that he called it his home. He raised his glass to me.

"There was a composition of his in the *Nation* a few years back," I said. "And I have that saved as well. 'Our New Ireland Beyond the Waves,' he called it. Kilpeder was always proud of Thomas Justin Nolan. A stalwart of 'forty-eight, as the man said."

"They found him a job with the water company in New York," Ned said. "Inspecting charges made to householders, that there might be no error made in the billing, but after that a better one, with the company that has the ferry service to the Jersey side of the river. It paid him eleven dollars a week, and we had a room close to the wharf."

I declare to God, it had never occurred to me that he would have had a living to make, like any other man. In my imagination, I had always seen him making a speech on a platform decorated with green and orange bunting, or seated at a desk, composing "Our New Ireland Beyond the Waves."

Ned must have read my thoughts. He was still smiling. "That was not his true life," he said. "His true life began at six, when he could join his chums in a tavern that they frequented, and in the last year or two before the war, I was old enough to meet there with him. And there were always committees and public meetings and the like. There was always a chair for him on the platform, but he was rarely asked to speak. I mind that once, when I was small, he introduced Thomas Francis Meagher, and Meagher described how he and the other fellows had escaped from the penal colony in Van Diemen's Land."

Thomas Francis Meagher, now there was a name to conjure with, and on the instant, I forgot Ned's poor father. Meagher of the Sword, he was always called in the *Nation,* and they would have engravings of him, a handsome man, with a uniform and moustaches.

"And John Mitchel as well," I said. "Would your father have known John Mitchel?"

"Not in the latter years," Nolan said. "Mitchel went with the Confederacy." He shrugged.

He drank off his tumbler as if it were water, and with as little effect upon him, and I poured him another. As he talked, his eyes moved about the room, and I reflected that although he may have come home, he was for all that in an unfamiliar land. He studied the heavy curtains drawn closed against the evening, the cabinet of books, the glow of the turf fire, the hearth rug of brown matting, the red-and-blue-patterned carpet, the prints and engravings on the walls, and one of the two oil paintings of which we then boasted, the meeting of the upper and lower lakes at Killarney, a sheet of blue water, edged by oak and myrtle, and in the distance the lovely three-arched bridge. My belief now is that to a stranger from across the water, what is likely to seem most foreign is that which is to us most homely and comforting, the way we secure ourselves against the winter within our small rooms, with red fire and drawn curtains, and the chairs drawn close together.

But then he said, abruptly, "As I walked here, I passed Tully's shop. That is where Robert Delaney works, is it not?"

"It is," I said. "And he lives there as well, in a room above the shop which Tully gives him as a portion of his wages." I was not surprised by his information, for Bob was head of our Kilpeder circle, as it was called, and would be the man to whom Nolan would report.

"I will need to speak with him as soon as it can be arranged," Ned said. And with his words, or rather with the tone of them, I felt the intrusive presence in the room of something hard and cold as metal.

It was now my own turn to smile, and I said, "That has all been arranged for you. Bob is having his tea here with us tonight. The shop will be shut by now, but he will have his chores to attend to, and he will be here then."

"Then you are friends, the two of you?"

"We are indeed," I said, "and Bob is here often for his tea. We are great friends, himself and me and Vincent Tully."

"Tully of the shop?"

"The son," I said. "Old Dennis has no hand or part in the organization, and if he was certain about Vincent he would skin him alive. Mind you, he must have his suspicions. Tis a small town."

"I noticed that," Ned said.

"We took the oath together, the three of us," I said. "Two years ago, we went up to Cork City, and took the oath from—"

"I know who gave you the oath," Ned said, cutting me off.

But then Mary came into the room with a platter of buttered bread, to stay our hunger, and the talk drifted off to other matters—the tall buildings of New York, and the rigours of a sea voyage in the late winter. It was clear to me at once, as it was ever afterwards, that he warmed to Mary, who had a great skill at drawing people out and putting them at their ease. Although with Ned she had her work cut out for her, as he sat there, stiff and awkward, with a slice of bread in one hand, and the other resting upon his knee. But Mary talked away, leaning forward in the small armchair which was reserved for her use, a trim, neat figure in her gown of brown stuff, tight-gathered at the waist, her smile and wide brown eyes coaxing him into conversation.

This she did by describing to him the America which existed in all of our imaginations, shaped a bit by Washington Irving and Fenimore Cooper, but most of all by the letters which came in hundreds to every part of Ireland from the multitudes who had fled there in the famine years, so that our phantasy was a jumble of virgin forests and moccasined redskins, tall ships at anchor, streets thronging with all the races of the world—Portuguese and Irish, Russians, Chinamen, Swedes. She had a great gift for vivid language, and it was all worthy of an essay by Elia, and also with Elia's gift for droll irony, of which Ned was not yet aware.

But presently Bob arrived, and with the pride of a discoverer, I made the introduction. As vividly as I can see the room in which I now sit, I can see the two of them standing for the first time together, Ned tall and dark-suited, and Bob of middle height, but compact of build, his face square and even-featured beneath close-cropped sandy hair, and with eyes as blue as Ned's were dark. There was history in their handclasp—not Patrick Prentiss's university history of grand, smooth marble, statesmen and statutes and the unfurled maps of battles waged upon wide plains, but the histories of our lives to come, theirs, and Mary's and my own, and a few score others.

"You have been long expected," Bob said, using almost my own formula of words.

"As well myself as another," Ned said shrugging. "It was the sensible thing to send me. Hugh MacMahon here and myself are first cousins. It will rouse few questions if I am here on a visit."

Bob shook his head. "I would not rely upon that, Mr. Nolan. For the past few months the Constabulary and the magistrates have been showing great interest in visitors from the States. The fellow below in Cahirciveen gave himself out as a returned local. John O'Connor."

"You are very free with your use of names in Kilpeder," Ned said. "So I have observed."

Bob laughed at him. "The Cahirciveen Barracks know far more than I do about John O'Connor. He is on his keeping now in Iveragh, to avoid arrest. But he has his circle intact. There has been no martial law declared yet, but twill be a matter of weeks."

"If it is weeks, that would be a fine gift to us from the British. Before then, the bastards will have more serious matters to attend to than mere martial law." He used the word forgetful of Mary's presence, for he was a man careful of his speech in the presence of women.

I glanced towards her with a smile, but she did not catch my gaze. She sat with her two hands resting close together on the chair arm, studying the two of them as they faced one another, Ned unknown to us as yet, and Bob with that brisk, wary confidence which he was to carry far into his middle years, and which was a part almost of his stance, like a pugilist's, shoulders squared and head drawn back.

[27]

"You bring news, then, Mr. Nolan," he said, "which is as welcome as you are yourself." And when Nolan said nothing to this, he added, "News that has been a long time on the road. A damned long time."

But to this Ned had nothing to say either, and instead took from his breast pocket a wide, folded paper and handed it over. "You will want to examine my credentials," he said. "You should by now have asked for them."

Bob read them, holding the paper close to the green-globed lamp on the table. "Captain Nolan," he said, and handed it to me.

"Irish Republican Brotherhood," it said across the top, in stylish letterpress, and beneath it a harp, with the motto "It Will Be Restrung." The handwriting was elaborate and leisurely, a bookkeeper's hand, and it directed Captain Edward Nolan to proceed to the town of Kilpeder in County Cork, and there to take command of all circles presently under command of Robert Delaney, who was to hold now the post of second-in-command. Captain Nolan was to maintain the strength and integrity of his command, to drill the command, to distribute such arms as might be available, and to instruct the command in their proper use. He was to execute promptly and thoroughly all orders transmitted to him through proper channels, and those orders only. There was much else which I did not bother to read—the copperplate filled the page, almost without borders—but which seemed from such stray nouns as caught my eye to be impressively martial.

Upon habit, I began to hand it to Mary, but Ned reclaimed it from me. "You have no questions about this paper, Mr. Delaney?" he said, and when Bob shook his head, he leaned forward, and placed it upon the fierce red turfs of the fire. For a moment, it shared that lurid, spectral life, and then became frail, black ash. Thus it came to us and then left us, harp and copperplate alike, abrupt intrusion from some remote and invisible generalissimo in Dublin or even, as events were to disclose, in Manchester. The integrity of the command, by God. A hundred-odd labourers, farmers' sons, public-house potboys whom we had been drilling on moonlit nights in the wasteland beyond Knockmany, more to maintain morale than to impart military craft, with half of them giggling, persuaded that this was some kind of nocturnal mummers' play.

"No questions about the paper," Bob said, "and there was scant need for it. Tis a soldier that is sorely needed for the task at hand, and not a shop assistant like myself. I have questions in plenty for you, but not about the paper."

With the unreflecting familiarity of a family friend, he picked up the whiskey jug, and refilled our three glasses. His relief was real indeed, as

I had good cause to know. He had even in those days a great fondness for ordering men and affairs to his own satisfaction, beginning with the wares upon Tully's shelves, but the task at hand had been a bafflement to us both, and to Vincent as well. We had found in a bookshop on the quays of Cork the translation of a manual of arms composed by a Frenchman who claimed to have served in Napoleon's Grande Armée, and of nights Bob would sit in this room conning it and cursing. And well he might, for what was no doubt of service upon the broad meadowlands of Leipzig and Austerlitz was of little use in the fields beyond Knockmany. There had been beside it in the shop blunter manuals composed in English, but Bob would have no traffic with the enemy. "Still and all," I had remarked once to him, "Wellington seems to have known what he was about."

"Wellington was an Irishman," he said.

The purity of our patriotism, to say nothing of its fanaticism! And yet because it was a part of our youth I see it now, in the warm amber light of remembrance, as an innocence. And it was riddled with inconsistencies which we took care not to notice. Was not Bob forever prating about the titanic energy of the English manufacturers as contrasted with our own slack craftsmen and merchants, but in the next breath lashing them as soulless materialists, with hellfire phrases culled from Thomas Carlyle, himself a stout Queen and Empire man? And as for me, was not my own special love the poets of England, Wordsworth and Keats and Tennyson? And perhaps the Fenian generalissimo in Manchester saw himself a second Marlborough.

"For three years I was a soldier," Ned said in a deprecating manner, to lighten our tone, "and with naught else to show for my days." He raised his glass ceremoniously, first to Mary, and then to the two of us. "No, I misspeak myself. I was two years with the ferry company that employed my father. I handled lines on the boat that went to Weehawken."

Wherever that was. On the New Jersey shore no doubt, with the great forests and prairies stretching beyond it, sprinkled with red men riding bareback like acrobats. But light talk did not come easily to him; courtesy alone it was that forced him into sociability. Mary it was, as always, who brightened the evening room.

"We can go in now to our meal," she said, "and may it be the first of your many with us, Mr. Nolan."

I am almost certain that there were slices of cold ham, and cabbage, and a bowl of boiled potatoes. A warm room, the kitchen, with the warm, seductive odours of cooking, and the dresser with Mary's best Delft laid out along its three shelves, blue and white against the polished yellow pine. On the wall which faced me, as I sat across from Nolan, was the Adoration of the Magi which we had bought in Millstreet for two pounds when Dr. Sugden's effects were sold off. Shielded by glass from kitchen steam and smoke, the Wise Men approached in awe and bafflement, gift-laden, their raiment rich and exotic.

Ned was a hearty trencherman, but as he plied knife and fork, his eyes moved about the small room restlessly, before settling, at last, on the hearth. It had been the same in the front room, and I believe for the same reason. Were it not sacrilege, I might suggest a kinship between Ned and the Magi. In all the years of his boyhood and youth in the streets of New York, and his years in the Federal army, Ireland had been a distant, unknown home, above which blazed a commanding star.

Later, when he had come to know and to trust me, much of what he said confirmed this. When, a small boy, he left Ireland with his father, he left behind a dead mother whom he could not remember, a tintype cut round and pasted to the casing of his father's watch, the face soft and indistinct, wide-eyed. His father's life had been more than the ferry office, copying accounts payable into ledgers. There had been the meetings and demonstrations and committees and the endless schemes of the 'forty-eight men. The very schemes, indeed, which in the fullness of time had led to the Fenian Brotherhood and to the plan which had brought Ned back at last to Ireland, and had set Bob and myself to work drilling hobbledehoys on the wasteland of Knockmany.

Bob waited until Ned had a fair bit of ham and cabbage tucked inside him, and then said, "Captain Nolan, bits and pieces of that letter we burned are a puzzle. 'To distribute such arms as might be available.' What might that mean?"

Ned chewed and swallowed, and then answered him with a question.

"What arms have you now?"

"A dozen or so shotguns and fowling pieces. Not a single rifle. I have a revolver myself, and Vincent Tully has an elegant pistol that he wheedled from his father. Hugh here has none."

"And for how many men?"

"Between sixty and seventy. Some dropped out in the course of the last twelvemonth, but others took their place. It evens out."

"Dropped out?" Ned said upon the instant. "They took the oath, and then dropped out?" He began to say something else, but instead said, "How have you been drilling them?"

"With pikes," Bob said. "We made pikes. We look like a band of croppies."

It was true. It was as though history had consigned the Irish to an eternity of pikes. Some nights, when I stood with my back to Knockmany Hill, and saw them against the horizon, nothing beyond them save branchy thorn, I felt that I had been dropped into history's deep well, and had come upon the levy of some starveling chieftain in the Desmond rebellion, or the country people who had marched to their destruction on Vinegar Hill in 1798. Owen MacCarthy, the Macroom poet, has a line in which he describes the pikes carried by the fellows of his day as looking like a forest in leafless winter. And it was the same with us, unchanged.

"Have any of them seen service in the army?" Ned said.

"Not one. There is one fellow, older than the rest, who was in the Constabulary in his youth, before they turfed him out for general incompetence. And bloody right they were."

Ned nodded, expressionless, and cut another bit of ham.

"I have drilled them with pikes," Bob said, "and with the promise that the organization would get arms to us before the appointed day. But I have seen none, nor has O'Connor in Cahirciveen nor Timoney in Killarney nor the man above in Millstreet."

"Then you will have told your men what I will tell them. That the organization has made plans for a general distribution of arms in advance of the Rising."

"Your organization is cutting it very close."

"It is as much your organization as it is mine. I know a bit of what they intend. I picked it up in Manchester."

"Do you know, Captain Nolan," Bob said, "how matters have stood for the past two years in places like Kilpeder, across the country? It was two years ago that Hugh and Vincent and I went down to Cork and took the oath, and then came back and gave it out to the lads. 'Sixty-five was to be the year of action. The country knew it and Dublin Castle knew it and the English knew it. James Stephens all but proclaimed it from the rooftops of Dublin, before they caught him and flung him into Richmond Gaol. And then it was to be 'sixty-six, so O'Mahony proclaimed in New York. And now 'sixty-seven. Do you know what it is like to keep sixty or seventy country lads together, drilled with ashplants shoved into metal, for two years, at the behest of an organization that cannot make up its mind?"

"Captain Nolan," Ned said. "The organization has made a captain of me right enough, but the words have a strange sound. It was a corporal I was for the three years that I was with the Federals, until near the very end, in Virginia, when I was promoted to sergeant. Tis much the same with the other Fenian soldiers who have come over from America."

Bob glanced over at me, annoyed, and then back at Ned.

[31]

"I don't mind about your bloody rank, but I mind about the question I put to you."

"I answered the question for you, as best I could. I am a corporal is all, a jumped-up corporal, and such fellows as myself and yourself are told what to do, and not why. You have been drilling your men, and sometime, within less than two months, we will be leading them out, you and I."

Mary had arisen, to clear the plates, but now she stood, stock-still, with a look that I could not read.

"Armed or unarmed," Bob said, but it was more question than statement.

"Tis but a scant look that I have yet had of the countryside," Ned said. "It must wait until tomorrow. 'Captain Nolan' will be fine and proper with the lads, but for so long as I can remember, I have answered to 'Ned.'"

And "Ned" he became to us, at that moment and forever afterwards. Even in the later years, when he had become notorious, and his name could be found in the papers, linked with Rossa or Lomasney or the dynamite men, there was always a brief, alien moment when "Edward Nolan" rested unfamiliar within the paragraph. A month or so he was with us, but he would be joined with us forever.

There was tea and a sweet to follow, and by an unspoken agreement between the two of them we talked of general matters. My schoolhouse, I told him, was not the one in which his father had been master, but that older one still stood, around the turning in what was still called School-house Lane, and was used by Dennis Tully as a warehouse.

"Your friend's father," Ned said.

"He is more than that," I said. "He is a merchant of substance. The fortunes of Dennis Tully are a wonder to the world."

Bob caught the dryness in my words, and said sharply, "He has been good to me. Generous."

"You earn your keep, Bob," I said, "and a bit left over."

"But no friend of ours," Ned said.

"You heard Hugh," Bob said. "A merchant of substance. And a pious man, he and Father Cremin are very close. And Cremin has denounced the organization from the altar and called down the curse of God upon it. There is no part of Ireland where the priests are more fierce against the Fenians than they are in Munster."

"I wonder," Ned said, in an oddly mild tone, "that such pious scoundrels dare to call themselves Irish."

"They are Irish right enough," I said. "All too Irish." Unspoken was my thought that they were more Irish, perhaps, than the fellows from

New York who had come to lead us, with their great square-toed boots and their boasts of as yet invisible rifles. Not Ned alone, but the entire crew of them, for so strange was the atmosphere of this strangest of risings that the air of Ireland was thick with talk about "the American officers," as they were called. Tis a nation of sheep that we have been until these latter years, at the bidding of Spaniards and Dutchmen and Frenchmen and Americans.

"How must the lads feel about all this?" Ned said. "It cannot be pleasant to have the curse of God called down upon you from the altar. Can they take the Sacrament?"

"They cannot, of course, but they all do, every man jack of them. I do myself," Bob said.

Ned's smiles were always unexpected. "That must call for some nimble theology on your part."

"Tis no part of a priest's duty to stand between my God and my country. The oath is the sticking point, though; that is the tricky part."

"The oath is sacred," Ned said with vehemence. "It is an oath made to God to free this country from oppression, and it is binding for life."

"Father Cremin is not of your opinion," Bob said mildly, and with a fleck of amusement.

"To hell with Father Cremin," Ned said. "A minute ago you told me that men took the oath and drilled with you and then drifted away. I was astonished that you had let them drift."

"Let them?" Bob said. "You can hardly hold a court-martial on Knockmany Hill."

"Why not?"

Bob and I stared at each other, startled less by the words than by the casual way of their utterance.

"Drag a fellow away from his home and card him for punishment," Bob said, "as the Whiteboys and the Ribbonmen do? Is that the meaning of your question? By the light of the next morning, you would have no Fenian circle in Kilpeder. Let me make a point to you, Ned, and I mean no disrespect to your rank. You have come back to your home, and you bear an honoured name, but you have come to a place unknown to you. On some matters, you would be well advised to take Hugh and myself for guides."

"The oath is for life," Ned said.

By God, I thought, you could carve the words on that fellow's tombstone.

"For life," Bob said. "But words must be tempered by circumstances."

Another tombstone motto. I thought often in later years that with those words, the two of them had spoken their secret names.

"And you asked me a minute ago," Bob said, "how the lads felt when they were cursed from the altar. Bloody awful is how they feel, frightened and bewildered. Potboys and labourers is what they are, simple men with no learning. And the cause to which they are pledged is condemned by the Church, by every bishop and nearly all of the priests. Not to mention most of the Catholics that they look up to as their superiors in rank, the merchants and the publicans and auctioneers and the rest of it. I have great respect for the fellows who come with us to the hillside, and even a kind of sympathy for the ones who fall away."

It was the simple truth that he was speaking, and the sincerity of his words had their effect upon Ned, who to the end was what might be called a fair-minded fanatic. But not the full of the truth, which it is not easy to put into words. Many there were among the merchants, and not a few among the priests, who condemned us with full lung and easy conscience, and yet nursed a secret hope that we would succeed.

"They go back from your Knockmany Hill," Mary said suddenly, "to the cottages of fathers and mothers who are as simple as themselves. Fearful men and women who remember the great hunger, and who know the power of the landlords and the magistrates and police."

She was pouring out the tea, and she spoke quietly as she poured.

"We all know their power," Ned said, as he took the cup from her. "The organization exists to put an end to it." But his tone was as quiet as her own, and his words those of one willing to end a controversy.

After our meal, we went back into the front room, and settled down to one or two glasses to round matters off, but it was clear that none of us was eager to make a long evening of it. Ned was something new that had come into our lives. But the talk was pleasant, and with no constraint save that of Ned's awkwardness of manner, which he was never to lose, not even after we had all grown very close to each other. It was as though within his mind was a world in which gossip and chat about weather and crops held no place. But he was also, as I only began that first evening to discover, a fellow of wide and curious reading, for all of his scant formal schooling. A jumble bag it was in time to prove itself, revealed in the odd reference, or in hillside conversation—Hugo's *Les Misérables*, Marcus Aurelius, Herodotus, the essays of Montaigne, *Uncle Tom's Cabin*, Patrick Henry, Cooper and Scott, some American who had sailed before the mast for two years. And Shakespeare. He was a great reader of the plays of Shakespeare.

Upon *Les Misérables* he for some reason spoke that evening in a way that was, for him, almost garrulous—not of the book itself so much as of the nights which he read in it, by campfire, at the great siege of Petersburg. He was not upon the soil of Virginia at all, he said, but in the labyrinthine sewers of Paris with poor hunted Jean Valjean. Jean Valjean was a great hero of his, he said, as he sat stiffly before us, hands gripping his bony knees.

I walked Bob to the gate, and paused with him there briefly.

"The cousin is an intense sort of fellow," I said. "Not the man to take to a race meeting with you."

"He is a good man," Bob said. "He has been sorely needed here. Tomorrow I can pitch that damned Frenchman's manual of arms into the fire."

"Do you think so?" I said, surprised. "I do myself, but I thought the two of you got off on the wrong foot."

But Bob shook his head, and with a clap upon my shoulder set off for Tully's.

Soon after, I picked up Ned's case, and led him up to the rere bedroom, which he would be using, the room which in later years would be the children's. And so much were the young things into our way of speaking that it was not their own at all, but rather "Ned's room." In those days, in the seventies, the Rising of ten years before had receded into the dim past, into legend, but the room was named for Ned.

He took the case from me, swung it onto the low bed, and opened it. Shirts and trousers he placed upon the coverlet, and then, rummaging deep, pulled out two objects wrapped in flannel. The smaller of the two he unwrapped.

"Bob said below that you lacked a weapon, Hugh. You are welcome to this."

I took the revolver from him cautiously, and weighed it in my hand, my forefinger resting not upon the trigger but upon the guard. It was heavier than I had expected, the metal cold to the touch. The chambers were empty, little black mouths. Holding it, I felt awkward and ill at ease.

"This is my own," he said, and unwrapped the other length of flannel. Guns have been no great love of mine, then or ever after. Sombre instruments of death they are, compact and brutal, with a sinister intelligence, as if knowing in their metal souls that an ounce of pressure, a moment in space, can send death upon man or beast, tearing into flesh, muscle, skin, fur. But of the dark species, I could see that Ned's was a beauty.

"This is a Colt," Ned said, the word holding within itself the image of a young horse running wild in a meadow. "'Tis the newest of their designs, a single-action .44." Holding it in his right hand, he ran his left along its long-barreled length, a lover's stroke.

"It is the weapon you carried in the war?" I said.

"This fellow? This fellow was never issued to corporals." He carried it over to the candle which Mary had lit for him. By soft, homely light it glistened, sleek and ponderous, but with the indwelling grace of all fine machinery.

"Three nights before I set sail, twas given me by a fellow named Rafferty, who had been a major with the Engineers. Not a member of the organization at all. I was having a meal that night with two of the lads, and he walked across the restaurant and handed it to me, wrapped in brown paper and tied up with string. 'I know who you are,' he said. 'I intended this for Joe MacGuiness, but I can't find him. Has he shipped out?' 'Who is Joe MacGuiness?' I said. And he laughed, and clapped me on the back, a loose, heavy man, with a red face and thick brown moustaches. 'Good for you,' he said. 'The less said, the better.' "

"How did he know you?" I asked.

"The organization is the common gossip of New York. A cheap sacrifice it is to hand over a revolver which you no longer need. The amusing part is that I had never heard of Joe MacGuiness. For all I know, he had indeed shipped out, and is here now, somewhere. But it's an ill wind."

He hefted the revolver again, and then placed it carefully on the table, beside the candle, where the flame flickered along its flank.

"'Tis not the softest bed in the world," I said.

"It feels grand," he said. He pressed down his palm upon the straw mattress.

By the time that I had completed my few chores, Mary was in bed, her hair unbound, and her hands joined upon the coverlet. I placed the gun he had given me on the chest of drawers.

"A gift from Ned," I said.

She looked at it without speaking. I doubt if she had ever before been in the same room with such an object.

"I can see that," she said in a small voice.

"Well," I said, "what would you have? It is what has been preparing itself these two years."

"I know that," she said, but her eyes did not leave the revolver.

"On the appointed day," I said, "there may be little cause to use it. There is naught save the police barracks between ourselves and control of Kilpeder, and they are sensible men, Sergeant Honan and his lads."

"You know better than that, Hugh."

"Well," I said again, "what would you have?" and with an edge of irritation in my words.

But instead of answering, she turned her head towards me. "He is a frightening fellow," she said. "He is not like any of us, is he? Nor like Sergeant Honan, if it comes to that."

"He is a likable fellow," I said. "I took to him at once, and so did Bob."

"He is indeed," she said. "Tis not Ned that frightens me, but what he has brought to Kilpeder." And said no more.

Nor had she need to say more: I knew what she meant, and felt it myself. We had drilled and practised, and Bob had instructed me in the use of his own revolver, which although of English manufacture was doubtless similar in operation to the one upon the chest. But the guns Ned had brought to us were as much messengers as weapons.

I walked to the window, and Mary spoke to my back.

"It is very close now, is it not?"

"Very close or not at all," I said. It had seemed very close in 'sixty-five, the year of action, but the year had come and gone. "But if it is close, twill be a matter of weeks." I must have sounded learned upon the subject, but in fact we knew nothing, and I doubt how much the men in Cork City knew. It was unreal, a kind of phantasy, unlike Ned's revolver. Even the loyalist newspapers knew more. It was from them we learned that Stephens and O'Mahony had been thrust aside by men determined to act. Men without names or faces for us, although later, of course, we knew the names of Kelly and McCafferty and the others. But until the end the names were remote to us, even when we stood in the courthouse in Cork and heard them named as those upon whose orders we had rebelled in arms against Queen Victoria, her realm and person.

Faintly I heard—or sensed, perhaps—the sound of Mary's brush, as she moved it through her thick brown hair, warm, familiar.

"Unreal," she said, in echo of my thought. "Evenings when we talked together, ourselves and Bob and Vincent, it was all very grand and cloudy, like an opera. And now it is a gun upon a chest of drawers."

The street below was pitch-black, with only the two spires to be faintly discerned after my eyes grew accustomed to the darkness. There were no streetlights in Kilpeder in those days. The taverns would still be open, but they were around the turning, or too far down the road for their lights to travel. But one could sense the town's full being, shops and market house, the wide square. And beyond the town, Lord Ardmor's deer park and the surrounding hills. In the barracks, the constables were asleep, or gathered for a last cup of tea, against a wall their rifles more deadly even than Ned's revolver. In the room above Tully's, Bob would most likely still be awake; square bare room, bed, table, shelf of books; perhaps, by bedside, a guttering candle. In the shop beneath him, wares and provisions piled in profusion, tea and candles and baling hooks. Hours hence, morning light, fresh and confident, would wash darkness away, restoring the familiar, which has always the face of permanence. But now, to my eyes and senses, darkness filled our world with wonder and with tremors of possibility.

3

[Patrick Prentiss]

And when Patrick Prentiss, in London a year later in the winter of 1905, once again in his rooms in Pump Court, was writing his history of the Fenian rising, he too held in his mind an image of the somnolent market square of Kilpeder.

It was a winter as cold almost as the one of which he was writing, the winter of 1867, with light snows, and grey, overcast afternoons, darkness coming early and almost welcomed, for with darkness the city turned inwards, to lighted rooms and brisk coal fires. In the garden beyond the court, the earth was frozen hard, and the leafless branches had a brittle look, as though they might easily be snapped.

He was well launched now upon his work, with his notebooks and journals stacked on a long table beside his desk, meticulously labelled. Accounts of conversations held in Dublin or London lodging houses, saloons and restaurants in Boston and New York, with men for whom, as for Hugh MacMahon, the Rising had been a bright-coloured morning in uneventful lives, and others, like Devoy and Rossa in New York, conspirators still, the drama long before played out: Devoy tight-lipped and sardonic, grey close-cropped beard, and eyes like slits, and Rossa, aware that his life had once been legend, song, but hard-drinking and boastful, hints of "actions" by his Skirmishers stretching into the eighties and nineties, a landlord murdered, an informer executed. Looking into eyes hardened by wariness or made watery by whiskey, Prentiss had tried to recover distant springtime.

At five o'clock, more days than not, he would take a walk through the gathering darkness, to the bustling Strand, streetlamps a soft pearl, fog-swaddled; shop windows glowing; a jostling crowd along the footpaths; heavy traffic of cabs and trams. Or else along the Embankment, the Thames dark and oily beyond moored barges, towards Westminster Bridge and the Houses of Parliament, pinnacled and mullioned, a vast expanse of nineteenth-century exuberance, transformed by London fog and evening light. Measured against that scene and the empire which served it, the incident of which he was writing shrank to insignificance, tainted by comic bravado, whiskey oaths. Once, on another winter night, in 1884, a veteran of the 'sixty-seven rising, William Lomasney—the Little Captain, who, with a score of men, had attacked the barracks at Ballyknockane, and had suffered with Nolan and the others in English prisons—rowed with two men to the buttresses of London Bridge, down the river, and in a bungled dynamite attempt had blown themselves into fragments. Faint, futile scratch upon the stones of the great city, washed away by the waters of the rich, dark river.

At his club, the Savile, over a mutton chop, a glass, a game of whist, he would be asked about his book, and he would answer, vaguely, that it was about life in Ireland in the last century. "Good God!" they would say. "Ireland!" But more than a few would have Irish connections, of one sort or another—a fishing lodge in Connemara, a daft cousin from Kilkenny who had gone into the army. They tended to forget that Prentiss himself was Irish; nothing Irish in his manner or his accent. Dealing the cards, he would suddenly recall Rossa leaning across the table. "No one knew Ned Nolan as I did. I knew him as I know this hand." He held it out for inspection, and Prentiss wondered at its biography, a hand which had held a pickax in an English prison, held dynamite caps, signed letters that sent men out to assassinate, bullet from behind hedgerow, explosion of city brick. Or he would remember first light on the Derrynasaggarts, when he had walked from Kilpeder to Killarney to feel the texture of his territory as a good historian should, light striking dully at first upon stone and furze, then brightening, hills too bare for grazing or habitation, ghost-peopled. These he remembered as he dealt out the cards to waiting hands, smooth, cuffed in immaculate white.

But later, perhaps in the cab riding home through darkness, he would remember Kilpeder, seeing it from the doorway of the Arms in morning quiet, or at night, passing through the falcon-guarded gates of the Castle, after an evening spent with old Lionel Forrester, moonlight falling flat upon market house and obelisk. Along the street, and then the Macroom road, indistinct forms moved towards the police barracks, the scene held within the glass globe of his imagination, in London, a toy.

It was not that he saw the rising in Kilpeder as the centre and focus of the rebellion of 1867; for that rebellion, as he had come to learn, had no true centre: a confused command, informers, poor communication, snow, scattered futile attacks upon barracks, coast-guard stations, railways, marches and countermarches, humiliating defeats, English prisons waiting at the end of the road. It was rather the reverse, with Kilpeder as a characterising action, peopled with actors who took on faces, identities, destinies, as he learned of them through his two Virgils, MacMahon and Forrester, a retired schoolmaster and Lord Ardmor's older cousin, voice dry and sardonic.

For of those still-living men with whom he had talked, and who had been close to the centre of things, when there had been a centre, few had actually been "out" in the snows of March. Many had already been caught up in the government sweeps of 'sixty-five and 'sixty-six, and were in their English cells, or in Dublin gaols awaiting transportation—Devoy, Rossa, O'Leary, Luby. The insurrections had been local, at the orders of men shadowy then and still shadowy: Kelly, McCafferty, a few French colonels on half pay hired as mercenary leaders. Those who had been out remembered bits, fragments: a running hillside gun battle fought with bewildered, Wild West bravado, a thousand men waiting out the night in the Dublin foothills, beyond Tallaght. But *why?* The question nagged at him incessantly. Why had those men, scattered across the towns of Munster, from Kerry to Waterford, marched with their few stands of muskets and rifles, with their pathetic handcrafted pikes, through snow and into massed fire, in the service of a patchwork conspiracy?

He began work early each morning, at half-seven or eight, while most of London was still asleep. Strong tea, unsweetened, close to his hand, the hand moving, not steadily or smoothly, as Macaulay or Michelet might be imagined at work, but fitfully, a paragraph or two, and then the pen laid down upon its stand of silver and onyx, a gift from his father, the Dublin barrister, who saw history as a series of briefs, economically composed, cased, ribboned. In those pauses, he would rummage through files, ledgers, notes untranscribed from memorandum books, conversations, court records, newspaper cuttings.

It had begun, what historians (if he should ever finish his history) would someday call the Fenian rebellion, long before 'sixty-seven or even 'sixty-five—a decade earlier, in 1856. It had begun when James Stephens—veteran of the 1848 rising—returned to Ireland to take the country's temperature. For months he tramped the roads of the four provinces, disguised as beggarman, casual labourer, commercial traveller, talking to the young and the disaffected. His three-thousand-mile walk, he called it later; by that time he was the legendary "Number One" of the Fenian conspiracy. In 1865, holding the strings of insurrection in those hands which everyone remembered as small and ladylike, he was the hero of the famous escape from Richmond Prison; in 'sixty-seven, he was a leader discredited, sentenced to more than thirty years of garrulous recollection, long-bearded by then, a shabby sage living penniless in a suburban lodging.

But in 1856, in the year of his ramble, James Stephens had been a will-o'-the-wisp, never forgotten, dimly remembered. *An seabhac,* he was called in the Gaelic-speaking districts, "the Hawk," and that passed over into police reports as "Shook," "Mr. Shook." "It is reported," wrote the sergeant in Castletown Bearhaven, harbor town in a spur of West Cork, "that Shook, who was last month reported in Waterford by the *Gazette,* has been this week in Castletown, and met with a score of men in the shop of a farrier named Grady. What he said to them is not known, but they were men of a lowly condition, except for Grady himself, who is known for his intemperate habits." It was a decade after the famine, the great hunger, and Mr. Shook visited the districts more sorely damaged, Skull and Crosshaven and Skibbereen, where he talked to a young hothead named Jeremiah O'Donovan, who claimed that lineage entitled him to call himself "O'Donovan Rossa."

With difficulty, Prentiss sought an image of that early Stephens, unsmeared by gossip, failure. He saw him at nightfall, cresting a hill, before him a village imperfectly cradled against sea winds, huts straggling towards dull water, a darkening strand. In beggar's disguise, long greatcoat, boots patched and dusty, canvas pack strapped to his back, he pauses. Here, in the village before him, ten years earlier, the dead lay untended in their cabins, and beyond them, in the fields, the crop of potatoes rotted black and putrescent. Their stench clings to the air, invincible against seaborne freshening winds. He remembers, perhaps, the Tipperary peasants of 1848, polite and apathetic, puzzled, as Smith O'Brien preached resistance to them, mild-voiced patrician strayed into rebellion, counting out for them on delicate fingers their numberless wrongs. In the front of the small crowd, a cottier hawked, spat precisely between his boots, nudged his neighbour. A fairday treat, these gentlemen from Dublin, frock-coated, preaching a genteel rebellion, constables to be halted on the road, disarmed without injury to their person. Young Stephens stood among them, not of them, loaded carbine resting on forearm. Beside him O'Mahony, chieftain of the Comeraghs, a Tipperary man known to them, bred of fighting stock; a tall, handsome man, his coat open and two pistols shoved into his waistband. O'Mahony could have led them, or Stephens himself, but not these gentlemen from Dublin. It was over in a few hours, that rising in 'forty-eight: an attack upon a barracks, a rattle of rifle fire, and two men dead in a field. Never again, O'Mahony and Stephens vowed in Paris exile, exhilarated by talk of Blanquist barricades, dark-eyed *carbonari* in ill-lit cafés off the Boul' Mich'. "Use the faction fighters," Stephens said, "take hostages, tear up the rails." And pushed the bottle of wine towards O'Mahony, who, temperate in those Paris years, smiled, and shook his head. But later, from New York, O'Mahony wrote to him of hundreds of thousands of famine Irish, washed up on the shores of Boston and New York, bewildered, wrathful, peasants unused to brick and asphalt and clanging horse trams, saloon bullies, their minds clinging to sun-shadowed hills, bog cotton, a twist of road, the voices and heat of winter taverns. "A second Ireland here," he wrote. "Unbroken. They can send money, men. England drove them from their homes, and well they know it." They must have a sign, he wrote; they must know that the country is not dead.

And so Stephens set out upon his ramble, his trail left behind him in scattered, puzzled police reports, in memories of old men swollen and magnified by time, by pride in their own vanished youth.

"Now, in my town, in this town," an old Cahirciveen man had told Prentiss, toothless, cheeks like veined crab apples above unshaven stubble, striped work shirt neatly pinned at the collar, "we were a tinderbox waiting for the spark, and James Stephens was that spark—Mr. Shook, he was called, *an seabhac*, the Hawk. He met with us in Pat Sullivan's licensed premises, under the noses of the peelers in the barracks across the road. I was at that time sixteen years of age, and was the youngest man in Cahirciveen to be sworn by Mr. Shook. That is a fact, Mr. Prentiss, and should be written down." Pat Sullivan, Prentiss thought, the name sliding into place: with O'Connor when the coast guard was attacked; penal servitude for life. The old man sat flanked by daughter, son-in-law. The daughter plied Prentiss with tea, bread, the bread raisin-studded, glaze of sugar. With embarrassed pride, wary eyes upon the old man, they nodded. "Stephens was a well-built man, sturdy of limb, and with eyes black as coals. I mind him well, and a black beard. A clever man, who had long before been an engineer with the railway. At Killenaule, in 'forty-eight, he had been wounded and left for dead. He crawled behind a hedge and lay low. Did you know that, Mr. Prentiss?" Yes, Mr. Prentiss knew that. Two prints faced each other. The Sacred Heart—chalk-white and vermillion, index finger resting on heart miraculously naked—contemplated, with eyes melting, tender oval photographs of the Manchester Martyrs, Allen, Larkin, and O'Brien. Above their heads, a scroll, "God Save Ireland," and beneath it the date of their hanging, side-by-side on a triple gallows, "November 23, 1867."

"Six months of hard labour he was given," the son-in-law said proudly, flourishing an invisible campaign ribbon, "picking oakum for twelve hours a day in Kilmainham, sewing mailbags. It is said in the family that his fingers were never right." Fingers that had stitched Her Majesty's mailbags rested upon bony knees.

"It is of James Stephens that Mr. Prentiss would hear," the old man said, "but I have nothing more to tell. I saw him but the once. He never returned to Cahirciveen. He never returned anywhere. That was his way, he was a hawk in flight. He was too swift for them, Richmond Prison could not hold him."

"He is but recently dead," Prentiss said. "If I had begun work four years ago, I could have talked with him."

The old man sat as if unhearing, deaf to news about a man older than himself, a man forgotten, withering behind walls of Blackrock stucco. He saw a young hawk in flight, dark against a morning sky.

But Hugh MacMahon was, characteristically, more acerb. "There was not one man of the Kilpeder circle whose oath ran back to the time of James Stephens's ramble. Bob and Vincent and myself were the first, and we brought back the oath from Cork. He was never in Kilpeder, that I have heard, although tis said that he was in Macroom. At the time of his ramble, we were all of us schoolboys at work on our spelling and our sums. Long after, I met men who claimed to have met him, to be sure, and some who claimed to have been given the oath by Mr. Shook himself. But by 'sixty-five, Stephens was Number One, COIR was his title, Chief Organiser of the Irish Republic, and he was everywhere at once, in New York, in Paris, in London, in disguise in Dublin itself. But I remember the escape from Richmond Prison in 'sixty-five. It was the talk of all Ireland, and London as well, I have no doubt. Man, it was prodigious. There they had him caught at last, on the very eve of the Rising, as we then believed, the Hawk netted. The government made great play of it, and the lackey newspapers, as we called them. They had drawings of it, to drive home the point: James Stephens with shirt collar unfastened, manacled wrist and ankle, being led through the entranceway of sombre stone. Dame Street was thronged for his arraignment, and all the gentlemen and ladies were down from the viceregal lodge to get a look at him. 'I deliberately repudiate the existence of British law in Ireland,' he said, 'and I defy any punishment it can inflict on me. I have spoken.' " MacMahon's laugh ended in a dry cough. " 'I have spoken.' Brave words, by God, but they put us in a panic. Bob and Kevin Mangan, who was in command in Macroom, rode down to Cork, but of course they knew no more than we did, and Bob rode home in a fury. 'Never fear,' Jackie Keegan had said to him. 'They have not yet built a cage strong enough to hold the Hawk.' Then he put his hand on Bob's shoulder. 'They all talk like penny dreadfuls,' Bob said to me, but we put on a brave front for the men, and if I remember aright, Bob borrowed Jackie Keegan's words with a clear conscience. And by the living God, wasn't Keegan right? They arraigned Stephens, but they never tried him. Two weeks later, he was free as a bird. It was a great sensation, and the effect upon the movement was prodigious."

It was indeed, and for this Prentiss had needed only to consult the yellowing files of newspapers. But in fact, the escape had been described to him in New York by John Devoy himself, who led the band of men waiting outside the prison walls. Straight and inflexible as a poker, like Ned Nolan one of the unforgiving men, wedded to the oath, gaolbird, conspirator, looking not Irish but like a Yankee colonel, retired. "It was simple enough," he said, "and why not? An inside job, as they say over here. The two warders on his block were sworn Fenians, Breslin and Byrne. They moved him through the inner wall and across the courtyard, and Kelly and myself and a dozen lads were waiting beyond with rope. I mind that when we reached the North Circular, a fellow named Ryan said to me, 'John, we have tonight witnessed the greatest event in history.' So much for the Crucifixion."

"And what did Stephens say?" Prentiss said.

Devoy smiled grimly and relit his cigar, moving the match carefully, from side to side, twisting the cigar. "Stephens? He had little enough to say that night, although I think he inclined towards Ryan's view of the matter. He was a vain man; it was his besetting sin, and it proved fatal a year later. But what the devil, it was *felix culpa*, without vanity could he have managed what he did ten years before? A man on his own, walking the roads of Ireland, scattering the seeds of revolution. It was spitting rain that night, the dark rain of late November. The one thing we hadn't remembered was an overcoat for Stephens, and so I put my own around his shoulders. You cannot have the Chief Organiser of the Irish Republic shivering along the Royal Canal. But first I transferred my revolver, and until we reached the safe house in the North Circular, I was worried lest the rain damp the cartridges."

"You would have used it," Prentiss said.

Devoy exhaled fragrant Havana smoke. "If a peeler had so much as asked us our destination, I would have blown him out of his boots. I'm sorry it didn't happen. No blood had yet been shed, you know, and that might have tripped the wire. By God, the night that James Stephens flew Richmond, we could have raised half Dublin. Or from then through the Christmas season and into the spring of 'sixty-six. After that came the arrests, and the organization fell apart. Nor would there have been a rising in 'sixty-seven, had not Stephens been deposed. It was simply done. McCafferty put a cocked revolver to his head, and said, 'Mr. Stephens, you are deposed.' McCafferty had a wonderful simplicity of manner—one of the American officers, a Confederate guerrilla with Mosby. But of all that, I have heard talk only. By February of 'sixty-six, I was myself in Mountjoy Gaol."

"Then in 'sixty-seven," Prentiss said, "when the Rising came, it was McCafferty gave the word? By then McCafferty was Number One?"

Devoy smiled again. "There was never but the one held that title. James Stephens. Mr. Shook. But it would not have been McCafferty. McCafferty was organising the raid on Chester Arsenal. Kelly gave the word, a solid man. I mind the day of the Rising, you could feel it among the warders, and one of them, a decent skin named Clanahan, told me that there were a thousand men in the Dublin hills up above Rathfarnham, and the troops had gone to face them down. Later, we heard about the risings in Cork."

"The Kilpeder rising?"

"The Kilpeder rising, yes, Ned Nolan's rising, but the other ones as well—Ballyknockane and the others. A bloody waste. In the back room in Grantham Street, in January of 'sixty-six, I told James Stephens that it was then or never. I have heard it said in later years that when McCafferty had the hammer cocked he should have finished off the job and squeezed the trigger. But I would never have had part in that, nor would Burke or Kelly. We owed everything to Stephens. He botched it, and he was thrust rightly aside, but we owed him everything. Sorry decades he had of it after that, poor devil, but the funeral was a great occasion, I am told." Devoy drew again on his cigar, and grinned at Prentiss. "Fenians specialise in grand funerals, Mr. Prentiss. We dug up poor Terence MacManus, and shipped him across the world from San Francisco to Glasnevin."

Hawk in a rainy night, Prentiss thought, in borrowed overcoat, the leafless trees dripping, led by armed young men through streets of brown and red brick, along the banks of the dark canal, rain-pattered. He died then, not sorry decades later, brought down by history's fowling piece, far behind him his long ramble through Munster and Connaught, the years of scheming and contriving, cadging funds from New York immigrants, riding the cars to address Irishmen encamped with the Federal troops in Tennessee, Virginia valleys. Ahead of him lay only his own months of indecisiveness—terror, perhaps, at the prospect of what he had himself summoned into being, and then moss trooper McCafferty's wide-mouthed revolver pressed against his skull.

"My own specialty," Devoy said, "was the recruiting of Irish soldiers among the British regiments, and a brisk traffic it was. I gave the oath to hundreds of them. But the British aren't fools. By the spring of 'sixty-six, the regiments had all been replaced by true-blues from England, and myself and my recruiters were behind bars. Stephens had given me a title, Chief Organiser of the British army. He was a great man for inventing titles. When they arrested me, I was at the task, with two sergeants in the back room of a public house. I was shopped by an informer."

They had had dinner in a restaurant in the West Twenties, around the corner from Devoy's Fenian newspaper. Coffee sat cold before them, and empty wineglasses.

"They gave you a life sentence, as I recall," Prentiss said.

Devoy shook his head. "Fifteen years' hard. I had never had a chance to fire that revolver I spoke of. That is why I was eligible for the amnesty in 'seventy-one, myself and Rossa. Lads like your man Nolan had to linger on a few years. When Nolan came over, we were here to welcome him."

"Had you known him before," Prentiss said, "in Ireland or in prison?"

"Not at all," Devoy said. "Ned was sent over late in 'sixty-six, or early 'sixty-seven, on the eve of the Rising. And afterwards, I was in Millbank and he in Portland. He had the worse of it. Millbank was accounted a model prison, but Portland was bad. Men went mad in Portland. Not Ned, though. It hammered Ned into hardness. That is the way of it. Prison turned poor Rossa into a fanatic, and Ned into—well, what he became. You know what he became."

But Prentiss did not. They all moved in courses beyond his experience or understanding. Russian nihilists, perhaps, or anarchists, meeting in their Whitechapel clubs and coffeehouses, dark-faced, gesticulating, wide declamatory Slavic sweeps of arm. Not Devoy, close-buttoned, spare, a distant, polite courtesy, devoid of affability. "These days?" Devoy had said to him when they commenced their meal. "These days I am a most respectable old party. My paper tried to keep alive an interest in Irish affairs; we have a Dublin correspondent; there are many fraternal organizations, here and in Jersey. Clambakes, commemorations. Ireland is very quiet now, you know, very constitutional. She has entrusted her future to Mr. Redmond and Mr. O'Brien and Mr. Healy."

Prentiss knew better. Even now there was a shadowy Fenian organization, and Devoy was close to its centre.

"Mr. Healy," Devoy said mildly, "the man who betrayed Parnell. And little Johnny Redmond. There are no Ned Nolans now. All that died in 1891, in the hills of West Cork."

Throughout the meal—clear soup and mutton chops for Devoy, the price of dyspepsia—the old man had been casually informative about the 'sixty-seven rising, an event closed and sealed into the past. But his references to more recent history were evasive, tortuous, touched with an occasional sulphur—factions, schisms, Sullivan and the treacherous "Triangle" wing, the Invincibles, Rossa's Skirmishers.

"Lomasney," Prentiss ventured, "the man who set the explosives beneath London Bridge, he was sent out by Rossa?"

"William Mackey Lomasney," Devoy said. "The Little Captain, his men always called him. A compact man. I know his widow well, she lives over in Brooklyn."

"By Rossa?" Prentiss repeated, amused.

"Don't be too certain of that, Mr. Prentiss," Devoy said, hard grey eyes fixed on him, fork and knife held poised above chop. "The organization mounts a campaign of its own from time to time." Fork skewered, knife cut decisively. "Lomasney and your man Nolan were pals, and neither was close to Rossa's operation. Or so I have been told."

"Why Ned Nolan?" he said later, tasting wine with temperate care. "Why write about Nolan? A good man, but never a leader, you know. Save at the setting forth, save at Clonbrony Wood."

"Perhaps that is why," Prentiss said. "Or perhaps because I cannot understand a man like Nolan, his mind hardened to a diamond point. He is like one of the men in Plutarch."

"Plutarch," Devoy said, testing the heavy vowels upon his teeth like a bit of mutton. "If I recall Mr. Plutarch, his aim was to make men's lives as clear as glass, the rogues and patriots of Greece and Rome."

But it was Devoy himself who had put Prentiss in mind of Plutarch—

exiled, unbending patriot, with a clean, aseptic tang, cigars, two whiskeys at night. As much as Nolan's, if less disastrously, his mind had been hardened to a point. An elderly bachelor now, picking his way among factions, holding his secrets like a poker player, bland, unyielding smiles.

"We worked closely together at times," Devoy said, "but we were never close to each other, if you take the distinction. I trusted him. He broke with us when Davitt and I made the compact with Parnell. He was one of the irreconcilables. He drifted away thereafter to the hard men, the men at the far edge—dynamite, revolvers. History has proved him wrong. Ours were the methods that smashed the landlords."

Prentiss waited, not speaking. He twisted his wineglass on the white, stiff damask.

"Broke with us, I said. But we were the men managing the plan of campaign. Ned was . . . obscure. He was a courier between this place and that, and half the time the organization had a bit of salary for him. But for the most part, he supported himself as best he could. For a time he was with the streetcars here in the city, and for a time in the late seventies, Tom Bonner had him as a straw boss in a brickyard up the Hudson, near Verplanck. 'Sixty-seven was a long time ago."

Hero on half pay, Prentiss thought. The past pale and dead as the snow of Clonbrony Wood. But not at the end.

"The man who emerged from Clonbrony Wood," Devoy said, "was Bob Delaney. There was a lad for you! I can remember him from the time of Parnell's visit to New York, Parnell as cool and handsome as a pedigreed earl in a stage melodrama, and Dillon beside him, and Bob Delaney two paces behind. I took to him at once, a man able for any contingency. That little rat Healy was with them, the Judas who betrayed his chief. But not Bob Delaney, by God! Delaney stood by Parnell when the combined powers of England and the Church were set to crush him."

"His last years were unhappy," Prentiss said. "A country solicitor picking up odds and ends of work. Back where he began, back in Kilpeder."

"Yes," Devoy said. "And we know why. He shared a weakness with his chief. A certain fatal weakness."

"It was more than the woman," Prentiss said. "You said it yourself. The men who stood by Parnell went down with him."

"Not all of them. Johnny Redmond thrives. It was an open scandal, as bad in its way as Parnell and Katharine O'Shea. Worse in its way. Delaney was a married man with children, and that woman's husband was a friend of his, a decent fellow. Parnell was an aristo, a Protestant. Bob Delaney was one of our own."

Prentiss shrugged. "It was a private matter, surely."

"Private?" The teeth in the thin-lipped face were bared. "It was adultery first brought the English into Ireland. Dermot and Dervorgilla—learn the history of your people, Mr. Prentiss. It is the worst of sins, the sin of the flesh. Delaney's future lay all before him, before he strayed into those perfumed sheets."

Bachelor, wed to Ireland, jealous of her rivals. In the cold grey eyes, Prentiss saw for an instant flecks of remorseless, private wrath. Then, "No matter," Devoy said, "he is gone now. May the earth rest lightly on him."

"He must have described to you the action at Clonbrony," Prentiss said. "Edward Nolan, I mean."

"Described it? Yes, I am certain he must have, sometime over the years. I cannot recall, to be truthful with you. Ned was never a blowhard like some of them. I mind that when he landed here, after Portland Prison, he was bitter enough, at the bungled orders, and the cravens in this place and that, and the informers. But sure, we all were. He was in a cold fury about the informers. And he lost men in that wood, you know. Four of his lads shot down, and another left dead in the streets of Kilpeder. Four, I believe it was."

"Yes," Prentiss said. "Four."

Later, they stood in the evening of a Manhattan winter. Powdery snow wind-driven within the yellow glow of streetlamps, a briskly moving traffic of pedestrians. In the street, a crowded trolley, yellow-sided, moved westwards, towards the river. A patrolman, recognising Devoy, touched hand smartly to helmet, and Devoy, hands buried in the pockets of his short overcoat, nodded in return. No peelers in this city—a police recruited from shiploads of strapping lads from Mayo, Leitrim. Devoy, a man of resources, knew their masters, downtown in Centre Street, had his Clan na Gael circles within the force.

"I would give much, Mr. Prentiss, to have been with Delaney and Ned Nolan in Clonbrony Wood." He had lit a fresh cigar, and held it, firm-jawed.

"A fiasco," Prentiss said sceptically. "A running gunfight in the snow, and five country lads dead. And in the heel of the hunt, walking out to the constables, hands in the air."

"The one blow struck since Emmet's rebellion," Devoy said. "Never after that."

In iron winter air, softened by snow, by gaslight, he stood in his forty years of exile, capable and shrunken, implacable. Around him, the streets of a city which had become his own, their smells and noises by now his own. He smiled and extended his hand to Prentiss. The white, even teeth were false, the hard lines of plate masked by trim, military beard.

But Prentiss, in a different, Thamesside winter, remembered more vividly West Cork's late spring, and Hugh MacMahon's voice beside him, as they walked into the hills. Hedgerows were in early leaf, pale green, translucent, and the sun fell upon distant boundary fences, cross-hatching the green of pasturelands where cattle grazed.

"I remember well the night," MacMahon said, in the courteous tones of one to whom it does not really matter if he remembers well or ill, so long as listeners are satisfied, the past brought forward, a trophy redolent of his own lost time.

4

[*Hugh MacMahon*]

I remember well the night that Bob and I brought Ned Nolan out to the Knockmany wasteland that he might meet the lads and gain some notion of how we had been drilling them. Bitter cold it was, for the time of year that was in it, the ground beneath our boots hard and unyielding. For a mile or so, our path followed the Derrybeg, a bit of stream that feeds into the Sullane, and the clouded moon glinted now and again from its icy edges. We walked without talking, the three of us and eight or so lads from Kilpeder itself, and there was another quartet waiting for us at the boreen that drops down to the Derrybeg from the near side of Knockmany.

At the appointed place, as we had grandly named it, all but a thin, brief curve of the Derrybeg was lost from view, glinting at us now and again from beyond a few bare-branched thorn trees. Twenty were awaiting us there, talking in twos and threes, or walking up and down, swinging their hands to their oxters to fight the cold. And we had a good half hour to wait until the full complement was there, the others drifting in on their lone or more often in threesomes. We could hear them before we saw them, country fellows walking their way in heavy boots across winter earth. At last, as I made the tally, there were sixty-two of us, and a fair account given for the ones missing—Bob Prendergast was up with an ill heifer and the like. Vincent Tully was the last to arrive, though he was one of the very few to come by horseback, on the dappled mare that had been his father's Stephen's Day gift, riding across the lads and straight to where Bob and Ned and I stood together. He swung himself to the ground, and said, although whether to Ned or to Bob was not clear to me, "I am late, General, but through no fault of my own. The old fellow kept us at our rosaries for a solid hour. My knees are kilt."

He was wearing a short riding coat which I well knew and envied a bit, of soft, heavy black wool, with a cape to it, and he had the lapels flung back, despite the weather, so that in the darkness there was a gleam of shirtfront. His stiff hat was pushed up from his forehead, and he smiled, impartially, at the three of us, that heart-quickening smile he had, as though he would draw anyone to whom he spoke into some easy, unthreatening pleasure.

He took Ned by the hand, easily, as though we were meeting for the hunt some autumn morning, leafy trees russet and the pack baying at our knees. It was a way that Vincent had with him always, of giving light to a scene. Some there are, as Edmund Burke would say it, who possess an unbought grace of life, and this Vincent had in abundance, a fact not without its irony when it is held in mind that all flowed from the hard, sweaty-palmed bargains struck in Dennis Tully's shop—dappled mare, soft white linen, all. But this is unjust of me. Some lives there are that move in music, lucky lives, and some, most, that do not.

Ned's did not. He held Vincent's hand in his a moment, for politeness' sake, touched his upper arm, and then turned to Bob and nodded.

We had the men drawn up in file, standing awkward and silent, hands pressed to their sides, the coarse jackets in which they had performed a long day's labour softened by darkness, and their shapeless hats softened by seasons of rain and wind. Bob had sent them word not to carry their pikes with them this night, or the few guns that we could boast of. There was not one of them that I did not know by name, but not above five or six with whom I was on what might be called terms of familiarity—fellows, that is, with whom I had taken drink of an evening. And of those few, all were men with small holdings of their own; for the others were labourers: a lad who worked for the farrier, young Joe Harrington, who helped at the livery stable. So great a gulf there was in those days, God help us all, between a schoolmaster and other people.

Bob walked over to them, with that confident bounce he had to him always in those days, and Ned beside him.

"Lads," Bob said, "there will be some of you who know who is this man with me, because you may have spied him the past few days in the streets of Kilpeder. He is one of our own, a Kilpeder man born, and the son of Thomas Justin Nolan, whose name all of us revere. One of the heroes of 'forty-eight."

Vincent and I had not moved forward, and although I craned my neck, I could not see Ned's face. His back was to me, angular and stiff.

"And so he is Hugh MacMahon's first cousin as well." In my position as first cousin, I nodded, and without seeing it, could feel Vincent's smile.

"What is more to the point," Bob said, "he has come down here to take command of Kilpeder. Ned is Captain Nolan of the Army of the Irish Republic, and Hugh and I have seen the document which puts him in command. A proper document, with a seal and a motto and the rest of it. The organization has done everything in proper military fashion."

The men stood silent, motionless, for what, after all, was there to say. But I fancied that I could sense a movement through them as wind picks at the surface of a pond. That was for me as odd as anything of those weeks, and proof were any needed that warfare is a bizarre enterprise, the way lads different the one from the other are changed to some unknowable organism when once they were placed in files. Not that we were much of an army, God knows.

"And he is more than that," Bob said. "We have been hearing in this place and that of Irish lads who served in the great war in the States that now has ended, and attained high rank some of them, generals and colonels and the like. But who in West Cork has seen a one of them? Well, by God, the man stands before us. Ned Nolan is to be our commander for good reason. Three years he served in the Union army, and fought bravely in that great conflict. He knows the ways of armies better than any red-jacketed Englishman strutting the streets of Cork or Fermoy, who knows only the ways of lording it over naked Hindoos or the savages of Africa."

The sapling offers true promise of the tree it will become. There would be times, fifteen years in the future, when I would stand one among thousands, or at least many hundreds, to attend the oratory of Bob Delaney. Oratory, it was called always in the nationalist press and never a mere speech. He was to have in those days a raised platform at his disposal, draped with buntings of green and white splashed with yellow sunbursts, and dignitaries seated behind him, stiff-collared, tall brushed ebony hats resting on knees. The flaring pitch of torches would make splendid the scene, streaks of orange flame lurid against the blackness of a provincial market square. And faces, my own among them, turned upwards towards him. But the knack rests folded within the acorn.

"There you are, now," he said. "We can chuck out the drill book of that jackanapes Frenchman, with his piquets and right-about-faces and dancing-master commands. Captain Nolan can show us how Irish fellows did their marching up and down the valleys of Virginia." He reached up a hand, and took off his stiff billycock hat that he had purchased a year before in token that he had become Dennis Tully's shop assistant, and swept it down to his side, not a salute, and with a touch of self-mockery.

One of the men gave a kind of shout of welcome, and then the others took it up, ragged and brief, more a courteous noise of welcome than anything military, and then there was a silence again. After a pause, Ned stepped forward, away from Bob and closer to them.

"I am happy indeed," he said, "to be back home where I belong. In West Cork. What Bob Delaney said to you is the fact. I was with the northern army in the war, in the Irish Brigade, as it was called, and I was well trained by them in the ways of war and was in some of the fighting. But I was no general or colonel. I was a private soldier at first, and then for most of the time a corporal, and when things were winding down, I was made sergeant. But that is no loss to us here. For what will be expected of us here in Kilpeder on the appointed day, a general would be of no more use than an archbishop. It is sergeant's work that is asked of us, or a lieutenant's at most. I hold the rank of captain in our army, as Bob has told you, and it is best if you use that title in our dealings. But so much about rank, and there is the end of the matter. A commission is but a word upon decorated paper. The matter to keep in mind is that we have all of us sworn an oath to the Irish Republic, now virtually established."

What the lads had been expecting, I cannot say, but I doubt if it was Ned's flat, unemphatic words. Over the months, Bob had of necessity perfected a line of sunburst eloquence that would have done credit to Dan O'Connell, the Liberator, and they may well have expected yet greater grandeur from this emissary from distant battles. Perhaps not. Perhaps they were alarmed by this evidence that we had all enmeshed ourselves in the toils of an organization whose roots were far from West Cork. Ned might think himself back home, but to the lads he was a stranger.

"Bob Delaney here I have made my second-in-command. And Hugh MacMahon and Vincent Tully are the two adjutants. This means that whatever commands they give, you may take as coming from me. And my commands you can take as coming from the staff of the Army of the Irish Republic. They are to be obeyed promptly and without question. Now then."

He walked slowly along the line of men, and then turned and walked back. As he turned, I could see his face a bit in the darkness, high cheekbones and lantern jaw and nothing else.

"Bob tells me that in the past, last year perhaps, there were men who took the oath and drilled with you, and then drifted away. I can understand that. We have had a long and maddening time of it, the lot of us. But that time is past us, thank God. There will be a rising; the appointed day has been set, and it is near at hand. There will be no more drifting away. You have taken the oath, and if you drift away you will be judged by the Kilpeder column as a deserter in time of war. Do you all know what is the punishment for desertion used by all of the armies of the world?"

This was the first time that any of us had heard used the word *column*. But for the moment we had no mind for such niceties. There fell a bleak silence which Ned, it was clear, had no intention of breaking, for he commenced again his pacing this way and that.

"'Tis well known to all," someone said at last, and the men in the front rank turned their heads towards him. His name was Pat Dunphy, a small farmer westwards on the Kerry road, and well respected by the men of his locality, a powerfully built fellow in his thirties with hair thinning towards early baldness, a great man alike for the dancing and for the harvesting.

"It is," Ned said, and faced him. "And what is it?"

"Deserters are shot," Dunphy said. "Or hanged, whichever it is."

"From what Bob has told me," Ned said, "we should not be wasting our lead. The Kilpeder column should hang a wretched fellow like that, would you not agree?"

After a pause, Dunphy said in a low voice, the first words rumbling in his chest, "There was no word of hanging or of shooting or of desertion when Bob Delaney was our leader. And here we are this night, at risk to ourselves, and we are here to risk more. You have no cause to use such speech, Mr. Nolan."

"Captain Nolan," Ned said.

"Captain Nolan, so," Dunphy said. "It is from Bob Delaney that we have expected the word."

Bob stepped forward, but Ned heard his footfall and shook his head. "Bob Delaney gave me a quite proper caution," Ned said. "He

[56]

cautioned me that you are all men well known to one another, and that I am a stranger to you. Tis true. But I am a stranger sent to you because I know what will be needed and how it must be done. And at the top of the list is understanding what we are about. The organization intends to take control of this country by force of arms. We will be attacking the British army, and the Irish Constabulary, which is a part of that army. Some of them will be killed and some of us. Make no mistake about that. All that need concern us is the Kilpeder area. We will have certain tasks to perform here, and then, if we succeed in them, we will march north to a certain point of assembly and place ourselves under a higher command. I intend that we should succeed, and for that I need proper soldiers, and not farmers."

"Farmers is what you have," Dunphy said. "Soldiers are fellows with guns."

"So will you be," Ned said. "I have no intention of beginning operations without arms. But that is not what makes soldiers. Soldiers are men who take an oath and obey orders whether they like them or not, or however they feel about the man who gives them. As a matter of interest, Mr. . . ."

"Dunphy. Pat Dunphy. And I have been two years a sworn man."

"As a matter of interest, Pat Dunphy, how do you feel about me?"

Dunphy waited before answering. "I think you have the nerve of a Limerick cattle jobber."

"Fall out," Ned said. "The way you do that is, you step between the two men in front of you, and you walk over to me."

For a long moment, while I held my breath, Dunphy stood motionless, and then, with a shrug, he shouldered a man aside, and stepped towards Ned. I could see him more plainly now, one of those big countrymen who hold themselves with ease, heavy-muscled but not fleshy. His eyes were hidden from me, but I knew the dangerous, casual step of such men. I have seen such a man put down his pint carefully and with exactness, and with his freed hand, anger flowing at need to his fingers, seize a fellow by the throat.

"And if I gave you an order?" Ned said.

"You spoke the word yourself, Captain Nolan. I took the oath. But by Jesus, you do not make it easy for me to do it with pleasure."

"Indeed I do not," Ned said, and turned to Bob. "Is this fellow of any use to us at all, or have we just had a fair sample of him?"

"There is no better man here," Bob said. "There are three other Lackan men here this night, and they are here because of Pat."

Ned nodded. There was not a man who was not with his eyes fixed upon the two of them. Ned's hands were buried in his jacket pockets, his heavy coat of foreign cut flung back.

"Very well so," he said at last. "Pat, the one lack that we have aside from weapons is a sergeant, but we can remedy that straightaway. You are sergeant now of the Kilpeder column."

"I am the sergeant?" Dunphy said.

"You are," Ned said. "You have no choice in the matter. I have been a sergeant myself, and by Christ I do not envy you the rank. Tis the sergeants who rule men in battle, and not the colonels or the generals at all. Tis you the lads will end up cursing, and not Bob or myself. But I suspect that you have no reluctance when it comes to telling other men what to do and how to do it. Am I right, lads?"

There were a few of them who had begun to grin, but at Ned's question, a wave of laughs spread across the ranks, from one of them to the next. In the half view that I had of Bob, I saw him studying Ned with a new kind of interest, as though Ned had suddenly disclosed to him an unexpected quality. Vincent turned towards me. He was smiling, but not as the men were. "Our Mr. Nolan is a resourceful sort of fellow," he said.

Dunphy had begun to walk back to his place in rank, but Ned put a hand on his arm. "Not anymore, Pat. You must stand out here henceforth, and face the music with Bob and myself, and Hugh and Vincent. And when next we muster, I expect to find the men drawn up properly, an arm's length between one man and the next. Take a look at them there, like tinkers at a fair."

Much that Ned knew about tinkers, which are as rare as caribou on the streets of Manhattan. It was doubtless some phrase that he had picked up in a New York public house, or a Virginian encampment, for he had a full arsenal of these. As though by speech and manner he was determined to shape himself into the Irishman that he was not save by birth and the years of his infancy. What he was in truth was a soldier, and after that night, we had no doubts upon that score. And the first who would swear to that was Pat Dunphy, who was Ned Nolan's man from that night forth.

Night upon that quiet wasteland, the shoulder of Knockmany above us, humped and broad. I remember well that night. A wind had begun to rise from the west, strong enough to be carried to us over the Derrynasaggarts from the limitless sea, stirring winter's dry branches.

"There is little else that we need talk about this night," Ned said, his voice crackling. "You have been well drilled by Bob Delaney, I have no doubt, and Pat Dunphy here, Sergeant Dunphy, will keep you on your mettle. But keep this in mind. On the appointed day, we will not be playing soldiers on parade. In Kilpeder and on the march northwards from Kilpeder, I will ask things of you which you have never done, and which please God you need never do again. The town of Kilpeder is held by the Irish Constabulary, who are the armed soldiers of the English Empire, and who rule over us with their guns, for all that their jackets are not scarlet, and for all that they call themselves Irishmen. They are not Irishmen. There may be a decent fellow or two amongst them—small wonder at that, with not enough work in the land for strapping lads to set their shoulders to. But when you have taken the Queen's shilling and put her coat upon your back, you are England's man and do England's bidding. Remember that, because they will. They have taken their oath, and I doubt not that you have seen them at their work. But we have also taken an oath, an imperishable oath, which is to no queen nor empire, but to our own people and our own land. And when I order you to let loose your fire upon those who serve our enemy, twill not be me who gives that order, but the words of our oath speaking through me. Remember that oath."

Remember that oath. Learned men of the Middle Ages, the realists and the nominalists, used wear each other out disputing whether or not words and ideas have a true existence, as do chairs and stars and mountains. Ned could have resolved this conundrum for them. For all of his life, that oath to the Irish Republic which he had taken, which all of us there on that wasteland had taken, was as real and as certain to him as the nerves and tissues of his own body. Little thought had we then of how his life would be shaped by it, nor why, but there was no question of the power which it gave his words. As though we had all of us been bound within a brotherhood whose invisible webs stretched far beyond our mountains, sacred and absolute.

They were still within our ears, clinging to his harsh, unemphatic voice, when he dismissed the lads. Even Vincent, our resident wit, blithe and bonny, was quiet for a bit. He walked with Ned and Bob and myself to the road, as did Pat Dunphy, with the other Lackan men waiting behind for him, looking after us without surprise or curiosity, as though it was only to be expected that Pat should be entrusted with responsibility. Nor was it the Lackan men alone who had been won over by Ned that night. Ned, as I realised later, when I settled into my bed, and lay sorting things out before sleep, had seen that he must impress himself upon us, and had addressed himself to the task. He had made use of Pat as would a true commander, but his parting speech had had more in it than skill. There was iron in Ned, and he had shown us a glimpse of it.

Vincent walked beside us, leading his horse, and when we had gone a bit, he stopped, and drew from his coat a flask which I had seen before, a handsome object of hammered silver, with a design of whirls and spirals. He unscrewed the stopper, and took a pull at the flask, then handed it to Pat. "Sergeant Dunphy," he said. Dunphy took it without reflection, but when it was halfway to his lips, he suddenly stopped, and looked over at Ned. But Ned nodded, and Dunphy had a go at it, then carefully wiped all around its mouth with his sleeve, and handed it to Bob, and thus it went its way around our small circle. It was whiskey finer by far than any placed upon Conefry's counter, or all but the finest stock held in reserve at the Kilpeder Arms itself, smooth and with the barest touch of smoke upon it, caressing palate and tongue.

Ned was the last of us to drink, and before doing so he looked at each one of us in turn, then drank, more deeply I think than any of us had done, although the hardness for spirits of Dunphy's head was a part of his legend. Then he lowered the flask, and wiped off its lip, as Pat had done, and held it in his open hand, the fingers of his other hand moving in the darkness over its invisible traceries.

"Tis a fit container for such whiskey, Vincent," he said. "Kilpeder spirits can occasion no complaint."

"Kilpeder indeed," Vincent said. "Tis my father's private stock that he measures out when he has a bishop or a monsignor as visitor. Were he to know that we had used it to toast the organization, twould cause an arrest of his heart, poor man."

"Fine whiskey," Ned said, "carried in silver to a cold winter's night. It was welcome. And there, Vincent, is the end of it. Never, ever, for any reason, is whiskey to be taken to any muster or action of the Kilpeder organization." He handed the flask back to Vincent. "And no member of the column is to report for duty having taken whiskey. Do you mark those words, Pat?"

"I do," Pat said, firmly, though a bit puzzled by the way Ned had sidled into the order.

"Because that is your responsibility. I will answer for our officers, but the men are your responsibility. If I find that a man on the field has had liquor taken, by Jesus I will have him flogged, and I will set you to work with the rope."

"Yes," Pat said.

" 'Yes' is fair enough as the response to an order, but I want you to mind what I have said. We are an army without uniforms and badges and the rest of it, but by Jesus we will not be without discipline. As I have said, Vincent, that is fine whiskey."

And with that, he rammed his hands back into his pockets and set off, leaving us to catch up with him. Vincent watched him with a half smile, between amusement and admiration, and then stowed away the sinful flask, in whatever was its proper recess within his elaborate costume.

At the time it seemed to Bob and myself, who had been spared this mortification, that Ned had acted in a crisp and soldierly manner, and our respect for his exotic military ways went up yet another notch, for never could Bob have spoken so to Vincent in the days when Bob commanded us, and had he done so, I doubt not but that Vincent and I would have burst out laughing. Only later, from Ned's half sentences, scenes grudgingly sketched, did I learn more about his feelings towards drink.

I saw a boy standing beside his father, loved and revered giant, in a saloon bright with gaslight, sawdust-floored, after some public meeting perhaps, echoes of oratory carried by himself and his friends to be saluted by dollops of American whiskey. They stood in a semicircle, a half dozen of them, glasses in hand, standing their rounds, and the young barman, red hair of County Leitrim, putting up every third round on the house, his own glass decorously hidden beneath the counter, companionship warmer and snugger than air cloudy with cigar smoke. Ned's father held the floor, Thomas Justin Nolan, one of the heroes of 'forty-eight, a Young Ireland man, not driven to America as his pals had been, by failed crops and evictions, the famine Irish, but scourged away for his beliefs, the friend of Doheny and Meagher, a schoolmaster by rights, head stuffed with poetry, patriotic orations. But by the fourth round, or the fifth, the tongue would be thicker, the sweep of the arm broader. A cascade of language. They would walk home together, through the iron Manhattan night, perhaps one of his father's friends there to steady him, the friend telling Ned of all that the father had endured for Ireland, wet lips and watering eyes the badges of old battles, wounds and whitened scars. But in the morning the father would sit quiet and nerveless, cold tea before him, his hand gently shaking as he touched its rim. "A long, dirty night, Ned. Tis well for us that we are not often out, as my own father used say, your grandfather." His sidelong apology, the words formulaic as a litany. And young Ned would wait patiently for the return, in late afternoon, of the loved giant, full of wit, easy charm in the roll of a shoulder.

Not that my Ned kept the bottle always at a distance, as I was to discover in the early hours of the coming morning, but for him it was a silent and solitary weapon against himself, and I was never to see him with the effects of drink upon him, nor have I ever spoken with any man who did. Some men there are for whom hard spirits are not solace but punishment, and whether they are to be considered less rather than more fortunate than the rest of us, I cannot decide.

It was long after we had returned to Chapel Street, and the two of

[61]

us had made our good-nights outside my bedroom door. Mary was, of course, asleep, and I undressed quietly in the darkness and lay down beside her, conscious of the welcoming warmth of her body. In her sleep, she half turned towards me, and faintly I could see her face by the same veiled, pallid moon that had attended us at Knockmany, but it fell now upon quiet beauty, vulnerable and trusting. Her unclenched hand lay near my own, and I took it in mine, and so lay there, looking upwards, sorting out in my mind the events of the night. I drifted into a first welcome half sleep, and was content with it, for how long a time I cannot say, until I was awakened by a noise as of a chair being moved, below, and then, when I had begun to doubt my ears, it came again.

I rose up then, and not willing to waste time in searching the door hooks for my robe, pulled on my trousers, and went downstairs. Ned's door, I took note in passing, was open, and I found him in the kitchen, a candle lit on the table before which he sat, and the bottle beside him. He was still fully dressed, and he must have heard my steps upon the stair, for he was facing the door as though awaiting me, and he was smiling.

Now, ours was not to be the only late encounter of that night, for when Vincent returned home, as he was to describe to me the next evening, his father was awake and waiting for him. My mind, as Vincent told me his story, still held that kitchen scene, with its one source of light, weak and harsh, falling dead upon Ned, high cheeks and deep-set eyes, and that smile which introduced me, as it were, to some unfamiliar portion of his being, withdrawn and menacing. I withheld from Vincent an account of the words we exchanged, which is a most singular fact, for Vincent and Bob and myself were as close as the Three Musketeers of Dumas the elder, although it now occurs to me that Athos had his dark secret, undisclosed to Aramis and Porthos almost to the end. But then Vincent was intent upon his own narrative.

I use with deliberation the word *narrative*. Some men there are who lack all ambition to set words to paper, who have all the full gifts of the storyteller, save no doubt that of persistence. Vincent Tully was one. As a raconteur, he was a marvel, and it accorded well with his other charms. When Vincent was in form, only the most crass of philistines would interrupt him with questions or comments, and certainly not with some competing or corroborating anecdote. For if some few facts needed for enlightenment seemed missing, one could be certain that they were held back by design, and would make their surprising appearances at their appointed times. His stories were shapely, and you could feel the pleasure which he took from the shaping, his hands moulding them for you in the empty air. All that would be needed of scene and setting would be worked in: characterizations, tones of voice, the hesitancies or shrewdnesses or buffooneries, the look of a room, the noises and silences of a conversation—all present there for his listeners in phrases flung out, as it were, casually. And when all had been brought to its conclusion, sealed off with some deceptively offhanded phrase, "There now, lads, what do you make of that?," the story would float for a bit, invisible, and the pleasure of his listeners would be tinged, faintly, by the melancholy attending those arts which vanish forever within the moment of their enactment, the arts of conjurer, dancer, juggler.

It was so with Vincent's story that evening of how he had been confronted by Dennis Tully, and I marked then, not for the first time, of a danger that is given to the skilled storyteller with his gift. For the story may have its meanings packed within it, pregnant phrases and colours, and yet the meaning withheld from the teller himself, unlike the fables of Aesop and La Fontaine, which at the end obligingly disclose their admonitions and exhortations. Certainly as Vincent told me his tale of father and son circling each other like the great cats, a thumb hooked in his waistcoat of violet shot silk with its white sprigs worked upon it, he seemed almost to be asking me to riddle out for him its meaning, and well might it have been had I done so. But I was too intent upon a face in candlelight, and Vincent's voice carried me along with its tone of mischievous merriment.

It was past one when Vincent unlocked the hall door and stepped into the hall, dark now save for the band of yellow light falling into it from the open parlour, but which always, when I had occasion to visit, was a first messenger to me of the Tully prosperity, what with its rich carpeting, a bright rose with yellow squares and lozenges worked into it, and its elaborate coatrack, intricately branched like the antlers of some Highland stag, and the long table with its top of pink marble.

"Vincent," Dennis Tully shouted out to him. "In here. In the parlour."

When Vincent came into the parlour, he said, "I was intending to come in here, Father. I saw the light from the road. What ails you, are you ill?"

"I am not certain," he said. "I might be. I might be ill."

He was sitting, Vincent told me, in the chair the family knew as his, and which even strangers to the room were wary of occupying, as though a bit of his being had leaked into its cushions and heavy arms. A pot of tea stood by his elbow on the small, dark-wooded table. All of the room's gas lamps were ablaze, and the drapes of heavy green velour had been pulled across all but a narrow bar of window, beyond which was the faint-mooned night. It was the chair in which he used take his ease, his bald head with its nimbus of early grey resting against the starchy linen of a needless antimacassar, and his heavy-jowled face in repose, the cheeks full and pink, hands, faintly brown-mottled, resting upon heavy knees. From that chair, sitting thus, he would survey that portion of the world which was his family, his guests—Mary and myself it well might be each fortnight or so, schoolmaster and wife, and Considine, the Catholic doctor, and perhaps Mr. Roberts, the relieving officer. But tonight, he sat forward in his chair, his arms folded across his swelling paunch, and as he sat, he rocked himself gently, back and forward. His head was bent, so that the creases beneath his jaw pressed on one another. Vincent touched the teapot.

"Dear God," he said. "Small wonder. The tea is stone cold. It would sit like ditchwater within you."

"Mary Ellen brought the pot to me before she went off to bed. I had not asked for it, but you know your mother."

Vincent drew out his watch and held it to the lamp. "A glass of port," he said. "It is a sovereign remedy. And I will join you."

As he stood by the sideboard measuring out the glasses from the decanter, the port dark as ink, he talked the while about the lateness of the hour, and the strangeness of finding Dennis still up, sitting alone and silent beside cold tea. But as he talked, he thought.

"I know the hour," Tully said. "And with no help from your elaborate timepiece." Which indeed it was: Vincent had a fondness for flasks, watches, cigar cases. "I have been here, in the parlour. Where have you been?"

"In no respectable place," Vincent said. He carried the glasses with care, for he had filled them close to the brims, but he nevertheless splashed from one of them onto his fingers as he gave it to his father, not the colour now of ink but of plum. "And I had best tell you the truth of it. I was up in the mountains with some of the lads, at Laffan the distiller's. And my head is none too steady, if you must know. You might as well be drinking gunpowder and paraffin as what that lad brews."

"I wonder you have the stomach to put port on top of poteen."

"Where there's a will, there's a way," Vincent said, and sat down facing Tully, with the table between them.

"Who was it went up there with you? Twas a daft thing to do, in the blackness of night."

"By God, it was. But sure, yourself did as daft as that in your own day, no doubt, and worse perhaps."

"I did not. At your age, I was a married man and a father. And the shop to keep me to my task."

"No harm done," Vincent said. "Tis best that wild notions work their way out of the blood in youth. Not that it was so wild a notion as all that. We were after having the parting glass at the Arms, and one of us said, 'By God, the night is young, and there is lashings of drink up the mountain at Laffan's.'"

"And who were these ones you went off with?"

"The usual," Vincent said. "Bob Delaney and a few."

"I wonder Bob had so little sense."

"Sure, it was Bob's notion. There is more to Bob than what you see of him in the shop."

"And Hughie MacMahon?"

"He was not. Mary is not well, and he was the night with her. And as well for his reputation. Twas no prank for a schoolmaster."

Vincent told me that in the minute or two that he had for the contrivance of this fiction, there was another part of his mind picking away at it like a Crown solicitor. Had his father walked round to the shop, or past my own house? But once the horse was launched for the gate, there was no hope save in a cool head and a good hand with the reins. And he had been a practised contriver in such matters, for the father was a constant interrogator of Vincent's doings, with naught to distinguish him from a father confessor save the absence of a grille and the power to absolve sins. But perhaps, I thought, he possessed something akin to that power. Vincent's reckless ways—and I speak now not of rebellions at all, but rather of his ways with girls and horses and gaming tables—were matters into which his father probed and probed, but without wanting ever to know the whole of the truth.

"And this cousin of Hughie's, this Ned Nolan. Was he with you?"

"He was indeed," Vincent said at once, before allowing himself a sip of the port. "Although he has no head for the drink. A glass or two, or perhaps a third, for politeness' sake. But we were glad for his company. A most interesting fellow."

"Interesting," Tully said.

"And well he might be," Vincent said. "Three years he was with the Federal army, fighting in the valleys and mountains of Tennessee and Virginia. And as well as that, he has lived in New York. A travelled man."

"He is indeed. He has travelled now across the water to Kilpeder. Few enough make the journey in this direction."

"Travelled back might be the better word for it. He was born here, he is a Kilpeder man."

"I know that," Tully said. "Tom Nolan's son. I knew Tom Nolan. It was a bright day for Kilpeder when Tom Nolan took his leave of it."

"Perhaps," Vincent said. "I have heard Thomas Justin Nolan's name spoken with respect in this house by Dr. Considine, and by Father Cremin himself."

As no doubt he had, for that is the way of it. The Men of 'Forty-eight, as they were always called, were in those days much revered, as patriots and gentlemen who never sank to ruffian warfare, nor stirred up the violent and ignorant blood of mountainy men and slum dwellers. Unlike, of course, the Fenians, who were condemned by the respectable as so many *sans-culottes*. And yet I have lived to see the Fenians—by which, of course, is meant the "real" Fenians, the Fenians of 'sixty-seven, the Men of Clonbrony Wood, like Vincent and myself, God help us, held up as storybook heroes by which to condemn the Land Leaguers and the Invincibles and the Dynamiters. Time and failure, above all else failure, cast over the past a mantle woven of soft colours and textures.

"Dr. Considine never knew Tom Nolan," Tully said, "and neither did Father Cremin. They are strangers in Kilpeder, for all that they have lived here a few years. Blow-ins. I knew him."

A point well taken. For Thomas Justin Nolan had not contented himself with contributing impassioned essays to the *Nation*. He had done his best to rouse up Kilpeder, haranguing the evicted and the half starved of 'forty-eight to take up pikes and cudgels and sticks. And when that failed, he set off for Tipperary with a half dozen malcontents to join Smith O'Brien. Well would he have been loathed by the Dennis Tully of those days, young then, and by his father, old Malachi, the Founder of the Shop, as he came later to be called. For it was in those days, in the terrible days of the famine and its aftermath, that the foundations of the house of Tully were well and truly laid. And when, in the early sixties, Dennis built the great new shop on the square, he had a stone placed above that door not with that year incised upon it, but rather, the year 1846. Small use would Malachi and Dennis Tully have had for Thomas Justin Nolan.

But Vincent could see well enough the direction in which Tully's words were carrying them, and I could see it myself as Vincent sketched in the scene for me. I could see that parlour, crammed to overflowing with its trophies of Tully prosperity, the oil paintings in their frames of elaborate gilt, the sideboard, the armchairs like ships adrift upon a sea of Turkey carpeting, the overmantel like a cathedral front, the drawn and shielding velour. And I could almost see Tully himself, although he was a bit wavering and indistinct in Vincent's sketch, for although the father served Vincent often as a subject of his satirical portraits, there was within the man a deep and primitive power. What Vincent could not have foretold were Tully's next words.

"I had a visit this night, Vincent, from Sergeant Honan down at the barracks. He was late enough calling in; twas long after you had left for the Arms."

Vincent told me that he made no response, but sat quietly, without taking his eyes from his father, for Tully was one of those who believe that an averted gaze is evidence of wrongdoing.

"He inquired after you," Tully said, "and I said that most likely you were at the Arms with your chums, and from there would be apt to finish off the night at one house or another—Hughie MacMahon's, most likely. Or off into the hills to sample some of the poteen in this cabin or that one, that it is his sworn duty to banish from the barony. Tis a great comfort to a father to predict so well the things that his son will be about."

"If Sergeant Honan does not know about Pat Laffan's bit of poteen, then he is alone in his ignorance," Vincent said, light and wary. The port, which came not from Laffan's still but from the sunbaked hills of Portugal, was rich and cloying on his tongue.

"Ye are not alone when ye find Ned Nolan interesting," Tully said. "The Irish Constabulary are interested in that lad. Interested indeed. And in what friends he may be finding for himself in Kilpeder."

"He has found for himself his own first cousin, Hugh MacMahon," Vincent said. "And Bob Delaney and myself. By God, the Constabulary takes much upon itself, if they have taken to sorting out friendships among the men of Kilpeder."

"Well do you know what I mean, Vincent, and it falls well within their duty. Twas in the strictest confidence that Sergeant Honan spoke to me. Twas out of the goodness of his heart, and out of concern for yourself and for me."

"For me?" Vincent said. "And for yourself?"

"There are desperate men abroad, Vincent, who would bring grief and misery upon us all. You need not go to the barracks to learn that; you have only to go to Mass and attend Father Cremin. He has read them out from the altar, and he has read out the letters from our bishop denouncing them. Those desperate fellows, if they could work their will, there would be blood in the streets of Kilpeder and of every town in Ireland."

"And what has that to do with Ned Nolan?"

"Do you think your own father is a child, Vincent? Or that Dublin Castle is children playing at hurley? Ned Nolan is a known man. He is a sworn Fenian. That was known in New York, and what is known in New

York is known in Dublin Castle. They have been sending over their men for the past six months, ruffians and reprobates with no employment now that their war is ended."

"And Ned Nolan is one of them, is that what Honan came here to tell you?"

"He did more than tell, Vincent. He brought with him and showed me the report from Dublin, with Nolan's name spelled out. And the names of the miscreants who sent him out, and the day of the week that he came to Dublin. All that is known. And it is a report that he risked all by showing to me. 'Most Secret,' it had written above the top of it, above the coat of arms."

"Dear God," I said to Vincent, when he told me that, but Vincent shrugged.

"What else did we expect, Hugh?" he said to me. "The coming of the Yankee officers has been no secret; it has been in the *Cork Examiner*. And the Kilpeder Barracks knows more than that. They know that there is a sworn circle here, because they have listened to public-house boasting. But they are not certain how large it is. They think that you may yourself have been the Centre, but that Ned has come to replace you. Close enough to the mark."

Close indeed. And why I had not expected it, I cannot say. When it comes to agitation or sedition, your schoolmaster is a marked man. It was so in 'forty-eight, and it was to be so again, in the eighties, with the Land League. We are a peaceable lot on the whole, poor devils; indeed, if I needed a word to throw over the lot of us, it would be the word *timorous*, eager to stand well with priests and inspectors and similar dignitaries. But we are educated above our station, and we have our little vanities, our knowledge of Irish history, patriotic poems memorised, and speeches from the dock and all the rest of it. And I must confess that my local predecessors had not created a felicitous tradition, what with Thomas Justin Nolan, and long before him the wild poet and fornicator Owen Ruagh MacCarthy, who had gone off to join the Mayo rebels, and got himself hanged for his trouble. But that anyone should think me the leader of so much as a Temperance sodality gave me a low opinion of the Constabulary, although that was refuted by the document which Honan had carried with him to Tully's.

"But what of Bob and yourself?" I asked, to show a proper concern for the safety of my friends.

"Ah, now there," Vincent said, "we have been shielded by our characters. Bob is ambitious young Bob Delaney, Dennis Tully's shop assistant. And as for me, sure everyone knows about me, women and race meetings and that. A would-be gentleman, a shoneen. Bob is more a Tully than I am myself. All of Kilpeder says that; you have said it yourself. It is what my father believes, if the truth were told."

There was a bitter edge to his words, like a man biting into a sour rind of truth. It had been so almost from the day that first Bob had come down from his father's farm to take up employment in the shop, youngest son of a farmer in middling prosperity, a compact young fellow with the easy yet brisk manner that comes of confidence. I mind that Bob, a pleasing acquaintance who had not yet become a friend, in the Arms of an evening, or in Conefry's, quick banter and wry wit, and yet always that level look from eyes that would be putting a roomful of men into their proper proportions, a bit of himself standing apart from the banter. I mind him in the shop, and how Tully would watch him, pleased and faintly anxious, as might a man discovering that a workhorse of his purchase was a hunter, smooth and capable.

"But with a difference, Vincent," I said. "'Tis yourself that is the Tully by blood, his one son. 'Tis you that he loves."

"I know that," Vincent said. "And for all the fear that his words put into me, I knew that he sat there in grief and alarm. Cornelius Honan has by now his suspicions, do you see, and it was those that he had brought with him to the house. He came to warn me off from Ned and yourself."

"That was decent of him," I said. "He is a decent enough fellow, you know."

But Vincent shrugged again, the fleck of bitterness still upon him. "There are many in the Constabulary who are decent enough when they are let be. But he was more concerned to keep on the right side of Tully and Son. The Ardmors may believe that they own the barony, the Ardmors and the other gentry, with their big houses and their hunt and their pack of hounds, riding across fields with their shouts and flashes of scarlet, like John Peel. Before long, they will be scraped away like the frosting on a wedding cake, and beneath will be Tully and Son."

As he talked, I could see the two of them, Dennis Tully and Cornelius Honan, with their heads bent towards each other. Honan's tall helmet rested apologetically at his boots. He would now and again work in a thick forefinger to loosen his collar, with its stiffening of leather and horsehair. In his hand, he held the report from Dublin, message from a distant empire whose bidding he did. As he talked, he jabbed at it. "No harm in the lad, Mr. Tully. No harm at all, to be sure. A bit wild, as lads are inclined to be these days." Tully nodded, and studied Honan with the mild, clear eyes of a cardsharp. But behind the mild eyes was anger at his son, and fear for him.

[69]

"He drew me out then, Hugh," Vincent said. "He has done it before, on other matters. I know what you think of him, a gombeen man with no more conscience than a badger, but he is shrewd as a badger, like his father before him, the Founder. And the first Tully of all, with his tray of huckster's goods, threads and thimbles for the women." He might have been speaking of one of the dynasties of pharaohs. "He drew me almost over the edge, but I pulled back in time. I'm a Tully myself. But that isn't the proper phrase. He spoke out of what he believes is the truth."

"What I know, Vincent," Tully had said to him, "is this." As he talked, he grasped his fingers one by one, the little one first, as Vincent had often seen him do in the shop, explaining a billing to a farmer. "There is no one in this land wants trouble—the people do not, nor the Church, nor the gentry. We have all of us seen too much of trouble. There is no one wants trouble but the mischief-makers, and it is upon their own heads that they will bring it. There are police stretched across the length and breadth of this island, and very able and well-armed men they are, snug and secure in their strong barracks like the one here. And if the police are not enough, there is the army, and those lads with their bayonets will brook no nonsense. I do not know what these mischief-makers want, but I know what they will bloody well get."

"What they want is a free Ireland," Vincent said. "From all that I have heard."

"A free Ireland!" Tully said. "Yerrah, isn't freedom for the poor country what we all want?"

"Perhaps," Vincent said.

"Is not that what Daniel O'Connell the Liberator was toiling for all of his life? Were we not all enrolled under the banner of the Repeal Association, the priests and all? Toiling and agitating in an orderly and peaceable manner, with no thought of mischief."

"The Fenians have no great regard for your Daniel O'Connell," Vincent said. "He held his monster rallies in this place and that place, and when it suited the English to have done with him, they set the heel of their boot upon him and smashed his movement. And he left the people naked to the fury of the famine when it came a year or two later."

Vincent rose and poured himself another glass of port. His father, his own glass untouched, spoke to his turned back.

"Vincent, Vincent. You must not use such words. You had not even been born when O'Connell first roused up the people. He was a lion of a man. He gave courage to thousands; they sheltered within his voice. We were nothing. Despised. They despised us. He roused up the rocks themselves with his voice. You may speak foolishly in this house, if you must, where there is none to hear us, but I will hear no ill word spoken 'gainst the Liberator."

"He was exactly that," Vincent said. "He was a voice. You have named it. And he was nothing more."

We knew him, Vincent and myself and those our age, from the coloured engravings on our parents' walls, on the walls of public houses, from banners carried in parades and processions. Florid, meaty face, burly-shouldered, one hand on hip, the other raised aloft. As though a tribal chieftain had been crammed into modern dress.

"A voice," Tully said, puzzled.

"He came and he went," Vincent said. "And he left us where Jesus left the Jews. He died off there in Italy, did he not, in the odour of sanctity, in the famine times, while the starving of Ireland stood helpless as they watched the grain and cattle shipped off for the dinner tables of England."

"The famine was a terrible visitation beyond the remedy of man, but it is behind us now, thanks be to God. We are not doing so ill, boy, the Tullys and people like us. Look around you at the furnishings in this room, the tables and all, that many a Protestant would be proud to claim. In Limerick and in Cork City itself, tis said, 'The Tullys. If you intend business in West Cork, it must be with the Tullys.' We are on the move."

As Vincent quoted the words to me, an image rose up before me of the Tullys on the move, a triumphant and irresistible procession. And yet for the Ardmors behind their proud gates and for the other families of the gentry, Tully would always be "Tully the shop," the huckster's cabin remembered. And for the hillside small farmers, that procession would be no rousing spectacle. Gombeen men on the march. Still, you never know. Did not the Fuggers and the Medicis commence in a small way?

"You might fling all that away, Vincent, if you keep in the company of a lad like Nolan. But you must know that yourself, you are a clever lad. You have more within you than Bob Delaney, and a better education was provided you than the schoolmaster enjoys. Hughie MacMahon never saw the inside of the Queen's College."

"And Bob Delaney," Vincent said. "Will you have a similar warning for him?"

"More than a warning, by God," Tully said. "I depend upon Bob, he has been a good man for the shop, but he has no blood of ours. If he brought any disgrace or unrespectability upon the shop, I would turf him out without a pound in his pocket to pay his fare from Queenstown." The ruddy face was screwed tight, as if to hold back tears.

Affection, a heavy, slow-moving beast, stirred within Vincent. He set down his glass, and bending to his father, placed a hand upon his arm.

"The Tullys can never be bested, Father. You have said it yourself. One of us by the one road, and one by another."

"I know nothing of roads," Tully said. "But I know what is best for us." He put his hand on his son's, and held it tight.

And so Vincent left him and went up to his room. But he paused at the door. His father sat immobile. He sat with his head twisted away from the door, towards the heavy pink-and-white marble of the fireplace, as though the cool, pretty stone held reassurance.

"And there you have it," Vincent said to me. "He has his suspicions, but he dares not utter them, lest they should come to pass. He has his superstitions as well, you see."

"He loves you, Vincent," I said. "And he is frightened for you. He is right to be frightened."

"Is he not?" Vincent said. "But for once time is with us. You can feel it in the countryside. It is drawing to a head. By God, Hugh. What a day it will be!"

In candlelight, Nolan smiled at me. A death's-head.

"One Tully by one road, and one by another," Vincent said.

From his handsome cigar case, he took out two cigars, and as he held the light to mine, there was a flash of gold from his cuff link, in its setting of snowy linen. He smiled at me, at his father, at himself. He had the gift of grace. An unexpected gift, putting to shame the savants, with their charts of traits passing down from one generation to the next. A heavy, ponderous race, the Tullys, save for Vincent.

A dynasty of the pharaohs. When I call up Dennis Tully to memory, it is always in the shop or in the fine, crowded house that I see him, and never standing apart, with clear space shaping itself behind him. And yet I must often have seen him so, climbing down the church steps after Mass, or walking across the square, hat firmly anchored. Always, I see him moving among things, a thick atmosphere of objects.

The shop was choked with them—flitches of bacon, shovels and spades, barrels of flour, brooms, bottles of liniment, sweets for the children, jars of preserves, bolts of cloth, kegs of nails, boards, tea bins. Behind the long counter were rows of drawers and cubbyholes, cavernous ones by the floor, and ranging by size upwards towards the ceiling, at the top small and mysterious. Bob Delaney kept these neatly labelled, but Tully had no need for the writing. He knew the contents of each minute drawer by the graining of the wood, imperfections of varnish.

Bland and alert, he moved from keg to bin. Each transaction, however complicated, whatever its proportions of credit and cash, was a set of figures and a total prompt and exact in his brain. Those totals he would write out on slips of paper for his customers, of whom many could neither read nor write, frieze-clad or black-skirted and cloaked. But for Tully, those transformations of copper and shilling were not complete until Bob had entered them in one of the ledgers. All day, the duplicate slips would be skewered on a spindle, and an hour before closing time, Bob would take them to the ledgers. The ledgers were mysteries, for into them the interest was added, and then, regularly, compounded. And in this manner, things—nails and sweets and heels of tobacco—would be rendered wholly ethereal, invisible and impalpable, without odour save the faint perfume of dried ink. But in time it, whatever it was, would rematerialise, a kind of transubstantiation, would become a dinner service, a set of velour drapes, schooling at Queen's for Vincent and with the Ursulines for Agnes.

It was always said in Kilpeder that Tully took his first step into moneylending, into setting up as a gombeen man in the full sense of that term, by way of obliging a farmer named Matthew Dennehy, one of the Ardmor tenants, who had fallen four full quarters in arrears, and with his notice served upon him by old Everard Chute, who was in those days agent of the estate. I do not know if this is history or legend, but Dennehy was still alive when I first took the school, and it was my whimsy to study him as one might an historical survival, as one might, perhaps, some ancient half-pay captain who had once hurled snowballs against the infant Bonaparte at Brienne.

I imagined them sitting together, at night, a bottle between them, in the old shop at the end of the lane. And Dennehy, between sips, between cracks of his big-boned knuckles, is saying again that he does not know which way to turn. At last, delicately, frightened of the momentous step, Tully says, "You know, Matt, there may be a way out of this." And Dennehy, who has been staring at the dirt floor, looks up at him. "Tis how the shop has done well this year, thanks be to God, and I have the odd pound set by." And then, eyes slightly averted from Dennehy's beseeching gaze, he takes a deep breath. "But the way of it is, Matt, I would want a bit more back than I might be able to give you. . . . When you are back on your feet, to be sure. That is only right and fair, is it not? Tis no more nor less than what I do when I give out provisions on credit to yourself and the other lads." And Dennehy says at once, the words tumbling over each other in his excitement, "Right and fair indeed, Dennis. You have a family of your own to consider." Tully takes out a bit of paper, works out what the whole amount will be, the sum advanced and the bit extra, and passes it over to Dennehy, who screws up his eyes. Then he pours out another tot of whiskey for the two of them. Nothing is written out and signed. The whiskey sets the bargain.

But in the years that came, there were other clients, and in time there were notes to be signed, drawn up by Cornelius Hallinan the Catholic solicitor, with schedules of payment and specified penalties. That was the wonder and mystery of the ledgers. Paper made paper. Numbers communed with one another, coupled and spawned. And in time, Bob Delaney became the cute lad from the country with a talent for numbers, who could keep track of their breeding and their progeny. Tully, as Bob once told me, was made uneasy by Hallinan, a smooth, smiling man with irritating pretensions and social graces, guardian of the sacred laws of conveyancing. Hallinan kept his own carriage and team, was on terms of easy familiarity with Protestant solicitors and estate agents. But Bob had been a genie, summoned forth when he was most needed, as though Tully had given a chance rub to a magic jar strayed onto his shelves. And there was more to it than that, as anyone with eyes could see, although Bob never spoke the words aloud, neither to me nor to anyone else.

Tully must often have measured Bob and Vincent, the one against the other, and wondered which was the son. Vincent must have seemed to him an exotic graft upon Tully stock, reckless and generous, careless with money and words, and Bob the inheritor of the Tully shrewdness, who could manage numbers as ably as Tully, could unroll bolts of cloth, gauging their lengths against his forearm, or as old Malachi, the Founder, could sort out his trays of goods, his trinkets and his paper spills of sugar to sweeten the tea of cottiers.

A dynasty of the pharaohs. There were old Kilpeder men who remembered when Malachi set up shop in the cabin in the lane, which in my day served Tully and Son as a storehouse, as it still does. A huckster's shop, of a sort that may yet be found in a half-hundred towns, counter and a few shelves, ill lit, a smell of tallow, a trade in coppers and shillings, promises to pay, never a pound note handed over from one year to the next. It would have been in those years, the early years of the century, a dark lane, filth in the roadway, and the foulings of horse and ass, acrid stench of piss too ordinary to be noticed. The square beyond was already the glory of West Cork, with its handsome market house of cool grey stones where Ellen had once seen Art O'Leary, handsome and brave, but not then an obelisk for an Ardmor heir as yet unborn. And as yet no Catholic church, but a chapel only, the shadows of penal days dark upon it. The gates of the Ardmor demesne, falcon-globed, thrust themselves outwards into the square. Through them would roll the carriages of the gentry to their dinners and balls, and distant, invisible behind plantations, the tall windows of Ardmor Castle ablaze with candlelight, music unheard in dirty laneways filling the high-ceilinged rooms. In those days, it is said, the Kilpeder people would crowd themselves on either side of the gates to huzzah the splendid guests in their silks and broadcloths, a practice which was later to fall into disfavour. But on such evenings, the Malachi of my imagination would tarry within the shop, casting up his accounts as best he could, being unable to read or write.

And Malachi himself, whence had he sprung? Not from these baronies, surely, where the surname is otherwise unknown. A pedlar's son, perhaps, growing up on the tramp with his father, the father in the breeches and swallowtail of olden times, pack slung across his back, stout ashplant thrust before him, walking the roads of Munster, long-striding, and the young Malachi at a half run behind him, barefoot. Beyond that, clouded over by the mists of time, nothing.

"And there you have it," Vincent said to me again, studying his evenly burning cigar, pale hand steady. "An impressive man, our Captain Nolan. The genuine article."

"Tis the genuine article that we are in need of."

Fragrant smoke drifted between us.

I remembered standing at the door to the kitchen, where Ned sat with the whiskey, smiling, the room dark behind him.

"I thought you were long abed," I said to him.

"No more than yourself." He raised the bottle from the table, and held it towards me.

"A short one, perhaps," I said, and took a glass from the dresser. I sat down facing him, and he splashed whiskey in my glass and his own. "Good luck," I said.

"Yes," Ned said. "Good luck." He moved his glass in a circle on the table and then lifted it. His shirt was unfastened at the collar, and despite the chill of the room he had unbuttoned his jacket.

"Well, Ned," I said. "What do you make of us? A sorry lot of warriors, are we not?"

But he did not answer me. Instead, he drank off what was in his glass, and poured himself more.

"Those lads," he said suddenly. "You know each one of them, and I do not."

"Ach," I said, puzzled. "I do and I don't. Some of them I have known for years, and others of them I know the family well enough but not the lad himself. Is that what you mean? Do you mean can we depend upon them?"

"A day has been fixed, Hugh. If no orders come to us otherwise, we will take the barracks. We will leave twenty men behind to hold it, and the rest of us will move north, towards Millstreet. If we take it, that is."

"Why should we not take it," I said, "with yourself here to instruct us in the ways and means of it?"

He smiled at me again. "I know the ways and means of it. You do yourself, if you put your mind to it. We surround the barracks, and shout out to the sergeant to hand over. Then he unlocks the door, and he and his men come out and make a neat stack of their carbines for us." In candlelight, the long, narrow head nodded. "Tis a simple task."

"Indeed it is not," I said, appalled by what I took to be his innocence. "You would not say the like if you knew Cornelius Honan. There is not a sergeant in the Constabulary more proud of his stripes. He has been in for eighteen years, the son of a landless man in County Limerick."

"Are you friends, by any chance?" Ned said casually.

It was a curious question to put to a Fenian, and I began to answer accordingly, but then I paused. Honan was a heavy, solid man, as sergeants should be, tall and beefy, and although he had the makings of a paunch which no tunic could hide, his back was as straight as though made of oak planking. When he walked, the whole leg swung forward, massive as the trunk of a young tree, and the step set down firmly, and with deliberation. But the massive head, although moulded to scale, was not menacing. Indeed, there was often to the face a soft, questioning look, the lips parted in a half smile, and the mild blue eyes direct and candid.

Two score of times at least Con Honan and I had been together, schoolmaster and sergeant, passing the time of day in the market square, or after Mass on Sunday, exchanging affable, casual words. We had been six or seven times together when there was dancing and music at one of the outlying farms, the air busy with shouts and the sounds of the fiddle, and Honan standing against a wall with men his age, too dignified for the dancing, a pint of porter in one hand, and the thumb of the other hooked into his belt. Later, as well he knew, after he had left, there would be poteen from Laffan's or one of the other stills, an outlaw spirit, colourless and potent. It was one reason why he never tarried too late, a delicate tact belying his bulk.

"No," I said. "Not friends."

But at that moment, the moment of my response, I remembered such a night, at Michael Joe Grennan's, standing with Bob Delaney and a red-haired, hard-drinking man named Paudge Skerrett and Michael Joe himself. A young fellow with a lovely dark-hued voice had favoured the house with a song, and after the last notes had died away, I took it upon myself to explain to those with me why it is sung with one set of words in Connaught and a different set here in Munster. "Now, that is curious,"

[76]

said Honan, who had heard me, and now moved over to us. "Limerick is in Munster, but tis what you call the Connaught version that is sung in Newcastle West, but not entirely the same." And in a soft, low voice, which did not carry far beyond the five of us, he half sang and half spoke the words, in an Irish so pure as to have roused the envy of a Gaelic scholar. When he had come to his close, Michael Joe put a hand upon his shoulder, and said, "Good man yourself, Sergeant," the hand resting on the tunic of that uniform which was our own and yet not ours.

"We have drunk together," I said to Ned, amending my words, "but we are not friends."

"Then you will not mind killing him," Ned said. "Drink up," he said, splashing more whiskey into what was in my glass, and replenishing his own. "Tis with me that you are drinking now, and not with Sergeant Honan."

I looked up from our two glasses into his shadowed, half-hidden eyes, and thought of Mary asleep above, how her sleeping hand had rested in my own. Candlelight touched hearth, dresser. Beyond was darkness.

"Oh, yes," he said. "Why else have you been drilling men, and why else are we waiting for arms? Why else did we take the oath? Honan will not hand over the barracks to us if he has manhood in him at all. A few of his will be killed, and a few of ours. Honan himself perhaps, perhaps you, perhaps me."

I lifted my glass then, and knocked back the whiskey without tasting or feeling it. Ned was smiling again, the mirthless smile with which he had greeted me.

A score of times, at the drilling, I had heard Bob use words about dying for Ireland, and we had used them as often amongst ourselves, sitting in the parlour of this house, or had heard them in the songs that Vincent sang in his high, sweet tenor, to Mary's accompaniment, the two of them held in candlelight not harsh and lurid like this, but soft, touching hair, hands. The minstrel boy, his father's sword girded on, went out into the wars and to death; glory guarded the graves of Clanricarde and Owen Roe. The songs never spoke of killing for Ireland, never about killing, perhaps, Sergeant Honan, who had a song of his own, purer and more Irish than the ballads of Thomas Davis and Tommy Moore.

Ned nodded, the slow, grave nod of a master admitting a neophyte to a mystery, and put whiskey in my glass. A sacrament.

"Or perhaps a constable of his," he said. "A country lad like those we were with tonight."

"You spoke the words yourself tonight," I said, "at Knockmany. They are England's army in Ireland. Armed and uniformed."

"Yes," Ned said.

But the words as I spoke them were words only, rustling newsprint. A rebellion had shrunk to a town, and the town to a kitchen, the kitchen to two men facing each other across a table. Dark night covered us, and I felt an unreasoning spurt of anger against those unknown men in Dublin and New York, happy at their intrigues and grandiose plans, their mock-heroic paper campaigns and their sunbursts of oratory. My rebellion would be a kitchen table, a police barracks, Ned Nolan's American revolver.

"Easy enough for you," I said, without caring if my resentment showed. "A soldier trained and shaped in their great war."

I tasted the second glass, right enough, rough and unwatered, a strong fire in my mouth.

"But that is it, Hugh," Ned said. "That is it. I have told you. I was a corporal, a flea's jump above a private soldier. We were most of the time in encampments, or on the tramp between this place and that. And the battles were for us like skirmishes, firing off our rifles and fixing our bayonets and rushing forward when we were bid. It was not my life, but a dream into which I had tumbled. Wars are for generals and colonels, and young majors, perhaps, on their tall horses shouting out orders that no one can hear because of the cannon."

"You were a soldier tonight, by God," I said, and finished off my glass. "None of us had ever seen the like of it. Pat Dunphy would follow you to hell from this night on."

"Pat Dunphy *will* follow me to hell," Ned said. "Mind your subjunctives and your indicatives, Schoolmaster MacMahon."

He twisted his empty glass in his hand, and then held it towards me, and the hand was steady as a stone.

"Don't be a miser with your whiskey, Cousin Hugh," he said. "My father used praise to me the generosity of the MacMahons. The Nolans for liberality, he used say, and the MacMahons for generosity. Is that still said in Kilpeder?"

"I have never heard it," I said. "A short one for each of us, Ned. And then we will cork the bottle."

But it was a good measure that I poured for each of us, although when I had done so, I put in the cork, and gave it a hard rap with the heel of my hand. Ned glared at me, but then shrugged and nodded.

"Tis late," he said.

"Tis," I said. "And I must rise early to instruct the youth of Kilpeder in the uses of the subjunctive."

"*Should* and *would*," Ned said. "We would sit talking together but we should not. We would free Ireland, and therefore we should shoot Sergeant Honan. Should Sergeant Honan shoot us?"

"Tis late, Ned," I said.

"He put on the uniform of his own choice," Ned said, "and took his oath to Queen Victoria. He was not conscripted."

"True enough," I said, although I reflected that hardship is a good recruiting sergeant, and that for the most part the Constabulary occupied itself with innocuous tasks. It would require patriotism more sturdy than my own to think of them as spurred and booted Cossacks.

"You must remember that," Ned said. "You must all of you remember that."

But I knew, in that moment, that it was himself to whom Ned was talking. And I was in later years to remember it, when Ned Nolan's was a name with which to frighten the young, a hard man, as hard as the Invincibles, without mercy or compassion within him. What happened to Ned in Portland Prison is known to many, and what happened in the years of wandering that followed may be guessed at; but I know of my own knowledge that it was not so always. When Ned would lead us out upon the appointed day, there might some of us be killed, and we might kill others, and it would be at Ned's command. That is why he had been awake in the kitchen, with no company save for the bottle, and why he had given me that terrible, humourless smile.

"Time to draw the blinds, Ned," I said. "Time to call it a night."

"Right," Ned said, and drank off his drink. And he rose then to his feet as steadily as if he had been at work at a carafe of water.

An expression only, "to draw the blinds," for there was neither blind nor curtain to the kitchen window, nor need for any. Before blowing out the candle, I walked over for a minute to that window, and behind me I heard Ned's footfall as he left the room. The moon must have been behind clouds, for I was looking into blackest night, and saw naught save distorted light reflected from the windowpane. What history can ever be written truly, whether of the Fenians of Kilpeder or of the empire of the Assyrians? Young Mr. Prentiss never asks about conversations in kitchens, nor would he care that the words spoken in them have the feel of the table's oak beneath my fingertips, the taste of unwatered whiskey upon my tongue, nor that, later, the words spoken, the world beyond the windowpane was black and invisible, frightening: Kilpeder itself, the barony, the encircling mountains, and beyond them rivers, towns, cities, armies, ports, prisons, and oceans. Turning back into the room, I blew out the candle, feeling its warmth against my shielding hand.

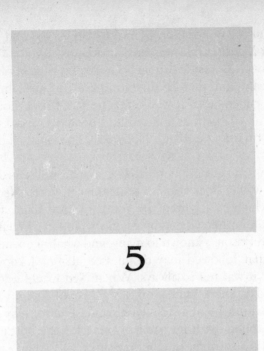

5

[Patrick Prentiss]

On a fair evening in the lime green of a Munster June, Patrick Prentiss walked for the first time between the globed and falcon-guarded gates of Castle Ardmor, putting behind him the town of Kilpeder as completely as though he had stepped from one planet to another. A minute before, he had been in the market square itself, an absent eye upon the Arms, upon Tully and Son, Henefy the butcher's, Conefry's public house, and a minute afterwards, he was within woodlands, oak and pale-leafed larch.

He passed, on his right, a gate lodge, no longer tenanted, minute but Palladian, with two small Doric columns supporting an ornamental porch. Old leaves lay piled against its door. Before him, a straight avenue drove through the woods, its surface broken by ancient carriage ruts, hoof marks. New grass sprouted within the ruts. Homing birds circled above the trees.

Where the woods thinned away was pastureland, enclosed by iron railing. Within, beneath two distant oaks, black cattle lay awaiting the herdsman. Beyond the pastureland, on his left, were other woods, and a stream which flowed towards the Sullane from a sheet of lake. A small, high-arched bridge crossed the stream, and beyond, at the far side of the lake, was a small stone pier, almost an ornament, although a boat rode moored to it, flat and low in the water. Beyond the lake, framed by a screen of elms, a wooden summer house, round, with a conical roof. It was a scene familiar to Prentiss from Japanese prints, and he knew that this was precisely the effect it had been contrived to create upon visitors when once they had driven past the woods. And contrived with something subtler, more artful, than mere carefulness. Stream, lake, bridge, pier, summer house, almost the very cattle restful beneath their wide-armed oaks, had been brought within a design at once deliberate and casual.

Ardmor Castle itself lay a good distance beyond, austere and graceful. It, too, had been created with an eye towards its effect upon the traveller, but an eye different from that which had employed bridge, pier, and summer house to provide a moment of Japanese astonishment. The tall Palladian windows, as Prentiss approached the Castle, held the last light of evening sun, soft and cool, a play of light between great Portland blocks. The avenue ended at an arc of gravelled drive, along which he walked to the entrance. But, close at hand, the white paint of the window casings was chipped and weather-stressed. The steps which he mounted to the door were streaked with dried mud, pale brown.

It was Hugh MacMahon who had suggested that Prentiss talk with Lionel Forrester one afternoon as they stood on a low hill with the Castle and its demesne in view. "He was here in Kilpeder in 'sixty-seven, you know. The Earl was not; he was off in Cambridge for his education. But Lionel was here, on one of his visits to the Earl's mother."

Prentiss smiled doubtfully. "There is little about the Fenian rising," he said, "that could be told me by the cousin of an earl."

"He would be a pleasant man for you to meet, all the same," Mac-Mahon said. "A bit of an historian, like yourself. A writer, at any rate. Essays and books of travel—a few romances. I have the most of them. A matter of local pride." But Prentiss shook his head.

As they walked, the Castle remained in view, its great bulk reduced in size to that of a doll's house, the lake an irregular mirror, green-silvered. There was no path from the hill, and they made their way through nettles and tall grasses, MacMahon swinging at them absently with his thorn stick. The Sullane flowed beyond the demesne's far wall, in sun or tree-shadowed.

"We are two worlds here," he said. "Ours and theirs. Their world is half the story." He paused and turned towards Prentiss. "You must know that yourself. Your story ends at Brierly Lodge."

Prentiss shook his head again. "Ned Nolan killed that man in 1892, a quarter century after the Rising." But stirred by curiosity, he said, "Was Forrester there that night, at the Lodge?"

"Indeed he was not. He was Lord Ardmor's cousin, and by then the houses of the gentry were closed to the Ardmors. A peculiar business. The Ardmors were the most grand of all the families. They still are. Belted earls. There was a time when they owned the town of Kilpeder, as casually as a man might own a pasture, or a fishing lodge in Connemara. But after the days of the Land War, certain doors were closed to them. It was a bitter time."

"You know him, then," Prentiss asked, "Lionel Forrester?"

"I see him no more than three, perhaps four or five times a year. He comes in autumn for the shooting, and then again in the spring. We exchange books. In the autumn, without fail, he sends over grouse, pheasant, and every year or two there will be some new book of his own with them. A lovely small book he has published on the hill towns of Italy, illustrated by himself. Lord Ardmor lives there now, in the hills below Florence. He is never here."

"Never?"

"He left Kilpeder for good in 1892, the year that his wife died, over in London. Twice he has been back, upon estate business, and when it was attended to he set off again. Save for a handful of farms, the Ardmor lands have been sold out up to the walls of the demesne. They were a great people once, the Ardmors, with farms stretching out along the county road to the Kerry border, and northwards towards Millstreet. They were once landlords to my own people, the MacMahons, and to the Nolans as well, if it comes to that. Times change, even in this wretched backwater."

They had begun to walk again, and now a plantation hid half the Castle from view, as though a cloud had passed over it.

"But you must be friends," Prentiss persisted, "yourself and Forrester. Why else would he send you his books, braces of grouse?"

"I have never mastered the preparation of such creatures," MacMahon said, "hanging and all the rest of it. The poor being lies there on my counter, with its plumage growing dull, and its open eye like a bead of dark glass. The books are more welcome, to tell you the uncivil truth. A great gift he has for bringing far-off places before you with but a stroke or two—the sun upon fishermen's nets, or the women in Sicily leaving Mass on a Sunday, dark and silent. No, not friends. There is his world, and there is mine."

They had come down from the hill by now, and walked across a field to the road. The smell of clover was in the air, and its flowers starred the grasses. They walked in a companionable silence, but Prentiss sensed that MacMahon was leaving something unsaid. He did not speak, content that his newfound friend, for so he had begun to think of him, should be alone with some past or other. Then, at last, with an elaborate casualness, MacMahon said, "But Forrester knew Bob Delaney well. You see, Bob and Ardmor were friends."

"*Lord* Ardmor?" Prentiss said incredulously. Ardmor Castle, and a room in the back of Tully's shop, the smell of provisions.

"Not in your time," MacMahon said, almost curtly. "Not in the time of Clonbrony Wood. It was much later, in the days of the League, when Bob was organising the farmers. In the days of the boycotting and the Parnell agitation."

A dry wall separated them from the road, unmorticed stones placed carefully, one upon another. Beyond the road, the turf smoke rose from a cabin, pungent yet sweet, an odour which always afterwards, in London, would summon Ireland from Prentiss's memory, speaking to him of roads, cabins, a curlew's cry. It was a mean cabin, the thatch old and discoloured. Outside its open door, hens pecked at a dunghill. The ground was level now, and the Castle and its demesne invisible. Only fields now, the cabin, the bend of road. The cabin was mud-walled, smeared with whitewash—a labourer's cottage, or a herdsman's.

"Bob Delaney of those years," MacMahon said, "I cannot say which of us knew him better, myself or Ardmor. And yet he was always, even at the end, the one closest to me, save for Mary. Closer, perhaps, than my own sons. But we took different roads out of Clonbrony Wood, Bob and Ned and Vincent and myself."

"Delaney's road took him to Parliament," Prentiss said.

MacMahon nodded. "To Parliament," he said, "and elsewhere. Twould be a great pity, Patrick, if you were all this time in Kilpeder and without talking to Lionel Forrester." He rested his hand on the wall, his absent gaze upon the cabin. "A great pity," he said.

And so Prentiss, from the Arms, had sent up his note, stiffly and formally written. Dublin barrister's son, Clongowes Woods College, scholar of Oxford. He had an uneasy sense that for all that, he, no less than a Delaney or a MacMahon, was approaching a half world that was not his. But the reply was informality itself, a scrawl on a half sheet of plain paper. "By all means. Come whenever you like. Tuesday evening, if it is convenient."

The bellpull sounded a muted clamour somewhere within, and presently the door was opened by a middle-aged woman in a dress of black stuff, thin-featured, her greying hair pulled back into a knot. Prentiss handed her Forrester's note, and without reading it, she said, "Good evening, Mr. Prentiss. Thank you. I will take you down to Mr. Forrester, in the library. He told me that you might be calling in. But you need not have walked; we could have sent the trap for you."

He followed her down the wide hallway, lighted only, through the arched window at its far end, by the declining sun. "It was a pleasant walk," he said. "The grounds of the Castle are lovely." He mocked his own words as he heard them, the language of an historical romance. But what else could they be called?

"Lovely indeed," she said, without turning back towards him. "There was once a time—" she said, and then broke off. "They will be yet lovelier in a few weeks, when the trees are at their full." It was an Irish accent, but not West Cork, a touch of harshness to it.

The paintings startled him, not at all what he had expected—gravy-coloured landscapes, ancestors in scarlet coats, masters and mistresses stiff upon terraces, beside them children, sober in velvet and sprigged muslin, clutching hoop or striped ball in proof of infancy. These paintings, even in dim light, were vivid and airy, splashes of weightless warmth. He paused before one, silvery mist on a half-hidden river, two figures, dimly visible, sexless, on the river's far bank. Beyond, buildings coloured peach, lemon, persimmon. River, buildings, figures alike were dissolving into mist.

"That is Lord Ardmor's," she said.

"French," Prentiss said. "He must be fond of the French."

"He painted it," she said. "All the paintings here in the hall are his, and those in the back drawing room as well. The Rose Room, Lady Ardmor used always call it. It is a great pity that these ones do not have better light."

She opened a door, then stepped back. In the room a man came forward from the library table beside which he had been standing. "Mr. Prentiss?" Forrester said. "You are most welcome."

The library, unlike the hallway, was what Prentiss had expected of Ardmor Castle—dark, high-ceilinged, a wall of tall windows fronting the terraces, and the other walls, deep-shadowed, shelved and book-laden, save for an immense stone fireplace, its marble bright against darkness. Flames danced within its cavernous recess.

"It is good of you to see me," Prentiss said.

"Not good at all," Forrester said. "More curiosity than courtesy. Historians are rare in Kilpeder. You may be our very first. Save, of course, for Hugh MacMahon. MacMahon is well? Still in his hermitage?"

A lean face, touched with red at the cheeks, pale blue eyes, brown hair flecked heavily with grey, the nose thin and high-arched. He was dressed in rough tweeds, blue tie loosely knotted. He smiled as he spoke, the smile, like his note, casual and distant.

They sat facing each other in deep chairs, beside the fire. Forrester offered a cigarette from a box of ivory and sandalwood, bazaar ware for tourists.

"You see, MacMahon wrote me about you. You are a fellow of prodigious learning, he tells me, for all your youth. Oxford."

"New College," Prentiss said, a bit stiffly.

"When I was at Magdalen, your shop had no great name for prodigious learning. Times change. Are you long down?"

"Three years," Prentiss said. "Four." He shifted in his chair. "Hugh MacMahon, I have discovered, is a man with ironies."

"Not on that subject. He has great respect for learning. Now, Tom Ardmor is Cambridge, he was at Cambridge in 'sixty-seven. I was here myself, though. By chance, almost. That is your"—he hesitated for a word—"your subject, is it not, the Rising and Clonbrony Wood, and the rest of it?"

"My subject is the Fenian movement," Prentiss said. "But it is a difficult subject to give a shape to. There are no records, in the proper sense of the word. My notion is that if I could understand Clonbrony Wood—"

"Yes," Forrester said at once, with a kind of eagerness.

"You agree?" Prentiss said, surprised.

Forrester waved his hand, scattering the plume of cigarette smoke. "About Clonbrony Wood? I know very little about Clonbrony Wood. How could I?" The gesturing hand spoke for him. How could this room, the hand said, know of the world beyond the demesne, the conspiracies of labourers and shop assistants?

"Eternity in a grain of sand," Forrester said. "Do young men read Blake these days? There was a cult of Blake when I was young. Rossetti's brother found him in a barrow, so the legend went. Found his book, that is. Yeats claims that he was Irish, like everyone else. But if, indeed, one could take a moment of history, a week, a month, and know it fully, perfectly, turn it in one's fingers until all the lights had played upon its surfaces. . . . That is what you have in mind, is it not?"

"No," Prentiss said, taken aback by an encounter with metaphysics in Kilpeder, "not really. You credit me with too much originality."

"Perhaps," Forrester said. "Or perhaps you do yourself an injustice."

The room was half light, half shadow, the tall books in shadow, but cool sunlight spilling in from the terrace windows. In the distance, beyond the windows, an horizon of mountains.

"They were very odd for us, those weeks in February," Forrester said. "Frightening, yet not perhaps as frightening as they might have been. We never doubted that the Rising, if it ever came at all, would be put down. Not after the army was moved in. It was what might happen before then. Our houses, the houses of the gentry, were scattered, you see. The army could offer us no real protection, nor the police, either. Isabel—Lady Ardmor, Tom's mother—would be saying at one moment that the servants should be armed, and at the next that they could none of them be trusted."

"And could they have been trusted?" Prentiss said.

"Oh, I expect so," Forrester said. "In the event, only two of them were out with the rebels. One of the undergardeners, and the son of the head gardener. Dinny—I think that was the lad's name—did six months in Richmond Prison, and then came back home. Isabel set him to work again with his father. It was that kind of time."

He was a tall man, sparely built, long legs stretched towards the fire. The weathered boots were beautifully polished.

"That kind of time," Prentiss said.

He could almost see Dinny, defeated hero, cap twisted in nervous fingers, and sheepish, uncertain smile.

"Or so it was here," Forrester said. "At Ardmor. But not everywhere. After the Rising, some of the lads who had been out were turfed out from their holdings. The smaller landlords were furious, as you can imagine. Nolan had raided them for arms, you know. Nolan gave a focus to their anger. Outside agitator stirring up the loyal peasantry. And in the next breath, they were denouncing every Catholic in Ireland as treasonous. A peppery lot, the minor gentry of Cork. Do you know them at all?"

Prentiss shook his head. But he imagined them, as a moment before he had imagined Dinny. Red cheeks and choleric voices.

"One night," Forrester said, "after the arms raid but before the Rising, there was a meeting of them at Christopher Pierson's. No, by God, no, it was not at Christopher's, it was at Johnny Boyle's place, Brierly Lodge. That is, in 1867, it was Johnny Boyle's place. When Nolan came back, a quarter century later, to do his killing, Johnny was long gone. Sold out and long dead, no doubt, or living in digs somewhere in London. A coincidence, though, for all that." He leaned forward, and tossed his cigarette into the fire.

"When Ned Nolan came back." First MacMahon, and now Forrester. As though the Rising had not had its ending on that winter's afternoon in Clonbrony Wood.

"I was there that night," Forrester said. "Representing the family, so to speak, in Tom's absence. In the old days, in Tom's father's day, we would have been meeting here at the Castle. But with Johnny in the Lodge, Brierly was more club than lodge. Johnny was a widower, both his boys off in the army. A decent fellow, ex-army himself. He couldn't understand why Government had let the thing go on this long, why they hadn't smashed the Fenian centres, and flung the leaders into gaol. None of us could, for that matter. And the arms raids had given us all a scare. Brierly Lodge itself had been raided, and Johnny held up at pistol point. His rifles and shotguns taken, and even his service revolver."

A portrait hung above the fireplace: a woman, slender, black-gowned. Prentiss was sitting too close to the fire to see it properly. Foreshortened, it was almost an abstraction: black, ivory, a splash of vermillion, the bright background indistinct, a warm peach. As Forrester spoke, Prentiss rested his eyes upon it.

"This is the sort of thing you will need to know, is it not?" Forrester asked courteously, a shade dryly. "The Rising, from a landlord's point of view?"

"It is indeed," Prentiss said quickly, as though Forrester had discovered in him some lack of manners.

"It is all I have that would be of use to you, I fear. When the trouble came, the battle of Kilpeder, as they call it now—in later years, I used to be certain that we had heard it all, here in the Castle: the gunfire, the attack on the barracks. I used to describe it, very vividly. Isabel and myself standing out there on the terrace, looking anxiously towards the town, the servants terrified. Perhaps we did. Certainly we should have heard the gunfire. It was a fierce fight of its kind. It was all long ago."

In Prentiss's imagination they stood together on the winter terrace, a woman of middle years and her nephew. Beyond them, terraced lawns, a lake edged with leafless willows, a sheen of ice. Beyond the demesne walls, perhaps beyond sight, although the Castle stood on a slight eminence, bands of men moved along the street towards the barracks. The sound of gunfire, and perhaps of shouts, a scream. But the watching figures, the woman and the young man, had but to step back inside the morning room and tea would be waiting for them by a fire, a rack of buttered toast.

But something nagged at Prentiss, disturbing the tableau, and he suddenly realised what it was.

"It was snowing," he said. "The weather bitter cold and a heavy snowfall."

"Yes," Forrester said. "The snow of the Fenians, the country people came to call it." And then, realising the point of Prentiss's words, he smiled. It was a smile of delight, and it brightened his face. He nodded towards Prentiss, and it was as though, at last, they had moved past courtesy to touch one another. "A very heavy fall of snow. It had begun the evening before, and continued all through the night, and through a part of the day itself. It was the snow that sealed the Rising into failure, people said, all across the south. Munster and Leinster alike. There was a high wind as well, and later there was a much heavier snow and the mountain passes were sealed off."

Prentiss waited.

"There would have been snow on the terrace, and we could not have seen beyond the nearest lawn. I remember the snow very clearly. I remember, I think I remember, standing by that window, right there, that one, looking out at it. But in my other memory, Isabel and myself on the terrace, looking towards gunfire, towards the battle of Kilpeder, there is no snow. There is a scattering of dried leaves on the flagstones, from the sycamores. Isabel is wearing a short jacket, brown or black, with fur at the collar. Her hand rests on my forearm. Through clear air, I am looking towards woods, naked branches, the lake."

A great gift for bringing scenes before you with a stroke or two, MacMahon had said of Forrester.

"Well, Mr. Prentiss," Forrester said. "Well, well. History."

"As you say," Prentiss said, "it was a long time ago." He hesitated. "Perhaps there is some reason why you remembered it as you did."

"Some reason," Forrester said.

The woman who had admitted Prentiss brought them tea, setting it out on the low table between their chairs, a service of elaborate silver, dull, spots of tarnish. The fluted cups were Chinese, a pattern of reds and browns.

"Shall I pour for you?" she asked.

"No need for that, Emily," Forrester said. "Thank you. We can manage."

"Toast," she said, "and a few currant buns that I had the girl heat up. Will that do you?" She smiled at Forrester.

"Will that do us, Mr. Prentiss? I think so, Emily. Yes."

"She is not a local?" Prentiss said, when she had closed the door behind her.

"Emily?" Forrester said, with his hand upon the teapot. "She is from

Westmeath, near Mullingar. But she has lived much of her life outside Ireland. And she is not the housekeeper here, Mr. Prentiss. Emily is my companion, and has been for many years. We are friends, Emily and I. Visitors to Kilpeder, on occasion."

Deftly, he poured tea, hot water.

"Emily and I travel light," Forrester went on, "but always with our tea. The Castle is closed, much of the year. When we are here, Evans, Tom's agent, sends up girls from the town to do for us." He stirred his tea. "Some reason," he said again. "What reason? Now, that meeting of the landlords at Brierly Lodge. You may be certain about that, at least; set down that as history. I found it curious, the way they spoke about the Irish, curious and a bit frightening. They were Irish themselves, of course, most of them. 'Anglo-Irish' has now become the fashionable term, a foolish term. I am Irish myself, of course. My father had a small estate near Mallow. I am very much the poor cousin, younger son of a younger son. But I had been to school in England, and then Oxford. Your own experience as well, perhaps."

But Prentiss had gone to Clongowes Woods, in Kildare, thick-wooded with elm, an avenue of lime trees leading to towered mock-medieval, and within, white-walled corridors, images of Ignatius, Xavier, Jesuit discipline. A school for the sons of aspiring Catholics—land agents, solicitors, judges.

"Frightening?" he said.

"As though they were in terror of their own tenantry. A deep, unbridgeable chasm between their world and ours. Do you ever feel that? There was a time when I did myself, I confess. Not then, but later, in the eighties, during the Land War and the boycotting. In the worst year of it, none of us went abroad unarmed. I carried a short-barrelled little American revolver, no more dangerous than a popgun, I suspect. I was riding one day across the mountains into Kerry. Late in the afternoon, I came to a cabin set close to the road. Its door was closed, and there was no sign of life inside, no smoke from the chimney. Two windows fronting the road like blind, staring eyes. But four men were standing by the gable end—an old fellow, about sixty, and three younger men. Two of them had shotguns, held in the crooks of their arms, as though they had come home from a day's shooting. As no doubt they had. But that isn't how it felt. It felt . . . sinister. They stood motionless, looking towards me, the four of them. I raised my hand to my cap, but they made not a move. The old lad was wearing a shapeless hat of some sort, but the others were bare-headed—thatches of dark, uncombed hair growing down towards deep-socketed eyes. And they seemed, all four of them, to have the same mouth—long, thin upper lip. A cruel mouth. I was soon past them, but I twisted in my saddle to look back. They were still looking at me, still motionless. Their race and ours, Mr. Prentiss. And at that moment, I was certain that they hated me, although they had never seen me before. They were violent times, you know. Land agents murdered. Men stripped and carded, their bodies flung into bog holes."

From the rack, Forrester selected toast, arranged the slices on bread plates, handed one to Prentiss. Beyond the windows, the air was thickening.

"It is different now, no doubt. A more quiet time. You have never had that feeling yourself, Mr. Prentiss, that they are a different race?"

"It is my own race," Prentiss said. "As such matters are reckoned in this country. My people are Catholic, native stock. I cannot explain our name; we have never been interested in genealogy."

But he knew what Forrester meant. Son of a Dublin barrister, grandson of a Dublin solicitor, beyond that a farm in County Meath, near Bective. On a hot August day, he had once visited the farm with his father, the carriage rolling north from Dublin into lush countryside, the grass an intense green. His father was in an expansive mood, silk-hatted, seals and watch chain glittering in the sun. A small boy, solemn and wide-eyed, Prentiss sat, listened. "The ancestral sixty acres," his father said, gesturing with ebony-handled whip held in grey-gloved hand. "Well to remember that, Patrick." Beside their carriage, the leafy, tranquil Boyne moved to the sea. But here, in mountainous Munster, Prentiss felt no bond joining him to rawboned peasants, slow-moving, their voices thick with a forgotten Gaelic.

"Indeed," Forrester said politely, wiping his fingers upon stiff linen.

"But that is how the landlords felt, that night in Brierly Lodge?"

"Oh, yes," Forrester said. "There must have been a dozen of us there, talking of every innocent matter under the sun, until Johnny's manservant brought in the two steaming bowls of whiskey punch, and set them down upon the table, and then closed the door behind him. And even then, we said nothing until we heard the creak of his boots as he walked down the hall. 'Galvin is safe,' Johnny said. 'I'd stake my life on him. He's been with us since my father's day. I helped his son out of a bad scrape a few years ago, saw him off to America, paid part of his passage money.' 'None of them is safe,' someone said. I think it was Sanders, a man named Sanders who was land agent for the Dennisons. 'Ask any of those misfortunate families who have taken shelter in Killarney,' he said."

Light was fast fading from the terrace windows. The room darkened, but fire kept the hearth bright, tarnished silver held its reflected glow. Above the fireplace, the enigmatic portrait was in shadow.

"Because, you see," Forrester said, "in Kerry, the Fenians had gone into action, attacked a barracks."

"A coast-guard station," Prentiss said. "Near Killarney."

"Was that it? The Kerry gentry throughout the countryside fled into Killarney, with their silver and family portraits loaded into carts. And word of this had spread across the mountains, of course. But our meeting came to little; those things never do. We all signed letters which a solicitor named Fortesque composed for us—one to the inspector of police, and one to Dublin Castle, deploring the dilatory measures being taken by Government, loyal subjects of the Crown being left defenseless against armed and murderous bands. But in the event, the army moved promptly enough, and the Constabulary as well. No, it was the mood of those men, my fellow landlords, so to speak, that frightened me."

The landlords of West Cork, some in the frock coats of the period, and others in rough shooting jackets. It had been as much tack room as drawing room, a widower's house, a stag's head above the fireplace, riding whips crammed into a stand near the door, scuffed, comfortable chairs. Against one wall stood the gun cabinet, empty, its glass doors open and one of them half torn from its hinges, the work of Nolan's Arms Raid. Long before they had finished their talking and their letter signing, both bowls of punch were exhausted, cloves and bits of lemon floating in the dregs. Boyle shouted down the corridor and had them refilled. They were less guarded now, in Galvin's presence. Forrester created it for Prentiss almost as a comic sporting print, fox hunters unbuttoned at day's end, or a chapter from one of Charles Lever's novels about the squires of Galway. Whatever had frightened him that night was not apparent from his words. He had written a few romances, MacMahon had said, and he seemed to prefer the narrative mode, stories whose meanings lay nestled beneath the surface.

Something of an actor, as well. Midway through his account, he jumped up, a spry, elderly man, loose-jointed, and walked across the room to the windows.

"Sanders was standing here, do you see, by Johnny's window, a great beefy fellow in a checked waistcoat. His notion was that we should arm ourselves, or rearm ourselves, to be more exact. He had a basketful of historical half truths which he shovelled out for us—we were a garrison who had held Ireland for the Crown for three centuries, and never with proper help from England. In 'ninety-eight, our grandfathers had known how to deal with rebels—the lash and the triangle and the pitch cap. As he talked he made great sweeping gestures towards Ireland, which lay somewhere beyond Johnny Boyle's drawing-room windows, in the black night. The whiskey had gingered him up. 'Your grandfather,' he said suddenly, jabbing his finger towards me, 'your grandfather commanded the yeomanry in 'ninety-eight. He knew how to deal with rebels.' 'He held the King's commission,' I told him, in the offensive Oxford accent which I affected then, 'and he acted under authority.' ''

Whether affectation or not, Forrester still had that accent, Prentiss thought, and found himself looking at the old man with amused respect. Something of a dandy in his heather-coloured tweeds, the blue tie knotted with studied negligence. Final light shone through thin, carefully combed hair, showing the long, narrow skull beneath. How must he have looked that night in 'sixty-seven, at Johnny Boyle's? The face thin then, as now, cheeks pink, high-arched confident nose. Prentiss saw an Oxford under-graduate grown old, with lightness of manner preserved as in camphor. Had he ever married? Prentiss remembered Emily, slender, middle-aged, standing by the tea service, "my companion."

"The houses of the gentry were never in danger," he said. "The plan was to seize the police barracks across the country, control the roads and railways, raise up the country."

"Raise up the country," Forrester said ironically. "As easily raise up the lake."

So it must have seemed from this room, this terrace, from a position so lofty that there was little to choose between peasant gunmen and squireens in loud checks.

Forrester opened the window by which he was standing, and Prentiss stood up to join him. But first he took two steps backward, and looked at the portrait above the fireplace.

It was extraordinary. A young woman, in her late twenties, perhaps, standing beside a small fireplace of her own, delicate, chaste marble. Above it, an oval mirror, edged with gilt. To her right, on a low table, a white bowl filled with roses. She was wearing a ball gown of black velvet, cut low and square at the neck, the waist pulled tight. One hand rested on marble. She was turned three quarters towards the viewer, so that the mirror reflected a portion of her face, but it reflected nothing else. The painter seemed to have caught her in suspended movement, as though she had paused for a moment before leaving the room, to look towards him, perhaps, or towards the viewer. It was a deliberate, almost a flamboyant exercise in arrangement: blacks, contrasting whites of skin and marble, shadows, the deep-burning red of the roses. But the woman herself warred against its cool formality of design. She was a woman of remarkable physical charm, although too slender, perhaps, for the fashion of her period: small waist and firm, small breasts, compact apples. The charm was in her face—even lips, straight nose, dark level eyes. Eyes which gave somehow an impression of intelligence and wit. I am late for another engagement, her face seemed to say, I cannot wait to be arranged into whites, blacks, grey shadows. The artist had recognized this playful malice, and, his revenge, had worked it into his design. Design and subject were held in a delicate, faintly erotic tension.

"It is a speaking likeness, as they say," Forrester said to him. "Sylvia Ardmor, Tom's wife."

"She—it—is very lovely," Prentiss said.

"Both," Forrester said. "Sylvia was lovely, and so is the portrait. It's Galantiere's, you know. People forget that he was English, because of his name and because he settled in Paris. But that was painted in London, in Tom and Sylvia's house in Cheyne Walk. She gave him five sittings only, short ones; that was the bargain they struck. It was a challenge, in a way. She and Tom and Galantiere were great friends at that time, but later there was a falling-out. I was there at one of the sittings. In the drawing room, Tom and Galantiere and myself drinking hock and soda, and Sylvia pretending to be furious with him because of his fussiness. It was a foggy morning, yellow fog from the river pressing against the windowpanes. A Whistler morning, Sylvia called it, which didn't make Galantiere happy at all."

Forrester laughed in reminiscence, as though remembering a scene and a time when he had been more at home than he was here. With an effort, Prentiss turned away from the painting. He was embarrassed, and he knew why: the eroticism was faint, discreet, but it was a part of the painting's texture, and he had responded to it.

"An arresting portrait," Forrester said, as if exonerating him. "Everyone thinks so. Sylvia always pretended not to like it, but that was a game she was playing, with Galantiere, or perhaps with Tom. 'I look cheap,' she said once, 'like an artist's model dressed up in the gown of somebody's mistress.' Tom used to paint. The paintings in the hall are his."

"Yes," Prentiss said, "I know. Your— So I was told."

"Tom was talented," Forrester said. "I envied him his talents. Painting; tried his hand at engraving; poetry. At one time, he and I worked together on a book, but he lost interest. I finished it myself, but one section is his, and it was singled out for praise. He was a talented man."

He spoke as though Ardmor were dead, and not somewhere in Italy, in the hills south of Florence.

"He designed the avenue," Forrester said, "the approach to the

Castle through the woods. Not the gardens, of course, or the terraces. They go back more than a century, and Tom had great respect for them, but he thought them too formal, cold. Tom took delight in arranging the spontaneous, if that isn't a contradiction, an Irish bull."

"Lady Ardmor," Prentiss said, "was she English or Irish?"

"Oh, Irish," Forrester said. "Irish. She was a Challoner, County Westmeath. Like Emily. When I first knew Emily, she was in service to the Challoners. She came here to Kilpeder as Sylvia's maid. Does that seem possible?"

Prentiss could not think of a reply. Forrester, he concluded, drew quiet pleasure from keeping him off-balance.

"The prospect from the wood's edge is attractive," he said, "the lake, and the summer house beyond it."

"An arranged spontaneity," Forrester said. "That was Tom's design. But in the very old days, when I came here as a boy, there was a herd of red deer in the park. So tame that they would let you walk very close to them. In those days, Kilpeder, the great object of your research, was a huddle of shops outside the gate. On Sundays, we would cross the square to service at the church. The hunt would meet outside the Arms, gentlemen in pink coats, the dogs yelping. Old Gilmartin would bring out sherries for the riders. Tom's father was master of the hunt, of course. So was Tom, for a few years, after he succeeded. But not for long, although he managed the hunt well. He was a fine rider, reckless. But good hands. Towards the end, of course, he did not ride with the hunt at all. Towards the end, there were not above five gentlemen in the barony with whom he was on speaking terms."

"The end?" Prentiss said.

"You must see the prospect from the terrace," Forrester said. "Before it grows too dark."

Darkling. The lawns a dark green now, the stones of stairs and balustrades shading towards black. Beyond, elms cast long shadows upon the lake, its waters ruffled by faint wind. Near the avenue, a workman stood motionless, leaning with both hands upon a rake. The woods were dark. The river, into which the lake issued, was barely to be discerned beyond the woods. Set against it, the demesne wall of dressed stone; beyond the walls, the first lights had been lit in Kilpeder. The steeples of the two churches broke the darkening sky, Protestant to the left and near at hand, low and prim, and to the right, farther off, the tall, assertive spires of Saint Jarlath's, knobbed, Italianate, Catholic.

"The object of my research," Prentiss said, in tribute to Forrester's irony, nodding across darkness towards the lighted town.

"You could call one or two of my own little books histories," Forrester said. "I do myself, but historians would not. Colour distracts me, sentiment, heightened sentiment. I have a fatal weakness for pattern."

"Like Galantiere," Prentiss said.

The prospect was inviting, cool. What must it be like, he thought, to lay claim of ownership to all this—castle, terraces, lake, a herd of red deer, a town? Kilpeder seemed, for the moment, thrown out of proportion, a graceless pendant to the walls which encircled the demesne.

"What is it that the ballad says?" Forrester asked. " 'Full sixty men from Kilpeder town, to the hills above did go.' " He spoke the words without irony, for the irony was in the scene itself. The hills were invisible, blanketed in darkness.

Years before, a house in Chelsea, fog along the Thames, river traffic moving warily, two men drinking hock, at ease, joking. A young woman, dressed for the ball, rested a hand upon white marble, looked towards them. The artist spoke to her, impatiently, and she replied. What words had she used, what voice? Ardmor left Kilpeder in 1892, MacMahon had said, the year that his wife died, in London. Towards the end, not five gentlemen in the barony were on speaking terms with him. The end of what?

"I come every autumn," Forrester said, "and then for a few weeks in June. The shooting is still good—partridge, plover, pheasant. We shoot over Clonbrony Wood, among other places. Tom still owns Clonbrony. Curious, that. 'And death was waiting in the snows of dark Clonbrony Wood.' Waiting now for the poor birds; elderly gentlemen in tweeds and gaiters."

The terrace was dark, and darker still, so Prentiss would have thought, the library behind them, but when he turned his head, he saw that lamps had been lit, pools of light falling upon dark wood, carpeting.

"It was good of you to see me, Mr. Forrester."

There was a pause before Forrester replied. The face was in shadow, mild eye and fierce, military nose. "The estate is in retirement, so to speak. One of these years it will be sold off. The Guinness family are great gatherers of castles and titles, great restorers of parklands and grottoes and Norman keeps. You must one day have a look at our keep. It was the original castle, you know, back in the days of the O'Donovans. Those O'Donovans are waiting in the shades for the Forresters. Nothing lasts in this country. It wasn't good of me at all, Mr. Prentiss. Good talk is rare in these parts. I am determined that we should know each other better."

"I should like that," Prentiss said. Forrester's melancholy seemed to him too lightly held, like his moment's pose as a tweedy squire, shooting over Clonbrony Wood.

"Would you believe," Forrester said, "that Ardmor was once famous for its balls? They were the events of the season, back in the days of the old earl, Tom's father. I remember one from my boyhood. A great blaze of candles and gaslight, musicians down from Dublin. I remember odours, perfume, candle wax, oaks from Clonbrony flaming in the fireplaces. The Ardmor Ball was always in the spring, the countryside beginning to grow warm, the earth softening. Winter would be behind us."

"Winter is behind us now," Prentiss said.

"Yes," Forrester said.

Prentiss declined an offer to be driven back to the Arms by someone called Tim. Emily, "my companion," was nowhere in sight, and Forrester saw him to the door. But the hall was lighted now, and as they walked along it, Prentiss found himself staring in haste, like a tourist hurrying along a gallery of a museum on the Continent, at the paintings by the absent, talented Tom Ardmor—indistinct forms, bright pastels, noonday sunlight.

6

[*Hugh MacMahon*]

So far as County Cork is concerned, the Fenian rising of 1867 began with what is known to this day as "Nolan's Raid," which took place on the night of February 20. And if it had had no end in view save that of spreading dismay and consternation, it would be accounted a military triumph worthy of Hannibal or Murat. Ned being Ned, however, his purpose was less complicated. We needed arms and we needed them at once. By the twentieth, it had become certain that no supplies from Manchester or from Dublin would come to us in time.

He set up headquarters in the foothills of the Boggeraghs, in the cabin from which Pat Laffan operated his still. Bob and Vincent and I were there with him, of course, and it was our task to send out the squads to the various houses which we had marked out, but it was Ned who directed the operation, and no one was left in doubt on that score.

It was a humble dwelling, in all truth: a cabin of two rooms, thatched of course, set upon a slight rise, with windows on either side of a half door, staring out across wasteland. Laffan was by way of being a farmer as well as an illegal distiller, and there was a barn set closer to the gable end than might have been desired by the fastidious. The air, within even the cabin itself, was drenched with the thick, heavy odours of beasts, piss, excrement, damp straw. Odours which from that night forth I have associated with poteen, and in his case most unfairly, for his distillations had the craftsman's touch, pure and smooth upon the tongue, and, although almost colourless, with the faintest sheen of pearl, as though he had bottled the moon's very light. No, the aversion bred in me that night had about it something primordial, frightening, as though, town dwellers for the one generation, we had journeyed backward to the dark abysm in which our grandparents had dwelt and the generations before them.

Laffan was a slow-moving man, heavy of shoulder and haunch, and so taciturn as to seem sullen. Although there was little for him to occupy himself with, or to talk about. He knew what we were about and had willingly turned over his cabin to us, and for him that was the end of the matter. He stood watching us, for minutes on end, arms crossed and those meaty shoulders leaning against the wall of stone and mud. Then he would step outside, into a night which was darkening as we began our labours, and then once again, when the operation was fully under way, as black as pitch save for a faint, clouded moon. Once or twice, I walked out to join him, and we stood together in a silence which was trusting but not at all companionable.

Along the twisting boreen which led down to the road, we had posted three men with lanterns, in part to act as lookouts, but more to give light to the lads as they came up with their laden carts. Six squads of them we had sent out, with five or six lads to each squad. From our point of vantage, standing outside the cabin, the lanterns were like fallen stars, lonely and unconnected. But the watchmen were within earshot of each other and of us. One of them would shout out and another answer him, young fellows caught, like ourselves, between excitement and fear.

Peg Laffan, the wife, was as morose as himself—their evenings together must have been a giddy round of silences—but she had at least the task of tea making with which to occupy herself. The kettle above the fire was kept at the boil, and the tea itself was strong enough to trot a mouse across it, in lantern light the colour of mahogany. There were not cups enough for all of us, but she kept her eye upon them, and when one of them was empty, she would fling out the dregs into the fire, give the inside a swipe with her apron. I had more than once a wish that I were safe in my own kitchen, with Mary setting out for us the blue-and-white Delft, and a kettle of Christian ancestry singing on the hob.

There were young Laffans as well, behind the drugget curtain which divided the rooms, and with all the comings and goings, the poor things had little sleep that night. There would be quiet for a bit, and then one of them would commence, and set off the others. Presently the mother would go in to them, and remonstrate in some fashion or other that accomplished little, and then, at last, Laffan himself would go in and thunder out some sort of roar, in which words as such played no part, and at once quiet would descend for a bit, as the poor creatures lay there cowed and nerveless.

"Merciful God," Vincent muttered to me once, as we stood together by the door. "It might not be a good idea to liberate this lot."

"The finest peasantry in the world, Daniel O'Connell used to say."

"Barring Sicily," Vincent said.

But the two of us were ashamed of our shopkeeper's scruples, as we knew from the awkward glances which we then exchanged. In truth, we were as lonely beneath the immense black night as the lanterns on the road. And we had cause enough for our fear; for by this one night's work, Ned was taking us far beyond the swearing of an oath, however seditious, or the giving out of the oath to other men, or even the nights of armed drilling. For Vincent and myself at least, and no doubt for Bob as well, the foetid cabin far from any other farmland, the woman and man who seemed seldom to have need of speech, the close, rough walls of the mean room, the dirt floor, seemed theatre and emblems of an unknown world across whose borders we had strayed.

No doubt for Bob as well. But for the first part of the night, Bob was too intent upon his task to think of such matters. He and Ned sat side by side on a settle drawn up to the deal table, with the quarter-inch ordnance survey map of the barony spread out before them, one side of it pinned down by a block of wood and the other by an earthenware crock. Bob had put an X upon each of the estates and farms where we knew that there were arms for the taking—shotguns or rifles or pistols or whatever— and he had worked out the route which each of the squads was to take, and even the time which they should allow themselves for their "visits," a word that he used less from delicacy than from want of a better.

It was a task that Ned, who was ignorant of the barony, left to him, and he performed it in a manner which I found awesomely workmanlike. He might have been back in Tully's shop, sleeves rolled up and apron tied about his middle, listing up kegs of nails and sacks of sugar. Once or twice, I leaned over, between them, and watched his pencil moving across the map, touching first this X and then that one, skimming over the blue lines of streams and the red ones of roads. Our world was set down there upon that great rectangle of paper, encoded as squares and circles and oblongs and cross-hatchings. The whole of the map was coloured a pale, yellowish brown, the chalky brown of rain-dampened clay.

But of the fellows whom we were sending out, the most of them had never seen a map before, and Bob might as well have been consulting occult and sinister hieroglyphics. He would translate for them marks upon paper into roads, streams, a lump of hill, a crumbling keep set in a pasture, a humpbacked bridge. It was no easy task that he had set himself, for when it was possible, we sent them out towards townlands where there would be less likelihood of their being recognised, and thus along roads less familiar to them than their own. Once or twice, he was able to catch a slip he was about to make.

A fellow named Brendan Casey was to take his men to an estate called Thatchcroft, the property of a Major Singleton, a retired Indian officer, with a well-stocked gun room, so we had been told by one of his stableboys.

"Have a care with that one," Bob said to him. "I have had dealings with him; he is a peppery bastard. In his mind he is still back in India, giving the toe of his boot to the poor Hindoos."

"Ach, I will mind Major Singleton well enough," Casey said, and grinned. He was a lean fellow, about thirty, with most of his front teeth gone.

"Take care you do," Bob said.

"Sure, I have had Singleton in mind for the past two years, since he had the law about the beasts I used turn into that other pasture of his by my own place. There he sat, the hoor, in his gig, with his high starched collar, and Constable Belton from the barracks beside him to give weight to his remarks. Sure, the man before him never troubled me, a decent old skin who lived off in Cavan."

Ned jerked his head up and looked at Casey, but Bob rolled his pencil back and forth on the map for a bit, and then said, "A soldier from India, Brendan. Even with the five of you, fierce fellows with blackened faces, he might put up a fight."

"Twould be his last fight, by God. You can depend on that, Bob."

"Yes," Bob said. "But there will be no need. One of the other squads can attend to Major Singleton."

"Casey is your name?" Ned said. "Were you attending me, Casey, when I spoke to the lot of you, not two hours ago? Not one hair is to be harmed of these people, any of them. If there is trouble, back away from it. Use your weapons only to fight your way out, if need be. Do you remember my saying that?"

It was clear that Casey did not; he was beside himself with foolish excitement.

"You have a squad," Ned said, "because Bob Delaney praised you to me as a man of good sense, respected by others. Give me some evidence of it."

"You can rely upon Brendan," Bob said, and gave Casey a quick, reassuring smile. "I would stake my life upon him." Which was going a bit far, but they were welcome words to Casey, who nodded and swallowed, with great activity of the Adam's apple.

"It is not your life that is at stake," Ned said. "Tonight's work will be like poking a stick into a hornet's nest. And I will not have it said that the Fenians began operations by setting Irishmen to the murder of other Irishmen, or battering them bloody and senseless in their own halls. This is a requisition of arms for use in the impending warfare against the common enemy of all Irishmen, the forces of the British Crown."

"Can you remember all that, Brendan?" Bob said dryly, but with the same easy smile. "A requisition of arms."

"By God," Brendan said, making a last stand to preserve his dignity, "the lads who rose up in Kerry last Wednesday were less nice about matters. When they encountered the police on the road, they cut loose with their rifles."

"Never mind about the wild rapparees of Kerry," Ned said. "Kilpeder is under my orders, and you can depend upon it that if my orders are not attended, I can make your Major Singleton look like a suckling babe."

Bob had been moving his pencil from point to point on his map. "Here you are now, Brendan," he said. "A mile beyond Thatchcroft, just beside the bridge. Mrs. Heatherington, a decent Methodist widow, with a son up in Dublin studying Greek and the Scriptures at Trinity. A great lad for the shooting of snipe and plover, and the father was before him. I have often seen them myself, blazing away. Call in on Mrs. Heatherington, and don't forget to take the shells away with you. You can leave their collection of tracts; we will not need salvation this night."

Casey grinned back at him, showing us his collection of missing teeth.

They were a serviceable matching pair, Ned Nolan and Bob Delaney, Ned all metal and sharp angles, and Bob easy and affable for all his briskness. I wonder did Ned ever understand our nature, but to Bob it was all bred in the bone, the way he could give an order and it would be taken,

[101]

because he never stood himself upon a height. They would have been a delight to Plutarch, the pair of them, had he been so foolish as to wander into West Cork. Or perhaps Machiavelli.

It was those lads in Kerry and their mad endeavour which had swung Ned into action, and sooner than he would have wished, and it was debated for years afterwards, what they had been about and whether they had been wise or foolish. The matter is one upon which chance has permitted me to speak with authority, although how much weight my words may carry is another matter, for when I set forth my account to Patrick Prentiss, he ceased his note taking, although encouraging me to continue. I cannot blame him.

There was not a man in Laffan's cabin that night or out upon the roads who did not know that Kerry had risen up, although what had taken place there was a matter of wild speculation. But it gave to our own enterprise a fine, tense edge, a sense that we had at last begun. Ned, when he spoke to the men at the commencement of the night's work, had made mention of it, and although he spoke of it in guarded terms, it let loose a cheer. Killarney and Cahirciveen were the two of them under attack, it was believed, and the Iveragh peninsula sealed off. But the truth was otherwise, for it was brought into the barony on the Friday by two of the fellows who had been there, and had crossed over the mountains in search of refuge with a cousin who lived in Graney, a man named Phil Larkin. Larkin sent a message in to Bob, and Bob and Ned went out to visit him.

The two fellows, brothers named Egan, Cornelius and Dennis, were not the best of war correspondents. They were young lads, Cornelius no more than eighteen and the brother a bit younger, and they were frightened out of their wits, at once boastful and terrified. It was at Cahirciveen that they had risen up, hundreds of them, under the command of a colonel named O'Connor, a returned Yank like Ned, and there were other Americans with him. O'Connor was apparently Hector and Ulysses rolled into one, fearless and wily, and with a white cock's feather stuck into the band of his soft black hat. Young Dennis was much taken with this feather, and with O'Connor's skill with a revolver. But they had little understanding, either of them, of what had taken place or why. They had captured the police barracks at Cahirciveen, and then marched along the Glenbeigh road to the coast-guard station at Kells, which had also fallen to them, together with a supply of arms. Then they made march for Killarney, and on the road encountered a detachment of police to whom they gave battle. All of this was but triumph after triumph, with O'Connor leading in the van, his plume like a white flame.

It was stirring stuff, especially in the disjointed and tumultuous account rendered by the Egans. Bob knew the Glenbeigh road, and as they gave their reports, he could see the column of men from Cahirciveen, on the march along the dusty road, with the wide and lovely bay to their left, and beyond it, distant and blue-hazed, the mountains of Dingle. It was no small matter to us, Irishmen on the attack for the first time since the poor doomed peasants of 1798 had raised up their banners in Antrim and Mayo. But at that point, after the defeat of the constables, the story the Egans had to tell fell apart, with O'Connor sending some of the men back to Cahirciveen, and leading the others up a mountainside.

The Egans had been with him on the hill, where they had spent the night and all of the day that followed, until, towards that evening, an evening of chill, damp rain, when they were famished for the want of food or drink, the hill was surrounded by British soldiers who commenced the climb up towards them. They were Scotchmen, kilted and bonneted, a breed that none of the Kerrymen had ever seen before, and ferocious in Cornelius Egan's description—swift-blowing mist, and the kilts swinging above great bony knees, with enough sun shining through to catch a glint or two upon the steel of fixed bayonets. What was as eerie as any of it was that the Scotchmen shouted out to each other in Gaelic, the coarse and barbarous Gaelic of the Highlands, which the Kerrymen could but half understand.

By first this tack and then that, Ned and Bob pressed the Egans for an account of how all this had come about, but it was no use. They were decent ignorant country lads, boys rather than men, and their story fell into two halves which could not be joined. They were at one moment storming the coast-guard station, which I could well see in my mind's eye, a pretentious construction with false, useless turrets pointed like minarets. And the next, they were crouching there amidst rock and mist and furze. It was useless. "God damn you," Ned said, grabbing hold of Cornelius by the front of his jacket. "O'Connor must surely have told you why he commenced operations when he did." But Cornelius stared at him with the mild, terrified eyes of a mountain hare. In the heel of the hunt, the Egans were left under the guardianship of their cousin Larkin, with strict orders that they were to be let speak to no one. Larkin agreed with ill grace. He was ready enough to give refuge to his kinsmen, but he was not an oath-bound man, and passing along the word to Bob was as far as he intended to go. "Oath or no oath," Ned said to him, "you have been given an order by the Army of the Republic of Ireland." Larkin was an alert, sardonic man, and he gave Bob a bitter, amused look, and then said to Ned, "The Irish Republic. Well, la-di-da!"

But Ned's precaution was useless, for other Cahirciveen men drifted in, from across the mountains, and with stories equally portentous, which swelled up with each telling, so that it was a great puzzlement how this mighty host had declined into stragglers on their keeping. But by then, Ned had decided that Bob and I were to go down into Killarney to see what could be learned. "You should try to find O'Connor," he said, "but I doubt if you will. And that failing—"

"I know the beat," Bob said, interrupting him with his easy smile, for Ned had forgotten that until his own arrival, Bob had been our Centre, and had consulted with the Kerry men.

"A bloody goddamned colonel," Ned said, "and he leads his men up a mountain."

"If that is what happened," Bob said.

Bob was a wonder to me. Ned lay beyond my understanding, an exotic. But Bob, the companion of my bosom, was proving his match, sensible and unruffled.

We set out early the next morning, a clear, crisp winter's morning, nourishing to the spirit, on horses that had been found for us, in a manner of speaking, by Joe Gaffney, an oath-bound young lad who worked in Trainor's livery stable. Westwards out of Kilpeder we rode, and over the county road which led across the Derrynasaggarts and then dropped down into Kerry. A half dozen times in the past, we had made that journey for the pleasure of it, and more than once, Mary came along with us, and we had made a holiday of it, with chicken and ham in a hamper and the rest of it. But never had we had a day more lovely for it, and human nature being what it is, we put from our minds for long stretches of the road the purpose of our ride, pleasured by the day and by each other's company. Or I did, at any rate. With Bob you could never be certain. He could chat away, or deal a hand of cards or stand his round in a public house, but always with some centre of his mind a cool, well-swept room, and Bob balancing, weighing, judging.

Rich pasturelands fell away towards foothills, the grasses long and rank, deep green with the morning wet upon them, rock-strewn, sheep distant drifts of white. And from foothills, we rode up into the mountains themselves, broken and rocky, touched with gorse which had just begun to purple, a pale, pinkish sort of purple. We had them to ourselves, no other riders on the road, not even the occasional farmer with his cart or his donkey, creels slung to either side. It was an utter solitude, and from the crests of high hills we could see for great distances, the far hills which held Kerry yet from sight, or, if we twisted around in our saddles, West Cork, Kilpeder hidden now from view, although we could make out Knockmany, which stands above the town. At this height, birds only were our companions, hawks; we once saw three of them, close together—an unusual sight, for the hawk is a lonely hunter. Bob reined in, and sat watching one of them as it wheeled above us, the broken edges of its outstretched wings like fingers. It swung in long, searching arcs, and then hung motionless against the wintry sun, then plummeted beyond our sight.

We rode down into the foothills on the far side, down into Kerry, and the earth quickened again for us. A strange, history-haunted place is Killarney and its lakes, and the history never guessed at by the summer visitors who throng to it from far places, from England and the Continent. Small need has the visitor to know that the wars of Elizabeth and Cromwell raged through this part of Kerry, the Desmond rebellion and its terrible aftermath, and the days of the great hunger, a desolation which there are those still alive who can remember.

For myself, I have rarely ridden down into Killarney without reflecting on all this, fine sonorous reflections, phrases half forming themselves in the mind, touched with the shadowy, flavoursome melancholy of the past.

Yet some are shielded by temperament from the seductions of the past. "Gone are the glories of the great O'Donoghues," I said to Bob, quoting, "and gone the glories of MacCarthy Mor." We had come to a last rise of hill, and the town of Killarney with its spired cathedral lay before us. Sunlight caught a ribbon of water.

"Long gone, by Jesus," Bob said. "Long gone and best forgotten."

"You have been too long behind Tully's counter," I said, to get a rise from him, "with your nose buried in his brutal ledger. Look about you, man. Our past lies buried here, as Owen MacCarthy tells us in his verses, in the monuments of our poets and of our mighty dead."

"Let it stay buried, so," Bob said. "Owen MacCarthy has no chiselled monument in Muckross Friary. They gave him the rope's end above in Mayo, and set his tarred body on the gibbet to frighten crows."

It was a fitting terminus to my dreamy musings, no doubt, and yet I recall that on a day when Bob and Mary and Vincent and myself came to Muckross, and Mary spread out her white, laundered cloth upon the grass, Bob had shared with us the feelings of that evening hour, the sky a delicate darkening green, and heavy-branched willows trailing against faint-lettered tombstones. It was a mood of the moment that was upon him now, an irritable fear of the past which reaches out towards us in this country, bony fingers clutching at our ankles.

But the town itself brought me back into the present, and no mistake about it, for nothing that we had learned in Kilpeder had prepared us for it.

The streets were crowded with soldiers, or so it seemed to my untutored eyes, and wherever the eye turned one saw the scarlet splashes of their jackets. They were in the streets and standing in knots outside the barracks and the courthouse, and standing on the steps of the cathedral itself. As we learned later, they had pitched their tents in fields on the far side of the town, and there were the half of them still on the hunt for O'Connor's men in the hills beyond, and the other half had been given the afternoon and evening free to amuse themselves in Killarney. As Bob and I stood looking about us, four of them came out of the public house across the road, their pillbox hats pushed back on their heads, and the fastenings of their collars undone. They appeared harmless enough in manner, with drink taken but not rowdy at all.

But it was an unfamiliar spectacle to Bob and myself, and we stepped aside from the road to lean our backs against the window of a huckster's small shop. Down the road from the direction of the cathedral what seemed at first an entire regiment of them came ambling, fifteen of them at least, boisterous and shouting, and the four fellows who had emerged from the public house stood looking at them, as we were ourselves. "Tom," one of them shouted out to a mate whom he recognised, "have you and the lads been to evening services? You'll fare better in here." He jerked his head to nod at the tavern behind him, and his cap caught a glint from the slanting sun. He had close-cropped, sandy hair, and he was not young, a man about thirty, with the two broad stripes of a corporal.

"Merciful God," I said. "The entire British army has been sent up to Killarney."

"Brutalised populace cowers in terror," Bob said, nodding towards three girls who stood close together at the corner opposite, leaning so that their shawled heads almost touched. They were giggling, all three of them. The tallest of the three was also the boldest. She had one hand resting on her hip, and the other touched the border of her shawl. As she looked towards the soldiers, she said something which set the other two into fresh fits of giggles. She had wide, dark eyes and high cheekbones. A fringe of hair beneath the shawl was black.

"The parents of those lassies have scant thought for their responsibilities," I said. The littlest of them was fairly jigging with excitement, her feet moving in a pattern.

Bob grinned at them, his eyes fixed upon the tall, black-haired girl. "The British army may leave a memento or two behind it, if care isn't taken. Those lassies should be skelped to their homes by a priest from the cathedral." But his words were more harsh than his glance. He caught her eye for a moment, but she twisted her head away from him. The young men of Ireland stood little chance that day in the streets of Killarney.

Truth to tell, the chastity of Kerry was the least of my concerns. The British soldiers who crowded the streets of Killarney, or to my eyes seemed to crowd it, were harmless enough for the hour, and many of them Irishmen themselves no doubt, but there was no mistaking the meaning of their presence. I could read it in one lad who stood for the moment by himself, outside the public house, at his ease, uncertain where next to wander, his two thumbs hooked in his white belt. He was a private soldier, no wide arrows on his sleeves, a lean, hungry-looking fellow with a prominent Adam's apple. Up the street and then down it he looked, his glance taking in the two of us, and resting on us for a moment. He wasn't smiling at all, and the corners of his long, thin mouth were turned down.

"This is by no means the lot of them," Bob said. "The Egan brothers spoke about Scotsmen, red-shank Highlanders."

"But how in God's name did they get here?" I said. "How could they have come from Cork and not taken the Macroom road through Kilpeder?"

"The British army is everywhere and nowhere," Bob said. "Like the Holy Ghost or the circumference of the circle, whichever it is. We had best find out."

He pulled his shoulder away from the huckster's window, and the two of us set out, along the road of red jackets. It was a holiday spirit, almost, in the town of narrow streets, and if it was the red jackets that lent such an appearance, the townspeople and the people in from the country could not be said to be glowering at them. At the railway station, the plan of the town opened up. There was a market square, with shops and public houses and no fewer than four hotels fronting upon it, and farther along, set at an angle so that its well-kept lawns touched an edge of the station itself, the great railway hotel, to which in summer the holiday makers thronged. It was thronged now as well, and unseasonably so. Broughams, landaus, and gigs stood in the curved carriageway, and gentlemen and ladies walked up and down beside them, talking, the long gowns of the women sweeping upon combed gravel, so that had we been standing closer we could have heard the *swish, swish,* a sound luxurious and erotic. The army was here as well, but not public-house corporals and private soldiers. Beneath the white portico, two ladies and a gentleman stood surveying the scene, the ladies in wide-brimmed hats tied beneath the chins with scarves, and the gentleman short and corpulent, silk-hatted, his hands clasped behind his back. On the steps, talking with them, were two officers, youngish and bareheaded, their caste proclaimed less by insignia than by carriage. One of them, a handsome, youngish man with long downward-curving moustaches, stood negligently, arms folded, a black, polished boot resting on the top step. The other, a head shorter, divided his attention between the conversation and backward glances towards the town. Someone said something, I imagined it was the young officer, and they all laughed. The silvery laughter of women was carried to us across close-cropped lawns, circular beds of winter shrubs and plants.

"Officers of the Second Blankshires reassured the alarmed people of Kerry," Bob said. "Their spruce and cheerful appearance was to many a welcome sight."

"You would have a great future in journalism," I said, "if you could but tear yourself away from Tully."

"Perhaps the Second Blankshires have made other plans for us," Bob said. "They seem a benevolent lot."

We stood exchanging such banter, as though displaying our manly lack of concern, until we noticed that the younger of the two officers had fixed his eye upon us, and why this alarmed us, I cannot say, for we were a respectable-looking pair, a schoolmaster and a shop assistant with the pallor of the indoors upon us. They made a pretty tableau, the five of them, the two ladies and the portly gentleman and the two officers, and in the evening air I imagined a waltz floating out from the assembly room, violins and a piano.

"A scene more suitable for Vincent than for ourselves," Bob said. "Let's away."

Beyond the square, the streets narrowed again. Timoney's public house was down one turning to the left, halfway the length the street—a decent-sized house, with clear glass above and dark red glass below, and his name blazoned above all, "Martin Timoney," gilt paint upon crimson.

It was a public house's quiet time of the day, the early evening. At the counter, near the door, two old fellows were drinking, one with the pint before him on the oak, and the other holding his in a long, claw-thin hand. The barman, young and growing bald, stood before them, behind the counter. Sunlight, falling through red glass, stained the floor. A public house has at that hour a recessed quiet, without even the lingering ghosts of the night's revelers. There is a touch of the confessional about it, or the pleasures of melancholy meditation.

Bob walked past the two old ones to the far end, and perched himself on a stool. We waited for the barman to come down to us, Bob with his hands folded before him.

"Is life quiet these days in Kilpeder?" the barman asked him.

"Dennis, is it not?" Bob said. "'Tis always quiet in Kilpeder, Dennis, save upon market days and bonfire nights. Over the mountains to Killarney, if 'tis excitement you want. Or Killorglin, of course."

"Killorglin," Dennis said with disdain.

"My friend Hugh MacMahon," Bob said. "He is master of the school in Kilpeder."

Dennis held out to me his soft white hand, damp from the swabbing out of glasses. "I had best mind my words and my grammar," he said, "in the presence of the master."

"Two short ones, Dennis, if you will," Bob said. "And a drop of water, if you have it to spare. The railway hotel is thriving for the time of year that is in it."

Dennis smiled, but said nothing until he had measured out our whiskeys and placed them before us.

"You observed that," he said, the elegant word no doubt chosen for my benefit. "Half the gentry of the barony are at present in the town. There are some of them staying with the Kenmares, and some with friends out towards the lakes, and the remainder are crowded into rooms at the hotel. They commenced their journeys here when once word was out that the barracks at Cahirciveen had been attacked. And more of them came pouring in after the Kells station was taken. There were some of them came with laden carts, silver tea services and portraits in gilt frames and tall candlesticks of gold and silver. Tis a mercy to God that the tinkers are not in town."

"Your health," Bob said, and raised his glass.

The glass of spirits was welcome after the journey, cool to the senses, like the cool, quiet room.

"We left off our horses at Brick's stable at the far end of town," Bob said, "but Jeremiah himself was nowhere in evidence. There was only the wee lad of his."

"Jeremiah has been away from the town these past few days," Dennis said. With his bar rag, he polished away at the oak before him. A useless labour. Ancient rings of porter glasses and whiskey glasses had become parts of the wood's texture. "Tis not known when he will return. A fair number of the lads of the town are away from their familiar haunts."

"We had a quiet journey of it across the Derrynasaggarts, Hugh and myself. Not a soul to be seen, barring the occasional hawk."

"If hawks may be said to have souls," I said.

Dennis was not of a speculative turn of mind. "You would not," he said. "Beyond, in Iveragh, in the hills towards Cahirciveen, there is great movement and excitement, tis said."

"Is your father about, Dennis," Bob asked, "or is he off with Jeremiah Brick on their holidays?"

"He is not. He is above. You will want to be talking with him, I expect. Do you see those two old ones down there?" he said, at once lowering his voice and giving a savage edge to it, a knack which publicans acquire before ever they can pull a decent pint. "Small farmers the two of them, from beyond Gortrelig. The one of them had need of tobacco, and so they decided to make a day of it in Killarney. George O'Riordan's shop purveys a class of tobacco to which he is partial, he says. Trafalgar Blue, tis called, with a drawing of Lord Nelson, coloured blue, on the wrapper. The two of them, nursing their pints. If the earth itself opened up, the two of them would give it no heed."

"That is what has happened, Dennis, is it not?" Bob did not change at all the tone in which he had been speaking, and yet the room seemed more quiet. Only the soft *sss-sss* of the tobacco fancier and his chum broke the silence. "The earth of Kerry has opened up, it would appear. Two lads from Cahirciveen are now with a cousin in Kilpeder, young brothers named Egan, and I have been talking with them, myself and a certain friend of ours."

Dennis said nothing. His hand, with the bar rag beneath it, rested motionless on the oak.

I touched the rim of my glass. "Let us try the second half, Dennis," I said.

Bob looked down at the old fellows, and then at a print hanging on one wall of Robert Emmet in the courtroom, in his uniform of green and white, one hand flung up as he orated. With his eye resting idly on the print, Bob said, "What class of fucking madness have the Fenians of Kerry been about?"

"Dennis," I said, prompted less by thirst than by a human wish to ease the moment. "The other half, and pour one for yourself while you are about it."

But he did not. He poured out our two whiskeys, and moved closer to my hand the jug of water. From the coins in my pocket, I sorted out a shilling, and placed it beside the jug, where it rested, unnoticed.

"Tis a question which you should be putting to my father, so, and not to me."

They had been matching numbers, Martin Timoney and Bob Delaney, the Centres for Kilpeder and for Killarney, until the arrival of the American officers.

"Yes," Bob said. He picked up the jug and measured out water until the deep-banked brown of the whiskey had softened to pale gold.

He waited until Dennis had left the room, and then lifted his glass.

"The Timoneys are not on their keeping in the hills of Iveragh," he said. "For prudence, commend me to the publicans of Munster."

"For Jesus' sake, Bob," I said. "Martin Timoney is a cripple who walks with two sticks. And he is fifty if he is a day."

"Dennis is agile enough," he said. "Soft but agile, like a tabby cat." He drank off his drink in two swallows, and set down the glass smartly upon the counter.

Without appearing to do so, or so I trusted, I studied Bob in the well-scrubbed mirror behind the bar. It had been my mistake to admire him for his calm. His square, capable face was calm enough, jaw set and level blue eyes at ease, and his manner, save for that one crack of the whip, was easy. But he sat rigid, and the outstretched fingers of his free hand were arched. I turned away from the mirror and looked at them, pressed against the oak, the tips white.

Dennis was back almost before he was gone, relieved, no doubt, to be acquitted of his mission, and nodded to Bob, who rose up and walked through the door, which led to a flight of steep stairs. I followed after him.

Martin Timoney was waiting for us on the small landing, the heavy weight of his body pressing down upon sticks held in his either hand.

"There was no need for you to rise up for us, Martin," Bob said.

"Small matter," Timoney said. "I am up and down those hoors of stairs a dozen times a day. Why would I not be?" He was a great, beefy man gone soft with the years, heavy belly pressing against thick belt.

He led us into one of the two front rooms above the shop, where a second man was seated, lean and wiry, with long, straight hair, black almost as Ned's, but not otherwise resembling him.

"Captain Eugene Reilly, this is," Timoney said. "He came to us with John O'Connor."

Reilly was seated at a round table of black oak, and Timoney motioned us to join him there, with a gesture of one of his sticks. Then he swung himself into one of the chairs, let a stick drop to the floor beside his chair, and sat facing us with his two hands resting on the knob of its mate.

"Ned Nolan has spoken to us of yourself and Colonel O'Connor," Bob said politely. "Ned Nolan is our commander in Kilpeder."

"I know that," Reilly said. "But I don't recollect Nolan at all. There are too many of us here at the moment. Who was it that Ned Nolan served with? There was a Nolan with Meagher, but he was a Eugene Nolan." His voice, unlike Ned's, was pure Yankee, heavy-timbred and yet nasal.

Bob shook his head. "He told us, but I have forgotten. He was in the fighting in Tennessee and Virginia."

"A number and a name," I said. "The Seventh New York, or some such."

"No matter," Reilly said. His hands were shoved, palms down, into his trousers pockets, a trait which he shared with Ned. "Well, lads," he

[111]

said. "There is scant resemblance between Kerry and Tennessee, save for the hills. The battle of Kerry will never be written up in the annals of warfare."

"What happened, in God's name?" Bob said. "Tis why Ned has sent Hugh and myself down into Killarney. I am under orders from him to speak to Colonel O'Connor."

Martin Timoney laughed without pleasure, and looked over at Reilly. "*Colonel* O'Connor, is it?" he said.

"John O'Connor is on the run," Reilly said. "He is safe enough outside Sneem, with friends of ours. But there are army patrols and patrols of Constabulary out upon all the roads into Iveragh. For the moment, I am in command in Killarney. It's all over in Kerry, lads. That's the long and short of the matter."

"In Kilpeder, we know nothing of what happened here," Bob said, with his deceptive patience. "The Egan boys are on their keeping there. You raised up Cahirciveen, and took the barracks, and then you took the station at Kells, and then you fought the police, somewhere between here and Sneem. That is what we know in Kilpeder."

"Fought the police," Timoney said, his voice edged with disgust. "By God, they did. And brought the whole bloody army down upon us. Have you walked through the streets of Killarney?"

"John O'Connor raised Cahirciveen," Reilly said. "Colonel O'Connor did. Not me. Nor can I tell you why he raised it. He sent out to me a message that he had raised it, and that I was to make ready our lads. The next day I sent out thirty of our lads under Jeremiah Brick, and there are but seven of them back in Killarney." And then he took a hand from his pocket and rested it on the table. "I can tell you more than the Egans could, but not as much as Nolan will want to know."

"Are you at all hungry, lads?" Timoney said.

"Am I hungry, lads, is it?" Bob said. "Kerry is raised up and then sunken down and lost to us, and you ask, am I hungry, lads."

"Kerry is lost, right enough," Reilly said. "You have the right of it there."

Bob shook his head. "Hugh and myself cannot even understand how the bloody army comes to be here at all. There were no troops moved along the Macroom road."

"They moved south from Limerick Junction," Reilly said. "A general named Horsford sent them here. Sir Alfred Horsford, and a fine, prompt general he is. He paid us a visit of inspection. I have seen him from the window above, standing in the road with his aide, a little, peppery fellow with great moustaches. He commandeered whatever was in Limerick

Junction—jaunting cars, vans, gentlemen's carriages. Kerry is sealed off."

"So it would seem," Bob said.

"How could you not be hungry?" Reilly said. "I couldn't force down another bite myself. For three days I have been in this room, with Timoney wives forcing ham and chicken and meat pie into me. I think they are fattening me for the fair."

You never know about people. At my first glance of Reilly, I had taken for some reason a dislike to him, but I had misjudged him. There he was, like Ned back in Kilpeder, dropped down from the sky into a strange land, and with all his great plans frayed away, hidden in a room above a public house, with little for diversion save food and the occasional glimpse of a British officer with a scarlet jacket and fierce cavalry moustaches. But he had no more nerves than an icicle, and even a certain sympathy for Bob and myself, despite our rudeness.

In the event, a great tray of the ham and the cold chicken was brought in for us by Dennis's wife, a thin, short woman with a narrow face and a quick, nervous smile. Thick-sliced bread, and a plate of butter, a pot of tea. I buttered for myself two of the slices and placed ham between them, and then, seeing that Bob would make no move towards the food, I did the same for him, and poured us out mugs of tea.

"There are now British troops on either side of Kilpeder," he said. "In Cork, and now here in Killarney." This sombre fact had not presented itself to me.

"They are," Reilly said. "And so have they been from the outset. Whether westwards of you in Kerry or northwards makes little difference. Surely the men of Kilpeder don't expect to fight single-handed. What matters is that all the Centres will rise up on the sixth, and the British cannot be everywhere at once. What has happened here has sunk us in Kerry, but the rest of you are no worse off."

Bob and I looked at each other, and I remember yet the look of him holding the bread and ham in his two hands.

"On the sixth?" I said.

"Of course on the sixth," Reilly said. "The great puzzle to me is why John O'Connor jumped the gun down in Cahirciveen." Looking at the two of us, first at one and then at the other, he had now a fresh small puzzle on his hands, but this one he solved smartly enough. He had a fox's head, triangular and compact, with alert, close-set eyes. "Nolan knows that. Did he not tell you?"

"He did in a way," Bob said dryly. "He calls it the appointed day. Captain Nolan is not much of a conversationalist." He bit now into his bread and ham, and I was embarrassed for him. He was, after all, our second-in-command. But I had scant feeling to expend upon sympathy. The appointed day, as following Ned we had come piously to call it, was now in truth but a few weeks away, and this fact had not been given to us in cheerful circumstances. I consoled myself with ham and buttered bread, and wished myself back in my own kitchen.

The small, bare room was now darkening, with no lamp or candle lit. Martin Timoney, with his gross belly, and the cool, leathery Reilly sat shadowed. Men in the street below were shouting at each other, soldiers perhaps, or perhaps townspeople or fellows in from the countryside. Bob stood up and walked to the window.

"We gave a scare to the gentry," Timoney said. "By God, if John O'Connor and his lads did nothing else, they did that. Do you know who is now crowded into the railway hotel, amidst all the Protestants? The Liberator's family. The O'Connells of Derrynane and of Killarney. They are where they belong, by God, the bloody Whigs. Amongst their own at last." There was a small, sour triumph in his voice, as though his tongue probed an abscessed tooth.

"Three of O'Connor's men are in the street below," Bob said. "And a guard of General Horsford's redcoats to prod them along." Jesus, Mary, and Joseph, I said to myself.

"Yes," Reilly said. "That is how they have been brought in. In twos and threes."

"The battle of Kerry," Bob said, with his back still turned to us.

"The battle of Kerry," Reilly said. "I can tell you briefly what we now know of it, Martin and myself, and he can correct me if I go astray. There was no battle, in any proper sense of the word. The coast-guard station at Kells had been reinforced by the Constabulary, but they surrendered without firing a shot. O'Connor compelled them to carry out the arsenal of arms, and stack all neatly for distribution to the lads. Then he hoisted up a green flag of some sort atop one of the turrets, and they set out. It was from Kells that he sent out his messenger to Martin and myself. The messenger was cock-a-hoop with news of the great victory."

"The coast guard are English, the most of them," Timoney said, "but the constables are decent Irishmen. They refused to fire upon their own."

"So they told John O'Connor," Reilly said, "but they had a different story for General Horsford's ears, you may be certain. On the march here, near Glenbeigh, O'Connor encountered a patrol of mounted constables, and ordered them to surrender. There was a scuffle, and the sergeant in command, Duggan, tried to cut his way through. One of our lads let loose and brought him down. He was carrying despatches from here to Cahirciveen, and it was when O'Connor read these that he changed his plans, and took his men up into the hills. There you are. The battle of Kerry, to be celebrated in song and story."

Little did he know Kerry. The battle of Kerry is sung to this day beyond the mountains, the attack upon the station at Kells and the lads of Cahirciveen pressing forward with O'Connor in the van. There has been a print made of it, which shows us O'Connor in a uniform of some sort, and a great wide-brimmed hat with a plume, waving on his men with a drawn sword.

"The sergeant was wounded, so?" I said.

"A sore wound," Reilly said. "He was shot in the back at close range, and the bullet passed through a lung. He lay there on the dusty road in his blood, but he was conscious. John O'Connor got some brandy down him, but he choked on it. The men were unnerved by it, our lads and the policemen alike. John stood beside him and read the despatches, while the others tried to make him comfortable. He has died since, in the hospital here, and small wonder, jounced along that road in a cart."

The first blood shed in the Rising. I saw him lying there in the road. All the others were shadowy and indistinct: the policemen in their black tunics, and our lads in whatever they were wearing, and all of them looking at each other and at the man lying wounded in the road. But the man himself I saw clearly in my imagination. Someone had folded a jacket and placed it beneath his head.

"He was with the reinforcements sent down last month from Cork," Timoney said. "Not one of the local fellows at all. But the constables with him have not been able to say which one of our lads it was that fired off the ball, thanks be to God."

"And there we have it," Bob said. "One policeman shot down, and Kerry thick with soldiers. What in hell was it that O'Connor found in his despatches?"

"I will know that when I am able to talk with John," Reilly said. "I think that perhaps he sent off a messenger to us here, but no message arrived. John must be got out of the country. He is a marked man now."

"'Tis all quiet again in the street below," Bob said, "save for three young lads going into the shop for their pints. Twill not be their first tonight by the look of them." He turned away from the window.

"Trade will be carried on despite necessary alterations of the premises," Timoney said. "Dennis will attend to their needs. If tis a quiet life you seek, Dennis is the lad for you."

"He is indeed," Reilly said. "Dennis will not be sorry to see the last of me."

Bob walked across the room to the sideboard, where he picked up a bottle and glasses which were standing upon it, and brought them to the table.

He measured out drinks for the four of us, and raised his own to his lips without a salutation. Only after he had drunk did he sit down again beside us.

"You will be a marked man yourself soon enough, Captain Reilly. One or another of those lads who have been lifted will have a story to tell, to save his own skin."

"I have been giving thought to that," Reilly said. "As you can well imagine." He turned his glass in his hand, and then raised it. "An ignoble chapter in the history of the clan Reilly. Six weeks knocking about Killarney and never a shot fired off in anger. You never know, lads. I may turn up in Kilpeder, like a bad penny."

"No," Bob said. "Don't chance it."

"Shipments of arms were promised," Reilly said. "You know that yourselves. And where the hell are they? Arms were to have been landed on the strands beyond Cahirciveen. We were ready for them."

"No safer place in Ireland," Timoney said. "And has been time out of mind. Tis because of the smuggling that the coast guard was put into Kells, and they were helpless. My father put up many a bottle on the counter below that never earned twopence for Queen Victoria."

Kerry strikes another blow for freedom, I thought. I have heard it said in later years that both Reilly and O'Connor did indeed make an effort to cross over the mountains to us in the days that followed, but the Kerry men would not hear of it. They were kept in a safe house for a few weeks, and then smuggled off by boat from the famous Cahirciveen strand. Until a few years ago, I would get a Christmas letter from Captain Reilly, who settled in Newark, New Jersey, and became a dealer in hardware. In every letter, he would recall the evening when Bob and I had talked with him in the upstairs room of Timoney's public house, neatly composed letters written in a flowing script. "They tell us now," he wrote in one of them, "that the British knew all our plans, and that we were shopped by informers. But you know and I know that it was for want of arms. Kerry was ready, and so was West Cork." Like the letters, no doubt, that the exiled Jacobites sent back from Paris and Rome to the Highlands, as Prince Charles, their bonny leader, drowned himself in brandy and self-pity.

He was a different man that evening, not yet snug in Newark with the heavy paunch and growing family of the Christmas tintypes. Like Ned Nolan, he was that evening a man fit for great enterprises, as Bacon would put it, and in that respect did not greatly resemble the rest of us, save perhaps Bob himself.

To speak the truth, I would have tarried in that snug, dark limbo. I had no wish to venture forth once more amongst the redcoat soldiers who walked the streets of Killarney, carrying in my mind's eye a picture of Sergeant Duggan staining the road with his blood. But Bob, when once he had finished off his glass and its other half, and when he had satisfied himself that neither Martin Timoney nor Eugene Reilly had anything more to tell us, rose up and made his adieu, and I followed suit.

"Mr. Delaney—Bob, is it?" Reilly said, when we were at the door. "What happened here was one incident only. Sealed off, if you like, as Kerry itself is. It does not affect the Rising. It does not affect West Cork. Tell Nolan that."

"No," Bob said, with his hand upon the knob. "But it makes a damned sorry first act. Safe home, Captain Reilly." And with his boots clattering down the narrow stairs, he left it to me to speak to them more civil words.

That night we shared a bed at Jeremiah Brick's, a mournful establishment, with Mrs. Brick distracted by Jeremiah's absence, and ill equipped by nature or experience to understand the events which had swallowed him up. But this did not prevent her from setting out tea and decent plates for us in the morning, nor from favouring us with the sharp edge of her tongue. I had met her twice or three times before, and had thought her a harmless, inoffensive creature, and in this I was entirely mistaken. She was a termagant.

As Bob and I sat shovelling in our tea and buttered bread, she stood beside us, fists resting on hips, intent upon ruining our digestions. "Poor Jerry is wandering the hills, or dead upon them, or they will be leading him through the streets at the rope's end as they did those lads yesterday. But Martin Timoney is snug in his public house, you may be sure, and by nightfall, you will yourselves be safe in Kilpeder. I wonder that you have the heart to face nourishment, either of you."

"'Twas kind of you to set it before us," I said.

"Not for your own sakes, you may be certain," she said, "but in the thought that some decent woman in the mountains may be doing the like for poor Jerry. You thought that you could best the British army, did you, may God pardon you for ignorant children. They have been pouring into the streets of Killarney, strapping, handsome fellows who know the uses of guns and cannons."

"It has not come to cannon yet," I said, ever the pedant.

"My own brother is in the Munster Fusiliers, a corporal over them, and if the Munsters are sent here, they will make short work of the lot of yez."

"And Jerry as well, no doubt," I said, contriving by this stratagem to make a moment's pause in her tirade.

"The priests at their altars have denounced the lot of yez," she said, "and yet yez call yourselves Irishmen."

Bob had said nothing, working away at his plate. Now he pushed it back. "You have the right of it, Mrs. Brick. I wonder why did Jerry ever drift into desperate courses, when he might abide at home, enjoying the quiet of your chimneyside." Irony was wasted upon her.

But when we had saddled our horses and led them out, she was waiting for us at her open door, one of Jerry's coats flung over her shoulders against the morning chill.

"Safe home across the mountains," she said. "You are good lads, the two of yez."

"Jerry will be back to you," Bob said, touching his hand to his hat. "Never fear."

"God willing," she said. "And God spare you lads."

Jerry did come back to her, but it was for one week only. Then he was lifted by the police and tried at the assizes in Tralee and sent off to Millbank Prison in England, where he served two years. By the time he was released, the livery business had failed, for the Killarney gentry and the respectable tradesmen would have no dealings with a Fenian family. The fingers of his right hand were twisted and bent out of shape, some say from the work to which he had been set, but others say that it had been smashed by a guard's truncheon.

We had a quiet journey home, with neither of us in a mood for conversation. Several times I asked Bob for his opinion of what we had learned and had not learned, but he put me off. But then, as we were riding along the Flesk, he reined in, and sat looking at the quick-moving silver river. "As Reilly rightly asked us, Hughie, where the hell are the bloody arms?"

"He asked the wrong men," I said.

"Did he not?" Bob said in agreement. "It is to Dublin and New York and Manchester that he should put his question."

He might as well have said Timbuktu or Vienna, for all of me, distant dots on a schoolroom map of the world. But there was Bob, a shop assistant sitting astride a borrowed horse, dealing out the words like cards from a well-thumbed deck.

"March the sixth," he said, "the appointed day, and to learn that we had to ride down into Kerry. Bloody Yanks." Then he touched his heel to his horse's flank.

This time we did see soldiers on patrol, six of them, mounted. They were riding along a ridge to our right, distant by about a mile, in single file, the sun of noonday flat upon their scarlet. We proceeded along at our easy amble, and yet fearful that they would at any moment come riding down upon us. But although they saw us as plainly as we saw them, they made no move towards us, and we rode side by side, as it were, for a full half hour.

"They are minted in their thousands," Bob said, "like the tiny grenadiers and cavalry that you see in the windows of the Cork City toy shops."

But there was nothing tiny about these lads. The soldiers whom we had seen strolling about the streets of Killarney had been impressive evidence of the physical standards maintained by Her Majesty's regiments, and about these six dragoons there was something almost heraldic, silhouetted as they were against their ridge.

To come from Killarney back to our own Kilpeder was, on this one day at least, to pass from one world to another. The somnolence of the town, which so often we had cursed in our youthful high spirits and impatience, now seemed to us blessed. A farmer with his ass and cart came towards us, and touched a hand to his shapeless black hat, recognising the schoolmaster perhaps, or perhaps a more august personage, Dennis Tully's assistant. An old fellow, wizened pippin of a face, and dressed in the old fashion, breeches and high woollen stockings. We passed Saint Jarlath's and the priest's house, and then my own house and the school. At the barracks, there was no sign of Sergeant Honan, but Constable Belton was standing at the gate, chatting with two others, the three of them taking their ease. Strapping country lads crammed into uniforms, and not menacing at all, unlike the redcoat soldiers on the ridge above the Flesk.

But when we had passed the barracks, Bob leaned over to me and said, "Those two are not Honan's men. They are blow-ins." I looked back towards them, as casually as I could manage, and indeed I recognised neither of them. "Those idjeets in Kerry," I said; "because of them the barracks in Kilpeder has been strengthened."

"Because of something," he said, and rubbed the back of his hand across his mouth.

"Why else?" I said. "There was a pleasant balance of nature here between the peelers and ourselves. Tis shattered now."

Bob drew away his closed fist and smiled at me, and we rode gently along the market square to the stable.

And as gently strolled back again to my house in Chapel Street. The stone falcons of the Ardmor gates had their sightless eyes fixed upon us. The town seemed now a trifle less friendly, and worst of all was my sense that Bob and myself, and not the constables, were the discordant element.

It was a feeling which grew in strength when we entered the house. Ned had been in the kitchen, but our footfall summoned him. It seemed, for the moment, that he was himself the householder, and Bob and myself the visitors. The fire in the parlour had died out, and the air was chill. He was wearing the black suit which served him almost as uniform, and one of my own scarves was tied about his neck. His lank hair was uncombed, and between that and the long jaw and heavy cheekbones, he looked more than ever like a Red Indian from the American plains.

"Kilpeder has been growing by leaps and bounds," Bob said without preamble. "Tis not safe for Hugh and myself to leave the town unattended overnight."

"Fifteen of them," Ned said. "Mounted constables. They rode in yesterday afternoon, caped, with their carbines slung across their shoulders. They have a sergeant of their own, but an inspector came along to deliver them to Honan."

"The army itself has settled into Kerry," Bob said. "They moved south from Limerick Junction."

"It is our good fortune that they are not here as well," Ned said, "but only peelers."

"Only peelers," Bob said, with a deceptive mildness.

"We have our work cut out for us," Ned said, "from now until the appointed day."

"Until the sixth, that would be," Bob said in the same easy manner, and Ned stared at him fiercely for a moment, and then smiled.

"Yes," he said. "Until the sixth. The night of the fifth, to be precise. But we attack on the sixth, after dawn. They must be fond of talking, down there in Kerry."

"Such has ever been their reputation," I said.

"It was from no Kerry man that we learned the date," Bob said, "but from a Yank, like yourself. A man named Reilly. O'Connor is on his keeping in Iveragh, and his men scattered."

Ned nodded, and then, with his shoulder resting against the bookcase and his elbows held in his cupped hands, listened as Bob told him what we had learned in Killarney. Or rather, what Bob had learned, for I was astonished at how attentive he had been, noting the markings of the several regiments, and holding in memory what we had seen and heard. The furnishings of the room, secure and comfortable, reproved his words, as though he had ushered troopers and horses through the narrow door.

"But neither Reilly nor Timoney knows why he dispersed his men,"

Bob said. "And there are patrols out as far as the Derrynasaggarts. We passed one of them, but we were not hindered."

"Right," Ned said, almost with indifference. "Come back into the kitchen, the two of you." At the door, he paused and said, "Hugh, bring the *Examiner* along with you."

It was spread open across the chair in which I used spend my evenings, near the fire, and the page upon which my eye fell had an unfamiliar look to it, column beside column of the one account, with some of the paragraphs set in heavier type than the others. I took my spectacle case from my breast pocket, and fastened my spectacles upon my head. One of the bold paragraphs swam into my cleared vision, like a fish darting from murky water to the clear glass wall of its tank.

"They were dirty, ragged, wan, and shivering," I read, "as though the Poor Law Guardians had emptied out the skeletons of their sick wards upon the quays of Dublin. They were clad in the oddest and most motley clothing, and yet most had money about them, and a goodly number of revolvers were found where they had thrown them in their flight. The appearance which they presented was a curious mixture of the ferocious and the pathetic. From the crowd of ruffian onlookers who had been attracted by the spectacle, there came a few isolated shouts of rebel defiance, but these were not heeded by this cowed and dejected Fenian 'army.' "

Merciful God, I thought, what disaster is this? And folded back the paper so that I could inspect its first page. There were two stories, each with its headlines of tall black print, and I could make sense of neither of them, nor guess at a connexion between them. The one had to do with the capture of more than a hundred rebels on the docks of Dublin, after they had come ashore from the Liverpool boat. The other told of a "daring" and "villainous" attempt by the Irish Fenians to capture Chester Castle. And this baffled me utterly, for the only Chester of which I had ever heard was in England somewhere. Forgetful of my errand, I sank down into the chair, and fastened my glasses more securely.

Dimly in my imagination I saw such a castle as legend and song have furnished forth for us, massive and turreted, set in its lonely eminence, fierce seas pounding the rocks at its base. What had such a citadel to do with sullen scarecrows on the Dublin quays?

The *Examiner* obliged me with an explanation, as it had done so often in the past, upon matters of less moment. "Had the conspiracy gained its complicated objective," it told me, "the consequences would have been most serious. At least 10,000 rifles and a great store of ammunition is contained within the arsenal at the Castle. The rebels, close upon one thousand of them, had for the preceding several days been converging upon Liverpool, which lies fifteen miles to the north of Chester, and plans had been carefully laid to seize the Holyhead boat, and to destroy the railway and other lines of communication. Drogheda, on the Irish east coast, was the appointed port of delivery, and a number of arrests of Fenians in that city have been made by the Constabulary."

Far more pressing than my recognition of a disaster were my emotions of confusion and fright. We had always known, to be sure, that somewhere, far beyond the hills of Cork, there was a directory, or a supreme council, or whatever it chose, from month to month, to call itself. And we had known that somehow, perhaps by magic, it would provide us with arms. Perhaps, in our innocence, we had assumed that they would come to us from America, tall steamers bulging with rifles, gleaming and oiled. Never had we imagined an English castle smashed open, and boats and railways seized. I set to work again upon the *Examiner* but could not make sense of what I read. I then recalled that all that was required of me was to carry it into the kitchen.

But thus it was, in the homely pages of the *Cork Examiner*, that we learned of the ruined raid upon Chester Castle, which was to provide arms for the Rising. In the weeks to come, the *Illustrated News* and such journals would furnish their English readers with appropriate images, Chester Castle no longer a romantic bastion, save for one remaining tower, but a grim collection of utilitarian storehouses and the like, and our Fenians an ugly and reprobate lot with revolver butts protruding from their workingmen's jackets. For the present hour, my imagination was left to its own contrivances.

Ned and Bob stood side by side in the kitchen, with the ordnance survey map spread out before them on the table, and with mugs of tea in their hands. Bob had unbuttoned his greatcoat, but had not yet taken it off. I held out the newspaper, but Ned did not lift up his eyes from the map, and Bob it was who took it from me. It was clear, however, that Ned had already told him the gist of the matter.

"Troops," Bob read aloud, "were moved into Chester by railway in the hours before the intended attack, and were in position to repel any hostile action by the insurgents."

"In an excellent position," Ned said. "Our lads had revolvers only. It would have been bloody murder. Somewhere in there it says that five thousand troops were moved in."

"The tea is fresh-steeped, Hugh," Bob said, taking over Ned's task of putting me at ease in my own house.

"Had you known about these plans, Ned?" I said.

"We were to be armed before the appointed day," Ned said. "I knew only that."

Bob held his two hands cupped around his mug, as though for warmth. "This is all bloody nonsense, Ned. Murderous nonsense. And well you must know it. If those rifles had been landed at Drogheda, they would have well served the east. Dublin itself might have been taken on your bloody appointed day. But they could never have found their way to the midlands, let alone to Cork or Kerry or Galway. Reilly, below in Killarney, seems to believe that arms from someplace or other were to have been landed at Cahirciveen. That would have been helpful," he added in a tone of open sarcasm.

"It would indeed," Ned said, ignoring the tone. "Perhaps that is why O'Connor knocked over the coast-guard station. O'Connor may have had orders that neither of us knows about. That is how the organization works."

"No arms will be landed now in Kerry," Bob said. "And O'Connor will be a lucky man if he gets out of there with a whole skin."

I had scant wish for tea, but for want of something to do, I poured myself a cup. Whatever Ned's merits as a captain, he was a poor fist at the tea making. Weak, pallid stuff it was.

"We have two scant weeks left to us now," Bob said. "And you know what condition we are in. Small farmers and labourers with a scattering of duck guns."

"Why should I not know what condition we are in? I am in command in Kilpeder, Bob Delaney, and you would do well to remember it."

"I do not envy you your eminence," Bob said. "What do you propose to do?"

"A curious question, Bob. You know what we intend to do. Early on the morning of the sixth, we will secure the barracks and then move north to Millstreet. At Millstreet, we will become part of a much larger force."

"Without arms," Bob said, "and although fifteen men have been sent to strengthen Honan. Not sent, by God, but carried here by an inspector. Dublin Castle is on the move at last."

"Not without arms," Ned said. "When first I assembled with you at Knockmany, I pledged to you that we would not go unarmed into action. Nor will we. We have perhaps seventy men to be provided for, and the barony itself will do the providing."

So it was, over mugs of tea in a schoolmaster's kitchen, that the great Kilpeder Arms Raid—"Nolan's Raid," as the wretched ballad has it—was planned. Bob and Ned went over the map, inch by inch, with Bob translating its lines and squiggles into farms and estates and the names of men. He did not know all of them, by any means, any more than I did myself, but he knew a fair number, and he was able to give Ned's plan its launching. Presently Mary came home from whatever visit she had been making, and with her sleeves rolled back, set to work preparing us a proper meal, and an hour later, in time to eat with us, Vincent strolled in. What Mary, her back turned to us, thought of our conversation, I can but speculate, but it could not have made pleasant listening for her, acts of brigandage however justified by necessity.

But Vincent was a great help. He had even then, in his early years, a vast knowledge of the sporting life of the barony, and who among the gentry were best esteemed for their prowess with the gun, and which of them had seen service in the army. The notion that they should furnish us with the sinews of war struck him as a droll one, and he entered the task almost as though it were itself a sport, or at least a game of some sort. "Now, Saunders," he said, putting a white, precise forefinger upon the map, "I have heard make his boast in the Arms that his gun rack is unmatched this side of Mallow, his weapons lovely creatures shaped expressly for him by a gunsmith in London. I have longed to try them out." At this stage in his career, there were but a handful of gentry houses to which he had the entrée, and these mostly the houses of racketing bachelor squireens, wild, hard-drinking fellows. It was far different in later years.

From beginning to end, I do not believe that Ned had ever a proper grasp of Vincent. Ned had a pawky humour about him at times, and was ready at times to laugh at the droll or ludicrous side of human affairs. But at bottom, life was a serious matter to him, a weighing out of certainties heavy as lead or gold. And too much of Vincent seemed to him all froth and banter, silver flasks and flowered waistcoats, chat about women and horses. In this he was I think misguided by his long years of absence from this country, for by all that one hears or reads about them, Americans are a sober and industrious people, at work on their needed inventions and conquering their Indian-haunted wilderness. But the Vincents of this world are the very stuff of our national being, and we know them well. You will see them at race meetings, hats pushed back, cigars clenched between white, even teeth. Or a knot of them together by a tavern fire, a bowl of punch steaming before them against the winter's cold. Best of all, you will see them out beagling of a russet morning, in their tweeds and leggings starred with burrs, their shouts blending with the yelps of the dogs. And we know that beneath the froth and the banter there may be nothing, nothing at all, a cave of empty air. Or there may be a will hard as iron, and the cunning of a running fox.

At any event, Ned cut short with impatience all of Vincent's savoury anecdotes about the people whom we proposed to rob—"a levy for the national cause," as Ned put it delicately. He was interested only in Vincent's guesses as to what kind of arms we might expect to find, and which of the owners might be likely to offer us resistance. Vincent was not offended. He relished Ned as he did most new experiences, an untried sherry, or the arrival in the barony of a newly purchased brood mare. Bob made his notes of all that we were able to put together, and when that was done, he and Ned bent their heads over the map, and worked out our plan of campaign.

It was done as simply as that, the planning of "Nolan's Raid," "the Arms Raid at Kilpeder"—call it what you will. Two hours' work, and then the meal which Mary had all this while been preparing, the map folded neatly and put aside, and the dirty cups of cold tea carried out into the scullery, and the blue-and-white Delft plates set out before us. It is a great wonder to me, the distance between thoughts and their consequences, which is no doubt a good reason why I chose well in choosing a sedentary calling. For Ned and Bob, once they had marked out the likely houses upon their map and had talked a bit about the likeliest fellows to head the squads, all was settled and done, and they fell to their boiled fowl. Nothing more certain to them but that the plans would blossom out into actuality, as with those pellets from Japan that are dropped into water, where they unfold themselves into plants and small misshapen dragons.

And it came to pass, of course, three nights later. The same map was spread out upon Laffan's rough table, in the dark night, black and windy beyond the walls of the cabin, blackness broken by the fallen stars of the watch lanterns. It was a task that took the whole of the night, and on into the dawn hour. Each squad had its route assigned to it, four or five or a half dozen houses, and when they returned, if they had used their time properly and efficiently, they were rewarded by being sent out again. Not a squad but had one failure to report, or two. At Rosenalis, despite what both Bob and Vincent had thought to the contrary, there was not a weapon upon the premises, although two duck guns had been sent down to Cork for repair the week before. And Summit's Eye, the ramshackle farm of a squireen named Nagle, was reported by its squad to be fastened up tighter than a hogshead, as though Nagle had expected trouble. "We could have battered down the door with time and patience," said Kennedy, who led the squad. Then he added, sensibly enough, "But to hell with it, we said."

But our success was a substantial one. In fours and fives and sixes, the rifles and shotguns of one sort or another were carried up to Laffan's, and each one of them examined, first by Ned and then by Vincent, and then added to one of the neat stacks in the far corner of the room, by the gable end. Beside them, upon an upended crate, were placed the small wooden boxes of ammunition. One of these lacked a top, and I put my fingers into it, feeling the cool, oily cartridges, with their dark, sullen tips. There was a fair sprinkling of pistols as well, and a few revolvers, complicated instruments, self-important in their appearance, as though they knew more than any owner would of the ways of explosive death. And there was even, beautifully boxed in dark walnut, lined top and bottom in faded blue velvet, a pair of duelling pistols, with engraving upon the long, wide barrels, the floor of the case fitted to their shapes. It had been carried to us from Barrington's house, at Glencairn on the Millstreet road, whose father and grandfather before him had been celebrated upon the field of honour in the days when none dared call himself a gentleman who had not blazed away at his opponent and in turn stood his fire on a cool, foggy morning, seconds and surgeon in attendance, and flasks of brandy and coffee waiting in the carriage.

Ferdy Lynch, who brought the case to us from Barrington's, placed it almost with reverence upon the map spread out upon the table, where it covered many acres. It was plain that he considered it, poor fellow, the prize catch of the raid, although even I could see that the pistols were all but useless to us, elaborate contrivances with small wheels and mysterious devices. They seemed to me haughty and malignant emissaries from the world which we proposed to challenge, a world which could waste a hundred pounds upon a pair of murderous toys.

But Ned, with more tact and good humour than I would have credited him with, nodded to Lynch with approval. "Fine weapons indeed," he said. Lynch, like some of the other men, had blackened his face for the night's work, his features finger-smeared with chimney soot, and when he smiled, his strong teeth were white as rain-washed marble. His was one of the last squads in, and although the room was yet dark save for the guttering tallow lights, the air beyond the streaked window had begun to lighten. We were all of us tired, and no longer fully awake, and when Ned had gently closed upon the duelling pistols their cover of dark, smooth wood, he rubbed his knuckles into his eyes.

It was clear that he was pleased with his night's work, and he had reason to be. By Bob's tally, we had armed the Kilpeder column, with rifles, shotguns, revolvers, and with a spare armful or two to provide for accidents or for such recruits as we might pick up. As events were to prove, it might even be called the single most successful exploit of the 1867 rising, which no doubt is the reason why it was to appear so often in the wretched pothouse balladry of later years, together with Clon-brony Wood, and O'Neill's battle on the coast below, and the running gunfight that Crowley was to stage, a bit later, in Limerick. And yet at the time, throughout all of the long night, it was not prodigious at all. Perhaps because Ned was so workmanlike, sending out his squads as you might send out fellows to mend a road. Or perhaps because all the rest of us were so ignorant of what we were about, blind-certain that a sol-dier from America held in his two hands the ropes and reins of grand strategy.

The very last squad of all was Matty Brennan's, a light squad, because two of his lads, brothers, had sloped off when they came to their own farm, on the way back. "Sure, they are not to be blamed," Matty said, with a faint truculence, "when they could see the smoke from their own hearth, and knew that the old father was astir." Bob nodded, and bid Matty tarry for a bowl of Laffan's stirabout, which, curiously, Laffan was himself preparing, rather than entrusting the task to his wife. It was very good stirabout, hot and thick, with the taste of morning upon it. Into each bowl, as he ladled it out, he added an eggshell of his whiskey, and a knob of butter and a splash of milk.

I took my own bowl outside with me, to stand clear of the close, foul-smelling cabin. There were only the few of us left now upon the hill, but groups of men had all night been moving in and out of the room, sweating and cursing, spitting upon the floor and scarce deigning to grind the gob into the dirt with heel of boot. Their presence lingered, staining the air. Soldiers of the Irish Republic they well might be, but Laffan's cabin that night had been ripped out of time, and we might all of us have been Ribbonmen, or the Whiteboys of the century before us, cowherds and spalpeens bent upon acts of dark, bloody vengeance. For some, at least, of the lads that night, it had not been so much the arming of the Kilpeder column that we had been about as a bash at the landlords, and the first in many long years.

Truth to tell, there had been a part of me that felt the same. In my mind's eye, I had seen a dark drawing room, invisible the elegant, thin-legged chairs and sofas, the needlepoint fire screens; minatory upon the walls the silhouettes and paintings of fathers and grandfathers, cold, starched, imperious; silver and pewter on the sideboard. Shouts and a battering upon the hall door, and presently an enquiring candle carried down the stairs, and the door bolts opened, the door opened a crack at first, and then flung wide. And beyond the door, in chill night air, the universe unfamiliar as it always is when one encounters it at midnight, roused from sleep, Matty Brennan and his squad, dark clothes and faces blackened. Without a word, they push forward into the hall. And for the householder, an inherited nightmare: murderous peasants risen up from mist-shrouded bogs. Not Matty Brennan, as decent and mild a man as you would find in a day's walk, but a bog creature, and worse than he bunched up behind him. And Matty Brennan, for his part, seeing not Samuel Whoever of Whatever Lodge, blunt, careless, good-humoured, but a landlord frightened with good cause, fearful for his drawing room full of ormolu clocks and petit point and boastful heirlooms. There were dark passions at work within all of us in those years, as there would be again in the days of the Land War. Least of all do I absolve myself.

But the morning world outside Laffan's cabin was aloof from such concerns. They lay, all of them, somewhere below the twisted skein of boreens, beyond pasturelands still soaked with the night's slight rainfall. No other cabin lay within view, and with my back turned against rifles and revolvers, it was as though I had all Ireland to myself. All darkness had been bleached away, and the countryside was held in wet, pearly light. It softened the rank, harsh green of the grasses, and the black, glistening rocks. The boreen which led down from our cabin was thick-edged with hedges and slender trees, rowans and blackberries, leafless now in this month before spring. Far off, to my left, stretched a small bog with the mists still clinging to it, and beyond the bog, unexpected light struck a stream's ribbon of pale silver. And, farthest off of all, still dark, far to the west, were the Derrynasaggarts, sheltering us from the sea. It was a world without sound—no curlew cried, no darting wing broke the low, cloudy heaven.

Brief master of an unpeopled world, I stood thus for I cannot say how long, a few minutes no doubt, long enough to let the morning air chill my porridge. How often it is that one has the universe to oneself, and how easy of attainment, if one tarries long before going to bed, or rises up before others are astir. But on this morning, and perhaps because of the manner in which we had spent the night, it was mystery that I felt pressing itself upon me, and a great wonder at our lonely enterprise. Who were we, I asked myself, and under what authority did we rampage about in the night, pillaging households for guns with which to shoot at policemen and redcoats? And who were they, that they should march up and down across the land, holding us all in subjection to a distant queen and parliament? The answers lay somewhere soaked into the scene before me, which was the shape and form of Ireland, as urgent upon the senses as a song in Gaelic heard at nightfall, carried across a valley, or the sight of a turf cutter walking homewards in evening light or the time-softened stones of a shattered abbey seen against a horizon. Thus, alone, do we commune with ourselves, and the issue of all is guns fired off, and men falling down with great holes smashed into them.

But fortunately, I was not left long alone with such reflexions, for the others now came drifting out, first Bob and Vincent together, talking and laughing. Bob seemed neither sleepy nor tired, pleased as Punch by what we had accomplished, and his manner was brisk as he rubbed his hands together against the rawness of the morning.

"By God, Hughie," he said to me, "you look like Prince Hamlet there, perched like a black crow upon the crumbling parapets of Denmark."

"There is a professor below in Queen's College," Vincent said, "who believes that Shakespeare was an Irishman. How else could he have written such grand poetry? Tis a thought. Tommy Moore was a grand poet, and he was Irish. There is powerful logic on the professor's side."

He had taken a morning cigar from his case of blood-red morocco leather, and now he lit it with his elegant little machine of flint, moving the flame to and fro and taking gentle puffs.

Bob laughed, and clapped him on the shoulder. But Bob's words had come too pat upon my lofty meditations. Often it is not the grand, tumultuous scenes in Shakespeare which have the most effect upon me, but the quiet ones tucked away in odd corners of scenes and acts, so quiet that often they have been hacked away from such productions as find their way to the theatres in Cork. Somewhere upon a barren plain like the one before us, the armed men of Norway trudge along towards Poland to gain a little patch of ground that has no profit in it but the name, and a courteous captain, tarrying to chat with the black-crow prince, says that he would not pay five ducats to take the lease of it. Spoken like an Irishman; I have heard the same said often. But Hamlet pumps up these most sensible words into grand and resounding music, as is his inveterate habit, and turns Fortinbras, a machine for killing if ever one clanked along the earth, into a delicate and tender prince, puffed with divine ambition. Spoken also like an Irishman, but in the early hours, after a hard night session in convivial company.

"He has no great fondness for the Irish, this same Shakespeare," I said, "when he thinks about us at all. Rug-headed kernes. Has Queen's College taken that into account?"

"Deception," Vincent said. "Covering his tracks. Pretending to be the son of a Stratford tanner."

"Hark at you," Bob said. "The two of you. Holding a scholarly conversation, and Laffan's cabin behind you, crammed to the thatch with plundered firearms."

But as he spoke, he could not keep the pleasure from his voice, and Vincent and I, seeing this, grinned at each other. I wonder did Vincent guess then, as I myself did not until much later, at the sources of that pleasure. Ever since our visit to Kerry, the question of arms had been nagging at him, and it was a great relief to him to know that we had them now, safe within Laffan's. But I believe that there was more to it than that. What we had been about has passed into legend as "Nolan's Raid," but it was as much Bob's work as his. Bob it was who chose the squads, and chivvied and cajoled them into an understanding of their tasks, who hailed them at the door upon their return, and urged them towards the hearth to take away the chill of night and darkness.

Vincent walked to one of Laffan's boundary stones, a flat grey boulder with a dab of faded whitewash on it, and looked at it absently, as if trying to call something to mind.

"We are close enough now to the appointed day." There was for once no banter in his pleasant tenor.

"Close enough," Bob said, and looked back towards the cabin. And as he did so, the last of us, Ned and Pat Dunphy, with Laffan following, came out to join us.

Ned's heavy coat was hanging unbuttoned and loose, and his hands were jammed down, as always, into its pockets. He must himself have been as pleased as Bob, but his features did not show it, rawbones face, and dark, sunken eyes. Laffan, a loose-featured, slovenly man, was carrying a jug with him. He served us well that night, and would in the days to come, but I had no liking for him. He moved to some jagged and barbarous music of his own, set for him by these lonely acres, companion of hares and snipes.

"We could all of us do with a pull at that," Ned said, nodding to the jug, and Laffan, taking out the stopper, handed it to Bob. With a quick, surprised glance at Ned, Bob tilted up the jug and swallowed, then wiped the neck of it and handed it over to Vincent. When my own turn came, I took first a small, apprehensive sip, but it was one of Laffan's better concoctions, smooth as melted pearls, and I took a good swallow of it and then a second, to wash down the first.

We stood in a rough circle, the six of us, and the moment had the feel of ritual to it, as the whiskey moved among us. If there had been snipe or curlew to swing above us, it would have thought us small and insignificant, six men standing beside a cabin, and stretching out away from us in all directions the immensities of pasturelands and bog, reaching out towards mountains. Our voices, so confident and strong as we faced each other upon the ground, would bleach away into the silences of the upper air.

Ned was the last of us to drink, taking the jug from Dunphy, and when he had slaked his thirst, handing it back to Laffan, who restoppered it, and then, turning his back upon us, walked to his cabin with heavy-haunched tread.

"The men will need two long sessions to get the feel of those weapons," Ned said. "After that we will drill in earnest. Give them this night to rest, Bob, and bring them back here the night after. Each man will take his weapon away with him from that drill, and the rounds for it, and we will drill again, on the Thursday at Knockmany. Can you see to that?"

"I can," Bob said. "Pat Dunphy here and myself can see to it."

"The greater part of the lads have never had their hands upon gun or rifle before this night," Dunphy said.

"There is no great mystery to it," Ned said. "I can tell them in an hour all that they will need to know."

"Yes, sir," Dunphy said, in a voice heavy with doubt.

"My word on it," Ned said. "Firepower and men banging away is what we will need, and not sharpshooters."

Bob, I took notice, had a look as quizzical as Dunphy's, but he said nothing on that subject.

"The night's work will make a great stir in Kilpeder," he said.

"The stir will have begun by now," Ned said. "Honan at the barracks will know of matters within the next few hours, and then the district inspector, and those gentlemen will put it on the wire to Cork and to Dublin. You lads had best be in your homes by then. You had best brace yourself, Hughie, for brisk questioning from Sergeant Honan."

It was as though Ned had completed his reading of one chapter of a book, and had flipped over the page to the next one. His eyes peered at me from their heavy thickets. It was a book which could not be rewritten, as it were. The night was irrevocable.

"What would you have me tell him, Ned?" I asked.

He shrugged. "He will not believe anything you say. I had my meal with you last evening, and then walked out. You have not seen me since. He might arrest you or he might not. I am inclined to doubt it. Bob and Vincent will be safe. I am depending on that."

"Welcome news," Vincent said in a small voice, and he and I exchanged glances. He was holding his cigar between his lips, but it had died.

"They will proclaim the district," Bob said. "But that will take time. It must be done from Dublin. Until then, there must be warrants, and probable cause, and all the rest of it."

"Proclaim it they will," Ned said. "This comes hard upon the heels of O'Connor below in Kerry, and with only the mountains between us. Patches of the same quilt."

Vincent and myself, not to mention poor Dunphy, were like schoolchildren eavesdropping upon the conversation of masters discoursing upon matters too lofty for our comprehension. Or I was myself, at any rate. Vincent, I observed, had a small smile behind the dead cigar.

"To be honest with you," Vincent said, "I would feel safer outside the town entirely."

There was a pause before Ned responded, and then he nodded. "Fair enough," he said. "You can stay here with me, if you would like. I cannot answer for Laffan's fare. But not you, Bob, nor Hughie. I need you in place, there in Kilpeder, whatever the risk to you may be."

"Upon that you may depend," Bob said. "Hugh and myself have livings to earn. We are not gentlemen adventurers, like the two of you."

Which was true enough. In a few hours' time, I would be facing my ruffians, textbook in hand, and the switch nearby to suppress any servile insurrections, and Bob, his grey-and-white-striped apron tied neatly about his middle, would be attending to the needs of Tully's customers. The images did nothing to dispel the feeling of unreality which had taken hold of me. Is it likely, I asked myself, that Ireland will be freed by schoolmasters and shop assistants. Or by dogged, puzzled countrymen like Pat Dunphy, or imitation squires like Vincent. Someday, perhaps, in a century's time, the scene which we provided at the moment might make a handsome steel engraving, the Fenians of Kilpeder gathered outside a mountain cabin, with streams and hills in the distance, our features set in lines of calm resolution. But the simple truth was that Vincent feared not the Irish Constabulary but the wrath of Dennis Tully, and who could blame him? Myself it was who thought with despair of my Mary opening the door upon Sergeant Honan, and his men behind him with their carbines.

But a glance at Ned did much to dispel such misgivings. Not alone because he was capable and determined, but because he had come to us as the emissary of the organization, with its net spread across the country, and its Centres in Dublin and London and Manchester and New York. I think that for all of us, in those weeks, Ned had a meaning larger than his life and being. He embodied for us what was always in those days called "the cause," a term which has now an old-fashioned ring to it, although politicians have a fondness for it. "The cause for which the Fenians fought and died on the hillside," they will tell us as they seek our votes— O'Brienites and Redmondites, and Healyites, and the rest of them. I have always held myself aloof from their courtings, although I was briefly in demand as one of the hillside men, as we came to be known. Far different was it in those days. Perhaps it was youth.

"Well, now, Captain Nolan," Bob said, as we took our leaves of himself and Vincent. "You can look back upon a good night's work. We have begun well." And reaching out, he took Ned's hand. The two of them stood thus for a minute, looking into each other's eyes. Those two had ways of understanding which left me shut out.

"Bid Kilpeder good-morrow for me," Vincent said to me. He seemed as blithe as ever. It was almost as though he had chosen to spend the weekend with a friend, in the hope of a morning's shooting.

When Bob and Pat and myself had gone down a bit of the boreen, I twisted my head for a last look at them. Vincent was nowhere to be seen. Perhaps he had gone back into Laffan's to inspect his accommodations, God help him. But Ned was standing half turned away from us, bareheaded, a gawky crow of a fellow. He was facing northwards, towards Millstreet, motionless as a statue.

"A good beginning," I said to Bob, quoting back at him his own words to Ned.

"Here," Bob said. "It has begun well here. In Kilpeder." And said no more.

At Kiloughter cross, Pat left us, to walk the five miles or more to his farm. "We are equipped now, Bob, are we not, for the appointed day?" he said.

"We are indeed," Bob said, "when once we have learned the management of those blunderbusses and horse pistols and portable cannon."

Dunphy laughed, with legs spread apart, and hands pressed upon heavy hipbones. "One thing is certain, Bob," he said, "if all of the columns have commanders like Nolan, the poor old country will be free."

But when we were by ourselves, the two of us, I said to Bob, more bluntly, "What ails you at all?" It was clear morning now, the air bright and sparkling, the pale blue sky broken only by a few clouds, high up and fluffy as cotton.

"Nothing at all," Bob said, looking away from me across flat pastures towards a distant cabin. "Nothing at all, save abject terror and foreboding." He laughed then, and turned to me, to see the effect upon me of his words.

"You are not quaking," I said to him, "not so that it can be noticed."

"'Tis not my way," he said, which was true enough. "He is not constructed as the rest of us are," he said, "yourself and myself and Vincent. He is like one of those revolvers, back there at Laffan's."

When Bob spoke the word, I was back in the rere room of my house, that first night, and Ned, a stranger to me then, was holding in his hand the American revolver, bulky and dark-metalled, with its wide, murderous mouth.

"Tis what is needed," I said, and Bob nodded absently.

"Oh, to be sure," he said, and we walked along in companionable, troubled silence for a bit. But his words chimed with other feelings of my own, and they put a damper upon the bright morning.

"We have a fair chance," Bob said, to himself rather than to me. "That is all we ever hoped for, a fair chance." But in truth, we had hoped for much more. Two years before, on that balmy afternoon in March when we had journeyed up to Cork to take the oath, there had been great talk of men and guns and gold pouring in to us from America, when once their great war there had been ended. And so recently as last year, the loyalist newspapers had been whipping themselves to a frenzy that the guns were already here, and trained soldiers in their thousands, and Fenian agents subverting the allegiances of our Irish lads in the regiments of the British army. One of the great illustrated journals of London had given over an entire page to an imaginative engraving of a steamship hove to in some wild and desolate cove of the west, black storm clouds stretched across the horizon, and bulky, ominous mountains crowding down to the very edge of the strand. Boats were putting out to the ship, to carry away oiled rifles packed into immense cases the size of coffins. And all this had dwindled down into Laffan's cabin, and Ned's squads of five or six men carrying up an armful of duck guns in the vast, starless night, with meagre lanterns to light the way.

But it was now daylight, with the smell of wet grasses in the air, and Bob and myself for all the world like two idle young fellows walking the road into Kilpeder. The road itself is still there, of course, why would it not be, and many the time in later years I was to walk it, calling back that morning to memory. The road is there, and the pastures, the black-grey fences, and either the very cabins or else their successors. It is the past that has vanished, my own past and that of the land. Some there are who have described the events yet to transpire as "glorious failure," wrapping around them the tinted mists of legend behind which figures in motion may dimly be discerned. And others there are who make mock of them, calling those of us who went out in Limerick and Tipperary and West Cork ignorant and blundering men, deceived by callous and half-drunken adventurers, as the servant girls of New York and the navvies of Liverpool were deceived, handing over their soiled and folded dollar bills, their smeared shillings, so that the Fenian leaders might live safely and well in the hotels of their choice. Learned and judicious scholars, no doubt, will someday see us in a perspective as yet unimaginable, black ants the lot of us, crawling across the entablatures of history—Fenians and policemen and soldiers and landlords and labourers.

Once only, and for a few weeks, did my life touch upon the life of history. It was to be different for Ned Nolan and Bob Delaney. They were marked men: history chose them for her own. But I was to drift into history, and then drift out of it again, a man shaped for obscurity as others are shaped for great enterprises. Are not my inconsequential memories the evidence of this? I remember Bob and myself upon our morning walk into Kilpeder, air warming beneath the rising sun, the dust of the road and scatterings of cowslips in the verges, the spires of the town in the distance, and the silvery Sullane. Bob's spirits lifted as we approached the town, although he was still preoccupied, and he began presently to whistle, a tune which I did not recognise. It could have been one of a score, the plaintive haunting tunes which we townsmen identified with the Irish-speaking outlands of the Boggeraghs, tunes scraped upon fiddles or carried by the unaccompanied voice. Such tunes, even when they are sprightly or rambunctious, have always about them the loneliness of moorlands and bracken hills, a savoury and beckoning melancholy.

We were at last at the last cross before the town, which falls upon a slight rise, and but a twenty minutes' walk along the Macroom road to Chapel Street, beyond which, past church and school, lay the market square. There we paused, and Bob, turning towards me, misquoted Tom Moore, our favorite of our Thursday evenings, as we stood about the piano, Bob and Vincent and myself, with Mary seated before it, her hands upon the keys, and candles glowing softly to either side of her. "The valley lay smiling before us," Bob said, and smiled at me, as though he too held that memory, notes of music and flickering candlelight intertwined, and our voices holding us joined together in friendship. From where we stood, I could see our house, a warm and beckoning presence, far distant from Laffan's lonely hillside and the night's work that was behind us. But it is the night's work that was to be remembered, in the barony and far beyond it, history and human nature being what they are.

In search of arms he sallied forth, brave Dunphy at his side.
"Rise up, rise up, ye Fenian men, defeat I'll not abide.
With weighty lead and dauntless steel, we'll face them as we should."
Thus Nolan bold, 'neath green and gold, marched towards Clonbrony Wood.

It is thus, no doubt in the annals of all nations. Schoolmasters and shop assistants and squireens with sprigged waistcoats are not the stuff of ballads, but rather the gunmen who drift in and then away, and the good-hearted young fellows who in the heel of the hunt lie stretched upon the hard earth, blood staining the snow.

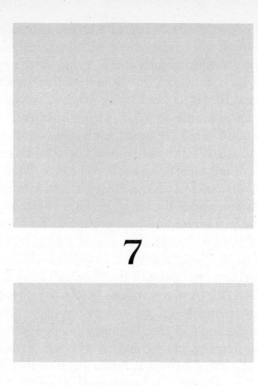

7

[Patrick Prentiss]

One summer afternoon, when Patrick Prentiss had put aside for a few days his manuscript, and the accumulation of notebooks and records from which he was constructing it, a memory floated, unbidden, into view.

He was spending the week with a university friend, Dick Leese, in a North Devon village a few miles from Taunton, a village which was as subdued and as comfortable as a Victorian sampler: church, vicarage, inn, greengrocer's, draper's shop, set upon a gentle curve of road. His friend, and his friend's neighbours, most of them, kept bees, and in the drowsy afternoon sun of late June, their sounds blended in his senses with the fragrances of clover and new grass. Kilpeder, with its shabby market square and ragged hills, seemed as distant as the Poles. Leese's garden ended, beyond leafy brambles, in a stream, beside which ran a sandy footpath. Downstream a quarter mile, a small bridge, humped but graceful, arched above the water. He would walk to it, in the hour before tea, an hour heavy with sound and odour, the heaviness of a secure and settled world, the church's square tower just visible above wide-branched elms.

On that day, a memory tugged at him, gently, without reason. It was summer, and, home from school, he was in his father's study in the house in Palmerston Park. His father, back to the window, was seated at his great desk, making notes in his precise hand, lifting it regularly to dip his pen in ink. His other hand rested flat upon the desk, but he raised it from time to time to his smooth, silken beard, yellow flecked with grey. Across the room, near the cold fireplace, Patrick sat on the floor, back resting against a chair. He was very quiet. This was their custom, ratified by unspoken compact. He was welcome in the study; his father liked him there, would from time to time look up towards him and smile. But he was not to talk, not until his father sighed, stretched, placed the pen back in its stand. He had the run of the books row upon row, the highest shelves beyond his reach, but the best ones close to the floor, tall folios describing journeys to the Levant, the Amazon, China, and richly illustrated. On the afternoon he now remembered, he had placed flat on the floor beside him an old, bound volume of the *Illustrated London News,* an immense volume bound in purple buckram, and on its cover, stamped in gilt, the Queen, with a tall, leafed branch in either hand, seated, and above her a semicircle of seven crowns. Or he assumed it was the Queen. He did not dare ask.

It was, as he came later to understand, the summer of Parnell, and by October Parnell would be dead. But all that summer, week after week, he would return to Ireland for his savage, desperate fight to recapture the cause which he had once commanded, speaking on shabby platforms, guttering torchlight, bodyguard of ex-Fenian toughs, and the crowds hostile, jeers and lumps of earth flung towards the platform, towards the tall, furious speaker, beard unkempt, voice hoarse with shouting. All that melodrama Prentiss learned of later. But it seeped, like wisps of autumn leaf smoke, into the house in Palmerston Park, at dinner, or occasionally at early breakfast, when associates of his father's would call in, before they all set off for the Four Courts.

"He has gone mad," his father said one morning—and that summer, the pronoun always meant Parnell. "I mean that literally. There has always been madness in that family. Tearing the party apart, the country apart. And who will profit from it? The Tories, of course. The landlords and the London bankers. We made him, by God, and if need must, by God, we'll show him that we can unmake him. Our own fault—ten years of treating him as a kind of uncrowned king."

"Ah well," a friend said one morning, holding towards the maid his empty cup, "he has now an uncrowned queen to console him." But Patrick's father, unsmiling, nodded in warning towards the listening boy.

The world lay spread within the purple buckram folio—a great ship being launched in New York, the Italian chamber of deputies, the Seychelles Islands, the Crystal Palace in London after a great snowstorm, heavy white mantles obscuring glass and iron, the Emperor and Empress of the French at the Tuileries, the Emperor uniformed, goateed, the Empress in tight-waisted crinoline, diademed. Now, a quarter century later, the French no longer had an empire, Napoleon III dead and his empress growing old, somewhere in England. The pages were brittle to the touch as Prentiss turned them one by one. The familiar lay suddenly before him, humble and puzzling.

A full page had been given over to what looked like any village in Ireland, meaningless in its familiarity. A dirt road, beside it a tumbledown wall, beyond the wall a square barracks, and beside the barracks a score of men black-caped, rifles on shoulders, lounging. A uniformed man, sword at waist, stood talking to top-hatted civilians. On the far side of the road, in a field, peasants stood gathered and were staring towards the barracks, the women shawled, barefooted, the men shabby-breeched, dented hats, one of them with a bit of pipe clenched between set lips. Beyond, the road straggled towards gable ends, a church spire, and, in the distance, a row of mean cabins. Against grey engraved sky, random birds—each two quick, double-arched strokes. Nothing more. Beside one of the cabins, a woman's huddled figure, indistinct. "The police barracks at Kilpeder, County Cork," the legend read. "Scene of one of the attacks by armed Fenians on March 6. The battle which began here ended that night at the neighbouring Clonbrony Wood."

He remembered asking his father, suddenly, "What was the battle of Kilpeder?" His father, preoccupied, looked up, rehearsed the words to himself, and said, "Kilpeder? In Ireland? There is a Kilpeder in Cork, on the Killarney road. A market town. There could have been a battle there in Tudor times. The Desmond rebellion, perhaps."

"No," Prentiss said. "It is here, in the *Illustrated News*. Kilpeder and Clonbrony Wood."

His father put down his pen, and looked at Prentiss, two white hands resting on the desk. "God bless us, boy. Clonbrony Wood. What have you there? Bring it here." It was an armful. "Put it there, Patrick," his father said. "Never mind the papers; they are safe enough."

The book open before them, Prentiss bending forward, father and son studied the engraving. By a trick of perspective, it was almost as though they stood together on the road, where the artist had stood, looking towards barracks, policemen, peasants, the wheeling, frozen birds. It was this that he remembered most clearly.

"I was at Trinity," his father said. "I was a few years older than you are now. The Fenian rising—I remember those days. Ballyknockane, Clonbrony Wood, Tallaght. The Fenian snows, gunfire down in Munster, in our own hills—here outside Dublin. And then everything seemed to die away. But it was all brought back to us before the year was out. The police van smashed in Manchester, and Colonel Kelly rescued. Allen and Larkin and O'Brien hanged in public, with a drunken English mob jeering at them. Clonbrony Wood. I may have seen this very engraving. As a young fellow at Trinity."

The young Prentiss could not imagine his father as a student. He had always been encased in authority, handsome worsteds black as ebony, tweeds soft and thick.

"God save them all," his father said. " 'They rose in dark and evil days.' Have you ever heard that sung?"

Prentiss shook his head.

"There were lads at Clonbrony Wood no older than I myself then was," his father said. "And what in God's name were they serving? The vanity of James Stephens and the greed of Yankee adventurers. Their wretched organization shot through with charlatans and informers. The price was paid by those poor lads who did the fighting. Do you know where the greatest of the hostings were, Patrick? Right here, in the mountains outside Dublin. Tallaght, Glencullen, Stepaside. Brave men. Misguided men, but brave."

Prentiss could not grasp the disjointed words. There was a touch in his father of the university don who had missed his calling. He loved to lecture, to unroll the past, at the dinner table, or on those long Sunday rambles in the mountains where once there had been a great hosting. Once, on a walk across the Scalp, high rock croppings and barren bogs on either side of them, his father had set out for him the entire career of Napoleon, from gaunt, hungry lieutenant to the ruined exile on Saint Helena, paunchy and lachrymose. But he was not lecturing now, and his words were choppy, weighed down with feelings which Prentiss could not understand.

"You know F. X. O'Brien, do you not, Patrick?" his father said. "He has been often to this house. F. X. was one of them. One of the Cork Fenians. Not at Clonbrony, but he was in Cork, fought there. They had a special fate for him. Hanged, drawn, and quartered, that was his sentence. The last man ever to receive that sentence in British law. The

[140]

sentence that was carried out on poor Emmet, right here in Dublin. But they lacked the nerve to carry it out. Have you ever noticed Mr. O'Brien's hand, how he uses only the one hand, the other one crippled, the fingers bunched together? Prison did that to him."

But Prentiss had never noticed O'Brien's hand. He remembered a man who seemed ancient, long thin beard streaming down almost below his waistcoat, avuncular, tedious.

"There is a man," his father said with sudden animation, "a man who has been twice to dinner in this house. No, three times perhaps. Your mother would remember. Now, he was there, right there, in Kilpeder and Clonbrony Wood. Stood his trial. Bob Delaney." His father stabbed the brittle page with his forefinger, as though angry that the artist had not sketched in Delaney, perhaps standing with the officer and the top-hatted gentlemen. But he would not have been part of that scene; for the scene must surely represent the aftermath of battle, a scuffle more likely, by the look of things, obscure and inglorious. Battles were fought on wide, windy plains, cavalry and lines of charging infantry on the run, cannon ringed with circles of engraved smoke.

"He was there," his father said again. "One of the heroes of Clonbrony Wood, as later they were called. Did him no harm at all, years later, when he stood for Parliament. Quite the contrary. Do you remember Mr. Delaney, Patrick—a brisk, well set-up man, clean-shaven?"

But Patrick did not. He would not have remembered F. X. O'Brien but for the Father Christmas beard. There had always been too many guests for him to remember them all—members of Parliament, barristers, Land League agents, judges, a few clients. They were a blur of faces above white linen.

One memorable night, years before, long after dinner, when the men were lingering over brandies and coffees, his mother had come upstairs to where he was lying half awake. "Put on your robe and slippers, Patrick. Mr. Parnell is here, and Father wishes you to meet him." No black wool, starched linen, but rough tweed, as though back from a day's shooting, a knit waistcoat of some sort. Beard and hair were auburn. Preoccupied, he looked at Patrick, nodded. "A fine boy," he said to Patrick's mother, "a fine little man." He nodded again, and there was an awkward silence.

"I brought him down for the moment only," Patrick's mother said. "He is half asleep."

"Have him reading for the law already, do you, Prentiss?" Parnell said to his father. "A young barrister?"

"In time," Patrick's father said. "All in due course. Best get him back to bed now, Ellen. He will remember this night, meeting Mr. Parnell."

At the door, Prentiss twisted his neck, looked back towards the table. Parnell was reaching towards the oval silver bowl of apples.

"He is the Uncrowned King," Prentiss's mother said to him at the foot of the stairs, her hand resting on the carved pineapple of black walnut. "There is a song about him that says that. The girls in the kitchen all know it. A handsome man, Patrick, as handsome almost as your father."

Katey knew the song. She sang snatches of it for him the next morning, as she kneaded flour for the bread, a fine sift of it on her sleeves, pulled back from the wrists. "For the uncrowned king of Ireland lies in Kilmainham Gaol." But what would a guest at his father's table have to do with gaols and prisons? Patrick tried to imagine him in a prison cell, stretched out upon straw, the cell in deep shadows, manacles and heavy chains upon the damp walls, rings and bolts of dark iron. "What else can you expect from them?" Katey said, and slapped the kneaded flour on the board. "Robert Emmet was a gentleman, and Lord Edward Fitzgerald was a lord. Prison and death were waiting for them, and tis waiting for Mr. Parnell again." On Sunday drives into the Phoenix Park they would pass Kilmainham Gaol, across from the park entrance, grey, massive stone, high shielding walls topped with shards of angry glass, armed constables at the sombre gates.

But that had been when Prentiss was a boy, and not the young scholar from Clongowes Woods who stood beside his father's desk, in the green-globe-lighted study.

"No," he said, "I cannot recall Mr. Delaney."

"A pity," his father said dryly. "He is unlikely to be dining with us again. Mr. Delaney has elected to follow Mr. Parnell into the wilderness."

Now, the now of Prentiss and his father talking in the study, everything had changed. Parnell was no longer the uncrowned king. Below stairs, he was no longer Katey's hero, for politics in Palmerston Park was monolithic. "There was the bad drop there," she would say, enigmatically, "the bad drop was there somewhere." Downtown in Dublin, on broad Sackville Street, beyond the immense statue of O'Connell, the Liberator, there would be scuffles between the two factions, those who supported Parnell in spite of all and those who opposed him, tall hats knocked off by staves of wood, and the mounted Dublin Metropolitan Police riding forward and back to keep order, leaning down and bellowing, swinging their long, leaded batons. Once, at teatime, Prentiss and his mother had watched a scuffle from the tall windows of the Imperial Hotel, facing the white-pillared General Post Office, themselves and the other guests standing appalled and fascinated at the windows, and the two mobs surging about Lord Nelson on his high pillar, with his great victories inscribed upon the four sides of its base, Trafalgar and the others. "There you are," one of the other ladies had said to his mother, "the country turned into a Donnybrook." His mother had not replied, and Prentiss, turning towards her, had seen that she was biting her short, full lip, and her eyes had brimmed with tears.

"It was far simpler for those lads," his father said. He moved the flat of his hand across the *Illustrated London News.* He turned the tall, wide pages.

"There," his father said, turning another page. "That was the battle here, in Tallaght." It covered the page. Beneath a wintry sky, a row of soldiers, or police perhaps, took aim and fired. Beyond them, shadowy and indistinct, beyond dark buildings and bare-branched trees, their targets were an indistinct mass. And in the distance, low upon a near horizon, the Dublin mountains. "That was the great Fenian hosting," his father said. "At Tallaght." Tallaght was very close to them, a short drive from Palmerston Park into the gently sloping foothills, a village, suburban villas. "The Irish Constabulary, as they then were," his father said. "It was as a reward for their services against the Fenians that the Queen accorded them their regal adjective. The Royal Irish Constabulary. Those are the lads who brought the Fenians low, not the army." There was one other full-page engraving, in the next number of the *Illustrated News.*

"Fenian Prisoners at Dublin Brought Out of the Lower Castle Yard on Their Way to Mountjoy Prison." A fine representation of Dublin Castle, the ancient battlemented tower, and the Chapel Royal. The yard was crowded with cavalry and infantry; beyond them, a throng of gaping spectators, necks craned forward. At the centre, almost obscured from view, double files of bayoneted soldiers on either side of them, a mass of coarsely dressed men, heads bent in sullenness or shame.

"Well indeed," his father said. "And there you have it." Absently, he closed the volume. Upon purple, the seven-crowned gilt queen reigned over the world's happenings. The past was locked away upon brittle pages, to be set back beside the bound volumes of *Punch.* But not entirely. For to the table at Palmerston Park had come white-bearded O'Brien, who had been sentenced to be hanged, drawn, and quartered, and Delaney, whom Prentiss could not remember, but who had now been lent, by his father's words, a dark glamour, a follower of Parnell, the fallen Lucifer.

Not entirely. His father nodded absently as Prentiss took the book back to its shelf. He tidied the papers of his brief, brushing from them the faint dust which had drifted from the dead pages. Now, although he seldom used them, he put on his spectacles, thin gold ovals.

"It was all hopeless, you see, Patrick," he said. "Scattered outbreaks, gunfire, some men killed. Like poor Emmet's insurrection, a half century before. When it was all over, and the poor devils dead or awaiting their trials, a ship loaded with arms arrived from the United States. At Sligo, of all places. The Fenian man-of-war, it was called. Surprising that the *Illustrated News* did not have a drawing of it." His father had a way of returning to his work, to let Prentiss know that a conversation had ended. But now his father seemed abstracted.

Sunlight of a summer afternoon fell into the room through an opening in the drawn drapes. Soon they would be going on their holidays, his father and mother and himself, and Elizabeth, his sister. Italy this year, where none of them save his mother had ever visited. A young girl, fresh from the Ladies of the Sacred Heart, she had gone there with her own parents, and brought back memories of narrow, hilly streets, cool, shadowed churches, the immensity of Saint Peter's.

"They suffered dreadfully in the prisons," his father said. "The English treated them barbarously. As a young lawyer, I served with the Amnesty Committee. I remember the first releases—O'Leary, Luby, Devoy." He saw that Prentiss was studying him, and smiled. "We are a curious people, Patrick. Small wonder that the English cannot understand us." He picked up his pen, touched a forefinger to its nib, and dipped it into the elaborate inkwell of brass and malachite. "Brave men," he said. "Brave, ignorant men." He bent his leonine head to his work.

But what Prentiss remembered most vividly was the moment shared by father and son, the heavy volume spread open before them. Such moments between them had been as abrupt and transient as magic, to be buried deep in the almost unrecoverable past. Almost, secure behind the heavy drapes of Palmerston Park, almost they had stood together on the obscure, puzzling road. And perhaps, he thought now, perhaps his present researches had begun there. Curious now, to think that he had first heard then the name of Robert Delaney, and with the sulphurous excitements of the Parnell years in the middle distance, obscuring from view the young man who had stood, revolver in hand, upon the actual road. One of the brave, ignorant men, as his father had called them.

The warmth of the Devon summer was almost palpable, a thick blanket of settled air. Church, bridge, stream, path, the motionless ferns, delicate deep-green embroideries, the sound of bees like the heavy air given voice, all spoke to him of an ordered world, an ordered history. The scene, with its unctuous harmonies, reproved the tattered narrative which he had been trying to piece together. Tea would soon be waiting in Dick Leese's parsonage, set at its discreet distance from the church; the table spread in the garden, near beds of roses, red, pink; and young Eleanor

Leese's hands, white birds, moving swiftly above the cups. The French windows which opened from the study would be thrown wide, and in the darkening room, shelves of books would lie in shadow, Church Fathers and the new novels from Paris standing side by side. The church itself was fifteenth-century, but Dick already had its history pat: the names of the builders, the Edwardian reformers who stripped away the statues and the altar screen, saints of stone and plaster touched with blues and gilt lying higgledy-piggledy beside the railings, the long eighteenth-century somnolence, with hard-drinking, red-faced parsons, the near-scandal of a ritualist from the Oxford Movement in the 1850s, Mrs. James in the 1880s who wore bright-coloured Indian shawls and went mad, her scholarly husband who never completed his parish history. In England, history was a benign sea creature, its movements sluggish and elaborate, its girth expanding layer by layer, iridescent plates. Irish history, his own history, was scraps, fragments, the tumbled stones of ruined abbeys, castles. No need for the late Mr. James's unfinished parish chronicle; it bloomed in the well-tended gardens, it whispered in the cool grey quiet of the church, whose services Prentiss had attended that Sunday, disguised Papist listening to the sermon of his Oxford friend, a mild, soporific commentary upon a scriptural text, around him the congregation, squire, solicitors and doctors, strong-farmers, servants.

Walking back now, Prentiss left the stream, set his back to bridge and steeple. The scent of roses came to him strongly now, and in the garden, as he had expected, his friend was waiting for him, worn jacket of light grey tweed, round, solid head, and features which had from the first seemed confident, enquiring, kindly. He was a part of this world, as Prentiss himself could never be, for all of New College, his London club, his rooms near the Embankment.

"It still seems formless to me, I must say," Leese said. "A shapeless farce." Deftly, he sliced open a muffin, heaped upon its half a spoonful of Eleanor's strawberry preserves. "Peasants and shop boys in a scattering of towns wandering forwards and back. And at the bidding of rogues from New York who were lining their own pockets with the pitiful half dollars of servant girls and navvies. Informers and charlatans. If you must have a rebellion, why not take a real one? Take Tyrone's rebellion—'the most formidable rebel that has ever risen up against this kingdom,' Elizabeth called him."

But Prentiss remembered Kilpeder and Macroom, streaky-thatched cabins, muddy streets.

"Those peasants and shop boys," he said. "Why did they take up arms, Dick? I don't know the answer myself. Not yet. They knew what they risked, you know. And they paid the price, a dreadful price. Some of them went mad in prison."

"Did they?" Leese said. "Know the price? This is the country of the Monmouth rebellion, you know. Right here. Bewildered peasants who hailed that silly young man as 'King Monmouth.' Jeffrey tried them over in Dorchester, batches of them in smocks and ragged breeches. The rogues who stirred them up knew what they were about—Shaftesbury and the others. Power for them. But the peasants thought . . . what? Preserving their true religion against Papists like you, perhaps. What they said at the trials and on the gallows has been ill recorded. Illiterate wretches begging forgiveness from God."

"The Fenians did not beg," Prentiss said. "They sought forgiveness neither from God nor from Queen Victoria."

On a Manchester gallows, a triple hanging: O'Brien, Larkin, and Allen had kissed, before standing quietly to await the dark hoods, the hemp. But they had accomplished their purpose: they had rescued Kelly, the man who had replaced Stephens as chieftain of the Fenian army. In the hell of Dartmoor Prison, some of the Fenians had refused a conditional pardon. Prentiss had talked with some of them in New York, old men now, boastful and clinging to tattered memories, bits of bright bunting. No more than Dick Leese could he understand what they once had felt, boys with pikes and stolen shotguns.

"It was a shambles, was it not?" Leese said. "That is all one knows of it now. The Fenian fiasco. Comic opera 'generals' and 'colonels' scurrying about, and then a few skirmishes."

"It was a mess," Prentiss said. From notes and old newspaper cuttings, transcripts of the state trials, from what the old men had told him—not much, not accurate—from the state papers that he had been allowed to examine. Vanity, blunders, desperation at the top; and at the base, fellows who had taken an oath at gable's end, shadowed corner of a public house.

It was managed from New York, he told Leese, from three thousand miles away, late at night after public meetings, in shabby boardinghouses off Broadway. O'Mahony had been shouldered aside. In his closet, dusty now, hung the uniform he had worn as a colonel in the Union army, a gesture made by the Yankee government to snare recruits from among the young Irishmen working on the wharfs of Manhattan and Brooklyn. In his head still swirled the mists of Celtic legend, Finn and Cuchulain, prodigious heroes. John Roberts, rival chieftain, with his own "Fenian House," staff officers lounging in a parlour equipped with its table of bourbon bottles, boxes of cigars, spittoons, plans worthy of Cuchulain himself: a man-of-war to prey upon British shipping, an invasion of Canada. The public meetings, of one camp or the other, were monstrous in size, with the New York Irish crowding in to be fed upon oratory and braggadocio, Roberts florid-cheeked above bushy beard, and on the platform behind him his veterans from the Army of the Potomac, lads in square-toed boots, blue tunics which once had borne gilt buttons, and at another meeting, in a lecture hall near Cooper Union, O'Mahony and *his* veterans, O'Mahony tall and pale, his downward-curling moustache at once fierce and melancholy, a man of honour, romantic and saturnine, nursing his secret knowledge that the hour had passed, if it had ever been.

Back and forth across the Atlantic, from France, from Ireland, moved Stephens, *an seabhac,* the Hawk, ten years in the past by now his walk of a thousand miles, up and down the four provinces of Ireland. By reports to the Dublin government from informers and rural constables, he was everywhere. A sergeant in Dungarvan heard that he was in Waterford, blind now, with a boy beside him as his guide. In Leitrim, county of bogs, wet pastures, reed-fringed lakes, he spoke to sworn men, mustered by night, bearded like an Old Testament prophet, armed. The time is now, he told them, the year is 'sixty-six. So the sergeant in Carrick-on-Shannon reported, laboriously writing in round, schoolboy's hand.

But whenever he in fact appeared, the legend would be shrunken back inside the skin of the man. He had raised the hopes of his followers by bluster and pretence, sustained by his assurances to himself that all would come right in the end, forces would be massed in their tens of thousands, armed and trained. But when they called upon him to act, the myth which he had brought into being would shrink to its true, icy proportions. In bleak December of 'sixty-five, in Kelly's Dublin lodgings, Devoy and his squad, armed with American revolvers, guarding Grantham Street, curls of yellow fog against claret brick in the sombre afternoon, Stephens had called off the 'sixty-five rising. A delay of a month, perhaps two, no longer than that. He must go over again to America, heal the split there, organise arms shipments. There had been too many arrests— O'Leary and O'Donovan Rossa in Dublin, Kenealy and Keane in Cork. The Centres must be reorganised. In twos and threes, the Centres were brought into the Grantham Street parlour by Kelly and Devoy, where he sat facing them behind a low table, *an seabhac,* the man of legend. A month, perhaps six weeks.

A fatal delay? For a half century, Fenians would argue the matter. According to Devoy, talking with Prentiss in a Manhattan restaurant, Stephens had thrown away the game. Government had now the leisure to replace the regiments of Irish soldiers whom he and Boyle O'Reilly had patiently recruited, administering the oath to red-tunicked privates and corporals in a Camden Street public house. By the end of February, *habeas corpus* had been suspended, and Devoy himself was in prison, and hundreds with him.

"He threw it away," Devoy said, implacable, unforgiving. "When Kelly and I broke him out of Richmond, the game was in our hands. I know that, Mr. Prentiss; that is not guesswork. Those months after Richmond, I commanded his bodyguard. The country was organised, Dublin was organised. We could have taken Dublin."

"Without arms?" Prentiss said.

"Arms? We had arms. Twelve thousand sworn men in County Dublin alone, and arms for a thousand of them. There were entire regiments pledged to turn upon their officers. The Pigeon House Arsenal on the North Wall was loaded with arms, and it was ripe for the plucking. But after February, they were shipped off across the water to Chester Castle. That is why McCafferty had to try the raid on Chester a year later."

A year later. Until May of 'sixty-six, Stephens lay low in Dublin, and then made his way back once more to New York. 'Sixty-seven, he promised now, would be the year. In November, he spoke to a meeting of fifty thousand. "My last words," he said, "are that we shall be fighting on Irish soil in January and that I shall be there in the midst of my countrymen." That night, he repeated the promise to his lieutenants, Kelly and Burke and McCafferty and the rest of them. They took him at his word. It was then that the second wave of officers was sent over, and among them young Edward Nolan, called "Ned" by his friends, and by the friends of his father, dead now, who had been the eloquent Thomas Justin Nolan, faithful attender of monster meetings, circulator of petitions, distributor of handbills, savourer of bourbon whiskey, garrulous, thoughtless, loving father.

"A mountebank," Dick Leese said, in mild reproof, in the deep green of Devon's summer late afternoon. "Swaggering around from city to city, country to country. Breathing fire and brimstone on public platforms, but frightened at the sticking point. And living very well in New York, no doubt. Rooms in a good hotel and all the rest of it, oysters and roast beef."

"A decent hotel," Prentiss said. "He had a position to maintain after all. It was expected of him. He was the Fenian chief. Organiser of the Irish Republic was his title."

But warmed by Leese's steady, amused gaze, he smiled. "All right, then," he said. "It was a desperate farce. In 'sixty-five, Stephens was in Dublin calling off the Rising, and now, a year later, he was in New York, and at it again. But his luck—if you can call it luck—had run out. They deposed him then and there. McCafferty put a revolver to his head, and told him he was deposed. He cried, and they looked at him with pity and disgust. McCafferty and Kelly and Halpin and the others, hard young men who had fought as guerrillas in the war."

"Well they might," Leese said.

In mid-January, they set sail for France, where they were to make their way to London. They promised to take Stephens with them, an emblem now, a burned-out legend to those who had been dealing with him, but still, to the Irish peasantry and the British government alike, a man infinitely dangerous and resourceful. They waited for him at a Brooklyn pier, in the dark, bitter cold of a New York winter, and in the morning, until the sailing, they stood at the railing. Flecks of soft white snow fell from a grey sky. They sailed without him.

"That was then the high command of your Fenian army," Leese said, incredulously, "a half dozen or so young toughs with six-shooters, sailing off for Europe. Moss troopers looking for excitement and glory."

He lived out long decades after that, in France, back in New York, back to Paris again. At last, in his old age, he was allowed to creep back to Ireland, to a cottage on the bay south of Dublin, the long beard white now, patriarchal. He was a local curiosity. Prentiss, as a boy, might well have glimpsed him, riding with his father along the coast road to the pier at Kingstown. James Stephens, *an seabhac*, the Fenian chieftain. In Fenian legend, soiled clouds of romance which clung to the enterprise, on the night after the sailing, Stephens had visited the deserted Brooklyn pier, an inch of dirty snow on the cobblestones, cut by the wheels of carts, mired by dray horses.

"The organization was in place in Ireland," Prentiss said. "Not in New York or London. Centres in Dublin and Cork, in towns scattered across the south—Tipperary, Kerry, Limerick, Waterford. They had been waiting for two years, drilling, waiting for arms and trained soldiers from America. But they could not be held together beyond that spring of 'sixty-seven. The country was under martial law, scores of men were in prison, there were rumours of informers, police spies. It was then or never, so Kelly and the others reasoned. The date was fixed for March sixth. McCafferty's raid on Chester Castle was their last chance for arms."

"And they proposed to overturn the kingdom, sever the Union, establish a republic," Leese said. "Anything else? Or is that the full shopping list?"

"A minimal list," Prentiss said. "They were agreed upon that. Some of them thought that the estates should be broken up and distributed among the tenants and the landless men."

"Jack Cade, in fact," Leese said. "A peasant revolt, with steamships and telegraph and American revolvers."

Eleanor Leese came to them through the opened French windows, her skirt trailing the grasses. She carried with her a wicker basket, empty save for gardening gloves. Auburn hair was pulled back from a high, pale forehead. A small gold watch was pinned to her shirtwaist. It lent her a mock touch of the schoolmistress: she was not schoolish at all, a light, bantering young woman.

"Patrick has been telling me about his Irish revolutionaries," Leese said. "A desperate crew."

"You must not tease Patrick," she said.

"Desperate men," Leese said. "Gunmen and incendiaries. Eleanor and her family had a summer place in Ireland, Patrick. Did we tell you that?"

"In West Cork," Eleanor said. "On the coast, near Glengarriff. My brother keeps it as a fishing lodge. When we were children, we thought it magical. The sea, and the mountains purple with gorse. Father's parish was in South London, you know. In winter it would be dark by four in the afternoon. By February, our thoughts would all be upon Glengarriff, even Father's. All soft air, and the rains fine as mist. The light is always changing, lovely for watercolours. And the people are lovely. I don't mean the county families, Patrick; I mean the ordinary people, the farm people. You must know Glengarriff, Patrick."

"Yes," Prentiss said. "It is very close to the market town which I hope will give my book its centre. A town called Kilpeder. There is a road to the north, through the pass of Keimaneigh, and past Gougane Barra. The mountains rise and then fall, and Kilpeder is set among them. A very ordinary place, not at all like Glengarriff."

"Glengarriff," Eleanor said again, seating herself between them, resting her basket on the grass. "It will be chill soon, but isn't it lovely now, just this hour, this half hour? With the first long shadows across the grass? These disturbances you intend to write about, Patrick, surely they did not touch Glengarriff. I never heard mention of them. We had friends there, Irish friends. The Butlers and the Armours, and a wonderful old man named Hassett who lived by himself, high up on a hill with a splendid view of the bay. It was purple at sunset."

"Oh yes," Prentiss said. "Glengarriff as well. There was an attack upon the constables in Glengarriff, but it was fought off. West Cork was Fenian. That is why I chose it. There are traces of it, but summer visitors would not notice them."

In Skibbereen, a famine grave, in a churchyard above the river, the earth sunken. Anonymous, no names incised upon stone. Bodies had been taken there from the workhouse, stiffening in coffins of cheap pine. An untended grave, a field in size, unweeded, a shameful history obliterated from memory. "Poor landless people," an old man had said to him. "Five acres they had at best. It was the sickness took off the most of them, the fever. So I have always heard." A Sunday afternoon. He had come with children, grandchildren, bringing flowers to their own well-tended plot, low iron fence ankle-high, statue of the Virgin, head bent, mantled, arms outstretched. Spring flowers grew from bright grass. His sons, heavy-shouldered farmers, neatly dressed, watched with embarrassment as he explained the grave to Prentiss, the famine a shrouded legend. The Fenians now legend as well, a brighter legend, hillside men armed and reckless, time-softened. But Eleanor and her father, his clerical collar set aside for his holiday, would have heard little of this from their friends the Armours and the Butlers. Nor from the locals, polite and deferential. Soft day, your honour, sure the trout will be lepping to the lure.

"Disturbances," Dick said, echoing her word in affectionate mockery. "Our Patrick has a full-scale rebellion on his plate. High treason, armed rebellion, rifles from America."

"The rifles never arrived," Prentiss said.

"There were boycottings," Eleanor said. "We heard about those. Were those the Fenians?"

"Boycotting came with the Land League," Prentiss said. "With Parnell. In the eighties."

"It all sounds very romantic," Eleanor said. "Like a novel. I cannot imagine why Dick teases you. Why do you tease him, Dick?"

"I am worried about our Patrick," Leese said. From a sagging pocket, he took out pipe, leather pouch. Pouch carried across years from Oxford to Devon; Prentiss remembered it. Our Patrick. "I sense the stirring of tribal blood. Scratch away the New College paint and polish, and we have a fierce Irish rebel sharing our table and our garden. A dynamite man, ready to blow our poor little bridge to smithereens. Like that chap who tried to blow up London Bridge. Patrick even knows his name, I'll wager. What was his name, Patrick?"

"Lomasney," Prentiss said. "William Mackey Lomasney."

"There you are," Leese said to Eleanor.

"He is a part of my story, in a way," Prentiss said. "It was Lomasney who attacked the police barracks at Ballyknockane in 'sixty-seven. He was in prison with Ned Nolan. Ned may have been with him at London Bridge. I don't know that yet."

"There you are," Leese said again, grinning as he held the pipestem between strong, even teeth. Gently, he moved a match flame back and forth across the bowl. "Patrick is much taken with this Mr. Nolan. He was with us, so to speak, longer than most of them, was he not?"

"So to speak," Prentiss said. "Thirteen years ago he killed a man. There, in Kilpeder, where it began."

Eleanor placed a hand to her throat, and looked at Prentiss with widened eyes, as though he had dropped a clump of turf upon the table, among the teacups, the plate of sandwiches.

"There you are," Leese said, a third time. He had been the same at Oxford, a prober more implacable than Prentiss's tutor. "But why do you want to do that?" he would ask some inarticulate hearty with no other scheme in life than to sail off to join the family firm. "Why Ceylon? Why tea?" "Why the Church?" Prentiss had asked him once, rounding upon him. "Why spend your life baptising the children of farmers and burying their maiden aunts?" "Oh," Leese had said, suddenly evasive, "there is more to it than that, you know." And here he was, in his vicarage garden, confident as ever.

"It is so unlike you, Patrick," Eleanor said. "Really." She rested her chin upon the hand which had moved to her throat, and smiled at him. "Is it political? Do you see a career for yourself in Irish politics? I shouldn't think the Irish would like to be reminded of their gunmen and their murderers. Or would they?"

"They might," Prentiss said. "You would find them a curious people, Eleanor. One of the Kilpeder gunmen went into politics. He helped to organise the boycotts you were speaking of, and later he was in Parliament with Parnell."

"In short," Leese said, "made a good thing out of his treason."

"Perhaps I hope to make a good thing of it," Prentiss said. "Make my name as a historian."

"Not ruddy likely," Leese said. "Try the War of the Roses. The court of the Sun King. Not gunmen and Irish police barracks and constables shot down from behind hedges. Good sensational stuff, that, but it isn't history."

"We have no other history," Prentiss said. "Ambushes, demagogues, famine graves. That is our history."

"We," Leese said. "Our. Now we are getting to it. Is that how you think of it? A bit romantic, if you want my opinion of it. Your father was scarcely a gunman, was he? A most respectable barrister, as I recall. And Oxford, like you?"

"Yes," Prentiss said. "Most respectable, a king's counsel. Not Oxford, though. University of Dublin. A Trinity College Catholic. He was a supporter of Parnell, until the Split. Men who had been Fenians in their youth were guests at our table. I met Parnell once; he was our guest at dinner."

"But no gunmen," Leese said, gently, insistently.

"No," Prentiss said. "No gunmen."

But Hugh MacMahon, a man of his father's generation, had stood beside him on Knockmany Hill, pointing out the field on which Nolan and Delaney had drilled their men, and MacMahon himself among them. Ragtag army with a few score of plundered shotguns and sportsmen's rifles.

"And that final dawn we mustered here," MacMahon said, "the famous dawn of March the sixth." He gave a rope twist of irony to the phrase.

"And the snow," he said, "the famous Fenian snow. It had begun latish on the afternoon before, towards evening. The sky had darkened in preparation for it, with heavy, low-hanging clouds of dirty grey, but there was naught of grey about the snow itself when it came, large, lovely flakes of drifting white. I can remember to this day that snowfall, it is mingled in my mind with what was to follow."

"Yes," Prentiss said. "I know about the heavy fall of snow."

"Well now," MacMahon said. "I would not go as far as that. Tis in the ballad, right enough. 'When the snow fell fast in each mountain pass, from Cork to Aherlow.' Ballad makers are a tradition-minded class of people. Twas not a thick snowfall, as the legends have it. I doubt if the passes were clogged. Later they were, with the second fall of snow. Not that we were given the chance to move up into them, not the Kilpeder men, at any rate."

"Tradition-minded," Prentiss said, putting the word in his storehouse of phrases.

"Tradition holds that history has allied the weather itself against us, the clouds and winds. Have you not observed that? The winds that shattered the ships of the Armada against our shores, great storms at sea. Wolfe Tone in Bantry Bay in 'ninety-six. There were gales that Christmas as well. From the deck of his ship, he could see snow upon the tops of the mountains."

The field, thick-grown, sloped eastwards towards a small bog, red-brown. History, upon the hill, was a stitching of tattered legends.

"Mind you," MacMahon said, "the snow bore down upon us, right enough, but in a curious sort of way. We had no notion, you realise, of what the lads in Tipperary were about, or Limerick, or even O'Brien in the east part of our own county. And Dublin, which all held would be the centre of action, as the saying went, was as far from us as Constantinople. The snows spoke to us of this. We were sealed off from the world. Below down there, just there"—he stabbed with his spiky blackthorn—"we stood towards dawn, waiting, and the world was ourselves and the snow."

"But surely," Prentiss said, "there must have been messages sent back and forth between Cork City and yourselves?"

"There were, to be sure," MacMahon said dryly. "Precious communications and precious few of them. On the morning of the second, which was the Saturday, a man arrived from Tumulty and met with Ned and Bob to say that the Rising was on and there must be no faltering. The night of the fifth, or first light on the sixth. And never mind about what had happened in Kerry, or the disaster at Chester Castle. Then he went on with the same message to Millstreet and then to Mallow. Damned hard of hearing the lads in Mallow proved to be. Ach—" He broke off with a laugh. "Good sense they had, all things considered."

It was on the first day of March, as Prentiss already knew, that Massey, who was to command operations in Munster, arrived in Cork City. One of the Punch-and-Judy Fenian adventurers, Godfrey Massey, bastard son of a Castleconnell squire by a peasant girl, commercial traveller, colonel (perhaps) in the Confederate army, friend of John O'Mahony and Thomas Justin Nolan, lounger about Fenian headquarters in Manhattan, fire eater.

But MacMahon said, the words falling hard upon Prentiss's thought, "A man who had been a general in America would command us in Munster, so Ned told us after he had spoken with Tumulty's messenger. We were to secure the barracks in Kilpeder, cut the wire and rip up the road, and then move north, over the mountains. The other columns would be doing the like, and we would move, all of us, towards Tipperary, where the man who had been a general would take command of us."

"But something happened," Prentiss said mildly, falling into Mac-Mahon's habit of understatement.

"It did indeed," MacMahon said. "Something happened."

"That dawn," Prentiss said, "in the hour after the dawn, when you were waiting for Ned Nolan to give the word." He tried to imagine it, but the ugly, weed-choked field thwarted him. He had nothing in his imagination but a woodcut, men with shotguns and pikes, a green banner perhaps, and Nolan prowling forward and back, face hidden by the wide-brimmed hat. "Can you remember what you thought, what the lads said to one another? Were they exalted, or fearful?" They would be firing those guns, being fired upon, farmboys and labourers. Surely they were reproved by the wide, rock-strewn fields, the sullen bog, low clouds, last lingering darkness.

"We remembered the snow," MacMahon said. "In the years afterwards, we would remark upon it. It brought fear to us, and that sense of being cut off from all the world. Before marching off, Ned squared us off facing south, facing towards the town, of course. What was to happen two hours later, in the town itself, is a different matter. Each of us had his different memories of that, jagged and raw-edged. But from the field below Knockmany, the field you see before you there, we remembered the snow, and our—our innocence, you might call it. A few weeks later, in the prison yard, we would meet lads from other towns who told us the same. But there were towns, do you know, that never rose at all. The snow fell upon empty fields. Or upon fields where five men gathered or six, and waited there together a few hours, looking sheepish at each other, and at last sloped back to their homes. Ach, who can say what should have been done, or what should not?"

He leaned both hands upon his stick, pressing it down into turf softened by an early morning's rain. Thick-knuckled hands, white as schoolroom chalk.

"You have a different weather here," Prentiss said, sitting with his friends in the vicarage garden, at twilight, in Devon.

"Oh, I would dispute that," Leese said, comfortably. "A garden in Cork and a garden in Devon must be very much alike. There is something gnawing at you, young Patrick Prentiss."

Debate in a garden. Late at night, at Oxford, Leese, tankard in hand, deep-ensconced in leather armchair, with a kitbag of innocent Socratic questions. Here, when there were no visitors, perhaps he practised upon Eleanor, who seemed ready for him. Prentiss smiled at them both, but shook his head at Leese, declining debate.

"If it is," he said, "I am fortunately unaware of it. What happened in Clonbrony Wood one day in the March of 1867, and what happened there on a winter evening, a quarter century later—there is nothing gnawing at me but that."

That, and what had happened in between—prison years; the Land League and the boycotts; the rise and fall of Bob Delaney; Vincent Tully's "merry jests" and primrose-sprigged waistcoats; the absent master of Ardmor Castle upon whose lawns, ill tended now, red deer had once roamed; a woman's portrait, white and black with a splash of enigmatic colour; a young Hugh MacMahon in the seventies, rebellion now scattered mists, negligible, gathering music, songs, shards of Gaelic poetry in remote mountain villages, faces of old singers, round and wizened as crab apples bent towards red hearths; his own father, smoothly broadclothed, glint of gold near waistcoat pocket, white, long-fingered hand smoothing down a silky beard; a dinner at Brierly Lodge, the double door burst open and revolver shots; Ned Nolan, who once, young, had mustered men in a field below Knockmany, wandering, wounded, beyond Clonbrony to rain-shrouded hills.

Darkening shadows, elongating. Against them, grass and thick shrubbery, flower-starred, a deep, lingering green. Here, now, it was not Ireland's own, intenser green which he remembered: dew-drenched, rain-sodden pasturelands, clumped straggling hedgerows, the leaf-laden trees of summer. He remembered boglands, red bogs and black, dead vegetation, fibrous, worked upon by the secret juices of old centuries. On headlands, or set now within meadows, half-demolished keeps and towers, bits of abbeys, friaries, a ruined chancel, the jagged tracery of a shattered transept. In early light, grey, streaky, an abandoned cabin, doorless, its entrance a gaping mouth. A curlew's cry beyond a lake fringed by winter's dry, rattling reeds. He remembered his country as slovenly, distracted history.

Eleanor Leese returned his smile, and, preparing to rise, placed a hand upon the high wicker handle of her basket. She favoured, even in traditional Devon, skirts faintly Bohemian, bright reds or greens, contrasts to her decorous shirtwaists. Leaning towards the basket, waist and hip were a smooth, supple line. For a moment, incongruously, Prentiss remembered the portrait in Ardmor Castle, black velvet and white, troubling flesh.

"I envy you, Patrick," she said, "rummaging in the past. But it never holds still, does it? It is like those kaleidoscopes we had when we were children. Such lovely patterns, but then a turn of the wrist, and the bits of colour would fall about, and make an entirely new one."

"Be careful, my dear," Leese said. "Patrick will remind you that that doesn't matter. What matters is that there can never not be a pattern. Kaleidoscopes and historians are patternmakers. That is why we cherish them."

But Prentiss, at that moment, wished only to look at Eleanor Leese, a young woman at twilight, in a garden of darkening flowers. He envied Leese his casual succession of such evenings, and the certainties which they implied. The evening was thick as butter, the air heavy and benign. And yet Eleanor, waist and flank firm, sensuous and slender against linen, did not seem fully wedded to its imperturbable quiet. Or so, patternmaker, he imagined for that moment. But in the next, she was rising from her chair, and, both hands now upon the empty basket, looked gravely down at him, his friend's wife. Once, years before, a young man named Bob Delaney had looked, circumspectly, no doubt, at a woman as Prentiss had found himself, without volition, looking at Eleanor Leese, and from that moment Delaney's fate had been teased out, Troy compressed into a tattered Irish town. Or so Prentiss imagined.

"Time to think of leaving," he said, to both of them. "Tuesday, on the morning train."

"Leave this?" Leese asked, in mock-surprise, gesturing with pipe towards the garden, and, beyond the garden, trees, stream, village, church, bridge. "Leave this for notebooks and jottings and those Irish brigands of yours, shop boys with pistols?"

"There you have it," Prentiss said. "Exactly so. The Centre of my Kilpeder rebels was a shop assistant, a young fellow in his early twenties. And a most remarkable one. He became in more quiet times a member of Parliament, one of Parnell's lieutenants."

Mock-surprise turned to mock-sorrow. Leese shook his head. "A noble career," he said. "Ending his days with that gang around Parnell. Jobbers, country auctioneers, penny-a-line journalists. Very well, then, Patrick my lad, back to them if you must. What can we do with this fellow, Eleanor?"

"Do?" Eleanor asked. She was looking towards her roses, masses of indistinct colour. "Patrick seems to be managing nicely. Better than my roses. They need rain, poor roses. Was he happy in Parliament, Patrick, your shop assistant?"

"Happy in Parliament," Leese said. "What a question! You'd never make an historian, would she, Patrick?"

"I believe he was," Prentiss said to her. "At first. But he ended his days back in Kilpeder. At the end, he was a country solicitor in a small way, drawing up wills, a bit of conveyancing."

But Eleanor had gone to her roses, her skirt trailing across the even, close-cropped grass. She bent towards them, solicitous, and touched a blossom. Prentiss and Leese studied her, fondly. Full evening now, the air fragrant, flower-scented.

A few days later, back home in London, in his rooms in Pump Court, city noises floating towards him, muffled and indistinct, Prentiss would remember darkening air, a slender woman bent towards flowers, would remember his own memories of that other island, that other town, market square, Tully's shop where once Delaney had worked, where Dennis Tully had puzzled, knuckle-gnawing, over his ledger books, the police barracks, unchanged for a half century, upon which a band of men had moved in snowy March.

8

[Hugh MacMahon]

At two o'clock of the morning, I rose up and dressed by candlelight. Mary was breathing quietly and evenly, and I judged her to be asleep. Thus, although I wished dearly to kiss her, I dared not take the risk, and accordingly, the last thing I did before I left the room was to take from the dresser the revolver that Ned had given me, in its roll of flannel, and the box of cartridges, and I went down then to the kitchen with the thought that there would be time for a cup of tea before Bob called in with the horses.

But at the foot of the stairs, I had another thought, and opened the hall door to see what sort of night it had become. It took a minute or two for my eyes to accommodate themselves to the light of a clouded moon, veiled by the softly falling snow. Nothing, of course, was astir, and snow made the silence more perfect. Neither up Chapel Street nor down it, to my left or my right, could I see farther than a few feet, but the spires of Saint Jarlath's, across the road, were dark, faint eminences. Always, whether back there in that house of Mary's and mine, or here, in this small house upon the hillside, whenever I am moved to open my door upon black night, I am seized by the immenseness of the universe of stars and gusty winds. But upon this night, needless to say, it was as though the rooms at my back held all of the security that I had ever known, and beyond me lay an uncharted life.

When the fire in the hearth was glowing, I set the kettle to boil, and then, drawing up the bench to the table, unwound the long roll of flannel and sat motionless, looking at Ned's gift to me. The yellowish glow from the paraffin lamp fell full upon it, a dark, lethal instrument, long-barrelled, with a wooden grip which, presently, I ran my fingers along. The walnut was smooth and oily to the touch, but the sensation was curiously pleasant, as though the revolver held within itself an authority which leaked out to me. With confidence now, I picked it up, broke it open, as Ned had instructed me, then placed it back upon its flannel, opened the box, and shook heavy cartridges into my palm. As, with my thumb, I drove each one snug into its metal nest, I felt a sense of growing sureness, as though commencing at last a task which I had long held in contemplation. When I was done, I pointed the gun towards the poor innocent kettle, drew back the hammer, held it so a moment, and then eased it to its rest. Then I placed it back on the table, and looked towards the window, which was black save for the faintly reflected room.

I was distracted by the singing sound of the kettle, but as I looked up, I saw that Mary had come into the kitchen, and was standing with her shoulders resting against the doorframe, holding her two elbows. She had put on her robe, and her long brown hair, unbound, fell upon it. She could have been there for but a moment or two, and yet it was as though she had been watching me as I loaded the revolver. The kettle began to scream at us, and I made a move to rise, but she said, "I will make us our tea."

With a silence between us, she set to the task, busying herself with pot and cups, sugar bowl and pitcher. Presently she sat down on the bench facing me, and with steady hand poured out our tea, but her features, I saw, were strained, and her lips pressed firmly together.

"I tried to slip away without waking you," I said.

"I was not asleep," she said. "'Tis snowing. Have you looked outside?"

"I have," I said. "Soft, feathery stuff. Windblown. God help the poor sheep."

"That is a ferocious great cannon," she said. "Have you mastered the use of it?"

"I was wondering, do you know, where would I carry the bloody thing. Tis too big for my jacket pocket, and if I shove it into the band of my trousers, I might blow off my own knee. I am a sorry excuse for a soldier."

"You are none of you soldiers," she said. "Faction fighters is more like it. Or like the Whiteboys, who were hanged in Macroom in the days gone by."

"We are like neither of those," I said. "And well you know it."

"I do not," she said. "At the outset, two years ago or three, it was a vast rising that was spoken of, from one end of the land to the other, and great ships from America with rifles and soldiers. And now it has all dwindled away to a few Kilpeder lads going off into snow and blood."

"It may look so," I said, "here in Chapel Street, in the middle of the night. And it may look so in towns scattered across Munster, in Waterford and Tipperary and Limerick. Every great enterprise, perhaps, may look so at the outset."

But I took an end of the flannel, and flung it over the Yankee revolver, which together with Ned's gun was the only armament from America of which I had certain knowledge. As Ned, O'Connor, and Reilly back in Killarney were the only returned Yanks. It was Mary's words, rather than my own, which the more truly spoke my own feelings. Common reasoning might tell me that men in other towns depended upon us, as we did upon them. But what has common reasoning to do with a man sitting in his own cold kitchen, his hands wrapped for warmth around a cup of tea, and on the table before him a loaded revolver which he has sworn to put to deadly use? A gust, sudden and brief, shook the ill-framed window, a messenger to us of the raw night beyond. I looked towards it, but Mary did not; she continued to hold her gaze upon me, a gaze which I could not read.

"What would you have me do?" I said at last, and crossly. But she made no reply, save to shake her head.

"If tis not done now," I said, "it will be left undone. Two years of delays and promises that were not kept. Whatever rising there will be this day is all that there will be in our generation. Men have been drifting away, you know, a few here but more in other places. And who can blame them?"

"Who indeed?" she said. And standing up, she said, "I will put together some ham and bread for you. There is no telling when you will next sit down to a meal; you had best have something with you."

"Tis already done," I said, and nodded towards the larder. "Bread, cheese, ham, those slices of lamb. I prepared all last night, after you had gone up to sleep."

"I did not sleep," she said. "When you came to bed, I lay there quietly, but I did not sleep."

But it was as if she had slept, and in the sleeping a change had stolen over her, as in the old tales that country people tell. A quiet, easy evening we had had, talking of this thing and that, and skirting the morrow as one would a bog. We had whiled away the long hours after tea in the front room, where lamplight, soft and yellow, fell upon books, upon the small piano which was her great pride, upon her sheets of music. I had described to her yet again the almost invincible ignorance of the Dennehy brothers, twin sons of a mountainous small farmer northwards of the Macroom road, who would the two of them be better off at home with him rather than cracking their thick skulls upon fractions and decimals. And she had proposed, as she always did, pedagogical strategies. But this was a different Mary, and one new to me. I think now that perhaps I was seeing in her the mirror of my own fear.

"God speed the work," she said dryly, and at that moment we heard Bob give a rap to the hall door and then open it. Down the short hall came the quick, confident sounds of his boots, and then he was in the room with us. He was wearing the heavy tweed greatcoat that had been his Christmas gift from old Tully, with a half cape falling from the shoulders, and he was hatless. A tall belt was buckled about it, and from the belt hung a leather pistol case.

"God almighty, Bob," I said. "You look like Rory of the Hill. Where did you come by that rig?"

He grinned at the two of us. "Twas liberated by the lads the night of the raids. It comes to us through the kindness, you might say, of old Nicholson of the Rise. Twould be nice to think that its leather had been baked by the hot sun of Afghanistan, but I doubt that greatly. Nicholson does not have the look of a battle-hardened veteran. A fearful morning, Mary. Snow and wind."

"You will have tea, Bob," Mary said.

"I will indeed, thank you. A cup on the run. I'll take it standing, and then Hughie and I must be off."

"A quiet night," I said. "From what can be seen of it."

"It is that. But young Neafsey was at the stable at the appointed hour, and with horses saddled for the two of us. I sent him on ahead, to Knockmany. He had tea cooked, but I declined, having a preference for your own, Mary." He took the cup from her.

"A small enough compliment," she said, with a dash of her old manner. "That you have a preference for my tea over that of a stableboy." And indeed she managed a smile, and at that instant I longed to hold her to me, to cherish her.

"No other life?" I said.

He took a long swallow. "I would not say that. I took a gander at the barracks. There was a light burning in an upstairs window, and two constables walking back and forth, outside the gate, with their rifles slung over their shoulders, swinging their arms to and fro against the cold."

Mary's hand went to her throat, and was there a moment before she dropped it, awkwardly, to her side.

"Troubled times, Mary," he said. "It was to be expected."

"Mary says that we are the Whiteboys of Macroom come to life again," I said. "By God, Bob, you have the look of one." As in a way he did, greatcoated and belted and pistolled. But he had not a Whiteboy's face, or at least not as in boyhood I had imagined them, half heroes and half ogres, brutal and ferocious peasants, houghers of cattle, torturers of bailiffs and tithe proctors.

"We could use a few of those lads this day," Bob said. He drained off his cup, and set it down upon the table. I took this as the message it was, and rose up to join him.

"Do not forget this," Mary said, and handed me from the larder my parcel of food. "Enough here for the two of you, by the weight of it."

In the hall I struggled into my own serviceable overcoat, and discovered then that one, at least, of my problems was solved, for the revolver fitted easily into its wide, deep pocket. Bob politely walked down the short garden path, so that I could take my good-bye of Mary, and this I did by holding her tightly to me, and then kissing her. There was not enough light for me to see her face clearly, but I ran my fingers across her cheek and mouth. She took my hand in her own two, and held it closely to her mouth, kissing it, and I pressed it tightly and stood a moment motionless. Then I joined Bob, and was careful not to look back.

The silence of the night was extraordinary, or so it seemed to me. And the moon, despite the snow, gave a decent enough light. We mounted, a bit clumsily the two of us, and set off for the half mile of the Macroom road, before the road which would lead us up to Knockmany. But we took care to ride to it by way of Skinner's Lane, avoiding thereby the barracks, which we would soon enough be visiting. Who Skinner was has been lost in the mists of time—a Protestant, by the name of him, or perhaps there had been a tanyard there in the old century; but it was now a lane of mean hovels, eight or ten of them, dirty-thatched and sullen. Not a Christian was astir within them, and so narrow was the lane that I almost could feel the warmth of the bodies asleep within, families huddled together in single rooms to the point of decency and beyond it. But the falling snow was cool and white against my cheek.

Once we were beyond the town and on the road, we felt more secure. The town straggled to a conclusion of cabins scarce better than those in the lane, and in one of them, almost the last along the way, there was a dim, small circle of candlelight. Bob nodded towards it. "Deeny Lawlor," he said. "Good lad. How in hell did he know when to awaken, without clock or watch to his name? I am not altogether certain that he can tell time."

He was a good lad, Deeny Lawlor, as Bob had said, the oldest boy of the Lawlors, about nineteen, with a mop of carrot-coloured hair and two of his lower front teeth missing, the consequence of some accident or scrape, although he was quiet enough in his ways. He had been seventeen when Bob and I gave him the oath, against the gable end of Hartigan's, and I remember wondering, with the same snobbery that Bob had just now shown, what he understood by the word *republic*, which he was swearing to uphold. But his head was crammed with a half history which he had somehow managed to acquire—Daniel O'Connell and Brian Boru and all the rest of it. And now, what with the ballads and the history and the Fenian oath, he was dressing by candlelight. Sixty-six of us fought, if that is the word for it, the battle of Clonbrony Wood—and the cause that held us together a cloudy abstraction.

We swung left off the Macroom road, at not yet three in the morning, and rode at an easy amble, saying little enough to each other. It was a narrow road, and I let Bob take the lead. We were, the two of us, practical rather than skilful horsemen, and he jounced a bit as he rode; but there was a purposefulness to his back that in my present mood I found comforting. The wind had died away.

Within an hour, or surely within two, Bob reined in, and when I joined him, he took my arm and pointed. Three lights glowed before us, two at a distance, and one closer at hand. "There you are," he said. "Ned's lanterns of welcome. The resourceful man." We rode towards them, and came soon enough upon the first, with a fellow standing beside it. He bent down and swung it up, and its lurid light fell full upon his face, Donal Cassidy, a drayman. His free arm he swung up in a kind of salute, something I had never seen him perform. "Bob," he said by way of greeting, "Master MacMahon." Wonderful the respect that schoolmasters command.

"Soft morning, Donal."

"'Tis indeed," Cassidy said. "I was one of the first here. There was but Captain Nolan and Vincent Tully and a scant half dozen before me. There is by now a full twenty of us." He said it with pride, as though, like myself, he had entertained doubts.

The twenty men had gathered in the exact center of the Knockmany wasteland, and they were lighted for each other by the two lanterns. I would have recognised Ned at once, had he not come forward to meet us. He was a dark figure, in his black American overcoat, and with his wide-brimmed, soft hat pulled well down upon his head, and canted to one side. He held out a hand to Bob, who was the one closer to him, and helped him from his horse. I made my own way to the ground. But Ned was beside me the next minute, and took my hand in his, and put his free hand on my forearm.

Still holding me so, he turned his head to Bob, and said, "The town is still quiet?"

"For the most part," Bob said. "One or two of the lads making ready to venture up here. And two constables on night patrol at the barracks. An unusual sight, that."

"And a lighted window, Bob tells me," I added.

"Cornelius Honan studying his book of regulations," Vincent said, strolling up to us. "A studious man, Sergeant Honan, eager for advancement." He had a cigar clenched between his teeth, and you might have thought him taking his ease at the course, between races, inspecting the entries.

"Whatever about his habits of study," Ned said, "he is a prudent man."

"Might he be expecting a visit from us, Ned?" Bob asked.

Ned paused before answering, and then said, with a brief shrug, "He might. The Constabulary must surely know that the organization intends to act within the month. They know that West Cork is disaffected, as they call it. Why else would they have strengthened the barracks here and at Macroom and at Millstreet? But guards posted or not posted, we can take Kilpeder, and that is all that need concern us."

In lantern light, orange glows that sent circles forward, the snow glittered faintly upon the ground. I studied it, and held my mind at a distance from Ned's words.

Next to arrive were Pat Dunphy and the other three men from Lackan, with Dunphy in the van. Dunphy and two of them were carrying shotguns, and the third fellow a scythe, as though he were setting out for a day's work in the field. For an instant, it caught the lantern light at an angle, and glittered more brightly than the snow, metallic and fearsome. I would long afterwards see in my mind's eye that scythe; it had the force of an emblem.

"Vincent," Ned said, as Dunphy walked towards him, heavy-haunched and stolid, "have you any of those cigars of yours left on your person?"

Vincent smiled. "Never without," he said, and drew forth from some inner recess of his caped coat his case of handsome morocco. I was standing beside him, and could see that he had the one left; but he drew it forth with a flourish and handed it over to Ned, as though from a bottomless supply. He reached then for his tinder, but Ned, shaking his head, bit off the end, spat it out, and held the unlit cigar between his teeth. He held his hand towards Dunphy, and said, "Good morning, Sergeant. I had expected you before this."

"Tis a foul morning," Dunphy said.

A fellow like Dunphy, now, or the other Lackan men—what was it that had brought them out to join us? Bob and Vincent and myself I understood well enough, and even Ned, that obsessed and driven man. But lads like the men from Lackan. For every countryman who joined us, here and elsewhere in the island, there were ten who did not. Had this not been the case, we might have fared better. Your farmer's true loyalty is not to nation but to his own bit of land, and little else matters to him. To those few acres he clings and holds fast, by whatever means seems best to him, in one year banded together with others to torture and terrorize bailiffs and grabbers, and in the next year crawling and fawning before his landlord, addressing him in the abject and disgusting accents of servility. And the Church is forever at his Sunday ear, preaching a necessary submission to authority and the evils of agitation. Farmers' sons themselves, those priests, but risen now in the world a bit, holding stations in the homes of the graziers and auctioneers and land agents and comforted by great Sunday meals, beef and roast lamb, washed down with red wines. And the priest has his older brother, the strong-farmer in the Galtees, and his younger brother, the Irish Constabulary sergeant in Limerick. Christmas they have together in the Galtees, strong-farmer and priest and policeman, at the long table, with goose and turkey, with the women carrying round the steaming bowls of cabbage and potatoes in their sleekly buttered jackets. Later, in the seldom-used west room, there is whiskey and hot water, and the melodies of Thomas Moore, sweet and acquiescent, and perhaps a fiery touch of "Clare's Dragoons."

Speaking thus, I may seem the unrepentant Fenian that I am accounted in Kilpeder, although affectionately so in these latter days, with Fenian guns and English prisons faded into the romantic past, and "The Battle of Clonbrony Wood" added to the repertoire. Yet nothing could be farther from the case. In that thick, close-woven blanket which is the life of our people, priest and publican, auctioneer and tenant seem to me the strong and certain strands, and our fierce ideology, our talk of republics and the rights of man but the glitter of strange threads. And yet, and yet! . . . Pat Dunphy and the Lackan men were with us at Knockmany on that morning of snowy March, and sixty others as well. They were, the most of them, unmarried men, which may explain a bit, but by no means all of them. Dunphy himself had left a young wife and three children behind him. Young lads, like ourselves. There would none of them have been among those who ten years before had seen James Stephens, *an seabhac*, who, or so many of us believed, had flown back to Ireland for the day of the Rising, although in fact he was safe in Paris, deposed and sulphurous. Bob and I had read out the oath to them, mouth-filling words, and they had held their hands raised. Perhaps Mary had the right of it, as she had of so many matters, that these were the grandsons and great-grandsons of the Whiteboys, stirred by some legacy within the blood, loyal to some crazy tribal instinct.

Be that as it may. It was to Ned that they looked that day, as truth to tell I did myself. Morning, cloudy-grey behind snow, had come before the last of the fellows arrived, a file of five, with the easy, quiet stride of countrymen. And in all of that hour of waiting, and whether he was talking with us or not, there was about Ned a remove, a distance from us. And he would often, in fact, be by himself, standing beyond our crowded circle, at the edge of the lamplight, with his hands buried deep in the pockets of his coat, and the unlit cigar jutting from his angular, hard-boned face. There were fellows in other towns of Munster and Leinster who mustered that morning, and after talk and dispute and bluster, dispersed and drifted away, appalled, no doubt, by the frightening loneliness of their circumstances, and persuaded that the snow had fallen as a blanket over any rising. And to confess the truth, I have wondered how we would have acted had it not been for Ned. In later years, when all was misted into legend, it was said that Ned's military experience held us together and carried us into action. I doubt that. He had been but a corporal in America, one of those to whom orders are given, and with no learned notions of authority and command. What held us to the line was that fierce certainty of his, whatever may have been its sources. And however fanciful, I have the thought that some uncanny portion of his being knew that he was forging in these hours the shape of his life for all the years to come.

At last, he walked over, and called to him Bob and Vincent and myself and Pat Dunphy, and went over with us yet once again his instructions as to our tasks, and his advice as to how we were to proceed if things did not advance themselves as we hoped. He was almost painfully patient in the performance of this, as though he regretted leaving any part of our errand out of his own hands. Bob caught my eye once and smiled. And indeed there was something of the schoolmaster about Ned at the moment, earnest and pedantic, anxious for clarity.

Then he bade Dunphy muster the men into order, in their files of ten. The lanterns we snuffed out, for there was no longer need for them. The men stood nervous and quiet, with their weapons sloped at a wide range of angles, the rifles and shotguns, and some scythes, and even, so I saw with astonishment, two weapons which looked more like pikes than like anything else. These last lent to the occasion, to my own eyes at least, a forlorn and sinister colouring, as though they had been bequeathed to us by our wretched history. Scarecrow revenants from 'ninety-eight, and shadowy behind them, the levies of the Desmond wars, who had marched through these very valleys—no, not marched, but clung to the edges of now vanished forests, leaderless at the end, hungry, pale-visaged behind matted beards, hunted down.

"Now then, lads," Ned said. Vincent's cigar he had placed carefully in the inner pocket of his coat. What meaning it had for him, I cannot say: perhaps he remembered some Yankee captain in those distant Virginia and Tennessee mountains, seasoned commander of seasoned troops. "Now then, lads."

He walked along the front rank, with Bob and Vincent and myself following along after him, and Dunphy standing off a bit, to one side. I cannot forbear remembering how young we were, a few of the men in their thirties, but very few of them. At the centre of the rank, Ned turned to face them.

"This morning," he said, "across the width of this island, the fight has at last begun for our freedom. It may not have the feel of it here, this small lot of us here, assembled on a wasteland, and with a lonely task before us. But you must be clear in your minds what is happening in the many other places. I will tell you what I know of it, but that is not much. Captains are lowly creatures when all is said and done, and the men who have spent long months in the planning of this day have had more matters on their minds than the town of Kilpeder. We ourselves will attend to Kilpeder, and then we will march northwards to the place of assembly for Munster, and the other towns will do the same, God willing. We will thereafter be a great host, but not the greatest one. There are men assembling now, at this hour, in their thousands, in the hills above Dublin. There the chief fighting will be waged, but there will be fighting enough here for all of us, and the Dublin men will be depending on us. And as well they might. In the centuries gone by, was there ever fighting and this county not a part of it?"

"Captain Nolan," one of the men called out to him.

If he was annoyed at the interruption, he did not show it. "Yes, Paudge," he said. Paudge Callaghan, to be sure, from Inchigeelagh, well to the east. It was a wonder how easily all of their names came to him.

"Will *an seabhac* be here with us in Munster, or will he be with the great army in Dublin?"

His words were so thick that it took a bit of straining to make them out. Inchigeelagh is Irish-speaking, or was then at any rate, and the wonder is that he had English on him at all, and that he was there with us that morning. Years later, when I had come to know his people, they seemed to me dwellers in a world of their own, untouched by risings or agitations. But you never know. I myself gave Paudge the oath, and he carried it back with him to Inchigeelagh, although there it was seed scattered upon rocky soil.

Ned paused before he answered, and then said, "He may be with us in Munster, or in the hills and streets of Dublin, or he may be in some other place entirely. What other meaning has the name that was given him ten years ago? He is the wild hawk, and he flies at his own bidding.

"Have you other questions?" Ned said. "Any of you. Now is the time to ask them, and not later." When no one spoke, he said, "You asked will James Stephens be here. I can tell you who will be, it is but right that you should know, and there can now be no harm in speaking the word. A gentleman named Massey is one of the chief men in the organization. Like myself he was trained up in the American war, but he was a colonel in it, and not a poor corporal as I was. And he is a general in the Fenian army, a general in the Army of the Irish Republic. He paused first with the lads in Cork City, but he is by now in Tipperary. General Massey will lead us, and we could have no better man."

This made a visible impression on them, as well it might, or at least upon those of them given to reading the *Cork Examiner* or any of the other journals. For the most part, the newspapers had had nothing to report but wild rumours and statements from Dublin Castle, but Massey's was one of the names often mentioned in these, like Stephens's and Kelly's and that of the French general Cluseret.

"So much, then," he said, with a sardonic flicker upon the words, "for grand strategy. Our own task is a simpler one. Mark your place there in rank. We will come to the town from the Macroom end. But when we come to the first houses, we will divide. The first four ranks of you will be under my command, and Vincent Tully and Pat Dunphy will be with us. The rest of you will be under Bob Delaney's command, and with Hugh MacMahon as his seconder. And you know what we will be about in Kilpeder."

He paused then, deliberately, that they might reflect upon his final words. He stepped back a few paces, so that he was standing beside Bob.

Then, when the pause had lasted long enough, he said, "The police barracks in Kilpeder, and in every town along the line of march north from Cork, must be taken. We need concern ourselves only with this one. And we must be brisk about it, no drawn-out siege. Sergeant Honan and his constables must turn that barracks over to us, and themselves as well, and their arms. They will not do so in answer to our pleading and coaxing, however eloquent. They must be driven out, and it is most likely that they will put up a fight. Now you will have questions. Where are they?"

But there were none. The men exchanged glances with each other, nervous glances some of them seemed to me, but no one spoke. This time, however, Ned did not resume his speaking. He stood almost motionless, his long arms at his side, and waited.

"Captain," one of them said at last, "you know that more constables have been brought into the barracks."

"I do, of course," Ned said. "Fifteen of them, under a sergeant of their own, to keep Honan company. Capable, strapping fellows they look, and each one with his carbine. But even so, the barracks has not the strength to hold us off, if we are determined and if we obey our orders. Some of those fellows may be decent enough, off-duty, for all I know, but they are soldiers holding Kilpeder for the Queen, against whom we have this morning declared war. And bear that in mind as well. This is not Stephen's Day mumming."

It was full morning now, and even in that dreary wasteland, with the bog to one side of us, there were birds at their chattering, without my having taken notice of it. But I heard them now, in the silence which Ned had arranged.

He suddenly turned his head, and said, "Have you anything you want to say to the lads, Bob?" Bob commenced to speak, but then put his lips together, and shook his head. He was looking neither at Ned nor at the company of men, but off towards the small copse where the birds were at their work. Apparently no address to the troops was expected from Master MacMahon, which was all for the best. There was still that wondrous silence, of which I do not know if anyone save myself was conscious.

"Then there is but the one thing left to say," Ned said, "and I will say it quickly. We have had enough of talking in this country, too much of it, from the spouting of O'Connell in our father's time until the present hour. Scant good it has done us. These valleys were twenty years ago black with hunger and fever and death. There are few of you standing here this morning who lack kinsmen destroyed by the great hunger. The people of these valleys, and of the valleys and hills across Ireland, died in their cabins or begging to be admitted to the workhouses, and their uncoffined bodies were tipped into the famine graves. Many more took leave of their homes, and at Queenstown boarded the coffin ships for New York, where the streets are paved not with gold but with work and loneliness. And in those terrible years, the spouters of words did nothing. O'Connell carried his beggar's cap to the English in their parliament, and the poets of Young Ireland wrote fine words in their newspaper. And it would be the same, it would be the same, if the blight were to come again."

It was extraordinary. I have not forgotten a word of that moment. There was nothing he said, not a syllable of it, that had not been said a hundred times in shebeens and in the ill-printed Fenian papers. The words had even become, in ten years, a cant of their own: O'Connell's begging cap, and the famine graves and the coffin ships. What was extraordinary was the sudden, unexpected passion that Ned Nolan brought to their utterance. There had been something hard and opaque about him, something dangerous, like his long-barrelled revolver. He had come to us buttoned up within his long dark overcoat, and although he was a pleasant, friendly fellow when you came to know him, there was a centre of his being which he kept hidden. It flashed forward now for a minute, and would be soon covered. Bob and Vincent did not seem conscious of it, and when I questioned them in later years, they said that Ned had made a fine speech, giving to all of us a sense of what we were about, and there was the end of it. But for me, it was as though he had revealed himself, and nothing in his latter years was to surprise me, not even when he was spoken of as a dealer in knives and dynamite and mindless terror.

The men had their eyes fixed upon him as he paused. He was standing motionless and rigid, a tall scarecrow in winter snow, with a scarecrow's soft, floppy hat.

"It would be the same," he said for the third time, "save for two things. One of these is the oath that we have all taken, the Fenian oath, which is binding upon all of us for life. You have heard that oath called sinful, but I tell you that it is sacred. We have sworn to drive from this land the strangers who enslave us, and to silence those miscreants of our own who serve the strangers, be they constables or landlords or bishops of our own holy church. There is no other way, no other way, to make certain that we will never stand hungry and cold, as our fathers did before us, upon the hillsides, looking down upon the carts of ripened corn moving along the roads to the quays of Cork City, and the herdsmen driving the long lines of cattle which would put meat upon the tables of London and Manchester."

He could have chosen no image more certain to explode within the mind and ignite there an unreasoning and unanswerable rage. Few indeed of those standing there upon Knockmany wasteland were old enough to remember those days in 'forty-six and 'forty-seven, but we had all of us heard of the wagons of corn, and those who had watched with empty bellies. A shameful image, and the shame stoking our passions, as if, by not falling in fury upon the wagons, those skeletal wretches had shamed themselves and us.

"The oath," he said, "and one thing else." He reached to his side, unfastened the thong which held his revolver in its scabbard, and drew it forth. He held it aloft, not as though to fire it, but cradled in the palm of his hand, with his fingers curled around it. "Without this," he said, "and without the weapons you have brought with you this morning, the oath is without meaning. The oath without this is empty words, a ballad in a shebeen or a spouter spouting words on a platform draped with green bunting. But the two together, the Fenian oath and the Fenian gun, and our brothers across Ireland this morning, bound by the oath, and strengthened by the gun, will throw off the yoke of England."

He replaced the massive gun, and with care, taking his time about it. Then he looked up again at them. "I have been too long about this," he said. "I have too long been making a speech of my own. It is time we moved down upon Kilpeder. Your own town it is that is waiting for you, and the town of my own people in the days gone by. We have a brisk winter walk before us, Pat. Best begin."

Dunphy had the makings of a sergeant, right enough; Ned had chosen well, and the wonder is that Dunphy had wasted his time on his Lackan acres, when the English could have put him to good use in their army. He filed off the fellows so that the bulk of them, who would be under Ned's command and his own, were in the van, while the twenty who were to take their orders from Bob made up the rere. As we walked towards our horses, I tried to read the faces of the men, but it was a profitless endeavour. All shapes and sizes of faces were there, and if one seemed to me bellicose and another apprehensive, this may have been but my own imaginings.

Ned and Vincent took their places at the head of the column, and Bob and I came last of all. We might well have looked like harvesters coming in from the field, or fellows setting off for the hiring fair. We had no banner. In the coloured lithograph of Clonbrony Wood which can still be found, flyspecked, in the public houses of County Cork, there is a great

Fenian flag flying above us, green and silky with a great gilt harp, but that is all mythology. Neither were there voices raised in song. The fellows trudged along, talking with each other, some of them, and you would on occasion hear a sudden, nervous laugh, but that was all. It was a narrow road, scant better than a boreen, but the fellows were able to foot it three abreast and to keep in fair order. Snow hung upon the hedgerows to either side of us, but it had almost ceased to fall, which is another contradiction of the lithograph. The print makes fine, dramatic use of a blinding snow.

As I have recalled over the years that final hour, men moving along a familiar road between snow-mantled hedgerows, I have thought of the strange space which is perhaps in the mind, perhaps in the universe, between the thing willed and the deed done. For with the doing, all is transformed, and yet, but the moment before, all is possibility, subject to revision, whim, reflexion, timorousness. And a moment later, a moment I am about to relate, a boundary is crossed from which there is no return. Such reflexions, I tell myself, are a measure of my own eccentric being. I doubt if they passed through Bob's mind as he rode along beside me that morning, and yet Bob was a man more clever than myself, in all likelihood, and in most ways more supple of mind.

Thus, when I now said to him, because the words echoed in my ears, "A curious speech that Ned made to the lads," he did not take my meaning.

"He made a speech about not making speeches," Bob said. "But it served its turn. It would have been indecent to march off without a word spoken." But then he moved his eye across the white-covered fields, the mantled walls, and turned towards me. "It was curious, right enough," he said, nodding. "We never talked with him about such weighty matters. He came to us with a revolver, a man who knew how to drill men."

But that was not at all what I meant.

There was little else of note that Bob and I had to say to one another on that advance upon Kilpeder. But he was welcome company, my dear friend from my first year in the town after the three dreary years of my apprenticeship in Mitchelstown. He had a firm hold upon the ropes of life, or so it then seemed to me. But one word of his I do remember.

At the cross, we swung right onto the Macroom road. A wide road, and entirely quiet in this early morning hour. There were no marks of cart or hoof upon it. Rather, it was a broad, long blanket of soft, exotic stuff spread pure and puzzling upon a familiar scene, chill and enticing, with faint, shifting sparkles here and there. Before us rose up the tall twin spires of Saint Jarlath's, and, set off to their right, recessed from them, the demure single spire of the Protestant church. Coming home to Kilpeder, from Macroom or from Cork City, these were the welcoming thrusting signs against the low horizon of distant hills. The hills could not be seen this morning, obscured by the low clouds, although the sky was beginning to brighten.

Before one has reached the town, there is a steep rise in the road. Ned halted the column before it, and twisting in his saddle, beckoned to Bob and myself to join him. Bob looked at me, and said, "Farewell content," one of those tags from Shakespeare with which we used to amuse ourselves, and urged his horse forward, but keeping it to a walk. I joined him, and we rode towards Ned and Vincent, along the lines of men who stood waiting. They were all of them looking either towards us or towards Ned. It was then that Bob made the remark to me that I was to remember. He intended a casual, flippant tone, but his words were strained and constricted, his calm surface more brittle than I had supposed. "And if we win, Hughie," he said, "there will still be men walking and other men on horseback." I stared at him, too startled to make response, but he shook his head.

"Right," Ned said to us. He was himself again, so to speak, quiet and purposeful. "When we rise the small hill before us, we will be in view of the town and the barracks. The two men who are on patrol are of no concern, the barracks itself will be astir by now, and their tea on the brew. We will dismount and take the men in at a quick walk. But not a run, there will be no running. And we all know what we are to do and how we are to do it. Good luck to us all, and God be with us."

As he spoke the last words, he raised his voice, so that they could be heard by all. The men responded now not with silence, as to his speech at Knockmany, but with a shout, ragged at first, four men or five, but then the full company of them. When it had died out, one of them called out, "God be with us." When he did, a number of them made the sign of the cross, and to be honest, I touched my chest, where, buried beneath tweed and layers of winter flannel, next to my bare skin, hung a scapular which had been with me for ten years or more, bestowed by a missioner, shoved for most of that time in a drawer behind rolled-up stockings. The words had, to be sure, their irony, available only to retrospection, with before us the spires of the two churches, set hard and ferocious against our criminal enterprise. But Ned nodded, and then, because I was closer to him than Bob, he clapped his hand upon my shoulder.

We cleared the rise, all in good order, and commenced our brisk walk. At the first of the outskirting cabins, we halted again, and divided our force into its two unequal parts. Bob and I led our men out first, as was the plan agreed upon. We were now but some four hundred yards or so from the barracks, and we advanced upon it. It stood upon its own grounds, a solid, three-storeyed building, of good grey limestone, with iron bars guarding the ground-floor windows. A short path ran straight from its heavy door to the street, and to its either side the garden which was Cornelius Honan's pride. His rose bushes had now their covering of snow upon them, but they put me in mind of the summer evenings when I had seen Honan at work upon them, his tunic off, and his sleeves rolled up. The roses had names, but I have never had patience for such affectations, although his knowledge as to their nurturing was admirable. It was in a different world that he had tended his roses, not the world of this white March morning.

When we had come abreast of the barracks, we did not halt, although I could not take my eyes from it. Either the sentries had been called in or else they had seen us and given the alarm. But there was no movement visible to me behind the unshuttered windows, although, when we were past, and had the building at an angle, I saw the faintest of grey plumes at one of the chimney pots. Ned had been right; they were at their tea. We were by now at our own destination, a row of four cottages with common walls, across the road from the barracks, and twenty yards or so past it.

We halted then, and Bob, with a nod to me, walked towards the one nearest him, and raised up his closed fist to knock. They were labourers' cottages, all four of them, of men who worked in the Ardmor demesne, and I knew not a one of the families. There were gardeners and servants at the estate, and most of these sent their children to the school. Indeed, an undergardener's son was in the crowd with us this morning, back with Ned's lot. But for the children of these cottages, there was no schooling, whatever the National Board might assume.

I gathered to me the five lads whom Ned had assigned to me, and went to another door. As I stood before it, I hesitated, and looked up the road. Ned had halted his fellows at the far side of the barracks from me, and was pointing out to them a tumbled wall some ten feet into the field directly across from the barracks, and a doorless stone hut which stood at an angle to the wall. Vincent, standing beside him, had unbuttoned his greatcoat, and thrown back its flies. He had taken out his pistol, and held it away from his body, stiffly, pointing to the snowy road. As I turned away from them, back to my own task, I at last saw life within the barracks. There were two men at one of the side windows of the first floor. They were indistinct forms. I could not make out the faces, but I had the uncomfortable feeling that they were staring directly at me. Ned shouted something towards the barracks that I could not hear, and at the sound of his voice, the faces turned away from me. Down the road, two lads had been sent by Ned to cut the telegraph wires. One of them had already clambered up, and had drawn from his belt an implement of some sort, a small shears, no doubt. There, I thought, that will be the first act of war, slashing Her Majesty's wires. Beyond them, the Macroom road lay empty and white.

Here goes, I thought, with the help of God, and I hammered on the door. The blows rang loud and hollow in the cold air, and there was no response to them. I waited, and then began pounding again, ten or a dozen times, and shouted, "Within the house! Open your door!" The man beside me shifted his weight from one foot to the other. "Do you know who this is?" I asked him, but he shook his head. I lifted up my fist again, but as I did so, I heard a stir behind the door, and then it opened wide. He was an old fellow, sixty if a day, with thin tousled white hair. He dropped his hand from the latch, and stood staring at us, shifting his eyes from one of us to the next. I imagined that it was not our faces that he saw at all, but our guns, which, of course, the men did not hold pointed towards him, but had nevertheless a dangerous and alien appearance. Then he turned back towards me.

"Master MacMahon," he said.

"It is," I said. "We have come to borrow the use of your house for the morning."

"Master MacMahon," he said again, as though clinging to the one familiar element in the scene. It is well to be a village celebrity.

"I do not have your own name at the tip of my tongue," I said.

"Dominick Murphy," he said. "I am a labourer on the estate." His voice was croaky with sleep and bewilderment. In the darkness behind him, a form, perhaps white-clad, wavered.

"Well then, Dominick," I said. "Your day has had a rude beginning, I admit. But there is no help for it. Have you family within? You had best get them out of this, and yourself as well."

He kept looking, silent, first at me and then at the guns, and I kept peering into the cottage's single room. I now saw the bed, set against the wall, and the hearth, and the woman standing beside it, long grey hair, and arms crossed against her bosom, hugging herself. There was some fear in Murphy's stare, but mostly it was stupid bewilderment.

"Step outside for a moment," I said. "And you will grasp matters." But he stood as though frozen. I reached forward and put my hand on his arm and led him onto the footpath. "See for yourself," I said. Most of Ned's men were now moving to positions behind the wall and the hut. Dunphy was with them. But Ned and Vincent were standing facing the barracks directly, in the road, with seven or eight lads behind them, as if to give them cover, their rifles pointed directly at the barracks. From within, a voice was shouting out at Ned.

"Kilpeder has risen," I said to Murphy. "All Ireland has risen up this morning, and Kilpeder with the rest of it. The army of the Irish, the Fenian army, must take the barracks, and we have need of your house. We need it now."

The pale morning light and the scene which confronted him had a wonderfully tonic effect. He did not comprehend what was happening, but at least he was awake.

"'Tis not my house," he said, "'tis Lord Ardmor's. All of these cottages are the lord's."

"He need never know," I said. "He is away in England."

"Mr. Chute will know," he said, "and her ladyship, and the cousin from England, Mr. Forrester. Mr. MacMahon, have you gone mad?"

As he was talking, Ned shouted something to the barracks which I could not make out over the querulous whine beside me. Then, slowly, still facing the building, he and Vincent and their squad began moving backward, step by step, towards the field.

"Not yet, Dominick. You are welcome to stay in your cottage, yourself and the wife, but it would be a foolish thing to do. It could be dangerous here very soon. You are best gone."

At that moment, Bob came to me. His right hand was shoved into his pocket, but I could see that he was gripping his revolver. "Hughie," he said, "what in God's name are you doing?"

"Bob Delaney from the shop," Murphy said, to himself but aloud. It was as though he was furnishing out a nightmare with familiar faces.

"Dominick Murphy here and myself have been discussing the rights of private property," I said.

Bob gave me a brief grin, and then said, "Right. Murphy, from the estate. I know you." He grabbed Murphy by a shirt-sleeved arm, and said, "You take your wife and a warm jacket and go up to the market square. Now. Don't argue about it." Using the arm as a kind of crowbar, he shoved Murphy back through his door, and then turned to my men. "Two of you we will need—you two. The others of you get inside and take your positions by the window. Keep your rifles and your eyes fixed upon the barracks, but do not fire them off until you have been given the word." He craned his head into the cottage. "Move, God damn you," he called in. "That is my last word to you."

There are occasions when a brusque lack of courtesy will work wonders. Murphy and the wife were out on the footpath with us almost upon the word, Murphy in his frieze jacket, and his wife with a man's overcoat flung loose over a greyish shift. The poor woman's face was pinched with fear, and her deep-sunk, ringed eyes were staring wide. "It is all right," Bob said to her. "Go up to the square now with Dominick. There is the good woman."

Then the two of us, and the two men he had chosen, went up the road to consult with Ned. Bob took the crown of the road, and looked neither to left nor to right, but I had my eye on the barracks. I had expected to see the barrels of carbines shoved through the windows, but there were none in view. Ned and Vincent were standing before the hut. There were men positioned within and behind it, and others, the most of them, standing behind the low wall.

"We hold the row of cottages," Bob said. "The people have been cleared out, and Hughie and I have our lads in position."

"Good," Ned said. "Sergeant Honan and I have had a few words. I told him to hand over the barracks, and he told us to disperse."

"What will he do now?" I asked.

"What will *he* do?" Ned said. "He need do nothing. He is strong and secure within his walls. He expects that we will think matters over in the sober light of morning."

"At least he cannot signal for help," I said, thinking of the slashed wires.

"Perhaps," Ned said. "But if every barracks is on the alert, they may be expected to send a signal each day. Or perhaps twice a day. Perhaps."

"At least he cannot report upon how many of us there are," Vincent said.

"Or how few." Ned looked down the road towards the square. "From this town and all these townlands, sixty men." I followed his gaze. From our angle, the corner of our square was virginal, the shops and Conefry's public house quiet and closed in upon themselves. The squat obelisk commemorating the coming of age of the third earl had its cap of snow. Shortly, to be sure, knots of the curious would gather in the square, whatever the risk to themselves might be, but for this half hour we had the town to ourselves, we and the Irish Constabulary. Idly, I raised my eyes up towards the Castle. Nearly all of it was hidden by its heavy plantation of larches, but its uppermost storey stood yellowy white against the pure white of the snow upon the trees. "The town of Kilpeder," so ran the legend beneath the coloured print in the Arms, "property of the Earl of Ardmor, 1822."

"If we disperse now, Sergeant Honan says, it will not go too hard with us," Ned said. "Scant harm has yet been done, after all. A few score of excitable lads with shotguns and scythes." He looked straight at Bob. "A reasonable man, Sergeant Honan."

He turned around to face the men. "All of you," he said. "Get down flat on your bellies behind the wall. I don't want a head or an elbow peeping out until I tell you differently." To us he said, "Get behind the hut there. And leave room for me."

When we were all placed, he was the one man standing. He unbuttoned his overcoat, pulling back its sides against the constriction of the heavy belt which held his holster. He stood stock-still then, as though he were the one man facing the massy weight of the Irish Constabulary. Then he climbed over the low wall. He walked along the line of men sprawled out, and paused before the fourth man, taking from him his weapon. He stood upright then, placed the rifle carefully against his cheek, took aim, and fired.

It was the loudest noise that ever I had heard. In the nights of practice we had had, after the arms raid, I had found the explosions of the rifles maddening and fearsome. The shotguns had not been too bad, loud and roaring, but with a kind of flatness to them. The rifles, though, had an ear-shattering and always unexpected roar, the sound of death. There was a faint, sick odour of burned powder. There was silence. I could see from my angle, behind the hut, the most of the barracks. It had not changed, save for an immense, jagged hole, a wound, in an upper-storey window. By the time that I had turned back my head, Ned had moved down the line, and had a second rifle in his hands. I felt a grip upon my arm, and, looking, saw that it was Vincent holding tight to it. His lips were parted. A second time, more quickly, almost casually, Ned fired, aiming now, as it seemed to me, lower than he had done. Then he shoved the rifle away from him, and dropped down, crouching over one knee.

"That will do it," Vincent said. "Firing upon the Queen's men." He was smiling, but the nature of the smile I could not read, whether nervousness or delight.

There was more silence then, and after it a voice called out to us that I recognised as Honan's, but strained and unnatural.

"Nolan," he called out.

"Yes," Nolan shouted back at him.

"Nolan, you are on the edge of a cliff with a foot over it. No fault of yours, but there was no one hurt by those shots. You are in luck. Give over your bloody madness."

Ned rubbed the sleeve of his overcoat across his mouth.

Then, unfolding himself like a clasp knife, he stood upright, exposing himself from waist to head. Jesus and Mary, I said to myself, for I thought that he would be blown to pieces as he stood there. But I came in a calm later hour to understand that he and Honan were playing out the final two moves or three in a game of their own.

"Step out here where I can talk to you without shouting," Honan called.

"I can hear you well enough," Ned said. "And you can hear me. We are under orders to take Kilpeder, and take it we will. There is no need for the shedding of blood. Let you and your men come out peaceably. There are twice as many of us, and the most of us are armed." But when he had said that, he put his two hands upon the wall, and climbed over it. He took a dozen steps, which brought him close to the road. Then he waited. Presently, the barracks door opened, and Honan was filling its frame. His tunic was buttoned, and he looked fit and soldierly, although he was not wearing his tall helmet. His heavy face was florid.

"Nolan," he said, "have sense, man. The Constabulary is not in the business of handing over barracks to Whiteboys or Fenians or whatever it is you call yourselves. We have stout walls, and we are provisioned; we are better armed—with carbines, mind you, not a collection of stolen duck guns and duelling pistols. We can hold this barracks until Judgement Day."

"Judgement Day has come," Ned said.

"You are a bloody murderous fool," Honan said. He put his two cupped hands to his mouth, and shouted, "You lads there. Pay attention to me. There will nothing come of this save that some of you may well be killed. And after that, no life for yez, for any of yez, save prison and crusts of bread. That is what this man has in mind for yez. Do you want that?"

I looked around at the eight or nine of us who stood huddled behind the safety of the hut's wall. They were frightened, clearly, perhaps as frightened as I was myself, but not one of them moved. A bandy-legged man named Dermot Foley was staring at the trampled dirty snow before his boots, his eyes bulging, his cheeks puffed, and his jaws clenched.

"It is for you to say," Honan called. "Not this gunman whom none of yez knew a month ago. Come on now, lads, what do you say? Drift away, and scant harm done." His voice had taken on a tone sensible and cajoling, as he would have spoken to men ranting drunk who had come streeling out of a public house.

It was Vincent Tully who gave him his unexpected answer. He stepped past me into the open, pointed his revolver straight at Honan, and fired off two shots. For a moment all of us, even I think Honan and Ned themselves, were startled into bewilderment. Honan jerked his head back and forth between Vincent and the frame of his door, where one of the balls must have struck. Ned was the first to move, running in a crouch not to the wall, but to our hut. Honan leaped backward into the barracks, and some other constable slammed the door behind him. Almost at the moment that Ned gained our safety, a burst of fire came towards us from the barracks. From which windows they were firing, I cannot say, for I stood with my back pressed against the wall of the hut.

"It's begun," Ned shouted to Dunphy. "Give them a round and then hold your fire." And now, though admittedly safe behind the hut, there was rifle and carbine fire to either side of me, a hideous pandemonium of noise. Thus it was that the "battle," as it was to be called, began, with Clonbrony Wood, which was to give it a name, miles distant, its leafless trees awaiting us, and its carpet of snow as yet unsullied.

As though upon concerted plan, the firing ceased, from the barracks and from behind the wall, but my ears were still deafened by it, and I seemed to be hearing its echoes, as though I would never again not hear them.

Ned was holding his revolver in his hand, and he had thumbed back its hooked, deadly hammer.

"Pat," he called. "How are you?"

"All is well," Dunphy answered. "No harm done. The lads fired off a grand round, did they not?"

"They did indeed. We are doing well." Then he turned to Vincent, and in a lower voice said, "By God, Vincent, you are a bloody careless man. You could have had me killed."

"And myself as well," Vincent said. "Honan was calling over your head to the rest of us, and I gave him his answer."

"Fair enough," Ned said, after a pause. "The talking was useless. What did you make of it, Pat," he called.

"The windows were all manned," Dunphy said. "The bloody black barrels are pointing at us."

"We will give it another try," Ned said. "You lads. When Pat gives you the word, fire off two more rounds. But this time, I want all of you to take the same target. The window just to the left of the door where the sergeant was standing."

There was a wait of perhaps a minute, and then there was a burst of fire from our side, then a wait even longer, and a second burst. I looked up towards the square in time to see two men, whom at the distance I could not recognise, running across it. Shots came now back towards us from the barracks, not a concerted round, but a quick bark, a pause, and then two more, as though the constables, too, were picking targets. In my fear, all sense was drained away from me of the constables as men whom I had for years been encountering, with civil words for each other, Honan shirt-sleeved at his roses or teaching me the Limerick version of a folk song, the genial and far from brilliant Paudge Belton, heavy belly shoving forward his tunic. They were men safe behind stone, with well-greased carbines, and if I were to put my head into view, they would have blown it apart.

Ned risked it. He stepped swiftly into the open, and then stepped as swiftly back again.

"They are settling in for a long morning," he said. "Right, Bob. I am going to cut back to the lads behind the wall, and Vincent will hold these fellows here as a reserve. Hughie and yourself, make your way back to the cottages. The carts will be your duty, Bob, and they should be here and with us within the half hour. The cottages are your command, Hughie. You are to give us supporting fire, and you must use your own judgement about that. There cannot be more than seven or eight rifles with your lot, and each with a handful of ammunition. Unless you have the word from me, do not budge from where you are, whatever happens."

I stole a glance at Bob and one at Vincent. They roused in me an envy which was almost, for the time, an anger. Bob might have been behind his counter in Tully's, listening as a farmer rattled off his requirements. And Vincent seemed almost, I swear, to be enjoying himself, his large black eyes glistening with excitement. Well may he be, I thought, with the solid wall of the hut at his back. When I looked to Ned, I saw that his eyes were fixed on me.

"Are you clear in your mind about what you are to do, Hughie?" he said. "Bob will be back with you soon enough, after he has brought up the carts to me."

"Oh, yes," I said. "Tis clear enough."

But he continued to search out my eyes. "And one thing more. Tis unlikely that Bob will meet with a misadventure. But if he does, the carts become your duty, and I want them here whatever the risks. If you fall into great trouble of any sort, give me a shout, and I will see to you."

Beyond Ned, and from behind the wall, I saw a man raising up his head and shoulders to look about him, a tousled-haired young fellow. There followed two shots from the barracks, in quick succession, and the fellow dropped from view and let out a hideous screech. We stood looking at the wall and the screaming continued, wordless and shrill, a kind of sobbing. "His shoulder," Dunphy called to us. "All of his shoulder is shattered and bloody."

"There you are, lads," Ned called back. "There is how the Constabulary treats men fighting for their country. I will be with you directly." Some cool small portion of my brain took note of this as a fine bit of cynicism: as if Ned had not been banging away at the Queen's uniforms. "Right," he said. "Let us get this moving. That fellow screaming is doing us no good at all."

"You men," someone shouted from the barracks, "do you see now where this is leading you?"

"Off we go, Hughie," Bob said, and I braced myself to move out into that deadly road. But my body must have told Bob what I had in mind, because he shook his head. "Not in the road, Hughie," he said. "By God, you are a fool for bravery. We set off together, Ned and ourselves. Then you and I go down through Tunney's Lane. It puts us at the far side of the cottages."

I nodded. I felt that both Bob and Ned were looking at me curiously, as though my shameful fear was spread out across my face.

"Run at a crouch, Hughie," Ned said, "and I need not tell you to be fast about it. And remember that those lads are not duck-shooting marksmen, but country boys dressed up in stiff-collared tunics." He clapped a hand to my shoulder, and said, "Go!" Then he was himself moving forward, the black skirt of his coat flapping.

We were fired upon, the sounds falling upon my ears like boards being clapped together, but far more vivid to me was the noise of the screaming man. Bob outpaced me, and it was with a shock that I saw him stand upright and then pause to wait for me. I ran towards him, and he came forward.

"Take a calm breath, Hughie," he said. "We are beyond their angle of fire." He was looking past me, along the path we had taken, and there I saw our line of men stretched out flat, and Ned crawling along it, black and scurrying. It was to the wounded man that he had gone, and I saw him opening the poor fellow's frieze. The barracks looked as always it had, official and solid, but now with the black barrels shoved out.

We turned down the laneway, at whose far end, past the facing rows of wretched hovels, could be glimpsed a slice of the market square. The two of us were breathing hard. Ahead of us, a door opened; a man stood waiting for us. When we came abreast, he said, "Are the boys out, Bob, is that what it is?"

Bob paused to look at him. "They are, Batty. The boys are out, but you may as well go back to bed. Take the day off."

"'Tis very close to the barracks here. Should we move off from it, do you think? Which way should we go? Will the boys be moving into the square, do you think?"

"They might," Bob said. "We might."

"What should we do?"

"I don't give a damn what you do," Bob said, and strode off.

"Master MacMahon," the man said in a whine, "are you with them yourself?"

I nodded without speaking, and hurried after Bob.

"Damned little scut," Bob said to me from the side of his mouth.

"Good luck to the boys," the man called after us. "Up the Fenians."

Bob twisted his head around without breaking pace. "Up your arse," he said.

The market square had that morning an appearance which it had never had before. Its snow had the peculiar effect, at least upon me, of lifting it, provisionally, out of time. Not a soul was to be seen, although there were tracks, which gave to the scene a touch of Goldsmith's village. Nothing which had happened this morning seemed to me entirely real, and it was therefore appropriate that the familiar square—the piazza, the forum, of our social existence—should be white-mantled. Behind us, three shots rang out, two close together and then a third. No doubt someone, one of the lads or one of the constables, had incautiously presented a head or a shoulder.

"Hughie," Bob said, "I will take a couple of lads with me, and we will be about our task. Fifteen minutes, twenty perhaps. Joe Harrington should be waiting for me at the stable. Keep these lads in the cottages encouraged and brisk. As Ned said to us, use your own judgement." He turned to make his way across the square, and then turned back towards me. "Are you in as bad a state as I am? I am bloody terrified." It was shaming, the solicitude which he and Ned were alike displaying, and I saw myself in their eyes, fearful and indecisive, a thing of straw.

Bob set off, and I walked in the opposite direction, along the footpath, to the cottages. The door of the one closest to me hung wide open and defenceless, and I stepped inside. It was like stepping into a total darkness. The morning sun was still watery, and yet bright enough to strike up a sparkle from the snow, and my eye was assaulted now by the gloom within. But I could make out two men kneeling side by side at the window, their weapons shoved through it. Three others were beyond them, two of them sitting on the bed, and the third leaning, arms folded, against the hearth. A low turf fire glowed in the hearth.

One of the two on the bed said to me, "Good morning, master," and, my eyes accustoming themselves, I saw that it was no full man at all, but a lad of seventeen, Gerry Lawlor, who had been my scholar.

"Good morning, Ger," I said, walking over to him. He was hunched forward, with his arms wrapped tightly around his legs. The man beside him had a shotgun resting across his knees. "Where is your weapon, Ger?" I asked.

"I have none," he said. "I was going to bring the scythe with me, but it seemed a foolish thing to be carrying. But then I found that others had come with theirs."

"Yes," I said. I considered handing over my revolver to him, but thought better of it.

There came again a spattering of shots, and I went to the window.

"All right, boys," I said. "Fire away, at those two lower windows." They hesitated a bit, and then cut loose. Fearful as was the noise in the open field, it was nothing compared with this.

One of the men looked at his weapon almost in surprise, and certainly with respect.

"All this serves but scant purpose," he said. "The barracks is as strong as a castle. I mind the building of it, when I was a child. There were army engineers here, and men from the Board of Works. Great blocks of stone they used. My Uncle Dan was one of the labourers."

"Captain Nolan is firing to keep them thoughtful," I said. "Wait a bit."

I visited each of the four cottages, and in each one had the lads fire off a round or two, so that they might acquire a feeling for the occasion, and also that they might regard themselves as gainfully employed.

When I stepped out into the street from the last one of the four, I saw Bob and his men moving down along the far side of the square. They had with them from the stables two carts of loosely corded hay, a conventional scene which for me was rendered dramatic by the circumstances. Bob was a wonder to me, looking, even at the distance, matter-of-fact, as though rebellion were all in the day's work. He caught sight of me, and waved his arm in a wide, slow arc, and in response I touched my fingers to my forehead. Behind him, at the angle which formed that corner, was the prim, shut Protestant church—secure within its railings, its snowy grounds studded with white gravestones—and the gates which guarded the demesne of the castle.

Laboriously, his lads moved the carts along the white road. When they were abreast of Tully's shop, Bob halted them, and crossed over to the double door, taking one of the fellows with him. Some yards to the east of them, just beyond Conefry's public house, was a lane grandly called River Street, which had led directly to the river in the days before the building of the demesne wall. A small knot of men and women, ten or a dozen of them perhaps, had gathered there, out of idle and reckless curiosity. Bob took from his pocket his keys to the shop, unlocked the doors, and with the other man went inside, leaving the doors opened wide behind him. When requisitioning supplies for military enterprises, it is helpful to have keys to the premises of the principal merchant.

Soon enough they were again visible, each of them carrying by the handles two ten-gallon tins of paraffin oil. These they balanced atop the bales of hay, and then Bob did a most interesting thing. He went back and locked up the shop again. He was, after all, Dennis Tully's shop assistant, and many a time I had stood beside him as he locked up the shop, with perhaps an evening of music before us, gathered about Mary's pianoforte, or at the least, a quiet jar in Conefry's.

A fine genre painting they made, the shop and its earnest young assistant upon a snowy morning, behind the great bowed windows of leaded glass on either side of the doors, the squares and pyramids of enticing merchandise, and, emblazoned across the front with swoops and curlicues of gilt, "Tully and Son." But Bob was only a moment at his prudent task, and then he and his men again set off upon their journey, cutting across the square directly towards me.

At that moment, the barracks cut loose with a ferocious rattle, which for aught that I knew was directed at Bob's party, or even at myself. Without pausing to reflect upon the matter, I shouted out to the cottages to recommence firing, and plunged into the one that I had chosen for myself, less as a command post than as a hidey-hole. From behind the wall, Ned commenced firing as well, and for four or five minutes, the air was filled with murderous and bowel-loosening noises. I reached into my pocket, and wrapped my fingers about the revolver, letting my forefinger touch the trigger.

As though in concert, so far as I could judge the directions of the sounds, Ned and Sergeant Honan ceased firing, and I bade my own fellows do the same. The air of the cottage was heavy with an acrid stench. My eyes were stinging and filled with tears; I rubbed them, which made matters worse, but I could see well enough. The two lads who had been firing from the window turned round their heads to me.

"Good lads," I said to them, "good work," for want of anything better to say.

"Jesus, Hughie," the older of the two said to me. "Twas at us that they were shooting that time. If you step out into the road again, they will have your life off you."

"More likely they were after Bob and his fellows," I said, "so far as I can judge. But they should have been safe enough, save for some chance unlucky shot."

[185]

I waited as long as I could, until curiosity and a concern for Bob's safety had got the better of me, and I set off to investigate, leaving a deputy behind me. But first, I drew out my revolver, and held it away from me at an angle, being fearful of an accident. Then I burst out from the cottages, and ran for dear life. There were several rifle shots, but whether directed to me or not, I could not tell. When I reached the safety of the lane, I leaned against a cabin wall, panting and grateful.

There I was hailed again by Batty Collins, history's eternal observer.

"Master," he called over to me, "what are they about now, Bob and his lads?"

When I came abreast, I halted and walked over to him.

"We intend to burn Honan and the constables out into the open, where we can fight them on better terms."

"Jesus, Mary, and Joseph," he said in sudden shock. "Are you serious?"

"I am indeed," I said, "and I cannot tarry to chat with you."

But I had tarried, and I knew why. There had begun to press down upon me an awful and bewildering sense that I was living within two different realities, like plates of stained glass with different designs upon them, which had been flung down one upon the other. As we had for long months planned to do, we had risen up in rebellion. I could see that it was happening and I was taking part in it, but I could not fully believe what I saw and did, not even with bullets from police carbines whizzing about me or towards me or whatever. The revolver in my hand was real and yet not real, like the cutlasses and sabres issued forth to dramatic societies. It held within its chambers cartridges which upon explosion, upon the mere tensing of a forefinger, would rip through flesh, muscle, artery, smash bone, blow eye and brain into bloody messes. The lanes and shops of Kilpeder, my own town, were as they had always been, and the spired churches, the foolish pyramid with its grovelling words, the shop and Bob standing before it, keys in hand, shapes of familiar hills ringing the horizon, the shawled women who had stood peering out at our disturbances—all of this was a reality that stretched backward into time, the time of history and of my own memories. What we were now about held for me a dreamlike quality, and yet a dream urgent and dangerous.

"Burn them out, is it?" Batty said. He began to say something more, but checked himself. I could easily have furnished him with words. The Whiteboys of a time gone by might have done the same, for there was no deviltry of which they were not capable. But Batty's words, whatever his intention, came to me with a brute ugliness.

"They can give themselves up," I said. "They need but say the word."

"Ah well," Batty said cryptically, and vanished into the shadowy recesses of his cabin. He closed the door shut behind him, and I heard the snick of its latch.

Not running now, but at a quick walk, I went to the end of the lane, precisely as firing was resumed. The other reality, of hay carts and murderous carbines, claimed me again. From my coign of vantage, I peered round the corner. Bob's party was now within a line of fire from the barracks, and Ned and Vincent were giving them what support they could. Ned was crawling along the long line of his men, putting his hand first on this man's shoulder and then on another's, and Vincent was anchored at the hut. The sounds were as dreadful to me as ever, as though being flung into my head. The fellows with Bob must have been well aware that they were now the chief targets, but they kept to the task, and Bob was at one of the carts. He was shouting something, but I could not make out the words.

I stood unable to move, to go forward or to retreat back into the lane, and I became a watcher, as Batty was, and the shawlies in River Street. And as I stood watching, one of the men at the other cart gave a hideous screech, louder than the sounds of rifle and carbine, and was hurled backward onto the snow. He did not stop screaming, but lay there with his legs drawn up, and his hands clutching at his middle. Bob ran over and knelt beside him, as did two of the other men who had been with him. There matters rested for a minute or two, three men kneeling and motionless, like the Wise Men at the *crèche*, and the fourth man writhing and screaming. Then Bob shook his head and stood up, touching as he did so the shoulder of the man nearest him, and they turned again to the cart. For a bit, all firing had stopped, as though the barracks were as shocked as I was myself.

He lay there in the snow, and it was as though he were turning into an animal, the screams coming from some dark, awful place within the soul in which we are all animals, brutes in anguish. Once, a small lad, I had run with others to a labourer whose arm had been caught in a sawmill, and his screams had been like these. But the fact that we had all of us, all within earshot, run towards him made the memory now seem less dreadful. This fellow lay alone, and the backs of his chums were turned against him.

When I could stand it no longer, I turned round the corner, and ran to him. Perhaps I thought that I could be of help to him. I do not know. He was beyond help. Despite the month that it was, he was wearing only a jacket of rough, heavy frieze, and his fingers were spread wide across his belly. The cloth was sopping wet, and his fingers glistened with blood, bright and shiny. It was as though the screams came not from his mouth, but from the mangled belly. I knew him, although not well: Michael

Dermody, a labourer upon Major Clement's estate, a taciturn man with a deep, rumbling voice. Not taciturn now, and the wordless cries were shrill as a girl's. His eyes were screwed shut.

I had the revolver in my hand, and I suddenly was seized by the wish to fire it at the barracks, to shove lead into the men who had done this, to reduce them also to bloody, screaming animals. When pigs are slaughtered, it is done more cleanly. But instead, I put back the weapon into my pocket, and walking behind Dermody, I leaned down, and with my two hands, gained a purchase of him at the armpits. Then I straightened myself as best I could, and began to tug at him. It was no use. He was a far heavier man than myself, and I budged him not more than a few inches. And added to his agonies, perhaps, for I fancied that his screams grew more intense. Spasms shook his bent legs.

"Hugh! Hugh!" I heard someone shout, and looking up, saw that Ned had twisted around so that he was facing me.

"Let him be," Ned called to me. "You cannot help him."

It was true that I could not, but I stood irresolute, still holding Dermody by the shoulders. His screams were a terrifying reproach, as though I myself had done this to him.

"For God's sake, let him be," Ned called. "Get out of there. Get back to the cottages."

For the time that I was there in the field, not a shot was fired by either side, and for aught that I knew the only murderousness was that which raged within me. My arms were shaking, despite the weight upon them. Ned was not the only man staring at me. Along the line of our fellows, a dozen faces were turned towards me. The hay carts, for which Dermody had paid with his bloody belly, had by now reached the wall, and stood there side by side. For all my brave words to Batty, I had been sickened by the use to which Ned intended to put them, but I was so no longer.

"God damn it, Hughie," Ned called, "I have no time to waste upon you. Get clear. Now, God damn you."

I lowered Dermody to the snowy ground. He was beyond knowing was he saved or no, was he dying or no. He could not have known where he was, nor if anyone stood beside him, nor what had happened to him. He had become pain. I looked for a last time at the distorted face, beefy and unshaven, the mouth opened wide to show broken, blackened teeth. Then I turned away from him, and ran back to the laneway.

I went to each of the cottages, and explained what Ned and his lads would be about. They would need all the help that we could give them, but it seemed best to me that my fellows with rifles be left to their own discretion, to fire when they chose. We had little enough ammunition. Brendan Cosgrove, who held the cottage nearest the barracks, asked me who had been hit, and how. Even at the distance, we could hear him, but the screams now were not continuous. He would slacken off, and then commence again. Is it still pain, I thought, or is despair mixed in as well?

Beside the fireplace hung a large, coloured lithograph of the Sacred Heart. He was robed in white, and His face was tranquil, inviting, the beard auburn and silky. With a forefinger, He pointed to the mysteriously exposed heart, red and pulpy. Despair, they tell us, is that obscure, un-named sin against the Spirit, for which there is no forgiveness. Silently, I offered a prayer for poor Dermody, and then, since I was at the task, one for myself as well. In my house, not ten minutes' walk away, I imagined Mary standing motionless by the window, one hand resting, perhaps, upon the sash. More faintly than to me, Dermody's screams would come to her, and the sounds of gunfire.

There was gunfire now, suddenly, and I went out into the road, and took shelter in the shallow doorway of a huckster's shop, the mean dwell-ing of a widow named Neely, who doubtless was shivering within. The window beside me held a sparse, grubby display of tins and boxes, fly-specked, and with a film of dust upon them.

Stones had been pulled away from a section of the wall, and the carts pushed through them. Men, four of them to each cart, and crouched as low as they were able to and yet perform the task, were hauling them to the barracks. One of the men was Ned himself, as I could tell by his wide-brimmed black hat and tightly belted coat. I felt a quick spasm of anger against him for endangering himself, for if he met with misfortune, who would lead us? But I had scant time for such reflexions. The barracks was directing all its fire against the carts. I raised up my hands and waved them forward and back, as a signal to the men in the cottages.

An instant before Cosgrove opened fire, one of the men at Ned's cart stumbled and half fell. Ned grabbed hold of him about the middle, and hurled him aside. He rested a moment upon one knee, then rose up, and set off down the road towards me, to the safety of the cottages. He held both hands pressed to his side, at the ribs, and as he ran he lurched. My attention was fixed upon him, but was drawn suddenly to a blaze beyond him. Ned had set fire to the two carts, and had shoved them then against the barracks door. Now he and his men were running back for dear life to the safety of the wall. I stood gaping, like a spectator at a circus who sees wild animals driven through hoops of flame, and it was only rifle bursts from opposite told me that the lads in the cottages had more sense than myself. They were squandering their cartridges, no doubt, but they gave good cover to the running men, for none of them fell. When I was certain that all of them had gained the wall, I gave a signal to cease fire.

By now the wounded man had reached me, indeed fell against me, with his two hands still clutching fast to his side.

"Jesus," he said. "Oh, Jesus, Hughie, I am hurt bad." He knew my name, but for the moment I could not remember his. A fellow in his mid-twenties. Tears filled his wild, fearful eyes.

"Go into one of the cottages and lie yourself down," I said. "We will see to you as soon as we are able. We will fetch a doctor to you."

"Hughie," he said. "Don't leave me there to lie in my pain with the blood dribbling out of me, like poor Dermody. Am I bad hurt?"

"I cannot tell," I said. "You were able to get yourself here, which is a good sign." I propped him against the huckster's door, and holding his wrists, pulled his reluctant fingers away from the wound. "I cannot tell. Perhaps the bullet but grazed you, or perhaps it has gone inside of you. We will need a doctor. But if you value your life, man, go and lie down. The lads in the cottage can perhaps attend to the bleeding."

He gave a short sort of sob, and I put my cupped hands to his face. "Go along now to the cottage," I said. "There is a good lad."

His name was Matty Brennan, and he had been given a deep graze. The bullet had hit one of his ribs at an angle, splintering it. Later, after all of us had left Kilpeder, save for the wounded, Hickey, the Protestant doctor, ably attended him, patching and bandaging him, and making certain that he could stand trial with the rest of us at the assizes. In his latter years, he drifted away from Kilpeder, and I seem to remember hearing that he had been seen in the workhouse in Buttevant. But once, not ten years ago, he came to Kilpeder on a visit, and was feted in the public bar of Conefry's. He was then a shabbily dressed man in late middle years, bald and almost toothless, but one of the heroes of Clonbrony Wood. Towards closing time, he unbuttoned his cheap jacket and hoisted up his shirt. The scar was there, pale white and smooth against yellow, wrinkled skin. "And there is the man who was with me," he said, as someone handed him another large whiskey, "Master MacMahon." He lifted his glass to me with a shaking hand. I tried to remember the boy of that snowy March morning, wild, tearful eyes, a sob, hands pressed to a dark, spreading stain. I remembered him vividly, as I had held him against the huckster's door, pale face and red, wet lips. But he was not the boaster who stood before me, whiskey wet upon his chin's stubble. Only the scar joined them, surgical, unnaturally smooth, time's umbilicus.

Now, from beyond the far end of the wall, our men, about twenty of them, were moving out, and they moved in silent safety, for no shots were sped towards them from the barracks. For the present, the barracks had thought only for the flames which had been carried to them. Ned's fire was, from one point of view, a great success. The paraffin-soaked hay was a fierce blaze, the flames thrown high, and it was certain that the wood of the carts and then the great oak doors, iron-studded, would be afire. I knew, without having it explained to me, why Ned had sent out his detachment. If Honan was forced to lead his men out of the barracks, they could never use the front, which faced upon the Macroom road. The door would be an inferno, and the ground-floor windows were barred. If they tried to drop from the first floor, Ned's men could pick them off. He would have to send them out through the rere, which faced open fields sloping downwards towards the demesne wall. Ned was sending men to confront them there, although what he intended they should use for cover, I could not imagine.

I wonder now that I could so calmly have accepted the notion of seeing men trapped between flames and gunfire. The rage which I had felt as I knelt beside Dermody had abated, but it was not replaced by sympathy or human feeling. I think—but how after all these years can I be certain?—I think that I was moved by a chill fear, not so much for my immediate safety, but rather fear rising from my knowledge of what we were about. It was as though we had walked, step by step, deeper and deeper into a rebellion from which there could now be no turning back, whatever the consequences. My ride with Bob that morning to Knockmany seemed now many hours in the past, idyllic and tranquil, and then our mustering there, our march into the town. Hour by hour, minute by minute, we had been carried into what was by now a battle, a rebellion in arms, with three of our lads already wounded, and one of those most likely dying, and within the barracks it was likely indeed that our fire had found a target or two. We had but the one hope, that things were going well for us, not in Kilpeder alone, but across the island. And so I watched the barracks being set afire hoping only that horror and fear would drive out the constables, and that they would then have the good sense to surrender.

Much of what happened next happened beyond my sight. The door was now on fire, but if the fire had yet spread to the floors of the barracks, I could not tell. From behind the wall came every now and then a shot, isolated and unexpected, as though Ned, to conserve bullets, had told them to fire only at what they might glimpse moving behind the windows. There was no return fire from the barracks, and yet matters now rested with them, with what Sergeant Honan might decide to do.

Later, when we were most of us taking our ease in the Cork City

Gaol, awaiting our trials, Vincent told me how matters appeared to the lads sent out by Ned to circle round the barracks, for Vincent had been placed in command of them. Even then, even in the gaol, when his fortune, like everyone's, was at the ebb, there was a dash and a spruceness about Vincent that commanded my envy. His father kept him well supplied with cigars, and with delicacies of various sorts to supplement the abominable fare, and even in prison he proved most open and generous, sharing out what he had. We stood together smoking, he and I, one dank, chill afternoon, with our backs resting against the wall of the exercise yard. There was a greyness to the air, as though we were not men at all but figures in a lithograph, men walking together in twos and threes, or by themselves, squatting on their hunkers. There was a narrow walk which ran across the top of the wall, and policemen patrolled there in their short black capes, carbines slung over their shoulders. There must have been a good four hundred of us in the gaol, from Kilpeder and Knockane and Millstreet and the other towns, and wild, foolish rumours were in the air that an attempt might be made to break us out, of the sort which indeed was soon afterwards attempted at Clerkenwell.

But Vincent, by all that could be judged from his bearing and manner, might have been waiting for lads to join him for a morning's beagling, his caped overcoat unbuttoned, a bit dusty and wrinkled, to be sure, and his boots unpolished. I envied him, for the rest of us, even Ned and Bob, were sorry sights. Ned was like a great crow winged by a hunter's unlucky shot, dark in appearance and dark in manner, friendly enough, and with a show of cheerfulness for the young, frightened lads, but when he turned away from them, his face was like a mask, the eyes narrowed to slits, and the long lips pressed together. Somewhere along the way, he had lost that soft, wide-brimmed hat, and his lank hair went uncombed. He was by himself for most of each day's hour of fresh air, or else talking with Bob, and Vincent and I had each other for company.

"It took us a good ten minutes," Vincent told me later in gaol, "to move down the Macroom road, and then cut down Tully's Lane, and then move ourselves across the fields until we were abreast of the barracks. Position yourselves as best you can, Ned said to me blithely enough, but where we found ourselves, there were no positions at all. Directly behind the barracks is that garden of which Honan was so proud, cabbages and onions and potatoes, looking dead now with the blanket of snow lying on plants and dirt alike. Then scruffy, untended fields without so much as a rock for shelter, and at the far end, a kind of horizon framing the scene, a stretch of the demesne wall. The wall would have provided splendid shelter, to be sure, but it was too distant to be of use. Of the boys with me, two only had rifles, and the others shotguns, which would have been useless at the distance. For want of anything better, I bade the lads stretch out into a line, and then had them drop to one knee. By God, I thought to myself, if the barracks opens fire upon us, I will bid us cut and run, and scramble over the wall, and to hell with the Irish Republic. But there were no shots at all from the barracks. From far off, from Ned's line on the far side of the road, I could hear shouts that I could not make out, but nothing else. I could not understand the silence of the barracks."

Tully's Lane. It was curious to hear Vincent use, so casually, what was, in a manner of speaking, his own name. It was named for the huckster's shop out of which the family's fortune had been spun, like the gold of a fairy tale, the wretched hovel still standing, a warehouse attending the needs of the great establishment on the square, but where once Vincent's grandfather, like the widow Neely, had in dusty darkness pawed over copper pennies, tobacco, spills of tea. A lane named for a huckster's shop.

"Behind us," Vincent said, "was the demense wall, and, far behind the wall, the plantations of trees, their branches white with snow that held sparkles of sun, and beyond the plantation, one corner of the Castle was visible, an angle of lofty pediment. Do you know what I had time to remember, even at such a moment? That print in the taproom of the Arms, the town and river and the demesne laid out, and at the four corners, for decorative effect, the Castle, and a bend of the river, shaded by willows, and the old keep, dressed in romantic ivy. And the legend beneath it, 'The town of Kilpeder, property of the Earl of Ardmor, 1822.'"

"You forgot the fourth corner," I told him, "the knight-at-arms." In heavy medieval armour, two hands resting upon a tall shield, shoulder-high, bearing the arms of the Forrester family.

"Yes," Vincent said, grinning at me. "Property of the Earl of Ardmor." His slim cigar, the colour of autumn leaves, had gone dead, and he rekindled it with that silver contrivance of his, an incongruous twinkle of luxury in the exercise yard of the Cork City Gaol.

"But we had not long to wait," he said, "before we discovered the explanation of the silence. Across the length of the building, on the ground floor, there was spreading a rosy glow, like a captured sunset. I thought at first that we were looking through the wardroom to the burning door and the carts, but I realised then that those bales of hay had done all that was asked of them. The barracks was well and truly afire, and the police with no choice but to come out to us or die a horrible death within. Which meant, I thought, that we had won, for Con Honan was a sensible man, and not Horatio at the bridge. But it was a numb feeling, with nothing in it of triumph or even excitement. A house was burning on the snows and men trapped inside it. In our foreground was Honan's kitchen garden; he used boast in Conefry's of his damned onions. Honan was the enemy, to be sure, armed and black-caped, but it was also as if we had set fire to our own lives. Or poor Belton, with his shortness of breath and porter-heavy belly.

" 'Honan,' I shouted out upon sudden impulse. 'Honan,' and then waited. 'Honan, can you hear me?' There were forms moving behind the first-floor windows, although not so close that I could recognise them. But then Honan was standing there, looking out at me, still buttoned-up and formal, although I fancied a smear of some sort on his cheek. 'Honan,' I shouted, 'will you clear out of there, in God's name?' But he shook his head, and turned away from me. I could not believe what I had seen. I know now, of course, that he had his own reasons for hanging on as long as he could, and that he would do his parleying with Ned, not with some fellow trampling down his onions."

Or perhaps, I thought, as I listened to Vincent, perhaps it was in disbelief that Honan, too, had shaken his head, as he looked out the window upon the son of Dennis Tully, armed and bellicose, his lot cast with farm boys and labourers. Even here, even in the exercise yard of a gaol, Vincent seemed a visitor rather than a prisoner, in his handsome coat, fastidiously choosing his words. But it must in fact have been just then that Honan walked the breadth of the barracks to the front windows, and shouted out to Ned.

It was, so Bob was later to tell me, a fearful sight, for it was across the front ground-floor rooms that the fire, having its own ferocious will, had chosen first to eat its way. Honan stood above flames, and smoke was drifting about him.

"Nolan," he shouted, "we are leaving the barracks now, by the back garden. Stand clear of us, if you know what is good for you. There is a man dead in here, wearing the Queen's uniform. We have a dead constable to bring out with us. You have done murder this day."

Ned, kneeling beside Bob, stood upright. "We have our dead, Sergeant Honan. There is a man lying quiet in the field behind me. It was for our own country that he died, and not for your Queen off there in England. Clear out now from that murderous building, and bid your lads stack their arms when they are clear of it."

Honan stood there a moment, and then, so it seemed to Bob, gave a brisk nod before turning away.

"Damn it to hell," Ned said, "he means to make a fight of it, the bloody fool." He turned to Dunphy then, to call him over and give him his orders; but it was just then, at that moment, that the lookout came riding down into Kilpeder along the Macroom road.

I could see him myself from where I was standing. Ned had posted two of them, atop the hilly rise of the road just before it dipped down towards the town, and had given them the two horses which Bob and myself had ridden to Knockmany that morning. He looked like a scarecrow, a graceless fellow, all knees and elbows, wearing a shapeless hat which as I watched blew away from him. Unmindful of what shots might be speeding towards him from the burning barracks, he rode straight to our wall, and when he was abreast of it, reined in and slid from his horse. I watched him talking with Ned and Bob, and saw Dunphy walk over to join them. He kept swinging his arm in wide circles, and he was dancing with excitement, hopping from one foot to the other.

Presently, Ned and Bob stepped out into the road, and ran down it towards me, Ned's overcoat flapping behind him. When they reached me, he grasped my arm so tightly that it hurt.

"Bob says that the Castle has a watchtower," he said. His face had darkened, his eyes the colour of dirty slate, and the taut skin of his cheeks was suffused with blood.

"Watchtower," I said, confused, to Bob.

"The gazebo, he means," Bob said.

"Yes," I said, "the gazebo."

"Come along with me," Ned said. "I need it. Do they keep it locked?"

"No," I said, feeling myself puzzled and foolish. "Who would lock a folly?" His long fingers were biting into me.

"Go along with him, Hughie," Bob said. "You know it as well as I do, or better."

And this was true. The Ardmors were courteous and neighbourlike in such matters, allowing the townspeople to stroll the grounds of the demesne to admire the gardens and the river. A half dozen times, at least, I had climbed the winding stairs.

"Bob," Ned said, while at the same time pulling me away with his strong claw, "take the men from the cottages, and bring them around behind the barracks to where Vincent is." He tugged so fiercely at me that I stumbled against him, and I looked towards Bob for enlightenment. But Bob looked at me for but a moment more, his face as white as Ned's was dark, then turned his back to me and went over to the cottages, shouting as he walked.

At half walk, half trot, Ned and I set off, and went the full length of the deserted market square, past the Arms and Conefry's and Tully's and the saddlemaker's and the smaller shops.

"What is it, Ned?" I asked him, twice, but he may not have heard me, for he did not respond by so much as a shake of the head.

At the far end, the Protestant church, spired and smooth of stone, sat as though reproachfully behind its closed gates, the snow upon its grounds unsullied, and little nightcaps of snow upon its gravestones of granite and white marble. Close to it, at right angles, stood the pillared entrance to the demesne, with globes surmounting the pillars and, grasping each of them, a falcon with outstretched wings, snow-decked. Beyond the pillars lay the first curve of the carriageway and the entrance lodge, a playful bit of mock-Palladian. Ned nodded towards it.

"Is that likely to be manned?" He had paused in his onward march, but his body was straining to go forward.

"Dear, no," I said. "An old couple live there, named Rafferty. He was once Lord Ardmor's coachman."

But Ned walked to it, holding loosely his revolver. The door was ajar, and he walked inside, and a minute later came out again.

"They have cleared off," he said. "Is the tower far distant?"

"You can see the top of it," I said, "beyond the plantation to our left. If we walk along the carriageway a bit, we will come to its path." And so we set off, along the clean snow.

The invasion of Ardmor Castle. Haste had put him into a slight error, for the Raffertys in truth were there, huddled together in their tiny scullery. No word had come to them of the morning's work, either from the Castle or from the town, and for hours they had crouched on stools there, poor frightened creatures well into their seventies, listening to gunfire and distant shouting.

At a curve, just before the path we sought, the Castle came suddenly into full view. The blanket of snow which had fallen upon our world made it seem more than ever a scene of fairy-tale wonder. Nothing moved, no one was visible. Although Lionel Forrester was years afterwards to tell me that sometime during the morning he and Lady Ardmor, his aunt, had stepped out onto the terrace, through tall windows, and had stood looking towards the town. But I did not see them; neither did he remember seeing us. How would we have appeared to him? Blackbirds hopping upon snow, figures scribbled in haste by an engraver to give scale and proportion?

It was but a ten minutes' walk to the gazebo, along a winding path, with trees to either side of us, larch and elm. I had never walked it in winter, for a visit to the demesne grounds was a summer treat, the gardens bursting with colours and between them small paths of combed gravel, grey and tan, the woodland paths soft and leafy, and the elms huge-branched and heavy with shade. All now felt unfamiliar, snow obscuring the path, and Ned striding on ahead of me, coattails flapping, a giant rook.

At the clearing, where in summer a brief, pleasant lawn surrounded the gazebo, emerald green, he did not pause for admiration, but walked straight to the door.

It was called by most, gentle and common alike, the "folly," but I have my own pedantic preference for *gazebo*, a foolish little word, makey-uppy Latin; *gazebo*: "I gaze out upon." Like *belvedere*. The model, or so we all believe, was a campanile in some Italian hill town, but if so, it had been translated into our rough northern idiom, looking like a Norman keep, but far taller and more narrow, a daft, precarious building which took pride in its ornamental uselessness.

Ned put his hand to the latch, and the door swung open, the interior of the ground floor brighter than I had expected, with the pale, even sunlight of a winter morning falling upon its flagstones, and upon picnic tables and chairs swathed in muslin. The spiral stair began at one side of the room, and Ned went at once to it and began to climb, with myself following close at his heels. The wedge-shaped stairs were too narrow to be taken other than one at a time, and I felt his impatience. Five stories we climbed, past high, narrow rooms, the topmost one fantastically painted a dark, velvety blue, with a myriad of little, gilt, five-pointed stars scattered at random. The stairs ended there, but Ned, as though he had visited the gazebo in some other life, went to the small door, opened it, and with head and shoulders bent, climbed upon the squat, straight staircase into the belvedere.

When I reached him, I had a brief, giddy awareness of height. Our world—my world, rather, for Ned was always to be a stranger to it—lay all about us: the great hills, the Derrynasaggarts to our left and the Boggeraghs to our right, horizons of white mountains which had two days before been green, heather, black. Behind us, I knew, lay the Castle in all its comely, tranquil proportions. But Ned was standing rigid, his hands holding fast to two of the little stubby sandstone pillars. Beyond us, in the direction which held his gaze, flowed the Sullane, and beyond it the high demesne walls, and beyond them the town. As I moved towards him, the air was ripped by rattling gunfire.

Below and beyond us, the town was bulky and commodious, slate roofs and humbler straw, the market square a cloth of white, but the pattern which it offered in summer was twisted askew by the battle at the barracks. The fire within, terrible though it must have been from close at hand, was from here but a dull glow behind the lower windows. But the battle was spread out to be seen, our lads to the front of the barracks and to its back, Vincent's men, and now Bob's as well, kneeling, with their weapons to their shoulders. Although I did not know it, the quarrel was upon its hinge. Honan had bade his men give out with a burst of shots before they made their dash out through the rere, and into the open. The firing had from where we were a different sound—not terrifying blasts upon the ear, but angry, dry bursts.

And yet all this I saw but with a corner of my mind and eye, for my attention had been pulled at once in the direction upon which Ned's gaze was riveted.

Along the Macroom road, bewildering and terrifying as nightmare, came marching towards us a long column of soldiers, their red coats vivid against the snowy landscape and within the bright air. Marching, I have said, but not all of them were afoot, for in the van rode a troop of cavalry, not red-coated at all, but with long, dark capes falling from their shoulders. The troops were some distance yet from the low hill which sweeps gently to the even road into the town. Indeed, the cavalry could have reached it at once, almost, were the horses to be put to the gallop, but the column moved as one, with the horses held to a walk. It was this, my first shock over, which seemed to me most terrifying of all—that brisk but unhurried movement, with its air of certainty. There were three riders in front of all—the officers, no doubt.

They were gallant riders, the three of them, negligent and purpose-ful, broad of shoulder, with the cloaks flowing in smooth soft lines almost to the flanks of their mounts, and riding closely together as though chatting, gentlemen taking the late morning air, as though riding home-wards from morning hunt, from a view to a kill, and a meal prepared for them: gammon and shirred eggs, hock in tall fluted glasses. Behind them, men afoot and men mounted, a brave display, moved in silence towards our privileged eminence, which shielded us by distance from the thud of boot and hoof, clatter of metal, the creak of straining leather.

By distance and gunfire. Ned had one hand firm upon the foolish, ornamental parapet, and he was leaning forward, a gargoyle, as in the Doré illustrations to Hugo's romance of history. He had as fine a view of matters as any general might wish, Junot or Hannibal or Murat.

All of a sudden he turned towards me, and what I saw in his face terrified me. But I had too much to deal with at the one time: the murdering town and a room of velvet sky and glittering stars, the austere, benign silence of the demesne, soldiers the size of toy sets laid out in Prendergast's shop window in Cork City at Christmastime, the school-house and our own house beside it, grey slate and bricks the colour of low-burning turf.

He stared at me without seeing me, and began to turn away, but I laid a hand upon his shoulder.

"Bloody bastards," he said, spitting out the words like bullets, and he jerked his shoulder free.

"My God, Ned," I said to him, "are we done for?" Through all of the morning's work, from Knockmany's streaky dawn, he had had about him a certainty; he was a will bulging with purpose. Drained now, and a kind of rage was there.

My question called him back, and he saw me, as might an astronomer, bringing his instrument to bear upon the near-at-hand. "Yes, Hughie," he said. "We are done for."

They came shouting now from the barracks, and our fellows cut loose upon them. Stick figures they looked, and two of them dropped before my eyes, the one of them pitching headfirst upon the snow, upon snow-heavy vines, and the other dropping to his knees, a rooting animal. All this I saw transpiring beyond Ned's heavy shoulder. Beyond them, beyond the town, scarlet jackets crested the hill, dark-caped horsemen. In Honan's kitchen garden, above frozen roots and tubers, heavy boots, approved and issued from Dublin Castle, dug themselves into place. They had come out, pell-mell, but each man jack of them carrying his carbine, and dropped now, each hale and hearty one of them, to the one knee, as procedurally set forth in the *Manual*. And our own lads, if that is the proper term—for they were all of them Irish, intent upon destruction the one of the other—held fast.

"Oh yes," Ned said, "we are done for indeed." He had his back turned against the lot. Then, with a heave of his heavy-boned body, he said, "We must get out now. As many of us as can make it out."

Now, a clarion call, silver and liquid; a trumpeter from within the scarlet jackets sounded their charge, and their cavalry, who had been shielding screens upon either flank of the marching men, moved forward at the trot. Marvellous they looked to me, and invincible. But Ned had already turned away from me, and was clattering down the steep stairs. I followed, reading auguries in the hunched, bony shoulders.

9

[Hugh MacMahon]

It is set forth in Brailsford's *History of the Royal Irish Constabulary* that the police at Kilpeder bravely held their blazing barracks until forced out by the flames, and then, although outnumbered, gave battle upon open ground until such time as they were delivered from their peril by a "flying column" of foot and horse under the command of Lieutenant Colonel J. F. Sheppard. And all that is true enough. What sounds falsely upon my ear is the account of how the "rebels" "withdrew" from their siege, and moved northwards towards Clonbrony Wood. "Fled from the town in terror and panic" would be language coming closer to the mark, but Mr. Brailsford, no doubt, was at pains to make us seem formidable, the better to celebrate the victory, a habit of military historians since the days of Caesar.

In the time that it took Ned and myself to race out of the demesne and down through the deserted town to the barracks, the troopers had reached the outskirting buildings, where their officer, who for aught that I know was indeed Lieutenant Colonel J. F. Sheppard, brought them to a halt. Four abreast, they lined the Macroom road, with their long murderous sabres unsheathed and pointing heavenwards. The sounds of gunfire had ceased.

By the shop of Robinson, the saddlemaker, Ned stopped short, and rested his back against the door. We were winded, the two of us. Ned saw me staring, first at him, then down the road, then back at him, and suddenly, inexplicably, he smiled. "Well, Hughie," he said, "what shall we do now?" He wiped the back of his hand across his mouth.

The lads behind the wall had risen up to their feet, most of them, heedless of safety, and were looking towards the caped troopers. Distant, beyond the mounted men, the foot soldiers, scarlet and black, marched with easy, confident stride. One of the troopers shifted in his saddle, and sunlight struck a glint from his sabre.

"They have all the time in the world," Ned said, and then repeated himself, "all the time in the world."

"What do they expect from us, Ned?" I asked him. "Why have they halted there?"

He shook his head. "I don't know," he said. "Perhaps they want us to surrender."

It was a moment hinged upon silence, upon dreadful expectation. Later, it would be set forth that indeed Colonel Sheppard had determined either to take our surrender or else force us to make our stand somewhere beyond the town, upon open ground. But none of us could have known that, and certainly Ned did not. He stood leaning against the door, looking down at his boots and at dirty snow. Then he shook his head, briskly, as though to clear it. "Come along, Hughie," he said.

He walked with long, angular stride down the road, and when he was within earshot, shouted out to Dunphy, "Hold where you are, Pat. We are going for the rest of the lads." Dunphy, standing amidst a small knot of his fellows, was motionless, his elbows outthrust. There was no wind, and the sky was a clear, delicate blue. Beyond the wall, beyond the ragged line of men, beyond the empty winter fields, lay woods, and, farthest of all, the tall hills. We were at that moment so close to the burning barracks that I could feel the heat upon my face and neck, a sinister, out-of-season warmth.

When we had circled the barracks and come out into the fields behind it, I do not know what I had expected to see, but not, certainly, the kind of tableau which greeted us. Honan and his constables, Bob and Vincent and our lads, stood facing each other, but they had moved far enough away from each other to be out of the range of their rifles and carbines. Honan had drawn up his men into military formation, three ranks of them, with himself and the other sergeant standing a bit to one side, and with the useless barracks behind them. Bob and Vincent had fallen far back, almost within the shadow of the demense wall. And there they stood, the two lots of them, as though waiting for Ned or Colonel Sheppard or history to tell them what to do.

When we had come near to our lads, Ned dropped his stride to a walk, and stepped close to Bob.

"Jesus, Ned," Bob said in a low voice. "Vincent and I took a walk up towards the road. The entire fucking British army is moving down upon us."

"As much of it as is needed for the task at hand," Ned said. He was looking closely at Bob and then at Vincent, and could not have been reassured by what he saw, for I could read on their faces that they were as frightened and as bewildered as I was myself.

"What about the lads?" Ned asked.

Bob shrugged. "They are beginning to grasp what has happened. It is not easy for them. A half hour ago, we were in a fair way towards making ourselves masters of Kilpeder."

"Yes," Ned said, looking down the long field, snow-shrouded weeds, towards the lines of passive, watchful police, the burning building. "Well, Bob, what do you think? Vincent?"

"You know well what must be done, Ned. Hand over ourselves and our weapons, either to this lot or to the soldiers, I doubt if it matters which. We are untrained country lads, Ned, good enough to blaze away at a police barracks, but there it all is."

"Vincent?"

"If you have any doubts, Ned, go up and take a look at what is clanking along towards us. Our fellows wouldn't hold against them, they would cut and run. And small blame to them, I would rather be elsewhere myself."

Ned nodded, and then walked off by himself. For a moment, I thought it was over, that he had set off to make what peace he could with Honan. But instead he halted, some twenty feet or so away from us, hands buried deep in his pockets. He was a strange one, right enough. He looked at us without seeing us, and then beyond us to the horizon.

When he came back, he planted himself in front of the lads, his long, gawky legs spread wide apart.

"You all know what has happened," he said to them. "The English have called down upon us one of their flying columns, and there is no way that we can make a stand against them in Kilpeder. They would cut us into ribbons, that is the trade they are in. But we would be foolish indeed to surrender to them. Bob and Vincent and Hugh and I have discussed the matter, and we are agreed upon that."

So much for simple truthfulness. I stole a glance at Vincent, but he was staring at Bob, his large, dark eyes apprehensive.

"There are two reasons for that," Ned said. "For as long as we can hold those soldiers embroiled with us, they will be pinned down, just as we are. They will not be marching northwards to where the great battles will be fought. But there is another reason which is as good almost as that one. There have been men killed here this morning, on both sides. If we surrender, we will be placed under arrest, and the charges against us will be armed rebellion and murder. Not to mention such matters as robbery and arson."

He paused to let that sink in, and on me at least, it made its full impression.

"Our best chance is to move out. We will get ourselves clear of Kilpeder, and head towards the hills. And we will scatter. You lads here will go with Bob and Hugh, and Vincent and Pat Dunphy and myself will take the other lads westwards and through Clonbrony Wood, and towards the Derrynasaggarts. The soldiers will move out against us, but they will take their time about it; they will not be expecting it. Scattering us might suit them as well as it suits us. And if we reach the hills, either lot of us, we will have a chance of drifting away in our ones and twos and threes. Tis not that splendid a chance, but tis the best I can offer you. Take a minute to think about it. I am not ordering you to do it; we are past that, but I will lead you."

He paused then, and moved his eyes along them, while they looked at him and at each other. And in the pause, Bob, who two scant minutes before had been hell-bent on surrender, spoke up.

"Surrender, is it? I doubt would they let us surrender. They would be more likely to cut us down with their butcher's swords. Trample us down with their great war horses."

"We're for it, lads," Vincent said. "Ned knows the ways of armies, and we had best mind his words." He had regained a bit of his swagger, and was standing with arms akimbo, fists resting on hips. You would have needed to know Vincent as well as I did to tell his mood, the darting, gambler's eyes.

I did not at all share their enthusiasm for Ned's plan, whether real or feigned. When, minutes earlier, Ned had leaned against the saddler's door, staring down at his boots, he had spoken the simple truth. We were done for, and the sooner over, the best. I would as soon be shoved into a cell as wander over wild, savage hills. And I was filled also with a kind of sickening despair, a nausea of the spirit. Reality had come crashing against us. Crowns and judges and policemen and soldiers and booted cavalry had no intention of turning the country over to labourers and shop assistants.

"Master MacMahon," one of the men said, and although I heard him, he had to speak my name again before I turned my head towards him. He was a young fellow, seventeen or eighteen, and he had been in my school, I was certain of it, but I could not recall his name. He was in a dark jacket, with a muffler wound tight about his neck, and he carried an exotic, long-barrelled fowling piece of some sort. He was hatless, and pale red hair half hid his ears.

"Master MacMahon," he said. "Is that your own thought as well?"

I paused before answering, and in the pause, Bob walked over and stood beside me. Ned was tense and impatient, the massive Yankee revolver again in his hand. I was standing at an angle to the men, and a corner of my eye was aware of the blazing barracks.

"Vincent Tully spoke for myself as well, lad," I said. "Captain Nolan is the only one of us with an understanding of such matters." Then I turned sharply away from him, and let my gaze rest upon the lines of policemen. They seemed to be at ease and yet attentive, with the tide swung unexpectedly in their favour. Their world was coming right side up.

"Ned," I said, "you surely cannot believe that those fellows there will allow us to stroll away."

"That is the one thing of which I am certain," Ned said. "They have acquitted themselves well. Honan held the barracks until the soles of his boots began to smoke, and now he holds the grounds. Why should he risk his lads further when the British army has come to attend to us?"

Patsy Flavin. I remembered him now as a schoolboy, in the same sort of jacket, hunched over the desk, a brother beside him with the same carroty hair. Perhaps it was my teaching which had brought him here with us, to this scruffy field. Come to attend to us. Shouts, swinging sabres, and my own death perhaps; it was unimaginable.

"We will move down, staying close to the demesne wall," Ned said, "to the far end of the town, and where the wall meets the Protestant church, Bob will take you around past it, and down the Killeter road for a bit, and then you will strike out across the fields. At the church, I will leave you, and go back for the other lads. If you hear shooting or any disturbance, you are to pay no heed to it. Keep together until you are well beyond the town."

The men stood listening to Ned as though he were some faith healer or prophecy man, unfolding for them some sensible or inspired plan for their salvation, as well they might, so brisk and confident was he in manner. And yet it seemed to me little better than a counsel of despair, a prolongation of defeat which was already in my mouth, a bitter, metallic taste, like that of iron. I was ashamed that I had not had the courage to answer Patsy Flavin's question honestly, a guilty schoolmaster who had dragged his pupil into the way of danger. And yet I could never have done that, for we were all of us bound together by that place and that hour, and Ned was our will and our brains. In all of the latter years, when Ned Nolan was spoken of or on the occasions when we met, the years after he had been shaped into an ogre or else into a twisted kind of hero, depending on one's point of view, in all those years I would remember him as he was in this place and hour.

And the simple truth is that he moved us out of the wasteland beyond the barracks garden, and down along the backs of the town, and out onto the road which led to open country, so that the ballad makers had "Clonbrony Wood" and not "Kilpeder" as a name for their heroic jingles, although if any battle was fought that day, in the proper meaning of the term, it was the Fenian attack upon the barracks and the defence of it by the Constabulary. For what was to happen a few hours later in Clonbrony Wood was not a battle, not as I have been given by books to understand that word. Poets, from Shakespeare to Byron to ballad rhymesters, are savourers of the picturesque, and their fancy was captured by Nolan's Fenians moving through snowy woods, pressed hard by red-coated soldiers and dark-tunicked police, and halting then at last, surrounded, to make their final stand. But it was not a battle. A winter's hunt is more like it, with Ned's rebels as the quarry, brought at last to bay.

I remember how we moved out along the wall, with glances cast behind us, to see were the police holding their ground, and how they remained standing, at their ease, behind their ruined barracks. As Ned had spoken of the soldiers, they had all the time in the world. When, months later, Her Majesty bestowed upon the police the regal adjective in token of their loyalty and zeal during the Rising, so that they would henceforth be known as the Royal Irish Constabulary, Kilpeder was among the battles singled out for particular praise—both the skirmish itself, as it was called, and the service later tendered to the army by the policemen in the final pursuit through woods and across difficult terrain. Praise well merited. Scant hours before, as seen from within the barracks, armed and dangerous *banditi*, tentacles of anarchy and treason. Before their eyes, we were dissolving into more familiar shapes: ruffians, skulkers, Ribbonmen. They had long experience with the sorts that we were becoming. We had marched into Kilpeder, but we were moving warily out of it, and although it was but fancy on my part, for the distance between us was, thank God, too great, I imagined an easy authority swelling them, almost an habitual condescension.

All of this long stretch of demesne wall of smooth and comely stone, grey as a gull's wing, was heavy with ivy, the deepest of greens splashed with snow, spiky at the edges. The lads in the line closest to it could have touched it with outstretched arms, had they a mind to. That wall, now, in these recent years, is broken in places, patched with cement or with gaps bridged by rusted strands of barbed wire, but in those days it was perfectly attended by the groundsmen, a promise of the order which lay within, patterned gardens, the Castle itself, terraced, its tall windows catching the sun, guarded not by stone alone, by witty gate lodge, but by policemen, cavalry, quick-marching infantry, by lions and unicorns, stone-eyed falcons. To our other side, beyond stubble fields, thistles, and rank grass, were the backs of Kilpeder, weather-streaked brick and whitewash, peeling plaster. From rere windows above shops, behind grey curtains, our progress, if such it may be termed, was doubtless being observed, notations put to later use, when our shabby retreat was transposed into legend, rhyme. But at the moment, there were no shouts of encouragement.

At the narrow passageway which led out into the angle between demesne gate and church, Ned halted us. He drew Bob apart from the rest of us, and spoke to him so quietly that we could not hear his words. Bob told me, later, what he said. "There was no way to read his thoughts," Bob said. "You remember those eyes of his, Red Indian eyes we used call them, black as coals, and the long, thin lip, like the caricatures of Irishmen in *Punch*. What he said was plain enough, that the two lots of us, his and ours, should make our separate ways, and trust to luck and chance. And if luck was with us, we should seek to join up together in Clonbrony Wood. 'Luck,' I said, repeating his word flatly, but as a question. 'More luck than we will have,' he said. Time stood still, and there were only the two of us; the rest of you were blurs at the edge of my vision. Noises I heard, feet shuffling, and shouts which I could not puzzle out from the lads behind the wall facing the barracks, and then, from a distance, prompt as fate upon his words, the notes of a bugle, carried through the dead, windless winter air."

"I remember the bugle well," I said to Bob, "and it put the fear of God into me, that they were marching and riding towards us with horses and rifles and heavy boots, and with music itself." But that was a fanciful afterthought, for at the time the bugle call rose in me only a fear that my bowels might loosen. I could feel the wind and dark water roiling in my gut.

"It pulled me back into time, as you might say," Bob said, "and I knew that we must scatter before those marching men could move down upon the town; but I could not tear my eyes from Ned's face, as though he and not the British army were passing sentence upon us, until he struck me lightly on the arm with his closed fist, and said, 'We will move now, in the name of God.'"

And move out we did, out upon the east end of the square, where the stones of state and church—Lord Ardmor's blind, fierce-clawed falcons, the Protestant church's spiky steeple—confronted us. Beyond the full length of the deserted square, shops and inn and taverns, lay the gutted, ravaged barracks, and across the road from it, at an angle awkward for our vision, the wall behind which Dunphy waited with his men. I spared a bit of sympathy for them, knowing that for the full fifteen minutes or more that the rest of us had been conferring, they had had a fine holiday view of the British soldiers in their progress down upon us.

And so had we now, as well, for the square is not built flush upon the Macroom-Killarney road, but rather canted at an angle, so that from where we had for a moment paused, with the church railings at our back, we faced them directly, if from a merciful distance. It was as though a great scarlet animal, scaly and centipede, had crawled itself towards Kilpeder, unhurried scarlet upon the white-powdered road. Empty hills rose up behind it. To its left, nearer at hand, rose up the steeples of Saint Jarlath's, and close to it, shrouded from my view, my own house, and Mary within it, who must have heard the bugle call, and would have guessed its meaning. "Mother of God," said one of the men close to me, low-voiced, as though fearful of drawing down upon us the attention of the scarlet animal. The officers in command of the column sat their mounts easily, huntsmen out for a morning's kill in fine, clear weather, their air, unlike ours, tonic and bracing.

"All right, now," Ned said, "let us get to hell out of here and into open country." He had taken from its sagging holster of dull black leather his massive Yankee revolver, and was holding it loosely in his heavy-boned hand. "Vincent, you come along with me." Vincent stepped towards him at once. He seemed calm, but his face was white as schoolroom chalk, a handsome face, a touch girlish almost, with none of the fleshiness it was to gather to itself in later years, and I almost could fancy upon it a faint smile, perhaps of terror.

"Ned," I said quickly, "you'll not forget about the lads we posted in the cottages." Ned turned towards me, and then, suddenly, smiled, as though he had recognised something familiar. "We will not, Hughie," he said. "We will not forget the lads in the cottages. You will be seeing them again, God willing. In Clonbrony." And with that he turned on his heel, and with Vincent beside him, set off down the square. An ill-assorted pair, Ned in his outlandish American coat and wide-brimmed hat, and Vincent elegant in his coat with its half cape, bareheaded.

Bob wasted no time, but led us off at once, down the laneway which led out into the Killeter road. We were a strange procession, on the move out of our own town, for the cobbled laneway was so narrow that we could go but two abreast, and we were silent, the untramelled snow a cushion beneath our boots. Beyond us lay a byroad, with a scattering of farms set far back, and hedgerows to either side of us. The distance from the square, scant though it was, had given courage to one of the farms, and its people stood outside their cabin, staring at us, the man and woman, and several little ones, and an old, bent man, leaning on a stick. They did not wave or call out to us, as is the country custom. The turf stack beyond looked odd, with its cover of snow. One of our men raised his arm, as though hopeful of a responding salutation, but there was none. The cabin stood upon a rise, and from it they were doubtless able to see the scarlet soldiers.

Bob set us a brisk pace, and although taller by a head, I had to make my strides long to keep up with him. I could not make out his mood. Suddenly he said, in almost a snarl, not so much to me as to himself or to the white road before us, "Bloody mess and waste. Bloody filth." He often said such things, with his terrifying distaste for sloth and sloppiness and ordinary human slow-wittedness, keeping Tully's cavernous shop a miracle of tidiness. His words seemed homely, almost, save for the venom he put into them. He wanted no reply from me, and I gave none. After a bit, he turned towards me, whether to look at me or through me I could not tell, and I was shocked by what I saw. We were all of us frightened and bewildered, God knows what my own appearance must have been, but what I saw in Bob's face was a kind of sick fury so intense that it left no room for bewilderment. For the first time in that day of gunfire and flames, and flesh ripped by bullets, his eyes were murderous, as though he wanted to kill but did not have his victims within reach.

"Kilpeder is but one place," I said to him lamely. "Sure there are fifty risings this day. Tis the appointed day. All across Munster and up Leinster into Dublin." Thinking only to console him with these pious words, for in truth at that moment I cared not a threepence for the Rising, but only for my own skin and blood, or at the most for the skins of the lads with us.

He continued to stare through me. It was as though my words came to him slowly through the bright, brittle air. Then he said, "You fool, Hughie," and turned away from me.

And that, by mutual accord, suspended our conversation. I twisted my own head, to take a glance at the men behind us, and saw that they needed no urging to keep to Bob's brisk walk. Each step we took carried us farther away from the hideous scarlet thing that they had glimpsed upon the Macroom road. Their faces showed their fear.

It was a bit later, ten minutes perhaps, that we heard the shots, some half dozen of them, a first one, and then a second, then the others coming bunched together. At our distance, they had a dry, brittle sound, like the barking of dogs. And after them, nothing at all. They halted us, and on instinct we all of us turned heads towards the town, but of course there was nothing to see.

"It could not be Kilpeder," I said to Bob. By now, Ned and Vincent and their lads would have been well away from Kilpeder, and the soldiers could scarcely have reached it, even had they come forward at the trot. Bob shook his head.

"No," he said, "not Kilpeder."

What we were expecting, I cannot say, but there was nothing. Bare fields and leafless trees, wide-scattered, lay between us and the town on our one hand, and on the other, more fields, moving gently towards uplands, and far distant, giving us our horizon, the Derrynasaggarts, great mounds heaved up against a sky blue as a robin's egg, empty and perfect.

Bob shook his head, and then set forth again upon his stride, with myself beside him and the others close behind. Whatever may have been our look of soldiers in the early morning, as we had marched down upon Kilpeder, we were shedding fast. Those of our lads who had proper weapons, rifles or shotguns, carried them carelessly, sloped upon shoulder, or elbow-cradled. We must have looked more like fellows tramping to the hiring fair, dogged and mildly hopeful. But lads bound for the fair would have been joking one with another, and one of them would sooner or later have struck up a tune, with the others joining in, ragged-voiced and cheerful. We had as little to say as cattle being moved to the market.

And as we tramped along, the shots that we had heard echoed faintly in some chamber of my mind's ear, six shots lying within silence. Or so I now remember matters, but this may be an invention of my fancy, for of all that day's work in Kilpeder, the "battle" of Clonbrony Wood and all the rest of it, those were the shots that would have an afterlife of echo, in the newspapers and at the state trials, and after that in the wretched ballad. Those six shots stretched out two men dead upon the ground, one of them in the dark wool of the Constabulary and the other one in jacket of coarse frieze and heavy boots daubed with muck and dung: Constable Belton and young Jamesey Spellacy. Mr. Butt and Mr. Bourke at the trials, those barristers artful as Odysseus, contrived to weave around them a thicket of uncertainty and conjecture; but the ballad maker was in no doubt upon the subject, and it was from those few seconds of time, the time it takes for maddened and desperate men to fire off shots at each other, that the image sprang forth which Ned would carry with him to the grave, of a cool and reckless murderer, as black and implacable as a hillside boulder. But Bob and I were far away from those shots, we heard them and wondered at them, they touched us with chill fingers, and then we set forth again on our retreat, to give it a dignified name.

It was one in the afternoon, a full hour after we had set out from Kilpeder, that we came to the cross which placed us upon the Killeter road. Behind us, a long stretch of the boreen which we had walked ran straight and unbending, and it was empty. Tall hedgerows rose up on its two sides, snowy and tangled. As though we had moved along silence, across snow, from the confusion and mud and blazing straw of Kilpeder into wide, silent fields across which we had been sentenced to tramp forever. There was a farm at the juncture of boreen and road. The hedgerows gave way to a wall of rough grey stones, a slapdash wall with but scant artistry to it. The house lay far back from the road, a long, melancholy-looking structure in its solitude, with snow upon its thatch and its turf stack, and the pile of dung beside its door. Smoke rose upwards from its gable end, and the smell of turf rose towards me, familiar and pungent.

The road before us ran north for five miles to Killeter, a huddle of cabins at a cross, with one of them licensed to sell spirits, although I had never paused there to sample its wares—a vile-looking premises, of use, perhaps, to cowherds and to spalpeens moving southwards to the hiring fairs in Kilpeder and Macroom. But one of its roads swung eastwards, following the edges of low hills and touching, on its right side, Clonbrony Wood. We paused by the low wall, as though we had reached a station. And in that pause, the door of the cabin opened, and a fellow came out from it, and walked towards us across the snow-covered field.

We stood looking at him, the score or so of us, as though he were an emissary of some kind. He had brought out his stick with him, and as he walked, he swung it out before him, planting it on the hard earth and then raising it up again, a heavyset man in his late middle years, in frieze jacket and breeches of the old-fashioned sort jammed into tall boots. When he was close enough, he shouted to us, but I could not make out his words. He kept his peace then, and without breaking stride finished his walk across the field, pausing only when he had reached his fence, with only the stones themselves between himself and us. He spoke again, and I knew then why I had not grasped his words, for he had been shouting to us in Gaelic.

"What are you doing here at all?" he said. "Who are you?"

I rummaged around in my mind to find words for him, but Bob answered in that wretched Gaelic of his, which he had carried down with him from his father's farm into Kilpeder, and had kept in a clanking, rusty kind of use for his dealings from behind Tully's counter with fellows like this one.

"We have been fighting with the police in the streets of Kilpeder," he said, "and now the police and the soldiers themselves from Macroom and from Cork, perhaps, are in search of us. We are on the run for the hills."

He was a thick-faced man, with full, unshaven cheeks, broken-veined, and hard-muscled jowl. A rough boulder of a face it would have seemed, but for wide, staring eyes of palest blue, shielded by heavy brows. He paused before speaking.

"Great fighting that must have been," he said, and let the blue eyes rest upon the sloped rifles and shotguns. "What work were you at?"

"We are Fenians," Bob said. "It is the appointed day of the Fenians, across all of Ireland." Deliberately, or so it seemed to me, he spoke the word *Fenian* in English, placed into his Gaelic like a pit in a pudding. I glanced over at him. Knowing Bob, I knew that the rage was still working in him, but for the moment there was something else as well, a kind of bitter comedy. His tone was light.

"Well, now," the farmer said. "So that is who you lads are. There has been much talk of you fellows. Are you the fellows who smashed into Union Hall with blackened faces, and frightened poor Mary Tansell the servant girl and took away the lovely fowling pieces from London?"

"Ourselves, or friends of ours," Bob said.

"In the name of God," I said to Bob in English, "have we nothing better to do than to lean on a wall chatting with the gentry?"

"Gentry, is it?" the farmer said to me in brief English, and said then to Bob, in Gaelic, "And this is what all of the talk has come to, is it, plundered shotguns and a fight with the police of Kilpeder and nineteen fellows hurrying along the Killeter road?" I took notice that he had made count of us.

"Yes," Bob said, in a flat voice, without inflection, "this is what the talk has come to. They will be along after us soon enough, by the boreen or perhaps by the big road. I wonder that they have not found us by now."

The man nodded, and rubbed along his mouth the back of a hand huge as a young ham, a faint mat of greying hairs. "The low hills are almost on top of you," he said, "but the great hills are a long day's walk. You would be safe enough in the great hills, where there is naught save heather and wild hares and trackless waste."

Distant, the hills seemed unfamiliar, with their dusting of snow. Silence clung to them. In the middle distance, a hawk wheeled in the air, hovered. There were wild hares closer to hand. I imagined one, cowering in thicket, long, attentive ears pressed flat with fear, the slender body poised, low-crouching. In season, farmers would harry him for a morning's sport, crashing through hedges, climbing stiles, their boots tramping down tall grasses, their breeches thistle-starred.

"You will have from here a fine sight of the red soldiers," Bob said. "It will be as festive as a fairday. And perhaps a chat with them as well."

"Scant Irish or none at all do the English soldiers have on them," the farmer said.

"They will have with them the police, black hounds upon the scent. Sergeant Honan was reared upon Irish, in the savage wastes of Limerick."

The farmer took a look at his barn, and then turned back to Bob. "I have heavy chores awaiting me," he said. "I cannot spend the day at this wall, on the watch for red soldiers."

It was the first pause that we had taken, and the lads seemed now, for that moment, more at ease, caught within a familiar scene, a farmer standing by his wall. From farms such as these they had themselves ventured forth that morning.

"From the tallest of the great hills," the farmer said, "you can see the water on a cloudless day, beyond the hills of Kerry."

He turned then, and walked away from us, his blackthorn prodding the ground before him.

"Good luck to you," Bob called out to him, and without turning round to us, he nodded in response. "You might wish us luck as well," Bob called. "We have need of it."

He turned then. "I wish you neither good luck nor ill," he said. "You are nothing to me." He spoke with a chilling neutrality, and his words seemed to float across distance, perhaps because he had not bothered to raise his voice.

As we moved up the Killeter road, he stuck in my memory. I saw him as he stood, turned, and heard his final words, spoken in that language which is wedded, as English can never be, to our landscape, as though a tongue speaking for fields, scattered boulders, pools, red boglands. You are nothing to me, he had said, and it was the hard-packed earth that spoke, bare-branched trees tossing in winds from the sea.

Hills lay before us now, true enough, not the big hills towards which his words had gestured, but rising ground moving towards crests, crisscrossed with fences. In a distant pasture, a herd moved slowly across the unfamiliar snow, the small black cows of Munster, and apart from them, near a pair of bullocks, stood a lone thorn tree. It was a good road, wider than it had need to be. Along one stretch of it were hawthorns in early leaf, tips of furled green thrusting through snow. There was a great quiet, a Sunday stillness.

The men had begun to talk once more, I could hear snatches of what they said. "By God," Dinny Lacey said, "that lad had the right of it. We would not reach the mountains until nightfall, but an army would be safe there. Tis broken, savage country, so I have always heard said."

"I have no notion of what the lad was about," his chum said. "I have not a word of Gaelic, no more than my mother and father before me." He spoke with a flick of disdain: it was fast becoming a stigmatised tongue, fed by the elements, by history and the seasons, but by these alone.

"I spoke harshly to you, Hughie," Bob said, "and without cause. I ask your pardon."

"Sure, there is no need for that, Bob," I said. "Not between the two of us." Although the word had cut into me, more deeply than I would admit to myself. Fool.

"God alone knows what lies ahead for us. I expected that the army would be upon us before now. It might indeed be better to scatter and try for the big hills."

"Clonbrony Wood, Ned said," I reminded him.

But Bob, as though he had not heard me, said, "We shambled into this, and we are in a shambles now, right enough. Boys from farms and shop assistants setting themselves up as rebels, with the Church itself against us. That farmer back there, with his Gaelic like a mouthful of pebbles, has the right of it. We are but a drift upon the roads, to be blown away."

"We held Kilpeder," I said. "Ned gave Kilpeder to us, and had it not been for the soldiers in their hundreds—"

"Had it not been," he echoed me, in a low, ice-edged voice. "By God, Hughie, did you take a close look at those fellows? Those are real soldiers, the genuine article. And the rulers of this land know how to move them about, they have been doing it for centuries." He hunched his shoulders forward. "We will have a close look at them soon enough."

"Ned Nolan is a soldier," I said. "Twas a real soldier led us into Kilpeder."

"A real corporal," Bob said. "He was at pains not to deceive us on that score. He is a lad like ourselves, when all is said."

"Not this morning he was not," I said, stung by Bob's bitterness first towards me and then towards Ned. "He was a young general; we could not have asked for better."

"To be sure," he said. "The Napoleon of Kilpeder. A Hannibal of the hen coops."

"By Christ, Bob," I said, "we have every last one of us a right to be angry and frightened in this hour, but you have no cause to turn your wrath either on me or on the man who commanded us. Who still commands us. Put a guard on your tongue."

My voice rose as I spoke, and Bob put by instinct a hand on my arm, to caution me. But I could tell that the lads were giving no heed to our talk.

We had come to a place where the road rose up to a humpbacked bridge of two arches, beneath which moved a stream, the Awbeg, which flows down from the big hills to join the Sullane. The snow, which had been heavier in the hills, had swollen it, and it made a lovely sight, sparkling in the cold, clear air, with snow-bedecked bushes bending towards it.

Bob stepped to one side, drawing me with him, and pressing our backs against the hedgerows. He motioned the men to move forward, and so they did, up to the bridge and then across it. But when they were on the far side, they looked back towards us. Bob shook his head, and with a gesture of his outstretched arm motioned them down the road.

"Not a question out of them," Bob said. "Like a herd of fucking sheep. They will have questions for us soon enough, by God."

"The men as well, is it?" I said. "The men are fucking sheep and Ned Nolan is a barnyard general and I am a fool. That cleans your slate."

We had, as it were, the world to ourselves, the world and my anger. I would rather have been tramping with the lads, towards Killeter and perhaps towards Nolan, than to be with Bob in his present, inexplicable mood. An unclouded sun was warming the afternoon, and almost one could feel the snow melting into the grassy fields. He turned away from me, and walked to the crest of the bridge, where he rested his elbows on the stone of the parapet, and stood looking down at the Awbeg. I walked up and stood beside him, unwilling to speak. It was a handsome small bridge of dressed stone, from the last century, when landlords took pride in such matters.

Silent, our shoulders almost touching, we stood thus, two friends who had never before spoken harshly to one another.

"Hughie," he said at last, "I must a second time ask your pardon. I cannot get a hold on myself. I cannot trust my judgement. Sure, I have no quarrel with the lads or with you, and least of all with Ned. He was all that we could have asked of him, and more. Too much, perhaps."

But I made no response, and stood upright, stiff. He had to twist his head to look up into my face.

"It was a wonder that we performed in Kilpeder," he said, "and Ned showed us the way. A few score country lads with shotguns and scythes and a cartload of hay, and we laid siege to as sturdy a barracks as was ever built in Munster. If something that looks the size of a bloody regiment had not come down upon us, Kilpeder would be in Fenian hands, and the rest of us marching northwards to the hosting."

"And so may we yet," I said, "God willing." But I did not believe what I said.

"There will be no hosting," he said, "if I am right in what has been gnawing at me. I think that we have been shattered, and not in Kilpeder alone. The Rising is over and done with."

Beneath us, water clear as crystal flowed over a sandy-brown bed. Its sound was sibilant, whispering. Twigs floated upon its swirling surface, carried down, perhaps, from the high, distant hills.

"There is a dreadful thought, Bob," I said, jarred from my anger. "We know naught of the Rising save what has befallen us here."

"I know that," Bob said. "Did I not tell you that my mind is disordered? I am terrified of what may await us at the end of this day. Twas when we were on the boreen, and had left the town behind us, that the thought came to me, and it has not left me."

"Ach, well," I said, and shrugged. But he turned now away from the bridge, to face me directly.

"Those soldiers know what they are about," he said. "They expected our attack on the barracks. We had cut the wires, Honan was cut off. But the army was on the march towards us, and had been from early morning. Perhaps longer, if they were sent up from Cork. They knew, Hughie. They must have known."

Beyond his shoulder, I could see our lads, slowed now to a walk, an amble almost, with one or two of them, bringing up the rere, paused to look back at the sight we must have presented, two gargoyles on a bridge.

He took my silence for a question, and answered with one of his own. "How could they have known, Hughie? Can you tell me that?"

But I had no answer. There was nothing so far as the eye could see

[215]

but empty fields, a few scattered houses, a herd, black shapes upon a sheet of white, the low hills.

"They have been playing with us," he said. "Cat and mouse. Small wonder that centres across the length and breadth of the land were left unsmashed, and returned Yanks like Ned were let swagger in the streets with their wide hats and square-toed boots and Yank revolvers. They had the measure of us."

"You are a wonder, surely. We are on the run for our lives, and you are busy at work upon fanciful notions. What you have need of is Vincent's silver flask of whiskey. The flask is waiting for you, together with Vincent himself and Ned and the other lads. Take a look at the boys up the road there. They must think that we are plotting to desert them."

He stood looking at me, and then, at last, he smiled. "You have the right of it, Hughie. Come along now, or we will have to trot to catch them up." And he turned on his heel and set off, with myself behind him. He was himself again, or so I thought. To the last day of his life, there was never a way to read him properly. He kept always a part of himself in reserve.

And so we marched down into Killeter and into what would be for us the ignominious end of things, the famous "battle." In the months to come, and in the years that followed, the "battle," as we always—we patriotic Irish—called it, was a legend kept burnished, a shield which we tried to hold between ourselves and ugly truths. For Bob Delaney—standing upon the humpbacked bridge of Killeter, with men dead and a burned barracks behind us, and surrender an hour ahead of us, in an almost foreseeable future, a future no farther distant than a crossroads—had spoken with history's very voice, with Patrick Prentiss's voice, a voice that speaks of us in footnotes, kindly or derisive.

There were other shields, and they were to have their ballads as well. At Ardagh and at Kilmallock, in Limerick, the barracks were attacked, and there were hostings in Connaught as well, in Galway and Sligo. A thousand men rallied that night in the market of Drogheda. Resolute men in Cork captured the barracks at Ballyknockane, with F. X. O'Brien to lead them, and William Mackey Lomasney, and young Michael O'Brien. The Southern and Western was attacked, and the rails torn up, and the wires cut. The coast-guard station at Knockadoon was taken, and arms secured there. There were a score, perhaps two score of such actions. I grew weary hearing of them, for many of the lads came at the heel of the hunt to be lodged with us in the gaol in Cork City. We were like mirrors set up to take the reflexion of each other, the lot of us boasting in whispers to one another, and all with the one story to tell, of attack and straggling retreat and surrender. "Flying columns," they called the soldiers who were sent against us, and they were everywhere; but when they moved against us, they seemed not to be flying at all, but moving, like the red files on the Macroom road, with sure, invincible tread, lines of power which stretched outwards, from London itself, across water and dusty roads and snowy roads.

The Rising marked us all, all of us who had been out on that March morning, all of us save, no doubt, myself, a sedentary man who was glad enough to leave behind him his prison sentence, and the gunfire, the blazing barracks, and the men we left dead or writhing in their agony in the streets of Kilpeder, glad enough to have well behind me the unnatural silence of the snowy fields along the Killeter road, the indifferent verdict passed upon us in Gaelic, the low hills, and the sight which was granted us at last of Clonbrony Wood, glad enough to come home to Mary, limping from where the leg-irons had cut through tissue and blood to white bone of ankle.

And yet if Clonbrony Wood itself was a battle at all—but it came closer to being the running gunfight that it was termed by the *Cork Examiner,* a few days afterwards, before legend had time to cluster about it—neither Bob nor myself nor our platoon had part in it, although we heard its noises. Clonbrony Wood for us was anticlimax, ignominious and bewildering.

It was at about three in the afternoon that a rise in the road brought us into clear sight of Killeter itself, with its cabins scattered about the crossroads. The woods themselves began just beyond the road. They are thinner now, and have been since the seventies, when the Ardmors began working them for timber; and visiting them today, with their new growths, I have difficulty in recalling the presence which they once had, the heavy-trunked trees, with their branched intricacies, their darkness. To reach them would then have taken us a half hour's walk, perhaps, down the rise, and then through Killeter, and up the road. But we stopped short.

Between Killeter and the woods, spread out as if they would fill the landscape if they could, was the British army. Not, as I could judge matters, in formation, but rather holding, without advance, in a wide arc. There were two companies standing in ranks, at ease, on our far right, and mounted men to their left. It seemed a tableau set up by boys, lead soldiers daubed with scarlet, against a woodland. There were constables there as well, tall-helmeted. As we stood watching, the sound of a single rifle, an angry bark, came to us from the woods, and was followed by two others.

"They are in the wood beyond," I said, "and no place for them to move, save to the steep hills."

Bob said nothing. The lot of us stood clustered together.

"There is no counting of the numbers," a fellow named Larry Rodgers said. "They have come against us in their thousands."

But I said, "In their hundreds," correcting him as if upon instinct. Small difference it made.

"There was their road," Bob said, pointing. "Small wonder that we saw nothing of them." To the south, for as far as the eye could see, was ground lower than our own. In the distance, the steeples of Kilpeder were clear and minute against the horizon.

"What are we to do, Bob?" I asked. But he said nothing. He stood as though transfixed. His face was in profile to me, and I could read nothing from it.

"My Jesus, mercy," Larry said. "They will slaughter the lads in the woods, and then come raging against us."

"There you have it," Bob said. "Larry has a keen eye for strategy. Ask him, what are we to do. We will first fall back from this rise, and keep decently out of sight." There was gunfire as he spoke, and it urged us down from the low crest, and back onto level ground. We were but a rabble now—I can find no kinder word—and the weapons we carried seemed to me grotesque, as though some malicious fairy had transformed the loys and pitchforks which history had assigned to us. And the lot of us looking for a word of some kind from a shop assistant who was struggling to hide from us his own feelings.

"Right," he said presently. "You have seen for yourselves the way things are. Captain Nolan and his fellows are in the woods, and the soldiers have spread a wide net. They will be moving in now to close it. If I were Captain Nolan, I would stick a white handkerchief on the end of a rifle, and wave it in the air. But I am not." And as if to prove his words, there came now another rattle of rifle fire. I tried not to imagine the woods. There were a few narrow paths through it, matted with decayed leaves, but it was otherwise a tangle of trunks and high undergrowth, and the branches overhead so thick that even when leafless they kept the paths sombre and dark, with every now and then a shaft of yellow, mote-mottled light.

"They took no notice of us," Bob said, "not so far as I could tell. And that may be giving us the only chance we have. We will move back a half mile or so, and then we will strike across the fields and the low hills, and make towards the Derrynasaggarts. With the help of God, we can do it unnoticed."

No one spoke. I turned my eyes, as most of the others did, towards the distant mountains: great bare, jagged lumps, unfamiliar to us all, save as chance might have taken us along the county road into Killarney, and they were even then huge, alien presences, uninhabitable, rock-strewn, their steep sides barren or covered with rank grasses. Purple-patched in summer with the purple, tough-rooted gorse.

"Dear God," one of the men said, "there is naught there, Bob. Tis desert waste."

"I know that," Bob said. "There is one other thing we can do. We can set our weapons on the road here, and walk down to the soldiers and the police with our hands above our heads. We cannot go back. Kilpeder is held by the Crown. Choose for yourselves."

He stood facing us, as though indifferent, with his hands buried in the pockets of his greatcoat. "I did not care which they chose," he told me later, in Cork City. It had been a long day, and it was ending.

"Bob," I said to him, as though reminding him. "There is Ned there, and all of the lads with him, trapped in Clonbrony."

He shook his head. "We are of no help to Ned. The twenty of us. Getting ourselves shot down in a rush across open fields, is it? They would slap us flat, like men swatting bluebottles. Ned is done for, and we are about done for ourselves."

"Jesus," Larry said, "we are a sorry lot," but Bob did not bother to look at him. It was at me he was looking, as though he expected a judgement of some sort from me. I wanted dearly for it to have been a month before, or a week even, and myself in the lamplight-softened parlour, when a knock on the door would bring Bob to us, and an evening of quiet talk. But it was a knock that had brought Ned, dark against the evening sky, black wide-brimmed hat pulled low upon long heavy face, case with the two revolvers and their greasy cartridges.

"Tis your command, Bob," I said. "We will do as you bid us." For of all things in the world, I wanted least of all to move down towards the wood, towards those death-dealing men in their scarlet jackets, a purposeful multitude; but if we were to turn our backs upon Ned, I wanted Bob to say the word. It was as though I had seized hold of my conscience and held it deep within an icy pool where it could not move or feel.

Bob nodded. He has looked into my mind, I thought, and accepts what he sees there.

There were no sounds now coming to us from the woods. He took his eyes away from me, so that he could look at us all. "Is it an order you want? Very well so, you can take it as given. You know what I think is the one course for us. But tis the last order that need be given. When we strike out across the fields, we will be but fellows on the run, like sheep stealers or caravats. We will do best if we scatter."

"'Tis ended, then," Jack Reynolds said, a man of about thirty, older than most of us, a short, bandy-legged fellow, but with powerful, sloping shoulders. He put it as a question, puzzled.

"I don't know," Bob said. "'Tis indeed the end of the Kilpeder rising. You are brave lads, and Hughie and myself are proud to have been out with you." But beyond his shoulder, Clonbrony lay hidden by the rise, and I wished that he had not spoken of bravery.

"If they take us, Bob," Reynolds said, "what will befall us?"

Bob sought for an answer, and then shrugged. It was answer enough, and we felt the chill of the dreary afternoon. The bright, crisp sun of the morning had turned leaden. It was a time of day for strong, sweetened tea, and bread warmed at the hearth.

"There is naught there," the same man said. "Wild goats disdain it."

A single shot then, as though not from a "battle" at all, but some distant boy potting a squirrel, an autumnal sound, familiar as a curlew's cry.

"Best off," Bob said. "Come on now, lads." And, as though to show us how, he walked through the knot of us who faced him, and set off along the road we had taken, his fists still jammed in his coat.

I lingered, and was the last of us to leave. I watched them as they walked, not hurrying, certainly, but clearly ready to put a distance between themselves and Clonbrony. There were six or so of them quick-stepping, and Bob let them take the lead. He did not look back for me. The huntsman whom I had imagined had companions, for now two shots came almost together, too close to have been fired from the one weapon. Mercifully hidden from me, as was I from it, I imagined the wood as a tangle of branches, shadows, moving figures who could not clearly see each other, blurs of black, grey, scarlet. I imagined silence, broken by sudden, random explosions, by screams which would not at the distance carry to me. But I kept my back to it, and it was not long before, with loping strides, I had caught up with Bob and the lads, drawing warmth from our closeness together.

What remained of that day, or of the Rising, is scarcely worth the telling. We never reached the Derrynasaggarts. Close to the Killeter Bridge, we struck out across the fields, and, as we moved, we scattered, spreading apart from one another, moving slowly through hindering nettles and high grasses, clambering awkwardly over dry-stone fences. We reached, all of us, the low hills, which rose so softly that at first one was not conscious of them, but soon enough we were climbing past furze, and wide, flat rocks, half hidden by the snow. Larry Rodgers and I had fallen into each other's company, and from time to time we would pause to look to left and right, and would catch sight of others, lonely figures like ourselves. We had, all of us, two hours or three before the soldiers and the constables moved out against us, long enough for the leaden afternoon to shade into March's early evening.

By a long, narrow rock, Larry and I rested, and looked down towards the ones closest to us, a mixed lot of soldiers and police, strung out in a line, and at the one end of the line a caped horseman, his horse edging daintily through a patch of nettles. Larry gave a sigh. We were reluctant to move. It would have been restful to sit, country bumpkins at a spectacle, as farm lads watch beaters of an autumn morning, moving through stubble to drive into flight grouse, plover, plump-breasted pheasant. But we rose up, and commenced to climb. We climbed doggedly, like men at work upon a task whose purpose has dimmed, until we heard the sounds of their shots, and then we stood stock-still, and turned around towards them. One of the constables shouted words to us which we were too far off to grasp, his hands cupped around his mouth. I nodded, not to him, but to Larry and myself. I took carefully from my pocket the revolver that Ned had given me, my fingers touching by accident the cold metal of its barrel, and dropped it to the ground. Larry looked at me, pale-faced, with wide, staring eyes, and then, bending down, placed his shotgun beside the revolver. Then we walked down the hill towards them, with myself a few steps in the lead. When we were closer to them, the horseman shouted to us to throw our hands above our heads, and we did so.

As we walked, other soldiers, a half dozen of them, came towards us from the right, with three of our lads, whom they prodded forward with rifle barrels, in a matter-of-fact way, without cruelty. When we were three or four arms' lengths away, the horseman bade us halt, and he rode up to us. He was a young fellow like ourselves, in his early twenties, and with a face handsome and boyish beneath its helmet, eyes of cornflower blue and a short, full mouth. He was very serious, frowning. The three lads were shoved over to Larry and myself, and the five of us stood together, our eyes not meeting. He seemed to find us mildly curious, but his mind was elsewhere.

"All right," he said to the constables, "two of you take them down with the others." He nodded to his sergeant, and then rode forward, passing very close to us.

The two constables who led us back across the fields were unknown to me, even by sight. They were two of the new men who had been sent in to reinforce the garrison. The lot of us plodded forward in silence for a bit, and then one of them said, "Jesus, but they will be nailing a gallows together to accommodate you bastards." He had the thick speech of Connaught—Galway, perhaps, or Mayo. He held his carbine carelessly, in the crook of his elbow. No one answered him, and he spoke again.

"Stupid, ignorant men you are, the lot of you, and murderers."

"Give over," the other one said. "Give over, Mick. Leave it be."

"They will not be let be," Mick said. "By Jesus, they will not. There are three constables dead or as good as dead in that fucking wood, do you know that, boy?" He let fly with his boot, and caught Larry, who was closest to him, a hard crack on the shin. Larry stumbled, but kept walking.

"I told you, damn it," the other constable said, "leave it be."

It was as if Mick had not heard him. "And Paudge Belton of your own town shot down in cold blood, his poor fucking face blown away. Hanging is the least of what you deserve."

"Dear God," I said to Larry, without thinking, "poor Paudge Belton." He was the one of them that I knew best, save for Con Honan: harmless, jowled face and heavy belly; in summer, choked by horsehair-stiffened collar, the sweat would pour from him.

"Poor Paudge Belton," Mick said, mocking my tone. "Tis sorry I am that those bastards in the woods gave in at last. Shot down, they should have been, like rabid foxes."

"Tis over, then," I said. "Thank God, tis over."

"Not for you, you hoor," Mick said. "Tis but beginning for you."

"Shut up, damn it," the other constable said, "and you as well," and he grabbed me so fiercely that I felt his separate fingers through the thick cloth. "Shut up, the lot of you."

It ended so, the battle of Clonbrony Wood. Ned and Vincent and their lads were waiting for us, under guard. Then the lot of us waited, until Bob and the others were brought in, in ones and twos and threes. By the time it was all complete, and they had us on the march into Kilpeder, it was almost night, and lamps had been lighted in cabins which lay before us. As we walked, identity seemed to fall away from us, and we became something different from what we had been: prisoners. Even Ned, of whom I caught glimpses, seemed changed and diminished. He had lost his hat, and his right arm hung loose at his side, as if it had been shattered. No one spoke. I would have welcomed even Mick's raging malice, but the constables in files on either side were as silent as ourselves, and the only voices we heard were those of the soldiers, far ahead of us, as they drifted back, a shout now and again, and easy laughter.

It ended so, in scattered towns and hillsides, beside rivers, in barnyards and pastures, across Munster, and up through Waterford and Wicklow into Stepaside and the hills south of Dublin. The dead were not many from the Fenian rising of 'sixty-seven, some seventy or eighty counting the two sides, and of those most were Irish, rebels and constables and coast guards. Emblems were found, so the newspapers said, in the pockets of some of the dead, a green flag carefully folded, the oath of the Fenian Brotherhood written out, in copperplate and incongruously on the flyleaf of a missal. It was weeks before the men of Knockadoon were run to the end, and Peter Crowley shot dead in Tipperary. Lomasney's men held out for a bit, on their keeping, with few willing to help them. But for the most part, it ended elsewhere as it ended beyond Clonbrony Wood, farmboys and mechanics, a scattering of clerks and schoolmasters, tramping along under guard, scared and shabby.

Dark night had fallen when we reached Kilpeder. The barracks was beyond use, fire-gutted, our signal and solitary triumph, and we were taken to the market house. We entered by the Macroom road, and the lamps of the town were waiting for us, glowing behind drawn curtains. We filed past darkened Saint Jarlath's, its spires immense against a starless sky, past my darkened schoolhouse, my house with a lamp lit behind the parlour curtains. I turned my head away from it, a prisoner who once had been lover, schoolmaster, reader of dusty books, warm within unvalued comforts.

The wide double doors of the market house had been flung open in expectation of our arrival. It was by day a handsome edifice, much admired by visitors, commodious and yet chaste and simple in the fashion of the old century. Now darkness had robbed it almost of outline, although I could make out, poised against dark air, the heavy iron crane, bolted to the stones shoulder-high for the weighing of produce. It bore an uncomfortable resemblance to a gallows. As I passed through the doors, feeling the press of others behind me, I twisted round my neck for a last look at the town, but there was little to be seen save the random lights in windows above shops, although I did fancy that I caught a glimpse of dim, shielded light on the horizon, where Castle Ardmor sat serene on its low hill, dark quiet river and dark plantations holding it aloof from the town. But then the fellows at my heels were shoved against me, and I half stumbled into the shapeless black.

We were held penned there only until morning, when we were marched to Macroom, and then taken on the cars to Cork City. In Macroom we were given bread and mugs of sweetened tea, and by midday we were in the city, with the worst fears of the night behind us, and a faint taste of the tea still lingering. Soldiers, brisk and pink-cheeked, herded us to the gaol down wide, cobbled streets, and across the noble bridge which spans the Lee at Patrick Street, beneath us the dark, oily river, smells of rope, tars, coal. All yesterday, and today, and the days of the week to come, batches of prisoners like ourselves would be herded in, unshaven and weary. It would take time, months and years, decades indeed, for the balladeers and versifiers and statue makers to get to work upon us, scrubbing our faces and brushing our clothes, changing us by the magic of meter and marble into what we had not been. The people of Cork City had a clearer view of us.

Part Two

10

[*Patrick Prentiss*]

Patrick Prentiss had come to think of his reading glasses as his "Irish spectacles," although he had purchased them, two years before, from an oculist in Paris. He did not require them for ordinary reading, save for the occasional footnote, but for the purposes of his present research they were a necessity. After a few hours at work on old newspaper files, the reports of trials, of special and select committees, the print, wretched at best, would begin to waver and recede, diminishing. Still worse was it in those hours when, quite improperly, a friend in the Home Office allowed him to rummage through the copies of reports from magistrates and constabulary inspectors, on condition that he make no notes, nor ever cite them or make direct attribution. There would be the occasional bold, soldierly hand of some retired major or captain, the painstaking, round-lettered script of a pedantic sergeant, but there would too often be almost indecipherable scrawls, written in haste. The words would blur together, and were in any event jumbles of facts and surmises. They hinted at shadowy conspiracies, told of "information received" from some informer in Dublin or Liverpool or New York, identified only by initials, some A.B. or M.N., hunched over gin-palace counter, or coffeehouse table.

Prentiss would take the Irish spectacles, framed in thin, pale gold, from their case of red morocco leather, and the words would float into clarity, as though by magic. Occasionally his friend, a Scotsman of his own age named Alan Grant, would find something for him, and carry it over to the library table. "Here," he would say, "here is that fellow of yours again." "R.R. is also certain," the report would say in a middle paragraph, "that the funds which Edward Nolan drew from the Skirmishing Fund are intended for the purchase of explosives." The report would have day and month but not year, but a clerk in London would have stamped in a corner the date of its receipt, "August 11, 1884." "Yes," Prentiss would say, "there he is." And wonder, behind shielded eyes, if those were the explosives which had blown Lomasney to bits beneath London Bridge, a ten minutes' walk from the room in which he and Grant were sitting. "And here is your man Delaney," Grant would say, Cromarty and Cambridge at war within his consonants, "a fine respectable fellow, I must say." "Robert Delaney, a solicitor in the town of Kilpeder in this county and a most desperate secret Fenian and rebel, has been named to office in the Land League, with the connivance of his Brotherhood. He is in the confidence of M. Davitt, instigator of the League, a ticket-of-leave man from Dartmoor Prison."

Prentiss shook his head, and pushed the Irish spectacles up onto his forehead. "Does Government really believe such nonsense? Delaney had long before drifted away from the Fenians. The Fenians hated the Land League. Delaney was a prosperous solicitor by then, married into the wealthy merchant families of Cork."

Grant laughed. "How would I know what Government believes? Reports from policemen and peppery resident magistrates. Wretched informers paid by the piece. How do you know, if it comes to that? There were ugly customers in the Land League. Boycotts, terror tactics, land agents murdered, bailiffs murdered."

Prentiss shook his head again. "Not Delaney." He matched his tone to Grant's. "Why, he was a guest at my father's table."

"Ah," Grant said, "that makes all the difference." Fellow Celts, playing with Saxon notions of probity, code of the gentleman.

Hugh MacMahon had a photograph of Delaney and himself in the early seventies, schoolmaster and newly articled solicitor, standing stiffly together, each with a hand resting on a table which was covered in dark

cloth, fringed. Massive Bible, vase of long-stemmed ferns. Their suits—
MacMahon's dark, Delaney's light—looked new, and they wore them
awkwardly. Beneath Delaney's strong, square face, a stiff collar seemed to
be choking him. His free hand rested on his chest, fingertips hidden by
the lapels.

"What you really need, we'll never see, either of us," Grant said.
"Special Branch keeps all that under lock and key, over at the Yard."
Beside the Thames, the clumsy fake-Gothic of New Scotland Yard,
brown-turreted.

"Perhaps," Prentiss said. "More of this, most likely." He handed
back the yellowing report which had conjured a desperate Fenian out of
the figure in the photograph. But he had once, in youth, been desperate,
on a March morning, armed, one of the men of Clonbrony Wood, had
served six months in Portland. A brief trial, *Regina v. Delaney,* less than
a full page—Prentiss knew it almost by heart—but the trial of Edward
Nolan, on two counts of treason-felony, and for the wilful murder of
Constable Patrick Belton, ran on for pages.

The photographer's name was stamped in gilt on the photograph's
brown border—"Robert Emmet Cashman, Sunday's Well, Cork"—and
on the back, MacMahon had written the day, "February 11, 1873."

"Delaney became a member of Parliament?" Grant said. "One of
the ruffians that Parnell wished upon us?"

"Yes," Prentiss said.

"Some of those fellows brought over by Parnell were surely Fenians,"
Grant said. "Fenians at heart. Speeches breathing fire and destruction.
The Irish members had been a decent lot when old Isaac Butt ran them.
Butt was a gentleman. Parnell changed all that."

"It was Butt who defended Ned Nolan," Prentiss said. "At the Cork
assizes in 'sixty-seven. He saved Nolan's life. Nolan had a charge of murder
against him, along with everything else. A policeman named Belton shot
dead in a laneway beyond the barracks. Butt broke down the witnesses.
He was a savage cross-examiner, by all accounts."

"A different matter entirely," Grant said. "A barrister standing to
his brief."

It is not my business to judge my clients, Prentiss's father told him,
in the study in Palmerston Park; we have judges to do that, and juries,
idiots though they well may be. Satisfied fingers stroked the silky, grey-
flecked beard.

"Butt was a gentleman," Grant said again. "He respected the traditions of the House, decency. Parnell hated this country. He smashed poor
old Butt, brought in ruffians and gunmen like your friend Delaney."

Delaney had been many things in his time, Prentiss thought, not all of them pleasant, but never a ruffian. Grant, able young civil servant, Scotsman on the rise, son of the manse with parliamentary baton in his knapsack, had Delaney tagged and docketed, tucked away in stiff red folder, ribbon-tied: Fenian, rural demagogue, hanging to Parnell's coat-tails. As I have Grant docketed and tied.

"Before the assizes," MacMahon said, "I never had more than a glimpse of my chums. We were in different cells. Three of the lads from Ballyknockane were with me, and a witless poor creature seized up at Knockadoon; the five of us—straw pallets on the flagstones and the noisome slop bucket, bread and cocoa shoved into us, pannikins of stew with chunks of fatty lamb. We would all be together in the exercise yard, round and round in a great oval, four of us abreast. But we had our own clothes, of course, and our heads had not been shaved. That came later, after the trials. No talking was permitted, of course, but Bob and Vincent and I would contrive a kind of conversation with grins and winks, bobs of the head. Not Ned. He was like some wild creature brought into captivity, sullen and aloof from us all, prisoners and warders alike. Like some creature brought down by ropes and snares on the pampas."

"At the end of the day, Parnell learned his lesson," Grant said. "When he was down they all turned upon him, all the jumped-up shop assistants and ticket-of-leave men. He raised them up, and then they turned on him."

"No," Prentiss said, "not all of them."

There were no photographs of Delaney in those final years. Mr. Cashman of Sunday's Well never visited the dusty office to photograph the former member of Parliament. Briefless solicitor, bottle in desk drawer, back to dirt-streaked window. "One of Parnell's last public meetings was in Kilpeder, a little more than a month before he died. Delaney was with him on the platform. They were pelted with rocks, clods of mud."

"And all for the love of a woman," Grant said lightly, but beneath, serious and cold, spoke the Scottish clergyman's son, chilly Sabbaths in the manse, an angry heaven.

Prentiss stared at him, startled, then realised that he was speaking of Parnell. "So it would seem," he said. "He fell, surely, and a woman was part of it."

"Nothing else like it," Grant said. "Not in modern times. He had the country in the palms of his hands. Smashed everything for a bit of skirt, to be blunt about it. Ach, well. That is neither here nor there."

But Prentiss knew that it was. Bob Delaney, too, had been in love, and the love had been part of the skein.

"It can happen," he said to Grant. "It can happen to the most careful of men."

Walking home to Pump Court in foggy November, bridge and Houses of Parliament at his back, he would pass New Scotland Yard. Somewhere within, a few rooms with desks and files, no doubt, the Special Branch, which had once been the Irish Branch, kept its tabs on anarchists, the radical Jews of Whitechapel, poets of the bomb; sergeants and inspectors ran their lines of informers, painstakingly collated lies and boasts, swaggering accounts of conspiracies in Saint Petersburg, Cracow. A building some ten years old, its legend nurtured in the popular press. In the eighties, in the days when the Fenians and the Invincibles had run their dynamite war, the Irish Branch had had its offices in the old Yard, off Whitehall, in the shadow of Government. Nolan's name would have been in its files, Nolan's and Lomasney's and McCafferty's, and, no doubt, Delaney's as well, and O'Brien's and Sexton's, and twenty more at least of Parnell's lieutenants, the lot of them jumbled together: terrorists, Land League agitators, silver-tongued orators from Clare, sedate family friends of the Prentisses—for the Irish Branch, the very word, *Irish*, was an informal bill of attainder.

Find yourself rooms in the Temple, Prentiss's father had said to him. A bit of the law might rub off on you. I can send off a few letters if you'd like. It had proved good advice, in its way. Now, in a late afternoon with winter in the sky, he walked from government, through law, into history, savouring a past that was like fog, at once thick and impalpable. It was to these streets that Bob Delaney had come, twenty years before, his first youth behind him, Clonbrony Wood a legend, the indiscretion of an ardent patriotism, hero (to some) of the Munster boycotts, Tully by marriage, husband and father, member for Cork.

"I remember him coming home after that first session," MacMahon said. "Beneath his manner, he was awed and bewildered, and Mary and myself were awed on his behalf, so to speak. 'I crossed the bar,' he said, 'with a member on my either side to escort me, and signed my name in the book on the table, and the Speaker shook my hand, and a place was found for me on one of the benches which we claim. The Irish National party. And, by God, Hughie, I was as much a member as any of them, as much a member as Gladstone or Forster or Chamberlain or any of them. There in that great chamber, with the mace and all the rest of it. And all our lads on the benches with me—Dillon and Healy and Harrington.' 'And Parnell?' I said to him, taking from him the empty tumbler to refill it. His fingers were trembling a bit. 'Not that first night, nor the next. But on the third, late in the sitting, he walked in, in formal dress black as midnight and white shirtfront. He took the first place he saw, in the bench in front of my own, and after he had settled himself, he twisted around, and took my hand. "I am delighted to see you here, Mr. Delaney," he said. "You belong here." Then he settled his tall silk hat forward on the bridge of his nose, covering his eyes, and whether he was sleeping or listening to the speeches, there was no way of knowing.' 'There you are,' Mary cried in admiration. 'In their House of Commons itself, he keeps on his hat, to show them what we think of them.' She had a great distaste for strong spirits, but she had had first one and then a second glass of sherry, and her eyes were shining. 'Not at all, child,' Bob said, 'not at all. Tis a custom of the House. But by God, they know what he thinks of them. From time to time, first Healy, then Dillon, would move over to him, and the two would confer. Healy had a little list of items. And once, Parnell took a pencil and a scrap of paper from his pocket, scribbled out a note, and handed it to Healy. I could see the signature—C. S. Parnell. He was there for but an hour, and then he shrugged himself into his opera cape and strolled out, in the midst of Harcourt's speech, as though the House of Commons were but a music hall.' 'Which it well may be,' I said with my best worldly manner, Kilpeder schoolmaster passing judgement upon affairs of state. 'If so,' Bob said, 'tis the grandest ever built, great windows and massive carvings, the vaulted roof so high that birds might nest in it. Massive, Hughie, massive is the word for it.' 'A pity when Home Rule is won,' I said, 'and Mr. Parnell and the rest of yez will have to content yourselves with a few rows of benches in the old Bank of Ireland and nothing to be seen from the old windows but the dirty old Liffey.' Bob took my point and smiled, embarrassed and yet not perturbed. It was wicked of me to tease him thus, in the flush of his excitement, when he had made time to call in on us before hurrying off to take Agnes and himself to have dinner at old Tully's, where the Bishop of Kerry and himself were to be the guests of honour. But I think that he would rather have lingered away the evening with us, if truth be told."

It was an innovation of far-reaching consequences, Prentiss's father said, as he and Patrick walked down Rathmines Road, and not for Ireland alone. The *old* Irish party, Mr. Butt's party, was a party of gentlemen. Parnell changed all that, brought in solicitors, penny-a-line journalists, Land League agents, shorthand writers like little Healy, little Healy from Bantry, the Bantry band, ham-and-bacon merchants, auctioneers. Little Micksey Mackey from Waterford, there was a prime specimen to be left free to roam the lobbies and libraries of Commons, the terrace.

Patrick Prentiss, home from Oxford on long vacation, kept admiring pace with him. Opposite the Rathmines church, his father halted, back to the straight, narrow lane which led to the rere of Portobello Barracks. At the far end of the lane, two soldiers leaned against a red-brick wall, hatless, their collars unbuttoned. Prentiss's father rested his two hands upon the gilt, bulbous knob of his walking stick, ferrule pressing against Rathmines pavement. He smiled, sending small waves through the silken beard, spreading wrinkles towards the blue, pale eyes. "Our own lot, in fact, Patrick, unlikely as that may seem. Those country solicitors in salt-and-pepper suits and billycock hats are most eager to retain barristers of, shall we say, the older school. Especially if we are Catholic and just a bit patriotic. Ireland's governing passion, Patrick, is snobbery." Standing poised between religion and state, church and barracks, Prentiss's father swayed slightly upon his stick, delighted by his words.

But for all that, thought the Patrick Prentiss of 1904, walking through the Temple to Pump Court, few members of Parliament in the eighties had, even in forgivable youth, carried a gun against the Queen's soldiers, fired a police barracks, stood trial, heard sentence pronounced.

"It was that same evening," Hugh MacMahon said, "that Bob told Mary and myself of his maiden speech, late in the session. He spoke against the motion for a coercion bill, and Dillon and McCarthy had spoken before him. He was so nervous, he said, that he was afraid the words would fail him, although he had his headings written out on a sheet of foolscap. 'Gaolbird,' he was fearful they would shout out at him, 'Fenian.' But the House was courteous to him on that first occasion—tis a custom they have—and there he was, Bob Delaney of Tully's shop in Kilpeder, on his feet in the House of Commons, addressing the House. I visited him there once, you know, that one time I journeyed to London, and sat perched in the visitors' gallery peering down at him, but that was in a later session, when he was at his ease in the House, lounging back on the bench, as the others were."

But all that, Prentiss thought, was in the eighties; the Land League itself had not come into existence until 'seventy-nine, and there had been a decade of years after the Rising, the years in which Bob Delaney had risen from assistant to partner and son-in-law, had been articled as a solicitor.

"Ach," MacMahon said. It was on Prentiss's third visit down to Kilpeder, and, fulfilling a promise, he had taken MacMahon on a visit to Cork—a visit to the Opera House, a late supper at the Oyster, and then rooms at the Metropole. "Ach, they were the quiet years. Twas not too easy for myself at the outset, you understand, winning myself back into the good graces of the Board. Bob and myself were treated as lads who had run wild, and there were those in high places with their faces set against me. But old Tully was able to work wonders, even with Father Cremin, and with the Bishop himself. For the sake of our friendship with Vincent, he did it, or so I thought at the time, fool that I was." The weather was against them, a spattering rain drumming against the Lee and a low grey sky, and as they walked, the distinctive shape of Shandon, across the river, was blurred.

"I had expected him to be in a rage against the two of us, and Bob in particular, for having led Vincent into evil courses, but by God, did he not pay the solicitor's fees for all three of us, and not those alone, but the great costs of having us defended in court by Emmet Bourke himself, who was accepted by all as the most prodigious barrister on the Munster circuit, whether Whig or Tory, and of whatever denomination. Although he was a Catholic in point of fact, and therefore a Whig, the brother of a bishop." He walked against the wet wind as he might have walked down the hill from his Kilpeder house, in long, easy strides, the hem of his shapeless tweed coat beating against his calves, tweed hat pulled low.

"Now that was something," he said, "to be defended by Emmet Bourke, although at the time I was too frightened to savour the honour."

"But not Nolan," Prentiss said.

MacMahon laughed, an old man's phlegm-choked laugh. "Indeed not," he said. "Butt defended Ned Nolan. To old Tully, Ned was the devil incarnate. He might not have been too far from the mark."

Rain thickened. With one accord, they took shelter in a public house, cavernous, warm with the heat of bodies. Gaslight glowed through globes diverse-coloured, red, yellow, blue. The long back bar was a dazzle of mirror, reflecting the colours, rows of bottles. They found two tall stools, screened on either side by milky glass set in dark, scrolled wood.

"Most elaborate," MacMahon said dryly, and signalled the barman. "Emmet Bourke conferred one time with me," he said. "He sat facing me on a chair which was brought in for him, and Dripsey the solicitor standing beside him. A half hour then, and two hours in the courtroom. And a hundred and fifty guineas earned, so Vincent told me later. By God, the law is a splendid profession."

"The family profession," Prentiss said. "My father is a barrister."

As though caught in a lapse of manners, MacMahon took him by the forearm. "He is, of course. You must excuse my language. Butt was a different matter entirely. He worked wonders for Ned. By the time he had finished, the jury was half convinced that no one at all had killed poor Belton. But sure, I have no cause for complaint. Emmet Bourke gave value for money. Two large toddies against the day that is in it," he said to the barman, "with steaming hot water and lumps of sugar. And a few cloves."

"You could have had no complaints on that score," Prentiss said.

"None whatever," MacMahon said. "But I have heard it said that that was a fixed policy of Government. To throw the weight of the law against the fellows like Ned, the leaders and the Yankee soldiers who had

[234   ]

come over. And let the small fry swim about in prison for a year or two, studying repentance and the folly of accepting evil counsel. It makes sense. We could have driven the prisons into bankruptcy, feeding and lodging us."

"Yes," Prentiss said, thinking that they wished also to demonstrate that this had been no true rebellion, but rather mobs of ignorant men, the dupes of adventurers and confidence men.

"Mind you," MacMahon said, touching white, thin fingers to the hot glass which had been set before him, "there was great fury against us in England—the attack upon the police van in Manchester and Sergeant Brett shot dead, and the explosion outside London, in Clerkenwell, with those wretched innocent people killed, poor people like ourselves—how many were there?"

"Twelve," Prentiss said, "and a hundred or so wounded."

The white fingers drew back from the glass, as though burned.

The public-house door opened, admitting briefly to the room cold, rain-washed air.

It was a different air in this present London afternoon, late autumn now. A story, Prentiss thought, with its London resonances. Delaney, an apprentice in the House, leaning forward to watch a hand scribbling a signature on a note, "C. S. Parnell." In a London suburb, gunpowder explodes a prison wall, sending masonry on high, random arcs. Beneath London Bridge, not much farther from where Prentiss now stood than the curve through violent air of jagged masonry, Lomasney the Fenian destroys himself foolishly, although believing perhaps that in the final blinding moment London Bridge was falling down, falling down. And in Chelsea, in a house whose address was still unknown to the would-be historian who moved crabwise towards him, a house imagined as small, bow-windowed, fanlight spreading white tracery above the door, Delaney had met with his great love, the love which Prentiss could not yet imagine, would never perhaps imagine, a life lived within dimensions to which history had no access. Prentiss, a moment's fancy, felt himself caught within his own contrivances. The story which he had once imagined as having shape, coherence, symmetry even, as having its centre in the market square of Kilpeder, spilled outwards, a tide, a river, undammable.

He reached at last his door, and climbed the rough-wooded staircases, past chambers where, by day, briefs were read by barristers, content with fractions of the truth, fragments, for whom truth was measured by precedent, plausibility, statutes indexed by Roman numerals and the names of long-dead kings. In his sitting room, he lit the gas, and drew heavy drapes across the autumn evening.

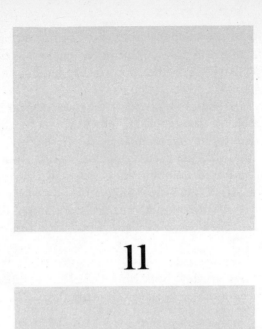

11

[Hugh MacMahon]

It is a curious fact that of all the circumstances of my trial, which by any mode of calculation must be accounted the most vivid incident of my life, there is none which I remember in more exact detail than that of my interview with Emmet Bourke, the eminent queen's counsel who, through the kindness of Dennis Tully, had been retained for my defence.

On the morning before the trial, I was taken from the cell which I had been sharing with the Ballyknockane men, and conducted along draughty white-walled corridors, and up two flights of stairs to a small retaining cell, which for all its frugality seemed, in the privacy which it afforded, the very height of luxury. From its small, barred window, I had a fine view of the exercise yard, and even, through a narrow, awkward angle, a glimpse of a city street, deserted at the first early hour, but by eight, I was able to watch workmen hurrying along it to their places of employment and drays lumbering slowly along, hauled by their straining horses.

It was close to noon when the warder, bearing with him a straight chair, ushered in Peter Dripsey, my attorney, whom I had come to know well, and Mr. Bourke. Dripsey was, I daresay, a decent enough fellow, a Cork City solicitor with a good practice in such matters as conveyancing and the probate of wills and the like, and a sister who was mother superior of the Presentation Convent. A lean, hollow-chested man, with a long, sorrowful face, and eyes that seemed always to be watering. "Dear, dear," he was forever saying during our conversations together, as a family doctor will say as he draws a sheet over the face of a patient lost, and this, together with the watering eyes, had given to our little talks a melancholy, autumnal tone.

Bourke was a different matter entirely, a well set-up man with only the beginnings of a paunch to mar his appearance, and clothes which even my country-bred eyes could recognise as elegant to the point almost of dandyism. His coat was black, and the broad tie above the pale waistcoat was a vivid blue. It was not, however, a dandy's face and head—rather, the face was full-fleshed, and the brown eyes were deep-set, shielded by thick, sandy brows. He was younger than I had expected of a man of such celebrity, the terror of opposing counsels and even of judges—surely a year or two under forty. He came of the right stock, there had been Bourkes practising at the bar since Catholics were first permitted to be called, in the 1790s, and Emmet's grandfather had been called in the same year as Daniel O'Connell, with whom he had been associated in the campaign for Catholic Emancipation. Emmet himself, however, wasted no time in displaying for me his hereditary qualifications, nor did he court my admiration by flourishing his accomplishments. In his presence, I felt myself a seedy provincial, as indeed I was, and a recreant one as well.

He swung himself into the chair, and gestured towards the bed, to which I lowered myself, so that I sat awkwardly facing him.

"Now then, Mr. MacMahon," he said, "I have gone over the particulars of your involvement in this wretched affair, and your situation seems identical with those of Delaney and young Vincent Tully. The three of you will go up for trial tomorrow, and I propose to deal with all three in the same manner. There are a few points only upon which we should all of us be clear in our minds. You are a schoolmaster; you have the rudiments, at least, of an education, and I doubt if I need belabour them."

He spoke in as matter-of-fact a way as he would in ordering a case of claret, and although I had not expected him to share my own deep interest in my fate, I was nonetheless taken aback. He seemed to notice this, and favoured me with a wintry but not an unfriendly smile. He rested his elbows on his knees, and his chin on his fists.

"You three lads," he said, "foolishly allowed yourselves to drift into a most dangerous conspiracy, which has now, let us thank God, been crushed. And crushed without difficulty, lacking as it did the support of a populace less foolish than yourselves. I am astonished, to be truthful, at the extent of your foolishness. A schoolmaster, of all people; a man who has in his care the education, and not merely the practical but the moral education, of the boys and youths of his locality. Father Cremin, I am happy to be able to say, is persuaded that you have discharged your duties properly. There is no evidence that you perverted your authority to seduce your scholars into unlawful acts."

"Indeed there is not," I said. "There was no thought of forming an infant brigade."

"Have a care there, Mr. MacMahon. If irony is to be employed in these proceedings, you will entrust it to me. You did not offer the oath to your scholars, but the oath was taken by young men who had been your pupils in earlier years. Mark that I say 'was taken': the passive voice is to be avoided in literature, but it is useful in law. And the influence of a schoolmaster extends beyond the schoolhouse. His example is heeded. A schoolmaster! And a young man from nowhere, a small farmer's son, who by diligence and intelligence has established himself as the valued assistant of the chief merchant in Kilpeder. And that merchant's son, a young man who has received an exemplary education, who has many friends in the county of the highest respectability, a young man of promise. And behold you now, the three of you! How may your acts, your wicked acts, be described as issuing from any fount save that of folly?"

"How indeed?" I said warily, having the hazy beginnings of a notion.

"I have spoken with that father, Mr. MacMahon. I have spoken with Dennis Tully. I do not use lightly so florid a word as *heartbroken*, but I use it now. Is your own father living, or your mother, perhaps?"

"They are not," I said, but added helpfully, "I have a wife."

"Unfortunate," Bourke said.

"And if I may, Mr. Bourke. I would like some protest to be made that I have been allowed but the one visit from her, and that one granted grudgingly."

"You must discuss such matters as that with Mr. Dripsey here. He is your solicitor. Your wife cannot help you in your present strait. Only I can help you." He lifted one hand to touch the handsome watered silk at his throat. "In law, Mr. MacMahon, wickedness, unfortunately, is not extenuated by folly. Unfortunately for you, that is; not for society. Foolish rogues are as dangerous as clever ones."

"No doubt," I said. My chances, slender at best, rested with him, and I was sorry to find myself developing a thin, sharp dislike for the man. He had too great a fondness for lapidary formulation.

"And yet, Mr. MacMahon. And yet. All over Ireland, on that unfortunate March morning, lads who had taken the very oath that you took thought better of what they were about, and stayed snug and law-abiding in their beds. Or else met at their gathering place, talked matters over, and quietly dispersed. This morning they are about their lawful tasks, looking forward to a quiet jar at the day's end, a chat by the fire. No doubt you envy these young men."

"I would prefer not to be in prison awaiting trial," I said, "if that is what you mean."

"Almost," he said. "I mean that you regret, in a most heartfelt manner, the course which you chose to follow."

"I regret most sincerely," I said, "that events took the course they did."

He smiled once again. "I have cautioned you once, MacMahon. Leave irony alone. And equivocation. You will find that Mr. Bodkin is a ferocious prosecutor. He lacks the faint, the very faint sympathy that I have for your misguided enterprise. Yesterday witnessed a painful scene in the courthouse. Edward Nolan stood his trial, and despite the efforts of Mr. Butt, one of the ablest barristers in this island, he was sentenced to life imprisonment. Had it not been for Mr. Butt's skill, he would have been sentenced to be hanged for murder."

No word of this had come to me, and I was stunned—less by the fact, for it was the verdict I had half expected, as by the way in which the word now came to me, in those polished syllables, savoured almost upon tongue and lip, and with Ned pressed flat into "Edward Nolan."

"In your own case, and in the cases of Delaney and Tully, we have contrived to have the charge lowered from treason to treason-felony, but that can carry a heavy sentence, a very heavy sentence indeed. I shall plead all three of you not guilty, but you know and I know and Judge Adams knows that you are as guilty as sin."

"Dear, dear," Mr. Dripsey said.

"Now then," Bourke said, "let us come to those few points I spoke of. Firstly, when did you take the oath of the Irish Republican Brotherhood?"

"In 1865," I said, "early in the year. In February it was, or March."

"And where?"

"Here," I said. "In Cork City."

"And who administered it to you?"

I gave myself what I trusted was but a long moment to think about that. "Do you know, Mr. Bourke, that seems as long ago as the Punic Wars. But I remember it clearly. Twas in one of the public houses down near the Coal Quay, in the back room. A fellow had come down from Dublin, a tall fellow with a crook in his back that made him seem shorter. That is how I remember him, but Bob and Vinnie may remember him differently; we took the oath together."

"Mr. Dripsey," Bourke said. "If you please," and held out his hand, a shapely hand, with a ring, dark-stoned, on a finger. Dripsey moved forward, and handed him the thick folder which he had been carrying. Bourke opened it, made a great display of leafing through its papers, then paused at one, and placed the ringed finger upon it.

"You are right as to the date, Mr. MacMahon. March eleventh. And it was indeed hard by the river, but not the Coal Quay. It was in the rere offices of one Joseph Tumulty, a ship's chandler, and the oath was administered by Tumulty himself."

I said nothing.

"I am not a necromancer, Mr. MacMahon. Not everything is disclosed in open court. Your prosecutor is better informed than your counsel. A deplorable circumstance."

High on the wall, just above where Dripsey stood, there was a dark discolouration, the size and shape of a man's head. I tried to concentrate my attention upon it, but I could not. Tumulty had been the Centre for Cork, to whom Bob at first and then Ned was answerable. And for that matter, Lomasney, and all the others.

"The Rising has failed, Mr. MacMahon," Bourke said, "and no harm can be done by discussing an organization which lies in ruins. People must save themselves as best they can."

"That may not be informing, Mr. Bourke," I said, "but it comes precious close. Is that the course you are recommending to me?"

"No," Bourke said. "Unfortunately, no." He was rummaging through the papers in the folder spread open on his lap. "An informer must have something of value to sell, and you do not. The entire pack of you were caught red-handed, and the testimony of the police is sufficient. Although they could not bring home against Nolan proof that he had shot the poor constable. Too many shots were being fired, and by both sides. Even there you would have been of no use as an informer; you and Delaney were by then moving to the Killeter road."

It was my first encounter with the law, and I was impressed by its singular relationship to the reality in which actual people lived actual lives. Months later, John Kenealey, who had been one of the lads behind the barracks, was to tell me of poor Belton's death—a foolish man excited by what had been happening, who with two others ran towards our fellows as they were moving off. He fell to one knee, and fired off his carbine, then rose up and paused, perhaps to reload. Ned turned and ran back towards him, and when he was not more then twenty yards, took good aim with his revolver, and fired twice. The other constables backed off. "I was with the laggards," John said, "and when the Captain fired, I was as close to him as I am to you. His face was very calm, with the lips set, and he took his time." "If you were with the laggards," I said, "he may have saved your life." "The second shot flung Belton over backwards," John said.

"Delaney commanded in Kilpeder until Nolan took over from him," Bourke said, "and you were his seconder. You have not given me an easy task."

I would have proffered him my sympathy, but thought better of it. His cautions against irony were sensible.

"But in fact Nolan did take command himself," Bourke said, "a hardened soldier. Not Irish at all, really. One of the Yankee adventurers, ruthless and bloodthirsty men."

"Irish enough," I said. "He was born here. He is my own first cousin."

"Is he indeed?" Bourke said, turning to Dripsey as though in reproof. "I did not know that."

"Does that make matters worse for me?" I asked meekly.

When he turned back from Dripsey, he was smiling. "For a man facing a long prison sentence, Mr. MacMahon, you are remarkably cool."

"Indeed I am not," I said. "I am frightened out of my wits. I cannot sleep at night, and I have watery bowels. I am in terror of the prisons of England, and the thought of years without my wife is an agony to me. I lie on my straw at night staring up into blackness, and say over and over that my course is run. I weep at night and keep the other lads awake. But I will not weep in the courtroom tomorrow, and I will not weep for you now."

He sat for what seemed an age, his hands spread flat across his papers, staring at me. Then he gathered the papers neatly together, and placed the folder on the floor beside his chair. He rose up, walked past me to the window, and stood looking out, with his back turned to the both of us. I looked towards Dripsey, but could not catch his eye. His lightly fleshed frame shrugged itself against the whitewashed wall in a manner which said "Dear, dear" without the use of language. It was a suave and worldly back, the wool admirably cut.

"It would not matter, Mr. MacMahon," he said. "Weeping would leave Judge Adams's withers unwrung." He turned round to us. "He is more amenable to other lines of reasoning. Our masters in Dublin Castle and in Westminster have no wish to impose back-crushing sentences upon the thousands, perhaps tens of thousands, of dupes who were caught up in this wretched affair. Their concern is with the ringleaders. There was one ringleader in Kilpeder, and one only. Edward Nolan. He has made a statement admitting as much, and in it he has specifically exculpated yourself and your friend Delaney. Not to mention the poor Tully lad." He hooked a thumb in a pocket of his waistcoat, and gave me one of his chilly smiles. "You follow me, I trust, Mr. MacMahon."

The window at his back bestowed upon the room a flat, late morning light.

"Not entirely," I said. "You were saying but a minute ago that your task was a difficult one. Twas Bob and myself who swore in the Kilpeder men, and before Ned arrived, twas us who drilled them. On the night of the arms raid—"

Bourke shook his head. "There is no arms raid in the bill of indictment. I have not been briefed upon an arms raid, have I, Mr. Dripsey?"

"You have not," Dripsey said, with a succinctness of which I would not have thought him capable.

"No," Bourke said. "And Nolan has made it clear in his statement that Delaney and yourself were reluctant to act on the sixth. In the weeks before that misfortunate morning, you argued against it, but he held you to your oath, that wretched oath. The Church is wise in the ban it has placed upon oath-bound organizations."

"We did?" I asked.

"Yes indeed," Bourke said. "Think back, Mr. MacMahon. Surely you will recall your efforts. It is important that you do so."

I shrugged. "It came more and more to seem a desperate enterprise, and when talking with Ned, we more than once said what we thought. But there was never a doubt but that—"

Bourke held up a hand. "You need say no more on the subject. Neither now, nor tomorrow in the courtroom. You are young, you were misled, and you are contrite. What we can make of that is my concern, not yours."

"Let us speak plainly, Mr. Bourke," I said. "All of the guilt is to be placed upon Ned Nolan's shoulders, and the most of the punishment with it."

"If you want plain speaking, sir," Bourke said, "you will have it. Nolan's case is a hopeless one; he knows that well. He has escaped with his life by a hairsbreadth. There is no reason for him to drag others down with him. His trial is over and done with, Mr. MacMahon. Remember that."

But perhaps, after all, my appetite for plain speaking was not a large one. Bourke's circumlocutions had had the kindly purpose of wrapping in cloths the blunt facts of the matter. Ned Nolan, it would appear, was to carry away with him the lion's share of the guilt for Kilpeder, but there would nevertheless be enough left to be shared out amongst the rest of us. Mr. Bourke, however, who plainly knew what he was about, had contrivances which would hold down our share of the pie to a decent spoonful. I was more delighted by this possibility than words can express, and yet it put into my mouth a thin, sour taste of guilt.

"And what of the lads, Mr. Bourke?" I asked.

"I have not been briefed with respect to the lads," he said. "You need not concern yourself about them, if that is the point of your question. They can look forward to a few months in gaol, which is a damned cheap price to pay for armed rebellion. A man named Dunphy can expect to stay inside for a bit longer. There are Crown witnesses to testify that he took aim and wounded a constable. Not seriously, thank God."

"We were all of us blazing away," I said.

"And wretched shots you were, most of you. That sort of thing is best left to the gentry. I doubt if we have anything more to discuss, Mr. MacMahon, unless you have questions." He made an elaborate display of drawing a heavy gold watch from his waistcoat pocket and holding it in his cupped hand. With a thumbnail, he flicked open its case. The gold casing, highly polished, flashed for a moment in the pale sunlight.

"Have you talked with Ned?" I asked him.

"With Edward Nolan?" he said, thumbing closed the watch and replacing it. "Certainly not. I have spoken with those upon whose behalf I have been briefed. Young Tully, and Delaney, and now you. I have spoken with Mr. Butt, however. Mr. Butt entirely supports the line which I propose to take, and I am delighted that this is the case. Isaac Butt is a formidable man of law, is he not, Mr. Dripsey?"

"He is indeed," Dripsey said. "A cunning fox in the courtroom, but a most amiable fellow. Too amiable, tis said by some. He has his little human weaknesses." Dripsey made vague gestures which might have hinted at drunkenness, lechery, sharp practice at cards.

"As who amongst us does not?" Bourke said, either with charity or with a light mockery of that virtue: he was not an easy man to riddle out. "My own are at any rate less reckless." He patted the gentle swelling below his waistcoat. "At the moment, a decent veal chop at the Oyster, and a bottle of Mr. Sugrue's claret. How are they feeding you in here, MacMahon?"

"Simple fare," I said. "I have no complaints."

"You will have to put up with it for some time to come, I fear." He bent down beside the chair and gathered up the parts of his brief. "One last point," he said, without looking at me. "You asked about your 'lads.' Commendable loyalty, however misguided. Young Vincent Tully was merely one of those lads. Unlike Delaney and yourself, he held no position of authority, despite the friendship which exists among the three of you. Is my point clear?"

"It is indeed, Mr. Bourke," I said after a moment's thought. "Were I to spend another day or two in your company, I might gather a usable sense of how the law works. It seems to be organised upon lines of its own."

He then did look directly at me. The brown eyes seemed to hold all at once malice, humour, and sympathy. "Perhaps, Mr. MacMahon, and perhaps not. I will add a weighty grain to your knowledge. You are indebted to Mr. Dennis Tully for my services, yourself and Robert Delaney both. Mr. Tully's affection for Delaney has suffered a rude shock, but it somehow survives. Why he has chosen to extend his generosity to yourself I cannot say. But the centre of his concern, and therefore of mine, is, of course, his son. That is but natural."

"A weighty grain?" I said, putting the words as a question.

"The laws of these islands, Mr. MacMahon, form a magnificent structure, intricate and impartial; they stand above us all, the guardians of our liberties and of our civil order. Lawyers, however—Mr. Dripsey, myself, all of us—are on hire; we are paid to secure the interests of those who can afford to hire us. A paradox. My brothers in the Four Courts would not like to hear me put matters that baldly, but there you are."

I did not like Emmet Bourke. For the next twenty years, until the day when, as Mr. Justice Bourke, he died of an apoplectic seizure while on holiday in Deauville, his name grew more solid and more luminous, with a kind of roundness to it, like those balls of tinfoil which schoolboys smooth and pat into shape. To this day, I am told, barristers on the Munster circuit, over ports and brandies in the assize hotels, will remind each other of good things which Emmet Bourke said or is remembered as having said—witty responses to opposing counsels, the delicate chaffing of crotchety judges, the ingenious citation of obscure statutes. Once I caught a glimpse of him, leaving the Opera House in Cork, on a night in September or October. Mist and fog had moved into the city. He was standing with friends on the steps, after a performance of *Maritana*—

black evening clothes, a black cape flung upon his shoulders, a tall, glossy hat tilted back. He was no longer clean-shaven, but had a sandy beard close-cropped, and the paunch was now heavy. He bore a faint resemblance to the Prince of Wales. As I passed him, he had said something which made the others laugh, and he enjoyed it himself, his head canted to one side, and the bearded face broken into a smile.

I cannot say why I disliked him, for there were no reasons of any consequence. He managed our cases well, Vincent's and Bob's and my own, and his confidence in himself was fortifying. He had a dashing courtroom manner, wearing his gown and wig, and a clerk to precede him and arrange upon the table foolscap and pens, a tumbler of water, lozenges. Perhaps because I was standing in the dock as I watched his performance, the dock itself a waist-high cell, and a warder standing behind me, indifferent, with folded arms.

Truth to tell, I had almost a preference for Hubert Bodkin, the Crown prosecutor. He was a runty, bald-headed fellow with a controlled snuffle that he made use of as punctuation. You knew where you were with Bodkin, a Protestant from Midleton; the family had had strong Orange connexions in the days of O'Connell's agitation. There had been a great-aunt, by repute no better than she should be, and on the hustings O'Connell had made sport with Shakespearean references to "a bare Bodkin." The Bodkins gave as good as they got: it was a Bodkin who first spoke of O'Connell as the Big Beggarman, and the King of the Beggars. But there was in all this a Munster savagery so deep-nursed as to be almost homely.

I have no doubt but that Bodkin despised me as a rebel and a traitor to the Crown, but then he regarded this as a disease, whether latent or virulent, from which all Papists suffered, a contamination of the blood like gout or jaundice. The prosecution of some half of the Cork Fenians had fallen to him, and to judge from my own experience, he performed his task in a workmanlike fashion, reading out the indictment and calling his two witnesses, Sergeant Honan and another constable. It had been a busy assize for him, and whatever zest he may have brought to his task had drained away by the time I came into the dock. He was now like a farmer clubbing rats in a barn—no friend of rats, to be sure, but with neither time nor energy to expend upon merely personal feelings.

So I may say in my calm present circumstances, but my feelings at the time were far different. My trial was the second that morning, following upon Bob's, and I was kept waiting in a small room below ground, from which I was summoned by a voice calling my name. The warder with me, a decent, phlegmatic fellow, opened a low door, and I climbed up a brief, narrow flight of stairs into the dock. After the dark gloom of the waiting room, the courtroom seemed vast and bright, with sunlight streaming in through tall windows. I was for a moment almost blinded, but could soon enough see, straight before me, the rows of spectators, fewer of them than my vanity had anticipated, although Mary was there, to be sure, in her good grey grosgrain, and its small, matching hat, sitting very straight, but with her nervousness hidden, and in the row before her, Dennis Tully himself, as bald as Bodkin, and seeming almost shrunken, hunched forward, staring at me, his hands clasped between his legs. The counsels sat at two tables, with a space between them. Along the wall to my left, facing the windows, in a kind of long box, sat the jury, the one jury that had been empanelled for us all, contriving, the lot of them, to look at once responsible and bored.

I had expected also a solemn hush, out of respect not for me but for the charge I faced, and here also the expectation was mocked, for there was a blur of voices, heavy chairs scratching against the floor, coughs, and movement as well, two spectators rising up together and crawling past reluctant knees to the aisle. Emmet Bourke arched back his shoulders in a stretch, and as he did so leaned to his left, and called something out to Bodkin, who looked up from his papers, startled, then grinned and nodded. Bodkin's wig was slightly askew on his bald pate. It was beyond doubt some trivial pleasantry, exchanged between learned brethren, but it made a poor impression on me.

Judge Adams, in his robes and long wig, with the tall bench separating him from the lot of us, seemed careless of the majesty of the law. He had invited some gentlemen of the county to sit with him, and these were talking among themselves, but as they did so they stared at me idly, another fish aswim in the tank. Adams himself, a small man overburdened by his costume, was hard at work writing, covering rapidly line after line, and pausing only to dip his pen into a tall, elaborate inkpot. He was hunched so far forward that I could not see his face, and I noted, a pointless detail, that he was left-handed, and wrote with the hand twisted awkwardly.

But he soon enough looked up, and I saw then a most extraordinary face, brown as a walnut and not much larger, brown eyes hooded by heavy lids but almost no brows, a long slit of a mouth. The immense wig framed and bullied the face. His looking up was like the cue which prompters hiss in the theatre. The spectators, novices like myself, were slow to silence themselves, but not the lawyers nor the jury nor the assortment of clerks and bailiffs. He looked first, absently, down the length of the room to the great closed double doors, and then, turning his head, as does a turtle, small head balanced upon long neck at once clumsy and adroit, he stared straight at me. He gave, then, a nod, which I supposed was one of recognition, but was instead a signal to the clerk of the court.

What next happened was that I heard my own name. It was spoken from not more than fifteen feet away, but in a voice which seemed to fling itself out into the echoing room. "Hugh Ignatius MacMahon," it said, "you are indicted upon the charge of treason-felony, against the peace of our Lady, the Queen, her Crown, and dignity. How do you plead?"

I said nothing. I was dumbfounded. All that I had seen and heard in those minutes—the whispering, rustling spectators, Bourke stretching back his shoulders, the judge's hand back-arched over his lines of writing, the sun-welcoming windows, the very air in the room with its faint odours of dust and wool, a juror's neck disfigured by a huge carbuncle, black gowns and fusty wigs—all this had been separate from myself, the machine of the world's business, grinding away, indifferent and impersonal, theatre, counting house. My name flung me into the midst of it.

"How do you plead?" the clerk said again, and this time his voice was low and matter-of-fact, as though he understood what had happened, and, moved to a mild brief sympathy, addressed me as one man to another.

"Not guilty," I said to him, and my eyes sought out Mary. My hand I kept resting firmly on the railing of the dock, for it was a matter of consequence to me that I not be seen to tremble.

Bodkin began speaking even as he was rising to his feet. "May it please your lordship, gentlemen of the jury," he said. "I appear with my learned friend Mr. Robinson for the Crown, and the defendant is defended by my learned friend Mr. Bourke. The case before you is identical in almost every respect with that which has just been concluded, the case of *Regina versus Delaney*. The accused, Hugh Ignatius MacMahon, of Chapel Street in the town of Kilpeder, comes before you . . ." I could recognise myself in what he was saying and would go on to say, and yet it was almost as though he were talking about someone alien to me and to everyone else, some legal fiction. Of the matters upon which Bourke had badgered me, not a word was spoken—when I had taken the oath, or where, or in whose company, or by whom it had been administered. The matter at issue, it appeared, was that I had taken part in an armed assault upon the barracks, and had been captured on the slopes beyond the Killeter road. It took Bodkin but a few minutes to set that forth, and then to call Cornelius Honan.

He cut a fine figure, erect and tall, his tunic clean and well brushed, and his chin rising above the stiff collar. In his right hand he carried a small black notebook, which he transferred to his left, in order to take the oath. He did not look at me, until Bodkin directed him to do so.

"He was with the men who seized the cottages down the road from the barracks," he said, "and facing the barracks."

"You could see him plainly from the barracks," Bodkin said, "and you could recognise him?"

"I could indeed," Honan said.

"And when you saw him," Bodkin said, "what was it that you saw him do?"

"I would catch sight of him from time to time," Honan said. "I saw him moving about from one side of the road to the other. I think that I heard him once shouting out, but I could not make out the words."

Bodkin looked down to his notes, and, with his eyes still upon them, said, "Was he armed?"

Honan paused before answering. "I cannot swear to that," he said. "But most of them had some weapon or other, shotguns and revolvers and—"

"Objection," Bourke said, and smiled at Bodkin.

"Was it your impression, Sergeant, that the accused was party to the attack on the barracks, or had he happened by some misfortunate chance to have wandered upon the scene?"

"He had not," Honan said. "He was in command of the men there in the cottages. Once, I remember clearly, he called to a cottage, and two men came out from it, the both of them armed as I well remember, with either carbines or shotguns, and he pointed towards the barracks, and the two of them cut loose at us. They fired off their weapons."

Bourke made a slight stir, as if he would again object, but, seeming to think better of it, he shrugged.

There were two dozen, perhaps, of such questions, and in his answers to them, Honan said nothing to damage the opinion I had always had of him as a man of fair dealing. He was stiff and awkward in his language, in awe, perhaps, of the occasion, but he said nothing to which I could take exception. He may even, for all I knew, have shared my own sense of unreality. Every so often, Bodkin would put a question or Honan make a response to which Bourke would object, and then Bodkin would put the question in a different way. It was a game that they played, a kind of shuttlecock, with Judge Adams attentive to the rules and the scoring. Far distant from that room, that city, the barracks glowed, a baleful red; the air was rent with explosions of gunfire; a man screamed without ceasing. Distant even from Kilpeder, in some world of things, passions, pain.

"Sergeant Honan," Bourke said. He rested his pen carefully beside his brief, and then ran a forefinger softly along its length. "You are an admirable witness, Sergeant. I admired your testimony in the earlier cases, and so I do in this one. You have given us, with the help of my learned friend, a clear picture of the unfortunate events which bring us together today. I have but a few questions to put to you." He raised his hand, and put it to the collar of his gown.

"Mr. Bodkin asked you, in a facetious way, whether you imagined that the defendant had wandered upon the scene by chance. And, of course, you did not. But I ask you this. Were you surprised to see him there?"

"I don't understand your question, Mr. Bourke," Honan said, and Bodkin said, "Objection," at the same time, his word cutting across Honan's answer.

"I accept that," Bourke said. "Let me try this instead. How long have you known the defendant?"

"I was posted to Kilpeder two years ago," Honan said, "and he was already the schoolmaster."

"Yes," Bourke said. "The schoolmaster and the sergeant of the barracks. Village dignitaries, representatives of learning and the law. In your two years, did you come to know each other well?"

For the first time since he made his formal identification, Honan looked over at me, and did so straight in the face. His own was impassive. Poor Belton, the constable shot down, had been his friend. I was glad that I could not look past the pale blue eyes.

"I thought I did," Honan said, and for the first time there was an edge to his voice.

"You knew him as a man of good repute, of good character?"

"He is an able master, from all I have heard."

"No doubt," Bourke said. "But I ask you as to his character."

"I never heard ill of him from the townspeople," Honan said, "if that is what you mean." He hesitated, and then said, "We knew him to be a man of advanced opinions."

"Advanced opinions," Bourke repeated. "In what respect were they advanced? Is he one of Mr. Charles Darwin's followers?"

This sent through the room a faint ripple of laughter among the well informed.

"Political," Honan said tersely.

"I see," Bourke said. "Advanced political opinions. And in Great Britain, we may all be thankful, that is no crime at all."

"Is that a question, Mr. Bourke, or a comment?" Judge Adams said. "The accused is not before us because of his opinions as to either politics or Mr. Darwin's speculation. He is charged, rather, because of the events which took place in Kilpeder on March sixth."

"With respect, my lord, the charge against him is treason-felony. One cannot be a traitor for a single day. It is a crime slowly nurtured."

Bodkin favoured him with an icy smile, and said, "My lord, if I may. One may give *proof* of treason in a single day, in a single hour."

"That would seem to be the case, would it not, Mr. Bourke?"

"If your lordship pleases," Bourke said, and tugged at his gown. "Sergeant, you have placed the accused on the scene, but you cannot tell us whether or not he was armed?"

"Yes," Honan said.

"He was one of some sixty-odd men who attacked the barracks. A participant with them."

"He was one of their leaders," Honan said.

"Indeed!" Bourke said. "He stood in a street and pointed. Have you other proof? Proof more compelling, if possible?"

Honan stared at him, began to speak, but then closed his mouth. You could almost sense him searching for words.

"Sergeant," Bourke said, "you behaved splendidly that morning. Yourself and every constable in the barracks. But it was a hot fight, gunfire was exchanged, the barracks itself was set afire. Can you indeed be certain that some one man was a leader, a man standing well down the street from you, a man who may or may not have been armed?"

Honan looked towards Bodkin for some kind of assistance, and then to the judge, but the two of them stared at him impassively.

"'Tis common knowledge—" Honan began, but Bourke cut him off.

"Common knowledge," he said, "cannot be called to a witness stand. Only witnesses can be called, and they can only speak to us of what they witnessed."

And neither, I thought, has common sense any place in a courtroom. If it was sympathy that Honan sought, it was to me that he should have looked, and not towards Bodkin or Adams.

"Very well, then," Bourke said. "If you have nothing further to add, let us move on."

"Before we do," the judge said. "Before we do, Mr. Bourke. The jury may have a firm sense of what you are about, but I am not certain that I do. Do you propose to argue that the prisoner did not take part in the attack on Kilpeder Barracks?"

"For the moment, my lord, I am concerned only to challenge the witness's rash assertion that the prisoner, to his knowledge, bears any responsibility more grave than that attaching to all of those arrested." He shrugged. "My learned friend may well be prepared to produce other witnesses, but—"

Adams held up a mottled paw. "You may proceed with your examination, sir."

"I will not detain the witness much longer, my lord. And if you will limit yourself, Sergeant, to what comes to you as your own, rather than as common knowledge. The attack upon the barracks was commanded by Edward Nolan, whose sworn statement I propose to enter in evidence. In the weeks of his residence in Kilpeder, where did Nolan lodge?"

"He lodged with the accused," Honan said. "With Hugh MacMahon."

"A sinister circumstance," Bourke said. "On the very eve of the insurrection, a notorious American Fenian arrives in Kilpeder, and takes up residence with the accused. Or perhaps not. Can you think of any reason for so doing, other than a sinister one?"

Honan drew a hand away from his side, and spread its fingers. "They were kinsmen," he said.

"Kinsmen," Bourke said. "Were they indeed? Distant kinsmen?"

"They are cousins," Honan said. "Edward Nolan's father and Hugh MacMahon's mother were brother and sister."

"That would indeed make them cousins," Bourke said. "Then he would as a matter of course have gone to MacMahon, unless he chose the excellent but perhaps costly hospitality of the"—he made a show of consulting his notes—"of the Kilpeder Arms."

"That is likely enough," Honan said.

"Thank you, Sergeant," Bourke said. He returned again to his notes, moving their pages about, pausing suddenly, and running his forefinger across several lines. Then he looked up, smiled pleasantly at Honan, and said, "I have no other questions, my lord."

As Honan stepped away from the stand, we caught by chance each other's eye. He may not have remembered the revolver which I had held in my hand that morning, but I remembered it well—its weight, the chill of its metal. I remembered holding it in my two hands and pointing towards the barracks, towards Honan, pull of forefinger, explosion of powder, steel. His uniform encased him, carried him through the hour which enfolded us.

Bourke called no witnesses on my behalf, but his speech for the defence I have heard described as vintage Bourke—not one of his great perorations, the luxuries which he allowed himself when his case was hopeless or when some principle of law or liberty was at stake. To the contrary, his concern was to call the attention of the jury to my shortcomings of character, a harmless schoolmaster of bookish and sedentary disposition, an enthusiast but by nature not a vicious one, my imagination giddy and ill ballasted. It was little less than a miracle of rhetorical contrivance, the manner in which he wove this picture from the brickyard straws of evidence. His manner of speech was negligent, and his tone faintly melancholy, almost patronising. I could scarcely recognise myself from his words, swept up by Ned Nolan into his brutal and sinister designs, cavorting upon the edges of violence. Twice he shrugged towards the jury, as though he and they, men of the world, must make allowances. And yet it was not a lengthy speech, and when he had brought it to a conclusion, he nodded to himself, sat down with a dowagerlike flourish of his gown, poured himself a tumbler of water, and addressed a whispered question to his junior counsel.

All this bit of theatre seemed at first to have been in vain, for the jury arrived at their verdict without leaving their box, and their judgement handed up to the judge. It was a verdict of guilty upon the charge of treason-felony.

There was then a pause which may have been but a moment, and yet seemed to me an eternity, and Adams asked me had I anything to say before his sentence was passed. It was my hour in history.

"No, my lord," I said.

Far above us, Judge Adams leaned forward. He had a habit of mouthing words to himself before beginning audible speech, savouring them or testing them upon thin, wet lips.

"Prisoner at the bar," he said. "You have been found guilty of one of the ugliest and most unnatural of all crimes. The very word, *treason*, is a repulsive one. The tongue falters upon it."

And yet he spoke it trippingly enough. Perhaps the number of times which he would be speaking it in the course of that assize had steeled him to its utterance.

"The Italian poet Dante places traitors in the lowest circle of his hell—the eighth circle, I believe it is."

He stole a swift, flickering glance towards Bourke, as towards one capable of responding to this wide-ranging reference. Bourke might perhaps have leapt to his feet in decorous protest—"The ninth circle, surely, my lord"—but he contented himself with a half smile.

"To turn upon one's own country, one's own sovereign, one's queen. This is the worst of all acts of betrayal. And it is the act of which you stand convicted."

At the time, I had not the patience nor the tranquillity of mind needed to weigh his words. They were but oratorical flourish, prefatory to my sentencing. In a debating society I could have refuted him easily enough, by turning his words against him. Victoria was not my queen, nor the monarch of England my sovereign; it was for Ireland, my country, that I had fought. Indeed, this court itself, and all its apparatus, from Adams himself to the benches upon which the jury sat, was to Fenian eyes a foreign imposition, an instrument of oppression, like the army and the Constabulary.

But it was not a debating society, and I said nothing. I missed my moment in history, which O'Leary and Rossa and Mitchel had seized, their words immortal now in those collections of *Speeches from the Dock* which patriotic schoolboys put to memory, the words given suitable illustration by the woodcut of an unrepentant Fenian in the dock, stiff-backed and with an arm flung upwards to heaven. Far from it, my appearance was described by the *Cork Examiner,* justly I have no doubt, as "hangdog." I was contrasted with the appearance of Ned Nolan, two days before, who had also said nothing, but was described as resembling "a chained wolf, murderous and sullen."

The truth is that caution and prudence guided my silence. I was about to be sent off to prison, and had no wish to provoke the man who was doing the sending, that monkeylike gnome swathed in the splendours of silk. But there was more to it than that. I must, I am certain, have sought out Mary's eyes and drawn strength from her, but of this I have no recollection. I cannot remember the forest of eyes fixed upon me as Adams went on with his harangue. I cannot remember how I stood, nor the feel of the wooden railing as my two hands gripped it. I remember a voice, a blur of scarlet, wigs and gowns, warders standing with folded arms, and I think, but am not certain, that I remember old Tully shifting his hams on the bench and drawing a handkerchief across his forehead. What I remember is a leaden sensation of being weighed down and broken by a universe of actuality.

The established order of things, before which I had been hauled as a felon, seemed at that moment overwhelmingly real, thick, deep-layered. And by contrast, the ideals and hopes which had carried me into rebellion against it seemed foolish and flimsy, as foolish as events had proved themselves to be—a scattering of attacks upon barracks and coast-guard stations, rifle shots fired out against handfuls of policemen, and across the length and breadth of Ireland the "cause," as we had piously called it, shot through and through with cowardice and base betrayal. In the streets through which we had been marched to the gaol, people had gaped at us as at a raree show. We had moved in a shadow world of half-formed ideas, boasts, posturings. I cared not a twopenny bit for England or for Queen

Victoria, but there had been treason, none the less. We had betrayed reality.

Most unlikely, you will say, that a frightened man receiving his sentence will pause to ponder matters of philosophic import. But this conviction came to me not as thought but as sensation, the texture of courtroom air, flat sunlight upon dark panelling, the rustling of papers.

"There is little evidence or none," Adams was saying, "to suggest that you played a conspicuous part in the dreadful events of March the sixth, and for this you have good reason to be thankful. You may be thankful as well that you are represented in this court by an advocate of remarkable resourcefulness and adroitness."

Here he gave towards Bourke by way of salutation a kind of bob of head and shoulders, and allowed himself a smile in which, so it seemed to me, admiration and malice were mingled. Bourke responded with a brief, restrained flourish, a fluttering upwards of his two hands to touch his white, starched collar.

"I bear this in mind. But I bear it also in mind that you held in your town the position of schoolmaster. Once again, there is no evidence that you perverted your authority to inculcate treason and disloyalty among the young of Kilpeder. Not in words, at any rate. But we can preach by example, and what you have offered to your town, to the boys and the young men of that town, is the spectacle of a person, supposedly possessed of some degree of education, who on that fateful morning abandoned his judgement and his conscience to the wildest and most debased of enterprises. Mr. Bourke has suggested that you fell beneath the sway of the miscreant Nolan. This may well be so. It does not speak well for your strength of character, and yet your reputation appears to have been a good one."

He paused then, and in a most unjudgelike manner rubbed his eyes with small, bony thumbs. When he drew them away, his manner had changed, was more brisk and matter-of-fact. The courtroom felt more quiet; it breathed a moment's attentiveness.

"Hugh Ignatius MacMahon, it is the sentence of this court that you be committed at Her Majesty's pleasure to one of Her Majesty's prisons for a term of imprisonment of not less than four years."

The air was murmurous again, and I stood swaying. It was the sentence which Dripsey, more or less, had led me to expect, the sentence which Bob had received earlier that morning. What he had not coached me upon were the customs of the occasion. I had supposed, in a hazy, unformed way, that there would be a chance for Mary and myself to embrace, and a moment or two, perhaps, for me to give to Emmet Bourke my thanks for his skill. As to the latter, there was small need for concern. Already Bourke's clerk, a glossy-cheeked young man, was gathering papers up from the table, and Bourke had strolled over to Bodkin, the two of them chatting together and laughing, Bourke with a hand resting on Bodkin's gowned arm. But Mary had risen up, and was moving towards me, her two hands pressed together.

I felt then the warder's hand upon me, not roughly, and knew that I was to descend the stairs that led directly from the dock. But I stood motionless as she neared the railing which ran along the well of the court, until we were so close that I could see her eyes wet and brimming. "Come along, now," he said. I wanted to call out to her, but I did not.

"There will be a time for you to see each other before you are sent over," he said, as he led me back to the holding cell. He was walking before me, and I nodded to his back.

That event of moment in the destinies of nations, the trial of *Regina v. Hugh Ignatius MacMahon,* had ended, and in the great arena above my head, clerks, warders, and barristers were busying themselves for the case which stood next upon the docket. The warder left me alone for a bit, swinging shut the heavy metal door with its small, barred window, the window with a small door of its own, which he left ajar.

He had paused before leaving the cell, unhooking from his belt a ring of keys.

"Twas far better than it might have been, you know," he said.

"Yes," I said. "I know."

He was a short man, sag-bellied, with a sallow face half hidden by moustache and close-cropped dark beard. He shifted the ring of keys from right hand to left and then back again.

"Yez meant well," he said, "the lot of yez." He had a Cork City speech. "What possessed yez?" he said suddenly, in a rush of words. "What in God's name were yez about?"

I shrugged and stood looking at him. "Ah well," he said, and left me, with a heavy, theatrical sigh. As he stood on the far side of the door, turning the heavy key in the lock, we looked at each other through the window, his face sectioned by the narrow bars.

12

[*Lionel Forrester*]

It is in early autumn that I am most often at Ardmor, and although I tell others, and at times myself, that I go for the shooting, that is but an excuse. Ardmor has become an autumnal world, and at my time of life, that suits me excellently. Most Septembers, when Emily and I arrive, the leaves will have just begun to turn. The mornings will still be warm enough for us to take our breakfast on the terrace, and we can look, beyond the lawns and gardens, to the plantations of larch, beech, rowan, and, beyond them, to the long avenue of elms which runs beside the river. The elms turn first, but if it is early enough in September, we will not mark this from the distant terrace, seeing only the heavy masses of dark green, and here and there, where there is a gap in the avenue, the placid, slow-moving Sullane.

But most mornings we breakfast very early, and often, before beginning work, I will walk to the river. For much of the year, now that Tom lives abroad, the Castle has but a small staff; but Tom insists on maintaining the gardens. Hatchey, the head gardener, will already have his boys at work. I pass them, and we greet each other, a few bobbing their heads with a sketchy, embarrassed civility; but the others will take off their caps or, if bareheaded, will give a tug of the forelock in the old-fashioned manner. They are the last conservatives: gardeners, gamekeepers, saddlemakers—Tories of the spirit. Beyond the terrace, the formal gardens are spread out across the lawns, in the simple and yet artful designs to which Isabel, Tom's mother, had given such attention. Once or twice I have almost felt her presence, remembering with extraordinary clarity the graceful arch of her back as she bent towards a flower bed, the sound of her skirt upon raked gravel. Her memory claims the gardens, as so much else in the grounds is claimed by the memory of Sylvia, a more complex shade.

And most especially along the elm avenue, where she loved to walk, and where I was often beside her, in those early years of the marriage, in mornings when Tom would be busy with a painting, or off in the country with Eddy Chute, the agent. Or towards evening, the three of us might walk here, her gloved hand resting on his forearm. Sylvia was accounted, among Tom's artist friends in London, a "great beauty," but what they meant by this was never clear to me, and I was more inclined to agree with her own London set, who called her appearance "striking," or even, said with affection, "puzzling." How did she see herself, I wonder, for she was conscious of the effect she created—was, in her own way, an artist of the personal. Evening suits her memory: tangled shadows falling from the elms upon the dirt path, fringed by grasses, the river beyond them, and the high demesne wall shutting Ardmor off from its town. She will be wearing, in my memory of her, a certain gown, dark plum, a purple with red glowing beneath its surface, simply cut, like all her gowns, tight-waisted, but falling loose and free to the ground, a shawl with the patterns of China across her shoulder. Tom will be talking, and her head will be inclined towards him, the long, dark hair framing her face.

Not that my memories are always of Tom and Sylvia as I take my morning walk, along the river, beneath the elms. I will be remembering, perhaps, some weightless, inconsequent moment of the past year—a play in London, an opera in Paris, a dinner with friends. Nor will my thoughts always be memories. In that half hour, I will often rehearse the scene or chapter at which I am at work. Perhaps one of those volumes of impressions which are my special pleasure—the delight which comes from delineating, in swift verbal strokes, some vivid scene: a Greek coastal town at hot noon; baked, shadowless streets; a few tables outside a *taverna*; the smell of fish, ropes, wet nets. But more often than that, alas, a chapter for one of those romances upon which much of my income depends: tapestries, rapiers, some cause splendidly lost, some Highland laird still faithful to the Jacobite cause, in service now to the French king, but remembering crags, heather, a harbour deep-sheltered by treeless cliffs.

I am not insensible of the irony in this. Many would think that I was myself enfolded within a romance, pacing the river of a ruined estate, an earl's estate, and the Earl himself, friend and cousin, self-exiled in Cortona, and Sylvia, his countess, the great beauty, a memory now, a slight figure walking beneath the trees of summer, a remembered voice, low and thrilling. But it is merely my own past life, lived then without thought of the shape which it was drawing to itself. "A ruined estate in Ireland"— there you have it—a jotting in a novelist's notebook. But not for me. I have always had, I pride myself, a clear, unworried sense of my talent and its severe limitations: a constructor of trifles, skilful at verbal colour, display, for whom distant scenes, dead times, serve as gaudy blocks, shapes, patterns, spilled from a box of children's toys. How could I speak truly of myself, let alone of Tom or Sylvia? Not writer but "man of letters" (odious phrase): spring and summer in London, summer-deserted city; winter in cramped, shabby rooms in Rome; autumn, a great saving in expenses, as the guest here of my absent cousin and friend, an estate almost bereft now of its sustaining farmlands, a sprawling, desolate demesne, sheltered by high walls of cut stone handsome once but broken now in places, the gaps bridged by rusting barbed wire.

The man of letters is well regarded in London, his name joined with those of others who ply a similar trade—Mason, Stanley Weyman, Conan Doyle, Walter Besant. A bit more in favour than they, perhaps, with the discriminating. Lionel Forrester, they will say, has a small, true talent for the evocation of scene; can be, when he chooses, a kind of Impressionist. But for this, you must seek out his thin volumes of sketches, reflexions. The romances—well, in their way, perhaps. But the romances make possible the season in London, the rooms in Rome.

Lionel Forrester is much in demand in London and in Rome, to fill out a table. He never married. There is a woman, but in every respect unpresentable. An Irishwoman. She began life, some can tell you, as lady's maid to Sylvia Challoner. Lionel and Tom Ardmor are cousins, you know. And, even now, the syllables of her name will stir memories. He does not keep the woman hidden; they go together to theatres, galleries, restaurants. You would never know—a reserved, well-mannered woman. A forbearing woman—you know Forrester's reputation until a few years ago.

Poor Emily. There might even be a romance there for someone,

Emily and myself, in the manner of George Moore, a lady's maid and a gentleman writer, in the best Moore style—broad, vulgar strokes with much attention given to fabrics, gaslit music halls, life belowstairs. All fiction tells lies, and at least Besant and I know that, even if Moore does not.

At Ardmor, it is easy to think myself a shade, with its sense of a setting from which life has been withdrawn. The formal gardens, Sylvia's lovely Japanese garden with its neglected teahouse and high-arched bridge, the choked pond, the empty sheds and barns, stables which are almost empty, save for the trap and my two mounts, the long avenue and the circular carriageway, the rookery and the plantations, the gardeners who, even when joking with each other, seem to me dispirited scene shifters, the great house itself with its closed wings. I have, as I have said, a taste for melancholy, and I envy young Patrick Prentiss, who, when he called upon me last week, encountered it as pure scene, at nightfall, unfamiliar to him. It may well have had for him its own order, the emblem in stone and grassy growth of a vanishing world. "Fall of the Big House," he would have thought. "The Irish gentry in decay." True enough in its way, no doubt; for I remember Ardmor in the days when I came here as a boy, in the days of the old lord, Tom's father, and especially coming once with my own parents, arriving on the night of the hunt ball, with myself sleepy from the long, bumpy journey, tired and cross, and then the Castle leaping up as in a fairy tale, every window lit, and the sound of music. But life does not follow the laws of historical generalization. There are big houses which have the look of Ardmor scattered across these baronies, the lands sold off, and the old families vanished into Cheltenham or Bayswater; but in as many, perhaps in more, life is unchanged—the balls, the hunt crashing, crimson, across the stubble fields, the county families visiting and revisiting, fishing and hunting lodges. It may well be the last act in our drama, part tragedy, part farce; but there are houses which would not accept so fanciful a notion.

No, the fall of the house of Ardmor had different sources, and if history destroyed us, it wore a mask. My great strength, the reviewers tell me, is my evocation of place, and I suspect in this a gentle, unspoken reproof, that my created characters are less real, pasteboard figures propped up against courts, cathedrals, waterfalls. But there may be here a perverse strength, an inclination to measure people not directly but rather as parts of a landscape. Thus, when I walk out into the town, perhaps for a late afternoon whiskey in the Kilpeder Arms, a figure exotic yet familiar in old tweeds, a dandy's tie of pink or pale blue, soft cap, it is as landscape that I see the people, try as I will to see them otherwise.

At the far end of the square, on the Macroom road, I will see the sergeant outside the barracks, his hand on the gate, and will see not him but his unknown-to-me predecessor in that long-distant scuffle which folk song has made into a battle, will imagine blows struck and shots fired. A foolish and vainglorious obelisk in the square will celebrate the coming of age of Tom's grandfather, and I will wonder at how young Sam Forrester was so worked upon by time as to become the old savage whose portrait hangs in the upper hall, mutton chops and small greedy eyes. The obelisk will not last forever: sooner or later, the town council will replace it with a ferocious, open-shirted pikeman, or Hibernia guarded by a concrete wolf-hound. In the Arms, I will be shown into the snug of the taproom, which I will have to myself, less by my wish than that of the proprietor and, no doubt, the customers, and there my whiskey and water will be set before me, an apron-scrubbed ashtray.

"The town of Kilpeder, property of the Earl of Ardmor, 1822," runs a legend beneath the engraving which hangs on the wall facing me. No longer. Even the ground rents of the town go now not to Tom but to the Tullys, the merchant princes of Kilpeder. Only the better sort drink in the Arms—solicitors, land agents, the town's two doctors, commercial travellers. From the snug, through its low, unglassed window, I can see and hear them, voices rising from deep within a world. Three or four times I have joined them, stiff occasions, our laughs too hearty, their eyes not unfriendly but wary, setting a distance, their manner a curious mixture of the deferential and the patronising. I have walked down to them from the Castle, through the falcon-guarded gates, a castle ruined in more ways than one, and myself a poor relation, of no fixed abode, accompanied by the woman, no longer young, who had once been Lady Ardmor's servant.

Often, I ride out into the countryside, the town falling quickly away, replaced by winding roads, hedgerows, the fields of small black cattle. When countrymen pass me—the men in shapeless jackets, tieless shirts buttoned to the collar, the women shawled, black-skirted—they will nod to me, or perhaps the women, especially the older ones, will sketch a curtsey. It is not as it is for me on the roads of other countries, even England. This is my country as it is theirs, for all that I do not live here, and these my own countrymen.

I will pass, if I am ambitious enough for a long walk, the gateposts of other gentry families—the Scotts of Cloud Hill, perhaps, if I take the Killeter road, which runs beyond Clonbrony Wood towards the mountains, or the Fitzherberts of Drimnagh, whose house stands upon a ridge beyond Knockmany, a small house and yet one of the few to possess a real distinction, designed by Francis Johnson in his best Regency manner. I will not call in upon them, neither upon the Scotts nor upon the Fitzherberts. The events of the eighties are long distant, of course, but here memories cling to the soil itself, almost, and the very rocks and trees remember. A few houses would welcome me, to be sure; but they would not return the call, not with Emily in residence.

It was far different before those "events of the eighties," in the first years of Tom's residence in Ardmor Castle, home at last from his brief, unsatisfactory experience of soldiering and his years in Paris, and far different, certainly, from his later return, with Sylvia. In those years, Tom, however ill suited to the role, was very much the grandee of the baronies, as his father had been before him, master of the hunt, magistrate. The spring ball, in those years, was celebrated, with guests from London and a few from the Continent, from Paris and Rome. The Scotts and the Fitzherberts were country cousins, the women's gowns either dowdy or too assertive, and the men standing together in awkward knots in tackroom and billiard room, awed and no doubt resentful, puzzled by the kinds of music which Sylvia insisted upon. The ballroom is sealed off now, of course, but one afternoon last autumn, Emily and I visited it, a wide, dusty room, cheerless, the paintings removed.

If I take the Kerry road, the Derrynasaggarts lie before me, distant and purple with gorse, the sun hitting suddenly upon a shelf of rock. In those days, in the eighties, there would be, in that direction, on either side of the mountains, villages which would be entirely Gaelic-speaking. They were, some of them, villages upon Forrester land, and I remember an occasion, in the late seventies, when Tom and I visited them with Eddy Chute. Some eight or nine mean cabins lay stretched upon the road, dung heaps before the doors, chickens pecking in the dirt, the thatch of the cabins ragged and discoloured. The peasants gathered about us almost before we had alighted from the carriage, their speech a Babel, a guttural singsong. Chute had a rough, serviceable command of the language, and he displayed this for us, talking affably with the men, and bestowing upon the women a decorous, remote raillery. They had the alertness of animals, matted hair, the women shawled and barefooted.

That chill, clear morning so many years ago has about it in my memory a quality of the legendary, of lives unchanged for centuries, locked within a secret tongue. It was the tongue of helots, and it is seldom spoken these days, save in the most remote mountains and moorlands. The old people speak it, and their children are ashamed for them. Or you will hear it shouted out on fairdays, from the tents where drink is sold, or perhaps a snatch of song. The people themselves associate it with ignorance, poverty, rough behaviour. MacMahon, the local schoolmaster, did as much as anyone to drive it out of our villages, and yet now, in the years of his retirement, he has become one of its enthusiasts, gathering up its tales and songs and superstitions before they vanish forever. But perhaps languages, like peoples, have their natural courses, and should not be kept alive by artificial means. So much more than language has changed here since the days of my young manhood, that vanished Ireland of the nineteenth century, landlord and tenant, master and man. Old Everard Chute, Eddy's father, had told him of the great famine, when villagers, at his approach, would fall to their knees, clutching at his coattails. In my own day, the famine was never spoken of among the peasantry, a communal shame, but the land itself remembered. It is strange to be separated from one's own people by language itself.

Very occasionally, I will ride up into the mountains, which are a world apart, unpeopled. It is a rough journey, along roads little better than goat paths, with gorse spreading out on either side, and no companion save a startled hare, the quick flight of snipe or widgeon. There are mountain pools, unreachable, their waters blue and tranquil. Mountains spread out beyond mountains, and on the very clearest of days one can look, it almost seems, across half of Kerry, and guess at the ocean hidden behind the farthest hills, steep cliffs and headlands, hovering gulls, gannets. Here, on a crest, I will rein in. There are few Irishmen, I suspect, who do not have a secret covenant with such scenes, such moments. Below, in the flatlands, in the fields and towns, patterns are jagged, warring, inconclusive, the parts of our world do not fit together. A weariness of political quarrels, ancient animosities, suspicions bred deep into the bone. Indeed, for much of my life I do not think myself Irish at all, save as a picturesque detail, and patriotic politicians and editors are certain that I am not. And yet. Alone among the mountain roads, the crouching hills, reed-fringed lakes, sensing the invisible shores, I will be seized by a deep, haunting certainty of place. Not entirely, perhaps, an illusion.

But on that day in 1874 when I paid my first visit to Tom, after he had taken up residence in Ardmor, it was a different world, a different Ireland. It was early spring, and Tom had taken a barouche to meet me at the railway station in Cork. There had been three of us in the first-class carriage, a Fermoy land agent, a fellow who was travelling down from Dublin to see Lord Midleton on some matter of business, and myself. Beyond the streaky window, the land opened out before us—the wide, green fields of the midlands, the hills of Munster, a flashing glimpse of ruined keep, a manor house half hidden by plantation, the battered, roofless nave of a lost friary or monastery. At each stop, there would be a small knot of country people waiting to board, the women talking to each other, holding bulky, shapeless parcels wrapped in brown paper, the men with hands shoved deep in pockets. I had not been back for four years, not since the death of Isabel, Tom's mother.

He was waiting for me on the platform, a long, tan riding coat flung loosely across his shoulders, and with the ends of his trousers tucked into boots. When we saw each other, he walked swiftly towards me, and seized my arm in welcome, then stood back a bit, as though to study me. "Welcome back to Ireland," he said, and smiled. He had kept the long moustache which he had grown in the army, but was otherwise clean-shaven, and his eyes were Isabel's, wide and pale blue.

We had seen each other last two years before, in Paris, and at dinner, after the opera, had sworn, the two of us, that Ireland had seen the last of us. In a student's restaurant in the Rue Bonaparte, a second bottle of Burgundy on the table between us, we had drunk to the decision, and in my liking for him, I had fought down a spurt of malice, for painting was a game which he could afford to play, young Lord Ardmor, with Chute managing the estate for him, and a thick book of cheques at his disposal, while as for me, I had only the four hundred a year and whatever else my pen might earn me. We had been in evening dress, of course, the only ones in the room; but the next morning, walking in the Luxembourg, he had worn a long jacket of brown velvet with a wide-knotted blue tie. "I know now what I want to do, cousin," he had said, his voice light and confident, and he walked with what he must have imagined to be an artist's negligent slouch; but the army had left its mark on him, whether he liked it or not. It was in the way he carried himself, held his head. Soldier and artist were gone here in Cork, replaced by an Irish squire, wider of gesture than would be his English counterpart.

It is a lovely ride, from Cork to Kilpeder, through the old market town of Macroom, with the mountains rising up on the horizon, and Tom drove with flair. He was always an excellent horseman, and I was not surprised to learn that he was master now of the local hunt. "Wonderful hunt country there," he said. "You know that. You remember when Father would take us out." I remembered. I am six years older than Tom, and I remember him, a small boy, beside his father, self-conscious, and yet with a precocious assurance, glances stolen towards his father for approval, the father seeming not to notice, a brusque man, heavily bearded, a commanding voice which almost bullied. He rode through life as he rode across fields, leaped walls and ditches, and he died before his time. I had last seen him in London, on his way to the races at Newmar-ket, and had given him a copy of my first book. It looked fragile and inconsequent in his large, mottled hands; he had taken out his spectacles, and, politely, turned a few pages. "Wonderful hunt country," Tom said, "and we are making it a decent hunt again, as it was in Father's day."

Tom reached out his long whip, and laid it lightly, skilfully, along the horse's flank. "You are indeed welcome, Lee," he said. "I cannot tell you how welcome." It was his boyhood name for me, and held memories.

"It is good to know that," I said. "Ardmor was always more to me than our own place, and now that Bert may sell out . . ." I shrugged. We had little in common with each other, my brother and myself, and although we both lived in London and had the same two clubs, we saw little of each other. Ardmor, in truth, meant more to me, as Tom did.

"Ardmor hasn't changed," he said. "You will see that. The gardens are the same. I am thinking of a ball next season. The county expects it. Difficult without a woman. But that will be a year away, and by then—" He stopped suddenly, and I looked over at him, but his head was turned away from me. "Look there," he said. "You remember the Rossiters? Old Rossiter still holds sway there. You remember Rossiter, Father's friend, fierce old tiger, fuelled on brandy." Behind the demesne wall, a thick plantation screened the house from view. I remembered, vaguely, a low, graceless barracks of a house, stables. Rossiter I could not remember at all.

"I'm damned glad I came back, Lee," he said. "Damned glad. I never expected—do you remember our toast in Paris?"

"Why did you come back?" I said.

The wheels, spokes yellow-painted, glistening, spun us along the Macroom road. The hedgerows were in their spring leafage, a delicate green; but the green of the pastures was already rich and heavy.

"I am not certain, entirely," he said. "There was no necessity, of course. Not with Eddy Chute here in the trenches. I've left the reins in his hands. It's his estate in a way, as it was his father's before him. He and the tenants are on excellent terms—a hard man but a fair one, and well they know it. But we work together, I am learning. We've turned the morning room into an office, and the two of us are in there for an hour or so most days. Do you have any notion of our rent roll? Ardmor is a kind of principality."

There was a nervous edge to his speech, as though he wanted to convince me of something, of some version of himself. Perhaps, I thought, that is why he brought down the carriage to Cork himself, rather than sending a groom. And then I reproved myself, knowing it to be an eager, casual mark of friendship. And yet there was something about him, about his manner and his dress—the rough riding coat, the heavy, dull-polished boots, the assertion of proprietorship. I imagined with difficulty Chute and himself working in harness.

"Do you know," I said, striking from an angle, "I can remember only one winter here—that Christmas I spent with your mother, when your regiment was marooned in India. It was a lovely Christmas—Isabel made it lovely: great logs from Clonbrony Wood blazing in the library, garlands of fir, a stream of visitors, steaming punch. On Stephen's Day, the peasants came round, young lads, dressed in straw. They were carrying a bird in a wooden cage, a wren, and they had an archaic rigmarole."

"Wren boys," Tom said. "They sing, 'The wren, the wren, the king of all birds.' It is all cheerful, but a bit frightening. Very old, and not native, I suspect. I think Raleigh's people brought it over with them when they settled Munster."

"No doubt," I said. Folklore is tiresome, morris dancing and letters from rural deans to *Notes and Queries*. Although late that night, in bed with a tumbler of milk punch and Florio's *Montaigne* as shields against the chill, I reflected that we Forresters, like the wren boys, were not native. We too had come over with Raleigh and Spenser, Wilmot and Mountjoy. Hacking out baronies for ourselves with cutlass and brand, knee-deep in bog water, slaughtering the native tribes, pushing them up into the scraggy hills. Our only signature upon the land a grotesque yuletide ritual, a bit of doggerel. The wren, the wren, the king of all birds.

"No doubt," I said to Tom. "But the brightness and warmth that Isabel brought to that Christmas was a flair of light in the darkness. Ireland in winter is wretched, do you not find it so? Treeless wastes, and the dark falling at four in the afternoon. Very little visiting between houses. The country closes in upon itself. The nights are long."

So, certainly, I had found it in my own boyhood, home from school, in that chill house in Midleton, a house without women, my father morose and devout, working his way through the Church Fathers, helped along by decanters of port, in the draughty library, and dear brother Bertie treating me as his fag. It was not a large establishment: a cook and a few slovenly maids, cowherds, a sullen, toothless brute of a gamekeeper. And stretching away from us, the dry, hard-packed winter fields, bogs, ice-coated pools.

Tom turned towards me and smiled. The smile broke through the new manner that he had shaped for himself, cut away layers of being—the army officer, the Paris lounger. He was once again, if briefly, the Tom who was, from first to last, my special friend, who is so even now, with the two of us old, and Tom in his curious exile.

"You have caught me out," he said. "I am here from spring to autumn, but Ardmor in winter I surrender back to Chute. I have kept the flat in Paris, and I venture south from there, to Italy. I have a special fondness for Venice in winter. Have you been there then?"

"No," I said. "In summer once," and I returned the smile. He had never, in those days, a sense of how privileged an existence those Ardmor rent rolls gave to him, to move about as he chose, which seemed to me the greatest of luxuries.

The road carried us, beside a stretch of the Sullane, towards Macroom, a town much like Kilpeder. Before us, I could see the spires of the two churches, and the battlements of the old Penn Castle. They are all much alike, those Munster market towns, shaped by landlords after the plan of English villages, but the plan never quite succeeding, a native wildness in the earth pushing itself upwards, destroying neatness. On market days, the peasants claimed them, driving in their cattle, the men in their long, muck-daubed coats, herding the beasts with willow wands, the heavy flanks of cows and bullocks pressing against shop fronts, overturning stalls, the trading people shouting out curses, and the public houses crowded, men with pints of porter spilling out into the road.

"I am still painting," Tom said. "I will show you what I have been doing. You will be surprised, I think. For a time, when we met in Paris, I feared that it would be an avocation, young gentleman uncertain of himself who takes up paint and crayon, a dabbler. There are hundreds of them in Paris. But now I know. I never showed you what I was doing then. Daubs, and I knew it. Not now."

I was pleased to hear this, but I could not follow the connexion of his thoughts. I said nothing.

It was not, mercifully, market day in Macroom, and we bowled through the town, down the road, divided at its centre by the island formed of market house and square, lines of shops and public houses, two hotels fronting each other, past the pretentious mock-medieval gates of the castle. We were observed by idlers, as how could we not be, the young Earl of Ardmor in his elegant yellow-wheeled barouche; but he seemed unaware of this, threading his way past carriages and donkey carts, handsome, his hair and moustache the colour of corn. It was of Macroom itself that he was speaking, but I was ill attentive, until we were safely through the town, with the road moving quietly past the demesne wall, a very long wall which seemed almost to be stretching itself to Kilpeder.

". . . and then brought before the magistrates," he said. "I am a magistrate myself now, you know. As Father was in his day."

As Father was. Landlord, master of the hunt, magistrate. As his father had been.

"I'm sorry, Tom," I said. "I wasn't really listening."

He smiled, in easy forgiveness. "I was saying that the Macroom landlords are having a few problems. Poor relations with their tenants—the old story. There have been a few ugly ejectments; the bailiffs now insist on being accompanied by armed constables. Last month a bailiff was knocked about by some thugs and left almost for dead. But we know who they are, it seems, and they will be brought up before the magistrates."

Beyond the wall, the Sullane was glistening silver beneath the sun of early afternoon, and the pasturelands were verdant. Beneath the wide-spreading arms of thick-trunked elms, cattle dozed or moved slowly, red-flanked. It was not only the dead, icy winter of this country that I remembered with distaste. I remembered ejectments and talk of ejectments in that airless, crowded library in Midleton, my own father and his friends. *Ejectment, eviction,* they were words with ugly sounds.

"They are a bullying lot, some of these Macroom landlords," Tom said, "and some are mortgaged to the hilt and have no choice in the matter. Things are better managed in Kilpeder. There has not been an eviction from Ardmor lands in the last ten years. Thank God."

Perhaps I should have pressed him on the point, but there was little need. The next few years would furnish me with a handsome if unwelcome demonstration of the relations between Irish landlords and Irish tenants. And not myself only. But in Ireland there is a heartbreaking discrepancy between its violence and the world which it offers up to the senses. These mild acres, robed in the warm, pale colours of spring, the air odourous, and the wide, pale sky, the clouds soft and indistinct, and the distant mountains purple, haze-bathed, a scattering of cabins upon rises, peasants in the fields as slow-moving as their cattle—pastel, a subject for watercolour, chalk. In a few years' time, journalists would be reporting as from a battlefront, their language lurid, splashed with blacks and scarlets. But the journalists were to come and then go off again, their notebooks crowded, knowing nothing, nothing whatever, of the land.

A curve of road brought the Sullane again into view, and Tom's eye brightened. "When you see that flash of river there," he said, "you know that the next bend will bring Kilpeder into view."

And so, in time, it did. The road rose as it bent, and of a sudden delivered Kilpeder to us, castle and town and the fields and woods that stretched out beyond them. Haze clung to them this day, although on others they would be, from this rise of the road, as clear as a child's toy world—the Castle with its lakes like bits of artful glass, the great house itself a toy, and the encircling wall, the shops and cabins of the town thrown together higgledy-piggledy. But despite the haze, the lakes glinted, and the spires of the two churches were distinct, severe in their separation from each other.

"Let's take the gate at the end of the village," Tom said. "Give you a peek at Kilpeder."

Small question but that Tom was a presence in the town. The labouring men, who had glimpsed the barouche, took off their caps and held them in the two hands, pressed against the chest, until we had passed them, and the countrywomen bobbed us low curtseys. In the Kilpeder of today, the Kilpeder of 1904, it is difficult to remember that such things used to be; and yet indeed they were, and not in Kilpeder alone. When someone has the power of life and death over you, you tend to treat him with deference, and to contrive some outward show of that regard. And the fact is that both Tom and myself took it for granted, would have looked upon a show of manly independence as suspect, sinister.

And yet the town seemed to have a life of its own, in which we had no part. The hotel had had a new coat of paint since last I had come to visit, a pale, startling blue, and its name was now proclaimed in an arch of gilt letters, "The Kilpeder Arms." Conefry's, the public house across the square from it, seemed to have been redone entirely, so far as could be judged from the exterior. It had once been a kind of cave, its outer wall pierced by two low, small windows, and a door about which darkness seemed to gather. But now, in the mode of Dublin and Cork and London, there was a front of polished wood and coloured glass, sheets of red glass and green, sparkling and inviting. Tully's shop still dominated that side of the square, and it seemed to me larger than ever, as though it might have absorbed smaller shops which once stood on either side of it.

As we passed Conefry's, two men came out from it, and stood stricken momentarily by the afternoon light; but one of them, recognising Tom, lifted his billycock hat. Tom lifted up his whip hand in response. "Considine," he said, "the Catholic surgeon." Irish country towns are furnished with two of everything, like Noah's ark—not male and female, but Protestant and Catholic: churches, clergymen, surgeons, solicitors, auctioneers.

Past the gates to the demesne, past the gate lodge, the long avenue, trees planted by Tom's great-grandfather, now shaggy-barked, long arms almost touching above the road. It was spring now, the leaves pale and translucent, but in summer they would be dark, and heavy, and the avenue kept in a kind of perpetual twilight, beyond which the sun would fall upon terraces, lawns, gardens.

Where the avenue met the circular, gravelled drive, he came to a halt, and said, "Let us walk to the house." We climbed down, and he tied the reins loosely to a post. The Castle was already in full view, a quarter hour's walk beyond us, and it was as though the haze was lifting, for the clear grey Portland stone of the façade was as bright as I had ever seen it, and the gardens, those round and oval beds which Isabel had planned with such care, were masses of spring colour, pinks and yellows and whites. Along the path farthest from us, between clusters of bloom, two peacocks picked their way, their spread tails just visible.

I heard a noise behind me and, turning, saw that a stable boy had appeared already, and was taking the barouche along a narrow path towards the carriage house. He was walking by the horse's head, a runty fellow with rounded shoulders.

"Your staff is attentive, Tom," I said. "Do you bully them?"

He laughed. "Not I," he said. "All that is Griffin's doings."

And Griffin, in fact, was standing at the foot of the stone steps to welcome us, beneath the *porte cochère*, as though he had been on the watch, as no doubt he had been. "You are most welcome here again, Mr. Forrester," he said, his heavy, pendulous jaw wobbling. He was something of a Forrester family triumph, a young footman whose skill at management had been observed by Tom's grandfather, and who, against all probabilities, had at last, in Isabel's day, become head butler, himself a grandfather by then, with four children in service to the family. Somewhere to the north, across the Limerick border, lived Griffin's kinsmen, and his voice retained a heavy Limerick accent, but in spirit he was wedded to the Forresters.

He flung open the hall door for us with a great, theatrical flourish, at once welcoming me, and presenting the house to me. It is the same house where now, more than a quarter century later, I write these lines, but the black-and-white lozenged marbles of the hall floor long ago lost their sheen, and the wide marble staircase is dingy now, its red carpeting frayed. In Griffin's day, there was time and staff and money enough for everyone. In the morning, one would encounter two housemaids kneeling on the stairs, and polishing the thin brass carpet stays. Ardmor Castle meant more in a way to Griffin than it did to us, for to him it was a magical translation from a cabin in a Limerick town which he never revisited, nor ever in my hearing mentioned. It is the sort of tragedy which is common when big houses fall, and yet it is never commemorated, "The Servant's Tragedy." Another possible subject for Mr. George Moore.

I had tea with Tom, and then went upstairs to rest before dinner. My room was always the same one, halfway down the long upper hall, a large, square room but sparsely furnished, with a splendid view of gardens, lake, river, the horizon of mountains. In the middle distance, the spires and slated roofs of Kilpeder. On visits in my childhood, Bertie and I would be crowded into the nursery with Tom, where, on ball nights, the sound of music would drift up to us, or an occasional, piercing voice. We would play games, Tom and myself invariably ranged against the world, with Bertie as an older, supercilious observer. But soon enough, Bertie and I were given a room of our own, with Tom banging on its door to gain admittance. Tom was the nursery's last child, for he and Sylvia had none, of course. It is in the wing of the Castle that Emily and I have sealed off, and I have no wish to visit it. I imagine it: the table and low chairs at which Tom would sit first with his nurse and then with his governess, the drawing boards and globes, an elaborate, extravagant hobby horse, by now sheathed in dust which, if scrubbed away, would reveal faded blues, reds, gilts. Tansie, the nursemaid, was Irish, a red-faced Protestant from Bandon, good-humoured and garrulous; but Henries, the governess, was the actual stuff of which governesses are made, daughter of a Derbyshire vicar who was the younger son of a baronet. Ireland was her place of exile, and nothing, not even an earl's palace, gave her solace. She kept a close, attentive ear upon Tom, ready to root out whatever Hibernian vowels he might have picked up from grooms or stableboys. Poor woman: she went on from Ardmor to a posting in Leitrim, near Carrick, moving deeper and deeper into the exile.

Between Ardmor and the house in which I myself grew up, the great contrast was one of space. Duhallow could properly, no doubt, be called an estate and Duhallow House a "gentleman's residence," but it was modest in size, bundled up upon itself, its rooms choked with the furnishings that my parents were forever hauling back from London and Paris. And when in imagination I would travel to Ardmor, or when I in fact would make the journey, its image in my mind would be one of immensity: tall airy rooms and the sweeping staircase, the ordered lawns and terraces moving towards the river, the scattered plantations, woodland paths dark and inviting, the hot, redolent stables, the deep encircling walls. This was in part the trick which the imagination of childhood plays upon size, but only in part. Ardmor was, in sober truth, one of the large estates of Munster, its own world.

Tom kept, I was surprised to discover, a formal table, even for the two of us, in the great dining room which I remembered from Isabel's day, with its Chinese wallpaper of white and emerald patternings, Manchu lords and ladies, stiff-brocaded, bending over small, arched bridges, pagodas, and in the distance, mountains not tumbling and savage like those outside the tall windows, but tamed, domesticated, a backdrop for civility.

The long sideboard was dominated by the wide, hulking punchbowl of silver which the Ardmor of that day had caused to be shaped in 1800 to commemorate the passage of that Act of Union by which Ireland and Britain were wed, becoming, at least in theory, one country. In many of the Irish big houses, you will come upon some similar memento of the Union, but few of them have the elaborate and swaggering vulgarity of the Ardmor Bowl. It could be argued that it was in very fact a swaggering boast, for historians have hinted that the Forresters were elevated from mere baronage by their support of the act. A wide mirror, with candle sconces, backed it, and the effect was a powerful one, at once impressive and amusing.

Tom grinned at me. "The tastes of our ancestors. People in London say that we are all too elaborate in these latter days. But there you are, judge for yourself."

"What people are those?" I asked. I sat quietly as Griffin and his attendant footmen served me. He brought to the task a perfected and highly wrought awkwardness, and the food, as always at Ardmor before Sylvia's time, was indifferent, slabs of burned beef, watery vegetables.

"Oh," Tom said, "people I have come to know. We must talk about them. We meet so seldom in London, Lee. That is strange. Cork, Paris."

"I know," I said. "London is my time for work. It earns Paris for me, Paris and Italy."

"*Etched upon Water*," Tom said. "A lovely book. But it could not have earned you many holidays in Paris."

"Scarcely a one," I said. "It sold a bit under three hundred. But the others, that's a different matter."

"The others," Tom said, with an embarrassed show of enthusiasm, but then halted, without words. It happens often, among my friends, and is a consequence of having friends who are more discriminating than are one's readers.

I extricated him by turning the subject with a flippancy, and brought him around, at last, to talking about his painting. He spoke in a way which was at once tentative and excited, and entirely without the affectation which I had noted in Paris. I wish greatly, and for more reasons than one, that I could remember with exactness the things he said. He was tentative, perhaps, because I had not yet seen his work, or else because the excitement was so much at variance with the country-squire role which he had assumed.

What he had to say was commonplace by the turn of the century, but was not then. Far from it. Those of Tom's paintings which are hanging now in the hall, which so stirred young Prentiss's admiration, would in the seventies, to British eyes at least, have seemed baffling and even grotesque, explosions of colour, curious perspectives, abrupt and arbitrary, subjects chosen almost by chance rather than design. So, I must confess, they seemed to me the next morning, when Tom showed me a few of them, and their predecessors, in his studio. And yet I have no reason to suppose than I am less responsive to art than is young Prentiss. Art, as we all know, has this extraordinary way of creating its own universe, governed by its own laws, and then drawing us into it, or so at least it seems to us laymen. I have been assured by those better able to judge that Tom was a true artist, and with an eye and a hand of his own. But that, finally, does not matter. What matters is the power that art exerted upon him as he spoke to me that night, art as a way of organising experience, colour, line, form, passion, intelligence.

"It must be the same for you, Lee," he said, "with words." And I assured him that it was, but I lied. Oh, at times, back in those days when I had serious literary ambitions, I might imagine that I had hit upon some felicitous correspondence of language with setting, with mood, and this would afford me a keen but transient pleasure. Nothing more. Nothing as compared with the emotions aroused in me by the setting itself, or by music, or starlight.

I envied him, but was also a bit frightened for him. It was as if he spoke to me of a new land, bright with parrot colours, streaks of light, plumages, and yet as he spoke, his words groped to find expression. Were I to set them down here, they would doubtless seem familiar, but hearing them then, it was as though he spoke from within some new revelation, some dispensation. He must have caught something of this from my expression, because he stopped short, and said, almost with hostility, "Enough of that, eh?"

"No, no, Tom," I said at once. "Don't misunderstand, I beg you. It is only that when a friend suddenly speaks seriously to us, we are taken off guard. I cannot tell you how greatly I look forward to seeing your paintings."

Mollified, he grinned, and was almost himself again. "See them you shall," he said. "Mind you, they are not yet what I have in mind, but they will give you a notion . . ." And then he was off again. I must confess that it became after a time a bit wearying, as religious enthusiasm does, or political fervour.

It was in any event something of a relief when Griffin brought out the decanters and a small cigar cabinet. Something about the brandy and port, the fragrant cigars, reminded Tom of where we were, and, by degrees, the landed proprietor came back, but still with that faint theatricality, as of a role which he was trying out, uncertain. It had been different when he spoke of art, of his art.

"Sometime soon," he said, "on the weekend perhaps, we should have Chute dine with us. He understands conditions here far better than I do. A cool head, Chute; the family has been fortunate."

"And a cool head is needed, I take it?" I said.

"Not for this estate," Tom said, "not really. But for the county, the country. There has been great worry about the prospects for this harvest. Not here, thank God, not in Munster. But above, in Connaught. And that kind of worry spreads, like wildfire. This country has not been the same, I suspect, since what happened in the forties. The peasants don't speak of it, avoid speaking of it, but it is rooted deep in the memory, a scar upon the land. It could happen again. I am certain that they never cease to think that. How could they?"

How indeed? But I marvelled at the ease with which we—all of us—spoke of the peasantry, of what might linger in its memory. Chute had dealings with them, and so for that matter had my father, a small landlord managing his own estate; but even they knew the peasants scarcely at all, save for the substantial farmers, the groundsmen, the servants.

Behind us, Griffin stirred. "Will there be anything else, my lord?"

"No, no, Griffin, nothing at all," Tom said. "You can go off to bed. Good evening, Griffin."

"Good evening, my lord. Mr. Forrester," he said.

They were Dutch cigars, slender and tawny, the taste sweet, aromatic. Occasionally, in London, I would buy one to smoke in my club. Always, it would remind me of Tom, times when he had visited me at Oxford, or once when I had dinner in his regimental mess.

"Do you ever miss the army, Tom?" I asked.

"What in the world makes you think of that? Good God, no. I hated the army—a foolish world, schoolboy rituals and appalling conversation. No, that isn't true, really. I had army friends, have them still; and there were bits and pieces of the life that I liked. Do you know, it's exactly like school: for a time it gives a shape to life, but after that it just isn't good enough. As though I were playing a role that I had outgrown."

"But now you are settled," I said, with a touch of malice that I had not expected of myself, "landlord and artist."

He recognised the malice, but did not respond to it sharply. "Just so," he said. "Such things have been known."

"Seldom in this country," I said, and, at the same moment, we both laughed. It had long been our conviction that Ireland, for all its loveliness, was at war with the imagination. Do you know, Tom had said to me once, in Paris, say Ireland to me, and I will tell you what I see. Hagglers at the Kilpeder fair, spitting on grimy hands to seal the bargain. A peasant driving home the herd. It is evening, winter, behind him a muddy road, leafless trees. A squire, alone in his parlour, half drunk, on the table before him, a bottle of whiskey.

"Ah," Tom said, light, protective mockery in his voice, "you will see. Ireland has never been painted. Not yet."

We took our cigars out onto the terrace. The night was mild, and there was a moon. Lawns and gardens were almost hidden, but beyond the plantations, moonlight glinted on lake, river, and, beyond the demesne, there were still lights burning in the town. The mountains were invisible. There was a faint, pleasant wind.

"Makings of a splendid painting there, I will grant you," I said; but he shook his head. "You could, in fact," I said, "make a vast historical panorama. *The Fenian Attack on Kilpeder.* Hundreds of rebels swarming around the barracks. Constables blazing away. The roof afire. Redcoats marching down the Macroom road. The Academy would hang it in a flash. Be a relief from those 'Siege of Lucknow' scenes, or else naked Africans with spears."

"I might," Tom said. "It isn't quite what I have in mind, but if you tease me enough, I just might. I could do it with accuracy, you know. The gardener's son was one of the Fenians. A few of the ringleaders are back in town. The schoolmaster, if you can credit that. The son of old Tully, the gombeen man. A solicitor, one of Tully's clerks, jumped up into gentility. All of them harmless, by all accounts. A year or two in English gaols put out their fires. I could consult them upon fine points."

"You could consult me as well," I said. "You seem to have forgotten that I was here."

"Good Lord," he said, "so you were. I had forgotten. I was away at Cambridge, and you were here with Mother. You wrote me about it. I have forgotten what you wrote."

"Nothing of consequence. It seemed then, from this distance, rather a scuffle than a battle. Of course, we could see very little, but we heard the rifle fire, and saw the barracks ablaze. And then, towards the end of matters, we could see the army cresting the hill from the east. I cannot even say that we were relieved, as the people at Lucknow were. There was never a sense of danger. I remember your mother standing, not here, but at the far end, in her morning dress and coat, and I can almost imagine a teacup in her hand. We had no sense of alarm, you see; it all seemed absurd. Even though there had been raids for arms a few weeks earlier, and there was considerable alarm among the landlords."

"Yes," he said, with a faint edge of disdain, "there would be. But how extraordinary that is. To stand at one's ease, upon one's own terrace, watching a battle."

"A battle in one's own town, if it comes to that," I said. "*Scuffle* would be a better word for it. But there were men killed, on both sides."

"Both sides," Tom echoed. "And what was their side? A republic, was that not it? An independent republic."

"So they said, but for many that was a formula of words. They wanted liberty. Freedom from England, perhaps from us as well. But they could not raise the country with such airy aspirations. In Kilpeder they managed to scrape together some fifty men. And this was one of the more impressive hostings. The fellow in command was a fire-eater. There is a ballad about him."

" 'Clonbrony Wood,' " Tom said. "Ned Nolan. He has become the local bogey man."

But what I best remember of that morning is Isabel, my aunt, standing beside me, her hair unbound.

As we stood there now, Tom and I, a light in the village went out, a star plunged into water. My aunt, I sometimes suspected, knew more than I would have wished of my feelings towards her. Or perhaps I did wish it, reading into our most innocent exchanges a dangerous flirtation. She was a clever and a virtuous woman. I would come to her for advice in problems of the heart. Of which, in those and in far later years, I was to have many. Nothing shocked her, provided only that it be given decorous expression. There was just that much difference in age between Tom and myself, so that I would see him in a fluctuant light, friend, cousin, nephew.

"And now they are all hard at work again," Tom said, "being whatever they were—schoolteachers, shopkeepers."

"Most of them," I said. "Not all."

Tom flung away his cigar, its glowing tip tracing an arc down into the shrubbery below the terrace, and rested his two hands upon the flat stone of the railing.

"I am going to marry, Lee," he said suddenly. "I would have written to you about it, but I knew you would be coming here on your visit."

He was in profile to me, and despite the darkness, I could make out his face.

"Why, Tom," I said, "this is splendid news. How could I have known nothing of it? Who is she?"

"We haven't made the announcement yet. I am very much in love, Lee, and I think she is as well."

"Quite proper, old friend," I said. "Quite proper." I felt a moment's awkwardness, as though now I played a role myself, the bachelor's bluff companion. "But once again, who is she?"

"You may even have met, may have heard of her. She is Irish, you know. Westmeath. But her people have a house in London, and they spend much of the year abroad. On the Continent. The Challoner family. They are distantly connected with Cork people, the Bowens and I think the Pendens. She is a great beauty. You may have met her. Her name is Sylvia. Sylvia Challoner."

He told me her name last of all, after speaking of her people, where they lived, kinsmen in another county. A lovely name. I must have started at the sound of it, for he swung sharply towards me.

"You have met, then," he said. "Sylvia could not remember a meeting."

"No, no," I said. "I would surely remember a great beauty with a lovely name. Why should you think so?"

"She writes a bit," Tom said, "she knows poets." Then in a rush of words, as though to shift the subject, "Her father is army, retired. Hubert Challoner. An early retirement. He is a brisk, humorous man; you will like him. The Westmeath lands are mortgaged to the hilt; no one will accuse me of marrying for profit. That is why they spend so much time abroad; the house is closed down. But they will be opening it for the wedding. And that brings me to my point, Lee. I am very much hoping that you will act as my best man."

I assured him that of course nothing could prevent it, that I would have felt hurt had he not called upon me, and all the while I was seeking out his eyes; but the darkness baffled me. The wedding was to be in late June, a bit awkward for me for several reasons, of which I said nothing to him. "A lovely name," I said again.

"Yes," he said. "I had best be on my guard. You are likely to fall in love with her, and you are known by reputation, you dog. Several poets have been bowled over by her, and they are not to be blamed. You will see."

"I am very happy for you, Tom," I said, and I was. There was an excitement in his voice which reminded me of his boyhood, when I had visited Kilpeder from Oxford, and he would be a schoolboy home from Winchester, liberated into the woods, the river, the deer park. And yet there was a faint wariness in his manner which I could not place. "Sylvia Challoner," I said. "You met in London?"

"I will tell you all about it," he said. "Later. We have an entire week before us."

I laughed. "From what you have said, that will scarcely be time enough."

And upon that note, we turned back into the house, and after a brandy in the library, made our way upstairs. Most of Kilpeder had preceded us to bed. The only lights glowing in the town came from its public houses. In the far fields and on the hillsides, one or two lights still burned.

Once, much later, it occurred to me as curious and perhaps even portentous that I first heard Sylvia's name spoken by Tom in the darkness of a Kilpeder night, as distant lights flickered and then vanished, with cool wind, faint and teasing, finding its way to us from the mountains. Even, indeed, that my memory of Isabel had prepared my mind for the sentimental. But then I was to have cause, in that later time, to search out glimmerings of Sylvia, anticipations, foreshadowings. Not a history of Sylvia, but rather a history of Sylvia in our lives.

13

[*Hugh MacMahon*]

It was in 'seventy, I believe, or 'seventy-one, that I commenced my custom of taking long Sunday hikes up into the hills. In those years, Bob would be with me more often than not, and often we would be joined by Vincent. But Bob was a busy lad in those days, for he was not only helping in Tully's shop but serving his required years as clerk to Cornelius Hallinan the solicitor, and, in such hours as were left to him, he was busy at the courting of Agnes Tully, who had returned from her schooling at the Ursuline convent in Cork, a slender girl with flaxen hair and cornflower eyes, as a novelist might put it, a graceful posture, and a quick, eager manner of speech. And yet the friendship which had long bound together the three of us was as strong as ever, and I believe that our Sunday tramps were a necessity for Bob, a way of getting his head clear of the smells of the shop, savoursome but heavy, and Hallinan's office, thick with the noxious smoke from the old man's pipe.

We were a custom of the town, the three of us setting forth after early Mass, stout sticks by our sides, and jacket pockets stuffed with bread, cheese, slices of ham, flasks. And almost always, before we were an hour's distance, there would be someone, on horseback or driving his gig, to call out as he passed us, "The Fenian chieftains!" "Are the lads risen up in Kerry?" he would shout, or "Jesus, will you spare my life, ye rogues and rebels!" For that is what it had come down to, a roadside jest. The awful months that Bob and I had spent in the hell called Pentonville Prison were behind us now by a few years, and we would speak of them to none save Mary, or to Vincent, who thanks to the wizardry of Emmet Bourke had escaped imprisonment, and was on that score a bit ashamed in our presence. And to the two of them, it was a softened tale that we told. It is not by way of rhetorical flourish that I speak of Pentonville as hell. The poet Shelley speaks of hell as a place very much like London, and I defer to his superior knowledge of his countrymen.

We were none of us yet the trumpery heroes that we were shortly to become. Time had not flung its shimmering mantle upon us; or, to speak more precisely, "Clonbrony Wood" and the other pothouse ballads had not yet been written. In Kilpeder, in Cork, indeed throughout Ireland, there was a patronising sympathy towards those of us who had been "out" in 'sixty-seven, coupled with the traditional feeling for all patriots, however misguided, who had fallen into the hands of the English. It was to this that we and several hundred others owed our premature releases, for stories of the barbarous and savage treatment meted out to us all slipped past the cold walls of Pentonville and Millbank and Portland, the beatings and the starvings, the special if unauthorised punishments reserved for the Irish, and Amnesty Committees sprang up. And yet side by side with such warm sentiments, the national temper being what it is, was a near universal conviction that we had made fools of ourselves, had risked our lives and menaced the tranquillity of the country in order to fatten the pockets of renegade leaders who saved their skins by turning informer. Ireland, with a smile and a sneer in the eye, to paraphrase the old song.

It was as though our deeds had sunk like rain into the earth. We took several times, on our Sunday rambles, the very line of march that Bob and myself had conducted, and I expected, perhaps hoped, that memories would prod at us and nag us, but it was not so. We passed the crossroads farm where the Gaelic-speaker had inspected us with savage neutrality, and the road leading towards Clonbrony, where we had heard the gunfire. All that we saw, we remembered exactly, and yet for neither of us did the scene have resonance. And this was as well, for we seemed, Bob and myself, to be settling down into respectable and quiet lives.

But for Vincent, matters were otherwise. For a time, at his father's urging, to be sure, he toyed with the idea of a career in law, and there were a few months when he and a rakehelly Limerick chum of his, Dinny Gilbert, spoke of going into some sort of commercial partnership, but nothing came of it. According to Vincent's embittered version of events, his share of the capital was at the last minute denied him by his father; but there was more to it than that, Bob confided to me, and Bob was in a position to know, having by now full access to Tully's ledgers and equally to Tully's hopes for his little dynasty. "He's a rum fellow, Dinny Gilbert," Bob told me. "I spent a weekend with Vincent and himself, above at his place in Askeaton, and twas on my advice that the old man withheld the funds. Mind you, we had a fine, frolicsome time of it—lashings of food and drink, a bit of beagling, and two nights the like of which you have never seen for wildness. But I would not trust Dinny Gilbert farther than I could hurl a forge. I made enquiries among a few commercial friends we have in Limerick City and friends at law, and what I heard was disquieting. Worse than that: he was never so drunk as he made pretence to be, which is the ultimate in human meanness." And was not Bob the shrewd lad, for in 'seventy-nine ruin was to stare Dinny Gilbert in the face, and he put a razor to his throat.

Vincent was a great one for knowing lads like Dinny Gilbert, and I believe this is why he was taken up by some among the gentry, that and his charm and his wittiness. At race meetings, Vincent was always much in evidence, brisk and ebullient, glossy hat tipped far back and cigar clenched, conferring when first you saw him of an afternoon with Lord Dunraven and an hour later with a stablehand and towards the close with a knot of disreputable fellows down for the day from Dublin.

"Friends we have in Limerick City" was the way Bob put it, meaning of course Tully and Son, towards which he had by now, and quite properly, a proprietorial attitude. He was no longer mere shop assistant in apron and rolled sleeves, a village boy having been taken on for those duties, but rather a kind of vizier to Tully, visiting him at close of day, after Hallinan had closed his office, and the two of them repairing to the small room behind the shop, the ledgers hauled down and opened. To speak of Tully's as it had become in these latter days merely as a shop was to do it an injustice, for Dennis's holdings in land and other considerations were now spread across the baronies, a patchwork of notes and mortgages, leases and lands owned outright and let to small farmers. Once Bob suggested to him that a map or chart might be of convenience, of the sort that estate agents employ, but from this notion he recoiled in a kind of superstitious horror.

The word was Bob's. "It is as though estate maps," Bob said, "belong to 'them'—and by 'them' he means the gentry, the Protestants, our betters, the Cromwellians, the other lot, however you want to term them. To surround himself with their badges and insignia would be to tempt providence. He does not put it that way, mind you, not even to himself, but there is the root of it. So long as it is but himself and myself, hunched together over the books, in that airless back room, then all is well."

It made sense. Indeed, beyond mere sense it accorded with my own notion of the Tullys as legendary creatures, possessed of instincts more certain than those of most men, a willpower blind as a mole burrowing underground.

But they were beings as fully of fact as of legend, and the Tully house, handsome and solid, its red brick by now half hidden by Virginia creeper, a fashion which had swept Munster, bulged with the evidences of their well-being: pianoforte and oil paintings; not one, merely, but two tea services of solid silver, shipped down from Weir's of Grafton Street in Dublin, the first set out to glint and domineer upon the sideboard and the second, so Vincent mirthfully assured me, wrapped in straw and stowed carefully away. The paintings, as even such country mice as Mary and myself could judge, were of a school of art known simply as "costly," and yet bringing to our northern and meagre island a sense of the great world beyond—skaters on a Dutch canal, red-cheeked and blithe; gondolas being poled along the Grand Canal, ruined grandeur to either side of them; a breathtaking panorama of the Alps, ice and snow stretching precipice after precipice towards infinity. They were windows, opening the world to us. Their frames were elaborately scrolled, gilded.

And yet I believed, both by common sense and by my sense of the Tully legend, that Vincent must have been a heart scald to the old man. Vincent, I believed in my innocence, should have been sequestered with his father in the back room, plotting and assessing, weighing and deliberating. But this was a mystery which delicacy forbade me to discuss with Bob, the accidental beneficiary of Vincent's harum-scarum ways. Plain it was that Dennis Tully looked upon Bob as a son, and that Bob was for this reason excused much, enormities even; for Dennis believed that Vincent would never have involved himself with the Fenians had it not been for the evil example set by his companions, Bob and myself. Yet in all other regards, or so it seemed to those of us who observed the drama, the son chosen by the old man was truer to family traditions than was the one sprung from his loins. It was a very long while, years indeed, before I came to a knowledge of how things stood between Dennis Tully and his son Vincent.

There were flashes, had I but interpreted them aright. I mind one evening, in those early years, after Agnes had returned home from the convent, when Bob and Mary and myself had been asked to supper at the Tullys. *Dinner* would no doubt have been the proper word for it, for there were lashings of ham and chicken, and a veal pie, and an enormous trifle, all of it served forth by one of the two country girls who had come into the Tully employ, in black with starched white apron. Vincent was to have been one of the company, but he did not appear, although the meal was kept waiting for him while Tully plied Bob and myself with more whiskey than was good for us, and while Mary made a valiant effort to chat with Mary Ellen Tully, a wan, taciturn creature, before turning with relief to Agnes, who was brimming with news of school life and the poetry of Mr. Browning, a writer of rare learning, it was held at the convent, although dangerously heterodox. "He is to be read in bits and pieces only, but some of the bits are gorgeous," she told me, whilst her father, for the fourth or fifth time, hauled out his great turnip watch and consulted it, and Bob studied Agnes uncritically, as though she had just now added literary acumen to the list of her virtues.

A place had been laid for Vincent in the dining room, and plate, silverware, and glass sat there reproachfully throughout the meal. When we were spooning up our trifle, he arrived. We heard him first, noisily opening the hall door and then walking towards us with heavy strides that were explained by his appearance, for he was dressed for the field, with heavy boots that stretched to his knees. Dark trousers of some sort had been stuffed into them, and above these he wore jacket and waistcoat of pale grey, stained and rumpled. He reached out a hand for a bottle of wine which stood near him, filled out a glass, and then sat down with us. It was clear to us all that he already had more wine than he needed, although at first his speech was unslurred.

"My apologies, Mother," he said. "Apologies, guests. Apologies, Father."

"We waited a time for you, Vincent," Tully said, "and then we sat down to our meal."

"Quite right," Vincent said. "Quite right." And said nothing more.

There was, of course, a silence after that, which Mary in her tactful way contrived to fill. Bob and I picked up from her, and the three of us chatted away, while Mary Ellen looked down at her trifle, and Dennis sat silent, looking at his son. Vincent, for his part, followed our remarks with every show of a polite attentiveness.

Then, of a sudden, he broke in upon us, to say, "I spent the afternoon with Jim Norris, Father. Walking the beat he has rented for his shooting. He seems a decent fellow."

James Norris was the ex-officer who had come recently to us as resident magistrate, a widower in his late middle years, and by all accounts as peppery as a curry, but, as Vincent said, a decent sort. I could not myself so testify: resident magistrates and village schoolmasters were not often in the same company, let alone ex-gaolbirds. Bristling beard and moustache, ginger flecked with grey, and heavy, orangey-coloured tweeds.

"That was pleasant for you," Tully said, in a voice midway between irony and wariness.

"Pleasant for me," Vincent said. "That was pleasant for me." He drained off his glass of wine and refilled it, holding it to the light to study its ruby depths. "And exhilarating for Jim Norris. Walking the stubble fields with a Fenian rebel, he said. 'Ex-Fenian,' I said, 'former Fenian.' But he would have none of that, slapped me briskly on the shoulder. 'Nonsense,' he said. 'If the call goes out, you'll be there again, Tully, me lad.' And as he spoke, he ran his hand along the barrels of the gun which nestled in his arm. But he was speaking in jest, Father. He knew, of course, that I am no longer a Fenian; he would never walk his fields with a Fenian."

"I should hope not," Tully said. "All that is over and done with. For the lot of yez." He jerked his head, to left, to right, so as to include Bob and myself.

"Under the bridge," I said. As indeed it was, so far as I was concerned, and Bob as well, more or less, although he had confessed to me that on the odd occasion he would send forward a pound or two, but as a sentiment only. We neither of us kept in touch with the organization, by now a furtive, pathetic creature, although still a hobgoblin of the Tory press. The Amnesty Committee was a different matter, in which the two of us were active, designed as it was to release from the prisons of England the many Fenians still within them, and still, from all that we could discover, in the awful circumstances which we had endured but for a brief few months. But then amnesty had the support of everyone, so it seemed, or at any rate, everyone in "our" Ireland, as opposed to "theirs." Dennis Tully himself had made a contribution of fifty pounds sterling, a prodigious sum, and several bishops had added their mites. The Irish are a generous people, when it comes to the support of lost causes and denatured patriots.

But for Bob and Vincent and myself, matters were different, and would be so as long as Ned was in Portland. There would every so often—every six months or so, let us say—be stories circulating about him. A batch of prisoners would be released from the prison, and would be welcomed in Dublin by the committee, a knot of men waiting for them in the grey, rain-streaked light of the North Wall, and then, a day or two later, a great dinner at Morrison's, or one of the other hotels. Ned would serve them as their absent champion, for he had become notorious, "Fenian" Nolan, sullen and unredeemable. Tales would be carried out, but would be denied by the authorities, that to break his spirit he had been cast alone into a cell, his hands manacled behind him, to eat like an animal from a tray set before him, and let wallow in his own stench and filth. There were others of whom such stories were told, of course—Rossa for one, and Dr. Corrigan. In the time of my own imprisonment, I was a stranger to such heroics, seeking to make myself as inconspicuous as possible, and I cannot in truth describe myself as worse treated than were the decent non-Irish housebreakers and footpads. But that prison is forever a part of my imagination: in sleep, its grey, cold stones float weightless into my dreams; I hear the nighttime footfall of a warder echoing down tunnel-like corridors. How much more dreadful must it not have been for Ned and those like him—hard cases, intractable.

And all this while, I held my classes, nodded in deference to Father Cremin and to Sergeant Dineen, the new man at the barracks, and in the evening stood at the pianoforte beside Mary, the globed light falling softly upon her face, her poised hands. And Bob gathered the law to himself, precedents and instruments, wills and conveyances, found time to walk out with Agnes, a girl for whom that rustic phrase was inexact. And Vincent had time for—for whatever it was that Vincent did: drinking, hunting, whoring, or merely, as now, thwarting and plaguing his poor stolid father.

"He suggested," Vincent said, "Jim Norris suggested, that I take a gun out with him one of these mornings, now that the pheasants are rising. And I had to remind him that I have a few years left to run on my bond, and cannot own nor discharge nor indeed set my hand upon firearms. The country has gone to hell entirely when resident magistrates must be called to their duty by Fenian rebels. We had a good laugh about it together, Jim Norris and myself. He is a decent old skin."

Whilst Vincent talked, he worked away at the carafe, which he had claimed as his own, pouring out a glass and knocking it back.

"You missed a pleasant meal," Bob said equably.

"Pleasant, you mean, because I was missing from it. By God, Bob, you have chosen the right path for yourself. You can carve up words as nicely as Emmet Bourke."

Bob shrugged. "If you say so," he said.

Vincent began to speak, but stopped, and wiped his lip with the back of his hand, a sudden, vulgar movement.

"Ask your pardon," he said. "Pardon, all," and rose to his feet, or rather attempted to, for he lost his balance. But in a flash, Bob was around the table to him, steadying him, and then helping him from the room. In embarrassed silence, we heard their steps upon the stairs.

"Ah, well," I said. MacMahon, the diplomat.

My eye rested for a moment, and unaccountably, upon Mrs. Tully, as she sat with her chair pushed back a bit from the table, and her hands at rest, nesting birds, in her lap. There was always about her face a grey placidity, the eyes grey and pale, and the cheeks, unlined for one of her years, pale. It was so now; but now, I saw, the eyes brimmed with tears which would not or did not fall.

Neither Mary nor myself ever came to know her well, nor did Bob, for that matter. Agnes and Vincent spoke always of her with affection, respect, and a faint embarrassment intertwined. She was one of the Dempseys of Charleville, a hard-bitten clan of shopkeepers and auctioneers. A few months after this dinner, when Bob and Agnes were wed, they descended *en masse* upon Kilpeder, the men ruddy-faced and plump-jowled, halfway between huckster and merchant prince, and the most of them with loud, blustering voices. Neither could the Dempsey women be described as downcast violets, for Dempsey men seemed to have a predilection for women large of bone, tall, gawky creatures, but full of energy and high spirits.

But our Dempsey, Mary Ellen Tully, Mrs. Tully, had no great resemblance to her breed. She was a pool of grey quiet.

Presently, Bob rejoined us, wearing an easy, social grin. "He's fine," he said. "He'll be right as rain."

"When the whiskey and the wine are drained out of him," Tully said.

"I am not so certain of that," Bob said. "He tells me that Norris and himself had a game pie at midday that seemed a bit off to him at the time, but he said nothing and ate up his portion out of politeness."

"Poor Vincent," Agnes said. "Ought we to send Biddy down the road to Dr. Considine?"

"Not at all," Tully said, quick, gruff. "No need at all. Rest is the best thing in the world for him. Twill smooth out the gut, and perhaps, should he wake up in the night, a touch from the black bottle."

It was not Hickey, the Protestant surgeon, who was Donald Considine's chief rival in Kilpeder, but rather the black bottle, which was kept in stock at Tully's, a villainous mixture, with a label bearing the face of an ancient and benevolent priest and a long list of the ills and abrupt seizures which it proposed to doctor. Quite effective it was, in many instances.

But there was no present need for either bottle or Considine, game pie or no, and from a glance that I saw Agnes dart to Bob, I could tell that she knew this herself. It was a glance and a half smile, bantering and provoking, the kind of language that courting couples share, quite different from the languages of marriage.

"God knows what ails that fellow," Tully said, speaking neither of wine nor of game pie. "Do you know, Bob? Hughie?"

"It takes longer for some to settle down than for others," I said, at my most sententious. "And they are the better for it, in some instances."

"Some instances," Tully said.

You settle down quickly enough if you are an apprentice schoolmaster with marriage in mind, or if you are a shop assistant from the back of beyond, youngest son of a small farmer. But what need, with an indulgent father ready to pour gold out upon fine clothes, hunters, the paraphernalia of gentility. What need, with Cork City but a few hours' ride distant, and Europe itself separated from Cork by but a mysterious and inviting sea.

Tully shook his head. "God knows, he will never know want."

There was tea later, served not as in the past, with the lot of us sitting round the table, but in the front parlour, with Mary Ellen Tully pouring out the cups, and Biddy carrying them round to us. The talk became general, and we put Vincent from our minds.

Agnes was prevailed upon to sing, with Mary accompanying her. She had a lovely voice, and the convent had trained it well. She gave us four songs, two from Moore's *Melodies,* and two from the operas of Donizetti, the lovely vowels of Italy flowering in our cold northern town, in the parlour crowded with its dark, heavy tables and chairs. They made a pair at the piano, Mary and Agnes, the dark girl and the fair, their heads inclined. Bob and I looked once away from them and towards each other, and the two of us smiled. Agnes, I thought, would be joining our small group, bound to Mary and myself by sisterhood, as she was joined to Bob by love. She had in those days a convent-bred pertness about her. It was easy to imagine her as the stellar turn at Saint Ursula's, with half the girls mad for her, and the rest raging with spleen and vexation. She had wit in those days, quiet but flecked with malice—a rare quality in women, I have observed, but a welcome one, a spice or relish against blandness.

Who could then have imagined what the future held in store for her, nor that Bob would himself be the agent of her transformation, who sat now bent towards her, hands upon knees? Old Tully, hands folded upon heavy paunch, Vincent for the moment forgotten, was well pleased with the world, the heavy face beneath the vast bald red-speckled pate soft and unguarded. Moore's *Melodies* wreathed around him, that delicate world of moonlit lakes, star-glittering night skies, an ancient, vanished chivalry.

Later, walking home, Mary and I paused, and turned round to look back. The lamps in the parlour were turned out, but the kitchen was still bright, where the two maids would be at work, scrubbing and scouring. My head was still crowded pleasurably with notes of music and perhaps a bit too much wine. Of a sudden, a light went on in an upper room, at first a soft glow, then brightness as the wick was raised, and there was Agnes, standing, I was certain, before a mirror which I could not see, her hand touching her hair. She turned then with a swirling motion and passed from view, as though dancing.

"Shame on you," Mary said good-naturedly, "to be peering at girls in their rooms, like Brendan Healy, who was thrashed by Mary Murphy's brothers."

Across the road from Tully's, empty and expectant, stood the house into which Bob and Agnes would move as man and wife—not in the exact sense of the word a present from Tully, and yet almost so, as Bob explained to me the terms of the lease which after a certain number of years would be replaced with a mortgage. "I prefer it this way," Bob said to me. "Tully had his ideas and I had mine, and this is the agreement which we hammered out. It suits me well enough and it suits him."

These rows of houses facing each other, seven on one side and nine on the other, the far end blind, and the roadway handsomely cobbled, were in those days what they have remained into the present time, the residences of our established citizens, those of them who did not prefer to live outside the town entirely, our solicitors and doctors, our auctioneers, and Conefry, our leading publican. To move into one of them from a room at the shop, as Bob would do, a gaolbird in however honourable a cause, a lad yet in years, an apprentice solicitor, was to make a broad leap. And yet the strange thing is that Kilpeder accepted it, even those who disliked Bob or were jealous of him, of whom there were many, as events years afterwards would prove. There was within Bob a blunt assumption of his worth, a casual confidence. On that night, the empty house lay there waiting for him beneath a faint, clouded moon.

That evening stays fixed in my mind, not because of Vincent's unfortunate performance, but rather because, despite him, it had been a warm, a solacing occasion. Our lives henceforth, I remember thinking, fatuously, would stretch forward peacefully and in harmony. Mary, although none knew this yet but ourselves and Dr. Considine, was carrying Brian, our firstborn, a source to us of great hope and wonder. And there had already begun to stir within my mind, as Brian stirred within her, my great ambition to gather and set down the poetry and the music of the

Irish-speakers in the mountains beyond us, and especially in the lost villages and townlands towards Kerry. I would be, I told myself at midnights, a Galileo, a Winckelmann, a Schliemann, carrying back to Kilpeder, as to Oxford or Padua, gems from the earth itself, that music of which Moore, for all his charms, gives but a faint shadow, and that poetry of which he knew nothing, locked within the perishing tongue of the Gael. And Bob, the Bob of my imagined future, would become one of the great men of our town. Of Vincent I was less certain, to say the least. And always there was the thought of Ned, in the pit where he had been flung. But he would be one day released, and before too long; was there not talk that even Rossa would be released, more implacable even than Ned, a catamount spitting defiance? And yet the future had a shape, or so I thought.

I remember that evening, strangely enough, more precisely and with colours more vivid than I do the wedding of Agnes and Bob, although that was a grand event by all standards, but without shape, although the marriage itself and its nuptial Mass were lovely, the church hushed and the altar banked with flowers. But the festivities afterwards had to my mind a clumsiness to them, a great mob of us crowded into the Tully house, which, big though it was, was too small for such an occasion, with half of Kilpeder there, and Mary Ellen Tully's people, and Bob's father and brothers, whom I had met but seldom, farmers, with Bob's own appearance of self-containment, quiet-spoken men with sudden flashes of sly wit. By nightfall, the party had spilled into the kitchen. I wandered in there myself, and discovered, against one wall, Bob's father and two of the brothers. They had struck up an acquaintance with a knot of farmers from beyond Cloneety, and they had all of them pints of porter save for a few with whiskeys. It was the usual talk of farmers, calculated to bore others to distraction, and yet in the sounds of their voices I discovered what I had been feeling.

A farmhouse is best for weddings, with the barrels of stout and porter wheeled in from the barn, and a fiddler to lean against the wall, the notes moving like quicksilver, in air heavy with tobacco smoke, the smell of food, drink spilled upon rough board or close-packed earth. A house too small perhaps to hold the celebrants, who stand chatting and drinking in the yard, and about them the natural world, the trees of summer, heavy-leafed. Evening darkens to night; voices thicken; the spirit, by spirits unchained, rises up; there is laughter, grace, clumsiness. A quarrel perhaps; a drift of insults, whiskey-fuelled, soon resolved. Song, alone or entwined with violin, almost unbidden, a sweetness piercing the air.

At the wedding feast of Agnes and Bob, all was meant for the best, and there was great good humour, but there was also a stiffness, a constraint. It did not touch them: Agnes was radiant in a gown of white silks and laces which would not have disgraced the Castle itself, her fair hair bound and coiled after the fashion of that year, and wearing her father's special gift to her, a necklace of interwoven gold and silver from which depended a fiery stone, intricately cut, and housed within elaborate gold, thin-hammered. "A bride of great beauty," I said to Bob, when we had a minute to ourselves, the two of us standing by one of the tall bowed windows which fronted upon the road, night fallen by now, and gaslight from behind us spilling upon the shadowy bushes of the garden. He smiled and nodded, and I touched my glass to his. There was nothing of the blushing bridegroom. He was a man with a foot poised upon the future, and he took in his stride the events of the day.

Looking beyond my shoulder, he smiled at someone, and raised his glass in salutation. "One of Vincent's chums," he said to me. "Sandy North of Buttevant. Vincent has done a grand task, turning out for us bankrupt gentry, scapegrace younger sons, the bastard sons of viscounts, as Sandy is reputed to be on excellent authority."

"You are a hard man, Bob," I said, "and on your wedding day at that. They are not all of them reprobates. Edward Chute is here to grace the occasion, and Mrs. Chute as well." I could see Edward Chute from where we stood, Lord Ardmor's agent, a short, plump man, his belly pressed against his waistcoat with demure, erotic urgency, bald-headed save for a fringe of red hair, and his round, full-cheeked face bathed in porter-stoked goodwill.

"Not one of Vincent's pressgang," Bob said. "Castle Ardmor has always done the decent thing. Sent along the estate agent and his good wife when the town's leading merchant married off his only daughter to his shop assistant. And we in our turn put up obelisks to them in the town square. The loyal tenantry." And all the while that he said that, very quickly, he was smiling towards poor gormless Sandy North, whose exalted parentage, so it has always seemed to me, was but romantic legend, although bastard he was beyond question and dowered with a small estate which he was frittering and gambling and whoring away. Bob turned towards me then, and it was his true smile, quick and mischievous.

It is always there in Irish life, the wrist's twist that flirts aside the decent cloth, damask or calico, and shows for a glinting instant the sharpened knife. It is not menacing at all, when you have lived your life with it. We would be lonely without our knives and our wounds.

"Well, well," I said. "The bold Fenian."

"Twas like a dream, Hughie. Not as it was, but as I remember it," Bob said. "Is that how you remember it?"

Beyond the window of leaded glass, starred by lozenges of colour, gold, ruby, emerald, the town lay lonely and deserted. A raggle-taggle few were no doubt abroad—casual labourers, stableboys, perhaps a few farmers wandering out from O'Hart's pothouse, whiskey-sodden. But respectable Kilpeder was within the walls, even Norris the R.M., and Sergeant Dineen from the barracks, in civilian garb, an ill-fitting suit of black worsted against which his powerful chest and shoulders pushed and heaved. No doubt they reported regularly on us to Dublin Castle, but there was little enough to report. Save, perhaps, that I might myself, two or three times a year, give a meal and a night's lodging to some scarecrow recruiter for the organization, some hollow-cheeked Paudge or Mick or Dinny, a copy of the oath tucked into an inner pocket, folded and refolded, fragile and dirty. "In the name of the Irish Republic, now virtually established . . ." They came in different shapes and heights, those emissaries of the metaphysical republic, but most of them shared—those of them who visited me, off and on, in the seventies—a fondness for the bottle, and most of them possessed the courtesies of the urban poor— Dublin, Belfast, Liverpool—low-voiced and sidelong, and an appetite on them, a bottomless capacity for cabbage and bacon, slabs of bread, cups of sugared tea.

"I am not certain how I remember it," I said to Bob the bridegroom. The barracks had been rebuilt entirely, within two months of the Rising, Government sensitive no doubt to its blackened walls, collapsed floors and ceilings. This new one was built to a larger scale and an entirely different design: yellow brick, rosy brick, blocks of solid stone, three storeys high, and at each corner a windowed turret, with a cap of slate. The four turrets give it a faint, exotic colouration, an imperial touch. Late one night in the Kilpeder Arms, a month or two after Bob and myself had returned home from our time of imprisonment, Vincent Tully unfolded to a delighted group of us, jars of hot whiskey on the table before us, his notion that the Ministry of War had confused two sets of plans, the one of the Kilpeder barracks and the other for a fort on the Afghan frontier. And now, he explained, our humble, dowdy barracks stands somewhere beyond Peshawar, puzzling the swart, mat-bearded Pathans. I laughed with the others, holding my glass, as Bob held his, in a hand rubbed raw by oakum and then callused over.

"Ah well," Bob said now, and gestured, with a hand again smooth and pale, an attorney's hand, towards the crowded room.

"You have my best wishes and my love, Bob," I said, "yourself and your lovely bride."

"Is she not?" he said quickly, the words tumbling out. "Is she not lovely?" His eyes sought her out where she stood laughing with two of her bridesmaids, lasses who had been at school with her. Later, when everything had gone wrong between the two of them, I would remember this moment, the quickness of Bob's words, and Agnes with the day's special glow upon her.

In more ways than one, the day marked the end of Bob's apprenticeship, for when they moved into the new house, it was as though he incorporated into his being some of its massy weight, brick and heavy-grained oak. As though he took possession of a kingdom, and indeed Dennis Tully seemed that day a petty sovereign, jowly head resting upon stiff wing collar, aureole of white hair.

A call went out then for Bob and Agnes to dance a measure, and nothing loath, he made his way to her, and took her two hands in his own. A space was cleared for them, and Mary at the piano, after an indecisive minute striking this note and that, commenced suddenly a mazurka, the notes, rich and silvery, flung into the room. Bob led his bride to the centre of the clear space, and without hesitation, one hand resting lightly on her waist, began the dance. It was a wonder to me, one of the many ways in which the Bob of those years had the capacity to amaze me. It was no surprise at all that Agnes had command of so genteel an accomplishment, but I had never seen Bob dancing save at crude rural celebrations, jigs and reels, athletic performances. Yet here he was, as assured as an aide-de-camp in Dublin Castle, light upon swift-moving toe, and Agnes following his lead, her head held slightly back and looking full into his eyes. I glanced towards Mary, but she was intent upon her music, her arched hands moving with swift certainty. They were alone within the cleared space, alone with the tumbling silver notes, and all eyes were upon them.

"By God, Bob," I said to him, hours later. "By God, you are a cool one." For answer, he opened to me his loosely closed fist, and there were four curved, shallow wounds there, where in his nervousness he had gouged with his nails the palm of his hand. He told me of how Agnes and Vincent had between them taught him the ways of polite dancing, training for parlour uses feet which had been shaped for barns and rude pastoral festivities. But that evening, you would never have known of such preparations, as the two of them moved and turned, their eyes upon each other, Agnes's face still and intent, a faint smile upon Bob's, touching the lips but not the eyes.

Thus it was with us in the seventies, in that decade of waiting, as some of our histories now speak of it, although it scarcely seemed so to us as we lived it. For a long while, those of us who had taken part in the Rising were content with what seemed history's humiliating verdict upon it, without even the rosemary smell of decent memories. It had come and gone, leaving scarcely a scar upon the land, leaving only a few score men locked away in English prisons. And when, later, a kind of cult of the Fenians sprang up, with banners and songs and shilling pamphlets, blurred photographs for tavern wall, the oleograph of the Manchester Martyrs on the scaffold, Allen, Larkin, and O'Brien, with "God Save Ireland" enscrolled above them, the three of them hands joined, their necks hemp-engirdled, above them an English sky, dark and rain-heavy, and beyond them an English mob, jubilant—all that seemed, to myself at least, a lurid phantasy, unconnected with reality.

Because reality was marriages, the birth of children, the teaching of mathematics, the keeping of shop accounts, furniture, a social drink in the Kilpeder Arms, and on Sundays, after Mass, a walk into the hills of summer, past rich meadows, quick-running freshets. The Rising was now less real even than fairdays and race meetings, the crowds pressed together, laughing and sweating, and from open tavern doors the smell of spilled porter. Once, I remember, I was one night walking past Grennan's on the outskirts, a shebeen patronized by casual labourers and the like, when from within I heard a voice boggy with porter roaring out that foolish ballad of Clonbrony, and thought, quite without vanity, that it was a song about myself I heard, an unrecognisable self, an oleograph.

Thus it is that history plays its pranks upon us; for in those years of the seventies, when the form of life seemed set forever, they at last released from prison Ned Nolan and the other hard cases, and we next heard of him a few weeks later, when he landed in New York, a delegation to meet him at the pier, and afterwards a banquet and the next night a great monster meeting at Webster Hall, reported not only by the Irish papers of New York, but by the *Herald* and the *Times* as well. The *Times* carried a print of him stepping down the gangplank, unrecognisable, bundled up in overcoat with upturned collar, but the *Irish Sentinel* displayed him on the platform of Webster Hall, with new-grown moustache, decent but ill-fitting jacket. Behind him, seated in a long row, were those who had preceded him, Devoy, Connolly, Lyons, Gaffney, and the others. His speech was applauded to the rafters, but it was not, surely, what they had expected. A short speech, which the *Sentinel* reprinted in full, without oratorical flourishes. Devoy made up for it, describing Clonbrony Wood as the one bright page in the dusty history of the Rising, and dwelling then upon the awful details of Ned's prison life. "Fenian" Nolan, the *Sentinel* called him, and the name stuck. It was a strange floodlit moment in his existence, between the darkness of his English prison and the obscure, murderous shadows into which he was to move.

"There you are, now," I said to Bob as we sat together in the snug of the Kilpeder Arms, the bundle of American newspapers spread out before us.

"Tis all over now," Bob Delaney, articled solicitor, said. "It was never over for us while Ned was locked away there."

"What will he do?" I said. "What can he do? He has no trade, only a few years of soldiering."

"His father's trade was oratory," Bob said, "but the son seems to have no aptitude for it."

" 'Fenian' Nolan," I said. "There could be a year of banquet dinners in that."

There was a bitterness to our jesting; it soured the lip of my glass.

Those were great days, the seventies, for sketches of released Fenians being welcomed, in Dublin or in Boston or in New York. Four from among the lot of fellows released in January 1878 landed at Kingstown at six of the evening of the twelfth, and Dublin went mad with excitement.

The harbour was illuminated against the dark of a winter afternoon, and, visible across the bay, bonfires on the summit of Howth, like the flames, as one paper suggested with blasphemy, which Saint Patrick had kindled on the hill of Slane, and bonfires to the south as well, at Dalkey. The *Freeman's Journal* had a sketch of the four of them leaving the mailboat, and it blurs in my recollection with the view of Ned in the New York paper. There were rockets set off, and no fewer than three brass bands, stretched along the length of the esplanade, to play "A Nation Once Again" and "God Save Ireland." But that was mere sample. When the boat train reached Westland Row, there were thousands waiting, and brass bands to the number of eighteen. The coach that drew the four prisoners to the European Hotel in Bolton Street was followed by a great mob, shouting but orderly. Night was full by then, and hundreds of torches flared and guttered. Three of the prisoners, as they had been until that week, McCarthy and O'Brien and Chambers, were soldiers who had been court-martialled in 'sixty-seven and sentenced to penal servitude for life. They bore the mark of the last decade upon them, their eyes deepsunken, and their steps faltering. The fourth man, prison-pale but handsome, a heavy moustache, muffled in a caped greatcoat presented to him by well-wishers in London, spoke for all four of them.

All this, of course, we read at the time, but my memory is refreshed by the pamphlet which was put out by the *Irishman*, reprinting its many columns of description, and the speeches of welcome, and the poems which were composed for the occasion. The oratory was lush as pomegranates. Major Purcell O'Gorman, member of Parliament, whom I met in later years, provided the juiciest—an immense man, almost spherical, and much prized for his speeches, although in private, whiskey-oiled, he could be blasphemous and obscene as a Turk. "You have made an offering of life and liberty on the altar of your country; and if by such sacrifices as yours her freedom has not been achieved, her honour has been saved, her manhood has been vindicated, and a fund of public virtue has been created amongst us which will yet redeem and regenerate the land."

"Thomas Justin Nolan risen from the grave," Bob said to me, reading snatches of O'Gorman with appropriate flourishes of voice and hand; and yet his raillery and my own concealed a craving that the words might be true, that the Rising had saved the honour of our people, and I think now that if a day, a year, is to be given to the passing of the Rising from grubby fact into legend, myth, a constellation in the heavens, then why not that winter night with brass bands and thousands in the streets, streaming rockets, and fires blazing on Howth and Dalkey? Never again would Irishmen take the field, armed, in their own land, and although we made but a shabby display with our scattering of rifles and carbines, our clownishness and poltroonery, we had for all that been in the field, had fired and been fired upon, had taken the oath. The Republic of Ireland, now virtually established, a lunatic phrase with its own lunatic nobility. Those lightly used by the Crown, cowherds and labourers, given contemptuous warning and sent home to their villages, and even those hundreds who, like Bob and myself, served six months, eight, a year even, came quietly home, into silence. But as the years lengthened, as years of grasses grew upon meadows where men had fought, the men yet in prison stood within a lengthening perspective of time, a reproach to our pacific years.

They stood together, the four of them, at a tall window on the first floor of the European, and for as long as they stood there, the crowd refused to disperse; so says the *Irishman,* which furnished an illustration: four men, indifferently distinguished the one from the other, a consequence of cheap and shoddy printing. Now, a quarter century later, the biscuit-coloured papers, brittle, crumble at my touch. Behind the four, shadowy, are forms whose identities can be divined, the organisers of the "tribute." Patrick Egan, John Dillon, James Carey, T. D. Sullivan— Fenians, members of the organization, respectable nationalist journalists and solicitors, and even, a blob of cheap ink, Charles Stewart Parnell, who had made certain that he would be present, travelling on the preceding day's mailboat, a mystery still, Wicklow landlord, aristocrat, Cambridge man, Protestant, fierce and inscrutable. If only that picture were more clear, for our lives for a decade to come would be shaped by those inkblots—a photograph, with every feature, every lineament sharp and distinct, hinting at character, perhaps even at fate. It would show certainly what was to be remarked shortly by others in the room: that two of the four men at the window looked wretched, pale and confused, their eyes sunken. That night, one of them, McCarthy, collapsed and died—as the coroner was to say, because of years of ill-treatment in prison. The other man, O'Brien, died a week later. They were buried in Glasnevin, but only the Carmelite church in Clarendon Street would receive their bodies, for there was still a ban against unrepentant Fenians, denied the Sacraments—hell, as Bishop Moriarty had remarked, being neither hot enough nor long enough for such miscreants, and yet national heroes.

The organization put McCarthy and O'Brien to good use, of course, with funeral processions to Glasnevin—the greatest, it was said, since the funeral of O'Connell, greater even than that for Terence Bellew Mac-Manus, before the Rising. The great competition for patriotic corpses had begun, which still continues in Irish life. Poor O'Brien and poor McCarthy—farm lads driven by poverty or restlessness into the British army, then, at night, in some Dublin kip near the barracks, given the Fenian oath, scooped up on the word of an informer before a shot had been fired, and shipped off to an English prison. In my own brief time, for what is six months but an extended holiday, I could tell in the exercise yard which of the prisoners were Irish. There was no talking, and we walked, three abreast, in a long oval, around and around, shaven-headed, for the first months, broad arrows on our jackets, properties of Her Majesty, and the lot of us looked the same—Fenians, footpads, sodomites, burglars. But the ones who got the warders' truncheons, pokes in the ribs, or the flat of the iron-hard wood slapped against upper arm, these were nearly always the Fenians. Why they so hated us, I cannot say, but it is fact. Long years of that O'Brien and McCarthy had, without conversation, without the Sacraments, and then suddenly, freedom like a sunburst, blinding, the shouting crowds, a bewildering, uncomprehended adulation, and men who must have seemed princes, governors or prison inspectors at the least, in frock coats and holding tall, glossy hats, praising them as heroes. Perhaps their hearts exploded.

They needed but to wait for a few weeks, a few months. They were forgotten soon enough, most of those Fenian heroes. From time to time, their names float to the surface, in letters from the States or in American newspapers: night watchmen in New Jersey, Chicago policemen. Not all of them, to be sure; not Devoy, not Rossa, nor Boyle O'Reilly, nor Ned Nolan. But most of them were chewed up by history and then spat out still breathing, like those survivors of the Light Brigade who until a few years ago were on display as Chelsea pensioners, long white beards cascading down crimson tunics.

Things were far otherwise with one of those four men. I study his blurred likeness, but it tells me nothing. To the contrary, I read into that faded ink what I now know of him, what we all know. In the comfortable warmth of the hotel, he has taken off the caped greatcoat, but the print does not show us the empty sleeve pinned into jacket pocket, the arm ripped off when Michael Davitt, a boy of eleven, was set to work in a Lancashire mill, child of the famine Irish, driven out from a Mayo cabin in black 'forty-nine, the stones battered down and the thatch set afire. He was to become famous throughout Ireland, and I was myself to meet and talk with him, for was Bob not to become a member of his party and Parnell's? But before that he had come here, to Kilpeder, at the time of the great boycott. He was by then already famous, although a scant three years out of prison, the man who, as the English papers said, "had set Mayo ablaze," never pausing to reflect that that blaze had been kindled in 'forty-nine, when a bailiff's agent set torch to a cabin thatch, and small children, Michael among them, stood watching helpless, their bits of furniture flung out into the road.

Now, in the now of that crumbling pamphlet, he is but a blur, and behind him, yet more shadowy, a blur among others, a committee, stands Parnell. Could either of them have achieved alone what they were to work together: a revolution? To say nothing of their effect upon our small circle in Kilpeder, in the strange years that were to open for us, with myself the only one left unscathed: schoolmaster, antiquarian, husband and father, watcher by roadsides, seated in parlour corners, shadowed.

An accidental triumph, that *Irishman* pamphlet. Davitt is there, and Parnell, Dillon and Sexton, who were to become Parnell's lieutenants, Biggar from Belfast—humpbacked Fenian, Fenians and moderates, joined for the occasion. In the far background, too unimportant as yet to be given pride of place, stands James Carey, beefy and walrus-moustached, could we but see him, member of the Corporation, master builder and speculator, who in a few years' time, disgusted alike with moderate and Fenian, would conspire to send the Invincibles out into the streets of Dublin with revolvers and derringers, into the Phoenix Park with long surgical knives to cut down Cavendish and Burke, Chief Secretary for Ireland and Undersecretary. All there, all within the shoddy *Irishman* sketch, indistinct. It lacks nothing, that sketch, to make it all-inclusive, save that one essential of every proper Irish enterprise, the informer, the betrayer. Ah, but there is one, you will say: for did not Carey, at the heel of the hunt, do double duty, first helping to organize the Invincibles, then helping to set them to murder, and at the end turning Crown witness to swear their lives away? What better can one do than that? But wait! The editor of the *Irishman* brings his text to a ringing close: after a dark night, he tells us, the first colours of new dawn touch our Irish hills and rivers, our rich pasturelands. And signs his name, the signature itself reproduced—broad, confident black ink, loops and swirls: *Richard Pigott, Proprietor.* Take your choice of Judas, Carey or Pigott, depending on your politics; two scoundrels for the price of the one pamphlet, a bargain even by Irish terms. But the signature is a nice symbolic touch, eerie portent; for it was by forging Parnell's name that Pigott would at the end of things, almost, seek to link Parnell, once his chief, with the Phoenix Park murders, those slashing knives.

How the pamphlet came into my hands, I cannot say. Perhaps I bought it in Cork, or perhaps Bob did and passed it on to me. But I will swear that it made no great impression on us at the time. What was to happen happened so suddenly, so it seemed to most of us. Davitt, to be sure, had had his seven years in prison to think things out, to make plans for the movement. And Parnell—but who has ever contrived to read his mind, then or later? His star had begun to rise: we would shortly speak, in all seriousness, of Parnell's star, as though he had made a compact with fate, with the zodiac. For a full year now, he had been in control of the Home Rule party, having thrust aside poor decent, gentlemanly Isaac Butt, who had defended Ned Nolan at the trial. All this we were aware of, those of us who read newspapers, and we knew also that he had earned the wrath of the House of Commons, Whig and Tory alike, by obstructing its business, night after night. The terms that were used about him in England were outlandish in their extremity—"cad," "bounder," "renegade," "savage hater of his kind"—and delightful to Irish ears. We knew that he was accounted, and accounted himself, Irish, but was not Irish as we were, his accent English and aristocratic, and his manner slouching and negligent, assured and almost arrogant. "An English sword, shaped for an Irish purpose," Davitt said later of him.

Davitt wasted no time. When once McCarthy had been decently buried—or indecently, depending upon your view of these patriotic carnivals—he was off to Mayo, which he had left as a child of four, with the train making stops at each station, that he might be acclaimed—Ballyhaunis and Claremorris and Castlebar, with the reception being organised by Fenians in each of these towns. At Castlebar, there was a great torchlight procession, and a host of men and women accompanied him the next day to the field where in 1798 the Mayo men and the French who had come over to fight by their sides defeated General Lake and his redcoats. All this was reported in detail by the *Connaught Telegraph*, and copied a few days later by the *Examiner* in Cork, and no doubt by the Dublin papers as well. It is curious the way attention was so fixed upon Davitt; for at that time there was little, one would have thought, to mark him off from other released Fenians. At the time of his arrest, in 1870, he had been a young fellow of twenty-four, a procurer of firearms for the organization, quick-witted and resourceful, but of no more consequence than a score of others. It was in prison, so he was often to say in later years, that he worked out the plan of campaign which he was shortly to launch; but nothing of that was known in the first days. And yet it was upon Davitt that eyes were fixed in those winter months of 1878, as though everyone sensed that he knew what was about to happen.

Whilst he was in Mayo, so the *Connaught Telegraph* tersely reported, he visited his ancestral home in Straide, or rather the site where it had stood. It was a brief paragraph. Years later, in Dublin, on the one occasion when ever we sat together, he described the visit. It was in Morrison's Hotel, in the smoking room, Bob and I sitting on either side of him, the two of us with glasses of port which Davitt had insisted upon for us, but Davitt himself nursing a tall ginger beer. He was more gaunt in life than in his photographs, the eyes deep-sunk within a narrow face, and the skin, above a black, close-cropped beard, taut over cheekbones. In all the years that he had travelled with it, he had never grown easy, so it seemed to me, about the empty sleeve, neatly pinned or sewn into its pocket. When he talked to you, he would twist in his chair, thrusting the good shoulder towards you.

"Yes," he said, "yes indeed. A visit to the family home, an affecting moment."

The smoking room was crowded. It was a popular hotel, favoured by Home Rule politicians and Land League agents up from the country, and by auctioneers and commercial travellers as well, loyalists and nationalists cheek by jowl. A month later, they were to arrest Davitt here for violation of his parole, and two months later the police were to come here for Parnell. Walnut and leather, the air thick with cigar smoke, sporting prints on the wall.

"Yes indeed," Davitt said. "My visit home."

Straide is but a hamlet on the road between Foxford and Castlebar, a scattering of small holdings, a crossroads, a huckster's shop and public house, a church. And an old abbey, Straide Abbey, roofless, with a few handsome tombs. He went there on a cold, clear morning, travelling by sidecar, with two other cars following. Uncles met him there, cousins. Beyond the abbey, where his house had been, and the houses of neighbours, the fields stretched bare and unmarked. Davitt and his Uncle Patrick walked across hard, close-packed earth. "It would have been here, almost," Patrick Kielty said; "when you faced the morning sun, the abbey was behind your left shoulder. I mind giving your father a hand with the harvest, in the last good year." "They tumbled the walls," Davitt said, "but surely the stones would still be here." He had been four then; he could not remember it. "For a time they were, of course," Patrick Kielty said, "but the landlord used those stones, and the stones from the other evicted houses, to make the new boundary walls." One of the walls ran along the road, towards the church. Some of those stones, perhaps, Davitt thought. Kielty stamped his boot. "Do you feel here," he said, "where the earth is uneven? The house might have been here, where we are standing." "The landlord," Davitt said, "Knox of Ballycastle. I mind my father speaking of Mr. Knox, of Ballycastle." In the ugly Lancashire city of looms and factories, where a boy of eleven had lost his arm. "Not Mr. Knox," Kielty said; "he's long out of it. The town belongs to Mr. Joynt now, an English gentleman. And that poplar there, I remember that. This is the place, Michael." The poplar's branches were spindly.

Davitt walked down the road to the abbey. Winter-brittle weeds choked the pathway. Clear light, cold, fell from slender windows in the north wall, and beneath the windows a magnificent tomb, ornately carved, the Magi, Christ displaying His five wounds, a kneeling bishop. Bits of broken statuary lay about the chancel floor. Davitt's father had spoken of the abbey. "The Jordans of Exeter built the abbey. In the thirteenth century. English people they were, a class of English that is called Norman."

A class of English, from Jordan of Exeter to Mr. Joynt of Godknowswhere, moving in quick after the famine, attracted by the bargains set on display by the Encumbered Estates Act. And now, in Davitt's first winter of freedom, Mayo was again on the edge of famine, a bad harvest in 'seventy-seven and a worse in 'seventy-eight.

"You don't know what famine is like, either of you," Davitt said, nodding first to Bob and then to me. "I scarcely do myself, an infant in long dress. I was told about it later, over and over. We had nowhere to turn. The neighbours fed us for a week or two, first one cabin and then another, but they were themselves hard-pressed. In the heel of the hunt, we walked to Swinford, to the workhouse. The youngest of us was two months, and my mother and sister took turns carrying her. My father walked ahead. He would speak to no one. I seem to remember that a bit, the long road to Swinford. We sought admission to the workhouse, but there was a regulation that if a lad was above three years, he must bide with the men. My mother seized hold of me, and swore she would die first on the roadside, and my father could not gainsay her. We were one hour in the Swinford workhouse, and twas a great shame in the family. We would speak of it together, in the cottage in Haslingden, but never to a stranger."

He snapped his fingers at a passing waiter. "A pot of tea, if you please, and a round or two of sandwiches would go well, this time of night. Some ham and some chicken; mix them up."

"Yes," the waiter said, "straight away, Mr. Davitt, sir."

Suddenly Davitt began to laugh, and setting down his glass, he slapped the flat of his hand on the table. "But only in Gaelic. We would only speak of our disgrace in Gaelic—our own tongue, but fit only for misfortunes, dirt, shame. By God, I hold it no shame. The shame is upon a land that will put women and children upon the roads, homeless. It was as well for us, perhaps. There are six hundred buried in a mass grave in the fields beyond Swinford workhouse, and naught but a plaque to mark the scene," he said. "You have seen famine or something close to it, in your own county. It is one thing to see it, and another to have no food, to see children of your own and they starving. It was the sight that my father and mother saw, before they saw Liverpool. Mind you, to write down what has been seen so that all may feel it. It is a rare gift."

He put his hand on Bob's forearm, for it was Bob he was speaking of, whose accounts in *Christmas in the Boggeraghs*, in that winter of 'seventy-nine, had been given wide circulation by the League.

Bob shrugged. "Hughie here was with me, and indeed the fine literary touches, as you might call them, were stuck in by Hughie."

I did not gainsay him. Bob had a forceful, driving style when he set pen to paper, and a lawyer's gift for marshalling arguments and facts. But you would not be inclined to call him a *belle-lettrist*. It was the grim and unforgettable chronicle of those mountainy wretches driven week by week farther towards starvation which made the articles a sombre wonder, and all that was of Bob's composition, as was the battering indictment of Bartholomew Colthurst, the landlord of those barren hillsides. The descriptions were mine, stuck in at Bob's request—the bleak, wintry horizons, the mud cabins within which families huddled gaunt and ragged, the bailiffs and emergency men with their battering rams. What I had brought back with me from the dreadful day that we had spent in the Boggeraghs was a pedlar's bundle of colours, odours, noises, the sense of a misery and despair deeper than words. But if men were roused to anger by the articles, it was surely by Bob's hard proof that the system by which land was held could on occasion be a form of persecution and manslaughter.

"I remember those fine literary touches," Davitt said. "Perhaps you have missed your calling, Mr. MacMahon."

"I have not," I said, shaking my head. "I was shaped by nature to be a schoolmaster."

"With time out for a rising and a term in prison."

"A few hours of the one," I said, "and a few months of the other. That glutted my appetite for heroism."

"I can believe that," Davitt said. What must they have been like, those seven years served out of a sentence of fifteen? Unimaginable. A mechanical existence—slops, iron bars, shuffling gait of the exercise yard.

"Two years ago," Davitt said, "in 'seventy-nine, when the League commenced, we were hard-pressed for intelligent men, resourceful men, to act as agents. Recruits like Bob here were rare enough in those days. Tis far different now. The League is on the move; we are an organization more feared by the English than ever O'Connell's Association was. And, what is more to the point, feared by the landlords, as O'Connell never was, a landlord himself, and solicitous of their well-being, for all his brave words."

"Mr. Parnell is himself a landlord," I said, trusting that my tone was a mild one, "with fine farms and rolling pasturelands above in Wicklow."

"He is," Davitt said, unperturbed, "but he has not swerved a jot in his fight for the tenants and the small farmers. There is one difference between Parnell and O'Connell, and I could name others."

It was a fair answer.

We are a curious people, as has been remarked often. The very cornerstone of the movement which Parnell and Davitt had hammered together, the two of them, fox-hunting gentleman and Fenian gaolbird, was that of war to the hilt against the landed proprietors, and yet was not Charles Parnell himself Parnell of Avondale, the master of broad acres, in the newspaper phrase, carved out by a Cromwellian's sword? And this delighted us, if truth be told. A race of snobs, every last one of us, from the hedge poets and strolling harpers of the eighteenth century, fawning before their new English masters, to the leader writers of our patriotic press. Davitt was one of us, but Parnell was apart, remote, cool.

"My point, Mr. MacMahon," Davitt said, "is that the Land League has no shortage of helpers in these latter days, but I have a preference for men I can be certain of, men like Bob here, and men of whom Bob is certain."

"I take your point, Mr. Davitt, and I am honoured by it," I said. "But I have had my full share of public life, my few hours and my six months. I wish you well and I wish your cause well. When a hand is needed in

Kilpeder to carry a torch for a League procession, or to help with the scaffolding at a meeting, you can depend upon me. But there you are."

"Yes," Davitt said, and smiled with courtesy, shrugging his good shoulder. It was as close as I was to come to great events in those early triumphant years of the League, although later Bob would again find a use for me.

But that night was in the great, rousing years of the early eighties, which none of us in the seventies—in the years when the children came to Mary and myself, in the years of Bob and Agnes establishing themselves, and of Vincent's colourful, disreputable adventures—none of us anticipated. But there now is one of those tricks which history plays, not upon ordinary people but upon historians. I have noticed it in Patrick Prentiss. In the history books, whether of the national or of the loyal persuasion, the seventies are spoken of as the quiet years, the silent years, the years of preparation, or some such rubbish; for historians are hostile as though upon instinct towards quietude, silence, seasons, the stars. For them, the League, the boycottings, Parnell's coming into command, the land acts, the final explosion into bitterness and division, the melancholy aftermath—such concerns are the stuff of history.

And yet, looking backward, I see the slow seed time of the seventies. We all see, perhaps, what we want to see. Bob, I think, was a man unburdened by history, quick and brisk, ready to decide and to act. Ned, too, believed that he had flung history aside, but he had not; it dogged his steps, a mongrel, sharp-toothed and slavering. It is fellows like myself, perhaps, quiet men who have made no covenants with history, who live most fully within it, and it is the quiet times, the silent decades, that we savour: the growth of children, the entanglements year by year of our outspreading memories, unpruned.

Thus, were I to look back upon the decade, the great event leaping before the screen of recollection would not be brought to me by newspaper or pamphlet, would not point, save ironically, towards the future. It would be the return to Ardmor Castle of Thomas Forrester, Lord Ardmor, with his lovely bride, Sylvia Challoner. They had been awaited for days, and word was sent ahead that they were taking the coach road north from Cork, having landed the night before in Queenstown.

Their tenants had built bonfires along the ridges, high above the road as it leads into Kilpeder, and when the coach was sighted, at a distance, the fires were lighted. It was not quite night then, but the pale far edge of the evening, and the flames burned pale against the sky. From my parlour window, looking beyond Saint Jarlath's, I could see two of the fires, rising high and narrow as a sharp breeze took them. Curious that a few of the Ardmor tenants had been Fenians, on the run in those hills, and now their brothers were tending fires of welcome for a landlord's bride. I stood by the window for what must have been a long time, walking once into the kitchen to tell Mary what I was about, but she declined to join me. Returning then, and watching darkness fall, the first lights lit in the town, and the hillside fires fierce, red, leaping.

Presently I heard shouts, and walked outside my door and down the path. The Ardmors were arriving, of course, by the west road, and would not be passing my door. Half the town, at least, had hurried down to the gates, and stragglers were now afoot to join them. I myself walked a bit of the way, that I might have the gates in view. There were fellows standing outside the doors of Conefry's, pints of porter in hand, and shawled women, in their twos and threes, laughing and chattering, walked past the shops. At the far end of the square, at the gates, where the crowd had gathered, were lighted tar barrels, casting upon the scene lights at once lurid and festive. A sense of position held me tethered: not for schoolmaster, any more than for auctioneer or solicitor, to swell a progress, although I wished them well, bridegroom and bride, whose presence was now, at that moment, marked by a shout from the people at the gates, and a moment later, I could see the carriage itself, an open carriage despite the chill of the evening, and the two tall-hatted coachmen. The two seated figures were indistinct, tarry flames creating a flickering illusion of greys, roses, shadows.

Through the gates the coach trundled, and into darkness, although, far off, where the rise of the park moved towards the castle, above river, above plantations, terraces, light fell from tall, distant windows. There was nothing left to be seen by the watchers at the gate, but they seemed reluctant to leave, lingering by tar-barrel warmth, their voices, jovial, floating back towards me.

It was a fairy-tale hour. From Perrault, perhaps, rather than Grimm, and not text but tall-volumed engraving: past peasants, past castle gates, through enchanted woods, dark, mysterious, a young nobleman bears homewards his lovely bride. So it seemed to me, but surely did not to Lord and Lady Ardmor themselves, nor to the sensible townspeople of Kilpeder, welcoming a bit of frolic, torches and tar barrels, beacon fires on the hills, and no harm done if a shout for the landlord were thrown into the bargain. It would be different in a half-dozen years, when the Land War was upon us, and fellows standing this night at the gate, bawling their lungs out, would indignantly and honestly deny that ever they had cheered so showy an instrument of oppression as the Earl of Ardmor. Their fathers, perhaps, or their grandfathers more likely, obedient serfs. But not them. Such are the ways and uses of memory. Although it would be more difficult for them to expunge from recollection's slate the great festivities of a few weeks later, with the barns thrown open for dancing, and barrels beyond number of porter and stout, and all the grounds of the Castle free for the people of Kilpeder to wander about in, the deer park and the river walk, and the gravel paths of the terraces and the ornamental gardens themselves, which had been the pride of the old countess, much remembered and loved. The shadows of a late spring afternoon darkened slowly, the heavy-branched elms of the river path stretching across darkening water, and the air filled with voices. In the barns long tables groaned beneath hams and chickens, cakes thick-coated with icings, slices of barmbrack slathered with butter. At night, after the dancing had commenced, the Earl and his countess came out upon the library terrace, where, their being seen, a great shout went up, and the dancing was suspended, dancers and musicians rushing out, standing upon the lawns, black by now save where made bright by splashes of light. The Earl splendid in evening dress, and his lady seeming, as more than once in those years she did, as queens are imagined to look in—as I have said before—fairy tales. One of the fiddlers began then to play, an air which I could not recognise, amourous and clinging, and so enticing, so skilful the musician's art, that all other sounds ceased, save for kitchen clatter. The notes floated up towards husband and bride, floated towards tree-branched river, smooth-grassed deer park where, invisible, slept Kilpeder's famous herd.

Presently, there being nothing more to see, the townspeople turned away from the demesne gates, falcon-guarded, and made their ways home. As I did myself. For a while I sat reading; it was, as I remember distinctly, the spring and summer that I made my way through all of *Don Quixote*, all seven volumes of it in the set which I had found, a great bargain, in Cork City, in the translation by Motteux, the pages uncut, the paper of excellent quality although yellowed a bit at the edges, and an engraving prefacing each volume, the mad skinny knight, dagger-bearded, and his shrewd, clownish servant, in some new, ludicrous misadventure.

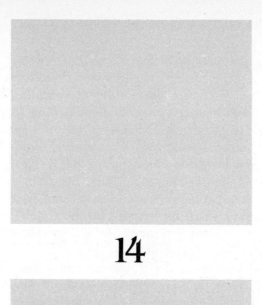

14

[*Lionel Forrester*]

I was visiting with the Emersons, in Limerick, when the note from Tom came to me, that they were back from Italy, and would be expecting me at Kilpeder. They had been away far too long, for my tastes, but we had several times missed each other narrowly, in Paris once, and in London, and I had been staying in Venice but a week before their arrival there. Tom wrote to me from Venice, a long, inconsequential, charming letter. They had taken the Casa Donati, which I knew well—its exterior at least: a gaunt, battered, attractive house on the Canal, just at the bend below the Rialto. He sent me sketches he had made, standing on their balcony: the *palazzi* across the Canal, gondolas, a distant glimpse of the Salute and the Custom House. The usual stuff of Venetian pilgrimage, no doubt, but all done in that new manner of his—swift impressions, puzzling at first, pen darts and blobs of ink, but then becoming clear, precise, but never, deliberately perhaps, vivid. I have saved them, somewhere, the Lord knows where. They were in love with Venice and with each other, Tom wrote.

There was a sketch also of Sylvia, this one in watercolours, not ink. She is standing on the balcony, in a salmon-coloured gown, cut low, but with a mantle of white lace flung over her shoulders, and she bends forward, both hands resting upon the marble railing, looking across the water, down the length of the Canal. It is late afternoon, so one would judge, slanting sunlight colouring water, stone, stucco. The technique which Tom used is by now a commonplace, but it was novel then—bold blocks of colour poised against each other. Even this sketch, an hour's work, perhaps, as he sat beside her on the balcony, has the energy of an argument. I do not speak from memory, for this sketch is not God knows where, but framed, hanging in my bedroom. Her face is half in shadow, half in the heavy, Venetian light.

I made my excuses to the Emersons, and hurried down to West Cork, the Emersons perhaps not all that unhappy to see me off, for I had been with them almost a fortnight, working with Jack on the small yacht which he kept at Kilrush, sailing her past Scattery Island, past Carrigaholt and Killbaha, and beyond the Shannon into the Atlantic. I felt light, unburdened, weightless; Jack is a skilful sailor, and there was little for me to do save haul on a line when he shouted to me. Passing out of Ireland and onto the open sea in that way is a curious experience. Looking back, towards Loop Head and Kerry Head, the country's intense green comes almost as a shock. Returning, if evening has come—an evening of mist and tenuous, frayed fog—the light at Loop Head seems a blurred luminescence, soft and welcoming. I was careful not to expound upon this to Jack, a hardheaded excise man who regards art and poetry as rubbish.

One of the Ardmor Castle traps was waiting for me at the railway station, and a leathery, taciturn groom named Leahy, his boots and top hat dusty and his dress negligent. He had brought with him sandwiches and a bottle of Sancerre, packed in a hamper. A note, tied to its wicker handle, said, "Welcome home to Kilpeder. Love, Sylvia."

And at the Castle itself, it was Sylvia rather than Tom who was the first to greet me. We had swung through the gates, and were riding down the long avenue, sun-dappled, when she came riding straight at us, across the meadows and through the trees, sitting a heavy chestnut mare, in a riding habit of dark green, a forest's colour. When she reached us, she swung the mare round, and Leahy halted the trap.

"Welcome home to Kilpeder," she said, as she had written on the note. I had seen her last in Westmeath, at the wedding, when she had looked as all brides look, white-gowned, radiant for the day. It was as though, I came later to think, she had, in courtesy towards us all, subdued herself to the role she played. But now she was herself, and this was my first clear sight of her. She held herself as though vain of her figure, and she had reason to be, a woman far more slender than fashion then preferred, but erect, thin-waisted, sitting her mount with easy confidence. She was bareheaded, and her hair was undone, falling loose upon the shoulders of the green jacket, and disordered after her ride across the fields.

I made to climb down from the trap, but she put her hand on my arm. "Later," she said. "Let us ride up to the Castle. We will surprise Tom."

And so we rode along together, pleasurably.

"Over there," she said, pointing across the meadows with her crop. "That is where Tom and I intend to make a kind of Japanese-y garden, with a stream and a little bridge and a little teahouse. Everything."

"Japanese," I said, puzzled. In a few years' time, half of London would be mad for things Japanese, but not yet.

"Oh, yes," Sylvia said. "And it will be mine, Tom says. When next you visit Kilpeder, I shall give you both tea in my teahouse, but you must ask my permission to come in, because it will be entirely mine, and not part of Ardmor at all."

"There is an engraving hanging in the estate office," I said. "It says that the town of Kilpeder, all of it, belongs to the Earl of Ardmor."

"And so it may, for all I care, but not the teahouse and the Japanese garden. They will belong to me."

"You could affix a plaque," I said. " 'Property of the Countess of Ardmor.' "

"No," she said. "It will say, 'This is Sylvia's.' "

Then we rode on for a bit, without talking, as the avenue took its sudden turn towards the curved carriageway, and brought Ardmor Castle into view.

Late spring, moving toward summer: it is the loveliest of Ardmor's seasons, so many think. So Isabel, Tom's mother, thought, and she it was who created the formal gardens, artfully arranging their blooms to move through all of summer's months, week by week. It was past the first tier of gardens, the lowest tier, that we were riding now, and I was taken by distant colours—pink, vermillion, rose, yellow.

"The gardens are always lovely," I said. "Always even lovelier than one remembers them."

"Yes," she said, a bit abruptly. "Look, there's Tom. At the portico. His back is to us; he doesn't know we are here." She touched her crop to her mare's flank, and bolted ahead, leaving Leahy and myself to jog along behind her.

When I reached the portico, they were standing together, her hand on his forearm. With his free arm, he embraced me, and then held me off by its length, pretending to study me. "You seem unchanged," he said. "Does he not, Sylvia?"

"You are the one who should have changed," I said to him.

The long hall seemed bare, and Tom caught my puzzlement. "I have taken down all those paintings that have hung there for donkey's years," he said, "all those Forresters dead and gone, in scarlet uniforms. And all those views of Flemish meadows painted with gravy. I am having the hall repainted, and then hung with paintings I have found in Paris, and one or two of my own, perhaps. Does that seem awful of me? I'll hang our ancestors somewhere else, of course. I won't banish them to a lumber room."

"You can for all of me," I said. "You were painting in Venice, then? You were inattentive to your bride?"

"He was most attentive," Sylvia said. "He painted me, and not the Bridge of Sighs or Saint Mark's." She turned towards him. "Tom, you should speak to Griffin about the groom who met Lionel. Leahy, isn't it? His collar was a mess, and his boots caked with mud."

Tom smiled at me. "This isn't London, my dear. It isn't even Dublin. Lee wasn't offended, were you?"

But before I could answer, she said, "No, but your next visitor might be. If you dressed him in a tweed jacket and a billycock hat, it might not matter, but if you want him in livery, you should make certain that he wears it properly."

It was a sensible enough objection, and yet it jarred a bit against an earlier image, a girl riding towards me across meadows.

"You have spent too long in London," Tom said. "You have forgotten Ireland."

"I never forgot Ireland," she said, and smiled. "Nor that I am Irish. I was not let forget it."

Her Ireland, Westmeath, was almost ours, although not quite. Her father, old Hubert, retired colonel, had opened up the house for the wedding, an older house than Ardmor, but much smaller. Queen Anne, warm red brick, two small drawing rooms almost bare of furniture. There must have been bad management in the Challoner family, several generations of it, to have ended up with a mortgaged estate in the richest farming county in Ireland, the soil heavy, and the grasses thick. Mortgaged, or else rented up to the walls of the demesne. But Hubert had had to have his army: all the Challoners had been soldiers. He was not your stock, *Punch* colonel, but rather a frail, delicate man, thin-boned—an elegant man, in truth—and his wife was as attractive, a poised woman with pale blue eyes, as pale as his were dark, almost black, like Sylvia's.

But they had lived so long in London, or abroad, that they seemed almost strangers in their own reopened house. One morning, a few days before the wedding, I had come upon Challoner in the dining room, standing by the window looking out over the fields, towards where, just at the horizon's edge, the sun glinted upon lake water.

"Good country here," he said to me. "Good land, isn't it, Forrester?" As though reminding himself, both pride and regret in his tones. His hair was silver, soft, brushed with care. But once, no doubt, it had been dark. Sylvia's hair must have come from him.

"Tea?" Tom said to me. "Or a whiskey?"

"Why don't we have both?" Sylvia said. "And in the library."

And so we did. The tea took a time to arrive, and as we waited, she poured us three whiskeys, as heavy a measure for herself as for us, pouring with a man's confidence from the heavy Waterford decanter, and then seating herself on the broad arm of Tom's chair, so that we faced each other. "To Lionel," she said, "to Tom's great friend Lionel," and she held up her glass.

"No, no," I said, "the toast should be mine. To the two of you. And my blessings."

"His blessings," she said, and sipped. Tom put his arm about her waist, and looked up at her, at her profile. She was looking straight at me, and smiling.

Light from the evening sun spilled through the tall windows, across the lovely, faded carpet, white, pink, pale blue, and touched the shelves of tall books unread for decades, perhaps never read. Turf in the deep fireplace was ready for lighting, great blocks from the bog, dark and fibrous. The room was more home to me than my brother's house, than my rooms in London. I remembered Isabel in this room.

She was a startling woman. Whenever someone describes Sylvia, he should begin with that word, for it is surely in his mind. Now, here in this room, the green riding habit gave her a dramatic presence. She sat poised on the chair arm, a slender woman but not at all a small one—tall, rather, and heavy-boned. She sat with back arched, Tom's arm encircling her, and one leg stretched forward, almost indecorously, the riding boot a glossy black. She held the whiskey glass in her two hands.

"A Japanese garden," she said. "I have been telling Lionel. It will be the first Japanese garden in West Cork."

"You may depend upon that," I said.

"And I shall serve tea there in the Japanese manner," she said. "We shall kneel upon straw mats, and I shall serve you tea in cups the size of eggshells."

"It is a very formal ceremony, I have been told," I said. "And wrapped in Eastern mystery."

"All form," Tom said. "No mystery."

"Mr. Whistler would not agree," she said. "I cannot make out Tom's notion of art at all," she said to me, "can you? I was certain, when first he showed me his paintings, that he would be a great admirer of Mr. Whistler, but not at all."

"I like them well enough," Tom said, "but it is not what I have in mind for myself. He is coming from another direction."

"From the East," she said, "from Japan. And not Paris."

Tom smiled and shook his head. "All that is nonsense, and he knows it. It is a game he plays. He is an elaborate man and plays elaborate games. He learned in Paris, as I am trying to learn."

I was still unpersuaded by Tom's new existence as artist. He was playing a game himself, like Whistler. But Whistler was also the genuine article. I had encountered him a dozen times at least, in one drawing room or another, one salon or another, a ridiculous dandy, spruce and corseted, with an affected way of standing and walking, and a sackful of epigrams contrived in advance. But he was the genuine article—a true artist, as I would never be a true writer. Nor Tom a true painter—as at first I foolishly supposed. And why need he be, an earl, with broad acres, and this extraordinary woman as his bride?

"Have you met Mr. Whistler?" she said. "Mr. Whistler and I are great friends."

"You are fortunate in your friends," I said. "He is a remarkable man. Very witty."

Tom gave me a sarcastic look. He was familiar with my evasions. But he said nothing. When, like me, you lived a month with one friend, a fortnight with another, you developed strategies, codes, private ironies.

"Yes," she said. "Did you know, we will give a grand ball. That wonderful ballroom will be used again for the first time in—how long, Tom, how many years? It looks so sad, Lionel, that great, bare box of a room, and sheets over the mirrors. We will have a grand ball, for all of our neighbours here, and people from Meath and Kilkenny and Wicklow and Dublin, and perhaps from London as well. They will stay for days and days and there will be paper lanterns in the gardens."

"A long, long time," Tom said to me, and I knew at once what he meant. A long, long time since we had sat together on the stairs, school-boys, and heard the music, the babble of voices.

"But first," Tom said, "and straightaway, the day after next, there will be the usual thing for the tenants and the Kilpeder people. A pity, Sylvia, that your teahouse isn't ready for them. Farmers like nothing better than a good cup of tea."

"Don't mock them," she said. "Or me. I think it is all wonderful, like a fairy tale. Lord and Lady Ardmor. The Earl and Countess of Ardmor. At your coming-of-age, was there a celebration?"

"I was away then," Tom said. "At Cambridge. Kilpeder was troubled then. They were troubled times."

"Troubled?" she said.

Mrs. Ledwich came in then with the tea, as I had remembered it from my childhood, in the service which had been a wedding gift to Tom's grandparents, and with plates of sandwiches, wider and thicker than they would have been in England.

"Where are you from this time, Mister Lionel?" she said. "Greece, is it, or the North Pole?"

"Farther off than that, Mrs. Ledwich. Limerick. With Jack Emerson."

"Limerick," she said. "God help us. I was once in Rathkeale."

"Nearer at hand than Wicklow," Sylvia said. "But we were in Wicklow last month, Lionel. At the Cardews. Do you know them, Lionel? He was at Cambridge with Tom."

I shook my head.

"A decent, empty-headed fellow, with a fine pack of hounds," Tom said. "There was another Cambridge chap staying with him. Charles Parnell, another great rider to hounds. He is thinking about Parliament, no less. In Isaac Butt's party."

"Yes," I said. "Butt has a decent lot with him there," and thought no more of it.

To my best recollection, that is how I first heard Parnell's name, that casually, a huntsman staying with a Wicklow chap named Cardew. In a few years' time, no one in Ireland would hear it with indifference.

Isaac Butt's name was, of course, a familiar one, and spoken nearly always with affection, whatever one's political allegiance. It was in Parliament, in fact, that I had seen him last, when I had called in to hear a humourous friend deliver a dull speech. I met Butt in the lobby: we knew each other slightly. One's affection for him began with his appearance, a plump man, below the middle height, a shock of disordered white hair, clothes carelessly worn, and a ready smile which did not play only about his lips, but lit up his eyes. He had a mischievous wit, without malice. He had had a few glasses too many that night. He often did—that was his failing, as everyone said, that and women. Between the two, they kept him teetering always on the edge of calamity. He joked about it. "The bailiffs," he would say, "the bailiffs and myself have become the best of friends. Old familiars. They know more about my house than I do myself. And why not, they spend more time in it."

"He is very handsome, your Mr. Parnell," Sylvia said.

"Not my Parnell," Tom said. "We have met a few times. We were together at Cambridge. Not my crowd, though. Hunted together a few times. Typical Wicklow squire, I would have thought him. Not Butt's sort at all."

"What is Butt's sort?" Sylvia asked. "Who is Butt?"

"A barrister," I said, "and a very able one. Or at least he was. And until a few years ago, a leader of the Orange gang, High Church, High Tory. And then he turned round completely, began working for amnesty for the Fenian prisoners, began something he calls Home Rule, to give us a tinpot legislature of our own, here in Dublin. He has formed his own little party, twenty members or so. Every so often one of them will rise up in the House and make a speech on behalf of Ireland. Harmless stuff, and some of his fellows are most amusing."

"But that is splendid of him," Sylvia said, as she poured. "Why do you mock them?"

"You keep yourself well informed, Lee," Tom said.

"You are quite right, Sylvia," I said. "It was wrong of me. Someone, God knows, should speak for this poor ramshackle country, and Butt has eloquence; he is no demagogue, no beggarman like O'Connell."

"And now handsome Mr. Parnell, the huntsman, aspires to be with him," Sylvia said.

"But not a very impressive addition to the ranks, despite his appearance," Tom said. "I should have thought him a Tory, a huntin', shootin' Tory squire."

"Butt was a Tory once," I said. "And a fellow in his party told me once that Kilpeder played its part in his conversion."

He looked at me blankly. "I have heard nothing of that."

"Butt took on the defence of some of the Fenians, in 'sixty-five and again in 'sixty-seven, at the Rising. Simple matter of the law; he had no sympathy for them. And there wasn't very much that he could do for them, although he did his best. Rebels in arms, not much material there for a defence. He defended some of the leaders, and a few of the rank and file. He appeared for Edward Nolan, the man who led the attack on Kilpeder."

Sylvia said, puzzled, "The attack on this Kilpeder? Here?"

"Oh yes," Tom said. "This Kilpeder. The attack and my coming-of-age. I was in Cambridge for both of them. I have been left out of history. But Lee was here; Lee saw the Fenian rising."

"Here in the Castle, that is," I told her. "There was little enough to be seen or heard from here. Rifle shots, and then, towards the very end, there was a glimpse of the soldiers moving along the crest of the Macroom road, at the end of the town."

"How thrilling," Sylvia said. "Were you all terrified, all of you here at the Castle?"

I took her question seriously, and tried to answer it. I remembered Isabel and myself on the terrace, beyond the windows of the room which now held us, Tom and Tom's bride and myself. Eight years before, no great chasm of time; and yet it also seemed locked away in an unrecoverable past. There had been snow on the terrace, and the day had had a winter's clarity.

"No," I told her, "not terrified at all. It all seemed to be at a great distance from us, from the Castle. It had been expected, you know—not that it would be here at Kilpeder, but that there would be a rising that spring. The local landlords were beside themselves with rage and apprehensiveness. And yet we all knew, somewhere within us we all knew, that it would collapse. Even the Fenians knew that, I think."

"They knew it," Sylvia said, "and yet they attacked. They went into rebellion."

"The wretched little affair here was one of their set-pieces," I said. "Men were killed. Fenians, a constable. Blood spilled. But a pattern for what happened across the country."

"But these were local people?" Sylvia said. "Your tenants? The people who lit bonfires for us and cheered us at the gates?"

"And will be coming round for the celebration," Tom said. "Not the very people, perhaps, but their brothers and aunts and fathers."

"Chute would know more about that than either of us," I said. "You should talk with him if it interests you."

"I will," Sylvia said, with a show of exaggerated decisiveness. "By George, I will. A rebellion at our very doorstep, and the two of you know next to nothing about it."

And the talk drifted off then to other matters, Venice perhaps, or friends we had in common. Or perhaps Tom and I told her the bits and pieces that we knew—Isabel and myself on the terrace, gunfire. Told her perhaps that the local schoolmaster had been one of the rebels, and the assistant in the town's big shop. But perhaps we did not. Sylvia was at the time less interested than she pretended. She was teasing us. No doubt she thought herself Irish, as we all did; but most of her life had been lived in London, with holidays at home. Being Irish was a plume for her hat, and what more Irish than faint, harmless echoes of a failed rebellion?

I stayed with them almost six weeks on that visit. Spring became summer, the elms along my favorite walk, beside the river, heavy with thick leaf, crowding out the sun almost. Sylvia would walk with me, while Tom worked and while I should have been at work, my manuscript lying, half finished, on the library table. It was another of my books of travel, the one on Spain, and had been promised to my publisher for that autumn. But talking with Sylvia was like visiting another country.

The demesne wall lies just on the far side of the river, and we heard noises from the town—shouts, the creak of cart wheels, Saint Jarlath's booming bell. It was in those weeks that I discovered Sylvia, as one discovers a country. Or thought I did.

Once we were sitting on a backed bench, about halfway down the avenue of trees, the morning air light and cool.

"Tom and I were not properly introduced, you know," she said. "We met at Galantiere's studio. The artist, you know. Every Wednesday and every Thursday, he would have people in for tea, but it was more often punch. I don't know why we had never met before. But of course Tom was in Paris, much of his time."

"And the army before that," I said.

"But then I would have been much too young," she said. "I cannot imagine Tom as a soldier. He would have been handsome—was he handsome?"

"Handsome enough, I expect. Like Parnell."

"I *like* handsome men," she said, in her mock-decisive way.

"It is a common prejudice," I said. "I have suffered under it."

"You, Lionel!" she said. "You are something better than handsome. You are . . ." She hesitated for a word.

" 'Interesting' is the usual evasion," I said.

"It is not an evasion," she said. "It is precisely right. You interest people, and it begins with how you look."

It would have seemed, in any other young wife, flirtatiousness, but not with Sylvia. Her dark, wide eyes were direct in their gaze, unsettling but not flirtatious. She was an unsettling woman. I liked her.

"Tom is fortunate," she said, "to have so good a friend as you. There is no one to whom I feel as close as you two seem to be."

A magpie sprang from one of the trees across the river and flew over our heads, towards a copse.

And once we picnicked, the two of us, taking a jaunting car out through the gates and up towards the Derrynasaggarts, a day now of full summer, with a haze upon the horizon, but the streams clear and sparkling, and the grasses a deep, fathomless green. We spread out our cloth in a meadow, beneath an oak, and from hampers Sylvia took out china, silver, glasses. Chablis was the colour of straw. Her summer frock was unbuttoned at the throat, and her flesh was clear, pale. She wore a hat of wide-brimmed straw, fastened beneath her chin with a ribbon; but once we were settled in the shade, she took it off, and rested it beside her, on the grass. The frock spread out, a pattern of small flowers, pale green, pale pink.

"Whose meadow is this?" she asked. "Is this Tom's? Our meadow?"

"Good Lord, Sylvia," I said. "How should I know? Ask Chute. Perhaps not. We are not the only landlords, you know—far from it. I think Tom's lands stretch northwards from the town, beyond Clonbrony Wood, in that direction. But there are scattered lands in all directions. This might be Tom's."

"Ask Chute," she said. "That is what Tom always tells me. It must be strange, not to know what you own. With us, it was the other way round. We knew exactly what we used to own, what we had sold off."

"And I," I said, "have never had it to sell. My brother has it all. Nothing like Tom, of course."

"On days like these," she said, "Father and I would walk the roads which spread out from the house. He carried a strange stick that he had brought back from one of those places—the Punjab I think—all twisted and warty, black as sin. We would pause at the rise of a hill, and he would hold the stick out before him, sweeping it in a great arc. And do you know, it was not the loss of the land or the rents that he lamented. It was losing so much of his stake here, so much of this country."

We are a curious people, we Anglo-Irish, English-in-Ireland, however you may want to call us. I could see Hubert Challoner from Sylvia's words, for I had seen dozens like him—soldiers, dons, colonial judges, traders in half the ports of China and the Levant, faces and necks burned red or brown. Soldiers, most of them. Ireland bred them for the Empire, their home the regimental mess, their traditions the traditions of the regiment. Call them Irish in the wrong tone of voice and there would be hell to pay. But for each there is a remembered scene—a copse, a freshet, a tumbled fence, or the music of an early morning, birdsong in clear, pale silence. Over the years, the estate will be sold off bit by bit, a farm to pay for a string of Indian ponies, a farm to see a daughter presented at Court or a son live at Oxford in proper style. Years can go by without a return to Ireland, or even a wish to. But in the end they come back, the remembered scene unfaded, unfindable, and with a bit of cash, a bit of luck, they will find a hunting lodge, rechristen it "Simla" or "Khyber Pass." The local news will not please them. A neighbour's son has turned Catholic in order to marry one of them. The government is not standing up to Fenian ruffians, Whiteboys, desperadoes. But on russet mornings, the hunt will wed them again to the land, at a race meeting, shouts, pounding hooves, a knot of peasants standing by a stall, a sudden wind; suddenly they will know that they are home again, that they have come home. We are not Irish, we Anglo-Irish, so the nationalist newspapers tell us.

But Sylvia, as she sat facing me, her dark eyes looking a bit past me, towards the hills, seemed not to have come from the world of Hubert Challoner, or from my world, or Tom's.

"Tom and his art," she said abruptly. "It is very strange, is it not? We expect people to be what the world expects of them. A landlord should be a landlord, or a soldier, perhaps, or a member of Parliament. Not a painter."

"No," I said. "Does that disturb you?"

"Disturb me!" she cried. "Good heavens, no. I think it is wonderful. I wish that I could paint or draw or sketch, but all I make are wretched daubs. I envy him."

"These painters he admires so, these Frenchmen of his, I have heard them called wretched daubers."

"Don't you believe it," she said with such fierce energy that I smiled at her. "They are changing the world, those Frenchmen of his."

"Art does not change the world," I said. "Nothing changes the world. The world changes itself, and there is nothing we can do about it."

"Well then," she said, "they are changing the way in which we see the world. Will you settle for that?"

"Gladly," I said, "although I am not sure that you are right. I don't myself see the world differently because of those chaps. I'm damned if I do."

"Now there is a man called Galantiere . . ." she began.

"I know there is," I told her. "I know him. Don't tell me that Paul Galantiere is going to change the world, because I will not for one minute believe you."

He was a society painter, a portraitist, with a skilful but, so it seemed to me, a showy technique, theatrical, masses of blacks and whites offset with single, dramatic splashes of colour, the crimson velvet of a rose, a yellow sash, a decoration. And I may perhaps have been unfair to him, because he was in truth changing the way in which people in that world of his saw each other, saw themselves; he gave them images of a new kind of elegance.

"No," she said, "I will not tell you that. But Paul understands what those new people are doing, those people whom he has no wish to imitate. And he showed me how to look at pictures. I had not known that there were ways of looking at pictures, at the world, at hills, horizons." She gestured briefly. "I was a very ignorant girl."

Her manner confused me. It would do so to the end, confuse and charm me. What she said was direct and candid, always, and yet there was a reserve, a sense of things left unsaid.

"Tom wants my portrait done, and I'm determined that Paul Galantiere is the man to do it. When we are in London for the season. We have a house in London now, you know. In Chelsea. Would I be a good sort of subject for him, do you think?"

I smiled at her. "Not as you are now, not sitting in a field with a friend, and crusts of bread spread about us. But as he will have you pose, yes, a fine subject."

"But you, Lee Forrester. If you were a painter, you would paint me as I am now."

She had leaned back, almost to her full length, and was resting her weight on an elbow. I could not, for that moment, imagine her anywhere else, nor looking any other way, and I envied Tom greatly.

In the end, of course, Galantiere did "do" her, the portrait which hangs above the fireplace in the library, but which was once, when he exhibited it, the sensation of a season. Perhaps he did catch some truth about her. He was not all artifice and melodrama, as I may have suggested. And he was especially clever about women. Then too, of course, he knew her well—far more intimately than I ever would. In his painting, she offers you a challenge as she stands there in half light, half shadow, her face, though pale, lighted as it were from within. But on that day in the upland field, with no shadows save those thrown upon her from oak branches, on that day there was no challenge, but rather a repose, the thoughtful repose of a beautiful woman in the presence of a man whom she has just begun to trust.

There were other days as well, of course, but they were all of a pattern, all like that late noontime in the field. Evenings had their pattern as well. That year, for some reason, we did not use the library after dinner, but rather went to the small drawing room which had been a favourite with Isabel, Tom's mother, and held her piano. Tom would sit reading in his chair and I in mine, our lamps making pools of light. Sometimes Sylvia would read, but not often; she was not a great reader. She might leaf through a volume of prints, or leap up suddenly and go to Isabel's piano. She loved Chopin, and played him with such feeling that I can still remember the sound of notes let loose in the room, moving towards the pools of light, towards windows beyond which drawn curtains and darkness hid the wildness of West Cork. Tom would rest his book in his lap, and study her, his profile towards me. The night bound us together— music, darkness, the sense of containment which the room held. I remember my own feelings as divided—my pleasure in our closeness together, and, distinct from that, my happiness for the two of them, and then, in its own complex abode, my sense of Sylvia, at once inviolable and sensual, lamplight full upon her throat and small, perfect bosom. Was there ever a time, then or later, when I was in love with her? Perhaps, but we never spoke of it, not even later when we were to exchange the most intimate of confidences.

Drawn curtains and the wildness of West Cork! So smooth a formulation, and therefore so deceptive. All around us a land and a people whom we did not know, save as servants, porters, coachmen, gillies, gamekeepers, gardeners. And these, a sardonic scholar might argue, were like those wild Indians of the American West whom the pioneers and cattlemen train to their service. They stare at us, those trained tribes, from photographs, a bowler hat with a feather in it, an ill-fitting frock coat, a manner— feigned or actual, who can say?—of docility; but the faces are savage, dark, the eyes hooded. So too, in my view, the servants and retainers of Ireland's great landlord families.

Not so very different, you will say, from circumstances in England or in France. And yet one feels the difference here, bogland and bare mountain enforce it. Once, Isabel and I stood upon a terrace, leaf-strewn, snow in the air, listening to rifle fire. Those fellows, those rebels, were, if you will, our trained Indians reverting to type—shopkeepers, stable-hands, gardeners' boys. English-speaking, almost to a man, their minds stuffed with the slogans of causes which had elsewhere grown stale, ill-written pamphlets, a porridge of crude and fallacious history, legends of an ancient oppression. But they had, for all that, risen up from the earth, from bog and mountainside. First and second cousins, most of them, of those Gaelic-speaking bog men who, significantly, had stood remote from those events, uncomprehending.

Now, in this year of grace 1904, there are few enough bookish people with whom one can talk of these or any other matters. The families of the small gentry, of course, would rather talk with Satan himself, or a Home Rule agitator, but these are in any event not bookish folk. They have their merits—honest enough, conscientious, sending off their sons to Trinity or the army or the bar; but they live within their round of dusty pleasures, enraged, one may be certain, that Ardmor Castle, which should by rights be the glittering centre of their existence, as Lismore is elsewhere, or Trevane Castle in East Cork, is dark, empty, abandoned, save for the yearly visits of a poor relation and his mistress, a former lady's maid. Tom, off there in Italy these ten years or more, is but a baleful legend at the club, like Beckford of Fonthill Abbey or Wilde of Reading Gaol. And, of course, they remember Sylvia, they remember that great ball which Tom and Sylvia gave to mark the fact of their wedding. That they will surely remember, as a token of the brilliance which could have been given to the town, to their lives.

Curiously enough, I myself scarcely remember it. It had no mark of Sylvia upon it, nor of Tom either, but was bustling, noisy, crowded with people who did not suit each other well: the local people, and the other great families of Cork and Kerry and Waterford, and then the people whom Tom had brought over from London who had never been to Ireland in some cases, although most had spent a few weeks fishing in Connemara, and were disappointed by our less showy scenery.

Sylvia liked it. I have one vivid recollection of her standing on the staircase, her hand upon the marble. A knot of people stood on the landing looking up towards her, and she was looking down towards them, eyes bright, lips slightly parted, an excited girl. I thought then that she was new herself into so large a life, child of mortgaged acres turned countess.

I could make friends, no doubt, with the local rector, Charlie Cummings, despite his disapproval of my ways, but to what purpose? He is, in his own timid way, a bit of a Liberal, keeping this well concealed, of course, for Liberals are universally regarded by our coreligionists as pawns of the Home Rulers. The pastor of Saint Jarlath's, the Catholic church, is impossible, a shambling, hairy-nostrilled lout, and his curate a red-cheeked enthusiast of hurling. Once, it is said, in the days before Catholic Emancipation, ironically, the priesthood attracted the sons of the old, decayed Catholic gentry, men of elegance, trained on the Continent, brimming with Fenelon and Bossuet. No longer. This leaves not the schoolmaster, a dough-faced little prig, but his predecessor, Hugh Mac-Mahon, a man of considerable tartness and savour, surprisingly well read, balanced in his judgements, and, most astonishing of all, one of the Fenian rebels of Clonbrony Wood. But why surprising, after all, for was not Bob Delaney himself a Fenian? Delaney, who as much as anyone contrived, almost by accident, our disaster?

We exchange books occasionally, MacMahon and myself. He will walk stiffly, self-consciously, up the avenue, the books always carried with great care, for he addresses them with the superstitious awe of the self-educated. Always, we meet here, in the library, with several, to me, most interesting exceptions. *Prodigious* is one of his greatest terms of praise. "Prodigious," he will say, tapping with long finger my copy of Schliemann's *Mycenae,* with its frontispiece of the Treasure of Atreus, close to the Lion's Gate, as it is termed, and its grandiloquent dedication to "His Majesty Dom Pedro II, Emperor of Brazil," with the "profound respect" of its author, Dr. Schliemann, at once discoverer and despoiler of Troy and latterly of Argos. "And with an introduction by Gladstone himself," MacMahon will say. "Extraordinary. A man of diverse talents, the late Mr. Gladstone."

"Yes," I will agree, extending towards him my box of Virginia cigarettes.

"A great student of history," MacMahon says, "and yet active in the world of practical events."

"All too active, perhaps," I say, and by way of answer, he bends forward to accept my lighted match.

Once, early one Saturday morning, I rode up to his small, pleasant house, and the two of us set off, afoot, into the hills. We spent the whole of that day walking and talking, pausing often, and once for an hour, for the lunch that he had packed, sandwiches made with thick slabs of bread, a cake. For that day and the next, and then only, MacMahon was able to put aside the stiffness imposed upon our relationship by class, by accent, and, no doubt, much else besides from a past which we both remembered.

"It is here, is it not," I said to him, "along this road, that Ned Nolan tried to make his escape, ten years ago?"

He walked a bit before answering, then shook his head. "No," he said, "not this road."

It was clear that he did not want the subject opened. But in my imagination, I placed Nolan on the road, ahead of us, a figure from the illustrated press, dark and menacing, long-striding, holding his murderous revolver.

We were bound for the mountain village of Kildaragh, where Mac-Mahon had arranged that we should have beds in the tavern. Late that night, we found ourselves, the two of us, sitting side by side in the tavern's crowded kitchen, close to the turf fire. Chairs of a sort had been provided for us, tokens of respect. The others, all of them peasants, lounged against walls or sat perched on upturned porter barrels. There was a fiddle in the room. Now, for the first time, I heard the music which MacMahon had described to me, and it truly was, in its way, extraordinary. Like most Irishmen, however imperfect we may be, I knew a few Gaelic songs well enough to recognise: "The Coolin" and "The Blackbird" and a few others; but I knew them in scrubbed versions, for drawing-room piano-fortes. Here, in this foetid room, with its floor of close-packed earth, lit by turf glow, by a few scattered candles, drifts of tobacco smoke in the air, the music seemed, as it were, to arise from earth itself, from the mountains invisible beyond the two small windows, from the immense night.

I stole a glance at MacMahon, who was keeping time to the music, his hand patting his knee. As much almost as myself, I thought, he is a stranger to these people. Especially did this seem so when he conversed with them in the Gaelic, his speech slower than theirs as he sought out the words. How must we seem to them, I thought, for although they seemed clumsy, awkward fellows, heavy and stolid, I knew this to be but a trick of culture, that within their own world they had their own alert-ness, their own ironies. Landlord, schoolmaster—visitors to be treated with courtesy.

The music, as I say, seemed to arise from the earth itself. But I have heard such singing elsewhere—in the mountains of Macedonia, once in a Calabrian village. It did not hold for me the magic which drew MacMa-hon towards it. It was as though the music held a secret about himself, spoke with clarity feelings which he knew only as muddled, muddied.

"It is all ending, you know," he said abruptly the next morning, as we walked down towards his house—a damp morning, the thick grasses wet, and the heather clumps of damp, wet purple. "The music, the poetry, the language itself. I helped to kill it, God forgive me. Myself and the other schoolmasters."

"History killed it," I told him bluntly. "Railways and schoolmasters and newspapers and a long list of things."

At his house, he made me a cup of tea, and as we sat drinking it, we gradually reassumed the manner upon which we had settled, friendly and yet formal, a bit distant. Tall cases of books leaned over us, and through a clear, polished window, small-paned, I looked beyond fields towards the hills where we had spent the night.

It was a bit later, as I was riding up the avenue—distant from me, just visible beyond a straggling plantation, the ruined Japanese garden—only then did it occur to me how similar were our circumstances, MacMa-hon's and mine. Ardmor Castle had outlived its time, so much was clear. Indeed, if one were to believe the editors and writers and the men who talked to you in clubs and at London dinners, all the Ardmor Castles had been sentenced by history. Buried, all of them, beneath a sea of mortgages, all but the largest ones, shattered by Parnell and the Land League, by agitators and terrorists. And now, most final sentence of all, the land bills which were making it tempting for us to sell out, pack up. But I have never been inclined to believe such people, with their theories produced upon demand, beside your eggcup every morning. I believe only what I can feel upon the fingertips, scent in the air, discover in the changing light.

Even with the wings of the house shut off, it is too large for us, too large for Emily and myself and the few servants. I walk, some afternoons, after I have finished work, from room to room, the chairs and tables swathed in dusty muslin, dirt-streaked. In the empty ballroom, my heels clatter noisily, *crack, crack* on the wood like rifle shots.

15

[*Ned Nolan*]

He thought of himself at times, drink taken, as a bird shot down with broken wing.

Once he left Manhattan entirely, and took work with an ex-Fenian named Tom Bonner, who had a brickyard up the Hudson River, beyond Peekskill. The work that Bonner found for him was neither demanding nor exacting, keeping him busy with tally sheets, checking up on loads of clay, straw, the wages of the workmen set down in a red-ruled ledger book. "I am fit for harder tasks than this, you know," he told Bonner. "I am not a cripple."

"You are not fit because you lack the craft," Bonner said. "Brickmaking is a craft ancient as Egypt."

Beyond the yard, beyond the kilns, crooked cobbled streets led to the village, fronting the river. A Catholic church of white-painted brick, raw and fresh, a churchyard with already a few gravestones in it, men from

Derry, Cavan, Fermanagh. Workmen's houses, built of the yard's own brick, a small wooden porch tacked on to each. In the evening, the men, coming home, would shout to the women who leaned upon the windowsills. The air, in spring, would be heavy with the smell of boiling cabbage, chops in a skillet. Nolan rented the back bedroom of a childless couple called Dennehy, and had his meals with them.

There were two saloons. He favoured the Shamrock, which was closer to the river. In the Shamrock, Terry Brophy, a Cork City man, served beer in tall, handled schooners, shot glasses of bourbon, rye. Nolan drank little. He welcomed the company, listening to the voices, Ulster and Connaught accents flattened out by the tones of New York and Brooklyn. They had drifted here, most of them, from the city. Brooklyn was a second lost home for them, or for some a first; some had been born in the States, and for these the Irish accent would be a faint whiff, picked up at home, in childhood. On Sundays, they would ride the cars down to New York to visit parents, cousins. After work, lining the long bar counter, their hands would be red with brick dust.

They never forgot who he was, that was the one bad part of it. Or rather, who they thought he was, wanted him to be. In New York, he could lose himself for days or weeks, if he had the money for it, and then slip back to his haunts. For a time, he had sat on the platforms with other released Fenians, in crowded halls, floors stained with tobacco juice. Once, his name, with Rossa's and Clandillon's, had been on a painted banner stretched across the front of the hall, lit by gas flames. "Nolan of Clonbrony Wood. On battlefield and in prison cell." Always, at the end, the crowd, large or small, would sing "God Save Ireland," and the hat would be passed around, "for the cause," or "for the lads still in England's grip." Nolan despised the self who sat on the platforms, put his signature to pieces of paper, or to the poor likeness of himself that was hawked at the door for a nickel. Pictures of Rossa went for a quarter, and for fifty cents you could buy a large cardboard with the likenesses, framed in ovals, of the Manchester Martyrs—Allen, Larkin, and O'Brien. "High upon the gallows tree . . ."

But at Van Brunt's Point, in spring weather, he could leave the Shamrock, and walk down the path which led from it to the river. It was a broad river, broad as the Shannon, with mountains in the distance on the far shore. In evening cool, ships moved north towards Albany or south towards the docks of Manhattan. Breezes, sweet-smelling or odoursome, would come off the water towards him. The river and the distant hills, his sense of mountains and ranges of mountains beyond those, forests and prairies, could fill him with a quiet happiness. But his years in the cell never left him, in dreams, in unbidden reverie, the walls pressing in upon him, the blackness, the sounds at night which were best left undeciphered. In the quarries, in winter, swinging mallet or pick, in silence, the light falling bleak and cold upon all of them, faces which now he remembered only from prison, the past wiped blank. But at night, lying upon straw and wool, he would fight off the past, remembering the clear pasturelands of Munster, and before that, the farmlands of Tennessee and Virginia.

Once, walking along the towpath which led to the brickyard's dock, he heard steps behind him, and turned to meet Bonner. Together, they walked to the dock's edge, where an empty barge lay moored, faintly moving in response to the strong current. Bonner picked up a triangular fragment of brick, and scaled it into the darkening water.

"Ancient Egypt," Nolan said, and Bonner took the point.

"And other things," he said. "You have a good pair of eyes, Ned. And a good brain. I could use a good straw boss. I've bought up river frontage across there, at Stony Point. Set out another yard. New York City is mad for bricks; there is no end to the building of that city. And the Irish have the word put in for them, at City Hall."

"You are on the road to fortune, Tom," Nolan said. "More power to your arm."

"But it would be a six-day-a-week job," Bonner said, "and late nights, a few of them in the season."

Nolan nodded, his absent gaze upon the spot of river where the scaled bit of brick had sunk.

"You know what I am saying," Bonner said. "You cannot hold down a decent job here or anywhere else, so long as you stand ready for any errand the organization sends you off on. Philadelphia, Chicago. You know what I am saying, Ned."

"Yes," Nolan said, "I know," admiring Bonner's discretion. He had been a wild boy himself, years before, with a past like Nolan's own, the emigrant ship and then the Yankee army and then the Rising. No longer.

"Mind you," Bonner said, treading on the heel of Nolan's thought, "I am a member myself of the organization, dues paid up and a bit over from time to time. And not too many questions as to where the funds go or how they are spent. But this is a different day and age. You won't free Ireland by sending over the occasional lad to put a bullet in a grabber. Nor by travelling off to Chicago to put paid to an informer."

"Is that what I do?" Nolan asked.

"I have no wish to know what you do," Bonner said. "I am not your judge."

He was at Van Brunt's Point, working for Bonner, the better part of six months, and from time to time he would go back for a few days—not to work, but drawn by the river, by its promise of freedom. For a year and a bit, he lived in two unfurnished rooms near the New York docks, a five minutes' walk from the flat in which his father and himself had lived, before the war. Walking those streets, which he could not quite remember, moments of that earlier time would recur to him: His father's florid, confident face, roseate above flowered waistcoat. Or his father coming home late from meetings no different from those which Nolan himself now attended. No difference at all—perhaps the banners and the bunting were passed on from one decade to the next—emerald green, harps, tinsel swords.

It was in that year that he had the girl from Cork who worked as a skivvy in Murray Hill. Thursday was her afternoon off, and they did not care how late she stayed out, if she was back at work by six. "It would be different if I was a full parlourmaid," she said. "They are most particular. They have a position in the household, like. But they don't care about slaveys, the Sturdevants don't."

"Is that your great wish," Nolan said, "to become a parlourmaid?"

"They have a clean, lovely life," she said, "waxing and dusting."

But she was always cleanliness itself when she came to him, her body scrubbed so hard that the smell of yellow soap became part of his erotic expectations. Later in the year, she was elevated to parlourmaid, and then they would have the afternoon and evening until eight. She would walk from bedroom to small sitting room, wearing only a tight-waisted petticoat of white muslin, her bare breasts free, the brown nipples brownencircled. Once, after they had made love, she saw him watching her from the bed.

"Do you think me shameless?" she asked.

"'Tis not that at all."

"I am filled with shame, letting you see me so, but I take pleasure from the shame. Can you understand that?"

"You must have long and interesting conversations with your confessor," Nolan said, and she did not reply. Her name was Margaret. Margaret Quill.

On the day before Christmas Eve, she came to tell him that a young American boy named Edward Reilly, a grocer's helper, had asked her to marry him.

"What did you tell him?" Nolan asked.

The windows of all the grocery shops and butcher shops were decked with red paper and green paper, and from hooks above the butchers' windows hung plump geese and turkeys. The corner confectioner had outdone himself, with flakes to represent snow clinging to the roofs of a small village, houses and farms and neat-spired white Protestant church. Before the model village, sweets and chocolates filled red boxes. There was a pond of glass, and small figures skating upon it.

"I told him that I would be honoured to be his wife," she said.

"He is a fortunate man," Nolan said.

She had removed her hat and heavy coat, snow-wet, and they sat side by side on the bed, their faces turned towards one another.

"It could be your good fortune instead," she said.

"No," he said, and reaching his two hands behind her inclined neck, began to unfasten her black gown.

"They say that you were a class of a general with the Fenians," she said, "and then you shot a landlord and were put away in prison."

"Something like that," he said.

Carefully, he undid the fastenings, which ran the length of her back, and then, picking up each hand, undid the fastenings at the wrist. Then he slipped the gown from her, and after it, the white embroidered camisole. She sat quietly.

"Two rooms the size of these," she said, "and the use of a kitchen. They could be made to look lovely. All clean and lovely, everything waxed and polished." When he freed her breasts, she said, "Next week he will take me to have tea with his mother, a widow who lives on the West Side." Her nipple, when his fingers touched it, was already erect. He put an arm around her shoulder and drew her down onto the bed.

He may have caught a glimpse of her a few years later, at the great memorial service for John O'Mahony, in Irving Hall. But he could not be certain. Young women who looked a bit like her were scattered throughout the cavernous hall. He was standing behind the platform, in the wings, with a dozen others waiting to be led out as warriors in the movement which O'Mahony had founded, twenty years before. But he was almost certain, her lips parted and her eyes bright. She was wearing a coat with a bit of fur at the collar, with a small round hat to match. There was a pleasant-looking, ginger-headed young fellow beside her.

A few years before, he had visited O'Mahony, who lived but a few blocks away, in wretched rooms, dark and airless. They sat together by a dusty window, looking down a long street to the river, which was blocked from their view by a warehouse. A chill day, and no fire. Nolan had brought a bottle; it stood on the table between them. O'Mahony's coat was buttoned to the collar, and he had a rug wrapped about his legs. The face was still handsome, fine-boned, and the down-curving moustache, although grey-flecked, was still dark.

"It could be an Irish day," he said, "a winter's afternoon."

He had been with O'Brien and Stephens at Ballingeary, in 'forty-eight. Thirty years ago. But he remembered Irish afternoons.

Above a table at the far side of the room hung the print which everyone knew, O'Mahony in his uniform as a colonel in the Federal army, hawk-nosed and militant. O'Mahony saw that Nolan was looking towards it.

"It is not there from vanity," he said. "Quite the contrary. It was not a grand military career, in command of depots and garrisons. We were waiting out the war, then ours would begin. Ach, what need to tell you, Ned. You were with us."

Carefully, Nolan measured more whiskey into the two glasses. "In Tennessee," he said, "under this commander or that one. But it was you I served."

O'Mahony lifted, in deprecation, a long, white hand. "We had begun even then quarrelling among ourselves while you were still off there in Tennessee. 'Sixty-five was to be the year. But on everything else we quarrelled. We are still quarrelling. They are. I am out of it."

He added water, a quick splash, to his glass.

"I spoke at your father's graveside, Ned. You know that. My remarks were widely printed, in the Irish papers of this country. Boston. Here. Chicago."

"I have them," Nolan said. "You were most generous."

"He gave his life to Ireland, I said. What does that sort of language mean? I no longer know."

"You have given your own life, Colonel," Nolan said.

It was true enough, he thought, sitting beside the shrunken man in the chair, lap-robed and shivering. A strong-farmer's son from the old Catholic gentry, the chiefs of the Comeraghs; he had thrown it away to ride into Ballingeary with revolver and rifle. A scholar, in New York in the first confident years he had translated Keating's old history out of the Gaelic; learned men had praised it. It was his scholarship which had found for them their famous name, from the warrior brothers in the ancient sagas: the Fenian Brotherhood. Now he had this, these rooms, a bottle brought as a gift. He was banished from the Council, like Stephens. But power had been stripped from him so long ago that he had been forgiven. They brought him out on ceremonial occasions.

The pale, long hand made a wide gesture. "I have disposed of my library," he said. "Clutter. Dead words, crumbling paper. I keep a few books in the bedroom, and read them over and over. O'Donovan's great translation of the *Annals*. Rabelais. Swift. *Tom Jones*. I would like to give you a copy of my translation, but they have all been given away, long since."

"I have your translation," Nolan said. "It is a noble work."

"Noble," O'Mahony said, with an underlining of irony. "Workmanlike, rather. You do not have the Gaelic yourself? It is dying out. A people without a language. You had a hard few years of it there, in that English prison?"

"Hard enough," Nolan said.

For a time they sat in silence. Nolan measured out more whiskey. He was not certain why he had made the visit, but the old man seemed comfortable with his presence, with the silence.

"Commanding General," O'Mahony said at last. "That was the title we gave me. I was the Commanding General, and Stephens was Chief Organiser of the Irish Republic!" Suddenly he began to laugh, but it turned into a dry, wheezing cough. "First I was shoved aside, and then the fellows who threw me over were thrown over in their turn. Informers, braggards, drunkards, cuckolds—my God, what a crew they had there in Fenian House, as they called it. We let you down; the whole pack of us let down the young lads on the hillside." He sighed. "A long time ago."

"What matters is the organization," Nolan said, "the organization and the oath. You gave those to us, yourself and Stephens. That is always remembered of you; it always will be."

"I hate cities," O'Mahony said, "and I have spent the half of my life in this one, save for the war. That ugly street below, the mean shop fronts, and the cobbles glistening in the rain. You are yourself deep in the counsels of the organization, I have heard."

"Not deep," Nolan said. "I do their bidding from time to time."

"You bear no great resemblance to your father. He was fair, and you are dark. We were gentlemen, or at least tried to be—Thomas Nolan, John Mitchel, Meagher of the Sword, Richard O'Gorman. But the fellows who are in it now—who the hell are they, can you answer me that? Devoy seems all right, I grant you Devoy."

"With respect," Nolan said, "it is not gentlemen who are required for revolutions."

For the first time that afternoon, O'Mahony smiled with what seemed genuine pleasure. "That may well be the case. Wolfe Tone was much of your opinion. There is a nice story told of O'Conor of Belnagare, back in the last century. He was of the great princely O'Conors, the O'Conor Dons. But between Cromwell and the Penal Laws, he had been crushed down, little better than a peasant. One day he and his son were ploughing together, and the son spoke to him with insolence. 'Have a care, sir,' said O'Conor, 'for you are but a ploughboy's son, but I am the son of a gentleman.' " He nodded. "You may well be right."

Spattering rain fell upon the window.

"I held things together as best I could," he said, "but that wasn't good enough. First Roberts split us in two, with his 'Senate' wing and that mad raid into Canada. Then Stephens and McCafferty at each other's throats, revolvers drawn. My God, boy, when a man's moment in history is over, he should vanish. In a puff of smoke. Or drop down the trapdoor in the stage."

O'Mahony here in New York, shoved aside. Indeed they were not gentlemen, the men from whom Nolan took his orders, not in O'Mahony's meaning of the word. Rossa, a shop assistant from Skibbereen; McCafferty, a bully who had learned his trade in the war, with Confederate irregulars.

Beyond the dusty window, Nolan could see an empty street shrouded by thin rain. The shops had turned on their lamps against an early darkness—a coal merchant, a greengrocer, an ironmonger. At the far corner, a saloon, its lamps globed in green and red, welcoming beyond rain, the chill of early winter.

"But I have yet a part to play, Captain Nolan," O'Mahony said. "Once I am dead, they can put me to work. I will return to Ireland then, Captain, and no mistake about it. Thousands marching along behind the coffin, ebony-draped. A quarrel, perhaps, for possession of the corpse, Fenians and Parliament men battering each other, with Her Majesty's constabulary to the keep the ring. And who at the graveside, would you think, to speak the panegyric—Dick Pigott, perhaps, or one of the Sullivans?"

Embarrassed, Nolan glanced away, and found himself looking again at the print of the uniformed colonel, poised and confident, a bit too theatrical.

"Oh, yes," O'Mahony said. "I know; no man knows this better than myself. I helped to bundle up the gin-soaked bones of Terence Bellew MacManus, and ship them off to Dublin. All the way from San Francisco. He was a useless sort of fellow in life, poor Terence; amiable but useless. But in death, by God, he put his shoulder to the wheel."

Nolan suddenly laughed, and turned away from the bright-coloured print, gaudy gilt insignia upon a tunic of midnight blue.

"It is best to look at things slant, Ned," O'Mahony said, "rather than head-on. It gives you a purchase upon life."

The lap robe had slipped to the floor. Ned knelt and tucked it about O'Mahony's knees. When he rose, the eyes, hawklike in the print, were half closed, and the still-handsome head was sinking.

"I will call in on you again if I may," Nolan said.

"By all means, Captain. By all means. Your father's son is always welcome. A splendid man, your father. Thomas Justin Nolan. He never found himself in this country. He was very proud of you, you know. I met him once during the war, at the Astor Bar. He had in his pocket a letter you had sent him, from Tennessee I think it was, or Virginia. He read a bit of it to me."

When Nolan was at the door, he turned around to speak, but O'Mahony was half asleep. In the street, he walked a block or two to a coal merchant's, and arranged to have a few bags sent up to the colonel. Then he walked westwards, in the distance the rain-clouded river.

O'Mahony's funeral went off as though he had himself drawn the design for it with a draughtsman's pencil: the service in Webster Hall, and the faithful gathered at the dock with black crepe armbands. In the hold of a steamship, coffin enclosed in sturdy planking, the first Head Centre of the Fenian Brotherhood returned at last to Ireland. Fenians and moderate nationalists vied for the honour of walking behind the coffin up Sackville Street to Glasnevin. It was raining that day in Dublin as well, the mean Irish drizzle of grey rain, but most walked with hats in hand, as token of respect. Newspapers were sent back to New York, with prints showing the crowd massed by the graveside in Glasnevin. Richard Pigott, standing beside the grave, read an oration sent from America by O'Donovan Rossa. "All differences set aside," Rossa said, through Pigott's lips, "we mourn today the death of the Chief, the Founder, gallant soldier, true Irishman."

"All differences set aside," Charlie Duignan said to Nolan. "That's a good one." They were in Hanafy's saloon on Eighth Street, waiting for Mick Coogan, the headquarters man. In the rear, by the door which led to the alley, at a small table, a beer before Nolan and a glass of whiskey before Duignan, his fingers curled around it.

"I will hear nothing said against John O'Mahony," Nolan said. He was facing the swinging double doors.

"Not from me," Duignan said. His family had come over from Limerick when he was three, and his speech was New York. *Thoid* he said for *third*, and *erl* for *oil*. Nolan was not fond of the accent, nor of Duignan.

"We've been destroyed by differences," Duignan said, "from the time of the Senate wing and the first big split. By God, if these fellows now won't see the sense of that, they must be made to see it."

"Something like that," Nolan said.

"Rossa has always been someone to march in his own parade," Duignan said, "with his own bugler blowing the praises of Jeremiah O'Donovan Rossa."

The swinging doors parted, but it was not Coogan. Two Yanks, one of them in coat and trousers of broad plaid, parted hair glistening with oil.

"He was not marching in his own parade in Dartmoor Prison," Nolan said. "In Dartmoor Prison he was a man in a cell, tormented. For all those years they were at him, but he would not be broken."

Duignan said nothing, and in the silence Nolan returned to Portland Prison. In blackness he lay on his pallet, that blackness unimaginable to others, the blackness not of night merely, but of a hostile, hating confinement, the sun closed off by stone and iron. Nolan remembered one night, early on, when he began suddenly to scream, the notes rising, a girlish, soprano scream. Up and down, to left of him and right, tin cups and slop buckets commenced to clatter, whether in sympathy or annoyance he could not tell. After that one time, he never screamed, but when he heard others, he would mouth, silently.

"He's straight," Duignan said, "Rossa is straight. But he's fucking crazy, and he can't leave this stuff alone." His forefinger tapped the rim of his glass.

Coogan pushed through the door, and stood within the smoky room, his head turning from this side to that, until he saw them. He was a Leitrim man, powerfully built, short, with heavy, squat shoulders, massive head set upon short, thick neck.

An abstainer, he took a glass of ginger beer at Duignan's insistence.

"The expenses you will have are in an envelope I will pass along to you. The railroad and lodgings out there and meals and the rest of it. It will see you through and a bit left over. There are so many Irishmen in Chicago that you can lose yourself amongst them. But stay clear of the organization. You are a couple of Paddies in search of employment."

"Ned here tells me that the organization has the goods on this fellow," Duignan said. "No doubt about it."

"No," Coogan said, "no doubt." Then, after a pause, he said, "Eh, Ned?"

"Not in my mind," Nolan said.

"Perhaps there is in your own," Coogan said to Duignan. "If there is, you should back off. I will send off no man on such a task if he has his doubts."

"No, no," Duignan said quickly.

They were days travelling on the cars between New York and Chicago. Duignan was excited at first, calling Nolan's attention to every town, low range of distant hills, water tower. But the monotony of the journey reached him at last, and he subsided. He wandered up and down the aisles, having conversations with strangers, and, once or twice, taking part in a game of cards. But Nolan cherished the wintry landscape, snow-covered fields, ponds covered with a brittle ice upon which sunlight fell pale and watery, houses and barns of timber, red-painted, bright against snow. Farm children, muffled and gloved against the cold, waved to them. The distances between towns was immense.

Dr. Sheehan lived in a suburb of the city, the frame houses sturdy and substantial, many of them with turrets and widow's walks, but the streets were unpaved and muddy. There were no gas lights. Nolan and Duignan waited in a byroad beyond Sheehan's house, in their hired car, the horse tired and placid. About ten that night, Sheehan's buggy came down the road, and he climbed out and threw the horse's reins over the hitching post. As he reached inside for his surgical bag, Nolan began walking towards him, with Duignan following.

"Dr. Sheehan," Nolan said.

"Yes," Sheehan said, startled. "Yes? Who is that?"

Nolan saw him in faint moonlight. The tintype had been a good likeness, a short, plump man with spectacles and a dark, close-cropped beard. The bag looked heavy. Sheehan shifted it from his right hand to his left.

"You know who we are, right enough," Nolan said. "You have been expecting us."

Sheehan craned forward. "Do I know you, lads? I cannot see you clearly."

"Kevin Timothy Sheehan," Nolan began, and Sheehan gave a long sigh, interrupting him.

"Yes," he said, "I know who you are."

"Sentence has been pronounced against you," Nolan said. "You are entitled to hear it."

"I am entitled to more than that," Sheehan said.

"No," Nolan said. "You were twice summoned to New York to answer the evidence. I wonder you did not do a flit."

"Once," Sheehan said. "I was called once by the Council, not twice. I could not leave my practice. I wrote to them."

The front windows of the house were lit, and Nolan could see a figure, Sheehan's wife or else the maidservant moving behind the drawn shade.

"It is all over, Doctor," Nolan said. "Talking is of no use."

"Give him his time, Ned, for God's sake," Duignan said. "An Act of Contrition and a minute to compose himself."

"He has a fair amount to be contrite about," Nolan said, "and time is short."

"Ned," Sheehan said. "I have you now. Ned Nolan. I saw you once in Hibernian Hall."

"And wrote me up in a special despatch to Mr. Anderson in Dublin Castle?" Nolan said. "Or did you save me for one of your trips across into Canada, one of your talks with Mr. Fleming?"

"Dear Jesus," Sheehan said.

For a moment, no one spoke.

"I have my rosary," Sheehan said. "An Act of Contrition and a decade of the rosary. To Our Lady."

He reached his hand into the pocket of his overcoat, and as he was drawing it out, Nolan raised his arm and shot him. He was hurled backward, and as he began to fall, Nolan shot him twice more, full in the chest.

With a wary eye upon the house, Nolan knelt beside him, and Duignan joined them, not kneeling, but with his hands pressed down upon his bent knees. He stared at the smashed chest, the open, staring eyes, beard-framed gaping mouth, and then, turning his head swiftly to the side, vomited.

Carefully, Nolan drew the hand out of Sheehan's pocket. The fingers were still curled loosely about the revolver, and he drew out hand and revolver together. When Duignan, coughing, had placed a handkerchief across his mouth, Nolan said, "There is your rosary."

"Oh God," Duignan said. "Oh God, oh God."

In the city the next afternoon and well into the night, Duignan got himself drunk. Nolan sat beside him, first in one bar and then in another, taking one careful drink to Duignan's four or five, and monitoring what he said. In the early hours of the morning, he saw him back to their lodging house and put him to bed. Two days later, they went back to New York. By the time they reached the terminal, Duignan was almost himself again, and beginning to swagger a bit, to hint at secret errands.

Nolan sought out Coogan, and said, "Never again give me that sort of task. I have no stomach for it."

"But you did it, Ned," Coogan said. "A neat, clean job, and it had to be done."

"Not by me," Nolan said. "Not again."

It was not until the eighties that he broke that oath, but the killing of Dr. Sheehan was enough to set the seal upon his reputation. The murder was never solved, but the rumours about Ned Nolan spread in Fenian circles, that he was one of the hard men, one of the irreconcilables. "He carries a gun with him," they would say, "and he has used it more than once." "Small blame," they would say, "after the things that were done to him in that prison." In those days, the organization was a spectral being, moving behind the façades of mass meetings, parades, patriotic holidays on the shores of New Jersey and Long Island, more bunting, and immense portraits of Washington and Robert Emmet in twin ovals. It called itself now the Clan na Gael, and judges and congressmen were among its members, Tammany sachems, lawyers, assemblymen. But somewhere within the Clan was the unnamed Supreme Council. Devoy controlled it, perhaps, or O'Donovan Rossa. Or perhaps they took their orders from Dublin, or Belfast. It fed itself upon mystery, upon the legends of the 'sixty-seven rising, the men hanged in Manchester, the men tortured in English prisons. Nolan was part of that. At Clan na Gael picnics on sandy beaches, children shouting, speeches and then a game of ball, New York policemen and firemen with Irish names would nudge each other and nod towards him. But he went to such affairs because Devoy thought they were good for morale. Black-jacketed, a crow among fleshy, perspiring men in candy-striped shirts.

His cousin Hugh MacMahon wrote regularly to him, and there would be once or twice a year a letter from Bob Delaney. They would have written more often, but Nolan did not always reply. When he did, his language was stiff, constrained, unlike MacMahon's genial, calculated rambling, and Delaney's crisp enthusiasms, sardonic accounts of his own successes, local follies. But he saved all the letters, and would once in a while reread them. The few weeks which he had spent with them in Kilpeder expanded into one of his centres of imaginative being. He recalled MacMahon's parlour, Mary at the pianoforte, a long Sunday walk with Delaney, Vincent Tully's yelping laugh as he unscrewed a flask. The distant Munster town he remembered in such odd, random moments, domestic and at ease. The crash of rifle fire, Clonbrony Wood, shattered the memory. Beyond the town, beyond Clonbrony, beyond the hillside cabin from which he had sent out the raiders, lay the hills which he had never visited, brown or green or purple in the constantly changing light. In imagination he walked them, along thin, forbidding paths, beside pure, icy rivulets, gorse, rocks scrubbed black and shiny as anthracite by rain and mist. Turning, in imagination, Kilpeder would lie spread before him, spired, populous, unreachable.

16

[*Hugh MacMahon*]

In memory, I can hear a Dublin hawker of ballads, his voice nasal and whining, as he offers to passersby his latest composition. He sings, "For the uncrowned king of Ireland lies in Kilmainham Gaol." I can remember nothing about the man himself, nor the time of day, nor what others heard him sing as they stood listening or hurrying past, but only the voice itself, and it does not carry more to me than that one line. But it fixes for me a time in all of our lives. It was in October of 1881 that Parnell and the other leaders were arrested and imprisoned in Kilmainham, and they were there until the following May, after the "treaty," as it was called, had been signed. And in the Christmas week of that year, I went up to Dublin to pay a visit upon Bob Delaney, who was in Dublin upon Land League business or his own or Tully's business, off and on for the most of that winter.

Once during that week, Bob's affairs took him into Kilmainham itself, to consult with Parnell and Egan, and I went out with him in the tram, a lovely brief journey, with the Phoenix Park just beyond. He would be several hours at least, and so I walked through the wintry park, its trees bare-branched, lining the long stately avenues, and then, with little longer to wait, settled down in the public house across from the prison entrance. It is a fierce, forbidding building, its stones immense and sullen.

There were no ballad hawkers outside Kilmainham, you may be certain, but the song is nevertheless entwined for me with my view of the prison itself, as I sat looking out towards it, nursing my pint of porter. A cold day, a damp, Dublin cold which the turf fire fought in vain, and I sat huddled within my overcoat. "By God," Bob said when he joined me, "they have a grand life of it in there, Parnell and the others. A sitting room as big as this tavern, and Parnell's bedroom, it could not be called a cell, leading off from it. They are being confined in great state." He signalled the barman, holding his two hands to signify that he needed a tall one. He was in great good spirits.

And there, in those words, the special flavour of those miraculous years is defined for me. Parnell was in prison right enough, and his chief lieutenants with him, but there was no way in which the British could keep him there forever. The ballad, with its air of weepy lamentation, was an expected ritual, a dutiful grieving that yet another Irish leader had been flung into a dungeon. But this was no four-for-a-tanner leader, this was Charles Stewart Parnell, whom we had indeed come to regard, in a few short years, as our uncrowned king, negotiating, from within a gaol, with Gladstone himself, the parleyings of equals. It is painful now to look back on those years.

After the long, bleak decade which stretched outwards from our wretched rising, everything suddenly tumbled upwards from wherever it is that history keeps her energies concealed. Young Patrick Prentiss, perhaps, could find a pattern in it, but I find none. The fearful, black harvest of 'seventy-nine, when it seemed that another famine was upon us, Parnell's seizure of political control, Davitt and the Land League— everything seemed to be happening at once, and all the parts of it feeding one another. Suddenly, or at least so it now seems, suddenly we were moved from lethargy, from a kind of casual and painless despair, into excitements, hopes, torchlit processions, cheering crowds. Later, in those final years of his, when Bob had ample time to talk and reflect, we would turn, the two of us, to the question of why, of how it had happened, and of how, because of it, the country was changed, forever it would seem. But Bob had no better answers than I had myself, although Bob was drawn close to the centre of events, and I was myself but one of the hurlers on the ditch.

"The uncrowned king," he said to me, in one of the late years. "A mysterious phrase."

"A good phrase for the hustings," I said, "for ballads, newspapers." I was affecting a bitterness to match his own, but which in truth I did not share. For those of us who stood at the foot of platforms looking upwards, at meetings held in the long, light evenings, but with torches and pitch barrels flaring, looking upwards at the rows of county councillors crammed into ill-fitting suits, local dignitaries, Land League agents, the occasional bland, smiling priest—for us he was an uncrowned king or something of that sort, well-tailored clothes ruined by the careless manner in which he wore them, a knit shooting waistcoat, rough and well-used beneath dark, rich broadcloth. He was a handsome man, as even his enemies allowed, but his vanity did not run to physical appearances, and he never seemed conscious of his even features: the black, deep-set eyes; high, arched nose; the silky, auburn beard. We always remembered his voice. Not that what he said was memorable; far from it. He had a gift for ordering an argument, and one for spare, unornamented energy of language. There were times when what he said was electrifying, as in the famous speech at Ennis, which in effect declared war upon the government. Bob was in Ennis that day, not yet a sitter upon platforms, but standing close to that one, and he came home to tell me that Parnell spoke out his words flatly and without gestures, his hands at his side curled tight, as though oratory was a trial for him. No, what we remembered of his voice was its manner and its accent, which was for us the accent of landlords, fox hunters, indolent indifferent men on horseback, their voices carrying the unmistakable authority of overlordship.

"And he looked like a king in command," I said to Bob, light mockery, self-protecting, quoting a line from one of the ballads. "So he did," Bob said in that late year, "so he did." We were sitting in his solicitor's office, which fronted on the market square—a large, square room which had once been in constant bustle, Bob shouting out orders to his clerk, Jamesey Gannon, and Jamesey shouting out a mock-insolent rejoinder, a pair of clients in the room perhaps, strong-farmers, fleshy and red-faced, and the wide mahogany desk strewn with papers, joined by some mysterious order known only to Jamesey, but the room dusty now, the desk bare save for brass inkstand and whiskey decanter, and the window dirt-streaked.

"So he did," Bob said. "Like a king in command. Do you know what they are all saying now, O'Brien and that little cur Healy and the rest of them? Each of them in turn comes forward to say that Parnell was simply 'Parnell' to him, but 'Mr. Parnell' to the others. God, the gobshite snobbery of the Irish. To desert a man, and then stand firm upon a point of social precedence."

"And which was it for you?" I said. " 'Parnell' or 'Mr. Parnell'?"

Bob smiled, and measured whiskey into our glasses, lovely Waterford tumblers, cut like diamonds. "We never knew him, you know, none of us. Healy was close to him, by way of party business, but he never mingled with us after hours, so to speak. Old stagers with a bit of gentility clinging to them, they saw a bit of him: O'Gorman Mahon and a few of those. He was as much a mystery to us as he was to the rest of the country. He made use of that mystery. He would stroll into the House late at night, well after the dinner hour, and take his seat, with his tall hat pulled down over his eyes. They hated him, the Liberals as well as the Tories, make no mistake about that. They could laugh at the rest of us, call us counter-boys and bog-trotters, but they could not laugh at him."

And though I had talked with him once, had shaken his hand; though I had been to a dozen of his meetings; though, at the end, at considerable personal and professional peril, I had stood beside him, myself and thirty or forty others, in a windswept town square, with a mob hurling taunts at us, at him, he was for me in life what he is now in memory—an outline, a shape, into which we had poured our hopes.

A dreary decade, I have called the seventies, and so they were from the point of view of fellows like myself and Bob, who were what the cant phrase of the time called "advanced nationalists," by which was meant Fenians who had been so tempered by experience that they were unlikely to shoot at you from behind a ditch. But for others, by which is meant the great majority of ordinary people, rich and poor, it was a golden season of fine harvests. It is as though the Rising, like the famine earlier by two decades, was a wound healed over, a whitened patch of flesh without pain or feeling. Below us, in towns like Skibbereen and Schull, the famine graves lay neglected, mass graves of the nameless dead, a shame and scandal to survivors that we had ever, and well within memory, sunk so low. In Cork, at least—I cannot speak for other counties—the famine had cut a clean swath, and the poorest of the poor were gone, the fellows of one or two acres, or no acres at all, but perched for a season on some scrawny hillside that could furnish forth a lazy bed of potatoes, gone to the famine graves or the workhouses or the emigrant ships. There were few now who did not have their twenty acres at least, and the number of substantial farmers had grown mightily.

All that was to change, all that warm late summer of contentment. And the change began with the three wretched harvests which ended the seventies. The summer of 'seventy-seven was wet and cold, the skies low and close, and there seemed a constant drizzle of rain. There was a break in the bad weather, just long enough to let the farmers save the hay, and although the prices for crops fell, they held for cattle and there was the best yield of butter that had been seen for years. But the following year was worse: there was no respite for the hay, all prices fell together, and most frightening of all, the blight returned to the potato, and the heavy rains and floods helped to spread it. It was like early winter, that summer of 'seventy-eight, the heavy air sweet with the smell of burning turf. When you walked into one of Kilpeder's public houses, you would see there farmers standing together, talking little. The weather that summer cut short my Sunday rambles, but once, with a few hours of rare, bright sunlight, I set out towards the hills, and as I neared the Killeter crossroads, I came upon a long, wide field of potatoes which the blight had touched. I was separated from it by a high fence of stone, a dry wall. There was no one in sight, although smoke rose from the farmhouse, a neat, prosperous-looking building, handsomely whitewashed, and with the doors and window frames painted a bright, fresh blue. In a far pasture, a herd rested beneath wide-spreading oak branches. Beyond that, far to my left, a stream tumbled down a rain-choked hill, with no sound coming to me from that distance. A scene for Constable, you will say, or Stubbs; but the white substance, splashed across the potato plants, at random, sent a shiver through me. It was like the emblem of an ancient terror.

It was then, in that second of the bad harvests, that the farmers began asking the landlords for abatements of the rents, and with such success as may be predicted; and to make matters the worse for them, there was a great tightening of credit at the banks. And a tightening of credit as well with regard to those less formal transactions which farmers had been in the habit of using. But the firm of Tully and Son was an exception to this, with the old man standing ready, as often in the past, to carry over an account, whether a large one or a small, and to make the prudent loan. It was no longer a matter of a handshake in the back room, or of an X scrawled upon a sheet of paper, but all was done in a proper and legal manner, and in Bob's office, with legal documents crammed with Latin obscurities and the signatures of witnesses, and seals of red wax.

Once, when Mary and I had gone for tea to the Delaneys, Bob left the two women to talk together of this thing and that, and drew me into the room which held his books. The tall window looked out across the road to Tully's house, a proud, bullying building of three storeys, which you would be more likely to see in Cork City or Limerick, set solidly upon its own grounds. From a leather box on the table, he drew out two cigars, and the two of us stood together by the window, the air fragrant with good tobacco.

"That fellow," he said, "is more solid than many a small landlord in this barony. There is a thought for you."

But it was a thought which had often occurred to me, and I could think of nothing by way of a reply.

"Lands, leases, notes, tenancies. When he reads, his lips move silently, and his eyes squeeze almost shut. And yet he is by now more banker than shopkeeper. By God, Hughie, is he not a wonderful being?"

"He has wonderful assistance," I said, from truthfulness rather than courtesy.

"Even there, Hughie, even there. He has the gift of foresight, as all great commanders have, Caesar and Bonaparte and Sheridan. A small farmer's son comes to him as a shop assistant, and he sees in him the makings of a solicitor." He turned away from the window and looked towards me, the cigar clamped between his teeth in a manner that Vincent would have carried off with an air, but which with Bob seemed but vulgar. He grinned. "He looks at a Fenian back from six months of hard labour, and sees a son-in-law. He has the gift of divination, of prophecy."

He made me uneasy, as though, against his own nature, he had moved into a vein of coarse and unappealing cynicism.

"I am in his debt, Hughie. What do I not owe to him—this house, my solicitor's articles, my law books, the chance to move out from behind a counter. Not, mind you, that I am not now well able to pay my own way. My practice extends each year. I would have a comfortable income if I did not do another stroke of work for Tully and Son. But there is a heavy debt there all the same. He has no need to remind me of it."

"But he does find ways to remind you?" I asked.

"No, no," he said at once. "I would do him an injustice were I to suggest that. He is a generous man, when he has a liking for you. But it is an oppressive feeling, for all that. Ach, what am I saying, can you tell me that?"

But I could not. I had my own private feelings about the Tullys, as I have earlier set forth, although I exempted Agnes and Vincent, who seemed not to be Tullys at all. And this seemed a conversation in poor taste, with Agnes sitting distant from us by but the thickness of a wall. But between Bob and myself there had rarely been secrets and reticences, and perhaps now I should have pressed him as to the causes of his unease. Instead of which, we smoked down our cigars in a companionable near-silence.

"He is a godsend, certainly," I said at last, "at the present moment.

If the talk in town is to be believed at all, there are twenty farmers at least who owe it to Dennis Tully that they have this day roofs over their heads, and he has been most generous in extending credit to the small fellows as well."

Bob shot me a look that was almost one of anger. "As I have said," he said dryly, "he is a generous man."

"All right, then," I said. "He has his own reasons for what he does. A grand house like the one across the way is not conjured out of the empty air. The fellows who have borrowed from him will have a heavy sack of debt. But he will give them time, and the landlords would not, and the banks would not. If there is a Tully flourishing in Kilpeder, it is because he is needed."

"I know that, Hughie," he said. "I know that. But is not this barony in a sorry state if two bad harvests can wedge the people between the landlords on the one hand and the gombeen men on the other."

It was an ugly term, and rarely had I heard Bob make use of it, although its use in the streets and public houses of Kilpeder was casual and universal. It was a term from the Tully past, from the huckster's shop in the lane, a clod of muck flung against the tall house of bow windows and rose-red brick.

"Two bad harvests," I remember him saying, and that would place his words in 1878, with terrible 'seventy-nine yet to come. In the first two years of the bad harvests, at least the prices held for store cattle and for butter. But in the year that followed, the harvest was wrecked again, first the hay and then the grains, and a winter followed that was the worst in memory, with the cattle suffering and many sheep dying. If the farmers, and the labourers who depended upon them, had been grim in the years before, they were now petrified with alarm, and small blame to them.

The summers of those years were but a milder form of winter, the days even of July and August chill, and the rain almost constant and steady, the skies low and masked by dirty grey cloud. In the summer of 'seventy-eight, the potato blight appeared again. Although it was but local and transient, it was like a messenger from the unspeakable past. Once, of a wet chilly August Sunday, I walked out for a few miles along the north road. The rain would come in spattering gusts, and I would take the shelter of a hedge. Then it would clear again, for a half hour or so, and the clouds in the western sky would shift, but there was no clear, bright sunlight. The smell of wet, heavy hay was sweet and cloying.

Those few of us who had our lives and beings in the town—doctors and solicitors and schoolmasters and saddlemakers—fancied ourselves men of the world, readers of newspapers, discoursers upon events. But not one of us was far removed from the land, and in our boyhoods had learned to read skies and roots rather than journals. Indeed, even in our present lofty existences, the wrecked harvests had their effect. The publicans were discovering that the strong-farmers were no longer summoning up rounds of drink in the old lavish way, and the saddlers that they were making do with what they had, mending and improvising. There was less call now upon Donald Considine, the Catholic doctor, for the treatment of every ailment: now the country people were once more content to apply themselves to the "black bottle," which had never lost favour with the old, that potent mixture sold not in the chemist's, but across Tully's counter, in a jet-black bottle, the ornate label bearing a wide-ranging list of afflictions.

"You see now how it is," I can imagine Bob saying to me. "The very heavens conspire with the Tullys. The potatoes rot at the stalk and up go the sales of Father John's mixture."

That observation I imagine rather than remember, but in truth I recall from those years the ruinous economy and Bob's ill humour as intertwined. He was in a kind of rage which moved out first in one direction and then in another, and once or twice against me. Never, so far as I could judge, against Agnes, although who can say how married people deal with each other behind closed bedroom doors? Yet surely his manner towards her in public was not merely courteous but affectionate, and such matters are not easily feigned before close friends. Agnes doted upon him, so Mary more than once informed me, and I had no need of the assurance, for when he handed a book or a cup, her small white hand would linger upon his a moment or two, and her wide pale eyes would seek out his.

The nuns in the Cork City convent had given Agnes a dutiful love of fine music, and the skill to play and to sing it with a winning sweetness. Once or twice she had played for us, coolly and accurately, sitting erect in one of those dark gowns which she wore by preference. When it came to the piano, my Mary was ready for anything, tearing into Chopin or Tom Moore or one of the tunes which I brought down with me from the Derrynasaggarts, and what she lacked in authority, she made up for by energy and wit. But Agnes, plainly, was fulfilling a social obligation and drawing scant delight from it, so that after a bit, we ceased to pester her upon the subject. And yet when Mary played, or Vincent, she would attend with a sweetness that won our hearts, Mary's and my own, and her eyes rested with pleasure upon each of us, but settled at last, always, upon Bob. And if the instrument upon which Mary was playing, or Vincent, was not ours, but rather the awesome instrument which had been brought to the Delaneys from Dublin, by sea to Cork City, and then, by careful stages, to Macroom and then Kilpeder, its sleek, sumptuous wood the visual texture of satin, but warm and living to the touch, then Agnes's pleasure would move beyond this circle of friends, to encompass the rich room itself, the heavy hangings at the windows, woods glowing in lamplight.

"Jack of all trades," Vincent would say, as he rose up after playing "The Rakes of Mallow" or "The Kilruddery Hunt," or occasionally, without warning, catching us, Schumann or Schubert, playing very well indeed for one without formal training, with both feeling and intelligence, but with an eye cocked towards us, as though to say, "What think you of this, lads?" But he was with us less often than we wished, for it was on the Friday night or the Saturday that we would gather, ourselves and a half dozen others, Donald Considine and his wife, Brian Roche, the town's other Catholic solicitor, and Larry Saurin, the lesser of the two Protestant solicitors, a decent, dim fellow, with a fund of faded pleasantries. And on the weekends, Vincent was most often otherwise engaged, visiting, in accordance with the season, at fishing lodges or shooting boxes through the county, indeed throughout Munster, and on occasion ranging far afield to Connemara or Donegal. At times he would be away for weeks upon end, to Dublin or London or the Continent, whence he would return with funds of anecdotes, hints, winks for the men, and for the ladies, for Agnes and Mary, accounts of fashions and boulevards, churches tucked way in odd corners of the countryside outside Paris, or a description of Versailles, myriad-roomed, a Babel of vanity touched by the vengeance of man, not God.

"I was once," he said—to Bob and myself, that is—in the snug of the Kilpeder Arms, "I was once upon a small tour of Versailles, and the very next week I was in London, walking along the Thames, with the Tower behind me, facing Parliament and the Abbey. A bracing experience. It teaches one who rules the world in this century, a walk along the Thames does. Lads, how did we ever bring ourselves to think that we could face up against the English, can any one answer me that?"

"We were younger," I said. "Fellows in our twenties."

"Even lads in their twenties should have better sense," Vincent said. "But sure the cause was a good one. I have no regrets; none of us has. 'Out and make way for the bold Fenian men,' as the song has it. You know that song, do you not?" he said to the ginger-headed young barman. "Well, here are three of us, the bold Fenian men."

The barman looked up from the glass he had been polishing, and smiled at us.

"Can you answer me?" Vincent said in challenge, almost with an under edge of anger, to Bob.

[344]

"As Hughie says," Bob said, in a tone which gave a full stop to our words, "we were younger."

Bob walked me home that night, for I had taken a pint or two more than was convenient, so pleasant had the evening been, in the warmth of the snug, the warmth of masculine friendship. It was a winter night, crisp and cold, and the heavens starry. "He is forever in Paris, that fellow," I said, "if he isn't in London. Tis well for him. Operas and theatres and museums all spread out before him."

"Opera, bedad," Bob said with a delighted yelp of a laugh. "Tis the women of Paris that he has spread out before him, one by one for the most part, on soft mattresses and creamy sheets. Sure, who among us would not haste away with such a goal beckoning?"

"Do you think that?" I said, disbelieving and with an obscure fear. Vincent to be sure was great for talking about women—"a certain pair of dark eyes in Paris," that sort of thing—but always with a music-hall twist to it, a joke, an affectation of manliness. But there was a bluntness to what Bob said, more in his tone than in the words themselves.

We had paused, just at the point where that side of the square becomes the Macroom road, and a bit before the turning into Chapel Street.

"Of course I think it," Bob said impatiently. "Why should I not think it? Vincent is unmarried and he has the usual equipment, and enough money to carry him to the brothels of Timbuktu, never mind Paris, should he fancy something a bit out of the ordinary. But Paris suffices, or so he tells me."

"He tells you," I said, foolishly repeating him. "He was having sport with you most likely."

"Having sport indeed," Bob said, "but not with me, I thank you."

To this day, I can remember the feelings which suddenly took hold of me there, as though Bob and Vincent had moved swiftly a far distance away from me, and there was naught between us but empty space. And I remember my feeling of foolishness, of appearing foolish before Bob, like one of my own pupils.

"It would not be exact," Bob said, "to speak of him as a whoremaster. He has too many other pursuits—hunting and shooting and squiring ladies. But our Vincent is a lively lad, and what the ladies will not proffer to him freely, he does not scruple to buy. Like many another."

"Yes," I said bleakly, and it was only then that Bob recognised my unease. He scarcely could study my features, in the moonless night, but he caught my tone.

"Good God, Hughie," he said, "I have shocked you. That was surely not my intention. I thought you knew, but how could you?"

"Vincent and I have never talked of such a matter," I said, "although I thought that we kept nothing back from one another."

"Then once at least," Bob said, "that took an effort on his part. Twas the year before last, when he came back from London with a dose, and he was up to Dublin once a week to have it attended to. He didn't dare go to see Considine, and he was trembling lest old Tully learn of the matter." He laughed. "There was no other matter that he would talk of with me, morning or night."

"Ah," I said, "and did things come right in the end?" It was, I trusted, a manly, offhand question.

"So it would seem," Bob said. "At any rate, he stopped talking about it, thanks be to God. The symptoms are most unappealing, at least to fastidious chaps like ourselves."

He slapped me on the back, and the awkward moment passed. We resumed our walk, for the short distance that was in it, but found little to say, a companionable silence.

Rural Ireland, whatever may be said on its behalf by sanctimonious patriots and mission priests, has its full share of human nature—couples courting behind the hedges, and on occasion carrying courtship too far. We had our share, that is, of marriages arranged by circumstances, and on occasion a terrible fate awaited a frightened girl who struggled to give birth alone, in darkened barn or in shed smelling of rotten hay and rusty iron. We had worse indeed than that, things unmentionable but of which all of us knew. And as for the gentry, the legends which clung about them were sulphurous—of riotous parties, and of squireens with their tally women—and few were the baronies of Munster which did not have a story left over from earlier times, from the bad, ended century, of some landlord who did not scruple to exercise the *droit du seigneur.* The story is told about a desolate manor house halfway between here and Macroom, derelict and windowless, the chimney fallen, where girls would be taken, bound and lamenting. No, I had my full knowledge of such human nature as might come to a fellow living in the countryside, and yet, absurdly, I had not imagined it within the circle of my days. For a married man, I must have seemed, to Bob and Vincent, absurdly innocent.

At my gate, we paused, and although I asked Bob in for a parting glass, we both knew that it was late, and he declined.

"Hughie," he said, "I have been talking out of turn. You will not think the less of Vincent."

"No, no," I said. "It is not that at all. Not that at all." Nor was it. What troubled me was outside reason, and had no name. It was as though Bob and Vincent shared a world of experience, sensation, textures almost, from which I was excluded. I wanted no part of it, and yet I felt shut out, a breach in our friendship.

"I wonder," I said with malice, "that you could not contrive reasons to take yourself off with Vincent, to Paris or wherever."

He answered my malice with a bluntness that had its own edge. "I am a married man, Hughie. And in the days before my marriage, I could scarcely have afforded a trip to France. I contented myself quite comfortably with the whores of Cork City." And with that he turned upon his heel, and walked off to his handsome and well-appointed house.

It was as though we had been caught in a mysterious quarrel, the terms of which were known to neither of us. When next we met, we made no reference to it, but were our old intimate selves, and yet such passages always leave marks upon a friendship, like scratches on a varnished surface. That night, late or not, I poured myself a good measure of whiskey before climbing up to bed, and sat quietly drinking it, in darkness.

The third of the years which rounded off the decade was the worst. The September fair of that year was crowded, as always, with men and beasts and noises, but there was little of the laughter and jesting of other years, the human warmth, the sportive malice and delight in sharp trading. Some of the fellows who stood that day in the market square had been travelling about that month, from fair to fair, from Millstreet to Macroom and from Macroom to Kilpeder, looking for what other years had schooled them to think a decent price. But the bottom had fallen out of the market, and there was now an unreasoning anger of one man against another, farmer against farmer, farmer against dealer. When a bargain was struck that September day, the old custom was but seldom observed, the two fellows spitting each one into the palm of his hand, and then the two clasped hands. This day it was more often a curt nod upon each side, and the dealer making a scribble upon his folded square of paper.

That year, the dealers drank in the Kilpeder Arms and the strong-farmers in Conefry's, with little traffic between the two. Along the sides of the market square, as always, hucksters had set up their stalls, with ribbons and thimbles for sale, religious pictures in heavy ochres and magentas, save for the Virgin in her white and pale blue, bags of boiled sweets for the children, chapbooks with the "prophecies" of Columkille and Pastorini, small wrappings of sachets to bring home to wives and sisters. The women whose stalls they were would have places allotted to them by tradition, and for the September fair, some of them had come from Killarney and from as far away as Kanturk and Dunmanway. They had a great way with them—great strapping women, the most of them, with black shawls and red petticoats, and leather lungs with which to bawl out their wares. But that year, they shouted in vain, and their customers were few—a strong-farmer swaggering out of Conefry's with a bladderful of porter, or a foolish labourer. They gathered together towards evening, therefore, in their twos and threes, arms crossed, to discuss the bad season. With nightfall, the drizzle of small rain became a steady pelting, and they flung cloths over their barrows and trundled them away. The public houses and the hotel had still their trade, but the square now was empty, with the rain beating down upon it, a cheerless spectacle. It was the same that autumn across the breadth of Munster. Across the Shannon, in Connaught, it was worse yet, as we were shortly to learn.

"Next year" was a phrase much used that year—next year things would come right again, the summer clear-skied and bountiful and the distant markets eager once more for Munster cattle. And next year, 1880, was indeed to be different, although in ways that few of us expected. I have seen it set down in print that just then, in the very months and weeks of which I have been speaking, Ireland moved out from her long, shadowed night and into the daylight glare and noise of history. A foolish notion indeed, for the eighties did to be sure bring us noise and glare enough, and at their close few upon the island had not been altered in one way or another, in fortune or in mind; but it had shadow as well as light, mysteries, and unexpected turnings. At the time, of course, we had no notion of what was beginning.

For us, if I were to name now a beginning, it would be in early October, a few weeks after that wretched, comfortless fair, when Bob was summoned to the police barracks, where a fellow named Mick Docherty was awaiting his removal to the gaol in Macroom, upon a charge of attempted murder. In the event, he travelled himself to Macroom the next day, riding there in advance of Docherty and his guards, and returning at about nine that night. He went first to the barracks, and then to the Kilpeder Arms, where he had a cup of tea laced with whiskey, and then to my house, where I poured him a second whiskey, while Mary went off to the kitchen to boil an egg for him and to cut a few slices of bread.

Neither Mary nor I thought it curious that it was to us rather than to his own house that he came. Indeed, we had been expecting him, without quite knowing why. By now, all of Kilpeder knew of Docherty's arrest, and knew also that he had fired the two barrels of a shotgun at another Mick, Mick Tobin, at close range, one of the charges smashing Tobin's shoulder into a mess of blood and meat and splintered bone. Conefry's had been full of talk of it when I looked in earlier that night, and with each telling the explosion resounded more loudly, and the gouts of bloody flesh leaped higher.

"Conefry's patrons are an imaginative lot, no question of it," Bob said, when I described the scene to him. "In truth, there were no witnesses at all. Docherty walked across a wet field to Tobin, and when he thought that he was close enough, he shouted and then cut loose with the shotgun. After that he walked back home. Tobin lay there bellowing like a calf until one of his sons found him."

"How is he?" I asked.

"Which one? Tobin? He will recover, Considine tells me, but the shoulder will not. He is badly maimed."

"Dear Jesus," I said.

"Exactly," Bob said dryly. "And how is Docherty? I left him sitting in his cell, with his hands on his knees, staring straight ahead. He is in a bad way, but he drifts in and out of his senses, and I got a good account of what happened."

"And in the cell he will remain," I said, "until the assizes?"

"And in one cell or another for long years afterwards," Bob said. "When the sergeant went out to his farm to arrest him, he made a clean breast of the matter, and he made a statement in the barracks and signed it." He shrugged, and held up his empty glass to me.

"What possessed him?" I said. "Had they been quarrelling?"

"They had indeed," he said, and then, just as I was refilling our glasses, Mary called to us, and we carried them down with us to the kitchen.

"Yes," he said, carefully tapping the egg with his spoon, as though the shell held mysteries captive within it. "They had been quarrelling. Docherty is to be evicted from his farm, and Tobin intends to take up the lease. Now that I reflect upon the matter, it may have become moot. The law has removed Docherty away from Kilpeder entirely, and from what the police and Considine tell me, Tobin has been ruined for the ploughing. His sons are too young."

He smiled at me, and I could not resist a grin myself.

"I am ashamed of you, the two of you," Mary said. "'Tis no subject for jests. A man shattered in body, and a neighbour sitting in a gaol cell. You have been in cells yourselves, the two of you. Did you relish the experience?"

"We did not, Mary," Bob said. "Not at all."

"I do not think I know them at all," Mary said. "Neither of them. Has Docherty a family as well?"

"Oh, he does," Bob said. "He does indeed. A wife and seven children, and he still young, more or less. And he has a brother off in America. Chris Docherty. Christopher. Does that name sound familiar at all to you, Hughie?"

I shook my head. "There are two of Tobin's lads in school to me, and two of Docherty's. Lately there has been bad blood between them, and I never thought to ask the cause."

"I can tell it to you easily enough," Bob said, as he cut in two one of Mary's immense slices of thick-buttered toast.

Mick Docherty was one of Lord Ardmor's tenants, as his father had been before him, holding on lease a farm of thirty acres southwards of the Killarney road. Where they had come from before that, no one knew. In the early years after the great famine, when all that region was depopulated, Pat Docherty appeared in Kilpeder, a young unmarried man, with enough cash on him to persuade old Everard Chute, who was then the estate agent, to make over a lease to him. The cabin on the holding was still standing, and into it he moved with all his possessions crammed into a bulging bag made from carpeting—a vest, some shirts, a missal, a rosary, and a leather bag of gold guineas.

Within days of the shot that he fired in Tobin's field, the history of Mick Docherty's family had become Kilpeder legend, and even today, with all of them long gone, you can hear it rehearsed. The missal and the rosary and the leather bag I am inclined to mistrust; they are the stuff of fairy tale, like the legend of the first Tully rising up out of the mist. But that old Pat Docherty was a stranger to Cork I can well believe. It is not a Cork name at all, nor even a Munster name. It was a family that kept to itself, and when it came time for him to marry, he left Kilpeder for a month, and came back with a girl from Adare, in Limerick, whom he had all along intended to marry, and who told neighbours that they had met some years before, when Pat was a gamekeeper on Lord Dunraven's lands. But there was little else that they learned from her, as though Docherty had put a stopper on her tongue.

"They were a curious people always," I one night heard one of the neighbours, Dinny Loftus, say in Conefry's. "Decent, helpful people always, and courteous. But they kept themselves to themselves, if you know what I mean. It is strange how first they came into these parts, the old man walking through a wasted countryside, picking and choosing from among the farms of those who had died or had been swept away, God rest them, and then walking with his bag of gold to the gates of the Castle."

"'Tis said that luck never follows a grabber," one of the drinkers said to Loftus, "and now, in the heel of the hunt, there is Mick Docherty in Macroom Gaol for shooting a grabber."

"He was no grabber," Loftus said fiercely. "By God, old Pat Docherty was no grabber. My own father took up the fields which marched beside Docherty's, and you nor no other man will call my father a grabber. The poor souls had all been swept away, I am telling you, and the fields had gone back to nature. They are buried in the famine graves at Tullynally, the men who had worked those fields."

"Ach, to be sure, to be sure," the drinker said. "I intended no offence whatever, Dinny. But Mick Tobin, now," and the drinker swivelled his head, hat-crowned, to left and to right, lest any of Tobin's chums be in earshot, "he was prepared to grab."

And so he was. A part of the story as Bob told it to me that night, the plate of crusts and hardening yolk thrust back, and the bottle brought down from above to the table, he had already known, and the rest of it Mick Docherty told him in Macroom, sitting almost motionless, looking ahead of him. In 'seventy-seven and again in 'seventy-eight, Docherty, like others, had sought an abatement of his rent, but Edward Chute had refused all of them. He was not acting alone; the estate agents of West Cork and some of those in Kerry had been consulting on the matter, and had concluded that abatements were not warranted, not yet at any rate. And the same judgement was made for this, the third year.

I can imagine easily the two of them, Chute and Docherty, in the estate office: tin boxes of papers, deeds, letters, yellowed notations a half century old, a century, piled forehead-high, Chute's desk a warren of crannies, slots, drawers with small knobs of grimed, unpolished brass, and on the walls—framed in walnut and scrolled, heavy oak—estate maps, builders' elevations, and, of course, the print of the town of Kilpeder whose legend declared that the town, and doubtless all who dwelt within it, were the property of the Earls of Ardmor. I know that room well. There is but one tall window, facing eastwards, with a view, beyond demesne, beyond walls, beyond fields, of the distant Boggeraghs.

As Docherty described the scene to Bob, Chute invited him to be seated, and so the two men sat facing each other, their knees almost touching. Chute was a fussy, precise man, the caricature, almost, of an agent, with a fringe of bright red hair and high, polished skull, a heavy, pear-shaped body. In those years, he wore a suit of orange-hued tweed, and the links of a gold watch chain stretched across the belly. Docherty I cannot see clearly, for we never met. He was a large man, Bob said, and youngish, in his middle thirties, with heavy head and flat face. It was now that Chute told him of the decision he had taken, that an order of ejectment was being prepared. It would not be the first eviction that year in Kilpeder—there had been four or five others—but it would be the first from Ardmor lands. Patiently, Chute rehearsed the matter with Docherty, proving to him as one proves a theorem in Euclid that the estate had no choice in the matter.

" 'Patiently' is Docherty's own word," Bob said. "Docherty has no quarrel with Ardmor or with Chute. His rage is all against Tobin, who had already come to his agreement with Chute that he would take up the farm when once Docherty had been removed from it. He is still in a rage, and vowed he was in grief that Tobin is not dead. I told him to put a sock in that; things are bad enough for him as they are. But was not Chute the cute hoor, if you will excuse my language, Mary, to do a deal with a grabber before making his move."

"Less cute," I said, "for him to give out Tobin's name to a man in a fury."

"Docherty badgered it out of him. He told Chute that there was no man in Kilpeder so mean or so foolish as to grab another man's land. Leave such tricks to other baronies. 'Very well, so,' Chute said at last, out of patience. 'Tis Mick Tobin.' And there we are."

"And off he went then," I said, "to his own place for his gun."

"Not quite," Bob said. "He went first to Tobin's house unarmed, directly he left the estate office, and he and Tobin had words, as you may well imagine. Tobin is not in such pain that he has not given a statement to the sergeant. When they broke off, Docherty walked away, towards the road, and then turned back and said, 'I will do you, Mick. I will blow you apart.' " Bob picked up his glass. "Tis then that he went off for the gun."

"It will go hard for him," Mary said.

"It will. Finding a barrister for him is an expense which he can ill afford, and which will serve little purpose. He will at least be snug and warm in prison. Better than walking the roads." Bob drank off his whiskey without watering it, and slammed down the glass on the table. "Tis a wretched, ugly system," he said, "and Tobin and Docherty and Chute himself are but cogwheels that keep it moving round and round. There will be more ejectments, how can there not be? One more harvest season of rain and cold will destroy this barony utterly. Who has the conscience to blame Mick Docherty because he was maddened beyond endurance and did what anyone might have done. But that is no defence in law."

He pushed back his chair suddenly and stood up. "I am but a rude, graceless guest, Mary, and I have a home of my own in which to be sullen."

"No, no," she said, and put her two hands upon his arm.

"Where the hell did Tobin find the money to take up the lease?" Bob said. "There is the only mystery in the affair. That miserable farm of his own is half wasteland. Small wonder he plotted to claw his way free of it, the bloody grabber."

"Twas a small enough ambition," I said, "and look there at the price that he has paid for it." A farmer with smashed shoulder, useless dangling arm, was in a poor way.

"I know, Hughie," Bob said. "I know." He patted Mary's hand with absent affection, and drew his own arm free.

I walked him to the hall door, and as I was opening it, he said, with a dash of his usual manner, "You would make a poor lawyer, Hughie."

"I would indeed," I said.

"A lawyer," Bob said, "or a magistrate, would ask how came a fellow like Mick Docherty into possession of a shotgun. And a handsome one at that, an over-and-under which would do credit to Vincent or to Major Townshend, with a stock of lovely walnut soft as velvet. And do you know the answer, Hughie? By God, tis a lovely one." He stood framed against the open door, light falling obliquely upon him from the open parlour. I shook my head.

"Tis a Fenian gun, Hughie. Chris Docherty, the brother, was there with us. He was one of the five or six fellows who contrived to slip away, do you remember, at the very end. He made it across the mountains, and in good time crossed over to the States. When things had quietened, his chum in Kerry got the gun back to the Dochertys. The old man never used it; he kept it hidden in the thatch. But Mick took it down a few years ago, and oiled and cleaned it. God knows whose it was first off. Major Townshend, perhaps, in very fact. We sent the lads out to Deep Dene, do you recall?"

"I can recall no Chris Docherty," I said.

"No more can I," Bob said, "and I have been racking my brain. Chris Docherty, I say, in the hope that a face will pop up, or a tone of voice. But the matter is beyond doubt. I met Ginger Hassett in the road today, and put the question to him. He remembers Chris clearly and exactly, and even knows what became of him. He became a policeman in a New Jersey town called Passaic."

"A policeman," I said. "Fine training for that we gave him."

"I know," Bob said. "Tis like when I was summoned yesterday to the barracks, and I thought how we had helped to bestow a new barracks upon Kilpeder by burning down the old one."

For a moment, in mottled light, we smiled at one another, sober men in their thirties, recalling an extravagant youth. It was from this door that I had set forth for the Rising, that March morning.

"Not that Mick has or had any part in the organization," Bob said.

"Fools, he called us, as he sat in his gaol cell in Macroom. I measured the judgement by its source. It seems that Chris was the older son. If he had not taken the oath, he would today be in possession. You'd think Mick would show a bit of gratitude."

"He has worries of his own," I said. "Safe home, Bob."

But that night, as I lay waiting for sleep, the room black, and no sound save Mary's quiet breathing, and faintly, the stirring of mountain wind, distant, a rising and falling sigh, I thought of Docherty's shotgun. Almost, for all my dislike of weapons, I could see it, touch it. For a decade, it had rested in Docherty's thatch, at last to be hauled down, oiled, polished, and used for what—against birds, farmyard vermin? And now by a man driven to desperation. Eviction would indeed have set him out upon the road. He might perhaps have somehow scraped together the pounds needed for passage to America, but perhaps not; perhaps there was only the workhouse.

In my mind, in the sleepless night, I could see him, a man I had never seen, heavy-headed, Bob said, with a flat face, walking towards Tobin's, the gun awkwardly cradled. My sorrow, a distant sorrow without pressure, a sentiment, went out to them both, to both Micks, Docherty and Tobin. The sound of the wind slowly eased both of them from my thoughts. A gentle wind in the streets of Kilpeder, but carried down from hills where it beat fiercely from the ocean, tearing at furze.

17

[*Patrick Prentiss/Myles O'Clery*]

"I not only remember Bob Delaney well," Myles O'Clery said, "I remember the first time that ever I saw him, at Morrison's Hotel, in Dublin. A fellow bursting with energy—they were all there in that first year—Parnell, Davitt, Bob, William O'Brien, J. J. O'Kelly. I was with them, of course; mark me down in your book as a 'Parnellite,' whatever you decide that means. I was with him at the start, and I stayed with him to the close, which damned few did, as you know. But I was a bit older than the others, remember; older than your father by six years or so. I remember when your father was called to the bar—a handsome man, your father. But so, by God, was Parnell. He could have made his living on the boards, playing cavalry majors, Hungarian barons, elegant French lovers, that sort of thing. Now that I think of it, I would call Charles Parnell and your father the two best-looking Irishmen of their day. They could never have said that of me. Tim Healy, God curse his mean little heart, used say that I put him in mind of one of the walruses in the zoological gardens. Close enough, I daresay."

O'Clery was an aging walrus now, his days at the bar and on the hustings far behind him, enjoying his long summers at the rambling fishing lodge in Connemara, surrounded by barrister sons, solicitor sons, the one son professor of classics at the Royal University, daughters-in-law, grandsons and granddaughters. In Connemara, he wore rough tweeds the colours of the landscape, heavy brogues, long woollen stockings, but impeccable white shirts, neat ties of black silk.

He had met Prentiss's train in Clifden, the capital of Connemara, on a day of improbable sunlight, the distant Twelve Bens glittering, the air bright, the sky a delicate blue, cloudless.

"You'll not mind, I trust," he said, "that I am putting you up at the Highlands Monarch; it is a very decent hotel, of the old sort, if you know what I mean. Johnny Lavelle manages it, a decent fellow. Two weeks ago, I could have put you up at the lodge, but now every nook and cranny of it is filled with the generations of O'Clerys. If I could find a bed for you, the noise would drive you mad. You have brought no rod with you, I see. No matter; we have them by the score. My God, what weather you have brought with you, would you look at it? Is any place as fine as Connemara? I bought the lodge in 'eighty-one, on the strength of my fees from the Sherlock case. *Sherlock versus Sherlock*. The Irish equivalent of *Bleak House*. It went on for years. Your father found a few guineas wedged between its ribs."

Prentiss was at home with the old man. He remembered, from childhood, driving over to the lodge with his parents, from their own summer place on Lough Corrib, near Oughterard. A younger O'Clery, the swellings beneath the tweed more restrained, would be waiting for them on the steps. The voice was the same, a voice anything but ponderous, a grasshopper's voice, thin and sprightly, leaping from one point to the next, delighted with itself and with the world. Once, home from school for the long vacation, as their carriage rolled along the miles from Oughterard to Clifden, beside them the lovely, reed-fringed lake, Prentiss had said, "He is full of fun, Mr. O'Clery is."

His father, reins held loosely in long, skilful fingers, had looked at him slantwise and smiled, a bit grimly. "Fun, do you say? Indeed, indeed. We are old friends, Mr. O'Clery and myself. But have a care with him. He is as cute as a . . ." His father paused, as though baffled for a simile. "We marched forward together, Myles and myself. He was just gone from Clongowes by the time I got there, but we picked up a friendship, first in London and then here, in the law courts."

Curious, Prentiss had thought, his father and Mr. O'Clery school-boys once at Clongowes, as he was now himself, walking the same cold, whitewashed corridors.

"Saw eye to eye in politics, as well. Or at least, I thought we did. But the Split found us on opposite sides. Without damage to our friendship, thanks be to God. More than most can say. That break will never heal. It will ruin the country. Ruined it already." His father had fallen silent then, biting his lip, and laying the whip, absently, against the flank of the lead mare; but in Connemara his spirits were rarely depressed for long. "Myles O'Clery," he said with jovial vehemence, and he peered ahead through light, silvery, sun-flecked rain, towards Clifden.

Now, on the second lap of that journey, from Clifden to Bal-lyconeely, Myles O'Clery spun out a companionable web of words, no need for a response.

"But we shall have time to talk," he said, "all the time in the world. I have laid down orders to the O'Clerys. And you'll be taking your meals with us, of course. I should from the start have picked you for a scholar, Patrick, but your father was always so certain that you were destined for the law."

"I may yet," Prentiss said. "There is time."

"All the time in the world," O'Clery agreed.

It was as though his father sat beside him, distant, appraising, courte-ous.

"It has been a splendid summer," O'Clery said. "More like Tuscany than Connaught. If the weather holds, there will be a splendid harvest. The farmers here can use it, poor devils. At the best of times, Connemara is better for holiday visitors than for the poor locals. But this year is grand, thanks be to God."

Beyond the lake, the hills were blue; sunlight struck from flat, rain-polished rock. Bogland ran beyond the far shore.

"Not like 'seventy-nine," Prentiss said.

" 'Seventy-nine," O'Clery said, puzzled, and then his brow cleared. "Ah," he said, "the scholar at work. No, no indeed. I did not see Con-nemara that summer, but the stories were pitiful. I was in Mayo that autumn, and that was bad enough. Donegal was in dreadful shape. 'God spare the poor Donegals,' they still say in Tyrone and Fermanagh. It was famine or close to it here in Connaught, and parts of Munster were hard-hit. People like ourselves, Patrick, we have no notion of what a season or two of ruined harvests mean to these people. The O'Clerys have never lacked for a roast on the Sunday table, nor the Prentisses either."

"Davitt brought you to Mayo?" Prentiss said. "You were there from the beginning of things?"

"Not quite," O'Clery said. "Not quite from the beginning. I travelled down to Mayo with Parnell. By rail to Castlebar, and there was a crowd there waiting for us, with banners that had been run up in haste, green every last one of them, a colour that Parnell had a superstitious dread of. And a band, of course, playing 'The West's Awake.' As we climbed down, he asked me did the tune they were playing have a name to it. He was unable to carry a tune, and he had no poetry at all in his being."

"The poetry was there somewhere," Prentiss said. "What happened is proof enough of that."

Eyes suddenly narrowed, O'Clery looked at him with canted head hunched towards shoulder. "You take your politics from your father, I see. Tis only natural."

"No," Prentiss said, "not on that subject, at any rate." A boy, he stood once more with his mother at the window of the Imperial Hotel. Crowds were shouting beyond, in Sackville Street. His mother was crying, quietly, eyes hidden by a square of lace.

"Not on that subject," O'Clery said, laughing. "As though for men of your father's age and my own, there were any other. It has marked us all for life. Did we stand with Parnell or did we not. There were good men on both sides of the divide. I can see that now. Mind, he was a strange man, as strange a man as ever I have known. Did your father ever tell you of the testimonial fund? In 'eighty-three, that would have been. We were all of us Parnellites then, your father as much as myself. Indeed, two times or three, it was to your father that he turned for advice on matters of law."

Far off, towards the Twelve Bens, it had begun to rain, the air a mist; but the sun was bright upon their road, the wonderful sunlight of the far west, remembered from childhood. It glittered upon strands of coral sand, waters of aquamarine, darkening, band by band, as the eye moved out, beyond the empty bay, to the Atlantic.

"Yes," O'Clery said. "In the spring of 'eighty-three. In Parliament, there were Tories branding us with the Phoenix Park murders. They as good as claimed that Parnell had furnished the Invincibles with their surgical knives. And in the midst of it all, don't we discover, almost by chance, that he had petitioned the Landed Estates Court for the sale of his property in Wicklow—the estate at Avondale, the shooting lodge, everything. He was done for, mortgaged to the hilt and nowhere to turn. And so a fund was set up, committees formed, money coming in from the four corners of Ireland, and from England and America as well. By the end of the year, there was nearly forty thousand pounds collected. The great Parnell National Tribute."

O'Clery began to laugh, a deep rumble welling upwards from a massive belly. It exploded as a high-pitched "hee-hee," and he drew an enormous handkerchief from his pocket, shook it loose, and held it to his face. "Hee-hee," he said again, and stopped the jaunting car, drawing away the handkerchief to look out across the water, a delicate blue. His eyes were dry.

"The Parnell National Tribute," he said again. "A great banquet was organized for the presentation. We were all there. I remember your father was there. The lord mayor began to speak—he had been practising this for days. And no sooner are the first words out of his mouth than Parnell says, 'I believe you have got a cheque for me.' Your man is a bit taken aback, but he nods and commences again. 'Is it made payable to order and crossed?' says Parnell. 'Yes,' the poor mayor said, 'it is.' 'You may hand it up to me, then,' says Parnell. And so the man did. The cheque had been fitted into a large square, with shamrocks and round towers and perhaps a wolfhound or two painted upon it, the lakes of Killarney and so forth. All business came to a halt as Parnell carefully drew the cheque free from its surround. It gave him a bit of trouble, and he rose to his feet, but at last he had it, and he folded it twice or thrice, and tucked it away into a waistcoat pocket. Then he glanced up and saw the mayor standing there, open-mouthed, and he said, in the most courteous manner imaginable, 'Sit down, sir. Sit down. Enjoy your coffee and your cigar.' Your father and Sexton and myself chanced later to leave the banqueting hall together, and Sexton was raging. 'A labourer,' he said, 'would acknowledge the loan of a penknife more gratefully.' And so he would."

O'Clery touched the horse with a light flick of his wrist, and left Prentiss to speculate as to why he had told the story. It was one of those episodes which had passed into legend, as though containing some truth about Parnell more absolute than language.

"I met him once," he said, "at my father's dinner table. I was brought down to meet him, then I was sent back to bed."

O'Clery nodded. "And never forgot the moment, I daresay. Tis like that gravestone of his in Glasnevin. A vulgar necropolis, gimcrack angels and shabby memorials; then, suddenly, you round a corner, and there, upon clean, decent turf, is a boulder of Wicklow granite, and the single word *Parnell*." He turned towards Prentiss and smiled. "In death itself there was a kind of grace to him. A mysterious grace."

But not by the account given once of him as he was in that final year by Prentiss's father.

"The granite boulder was your notion, was it not, Mr. O'Clery?"

"Ach," O'Clery said, "myself among many others. A large committee, the usual sort of thing, do you not know. But we did it properly, somehow or other. An appropriate memorial."

There was a finicking fondness for the appropriate detail which Prentiss, in earlier years, had not observed in his father's friend. It comported oddly yet attractively with his girth.

"Do you know what I like best about Connemara?" O'Clery asked. "Aside from the fishing, of course? The scenery, you might well reply, renowned throughout Europe, and drawing here Anglican vicars from Surrey, and globe-trotters from Bavaria. Would you not think that the Alps would suffice for them? Tis the eerie and lovely silence, others will tell you, as silent as the Highlands of Scotland, but without their menace, their dark and sinister glens. True enough, but what draws me here, summer after summer . . ."

They had come now to the boreen which led off from the Ballyconeely road to O'Clery's fishing lodge. Seven o'clock in the evening of a Connaught summer. The air had a still, intense poise, and the visible world was luminous. On either side of the road, hedges, tangled and leaf-heavy, shielded reed-fringed lakes, wet fields.

". . . summer after summer," O'Clery said, "is that there is no damned history, no history at all. History is the curse of this country, Patrick, and tis sorry I am that I must be the one to tell you. Who would settle here when there was anywhere else upon the globe to settle? The O'Flahertys settled here when they were beaten out of Galway by the Martins, and then the Martins settled here when they were beaten out by Cromwell. And there is the beginning and the end of the history of Connemara. Gone now, the lot of them. There is a ruined O'Flaherty Castle beyond Ballyconeely on the Roundstone road, and there is Dick Martin's house at Ballynahinch. But the Martins are gone. In September, when we take the train back to Dublin, I shudder—history closing in upon me, like these hedges to our either side here."

The "lodge," as the O'Clerys insisted upon calling it, as Prentiss himself had called it from boyhood, had been built sometime in the 1820s by a Loughrea grazier, a Protestant, named Ticknell, who had been told of the beauties of Connemara by his friend, Captain John Darcy, the founder of Clifden. Old Dick Martin was dead by then, but his son was in possession, master of Ballynahinch, and there was a thin scattering of smaller landowners huddled near Oughterard. But there were few roads and those few abominable. Ticknell was the first man to build in Connemara a house for the pleasures of summer, a lodge, vaguely Regency in design, white-fronted, with two frivolous mock-turrets. He went bankrupt in the early 1850s, and the lodge, sporting then the name Walton's Rest, passed to a Birmingham factory owner, who rebaptised it Erin's Repose. By the eighties, when his young grandson sold it to Myles O'Clery, ivy had begun to work its way beneath chipped plaster, and the black flag-stones which led down from the rere of the house to the lake path were cracked.

By then, Connemara had been written up in all the guidebooks as "The Irish Highlands," and it might have seemed dotted with such lodges were its vistas not so immense, its silences so absolute. Germans and Frenchmen came there for the season. The extension of the railway from Galway through Oughterard into Clifden made travel far easier. Families in groups and sporty bachelors in small parties would debouch at Clifden, where sidecars would be ready for them. They would have valises with them, cases made of carpeting, gun cases of dark polished wood, fishing rods wrapped in canvas, the children carrying nets and wearing hats of wide-brimmed straw. They would pile into the sidecars, or if the party was a large one, on either side of an outside car, and Connemara would begin for them with the driver, in his old-fashioned swallow-tailed coat, breeches legs tucked into long woollen stockings, his speech thick and alien but comforting as hot porridge on a chill morning.

The fishing hotel in which O'Clery had booked a room for Prentiss was two miles away from Erin's Repose, a comfortable, rambling inn, with windows upon the same lake. At night, from his room, Prentiss could see lights, and in early morning hear the shouts of gillies. He took his breakfasts in the hotel, listening to the voices at other tables, loud confidences of the English, the gentler, conspiratorial complacencies of the Irish. Then he would walk over to Erin's Repose for more tea. If the weather was good, the O'Clery sons would already be gone, no need for gillies. Hours before, they would have slipped away, past rushes, in early pearl-coloured light, a mist upon the water.

Erin's Repose boasted a dining room, with two tall windows looking out upon Mannin Bay, beyond hedgerows thick with heavy greens, with the reds and whites of late, fading blossoms. It was there that they took their tea. The O'Clerys kept no servants in Connemara. When the teapot was empty, O'Clery carried it to the small, crowded scullery, walking with heavy grace. "I think," O'Clery said, "that I first saw Bob Delaney the day after Parnell and some few others of us had come back from the Limerick meeting, which would put it at the very end of August or else the beginning of September."

They were terrible weeks of low skies and rains, and by now there was the certainty of a wet, ruined harvest. I can remember, as though it were but a week ago, staring out the window as we travelled eastwards by rail, with the heavy rain commencing again at Limerick Junction, streaming down the glass, and upon the fields of tall, uncut hay and corn. The compartment was heavy with cigar smoke, and we had little to say to one another, the six of us, although we were tense with excitement. In those first weeks of the League, we could scarcely believe what we were saying or doing. All of us save, of course, Parnell.

He was sitting nearest the window, in his suit of salt-and-pepper tweed, smoking one of his long, thin cigars from Fox's of Grafton Street, with a pad of paper balanced on his knees, writing, pausing a minute, and then returning to the task. There may have been others in the compartment who imagined that he was composing a deathless oration, but I had reason to know that he was at work on one of those unpublishable scientific, as he called them, papers of vague geological import, efforts to prove that veins of gold ran beneath the soil of his native Wicklow. These papers were his only gesture towards a prudent management of his Avondale estate. But it could be argued that in Limerick he had made, or rather had repeated, a deathless oration. Certainly it echoes with us to this day. "Keep a firm grip on your homesteads," he said there to the small farmers, the words coming very close to an actionable incitement to sedition. He had been saying as much, in one form or another, across Connaught and now into Munster.

It had begun in June, with the meeting at Westport, in Mayo. Archbishop MacHale had warned his flock against attending a meeting "convened in a mysterious and disorderly manner" and "organised by a few designing men." An astonishing man! Eighty-nine years of age, a half century as archbishop of Tuam, but his hand had lost nothing of its cunning, a prelate cut along lines of the High Renaissance bias. The meeting had been called for Sunday, the eighth, and his lordship contrived that his letter should appear in the early Saturday edition of the *Freeman's,* so that every parish priest in Mayo and Galway could digest it with his lamb and cabbage. Parnell had come over from Westminster on the mailboat, and Davitt hurried over to Morrison's to meet him. It was an awkward moment for Parnell, a Protestant; and invited speakers,

Catholics the most of them, had all morning been backing away. "Will I attend?" Parnell said to him. "Yes, certainly. Why not? I gave you my promise." At the door out into Dawson Street, Davitt almost collided into me. "By God, that is superb," he said. "That man is afraid of no one or nothing."

There were ten thousand at least, at the Westport meeting. Five hundred of them were young fellows on horseback, "cavalry" they called themselves, who escorted Parnell from the hotel to the assembly grounds outside the town. For most of those fellows, riding along before the carriage or behind it, Parnell was still but a name, lauded in the press as a quixotic sort of parliamentary moss trooper, remote Protestant gentry, benign supporter of Home Rule, a cause which meant little enough to the farmers of Mayo in that June of 1879.

It was a splendid day, one of the few fine days of that wretched spring. For two or three months, certainly since the Irishtown meeting in April, Davitt and his Mayo chums had been staging these Sunday meetings, and for better than half of them, the rain had begun to fall before early Mass, and by afternoon the field in Claremorris or Ballinrobe or wherever was soft and squelchy underfoot, and the green bunting sodden, cheerless. But this day was what soon the papers would be calling "Parnell weather," Clew Bay sparkling beyond pastures green as limes, its score of islands standing out clear and distinct. Croagh Patrick loomed above us, a shaggy brown giant.

Davitt and Parnell met that morning for breakfast at the hotel, and Parnell had me posted between them, a kind of buffer. That is how most often they met in the first year or two, at breakfast in a provincial hotel, or in a tea shop near Westminster, or in the smoking room of Morrison's in Dublin. And it is thus that I remember them most clearly, as upon that late morning, Davitt calling in after Mass, and in the close distance the jovial shouts of the "cavalry" mustering with perhaps a Sunday pint taken but no more. We sat at a table close by tall windows which looked out upon the town's handsome mall, designed by Wyatt in the old days, when landlords cared about the look of a town, as with the Parsons and the deVescis in the midlands, the Ardmors below in Kilpeder. God forgive us, we pulled down the power of the landlords, and a bit of the good went down with them, a bit of old decency. What have we left now but our own scruff? And if the campaign against the landlords had anywhere a beginning, it was there in Westport, that Sunday morning in June, with the shouts drifting towards us, and Charles Parnell and Michael Davitt facing each other across the teapots.

A kind of buffer, so Parnell thought me. In those days, as again at the end, he had need of me. I was in those days one of the youngest of the Irish members, and a bit more svelte, a bit more sleek than the present finds me. A Home Rule member, to be sure; but what did that mean? Family is everything here, or all but everything, and my credentials were solidly Old Catholic Whig. My father's credentials stood me in good stead: old Maurice O'Clery, Clongowes Wood College, a pal of George Henry Moore of Moore Hall, barrister, member for Meath, on circuit with Isaac Butt, a bagful of Latin tags, references to Ronsard and Rabelais—wide European culture, as it was called. A Catholic but a gentleman, as it were.

It was a pleasant life at Westminster in the seventies, especially for a member of Isaac Butt's Home Rule party, if it is to be called a party. We had our principles, firmly adhered to: amnesty for the Fenian prisoners in English prisons, and a reasonable reform of the iniquitous system of land tenure, and of course, as our ultimate object, the restoration to Ireland of a measure of self-government. At the same time, to be sure, we made clear, or sought to make clear, our loyalty to the Queen and to the Empire. Indeed yes. We were a rare flock, and the House took great delight in us. Disraeli, for example, had a great fondness for Butt, and the two would have a glass of hock on occasion. I remember coming suddenly upon the two of them one night in the library of the House, heads bent and almost touching, bathed in green-globed lamplight. A brace of contradictories, I thought. There is the arch-Tory, rhapsodist of the Queen-Empress, and he is no Churchill, no Bolingbroke, but a converted Hebrew, the son of a Hebrew bookseller, and the very effigy of his race as he sits facing me in profile—hooded eyes, beaked nose, the wispy beard of a high priest. A dandy once in his youth—waistcoats of puce and mauve, high rolled lapels of watered silks—but cool now in his dress: severe greys, more clerical than dove, and one hint of colour at the throat, flash of discreetly covered ruby at the wrist. And, head almost touching, shock of grey unkempt hair bristling into points, full, fleshy face, the leader, so England thought him, of rebelly Irish Papists, but in fact Protestant, an Orangeman in his youth, arch-Tory by birth.

The Fenians converted him, so he often said, in those months of 'sixty-seven when he was defending them. Not to their cause, for Butt to the last day of his life was a Queen-and-Crown man, but converted rather by their sincerity, their certainty that nothing could help us save the pike and the rifle and the ambush. And, of course, in a way, the Fenians converted Gladstone, persuaded him that something across the Irish Sea was dreadfully in need of redress. They were allies in a way, Butt and Gladstone, working for moderate reforms, whereas Butt and Disraeli, on the floor of the House, were at daggers drawn. But, in truth, the two of them had more in common with each other, the same playfulness and wit, the Tory Jew and the Orange Fenian.

A bit too fond of the ladies and the bottle, a bit too careless with his purse. Poor old Butt. More than once, the hat had to be passed round to keep him from debtor's prison, for all that he was leader of a parliamentary party and a queen's counsel with a thriving practice. I have seen him sitting so muddled by brandy that he scarce knew where he was, twisting and retwisting his spikes of hair, his mouth open. But never in the House, mind you, and never at the bar. He was a gentleman, a decent man of honour, and he loved Ireland, in his way. That was our weakness as a party, so it seemed in a few years' time, after Parnell had turned everything around. We were a party of Irish gentlemen, and the English made fools of us. At the end, we broke him. Not England, *we* did it. It had to be done, and Parnell stood aside and let us do it. When the end came—the end for Parnell, that is—I stood with him, and I remember that once he said, "The English need not destroy us; we kill each other." And I thought, You showed us the way. We sent poor Butt to his grave, broken, rejected. It had to be done.

I remember Parnell's first evening in the House, Butt leading him forward by the hand, pleased as Punch, the new member for Meath, and exactly the sort that Butt liked to see representing the country—master of his Wicklow hunt, high sheriff for the county, family with a decent name for a century or more. And there, I thought, rests the full total of his qualifications. And for all his handsome appearance, tall lean figure— he could have had any woman he wanted, why in God's name did he make the choice he did? He was nervous and hesitant for all of that session, scarcely saying a word. Well, thought I, he will go down in history as "Single Speech Parnell."

Once, your father and I came home on the mailboat together, and found ourselves joined by Old Major O'Gorman. Now, there was the old party in its finest flower. The old major, twice as fat as I am now, I give you my word; but suits of the finest black woollens admirably cut, and a beard like Saint Nick, white as an angel's wing, and above the flowing hoar moustaches, a nose of somewhat the proportions and precisely the colour of a pomegranate. Purcell O'Gorman that was, mind you, not The O'Gorman Mahon, as he called himself, the member for Clare. We took a stroll on deck, the three of us, your father and myself flanking the "bould" major. He walked with a swagger for all his heft, the belly flung forward like a fortification, and a stick almost as tall as a shepherd's crook, ebony, with a ball of carved ivory. "The man," he said, "is a disgrace. A disgrace and a mystery."

It was as calm that night as the crossing from Holyhead ever is, but there was a thick fog, and the deck was slippery. "Night after night, that man stands on his hind legs in the House and disrupts its proper business. Butt has talked to him, but it is no use. Himself and that popinjay O'Donnell and Biggar, the vulgar little bacon wholesaler from the North. My god, what a trinity!" That, of course, was how at first most of us responded to Parnell's policy of obstruction, as he called it. One night, I recall, after he had been talking for hours, for hours after long hours, he moved an adjournment of the debate on the grounds that he was not being heard with the proper attention. "You are right there, Parnell," Biggar called out in that uncouth Belfast voice of his, a bulky-shouldered little hunchback. "I had begun to drift off myself. You have a most melodious voice. Best to adjourn, and then do the entire thing again." And this, mind you, was the debate on the army estimates.

Back and forth we paced, the three of us, the major and your father and myself, with the lights from the saloon splashing pale yellow into the fog. The major, almost, in the darkness, one could sense the quivers sweeping across his mountainous flesh. "The forms of the House, lads, the forms of the House!" Parnell, do you see, and the small band he was gathering around him, had no respect whatever for the mother of parliaments, cradle of constitutional government, all the rest of it. One could expect little better from the others—Biggar and O'Connor Power. What were they but Fenians, sworn members of the Revolutionary Brotherhood? But Parnell! Look and manner of a gentleman, Cambridge accent. Butt sought at one point to disavow him, rose up one evening to declare that he could not control the conduct of the member for Meath, disapproved of it entirely, apologised to the House on behalf of the nation of Ireland. And Parnell, in the coolest manner possible, although not insolent, replied that it was to the nation of Ireland, and to that nation only, that he was answerable. "Damned puppy!" the major growled into the fog, stabbing the planking with the ferrule of his stick.

Your father and I made noises of assent. The major was a bit of a joke in the House, with his girth and his puns and his stories of dusty campaigns against Afghans; but he was one of our seniors, and we were a bit flattered. And yet a few hours later, in our cabin, your father said to me, "He is right, you know." "Who, the major?" "No," your father said, as slowly as possible, as though with reluctance, "I mean Parnell." His words came so pat upon my own thoughts that I was startled, and I began to tell him so, but he paid scant attention to me at first. "The English care not a damn for us; they never have. If you want an Englishman to listen to you, you have to seize him by the throat. That is what Parnell is doing, Parnell and Biggar and O'Donnell, that crew of his."

Good heavens, Patrick, here you are, rooting about in some obscure town in West Cork, hoping to dig up history like a truffle, and all the time it was at home with you. Historic scene: young Prentiss and young O'Clery avow conversion to Parnell on night boat to Kingstown. Fog covers Irish Sea.

For me, and I told your father this as soon as he gave me space, it was a night in late May of 1876. Some few of the Irish members were speaking for amnesty for the lads still in prison because of the rescue at Manchester, and also for a fellow who had long been suffering under harsh conditions in Dartmoor Prison, a one-armed labouring man named Davitt. Butt was strong for amnesty, mind you, but with the ill fortune that dogged him at the end, he had left the chamber, when Hicks-Beach, who was speaking for Government, made a sneer about members of the House who defended murder. "No," Parnell said, in a sharp, clear voice. "No!" "I regret to hear," Hicks-Beach said suavely, "that there is an honourable member of this House who will apologise for murder." This would have been for poor Butt a splendid opportunity for a half-hour disquisition upon evil conditions at home, the repugnance towards murder felt by every true Irishman, and so on. But what Parnell said was so brief and so startling that I have remembered every word of it. I once refreshed my memory by consulting Hansard.

"The right honourable gentleman," Parnell said, "looked at me so directly when he said that he regretted that any member of this House should apologise for murder, that I wish to say as publicly and directly as I can that I do not believe, and never shall believe, that any murder was committed at Manchester." I can see him as clearly as if it were yesterday. Like many members, he had an engagement later that night, and he was in formal dress, black worn carelessly, and the burden of his words was almost mocked by his tone, matter-of-fact and almost casual. But he had placed a powerful piece upon the board, for if no murder had been done at Manchester, then Allen and Larkin and O'Brien had been unjustly tried upon a capital charge, and unjustly hanged. He sat down then, stretched his legs out before him, and put on his tall, glossy hat. I was sitting aslant of him, so that I could see but a wedge of his face, yet I thought he was smiling towards Hicks-Beach, who had the look of a man just poignarded. It was as though a band of Fenians equipped with torches and scaling hooks had smashed into the House. We did have a few suspected Fenians, Biggar and Power, and they too were looking towards him, as though seeing him afresh.

And that, in my own judgement, is why he said it. Where that Wicklow fox hunter drew his political shrewdness from is as much of a mystery as everything else about him. He was not speaking to Hicks-Beach at all, but was sending back a message to Ireland. "Trust me," he was saying to the hillside men, to the thousands who ten years before had mustered by the shining rivers with pikes and stolen rifles. "I am no gentleman like Butt, no timeserver like O'Gorman, no timid Catholic landlord, no lackey." Small wonder the rumour spread that he had himself taken the Fenian oath. But of course he had not. In the years to come he had dealings with the Fenians, no hesitations about meeting with them in this quiet place or that; but it was a marriage of convenience. They used him, and he used them. And if there was loyalty at all, it came into play only at the end, when he was a hunted man, his back against the wall. Then they came down from the hills, as it were, to stand beside him. The Fenians had by then become addicted to lost causes; but not Parnell. He played to win.

Holyhead to Kingstown. In morning light, pearly-grey, soft through a thinning fog, the mountains rise up to you, Dublin mountains and the mountains of Wicklow, and the city buried somewhere safe from view, between water and gorse-purple hill. How much of our lives are spent upon that voyage, Holyhead to Kingstown, Kingstown to Holyhead, Dublin to London, Ireland to England, and then back again? Your father and I saw the sky lighten. We had gone back on deck, and spent an hour or so walking forward and aft, unencumbered by the major. Your father was not in the House, of course; he was taking his dinners at the Temple, but was almost as involved in politics as I was myself. And we resolved, the two of us, that I should throw in my hand with Parnell, even shook hands upon it, a pair of pompous young patriots. Mind you, I could afford the gamble. I held a safe seat, as my own father had held it before me; the O'Clerys have always been an unbudgeable family. And as we talked, Ireland rose up before us, to the west, the western isle, a faint line upon a broadening sky, brown beneath the pink of coral, beneath salmon.

Impossible, now, in the holiday stretches of 1904 Connemara, for Prentiss to see in imagination the scene which O'Clery pressed upon him: barrister and member of Parliament in mailboat, dawn upon the Irish Sea, lean against oak rail, peering through fog, through darkness, for a first sight of the hill of Howth, the Sugarloaf mountain. Now, looking at O'Clery with family affection, scholarly caution, he could see only Major

O'Gorman carried forward into modern times. Impossible to see through flesh with spectroscopic eyes to the young man who had gone back to the next parliamentary session, the session of 1877, a sworn member of Parnell's crew, sworn to wreck Butt's policy of moderation. And yet it was all there in Hansard: Biggar talking to the point of exhaustion, and then O'Clery taking over from him, the business of the House suspended for days at a time. He even earned himself a *Vanity Fair* cartoon by Spy which had hung in the library of Prentiss's home—"Obstruction O'Clery," Spy called him, a sleek young man, gently swelling paunch beneath trim waistcoat, bald patch the size of a golden guinea. "Mr. O'Clery," said the facing letterpress, "who is one of Mr. Parnell's brave band of Hibernian speechifiers, prepared to liberate their beloved island by putting the House of Commons to sleep."

Yes, said O'Clery, this was in the smoking room of Morrison's, at the corner of Dawson and Nassau streets. Parnell rarely stayed anywhere else, and so for a decade at least, its smoking room was an informal local parliament house, which did not entirely please the manager, because now the county families shunned it, limiting their patronage to Russell's and the Shelbourne and the Royal Hibernian.

Bob Delaney had written to Davitt, and Davitt had sent back a note to him. Not that Davitt was stopping at the hotel, not then nor for years afterwards. He was living on short rations in those days, a bit of cash that he had been advanced by the organization and whatever he was able to get by lecturing here and there on his prison experiences.

When Bob came in, I was sitting with Davitt and Sexton and Egan and a few others at the large round table in the corner. At the door, a waiter pointed out our table to him and he came straight to it. Not that he would have had trouble finding Davitt, who sat as he always did, at an angle to the table, so that the empty sleeve was in shadow. There were port glasses before the rest of us, I rejoice to say, and a bottle, almost empty, of that very decent crusted port that Morrison's used to carry. You don't find it there anymore. I don't know why. But Davitt had his tall glass of ginger beer, a fierce temperance man. If prison does that, God shield us from it.

Delaney introduced himself, and Davitt invited him to join us. He was wearing a dark suit of which he seemed rather vain—proud, no doubt, that it was ready-made, and not stitched for him by one of those itinerant tailors who are the plagues of Munster. He was a pleasant, able-looking fellow, sandy-haired, with blunt, regular features, and despite his nervousness, a ready smile. We signalled to the waiter for another glass.

There was for a few minutes an exchange of trivia—the nature of the bad harvest in the southwest, and so on.

"There is a bad harvest in the west as well, so we are told," Delaney said. He had a quick, appraising eye, and it moved from one of us to the next, and round the room, taking in the draped windows and the tables, a party of commercial travellers at the far end. But it came back, always, to Davitt.

"A ruined harvest," Davitt said. "I saw one like it before, many years ago, when I was a lad. There can be no mistaking it."

For that moment, it was as though the boyhood in an English factory town, the years in prison, had been washed away. A small child, one of a ruined family, stood upon a road in Mayo. For a moment only.

"You are not a farmer yourself, Mr. Delaney?" Sexton said.

"I am not," Delaney said. "I am a solicitor. But my clients are farmers, the most of them. And my brothers. I am of farming stock."

"Who is not," I said, "in this country?"

When the waiter brought the glass, Sexton motioned him to pour it for Delaney, who accepted it with thanks, but left it sitting before him, untasted.

"Not always a solicitor, I believe," Davitt said.

"Not always," Delaney said. "I began my days as a shop assistant in Kilpeder."

"And not always a shop assistant," Davitt said. "Mr. Delaney has been a gaolbird, like myself."

"For a few months only," Delaney said. "Twelve years ago. Not like yourself, Mr. Davitt."

Davitt nodded, and studied Delaney with those dark, sunken eyes of his. He was not bearded in those days, but he sported a long moustache, which dropped to either side of his mouth. What must seven years in prison be like? Unimaginable. And yet he could speak of it easily enough: some incident might provoke a memory, and he would give it in a flat, uninflected voice. It was in that room, in the smoking saloon of Morrison's, that Davitt and Parnell met for the first time. "I would not face it," Parnell said, speaking to him of prison. "It would drive me mad. I would kill a warder and get hanged rather than endure such agony. Solitude and silence are too horrible to think of." Curious, that remark. I have often reflected upon it. We think of Parnell as a man of silences, of solitude, and Davitt, the Davitt of those years, as always surrounded by others, talking and arguing.

Of course, I thought, the words *Kilpeder* and *Delaney* clicking at last into place. In my mind, I heard snatches of the ballad "Full sixty men from Kilpeder town to the hills above did go." Delaney and another man, their leader. Twelve years before, I thought. Country lads, shop assistants, a handful of Yankee officers. Snow had filled the mountain passes, cut off their retreat. Nolan, I thought—that was it: Ned Nolan. "With brave Nolan to lead on the van." Now Delaney was a market-town solicitor, up in Dublin for the day. Why?

"As I wrote to you, Mr. Davitt," he said, "I would be grateful for an hour of your time."

"You are more than welcome to it," Davitt said, and uncurled his hand upon the tabletop.

"Perhaps," Delaney said, "at some more convenient time. If that is all the same to you."

"As well now as later," Davitt said. "These gentlemen and myself have been taking our bit of ease after a tiring few days."

But Delaney sat there stubbornly, without speaking, his legs spread a bit apart, and his hands pressed down upon his knees. After what seemed a full minute or two, Davitt smiled and said, "Very well, then, Mr. Delaney," and standing up, he led Delaney away from us to a small table set between screened windows.

"Gentlemen," I said to Egan and Sexton, "we have been snubbed."

But Sexton was an old stager. "No," he said. "But we are not members of the organization." He drawled out the word, with mocking inflexion.

In those days, or so I have seen it claimed, Davitt was not only still in the organization, but had been named to its Supreme Council. "The Firm," it called itself at that time. Davitt was a member of "the Firm." And Bob Delaney was still, in those days, a paid-up member of the brotherhood. It is ironical enough, in view of what was to transpire, but the plain fact is that when Delaney made his approach to Davitt, it was as one Fenian to another. And yet the organization, as the world was shortly to discover, was suspicious of the league which Davitt was bent upon organising, and would soon enough drop him from the Council.

By the time that Sexton and Egan and myself were ready to call it a night, Davitt and Delaney had pulled their chairs close together, and from time to time, one or the other of them would nod. Things happened easily in those few years, and much was improvised. But it nevertheless tells one something about Bob Delaney, that he should have taken it upon

[371]

himself to organise the Land League in West Cork, and that he should have gone straight to Michael Davitt for his support. Later on, in the late eighties, one would often hear it said that Bob Delaney was one of the coming men, that once Home Rule had been won and we had been given back our old Parliament House in College Green, he would be certain to hold high office. That is not unlikely, although things worked out differently, for the country and for poor Delaney both. But as I stood in the doorway, waving a good-night to them, I saw, I must confess, a country solicitor, at once shy and brash, his manner stiff. And Davitt leaning towards him. Our old party, Butt's band of "Hibernian gentleman," was being challenged, by these fellows from outside and by Parnell from within.

Prentiss had seen photographs of Delaney, mounted in a heavy album, mock-leather dyed red, or else in a box with others, lying loose together. One was a wedding portrait, Agnes sitting poised and thoughtful, small firm chin and level eyes, and Delaney standing beside her, his hand upon her shoulder, lightly, and his head inclined, looking towards her and not the camera. Another, his head and shoulders only, showed him as, by MacMahon's reckoning, he had looked at exactly this time, and wearing, no doubt, the very suit which O'Clery described, and a tie elaborately knotted, unruly light hair plastered down.

There was one group photograph of them all, beside the river: Delaney and Agnes, the two MacMahons, and Vincent Tully. "There we are," MacMahon had said, handing it over to Prentiss, "the lot of us." They were making a picnic, in what must have been full summer, the trees heavy-leafed, and a wide white cloth spread upon ground which sloped down towards the river. MacMahon and Delaney, hatless, were stretched out full-length, heads resting on propped arms; but Tully was standing, one hand resting against the trunk of an elm, his eyes shaded by the wide-brimmed hat which, MacMahon said, smiling, he had brought back with him from Italy. The two women sat together, stiffly, hands in lap. Mary MacMahon was smiling faintly, her eyes squinting against the sun. Dappled sunlight, leaf-fretted, fell upon the scene.

"It is curious," MacMahon had said, "how the camera falsifies the past by freezing it. There we all are, on an August Sunday in 1880. So we will always be, until, someday, someone throws away this box of pictures. A riverbank pastoral. And yet that was the summer when Vincent's serious quarrels with his father about money began, his father indulgent as always, but vexed, with Vincent showing no disposition to settle down, and badgering the old man for funds for trips to Europe, or for a shooting lodge in which to entertain his raffish county friends. And Bob, see him there, stretched out at his ease; but in those months the League was claiming all his attention. We had to badger him to take the Sunday off. There was an edge to the afternoon. It was not tranquil, although it may seem so here, elm-shaded. There is another picture that goes with it: all of us sitting in a line, stiff and self-conscious, with my two lads sitting at my feet, young Tom leaning his back against my legs, and Agnes holding Conor, a baby, his face invisible, hidden by an immense bonnet of lace. Where that picture is, I do not know. It was not a quiet summer, not for us, nor for the country."

"Not the summer of the great boycotting," Prentiss said.

"No," MacMahon said. "That came later. In 'eighty-one. But the wheels were turning. The Land League swept all before it, like flames in an autumn wood. It all commenced so suddenly—here in Cork, at any rate—and few of us had a sense of direction, of where it would lead us, or how. And 'eighty was a dreadful year for people, you know. The distress was terrible, and yet the landlords did nothing; there were few abatements. Across wide stretches of Munster—although not yet, thank God, in our baronies—there were evictions, and land grabbing, and the rest of it. Neither did Government do anything, but relied upon private charities to feed the poor. And always, for all of us, there was the terrible fear that the great hunger might be upon us again. But not upon schoolmasters and solicitors and the sons of merchants. We had our Sundays by the bank of the Sullane, the cloth spread, and meats and bowls of boiled eggs, and baked chickens spread out upon it. So the camera holds us, frozen in time, the paper yellowing."

"But he was a student of manners, our Bob Delaney," Myles O'Clery said. "A half dozen years later, on the floor of the House of Commons, he was a credit to his nation, as the phrase has it. Not that the edges ever fell away from that West Cork accent, and his speech never changed, quick and abrupt, challenging. He had a sly wit, you know; a sardonic chap. But he was at ease in the House, and he would not have been a disgrace in a Mayfair drawing room. Of course, by then he had the advantage of excellent instruction, although of that, the less said, the better."

Their road had taken them to Mannin Bay, distant from them by a stretch of coral sand. Early evening, and beyond the bay, on the darkening Atlantic, a trawler moved slowly towards Galway. Heavy clouds hung low upon waters, hills, the level fields which stretched to left and right of them. Despite sunlight, spattering rain fell upon them.

O'Clery consulted a watch, flicking open its cover. "Six," he said. "Kevin will be here with the trap in a half hour."

He held the watch towards Prentiss, detaching it from its chain of finely linked gold. "A handsome timepiece, is it not? A trifle gaudy, perhaps, but the devil with that." Prentiss felt its weight upon his palm; his curved fingers moved along the intricate traceries of the opened cover. The Roman numerals stood clear and elegant against white. A raindrop fell upon it, between III and IV. Quickly, Prentiss dried it, and snapped shut the watch. The tracery, he saw now, surrounded the image of a stag, at bay on mountain crest. He handed back the watch.

"Presented by our party, a few years back," O'Clery said. "A quarter century of service in Westminster, sacrifices made for our nation. Damned few sacrifices, if you want the truth of the matter, but it sounded fine."

He pointed across the road with his stick, towards a broad, flat rock. "Over there," he said, "we can sit and take our ease as we wait for Kevin. A good lad, Kevin, and a good mind for the law—sharp and clear and entirely without imagination." A grim paternal smile, part love, part derision.

The Galway-bound trawler was a shape upon the darkening horizon. In companionable silence, O'Clery and Prentiss sat watching it, as they waited for Kevin O'Clery with the trap.

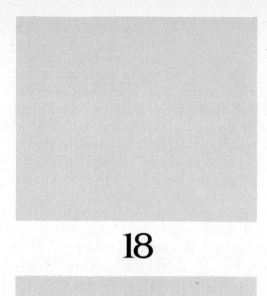

18

[*Lionel Forrester*]

Colours and shape. Soft browns, soft greys, delicate as the afternoons of autumn, and blues light as petals. The shapes seem imposed by the logic of necessity, lest the colours lose their purities, move against each other. But at a distance no greater than a few feet, colours and shapes resolve themselves, become river, path, an avenue of low-branched elms.

"It is our river, your river," I said to Tom, "the Sullane. Here in Kilpeder."

Sunlight lay, great blurs of light, upon the water, an apple green moving towards thick-textured forest green, and grasses studded with flecks of white, wild flowers.

"I like it," Tom said, "I like this one. That is why I wanted you to see it."

It was a fine room for painting, sunlight splashing in. Tom had carried the easel which held the painting to the tall windows which faced the terraced gardens, and beyond which I could glimpse the river itself, a stroke of silver in morning light.

"It is lovely," I said. And it was: lovely the colours he had chosen, and the ways in which he had placed them against each other. But I secretly felt something to be lacking, not in this painting alone, nor merely in all that Tom had shown me of his work, but in the entire school to which he looked for guidance and direction. And thereby I confess myself an utter "Philistine," a shameful confession for someone who prides himself upon being a bit of an artist in words, and who chooses words, his pigments, with a due regard for their weight, their colours, their legendary histories.

Tom gave me his quick, crooked smile, as though he had heard not merely my word of conventional praise, but as well its unspoken qualification. The room was chill, and he was wearing a short tweed jacket, the sleeves pushed back as he stood over his cluttered worktable, cleaning brushes. The top of the deal table bore an accidental heraldry—splashes of cobalt, vermillion, obsidian, ochre.

He pointed with a brush towards the window. "Beyond there," he said, "beyond the real river, as you would call it, one of our tenants has been shot. A man named Michael Tobin. A dispute about land."

"It is always a dispute about land," I said. And so it is, whether here or in Sicily or in the high Pyrenees.

"Yes," Tom said, "but this time we are involved, in a way. Chute proposed to evict a peasant named Docherty from another of our farms, a better one, and give the lease to Tobin."

An ugly word: *evict*. In Ireland, its latinity had long ago been bleached out, and what leaped to the mind was the "crowbar brigade," with their pickaxes and sledgehammers, three or four mounted constables to guard them, men and women standing on the roadside, the women barefooted, perhaps, children clinging to their skirts. At this point, I had never myself stood witness to such a scene, nor was there need to. Evictions were a part of the iconography of our imaginations, all of us.

"The man who shot him is also called Michael," Tom said. "Michael Docherty. He is in Cork City Gaol."

"Do you know him?" I said. "Either of them?"

"I know none of them," he said, placing the brush in its jar. "I know the servants, coachmen, the gamekeepers, bailiffs, the river walker. Not the tenants. When Sylvia and I came here, after the wedding, when the grounds were thrown open, porter and jugs of punch laid out on tables in the barns, they were all of them here, and Docherty and Tobin with the rest of them, no doubt. The best of friends. No, I do not know my tenants. Did you know your father's?"

"Oh, yes," I said. "Yes indeed. But ours is a small estate, of course."
Once, a small boy, I had gone with my mother, in the dog cart, to visit
a sick tenant, an old woman named Harris. My mother brought her a
hamper stuffed with cakes, jellies, preserves, a roast chicken. The old
woman's bed had been placed close to the fire, and she sat propped up.
Thin white hair lay upon the pillow. Her eyes were rheumy. She frightened me. A woman of middle years, daughter or neighbor, sat beside the
bed. When we entered, she leaped up and curtseyed, a full curtsey,
bobbing low. I hung behind my mother, who said, "Now then," briskly
and cheerfully. She took the woman's bedside chair. On a table by the
bed lay a water glass, rosary beads, a photograph framed in wood. It
showed a fierce-moustached private soldier, froggings and tall, stiff collar.
While my mother talked to the old woman, questioned the younger one,
I kept my eyes fixed on the soldier, imagining lands where he had fought.

"Chute and I have had a talk about it," Tom said. "Not entirely an
amicable talk, I'm afraid." He smoothed down his sleeves, and straightened his collar. "Chute is a decent fellow, as you know—honest, fair in
his dealings with people. But he's a bit of a landlord himself, most agents
are, and apparently they have banded together, to resist any abatement
of rent. That is what caused the trouble, is why Docherty shot Tobin."

We walked down, then, to join Sylvia in the morning room, but as
we stood at the door, Tom turned back, to take a look at his studio.
Perhaps his true life was in that room, a life of oils, pigments, brushes.
Paintings by two of those Frenchmen of whom he was so enamoured hung
on either side of the tall, undraped windows, colours and shapes, shapes
and colours. When he left that room, he left himself.

The morning room was bathed in morning light. It touched the
delicate wallpaper which had been there as long as I could remember, the
choice of another bride, Isabel: pagodas and small, high-backed bridges,
parasolled ladies, their faces riced, swift-sketched. Sylvia was not there,
but one of the maids came in behind us, carrying a china coffee service.
She rested it upon the long, low table. Tom seemed not to notice her. He
had gone to the window, and was standing there, one hand upon its white
frame. I thanked her, and she bobbed, a young, pleasant-faced girl.

Beyond the window, I could see now, as I walked towards it, that
Sylvia was coming towards us, through the gardens. She held a book in
one hand, and with the other had caught up her skirt. Her dress was dark
rose in colour, a morning dress, and she was wearing a wide-brimmed
straw hat, tied loosely. A long riding coat lay upon her shoulders, unfastened.

An autumn garden. Yellowed leaves and petals, wind-sheared, lay
strewn upon the gravelled paths. Morning mist had not quite cleared

itself; it clung to tall, bordering shrubbery. Sylvia was walking slowly—sauntering, rather—and now she stopped, bent down to a rosebush. She rested her book upon the path, and touched the bush with both hands. Autumn became her. All the seasons of the year became her, save winter.

We waited for her, and when she was with us, she poured the coffee, then, leaving the saucer on the table, held her own cup in her two hands, and as she sipped from it, looked over at me. "Other visits you never rose so early, Lee," she said. "You have learned bad habits somewhere. Not in Italy, surely?"

But before I could answer her, Tom said, "I have been talking to Lee. About Chute, and about Docherty and Tobin."

"Oh?" she said. "You do not surprise me. He has talked of nothing else, Lee, for all of the past week."

"Well," Tom said, "it is a sorry business. Why should I not be concerned? One of our people shot and another in prison, and it is because of us, in a way. Because Chute—in our interest, mind you—proposed an eviction, and because this wretched Tobin was willing to . . ."

"To grab the land," I said. "To be a grabber. It might have done him little good. The people have a superstition, that a grabber's land always fares poorly. I remember that on an estate close to ours, when I was a boy . . ."

But I stopped for a moment, because by accident, Sylvia and I had caught each other's eye, and I knew, as though by the occult, what we were both thinking. And she did as well, for she smiled. We were thinking, the two of us, that we were the children of small landlords. My father had had no agent; a bailiff sufficed him, as at present it did my brother. And Sylvia's father, during his years in the army, had put his affairs in the hands of a town solicitor. I remembered the "grabber," as they called him; whether or not he was really one I cannot say: a slack-shouldered, bearded man, constantly smiling, at least when he talked with us. Cook told me once that at Mass he and his family knelt by themselves, in the one pew, and that he was never in the public houses, save for a shebeen on the Mitchelstown road, which cared not who was served. And there, twice or three times a year, with his two older sons to tend to him, he would drink himself first into rage and then into stupor. "And he has had never the day's luck," Cook told my brother and me, "from the day he took up that farm." But he was smiling whenever we saw him, and if our trap passed him on the road, he would whip off his hat, and hold it to his chest with his two hands, the smile pulling at the black, matted beard.

"Yes?" Tom said, impatiently. "When you were a boy?"

"I must be getting old," I said. "Drifting into anecdote. But surely, Tom, Chute is not a harsh man. He is fair; you say so yourself."

"Docherty was badly in arrears," Tom said. "Two years. And nothing for this quarter. We have had these three wretched, ruined harvests in a row, and they did for him."

"But not for Tobin," I said. "Docherty did for Tobin, not the weather."

"It is a wretched system," he said.

"It is indeed."

"But not of your making," Sylvia said. "Not of our making, any of us—or Chute or those two poor fellows."

He was looking away from us, beyond terraces, garden, river, the town itself. "The system," he said. "As though whatever we do, is done by us or to us, is to be referred back to the system—a failed harvest, evictions, gunshots and men wounded. Mortgages and bankruptcies, lads taking up the shilling to go off and fight the Zulus, a derelict estate, a bog reclaimed. It is all the system."

It was, as phrased in those outlandish terms, a caricature of these eighteenth-century machines contrived for the betterment of mankind, all wheels and shafts and sprockets, which at the far end spat out dandies, mechanicals, chimney sweeps. Derelict estates, he had said, and I remembered one near my home: pier gates with festive sandstone monkeys couched upon them, paws to eyes, and thence down a short curve of drive to a roofless manor house, its windows shattered by the stones of urchins, a rain gutter hanging loose.

"All the system," Tom repeated. "You know what we have here on our hands this season? Another hunger, the famine come back again if we are not careful. There are all the signs of it. I can remember my father talking of those last months, when it hung poised. The system. It has crippled Mayo already, and it will move south. Not the blight this time. And Government is again unwilling to do anything, nor the landlords. Private relief—Good God! The Duchess of Marlborough is taking up a collection in London, holding musicales. Good God! The system, you see, is not unduly disturbed by private charity."

I had never before heard him so vehement, nor so concerned upon a public issue.

"A wretched system, Tom, no doubt of that. But we have no other."

"Have we not?" he said. His back was still turned to us. "Have we not? I have instructed Chute that there is to be a forty-percent abatement of all rents upon Kilpeder lands, that rents in arrears are to be excused for one year, and that there are to be no evictions for six months. Let us see what that does to the system."

Neither Sylvia nor I said a word, although I could sense Tom straining for a response. Presently, as though but to break the silence, I said,

"I am no authority upon the system, Tom, no professor of political economy. But I can tell you what it will do to Kilpeder. Save for two or three great personages like yourself, the Blakeleys of the Grange and the Pendletons, the landlords of these baronies are in a small way of business, and they are mortgaged to the hilt. Poor Mouser Lambert was not able to give a ball this year for his daughters. And those carpets of his a filigree of holes, like Dr. Johnson's definition of a net. If he were to follow the course which you propose for yourself, you would some morning see the last of him, his wife, and his daughters, and behind them a cart with what they had not sold off at auction. Is that what you want for a man whose father was friend to yours?"

"I propose the course for none but myself," he said. "Ardmor can well afford the loss. We are solid. Chute admits that."

"Oh, Tom," Sylvia said at last. "Can you not see beyond your nose? Kilpeder can be nothing by itself. You are the great family here, and everyone looks here towards Ardmor for a lead. Every small landlord in three baronies will have it flung in his face by his peasants that they are entitled to the arrangements that the Earl of Ardmor, God love him, has come to with his tenants."

"But conditions are quite different here," Tom said. "Surely they can see that."

I laughed—a bit rudely, I fear. "The tenants see what they want to see, and they are blind to the rest. And the landlords are the same. The landlords will see only that you have gone soft, gone rotten, same as if you had married a Papist named Bridget McGinn, that you sold them out, because you could afford to."

"You would be a standing reproach to them, Tom," Sylvia said. "To your own kind, as they would phrase it. And surely you could not ask Chute to carry out such a policy, measures that would bankrupt him, were he to apply them to his own lands."

"And there is a bit more to it even than that," I said. "A shotgun was fired to bring this about; a man is wounded and another awaiting his trial. And in the aftermath of that shot, the great landlord of the barony, the big lord, abates his rent. There is a geometry which the peasants can construe without help from Euclid."

Tom looked from one of us to the other, a kind of witty fury in his eyes.

"As you say, a system. And with nothing for any of us to do, high or low, save bow down to it. Perhaps the system is but a totem. But our own eyes need not be blind, Lee. Ride out towards the Boggeraghs some misty morning like this one; take a look at those wretched fields."

"I have seen them," I said, and shrugged helplessly.

"In this house or that one," Tom said, "once in a great while, you will hear a word spoken, in passing, of the great hunger thirty years ago. Or one may ride past a famine grave some morning, coming home from the hunt. We have done it together, Lee, you and I. An ugly depression, and a single headstone set for a marker. But I will wager you that it is never spoken of in the cabins; there are few legends that have sprung up about those days. Folk tales traffic in the terrors of the mind, nightmares, not the actual terrors of history."

"I have seen the fields, Tom," I said, a bit put off by his easily purchased virtue. An hour before he was debating one depth of magenta against another, matching up leaf shadows. "You cannot decide lightly a matter of this sort. It will have its effects upon the baronies, effects that you have not measured."

"Not lightly," he said, "not lightly at all. I proposed a meeting of the men of property, and as coolly as you pleased, was informed that they are determined, all of them, to sit tight. Next year, perhaps, we may offer abatements. Next year, if there is another ruined harvest. But four in a row is unheard of, it would seem. One would suppose that they conducted their business out of Old Moore's Almanac."

"They do," I said. "Some of them. Tom, some of those fellows are mortgaged to the hilt. They are as ill off as their own peasants. If they don't have their rents, they will go to the wall."

"But I would not, and yet Chute chose Ardmor Castle for the first of the evictions. I will not stand for it."

Sylvia had been watching us quietly, hands at rest in her lap. "Tom," she said. "We do not know our neighbors well. Not yet. We are too often abroad, and for too long."

"You are not likely to know them," I said, "if Tom pushes ahead with this. The landlords are a part of your bloody Euclid, Tom."

"What would you have, Lee?" he said quietly.

"I was here twelve years ago," I said. "That March, the March of the Rising. You were away at Cambridge. A meeting of the county families was called, and I went along, your deputy, as it were. It was after the Arms Raid, and everyone had the wind up. I suggested to them that the Constabulary and the army seemed to know their business, but they would have none of that. They were persuaded that red anarchy waited upon the doorstep, and that I was prepared to temporise with it."

"Yes," he said, expelling the word as an easy sigh. "Yes, I know."

"I am not certain that you do," I said. "You have an estate which is immense by all standards save, perhaps, the Hungarian, and it has been well managed for the family for three generations at least. You are not hanging on by your fingertips. After the great famine, twenty small landlords at least were swept away from my father's neighbourhood, and I daresay that the Encumbered Estates Act fell upon Kilpeder as well. These fellows—Chute and his chums—aren't villains from a melodrama."

"I ask you again, Lee. What would you have me do? By next quarter, Chute will have a budget of names for me. Candidates for eviction. Shall I evict them? Send them to the workhouse or out onto the roads? Tell me."

"You cannot do that," Sylvia cried suddenly. "Tom! Lee! My God, you cannot do that!" Her hand was at her throat.

"No," Tom said with a quiet anger. "I will not do that. My father did not evict, not in the worst of times, and no more will I."

No, I thought, Tom's father did not. But what of his father's father, who was my own grandfather as well, and our great-grandfather, and so backward in time to the first freebooting Forrester, with a commission from Elizabeth that amounted to a letter of marque, ratified in God's good time by Petty. Compassion came late to this land, perhaps to all lands.

"It was clever of Chute, was it not," I said, "to see to it that the first eviction would be from the Ardmor estates, and not one of the farms of the small landlords? He has a sense of hierarchy, Eddy Chute does."

"So have I," Tom said.

We fell then, by common accord, the three of us, to talk of other matters; what I cannot recall. It is curious how clearly I can remember the china coffee service, and Sylvia's hands moving above it, as clearly as I can that conversation, which was to have momentous consequences. It is not, I am persuaded, that memory is random, brutally indifferent, but rather that it has its own strict hierarchies, which are hidden from us.

It was a week or so later, when I was in Dublin on business, that I encountered Johnny Lynam in the Kildare Street Club. Why I kept up my dues, I cannot imagine, for I was so seldom in Dublin that I made almost no use of it. Because my father was fond of it, no doubt, and took me there for meals when I was home from Oxford. It reminded me of him—not in its appearance, God knows, but merely because we had been there together; and perhaps it did in fact have a smell which brought him back to me: good tobacco, and properly tended leather, and, in the cheerless dining room, the smell of joints, beef, or mutton, the steam rising from potatoes, a rice pudding which he always pushed upon me. Nowadays, I daresay, if I shoved my head through the door, the first member to catch sight of me would belabour me with a jambok brought back from the South African War.

There was a slight flavour of that future in my brief words with Johnny Lynam. I was in the library, as it is laughingly called, reading the *Saturday Review* and enjoying a cigar, when I heard the sound of someone flopping himself into the chair, close by, which, like my own, faced upon Nassau Street, with Trinity's cricket pitch visible beyond the tall iron fence of the college. I looked up to see Johnny glaring at me.

"Heard you were back," he said. "Staying with that cousin of yours." Why Johnny Lynam should have ventured into a library of any sort I cannot say, unless in search of a treatise on fly casting. Any more than I can explain his habit of telegraphic speech, chary of pronouns, and typical of his class. Perhaps it has been taken over by the squirearchy from the army, messages scrawled in haste and sent off by cleft stick.

"Yes," I said, in unnoticed mimicry, "been back a month almost."

"What's he up to? What's Ardmor up to? I'm not the only one who'd like to know that."

I guessed at once what was on his mind, but I looked at him blankly.

"Doesn't seem to realise that we may have a land war on our hands before too long. It has begun in Mayo. I would call what that fellow Davitt is about an act of war. And what can you expect—turn a Fenian rebel loose upon the country, and what can you expect?"

"You are moving a bit too quickly for me, Lynam," I said. "We were talking about my cousin Tom. Tom isn't a Fenian, in gaol or out. He is a peer of the realm, as the saying has it."

"May be wrong, Forrester," he said. "You could set me straight. Be happy to make my apology. But what I have heard, in this club and down in Waterford, with my own people, is that Ardmor has chosen this as the proper time to go against the other landlords in his barony. Damned rotten timing."

"These are bad times," I said, "bad for landlords and agents and banks and moneylenders, but infinitely worse for tenants. There will be hunger before the winter is out. I cannot speak for Waterford, but I can speak for West Cork. I came from there this morning."

"And can you speak for North Cork as well? Is your brother following Ardmor's generous example?"

"No," I said, "and perhaps I should not have spoken as I did. I am not a landlord, after all. In strict fact, I can only speak with authority for whatever chair I may happen to be sitting in."

Which was not entirely true, of course, for although I did manage to support myself by my pen, more or less, there were a few properties scattered about Doneraile and a few others close to Mitchelstown which made a considerable difference as I cast up my accounts each half year.

"Mind you," Lynam said, "these are bad times indeed. You are quite right. We all know what happened"—and he paused, in search of a word, his eyes straying towards the window, towards Trinity's forbidding wall and railings, its bare-branched trees, the cricket pitch chill and deserted— "what happened *then,* back *then.*"

But our generation, mercifully, did not. We were unborn then, or boys away at school. Few stories were told to instruct us. There were the unmarked famine graves, mountainside hamlets of scattered, empty cabins, the thatch rotted and wind-scattered. Cryptograms.

"Back then," I said.

"Not now," he said. "We learn from the past. And a ruined economy would serve no one's needs. Not ours, not theirs."

"Not even the moneylenders'," I said.

He thought a moment, and then laughed. "No," he said, "not even theirs. So take yourself back there to Kilpeder, and tell Ardmor to be a decent, sensible chap. He may fancy himself a—what is it, fiddler? painter?—but he has a position to consider. Time for all of us to hold the line, eh?"

"Yes," I said, "I will tell him of our chat," and buried myself in my *Saturday Review.* The tiresome fellow had a point, of course. If Tom's plan to abate the rents had become already a story blown across Munster, then he had stirred up for himself a wasp's nest of ill will.

Johnny was still sitting there when I rose to leave, but his mind, a fragile barque, had drifted to other matters. "Spent three happy years over there," he said, nodding across Nassau Street towards Trinity's grey stones. "You took yourself away, off to Oxford, wasn't it? Glad I stayed here. Can't remember learning a damned thing, mind you, but it would have been the same at Oxford." Burke, Swift, Goldsmith, Johnny Lynam—Trinity's mighty host.

As I was reaching the door, he called out to me, "At least you didn't go to Cambridge. Cambridge had the honour of suckling that beast Parnell. Been in Morrison's recently? Be worth a visit. Better than the Zoological Gardens. I looked in one evening—gang of solicitors, journalists, ticket-of-leave men—and there in their midst, puffing on his cigar, the master of the Wicklow hunt, former high sheriff of his county." Johnny shook his head, baffled. "Beyond me."

I was not stopping at the club, but rather at the Shelbourne, a two minutes' walk up Kildare Street and onto the green. In Dublin darkness often brings with it a damp mist, breeder of melancholies, fragments of longing. The yellow light from our windows, the curtains not yet drawn, fell upon the club's front, an endearing phantasy in what is called, in all seriousness, "the Venetian style," with stonework showing monkeys playing billiards. Eighteen sixty it was, the year the new club was built, that I first went there with my father, to test the pudding.

Beyond the club, towards the Library, although the street was almost deserted a ballad hawker was trying his luck, a pile of broadsheets at his feet, and his choice new specimens tacked to the board which rested against the wall. He looked as melancholy as the evening, a tall, weedy chap in an overcoat that fell to his brogues, and a shapeless hat. He was holding fiddle and bow in one hand.

"Army ballads, sir?" he called out to me. "Name your regiment. The Fusiliers?" I smiled and shook my head, but dug into my pocket for a shilling. Encouraged, he said, "Songs of the hunt? Name your hunt, sir—Kilruddery, the Blazers, the Black and Tans. Or your countryside, sir. Every county in Ireland, I know them all. If I don't have them to sell, I have them to sing."

"Do you now?" I said, holding a handful of change in my pocket. "Have you songs of West Cork?"

"Begod, sir, do I not? The bold Thady Quill. 'Ye Maids of Duhollow.' I have that one here with me, gorgeously printed. A shilling the sheet, and a bit of singing thrown in. You must know 'Thady Quill,' if you are a West Cork man. A most comical song."

"No," I said. "Not that one. Nearer, say, to Macroom."

"Macroom itself I have," he fairly shouted at me, as though stunned by the coincidence. " 'The Flower of Sweet Macroom,' I have that one in print for you, and I will toss in a rendition of 'By the Banks of the Sullane, I Chanced Once to Stray.' Two shillings the lot. There you are now."

"Near to Macroom," I said. "Not the place itself. There are great songs of all that region that exist in the Gaelic, I have often heard."

He looked at me at last with a glance other than the professional. "I have heard that myself, sir. Not that I have Gaelic myself beyond *poteen* and *asthore*. And to be truthful with you, I have never been closer to the place than an excursion once to Cork City."

"A place called Kilpeder," I said.

Recognition flickered, pulled at the edges of his mouth, and then the eyes narrowed a bit.

"Kil*peder*, is it, sir? Begod, sir, there is Kil-this and Kil-that from one end of the country to the other, and I have snatches of song for twenty, perhaps, of them. But a Kilpeder, and in West Cork, is it? Now that is a new one on me."

"You disappoint me," I said. "We take great pride in our ballad, and tell ourselves that it is known far and wide."

A clever fellow, he risked a half smile, one that could be denied if need be. "Sure no one knows all the songs," he said.

"I'll tell you what," I said, and handed him a few coins. "There must be a florin or two at least, mixed up in there. If any of the words of it come to you, bawl it out before it is too late."

He jingled the coins, and touched to his hat, in salutation, the fist that held his fiddle.

I walked along, past the Library, and past the splendid mansion which the Duke of Leinster had built, in the eighteenth century, when it had seemed, for a few decades, that a history lay before us, and not merely behind, a lovely house, French in its proportions. I was strolling, and two young women hurried past me, respectable young women, so far as I could judge. Their skirts swept the damp pavement.

I had not reached the turning before I heard him, the voice raised so that it would carry but not bawling out the song—a pleasant baritone voice, not too badly misused. The notes of the fiddle moved among the shabby words. The trees of the green were dark, bare-branched, huddled together and shielding from view the small, ornamental lake. There was a line of hansom carriages between myself and the hotel, their drivers, top-hatted or bowler-hatted, gathered together for a chat.

"When the snow fell fast in each mountain pass, from Cork to Aherlow,
Full sixty men from Kilpeder town to the hills above did go."

It was an impressive effort. Sensibly, he did not extend it beyond those opening lines, and they lingered upon the air, calling to some fragment of memory. I turned around. A carriage pulled into Kildare Street, and at the same moment almost, the door of the club was flung open, spilling yellow light upon the mist. A party of noisy young fellows, six at least of them, came out from Molesworth, the most sedate of streets at most times, with its Bible societies and its Protestant mission societies. Sounds, the movement of people, bustling inconsequence, shattered the moment's silence.

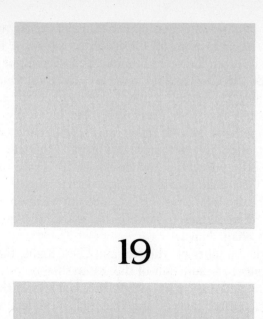

19

CHRISTMAS IN THE BOGGERAGHS
by Robert Delaney, Solicitor
The Square, Kilpeder, County Cork

Kilpeder, a market town in County Cork, will be known to all holiday makers who have taken the Macroom road over the Derrynasaggart Mountains into far-famed Killarney. Perhaps they may remember a straggle of low dwellings and then a square with an obelisk that celebrates the coming of age of an English-descended aristocrat. But most likely, their thoughts will be fixed upon the beauties lying in wait for them: the lakes and soft mountains of Killarney, the pleasures of a boat drifting upon waters of deep blue, the splash of the boatman's oar. They will not be looking towards their right, towards the more sullen mountains which are known as the Boggeraghs.

Our world presents a smiling face to summer visitors. By mid-September, they have all departed, and winter is gathering for its slow advance across the hills. Christmas comes to us, of course, in the dead of winter; but in Ireland, as in all Christian countries, it has its special warmth. In every cabin, however humble, a candle will be placed in the window to guide the Christ Child upon his way to us. One can stand at the head of a valley, at nightfall, and watch as first here, then there, a small light will leap into the mist. Presently, when it is dark night, twenty candles, thirty perhaps, will be fallen stars in the darkness. In most of those cabins, at midnight, as the eve of Christ's birth moves to His day, the families, kneeling upon the earthen floor, will say the rosary together. The morning, God willing, will be crisp, with sunlight glittering upon frost. And on the day following, the feast of Saint Stephen, the young lads will set off with their cudgels to hunt for the wren, "the king of all birds," as their curious chant has it.

But in wide stretches of Munster and Connaught, the recent Yule-tide brought a small measure only of the season's happiness. And with the rosaries were mingled prayers for succor. It is well known that Ireland has suffered a third ruined harvest, and it is rightly understood that great suffering for the agricultural poor will follow in its wake. It is to be wondered, however, how many there are, of those who no doubt are well disposed, sitting in Dublin or in Cork before cheerful blazes, who know, as hard and vivid fact, the nature and extent of that suffering. And it is to be wondered if they know how much this suffering, although brought by nature upon the people, is intensified by the harsh and savage system of landlordism.

The writer therefore solicits his readers to come with him in spirit upon a journey which he made a few weeks before Christmas, to visit hamlets whose families are as sorely pressed as any in Christendom.

Kilpeder lies, as had been said, upon the Macroom to Killarney road. But a half mile beyond the town, a second, and less known, road leads northwards, through the Boggeraghs, to Millstreet. For much of its winding and tortuous length, it moves through desert land, inhospitable to all save furze and mountain grasses, wild hare and mountain goat. High above, hawk and kestrel hang in the air. But the hills beyond Kilpeder are farmed by a sturdy and tenacious people who speak the old language, Gaelic, and who cherish customs older by centuries than the Christmas candle and the hunting of the wren. Their dwelling places are as primitive as those of the herdsmen of wild Tartary, cabins made of stone and mud, and these are shared by cow and goat.

The time which I spent among them, accompanied by a schoolmaster and local savant, who knows their language far better than I do myself, were days which oddly mingled a bitter discomfort and chill with the warmth that comes from an encounter with an instinctive hospitality. But what was borne mostly in upon me was a sense of a poverty such as I had never before witnessed, and which was now stretched to the extremity.

Here, however, I must make a distinction, one to which I shall presently return. The district which we visited, Aghabullogue, stretches for some eight miles, between hills, and its ownership is divided, roughly, between two landlords. To the south are lands of Lord Ardmor, owner of the town of Kilpeder and of much else besides, and to the north are the holdings of Bartholomew Colthurst, Esquire, of Dunmurray House. As between the southern and the northern halves of this region, there is little to choose, the both of them bearing every sign of landlord neglect. There does exist, however, one distinction, and it a crucial one, a matter, I make bold to say, of life and death. For Lord Ardmor is giving to these, as to certain other of his tenants, a full abatement of rent for the present quarter. His motive for so doing is unknown to me, and I prefer to believe that he acts upon a simple principle of Christian charity, in accordance with Scriptural injunctions. He would in that case be acting in a manner contrary to that of his ancestors, both remote and immediate, for the Ardmors have never been known as "good" landlords, whatever may be meant by that toadying phrase. It is sufficient that he has done so, and against the opposition of the other landlords, and also, it is believed, of his agent.

Mr. Colthurst, to the contrary, is at one with his class, sharing its selfish lack of concern. At this moment, he is no doubt looking forward to the comforts of the Christmas season, as these may be enjoyed behind the thick walls of Dunmurray House. Turf fires will be roaring in its fireplaces, and from its cellars will be brought up cheering bottles of sherry and crusted port. Mr. Colthurst does not employ an agent, and although he was not present at the eviction which I shall describe, it was doubtless while seated at one of these fires that he signed the order which brought into these mountains his bailiff and the bailiff's shabby crew of ruffians, and the constables who guarded these against the anger of the people.

But let me set forth our experience in a more orderly fashion. It was on a Friday evening, shortly after sunset, that my friend and I left Kilpeder, having arranged beforehand that we would spend the night with our friend Mr. G——, whose tavern lies some three hours' ride from the town. By doing so, we were able to set forth into the Boggeraghs by early light. To the north, the ground rises steeply to meet the foothills, and, after a half hour, we were able to pause and look behind us at the town spread out as in a panorama, its shops and churches dark silhouettes in the light of early evening, and, beyond its high walls, the great mass of

Ardmor Castle. At the crossroads hamlet, we were made welcome by Mr. G—— and his good wife, and after our meal, ten or a dozen of his neighbors came in from their farms to join us. We could watch them coming to us, their lanterns like slow, wandering comets in the blackness.

It proved to be a cold, clear morning, so that we could see not only the mountains which lay close at hand, but those stretching into the distance, dark and forbidding. The hamlets towards which we were riding were visible: wintry fields as brown as the slopes which lay beyond them, and pasturelands a pale green. A stream, the Navogue, flows between the two hamlets, but this we could not see until we were almost upon the scene. To our either side, the hedgerows were brown and lifeless.

North Aghabullogue, our destination, is a cluster of hovels, a dozen of them, and one a bit larger than the others which calls itself shop and tavern. It was eleven in the morning when we arrived, and the people had been long about their tasks. And yet, in truth, there are few tasks to perform now, in midwinter; but they keep themselves occupied, wall mending, repairing their work carts. So, at least, are most winters spent, perhaps even the present hazardous one. This morning, however, was a special one, and the men had come back from their fields. They stood, some of them, by the closed doors of their cabins, arms folded, and in some instances the woman of the house stood there, nervous as a mountain hare.

We had been seen from far off, and our progress studied. The men watched us as we dismounted, but without apprehension, for my friend the schoolmaster had been recognised. "Good morrow," he called out in Gaelic, and touched his hand to his hat. The man closest to us nodded, grave and unsmiling. My friend, Mr. MacM——, walked to the "tavern," past its stinking heap of dung, rapped upon the door, and entered, with myself following close behind.

We were in a dark, low room, with sacks and boxes upon the floor, against the walls. A turf fire was burning, smoky and acrid. Three men were standing beside it, cups of tea in their hands, and to one of these MacM—— addressed himself in English. "As you can see, Paddy, we are here on the morning, as I told you we would be." Paddy was a short, fleshy man, bald-headed, and in early middle age.

"It will be a busy day for Aghabullogue," he said, "more visitors than we have had in many years." His speech was so thick that an untrained ear might have mistaken it for Gaelic. Of the two others, one, Michael O'Tuoma, was to say, as best I can recall, nothing whatever in the course of the day, and might well have been a mute; but if so, he was not deaf, for when the conversation was in Gaelic, I noted, he followed intently, his small, deep-set eyes moving from one speaker to the next. But it was the third man, Joseph Haggerty, who was, so to speak, the melancholy occasion of our visit, for he it was upon whom sentence of eviction had been passed by Bartholomew Colthurst.

He was a tall, hollow-chested fellow, dark-bearded and with blood-shot eyes. Like the others, he was dressed in the old fashion, with turf-coloured britches and long wool stockings, and an overcoat of grey frieze hanging open and loose.

"Have you English at all, Joseph?" I asked him in my halting Gaelic, but he shook his head. And thereafter, we spoke Gaelic only, my own weak efforts being fortified by MacM——. Paddy brought mugs of tea to the two of us, strengthened by a copious addition of sugar. Poor Haggerty looked, expressionless, first at one of us, then at the other.

"It is a day of sorrow," MacM—— said to him, and although he heard the words, indeed nodded towards them, he said nothing, and his gaze was fixed somewhere beyond us.

"There are seven of them," Paddy said, "himself and the woman and the five children. Of the children, the oldest is a girl of nine."

"Merciful God," I said. "What is to become of them? Where are they to go?"

"There is room in this house for the two of them this night," he said, "and in other houses for the small ones. But after that . . ." He shrugged. "They were a small family. There was but Joe and an older brother. The brother died young, he was delicate." This last, this reference to delicacy, is how, in English, the country people will often refer to that consumption which is a chief source among them of early mortality. "Tis plain what he must do, poor fellow."

They have not even euphemisms for the workhouse, which to them represents, as in fact it is, a plunge downwards through untried air, bewildering and dreadful. It was for the Kilpeder workhouse, then, that Haggerty was destined—a broad, low building beyond the town, reeking of misery and misfortune. And worse: for terrible stories attach to it yet from the forties, from the time of the "great hunger."

"Where are they now," I said to Haggerty in Gaelic, "the children and their mother?"

He answered me with some difficulty, as though gathering his thoughts. "They are below," he said, "at—at the cabin. I will go now to them. She thinks that we should take with us the things that we have—the stools and the beds and all. But where are we to take them?"

I caught the eye of my friend MacM—— before he turned away from me and walked towards the door, and knew that our thoughts were the same. It was as though a great ocean separated us from these men and from their world. And yet this would have been the world of our own people a half century ago, our grandparents' world, a Gaelic world cut off from schools and newspapers and solicitors' offices. The tavernkeeper, Paddy, stood between Haggerty and myself, an emissary.

After Haggerty had left, Paddy took MacM—— and myself upon a tour of the hamlet. In summer it may perhaps have its cheerful aspects, but now, in midwinter, it lay caught in unmoving cold, the ground frozen, hedges and thornbushes bare. A cold wind came down from the mountains, shaking the branches.

It was several hours later that a shout from one of the cabins called our attention to the spectacle which we had come to Aghabullogue to witness.

Far below us, on the road which we had ourselves traversed, a small procession moved slowly, a cart with men in it, and some eight or ten men on horseback. The riders were in the van, with the cart, a long narrow one, bringing up the rear. From that distance, no sound came to us; but there was suddenly, briefly, a flash of light, as the sun struck upon a constable's carbine.

A knot of our villagers stood together beside the road, looking down into the valley. I could not read their faces, which were set, expressionless. They had, the most of them, long, sallow faces, and dark, lank hair falling beneath their hats upon their shoulders.

MacM—— and Paddy and myself walked down and stood beside them. The women and children, I observed, kept close to the cabins, the women's arms folded, and shawls drawn close, obscuring their faces. But the men were standing together. Haggerty was not with them. His cabin had been pointed out to me, and now, I saw, he and his family must have gone inside it, for there were none of them about. It was a cabin neither better nor worse than the others, a puddle before it with a skin of ice from which cold sunlight glinted.

Presently, the sounds of hooves upon hard earth came to us, and the creaking of cartwheels, but no voices. And shortly after that, we were able to make out faces, including one that I recognised, that of Sergeant D—— of the Kilpeder Barracks, seeming at this distance a toy soldier's face, eagle nose and fierce moustaches beneath the tall helmet.

But neither did voices come to us from the men beside whom we stood. They said nothing. One of them cleared his throat and spat.

When the procession reached the hamlet, we could see that the floor of the cart cradled a heavy log, to be used should it be necessary to force

[392]

an entrance. The bailiff's crew sat on either side of the cart, their feet upon the log. There were eight of them, and two only could I recognise as Kilpeder men. Eugene B——, the bailiff, rode with the sergeant, at the head of the procession, a short, corpulent man, wearing overcoat, muffler, and high-crowned hat.

He knew the house which was the object of his mission, as did the sergeant, and they led their men towards it. The men by the roadside turned then and followed them, and now the women, with the children following close behind, left the cabins and came out into the road.

"Joseph Haggerty," B—— called out, and then called again, the full name, "Joseph Haggerty." But there was no response from within, and thereupon, as though he had been expecting none, he took from his pocket the order of ejectment and read it out. Then he dismounted, and looked towards the crew in the cart and nodded. At the same time, the sergeant, with a motion of his outstretched arm, sent his constables to spread out in a wide arc that separated the villagers from the cabin. The constables were but performing their duty, without, so far as could be seen, either sympathy or ill will, and yet there was a menace in their very appearance—uniformed, caped, helmeted, armed.

"Haggerty," B—— shouted out again. "This is no good, man. Tis all over." Then, as though remembering, he called out in Gaelic, a Gaelic more fluent than my own. But from within the house came neither voice nor stir. He walked to the door and beat upon it with his gloved fist, dull echoing thuds.

When there was no response, he stepped back, and with a shrug that seemed to be speaking to us rather than to himself, he nodded to his crew. Its foreman, a broad-shouldered, bandy-legged young fellow, leaped lithely to the ground, and his men clambered down after him. With some difficulty, they contrived to lift out their weapon, a tree trunk which had been stripped clean of bark, and was some eight feet in length. Elsewhere, as we know, efficient battering rams have been perfected, set within frames and swinging from chains. Here we had the homelier and more traditional tree trunk.

As they carried it towards the cabin, I became aware of a murmuring about me, to the left and right, men speaking in low tones, either to one another or else voicing curses to the empty air. The crew stood before the door, three of them on either side of their weapon, holding it with an awkward determination. Their foreman looked towards B——, as if for some final instruction, and B—— moved his tongue across his dry lips. And at that moment, one of the women ran forward, seized up a stone almost the size of her fist, drew back her arm, and hurled it at the foreman.

It was a powerful arm, but she had had little practice or else was distracted by her rage, for the stone sailed well over the foreman's head, striking the cabin wall, near the door.

She was a young woman, and of handsome appearance, as the women of these mountains often are, slender and full-bosomed. Her unbound, black hair fell well below her shoulders, and the force with which she hurled the stone flung it to one side. I saw her in profile, high-cheekboned, and her eye blazing with anger. She had flung the stone, and stood in silence, her closed fists pressing upon hip bones.

Others in the crowd now moved to follow her example, stooping down to pick up stones or clods of earth. But Sergeant D—— moved quickly, swinging one arm towards his men, to draw them close, and with the other pulling at his reins, to swerve his mount towards three villagers who stood together, one of them holding a lethal-looking rock. "Now then," he shouted, riding down hard upon them, and one of the three, rage working against discretion, rushed forward and seized the reins. I saw him staring into the sergeant's face with eyes flooded by a frightening anger. At this moment, a small shower of rocks sailed over the heads of the constables, and this time one of them struck the foreman full in his chest, so that he staggered backward but did not fall. Reaching downwards with a long, sweeping movement, Sergeant D—— slashed out at the man holding the reins, striking him full in the face and with such violence that blood sprang from the fellow's nose in a scarlet spurt which fell upon his coat. The sergeant shouted something out to the man.

But now, all unexpectedly, the cabin door was flung open. For a breathless moment, we all stood looking into its darkness, obscure and dim in the winter sunlight. And then Haggerty came rushing out, holding in his two hands a long, murderous-looking pitchfork. Straight towards the bailiff he rushed, the tines of the fork pointed upwards. "No," B—— shouted, "oh God, no, Holy Mother." But before Haggerty could reach his target, one of the bailiff's men, quick of wit, threw a heavy shoulder against him, knocking him to the side, and a moment later, one of the constables, leaping from his mount, wrestled him to the ground, and a second one twisted the pitchfork from his grasp.

Haggerty began now, most terribly, to bellow—loud, meaningless sounds, like a bull calf's. The bellowing gradually raised itself in pitch, and it was as though he were shouting out words, but with such incoherence that they could not be understood. I was standing close enough to him to see that he was sobbing, the tears flooding his eyes and beginning to run down his earth-dirtied face. His mouth, almost toothless, was a wide, gaping wound.

I tore my gaze away from him, and looking towards his cabin saw that his wife and two of his children, flanking her, had come from it. She stood staring at her husband with the same helpless wonder that had seized us all; but the children, for whom it must have seemed an infernal moment, began now to cry.

Presently, but slowly, Haggerty's terrifying sobs died away, and he lay there. The two constables who had grappled with him stood a short distance away. One of the people, a tall, hulking fellow with a set, dark face, came forward now and helped the poor man to his feet. Haggerty looked around at all of us, as though seeing us for the first time. But when he saw his wife, he called out, "Come away out of that, now, Maire. Come over here with me, and take the children with you."

The young woman who had thrown the rock called out to the sergeant, "Let them back into the house, will you, so that they can take what they have."

"For why?" Haggerty said. "Where is there to take it?"

"My Jesus mercy," she said, "are you all turned to stone? There are children yet in the house. There are beds that they will need." And saying this, she strode into the house, passing me so closely that she brushed against my arm.

My friend MacM—— had gone to Haggerty, and had offered him the flask of whiskey that we had brought with us against the cold. He took it gratefully, and, tilting back his head, drank deeply. Then he wiped his mouth, and thanked MacM——. "There is but the one place for us now," he said, "and after that, there will be nothing." A man who had heard him shouted out to the bailiff, "Are you satisfied now, you son of a wh——?"

"He is not," another shouted. "He will have not satisfaction until the thatch is gone and the stones tumbled."

B—— stood stolidly, his face without expression; but the sergeant, it is agreeable to report, and several of his men were less callous, and the sergeant spoke out. "'Tis the law that is with the bailiff, and you all of you know that."

"A black law it is," the tall man who had helped Haggerty to his feet said, "and you should be ashamed to serve it. How can he pay his rents, how can any of us? Look around you, man. That law of yours will clear away all of us before it has run its course."

"'Tis the law nevertheless," Sergeant D—— said, "and the law can not be gainsaid."

"Best get on with it," B—— said, and struck his hands together, rubbing them against the chill.

I can now bear testimony that a family's dwelling place in the southwest of Ireland can be destroyed in less than an hour—the thatch torn off, and the walls pounded in with sledgehammers, pried open with crowbars—if a crew of men can be found heartless enough to perform the task.

Haggerty's wife and the two children had come over to him, and now these were joined by their other young ones. They stood together, close but not touching, Haggerty with his hands hanging loose at his sides, and the wife with her shawl drawn so close as almost to conceal her face. By the roadway, those who had gone to the young woman's assistance had placed, in a jumble, a cheap dresser, a few straw mattresses, some eight or ten shapeless sacks, two black iron pots, a creel, a few three-legged stools. Within the cabin, in their habitual places, they had no doubt composed a life, given the orderliness which the familiar communicates to us. Bits of wood, iron, straw: they had lived in the deep shadows of the cabin's interior. Now, in cold sunlight, they lay in squalour; a tinker would not have stooped to steal them.

And so too with the cabin itself. In less than an hour, it was a shapeless mound, destroyed, as is the invariable custom, lest the tenant sneak back into it, to warm himself and his family, when bailiffs and sergeants and constables and bailiffs' ruffians have left. A life can that easily be dashed into fragments.

All, after that, was anticlimax. The bailiff's men, their odious task accomplished, stood in a clump together, uncertain what next to do, but not greatly disturbed, for it was certain now that the villagers intended nothing more, for the moment, than to signal their anger and sorrow with dark looks and shouts. No longer was so much as a stone flung. The young woman herself who had commenced the battery, and who had set herself so bravely against the crew, joined now by a girl of her own age, her sister perhaps or her friend, stood quietly, although her shoulders and bosom heaved. There was on her face a curious expression, as though she could not understand what she had done, her lips parted.

Until Mr. B——'s crew was back in their long car, the constables remained in place, indifferent or embarrassed, who can say which; but then they too moved out from the hamlet, and down the narrow road, back to Kilpeder. The people of the hamlet watched them leave, as one might watch a storm from one's window, heavy shaking branches and scudding cloud.

I was standing, my helpless gaze fixed upon poor Haggerty and his family. MacM—— was beside me; we could find nothing to say to one another. "Now then," Paddy said, walking over to join us, "we had best take a drop to ease the chill of this." And we nodded, but Haggerty, when we went to him, would not join us. Neither did he look at us, or at his neighbours, or even at his family. His eyes first would turn, idly, towards the wrecked cabin, and then towards the procession dwindling away from us down the road—the crowd of wreckers, and the two files of caped constables, tall-helmeted.

"Leave him so for a bit," Paddy said. "There are neighbours to watch him. He will come to no harm."

"No," I said, when we were again within Paddy's walls, and holding, each of us, his tumbler of whiskey and steaming water against the winter chill. "He will come to no harm at the moment."

The workhouse lies on the far side of Kilpeder, on the Macroom road, a low, broad, graceless building, cut stone fronting upon the county road, but beyond that a higgledy-piggledy of whatever was left of the good stone, and then bits and pieces of fieldstone, rubble, brickwork, and beyond the central block, stretching away towards dull, useless fields, extensions made of brick of which one is an infirmary and one, set up in the years after the great famine of the forties, is the house for women and girls and infants. The windows on the ground floor are barred. Legend has it that in the worst days of the famine, when the workhouse already was filled to overflowing, the poor and the famished, who had come down into Kilpeder from mountainy villages such as Aghabullogue, suddenly, upon an impulse mindless as a wave, pushed themselves upon the few guards and then trampled over them, and swarmed inside in search of food or of warmth or perhaps of nothing more than something other than bleak grey sky above their heads. But there was nothing within, save peasants as wasted as themselves, hollow-cheeked, but frantic in possession, so that they fought each other, the weak and the starving pummelling each other, cursing, kicking, and flailing out arms.

Such stories from the great famine exist everywhere in Ireland, and in West Cork as abundantly as anywhere. Stories of the workhouses in Skibbereen and Schull, where the bodies would be found at the door in the morning, three or four of them, a family perhaps, cold and stiff. Or the stories of the famine graves, and of the cholera sheds at the outskirts of the town. Families standing bewildered by the sides of roads, or begging in the streets of cities and market towns. But this is not the worst: there are legends uglier than these, which are not fit to be set down, but which are known, which linger in the air.

In truth, the workhouses in these latter days are under the scrupulous examination of conscientious guardians, and the masters and their staffs are worthy gentlemen. We have advanced from the days of our parents and grandparents. But nothing can scrub from the imaginations of the country people those formless images of the workhouse as the place of ultimate shame, of the loss almost of name and birthright. It was this to which Joseph Haggerty and his family had been sentenced by Bartholomew Colthurst, Esquire, of Kilpeder, a gentleman of substance, a member of the Kilpeder Hunt, living upon his rents. The season of the year was Christmas.

Aside from MacM—— and myself, and Paddy, our host, there were perhaps eight or ten men gathered together by the fire. Most of them I recognised from among those who had made their protest with word or stone or else had stood in hostile silence. "He is cast forth upon the world," one of them said in Gaelic, "himself and his people. They are cast forth upon the world." "As any man among us might be," another of them said. "It could as easily be yourself or myself as poor Joseph." Which was indeed the case, for none of the cabins of Aghabullogue had made payment of rents for that quarter, and Haggerty, so far as could be told, had been chosen at random, to make an example.

I felt, more so perhaps than my friend MacM——, a sense of separation from these men, my fellow countrymen, although I had myself grown up upon a farm not fifty miles distant—a bit more prosperous, perhaps, and in an English-speaking region. I had grown up knowing Gaelic, which had been the language not of my parents but of their parents, and the language also of the casual laborers who would be with us at harvest time. A language falls away from one with disuse, becoming, when heard again, a rhythm, a wave of familiar sounds, meanings half recognised.

When the door opened again, it was to admit Haggerty himself. Beyond his shoulder, I had a glimpse of bare fields and hungry hills. He shut the door quickly, but a body of cold air had entered with him, a brief chill despite the fire's warmth. Paddy handed him a cup of hot whiskey, which he accepted gratefully, cupping his two hands about it. One of the others said something to him in a rushing tumble of words which I could not understand, and I looked for enlightenment towards MacM——, who shrugged. "There would in the old days have been a bullet for that blackguard B——," a fellow said, but using a Gaelic word coarser than "blackguard."

"There would not," a fellow rejoined. "There was not in those days a gun or a rifle between this valley and the next. But there would have been a number of men waiting for him where the road narrows between the rocks, and there he would have been cudgelled, a blackthorn to lay open his head like a rotted apple."

"Ach," Paddy said, "the peelers would have had a word or two to say about that. Tis not for sport nor for ornament that they carry their murderous carbines."

"What does it matter?" Haggerty said. "What is done is done. I do not know where to turn, God help me."

Before we left Aghabullogue, MacM—— and I made an opportunity to take him aside, and press upon him a sum which had been gathered in Kilpeder from some who did not know him but wished him well. He took it with embarrassment, his eyes not quite meeting ours, and it oppressed me to reflect that in months to come, if other misfortune followed, he might deal more easily with charity.

When we mounted, there was no one in the road save Paddy, who had come out to bid us farewell. To our right lay the ugly ruins of Haggerty's cabin, and a few of his possessions, although most of these had already been taken into the other dwellings. The air was still, and touched with that faint, brittle fragrance which is a presage of snow.

"What is to become of any of us here, if it comes to that?" Paddy said to us in English. But I could only shake my head. I had already resolved that I would set down what I had that day witnessed, and would see that it was printed. It might in that way bring some sense of shame, if not of Christian remorse, to Mr. Bartholomew Colthurst, of Dunmurray House, Kilpeder, a gentleman of substance. That failing, and I had little hope for an enterprise resting upon Mr. Colthurst's moral sensibilities, I might at the very least bring to the people of this county, and perhaps a few miles beyond this county, a sense of how things fare with us this winter, and why. To the north of us, in Mayo, resolute farmers, under the inspiration of the celebrated Michael Davitt but animated chiefly by their own fortitude and resolve, have banded together in a Land League. It may be that such an organization will spring up in the defence of those in Munster who till the fields and nurture the herds. This is devoutly to be hoped.

But it will be too late to be of much practical help to my friend Paddy and his neighbours in Aghabullogue. A Land League requires organization and meetings and planning. But Mr. Bartholomew Colthurst of Dunmurray House has his troops already in possession, his bailiff and his bailiff's men and his sergeant and his constables with their carbines, and behind them, the elaborate panoply of the law itself, with its writs of ejectment. It is true, of course, that the victory of his which I have here recorded may prove a hollow one. The eviction of Joseph Haggerty from his small holding does not of itself bring one shilling, bring one farthing, into Mr. Colthurst's purse. He has acted, it must be assumed, on the military principle by which mutinies are quelled, but in Aghabullogue, as we have seen, none was intended. No moneys are being withheld from him and secretly hoarded; indeed, the poverty of that valley is painful to behold.

In the weeks since I paid my visit there, there have been no more evictions, although there are rumours in the town of Kilpeder that these may be resumed. Joseph Haggerty and his family did enter the Kilpeder workhouse, but for a shorter time than I had feared: well-wishers in the county arranged for their transportation to New York. It is a path which thousands from our county have taken before them, a sea road to a far better existence than their own country can provide for them.

On Christmas Eve, in the warmth and security of my own home in Kilpeder, I remembered Aghabullogue, and the tumbled stones of Haggerty's cabin. He is a remembered name in that village, as his children are. But soon, in a year or two, the stones will have made their way to fences, to the walls of other cabins; what was his dwelling place will be but a low, shapeless mound, with nettles growing upon it. And his name will grow fainter, will drift away on the winter wind, will vanish.

It was a clear, cold Christmas in West Cork. At midnight, as we stood gathered by our front window, my family and our friends, we looked out upon a market square bathed in a faint, diffuse moonlight, and arching above all, a black, calm, starless sky. To the north, and the east, invisible, beyond farms and pasturelands, stretched the Boggeraghs, and, within them, sharing the vigil with us, the imperilled homes of Aghabullogue.

20

[*Hugh MacMahon*]

Even now, when I hold a copy of *Christmas in the Boggeraghs* and read again its final paragraphs, I can recall us standing together at Bob De- laney's window—Bob and myself, and Mary between us, and, a bit to one side, Agnes in the new winter gown that Bob had brought her from Dublin, dark, watered silk, and bits of fur at collar and waist. It was exactly the kind of night described in the pamphlet, cold and extraordinarily clear, with a thin powder of snow on the ground. I remember touching my fingers to the window, the glass frigid as the Pole, and I remember that we did indeed, in that room of Christmas warmth, think of Aghabul- logue and its tumbled cabin, folded within hungry hills.

How shrill that pamphlet seems now, with its lurid cover, a crude woodcut of burly men smashing in a cabin while, from the roadside, gaunt and pathetic peasants stare at them. In the distance, mountains tall and jagged as the Alps, capped with snow. But for the month of its appearance, it was a great sensation. Finneran's, the printers in Cork City, had three times to run off impressions of it, and it was mentioned in the *Cork Examiner* and in the *Freeman's Journal*. Bob was greatly embarrassed that by my insistence, his name only appeared upon the cover and the title page. It is still remembered, although long out of print, of course, and you will now hear it mentioned as the first shot fired in the Land War in County Cork. Which was, of course, precisely what Bob had intended.

There was, so he told me later, a small pile of the pamphlets stacked neatly upon his desk the morning that Bartholomew Colthurst came storming into his law office, bundled up in a heavy, caped greatcoat of broad plaid, and with a copy of the pamphlet clutched in his gloved hand. It was a bitter January morning, and he brought a blast of cold in with him.

"We do not know each other," he said to Bob. "We have never met."

"I know who you are, Mr. Colthurst," Bob said.

"Then you know that you have printed lies about me," Colthurst said, brandishing the pamphlet, "and set your name to them."

"Lies, is it, Mr. Colthurst? There are no lies in that. Have a care what use you make of words, or you will find yourself in worse difficulties. That is a serious charge you have made, but I can see that you are upset."

"Upset, is it?" Colthurst said. "I have a good mind to set the flat of a whip against you. Who the devil do you think you are, that you can safely slate a man in print?"

"First slander," Bob said, "and then the threat of physical violence. By God, Mr. Colthurst, you are making a busy morning of it. Would you care to wave a pistol at me as well?"

"There is no need for that with the likes of you," Colthurst said, "a jumped-up counterboy from Tully's shop. Pistols are for gentlemen."

"Gentlemen like yourself," Bob said, "who turf out families onto the roads of winter. Marvellous it must be, to be a gentleman. I wonder that you take exception to my celebration of your activities." And he let his eye fall upon his small stack of *Christmas in the Boggeraghs*.

"It was almost cruel of me, God forgive me," Bob said to me that night, as he poured for each of us a measure of whiskey, for Vincent and myself, as the three of us sat in that office, with soft lamplight falling upon the desk, and Kilpeder black as anthracite beyond the windows. His hand trembled a bit, with suppressed laughter.

"And cruel it was, no doubt," Vincent said. "He is not the worst in the world, poor Bat Colthurst. He is no bigot, and he is a fine lad for a day's sport. Many is the fine day's beagling that I have had with Bat

Colthurst. And now betwixt the two of you and your literary efforts, you have turned him into a raving ogre, a successor to Lord Clanricarde and Lord Leitrim, and the likes of those."

"He did his bit, Vincent," I said. "He collaborated in his infamy. He turfed out the poor Haggertys, and no doubt about that. Bob and I were there to watch it, and a bloody black day's work it was."

"There he stood, the little shite," Bob said, "between your own chair there, Vincent, and Hughie's, trembling with rage, and rummaging in his ill-stored mind for some savage insult to hurl at me; but he could think only that I had served my day behind the counter of the shop, that I have been a fetch-and-carry boy for your father."

"In short, you were goading him," Vincent said.

"Bloody little squireens," Bob said. "Half-mounted gentlemen, however you would call them. The ragtag and bobtail of Cromwell's crew. We will clear out that scruff to begin with—two or three years, that should take—and then, at our own good time, we can turn our attention to the absentees and the great estates."

As he said all this and more, he had a polished boot cocked on the open drawer of the great desk that had been brought down from Cork City, and a half smile that mocked his words and yet did not entirely mock them. It was a mood that had settled upon him now that he was Land League agent for the town of Kilpeder, and indeed a voice in the League councils for all of Cork.

"If that is your plan," Vincent said easily to him, "you have hit upon a sturdy skirmisher in Bartholomew Colthurst. He has damned few lands other than those at Aghabullogue, and his back is against the wall. But he has the friendship of the other landlords, and the kinship of Colthursts spread from Macroom to the sea. They will not see him bested to satisfy yourself and your Land League pals, much less the scarecrows of Aghabullogue."

"Or your father," Bob said, in a light, almost bantering way. For Dennis Tully had let it become well known in Kilpeder that he favoured the Land League, and would assist it in this way and that. From beginning to end, the Tullys never ceased to amaze me.

"Or my father," Vincent said in much the same manner, as though the two of them had lightly, politely, touched foils in a game of fence.

"Well now," Bob said, "let me tell you about Bartholomew Colthurst. I will read his fortune for you, and tis easily done, for he has little left."

He lifted down his boot, and sat squarely facing us. From the Waterford decanter, he poured measures out for the three of us, and added dollops of water. "He may be your beagling companion, Vinnie, and the devil of a fellow in the field or the bedroom or the County Club, but I am the great authority on his future, because his future is not being settled on the hunting field but in this office."

"In your office, is it?" Vincent said, in tones of mock-admiration. "Not even in Aghabullogue itself."

"Not even there," Bob said. "Ach, I grant you if Colthurst could find some starveling stupid enough to take up Haggerty's farm, there would be trouble. The people would toss him into a pot and eat collops of him for dinner, served up with nettles. But there will be no one to take up that farm, nor any second one, should he make a second ejectment. That miserable place is the arse end of beyond, and there was nothing sensible he could have done save take a notch in his belt as the people have done. But not him, not the great beagler; and now, thanks to Hughie's eloquence, the attention of all Munster is upon those wretched acres."

"It is indeed," Vincent said, and although he held his glass admiringly to the yellowish lamplight, it was Bob he was studying. "And I cannot believe that the landlords and the gentry of these baronies will allow one of their own kind to fall prey to a crew of agitators. You will excuse my using their term for the Land League. A crew of agitators."

"No excuse is needed. That is precisely what we are. A crew of agitators. But with a difference, as your friends among the gentry will discover. The gentry will make their stand against the League, I have no doubt, and they will have the government and the army and the Royal Irish Constabulary at their back. But they will choose their cases with care. They will not defend the indefensible, and they will not defend the hero of Hughie's pamphlet. If you fancy any of Bat Colthurst's beagle hounds, keep your eyes open. He will be selling out soon."

'Eighty. 'Eighty-one. 'Eighty-two. Those were Bob Delaney's great years of prophecy. That night, as Vincent and I stood in the square, the two of us—myself perhaps as much as Vincent, almost—were amused and a bit annoyed by the way in which he had taken to confronting life, crashing into it full-sail, and with an air of certainty. "*He* knows what the gentry will do," Vincent said, slapping his gloved hands together against the cold. "Who in God's name told him, the Land Leaguers above in Macroom and Cork? Have you ever seen such a pack—solicitors and *nisi prius* advocates, out-at-the-elbow journalists?"

"Ah, well," I said, to keep the peace and to get home out of the cold, for there was a thin, fierce wind coming down from the hills, "tis a new enthusiasm."

But we were quite wrong, the two of us, to be that light and mocking about it. In those three years of prophecy, as I came later to call them, I do not believe that Bob took a single false step. It is his public life of which I am speaking, of course. For in his private life, he was to fare far differently. But is it not wonderful to say of someone from Bob's beginnings, a shop assistant—Bat Colthurst had the right of it there—that he came to have a public life, to be one of the great men of the Land League, and a member of Parliament, and to be known as one of Parnell's young lieutenants?

There is such a thing as grasping fortune by the forelock, as the old writers would phrase it. But it is perhaps, rather, that there are moments in the lives of a few men when they are lifted out of their own obscurity, and welded onto the history of their people, so that the two are one. What I have called Bob's gift of prophecy in those few years was a sureness in action, a certainty that the great weighted pendulum of history was on the move, sweeping through time and space. A pendulum sharp-edged as an executioner's ax.

Poor Colthurst's affairs worked themselves out exactly as Bob had predicted. Before six months were out, he had sold up and gone to live with his cousins in their castle at Macroom, and from there he went on to London and was seen no more in this county. Once, a year or two later, Vincent encountered him above in Galway at a meet of the Blazers. The Land War was by then in full swing from one end of Ireland to the other, and in Galway and Mayo great estates were under siege. Colthurst, so Vincent was to report to me, was like the survivor of an early battle, spiteful and grumpy. "He tried to pick a quarrel with me," Vincent said, "sitting his borrowed hunter, and worrying the ends of his cigar-stained moustaches, but I would have none of it. And he had frequent recourse to a flask the size almost of a quart bottle, taking long pulls at it when he thought there was no one to observe. Thus are the mighty fallen, a family that has been here from the days of Cromwell at the latest."

It was a vivid picture, but more clearly still, as Vincent spoke, could I imagine Colthurst in his London lodgings, an exile, nursing his useless anger.

That is how the Land War began in our baronies, with the eviction in the Boggeraghs and the downfall of Bartholomew Colthurst. It was like a first brief shot fired at the commencement of a skirmish. The Land League, to be sure, made much of it, and in platform speeches in Millstreet and Macroom and elsewhere, it was spoken of as another Salamis or Marathon, and Colthurst as a second but more clownish Herod.

Now began the great days of the torchlit meetings and processions throughout most of the west and the south of Ireland, and in such matters

Kilpeder was not to be outdone. But there was an early one, a few weeks before the first of ours, in Macroom, and I journeyed down with Bob to attend it. For the week before it, there were placards throughout the baronies, of which I preserved one because of its picturesque diction.

"MUNSTER AWAKE!!!" it began. "Great Tenants' Right Meeting to Come Off in the Square of Macroom on Sunday Next." And the notabilities who were "expected to attend" were listed in their copious number, including a squadron of members of Parliament led by "Charles S. Parnell, Esquire, M.P." All that was, of course, but circus glitter, for Parnell and those other notabilities were holding back for a more strategic appearance; but the placard did state with truth that in attendance would be the hero of Aghabullogue, the defender of the poor farmers in our hills and valleys, the man in the gap, Robert Delaney, Solicitor. And there was a marvellous peroration: "From the China towers of Pekin to the round towers of Ireland, from the cabins of Connemara to the kraals of Kaffirland, from the wattled homes of the isles of Polynesia to the wigwams of North America the cry is: 'Down with invaders! Down with tyrants!' Every man to have his own land! Every man to have his own home!"

We set forth together, Bob and myself, and sat comfortably in his handsome trap, the sides a glistening black, and soft cushions upon the seat. Bob was wearing the new clothes which had been made for him, under Vincent's supervision, by Duffy the Cork City tailor—a handsome frock coat, black as the trap, and with black silk at the lapels. He was nervous—I could tell from the way he handled the reins—and before we reached Macroom he had smoked three of the long, pale cigars to which he had recently taken, holding them tightly between his lips.

It was evening when we arrived, and we went by arrangement to the Imperial Hotel, where John Stephen Murphy was waiting for us, a solicitor himself and the great man in Macroom for the Tenants' Right movement. Like Bob, he was well turned out, in frock coat and glistening white shirtfront with a neckpiece of watered lilac silk held neat by a small pearl stickpin. There were with him five or six others, and we had a meal together, while outside the square was being made ready. It was a grand meal. Girls were kept to the trot, moving to and fro between kitchen and dining room, carrying great serving platters of ham and sliced chicken, bowls of steaming potatoes in their warm brown jackets, and the tall glasses of porter and lager were kept filled.

There was about the meal that same sense of excitement, kept under fierce rein, that I had felt in Bob, and as I can look backward now upon it, I understand its sources as I did not then, although Bob had done his best to enlighten me. To myself, and no doubt to countless others, in those early months the Land League seemed a virtuous endeavour, and perhaps helpful to farmers in that woeful year. But never until now did I imagine that it would become the instrument that Parnell and Davitt would make of it, with the help of lads like Bob and John Stephen Murphy of Macroom. It was on this day that I began to have a sense of that future.

By the time that we moved forward to our tea and our slices of fruit tart, darkness had begun to settle down upon the town; but there was still light enough to see that a great crowd was gathering in the square. Barrels of pitch had been set alight, and from these some of the men in the crowd were drawing flame for their own pitch-soaked torches. You could hear now and then, above the dull noise of many voices, a sudden shout, unmenacing, jovial, and expectant—a man shouting across the square to a friend, perhaps, and then a fellow with perhaps one glass too many taken aboard shouting, "Up Macroom!" or "Up Cork!" as though at a hurling match.

But the League dignitaries took their time, awaiting the most propitious moment, and a bottle was put into circulation on the table. Bob and John Stephen, I observed, took but a tincture and filled their glasses with water, exchanging wry smiles. "To the Land League," John Stephen said, and raised his glass, and we raised ours. As if upon cue, a brass band in the square commenced to play. I had heard it warming up, the odd cornet note above the noises of the assembly, and the tentative thud of a drum. But it was ready now, and struck up the Young Ireland song by Thomas Davis, "A Nation Once Again."

> "And then I prayed I yet might see,
> Our fetters burst in twain,
> And Ireland long a province be,
> A nation once again."

Beyond in the square and within the dining room, the voices fell.

It is curious. The avowed purpose of the League was, for the moment, to relieve the pressures upon farmers large and small in this calamitous season, and to bring a halt to evictions. Beyond that, shimmering and dim, lay notions of the overthrow of feudalism and a peasant proprietorship. All this had little to do, seemingly, with political independence, and yet here was the band playing "A Nation Once Again," and every man in Macroom, whatever his politics, knew that the fight for land and the fight for nationality were conjoined, twisted together beyond the comprehension of logic.

In the square beyond, the crowd was singing out the words, for all of them knew them, and here, at the table, first the man who sat to my right, and then a man across from me, and then all of us were singing it, struggling a moment later to our feet, one by one, and standing with our hands to our sides, as though it were a national anthem, as perhaps it was.

"For freedom comes from God's right hand,
And needs a godly train,
And righteous men must make our land
A nation once again."

At the end, there was a roar from the square, but we stood silent at the table, a bit embarrassed, a bit cynical and a bit sentimental at the same time, the two states being close allies.

Of the meeting itself I best remember Bob's speech, of course, but I am not alone in that; for in the years to come you would occasionally hear a Macroom man say of Bob, "Didn't I have him spotted from the outset, from the Sunday when he stood with John Stephen Murphy on the platform in my own Macroom, and stepped forward, and gave the word that set the baronies ablaze? Wasn't I as close to him almost as I am this moment to you? A man making his first speech but as calm as O'Connell on the floor of Parliament?" But I was not myself that close to him, for although both John Stephen and Bob himself urged me to go up with the dignitaries upon the platform, I declined, and stood on the steps of the hotel, where I was joined by others.

John Stephen had the chair of honour, of course, with the parish priest and his curate to his right, and Bob to his left. But the meeting was not opened and neither did it close with a blessing from Father Maguire. That would come in later months, when the League had proved itself; for the moment, the Church contented itself with a show of benign interest. But I will grant to Father Maguire that he was benignity personified, a well-fed man of ample girth and jowl, and throughout these proceedings smiling broadly, and once or twice about to break into applause, although histrionically restraining himself—a message not wasted upon his parishioners, who like most Irishmen were adept at the reading of intricate clerical pantomime.

When John Stephen presented Bob to the assembly, with a floweriness of diction which proved him the author of the placard, Bob took off his tall hat, placed it carefully upon the chair, and stepped to the centre of the platform. He seemed calmness itself, but before he could speak a word, the band broke into "Clonbrony Wood." It was a come-all-ye at best, a bit of doggerel to be sung, not played upon instruments of brass;

but with time a species of instrumental version had been hammered out, and the crowd, familiar with it, joined in. It was shorter, thank God, than the versions sung out in public houses, and it was rousing enough for such public meetings as this one.

> *"Let all true Irishmen be good,*
> *And fight for what they hold.*
> *Like all those heroes brave and bold,*
> *Who held Clonbrony Wood."*

"He was one of them, you know," the man standing next to me said. "Bob Delaney was one of the men who held Clonbrony Wood in 'sixty-seven."

"So I have heard," I said.

"By Jesus," the man said, "isn't he the great lad? Would you take a look at him? The English may have us down in the dust, with their hands upon our throats, but we are not finished, so long as we have lads like that one." He breathed heavily, and a whiff which mingled porter and boiled bacon came towards me, a homely odour.

Bob waited, motionless, through the song and the cheers which followed upon it. "I recognise the song," he said. "And I seem to remember that I wandered myself into Clonbrony Wood a few years back for some purpose or other, I disremember what." He waited for the laughter and cheering which followed upon that.

"By God," porter-and-bacon said to me, "he's a droll lad, is he not? And a modest one."

"But I mustn't search my memories of that occasion," Bob said, "whatever it may have been. There's a couple of lads here this evening who will be marking down all that is said, and off it will go to Dublin Castle." He nodded towards two caped and helmeted constables, one of them with his pad and paper in hand. There was a muttering now, with an edge of uncertain menace, but Bob held up his hand.

"Leave them to their harmless task," he said. "There will be no word spoken tonight that will go beyond the bounds of the law."

"More's the pity, then," a fellow shouted up to him.

"No, no," Bob said. "Better the peelers occupy themselves with the copying down of oratory than for them to be at the other tasks which they do this year upon the landlords' bidding, standing guard whilst ruffians toss the thatch of poor cottagers, or carting off to prison some poor distracted fellow who has raised his arm against the destruction of his home. Scribble away, lads," he called out to the peelers, who stood beet-red beneath their stiff helmets, "scribble away. If I go too fast for you, give a shout."

Here was a Bob Delaney I had never seen before; his first public speech and he took to it like a duck to water, a born demagogue, if that is not too harsh a word to use of a friend. Dimly I remembered the words that he had spoken to our lads in 'sixty-seven, when he turned over the command to Ned Nolan—confident words, to be sure. He was a confident man from first to last; at the very end, broken and bitter, he was confident in his despair. But in 'sixty-seven, as we stood together the lot of us on the wasteland beyond Knockmany, his words had had a quiet authority, terse as semaphores. But who can say—with a man as skilful with words as Bob was from the first—who can say where artifice begins or ends?

"Times change," Bob said, and now that he had their attention, he risked speaking more quietly, although his words reached to the farthest men and women. "Times change, and plans and weapons must change with them. In the year 'sixty-seven, men rose up across Munster, and up through Leinster to the hills of Dublin itself. And with what results, we all know. Disaster, and the crashing of all our hopes amidst the laughter and derision of our enemies. Ah no, tis well we have our songs of the bold Fenian men, and the heroes who were hanged in Manchester. But we have seen how far pikes and rifles and pitchforks can carry us, and how far slogans and banners. We are met in a dark year and a cold season. Already you will hear talk that black 'forty-seven may be upon us again. God forbid that this should be so, and I do not believe that it is so. What I do know, and what every man amongst you knows as well, is that we have another ruined harvest, and that with a few decent exceptions, our overlords and masters—the landlords—will not take this into account. And we know their methods—the method of the crowbar brigade, the method of the tossed cabin and the families upon the road. The method of the farm being placed upon offer to whatever neighbour or blow-in will meet the old rent. And fine effective methods they are—the land was taken from us by force, by sword and cannon in days gone by, but it is held by cunning, by the setting of neighbour against neighbour, by the turning of honest men into land grabbers, protected by the carbines of the Constabulary."

There was a flimsy railing to the platform, and Bob rested his hand lightly upon it, and paused. I could see his eyes moving across faces, as though measuring them.

"But they need not be effective, those methods. It may not be pleasant for Munster men to look to Connaught for our instruction, but this once it may profit us to do so. In Connaught—in Mayo and in

Galway—the farmers large and small—mark that, large and small—have banded together, as you know. They are insisting upon a reduction of rents, and in town after town, the landlords have grudgingly backed down. And what is the weapon they have used? Not the pike or the musket, God save the day—"

"Tis a fit use for a rifle," someone called out. "Tis stronger than a speech."

There was some good-natured laughter and a scattering of satirical applause. The shout had come from somewhere across the square from our hotel, perhaps from the porch of one or another of the two public houses, where knots of men stood together.

"To be sure," Bob said, suiting his response to the laughter and the rippling applause. "There is the kind of observation that Dublin Castle will receive with delight. But the weapon that the Land League can place in our hands is protected by the law. We can act against the landlords, and there is naught that they can do. They cannot compel us to pay their rack rents, unless they can evict us. And evictions would ruin them as well as us, unless they can find grabbers. They will act to change the laws, you can depend upon that, but there is time needed. By then, we will have won, and Connaught and Leinster will have won. And that will be a battle only, not the war which the Land League has in mind. The land of Ireland for the people of Ireland. We will settle for nothing less."

The hills beyond the town were in darkness, but there was still a faint, greenish light in the west, towards Kilpeder. The square, though, was vivid with the guttering barrels and torches; their lights fell upon shops and market house, upon the square crowded with men, upon the platform. Bob was still speaking, and I half attended his words; but I was lured away from them by the spectacle. There was movement in the crowd, of course: a man wove his way through it, and walked down the road upon some errand; another craned his neck to look towards a friend. But it was curiously quiet. Even the bit about the land of Ireland for the people of Ireland, not a novel slogan by any means but usually good for a roar, had not jolted them. They were actually listening to what Bob said, and ever after that I believed that I had found out the secret of his skill as a orator. He had the knack of seeming to speak to each man there, and yet to be speaking to all of them.

It was only at the close, and knowing perhaps that it was expected—like the couplet that seals the poem, like the grace notes that are sent to linger in the air—that he rose to oratory. He had been speaking of the leadership of the League, with artful references to the local men, moving then to Davitt and Parnell, and Parnell's helpers in the Parliament—a handful as yet, but Parnell's name already known everywhere, even here in Macroom, although Davitt's was a name unfamiliar as yet.

"You will hear their names again," he said. "Mark them well. Charles Stewart Parnell is fighting the fight of Ireland on the floor of England's House of Commons, and he is fighting it well. And Michael Davitt has come from long years in an English prison to fight that same fight upon Irish soil. There has been a black pall upon Irish life since 'sixty-seven, but it is lifting, thanks be to God. Have a clear notion, each man of you, as to where your true interests lie. Give your trust to those men, as I have given mine, but do not give it blindly. The Land League asks for your help, so that it can help you. I do not know how it is with you in Macroom, but I know how it is in Kilpeder. You have most of you been in Kilpeder for this reason or that. You remember it. A town much like this town. At one end of the square, there are gates that are the back end of a great estate, handsome great gates, pillars of granite with globes upon them, and upon each globe, a fierce falcon, a fierce bird of prey. Beyond those gates, you can wander as in another world, a world that knows nothing of ruined crops, or evictions, or homeless men walking the hard roads. Beyond those gates, it is a pleasant world, stables for glossy hunters and yards for carriages, a castle such as we hear of in the stories, the abodes of princes. I wish no harm to the rulers of that world; but no longer, I promise you, shall they live at the expense of our world. It may be that you have gates like that here in Macroom."

As indeed they did, and from the platform he had a fine view of them. But for all that they knew them well, the better half of the crowd turned round their heads to look at the gates to Macroom Castle, a handsome but higgledy-piggledy building, half fortress and half mansion house, set not far back in its park, as at Kilpeder, but close at hand, a part of the town almost, lights at many of the windows, and almost, from a first-floor window, we could see people standing, as though drawn by the excitement.

Bob said nothing more on the subject, but let his lesson be absorbed in silence, as no doubt it was, for Macroom was to be a centre of Land League enterprise down through the Plan of Campaign at the end of the decade. Although John Stephen Murphy had far more to do with the matter—a prodigious organizer as events were to prove—at the end of things he and Bob would be on opposite sides, at the time of the Parnell split; and as everywhere at that time, the quarrel spilled over into the personal, and bitter words were spoken on both sides. But that lay far in the future. On this night, when Bob had finished, and before the men in the square had begun to give their shouts, John Stephen was on his feet, and his arm about Bob's shoulder. The two of them stood there together as the cheering commenced, and before I was aware of what I was doing, I myself was cheering. And the band broke out again with "Clonbrony Wood."

That was far from the end of the oratory, of course. John Stephen's was the great, anticipated speech of the evening, and was all that might reasonably have been expected from a man who could weave the towers of Pekin and the wigwams of North America into the call for a public meeting in West Cork. And yet I cannot but think, in the vanity of friendship, that Bob's were the words that sank in, speaking to farmers a language that they could understand, and rising only at the close to an image elegant, unforgettable, and a bit frightening—reminding all of us of the two worlds in which we lived, our own world and the world of those who ruled us.

When the meeting was ended, with the band playing "God Save Ireland," another of the Fenian songs, Bob and I went with the other notabilities into the back bar of the Imperial, where Bob at last allowed himself two decent-sized drinks, the first of which he knocked back, which was not like him.

"By God, Bob," John Stephen said, "you have the makings of an O'Connell in you. That was a damned fine speech."

"'Twas nothing to your own," Bob said politely. "I was too stiff. It came from saying my words over to myself, and making my poor wife listen to them in the middle of the night."

"You were fine the two of you," Father Maguire said. "Two styles of sermon, as you might say." He was holding a demure glass of beer, resting it upon his black, rounded paunch.

"More is needed than oratory, or even sermons," John Stephen said. "Am I right, Bob?"

"I can answer for Kilpeder," Bob said, and with that the two of them, heads inclining towards one another, turned to the real stuff and substance of the League, of which oratory was but the froth. It seemed an ideal occasion to give myself a few minutes of quiet air, and I made my excuses, but was scarcely heard by the others, save by Maguire, who made his own excuses and left with me, the two of us walking down the darkened hall, lit by but a single gas jet turned low, and out into the square.

It was curious to see the deserted square, which a half hour before had been crowded. The railed platform, beneath the wan moon, was skeletal, and the green and gilt bunting was beginning to sag. At the far end of the town, behind its gates, a few lights still burned in Macroom Castle.

"A mild night," he said.

"It is, Father," I said. "Thanks be to God."

"A significant night, perhaps," he said. "An important night."

"Please God."

"I have great hopes for the League, you know," Maguire said. "We all have. Tis the way to proceed. Your friend Delaney had the right of it there, in the first words he spoke. The Fenians were on the wrong tack: the people were never behind them, but only laborers, mechanics in the towns, a few ne'er-do-wells. Sure no one should know that better than Delaney."

"Or myself, Father," I said. "I was with Delaney. In Clonbrony Wood. We were not all of us ne'er-do-wells."

He gave a bark of a laugh. "Delaney is not, by God. He is doing very well indeed. And you are keeping well yourself, I trust."

"Well enough," I said. "Tis a strange enough thing to say, perhaps, Father, but do you know that I have never regretted Clonbrony Wood."

"Ah," he said, with an easy, tolerant sigh. "That is a matter for yourself and your confessor. I spoke hastily. There were good men with the Fenians, I do not hesitate to say that. My own brother above in Ballinasloe was with them for a bit, in his wild youth, and he is now a decent estate agent."

He rummaged in his pocket, drew out a tin of snuff, and after offering it to me, applied himself, taking a pinch between forefinger and thumb.

"Tis a dirty old habit," he said, holding the pinch a moment, and studying the pincers which held it, as though it were a soul being consigned to its destination, "and do you know, tis a confirmed clerical vice. Of the snuff takers I know, the better part of them are priests."

This was well observed, and as I was meditating upon it, he drew in the snuff, a bit for each nostril, great heavy, taurine snorts.

"I was in Rome that year," he said, "in 'sixty-seven. You can imagine how unpopular such events would be in that city. I was hard put to it, apologising for my misfortunate people, giving assurances to right and to left that we were law-abiding and God-fearing, whatever a misguided handful might be about."

"A misguided handful," I said. He laughed again, and pausing to brush his fingers, clapped me on the arm. "You take my point, Mr. MacMahon. But that was that, and this is now, and the brother is an estate agent, and yourself a respectable schoolmaster, and Robert Delaney—well, which of us could set a cap upon *his* ambitions?"

"His ambition at the moment," I said, "is that the League should carry the people out of the dreadful pit into which they have fallen. That is ambition enough for any man, I should think."

"My presbytery is but a five-minute walk," he said, "and tis a mild evening."

And so we set forth, the most respectable of men, schoolmaster and priest. The moon gave us just enough light, and mildness made walking a pleasure. He was a half head shorter than myself.

"Have you given much thought," he said, "to the position of the Church in this country?"

"From time to time," I said cautiously. "Perhaps less often than I should."

"Tis not a subject for a five-minute discourse," he said. "We are Irishmen, you know, Mr. MacMahon. Irishmen as well as priests. It was as Irishmen that we condemned the Fenians. Now there is plain speech for you. And it is as Irishmen that we are likely to look with favour upon the Land League. Likely, I say. Who ever knows what goes on in the minds of bishops?"

"I for one do not," I ventured.

"Nor I, for a second. But this I can tell you for a certainty. If there is any reason to believe that the Land League is controlled by the Fenians, then the League will be condemned, root and branch. Condemned by bishop's letter, condemned from the altar. I pray God that this is not the case."

"The Fenians," I said, "are more likely to fight the League."

"Do you believe so?" he said. He stopped, and wheeled around to face me. "Half the League organisers in Mayo are Fenians, tis said. The League is being organised by Davitt, a Fenian ticket-of-leave man, with the blessing of Devoy in New York and the Clan na Gael, which is but the Fenian Brotherhood with a Yankee accent. That does not sound to me like the Fenians fighting the League."

"If it is information you want, Father Maguire, or even a political analysis, you have come to the wrong man. I took the oath, as you know, and I did the things that were being done in the year 'sixty-seven, and served a bit of time in prison because of them. And from time to time, if I find myself with an idle few bob, which is not often, I send it in to the organization. Many do, many who were not out in 'sixty-seven. But there matters end. And as for the Land League, that is a matter for the farmers of Ireland. I am a schoolmaster."

"The farmers," Maguire said, "and Edmund Gavin in Castlebar, County Mayo, and Michael Davitt of Dartmoor Prison and John Devoy of the Clan na Gael and Bob Delaney. A fine lot of farmers they are."

"If you are concerned as to Bob Delaney," I said, "you should not have joined him on the platform at a public meeting, Father. You will excuse my blunt language."

"No offence taken," he said. "He has the support of Dennis Tully, and that is good enough for me. Young lads as you were then, the lot of you, Delaney and yourself and Vincent Tully, hot to strike a blow for your native land. Who is to blame you? Not like that mad fellow in the States, not like Ned Nolan."

But we had reached his gate, and although he courteously asked me in for a nightcap, I declined, and I doubt if his heart was in the offer. He had given me a message, and his task was completed. Perhaps, I thought, as I walked back to the Imperial, perhaps I should have made my assurances more forceful. For the truth of the matter was as I had told him, more or less. We had long ago taken the oath, and we sent in a bit, now and then, but we thought seldom of the organization, and then impatiently, with embarrassment.

The truth of that was borne in upon me forcefully less than a week later, when Jeremiah Mulcahy came calling upon us. Upon Bob, to be more exact; but Bob sent a lad along to my house to fetch me.

It was early evening, and there was a warm look to Bob's house, the bricks rosy in the clear air, and the garden neat and inviting. It was Agnes who answered my knock, looking cool and pleasant, as she always did, in a frock of sprigged muslin, a pattern of small flowers, and her pale, level eyes clear, her cheeks smooth but now with a faint flush upon them.

"They are within," she said, nodding towards the front parlour; but as I walked towards the closed door, she put her hand on my arm. "'Tis a man named Jeremiah Mulcahy," she said. "A Dublin man, by the sound of him." There was something which was worrying her obscurely, because the accent painfully instilled in her at school was gone for the moment, replaced by the Doric notes of West Cork.

But the name meant nothing to me, and I shook my head. "Go in, so, Hughie."

Bob was behind his handsome desk, his back to the tall, drape-hidden window. But from the windows to his left, late sun poured into the room, motes dancing in its broad bands, spilling itself upon the reds and blues of the Turkey carpet. Jeremiah Mulcahy sat in one of the two leather chairs which faced the desk. He had turned towards me at the sound of the door opening. His clothes were neat but clearly well worn, a suit of dark serge, and a shirt whose high, stiff collar was a bit tight for him. It had rubbed the skin of his throat raw and angry. They were each of them holding a glass, and Bob, nodding towards the bottle, asked me silently to help myself, which I did.

"This is Mr. Jeremiah Mulcahy, Hughie," he said, "and he has come from Dublin expressly to talk with us. And with Vincent as well, I would have thought; but he says that the two of us will do."

"Good evening, Mr. MacMahon," Mulcahy said, and held out his hand to me. His arm was short and muscular.

Even as I was settling myself in my chair, I had a dim, confused notion of what this was about. There was little these days that would have linked Vincent's name with mine and Bob's. Little save our friendship and one other matter.

"Mr. Mulcahy comes from the Supreme Council of the Brotherhood," Bob said.

Supreme Council—shadowy words out of newspaper melodrama: "sensational revelations, revolutionary underground." John O'Leary no doubt, and Charles Kickham, and added to those whatever names might occur to the journalist—desperate gunmen, hard-bitten. And here was the truth, in Bob's parlour: a plump, polite man with a tonsure.

"I was to be in Cork on my own affairs," he said, in a tone almost of apology, "and it was suggested that I might call in on the two of you. I am a commercial traveller by occupation." Agnes was right about the accent—pure Dublin, not Irish at all. Where did it come from, a conundrum for scholars.

"That was most civil of you," Bob said. "A great honour for the both of us, is it not, Hughie?"

I wondered had he had a drink or two before Mulcahy's arrival. There was an edge to his words, a faint danger, which I could recognise but Mulcahy could not.

"You are well regarded," Mulcahy said, "the two of you. Men who fought in Clonbrony Wood. Men who served under Captain Ned Nolan."

"Still a captain, is he?" Bob said, in easy, sociable tones. "I should have thought he would be a colonel by now, or an admiral."

Mulcahy smiled and looked down into his glass.

"There is a letter from Ned every now and then," I put in. "The odd Christmas. And I try to keep him posted about Kilpeder. He was born here, you know. Thomas Justin Nolan was his father, one of the 1848 men."

"I know that," Mulcahy said. "He died out there in New York. Without money, half forgotten, a ticket collector or something of that sort. But he must be a source of great pride to Ned Nolan. He took the

Fenian oath from John O'Mahony himself, and he stood by the oath, in fat days and lean."

"A family tradition," Bob said. He pushed the decanter towards Mulcahy. The slanting sunlight fell upon it, and the whiskey glowed amber. Then, remembering courtesy, Bob picked it up, and poured out a measure for his guest and one for himself.

"You may have guessed, Mr. Delaney, at why I have been sent to Kilpeder. You are still a member in good standing of the brotherhood, yourself and Mr. MacMahon. And it can be no secret that the brotherhood is determined to stand aloof from the Land League. We may wish them well, some of us, but we will stand aloof."

"Will we indeed?" Bob said. "It was my impression that Davitt is a member in good standing."

"You are mistaken, then," Mulcahy said. "I do not mind telling you that when Davitt came back to us from prison, he was put on the Supreme Council. But he has been removed from it, with regret on our side. He is still a member of the IRB, as you are yourself, but what he does now he does on his own, without our blessing. And I am here to impress it upon you that you are acting without our blessing."

"Very well, then," Bob said. "You may take it that I am impressed, and we may leave it at that, and enjoy a quiet jar together."

"Ach, Mr. Delaney," Mulcahy said, and he looked down at his thumb, which he was moving along the rim of his glass. "Mr. Delaney." Suddenly he looked up. His eyes were a pale blue, and they were staring at Bob. "It is not as simple as that, and you know that it is not. There are men serving this day in the London House of Commons who account themselves Fenians, but they are not. They broke their oath when they first walked onto that floor. They took a different oath then, to Victoria of England. And across Connaught and Munster now, there are men who account themselves Fenians who are active with the Land League. And you men, too, are in violation of your oath."

It seemed a century ago that we had taken the oath in Cork City, Bob and Vincent and myself. Had we ever been that young, to believe that we could overturn the Empire by drilling on wasteland, a few score rifles and revolvers, vague promises of shiploads of men from America? I remembered the room, the back office of Tumulty's chandler's shop, coils of rope and barrels loaded with bits and pieces of metal, a pleasant, musty smell in the room, the closed and bolted door screening us from the brackish smell of the river, the smell of tar.

"No," Bob said. "It is not that simple. But I would put it to you, Mr. Mulcahy, that the ranks of the brotherhood are not so top-heavy that you can afford to lose any of us. The fellows who have become M.P.'s, not that there are so many of them, and the fellows active in the Land League, and of those there are a fair handful, are in particular men of whom the brotherhood has need. History is on the march at last in this island, and if the brotherhood cannot read the lesson properly, it will be left high and dry. What the devil do you fellows on the Supreme Council think you are about?"

"What need is there to ask that? It is the Council that has sought to keep all of us true to our resolve, to fight for a free and independent country."

"Fight," Bob said, and said nothing more, content to rest upon that ironical echo.

Mulcahy sipped at his whiskey, and then added a splash of water to it.

"We are not children," he said. "There will be no fight made this year or this decade. We know that. But the day will come when this country will again be ready to fight for its liberty, and men will turn again to the organization. The members of Parliament and the Land League organisers—between the two of you, you will drain away the morale of the country."

"Have you ever been to a League meeting?" Bob said. "You might find it instructive. There was one in Macroom on Sunday, and there will be one here next month."

"With your assistance," Mulcahy said.

"More than assistance," Bob said. "I am secretary to the League in Kilpeder."

"You have had little to say," Mulcahy said, turning towards me. "What is your view of the matter, Mr. MacMahon?"

"'Tis no direct concern of mine," I said. "Schoolmasters stand clear of such matters. But if you ask as to my sympathies—"

"You did not stand clear in 'sixty-seven," he said.

"There has been too much said about that," Bob said. "Too much oratory, too many ballads."

"I daresay it comes in handy on Land League platforms," Mulcahy said. "Wave the Fenian flag and you can be certain of a cheer."

"If you ask as to my sympathies," I said, "they are all with the League, and I don't think myself the worse Irishman because of it. You tell us that you are a commercial traveller, Mr. Mulcahy. Surely you have seen the way things are for the farmers and the cottiers these past three years. The evictions have begun in this barony."

"Oh, indeed," Mulcahy said. "*Christmas in the Boggeraghs*, by

Robert Delaney. A fine bit of journalism there, Mr. Delaney. You have the literary touch."

"Look here," Bob said, "let us bring all this to a head." And with an air of determination, of bringing some matter to its conclusion, he poured Mulcahy and himself as large measures of whiskey as I have ever seen measured out in a respectable Christian household, and would have done the same for me, had I not gestured in time.

"The market squares of Ireland are filled Sunday after Sunday these last few months with Land League meetings. And with good reason. In part it is because of the hard times that are in it, as Hughie MacMahon has said. But still more because it is a fight for land. Land is what this country is about, and always has been, since long before Cromwell. Sixty-six men we had with us back then, in the Fenian time, when we attacked the police barracks. They are commemorated in that miserable ballad. 'Full sixty men from Kilpeder Town to the hills above did go.' Sixty men out of the many hundreds in these baronies. If they had come out in strength, we could have crashed them upon that barracks like a wave. If they had come out in strength across the length and breadth of Ireland."

"We are not going to fight 'sixty-seven over again surely, Mr. Delaney." Even after he had filled the glass to the brim with water, the potion was too strong for Mulcahy, and he sipped gingerly. "You know that sorry history as well as I do. Our chiefs bickering and fighting amongst themselves, and the organization spotted and flecked with informers. And worst of all, the Church dead against us, denouncing us from every altar. 'Hell is not hot enough nor eternity long enough'—you know the words as well as I do, Bob Delaney."

"I know them right enough," Bob said. "And they are resting in the sacristy of every chapel in the country, ready to be used again, if the organization sticks up its head too high. The Church will never support the organization. Never. And without the support of the Church, nothing can be brought forth in this country. Nothing."

"And that is now the claim of the League upon your loyalty, is it, Bob? You would throw over the organization for that, would you, for the support of the bishops?"

"The bishops," Bob said, "and the strong-farmers and the gombeen men. I know all of your objections. I read the *Irishman* every now and again."

The *Irishman,* despite a flimsy veil or two held up for the sake of respectability and the law, was neither more nor less than a mouthpiece for the organization, published by an eloquent near-bankrupt named Richard Pigott. It was ferocious in its opposition to the League, and in its denunciation of the alliance that Davitt and Devoy had hammered out. Although its rhetoric was shrill, it urged the pure, austere Fenian doctrine: no compromises, stay away from land agitation, await the Day when the Irish people will rise up and overthrow the tyrant by force of arms. Bracing, manly stuff. "The Fenians," as the saying went, "are not a transacting party."

"Take a look at the case you yourself have made," Bob said. "There is more to it than bishops. Do you think that all the informers died with MacNally and Nagle? The organization is honeycombed with them, here and in the States both. There is damned little that happens, whether here or in New York or in Chicago, that it is not known in Dublin Castle. And at times it is known in the Castle before it happens, if you take my meaning."

"There have been informers," Mulcahy said, "and there will be others of them in the future. And we have our ways of dealing with them."

"To be sure you do," Bob said. "A short march up a long laneway, and a bullet in the skull, if John O'Leary's delicate stomach can swallow such methods. But you won't get them all, and you won't get the worst of them. Have you ever thought that you might have one or two of them—"

"Have a care there, Bob," Mulcahy said.

" 'It did good work for Ireland /Did that old Fenian gun.' " Bob sang the line of street balladry in an affected gutty accent, a Dublin street accent. "Your Supreme Council can be as virtuous as Billy-be-damned, but you are dragging behind you a tail of thugs and assassins, of slanderers and poltroons."

His mouth was working after he had ceased to speak, and raising up his glass, he knocked it back, and poured himself more from the decanter. Mulcahy exchanged a glance with me, and put a balancing hand upon his chair seat, as though about to rise. But instead he said, "You once carried a Fenian gun yourself, Bob, yourself and Hugh MacMahon here. And Ned Nolan. That is remembered, and it is held in your favour."

"And yourself," Bob said. "Were you a bearer of arms in the great struggle for our nation's liberation?"

"In a manner of speaking," Mulcahy said. "I was with Peter Lennon at Tallaght. An inglorious affair."

"There was damned little glory to share out," Bob said.

"Damned little then," Mulcahy said, "and less now." He seemed about to say more, but instead he sat quietly, holding his elbows. The silence lasted long enough to be oppressive, and to break it I began to speak; but before I could, Mulcahy caught and held my eye. He became in that moment impressive in a strange way. The pale eyes were daunting.

"All right, so," Bob said at last. "It was courteous of you to call upon me, and not send me a skull-and-crossbones letter, or one of your desperadoes."

"No, no," Mulcahy said.

"But you have the sense of the matter now," Bob said. "I am clear as to what I intend. I have taken up the work of the League. You can read me out of the organization by bell, book, and candle, or whatever ritual you use."

Mulcahy sighed. "No ritual. We part company, that's all. I am sorry to see it happen."

"Myself as well," Bob said. He shook his head, as though to clear it. "Will you stay the night with me? There is a bed for you, and we can have a meal. Hughie here and his wife Mary might like to join us."

"We would indeed," I said, making one of my invaluable contributions to this event.

"I thank you, no," Mulcahy said. "I am booked into the Kilpeder Arms, and I will be leaving on the morning car. But I thank you."

It was now Bob's turn to sigh. "No," he said, "you will not. But surely you will have a parting glass with us." And he reached again for the decanter, whose level was not appreciably lower. Mulcahy clearly was on the point of refusing, but caught himself and said, "I will, of course, but a mild one, and a heavy splash of water."

We sat a moment, holding our glasses in silence, and then Bob raised his, and said, almost in a hectoring tone, "To Ireland."

Mulcahy thought for a moment and then said, "To old friends."

After he had left, Bob and I made a night of it: there is no other way to put it. The bands of sunlight that had fallen upon carpet, upon polished wood, softened, faded, vanished, and near-darkness stole upon the room. Bob applied himself steadily to the decanter, and although I nursed my own glass, not matching him drink for drink, we were neither of us, by nightfall, proper specimens of our learned professions. The carafe of water was emptied by nine, and we were drinking whiskey neat.

At sometime or other, we adjourned to Conefry's. The bar of the Kilpeder Arms was a more usual haunt for fellows of our standing, but not this night. The snug was deserted, and there was none save young Conefry, the proprietor's son, to notice the slur in Bob's voice as he called for two large whiskeys to be set before us. We stood so, without talking. Conefry seemed once about to address a remark to us, but I shook my head at him and shrugged, and he walked down to the public bar and its low roar of voices, a laugh, a shout as the pal came in through the side door.

"There you are," Bob said to me at last. "The oath broken. A foolish business. I am glad that it is over and done with. 'I Mickey Mud do solemnly swear,' and all the rest of it."

"To speak technically," I said, "you have not broken the oath. You have received an order from the Supreme Council, and you have refused to obey it. A different matter."

"A technical matter," Bob said.

As I raised the glass to my lips, I caught sight of the two of us in the long, discoloured mirror. A wretched sight we were, the pair of us, dressed up in the coats and waistcoats which were intended to denote our elevation above the lads in the public bar, and with our faces flushed, neckties a bit disarranged, and in our eyes the look, not easily specified but unmistakable, that denotes men with far too much drink taken.

Conefry came back to us, treading along the catwalk behind the bar. His bar cloth was tucked into the waist of his trousers, and he held several fresh-washed glasses by their stems, between his fingers.

"There is a lad below there, Mr. Delaney, Patch Grogan, would be honoured if Mr. MacMahon and yourself would accept a glass from him. You will know why, he says." Conefry grinned at us, and all but winked.

"Patch Grogan," Bob said, "who the—" But I put my hand on his forearm.

"We would indeed, Bart," I said. "Would you ask Patch to come in?"

Conefry nodded, with his cool publican eyes upon Bob, and turned back to the public bar.

"Jesus, Bob," I said in a low voice, "you surely must remember Patch Grogan, from beyond Knockmany. He was one of the fellows with me when we took the cottages, and he was with us on the march to Clonbrony Wood." That was what in time even Bob and myself had taken to calling it, "the march," which had been but the bewildered flight of terrified men.

Bob looked at me, eyes dulled, but a sober quarter of his brain was a bit shaken. "God help us, Hughie, the name means nothing to me." But there is no beating a politician, drunk or sober. "Hold that, Bart," he shouted out. "Hughie and I will have our jar with Patch and the lads. And gladly."

And tossing back the last of the whiskeys he had ordered, he took me by the arm, and the two of us went by the swinging door into the bar. There were twenty men at least, and the air was heavy with tobacco smoke, and the sweet, sickish smell of porter. Small farmers, the most of them, with a few labourers foolishly squandering their scant shillings. Patch Grogan was standing against the counter, and when he saw the two of us, he grinned widely, a decent fellow in need of a shave; the skin beneath the stubble was baked red, marked with tiny, broken veins. To solve Bob's problem, I walked up to him at once.

"Patch," I said, "this is a decent idea indeed."

"It is indeed," Bob said. "'Tis grand to see you again."

When Conefry had set the glasses down upon the counter, Patch made a small ceremony of picking them up, and handing them to us. The others in the bar were watching us, in a kindly manner edged with the faintly sardonic, the usual complex response of countrymen to anything out of the ordinary.

"Your health, Patch," Bob said, but in a clear loud voice, and with a gesture of the glass that included the room.

"To days gone by, counsellor," Patch said.

"Days to come, Patch. To come," Bob said.

"I heard you in Macroom the Sunday," one of the lads said. "By God, the country is on the move again. And once again, Cork is in the van."

"The vanguard county," Bob said, and took a pull at his whiskey.

"Tell me now, counsellor," Patch said, and he lowered his voice melodramatically. "The boys here and myself were disputing the point, some one way and some the other. The Land League, as you call it: Michael Davitt has put his hand to it, has he not?"

"More than his hand," Bob said. "His heart and his back as well. And John Devoy in New York, who can speak for the Clan na Gael. And Charles Stewart Parnell in Parliament, Parnell and O'Connor Power and Joe Biggar. If the Irish people have leaders today, they are the men who have taken up the Land League."

"To be sure," the same lad said, a lean, youngish man with an Adam's apple above his buttoned collar. "Parnell and Davitt and those."

"And the organization as well, no doubt, counsellor," Patch said. It was plain that the dispute had been between himself and the lean lad. "If Davitt heads it, then it has the blessing of the organization. Am I right, counsellor?"

"Ach, never mind that now, boy," Bob said. "There is no organization now as there was in your youthful days and mine. There is but a few cranky men disputing amongst themselves in Dublin, and a handful of gunmen in New York who have picked up bad habits from the Yanks."

"What matter?" another of the fellows said. He was holding a pint in his hand, a large, capable red hand. "'Tis the Land League that has the running now. 'Tis those lads will have the landlords and the English beat down into the dust."

"And there you have it," Bob said. "Bart, let us make it a great round while we are about it, and a glass for yourself as well."

"Jesus, counsellor," Conefry said, "the old fellow would rip the scalp off me if he knew that I took a drop on this side of the counter. But I will tell you, now. I will have the glasses poured for the lads here, and then I will step out and join you. This once."

And indeed, he had but the one glass. But when a publican on duty takes a glass, it is a certain sign of a wet, dirty night in his house. And so it proved. By half hour to closing time, there were two or three fellows with voices singing for us, and Matty Finneran, noted in the house for his elocutionary prowess, had recited for us "Did they dare, / Did they dare, / To slay Owen Roe O'Neill?" And I myself favoured the company with the lament for Kilcash, first saying the poem itself, and then giving a rough version of it in English. Some of the fellows were from the Gaelic-speaking district to the west, from near Ballyvourney, and their eyes brightened at the sound of the older language. And one of them was coaxed to sing, giving us a version they have there of the "Roisin Dhuv," but he did not have much of a voice.

Bob and I were by then sitting at one of the two small tables, its surface a litter of empty glasses and shells, the shells empty but crushed with the foam of vanished porter and stout. He had loosened his collar and unbuttoned his waistcoat, and sat with his legs sprawled out, the gas jet on the wall close behind us flickering upon his high-polished, glossy boots. He would not sing, he had no voice for singing; but neither would he recite, which was as well, for his speech was slurred, and he had reached that state at which silence is interrupted by flashes of unreasonable anger or spurts of lachrymose affection.

"All right, so," Bart Conefry said, when it was a full half hour after closing time. "The one song more and that will make it a night for all of us. Tim, you have the best voice amongst us. Give out, would you, give out with 'Clonbrony Wood.'" And he looked at Tim O'Driscoll, and then at Bob and myself, and then, almost as an afterthought, at Patch. It had been a grand night for Patch, a veteran of Clonbrony Wood, and drinking now with Kilpeder's schoolmaster and the town's Catholic solicitor, the three of us enshrined in the verses of a meaningless song. Tim O'Driscoll was as young as anyone in the room, a farmer's son in his mid-twenties, with a pure, light voice. He smiled towards our table, and

[425]

rested his back against the wall facing us, with the length of the counter between us.

"Jesus, no," Bob suddenly shouted. "That fucking ballad has been sung too often in this town, and in these baronies. Give it a rest, for Christ's sake. No more fucking ballads."

The fierceness of his words, drunk or sober, dropped a silence upon the room. Tim looked around uncertainly, gave me a glance, and Conefry, and one or two of his pals.

"Another song, so," Conefry said. "To round matters off. There are more songs than one." But he should have been more specific. Bart Conefry, I think, had some vague, confused notion of what might have been gnawing at Bob, but poor young Tim O'Driscoll did not. And he began to sing, the words tawdry, perhaps, but fiery with the meaning he put upon them, and the notes moving pure, silvery, through the fug of stale smoke.

> "In a lonely Portland prison,
> Where Ned Nolan lay in chains . . ."

"Good man," a fellow standing near me shouted out, but Bob's roar was louder.

"Give a stop to that, you mean little cunt," he shouted. "No more of that." O'Driscoll fell silent, in midword as it were, as Bob was climbing to his feet, awkwardly, his feet tripping over each other, and the weight of his arms, slammed down upon the table to balance himself, knocking off the tall glass shells, which crashed to the floor. "You mean little cunt," he said again, and made as if to go for Tim, across the length of the room. "What the fuck do you know about Ned Nolan. You were an infant in skirts in 'sixty-seven, and your father at home to mind you that morning, no doubt; a bad morning it would have been to venture into this town, with rifles being fired off. I am sick of them, sick of those rifles and sick of you."

O'Driscoll stood pale, puzzled, but one of his pals said, "By Jesus, Master MacMahon, you had best take Mr. Delaney home. He could do himself a mischief whilst in this state."

"You are right, so," I said. "A grand night, but it went on a bit too long." And I put my hand on Bob's arm, but he shook it off.

"Hughie," he said suddenly, and as if perceiving me through mist, after long absence. "What are we doing here, Hughie? Jesus, but we all made a night of it. There is a fellow with a fine voice was singing, did you hear him?"

"I did, Bob, I did hear him. A fine voice." And I smiled a bit towards poor young Tim, to draw him into the treacherous camaraderie of drink. And it worked, for the decent young fellow smiled back at me and shrugged.

"Out the side door, Mr. MacMahon," Bart said. "Twill be quieter so, and a shorter path to his house."

"Time now," Bob said to me, quiet, befuddled, "make my farewells."

"I've made them, Bob," I said, "for the two of us."

The chill night air came up to me like a naked sabre, cold and bracing. We stood in the narrow laneway between Conefry's and the saddlemaker's, uncertain of our footing. Bob rested his outstretched hand against the bricks, and took long breaths, in my experience a tempting but disastrous way of inviting sobriety. But it seemed in this instance to have a beneficial effect, for he said "My God" several times, and then stood motionless. I did little to help him, for there was nothing to do, and in truth I was a bit irritated with him. He looked at last away from the wall, and said, "I behaved like a fool in there, did I not, Hughie?"

"You did," I said, remorselessly.

"There would be no purpose served by my going back to make amends."

"There would not," I said. "At the moment they are drinking to celebrate our departure."

He managed a wan smile, which in the darkness I could barely make out, and wiped his lips with his handkerchief.

We walked along the length of the laneway, and out upon Bob's road—fine, solid houses, snug in the night's darkness, lights in one or two of them. Bob's front parlour was lighted; from a chink in the drawn drapes, a slash of light fell upon the garden.

"You are awaited, I see," I said.

"You may be certain of that," he said with a sudden, inexplicable bitterness of tone. "I am always awaited."

"You have no call to make yourself into a creature of melodrama," I said. "'Tis seldom indeed that you come home the worse for drink."

He began to say something, then changed his mind and said, "Your point is well taken. Do you . . ." and he stopped and turned to face me. "It was not Jeremiah Mulcahy, a harmless, pompous little fellow. There are times, you know, when my mind turns to Ned Nolan. When I think of the oath, I think of Ned, and that Red Indian face of his. When I put my hand to the present task, I turned my back on the oath, and I turned my back on Ned. And to mark the occasion, I got blind drunk and ugly."

"You have my vote, Bob," I said, "for what that is worth. Tis the Land League that is our one hope, the Land League and Parnell. The Fenians are over and done with."

"They are indeed," Bob said. "Make no mistake about that."

In the next few years, I used often to bring that moment to remembrance, Bob and myself as we faced each other beneath the faint, clouded moon, the lighted, comfortable houses to either side of us, and the night's silence. It was not the oath that Bob had betrayed, of course, nor poor Ned Nolan off in Manhattan. History had passed its verdict upon the Fenians, and those who could not accept it were doomed to poor Ned's life of impoverished conspiracy, vulgar meetings, and processions. But a man does not always get drunk for the reasons he supposes, and what Bob and myself were in truth mourning that night was the end of youth, of young manhood, and the opening of a new volume.

Clonbrony Wood had been our youth, even the rifle fire, the memory of open wounds mellowing in time, and the memory of the falling snow holding in a space of the imagination, unforgettable, foolish and yet pure. The shop assistant who had been Clonbrony Wood's second-in-command was a solicitor now with a rewarding practice, and the son-in-law of Kilpeder's merchant prince, wedded to the prince's fair daughter. Before him lay all that might challenge the spirit—a struggle against an old oppression, and the restoration of a land to its people. He had no cause for complaint.

And far less had I, with my solid marriage, and the two young lads asleep under the eaves. But youth falls away from us, crumbles and vanishes, and we do not know that; we believe ourselves to be in the thick of it, until one day, of a sudden, something will remind us that it is over, done with, swallowed up in Time's maw. We are all the tenants of Time, and whatever it is that reminds us, that thing we will convict as a murderer, like the messenger bringing bad tidings. For Bob, I think, it was the knowledge that Ned Nolan's day was over, that the brotherhood had become a shabby jest. The Land War, which historians like young Prentiss have begun to call the true Irish revolution, had just begun, and Bob was to have his place in it. He knew that from the first; he knew that as we stood in that street of comely and prosperous houses, of which one was his own—dark massive furniture, bits of Wedgwood and Spode, shelves of handsome books in leather binding, and his son Conor, not asleep beneath the eaves like my own two, but in a room of his own, the heir, the prince's grandson. He had no false modesty, ever: the country was on the move at last, and he was with it. But he remembered—remembered what? What moment clung with him most vividly? For me, it was a moment, five minutes or ten, when I had stepped outside Laffan's cabin, in the hills, in the clear air of that black night, and saw, stretching away from us down the boreen, the lighted torches, like fallen stars, which guided home our raiding parties.

"A hard night," Bob said to me. "'Twas decent of you to stand by me in all my infamy."

"Ach, go to God," I said.

But in the months to come, and from one end of County Cork to the other, there would be few could believe the Robert Delaney that Conefry and Tim O'Driscoll and the other lads had seen that night. There was to be no cooler head than his in the devising of League strategy, and when, a few years later, he stood for Parliament, one of Parnell's chosen lieutenants, it seemed to us all a fitting reward, and others to come, no doubt, when they had won Home Rule, and we had our own parliament once more in College Green. But this, of course, was not to be, the dream of parliament lying in ruins, hauled down by Parnell's disaster, and Bob brought down with him. But Bob was to have his own disaster as well, and were I Nostradamus or Pastorini, I could have foretold it from that drunken hour in Conefry's, when whiskey unlocked the heavy door, and gave us a glimpse at his furies.

21

[Rough notes by Patrick Prentiss on the progress of the
Land League, 1879–82, especially in County Cork. And on
various related matters.]

RIBBON FENIANS. The success of the Land League came in good measure
from the enterprise of the "Ribbon Fenians," as they were called. Robert
Delaney was typical of the ablest among them. The term originated with
"orthodox" Fenians, who used it as a reproach; but, as is often the case
in such matters, it was accepted with cheerful cynicism. It was held by
Fenians *pur sang* that land agitation was a base and vulgar distraction
from the cause of an armed rebellion intended to establish a free and fully
independent republican state. The strength of the League, they argued,
came from the primitive and bloody "Ribbon" societies, loose bandings
of agrarian terrorists whose origins were lost in the mists of time.

But at this time, of course, the Irish Republican Brotherhood was so
reduced in numbers, so finicky and doctrinaire, that it resembled nothing

so much as some Jacobite league of the White Rose or the Legitimist supporters of the Count of Paris or the Carlist pretender. And yet with a difference. A great fund of sympathy for the Fenians exists among ordinary Irishmen: as the words of the ballads have it, "they rose in dark and evil days." A few years ago, a Clongowes friend and myself were inspecting a statue to the rebels, erected in a Tipperary town: a villainous-looking fellow, short and murderous, pike in hand. "They rose in dark and evil days," my friend said, "and by Jove, they look it." But rise they did, and that is remembered in our latter day of bargains and banners and compromises and land bills. They rose, and they paid for their bravery or foolishness or both, in prison cells, in abominable mistreatment and cruelty. And so long as the organization exists, with its shadowy Supreme Council, that shadow will fall, elongated and fanciful upon our affairs. It is sustained, both here and in the States, by its very fanaticism, the legend of executions and assassinations, of "skirmishing funds," the dynamite attacks upon the cities of England, the murders in the Phoenix Park and in the cobbled laneways of Dublin.

In the light of that legend, then, it was an irony, perhaps an impudence, that the brotherhood should accuse men like Davitt and Delaney of achieving their triumphs by an alliance with the primitive and rural terrorists of the Ribbon societies. "And so was founded an agitation where some men pretended to national passion for the land's sake: some men to agrarian passion for the nation's sake: some men to both for their own advantage." So Mr. Yeats once put it to me, O'Leary's foster child in spirit.

RIBBONMEN. "Dear me, no," Hugh MacMahon said to me. "If ever I knew Ribbonmen, they did not make themselves known to me. There were Ribbon societies, to be sure; there are to this day, for that matter. With huge, mouth-filling oaths, about making drums from the skins of Protestants and all the rest of it. There have been government reports every decade or two for a century. Wild, alarming documents. But all it has ever been, whether you call it Whiteboys or Ribbonmen or some gaudier name, all it is is a hunger for land, a fear that land will be taken away. There is great ignorance out there in the countryside, ignorance and cruelty, as well as beauty, music. The Land League drew upon that, no question about it. Ugly things were done before it was over, to grabbers and bailiffs. Davitt could not control that, no more than Bob Delaney, or John Stephen Murphy in Macroom. That, and the fear that the landlords have always had of the wild peasantry."

LANDLORDS. Along the great central hall of Ardmor Castle, where now hang Tom Ardmor's paintings, there hung the paintings of ancestors, grandfathers and great-grandfathers. Lionel Forrester took me once to the room where they are stored, and pulled back the protecting cloth, sending clouds of dust into the room.

There was also heavily, ornately framed, a testimonial to Tom Ardmor's father, upon his coming of age. I have seen many similar, in the hallways of big houses, here and there, and this one was a model of its kind, declaring in a large, florid copperplate the love and devotion to the Honourable James Phillip Forrester of the people of his town of Kilpeder and of his tenants, the words glowing with an affectionate obsequiousness. An artist in Cork City had been called to the task, and across the top lay spread out a romantic version of Ardmor Castle in sentimental pastels, and across the foot, a frieze of tenants, looking upwards—rose-cheeked maidens and women, stalwart youths, bare-legged but decent, grave elders, white-bearded, frock-coated, with hats held in hand, and the women and girls curtseying. Along the sides were emblems—neat cottages, a shepherd and his flock, a fence and stile, flower-bordered. In the distance, mountains tame as calves. And this, no doubt, or something at best a shade more rugged, was how Ardmor Castle wished to see its world. But there was lurking, always, a nightmare version of that world, a world of savage, Gaelic-speaking peasants, dark, murderous, unknowable, a world of maimed cattle, tortured bailiffs and proctors, of bodies tumbled into dark bog pools. The world, in short, of the Ribbon societies as these existed less in fact than in the imagination of the propertied classes. Small wonder that Parnell, when he allied himself with the Land League, became in fact its president, seemed to his class a traitor of unfathomable malignity, mad perhaps, for there was madness in that family.

PARNELL. Less than fifteen years since his death, and already there are more than a half dozen biographies and "Lifes," hagiography mostly, one or two works of demonology, although Mr. O'Brien's, the work of a devout, nevertheless has claims to scholarship or at least to journalism of a superior order. But even Mr. O'Brien's, although sentence by sentence it claims accuracy as to what "Mr. Parnell" did or thought or intended, yet maintains the myth, the aloof austere leader, passion concealed by indifference. But what was the passion which drew into near-rebellion, into confederation with gaolbirds, midnight meetings with terrorists, this young handsome rider to hounds, who might have been at ease upon his Wicklow acres, high sheriff for the county, master of the local hunt. "Master Charley was born to rule," said his English nurse when he was six, incredibly named Twopenny. "He was arrogant," said a classmate at his English school. "He tried to rule us." Three years at Cambridge, cricketer, a poor scholar save in mathematics, then rustication. Gamekeepers and servants told him stories of 'ninety-eight, a rebel strung up outside the gates of Avondale, flogged until his bowels showed through, red and glistening. Mr. O'Brien makes much of this, but I doubt its importance. He was at Cambridge during the 'sixty-seven rising, at Cambridge when Allen, Larkin, and O'Brien were hanged in Manchester for the killing of Sergeant Brett.

He remembered them, ten years later, in one of his first remarks in Parliament. "I wish to say as publicly and directly as I can that I do not believe, and never shall believe, that any murder was committed at Manchester." *Sensation,* as Hansard puts it. The words leap out at one from Hansard's dry pages, as though some principle alien to English law, mind, thought, had been pronounced. "Ah, splendid," my father said, "splendid. But consider the circumstances. Parnell was ready, even then, to throw over poor Butt and take command of the Irish party. And we were ready with him, our friends were ready. But we owed much to poor Butt; he did not deserve this. A gentleman, to the backbone."

"Then Butt was a precedent," I said to my father. "Butt and his colleagues in the old party. Parnell wasn't the first Protestant gentleman to take up our cause." Said to Dominick Sarsfield Prentiss, Clongowes Woods, Master of Arts of the University of Dublin, king's counsel. We could tease each other at last, without hurt. "Gentleman!" my father said. "Ye rogue! There were Catholics in the old party, Butt's party, who could outgentleman Butt, an Ulster *nisi prius,* a Donegal backwoodsman, Orange stock. Protestant blood and an education at Trinity—there is Isaac Butt's claim to ancient lineage. There were Catholics of ancient lineage in Butt's party—The O'Donoghue, The O'Gorman Mahon. . .Ach, not that it matters. Protestant or Catholic, Parnell swept them away. You know what Davitt said of Parnell, after his first meeting with him? At the dinner which was given Davitt upon his release from that wretched prison. 'An English weapon, shaped for an Irish purpose.' Something like that." "He had an English accent, did he not?" "He did indeed. You met him once, you know. In our dining room. You were too young and sleepy to remember, a small boy. Your mother brought you down." "I remember." "No you don't," Father said.

THE PARTY. It is with us to this day, of course, the party that Parnell created, some eighty members strong. Frock coats and silk waistcoats, its best men squabbling with each other—Healy, O'Brien, Dillon, Redmond.

O'Brien has his tail of Cork malcontents, and Healy the Bantry Band of gombeen men. Some eighty Irish members, a dull, massive weight in Westminster. They carry the scars of past battles, arrests, terms in prison; they all remember the Split, when they turned upon each other. But the scars are faded now, hardened. What must they have been like two decades ago, when an ambitious young solicitor, ex-Fenian, came over from West Cork? O'Brien and Dillon had been firebrands in those days, storming the country from one boycotted estate to the next, defying the police, the army. O'Brien, refusing prison clothes, had lain weak and shivering in his cell. The "No Rent" campaign, the Plan of Campaign, it had been a war for a few years. Regiments had been brought over from England to overawe the countryside, but to no effect. "The landlords of this country," Finnerty said, "should be shot down like wood pigeons," but Davitt was more charitable. "Buy every one of them a third-class ticket to Holyhead and say good-bye to them." And presiding over them, cool and nerveless, a landlord.

WOODHAVEN. By the time Delaney entered Parliament, in the by-election of 1884, he was known far beyond the borders of Cork; not in England, of course. He came to Westminster as one of Parnell's backwoodsmen, an Irish roughneck. But in Ireland he was known as the man who had managed the campaign against Woodhaven, the largest estate in his baronies, save for the Ardmor lands. I have not, needless to say, been made welcome at Woodhaven. The Wilcoxes are no longer there, of course: George Wilcox moved out, bag and baggage, but Harvey Sanders, his agent, is a fierce true-blue Tory of the old school. We have met once or twice, and he managed to conceal his distaste, but imperfectly. He had learned, somehow—there are no secrets in Kilpeder—that Lionel Forrester and I have become friends, after a fashion, and this, were there no other reason, would suffice. The detestation which the local gentry feel towards Lord Ardmor has extended to his cousin, who is regarded as an exotic. That Forrester travels openly with Emily, his mistress, who once was Lady Ardmor's maidservant, does not help matters. Forrester finds this amusing, as he does most things.

And yet Woodhaven, despite all the Conservative predictions, is far from ruined, and Wilcox should make a tidy profit from the provisions of the new Land Act. Woodhaven House itself stands upon a rise, and Forrester and I rode out one morning for a look at it. From the steeply sloping Graney road, where we reined in, on a warm morning with sun burning off the haze, it looked as fine in its way as Ardmor Castle, although of more modest proportions, not dressed Portland stone like

Ardmor, but warm brick, rose-coloured in that soft light. "At times," Forrester said, "the demonstrations were carried to the gates of the house itself, straight before us there, do you see?" He had ridden out one day, along this road, to take a look at the excitement.

"Mind you, there was excitement enough and to spare in Kilpeder itself, and especially on any Sunday, when the 'monster meetings' were held, as they called them. And well named they are, Emily said to me once—collections of monsters. Emily comes from the gentle lands of Westmeath, you know. Sylvia brought her here. But when the boycott was at its height, every Sunday, rain or shine, there would be a monster meeting to keep up the spirits of the Woodhaven tenants. Davitt was here, O'Brien, Dillon, Parnell himself was here once, as I have told you. Nearly always, the meeting would be held in the square; but twice at least, as I recall, Delaney held it over there, outside the gates of Woodhaven House. By God, that chap knew how to work up a crowd. On the second occasion, there were two hundred constables. Two hundred. And a detachment of cavalry. I could see the platform from here, of course—a square island with the ocean of crowd lapping about it, and the caped constabulary; but I could hear nothing, no single voice, but the shouts of the crowd would roll towards me. I had my glasses with me, and I could make out the speakers. A tall, bearded man, stoop-shouldered, who was Dillon, so I learned later. And Delaney, in his short surcoat of brown tweed, hands plunged in his pockets. It was a war right enough, here in Kilpeder. The evictions were resisted in force, and the emergency men and the crowbar brigade worked beneath the protection of constabulary carbines. Two men died, a constable and one of Wilcox's bailiffs. The bailiff was never found, never will be unless they reclaim the bog."

"A war," I said. "Who won it? Woodhaven looks prosperous enough, from this distance." And indeed it did. The home farm might have been painted by Constable: hay wains, neat barns, a wide, deep meadow. At its far corner, beneath fat-branched trees, green against green, a herd lay at noonday rest, a heavy, silent thickness of sunny air.

Forrester shrugged. "A matter of definition. Something was changed, and forever. Did the tenants win? Some did, most of them did. But some were evicted, driven off. The funds that Delaney set up for them took care of them for a time, but the American money dried up, Clan na Gael money, half dollars from skivvies. The Americans liked to see results—a chief secretary for Ireland butchered, a dynamite explosion. When Delaney was waging his war against Woodhaven House, he had the eyes of the American Irish on him. But when a war is ended, who cares about the wounded veterans? They wound up in America themselves, most of them, an endless cycle. Delaney was concerned about them, mind you: credit where credit is due. But towards the end, he had other matters on his mind. Who won, you ask? The landlords lost, that much is certain. Delaney and Davitt and Dillon—they smashed us."

BOYCOTT. Like the names on a battle scroll—Lough Mask House, Portumna, Woodhaven—the great Land War battles. All of them fully reported upon in the London *Times, Daily News,* special correspondents, the *Illustrated London News,* and by the American papers, the *World,* the *Herald.* Marvellous engravings in the London journals: the military occupation in Ballinrobe, in Mayo; cavalrymen and infantry making their encampment at Lough Mask House, the emergency men marching under armed protection to gather Captain Boycott's harvest, and Boycott himself and his friends having their last meal at Lough Mask House, a few bottles of wine on the table, and Boycott standing, glass in hand, careworn, still unable to understand what had happened to him. Boycott was the first battle of the famous campaign, but Woodhaven followed close upon it. When Delaney opened war upon Woodhaven, in October of 1880, Boycott was still hunkered down in Lough Mask House, guarded by soldiers, his labourers and servants vanished, not a huckster in Ballinrobe so mean as to sell him food or a candle or a tin of pipe tobacco. So mean, or so foolhardy: men were beaten and maimed for dealing with grabbers or proclaimed landlords.

Seated that afternoon with Forrester, looking through soft light towards Woodhaven, warm brick, its back to the harsh, wind-breeding hills, it was difficult to recall its appearance in those journalistic engravings and sketches. There is one of the scene which Forrester mentioned—the League meeting outside the gates—and another of the First Cavalry en route from Cork to Kilpeder, caped and nonchalant; but the engraving which was famous for a time filled a page. Woodhaven House, in black and white, looks sinister and defenceless as well. Sir George and Lady Wilcox are standing on the steps, beneath the portico, and Sanders is beside them. Wilcox and Sanders are holding shotguns in the crooks of their arms. They are looking, all three of them, towards the gates of the estate, where no League meeting is in progress, but rather a hundred or more peasants, the women shawled and barefoot, the men in their old-fashioned swallow-tailed coats, and tall, battered hats.

"Extraordinary Events at Woodhaven House, Outside Kilpeder, County Cork." So begins an account in the *London Gazette*:

A combination equal in ferocity and determination to that which has been in operation against Captain Charles Cunningham Boycott in County Mayo has been organized far to the south, outside the small market town of Kilpeder, on the Macroom-Killarney road. For the past two weeks, Sir George and Lady Wilcox of Woodhaven House and Mr. Sanders, their agent, have been cut off from their tenants and from the townspeople of Kilpeder as effectively as if they were upon an ice floe at the North Pole. At the outset, a delegation of the tenants waited upon them, and offered, for the quarter which had fallen due, one half of the several rents set, such sum being in each case well below that fixed by Griffith's Valuation. Upon this offer being refused, the delegation then impudently gave to the Wilcoxes a "grace period" of twenty-four hours in which to reflect upon matters. That time having elapsed, the men returned, accompanied now by a spokesman, Robert Delaney, local secretary of the Land League. Delaney warned Sir George and Mr. Sanders that if the "fair rent" was not accepted, it would be paid into the League and there held in trust. Meantime, the estate would be placed in the same kind of "moral isolation" now being experienced in Mayo, and to which the novel term "Boycotting" has been applied.

Delaney was as good as his word. Upon a second refusal from Sir George, he made his way to the kitchens and then to the grounds, ordering the servants and labourers to suspend their work until further notice. "What would you have us do, Mr. Delaney?" the elderly gardener is said to have asked, not unreasonably; "the Wilcoxes have always been decent to us. I served the old gentleman, Sir George's father." "You can spend your time making novenas for Sir George," Delaney replied, "that he may come to his senses." And the servants were then led away, in a bewildered procession. Since then, save for a nephew of Mr. Sanders and various neighbouring gentlemen, the labours of this extensive home farm have fallen entirely upon the shoulders of the landlord and his agent.

Until the arrival of the emergency men and the detachment of cavalry and Constabulary, Woodhaven House was dependent for supplies upon the charity of the surrounding gentry. There is a large shop in Kilpeder, Tully and Son, but its proprietor, Mr. Dennis Tully, is an ardent supporter of the Land League—and, it should be noted, Robert Delaney's father-in-law. Tully is a man of average height, but massive in appearance, with a large, bald head, and small, sharp eyes. "Sure, the relations between this house and Woodhaven have always been of the most amicable, time out of mind. But it behooves a man to stand by his own people in hard times. And if it comes to that, Sir George is the ground landlord of the village of Graney. I am his tenant myself, and I am conscious of my situation." He was referring to a handsome villa outside the town which he acquired several years ago, and which is now occupied by his son Vincent. Neither Tully nor his son-in-law Delaney appears to be suffering undue oppression from "the landlord class," as they call it. They dwell across the road from each other, in spanking new houses, three storeys high, standing in their own grounds.

The *London Gazette* met with Delaney in his well-appointed office facing upon the market square. A solicitor, he is a cut or two above the average of the Land League agitators, lacking a university education, but nimble of wit, with a sardonic turn of phrase, and a certain amount of self-schooling. The phrase "Land War" is one which he accepts, and his views seem, on the whole, as extreme as those of his hero, Michael Davitt. "The land of Ireland," he says, "belongs to the people of Ireland. If the present landlords have any legitimate claim to it—and this I dispute, for it was taken by conquest and fraud—if they have any legitimate claim, it was long ago forfeited by their imposition upon the people of barbarous and oppressive conditions. Property, as you in England know, has duties as well as rights, and in Ireland, for centuries, since the days of Cromwell, these duties have been ignored. The claims are cancelled out, and the people are on the move to take what is theirs." "A man active in your movement," we said, "has declared that landlords should be shot like pheasants and wood pigeons." "Dear, dear," Delaney said, "no doubt he intended to say that landlords were *shooting* pheasants, rather than attending to their duties. The Land League is a peaceful organization, acting entirely within the law." He laughed suddenly. "The gentleman you quote has a broad accent. Perhaps he said that the landlords were shooting *peasants*. That *is* against the law. These days."

Delaney, it should be noted, was in earlier days less squeamish, and was then a local leader of the Fenian conspiracy. In March of 1867, he was second-in-command to the notorious Edward Nolan, taking part in the attack upon the barracks, for which he served a term in prison. He denies that he is any longer a member of the organization, and yet it is well known that Land League officials across Munster and Connaught have ties with the outlawed Irish Republican Brotherhood. On this subject, he is candid, up to a point. "I have never regretted my actions in '67," he says. "The Irish people are entitled to their full independence, and to strive for it, in the last resort, by force of arms. But much to which men are entitled in principle is foolish in practice. '67 proved that. I have the greatest respect for the I.R.B., but I believe that it is not suited to these times." "Have you the greatest respect for Edward Nolan, your old commander?" we asked. "I knew Ned Nolan for a few weeks," he answered, "long enough to know that he is a courageous man, and a cool, resourceful one. He has fought for Ireland, and may do so again. But perhaps you should put questions about Ned Nolan to the governor of Portland Prison, who knew him for seven years, subjecting him to barbarous and inhuman treatment in a vain attempt to break his spirit."

It is maintained by local loyalists to whom we spoke that for all his fair words, Delaney is still deep into Fenianism, and that the Land League itself is but a cloak for a new and perhaps more widespread conspiracy. The reader must judge of this from Delaney's words, and must also judge how far from the truth is his claim that the League operates entirely within the law. It is a question which Mr. Gladstone and Mr. Forster are doubtless pondering at the moment.

Sir George Wilcox was reluctant to speak with us, giving to us, in his civil note of response, an account of the harrowing circumstances in which he and Lady Wilcox are compelled to spend their days, and directing us, rather, to the recently formed Property Defence Association and to its chairman, Major Oliver O'Donovan.

Major O'Donovan, whom we met in his trim villa outside the town, is a man of middle years, Indian Army retired, as might be deduced from a brick-red visage and a crisp white military moustache. He is by nature, one would judge, a man of brusque but heartfelt geniality, but on the subject of the Land League and its agitators, and in particular Mr. Delaney, his views are fierce and uncompromising.

"Take my own case," he says. "A serving officer in India for seventeen years. A servant of the Queen, of the Empire, if you will. That is not yet a crime, I trust. Indeed, I was serving Her Majesty out there before she became Empress. And I supported myself, modestly enough, upon my rents, upon my rents and the thought that I would someday be coming home. This is my home, you know, sir, whatever the League may affect to believe. The O'Donovans are no Cromwellian blow-ins. We were here in Cork long before the name Delaney was heard of in Ireland. The O'Donovans have never had a name as rack-renters, not until the present year, that is. Now, as I understand matters, my lands have been marked by the League for their future attention. But I will not be driven off, sir, and neither will the other gentlemen who have banded together to form the Property Defence Association."

Major O'Donovan's lands have not yet been "struck," and the several labourers upon the acres which he himself farms seem well contented. On a stroll along a "boreen," or narrow path, we encountered his herdsman, Farrell, whom he called over for a few words. Farrell, capped and toothless, was firm although not clear-voiced in his praise of "the Major, sorr." It seemed achingly evident that Major O'Donovan, during his long years overseas, had cherished memories of his homeland, and had nourished himself upon the notion that he would spend here his declining years. So he may, but it seems likely that, for the present at least, his days will be joined in a battle unlike those he has known, and one whose outcome, at the moment, is much in doubt.

For the moment, the Property Defence Association, of which he has assumed the command, limits itself to extending such help as lies within its power to the beleaguered garrison at Woodhaven House. For the first local victim of the "war," Mr. Bartholomew Colthurst, no such succor was available, and the association vows that there will be no repetition of his fate. Major O'Donovan's language is appropriately martial, but he makes clear that it intends to obey all laws strictly. "A handful of Britons," as he says, "withstood ten thousand murderous Zulus at Rorke's Drift. We can deal with a few hundred Whiteboys by making use of the laws, the army, and the Royal Irish Constabulary."

It is a curious circumstance that, thus far, the chief landowner of the barony, and its first personage, the Earl of Ardmor, has stood aloof from the fray. It is his imposing residence, Ardmor Castle, which looms above the town of Kilpeder, screened from view by a handsome, thick plantation, and yet a constant presence. Lord Ardmor, through his agent, Mr. Chute, made at the outset an accommodation with his tenants, which less fortunately circumstanced landlords may have envied. At the moment, certainly, he can lay claim to no large portion of their affections. It is widely rumoured, moreover, although upon scant evidence, that, upon being offered the honorary presidency of the Property Defence Association, Lord Ardmor refused it. Major O'Donovan will not comment upon this.

Thus, at the moment, matters stand in Kilpeder in this exciting season. It is a nondescript town, neither attractive nor otherwise, and of interest chiefly as the veritable Platonic "form" of a dusty Irish market town. In addition to the taproom of the very decent local inn, it boasts a larger number and variety of licensed premises than would in England seem possible, save perhaps in the more Hibernian sections of Liverpool. There is a comely Protestant church, spired and shapely, at one corner of the market green, facing the entrance to the castle demesne, and, at the far end of town from it, on the Macroom road, an immense and assertive Catholic church, the size of a cathedral. The plans were drawn, we are told, by Pugin himself, but the execution, by a less gifted epigone, seems to the untutored eye a trifle garish.

It is between these two poles, church and public house, that the life of the country people becomes visible. In the evening, the women, shawled and black-skirted, will slip into the church to make their devotions, while the men will repair to the public houses. It is difficult indeed for the outsider to enter even a small way into their lives. In the church, Saint Jarlath's, in the claustral darkness of evening, a faint odour of old burned incense rising to brightly painted statues of Our Lady, Saint Joseph, other saints, the women kneel with bowed heads, beads moving slowly, as though with a life of their own, through work-hardened fingers. Their men, although no less devoted to their church, no less attentive to its prescriptions, repair rather to the public houses, which range from Conefry's spacious and prosperous premises to a high counter and a few lofty, uncomfortable benches in a huckster's shop.

Should one venture, not certainly into the shop but let us say into Conefry's, the patrons will reveal themselves as affable, courteous to a stranger, curious as to events in the great world beyond their mountains, and yet singularly and artfully uninformative. Some there must be in Kilpeder who view the Land League with a jaundiced eye—an auctioneer could have scant liking for it—and yet so entire is the social code of silence that little of value has been garnered after several hours of conversational negotiation.

Walking back to the inn, one's mind upon the morrow's pleasant train journey to Dublin, through warm and verdant noontime acres, there may suddenly come a sense of how enclosed, how secret, how menacing is this Kilpeder world. In the darkness, the encircling hills will be invisible, and yet one will be aware of their presence, an ancient enclosing and unfurling.

MERTON PATCH. Had lunch at the Reform with him, the "special correspondent" of the *London Gazette* during the Land War. Retired now, but able to keep up appearances, carefully combed silver hair, silver moustaches.

"Good God," he said, "how I longed to tell that story straight out. That battered old *miles gloriosus* now, that O'Donovan. In the weeks that I spent in Kilpeder, I doubt if I saw him once, just once, without a glass in his hand—tumbler, port glass, claret glass, the humble whiskey. He was half pickled in it, kept making lurid comparisons between the peasants and the Zulus. Not that it mattered—he was there for window dressing; the Tories love to turn up some staunch old Catholic Conservative to show their lack of bigotry. He did not matter; there were cooler heads in the Property Defence Association. The smaller landlords. And Eddy Chute was there in the background. There wasn't much he could do in the open, not as Ardmor's agent, and Ardmor swooning over the League, God knows why. But Chute was a landlord himself, and he knew the barony. Chute was a downy bird, but nothing for attribution, you understand."

ZULUS. Such comparisons were common, the imperial mind being much taken with the Zulu adventure—kilted Highland regiments striking out against the terrifying black warriors, a shower of assagais. Both Captain Boycott and George Wilcox were repeatedly compared to the heroic defenders of Rorke's Drift. The Land Leaguers had more difficulty when it came to identifying themselves with the blacks, although O'Connor Power, in one splendid flight upon the floor of Commons, described Cetewayo as "the O'Connell of his people"—a dubious compliment, coming from such a source. Interesting, that the comparison should come so readily to mind—a savage, murderous people, for so they are deemed, as an analogy for those who are supposedly members of the same nation as oneself.

APPARITIONS. As the school reader puts it: "On the east of Ireland is England, where the Queen lives; many people who live in Ireland were born in England, and we speak the same language, and are called one nation." On August 21, 1879, four months after the first meeting of the Land League in Mayo, a group of villagers in Knock, of that parish, claimed to have seen the Virgin Mary, Saint Joseph, and John the Evangelist. How in the world did they identify so specific a saint as the Evangelist? According to Mary Byrnes, the principal witness, she recognized him by his likeness to "a statue at the chapel of Lekanvey, near Westport, County Mayo." He was facing an altar, of divine origin, upon which was resting a lamb, on whose body "golden stars, or small brilliant lights, glittered like jets or glass balls."

It was a poor time for Knock and for all of Mayo, the third year of crops destined for ruin. On the night of the "apparitions" it was raining. In some of the testimony by witnesses, the Land League excitement is described as the work of "Whiteboys," a word which some may imagine as having vanished a century ago. By February, a journalist was writing: "Thousands of feet had come there, laden with the mud of the reeking highway, and multitudes had come and gone upon the surface of the enclosure, till every blade of grass disappeared and in place of a dry and smooth expanse there was left a place torn up as if a pitched battle had been fought upon the scene. At every step the foot sank ankle deep. Yet all who approached the gable knelt, and many prostrated themselves in audible or silent prayer."

Small wonder that English or foreign journalists, like Patch, return home to write books with, invariably, such chapters as "Superstitions," "Belief in Magic," and the like. And yet, there is scant difference between this and Lourdes. I refer not to the supposed manifestations—between credulous peasant girls in the Pyrenees and in the boglands of Mayo, there is little to choose. But surely the crowds who swarm into Lourdes are driven by the same blind, unreasoning faith which now carries them to Knock, and the devotions there equally vulgar and grotesque. Indeed, it has been argued by sceptics that Mary Byrnes and her companion visionaries were inspired by the example of Bernadette, a sermon upon her spiritual gifts and graces having been delivered in that church on the Sunday preceding. And yet the French are not taxed with being a nation preeminent for superstition and ignorance. Here, it would seem, the Irish are rivalled, if at all, only by the mountaineers of Macedonia and Transylvania.

Why do I write upon the subject with such heat? Why am I unable to see, whether at Lourdes or at Knock, an example of faith at its most innocent and affecting, a faith identical in kind with that which lifted the world from the dark night of idolatry and slavery? Even though it is a faith which I myself can no longer share. I try to think back, feel back, to the days when I had my portion of faith—of the Faith, as we always called it, the capital F almost visible upon the spoken air. I remember the chapel at Clongowes Woods, myself kneeling with the other boys, at Mass or Benediction, the evening air of Benediction heavy with incense, its smoke entangled in the slanting light passing through to us, touched by stained glass.

Nothing. I can remember the chapel, the other boys, myself kneeling beside them, the smell of polish on wooden pews, of candle wax, white clear candles sacramental, the feel almost of my hands joined in prayer, palm sealed to palm, head bent and bony elbows pressed against ribs. I could still rattle off the responses, a patter of fragrant Latin. I remember nothing at all of how I felt as I prayed. Nothing.

Behind all that I have thus far set down—conversations with schoolmasters, barristers, old revolutionaries, members of Parliament—rises up the high screen of that other world which exists for them as certainly as does this inkstand, the Thames which is invisible at this hour but of whose existence there can be no doubt. Thus, Hugh MacMahon has been in my experience of him a shrewd, wry man, sardonic at times, and no lover of the clergy. And yet, although the subject has never had occasion to arise, when I speak with him I know that I am with a man for whom the Faith is Christ's certain promise, a man devout in ways both simple and imaginative.

And if Hugh MacMahon, then how much more so the people who gather each Sunday at Mass, go on pilgrimages to holy wells, abase themselves on Station Island, climb Knock Patrick? How much more so the cottiers, with their holy, gaudy lithographs, candle flickering behind cheap coloured votive glass? Yet it is in some measure their story which I propose to tell.

PRESS CUTTING. An excerpt from the *Dublin Journal*, 20 September 1880—the story filed from Ennis, County Clare.

By this time, the vast crowd was in a state of extreme excitement, and in this was in marked contrast to Mr. Parnell himself, who stood calm and poised, bareheaded, with the evening sun falling full upon his handsome, auburn-haired face. He is not a trained public speaker, despite his years in the House of Commons, and his voice is insistent rather than musical. Often he will hold one hand tensely behind his back, or else will fold his arms. He had reached now the climax of his remarks. And yet he began this upon a note which was mildness itself, and thus belied the nature of his message.

"Now then," he asked this vast assemblage, "what are you to do with a tenant who bids for a farm from which his neighbour has been evicted?" The question, if rhetorical in intention, was not so received, and from diverse quarters, the shouts arose of which the most piercing and the most sinister were "Kill him!" and "Shoot him!" The shouts, although they may themselves have issued from the throats of idle ruffians, beyond question reflected a general mood or sentiment. Mr. Parnell waited, as though indifferent, until all was again quiet, and his final words, although he began them softly, rose to a thrilling conclusion. "Now, I think that I heard someone say, 'Shoot him!' " And as though upon cue, there were repeated shouts again, and he again waited for order.

"But I wish to point out to you a very much better way, a more Christian and charitable way which will give the lost sinner an opportunity of repentance. When a man takes a farm from which another man has been evicted, you must shun him on the roadside when you meet him, you must shun him in the streets of the town, you must shun him at the shop counter, you must shun him in the fair and at the marketplace, and in the very house of worship. By leaving him severely alone, by putting him in a sort of moral Coventry, by isolating him from the rest of his kind as if he were a leper of old, you must show him your detestation of the crime he has committed. And you may depend upon it if the population of a county of Ireland carry out this doctrine, that there will be no man so full of avarice, so lost to shame, as to dare the public opinion of all right-thinking men within the county and to transgress your unwritten code of laws."

REFLEXIONS ON ABOVE. The *Dublin Journal* of that year was sedately nationalist, by no means Parnellite. It is therefore instructive to note how early on, and from diverse points of vantage, Parnell was regarded in a romantic light, all of the makings of the legend already visible—passion shrouded by aloofness, a voice speaking from a distance, mystery. But there is a small genuine mystery here. In that extraordinary speech there is one false note: "moral Coventry" is not a term in common use by the farmers of West Clare: there spoke the public school boy, trained in English codes. That phrase aside, however, he was speaking with a directness, an accuracy, a knowledge of the Irish people and their ways which is uncanny. The Ennis speech was a declaration of war, and so it proved, a war in which victory would mean the overthrow of Parnell's class. When journalists, grudgingly or with enthusiasm, built up the legend of Parnell's glamour, did that thought float somewhere, unacknowledged, in their minds, that Parnell's triumph would be also a private act of self-destruction? His life, if that were true, would be tragic throughout, and not merely in its terrible final scenes. The thought is a useful corrective to the more common reading of his life, which reads it backward, peering beyond the shambles towards the buoyant, mysterious leader of 1880, declaring a new kind of war on the Ennis platform, a war whose first target would be poor foolish Boycott in Mayo, and then Sir George Wilcox in West Cork.

THE LAND WAR. It is the most convenient, the familiar term, and yet it was never, of course, a "war" in the conventional sense. Neither, in sober truth, did it begin with the Ennis speech. Fervent League journalists like William O'Brien plundered the arsenal of war correspondents, and talked of sieges, battles, plans of campaign—a species of martial rhetoric which the Fenians had made current. But it was surely war in some actual meaning of that word if the implications are accepted of Parnell's Ennis speech and of earlier ones by Dillon and Brennan. "Your unwritten code of laws," Parnell said. Already, in the weeks before Ennis, a land bailiff named Feerick had been shot outside Ballinrobe in Mayo, and near New Ross, in Wexford, a small landlord named Boyd had been wounded and his son killed by men firing from a ditch. At Clonbur, near the Galway border, Lord Montmorres was set upon by armed men and killed as he rode home from a meeting of landlords and magistrates. No arrests were ever made for any of these. At Carraroe, in the wildest stretch of Connemara, bailiffs and police were set upon by a mob armed with pitchforks, cudgels, and knives. Across Connaught and down into North Munster, neighbours working through the long day reaped the harvests of evicted farmers and carried away the produce, lest it fall to the landlords; in a dozen instances, they were protected by armed men.

Parnell and Dillon and O'Brien, of course, were not calling for this when, week after week, in market squares across the country, they praised the moral force of ostracism. But there is a fine line only between shunning a man and raising your arm against him, and the peasants in Mayo and Kerry lacked familiarity with such delicate points of moral casuistry. For that matter, in such a country as Ireland, there are worse punishments than a midnight carding, a tumble into thornbushes, a bullet. In that rich hive of a society, community clotted like honey in the comb, it must be a peculiar torment to be "shunned"—in the roadway, in the shop, in the marketplace, in the chapel itself. As though life had turned its back upon you, denied you not existence but identity.

TWOMEY. Was a kind of stableboy of Robert Delaney's; "retainer" or "dependent" might be better words. It was at Hugh MacMahon's urging that I visited him, in the hospital ward of the Kilpeder workhouse, a man younger than MacMahon but looking older by far, toothless and with bright, sunken cheeks unshaven, his eyes small bright dark buttons. "Poor Twomey," MacMahon said. "He used often to tell Bob and myself that he would have been with the lads at the day of Clonbrony Wood, but that the mother held himself and the brother fast to home, mending a wall. There is one of the secret crevices of history for you." But he served his part in the Land War, willy-nilly, and that was his claim upon Delaney. The mother was long dead by then, and the brother had died a year or two earlier. Twomey was working the bit of land himself, with the help of a few casuals brought in at harvest time. It was his bad luck that the farm lay in a townland beyond Lughnavalla, a place called Horseleap, which Chute's Property Defence Association had chosen for its counter-attack.

The "battle" of Horseleap was accounted a victory by the League, and so it was, in the sense that no one dared take up the farms of those who were evicted. It is miserable land, and to this day, although now for a different reason, it lies untenanted. No one wants it now, or needs it, and of the twenty cabins, only four or five have survived two decades of rain and wind, the thatch long vanished, but the walls standing: doorless, gap-windowed, floors of dried mud. The winds blow through them. But it was a League victory, for all that. The landlord, a company in London, sought compensation under the provisions of the act.

But the tenants of Horseleap, less fortunate, joined the ranks of those whom *United Ireland* called "wounded veterans of the war for the land." Homeless veterans, at any rate. For the better part of a year, they were maintained out of League funds, in cabins built for them in a wasteland christened New Horseleap. These cabins too have vanished: old Horseleap or new, luck was not in that jolly name. The subvention dried up, and the last of it was used to buy the families passage to Liverpool or Boston. But not Bill Twomey, who had no family, and moped about Kilpeder, discon-solate and bewildered, staying with this one and that one, mending and patching, until the day when Robert Delaney brought him to the house in Cork Street, with its small stable, and the cell-like room tucked against its gable end.

I had never before been inside a workhouse, and have no wish to repeat the experiment. The one in Kilpeder is the genuine article, built before the famine, and the scene, in those years, of such events as have seared themselves into the memory and dark imagination of our people.

Nothing can ever scrub away that mythic stain, but it must be said that this County Council has tried: the interior, though bare, is neat and seemly, the air oppressively burdened by an aroma which mixes boiling cabbage with carbolic soap. The inmates seemed cheerful enough, and the workhouse master, who showed me through to Twomey's bed, a decent chap, kindly and humane, manifestly well liked.

"That was my great day," Twomey said, "the day that Counsellor Delaney stopped me in the road, outside Tully's, and asked me would I mind giving him a hand with his horses, his two mounts and the chestnut he used for the trap. Later, of course, young Conor had his own pony and cart. I thought at first he meant some task or other that might take a day or two, cleaning the stable like, you know. But not at all! Twas as his groom he wanted me, and even that is not a fair description of my duties, for there were errands to do for him, and messages and the like. His assistant in all that did not involve the law, you might say. With my own wee room, and at mealtimes my chair to draw up to the kitchen table with Mrs. Gaffney and the two Lizzies."

"He had a great liking for you, Mr. MacMahon tells me."

"He did, I think. After a year or two, after we had come to know one another. But at the first, you know, I think it was not so much that he needed a groom as that he felt very bad about the people of Horseleap, almost as though he wanted to make amends. But sure, amends for what? Had he not fought for us, and raised up the standard of the Land League above our heads?"

I had brought him, with a few other things, a half pound of tobacco, and as he talked he worked elaborately at the task of filling his pipe, his hands arthritic and surprisingly small.

"If you knew Counsellor Delaney only in that unfortunate last year, the year of the Parnell carry-on, with the town murderous, and the counsellor in the thick of it, then you did not know him as he was when he commenced his progress. He was a farmer's son himself, you know, and proud of it, for all that he was a lawmaker beyond in London, pleading Ireland's cause, as they say."

"I never knew him," I said. "We never met. My father knew him."

Prentiss, Senior: A clever man, Patrick. An able man. A nice, wicked wit he had. But there was a flaw there somewhere, God knows where. Parnell was his master. "I would follow him into hell," he said to me. And by God, he did.

"The last year," I said, puzzled. "The year of the Parnell fight was 'ninety-one. That wasn't Counsellor Delaney's last year by a long chalk."

It was as though he had not heard me. With long, pulling sucks of air, he got the pipe lit, drew in smoke.

"I mind days when there were papers that I was to carry down to his office, and Jamesey his assistant would be waiting for me, but over his shoulder, a round-shouldered thin little fellow he was, I could see the counsellor at his desk, and the great personages of our world gathered around him. T. D. Sullivan I saw there once, the man who wrote the Clonbrony Wood ballad and A. M. Sullivan's brother, the chiefs of the Bantry gang. Tim Healy himself was there once, but that would be early days; they had a terrible falling out, those two did. And I have seen Michael Davitt in that room, a thin man with but one arm, empty sleeve tucked into coat pocket, and dark sunken eyes that would burn into you."

Long pause, while he puffed at the sweetish tobacco that MacMahon had specified, his rheumy, watering eyes unfocused, as he groped into the past's sweeter time.

"Once," he said, "and you know the tricks of memory, some bit of time will be held without rhyme or reason. I remember a day, in late autumn, during the battle of Horseleap it was, as you might call it, and I was down into Kilpeder upon errands of my own. Twas a day of great excitement; there had been trouble of some sort, and the police were moving forth from their barracks—I could see that at the far end of town—and others were standing to watch it as well. But I chanced without reason to look at the Ardmor obelisk, and there, standing beside it, were the counsellor and Vincent Tully, and the two of them laughing about something, so hard that one of them would strive to cease, and then he would catch sight of the other, and no use, twould set him off afresh. I see that so clearly at this minute, the two friends, those handsome, confident fellows."

"He was Mr. Delaney's particular friend, was he not?" I asked, carefully.

Puffs of puzzled tobacco. "I don't know as to that," he said. "Mind you, that was long before I entered into the counsellor's employ. But it seemed to me always that there were the three of them—the counsellor and Mr. MacMahon and Mr. Tully. And Mrs. MacMahon, if you can think of a woman being a friend. A fine, lovely woman."

"And Mrs. Delaney as well," I said.

"I have no quarrel with Mrs. Delaney," he said. "Twas only natural that she would later want a proper groom, and not a fellow like myself."

"That morning," I said, "the morning that Mr. Delaney rode off into the Derrynasaggarts . . ."

"The tricks that the mind can play on old men," he said. "I remember more clearly the two of them standing together by the obelisk, years before."

"That morning," I began again, "you saddled Mr. Delaney's horse for him?"

"I did, of course. Who else would have done it?" He shifted his outstretched legs. "Master MacMahon said once to me a curious thing about that morning of which you speak. He said it to me long afterwards, years afterwards."

"What was that?" I said.

"Twas when I was helping him move his possessions from the town up to his small house. The weight of books that man has! He is well known to be a learned scholar, acknowledged in Dublin and Cork City. Donovan the carter moved all of the heavy pieces for him, but this small piece and that, delicate like, he would entrust to no one but himself and myself. Three trips we made that day, from Kilpeder to the ridge upon which his present house stands. Twas a sweltering day in July. When the third trip had been made, and all unloaded and set into place, we stood, the two of us, with our jackets off and our shirt sleeves rolled up and welcome glasses of porter in our hands."

He shifted in bed, and looked beyond my shoulder, as though someone had come into the ward. But we were alone save for an old man in the far bed, asleep, his mouth hanging open. Beyond the tall, barred window lay the workhouse wall, spike-crowned; the Macroom road, dusty and quiet; a field of tall grasses shivering in faint wind.

"Twas a cloudless day, and in the far distance the Derrynasaggarts were plain to be seen. I have no love for them. As a young man, I travelled across them five times or six, on my road to Killarney, and if you cross them at the wrong time of day you would wish yourself elsewhere—great lonely rocks and wind."

"Ned Nolan," I said to him, prompting. But there was no need.

" 'I loved him,' Master MacMahon said, 'as Bob did. But I let Bob set out for him alone.' "

"How did you know that he meant Ned Nolan?" I asked.

But he had turned his head from me, and was looking past the old sleeper, across the Macroom road, towards the waving grasses.

22

[*Hugh MacMahon/Robert Delaney/*
Thomas Ardmor/Lionel Forrester]

It was strange, improbable from first to last, that Bob Delaney's life and the lives of the Ardmors, his life and theirs, should touch. But most strange of all, I believe to this day, must have been the autumn evening when he walked between the falcons at the gates, and set forth up the avenue to the house. For walk he did, and later I asked him why, for he had by now his two horses in the stable behind his house, and the trap of polished wood. "Sure, tis a mile at least," I said, "from the gates up to the big house."

"A mile is but a saunter, Hughie," he said. "We walk farther than that every Sunday."

I think that in very fact he had some notion like my own, that he was enacting a romance, in which the hero is always imagined as walking, through enchanted forest or broad sunlit meadow. But perhaps not; perhaps he wished only to prolong and savour the moment. I see him in imagination, although in imagination only, for that night he was so intent upon tumbling out before me all that was said at the Castle, and how it was said, that he had no time for such a trivial matter as how he felt as he approached it.

He had been seen from the Castle by one man at least, by Brian Griffin, the butler. Even as he was climbing the steps to the portico, the door swung open, and Griffin stood waiting to receive him. He was not a local man, but had been in Kilpeder for years, since the days of the old earl, and he and Bob knew each other a bit; once every four weeks or so he would walk into Conefry's for a pint, choosing always, of course, the saloon rather than the public bar, and exchanging civil greetings with whatever auctioneer or schoolmaster happened to be there. A dignified, silver-haired man with a soft Limerick accent. There was no "Bob" or "Brian" on this occasion, or subsequent ones. "Lord Ardmor will see you in the library, Mr. Delaney," he said.

"Would you not have gone around to the estate office rather than the main hall, Bob?" I asked him that night. "That would have been my own inclination." We were sitting, the three of us, Mary and Bob and myself, in our parlour, with a tea spread out before us, and a fire in the hearth against the early autumn chill. "It was to Ardmor that I wrote," he said, "and it was Ardmor who replied to me. Quite properly—my business was with him and it concerned Chute." He broke off a piece of toast and smiled at us. "He is but a man, you know, like ourselves and like Chute." But Chute was in the town often, in the taproom of the Arms or shopping in Tully's or in Robinson's the saddler's. Ardmor was more remote, and we would see him on more special occasions. On hunt mornings in the early years, when he was master of the hunt, leading the pack down the avenue into the marketplace, where the other huntsmen would be gathering, and old Gilmartin keeping his three girls lively, carrying out glasses of sherry and hot whiskey against the morning chill. And once a year he would inspect my school, exchanging awkward, embarrassed words with the lads as they stood at attention, ranged by height. The inspector and myself—the real inspector of schools, that is—would act as interpreters. "He is but a man," Bob said again, "but oh, Hughie, if you could but see that library you would think that you had died and gone to heaven. Great walls of books rearing upwards to the carved ceiling, and armchairs deep as wells facing a great fireplace in which you could roast an ox."

"A great reader, is he?" I said with democratic sarcasm.

"He is a painter," Bob said.

"A painter?" I said, confused for the moment by the unexpected reply.

"Yes," Bob said, "painter," and he waved his toast in the air like a brush daubing its canvas.

"Tis well for him," I said, still in my sarcastic vein, "that he has found a pleasurable way to while away his days."

But Bob shook his head. "He is more painter than landlord is the truth of the matter. There were three of his paintings on easels in the library, and later, because I had expressed my admiration for them, they took me to the room where he paints. Mind you, I was not seeing them in the best light, but in the yellowy light of evening. So they cautioned me."

"They?" Mary said, making a question of the word.

"Yes," Bob said, "they were both waiting for me there in the library, and later tea was brought in for us. This is my second tea this day."

"What is she like?" Mary said. "What was she wearing?"

Bob and I exchanged looks, and I began to say something, but Mary put her hand on my arm.

"What is she like, Bob? Tell us at once."

"Ach, Mary," he said, "how can I describe her or anyone upon demand? She is not a painter, there is a start for you. But by God, if worse came to worst, she could make her living as a model for a painter. She is very lovely, although a bit on the thin side. She had a gown of soft material, a very dark yellow, with figures on it, small flowers I think. Ask me no more than that. And lovely dark hair, worn long; hair almost black, and tied carelessly. No, I will put it differently. She had carefully tied her hair to give it a careless appearance. She is a civil, polite woman, and was most interested in what we had to say to each other, her husband and myself. She is a serious woman, I think, but given to smiling to herself. That is all I can tell you about her."

"You barely noticed her," I said.

"Ah but he did," Mary said. "Bob is a great noticer of women. You never knew that about Bob, did you, Hughie?"

"Be that as it may be," Bob said, and held out his empty cup to her.

"Is the tea bitter at all, Bob?" she said, pouring. "It might well seem so, after the fine China tea served in a sterling service, no doubt, at Ardmor Castle?"

By way of answer, Bob grinned at her, but his glance was wary and puzzled.

"Ah, sure, I had forgotten," she said. "You are well used to sterling in your own house. Agnes and yourself are no strangers to sterling."

"You had more to talk about than painting," I said quickly.

"We did," Bob said, with his puzzled, affectionate gaze still upon

Mary, "but I will tell you, Hughie, that those pictures dumbfounded me. They are like a private vision of what the world is, what reality is—trees, the water in rivers, riverbeds of sand and pebbles. And the colours—bright, warm. They confused me, those paintings."

"Unexpected, surely," I said.

"Yes," Bob said, "unexpected," and Mary smiled at him.

I do not know what I had expected. All of my life, our lives, "Ardmor" and "Forrester," title and family name, had been woven into the days of Kilpeder. At first, in the first years of their marriage, the world, so it seemed to us—the great world—had come to their balls, the wedding ball and the two spring balls that had followed upon it, carriages from all the great estates of the county, and from far beyond it, from Meath and Galway and Mayo, the lights of the Castle blazing; and in our imaginations we heard snatches of music, waltzes, imagined dancers, silk gowns sweeping floors of polished marquetry. He had been away for most of his life, at school and then at Cambridge, home for the holidays, and after that the army. Paris after the army, and now, for four months each year, Italy. But Kilpeder did not think of Paris as a city, Italy as a country; they were parts of "abroad," where families like the Ardmors went, as part of their lives, mysterious and alien as the migrations of birds. Later, of course, I was to learn that the years in Paris were spent in study, and that his friends there were neither Parisians of the fashionable *faubourgs* nor the British colony, but painters and writers, a few composers, his life a life of studios and cafés, excursions into the countryside, hampers of bread, cheese, wine. But that was for a few years only, and Italy was different. In Italy, they lived in grand, Kilpeder style, in a handsome Florentine villa.

"There are tall windows in the library," Bob said, "that open out upon a terrace. You could stand there upon that terrace, and look beyond the gardens, beyond the river, beyond the walls of the demesne, and look down upon the town of Kilpeder, see the lot of us bustling upon our duties or our pleasures, teaching young blockheads or writing wills for strong-farmers."

"As the engraving says," I said, " 'The Town of Kilpeder, Property of the Earl of Ardmor.' "

"What must it be like to own a town?" he said.

"Ask your father-in-law," I said.

For a moment, he gave me a glare so fierce that it was startling, and then he smiled.

"There is the work of art upon which Ardmor Castle rests," Mary said. "The engraving of the town they own, and us in it, and not paintings of rivers and sand."

"I declare to God," Bob said. "To judge by the two of you, I went up to the Castle to sell the funds and books of the Land League in exchange for tea and a few buns."

It was a comfortable hour after that brief passage at arms, and I still do not understand the edge that Mary and myself brought to our words, unless perhaps it was a simple, old-fashioned enviousness at work; for it has well been said that beneath every Irish rebel and incendiary there lurks a respect for the quality, an awe of their wide acres and lofty ways.

"Currant buns they were," Bob said, "and a rack of toast. They were brought in to us by Emily Weldon, the girl that Lady Ardmor brought with her from Westmeath. I think, Mary, that she wore black, with bits of white here and there, and a fetching white cap and apron."

"I know Emily Weldon," Mary said.

"The Earl is an easy man to talk with, did you find? He was stiff in his manner the few times we have talked—decent enough, but stiff," I said.

"Easy indeed," Bob said, "bearing in mind the subject of our conversation. He is an unexpected man—that is a good word for him. Do you know, if he were not a big landlord, I think that he would be with the League. He is not against us, surely. That much is certain."

There was a part of me that was not taken aback by this. It was well known that he had refused the chairmanship of the Property Defence Association, and that the year before, the year of the bad harvest, he had remitted the Ardmor rents, against the advice of his estate agent.

"Tis against nature," I said, "a landlord in support of the Land League."

"I did not say that he supported it," Bob said. "His circumstances are peculiar. His income in one room of his mind, and his conscience in another. It is no discredit to him surely that he has a conscience."

"My God, Bob," I said, "tis no discredit to him that he has an income."

"Parnell himself is a landlord," Mary said, firmly, as though that settled matters.

"They know each other, Parnell and Lord Ardmor," Bob said. "They were both at Cambridge University. Lord Ardmor says that Parnell was a devil for cricket; that is all that he remembers about him. Ach, but also that he was heaved out for some kind of scandal—brawling or a woman or whatever."

"Well then," Mary said, sighing, as though a burden had been placed upon her. "They are friends, are they, so?"

"They may be," Bob said with a shrug.

"You had no difficulty with your errand, then," I said, "not with Lord Ardmor so well disposed to the national cause."

"I said only that he was not against us," Bob said. "But no, there were no difficulties raised up. Far from it."

It seemed to Bob Delaney that the day was sinking within the library, in a splendour of soft colours—the slanting, heavy rays of sunlight falling upon the rich colours of the carpets, ochre and rose and the sandy brown of Arabia or Turkestan. The late sunlight fell upon the deep-set fireplace, with its surround of onyx black as ink, upon the row upon row of tall, leather-bound books, upon the tea service which caught and reflected the beams. It was too early for gaslight or candle, and the soft, fast-fading sun, the warm, glowing fire of turf gave the room its only light, transitory and challengeable. The far corners of the room were in shadow, soft-edged.

"That was your mission to me, Mr. Delaney?" Ardmor said to him. "Only that?" He wore a tweed jacket the colour of heather, a soft shirt, loosely knotted tie.

"It seemed mission enough down below," Delaney said, nodding towards Kilpeder, beyond the tall windows.

It had seemed best to put the matter before Ardmor, in plain terms. The League was not opposed to Ardmor Castle, had no reason to be, but it had reason to know that the Property Defence Association was being managed by Edward Chute, Ardmor's agent, and so was being managed, in a way, from the Castle. And in times such as these, there was bound to be talk, to be scandal.

"And scandal would never do, would it?" Ardmor said.

"It is never much help to anyone," Delaney said. "Anyone save scandalmongers, that is."

"That word has curious use in this country," Ardmor said. "It covers much ground. In England, *scandal* covers only matters of a very personal kind."

"And here as well," Delaney said. "But in extraordinary times such as these . . . You must know what has been happening, Lord Ardmor. Edward Chute has contrived to make himself much disliked by the plain people of Kilpeder. And you could well lose the good name that you enjoy if it were to be thought that you countenanced what he is about. Much less that you have a hand in it yourself."

"Does your league seriously believe that?" Ardmor asked. He seemed amused. Because he knows that nothing can touch him, Delaney thought. We can touch Bat Colthurst, and Woodhaven House, and Eddy Chute, and poor drunken O'Donovan, but not Ardmor Castle.

"I am agent for the League in Kilpeder," Delaney said, "and you might call this an official visit. But it is my own notion. My own mission, you would say. And friendly in its intention."

"I accept that," Ardmor said, "and I trust that you will accept in the same spirit that I will be dictated to by no one, neither by the Property Defence Association nor by the Land League."

"I did not have it in mind to dictate to you, Lord Ardmor. Nothing that I have said can carry such a construction."

"Carry such a construction," Ardmor said, laying a whip of light sarcasm upon the words. "You are a solicitor, are you not, Mr. Delaney?"

"Tom," Lady Ardmor said. She sat well back in her low, comfortable chair, and spoke the word from its depths, without moving. She was resting her chin in her hand, and watching each of them. Delaney had been aware of her, of her silence. "Tom," she said again, as if chiding.

"You have no cause for concern, Mr. Delaney. As I was about to tell you, Edward Chute is no longer land agent for the Ardmor estates. Not since the first of the week. I am surprised that that is not yet common talk in Kilpeder."

"It is not," Delaney said, fierce in his surprise. "By God, it is not. I pride myself upon my knowledge of Kilpeder, but I did not know that."

"It will be known soon enough. I intend to find another agent, of course, and have written off to my lawyers in Dublin. Until then, I will manage matters myself."

"It was a long association that Eddy Chute had with the Ardmor estates."

"Long indeed," Ardmor said. "He took over from his father."

"I remember the father," Delaney said. "Everard Chute. He was still alive and vigorous at the time of . . ." He paused.

"At the time of the Rising, were you about to say? A lively time for Kilpeder. I was away at Cambridge at the time, but you were here, I understand, Mr. Delaney."

"I was indeed," Delaney said, and smiled. "I invaded the Castle here, so to speak. That is to say, Ned Nolan and Hugh MacMahon climbed up to the top of your gazebo for our first glimpse of the soldiers on the march against us from Macroom."

"Edward Chute tells us that you and he were friends of a sort, for a few years," Ardmor's wife said, and Delaney turned towards her. The light in the room was changing, thickening itself. It fell upon her.

"Of a sort," Delaney said. "That puts it well. We were shooting together a few times, the two of us and Vincent Tully. He was a guest at my wedding, himself and Mrs. Chute. He will have enough to keep him busy, I am thinking, even without the agency."

"Oh, yes," Ardmor said. "He is a landlord himself, of course, in a middling way. And he has his association. Your league will keep him occupied, I suspect."

"Yes," Delaney said, and realized that he had not turned away from Lady Ardmor, had been staring at her. And she at him, as though her dark, level eyes were studying him. She smiled, and lowered her hand to her lap, resting it there.

"That is the Tully of the large shop in the square," she said.

"The son," Delaney said.

"Vincent," Ardmor said. "We have met Vincent, my dear. At the Rodgerses'. You remember him—a handsome fellow, pale, with thick black hair. The Tullys are one of the old established families of Kilpeder, are they not, Mr. Delaney?"

"They are," Delaney said. "May I ask, Lord Ardmor, if the League or the Property Defence Association was involved in the quarrel between yourself and Eddy Chute."

"I said nothing of a quarrel," Ardmor said. "There was no quarrel. There were a number of issues—ways in which the estate was being managed. We remain on friendly terms. Vincent Tully was in our famous rising, Sylvia, like Mr. Delaney here, and MacMahon the schoolmaster, and MacCaffrey who farms for us."

"Your famous rising," Sylvia Ardmor said. "And now here we are, the three of us, having tea on a quiet September evening."

The Town of Kilpeder, Delaney thought, Property of the Earl of Ardmor. If they had quarrelled, he would never tell a town solicitor, Land League agent. Eddy Chute was small gentry indeed, but he was gentry, Trinity College and a commission in the militia.

"You are my first rebel," Sylvia Ardmor said. "Were you sentenced to be hanged, drawn, and quartered?"

"I was not. But I served six months of a four-year sentence, and it was the making of me. I never looked back. A convicted rebel has a great future in this country."

He spoke without smiling, but Ardmor caught his eye, and smiled appreciatively.

"There were such sentences, Sylvia," Ardmor said. "Hanged, drawn, and quartered. The chap who commanded here in Kilpeder was given a barbarous sentence."

"He was given treatment that was as barbarous as the sentence," Delaney said.

"He was the famous one, Sylvia," Ardmor said. "Edward Nolan, Ned Nolan, Nolan of Clonbrony Wood. Not a local man, was he, Mr. Delaney, not a Kilpeder man?"

"His father was," Delaney said briefly.

"Safely away now, though," Ardmor said. "In America. Thanks to the amnesty campaign. What is he about in America, do you know? Do you ever hear from him?"

"He has settled in," Delaney said. "Working in a brick factory, I have heard."

Like two tribes, Delaney thought. Ardmor with nothing to say about that blackguard Chute, and myself standing yet with Ned Nolan, as though one small wedge of time were forever frozen on a March afternoon thirteen years ago.

"Ah," Ardmor said, as though receiving welcome information. "One hears rumors, in the sensational press, mossback Tories in the clubs— murders, dynamite."

"I wouldn't know," Delaney said. "I am not a clubman."

"More tea, Mr. Delaney?" Sylvia Ardmor said. "And do try one of these. Cook is proud of them."

T here was a time when I would find myself trying to imagine that scene, Bob Delaney's first visit to Ardmor Castle, his first meeting with the Ardmors—Tom Ardmor and Sylvia Ardmor, as he would in time be terming them to me, but only in the privacy of our deep conversation. To me they remained Lord and Lady Ardmor from beginning to end, remain so to this minute. Only Lord Ardmor remains, in his villa among the hills below Florence, which I remember in imagination as filled with the summer colours and odours of the Italy which I have never visited; but he lives there now the year around, and I have no postcard images of those hills in winter, and so imagine winds howling down the Alps and other fancies.

They talked, Bob told us, of this and that, the business of their meeting soon completed, but the Ardmors pressing him to stay, and himself nothing reluctant to do so. Perhaps they saw each other as emissaries from our two Irish worlds, ambassadors meeting to discuss a treaty, and that library, which thanks to the courtesy of Lionel Forrester I have myself since visited, the perfect setting for so lofty an encounter, blooming in the day's final burst of golden sunlight, light touching everything, touching the tall Chinese vases with their blues and mustard yellows, touching the peach and salmon of faded damask. How did they look, to each other, in that first sunlight of meeting? I imagine Bob, a bit stiff but, as was his way, masking embarrassment with a dry, distancing wit. And Lord Ardmor, whom I imagined then, although I know better than that now, as firm with the certainties of birth, class, wealth—certainties which communicated themselves in the way he sat, stood, talked. And Lady Ardmor, Sylvia Ardmor—her I was never, from first to last, to imagine with any clarity at all, not even the clarity of illusion. I see her only through what Bob was to tell me of her. It is a scene which does not easily compose itself in my mind, and yet I return to it more than once or twice, even now.

Lionel Forrester has shown me those of Lord Ardmor's paintings that hang in the Castle, and some of them, perhaps, may be the ones which stood on easels that evening in the library. "He is an artist beyond question, a very pure artist," Forrester tells me, "so I am assured by fellows who would know." When first I saw those paintings, a half dozen years ago, they seemed to me decorative daubs, bright and giddy as nursery toys, some of them, or swirls of luminous fog, bits and pieces of life, picnics, a hunt with scarlet cutting through russet autumn and the mists of the season, a man and woman standing motionless on a towpath, her hands at her sides, pressed against straight-hanging fawn skirt, but one of his hands reaching, hesitantly, almost furtively, towards her. I know better now: the whole world, I know now, is painting in the way that Ardmor was learning to paint in Paris, in his youth.

It was Forrester who taught me how to see those paintings, and who ransacked the deserted studio to pull out watercolours, charcoal sketches. I have never warmed to them, to be perfectly honest. I remember Bob and myself, that time in 1887 when I visited him in London, going round to the great galleries, where the glories of Renaissance Venice and Florence and Rome are spread forth; and for me these are indeed the splendours of art, against which the lads of our own day are to be measured and found wanting. Constable is to my mind a worthy inheritor of those giants, and Frith, who can bring all the excitement of great crowded occasions within a single vast frame, a scene so alive that you feel that you could plunge into it, and make a bet on a horse or whatever the occasion might be. Turner was a great fellow until he went mad. But Constable—there is all the genius of England in Constable, and they are a people of genius surely, that they could keep their own lovely landscapes intact and reduce ours to rubble and ruins.

In the great paintings of Constable, there seems to me a marriage of nature and man, the ways of man, his sowing and harvesting, his cathedrals and small bridges, his yoked and harnessed beasts of burden, wedded to the natural world of freedom, order, a wedding fecund and more tranquil than many, and the proof of that shining forth in the great depth, the green, shadowed, sunlit world of the paintings. There is little enough like this that I can find in the paintings hung in Ardmor Castle, although there are some, as even I can tell, which exist to celebrate sunlight or the greenness of grass, the opalescence of fog upon the great English river.

I cannot swear as to the words that Bob used that night—that the paintings were a vision of reality; that is how I remember it—but the words even now sound strange, affected. Perhaps my memory is confounding what Bob said with something that I picked up, much later, from Lionel Forrester. Certain I am, however, that Bob spoke of them with excitement, and that he spoke with a certain knowledge that the truth of Ardmor's being was there, paint upon canvas, and not in the estate office or on the hunting field.

A maid had lit the library lamps before Delaney took his leave. They had been standing, the three of them, on the terrace, and when they turned around, the lamps, milk-bowled or bowls of pale, glowing green glass, sent gaslight out to battle with the sun's final beams. That is how it must seem to artists, Delaney thought, like Ardmor here. We see, the rest of us, a room, chairs, tables, a fireplace, wall after wall of books, the light from the lamps a comfort, a pledge against darkness. But they see colours, colours and kinds of light.

Beyond them, beyond garden, river, high walls, lay Kilpeder, its slate roofs grey and black, heaped against each other, a jumble broken by the bare, empty marketplace, the town framed at the one end by the neat spire of the Church of Ireland and on the other, down a short distance along the Macroom road, the vaulting and assertive spires of Saint Jarlath's. Property of.

"Have you been in our little church, Mr. Delaney?" Sylvia Ardmor asked.

"Of course I have," Delaney said, mild surprise and mild vexation mingling. "I have Protestant friends, you know. A few. They marry. Their children are christened. They die."

Old Johnston, John Sinnot's law clerk, a decent old fellow, fingers inked with an ink so black that no soap could scrub it off but only soften it, briefly, to the blue of the sky. In the taproom of the Kilpeder Arms (a bundle of slates now from the evening terrace, deep grey and black as the sea at night), long ink-stained fingers, arthritic, drawing towards him a glass of port. "Ah, Delaney, ye rogue ye. You are great for the forms of the law and the Queen's peace and the rights of the subject; but beneath your expensive raiment, you are an unrepentant Fenian rebel. You would hang all the poor loyal Protestants from the boughs of trees."

He brought me into the Church of Ireland for a service, Delaney thought. Strange, that church, a church of absences. No faint smell of incense clinging to corners, no statues too-brightly painted—Saint Joseph in mild long robe of white, brown cape, Our Lady in blue and white, Saint Patrick in sacerdotal robe of emerald green—no confessionals. And behind the altar, no veiled and gilt-doored tabernacle, sheltering chalice and ciborium. Instead, an odour of cleanliness, clean as old dead Johnston, sunlight pouring in upon us from tall windows of clear, untinted glass.

"They are very different, the two churches," Sylvia Ardmor said. "I like the colours in Saint Jarlath's. The statues. When Tom and I are away, in Italy or in France, we often go to Mass. That would never do here, would it? Not in Ireland."

From this flagged terrace, Ardmor Castle could have looked down upon the Rising, Delaney thought. A scuffle in the street, distant shouts. But the rifle fire would have travelled in the clear, snow-scoured air.

"No," Delaney said, "that would never do here in Ireland."

Once again, he caught Ardmor studying him with an amusement which seemed neither hostile nor condescending.

"I have trespassed too long upon your time," he said. "And upon your patience."

"You have not," Sylvia said, and impulsively, she put her hand upon his arm. "Has he, Tom?"

"Not at all," Ardmor said. "Not at all. We know too few of our . . ." He hesitated for a word, and then said, "Our fellow townspeople."
Property of.

His arm remembered the sudden touch of her hand, withdrawn now.

She said good-bye to him in the library, but Ardmor saw him to the entrance door, down the long hall.

At the opened door, facing Ardmor, looking past him down the length of the long hall, Delaney said, "You are a historied family, Lord Ardmor."

"All families are historied," Ardmor said, with the same smile. "The native Irish are all descended from kings, so it is said."

"Not mine," Delaney said.

Shadows had lengthened. Tangles of shadow along the avenue as Delaney walked down towards the town, the tangled shadows of elm branch, oak branch, branch of copper beech.

When Ardmor returned, Sylvia had left the library. The doors to the terrace were still open, and he crossed the room and closed them, then settled himself before the fire with a newspaper.

Presently, he set down the paper. Before leaving the room, he crossed to the terrace doors, put his hand as though to open them, and then dropped it. There was nothing to be seen through the glass, blackness. His own reflection stared back at him, a slender man, fair moustache and wide, curious eyes, almost colourless in reflexion.

He climbed the weighty, curving stairs, steps muffled by thick carpeting spread upon milky marble, and walked down the hall to his dressing room. Once he paused, before one of his paintings which he had hung in Ardmor Castle, the oil of Sylvia in Venice. Beyond her bare shoulder, sunlight spangled the Grand Canal, a gondola a shadow upon the water, the Ca' Rezzonico dappled sun and shadow.

He changed from his heavy tweeds, but before knotting his tie, before putting on his dinner jacket, he crossed the hall to Sylvia's room and knocked.

She was at her dressing table, dressing gown hung loose, white, ribboned, her skin white against loose, dark hair. When she smiled, complicitous parentheses framed the wide, generous mouth. As she smiled at him, she set down the long-handled, curving brush and took up a small cloisonné pot, white as alabaster, flecked with flowers. He sat in the small, straight-backed chair close to her, seeing her in profile, but from the mirror she looked straight at him. An old mirror, silver-flecked but surprisingly vivid, ruthless. Small lamps flanked it, unwavering candles. He sat here often, watching her, a scene which seemed to him, somehow, inexplicably Venetian, and so reminded him of their early weeks there—not the Venice of fact but rather as, even when he was there, he experienced it most vividly in his imagination: a city of secrets, whispers, masks, deceptions, a tourist's Venice raised to a genuine perception. Perhaps.

"And there we are," he said, "Fenian and Land Leaguer. Ticket-of-leave man."

"And not at all what you expected," she said.

"Probably not," Ardmor said. "I am not certain what I expected. I liked him. Very much."

"I liked him very much," Sylvia said. "I, too."

"Yes," he said. "I noticed that. So did he."

"Do you think so?" she said, opening the jar. "Do you think he is observant in such matters?"

"Indeed he is, and you know it. I do not underestimate him, and neither should you. He may never have travelled farther than Cork and Dublin, but he will. Fellows like Bob Delaney are rising up in the land these days. His grandchildren may well be kings of the hill when this place is a ruin. Broken masonry and cobwebs."

Her long, pale fingers scooped cream from the pot, smoothed it across her forehead.

"We were rude," she said. "We asked him almost nothing about himself."

"He was curiously reticent about himself," Ardmor said.

"Is he married, for example? Has he children?"

"For example," Ardmor said, dryly. "Yes, he is married; he has a son. He married the shop, as they say here. He was Tully's shop assistant, and married the Tully heiress. Tully's own son, Vincent, is the apple of the old man's eye, but he is a playboy, sucks up to the small gentry and the half-sirs, shoots, hunts, gambles, goes off to London and Paris after whores. The old man has made Delaney into a kind of son, dutiful son, brought him into the family, paid for his education in the law."

"How in the world do you know all that?" Sylvia asked.

"Oh, Eddy Chute is eloquent on the subject of Robert Delaney. Delaney is everything Chute hates. Delaney is bounding up into the world, a fellow of no family."

Her fingers touching her temple, she looked over towards Ardmor, and smiled. "No, Fenian and convict. Chute would not care for that."

"To give Chute his due, he might be willing to think of all that as picturesque. The Irish—all of them—are sentimental about rebellions, once they have well and truly failed. It is success that they are suspicious of, and Master Delaney has all the marks of someone heading for great

[463]

success. As he pointed out to us, his rebellion was the making of him. By Jove, he was a pleasant surprise. Sardonic chap. And formidable."

"Them," Sylvia said, "they."

"Sorry?" Ardmor said.

"No matter," Sylvia said, "not really. I was thinking that when we are in England, or abroad, we call ourselves Irish. You do, I have always done. But here, at home, we speak of the Irish as 'them.' Like a plume that we can wear or not wear as we choose. Rakish, picturesque, like Mr. Delaney's gaolbird past."

"Poor Delaney," Ardmor said. "He has no choice in the matter. He must settle for knowing who he is. A sorry recompense."

She was spreading now the thin film of cream across her cheek, her fingers moving lightly, tracingly, across her skin. A movement of her arm brought forward the collar of the loose robe, half exposing a breast. Unnoticing, she continued to study her face and her husband's words.

"You are becoming impossible, Tom," she said. "You are becoming as ironical as Lionel. You know that I detest irony."

"No you don't," Tom said. "The only people who hate irony are the ones who are not able to recognise it. They hate it upon some ignorant instinct."

"Too clever for me," she said. "Lionel and you have always been too clever for me, the pair of you."

"But I am not really clever, you know, not like Lionel."

Her face was smoothed into quietness by the thin, colourless, transparent mask. She sat motionless, her hands folded upon her lap.

"Yes," she said at last. Her eyes sought out his reflected eyes. They were looking not into hers, but at her breast, a white, small, shapely breast. He stretched out a hand towards it, and her hand, white, quiet, moved to meet it, carried it to the breast. The robe fell open. Holding his hand in hers, she moved it across the breast, drew its fingers, circling, about the nipple.

"Dear Tom," she said, the lovely mask glistening in the silver-flecked mirror, their eyes again meeting. "Dear, dear Tom." She pressed his hand towards her body.

B y the time that I arrived in Kilpeder that autumn, the Land League's campaign of boycotting against Sir George Wilcox of Woodhaven House had given to the entire barony a sense of siege. Even in the Castle, we could feel it. Indeed, Tom himself was under a species of polite, restrained boycott on the part of the county families, a chill hostility which was to continue until he left Ireland, to grow indeed more intense. It continues, in its way, to the present day. An atmosphere of intense isolation clings about this place, isolation and, of course, in these latter days, neglect.

The hostility was fair enough in its way. The journalists and phrase-makers were right: the Land War was a war, and in wars there are no neutrals. Not on the battlefield, at any rate. Tom was not "for" the League, of course, but neither was he clearly and visibly its enemy, as the other gentry were, without exception. And Tom was more than gentry, he was nobility: the premier noble of the barony, a belted earl, whose grants of land had come straight to the Forresters from Elizabeth. Lord knows what stories about him that little cad Chute had carried to the club and the hunt. About all of us. Kilpeder was, after all, a provincial place. Most of the gentry, or those who passed as such, had been to London, had been to what they called "abroad," by which was meant a few weeks in Paris every decade or so; but there it began and ended. What they knew of the world came to them from *Punch* and the *Illustrated London News*, visits from English cousins-by-marriage as narrow as themselves.

If Tom and Sylvia had chosen to cast their nets wide, to entertain more often, they could easily have found company as worldly as them-selves. Some of the big houses of Meath and Cork and Tipperary had weekends as riotous as any that might have been found among the Prince of Wales's Marlborough House crowd. But neither were they worldly in that seedy way, smelling of scent and cigar smoke, slaughter-ing partridge and wood pigeon in the morning, sitting down to glutton-ous dinners followed by cards and then a discreet exchange of bedroom keys. They were worldly, the two of them, but in an elusive, gauzy, almost principled way.

It did their reputation no good, of course, that Bob Delaney, the local Jack Cade and Wat Tyler compounded, had become their visitor. The landlord fury against Delaney was, from the landlord point of view, en-tirely justified. Of all the Land League lieutenants, across the country, in those two embattled years, Delaney must surely have been among the most effective—adroit, clever, implacable, and with a fine line of lurid and incendiary oratory. At the beginning, I did not know him at all well, although I wandered down several Sundays into the square to attend him.

Thus I knew first his public self, a self illumined by fitful pitch-soaked scarlet and ruby flares, by the shouts of a mob pressed together in the market square, a band playing, between speeches, interminably, "Clon-brony Wood" and "The Boys of Wexford" and "Clare's Dragoons" and, unofficial anthem of a nonexistent nation, "God Save Ireland." On the first of those Sundays, Delaney's task was to introduce the dignitary of the occasion, William O'Brien, a figure at once wild and insignificant in appearance, pince-nez and scraggly beard, a backwoods Camille Desmoulins, with a justified reputation for bloodthirsty proclaimings, a high, harsh voice without music but able to work powerfully, on that crowd at least, pointing a preternaturally long finger towards the dark, distant hills beyond which lay Woodhaven House, "the dark and sinister fortress of your oppression," as he called it, and the crowd shouting—no, screaming—its approval. "Here is your man," O'Brien shouted suddenly, flinging a long, scrawny arm around Delaney's shoulder. "He led forth the men of Kilpeder once before upon a tragic day of snow and blood. And he leads you again in a new battle, against oppression and against landlords and landlordism." He made his free hand into a fist and shook it towards the hills. "We'll have the land for the people."

Delaney, not a tall man, a head shorter, stood quietly, with the negligible weight of that scarecrow arm upon him, waiting out a chorus of "Clonbrony Wood," and then stepped forward to speak, letting the arm of comradeship trail off from his shoulders. I remember not a word of what he said, save that he played his words off skilfully against O'Brien's. Delaney, when he chose, could rouse up the stones with brutal denunciations, but he had no intention of competing with O'Brien, instead spoke quietly, the back of the crowd, beyond the obelisk, scarcely able to hear him, his voice as much as his words expressing an implacable, seasoned determination. When he had finished, he took a step backward, as though to make certain that he did not seem to claim the position that belonged by rights to the visiting O'Brien. But the gesture did not carry: in Kilpeder, it was Robert Delaney who owned the platform.

When I first saw him at the Castle, it was not to speak. I had come back from a day's rough shooting, Glennon the gamekeeper and myself in a dogcart, when I saw him leave by the main hall, where a groom was waiting for him with his mount, a handsome bay mare. "That was Delaney, surely, the Land Leaguer," I said to Tom, as I helped myself to a whiskey.

"It was," Tom said. "Too bad you missed him. Another time."

"What in the bloody hell is the Land Leaguer doing here," I said, "unless to lead a mob to burn the place down about our ears?"

"Not at all," Tom said, "not at all. Sylvia is becoming fond of him. So am I."

"Small wonder, then," I said, and I flopped down into a chair facing him. "Small wonder that the county families are furious with you. And these visits of his are public events, I take it. He rides up the avenue on that bay, and tosses the reins to a groom. Perhaps the groom is his cousin, have you thought of that?"

"The groom is not his cousin," Tom said, annoyance in his voice. "I have never thought of you as a snob, Lee. Far from it, indeed. You have your own taste for low company of a certain sort, as I recall."

"Then that is how you think of Delaney? As low company that you bring into your house?"

"Don't try your tricks of language with me, Lee. Delaney is a man of substance in the town, a solicitor—a writer of sorts, in fact."

"A most effective writer," I said. "I have read *Christmas in the Boggeraghs*. You are the one being shifty, Tom, not me. The other landlords of the baronies are about as fond of you at the moment as they are of Charley Parnell. And they are your people, Tom. Remember that. Not Delaney. Not fellows spouting hellfire and revolution from plat-forms."

"They are?" Tom said, and then said, answering himself, "Yes, of course they are. My people, your people. Bat Colthurst and Eddy Chute and drunken, red-nosed O'Donovan, yes, our people."

"And the rector," I said, "the rector and Evaline Dewhurst and Charlie Patterson and his wife, and a hundred others. Not to mention your father and mother and my father and mother. Yes, our people. And at the moment, the Land League has us under siege, the lot of us, living and dead. You cannot blame your neighbours for not taking your own large-minded view of matters."

"But I don't blame them, Lee. I don't blame them at all. I want no part in this war, one way or the other."

"That isn't the appearance you are giving," I said, and finished off my whiskey.

"Damn the appearances," he said. "This is my house, this my land, and I will do what I wish upon it. Do what I wish and receive whom I wish. Those who don't approve can flaming well bugger themselves. Or each other."

Tom was, and is, less my cousin than my closest and dearest friend, a more than brother; but every ten years or so, I am brought up short against the knowledge than I am the younger son of a younger son, and that he is the Earl of Ardmor. He is not himself aware of the massiveness of being which this creates, a lordly conviction that what he does is right because he does it; it is a final stratum of personality, beyond friendship, beyond society. Even now, in the bleakness of his self-imposed exile, it governs him. It governs everything save his art, and his love of Sylvia.

"Nobly spoken," I said, and lifted my empty glass to him. For a moment, he glared at me with genuine anger, and then he grinned and took the glass, refilled it, and poured a drink for himself.

"I have often wondered," I said. "Is 'belted earl' an anachronism, or is there an actual belt that goes with the job? Can I see it?"

"There are robes," he said, "perfectly splendid. They cost the earth, or so Mother said when she bestowed them upon me. Father wore them a few times." He smiled again. "Derwater, in Galway, keeps his in a glass case, where he can see them every morning."

"I have met Derwater," I said. "He should be in a glass case himself. Better Delaney than Derwater."

He came one night after dinner, for coffee and a brandy. We sat in the library, the four of us.

"Chute has struck at last," he said. "A wretched place called Horseleap. Twenty or so small farms owned by something in London called the Munster Adventurers. It goes back to the days of Cromwell. They stand ready to evict, and why not? What should it matter to some company in London?"

"You intend to resist the evictions?" I asked him.

"With words, Mr. Forrester. Words and perhaps a few stones from lawless elements beyond my control. Small use against constabulary with writs of ejectment and carbines. It should be impressive—an entire hamlet cleared out, turned into a deserted village out of Goldsmith. It is their retaliation for the boycotting of Woodhaven House."

"It will be a defeat, then," I said, puzzled. "A defeat for your league."

"I do not think so," Delaney said. "It will seem so to the Property Defence Association."

"And to the poor wretches who will be turned out of their cabins," I said.

I looked towards Tom, and saw that he was looking not at Delaney, but at Sylvia. She was holding a small glass of Chartreuse, twisting it slowly, her eyes fixed upon it.

"This time," Delaney said, "we will be ready for that. There will be cabins for them, and support for them until they are on their feet."

"Ready for them," I said. "Ever since I arrived last week, I have been listening to military conversations. It is indeed a war."

Her glass caught suddenly the flame from a lamp; there was a flash of green, a wet gem; it vanished.

"I wonder, Mr. Forrester," he said suddenly, "that you have never written about this country. I have read your Spanish book. You have a great gift."

"Lee is more at home in distant places," she said, without looking up. "The near-at-hand bores him, does it not, Lee?"

"Perhaps distance makes for clarity," I said, "for orderliness of perception. What is happening here at the moment, for example, perplexes me."

"In what way, Mr. Forrester?" Delaney asked politely.

"It is a war of sorts," I said. "On that everyone seems agreed. What would victory be? For your crowd."

"My crowd," he said. "The Land League is open as to its goals. The land of Ireland for the people of Ireland, a peasant proprietary. The Home Rule Association seeks what its name implies, our own government and our own parliament."

"Tom and I were talking a few days ago, about his wonderful robes as an earl. What would happen to those?"

He sipped his coffee before answering, and then put down the cup and smiled.

"I will give you an honest answer. I don't give a damn. If the Irish people want their House of Lords, they are welcome to it. If they want Queen Victoria, they are welcome to her. I want the control of Irish lands and Irish life to return into the hands of the Irish people. Simple enough."

Simple enough to be misleading, as the two of us knew, and Tom as well, I have no doubt. He was the same fellow, I suddenly realized, as the young man who had led an armed band against the town, who had fired upon the Queen's constabulary and the soldiers of the Crown. But I understood, or thought I did—understood for at most a minute or two—his appeal for Tom and Sylvia. He was an unlikely man to turn up in an obscure market town: rural solicitor, local agitator. I turned towards Sylvia, to exchange a glance with her, and had one of the shocks of my life.

She had looked up from her liqueur. Indeed she had. And she was staring, openly staring, at Delaney, her mouth slightly parted. She sat at an angle to me, her free hand resting upon her hip. I remembered the first time I had ever seen that look, the spring when Galantiere was painting her portrait in the London house, on a morning when I walked suddenly into the room, and she was at the same angle to me, her lips parted, and her eyes upon him. He was mixing paints, not looking in her direction, humming absently, and suddenly she smiled. A slight smile, tender, affectionate. In that moment, beyond question, I knew fully, without condition, her relationship to Galantiere, and now with a knowledge pressing upon me, unformed and frightening, a knowledge of her relationship with Bob. And I was right, she told me later. We were to have

[469]

no secrets, Sylvia and I. She was smiling now; and then, perhaps feeling my eyes upon her, she shook her head, very slightly, and looked away.

We talked about it, three or fours days later, in that oblique way we had adopted in London, in the years of our deepening friendship. It was an unseasonably warm autumn afternoon, and we crossed the little Japanese bridge, the two of us, and walked along the shore of the small lake, beneath willows, to the absurd, small "boathouse" with its two punts.

We floated the punt, and faced each other above the clear, faintly rippled water. Briefly, the willows arched above us, pale-green, thick, with sunlight finding its way through the delicate bent boughs.

"Poor Lee," she said. "You are always finding me out." She had rolled her loose-fitting sleeves above her elbows, and now she trailed one hand in the water. Her forearm was pale, lightly freckled.

"Not by choice," I said.

"He is extraordinary," she said, "clever and strong."

"He may not have the kind of cleverness that he will need."

"True enough," she said, and watched the water slide past her wide-spread fingers. "Tell me what you think of him."

"Has Mrs. Delaney been to the Castle? She is very lovely, I have heard, in the Irish way, the light-haired Irish. They have a son."

"Conor," she said. "He talks about Conor. He has great hopes for him. I hadn't known that she is said to be lovely. Have you seen her? Who told you?"

"No one," I said. "I made it up to tease you. She is the shopkeeper's daughter. I know her brother Vincent; we have hunted together. A vulgar fellow. Overdressed and jolly. A climber."

"But Robert is not at all vulgar," she said.

"No, he is not. I grant you that."

"You will grant it to me? Were we having a dispute?"

"Not a dispute," I said. "One of our strange intimacies. Perhaps we should talk of something else."

"Yes," she said, "perhaps. But you want to talk of this, don't you? You are dying to know how far things have gone. Shall I tell you?"

"If you want to."

"Not very far, not nearly far enough. We have declared . . . an interest."

"If I were you," I said, "I would leave it there. A sentimental interest. No harm done."

I dipped an oar, and we moved out from under the willows. The sudden sun struck my forehead, but she was sheltered against it by her broad-brimmed straw, tied beneath her chin.

"Perhaps I may," she said. "But not for your reasons. It worries you because it is dangerous."

"You're bloody right it's dangerous. The lady of the manor and a League agitator."

"He and Tom amuse each other. He comes to visit. As you say, no harm done."

"Galantiere came to the house in Chelsea to paint your portrait. No harm done there either, I take it? At least Galantiere was a gentleman. Of sorts."

Her laugh was like the pond's surface, a ripple. "Tom is right," she said. "You are a snob."

"Perhaps I am," I said, "where you are concerned. This time, you could be hurt, really hurt. It isn't the way it was with Galantiere. Or that other chap."

"No," she agreed. "It isn't that way at all. It is as though Bob Delaney and I stood facing each other, with a deep divide between us."

"Tom could be hurt as well," I said, "and Delaney hurt worst of all. These people are not like us at all, Sylvia."

"I would never hurt Tom," she said.

"You would not mean to."

"You are a great admirer of Galantiere's portrait," she said. "I insisted on Galantiere, you know. Tom called him a society painter. Yes he is, I said, and that is precisely what I want, a mysterious society painting, all surface, black and white and a splash of sinful colour. And that is what Galantiere gave us."

"In fact," I said, "I have come to prefer Tom's portrait. I take it that Delaney has not seen it yet."

"No," she said, mock-prim. "Not yet. If he does, he will not know it is my portrait. He is very simple, poor dear. It would never occur to him."

When I stayed at Ardmor, I passed that portrait every day, morning and evening and night, at the head of the staircase, just after one turns towards the bedrooms. He painted it six months after Galantiere did his, and in its way it is a response. But it is unlike anything else of Tom's that I have seen—naturalistic, precise, and yet remote, mannered. As though he wanted to beat Galantiere at his own game, which, of course, he could not. Galantiere was a master at what he did: an artful, superficial master. Unlike too, though, in that the background is painted from memory, a scene upon the Grand Canal, as though the painting were done in homage to the first months of their marriage, a background entirely conventional in composition and attitude: gondolas, palaces on the far side, dappled Canaletto water. In the foreground, a woman sits at the tall window,

[471]

shielded by half-drawn blinds, the late sun falling on warm flesh. Her head is turned away from us.

But there is nothing conventional about the woman. She sits, half disrobed, her clothes gathered loosely in her lap. She is naked to the waist, her breasts small, precise, shapely. One hand rests lightly on her bare hip, in a gesture which is unmistakably Sylvia's.

"After all," she said, "it could be anyone."

"It could not," I said. "It could only be you."

"Why do you prefer it?" she asked. "Does it inflame you?" She made a mocking, satirical flame of the word.

"Yes, it does a bit," I said. "To tell you the truth. I am a very impure student of art. It must shock the servants."

She laughed again. "It does shock them, so Emily reports to me. Mrs. Sheridan, who is the lawgiver in the servants' hall, tells them that it is one of 'those Italian whores who pose for such things.' Emily does a wonderful imitation. Emily is very nice, don't you think, Lee? A handsome young woman, and barrels of fun."

"Very handsome," I said.

"I thought you had noticed her. We're a pair, aren't we, Lee? Incorrigible."

"Not quite," I said, "not a matching pair."

I rested the oars, and we drifted a bit, towards the other shore. She leaned back, and with the white leghorn shielding her face, closed her eyes, her one hand still grazing the water, and the other resting on the gunwale. Half unwilling, disliking myself, I imagined her sitting now, with me, in the punt, half naked, the sunlight upon bare breasts, slender hip with its high, arched bone. Tom's fault in a way. He had painted a portrait which declared its erotic intention; there was no other way to respond to it. Not Sylvia's fault, not really.

In the distance—beyond river, wall, town, invisible from the lake, willow-screened—the Boggeraghs rose up, brown crouching beasts. At my back, the distant Derrynasaggarts, framing the Castle. My imagination drew itself suddenly to some height from which I could look down upon a mountain-framed world, within the frame pastureland, cabins, strong-farms, churches, a town, a girdling wall, a castle, and, at the precise center, perfect, blue-green, bough and leaf-fringed, a lake, small and artificial, therefore shapely, and a boat upon the lake with two figures, one a woman, eyes closed, face lifted to the sun.

23

[Patrick Prentiss/Hugh MacMahon]

On December 22, 1880, when Sir George and Lady Wilcox left Wood-haven House, as they thought for a winter on the Mediterranean but in fact forever, their departure betokened, so in later years it would appear, the fall of feudalism in Ireland. Captain Boycott in Mayo, Bence Jones in Clonakilty, George Wilcox in Kilpeder—the attention of two islands had been drawn upon them, and the voices of property and authority had declared them to be the battlegrounds of a contest between civilisation and anarchy. The sounds of their crashes echoed against each other, rolling thunder beating upon hills beneath a livid sky.

Boycott quitted Lough Mask House on November 26, bundled with his wife into a windowless military hospital van, escorted by troopers of the Nineteenth Hussars and First Dragoons, by the Eighty-fourth Regiment of Foot, and by two hundred armed constables. It would have been a melancholy sight, had there been isinglass windows for Boycott to peer through: a low, overcast day, the van creaking along the untended estate avenue, on either side the ruined gardens, and, far off, sheeted by November drizzle, the windrows of rotted hay. Past the estate gates, the long road to Claremorris, along which Boycott and his escort travelled, was deserted. By orders of the Land League, at the sounds of the approaching caravan, creak of leather, roll of wheels, sergeants' shouts, hooves and boots upon the roadway, the people vanished from sight, behind walls, into farmhouses and cabins. In the villages, the shops were closed, shuttered and bolted; in not one of them could the Boycott party have bought a twist of sweets or sixpence of loose tea. At the train platform in Claremorris, Colonel Bruce of the Royal Irish Constabulary made a short speech. Boycott nodded his thanks, climbed into his compartment, and left for England by way of Dublin. Nally, the Land League organiser for Mayo, was observed by the correspondent for the *Times*, leaning against the station house, arms folded, a wisp of hay between his lips.

On the fourteenth of December, Bence Jones's sheep and cattle were wandering untended through Cork. The few drovers willing to serve him had, under threats, abandoned them; no dealer in Cork would accept them or feed them, and the bellowing of the calves and lambs was described in an otherwise bleak report by the police as "heartrending." One of his servants, an Orangeman, disguised himself and sought to buy provisions in Skibbereen, but was recognised and beaten; a Samaritan, braver than others, trundled him back to Lisselan with a note pinned to him: "Exterminators beware." Afterwards, he was never right in the head. With the help of the Property Defence Association, Bence Jones struck back against his labourers, evicting all of them. By this time, he was hysterical with rage and grief, uncomprehending.

He was a product of Harrow and Cambridge, a barrister, and had been in residence on the family estate since before the great famine, a loquacious, sententious man, who had written, that very year, a book which he called *The Life's Work in Ireland of a Landlord Who Tried to Do His Duty*. It seemed to Patrick Prentiss, when later he had occasion to read it, a small monument to human fatuousness. Like some latter-day Adam Smith, he described in glowing detail the bargains he had made and the economies he had effected by consolidating farms left vacant by the famine dead and by those driven overseas in the famine ships. He was able, so he boasted, to demand and collect the highest rents in Ireland. Those tenants unable to meet such rents were victims of the congenital mental and spiritual limitations of the aboriginal Irish—"drink, indolence, debt, and scheming." It was as though he had prepared for the Land League a text upon which they could draw for their sermons.

And throughout the entire course of the calamity which descended upon him, he could not fathom the malignity of either his enemies or his fate. He became a tireless letter writer to the press, moving slowly towards acceptance of a mythology which was taking shape: the aboriginal Irish, a compound of viciousness and sentimentality, steeped in whiskey and pickled in Romish superstition, had been a weapon placed in the hands of a renegade aristocrat, Parnell, a latter-day Catiline. Even so, all would not have been lost had it not been for Gladstone and Forster and the Liberals, who had entered into a secret alliance with Parnell, the end of which could only mean the destruction in Ireland of the English interest, the security of property and life, and the cause of civilisation itself. But at this point, Bence Jones faltered. Neither he nor the Tories of the Property Defence Association could fix upon a motive which might adequately explain Gladstone's sinister conduct.

It was one thing to talk over such matters after dinner in a London club, but poor Bence Jones was sending off his letters like battle despatches from the front line. On the day that Samuel Greene, his maimed and battered servant, was delivered to his door, he tended Greene's cuts as best he could, poured him a large tot of whiskey, and then locked himself in his office, surrounded by ledgers and estate maps, and wept with fury and grief.

More maps than were needed, for some were of merely historical significance, tracing the process of consolidation from before the famine. On the very earliest map, which hung above the broad, ledger-laden desk, the names of tenants were neatly inked in a minute hand, tenants and subtenants and sub-subtenants upon two acres—Sheerin, Tuomy, Collins, Donovan, Barry, Breen, Treacy. A roll call of the vanished, on coffin ships to America, or vanished into the workhouse maw, or into the mass famine grave beyond the chapel and up the hill. They had all of them, as explained in his *Life's Work*, "gone away of themselves," as, in a sense, they had. But that was not the way in which their disappearance was remembered in Clonakilty. Standing on a platform in Clonakilty, a Land League priest reminded his listeners that the demesne itself, visible beyond the marketplace, had once held "the homesteads of many a happy family who now are scattered to the ends of the earth." It had not been that way, Bence Jones knew, not that way at all. He was no exterminator; it was no crime, surely, to bring the land into full flower, the shabby cabins scourged away, doorways sunken into mud and muck, mounds of human excrement, and in single-roomed cabins, filthy, the hot breath of cow, sheep, pig. Happy families indeed! It was not the vanished dead who were now rising up against him, but those to whom he had leased out the consolidated farms, who had no cause for reproach, who had profited as he had, in proportion, from the smashed cabins of the vanished Breens and Treacys and the rest of them. No cause, and yet they it was who flocked to the square to hear Delaney of Kilpeder, the jumped-up assistant of Tully the gombeen man, who came one Sunday, taking off time from his persecution of poor George Wilcox, to recite yet another time the sorry calendar of grievances of the Clonakilty tenantry, dipping for cheap satirical effect into his copy of *Life's Work*, his own life only now beginning, building up a following, strengthening his legal practice, and poor Bence Jones, self-pity now his only consolatory dram, who had indeed by his reckoning of matters, given his life for Ireland, a life of work and prudence, reduced to bandaging the cuts of a servant and weeping behind a closed door, the tears coursing down parchment cheeks to a patriarchal white beard.

Patrick Prentiss, when he came to consider the triumph of the Land League in Kilpeder, that triumph which set the seal upon Robert Delaney's career—first Boycott far to the west in Mayo; then Bence Jones in Clonakilty to the south, in Cork but separated from Kilpeder by valleys, ranges of hills running east to west; and at last Kilpeder itself: three bell beats, each stronger than the last, the fall of feudalism in Ireland—Patrick Prentiss could not have known of Bence Jones's hour of angry, enraged tears. But he did have two accounts, one from Hugh MacMahon, one from Lionel Forrester, of the downfall of Sir George Wilcox, of the fall of Woodhaven House. Two parts of a world, spyglasses, acutely angled one from another, trained upon a single scene. And, of course, he had Woodhaven House itself to inspect, derelict now for some twenty years, the furnishings shipped off to the small, comfortable home in Cheltenham or else sold at auction, the stables empty and the stalls rotting, the ammoniac scent of horse piss long vanished, and the rooms of the house itself untroubled by memories. The Wilcoxes, George and Caroline, had vanished from the Irish earth.

H e wasn't the worst, old George Wilcox, not a certified exterminator like Bence Jones nor yet a foolish and choleric old soldier like Boycott. The Wilcoxes had always been generous towards the Kilpeder schoolchildren, and at the time when the Protestant church was refurbished, they saw to it that a stained-glass window would be placed in Saint Jarlath's, depicting, it is said, the arrival of Saint Columba on the island of Iona. They had come home from India burned the colour of old brick, the two of them, the back of Sir George's neck a crisscross of lines and gullies, like a map of the Punjab. I could well believe that in those sunbaked years their eyes of affectionate imagination were fixed upon the wet fields of Woodhaven House.

Sir George walked with a limp, nursing a game leg with a tall, intricately carved stick, its head a massive knob of ivory, and at cattle markets I would see him flourishing it at cattle dealers in mock-anger, and they, taking it for the friendly gesture that it was, their hats shoved back and sun beating upon freckled foreheads, would laugh him out of his pretend rage, and then the bargain struck with gobs of spit. Then he would move off through the fair, swinging the long stick to clear a path for himself, humming tunelessly, an Odysseus returned home. He wasn't the worst, old George Wilcox, and so I told Bob Delaney.

"Indeed no," Bob said, "far from the worst; but that agent of his is a right bastard and gave him the worst of advice. But that is not why the League went after him. The League went after him because he was vulnerable. Twas well known that bankers in three cities held his paper. The League knew that it could break him, and break him it did."

"The League," I said. "You have grown modest, Bob. You are the League in Kilpeder, yourself and Father Mullane and a few of the others."

"Very well, so. *We* broke him. Tis not sport, Hughie. Tis in earnest. There can no truce be made with the landlords until their power in the land is broken, and until we can show that to the people. And tis always best when you can yourself choose the battlefield, and not leave that privilege to the other fellow. What happened in Mayo was big; there were journalists from London and New York and Paris, and books are being written. It will happen here too. George Wilcox is against the wall, and there will be no letting up. Not for the sake of a few bits of stained glass that he bought for us from his rack rents. You know that yourself. Who was it wrote the description of Bat Colthurst's tenants homeless upon the roads of winter?"

"Sir George Wilcox is not Bat Colthurst," I said, although my heart was not in this minimal defence.

"Worse," Bob said, "worse than Colthurst. Colthurst had at least the decency to do his own dirty work and not hide behind an agent. Wilcox had his chance. Three times we offered to fix with him upon a fair rent, and three times he refused, and the squireens of the Property Defence Association pounded him on the back and called him a stout fellow. Let him look to them for his rents and his acres."

And so it was that Sir George and his good lady left Kilpeder much as Charles Boycott had left Ballinrobe, ignominiously, and with the stain of defeat upon them. It was raining, the thin cold rain of December, spattering upon the fallen leaves and the tangled, leafless hedgerows. There was a breakfast of sorts at Woodhaven House for the neighbouring gentry and the officers of the cavalry and infantry detachments, the magistrates, and the RIC inspector, the gentry arriving very early in the morning, each gig and carriage carrying a hamper of food, for of course there were no servants left at Woodhaven House—cook, parlourmaid, bootboy, swineherd, all had long since vanished upon orders from the League. Neither would any servants of the neighbouring gentry ride up the avenue to the house, and there would have been no tea at all had not Nessa Chute and two other ladies rolled up their sleeves and set to work. A melancholy breakfast it must have been, and unlike those years when the hunt met at Woodhaven, riding back from a kill across trampled fields, with the odours of ham and bacon rich upon the autumn air.

But to this day, and despite Bob's words, I cannot but feel that the Wilcoxes deserved from us a bit better than what we gave them: a journey through a landscape without figures to the railway station in Macroom. In Kilpeder itself, there was no one to be seen. They rode through the town in their small brougham, the reins in Sir George's fingers, and with a squad of cavalry before them and behind, caped against the rain, the capes sodden. The door of every shop and public house was shut against them, and even the doors of the Kilpeder Arms.

In my schoolhouse we could hear the jingle of their approach, and the hoofbeats upon the rainy road. The lads knew well what those sounds meant, and commenced looking at each other and at me and giggling. "Pay attention now to the task at hand," I said, "and not to idle noises in the road."

"Please, master," Pascal Quinlan said, a bold impudent boy, "may we not go to the windows for a glimpse of the military procession? Twould do no harm."

"You will do as you have been bid," I said, picking up my rattan and flexing it, "unless you have a wish to go home with your sore hands tucked under your oxters." They looked at me startled, and I was startled myself by the anger in my words and my tone.

"There is a history lesson for you, boys," I said. "The history of which we are ourselves a part. One of the evicting Englishmen is leaving us, for a time at least. And there is not one of you so young as not to know that the people of Kilpeder have risen up against him. It is in token of this that our Land League has given orders that we are to turn our faces away from him this morning. So much now for history, and get yourselves back to your sums."

Who, then, am I to protest that an insufficient charity was shown that morning when the Wilcoxes left us forever, their solicitors' letters coming to them in their small villa in the south of France to advise that not even an abatement would help them now, but they would do best to sell out. The London solicitors and their associates in Dublin managed all for them, and the local auctioneers. More than a year had passed by: it was March of 1882. Kilpeder made a treat of the auction, gentry and people crowded together in what had been the drawing room, bidding upon andirons and bulldogs of painted china and embroidered fire screens, but not the barbaric Hindu and Moslem shields and encrusted sword hilts and daggers: these had been shipped over to Cheltenham, which I saw in my imagination as a tidy, picture-postcard English village, bricked and ivied, where servants of the Empire came at last into safe haven.

I was told of the auction, I did not attend it. I had done my bit for the cause when I turned my back upon the old couple, and schooled my pupils to do the same. Neither did Bob Delaney attend it, for he was at that time in Kilmainham Gaol, with Parnell and the other leaders, upon charges of seditious utterance. No, the news of the auction came to me from Vincent Tully, who would never have dreamt of missing such an event, and who attended it with a few of his raffish friends.

"Melancholy, a melancholy afternoon it was," Vincent told me. We were walking out towards Clonbrony that Sunday. With Bob in prison, I lacked companionship, and especially I missed our Sunday excursions, when we would talk to each other of everything under the sun. And so Vincent came forward: he was in such matters as sensitive as any man I have known.

"But then most auctions are a bit melancholy," he said. "Not the large machinery and the traps and carts and wagons, and not the china services and crystalware that are bid for by the sharp lads from Dublin and Cork City. No, but the small, trifling thing that has a life within it, almost, and it is stripped away in a moment as the auctioneer's helper holds it up. 'Turn it all the way round there, Dinny, let the ladies get a look at it fore and aft: no cracks nor chips to be discerned, the finest specimen of a pressed-glass fruit bowl.' And the poor plump bowl is turned round by Dinny's lascivious hands like a naked Christian on the slave block of Constantinople.

"But I would not have missed it for worlds. I attended with Sylvester Prendergast from Millstreet and George Hoban, a decent Macroom Protestant. Things are awkward at the moment, you know, Hughie, for friendships between the two creeds—the two contending creeds, as old Father Murphy used call them in the days of my boyhood, before ever you saw Kilpeder. The two contending creeds. I used imagine them as pugilists, bare-knuckled boxers, the Protestant champion dapper and agile, and the Catholic champion looking a bit like Murphy himself, hairy of ear and nostril, but strong with the secret powers of the earth, and in his eye a fierce, invincible Catholic light.

"The two contending creeds. We were both of us on duty at Woodhaven House when poor Lady Wilcox's accumulation of bits and pieces went under the hammer. But now chaps that I have been riding with for ten years cut me dead, as though I were still a Fenian organiser, or perhaps deserved a cell in Kilmainham with Bob. To be sure, there are many Catholics to whom they give a clean bill of health—magistrates and solicitors. But not to the son of Dennis Tully. Ah, well. Mind you, I took good care not to bid upon anything. I had no wish to give them a weapon, chat at the club in the evening over a game of whist: 'Tully's son was there, snapping up this piece and that piece, no doubt for resale at profit in Cork City.' Ah, Hughie, in this world, the way of a usurer is hard; none hold us in affection, but where would they be without us?"

Where indeed? I had a mind to make response to him. But you could never be irritated with Vincent for long. He was a witty man, and could sketch a picture of himself so exact that he disarmed his critics in advance. A heavy bill of particulars could in those days be drawn against Vincent: that he was an idler and a snob, that there was something appalling in his detestation of a father who doted upon him, that he was a libertine and a seducer, that he wasted upon trivial pleasures a fine, sharp brain. But Vincent was always there before you, with a satirical picture of himself more ruthless than any that Spy or Ape might do for the pages of *Vanity Fair*.

In the event, he survived handily the brief coldness with which he was visited in the early and fiercest days of the Land League. By 'eighty-three or 'eighty-four, he was again in the graces of some of the county families, again out with the hunt, and one of the handful of Papists welcomed at the club. There were rumours, I heard them and so did Bob, that Vincent earned his passage into that world—a loan of the odd thousand pounds to this fellow or that one, and not at Dennis Tully's usurous rates, but help to a distressed gentleman; and it was said that when young fellows went off with Vincent for junkets to London or Paris, he was ready to take them to pleasurable addresses. Why the company of such fellows meant so much to him, I cannot say. Old Dennis, of course, was delighted—not by Vincent's idle, roistering way of life, but by his acceptance into good society; for Dennis was not an exquisite judge of such matters, and never saw that Vincent was on the edges only of that world, or if he was on occasion asked into the "best" houses, it was seldom for the "best" dinners or dances, and his wit and wild humour was his card of admission.

So it was, upon that brittle, cold winter Sunday, the two of us walking off the miles at a good clip, with Mary's lamb sandwiches in our pockets and pints awaiting us at Grennan's, that we celebrated, with Vincent's jests and my moralisings, the downfall of Woodhaven House, which was yet another bell note struck to mark the passing of the old order in Kilpeder. Bob, who had done as much as any man to accomplish that downfall, was not with us; but this was an occasion for concern and regret, rather than anxiety, for it was well known that the government, Gladstone and Forster, had clapped the Land League leaders into Kilmainham out of frustration and bafflement rather than any deep-set intention to seal them away. In two short years, Parnell and the Land League had made Ireland ungovernable, save upon terms acceptable to them. Small wonder that most of Ireland knew the street singers' ballad "The Uncrowned King of Ireland Lies in Kilmainham Gaol." The song laid on the misery and suffering with a trowel, such being the way of street ballads, but we all knew that the uncrowned king would not be lying there long, and that in the meantime conditions in the prison were not especially grim. Mr. Forster, however reluctantly, had seen to that, and I discovered the facts for myself when I went up to Dublin to visit Bob.

Not that Bob's arrest was anything to be taken lightly, for he was a ticket-of-leave man, who had served six months only of a four-year sentence. But in later years we would jest with him that he had furthered his career, by contriving to be one of the few local Land League agents to be "lifted" and carted off to Kilmainham, like Parnell and Dillon and the rest of them. For Bob went out of his way to court prosecution, although he chose his own time. The others were arrested in October of 1881, and Bob not until February of the following year. It is my own belief that this February arrest in deliberate violation of the law was arranged on that earlier trip up to Kilmainham that Bob and I took together, Bob representing to Parnell and the others that he wanted time to sort out the mess that Chute had created at Horseleap, but thereafter he would be available for martyrdom, and, indeed, anxious for it. In Land League days, a term in prison was a *sine qua non* for rising politicians.

He kept in after years, as a memento, the warrant under which he was arrested, as he sat in the taproom of the Kilpeder Arms, on the evening of February 4, 1882. In his final years, when he was making a bonfire of such papers, he was about to add the warrant to the fire, but I saved it. Its language is mild. "Robert Lacey Delaney is suspected of having, since the 15th day of December, 1881, been guilty of a crime punishable by law, that is to say: inciting other persons wrongfully and without legal authority to intimidate divers persons with a view to compel them to abstain from doing what they had a legal right to do, namely to apply to the land court under the provision of the Land Law (Ireland) Act 1881 to have a fair rent fixed to their holdings committed in the County of Cork and being the inciting to an act of intimidation and tending to interfere with the maintenance of Law and Order."

Inspector Pritchard had himself brought the warrant from Cork, and carried it into the Arms, with Sergeant Dineen from the barracks and one constable standing awkwardly just inside the door of the taproom. The warrant was served there and at that time by arrangement, and Bob, Vincent, and myself had come three quarters of an hour early, that we might have a parting glass.

"Will you not join us for a glass, Inspector?" Bob asked, as he took the warrant from him.

"I thank you, no," Pritchard said. "We should be setting out at once for Cork." But he rested his hands casually upon the back of a chair, while Bob took out his spectacles and read the warrant.

"This is very carelessly drawn up, Inspector, in my judgement. There should be language specifying that I compelled divers persons to refuse to *pay rents lawfully due by them*, or words to that effect."

"No doubt," Pritchard said, with a faint edge of smile, "but I have also no doubt that the language as it stands will serve its purpose."

"Nor have I," Bob said, "nor have I."

"Have you your manacles waiting outside," Vincent asked, "and your leg-irons?"

"No need," Pritchard said easily. "Mr. Delaney is a sensible man, a lawyer."

"Whoever drew up the warrant made a hames of it," Bob said, draining off his glass. "Was 'Buckshot' Forster the author, or some little fellow at the Castle?"

"Some little fellow at the Castle," Pritchard said, the smile broadening. "They will be the death of us."

"Some of us," Bob said.

A crowd had been gathering outside the Arms for the hour, and when we went outside, there were several hundred of them at least. When they saw Bob, they gave a roar. He and Pritchard went outside together, with Vincent and myself following, and Dineen and the constable drawing up the rear. A half dozen constables were waiting for us—not local lads, these ones, but mounted constables who had come up from Cork with Pritchard. They had not dismounted, and sat beside the jaunting car.

"Say the word, Bob," someone in the crowd shouted, and he was taken up by others. "Ye hoors," a fellow shouted, "you'll not lift Bob Delaney from the town of Kilpeder." "Up Parnell," someone shouted, and someone else shouted, "Up the Fenians." As though the notion had but now occurred to them, they moved to surround the cart and the constables, who looked stolidly down at them from their mounts, not moving a nervous hand towards baton or carbine. They looked, rather, towards Pritchard. "Down the exterminators," one voice shouted, and there were several more "Up Parnells," but "Up the Fenians" was winning the day, the most of the crowd shouting it, but not in unison. "Up the Fenians."

"There will be no foolishness, Mr. Delaney," Pritchard said. "I can rely upon you, I am certain."

"Ach, don't be too certain," Bob said. "I feel my Fenian blood rising up. Once a rebel, they say. We bloody well took the town of Kilpeder with fewer men than are now in the market square. I feel my Fenian blood commencing to boil, and tis the same, no doubt, with Tully and MacMahon here."

"Say the word, Bob," Vincent said, lighting his cigar.

"As I recall," Pritchard said, "you did not take the barracks."

"A telling point," Bob said, and held both hands above his head—for a moment, I thought, in mock-surrender to Pritchard but in fact to quiet the crowd—and held them there until there in fact was quiet.

"No, no, lads," he said. "We'll not play their game, but our own. The Chief is in Kilmainham Gaol, with the rest of our leaders, and Queen Victoria has sent me a copperplate invitation to join them there. It would be most impolite to refuse that hospitable lady. But do you know why she has been sending out these invitations, including the one that has plunged Michael Davitt back into the black, stinking hole of Portland Prison? It is because she thinks, and Holy Willie Gladstone thinks, and Buckshot Billie Forster thinks, that if the leaders are shut away, the Land League will thrash helplessly about, and then perish. That is their game. And here now is ours. Keep a firm grasp on your homesteads; that is the message which the Chief sent forth to us when we commenced our war for our land and country, and it is the message which he sends to us this day from Kilmainham."

"Bear in mind, Delaney," Pritchard said in a low voice, "you are here to be arrested, not to make a speech."

"Are you daft, man?" Bob said, in the same tone. "I cannot answer for these fellows should you muzzle me in the full spate of my oratory."

"Carry on, so, ye hoor," Pritchard said. He was well known to be blessed with a sense of humour, and he had need of it at the moment.

As Bob spoke, I stepped away from the portico of the Arms, and circled around the crowd, so that I could stand and look at the scene, which I kept telling myself was an historic one, and yet I could feel nothing of the proper emotions which are to be brought to historical occasions. A few years later, when Timothy Keegan published *Lights and Shadows of the Land War*, there, one among the copious imaginative though vilely drawn engravings—Parnell at Ennis, an eviction in winter, Boycott at bay—there was "The Arrest in Kilpeder of Robert Delaney," created for the edification of posterity: Bob addressing the crowd, whilst menacing constables point their carbines at him, and a version of Pritchard, complete with upturned moustaches, points at him an harassing forefinger. Bob has one arm and hand upflung, in an oratorical flourish.

And yet Bob's speech was not empty playacting, far from it. Across the countryside, in those months, all of the authority of the local League leaders was needed, lest the agitation crumble into anarchic violence. As it was, even in Kilpeder, we had our shots fired, and cattle maimed, and there were two deaths by violence, for which no indictments were ever brought in. "Who will take your place?" Parnell was asked, as he entered Kilmainham, and with a grim smile, he replied, "Captain Moonlight." He was not an actual person, the good captain, but a name printed in sprawling letters on the bottom of threats and warnings. "Grabbers Beware. Let John Fallin give up the farm which he has grabbed from his neighbour, lest harm befall himself and his sons. Signed, Captain Moonlight." Or "The Right Men of the Barony," or "The Sons of Captain Rock." But "Captain Moonlight" was the one that had become notorious, and Parnell, merely by speaking his name, half in threat, half in prophecy, had conjured up a century of terrors—bailiffs stripped naked and tumbled into pits of briars, proctors with cropped ears, burned barns and scorched crops, maimed cattle, landlords shot down from behind hedges. There was little that the Constabulary could do, and in wide stretches of the countryside—in our own Munster, but far worse in the starving and congested west—the only restraint was that exercised by the Land League itself, a most equivocal restraint, for the League had its rough customers in command in some baronies—Fenians and the sons of faction fighters. "Captain Moonlight," Parnell had said, and then stepped through the heavy stone entrance gates into Kilmainham.

But the government seemed to have a meagre grasp of life as it was lived in the "wild west," as it was called, and on October 20, 1881, the entire League was declared an illegal organization, and the necessary steps taken for its suppression. Across the length and breadth of the land, in the months that followed League presidents and secretaries and agents— "suspects," as they were called—were arrested, although only the most dangerous of them were actually imprisoned, and of these, a handful only were sent, as Bob was, to Kilmainham. And the effect of all this was indeed, as Parnell had predicted, to turn over the countryside to Captain Moonlight.

And, of course, the government and its police, in their "swoops" upon Land League agents, tossing them into gaol for the odd few weeks or months, did far more harm than good. On the twenty-second of February, the very month of Bob's arrest, a small landlord named Cotter, then in the eighty-second year of his life, and a bit off in his head by some accounts, was riding down to Kilpeder from his home in Macroom, accompanied by his elder son, a sprightly lad of sixty, and a grandson of forty, known locally and with good reason as Randy Cotter. Just before the road makes its slight rise before Kilpeder, they were set upon by a party of men with blackened faces, the one of them carrying a revolver, and the others staves, cudgels, and stones. The son died first, the revolver being fired into his face, and the old man was beaten to death.

Randy Cotter was then dragged down from the car, and killed in a slow, methodical manner. His screams were heard in two nearby farms, but few, of course, were so foolish even to consider coming to his help. His arms and legs were beaten into raw meat; then his breeches were drawn down to his bloody boots, and his organs of generation were hacked off. At some point in the process, he was murdered.

There, now, was Captain Moonlight at work, and he was a busy soul, lively in Connaught and Munster, and eastwards into Wexford and the midlands. And in this instance, one out of a hundred, which I specify only because it took place but a mile or two from my school, what principle of justice or tactics or simple vengeance was the good captain serving? Cotter was a landlord, but he was also, and recently, by way of being a tenant as well, for he had taken up two farms which marched beside his own lands, and he was thus a "grabber" and had been so declared in a placard affixed to his gate. That was his crime, and death for himself and his son and grandson was the punishment exacted for it. As for the special attentions which were bestowed upon Randy Cotter, rumours which spread rapidly from Macroom ascribed these to a brother bent upon avenging a young girl's dishonour. Which might well have been the case, a bargain vengeance, two crimes atoned for at once.

But there has always seemed to me something blacker and darker at work, a kind of primitive, tribal rage which ascribes to the masters of the land an absolute power in the most intimate as well as the most public parts of our lives, and for which none save the most primitive of retributions will suffice, the gelding knife and the bloody handful tossed into the roadway. At all odds, this piquant circumstance gave to the Cotter murder a celebrity all its own. Even without it, the nation was in no doubt that the countryside had indeed been handed over to Captain Moonlight, and that we were drifting towards the days of the Whiteboys and the rapparees.

It was in late April that I visited Bob in Kilmainham Gaol, going up to Dublin on the afternoon train, and booking a room for myself near the prison, an immense and notorious pile, with dark memories of the rebels who had been confined there in 'ninety-eight. It was to my considerable surprise and relief, therefore, that I discovered the chief "suspects" lodged, not perhaps in comfort, but certainly in circumstances not too far removed from it, wearing their own suits, and each two prisoners having their cell, with proper beds, and two chairs, and a table. They were given full access to such reading material as was sent to them, and the tables in most of the cells were piled high with books and journals and newspapers. Not to mention food. At first, Bob told me, there was an attempt made to restrict them to prison fare, and there was one hideous occasion when Parnell and Dillon, who prided themselves upon their skill in the practical concerns of life, had attempted to contrive a stew out of beef chunks and ship's biscuits and a watery vegetable soup, together with bits of boiled bacon which they had been saving for the purpose. The results were lamentable. But now the Ladies' Land League and similar organizations were attending to such matters, and prison fare was abundantly supplemented.

The finest cell was, of course, Parnell's, a large room, curtained, with barred windows looking out upon a courtyard which the suspects used as an exercise yard. It was in that cell, which served also as office, that Bob introduced me to Parnell. Dillon and Sexton were with him when Bob brought me in, and they all three of them greeted me most courteously. He—Parnell I mean, of course—was wearing heavy tweeds and a woollen cardigan and what looked to be a skullcap or fez, made of black, with a white design stitched into it. But this comical adornment took naught away from his appearance. He was as handsome a man as I have ever seen—tall and fine-boned with auburn beard and moustache, and searching eyes.

But there was little light to be brought into the room, too early yet for gaslight, and tall narrow windows, deep-sunk into heavy casements, looked out upon the cheerless, shadowed courtyard.

"You are no stranger to prison cells, Mr. MacMahon," Parnell said. "We all know of Clonbrony Wood. The felons of our land, is that how the song has it?"

"It is," I said, and exchanged a glance with Bob, for the Fenian imprisonments after the 'sixty-seven rising had few indeed of these present amenities. But Parnell took my point, and nodded briskly, as though settling a detail.

"Dillon here has known prison as you have known it," he said, "and Kenny has known it. But not now, not for the moment. Whatever may be Mr. Forster's view of the matter, or Mr. Harcourt's, Mr. Gladstone is a man of fine political instincts, and he is taking great care not to make caricature martyrs out of us, with broad-arrowed jackets and tin mugs of weak cocoa."

"I am unable to this day to take enjoyment from hot cocoa," I said, "nor from fried bread."

"Exciting days in Kilpeder, so we understand," Dillon said, a man handsome himself in his curious way, a Spanish way almost, sallow and long-bearded, with deep-set eyes.

"Troubled days," I said. "There is no law worth the mentioning. An ugly job of butchery on the Macroom road, and a grabber left for dead in a farm below Knockmany."

"A wretched business," Dillon said, speaking directly to Parnell. "A vile business."

"Yes," Parnell said calmly. "Yes."

There were times in the weeks and years to come when I was asked about that room, for of course it was made immortal not only in *Lights and Shadows* but in various patriotic publications, and William O'Brien printed a large engraving of it as a supplement to his *United Ireland*. It was duly hung in hundreds of parlours and public houses—"The Chief and the Leaders of Our People Hold Council in Their Prison Cell." Accurate enough, and I used often to study a copy, gaudily coloured, which hung behind the counter in Conefry's for a decade almost, gathering dust but the colours too violent to fade. History banished it, not time nor the scourings of sunlight. In ten years' time, the "leaders of our people" were at each other's throats, with Dillon leading the fight against Parnell.

But there I was, basking in my five minutes' worth of history, until Bob and I could decently slip away for a stroll in the courtyard, up and down, then this side to that side, then up and down again, a warder having escorted us there and standing now politely out of earshot, and a great greasy smile to show us that he was as good an Irishman as the next fellow, and jobs were not easily come by.

"A wretched business, Mr. Dillon calls it," I said. "Janey Mack! Do you know what they did to Randy Cotter?"

" 'Mutilated,' said the *Cork Examiner,*" Bob said.

"They hacked off his balls with a gelding knife," I said.

Bob stopped dead in his tracks and turned to face me. "Dear Jesus," he said.

"There you are," I said, "the code duello as practised by Captain Moonlight."

"Ah well," Bob said, "the Cotter farms were up the mountain, and his tenants ignorant Gaelic-speaking gobshites. And there was no girl safe from Randy Cotter, Gaelic or English, church or chapel."

"They are safe now," I said.

"I wonder," Bob said, "was it the entire man that they buried. That could have affected the number of mourners. There are a few lasses now virtuously wed who found him a man of parts."

"Nevertheless," I said, "tis back, bloody murder beyond there," and jerked my head towards the grey prison wall. Beyond it, the river flowed into the city from distant valleys and villages, the safe and tranquil villages of the Pale, Lucan and Chapelizod and the rest of them. But beyond the Liffey, beyond Dublin and Kildare and Meath, beyond the fat, grassy meadowlands of peace, lay mountains and gorges, the multitudes of farms and cabins, lights winking to each other after nightfall, a world of violence darkening towards the early nights of May.

"If they will have it so," Bob said, serious upon the instant. "We struck up the music and commenced the ball, but tis Government now must end the tune. Gladstone and Forster and Harcourt and company. We will come to terms, you know, Hughie. Parnell and Gladstone will."

I smiled at him, delighted by the confidence in his words, and he caught at once the meaning of the smile.

"Not Parnell and Delaney," he said. "I declare to Jesus, I have no notion why they sent me here, and not to Cork City or Clonmel or Maryborough with the other lads. I sit round the table and nod politely, and there is the beginning and end of my contribution. They are most decent about it, Parnell and Dillon and them all. 'Would you concur in that, Mr. Delaney?' Dillon will ask, with his grave, hidalgo courtesy. 'I would, Mr. Dillon,' I reply. And I do."

"Nevertheless," I said.

"You are all well at home?" he said. "Agnes writes regularly to me, with messages from Conor scrawled across the sheet. And Vincent has a fine, carefree pen."

"All well, Bob," I said. "You are missed, of course."

"Not for long, please God," he said lightly. "There is a treaty, as you might call it, in the works. We will all of us be in our native counties before long. This is between the two of us, Hughie," he said, in a low voice but conversational manner, smiling towards the warder, who politely held to his far corner, still with his faint, affable smile.

"By God, that is fine news, Hughie," I said. "That is the best news ever."

"It will be hailed so," Bob said. "I have no doubt that William O'Brien will contrive an entire new type font for it. GREAT VICTORY AGAINST THE ENGLISH FOE. BRIGHTEST DAY SINCE BEN-BURB." He shrugged and looked away from me. "Pay no attention to that, Hughie. It will be a good day for the tenant farmers, and they have long been in need of one. The violence will quieten down for a while. Randy Cotter did not make his sacrifice in vain."

It was there, in the grey, sunless exercise yard of Kilmainham that I first heard of what was to be called the Kilmainham Treaty, and which has been a bone of argument from that day to this. Had I but known what I was hearing, for that matter, or had Bob chosen to speak more bluntly, then I might have had a glimpse for a moment at the real workings of history, behind the bright tapestries and Christmas pantomimes. But instead, I thought only that Bob had fine news, and that I was privileged to be its early auditor.

It was grey evening when I left him that day, a yellowish fog coming in from the sea to settle upon the city of rose-red brick and cool, cut stone. When I came to the river, I walked eastwards along the quays, crossing over at the Metal Bridge. I paused at its arched center, and looked at the Four Courts to my one hand and the Custom House to my other, great confident, elaborate structures, arrogant and assertive, with the swaggering authority of the old century in them, when the power of the old order was intact, asserting itself in such toplofty architecture. However comfortable may have been the circumstances of the state prisoners, as they were termed, Kilmainham bore the odour of every prison house, a stench, a smell compounded of sweat and cabbage and damp stone, mud-caked exercise yard, slop buckets, the rancid misery of those hidden away in windowless cells. Far better the fog-wisped air.

Ensnared as always by history, I wandered through the streets and laneways which stretched out, a web, north of the river, taking a careless, winding route back to my lodging house, which I was in no great hurry to reach, a glum establishment presided over by a vast, aproned widow, who spoke with so thick a Dublin accent that I could barely understand her. Save for Sackville Street itself, fashion had long since moved south of the Liffey, and the streets to the north, which in the earlier century had been scrubbed and polished, were tarnished enough now at their best, and at their worst, discoverable without warning, upon turning a corner, as ugly and impoverished as any in Europe, the fanlights of what had once been the town houses of barons and parliamentary orators smashed in, children spilling out of the laneways, unwashed and, by the look of many of them, ill fed. A shadowy, dead city lay behind that poverty: sedan chairs, ladies in taffeta, duellists, gamblers, candle-lit balls in what now were slums. It was scripture among us Fenians that all had been changed, curdled, shrivelled, when Ireland lost her parliament, a nation reduced to a province, her noble parliament house transformed into a bank. We were right, no doubt. Without a parliament to attend, the lords and their hired hacks and delegates, their attorneys and conveyancers, had no longer reason to visit the handsome city that they had reared up astride the Liffey. But as one walks the streets of modern Dublin, that answer seems too pat. The grit and stench of the poverty is too actual for any of history's notions.

I was pleased enough, with night fast approaching, to turn away from the century's ruin, and seek out the drab decency of my Dorset Street lodging. It was to celebrate this that I allowed myself to be drawn to a brightly lit public house whose name I can yet remember, Patrick Hanratty, the name illuminated in the dusk by flickering gas jets. There was both a saloon and a public bar, and I went, of course, through the door which led into the former of these. I had had enough of poverty. There was carpeting upon the floor, and reproductions of paintings set in ornate frames, a Highland stag at bay upon a mountaintop and another of Strongbow's wedding to Aoife, MacMurrough's daughter, a riot of historical improbabilities, with armoured Norman knights and saffron-kilted Gaelic chieftains. There was a scattering of customers, sitting in quiet twosomes or on their own, chatting or reading the evening papers, at tables along the wall below the frosted windows, or else at the bar, clerks by the look of them or petty officials, perhaps a schoolmaster or two, like myself. I took my place at the bar and asked the curate for a hot whiskey, which he presented to me almost at once, for there was water at the boil against the evening chill.

I exchanged desultory meteorological speculations with the fellow nearest me, but although not rude at all he seemed more interested in his ham sandwich and his pint of porter, and I was at liberty to inspect the shop. There is a curious alliance between taciturnity and middle-class respectability, and although two fellows at a table were in spirited controversy, the other customers were either on their own or conversing in low tones that were muffled by heavy drapes, and by the thick, liver-coloured carpeting. But in the public bar it was otherwise, and not only did their voices come to me, cheerful with raillery or argument, but the long mirror behind the bar, projecting slightly, gave me a full view of it.

It was a large, plain barn of a room, uncarpeted of course, and with wide, dark flooring whose varnish was peeled in places, and its walls heavy with prints tacked to the walls or else glassed into thin frames of oak. It was still a bit early in the evening for steady artisans, but there were a number of them, all the same, and casual labourers, with kerchiefs knotted about their throats and shapeless caps. The air was heavy with smoke.

If I remember that public bar in such detail, it is with cause, for it is there, after fifteen years, that I again saw Ned Nolan.

At the angle where the counter met the wall, there was a snug, a small private room, as it were, with its own door, but with walls that came no higher than the shoulder. It was private enough from the bar, but the mirror which stretched across the lounge, behind the counter, was canted at just the angle to give me an imperfect view of a half dozen men sitting three on either side of a table, with glasses before them. He was seated in the middle of the three men facing me, and the talk was between himself and a man whose back was to me. It was as though Ned was putting questions, brief ones, and the other fellow was answering at length. The others, at least the two flanking Ned, were silent, their eyes first upon Ned and then upon the other lad as he made his responses.

I say Ned, but at first, of course, I did not recognise him. It is a long time, fifteen years, and much had happened. I recognised the face as one like his, an extraordinary face, rawboned, the cheekbones high and prominent, the eyes deep-set and shielded by heavy dark brows. But he was wearing thick moustaches now, the ends down-turning. His coat was dark; his hands were resting on the table, motionless, and his watchful eyes were fixed upon the speaker. He is very much like Ned, I thought, as Ned must be, and I thought that it would make a story to bring home to Mary and to Vincent, the tricks of the mind: that I had visited Bob, and so imagined that I had seen Ned, two hours later, in a Dorset Street public house.

And at that moment, as though ordained, he chanced to look up, and he gave a start, for he was staring at me in the mirror; our eyes were locked, and we knew each other. It was a moment or minute, measureless, and then he shook his head and returned to his companions; but I had read him aright, and sat where I was, ordering for myself another hot whiskey.

He came to me a full ten minutes later, not using the connecting door, but going out into the roadway and then in through the saloon, and he did not sit on the stool beside me, but stood. I saw him check the mirror, as though to make certain that he was blocking me from the view of his companions, or else blocking them from my further inspection.

"Can we meet, Ned?" I asked, and he nodded, as though pleased that I had cut at once to the point.

"We can, of course," Ned said. "Two old friends cast up together in the streets of a big city. Hugh MacMahon and Edward Lacey." There was more Yank in his speech than there had been, the vowels levelled flat.

"But not now?" I said as a question. "You are with your friends. You have not time for a short one on your own?"

"With my friends, yes," Ned said. "I would not want them to be restless. There is a pleasant morning walk I sometimes take. In the south of the city, along the towpaths of the canal. Do you know the bridge across the canal at Mount Street?"

"I can find it," I said.

"An early walk," he said. "Half-nine?"

"Half-nine," I said. "Will you bring your friends?"

He had a rare smile. I remembered it from the old days. "Mary is well?" he asked. "I have all your Christmas letters. I keep them. They are back—where I am now." He jerked his head towards what may have been the direction of the Atlantic and the broad continent at its far shore.

"She is well," I said, "and speaks of you often. We all do. Bob is in Kilmainham, you must know of that. Tis why I am here in Dublin."

"How could I not know it?" he said. "The papers are giving great play to the patriots in Kilmainham—Parnell and Bob and the rest of them." He spoke with a flatness that lay on the far side of sarcasm, which I would not have detected save for the word *patriots*.

He picked up my glass, and sipped the cooling, clove-scented whiskey.

"Mount Street Bridge," I said, and he nodded. "Good evening to you, Mr. Lacey," I said, and he smiled a second time. Beneath the rough, gold prospector's moustache, his teeth were white and large.

It was but the year before that Lord Ardilaun had furnished forth Saint Stephen's Green, and presented it with his compliments to the people of Dublin, but I had not yet had occasion to inspect it. It was a most handsome gift, and all the papers had carried illustrations, the *Cork Examiner* being pointed in expressing the hope that one of our own local brewers or distillers might be tempted to follow suit. But then, the Guinnesses, with their titles and peerages, were a law unto themselves. Now, in these latter days, they have also provided, far from Stephen's Green, beside slums in the Liberties, handsome homes for indigent old men reduced to poverty by a lifelong thirst for Guinness, thus proving the circularity of human existence. But this is ungenerous of me, for the Green, as I discovered that next morning as I walked towards the Grand Canal, is comely and benign, with walks and lakes and sentimental bridges, shaped with elegance and style.

The Green lay to my right hand, and on my left handsome town houses and the clubs of the gentry and the Shelbourne Hotel, scenes as far removed as may be from the slums which lay a mile away or less in any direction. As I walked past, a carriage pulled away from the hotel, its seats loaded with young fellows out upon some morning's sport or diversion, grey coats or coats of fine rich black buttoned against the morning's chill, their faces shining from a full breakfast, joking with one another and shouting to the coachman. Off to the mountains, perhaps, for it is Dublin's finest feature that her mountains lie so close at hand, reproof and invitation.

Ned was waiting for me, by the elegant small bridge that arches over the canal at Mount Street. There was water traffic, despite the earliness of the hour, barges from as far away as Athy, and with the feel and look to them of the countryside through which they had passed, messengers to the city of wide, green pasturelands, dark, treeless hills, deep glens. He stood upon the bridge, his folded arms upon it, but he had seen me coming, and his head was turned towards me. When I reached the towpath, he walked down to meet me, and put his arm awkwardly across my shoulder. I minded, as though the years had not separated us, how hard it had been for him to make such gestures, to touch a friend.

"We can walk down along the path towards Rathmines," he said, "and then up a ways into Rathmines village. They have a great barracks there, with the back of it against the canal. Portobello Barracks."

"Are you long over here?" I asked.

"Two weeks," he said. "No, closer to three. But mind you, Hugh, I am not here at all. I may be doing you no favour by putting you in my company."

"I would risk a good deal, Ned," I said, "for the chance of a chat with you. You are greatly missed by us—Mary and myself, and Vincent, and Bob."

"Married—the pack of you," he said, in what was for him a bantering voice, a voice warmed by affection but not quite at ease, "yourself, and Vincent and Bob."

"You have not read my letters with care," I said. "Vincent is as ever he was, a handsome wild rogue of an unmarried man, the terror of fathers and a few husbands."

We had begun to walk, and Ned scuffed his boot against close-packed earth.

"Bob is married," he said, "and married well. Every town lad's hope, to marry the shop."

"The shop is in his past," I said, "although he still acts for the old man as solicitor."

"That should occupy his days," Ned said. "There was a lad came over last year from Macroom and lives now in New Jersey. He tells us that old Tully has become a man of property, the odd farm here and there. There must be paper work enough in that for Bob."

"It is not paper work for Dennis Tully that has put him in Kilmainham Gaol," I said.

"The Land League, the Land League and the bloody New Departure, as they call it. Are you with them in that, Hughie? Green bunting and processions and all that?"

"I am with an old friend," I said to him, "on a fine day in early spring, and I was yesterday with an old friend."

He gave me a quick look, and then he nodded. "Fair enough. And Mary," he said, "and the lads?"

"You would not look for better," I said. "Brian is a practical sort of little fellow; there is the makings of an engineer in him or the like. But Tom, now, Tom is the lad for reading. There is a schoolmaster in him at the least, but I have loftier thoughts for him. The university."

"You wrote me that," Ned said. "That you had named him Thomas."

"That I had named him Thomas Justin MacMahon. After his great-uncle, Thomas Justin Nolan. After your father."

"Yes," Ned said.

At Baggot Street there was a bridge and another at Leeson Street. They sparkled in the morning light, and there was to the scene an air of briskness, the lock tenders shouting to the bargees, and across each of the bridges a stream of morning venturers into the city, in gigs a few of them and mounted a few, but walking, the most of them, tradesmen and artisans alike. In the distance, the Dublin hills lay in their haze, and closer at hand, towards which we walked, the great dome of the church in Rathmines, a Protestant township as such matters go, but bullied by the great Catholic dome.

"Ontario Terrace," Ned said to me, with a jerk of the head. "Where John Mitchel lived."

"I declare to Jesus, you are a wonder, Ned. I have lived all my life in this country, and I had no notion where John Mitchel lived."

"He lived for a time there," Ned said, "before they tossed him aboard ship, and carried him off to the prison colony in Van Diemen's Land."

"A hard man," I said. "Van Diemen's Land could not hold him." Cut from the same mould, the two of them, Mitchel and Ned. Smith O'Brien and Ned's father and the rest of them had been preaching a gentlemanly protest in 'forty-eight, but Mitchel had been for hard war, tooth and nail, sharpened pikes and vitriol flung from city rooftops.

"I have maps, Hughie," Ned said, speaking with a sudden, self-mocking urgency, "a Saratoga trunk full of them, and albums of pictures, photographs and all the rest of it, like some bloody Yank with an Irish grandmother."

"Two Irish grandmothers," I said, "and one of them my own."

Suddenly, Ned laughed, and touched his hand to my elbow, a gesture more natural in its feel than his earlier one.

"One night," he said, "I was talking to a Clan na Gael fellow in a pub—'saloons' they call them over there—in Scranton, Pennsylvania. A Yank born and bred, but fierce Clan na Gael, the son of a Leitrim man turfed out in black 'forty-seven, in the famine year. Scranton is anthracite country, Molly Maguire country, a rough lot. 'Tell me,' he says, 'what is Dublin like?' 'I was there but a day or two,' I said, 'in 'sixty-seven, on my way from London to Cork. A fine great city, with the most splendid of the world's parks, it is said—the Phoenix Park—and handsome public buildings, elegant squares, a river flowing through the midst of the city.' 'To hell with that,' he says, 'how is it for ambushes?' "

I burst out into laughter, and the two of us walked along in companionable silence, with Ned smiling at my laughter; but behind all that, I was thinking of how little there was that I knew of Ned's life. I conjured up a mining town, the air gritty with flecks of black, tunnels blasted through mountains, faces beneath flickering kerosene, they call it, black as Hottentots drinking away in saloons the moneys doled out to them by straw bosses, Irish men and Polish men and men from stretches of Europe that had no proper name. Ned drinking there, and why? Did the organization send him there or was he earning his keep? But at what? For he had no skill at the dirty craft, but only, so far as his few letters told us, a stretch on the ferryboats, and a long spell with Tom Bonner on the brickyards up the Hudson River, and a year or two in the printing shop of a newspaper in Brooklyn.

We had come by now to the Portobello Bridge, where we could turn to our left into Rathmines; but Ned paused, and pointed ahead. "Up ahead there, now," he said, "if you will take instruction from my trunkful of maps, is Harold's Cross, and it is there that they caught poor Emmet."

"Just there?" I said. "Ahead of us?"

"Up the Harold's Cross road a short distance," he said. "The house is no longer there. But Major Sirr had a guard posted at the bridge just ahead of us."

In 1803. For Ned, 1882, and the 1840s, when John Mitchel was living in Ontario Terrace, and 1803, when Sirr and his yeomen came for poor Emmet, shopped by informers, young hero down from the mountains, doomed rebel on the run—for Ned all this was now, not the past, not the present, but now, the timeless life of Ireland: ugly truth, splendid legend, whatever.

"Poor Emmet," I said, and meant it. So pure and simple an image, and so far back into our past, a century almost, a coloured engraving known to all of us from childhood: Emmet in the dock, towering above the tall bench, Norbury the bullying judge, but Emmet unafraid. Three generations knew his words. "Let no man write my epitaph; for as no man who knows my motives dares now vindicate them, let not prejudice or ignorance asperse them." Romance brought him down into the city from hillside safety: Sarah Curran, a cameo, cut into ivory, high forehead and small shapely chin in profile; she dwelt in a Rathfarnham villa, gardens and an orchard, white petals, rose-tipped. He was hanged in Thomas Street on an improvised gallows, planks laid across barrels, two posts and a beam. "This is the head of a traitor, Robert Emmet," the headsman said. Dogs lapped at the blood, but soldiers, Highlanders, drove them away.

"That bastard MacNally," I said, "defending him in court by day, and a government informer by night, so much paid out to him per month."

We turned into the Rathmines road, on one side of us the immense Catholic church, not there in Emmet's day, before emancipation. Across the road, soldiers in garrison undress strolled towards a laneway.

"There is no one prescribed form of treason," Ned said. "They come in all shapes and sizes and colours. MacNally was a young barrister struggling in dark and evil days, and perhaps with a wife and young ones to feed. I read somewhere that he had a lovely tenor voice."

"He betrayed a trust," I said, "the sacred trust between a man on trial and his counsel." Mild sunlight graced the laughing soldiers, a lance corporal one of them. "Dante has such lads blistering their arses on hell's hottest bricks."

I had refused Ned's heavy irony, and so he swung upon me. "He did worse," he said. "He betrayed his oath. He took the oath of the Society of United Irishmen, and he betrayed his oath. Not at the beginning, they say. He drifted into treachery."

A rose-red village, Rathmines, no older than our present time: handsome small houses for the middle classes, parlours and return rooms, and a small dank room for respectability's one essential badge, a skivvy, country girl run off her feet, fires lit with first morning blush.

We walked towards the village, towards distant mountains. I felt him beside me, after the years, hardened and yet unchanged, his secrets so long kept that he carried them with ease, negligence almost, a veteran's knapsack.

Perhaps he was right about MacNally, who knows? Treachery blossomed in those days, like the roses in Sarah Curran's Rathfarnham garden, at the far end of the road from Harold's Cross, between ourselves and the mountains we faced.

Nervous, worried, terrified perhaps. Who could blame him? With the net closing in on all the 'ninety-eight men, and himself a marked man, swaggering barrister toasting the Rights of Man in taverns on the Dodder, in the inglenook, a police spy, one of Higgins's men, Major Sirr's men. And afterwards, a quiet little chat in Dublin Castle with Mr. Secretary Cooke.

It had little to do with us, or should have had, strolling in the spanking new village. "They rule us yet," Ned said, "as they have done for centuries. Gladstone and bloody Mr. Buckshot Forster. It serves the purpose of this new lot, Parnell and his crowd, to sit out a few weeks in the comfort of Kilmainham, but in the heel of the hunt, they will cut their deal with Queen Victoria. Queen Victoria and bloody Mr. Buckshot Forster."

"As I understand matters," I said, "which is not very well at all, there is more to it than Parnell and his crowd, as you call them, meaning Bob Delaney amongst others. And if they have fought their way through to a bill that will give the people a hold upon their acres and a weapon against the landlords, then more power to their arm.".

"A bill," Ned said, with his quiet contempt, "and a nice little coercion bill to go along with it—a carrot and stick for nice little Paddies."

"Devoy is with them," I said, stung by his tone. "What is being done now was hammered out in New York by Michael Davitt and John Devoy. Everyone knows that—it has been in every newspaper, green or orange. The organization stands behind it."

He stopped upon the instant and turned to face me. He was furious,

I could tell, but his face was the mask that I remembered. Sioux or Comanche.

"Devoy is not the organization," he said, "no more than O'Donovan Rossa is, but at least Rossa acts. He has a skirmishing fund and he uses it, by God. Davitt and Devoy went meek as mice to the organization to seek permission for what they are about, and they were turned down flat. The organization is not a transacting body. We do not transact business with anyone. We make no arrangements."

"Ah well," I said. "Anything for a quiet life."

"You are a droll fellow, Hughie," he said, smiling in spite of himself. "It must be the MacMahon blood."

And so we spent the pleasant morning, walking back at last to the Merrion Row side of the Green, where we parted company. I remember the day, and I remember thinking afterwards, Was it by chance only that Ned had chosen a walk for us in the south side of the city, with a route that carried us back through elegant and comely squares, Merrion and Fitzwilliam, nursemaids with their charges, gentlemen and ladies of fashion, rather than across the river and into the Phoenix Park, a chosen pleasure ground for strolling friends? We said good-bye to each other, standing there at the turning, and I knew that there was little point in asking whether we would be seeing each other again soon, or if he might be drifting down to Kilpeder, nor indeed how long would he be staying in the city.

Again and again, in the weeks and then months and years, and indeed, until this present day, I have thought of Ned Nolan standing there as I turned to wave a good-bye to him, and of the Phoenix Park as I remember it, and of Bob's return home a week later, discharged from Kilmainham with the other prisoners. Ned stands, and stands unfairly perhaps—I would wish it so—at the heart of that jumble of memories, in the dust-flecked light of a Dublin noontime.

It was on the second of May that the prisoners were released, and the newspapers were, of course, filled with the news of it, heralding it, in accordance with their political predilections, as a great victory for the land and people of Ireland, or else as a craven surrender by Gladstone and his government to the band of agrarian arsonists and torturers who followed yelping at the heels of the demented aristocrat who led them. And that afternoon, Gladstone announced in the House of Commons that miserable, confused, infuriated old Buckshot Forster, the chief secretary for Ireland, had resigned in protest. By Thursday, the fourth, Parnell himself, and Dillon and O'Kelly with him, were back in their own places in the Commons, and Lord Frederick Cavendish had been announced as

Forster's successor. On Saturday, the sixth, Davitt was released from Portland, and Parnell and Dillon were at the gaolhouse gate, waiting for him. Together, they set off by train for London.

It was on the night before that Bob set out for Kilpeder from Dublin, taking the evening train, and it was on that same night that Lord Frederick travelled with Lord Spencer, the new viceroy, to Ireland. The papers would within hours be filled with his every motion, and they are burned into my mind, as into the minds of thousands in Ireland and in England. He caught the 8:20 boat train to Holyhead, and the next morning he was on the job at Dublin Castle, learning his duties from Burke, the under-secretary.

But in Kilpeder that Friday night, there was thought but for two people, Bob Delaney the one of them, and the other one Charles Stewart Parnell; and now it was that it became throughout Ireland a commonplace to speak of Parnell as the King or the Uncrowned King, the latter with a finer ring to it, a faint Jacobite romance. Father Mullane, who had been acting as unofficial agent for the League in Bob's absence, had arranged a small festivity in the parish hall, and the brass band was outside it, playing "A Nation Once Again" and "The West's Awake."

"We have beaten them, lads," Father Mullane said, a fine, rosy-faced curate. "The plain people of Ireland have beaten them. The Land League has beaten them. The felons of Kilmainham Gaol and Portland Prison have beaten them. And Bob Delaney of Kilpeder has beaten them."

"Bob Delaney of Clonbrony Wood, you mean, Father," someone shouted, and Mullane, although discreetly he said nothing, smiled demurely. Bob was all for Mary and Vincent and myself walking up together with himself and Agnes for a celebratory jar at his house, but Agnes would not hear of it, a prisoner discharged from prison, and then with two days' business behind him at League Headquarters in Dublin, and then the journey home to Kilpeder. She was proud of him, you could see that plainly, and had rightly dressed as for a celebratory occasion, in grey, and with a hat trimmed with grey feathers. She kept a forearm resting lightly upon his shoulder. And why should she not have been proud, for the shouts from the crowd had been no better or worse than the fact: we had by God beaten them, and the Land Bill hammered out in all of its details, and Buckshot Forster sent back home with his tail between his legs. Oh, there were signs, to be sure, of adjustments that need be made, for in Mayo a crowd delirious with excitement had rioted, and a nervous constabulary had fired into them, killing two boys, and some men wounded and a woman. Lord Ashton, riding home from a friend's in his carriage, was fired at, and although the assassins missed him, his wife was shot dead.

"A week," Bob said to Vincent and myself when we had a moment alone in a corner of the hall, above our heads bunting emerald and gilt. "A week to get the reins back firmly in our hands. Not all agents of the League are as pacific as the good father here. But we can whip them into shape. We've won, lads." Suddenly he laughed. "We are not used to winning, lads. We will not know how to behave."

Later, with Mary and myself alone in our kitchen, and the water on the hob for tea, I stood beside the window, looking out into the dark, making out, if barely by faint moon, the branched apple tree, its young leaves invisible.

"I mind once," Mary said, "when you stood there, and I here, by the morning fire, before you set forth to Clonbrony Wood."

"To Knockmany wasteland," I said, "and thence back into the town. The bold Fenian men of Kilpeder. Clonbrony was an afterthought, you might say."

"'Tis Clonbrony that is remembered in the ballad," she said.

"It would be," I said. "Bob has the right of it. We are not used to winning. We will not know how to behave."

Oh my name it is Joe Brady and I'm called the Fenian blade.
From the chapel in North Anne Street I set forth one pleasant day,
To strike down a cruel tyrant in the Phoenix Park so gay.

It was Father Mullane himself who brought the news of it to me, so agitated in speech and appearance that I could make out no more from him than a jumble of words, of which most proved right, but some of them wild tangles of speculation. It was to be that way for all of us for days. I spoke a word to Mary, leaving her puzzled and frightened, and walked down with Mullane to Bob's office. Dennis Mullane was a head shorter than myself—he still is, poor man, in a home now for retired priests in Greystones to the south of Dublin—but he did not look up towards me as we walked along, as was his custom, but spoke straight into the air, the rising wind from the hills. "Slaughtered," he said, "cut down, the lot of them, chopped to pieces with knives, and their throats slashed with baling hooks. The bloody Fenians," he said, "the bloody Fenian murderers." Then he heard what he had said, and to whom, and he stopped short, and put a hand on my arm. "God forgive me, Hugh. I was not thinking. This has naught to do with you or with Bob or with any of the lads from those days. Dear God, what news to come to us on the Lord's day."

"Who can say?" I said. "In God's name, what has happened?"

We had reached the corner of the market square, and it in its morning light, habitual and flat, shops and obelisk, and falcon-guarded gates, prim-spired church. In the direction against which we would in a moment set our faces lay the Macroom road, Saint Jarlath's, the constabulary barracks.

The news must have come over the wire to the sergeant. I glanced up for a moment at the wires, strung out their mile upon mile between ourselves and Dublin, carrying every day the news of journeys delayed and babies born and decisions to return home from Australia, and now this.

Bob was standing by the window of his office and saw us hurrying towards him, and nodded but did not move away. His hands, as I could see, were buried in his pockets. His clerk was in the front office with him, and three or four of the unpaid League organisers, and Vincent, and, of all unlikely people, old Tully, Dennis himself, in his salt-and-pepper suit, the wen or carbuncle or whatever it was on the side of his bald head glowing livid.

"There you are," old Tully shouted at me, his face screwed up, and in his tones the whine of repetition, as if he had begun the day with Vincent and then continued the shouting at Bob. "There are the lot you cast yourselves with in the golden days of your youth. Butchers. Butchers like Dowling in the shop with blood on his apron and offal clinging to his boots."

"Dear Jesus, Father," Vincent shouted, with an anger he had often felt but that I had never heard him express with such vehemence, "will you give over? Be quiet for a bit, or get out. Go back home or to the shop."

I walked over to Bob.

"The Chief Secretary has been butchered," he said, "and Burke along with him. Yesterday evening. They finished work in the Castle, the two of them, and strolled across the Liffey and into the park. On their ways home, I would think. A gang was waiting for them there and killed them. 'Butchered' is the word for it, right enough. The first wire that came in to the barracks said that the Viceroy was done as well—Spencer. But there is no truth to that. This is not the end of matters. The damned thing was planned, and planned well."

"He cannot be," I said stupidly. For so long, "Chief Secretary" and "Buckshot Forster" had been names for the one man.

"Cavendish," Bob said. "Think a bit, Hughie, for God's sake. Cavendish. Lord Frederick Cavendish."

"He is not here yet."

"He is here right enough," Bob said. "What is left of him. He caught the boat train Friday night, and arrived here just in time to be murdered."

"They meant Forster, surely," I said. "If the thing was well planned, it was as an attack upon Forster. These things must take time to plan and prepare, surely."

"They planned for Forster," Bob said. "No doubt of that. But they knew that they were getting the new man. Gladstone announced the resignation almost a week ago." He gave a bark of a laugh. "They let us out of Kilmainham just in time for us to kill Cavendish and Burke."

"Bob!" I cried. "This is not matter for your humour!"

"Humour, is it?" he said bleakly. "There were those of us there in Kilmainham who have served terms in prison for crimes of violence. Myself among them, you may recall. And the rhetoric that we have been pouring out, the lot of us, to ginger up the League has been bloody-minded stuff, some of it."

"There is a far cry from that to this," I said, "from fiery words on a platform to butchery in the Phoenix Park."

"What difference does it make, Hughie?" he said with impatience. "You are talking like some bloody moral theologian up in Maynooth. What matters is that we will be tarred with the brush, there will be no escaping it. Not even the Chief—the *Times* and *Punch* will have a field day with it. You have seen the pages they give to us in *Punch,* the Chief unctuous and parliamentarian, all Savile Row and Cambridge, and behind his coattails, the lot of us, with monkey jaws and grins, clutching revolvers and knives. Knives, mind you; twill be our image from this day forth."

I had never seen him so badly shaken, not at Clonbrony nor in the hours after it.

"Let them, Bob," I said. "Let them say what they will. Tis to Ireland that you are answerable and not to England or to its House of Commons. Mr. Parnell has said that often and often."

"Saying things costs nothing," Bob said. "It is the fact of the matter that we could not have got moving if we had not won the Church around to us. And we could not have won the Land Bill without Gladstone and his lot to back us up. There are the facts behind the speechmaking. How do you suppose Mr. Noble Christian Gladstone is feeling this fine Sunday? My God, Cavendish was some kind of kinsman of his. A nephew by marriage, or something of that sort."

A week later, a week later to the day, Mass behind us, Bob and I took our Sunday stroll along leafy lanes, towards the hills.

By this time, a bit more was known, by us and by the world. Parnell and Dillon had issued their denunciations of the deed, and so, for that matter, had the Supreme Council of the organization, and Devoy off in America. William O'Brien had issued his cry of horror in the *United Ireland* itself, black-bordered. All of the newspapers, not those in London and Dublin and New York alone, but the newspapers of the world, had issued their maps of central Dublin, for all the world like something out of Creasy's *Fifteen Decisive Battles,* the Castle and the Liffey, the park with its entrance gate and broad avenue running past the viceregal lodge, and the Polo Grounds marked out; for as everyone now knew, it was on the road, beside the Polo Grounds, that the thing had taken place. As Vincent had said, "At last we have made our mark in the world." But even Vincent was shaken: it was a curious response, affecting each man differently, but curious in its depth, as though at some outrage so enormous as to have no name, as though the crime statistics of the west and south— murder included with them, of course—had not been rising week by week through 'eighty and 'eighty-one and on into 'eighty-two. But this was different.

We knew now that they called themselves the Invincibles. The Irish National Invincibles. They had left their card, black-bordered, at the offices of the newspapers.

We knew also, the country knew, with that hallucinatory exactness with which an event can be known at which few were present—but there was in truth a crowd there, at the Polo Grounds, watching the match, and few of them heard more than shouts, a scuffle—what had happened. The very day of his arrival, that Saturday, poor Cavendish had set about learning his craft in that warren of offices and upper yards and lower yards which for centuries we have called the Castle. His own new office opened upon that of Thomas Burke, his undersecretary, and a passage led to the offices of the Lord Chancellor and the Solicitor General and the Attorney General.

There was much else, to be sure, in the Castle—chapels and the rest of it, and even one construction that could properly be called a castle, the tower from which our young hero, eagle, Red Hugh O'Donnell, had escaped in the days of Elizabeth, bringing north with him the brand which set aflame Tyrone and his own Tir-Connell and at last all Ireland. Up a staircase of stone, the offices of the inspector general of the Royal Irish Constabulary and the commissioner of prisons, busy men these days. And in the Lower Castle Yard, the headquarters of the Dublin Metropolitan Police, a fine body of men, height and rude health being among the chief criteria. There was even a sumptuous Throne Room, in which young ladies of family—Protestants, but with a fair scattering of Catholics in these more politic times—were presented to the Lord Lieutenant, for was he not the Viceroy, surrogate for Victoria herself?

Few Irishmen there were who were not bound to the Castle by some humble string or other. Myself included, for was it not the Chief Secretary, in theory, who arranged for the financing of schools and the scheduling of examinations and inspections, and who kept a benign eye and ear upon what I imparted to the young? The Chief Secretary was at the centre of one of those great webs which were spun outwards from London to span the Empire, the globe.

But there was another Castle, which had little to do with the setting of examinations and the presentation at Court of young gentlewomen. Thomas Burke knew that other world; a Catholic small landowner, half gentry, second or third or fourth cousin to the great Emmet Bourke, undersecretary since 1869. A "Castle hack," of course, as William O'Brien called him in our newspapers; a "Castle bloodhound," as Bob and others had called him on platforms across Munster and Connaught. Not without reason. Burke knew that other Castle—policemen, magistrates, the ear ready and cocked towards the informer, the purse open a bit, not too wide. Payment upon results, a nod as good as a wink. Dark and sombre in the imaginations of all of us on our side of the divide, that other Castle.

For all of that Saturday, Cavendish had journeyed with Burke, his Virgil, cicerone, into offices, along passageways, down narrow stone staircases and up them, sat before tables piled high with papers, dabs of red sealing wax. And then, in full evening, about six but not dark in Dublin's springtime May, he had set off on foot from the Castle to his lodge, and then across the King's Bridge to the Park Gate. At the new statue to General Gough, bold uniformed equestrian, Burke caught up with him. On their right-hand side the Nine Acres and on their left a game of polo and one of cricket, games of empire, the English countryside, the sports of gentility. They were dead, weltering in their blood, by the time help reached them. A gang of men had butchered them, and by the judgement of the coroner, they had been killed "by pointed weapons of great sharpness, keenness, and strength, but not very large, not very wide, and not much longer than ten inches or twelve." It was said at the time that they were American knives, of the type known as bowie, but we know now that they were surgical knives, furnished forth to them in Dublin by a surgeon well disposed to their cause. Such as it was.

"And they are not finished yet," Bob said. "Not by a long chalk. They had a go at a judge in Dublin two days ago, and there is a fellow killed who may have been an informer upon them. The Irish National Invincibles! Mother of God, what a name they found for themselves."

It was strange to be walking that leafy road, with the scent upon it of rained-soaked meadows drying in the Sabbath sun, and to be talking of such matters. As though a knife lay glittering upon the road.

"It will drift away in time," I said. "If there was a gang of them, there will be more informers than the one. You may depend upon it. It is the constant of Irish history, our only comfortable continuity."

Bob paused, broke off a branch from a hedge, and touched its flowers, pink-tipped. "I could name men to you, Hughie, who may well move between our lot and those people—Byrne for one, and Hogan for another. And that fellow Sheridan—oh, by Jesus, that fellow Sheridan." I listened to him with dismay, for even to an outsider like myself, two names at least of that trinity were known from newspapers and from a casual word from Bob, now and then—Patrick Hogan, a pal of Davitt's who had resigned from the Supreme Council and had helped organise Mayo for the League. And Frank Byrne, Liverpool and ex-Fenian, a man of guns in his early, salad days.

"Dear God, Bob," I said, suddenly, "is not Frank Byrne now the secretary of the entire Land League?"

"He is," Bob said wryly. "At the moment, at any rate."

"And now you are telling me that he knows more than he should know about that bloody shambles in the park?"

"*May* know," Bob said irritably. "May know. You know the way of it, Hughie, an organization like ours—we pick up this fellow and that one. A few odd birds. Untamed birds, might be a better phrase. And I have only my suspicions, do you see?"

"Not entirely," I said. "A strange impulse it was ye all had to make a secretary out of an odd bird."

"I grant you that," he said. "But he keeps neat records and minutes, and he does a nice line when it comes to keeping them away from the eyes of the Castle and of Scotland Yard."

"God send he does not do a nice line in surgical knives as well," I said. "Or butchers' cleavers."

"Damn it, Hughie. Isn't it bad enough without your spoiling a Sunday walk with your sarcasms? They would have been acting on their own, people like Hogan and Byrne and Sheridan. The Supreme Council has condemned them, has condemned the Invincibles root and branch. And as for us, we are as good as ruined if the Castle can prove links between ourselves and those gutter rats up in the Park. I doubt if they can. Odd birds but clever ones. We will get shut of them."

The fiendish park, I thought. As good a name for it as any other. Once there had been a priory there, with a spring of water, *fionn uisge.* In time, the Gaelic words were transformed into *phoenix,* and there is now a lovely statue to the mythological creature herself, set up long ago by Lord Chesterfield, a viceroy who adorned the office; a lovely notion, a linguistic error transformed into a myth. The national history. I could sense in Bob that following that outburst, he would welcome silence, and so we walked along, with Bob pulling the branch between his fingers, so that buds and young leaves were torn away. We were far away from the scene conjured in our minds—the same scene, I have no doubt, in the greys and blacks of newspapers and journals, some final, unconsoling distance from actualities of blood and ripped tissues, muscle.

And yet. Was there not always, for all of us, some tiny thrill that came from an unspoken knowledge that "Ribbon Fenians" were for all that Fenians in a way, that if the peelers were to be too rough in some protesting village, if some landlord proved himself too much a brute, if silence and Coventry and boycotting and the rest of it were scoffed at by some snatching little grabber, if, if, if . . . Why then, the last guns had not been put away, the last billhooks rotted and crumbled. We knew it and we did not know, and were content to leave it so, neither better in this respect nor worse than Mr. Forster in Dublin Castle or Mr. Gladstone in Downing Street. Violence, it may be, is not a stain upon the stuff of life, but a part of the fabric.

And I had now my own tale to tell to Bob, with an acknowledgement as well that time had gone by without my speaking it, without knowing whether to or not. We had come to the small fine bridge which arches over a curl of the Sullane, and paused there by silent accord. I remembered a bridge across a Dublin canal, the noise and sounds of water traffic, road traffic. Here there was a great and perfect silence, meadows and a gentle stream.

"When I was up to Kilmainham to visit you," I said, "afterwards I saw Ned."

"Ned," he said, as though he had not heard me correctly, but I said nothing. "Our Ned? Ned Nolan." And I nodded.

"There was all the excitement and pleasure of your return," I said. "Several times that evening I was of a mind to tell you, but there was always something that would intervene."

"Yes," Bob said, taking my point more quickly than I might have wished. "A full week ago, and tis now that you speak of an old friend, one of the friends of 'sixty-seven. You saw Ned, how do you mean that? Saw him to talk with him, do you mean?"

"I saw him by chance in a public house off Dorset Street, and we made plans to have a good chat the next day, and so we did. We took a long morning's walk along the canal in the south of the city."

"And how is Ned?" Bob asked, in a voice which curiously mingled affection and fury. "How is our Ned?"

"The same as ever," I said. "He was happy to see me, and he asked for you, for all of you. He misses us, I am certain, but he is as hard to read as ever. That fellow is a Red Indian, I swear to God, and not a County Cork man at all. Straight out of Fenimore Cooper," I added, to make light of matters.

"The day you visited me in Kilmainham," Bob said. "The timing is right. Was he on his own in the pub?"

"There were fellows with him, a half dozen of them. He left them to speak with me, and then went back."

"What were they like?" Bob asked.

"Ach, sure, what are they like, the fellows you talk with in a pub. Workingmen in scarves and caps, and a few small tradesmen or the like, more respectable, with stiff hats, one of them with a full, curly beard. No, wait. There was one of them you could never mistake, a fellow with the build on him of a young Hercules, a navvy or the like, with a clear, open face. You could not help but admire him."

Bob put a cautioning hand on my forearm as it rested on the bridge. "That is as much as we know of them, Hughie. More than we know. Have you spoken to Mary of this?"

"I have not," I said, and as I came into the open with those words, I knew that I was speaking to myself what I had refused to speak, why I had waited a week, until my walk with Bob. "I told her only that I thought I had seen Ned, but that the whole of the story could wait for your return. Mind you, that was only my liking for the dramatic; that was before what happened."

"Jesus, Mary, and Joseph," Bob said.

"Dublin is a huge wen of a city," I said, "and there are such things as coincidences."

"Hah," Bob said. "You talked of politics, I have no doubt, especially with myself in Kilmainham. What had he to say?"

"What you would expect. Ned does not change."

"He was over here on the business of the organization," Bob said. "You have no doubt of that?"

"He was," I said, picking my words with truthfulness and care, "and he was not. He has scant use for your lot, scant use for the Land League. But he spoke with disrespect of the Devoy lot in the States, and of the Supreme Council itself."

"No," Bob said, with a brief flash of genuine amusement. "Our friend Mr. Mulcahy would not impress him as a saviour of Ireland."

"He has respect for Rossa, and for others whom he would not name to me, of course. He had said too much, you could see that. The men who take the war into the camp of the enemy are the men who keep the oath."

"The oath," Bob said. "That fucking oath. Jesus, Mary, and Joseph."
A fine bit of blasphemy.

We stood without speaking, side by side, hands upon cool stone of another century, time-softened, and looked down into green slow-moving water, shallow.

"As you say," he said at last, "there are such things in nature as coincidences. He is a legally discharged ticket-of-leave man, and no doubt is legally in these islands. That is no concern of ours. Neither are you under compulsion to go about describing how you spend your holidays in Dublin, nor myself to recount the substance of conversations on rural bridges."

"William O'Brien has said in *United Ireland*," I said with mild malice, "that it is the duty of every patriotic Irishman to bring forth whatever might be of help in the unearthing—"

"What William O'Brien writes in *United Ireland* is binding neither in law nor in morality. And O'Brien and yourself can rest easy on the only real point at issue. You may be certain that the wretches who did this, your precious Invincibles, have at least two or three informers at work upon them already. And Anderson and Mallon at the Castle are not blunderers, far from it. They will pick the likeliest of the rogues and put the screws to them. There is no need to crawl into the sewer with them."

"A wonderful machine, the law," I said.

"It is wonderful because it creates choices, Hughie. For example, you may choose, if you prefer, to go back down into Kilpeder and tell Sergeant Dineen what you know. Or rather, what you think you know. What you perhaps suspect."

"A wonderful machine," I said again, and then said, "And you yourself, Bob. Forget the law: we both know that I would never go to the Royal Irish Constabulary and shop the man who led us at Clonbrony Wood. But Bob Delaney to Hugh MacMahon, what do you make of it?"

He shrugged: more a heavy heave of shoulder, as though to shove off a burden. "We don't know enough yet about these Invincibles, though we will soon enough. They are breakaways, for whom the ways of Kickham, O'Leary, and Mulcahy, Limited, are become too genteel. Even Devoy in New York is tainted in their eyes. And mind you, there is one thing of which we can be certain: they have acted not because Parnell and the League have failed, but because we have not. They see us as opportunists who are buying off the Irish people with a few acres of pastureland for graziers and the vague promise of some kind of talking shop in College Green that our masters will allow us to call an Irish parliament. Or to be more exact, Hughie, if I were myself an Invincible, that is what I would be thinking."

He turned his head away from the bridge, and laughed, flecks of light in his eyes; he was grinning.

"There is what I think, Hughie, and there are better matters that we could be talking of."

"About Ned was my question, Bob."

"I know no more than yourself. You talked with him, heard his tones, looked into his eyes. Ned is a gunman, Hughie, whatever craft he may work at the odd week. He is a gunman, and unlike most of them he has a clear, hard intelligence. The oath and this bloody island are his shrine and his church and his theology. If this was organised from over there, Ned is the man they would send—Ned or perhaps Lomasney or McCafferty. But my money would be on Ned."

He walked away, over the bridge and back towards the town, turning his head. "We don't dare be late for our Sunday tea, or Agnes will be raging."

On our return ramble, it seemed to me that Bob was determined that our conversation be sheared away from the Invincibles and from Ned, once he had from me every word of Ned's that I could remember. But I thought often of the matter in the months ahead, and most especially when the arrests were being made, and the names of Hogan and Byrne surfaced in print. By then they were safely out of the country, the two of them, and when there was speculation as to an American connexion, Ned's name was mentioned, of course, together with Lomasney's. By that time, the campaign of dynamiting had begun.

"It was the best compromise that we could get upon the bill," Bob said abruptly. "There were cheers in the country when we signed the 'No Rent' manifesto, and sent it forth from Kilmainham. But Forster had us crippled with his coercion acts, and our agents in detention across the length and breadth of the country. What Forster could not stop nor the RIC itself was 'Captain Moonlight,' as the Chief had predicted at the gates of Kilmainham. Grabbers shot dead and emergency men, and the lads of Forster's crowbar brigade dragged from their beds to be carded and thumped and tossed naked in the ditches. And the boycotting went on, of course."

"It did indeed," I said, "and does. And in Kilpeder and Macroom as well as elsewhere."

"You can count upon an end to that," Bob said. "That was a part of the bargain. A favourable interpretation of the Land Bill from Gladstone, and an end to 'unusual' as they are called, 'unusual' methods by the

League. We won, Hughie, we won. But not the war, as some believe. What we won was a first battle."

And so that is how great matters resolve themselves in our new world, I thought. Not with corpse-strewn battlefields, armies with banners and pipers and gaudy standards, but arrangements between a politician in a Downing Street mansion, you could call it, and another in a Kilmainham prison.

"Arranged," Bob said, as though reading my thought, "in the approved modern manner, messages carried to and fro by the approved new style of Mercury, Captain William O'Shea."

It was the first time I ever heard the name, and it made scant impression on me. "A member of the party, is he?" I asked.

"Of a party," Bob said. "Not ours, not yours or mine. But he is a Parnellite, you might say. A Parnellite and a Gladstone-ite. And an O'Shea-ite. Above all else, an O'Shea-ite."

He spoke with an angry vehemence for which I lacked the key. But we had by this time reached the crest of the road where it arched the hill, and we could see Kilpeder spread before us. The Sullane was a glisten beyond the walls of the Ardmor demesne.

"The fair world lies all before us," Bob said, in rough paraphrase of Milton.

"And the summer in it," I said. "With the countryside quietened down, we might give thought to one of our Killarney jaunts. How long has it been, four years or five? Agnes and Mary would enjoy it, surely."

"Killarney," Bob said, and as he spoke the word, I saw the upper lake, and the soft fringed shore, Muckcross Abbey, its soft, broken walls, and wild flowers scattered in the tall grasses. I saw our own youth, for we had begun going there long before Clonbrony Wood.

A fancy that I had, years since, is that on that particular Sunday, in the warm air, mild leaf-stirring wind, Bob had had it in mind to unburden himself to me as to the great matter which was on his mind, the passion that had taken root in his heart. When he did at last tell me, disaster was still far in the distance, a possibility only; but there was danger in the air, like the thunder before storm. Only once that day did he touch upon it, and then so obliquely that it could not be read.

"It is said by some," Bob said, looking straight down upon Kilpeder, "that Captain O'Shea has become a convenient go-between because he is the husband of Parnell's mistress." He spoke in so flat a voice that his words came to me as enigmatic as well as abrupt.

"Well," I said. It was as though two incommensurate facts had been crammed within the one sentence. Or rather, as though the language of two literatures had been—life and books. For Bridy Heron, who lived with

Carmody the cattle dealer, making the wan pretence of being his housekeeper and thus preserving for herself the Sacraments at whatever cost to her soul in the confessional, was Carmody's "woman." And Helen Squires, at Arbutus House, was old Major Armstrong's "woman." *Mistress* was a word from a planet different from ours, and the word *Parnell* from a third.

"I heard but the hint here and there," Bob said, "and a conversation between Dillon and O'Brien that I should not have heard, for I am not in their inner councils by any means. They are as shocked as you are, Hughie, if that is a consolation to you. Dillon is furious that Parnell should involve his personal life in the work of the party. And he takes a dim view of the entire matter, if it comes to that. Sturdy Irish Catholic stock, the Dillons, for all their lofty education."

"I see," I said, in a pretence at worldliness.

"What would you have, Hughie, for God's sake? He is a handsome vigorous man in his thirties. Would you have him a monk?"

"No," I said, "of course not." But a moment later added, with tartness, "Nor the wife of this Captain O'Shea in a nunnery, if you take my meaning. What sort of a captain is he, at all? They are supposed to be fierce gallant creatures with their women well under control."

"How the hell do I know?" Bob said. "I have barely heard his name. And once heard, tis best forgotten—there are such names."

"Nolan, for one," I said.

"Yes," Bob said. "Vincent has the name for wit and badinage in our select circle, but, by God, my own election lights upon you." He had all this time been carrying with him his branch, stripped naked now, and he flung it away from him.

"There is no one," he said suddenly and fiercely, "who can know what lies in bed with a man and a woman. No one. And no one has the right to judge."

"No one save God," I said, ever the logician.

"I grant you the exception," Bob said. "There are no others."

"Well enough said," I replied to him, thinking not all that much about the matter, but my thoughts, rather, adjusting themselves to a Parnell different from my foolish imaginings of him; for we see our heroes, no matter what our age, as coloured plates in a book of moral and civic edification. I was schoolmaster as much by nature as calling.

"It is often," he said, "no matter of right or of wrong, but of mystery, a puzzle for which we have lost the words or lack them or are too shy or too cowardly to speak them." His own speech now was slow, as though selecting rounded, harmless small stones from a clear stream.

But if he was speaking to me, as I now know he was—speaking less of Parnell than of himself—I lacked the loving skill to listen to what a friend's voice was telling me, beneath the sound of his words.

"Ah well," I said, "a lively discussion." For there were times often on those Sunday walks which meant so much to me when we would walk for an hour or more in a companionable silence, our thoughts upon separate matters, no doubt, but feeling the same weather, mild wind, spattering rain, seeing the same fields, plumes of turf smoke rising from the same chimneys. Never once that afternoon did I imagine that life might be pulling all of us apart, like fallen twigs in rushing water broken by sudden rocks. Nor imagine it later, at our tea in the Delaney parlour, with Agnes mistress of her tall silver pots, with their attendant trays of silver bearing water steaming, rich heavy cream. Later, Mary would play for us, but now she sat smiling, happy that Bob was back with us again, laurel-crowned, smiling then upon myself and upon Vincent, he smiling as well but with an anticipatory glint in his eye for the drop of whiskey which would follow the tea, a glint matched once for a moment by the silver flash of his cigar case as he unbuttoned and eased back his jacket. My Mary would not play until later, but in anticipation, as Vincent—and myself as well, to speak the truth—anticipated a splash of amber in clear Waterford, I heard the notes falling one by one into the room, melodies twined and intertwined, binding us together, an invisible silver, untextured and unweighted.

24

[*Lionel Forrester/Patrick Prentiss/
Hugh MacMahon/Robert Delaney*]

It is often in bed that we learn of other beds. After lovemaking, the mind drifts, in a delicious, erotic muddle, through a half world of beds, bodies, satisfactions, and there is an impulse to talk of them.

"They are sleeping together, you know," Emily said. "Sylvia and the Land Leaguer."

"Sylvia," I said. "I had not known it, but it does not surprise me."

He had come to the Castle, once upon business, then often for dinner, after Tom had gone off to Paris, and there had been only Sylvia and myself to entertain him.

"Sylvia has not told you?"

"Not yet," I said. "She will. We are very close, the two of us. As Tom and I are, if it comes to that."

As Sylvia was friends with Emily, the maid whom she had brought with her from Westmeath and London. A curious friendship, and conducted by Emily with an admirable punctilio. Only when we were in bed, she and I, would she speak of Lady Ardmor as Sylvia, and Tom was always, at all times, even then, "his lordship," or "Lord Ardmor." Save, of course, when she and Sylvia were alone, in the morning, or at night as she brushed Sylvia's long, rich hair. "And me?" I said to her once, when we were talking of the matter. "What do Sylvia and you call me, when you are alone together?"

"Ah," she said, "why do you think we would ever talk of you?"

"But you do," I said. "You have told her of the two of us, I am certain of that."

"Are you indeed?" she said.

"You have forgotten," I said, "that she and I are friends as well, you know. Closer than the two of you, perhaps." In the blackness of the night, I felt her smile.

Now, this night, we were not sheltered by blackness, but had left candles lit on the tables at either side of the bedhead. Flickering flames fell upon books which lay scattered on the near table, fell upon the dull gold of my watch, its coil of chain.

"Did you never fancy her yourself?" Emily said.

"What a curious question to ask," I said. "Now. I mean, after all this time. Why now?"

"I don't know," she said, flat midlands in her accent. "I have thought it before now."

"She is Tom's wife," I said. "And he is more than a cousin to me. We are friends."

She laughed. "Much that means in your world. Friendship would add spice to it in your world."

"Not for me," I said. "And if you do not know that by now about me, then you know damned little about me, for all that the same sheet covers us."

"I did not ask had you tried taking her to bed," Emily said. "I asked only have you fancied her. An innocent question."

"Innocent," I said. "Yes, of course I have. What man would not? She is a great beauty in her way, you know, and a sensuous woman. She must know her body, and how men respond to her. It can generate an excitement, a desire, if that is what you mean. For the instant only—a candle flickering, a bosom bent forward. If that is what you mean."

"Long ago," she said, "I was standing by the window in Sylvia's room, that small room of early sun that she claims for her own, with the small dressing room between it and Lord Ardmor's room."

"An extraordinary way of describing a bedroom," I said.

"Whatever. And far away from the Castle, far beyond the terraces, upon the small lake, there were the two of you, Sylvia and yourself, drifting, facing each other. Her hand trailed in the water. I fancied then, for that moment, that you were lovers, the two of you."

"Fancied," I said. "It is a great word with you, Emily. I remember that day. We were talking of—"

"It is a servant's word," Emily said. "A maidservant's word. What else do you expect from me?"

"We were talking that day," I said, "of her feeling towards Robert Delaney, our friend the Land Leaguer."

"That is as good a way as any to excite the blood," she said. "To talk of how one feels towards—"

"You are contriving it yourself at the moment, Emily," I said, "but not in the way you mean. What the devil are you about?"

She laughed, and raised herself up on one elbow, to look at me the more directly. The sheet slipped away from her, and her breasts, in the innocent, affectionate openness of lovers, fell free in the warm late summer night.

"I asked only if you ever fancied her," she said. "A simple question."

"Yes," I said, more irritated than I had expected to be, "of course I have. As she will lean towards me at dinner, when I help her over a stile. It could never be more than that."

"Not after knowing about Galantiere and Van Zandt?"

"By God, but you can be a perverse minx when you've a mind to be."

"She is no bigot," Emily said, "Galantiere a Frenchman of some sort and Van Zandt a Yank, and now a jumped-up Papist counterboy, one of the hillside men was out spreading death and destruction in the year 'sixty-seven, and at this very moment may be busy at his new career of barn burning and insulting Her Majesty."

"Oh there we have it," I said, "there we have it. The very Protestant Miss Emily Weldon is alarmed that the Countess of Ardmor has taken a fancy to a Papist. Give us a few bars of 'Lilliburlero,' Emily."

"God almighty, Lee," she said. "You know that there is more to it than that, and that I am concerned for Sylvia, as you are yourself. I have no doubts upon that score."

"Do you know," I said, "what theory is held by the Papist country people about Protestant women? Not the men, mind you, but a theory that is held about the women?"

"You are a grasshopper," she said, "when it comes to leaping from one notion to the next."

"You must have heard it," I said, "coming as you do from the grassy

[515]

plains of Westmeath, where rural pleasures do much abound, as the poet has it. That the skin of Protestant women is less white than that of the Papist women."

And I twitched the muslin sheet away from the two of us, and held up the candlestick, to make certain of the matter.

"Less white is not what they say," Emily said. "The saying that they have is that Protestant women have yellow skin. Is that the truth?"

She lay resting, as she had been upon the elbow, and now pulled gently, idly, upon her long lower lip, her half-opened mouth. A long body, clear of outline, not voluptuous, and yet sensuous, the flat, hard muscles of the stomach sensuous, the long legs, narrow, gently rounded thighs.

"Is that the truth?" she said.

"How am I to say?" I answered her. "Such times as I have slept with Catholic women—Catholic we must assume—it was on the Continent, French women or Italian. They come from tawny countries, you might say, warmed by the sun, dark-ripened."

"Such times," she echoed me, bantering, mocking. "It must be grand entirely to be a man, and have ranges and stores of comparison, women and their bodies but half remembered. Someday soon, will you but half remember me? Sylvia Ardmor's maidservant that you took to bed."

"You are becoming more to me than that," I said. "You know that." I spoke the words not to her but to her breasts, but I spoke the truth and she knew it.

"What does that matter?" she asked. "What is there for us?"

"We will see," I said. "More than we know at this moment, either of us."

So it was to prove. She is with me yet, as much wife as mistress; no, better than wife, to know that the bond was first set fully with the flesh—affection, love, trust flowering from lust, tissues, candlelight falling upon breast, flank, tuft of wiry, fair hair.

"The Orange flute indeed," she said, and her free hand stroked me, fingers sure and certain of purpose.

But later she said, "Still and all, Lee. He is becoming more to her than he should, and she to him, I doubt not. It could be very bad."

"They are level-headed, the two of them," I said. "I doubt if there is cause for—"

"Level-headed!" she cried. "Sylvia!" And she gave a short burst of laughter, exasperated. "You know very little of her if you say that. And you don't know her now at all. She has never spoken to me before of anyone as she speaks now of Delaney."

I said nothing, unpersuaded by her concern, although the circumstances astonished me more than I was willing to admit to myself. A most unlikely coupling.

"She was mad with grief and worry when he was in that prison in Dublin. It is an astonishment to me that Lord Ardmor did not observe it. *Distracted* is the word for it. Grieving for a murderer, an assassin."

"He is neither of those," I said. "And well you know it. You are a sensible girl."

"Sensible enough to read the newspapers and to hear what is said. If that lot did not do the murders in the Phoenix Park, cut down poor Lord Frederick and a man doing his duty, then they bought the knives and sharpened them, and put them in the hands of the butchers."

"We will know soon enough," I said. "But I know Bob Delaney a bit. We have had dinner here together, and have taken rambles together. He is not the ogre you make him out to be, an incendiary from the pages of *Punch*. It is dangerous enough that the Countess of Ardmor is having an affair with a town solicitor. *There* is the danger of the matter."

"You and I," she said, anger masking itself as unconcern. "That does not matter. A servant girl in a gentleman's bed."

"The other servants?" I asked her, and she understood the question.

"Perhaps," she said, "probably. Who can say? I am not in their confidence." Emily, Griffin, and Mrs. Ferguson the housekeeper: three Protestants in a household of Catholic servants, privileged, a distance always that did not exclude friendships. A novel there, perhaps, but who would have the knowledge to write it, a world secret from us?

"If they know it," I said, "Kilpeder will know it."

She laughed again. "It is so mad," she said, "that if they know it, I doubt if they believe what they know."

And I took her again into my arms; but we were tired, the two of us, and but lay together, our arms about each other. I stroked her buttocks, intimate and cool.

Presently she said, "It is time now." As I looked out the window, it seemed still, for a space, coal-black, but the black turned then to grey, and I could see the edgings of trees, spring-branched, far beyond the gardens and terraces, and a light, faint-off, in the eastern sky, which my window faced.

"Time," I said, and she disengaged herself from my reluctant arms, and slipped to the chair beside the window on which, hours before, she had flung her plain nightgown and flannel robe. She stood by the window. "An hour from now or two," she said, "and the gardener's boy will be out with the new roller, making the world comely for them, for Sylvia and for his lordship."

"And for the rest of us," I said. I always admired her natural ease with her body, her casual unconcern with such matters as dress and nakedness—unusual, I have found, in her class, even in intimacy.

Faint light from our two candles displayed her to me, the long, straight back, the slender buttocks whose texture lingered, ghosts, upon my fingertips.

"He is far different from Galantiere," she said. "There is that to be said for him." And picking up her gown, she slipped herself into it.

"As men, no doubt," I said. "A Cork solicitor and a painter of decorative portraits. We neither of us know what they are like in bed, or, for that matter, what it is like to be in bed with Sylvia."

She adjusted her gown, but left it unfastened, and walking across to my bed, picked up her candle. Suddenly, it flared upon her high-boned face, wide generous mouth, a thin, straight face. "*You* do not, and I believe you. In any event, Sylvia would have told me."

I took the wrist whose hand held the candle, and she made no effort to draw it away.

"What are you telling me," I said, "that you have been to bed, together, Sylvia and yourself?"

"Would that be so uncommon," she said, "a lady and her maidservant, in those cold draughty houses where Sylvia and her father made their rounds of house parties, a needy colonel and his daughter, an old man zestful for a lively party, a day's shooting? Bang, bang, and birds fallen to the weighty guns."

"You know what I mean," I said. "Sylvia has made love to you?"

"Or I to her. How are such matters decided? We have loved. It is why my feelings for her are so close, why I am so concerned for her. Had you never wondered?"

"No," I said, and I released her wrist. "I had never wondered, nor come close to it."

She sat lightly, for the moment only, bird upon perch, on the edge of the bed, the candle still so held that I could see her clearly.

"What are you thinking now?" she asked.

"Not thinking," I said. "What do I feel? I am not certain what I feel."

"What do you want to feel?" she asked.

"And how are things now between you two?"

She smiled and touched a cool hand to my lips, held it there, then drew it back. "It was a long time ago. After Galantiere. She was desperate then, unhappy. I could not bear it." And bending down, she kissed me, bending so swiftly that the candle's small flame guttered and went out. It was a passionate kiss, for her, for me.

Then I relit her candle from my own, and she left me. At the door, I called out, softly, her name, questioningly. She turned and smiled, mischievously. "Ah, but that is something you will never know, will you? You only fancy her a bit, you tell me, and then there is your great friendship with her husband. Poor Lee."

She closed the door so quietly that I could not hear the sound.

I can imagine no public event in my lifetime so shocking to England and to Ireland as the killings in the Phoenix Park, and young Prentiss tells me that he has heard the same from everyone.

That weekend, I remember vividly, I was staying with Jack and Lillie Holloway at their place in Wicklow, a full party of us, and the news came to us at breakfast time on Sunday, the sun streaming in upon the long table, and chafing dishes at the ready along one wall, steam rising towards the glass-protected paintings of long-vanished hunts, pink coats and belling hounds, a broken wall, an autumn landscape on a May morning. There were a half dozen guests already at table, gathered together at its far end, beyond which tall windows opened upon the Wicklow hills. My first response, I well recall, was that of countless others. "It isn't possible," I said. "He's not even here yet."

"Oh yes," someone—say Boy Heathcoat—said. "He came over that morning, yesterday morning, and before the sun had fairly set, they had him butchered. In the park, by the Polo Grounds." By the Polo Grounds—for some reason that was to stick in everyone's memory.

"Cavendish," Heathcoat said, "and the Undersecretary, fellow named Burke. I remember Burke, met him a few times. Hardworking fellow doing ten different kinds of nasty jobs at once and doing them well. Power-behind-the-throne sort of fellow. Forster would have been lost without him. By God, I'd like to hear what Forster has to say about all this in Commons tomorrow evening. He predicted it, you know, predicted something like this."

"It isn't Irish at all," Jennie Chambers said, her fingers touching the collar of her sprigged morning gown. "Not knives. Even the worst of them don't use knives!"

"Don't they just," her husband said. "Knives, billhooks, dung forks, whatever they can put their hands on. Read the newspapers, my dear. Happening every day."

That is how I heard of the detail, of this detail, and bit by bit the rest of it came out, as I poured myself a cup of tea and buttered some toast.

Billie Chambers was right and he wasn't right. Of course, we had been reading, week after week for close on to three years, of the killings in Ireland: *Land War* wasn't entirely a phrase invented by journalists. Bailiffs, constables, emergency men, land agents, the occasional landlord or perhaps a misfortunate wife and daughter who might be sitting with him in the carriage, bowling back from church of a Sunday, mild hymns still fragrant in their minds, and then a shotgun blast from the hedge. Or we would read, of course, in other journals, other fonts of type perhaps, of archdukes murdered, tsarist ministers blown to smithereens, bemedalled Austrian field marshals falling with thin steel wedged between the ribs. That is what Jennie meant. She meant that people one knew, or knew of, did not die that way, not the Duke of Devonshire's son, Hartington's younger brother, Mrs. Gladstone's nephew. Not to be learned of on a county weekend, as we spread smooth Wicklow butter across toast.

Pat Nugent was standing by the tall windows, facing towards the hills, hands clasped behind his back. "There," he said suddenly, unclasping them, and jabbing a forefinger.

It was pointed beyond the hills, in the general direction of the vale of Clara, where Parnell's house, Avondale, lay a mile or so to the south. Or so at any rate I judged, and judged correctly, to be the purport of the indicting finger.

"Where is he now?" he asked. "Where is he on this particular Sunday morning? Bloody madman turning against his own, and at last putting knives into their hands."

We know now, of course, where he was. He had spent the night with Mrs. O'Shea, at Eltham, where in theory at least he could not be reached, and he learned about the awful business when he bought a newspaper in Blackheath Station.

Curious, the way in which we respond so differently to public and to private disasters. We were shocked, truly and deeply, and yet had no intention that a weekend should be ruined, even though Pat Nugent, and Jack Holloway when he came down to join us, were less certain that the two could be disentangled.

"Fellow still rides to hounds, you know," Pat said.

"Seen him," Jack said. "Good hands."

"Parnell's carrying the horn now," Pat said. "He's laying his pack on the line, and they're running it like wolves."

"Doing a bit of a line himself these days, so I've heard," Jack said. "Wife of some half-pay officer in the Hussars. I simply cannot believe this other thing, Pat," Jack said. "I know the chap a bit. Odd sort, but he wouldn't involve himself with footpads and murderers."

"Would he not!" Pat said, swinging around. "It is the Land League that has been harrying the countryside, murders and maiming, counties proclaimed, and who do you think is the president of the bloody Land League?"

"Do sit down, Pat dear," Lillie Holloway said. "Have an egg, for God's sake, and a cup of tea. You must try to keep up your strength," she said sardonically, as though anxious lest his concern for the public weal might debilitate him, although few in the room, and probably not Jack Holloway, doubted that she had spent the night with Pat, slipping away at some decorous hour.

And that is how I learned that on Saturday, the sixth of May, 1882, at about six of a mild evening, clear but with a touch of low-clinging mist, as they walked along the wide handsome avenue towards the lodge, Frederick Cavendish the newly arrived Chief Secretary and Thomas Henry Burke, permanent undersecretary in the Irish Office, as ran the nouns and adjectives of their offices, were butchered by a band of ruffians who were later to make themselves known as members of the Irish National Invincibles.

It was a pivot, I think, a pivot in the way in which those of us who came from "our Ireland" came to think about the country: illogical, perhaps, but there you are. After Phoenix Park, it was a bit less "ours."

And there you are," Dominick Sarsfield Prentiss said to his son Patrick. "Frank Byrne. Byrne was secretary of the Land League organization in Great Britain, and Parnell had met with him when he was on leave from Kilmainham the month before, Parnell and poor Justin McCarthy, as genteel a chap as you would want to meet—would faint in the face of violence, much less naked steel. But it was Byrne who bought the surgical knives that did the job, and his wife smuggled them over to Dublin in her skirts. Boasted of it later. He was paymaster to the Invincibles, got them their running accounts from those bloodthirsty Clan na Gael blowhards in America. How close do links have to be? It all came out. Hogan and Byrne got safely away, of course; their sort always does."

They were far to the north of Phoenix Park themselves. The Prentisses father and son, on a Sunday stroll along one of the paths which ribboned across the Hill of Howth, with the city spread out before them, and the Irish Sea. On a very clear day, from where they walked, Wales itself could be seen in the far distance, an edge of low horizon.

"And it all came out later, of course, much later," Dominick Prentiss said, "when they tried to tie in Parnell, those fools of Tories. Hogan actually brought Le Caron, the bloody British spy, into the Commons to meet Parnell, had a few minutes' chat in the Gallery. 'One of our friends from America,' Hogan said. 'Ah, yes,' Parnell said, 'our American friends. Good lively sorts, good Irishmen.' And of course Le Caron hurried the good word to the Home Office. How the devil could we know they had butcher's knives in mind, dynamite, bloody murder?"

At hand, far below them, the mailboat moved towards Ireland, and beyond it, in the sun-sparkling bay, light-winded, pleasure yachts, elegant as herons, skimmed the water.

"Mallon had clear notions from the first as to who the knifers were," Prentiss's father said. "Damned good policeman, John Mallon was, not that he needed to be. Every fifth Fenian in Dublin was on the police payroll. Same as it was in the sixties. Same as it is today, for that matter. Mallon knew the knifers—Joe Brady, Fitzharris, Curley, the whole miserable crew. But of course, he wanted to get to the men above them, the men who sent down the orders. At the very least, he wanted to get the goods on Hogan. Put Hogan in a cell and turn the heat on him, and Hogan would lead him straight to Parnell. Straight to all of us, no doubt."

A man named Tynan was the go-between, Patrick Prentiss knew, bustling and self-important, carrying his messages from London to Dublin and then back to London again. "Number One, that is how I was called," he used to boast in later years, safe in New York. "Number One of the Irish National Invincibles," and always a drink for Patrick Tynan on the strength of that Number One of the Invincibles. By then, by the nineties, the Invincibles had become heroes of sorts in the saloons of New York and Chicago. A man of nods and winks, references to certain "higher-ups," a name or two that might astonish you, and yes please, the same again. But Superintendent Mallon had more sense than to fish with bait like Tynan.

The park murders, even though Forster rather than Cavendish may have been the preferred target, were planned with care—a military plan, with an escape route, and an alternate route should that one be blocked. Tynan was the go-between right enough, and League officials were involved. American money was involved. Orders had gone out from America, from Rossa or from Alexander Sullivan or from John Devoy—but

Devoy was too cautious a man, ruthless but longheaded. But somewhere, at some intersecting street and avenue of the web, was someone with military training—some fellow who had done his time as sergeant in some British regiment—Irish or Highland or Welsh, no doubt—or more likely, one of the Fenians of the old guard, a bit grizzled by now in hair and beard, who had seen service with the Yanks in their war over there. Mallon thought so, and so did E. G. Jenkinson, newly appointed as assistant undersecretary at the Castle, especially to deal with such matters, for no one believed that they would end there, not if these people called themselves invincible.

"They were exciting days, Patrick, by Jove they were. George Trevelyan came over to take Cavendish's place, you know. George Trevelyan. You know the chap, an historian, like yourself—isn't that what you call yourself?"

"It is what I call him, certainly," Patrick said. "A very distinguished historian. But not my sort, not at all."

"Talk to him," Dominick Sarsfield Prentiss said. "He used to ride about Dublin with a robe flung over his lap, clutching a revolver. And Lord Spencer surrounded fore and aft by entire companies with rifles at the ready. One might suppose that the Trevelyans had had enough of Ireland." His father laughed suddenly, the gold of the beard dark now but still gold, touched with grey. "His father managed the famine in the forties, as you know. Managed it! Created and sustained it, if John Mitchel were to be credited. But talk to George. A Macaulay on his mother's side—family of historians, you might say."

"Brilliant, the way he cracked Carey." Superintendent Mallon, Prentiss's father meant, not Trevelyan. "They were after Mallon too, you know. They knew Mallon was hot on the trail, and Brady had his plans set to do for him. There were a dozen attacks in the weeks and months that followed Phoenix Park, and nearly all of them in Dublin, and most with Brady's mark upon them. A bull of a man. Say what you will about Joe Brady, he came out of one of the old sagas, Finn or one of those, dressed up as a workman."

Sunlight glistened on the mailboat far below them, and quick, unexpected wind brought the scent of flowers from Howth Castle, fragrant and complex.

"What did for them, you know, was the law, that marvellous instrument which I cannot seem to bring you to respect, you bookish young rascal. Law books, those are the books with power. Dynamite, if you will, and iron chains. And, occasionally, a key to unlock a door. And in particular, with respect to those damned Invincibles, who almost destroyed us

[523]

all, daubed us all with their blood, the book was Section Sixteen of the Prevention of Crimes Act, as read by the Honourable John Adye Curran."

It was almost a year—it was not until February—that Brady and Carey and six others were brought into the courtroom at Kilmainham and charged that "they did, on the sixth of May, 1882, feloniously, wilfully, and of malice aforethought, kill and murder Lord Frederick Cavendish and Thomas Henry Burke." But it was not enough. Mallon and Curran were hunting bigger game, and it came once or twice under their sights, but would not stand still. Carey was the most respectable-looking of them, prosperous, a building contractor, city councillor—not a stonecutter, or a bricklayer, or a blacksmith like the others—and Carey was the one they used as Crown witness, taking his place not in the dock, but in the witness box, his name to be a curse word in the Dublin slums for decades to come: self-righteous, impudent, lost, as even his employers attested, lost to all honour. After Brady had been hanged, he wrote sanctimoniously in the prayer book which he sent to Brady's family, "After everyone betraying him he saved himself and many others."

Wrote it about himself, of course, not about Brady, the lion, who stood defiant in the dock. But there was no way to get beyond Carey, who could tie one Land Leaguer at least to the conspiracy, and who could swear that "Number One" brought their orders to him and to the others from London. Hogan and Byrne were safe, in France and in America. There was an American, Carey knew—or rather, an Irishman from America, one of the Civil War Fenians—and he had come over with orders and had been in a position to give orders of his own and to make plans and then see that they were carried out. Hogan and Byrne had met with him in London, and in Dublin he had met Brady and others in certain public houses and residences, on the north side of the city, as he understood. Brady would know, but Brady would say nothing, in the dock or out of it, broad-shouldered and contemptuous.

Mallon, in the Castle, placed before Carey photographs of Fenians recorded upon their arrests in 'sixty-five and 'sixty-seven, photographed full to the camera, or sitting sideways to it—young fellows, most of them—still bewildered by what had happened: scattered gunfire, confusion, arrest, mistreatment mingled with contempt. But other photographs as well, gathered with more difficulty—tintypes and studio portraits, never intended for Castle use. The big ones were there, of course: Devoy, Sullivan, O'Donovan Rossa. But fifty others, at least, cleared or smudged, one of them a wedding portrait, the groom awkward, stiff, the bride done up in white and holding a bouquet but looking like a skivvy on her night out. The groom was Dennis Florence Patterson, known to the Castle and to Scotland Yard as a killer, a mineworker in Montana for a few years, skilful with explosives. But Carey shook his head. "There was a Yank," Carey said. "But I declare before God, Superintendent Mallon, I never saw him nor heard the name. Tynan did, by Christ. Tynan did and Brady, but they liked their secrets. 'Number One,' Tynan would say to me. 'Don't call me Tynan, call me Number One.' He would say to me, 'Informers are everywhere.'"

"Suspicious sort of chap, wasn't he?" Curran said, and smiled at Superintendent Mallon.

"Never saw this beauty either, did you?" Mallon said, and turned over a photograph seemingly at random: a man standing in a shadowed doorway, tall, gaunt-shouldered, a moustache.

Carey smiled up at him. "I'd have known him. I'd have known Rossa, and I'd have known him."

"One or two sources place him in Dublin about then, but they are vague, damn it. People are always seeing him, like Boney or Titus Oates. You recognised him straightaway. Not a very clear likeness, I would have thought."

"There was a time," Carey said, "when the Clan na Gael sold tintypes of him for ten cents. Ned Nolan. The man in the gap. Nolan of Clonbrony Wood."

"He is in with a strange lot now," Mallon said. "Not quite Clan na Gael. More your sort of thing."

"Ah, now, Superintendent," Carey said.

"He has one chum at least in the League," Curran said, "a solicitor down in Cork, a place near Macroom called Kilpeder."

John Curran himself had told Patrick Prentiss of that conversation in the Castle, Curran a distinguished K.C. by now, thinking about retirement, staunch Tory but not a fanatical one, friend of Dominick Sarsfield Prentiss despite their politics. "There are legends," Curran said, "legends upon legends about the Invincibles. Built up even before they were topped on a gallows at Kilmainham. One spring, they were execrated, no corner-boy in Dublin so vile that he had a good word to say for those butchers. And by the next spring, Brady is a hero, the Fenian blade, and everyone's hate concentrated on Carey, the informer. Not upon Mallon and myself, thank God. We were simply Castle hacks, doing England's business. But Carey was a marked man. And, of course, they got him in the end. Shot him to death. Small loss, to tell the truth, although he served his purpose. But there were legends; you heard them, surely."

That Brady's mother visited him in his cell, the night before. "Joe, if you know anything, don't tell it. Bring your secret to the grave." Brady

was the first one hanged, of the five. On Whit Monday, May 14, 1883.
Crowds were waiting outside Kilmainham, and when the black flag was
raised, they fell upon their knees.

"What harm could it do, at this late date in the history of mankind?"
Hugh MacMahon asked Patrick Prentiss rhetorically. "I will tell you,
Patrick, as someone I have come to feel a friendship for. But as one friend
to another, and not for the book you are engaged upon. And there is the
condition. I am sorry for it. I am a bit of a scholar myself, and it goes
against my own grain."

"Yes," Prentiss said, "of course." But with a mental reservation that
he intended to raise later in the evening. A phrase much savoured and
used at Clongowes Woods: a Jesuit delicacy of conscience.

"There were but the two men that I remember of a half dozen sitting
with Ned in that snug off Dorset Street. There was one of them might
as well have been Tynan as anyone else. America was plastered with
likenesses of him after he had decided that he was a hero—posters and
drawings and all the rest of it—but there was damned little that the artists,
unskilled wretches that they were, could do to make him look like one.
Prim and tidy, with well-coiffed hair and curried, patriarchal beard. And
pince-nez, on a chain fastened to a collar stud. Has the world ever found
a hero with pince-nez? But of course he was equally concerned to demonstrate how genteel he was, how elevated above the mere working-class lads
who did the deed in the park."

MacMahon smiled at Prentiss, and then towards the gentle hills
beyond which lay the fierce Derrynasaggarts. He had kindled a turf fire
against evening chill; it made Prentiss a bit too warm, but he could tell
that MacMahon's shanks welcomed it.

"But there was no doubt at all about the other chap, Patrick. He was
a fellow you could not forget, and it was Joe Brady. I am not so lost to
reason as to sentimentalise him. He was a killer, whatever as to his reasons,
and it was Brady who knelt down over Cavendish and slashed away with
the surgical knife, to make certain that the fellow was done for."

"What was it about him, then?" Prentiss said. "A stonecutter in his
mid-twenties. The craft is one that calls for strength, but Dublin is full
of powerful fellows who follow such callings."

"Ach," MacMahon said. "Even the Tory journalists from London
at the trial were forever calling him 'resolute'—'quiet ferocity,' that sort
of thing. He was not a man you would forget in a hurry, leave it at that."

"A bit like the young Ned Nolan," Prentiss said lightly.

"No!" MacMahon said, with sudden, unexpected fierceness. "I

would think that by now you would have your sense of Ned Nolan as we knew him first, the Ned Nolan who walked upon that first evening into Kilpeder and knocked upon our door. It was not even Clonbrony Wood that changed him, or the killings that came to rest that day upon his hands. It was Portland Prison, the long years of it, years spent in silence, months in darkness with his hands chained behind him. Those are the years that made the other Ned Nolan, the one the newspapers talk about."

Prentiss, a young man, strove to imagine the others as young: MacMahon, Delaney, Nolan, Tully.

"What harm, then?" Prentiss asked, an hour or two later, as they sat with their hands wrapped about mugs of whiskey-laced tea. "What harm in my setting down in a book that Ned Nolan was seen by a friend in Dublin at about the time of the Phoenix Park killings? His name has been guessed at often enough—Nolan or Lomasney or McCafferty, with McCafferty in the lead."

"Guessed at in those papers they have over there in America in the Irish cities—Boston and New York. McCafferty used to make his hints now and again that he was the man. Let the triumph rest with him, such as it is."

"But Nolan never made the claim?"

"Ned Nolan?" MacMahon smiled in easy, condescending amusement. "No," he said, "Ned Nolan was not a man for making claims." He shook his head, disposing of Prentiss's mental reservation. "Let it rest there. There is blood enough on Ned's hands. He died with blood on them."

Now, Bob Delaney was a different matter entirely, to put matters at the mildest. I cannot blame Patrick Prentiss entirely for his lurid view of Ned. Had I not shaped it for myself in good measure? But Bob—Bob was like a fellow who had stepped out of the pages of Balzac—Lucien de Rubempré or one of those. I have had always a great fondness for those novels. Poor Vincent Tully said to me once, in a moment of exasperation, that I "had been ruined by your wife and by Balzac." What he meant exactly I cannot say, but it had the feel of accuracy to it.

In the September, the early autumn that followed upon their springtime release from Kilmainham, Parnell called a meeting at his estate of

Avondale, in Wicklow, to reorganise the Land League, and although, of course, it was the great men of the organization who were there—Davitt and Dillon and Healy and the others—there were a few other, lesser, chosen ones as well, and of these Bob was one. When the new League was formed, the Irish National League, there was a vague grandness to its title which now seems to me deliberate. More than land itself was now at stake, and independence was placed at the top of the banner, not for show merely, but as the next battle in the plan of campaign.

The plans were drawn up at Avondale, but they were presented to the rank and file, as you might call them, in Dublin in the following month—a miserable month October is, with its certain statement that the summer is over, and the dank blanket of winter drawing itself upon us. Bob had carried back to us an ebullient account of the September meeting, but it was a meeting a month later, a smaller one—himself and Parnell—which was to make upon him a impression which he did not pretend to explain.

It was a surprise to me, Bob had said to Hugh, when he came back from Avondale in September. A handsome house, a big house you would surely call it, from the old century, but not all that large, nothing at all like Ardmor, of course, or a half dozen others in this barony. It is set within trees, a great park of them, and with the first touches of September upon them, the leaves yellowing, and within are fine fireplaces of Italian marble, and windows which look beyond the plantation, across meadows, towards the river. There is to one side of the great hall a library which would make your mouth water, great inlaid shelves of dark wood reaching from floor to ceiling, and sets of books in bindings of tooled leather, maroon, black, brown. I snatched a look at a few titles—Montesquieu and Hume, Gibbon and Robertson. "There is a wealth of history in this room, Mr. Parnell," I said to him, as he showed me through the house; for he is courtesy himself, a man of excellent manners—you would not guess at that from the arrogance which gave him his legend—and as thoughtful of me and of Ignatius Brennan and our like as of Dillon and the grandees.

"I daresay there is," he answered. "I have taken down a volume once or twice to take a try at it, but it never held my interest. Do you know, Mr. Delaney, I suspect that they were bought by the foot-shelf, like the wood they rest upon. A proper house must have a library and a library must have books, and there we are." He clapped his hands together. "Come out here," he said, "and I will show you history, if you like that sort of thing."

And there in the hall, hanging from a kind of minstrel's gallery, high up, were faded flags and banners. "The flags of the Volunteers," he said. "The Parnells commanded in the Volunteers, back in the old days, back when we had our own country, our own kingdom, our own parliament. We fought the Union, you know, my great-grandfather did, one of Grattan's crowd. And my mother's father fought the English themselves, in the Yankee navy, fought them and smashed them on Lake Erie. I have his sword. If you like history."

"I have a friend," I said, "back home in Cork who has a great passion for history. I am remembering all of this for him."

"A passion for history," Parnell said. "An Irish failing."

After a bit, with all the work that lay before us, I forgot almost the grandness of Avondale, forgot even that I had stood chatting with the Uncrowned King.

But the hard work, the work with coats off and sleeves rolled up, that was organised by Healy and Harrington, but mostly by Healy. There is a wonder for you, that Healy.

So Bob told me that September evening after Avondale; and I thought in later years of that first description of Tim Healy, for in ten years' time or less, much less in fact, he would be speaking of Healy in terms less complimentary.

"As clever a man as you would expect to meet," Bob said, "and if he has one limitation it is that he looks clever; your truly clever man contrives an artful appearance of dogged bewilderment, like old Tully."

"He comes of a family of Tullys, does he not?" I said, to bait him a bit. "In a manner of speaking, to speak metaphorically."

"He is one of the Sullivans," Bob said, "on his mother's side. That does him no harm. His father was but clerk of the Poor Law Union in Bantry. He is a Cork man like ourselves. He learned shorthand to work in the offices of the railways in England, and sent sketches back to Ireland of what was going on in the Parliament. It was those sketches in the *Nation* that gave all of us our sense of what Parnell could do for us. You know that yourself, Hughie. We used read them out to each other."

"The *Nation*," I said, still baiting, but lightly, although that is not how Bob took it up. "Which oddly enough is owned by T. D. Sullivan."

"Jesus Christ, Hughie," Bob said. "There is no law that says a man cannot have uncles. You are proud enough of your own."

"My own," I said, "was Thomas Justin Nolan, not T. D. Sullivan."

"Your sardonic opinion is not shared by the Chief," Bob said. "When the Chief went off to America in 'seventy-nine, it was Tim Healy that he brought to assist him. He was a member of Parliament a year later, and a man of high standing in the movement, and he is still a young fellow in his twenties, a far younger man than we are ourselves. He has gone far and he will go farther."

And has he not! But it was not really Tim Healy that was on Bob's mind that autumn, and it was near the beginning of November that he and I had the talk which told me of one of the two great changes which came now into his life. The conference which established the new League—the Irish National League—was held in Dublin on the seventeenth of October, 1882, but it was not until the beginning of November that he came back to Kilpeder, and in that time there was no word from him, not to Agnes and not to any of us, although his name appeared for four days running in the national press as a member of the organising committee.

Healy chanced to be the man who told me that the Chief wanted to talk with me, in his room: Healy was the first man to call him that, if I remember aright, and then a number of us took it up—younger fellows, or else like myself fellows from the country. He had had his eye out for me that afternoon, but it was a slack day and I had taken a walk along the quays, and was returning to Morrison's Hotel along the far side of Nassau Street, beside railings of Trinity.

"He is in his room," Tim said to me. "He has been all day in his room."

"By God," I said, "he is entitled to his rest," for he had carried all before him at the meetings which presented the new constitution to the members, and told us (not for the first time in my own case, of course, for I had been at Avondale for the draughting of clauses and the planning of strategy) of plans to bring into Parliament ninety Irish members, and "Irish" according to our definition of that slippery word.

He was seated by the window, in those country tweeds of his, a fire working briskly upon the chill of the room, and a heavy travelling robe of blue plaid flung across his shoulders. But he half rose to greet me, with his habitual courtesy, and then again seated himself. The afternoon, as seen from that window, had a melancholy look which it had not possessed for me ten minutes before, the leafless trees in the College Park, and the gaunt eighteenth-century blocks of grey stone, where Swift and Burke had been students.

At the far side of the room from the fireplace was a table which he and Healy had been using as a desk, with papers stacked neatly upon it, a pot of ink, two ledger books resting one upon the other, a large one and a small. The chair that he motioned me to was awkwardly placed, a straight-back chair, parallel with his own, so that the two of us sat together, looking out upon that suddenly cheerless scene.

"I have a request to make of you, Mr. Delaney," he said. "You are a man of sense and judgement, and you can see what is happening. Government, for their part, is bringing harsh coercion laws down upon us, and these we shall fight tooth and nail. Some of them are out for our blood, and who can blame them, a juror stabbed yesterday five minutes' walk from here, and a grabber beaten to death last week in County Monaghan. Who can blame them? But we can win Gladstone around if we play the game aright. And the game henceforth, Mr. Delaney, for the next few years, will be played in London, against the politicians, not here, against the landlords. I need not tell that to you, a man, as I say, of sense and judgement."

Later, when I gave an accounting of this to Hughie and Vincent, I could see them exchanging amused glances. I was not without my vanity in those days, and I confess it. But beyond their amusement, I could see the look of men who were for once having a glimpse behind history's curtain, for the talk in all of the rural meetings, and in the nationalist press, had been of the Land War recommencing itself; but Parnell and young Healy and myself, in the darkling Dublin room, had been discussing a different kind of strategy indeed, one which in the end would outdo the League. Almost to the end, to speak more properly.

"It will not be a popular policy, Mr. Delaney," he said. "Not at first, not until it begins to show results. Dillon will not be all that happy, nor William O'Brien—oh, mind you, they will speak and write in its favour, act in its favour. Loyal men, the two of them. But they are anxious to take the fight back to the land. And it will go there—but at the right time, and on our terms."

"Yes," I said, as though I understood, but I did not, not entirely, although I had a glimmering. Healy was . . . beaming at me, or grinning—it is difficult to say which—as though I were being put to a test which I should have been mastering with ease.

"The organization will need a secretary in London," Parnell said. "In Westminster, to be more exact. Not the year round, God knows, not even for all of the time that Parliament is in session. But there will be times . . . We can manage a staff for you, a bright lad or two. Healy used to be able to manage for me with one hand what I am proposing to you; but I have other needs for him now, and he is himself a member of Parliament, and that takes away a bit of one's time. Not as much as is supposed. Not if you are an Irish member."

Dark had come into the room with that Dublin swiftness which can affect the spirit, and Healy, rising up, lit the gas jets, and then, at the desk, lit one, two, three, four, the candles which shed their lights upon his papers.

That is how it came to me, a latter-day Dick Whittington, the country boy upon the road to London and to his fortune and fame. Sylvia had called me that in the house in London. " 'Turn again, Whittington, Lord Mayor of London.' That is what the Bow Bells said to him. We can almost hear them from here, from Chelsea. Those are different bells, the ones we hear now. He had a cat, Dick Whittington did. Am I your cat, Bob?"

"He was a scullion," I said to her as we nestled together, apostle spoons, spoke into her ear, tangled hair. "He was a scullion who had a fight with the cook and ran off to legend."

"Ran off to legend," she said; "I like that."

"It need not affect at all your legal practice in Cork," Parnell said, "in Macroom."

"Kilpeder," Healy said from the desk.

"Kilpeder, of course," Parnell said. "I was thinking of that speech you made in Macroom, at the time of the boycotting. Your father-in-law could spare you for a few months a year, the odd month now and then."

"I manage Dennis Tully's legal matters for him," I said, hearing the stiffness in my own voice, "as well as those of others—farmers, graziers, merchants in other towns. And I have made time to serve as agent for the League, as you know, Mr. Parnell."

"Yes," he said, "you have indeed. That is what brought you to our attention, is it not, Healy?"

"I would be honoured," I said into the darkness, twisting in my chair to address a handsome, shadowed profile, bearded. Beneath the robe, I sensed, his hands were folded.

"Good cricket pitch over there," he said, nodding towards the darkness-shrouded grounds of Trinity. "I was a jolly good cricketer. At Cambridge. Only thing I did well at Cambridge. There was a Cork fellow at Cambridge with me, Tom Ardmor. Lord Ardmor. Family name is Forrester. He is from your very part of the world, is he not? Kilpeder?"

"Kilpeder," I said. "Ardmor Castle. And no need for a boycotting there, nor ever was. He reduced his rents the first bad year, before ever there was a League."

"Good," Parnell said, carelessly. "Good man. I cannot recall him clearly."

"As much cannot be said for his former agent," Healy said. "As much cannot be said for little Eddy Chute of the Property Defence Association."

"Chute," Parnell said. "Limerick name."

"Not this fellow," I said, "nor his father before him. West Cork agents born and bred."

"Write out a letter of appointment for Mr. Delaney, Healy. Make everything proper. By God, we have had some dicey agents in the past, Mr. Delaney—Hogan, Byrne. Don't happen to own any surgeon's knives, do you, butcher's knives?"

"I expect that you have looked at my record, Mr. Parnell. I served six months in prison. I have been a Fenian. I have taken up arms against Her Majesty, and have fired them off against her servants—Irish Constabulary and soldiers alike."

"It has served you well on the hustings, Mr. Delaney."

"On the platform, sir," I said. "Not the hustings."

"I am being premature," he said. "But only by a bit. What was that thing you told me, Healy, that Boney had said: 'A baton for every private'?"

Without looking up from his writing, Healy said, "That every French soldier carries a marshal's baton in his knapsack. He has to earn it, of course. There!" he said, and blotted the paper with so wide and dramatic a sweep of his arm that one of the four candles guttered and went out.

Almost immeasurably, that part of the room lay in deeper darkness, in near-night. Parnell measured it.

"My God, Healy," he said, in a strange, small strangled voice, a boy's voice almost. "Get it lighted. Or blow out another one. Quickly, man, what are you thinking of?" But Healy was almost before him with a box of matches, and the candle was relit. Foolish, I thought, for the three candles gave enough light for his work and more. It was not midnight.

I could hear Parnell's sigh of relief. "Nothing is worse than three lighted candles, you know that, Mr. Delaney, you must. In the hills of Cork such matters are known. There are few things more unlucky than three lighted candles; flames of death, they summon up spirits. And no month of the year so unlucky as October—dead leaves, dead skies, the feel of death in the air. I did all I could to put all this off until November, but we could not delay it. An unlucky month, Mr. Delaney; do nothing in October that you need not do. It comes out badly nine times out of ten."

But by the time I had bade him farewell, not ten minutes later, he was himself again, subdued, but courteous. He rose from the chair, the robe shrouded about him. "We will do well, Delaney," he said. "All of us together." He nodded: behind him, Dublin was again visible, for the lamplighters had been at work. Globes of pearly light, along Nassau Street.

"Pay no attention to that last bit," Healy said to me when we were in the carpeted corridor, walking towards the stairs. "He has superstitions that would do credit to a Kerry bonesetter."

Healy suddenly began to laugh; it shook his nervous, wiry frame. "Do you know the worst them all? I swear to God this is true. He has a mortal terror and loathing of the colour green. The greenest country in Europe, in every sense of that word. Green the national colour, green tacked up upon every platform he ever stands upon. The colour green."

"Whatever about green and candles and the month of October," I said, "it is a great honour to serve him. And I am in your debt for whatever good word you may have put in for me."

He paused, and put his hand upon my forearm. "Don't mistake me for a moment, Bob; don't ever mistake me on this point. The Uncrowned King, the Leader, the Chief—all that was my doing—phrases that I coined and sent home to the *Nation*. We were badly in need of someone like that, and now we have him. But there are no bricks without straw. I could not have done it without him being what he is—he is a remarkable man, clever and fierce as some animal in the jungles of Asia. But he is a strange creature as well. You caught a glimpse of that just now."

He was a remarkable little chap himself, eyes bright behind pince-nez, and a trim little beard, quietly dressed, but with a bit of dash to the cut of his long-tailed coat. A member of Parliament, after all.

"I put in a good word for you, Bob, I will not deny it. We are on the lookout for chaps like you. There is still old, dead wood in the party going back to the days of Butt, and tricksters out for a career, and some bog-trotting Land Leaguers from the wilds of Mayo and Donegal. But they will be gone before long; we are reshaping the party, the Chief and myself."

As we walked, he kept his hold upon my arm, as though he had forgotten his hand was there.

"But the Chief noticed you himself, you know, and Davitt and William O'Brien. Stirring times, Bob, stirring times. There is no telling where we will all find ourselves, what palmy coast. And old Ireland with us, of course."

But at the wide stairhead which led down into the lobby of the hotel, he paused again, and squeezed my arm almost with fierceness before dropping it. "Did you happen to notice the last word that he addressed to you? 'Delaney,' he said. 'Good evening, Delaney,' or something of that sort."

"'Tis my name," I said.

"Ah, but it had been 'Mr. Delaney,' you see. 'Mr. Delaney this' and 'Mr. Delaney that.' Until you had agreed to serve him, until you had gone into his service, so to speak."

Voices were now coming to us from below, and he lowered his own accordingly. "As I am 'Healy' to him, do you see, and Davitt is 'Davitt.' They are all alike, Bob, the gentry are, whichever side they may find themselves upon, and they never let us forget it. And how, by the way, is your good father-in-law?" He led the way down the stairs. "He is a prodigy, that fellow. A solid man. 'Tis around men like the Tullys of Kilpeder that we will build up the new Ireland. They are the new princely families."

And the Sullivans of Bantry, I thought. The Sullivans of Bantry and the Dillons of Julia Duff's shop in Ballaghadereen and the Lucies of Cashel and the Tullys of Kilpeder. Of whom I was one myself.

Later, years later, in the house in Chelsea, as Sylvia and I were having tea, a warm spring day, with blossoms on the cherry trees beyond the window, I remembered that night in Morrison's Hotel, and said, "Have you ever thought of calling me 'Delaney'?"

"Calling you what?" she asked, puzzled, and put down the book she was reading, marking the page with her finger.

"Delaney," I said, and told her the story, but by the end of it she was laughing.

"That would sound very odd, would it not?" she said. "A lady to call a member of Parliament by his surname, like a groom?"

"I was not when we first met," I said.

"You were not," she said. "We did not know what to expect—a wild Fenian, perhaps. Or a Land Leaguer with a pistol and a mouthful of Gaelic."

"I have been both of those," I said. "In my time."

We. It was a word which from first to last, almost to last, she used with careless ease, meaning, of course, her husband and herself. "Tom and I." "Tom often says." But there was great awkwardness for me always in speaking to her of Agnes, doing it as seldom as possible and finding circumlocutions. "My family" is the one we had settled upon. "I must go back to Kilpeder," I would say; "there is illness in the family." "Not young Conor, I trust," she would say.

Throughout all of the winter and spring of that year, he was away, at their villa in Cortona, but his presence was there. The walls were hung with his paintings, and those by friends of his whose names have become famous, were famous even then, one or two of them. Room after room of them, in no room crowded together upon the walls, as was the custom in other households of wealth, but one or two, chosen to hold with each other a conversation too subtle for me to overhear it.

When first I had seen such paintings as these, that first evening at Ardmor Castle, I attempted afterwards to explain to Hughie MacMahon their effect upon me, but I could not; and for all his interest in the mind and his natural instinct towards grace of feeling, I knew that he heard me out with a mixture of affection and incomprehending amusement. Later, of course, I might have been able to talk to him of them, but all that part of my life, which had become in most ways its centre, he listened to with nervous disapproval, concerned only for my safety, a friend's safety.

Not that Sylvia ever instructed me in art, or colour, or form: what knowledge she had of that was not a matter of words but of feelings; but I was always impressed by a quality in her which was noted also by our London acquaintances, who were artists for the most part, or on the fringes of that world, men and women whom I never saw save when she and I were together. She was reckless in that regard, and I followed her lead. It was a quality which allowed her to respond to painting as she did to the natural world, to sunsets upon rivers, to fog-shrouded streets, to a pear or peach, to the pleasures of the bed, with a swiftness so certain of itself that it was as good as accuracy, if not better.

"Tom said to me that first evening," she said to me upon that much later evening in Chelsea, "Tom said to me, 'He has the reins of life in his hands.' Tom is a splendid rider, did you know that? He doesn't ride or hunt these days as often as he did, but he is a splendid rider."

"I knew that," I said. "Master of the local hunt in the old days." The riders gathered at the falcon-guarded gates, the dogs restless in early morning light, scarlet-coated riders, masters of horse and scene. Down the full length of a dusty square, past the gilt lettering of Tully and Son.

"Do you know Robert Delaney?" she would ask, at one of the

"evenings" she dared for the two of us. *Bohemian* was the word then coming into vogue: it was an evening a bit "Bohemian" is how I would have named it to Hughie. "Mr. Delaney is a friend of ours. One of our fellow townsmen back in Kilpeder. But he is more than that: he is one of Parnell's bold fellows in Westminster. Mind yourselves now, we have an Irish rebel in our midst. Tom is very fond of him. We both are." But few of the guests at Mrs. Merihew's party cared about politics, English or Irish. There was a Mr. Merihew, it appeared, but he was away, governing some part of the Empire too tropical for Mrs. Merihew to endure.

"You are fortunate, dear Sylvia," Mrs. Merihew said, "to have such handsome fellow townsmen."

"Yes, dear Lucy," Sylvia said, "am I not?" And smiled, because malice was another of her pleasures, like fogs and rivers, a malice devoid of meanspirited intent, a savour.

"Not the only decent-looking fellow in his party," a very young man, not more than twenty, twenty-one, said, just down from Oxford, I had been told; he wrote things. "That chief of yours, the most handsome man in Commons, by God. My old fellow fumes at him at the breakfast table, over the *Times*. 'Damned renegade, that's all he is,' my old fellow will say; 'ought to be hanged like the murderers he has at his beck and call.' 'He is far too good-looking,' I say, and my old fellow turns purple behind his *Times*."

"He is most extraordinarily handsome, everyone says," Lucy Merihew said, "an unmarried man in his thirties; not much money but a good estate in Wicklow. Curious that he has not been snared; is that not curious, Sylvia?"

"How in the world would I know?" Sylvia said. "He is most attractive in his photographs; even the Spy caricature is attractive. You must ask Tom. Tom was at Cambridge with him."

"They knew," Sylvia said to me on the cherry-blossom evening in Chelsea, which was a year later, in 'eighty-five, before that damned Galway by-election which brought it all a bit out of the shadows, into a kind of half-light. "That night at Lucy Merihew's: those people knew that Parnell was keeping a woman, and if that lot knew, everyone does."

"Keeping a woman!" I said. "Not put with much delicacy, love."

"They knew far less than you have told me," Sylvia said.

"He is in love," I said. "And she is married. As you are. As I am."

"Not as I am," she said, with her sudden, mischievous laugh. "Very few are married as I am married."

"But you take my point," I said. "I do not find it easy to make sport of Parnell."

"Or marriage," she said. "What will I ever do about you, poor dear?"

"What you have done for me," I said. A bowl of flowers stood upon a low table between us, copper catching last sun, and above it a painting of winter sunlight. There is no other description: hills, light caping of snow, two vague, distant figures; but it was a painting of winter sunlight. I had learned more from her than love; from her walls, their walls, I had learned a way of seeing. Useless.

I spent almost all of 'eighty-five and 'eighty-six in London, good seasons and poor, sunlight and wretched yellow fog, and the worst London months of all, so they have always seemed to me, February and March, when winter seems to have been ratified as an eternity. But there was no help for it. Tom wrote not once but three times, urging me to join him in Cortona, that after all I could write there as easily as in England, more easily indeed without chill-cramped fingers, without huddling over a stove or beside a fireplace. But there was no help for it. I had two books upon the stocks, on which my income absolutely depended, and both of them held me bound to the British Museum, with the occasional train journey to Oxford.

Sylvia was the one unalloyed pleasure to me for all of one of those winters and well into the spring, for she had chosen not to travel to Cortona with Tom, and would have had no keen wish to spend by herself a West Cork winter. And so she stayed in that small, lovely house in Chelsea, on Cheyne Walk, which always seemed to me, still seems, closer to her in spirit, in manner of being, than most of the other places in which I have seen her.

But of course it was because of Robert Delaney, who was now a Parnellite member of Parliament, that she stayed in London. At first he was called by the wits a Tullyite, meaning by that term, which will not be discovered printed upon the parliamentary returns, a Parnellite pledged to keep a special lookout for the concerns of the Tullys, the Lucies, the Binchys, and the others. He was never that at base, of course, as events were to prove in crashing and irretrievable form; but the popular misunderstanding was a natural one, for he came to Parliament in 'eighty-four, hand-picked by Parnell to carry a by-election in a remote county. But 'eighty-six was the year in which Parnell and the Nationalists swept the board, smashing the old Whigs and Liberals and Buttites in Ireland, such as remained, and carrying to Westminster a party so large that it held the balance of power between Liberals and Conservatives. This time around, Bob's electoral expenses were paid for neither by the party nor by the Tullys, but by himself, and he made this known. For all that, however, he was regarded as a contradiction of qualities and histories—Fenian, small farmer's son, Land League agitator, and, inevitably, as the Healys and the Sullivans were "the Bantry Band," so was Bob Delaney the representative in the House, the first but surely not to be the last, of "the Kilpeder Clan."

So much I report as was common in the journals of the period, or in Sir Henry Lucy's malicious, lighthearted accounts, year by year, of parliamentary life. After 'eighty-six, though, Harry Lucy began to take the Irish members more seriously. In his early volumes, they are there as comic relief, with their bog-and-whiskey voices and oratory, their blunders, their droll turns of speech. Parnell was a different matter. He was no bog-trotter and he was a puzzler, a gentleman like George Henry Moore and The O'Conor Don, but ranged on the side of the moonlighters and the hillside men, capable of every sort of irreverence to the traditions of the House, drawled out in the tones of Cambridge and the best county hunts. But after 'eighty-six, after Parnell brought back his party of members, pledged to the point of being oath-bound, with the League at his back, and most of the bishops, and, in the judgement of many, with the unspoken, shadowy support of the dynamite men and the Fenians, Harry began to write of the Irish in different terms, mourning the passage from the scene of gentlemanly Irish from the old fighting families, true patriots if you will, a bit comical but lovable. About Parnell's eighty, there was nothing that Harry found lovable: Delaney was one of those whom he chose for one of his acid-tipped pen portraits.

But weeks of visits to Sylvia passed by, and I was a frequent visitor, before I encountered Delaney there. There were stray clues to a man's occasional presence, there always are—a pipe forgotten on a chimney piece—and there was little else of which she really wanted to talk, although we discovered a hundred different things. I always loved talking with Sylvia, because she was a lovely woman, of course, witty and sensual—an unlikely combination in my experience. That quality in her voice which I have described as that of silver—for, ransacking my mind, I can think of none more exact—was a quality of her being, bright, glinting, attractively tarnished, shining here and recessive there.

"Emily is not with me here, Lee," she said the first afternoon, after the parlourmaid had shown me in. "I am dreadfully sorry about that—on your account of course; but she is back in Westmeath, attending that poor brother of hers. Later on—a few months, perhaps. He has bad lungs, you know."

"I knew, Sylvia," I said. "Don't distress yourself."

"How strange Emily and you are together," she said. "I have never heard of quite the same sort of arrangement."

"You surprise me," I said. "Emily and you have no secrets, so I have believed."

"We have many," she said. "Shall we have tea?"

"I would rather have a whiskey," I said. "It is a raw afternoon."

She smiled. "What a good idea!" she said. "I'll join you." And so she did, pouring us two very stiff tots of Irish whiskey.

"Lee," she said presently, "will you take me to the House some evening, so that I can hear him? I want so to see him there, in that other life of his."

"I will take you, my dear, of course," I said, "but I will be taking you to the dullest place in London, this side of a nonconformist chapel."

"I would not find it dull."

"No, of course not. But he might not be speaking. Even the Irish keep quiet once in a while. Or he might be in the library, sleeping or writing you a letter. Perhaps he might be writing home."

"No," she said, "he will not. We will arrange it. He will tell me a good night and I will send you a note."

"His other life," I said. "A curious phrase. Surely he has several at least. He has Kilpeder. And he is still thick in League matters—dangerous matters some of them, member of Parliament or not. He could wind up in a gaol cell again for six months or so. It has happened, is happening."

She rose, in a single, graceful movement, and went to the window, looking out into the garden on her cherry trees, leafless now, delicate-branched. She was holding her glass in both hands, and then, in a sudden move, she took a deep draught of it, as a man would.

"This is his life," she said. "Here. And this is mine."

It was at that moment, with the air still holding her words, that I realised how serious it had become.

"Oh my dear," I said. "Oh dear Sylvia."

"Why 'Oh dear Sylvia'?" she said, with her long slender back to me, talking to the window, to the bare trees, to herself. And then, but to me now, although without turning, "Why, Lee? Why 'Oh dear Sylvia'?"

"Because you are in love," I said. "The two of you, you and Robert Delaney."

"Yes," she said, "we are. He in his way and me in mine; they are different ways, but yes, we are in love."

"If you mean that in the way that I know that you do, then it is a dangerous matter. Could be dangerous. You are going outside the rules."

The rules are still with us, elaborate rules—whether the visiting gentleman leaves his hat and gloves on the hall table, how guest rooms are disposed on country-house weekends—rules intricate as some game contrived by Persians or Chinese, but workable, by and large.

She turned now, and looked straight at me. "Tom and I have a marriage that is quite far beyond the rules, wouldn't you say?"

"Not outside the main rule," I said. "The main rule is don't get caught out, as you damned well know. And love can play hell with that. Love, need I remind you, is a passion."

"Tom and I love each other. He in his way and me in mine. We haven't—what was your vulgar phrase for it?"

"Tom and you have a love which I suspect is stronger than the way you feel about Delaney. But *passion* isn't a word that comes to mind."

She stood motionless for a moment, as though checkmated, and then poured herself another Irish, adding a splash to my own glass almost as an afterthought.

"Bob's leader," she said, "from the bits and pieces that I have heard—that isn't a mistress that he has, some vulgar tart in silks hidden away in Saint John's Wood. He is in love with that Mrs. O'Shea—so some people say. That is dangerous, more dangerous."

"It is indeed," I said, "if true. But it is beside the point."

Which should put an end to the absurd notion that the relations between Parnell and Katharine O'Shea were scarcely known until shortly before the scandal broke. Sylvia would have known about it from Robert Delaney, of course; but not me. I knew because it was common gossip of the House among Liberals and Conservatives, and from the House it had spread, years before, to the clubs, and from the clubs to drawing rooms and bedrooms. Katharine O'Shea had even served a few times as go-between, carrying messages to and fro between Parnell and Gladstone, and so had her husband, incredibly enough, a wretched little ex-officer who clung to his captaincy as a mark of respectability—Captain William O'Shea, "Willie." And a messenger, Willie was, to Joe Chamberlain as well. A squalid little triangle, which made gossip only because it seemed so difficult to reconcile with the Parnell of legend.

"And Delaney," I said. "How does Delaney feel about the dangers in all this—the dangers to him? As well as to yourself."

" 'Robert,' " she said, "I want you to call him 'Robert.' You are my great friend, Lee, and I want you to be friends with him."

"Willingly," I said. "I am greatly taken with him. And I have seen him in action, outside the gates of those boycotted estates—the estates of your neighbours and former friends, by the way. A formidable fellow. I'm not puzzled that you have been drawn to him; that isn't my concern."

She sipped at her whiskey, and then, sitting down again to face me, gave me one of her Sylvia smiles: irresistible, beyond argument, logic. "I think—mind you, Lee; I say I think—that I am very happy. I cannot be certain because I haven't known much of it. Not that I have been *un-*happy, but—you know what I mean."

Beyond argument, logic? I think so still, but cannot be certain, and know only that I never again tried to argue her out of it. Perhaps I should have—friendship urged it upon me; love, for the two of them, for Tom as well as Sylvia; family loyalty—everything urged it upon me. But it would have been useless. Who can argue against happiness; what weapons can prevail against it?

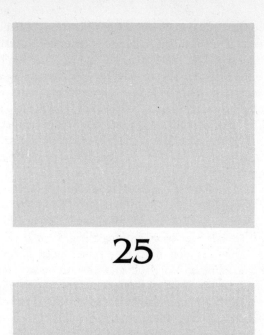

25

*[Patrick Prentiss/Hugh MacMahon/
Robert Delaney/Lionel Forrester]*

Patrick Prentiss knew, of course, that first reference to Robert Delaney, reprinted by Sir Henry Lucy in his *Diary of the Salisbury Parliament, 1886–1892*. It was, in fact, the first of a number of references to Delaney, but it set the tone, written in Lucy's best or worst manner: chattery, condescending, snide.

> An obscure paragraph in the morning newspapers tells us of the death of a man who once filled a large space in the House of Commons, Major O'Gorman. He was by far the biggest man in the house, big in girth, big in heart and spirit, and the primest favourite. He was indescribably funny, the real Irishman of flesh and blood (and a good deal of both) whom Charles Lever used to draw, and a source of unfailing amusement to Mr. Disraeli. It was a study to watch Mr. Disraeli with his eyeglass screwed in his eye, and his face taking on new wrinkles with unwonted laughter, as he watched

the Major in the paroxysm of his oratorical passion. But there was more to the Major than an elephantine ponderosity. He was the best of the old Irish school, save for Mr. Butt, his leader. He had won his title honourably, had appeared on the field of battle on behalf of Her Majesty, wearing her scarlet uniform. And more than once had appeared upon the field of honour, where, granted his dimensions, it is little short of a miracle that he survived the encounter. But perhaps he was in youth more slender, or perhaps he was protected by those medals of the Virgin which, it is said, he was never without; for he was, of course, a zealous although never a bigoted son of Holy Mother Church.

And whom shall we select out as representative of the band which has replaced Butt and Shaw and O'Gorman and The O'Donoghue—Mr. Parnell's choice crew? Shall it be Mr. William O'Brien, the penny-a-lining journalist with a taste for bloodcurdling rhetoric, or tricky little Mr. Tim Healy, Mr. Parnell's lapdog, but a lapdog no longer, so rumour has it, and in any event a feline sort of lapdog, with cruel claws and a razor-sharp tongue? Shall it be Mr. F. X. O'Brien, who bears the distinction of having, in 1867, been the last man in this kingdom sentenced to be hanged, drawn, and quartered? Shall it be one person or possibly two of whom it is whispered that they know a thing or two more than they ought of that butchery in the Phoenix Park of which Mr. Parnell professes such horror?

No, these are cases rather too special, or, in the last instance, too delicate. Let us, rather, take Mr. Robert Delaney, member for County Cork. A brisk, confident sort of fellow is Mr. Delaney, the nervousness of his first session behind him now, of average height, sturdily built and not ill favoured, with a thick brown moustache. He will appear in the House on occasion in the roughest of tweeds, as what member will not from time to time, but these so Connemara rough that one might expect snipe to fly from the pockets. For the most part, though, and unlike the great majority in Mr. Parnell's "Tail," he is quietly, indeed elegantly dressed, as though some firm hand—or, shall we not say, some gentle, feminine hand—has guided him to a decent English tailor.

Like the late Major O'Gorman, Mr. Delaney has worn the Queen's uniform, but one of quite a different cut and colour, with broad arrows upon it, earned not by serving the Queen, but rather by taking part in the ludicrous, but alas murderous, Fenian uprising against her. It has served him well, those few hours of rebellion, and the months of skulking and plotting which preceded them, no doubt. He is indeed the "hero" or, rather, one of the "heroes" of a ballad based upon the episode, one which enjoys popularity in Ireland upon political or bibulous occasions, to the extent that these may be distinguished from each other.

Mr. Delaney is deep in the counsels of the Irish National League, and most especially of its agrarian flank, the flank whence issues its moonlighting, whiteboyism, maiming of cattle, murder of landlords and disputatious tenants. He is a natural ally, then, of such as Mr. Dillon and Mr. O'Brien, but it has been marked from the outset that he has a particular sense of loyalty to his leader. No other Irish member, save only Mr. Healy at the outset, shows a readier ability to discern and carry out Mr. Parnell's wishes. And Mr. Parnell, for his part, has been observed to display towards Mr. Delaney some faint measure of warmth, far removed, of course, from actual camaraderie, but something other than the icy remoteness which he has made so effective an aspect of his political being.

In Mr. Delaney, it might in summary be said, we have an example brought almost to perfection of the new Irishman, as that genus is being shaped by the conjoined pressures of history, of the strange aloof figure who has risen to mastery over them, and, of course, of ordinary, old-fashioned ambition. For Mr. Delaney is an ambitious man, let there be no doubt of that: a shop assistant turned rebel turned solicitor, turned land agitator, turned member of Parliament, and married into one of the great mercantile families—or, as they are known in that island—one of the great "gombeen" families of Ireland, the Tullys of West Cork. He has even that one quality which alone distinguishes both the old and the new Irishman—a dash of the dangerous; for was not his leader in the Fenian uprising "Ned" Nolan, "Dynamite" Nolan, by common repute involved if not in the Phoenix Park horrors, then certainly in the recent series of explosive outrages and attacks upon property and life in London and other English cities? And if Mr. Delaney has repudiated his erstwhile leader, it has not been in the hearing of this writer, and certainly not in the House.

"Surely," Patrick Prentiss said to his father's friend O'Clery, as they sat together in the Stephen's Green Club, the club favoured by Catholics and the more genial sort of Protestant, "surely," he said, speaking of a brief later entry in Lucy's *Diary*, "that was cutting close to the bone."

The slight degree of warmth which exists between Mr. Parnell and that most unlikely object for it, the member for County Cork, Mr. Delaney, may be less mysterious than we had at first believed. Their personal lives are lived far indeed from public view, and this, slender though it may appear, is something of a bond, perhaps. The House, by the way, is as we know now graced by the new member for Galway, Captain William O'Shea, a dapper, ex-military sort, with glinting monocle and neatly waxed moustaches. The dramatic circumstances which led to his imposition upon the unwilling voters of Galway will be well remembered. Mr. Parnell is apparently indebted to him for some favour or other, and as an Irish gentleman he is, of course, punctilious in the payment of debts.

"Close to the bone indeed," O'Clery said. "But that wretched Galway by-election in 'eighty-six set every rumour flying, far beyond the party, and at last finding their way into printed hints and innuendos and all the slimy mess of it. That little swine Stead, the canting, sanctimonious nonconforming gutter journalist, had his little hint or two to make. Lucy was being relatively decorous, in fact."

They sat by the tall windows of the club, watching strollers on their way to the Shelbourne or from it. Across the road, Stephen's Green was heavy with summer leafage; ducks floated upon the toylike lake, studied from benches by children and governesses. A small girl dashed to the water's edge, frightening the ducks, but she scattered crusts of bread, and they swam back.

"The touch about Delaney, I meant," Prentiss said, and quoted the words again from the card on which he had written them.

"That! I hadn't considered that, for the moment. And I wonder if I did then. No, it could not have been known to many people at the time, Irish or English, Whig or Tory. Even though Delaney had become a man to watch. No, it was not known for several years. Does Lucy try it on again?"

"No," Prentiss said. "Not once. Not until the end, not until everything crashed."

"Extraordinary. Some little bird whispered once, and once only, in Harry Lucy's delicate ear."

"He had become a man to watch, you say."

"Oh, yes, indeed yes. Not Dillon's calibre, not yet at any rate; but he was moving there. A comer, like young Johnny Redmond, and you see how far he has travelled. No scandals at Johnny Redmond's coattails, though."

"He was so often home, to Kilpeder," Prentiss said. "Perhaps that—"

"On League business; and the land agitation went on apace, you know. He was active with Dillon and O'Brien in the Plan of Campaign. And he was a solicitor, after all, with a busy practice. Though towards the end, he was sharing that out with Dan Mulkerns in Millstreet; they might have formed a partnership, if everything had worked out."

O'Clery raised a ponderous hand from the arm of his chair and motioned to the waiter, who had been standing quietly, half asleep, resting against the wall of the otherwise deserted room.

"But really," O'Clery said, "or so I have heard, he came back to see that boy of his. Dermot, his name was. No, Conor. He worshipped that boy, they say. I am not the man to ask about Delaney's life at home, of course. We were allies, in a way, in the House. But never close. That schoolmaster pal of yours, back in Kilpeder. He's the man to ask."

Not Conor, certainly. Prentiss had made an approach to Conor, and had been received with wariness. Conor had no wish to talk about his father, not to Prentiss, not to anyone.

By the time the waiter had brought them their morning coffee, other members had drifted in, two or three groups of them, and a man on his own whom Prentiss recognised: Blake-O'Ferrall, another barrister, like O'Clery, like his father. This was his father's world.

"After that Galway election in 'eighty-six," O'Clery said, his voice a murmur, "when Parnell rammed Willie O'Shea down our throats, like it or not. 'The O'Sheas will be your ruin,' Joe Biggar told the Chief. A fierce, honest little Ulsterman, Joe Biggar."

"But Delaney's ruin, if we can call it that . . ." Prentiss began.

With a swiftness that surprised him, the ponderous old hand reached out, and grabbed his arm. "Softly, Patrick. A bit softly. This was fifteen years ago, or less. We are not talking about the Third Crusade, you know, or life at Versailles. Blake-O'Ferrall over there knew Delaney well, but I wouldn't ask Blake-O'Ferrall about him, if I were you. Get a string of oaths for your trouble. Blake-O'Ferrall and Healy are pals; they were fierce against Parnell. Your father was on their side, you know, but never fierce about it, I trust I can say. Good God, the man had to go, for the good of the country, good of the party—that was your father's stance. But you can't fault a man for gallantry, eh? A bit of petticoat."

"We were speaking of Robert Delaney," Prentiss reminded him gently.

"I saw her once," O'Clery said. "Not with him, of course. She was riding in the park. With her husband. God, what a woman, Patrick! Do you know who she reminded me of, as she sat her mount—I remember the mount, a chestnut, and her black riding habit, back straight but at ease? Elizabeth, the Empress of the Austrians. She came over here to ride, you know, Elizabeth did. Had a lover here. No, no, Patrick, you could never call Sylvia Ardmor a bit of petticoat."

"She was called as much," Prentiss said. "In Kilpeder. I have heard a phrase that Healy had for her."

"Healy!" O'Clery said, and left it at that.

"Loved," Hugh MacMahon replied to Prentiss, "why of course Bob loved Conor. Why would a man not love his own son? And when Conor was little, he worshipped Bob. You could see him staring at Bob often, wide-eyed. Once, when Bob was on the platform in the town, during the Plan of Campaign it was, I chanced to glimpse Conor, standing in the crowd, on his own—Agnes had no taste for popular demonstrations—and it must have been during the long vacation; at any rate, he was home from

Clongowes Woods, and he was looking up at Bob, who was not even, at that moment, speaking; he had just introduced O'Brien. That boy worshipped his father. Then. You would not guess that now, would you, Patrick?"

"I might," Prentiss said. "The end came as a great shock to a boy who felt that way. And in the final year, Delaney was no joy to any of you, I gather."

"You could say that," MacMahon said dryly. "Of course now, Bob had his own way of showing that love. It was because he was burdened with so much that he had not the proper time to give to the lad. 'Yes, boy, what is it now?' he would say—that sort of thing. And as often as not, when I took my own lads fishing, I would take Conor along with us, because Bob was in London, or fighting some cause elsewhere in the county or in Tipperary or wherever. But that never fazed Conor. 'My father is a soldier for Ireland,' he would say, 'and soldiers are away fighting their wars. That is the way of it.'"

"Was there a physical resemblance?" Prentiss asked, and MacMahon gave a sudden whoop of laughter.

"Indeed there was not. Where in the world is there blood that can contend against the blood of the Tullys? Blood cells like bull elephants, they must have. And it is in the heart and brain as well: if you are a Tully, sooner or later it will emerge, strong as granite."

"Except for Vincent," Prentiss said.

"Yes. Except for Vincent."

But what I could not bring myself to tell Patrick, among many other matters no doubt of far greater consequence, is that Bob seemed to me neglectful of Conor. On the rare Sunday that he would find himself in the town, the two of us would have our customary walk into the hills, and this was a matter of importance to him, as though he found his bearings less in what we said to each other, than in the trustworthiness of our silences, and perhaps he took his bearings from geography, for we had our set walks, four or five of them, one towards the distant townlands from which the Delaneys had sprung, from which he had long before ventured down to find employment. And another towards the distant Derrynasaggarts, beyond which lay Kerry. And we had never, either of us, forgotten that mission we had taken in 'sixty-seven, to get the lay of the land on the eve of the Rising, and the chill it had given us to see the British army assembled there in its might and dignity, each of us knowing at that moment when we stood outside the railway hotel that the Rising would be hopeless but neither of us saying it to the other. And we had a walk which we would make into Clonbrony Wood, where pulsed away the heart of all that happened afterwards.

"They mean to get us, Hughie," he might say to me suddenly, "and they cannot do it by fair means, so they will use foul." That is the manner in which I would get news from him of the great world in which he now moved.

"Ach, wisha, Bob," I would say, all worldly wise. "You have them on the trot. Tis the other way round entirely. Eighty members in their House, oath-bound, loyal one to another. You hold the balance of power in the bloody kingdom. Every paper says so, even the *Irish Times*, although it says it with fury."

"That is why, do you not see?" Bob said. "The British government, Tory or Liberal, will not stand still and let itself be bullied and robbed by a band of Irish highwaymen. Brennan on the moor!"

Bold, brave, and undaunted was young Brennan on the moor: how simple life is as it is lived in ballads. To myself, and to most fellows of my sort—"decent Irish nationalists" is how we would fondly describe ourselves—there was in the air a kind of giddiness of victory for which we had had no ancestral training, no taste of victory lingering upon the racial palate. It was a novel and savoursome experience. This walk of ours, upon this particular Sunday, was towards the village of Graney, in the hills, a village famed in song and story, if you include among famous songs the "Ballad of Clonbrony Wood" and "The Flight of Ned Nolan"; for at the end of the walk, whatever the hour, and Sunday or not, there would always be a shebeen whose door would be open to our discreet and ritualistic knock: two long, two short. And the time, of this I am almost certain, would be the Christmas season of 'eighty-six.

In London, Parnell had made his alliance with Gladstone—not as a supplicant, as Butt might have done, nor as a crafty, O'Connellite bargain, but rather as a chieftain at the head of his people; and so he appeared to all of us, to Irish and to English alike, aloof and resolute, a creature, so the Tory press had it, of Satanic pride. And well they had cause to know, for he had dallied with them for a bit, to make Mr. Gladstone nervous. And in the autumn, at home, the Plan of Campaign had been announced, and by now, by Christmas, was in full swing, to complete what the Land League had done four years earlier, what Bob's *Christmas in the Boggeraghs* had helped to do: to destroy feudalism in Ireland.

"That is why," he said again.

A light snow had fallen in the night, and it was difficult to put away from my mind the events of twenty years before—a wintry landscape, the ground hard beneath us, close-packed by frost. But we neither of us spoke of it: buried in the past, travestied in song.

"They are still sniffing the ground," he said, "for some trail that will carry them from us to the Invincibles. Or if that won't do, connecting us with the moonlighters and the Whiteboys. And they might just manage that—some of the League fellows in Mayo and Tipperary are indelicate creatures, and there have been murders. Balfour could bring in Coercion measures against us so ferocious as to shut us down entirely, put us out of business."

"What matter what the English do," I said, "if you have our people behind you. Our people and the Church."

At Mass that morning, winter sunlight falling upon altar, pews, through panes of coloured glass, green, red, yellow, I had been moved to think, not of Christ and His sacrifice, but of the community of feeling which held us bound together and of what it augured. For twenty years before, the year of the Fenians, the year of Clonbrony, we had done what we did—Bob and Vincent and myself and Ned Nolan and the others of us—with the words of priestly condemnation in our ears, although we stuffed our ears against them. But the Church was in support of the Plan of Campaign, as it supported Parnell and the cause of Home Rule— Father Meagher made this clear to us in his discreet, soft manner, hands folded benignly beneath his chasuble, speaking what had become in Ireland the Church's other language, rival to Latin, English, Gaelic, phrases that we had all, through decades, learned to read: "the just and lawful measures which an unarmed and peaceful people must employ if they are to protect their small homesteads, their hearth fires" . . . "wise leaders have devised for you, leaders in our town and far beyond it, a plan for your protection and for the protection of young families upon their own soil—a plan of campaign, I might dare to call it, if that did not have a political ring to it, out of place in a house of worship."

By "leaders in our town," he meant Bob, of course, and the two who deputised for him in his absence: Father Mullane the curate and Brendan Fogarty, the town's new young Catholic solicitor. Bob was in the pew directly behind that of the Tullys, Bob and Agnes and Conor, and beyond his shoulder I could glimpse old Tully, his polished, dull-pink skull, with the purplish wen at its side, above an ear, the size of a robin's egg.

"Yes," Bob said, in his blunt, irreverent way, "the Church has been surprisingly good in this matter. It has come up to the mark. Perhaps I was wrong to have misgivings: the Church can smell out victory as the beasts of Europe are sent to hunt for truffles." With his blackthorn, he made a slash at dry hedges. "The training of centuries. It pays."

"You are as great a cynic as Vincent," I said, scandalised and amused. "But you save it up for private conversations."

"Private irreverence would not serve Vincent's purposes," Bob said. "His goal in life is to shock the old man."

"A modest goal," I said, "easily attained. You did not take the Sacrament this morning, I chanced to observe."

"Private life in Kilpeder is close to impossible," he said. "No, I did not. I had not been to confession."

"I was not being intrusive," I said. "A friendly word only. The doings of a member of Parliament are remarked upon. We don't have all that many of them, and few in the past have been our own."

"Your point is taken," Bob said.

L ater, much later, when Bob Delaney by preference did his drinking alone, neither in shebeen nor friend's sitting room, the spired church visible beyond the lace-curtained window, he once remembered, out of all their walks together, that winter's walk with Hugh MacMahon, remembered it for MacMahon's light, well-intentioned words: "You did not take the Sacrament this morning, I chanced to observe."

"No," Delaney answered him, sitting alone, measuring out whiskey from a smeared Waterford decanter with shaking hand, in the dusty office which few visited save farmers who remembered him from the old days, and had unexacting work for him—a document to witness, a bit of conveyancing, "no, I did not."

I could have told him then, should have. But how could he have understood? He would have understood, shocked and angry, had I told him, shall we say, that I had misappropriated League funds, or had kept quadruple books for old Tully, siphoning off into my own funds from his supply of crumpled pound notes. But not that I felt nothing for Agnes, had not for years, that my true life was in London, in a slender handsome Chelsea house which was even then waiting for my return, a fire banked warm and secure against Thamesside fog, and, above, a bed where my true life lay within her arms, her opened legs, thighs, the warm soft nest of love.

My love for Sylvia lay beyond his understanding, so I thought. And was I not right? For when I did tell him, a year or two later, blurting it out, the whiskey doing the speaking for me, did he not respond as I had expected—shocked, you could see the stiffening of shoulder, arm, almost see the withdrawal of spirit, sympathy. "Tell me no more of that," he said.

"Whom am I then to tell," I asked him, who was the dearest of my friends, "tell Vincent? Tell Father Meagher?"

"Tell God," Hugh said to me, "or whisper it to the reed, like Midas of old."

My conscience, such as it was, was best left untended, or else battled over with the Scottish-born priest of the church near my lodgings in Pimlico, an area much favoured by the M.P.'s in our party, being sufficiently grim and cheerless to satisfy the national taste in such matters. "Dear, dear," Father Simpson would say, a voice coming to me through the grille, through the darkness. "Oh dear, what a muddle."

It was in the early spring of 1887 that Sylvia asked me to a late supper with Delaney and herself, served before the fire in the room facing out upon Cheyne Walk. A busy month, a busy season of that year for Delaney, moving constantly forward and back, by that wretched mailboat, between London and Ireland, with the Plan of Campaign under way, the Land War begun anew, first Clanricarde's estate at Portumna in Galway, and then De Freyne in Roscommon, Lansdowne himself the great grandee at Luggacurran, Brooke at Coolgreaney, Massereene in Louth. And, of course—fatally, as it was to emerge—Kingston in Mitchelstown. Locals led the agitations, but the strategists of the campaign were O'Brien and Dillon and Delaney and a few others. Every Sunday found one or another of them on a platform, hung with green bunting, in some landlord's town, the big house besieged in one form or another.

"No," Delaney said in answer to my question. "I had my Christmas in Kilpeder."

"He was visiting his family," Sylvia said, mock-demure, as she poured our coffees into slender china cups, fluted, designs of blues and reds.

"I wonder you did not find an occasion to combine business with pleasure," I said. "The boycotting in 'eighty drove out poor old George Wilcox, but there is always Ardmor Castle."

Bob smiled, and picking up a humidor from a side table, opened it and offered me a cigar. I looked towards Sylvia and she nodded.

"We are quite domestic, you see," she said. "Supper by the fire, a cigar. Darby and Joan."

"It is not a game, Mr. Forrester," Bob said. "The proprietor of the Ardmor estates has made his terms with his tenants, as I am certain you have reason to know. But not every landlord in the barony is so sensible. The Plan will reach Kilpeder, have no fear."

The proprietor of the Ardmor estates: a nice formality.

"Call him 'Lee,' " Sylvia said, "and Lee is to call you 'Bob.' I want you both to be great friends. You are my two great friends."

"Eddy Chute is bustling about with his Property Defence Association, and this time there will be a Tory government back here in London to whisper in his ear. He has already been busy in Mitchelstown."

"To be honest with you, Delaney," I said, "I am shamelessly lazy when it comes to politics. I scarcely read the newspapers."

"Lee is writing a book," Sylvia explained to him. "Two books, in fact. When he writes his books he lives in them."

"Not quite," I said.

"What sort of books are these ones?" he asked, politely, but out of what seemed a genuine interest. Sylvia had hit on the right phrase: Darby and Joan. And yet an odd one in its way, for she had never looked more alluring: domesticity agreed with her, or adultery, or the pleasures of the bed. All three, most likely. But perhaps, to be fair about it, it was Delaney, who in those years was impressive in his way, intelligence and energy. And self-confidence.

"Two very different kinds of book," I said. "One for pleasure, which may sell a few hundred copies and receive respectful, unhelpful notices. Travel sketches, written up from notes I made ten years ago or more, Venice, Bergamo." I shrugged. "I don't want it to be the usual thing—gondolas, shadows on the canals, crumbling buildings, Casanova. It is a pleasure to write, but it has been promised for the spring."

"Tom and I spent months in Venice, after our wedding. Lee should have visited us there. We could be in the book. Leaning from a balcony, dreaming into the Canal."

"And the other book?" Delaney said.

"Not worth talking about," I said. "It should make pots of money. The last two did. An historical romance of sorts. Swords and simple honesty, powerful villains confronted, treachery unmasked."

"Don't you believe him, Bob," Sylvia said. "He is very careful with his romances. He keeps himself chained to a desk in the British Museum. Like that German Jew you told us about, Lee, who sits there every day, plotting our destruction in our own museum, using our own books."

"He is dead now," I said. "It was years ago that he was using the

Museum. When I was a young man. He is very famous, or else notorious. Really, Sylvia, do you never read?"

"The books of friends, poems by friends. It keeps me busy."

"Delaney here—Bob here—is held by some to be plotting our destruction. The present ministry is much of that opinion, and many on the other benches."

"And Eddy Chute," Delaney said, smiling, at fireside ease. He was enjoying his cigar.

"And poor George Wilcox, and Boycott up in Mayo and Mrs. Blake and all the others," I said. "You are plotting their destruction, in a way, are you not? I ask out of a disinterested curiosity."

"The proprietor," he began, and then, as though realizing the stiltedness of the language, said, "Lord Ardmor's destruction is not held in contemplation. He has twice come to terms with the Ardmor tenants, in the bad year of 'seventy-nine, when the Land League was being formed, and again now, under the Plan of Campaign."

"He can afford to," I said, "but the smaller landlords cannot."

"Enough of this," Sylvia said, seriously but in the tone of a mock-fury. "Politics after a meal in front of a winter fireplace. I will fall sleep directly, with the two of you droning at me."

What she said was the truth, but not quite the truth; for politics did indeed bore her, almost as much as they bore me, and she had no especial interest in that side of Delaney. She saw the other side, the conspirator, ex-gaolbird, the man who led mobs of tenants to demesne gates, nighttime torches blazing like those of arsonists, the man who spoke language upon platforms which came a subtle hairsbreadth short of the criminally incendiary. She liked Delaney of Clonbrony Wood. No: loved him, of course.

That night, a few weeks earlier, when I had taken her to the House, upon Delaney's promise that he would be speaking, I glanced at her from time to time as she sat in the Ladies' Gallery, leaning forward gracefully but a bit less than ladyish, her elbow on knee, chin resting on small fist. She sat in profile to me, her face a cameo beneath the swooping and dramatic hat, a coil of hair fallen free from it.

Delaney was badgering Arthur Balfour, Salisbury's nephew and the new Chief Secretary for Ireland. Not that Balfour, a languid exquisite, is easily badgered; and for all his affectations and literary flourishes, he had been taking a Caligulan delight in flinging Plan of Campaigners into prison, including a few with whom Delaney had stood upon platforms. Although the two of them, the exquisite and the shop assistant, abided by the decorum of the house, their detestation of each other was evident.

"The Chief Secretary," Delaney would say, disdaining such hypocrisies as "my honourable friend," or the more distant "the right honourable gentleman." "The Chief Secretary," Delaney said, "is determined to fill the prisons of Ireland with those who dare to speak out for the poor evicted tenants of Ireland. Exactly as he and those who went before him were determined that the workhouses should be filled with the evicted, the workhouses and the coffin ships to Halifax and Boston and New York. But some of those ships stayed afloat, and their cargo have planted in the United States and in Australia an Ireland Abroad, which has shaken greatly this kingdom, and will continue to trouble it, until Ireland has won measures which secure life for the lowliest of her paupers."

"The member for Cork," Balfour drawled, "has a knowledge of the activities of the American Irish to which I willingly defer. And I would be most eager, as would the Home Secretary, to learn from him the much that he can doubtless tell us about the activities of those Yankee Irish friends of his, his former comrades-in-arms, may I call them."

"Call them what you will," Delaney said, with a flash of anger. "They don't give a damn what you call them, and neither do I." He sat down, the anger having played havoc with his customary skill at debate, and folded his arms.

Healy came to his rescue.

"Perhaps the right honourable gentleman has also an interest in what he himself is being called in the newspapers of New York and Boston." He was being called everything just short of being called a catamite— "Bunthorne" was a frequent term among those literate enough to have heard of Gilbert and Sullivan, "delicate flower," "mincing Miss Arthur." Not that any of this bothered Balfour, who smiled at Healy with an almost affectionate contempt, for he rather savoured the readiness of Healy's gutter tactics.

But when Delaney spoke again that night, he was in control of himself, and, as with a few others among Parnell's lieutenants—his "new men," as they were called—he impressed me, as he did most who heard him: his arguments marshalled like battalions in support of his invective, speaking this time, as he had not when Balfour got under his guard, with a deliberate and angry certainty. And all that while, on both of the occasions, Sylvia's cameo profile had its own story to tell to anyone with eyes to see.

As for Parnell himself, in those days he would be missing from the House for weeks at a stretch, adding greatly to the air of mystery which had attached itself to him, and which persisted even among the many who knew or guessed by now as to the reasons for his absences. But it was equally certain that he remained the master of the party, directing its every move, save, Delaney once admitted to me, for some aspects of the Plan of Campaign. But tonight, he condescended to drop in, very late, slipped into an inconspicuous seat, and sat for an hour, hands buried deep in the pockets of his Norfolk jacket, rough tweed, half buttoned over a cardigan. Presently, he sent notes to two or three of the members asking them to talk with him—Delaney himself was one, Healy another, and Justin McCarthy. They followed him when he rose and sauntered down the gangway, a tall, slender figure. He was wearing, incongruously, a white rose as a buttonhole.

That was one of many evenings or nights that I spent with them in Chelsea; and Sylvia was right: I did develop an affection for Delaney—a kind of friendship, it could be called, although not a deep one; for there was too much separating us—tastes, interests—and I have always been a bit put off by ambition, however nicely it has been arranged or concealed. But I preferred, much preferred, my afternoons alone with Sylvia, and especially as winter, even London's winter, warmed into spring. She was pleased to see me always, in part, I suspect, because I took so much for granted, even, or perhaps especially, Tom's ever lengthening sojourns in Cortona. Our friendship was genuine and deep; but there was a time when Sylvia really was in need of my company, because Bob was back in prison—not the genteel confinement of Kilmainham this time, but hard planks for a bed and the wretched food of a county gaol.

But often I wonder—never anxiously, I confess—about Emily's question to me, in bed that dawn at Ardmor: did I ever fancy Sylvia? Yes, of course, of course I did, but in a complicated way; and yet beyond question there was a quality of the erotic in our friendship, like a room touched by light of some certain colour, impalpable, affecting all that is palpable, evanescent.

A nd Mr. Lionel Forrester, call him Lee Forrester, Robert Delaney said once to himself, at the end, sorting things out, not drinking that afternoon, but sitting in the dusty office, his back to the market square, his hands resting flat upon the handsome, dark-wooded desk, a small pile of unattended, unimportant solicitor's papers pushed to one side. A decent enough fellow, as such fellows go. Like her husband, like Ardmor. No, he was more than decent. He had an easy way with him that I admired, wanted almost to emulate, but had too much sense. He knew how to take life easy, as the old song about the sally gardens has it. It is a trick, taking life easy. The gentry have it, and corner boys, the occasional drover; but it is one which I have never mastered.

As he looked back upon those years, the Dick Whittington years, as Sylvia called them, he remembered that quality which all who knew him then remarked upon, his sense of certainty; but he remembered also a fragmentation so deep, along lines of fissure deep as ravines, that he wondered now how self-confidence could have accompanied it. Kilpeder and the Tullys, his evenings with Hugh and Mary, Vincent on occasion, walking down each morning when in town to make his duty call at the shop for a chat with old Dennis, walking down needlessly for their houses faced each other, they could have breakfasted together but custom dictated otherwise, walking into the shop, a grand edifice by now, with a boy and two girls, young persons they were called, sisters, Brid and Norah Murphy, all three of them to do what he had done himself, and through the shop, past bolts of drapery, tinned goods which were now available in great quantities and varieties, beet root and American baked beans, hoes and rakes stacked together, to the office where old Tully now sat at his ease, facing a glass-frosted door and a half wall of ledgers, his thumbs hooked in the sides of his waistcoat, or hands clasped behind his head, that shining dome which Hughie always spoke of as old Tully's fleshly emblem, flesh stretched across bone, and the wen of knowledge above his ear.

"A soft day, Robert," he would say.

"It is," Delaney said.

"It should be a busy one," Tully said, "for yourself as well as for me. No rest for the weary, as the saying has it."

"That is why they are weary," Bob said. "He is sorting things out for you nicely is he, young Brendan Fogarty?"

"Well, now, he is, Robert. I have no cause for complaint. But of course, he will never be the solicitor that you are. But he tends nicely to all of the business of the shop, keeps all the books Bristol fashion, all of the algebra that was Greek to me until you came along. And a certain amount of my other concerns, the loans, do you know, a great many of them out now in these dreadful times that are in it, and I do my best to help out. But as you know yourself, Robert, it was true long before your affairs drew you elsewhere, more and more, land and property are becoming my great love. And isn't that the Irishman in all of us. We may be born to the shop, but our heart is in the land."

"So they say," Delaney said, "and it seems very much to be the case."

"And for that, something more is needed than a wee chap like Brendan Fogarty. I was talking the other day to Binchy above in Charleville, and he speaks highly to me of Dermody and Cox in Cork City. I have been meaning to ask you, Robert, have you an opinion of them?"

"They are highly spoken of," Delaney said, "and for a century or more. They were among the first Catholics in Munster to be articled as solicitors, a Dermody and a Cox. It is a formidable firm, skilled in the law."

"And both Catholics, you say. That is one of the points that was troubling me. With a name like Cox, you can never be certain."

"There was Watty Cox," Delaney said. "Some say that he was a Catholic."

"The same family, is it?"

"Not at all. Watty Cox was a Dublin man. He was one of the United Irishmen in 1798."

"Ah." Tully expelled a patriotic breath. " 'They rose in dark and evil days, to save their native land.' "

"They say also that he was an informer."

"Merciful God," Tully said, "let us hope there are none of those below in Cork City, in the offices of Dermody and Cox."

"They would find informing difficult. Most of the cases they handle are those of landlords besieged by your son-in-law. But I have come to know John Cox. A decent man indeed. We have had meals together after battering each other beneath the eyes of the law."

Tully laughed, as though delighted by this glimpse of life in a different craft, its roles and masquerades. But then said, with seriousness, "I am with the Plan of Campaign, Robert. With all my heart. You know that. There is little a shopkeeper can do, but it is perhaps of comfort to men like O'Brien and Dillon and yourself to know that the solid Catholic respectability of Munster stands behind you. The convict garb that they force upon those of you whom they toss into prison is a uniform to be worn with pride."

He had taken a different view of that uniform in 'sixty-seven, Delaney thought. But times change, men change, the Church itself changes, whatever it boasts to the contrary.

"I have no wish to change my own clothes," Delaney said, "nor to exchange my comfortable bed for one of plank. I am being careful."

"Lonely work it must be for you, off there in London among the English. Two rooms is it you have there in Pimlico, and ruining your digestion in cheap eating houses."

"No need for loneliness," Delaney said. "There are more than eighty of us now. Nor for cheap food. My practice gives me the comfort I require, which is little enough. And, of course, my shares in the shop here."

"That's grand, Robert. Grand. Lonely without Agnes, is what I meant. Agnes and young Conor."

My family.

"That is one reason why I am so often home," Delaney said. "That and the Campaign."

Vincent might, in the ordinary course of things, have been someone to talk with, and would in fact, with a delight that in Vincent's case was entirely innocent, have quizzed him endlessly about the pleasures of London at night, in wanton fog, gaslight. "Good God, Bob, no need to act the prig with me. Many a fine night I have begun myself in the Haymarket, or at the music halls. Have you forgotten our own fine excursions to Paris, in the old days? A fellow like yourself, tramping the lonely streets of the Great Babylon, they call it, from Westminster to Pimlico. Cook yourself a chop, read a bit in Thomas à Kempis, and then off to an untroubled sleep." No, it would not matter a bit to Agnes's brother if Delaney found for himself a bit of skirt, or even moved up some notches and installed a regular in one of the villas in Saint John's Wood. "I would myself, Bob, to give you the God's honest truth. It saves money in the long run—you know what you're getting—and a woman like that can be kept clean. Take her over to Paris for a weekend, now and again; let her get a sense of developments in the field. An inventive people." But Agnes's brother could never know, could never wish to hear, that Delaney and Sylvia Ardmor were in love, and that his life was with her. A part of his life, the part that mattered so deeply that he had no need to think about it, beyond knowing that it was there.

As for Vincent, he ran as wild as ever, like a lad in his twenties rather than one coming into middle age—a great beagler, swift of foot and with a sense of dogs, of all animals, dogs, hares, badgers. And a sense, as always, of a dashing appearance, careless-seeming but planned: fine clothes worn carelessly, ill buttoned; hat cocked to the back of hair rich and close-curled, not a fleck of grey in it. He took delight in his arsenal of useful contrivances, over-and-under guns imported from London, walnut-stocked, the metal rich, deep grey, with the attractiveness of an explosion's blaze, the later coolness of steel, quiet and dangerous.

It was but the December before, Christmas of all seasons, that Delaney had had to brief a barrister to defend Vincent against a breach-of-promise suit brought by one Marie Sinnott, spinster, of Mitchelstown. Vincent had escaped, but it was a close-run race. "I had relations with her," Vincent said, "I will not deny it. But I never promised her marriage.

I told her there was in my own conscience an impediment, an obstacle." "An impediment indeed," opposing counsel said; "you are unmarried, I believe, Mr. Tully." "I am, but there are three natural children, girls all of them, that I have engaged to provide for." "And is their mother living?" "All three mothers, thank God," Vincent said. "You know, Vincent, do you not," Delaney said as they walked away from the courtroom, "if the women of this country ever revolt, they will take after you with a pair of shears." "Cut off your nose to spite your face," Vincent said.

Old Tully had not been present in the courtroom that day. There were many things that he could fathom, but Vincent was not one of them. "What ails the lad?" he said to Delaney once. "Will he never settle down?"

"Lad no longer," Delaney said. "He has found a life for himself, a fine, racketing life, hunting with the gentry, visits to the occasional big house, he has his beagling. The lodge that you bought for him is comfort itself—a stable, a housekeeper, and always an attentive housemaid. Many would envy him."

"I did not buy the lodge for him," Tully said bluntly. "He used money to which he was entitled. Not all would envy him, Robert; you and I do not."

"No," Delaney said.

"Is he a Tully at all," Tully said.

That life, in Kilpeder, and the life in Chelsea, the bed cool and the feel of skin against fingers, and the life upon Campaign platforms, with arrest an hour away, the constables, caped, half apologetic and half angry, eyes upon the resident magistrate, waiting for his nod, and the life in Parliament, which seemed the strangest one of all, the one most remote from whatever was the centre of his life, the abiding centre somewhere deeper even than his meetings with Sylvia.

Once, as he walked along the Embankment, he looked up towards the Houses of Parliament, Westminster Bridge, in late afternoon, the setting sun behind them, and remembered the passage, somewhere in Macaulay, of some survivor of the twentieth or twenty-first century, some New Zealander who survived a new Flood or cataclysm, standing where he stood now, in wonderment. Inside the House, on benches ranged against each other, sat fools and near-bankrupts, a few members who were mad as March hares, backwoodsmen from remote counties with crotchets, pet bills; but there were also the men who controlled not Parliament alone, not the United Kingdom alone, but an empire larger than any that had been known, larger than Alexander's—Gladstones and Balfours and

Chamberlains and ghosts who sat beside them, Pitts and Foxes and Peels and Palmerstons. And Robert Delaney of Kilpeder.

It was not that the fragments of his life, any one of them, were unpleasant to him—far from it, save only the guilt which he felt when he returned to the wide, bullying house in Kilpeder, a hug from Conor, and from Agnes a kiss cold as frost, her body tensing within his arms. Only that it was a life of fragments itself nagged at him, tell himself as he would that most men lived in fragments, and few of them able to clutch fragments so savoursome.

When, therefore, on April 11, 1888, he stood upon the platform erected outside the gates of Lughnavalla House, six miles beyond Kilpeder town on the Killarney road, and deliberately, in accordance with Plan strategy, instructed the tenants of Mr. Joseph Judkins to break the law; when, having done so, he saw the resident magistrate nod to the sergeant, he felt a curiosity, a remote exhilaration.

"Let them through," he said, "let them through, lads. They are but minions, doing as they are bid. We have a better game in play, in which they have no part."

"Mr. Robert Delaney," the sergeant said, a burly red-faced sergeant who might have walked out of a *United Ireland* engraving, features exaggerated, but his voice stiff with embarrassment, "it is my duty to inform you—"

"We may take it as read, Sergeant," Delaney said. "I know the formula."

A brief sentence to follow in a month's time, a few months in a gaol not so comfortable as Kilmainham but far better than one in which, a young man, he had spent six months although expecting to spend four years, useful material now for the Campaign, O'Brien and Dillon upon other platforms, "our imprisoned comrade, imprisoned for speaking the truth," a question to be drawled by Parnell, and then, at the end of the few months, banners outside the gaol, a brass band playing "Clonbrony Wood."

26

[Ned Nolan/Gerald Millen]

Nolan brought young Jim Morrissey to a tavern that he called in on from time to time, a bar and a few tables, near the Manhattan docks along the Hudson. He knew it from years before, when he would come down to the city on one of Tom Bonner's brick barges, docks high up on the river, built for the river trade. Inland from them, a warren of mean houses, tenements, muddy streets. Irish used the tavern—it had an Irish owner, Gleason, and a saccharine Irish name, The Killarney Lakes—but Swedes used it as well, Germans, Bohemians. Despite the name and owner, it was but a docker's tavern.

"We'll have a bite to eat," Nolan said, pausing inside the door. "But it is a raw night. Will we have a jar or two of the hard stuff, to start us off?"

"If it's all the same with you, Captain, a schooner of beer with our meal would do me fine. I don't touch the hard stuff, to tell you the truth."

Nolan nodded. "Neither do I, Jim. Neither do I. And I don't use men who do. Not any longer."

"It is an honour, Captain," Morrissey said, sitting stiffly in the chair that faced Nolan, and he picked up the heavy, weighted schooner of beer, its colour indistinct in the muddy darkness of the tavern. "I have heard of you for as long as I can remember. I have met Rossa, of course, and have shaken hands with Devoy. Once, even, I spent an evening with poor Lomasney. Your name often is brought forward."

"Too often," Nolan said.

"Clonbrony Wood," Morrissey said. He was younger than Joe Brady, but he reminded Nolan of Brady, less powerful of build but the same square shoulders, forthright expression. A more simple lad than Brady, though; whatever legend had built out of him, Brady had had a head on his shoulders.

"A long time ago," Nolan said. "A different time."

"Oh, but by God, it did not stop there. Yourself and Lomasney—the Little Captain was Lomasney, and now there is but the Tall Captain. That is how you are described, the two of you, when names are not to be used; but sure, we all know who is meant."

Nolan put a restraining hand on Morrissey's forearm, until the waiter had set down before them plates of beef, potatoes, skinned in the American way, huge as grenades, mounds of watery cabbage.

"You talk American, your accent," Nolan said. "They will be on the watch over there—Yanks with Irish names, working-class fellows. Scotland Yard has taken a dislike to us."

"I am Irish-born," Morrissey said. "Limerick. My father was put into Dartmoor in 'sixty-seven, the time you were yourself put into Portland. The mother took myself and the sisters to New York. It was here that the letter came that he was dead in Dartmoor Prison. The bastards, they murdered him."

"I know about your father," Nolan said. "A good man. Be you as good a son."

"With the help of God," Morrissey said, and Nolan, brief, bleak smile, looked into a face incapable of irony. "God's help and your own, Captain. You have yourself a father to be proud of, Captain—Thomas Justin Nolan, one of the great old patriarchs—John Mitchel and Smith O'Brien and Meagher of the Sword. And Thomas Justin Nolan."

"We should all be proud of our fathers," Nolan said, cutting into tough, overdone beef. "These knives are bloody dull," he said. "Mine is." His father—coat unbuttoned to display a waistcoat once flamboyant, now faded, dabs of dried gravy upon it—his father leaned across the table in their room in Greenwich Village, beaming with whiskey and post-platform exhilaration.

> O my name it is Joe Brady and I'm called the Fenian blade.
> From the Chapel in North Anne Street I set forth one summer's day
> To strike down a cruel tyrant in the Phoenix Park so gay.

"This will be a five-man operation," Nolan said. "I am in command."

"Indeed you are, Captain," Morrissey said. He had not touched his beef. Who could blame him? Nolan thought.

"The second-in-command is in place, in London. He has been there for years. The Yard knows about him, but they think he is on the fringes, a blowhard. Far from it. He is a hard man. I have used him before. And another man in London, a Liverpool-born man. Yourself and myself and one other will be drifting over in the next two weeks."

"At your word, Captain. There is only one difficulty in the world, and I am embarrassed to mention it."

"No need for embarrassment," Nolan said. "Do you imagine that I have myself the dollars for a steamship ticket to England? All that is being dealt with, and our keep while we are there, and safe houses. We are soldiers in an army, Jim, never forget that."

"Why should I?" Morrissey said. "I have taken the oath."

"If all those kept the oath who took it, from the time of James Stephens to the present hour, there would be an army at our back larger than Napoleon's or Sherman's. The thing to remember, Jim, is that we are not soldiers in the eyes of the English but common murderers, and so we are dealt with."

He looked intently into Morrissey's eyes, but saw no flicker there, no shutters banged down to hide a moment's fear. He nodded.

"Eat your meal, boy. The gravy is very good."

While Morrissey plied his tools, Nolan took deep, steady swallows of his beer, for once savoring what he drank. Good beer: workmen demanded it, longshoremen, Germans.

Nolan's hair, long, roughly combed, was still black, but streaked with grey at temples, above the ears. The heavy, downward-curving moustaches were untouched by grey; they guarded their long, thin lips.

"They call us common murderers," he said, "but they know better. When Dr. Gallagher and his squad were brought to trial, it was the charge upon which they stood that they sought to levy war against the Queen. Those were the words. That was in 'eighty-three. They are in prison this day, and will be until they die. One of them was a lad your age, Tom

[564]

Clarke. He will have years of prison work ahead of him before he wears out. And there are ropes waiting should they care to use them."

He drained off his stein and set it down on the table. A good pint: he felt a harmless, soft lifting of spirit. Not another drop this day: a pint of beer was his quota.

Morrissey was enough at ease now to smile. Joe Brady's smile, quick and open.

"You are a wonder at your task, Captain. Lomasney dead, Gallagher in prison, but yourself still at large, contriving. But you wouldn't make the best of recruiting sergeants. You don't paint a rosy picture."

"I do not," Nolan said. "This is a hard dangerous craft, with small thanks even from many of our own, and the odds running against us. Chance, ill luck, not all of them at their Scotland Yard are fools, and informers above all else. There is an old saying: 'Put an Irishman on a spit, and you can find another one to turn it.' But never free of charge, mind you."

Two squareheads sat at the table next to them, talking in singsong Swedish or Danish. What would they make of all this? Nothing. Russians might, or Poles, bombs and pistols to fight tsars, Cossacks with long, swinging sabres, prisons worse than Portland or Dartmoor, frozen plains, ice-sheeted. Here, among the Yankees, only the Irish knew that England's empire was as cruel, her grip as iron, talon-fierce. Half English themselves, the Yankees. No Irish need apply.

Nolan said good-bye to Morrissey in the road outside the eatery. Two blocks to their west, past warehouses and docks, the Hudson flowed, darkening, the lights of ships and barges scattered upon it, slow-moving. The New Jersey shore rose straight up from the water. Suddenly, Nolan remembered the Thames that December evening in 1884. There is a river in England and a river in Macedonia, as the Welsh soldier said in Nolan's battered, imitation-leather copy of the *Complete Works of William Shakespeare.*

On the cars, riding down Broadway, he recollected bits and snatches of the scene: at Agincourt, greatest of the English victories, the French on the run, Fluellen, Welshman and professional soldier, shouts that the French have killed the boys in the camp, expressly against the laws of war. "The poys," Shakespeare has him say, his accent a joke, behind it the ghost of a gibberish Celtic speech. But Henry makes the Frenchman pay, slits the throat of every prisoner. "O," says Shakespeare, " 'tis a gallant king!" The laws of war.

The docks were far behind him now. On both sides, here in midtown, the bustle of the American city which he knew far better than his own country, could thread his way through blindfolded. And yet he still felt himself a stranger. At Twenty-eighth Street, he climbed down, and walked east, the city growing more genteel as he walked, putting working-class neighborhoods behind him, saloons with garish coloured lights, blue, green, doors swinging outwards to carry briefly into muddy streets smoke-stained laughter, shouts. Two whores accosted him, but he shook his head, brushed past them. One of them had a likely look, though, wide mouth and upturned face beneath a dark hat tricked out with long, waving white feathers. Once, years before, he had had a girl who looked a bit like her, a skivvy in a Murray Hill house a few blocks to the north, uptown. Married now, to her grocer, butcher, whatever he was, a squadron of children around her knees. Generous mouth. An Irish skivvy, witty and bitter.

Gramercy Park might be fashionable Dublin, where, in those weeks in 'eighty-two he had walked on his way to the Canal, far from the Phoenix Park, his place of business as it were. Fine, locked park, empty at this late hour, no nursemaids, portly elderly gentlemen taking their evening stroll to activate their bowels. Beyond the park, in the appointed street, he began counting numbers. The early brick elegance of Gramercy was behind him now, no fantasies of Dublin; a long street of substantial brownstone houses, each with its flight of steps, its small stoop, as New Yorkers called them. "Brownstone!" Tom Bonner said to him the year before, when he was resting up with Bonner, in the yards beside the Hudson, in Bonner's rambling house above the river, an Irish triumph over Yankees. "Brownstone, cursed dung-coloured muck that it is! Why in God's name would anyone with cash in his pocket build with it?" "I want to know nothing, Ned," Bonner said to him on the first evening, as they sat together on the veranda, looking past woods, a patch of the yards, kilns, to the slow-moving river. "To know nothing. I have given not a penny to the Skirmishing Fund nor to the other outfit. Tis as my friend that you are here." Curious, New York and Fermanagh entangled in Bonner's speech.

"I have nothing that I would tell you, Tom," Nolan said.

Monmouth—that was it, of course. For Fluellen, a river in Wales, not England. "There is a river in Macedon, and there is also moreover a river at Monmouth." "I am Welsh, you know, good countryman," King Henry tells him. They were at it even then, the English. Victoria, they say, wears a sprig of shamrock on the saint's day. Fluellen should have kept an eye on Falstaff, marked how that lad rewarded his friends, let alone Welsh gabbers and singers.

At number 67, he climbed the steps, tugged at the bellpull, and waited.

Footsteps, heavy and ponderous, sounded, and the door swung open. He could barely see the man in the unlit hall, tall, bulky. "You are the man that we have been waiting for," he said. It was a question.

"Edward Nolan," Ned said.

"The very man!" A jovial voice. "Michael Tierney, Captain, at your service." A wide, soft hand reached out, took Nolan's, drew him in, into darkness, closed the door behind him. "I've given the skivvy the night off, Captain, and Mrs. Tierney has decided to make an early evening of it. Not that she was not bursting to meet you, Captain; she has a great admiration for you. But privacy seems the ticket, eh?" Not a ghost of Irish in his words, less than there would have been Welsh in King Henry's.

But the parlour, drapes drawn, was well lighted, a room heavy with furniture, dark rich woods, paintings, indistinct as ghosts of cattle-dotted pasturelands, hung from every wall. There was a small cabinet of books. Arthur Millen, who had arranged this meeting for Ned, was standing beside it, holding an opened book in his hands. "Savage's book, Ned," he said, " 'Ninety-Eight and 'Forty-Eight. He quotes a speech that your father made in Conciliation Hall."

"A drop of the creature, Captain," Tierney said, "as they call it back home?"

Back home.

"If you don't mind," Nolan said, "a glass of ginger beer would be welcome."

"Ah," Tierney said, "on active duty, eh? Quite right."

When they were sitting together, by the fire, in chairs that Nolan found uncomfortably soft, cushions one sank into uncertainly, as if forever, he had a better look at Tierney. Not soft, really. The hand had been misleading. How could he be soft, to work his way up to this house of dung-coloured muck and heavy furniture, hand-painted paintings? From working on the roads with pick and shovel to selling the material for them to the city. The New Hibernia Asphalt Company?

"As I told you, Ned," Millen said, a prompt man for business, "Michael has been as generous as any friend that we have had these six years past. Fair-weather friends, many of them, scared off by a whiff of smoke. Not Michael."

"Not Michael Tierney," Tierney said. "By Jesus, no. The Tierneys came here in black 'forty-seven, Captain, driven out by the famine that Mother England arranged for us. I haven't forgotten that. See that painting there? That was painted specifically for me, for Philomena and me,

[567]

that is, by an Irish artist. That is where the Tierney homestead stood."

Stretches of pastureland, a low fence, clouds, pink-tipped, hung upon distant green hills.

"The artist offered to paint in the homestead for me as it was, as I remember it, a small boy, a fine strong farmhouse, nothing special, with a rose garden. But I said no, I want to see it like this, the way it is now."

"He is a reliable man, Ned. I vouch for him personally, and the organization does."

Millen's organization does, Nolan thought. All of them in competition. Sullivan's Triangle. Rossa's Skirmishers. Only Devoy spoke for the organization, what was left of it. And Devoy was compromised by dealing with Davitt.

"The Council of your organization does?" Nolan said. Millen nodded.

"I am acting for them. I am not chief of the Council, you know, but one of its members."

"This is good enough," Nolan said. "I have spoken with your chief."

"By God," Millen said, "you are a careful man."

"On the Tuesday," Nolan said, "I was given the authority to recruit and the assurance of funds."

"The assurance came from the Council," Millen said, "but the funds are coming from Michael here."

"And I had, for this one time, a wish to shake the hand of the man who was going over. I never met poor Brendan Horgan," Tierney said. "I was able to help out a bit, outfitting the Horgan team, but I never had the chance to meet him. And now I never will, poor fellow."

Nolan looked over at Millen, who shrugged faintly, almost imperceptibly. "Michael is absolutely reliable, Ned. What harm is there in talking now about the Horgan team? There is a new camp of the organization in New Jersey; it calls itself the Brendan Horgan Camp."

Better the neglected grave of Thomas Justin Nolan; a small sum that Nolan paid in, in perpetuity, kept it trimmed and weeded.

"There is little for you to know, Michael," Nolan said. Christian names seemed the road to trust. "I have the authorization to act in England, to take military action, as an officer accredited to the organization. I have not named my objective, not to the Council, not to the Chief of the Council. There will be a team of five. When we are assembled, in London, I will tell them our objective, and our plans."

"And there it is," Millen said dryly. "Now you know as much as we do, Michael. Would you deliver asphalt upon such terms?"

"We are not talking about asphalt," Tierney said, a bit downcast but still resolute.

"No," Nolan said, "you cannot shake the hand of Brendan Horgan, nor of Dr. Gallagher nor of William Mackey Lomasney. Lomasney died by accident, in the line of duty. But Gallagher, and Horgan, and Ryan were stagged. They and their teams."

"Stagged?" Tierney said, puzzled by the word.

"Shopped," Millen said, "informed upon. Betrayed."

"In Gallagher's case, it was no secret," Nolan said. "Anderson's agents and Gosselin's and Jenkinson's came into the witness box and told their stories. But it is widely known that Horgan was shopped as well, and I have my own suspicions about what happened to Mick Ryan."

"If it were not for informers," Tierney said, "old Ireland would have been free long ago. From the days of MacNally and Reynolds."

"You know your Irish history, Michael," Millen said.

Long before that, Nolan thought. In Tudor days, heads shipped up to Dublin in brine, cash on the barrelhead. In lonely fens, starveling chieftains listened, attentive as hares, for the sounds of boots crashing through weeds, the swish of cutlasses.

"The organization knows how to deal with informers," Tierney said. Neither Millen nor Nolan answered him. "So the story goes," he said hastily. "Carey, the man who betrayed the Invincibles, stalked all the way to South Africa, where the English meant to hide him away."

"Patrick O'Donnell," Millen said. "He followed Carey, sailed with him aboard the *Kinfauns Castle*, shot him in Cape Town. They brought O'Donnell back to London and hanged him. He has a ballad."

They all have ballads, Nolan thought. And with luck an ornate gravestone in Glasnevin, slumbering wolfhounds and a thorny cross.

> *I am, you know, a venomous foe*
> *To traitors one and all.*

"With luck, Michael," he said, "I can scrape through without a ballad."

"You have one," Tierney said. " 'Clonbrony Wood.' "

"It can see me through, then," Nolan said. "One is enough." Even a wretched one, lies contrived to fit a singsong rhyme scheme.

Tierney, for his part, was uncomfortable, did not know what to make of Nolan, who was like and yet unlike what he had imagined. Black-coated, shabby-genteel, polite and yet distant, not scornful, impatient to be here, in this room. A dangerous man; without odour, a spiritual state, gunsmoke clung to the black coat. Since Clonbrony Wood. There were those who said that he had sent the Invincibles into the Phoenix Park. And there was no doubt as to where he stood among the dynamite men. Not like Rossa's Skirmishers, half trained, reckless or timorous, sent out to their deaths while Rossa sat safe in New York, remembering prison barbarities over hot whiskey. Nolan was careful, resourceful, like the Little Captain, Lomasney. But even Lomasney had died, blown apart in the River Thames in London, in darkness.

On the whole, Tierney was glad enough to say good-bye to them, standing in the dark hall, the door open. A story to tell his children, his boys. A part of one of the Nolan teams, impossible without his help. What good is asphalt by itself?

"He means well," Millen said in the street. "He has good intentions."

"Hell is paved with them," Nolan said. "Intentions or asphalt. A friend of mine says that asphalt and brownstone are sending us all to hell in a handcart. Brick and granite are your only men, he says."

Millen laughed, and touched a hand, lightly, to Nolan's shoulder. "Safe home, Ned," he said.

There was one more visit that Nolan had promised for the night, and he walked to it, less than ten blocks to the south and a few avenues over. In the Village of his boyhood, the docks, streets had proper names, but numbers here, and numbers for the avenues this far east.

Devoy was making a late meal of it at Devaney's restaurant, a chop and mashed potatoes, a glass of milk beside his plate. A cigar, half smoked and carefully extinguished, lay in a tray beside his plate.

"Signed on with those Delta chancers, have you?" he said, coming at once to the point. "Charlie," he called out, "bring a pot of tea for my friend here."

"For a mission," Nolan said. "A specific mission. I proposed it to them and they accepted it. They are funding it. Is there anything happens and you do not know about it?"

"I trust not," Devoy said, glancing mildly from one empty table to the next in the sleepy restaurant.

"Do you have objections?" Nolan said.

"Misgivings only. They are a bad lot, but I will grant you that they are businesslike. When last I talked with Rossa, his hand shook so badly that it was an embarrassment to him, bringing the shot glass to his lips."

"The excuses for Rossa still stand, as well you know," Nolan said. Abominable, in the blackness of his cell, hands locked behind him, his ankles chained, hobbling, stumbling, crawling like an animal towards the smell of food, watery stew poured into a bowl upon stale bread.

"I have never said otherwise," Devoy said. He was a meticulous eater, cutting the veal into small bites, chewing as he cut the next one, his dentures working evenly behind the handsome, cropped beard, grey too early. Devoy had had his bad gaol years as well—it was a bond, Devoy, Rossa, Nolan.

"Lomasney and yourself," Devoy said. A bit of potato scooped up, a bit of meat skewered upon the tines. "Entrepreneurs."

"Never without the sanction of the organization," Nolan said. "We took the oath, and by Jesus, we have held to it."

" 'By Jesus,' " Devoy said. "You have a nice taste in blasphemy. The organization. What organization, which bloody limb of it? The oath. Which bloody oath?"

"You did not bring me down here for some class of seminary catechism, John. There is one organization, the Republican Brotherhood. And there is one oath, the one that I took a quarter century ago, as you did yourself. If you have a word, speak it to me, be it yea or nay. There is one organization, and so far as I am concerned, you speak for it."

"Have some sense, would you, Ned? That is excellent talk, and I certainly encourage all the whispers to that effect. But we are all of us warring against each other. The IRB at home, and who speaks for it? John O'Leary does striking poses out of Plutarch, and that child bard Yeats writes a sonnet about the pose. And the Clan na Gael here, with Sullivan's hands upon one part, and my own on the other. Those crawthumpers in the Order of the Irish Race. They would have burned Protestants like Tone and Emmet at the stake, and tossed Mitchel in the flames for good measure, a fierce Protestant."

When the waiter brought Nolan's tea, Devoy said, "I am ready for my own, Charlie, and would you place beside each saucer a single, small brandy. No, no, Ned, you will not contradict me on this. John Devoy is not the man to lead you down the primrose path."

When Charlie came back, Devoy lifted his glass. "Good luck, Ned. Hit the bastards. And hit them so hard that they cannot scramble back on their feet."

The taste of the brandy was complex upon Nolan's tongue. Charlie brought it out from Devaney's special supply, that was certain. Juice of the grape, juice of the wine, lickerish and summoning. A fool would have a second. Not Nolan.

"Mackey was a chivalrous fellow, was he not?" Devoy said. "Contriving and contriving, and dynamiting and dynamiting, and always making certain that no human English life would be endangered. Public edifices at night—a bit of a risk for the occasional watchman, no doubt. But no plan is perfect. It did for him in the end, of course. But why need I tell you about the fate of Captain William Mackey Lomasney? Am I right, Ned?"

"He acted under authority," Nolan said.

"Not mine," Devoy said, the dentures clamping unevenly together.

"Authority," Nolan said.

"You are fond of that word," Devoy said. "That must be helpful to you, in your line of work."

Nolan walked westwards again, towards his rented room in Hell's Kitchen, his back to one river, facing the other. Happy the city that has two rivers to boast of, its two flanks protected. For a week or two, he would have nothing to do, no place to go save the room: a cheap valise, a handful of books set upon the sills of two windows which looked out upon a row of buildings identical to his own, darkened at night the most of them to save on paraffin—kerosene, they called it here—no central lighting, unheated, the fireplaces treacherous.

A winter evening in London, six years earlier, mid-December, a fortnight before Christmas or a bit less, about six o'clock—the same time to the moment, almost, of what had happened in the Phoenix Park, a flash of surgeon's knives—on London's river, wide and darkening to ink. Existing for Nolan in imagination only, newspaper reports, a few words spoken; but hours earlier, a day or less, he had spoken with Lomasney, a short, slender fellow, one of the 'sixty-seven men, a lisp, quiet voice, sweet-tempered for all that had been done to him in their prisons—none of Rossa's bourbon-soaked self-pity, Davitt's humanitarian humbug—a slight, implacable man.

"You can go with whatever blessing you may need," Nolan had said to him, in the mean rooms off the Strand that Lomasney had rented for his team, a sitting room not larger than a matchbox, and the other room with its sag-mattressed bed where they slept two of them lengthwise and two athwart its foot—Lomasney and Fleming and the other two. "And when your London Bridge is blown up," Nolan said, "what will happen then? Will the Tower and the Houses of Parliament and all the rest of them tumble down after it into the Thames?" "It will be observed," Lomasney said; "one after another their images and symbols will be smashed to smithereens." The lisp cast itself upon his words, always, mocking them. But whatever he said he would do, he did, and he had been that way from the first, from the raid on the Ballyknockane Barracks in 'sixty-seven. "A small man," so ran the report given later by the besieged garrison, "but he appeared to be in command." And so he was. O'Brien was by theory in command, was tried as the Ballyknockane commander while Lomasney was still on the run, raiding for arms as though 'sixty-seven had not been smashed. J.F.X. O'Brien, last man ever sentenced to be hanged, drawn, and quartered, but spared, amnestied out with the rest of them, white-bearded and patriarchal now, one of Parnell's M.P.'s, a makeweight, docile and gentle-mannered, a beard stroker, rememberer of his past. And Lomasney, for his part, was close to Westminster himself on that last night, in a boat tied up beneath London Bridge.

Bungled at the last. The buttresses of the bridge had for months been shielded against such an outrage with iron gratings, and Lomasney lashed his explosive to one of these. The explosion, ill timed, did little more than shake the masonry, putting it off-base, but blowing the grating sky-high, and Lomasney's team along with it, although this was not known for days to the police, so small were the bits of wood and flesh, drifting swiftly downriver into oily darkness.

Two days later, Nolan, "one of the many curious," had visited the scene, in the same gathering darkness, wan pearly gaslights already a shrouded glow across the broad waters which had carried away Lomasney and his team. There must be no violence against people—Lomasney's credo. He paid for it, two nights before. "Bloody Fenians," a fellow beside Nolan said, cloth-capped, muffled against December chill, dun-coloured coat, his speech Cockney. "At least, no one was killed," Nolan said; "this could get worse." Puzzled by Nolan's own accent, the fellow twisted towards him a small, peak-chinned face.

Moving westwards, towards the Hudson, towards home at last for the night, towards what was this month's home, Nolan pulled his memories away from the other, the English river, looked at faces in crowds, moving towards late suppers, perhaps; hansoms jingled past him as he stood on street corners, leaping back from splattering slush. Towards dark streets again.

Gerald Arthur Millen, who the week before had brought Nolan authorization from his wing of the organization, who had met with him that night at the home of Tierney, the long-distance patriot, had not so long a journey to his apartment, on the far East Side, a floor-through in a brownstone. Marie, whom he had been with so long, eight years now, that he thought of her as his wife, was waiting to make him coffee. Toast to go with it, cut into long strips: "soldiers," she called them in her old-country way, a Cavan woman, the core of her speech northern but with Shannon water drenching its edges, softening.

"It was at a meeting you were, then, Art," she said.

"Of a sort," he said, easing tired feet from tight glossy leather, mud-streaked, into carpet slippers. "Bringing two men together, one a giver and one a taker. I am not certain which was which. Save with regard to money. On that score all is clear." He shuffled to the desk, small, paper-strewn, a cheap sideboard pressed into service, feeling his toes expand. "You need not wait up, pet," he said. "I have a letter or two to write."

"I don't mind," she said.

"Very good, so," he said. "But I will need a half hour, a bit more, perhaps. This requires careful writing, and thought." He drew up his chair, and opened the bottle of black ink, black as midnight in dim gas illumination flung from the wall towards paper.

First, as he always did, from habit become superstition, he addressed the envelope: "Robert Anderson, Office of Irish Affairs, Scotland Yard, London, England."

The letter took him close to an hour, because, an honest craftsman, he added whatever else he knew, with an assessment of its likelihood; but all that was essential, all that persuaded him to write the word *urgent* in capitals across the top of the sheet, above the superscription, was contained in the first paragraph or two.

Edward Nolan has received authorization from the Delta Council on which I serve to organize and arm a team, take it to England, and strike there. He will set sail himself within the week, but I believe that he means to travel by way of France, and in any event it will be a month at the earliest before he will have brought the team into the field. The nature of the outrage he contemplates I cannot tell you, nor whether it will be in London or Liverpool or Manchester. It is my impression that it will be an outrage against persons rather than buildings or institutions; on that score he speaks with mingled affection and contempt of Lomasney's so-called "scruples" and "warfare in the open field."

You should bear in mind, Mr. Anderson, that I had no power to block the vote of my Council, on which I am but one member. And remember also that Nolan has become a man known for his taciturnity and his lethal nature. This is what impressed the Council. He is a very dangerous man. This letter will come to you in the wake of a cable which I will fire off in the morning. If any news to the point comes to me, I will cable, or in great emergency report to Mr. Heathcoate at the Consulate here, but would greatly prefer not to use that route. I doubt if I will learn anything more. The only New York man whom Nolan trusts is Devoy, who does not trust me, and in any event is more close-mouthed than Nolan himself.

"There," Millen said, carefully folding the letter, and slipping it under the blotter. "All done."

"You work too hard, Art," she said.

"Man's work ends at set of sun," he said, "but woman's work . . ." He patted his knee, and she walked towards him, an uncertain smile. "You must be very tired," she said, but settled herself into his lap, resting her head, tight russet curls, on his shoulder.

Near Hudson Street, a streetwalker accosted him, and he drew her by the elbow, under the streetlight, to get a better look. She had dark eyes, mascara-lidded, and a small, upturned nose, a country girl. "You look like an Irish girl to me," he said. "I know too many Irish." But she looked at him without comprehension. "Your country," he said. "What is your land, your nation?"

"Oh," she said, and shrugged, amused. "I am Swede."

From cold northern shores, pine trees, clean snow forests. She should have had light eyes.

"Good," he said.

"I live near here," she said. "You come?"

"Yes," he said, "I will come with you."

He left her less than an hour later. They had talked little, striking a price as they walked. The room was small, cluttered, a butt-sprung bed with a coverlet flung across it, a basin and towels on a stand, a chamber pot behind a dim-coloured screen. A small window looked out upon darkness, an unlit street. Sudden, harsh light as she turned on the gas jet.

"You need more heat in here," he said, "this time of year."

"Is not mine," she said, "I use." She pulled down the coverlet, rough blankets, and began to undress, quickly and without fuss. "How you like?" she asked.

He sat on the bed and began unlacing his boots. "As it comes," he said, "as it comes."

"What?" she said. "What kind is that?"

"Any kind," he said, and was erect before she had unfastened a camisole of some sort, climbed in beside him. There were no sheets, and the blankets scratched comfortably, a contrast to her dead-white skin. She was thin.

A bit later, in boots and trousers, but shirtless despite the cold, he stood by the window. The smoke from tobacco drifted towards him.

"You like a smoke?" she asked him.

He shook his head. "That place you came from," he asked her, "do you remember it?"

Puzzled, she paused to think, and then made the noise of someone spitting. "Little girl then. Mud, streets of wooden planks, pigs."

The blackness was almost absolute, but he could make out, presently, a row of tenements, and at the end of the block a large shape like a warehouse. In such darkness, looking out such windows, in Pennsylvania, Liverpool, Manchester, Chicago—once, on a mission, a window in Belfast's Falls Road—he could look into city-hard blackness and imagine the hills of Cork, and Kerry invisible beyond them, a marketplace, friends gathered around a piano, a woman singing and a man's tenor taking up the melody. Along a road winding upwards towards gorse-covered hills, roadside flowers reached towards hedges, purple, crimson, white as a bridal veil. In winter darkness, along that road, men retreated, frightened and desperate, towards a snow-laden wood, black naked branches. He saw the woods, both flowers and naked-branched snowy winter, in the mind of his memory, and heard the song-entwined voices.

"Ach," she said, as if seeing him for the first time, yellow gaslight flung across him. "Your back. You had bad accident once."

"Once," he said. "A long time ago. A cat did that to me. A cat with nine tails. Did you ever hear the like of that? A cat with nine tails."

"You were in prison," she said. "I know prisons. People tell me."

"A long time ago. I have forgotten about it."

"Good to forget," she said.

"Some things," he said, "if you can. Good to remember other things." Why remember wooden planks, pigs rooting in muddy barnyards, when the world lies all before you, various and new?

He heard her stirring, jumping to her feet, the rustle of her clothes. In a different voice now, the voice she had used earlier, she said, "Time to go now. Time to leave. You live far from here?"

"I know how to get there," Nolan said.

Part Three

27

[*Patrick Prentiss/Hugh MacMahon/Robert Delaney*]

Every so often, Patrick Prentiss would imagine that he had the story complete, a circle rounded, the halves of a globe joined, the seam faint and even, like a line traced upon porcelain, but fainter even than that line, the web marks of his joinery, bits and pieces fastened together, some missing forever and their places taken with bits of paste glued in place by his imagination, it was so complete, at least to his own satisfaction, and he was so satisfied with his image, the image of his reconstructed world, that he could almost see the globe resting upon his desk in Pump Court, near the Thames, indeed near that stretch of the Thames in which Lomasney had blown himself to pieces so small that they were never found, neither his pieces nor those of his team nor of their hired skiff.

He would walk, of an autumn afternoon, to the Embankment, and look to left and to right, pleased beyond reason that he lived halfway, almost to the yard, between two bridges, two English bridges, Westminster and London, which were icons of their fates, Delaney's and Nolan's. Nolan had been in London the evening of the Lomasney explosion, that much Prentiss knew, and perhaps had been standing on the shore, in shadow, looking out into a darkening river, fog-girt, a Whistler nocturne, or closer to the moment, the Thames in those final Dickens novels that no one read any longer, a river of scavengers and corpses, figures bent from skiffs or rowboats upon dark errands. And the sudden explosion, ear-shattering, a moment's blinding light. Prentiss could imagine Nolan standing there, at once bewildered and comprehending, while a thread inched through his brain carrying a child's mocking song: *London Bridge is falling down, falling down, falling down . . .*

Above that bridge, above Southwark and Blackfriars and Waterloo, was Bob Delaney's bridge, Dick Whittington's bridge, Westminster, with just beside it—stretching, it would seem, almost without end—the vast, nineteenth-century, self-confident Gothic of the Houses of Parliament, of which, after that first visit, Delaney had brought back his account for Hugh MacMahon, chamber and throne room and council hall of state, designed to overawe and serving that purpose; so that to stand opposed against it was to be dwarfed into insignificance, ignorant tribesmen, ochre-striped Zulus, peasants from West Cork. But Delaney had gone back there, session after session, Whittington Redivivus, walking at last with casual knowledge through vast lobbies, taking his seat in the Council Hall itself, separated from the rulers of the day by the width of a table only, on which lay an elaborate encrusted mace and a leather despatch box. And below the House, below abbey and famous hour-tolling clock, lay the narrow, graceful house in Chelsea, within which lay his true life, the true quick of his being, as at last, with reluctance, he told Hugh MacMahon, and as at last, years later, with a reluctance almost as great, MacMahon told Patrick Prentiss, MacMahon still incredulous that a life could turn upon such a circumstance.

In those final years, from 'eighty-seven to 'ninety-two, events crowded so fast and tumbled: melodrama, farce, tragedy, and at the end something for which Prentiss could not find a ready term from that vocabulary—the Plan of Campaign, and then, in April of 1887, on the day of the second reading of the Coercion Act designed to destroy the Plan, the publication by the *Times* of the proof that Parnell was linked not merely with terrorists in general but with the butchers of the Phoenix Park, with the Invincibles.

"Of course I remember," Prentiss's father said, "read it at breakfast the next morning. *Times* was always a day late. *Freeman's Journal, Irish Times,* and then the London *Times* one day late, laid out beside the toast rack. Proof of our colonial status, eh? But we heard about it at the Four Courts that day, and how the Tory barristers crowed! Carson was beside himself with glee. Read it at breakfast, the facsimile the *Times* published. Do you know, I think I can quote it to you verbatim. Hold on a bit." He closed his eyes, brought barrister's memory to work, and produced a fair version of it.

15 May 1882

Dear Sir:

    I am not surprised at your friend's anger but he and you should know that to denounce the murders was the only course open to us. To do that promptly was plainly our best policy.

    But you can tell him and all others concerned that though I regret the accident of Lord F. Cavendish's death I cannot refuse to admit that Burke got no more than his deserts.

    You are at liberty to show him this, and others whom you can trust also, but let not my address be known. He can write to House of Commons.

Yours very truly,
Chas. S. Parnell

"All wrapped up in a red ribbon with a bow, eh?" Dominick Prentiss had said. They were themselves at breakfast, father and son, in the house in Palmerston Park, morning sun falling upon teapot and toast rack, his father at work on the two eggs broken into his bowl, heavily peppered; fastidious, with each mouthful he dabbed at the silver-streaked beard. "Everything necessary to do the job, even that 'Let not my address be known'! A line out of melodrama, Boucicault or Clyde Fitch. You could read it whatever way you chose. Something shifty about a man who won't give you his address, and for those in the know, a reminder of Mrs. O'Shea's snug establishment in Eltham. Neat, eh?"

"How did you feel when you read it," Patrick Prentiss asked his father, "yourself and your friends?"

"Feel, how did we feel? Proper word. We felt before we had a chance to think. And what I felt was my backbone turning to ice. There was no clue as to whom Parnell had sent the letter, and there were some dodgy characters mixed up with us, we know that now—Hogan and Byrne and worse than those. And we know what Parnell said to that bastard Le Caron in the lobby—all that came out later. There was no suggestion that the body of the letter had been written by Parnell, but the signature only, and I could have sworn to that signature. But common sense took over. You could never get Parnell to put anything in writing, much less a murderous self-indictment like that. Absurd!" Dominick Prentiss jabbed a spoon savagely into egg. "What matter to them? Not for a while. They got their damned Coercion Bill, and among the fruits of it were first O'Brien and Mandeville in prison and then your friend Delaney." *Pat-pat* of damask upon beard, the calm motion belying the heat of his words.

Across Ireland, from Galway to Waterford, Plan leaders were arrested in accordance with the provisions of the new act. But the most famous arrests were those of O'Brien and John Mandeville, for speeches made to the tenants of the Earl of Kingston in August of 1887, and of Robert Delaney, for a similar speech made in the following April outside the gates of Lughnavalla, six miles beyond Kilpeder on the Killarney road.

Mandeville and O'Brien did not appear before the Mitchelstown magistrates in September, as they had been ordered to, but a crowd was there, nevertheless, boisterous and angry: the police fired into them. Three people were killed, and there were a number wounded. How many had in fact been shot in the Mitchelstown Massacre became a matter of controversy.

When they came for O'Brien, he was holding an illegal meeting at midnight outside the notorious Clanricarde estate. He burned a copy of the Lord Lieutenant's proclamation, a small brief flame competing against paraffin-soaked torches. O'Brien and Mandeville refused to wear prison clothes, sat shivering undressed beneath blankets. Mandeville paid for it with his health, but O'Brien, tubercular and scrawny, was made of sturdier stuff, a Marat, thriving upon oppression, headlines, leading articles in his own newspaper. Neither of these was in Delaney's style, neither Mandeville, honest strong-farmer, local leader bluff and forthright, nor the thespian O'Brien, eyeglasses and journalist's pen ready to fight for Ireland.

In May, sardonic and courteous, Delaney received his sentence in the courthouse in Macroom. The RIC inspector, wiser by far than his counterpart in Mitchelstown, gave Delaney leave to address the crowd. The magistrates stood in shadow, in the doorway, but Bob stood in the sunlight of the courthouse steps.

Light and shadow. The allegory was not wasted upon the illustrators for the nationalist press.

"This is becoming a habit," Delaney said, in a voice trained now for public speaking. "But there is a difference now, lads, and mark it well. That first time the RIC carted me off to Macroom, back in 'sixty-seven, back when many of you here in this crowd were so young that you were still in girls' skirts lest you be carried away by the good people—"

"There were a few of us old enough to carry rifles that day, Bob," a Kilpeder man named Matty Hoskins shouted.

"Day by day he was learning," MacMahon said to Patrick Prentiss. "Remembering names was important. A damned waste it was all to prove, was it not, Patrick? Every art and skill of the statesman, every stratagem and lovely artifice; by the time the end came, he had them all, and then he threw them away, as you might say."

"History threw them away," Prentiss said, "and Delaney along with them."

"You are great on history, Patrick. Tis an idol of yours that consumes all, everyone, like Moloch of old."

"There were indeed, Matty Hoskins," Delaney had said. "There were indeed a few of us. Sixty-six, to be exact. And thousands of them, with their rifles and their cavalry, and, if need had arisen, their cannon. We are wiser now; there is one difference. And we have them on the run; there is the other difference. We'll not play their game, lads. An hour ago, when I went in this place, I heard someone shout, 'Remember Mitchelstown.' I want no one to ever have to shout 'Remember Macroom' because there was blood spilled here this day."

As his foot was on the step of the police van, someone began to sing "Clonbrony Wood."

"Oh, and one thing more," he said. "I don't want to come home to discover that some local Thomas Davis has composed 'The Ballad of Bob Delaney's Long Months in Gaol.' Think of my dignity, lads. A member of Parliament."

MacMahon was right, of course, Prentiss knew. Instinct and style had carried Delaney far; style and intelligence, ambition shrouded by wit and good humour, like a park of artillery screened by infantry. And that day on which he entered prison, May the fourteenth, 1888, might well have been the peak of his career, although it must have seemed to others, to MacMahon and Vincent and old Tully, a foothill only.

He had managed the crowd adroitly, and they even backed away to let the police van clear.

A day later, as MacMahon was walking away from his schoolhouse, where he had left his pupils to their sums, he met old Tully, walking home to an early tea, with, as MacMahon told Prentiss, the coat black as a raven's wing, which was his customary garb, but no doubt was one of several, for it was never shiny at the elbows, which is the curse of serge.

"We chose well, Hugh," he said to MacMahon, "you your friend, and I my son-in-law. There is the lad to stand up to Balfour and Carson and their battering rams. If only he was able to spend a bit more time at home!"

[583]

"Be of good heart, Mr. Tully," MacMahon said. "Once Home Rule is ours, there will be no need for either prison or London. We can have him all to ourselves, Agnes and Conor and yourself and his friends." He had but half a mind on what he was saying, trying with the other part to shape the lesson which lay before him, cramming the War of the Roses into minds that cared little for such matters.

"To be sure," Tully said, "to be sure."

"As the song has it," MacMahon said, " 'When brave Parnell brings Irish rule back home to Dublin town.' "

"Brave Parnell," Tully said, seizing quickly upon the word. "Bold Parnell might come closer to the case."

"Brave or bold," MacMahon said. They had come to the turning, down which Tully's and Delaney's broad, handsome houses, rosy-bricked, faced each other. "Whichever suits," he said absently.

"He is a bold man," Tully said, standing firm and opaque as a horse block, "who would seduce the wife of a follower, and take her into his own bed."

For a moment, the words, as Tully spat them forth, were themselves opaque.

"It is not gossip, Hugh," Tully said. "I am not the man to pass along gossip of that nature. But I was visiting in Bantry a fortnight ago, and I heard more there than I want to hear. A fine leader we picked for ourselves. And now we are bent beneath his yoke, like plough horses."

"You hear things, I hear things," MacMahon said, temporising. "'Tis best for a plant not to rise too tall in this country, or a blackthorn will whack it low. O'Connell himself was not safe from talk of that kind. And a more God-fearing man than O'Connell never lived, by all accounts. A frequent and fervent communicant."

"What was said about the Liberator," Tully said, and although they were alone, he dropped his voice, "was that he dared not toss a stone over the wall of the workhouse in Cahirciveen, lest he hit one of his bastards. I do not say that that is so or is not so, but it is in Kerry itself that this was said."

"Kerry," MacMahon said tersely, as though the mere word carried an indictment against itself.

"But this is something different entirely," Tully said. He was hatless, and the pigeon-egg wen seemed to MacMahon's worried eyes to be drawing blood into itself. "This is a defilement of the marriage bed. I have not heard this as public-house filth, nor as a jeer from some Protestant. I have heard it from Tim Healy himself."

For a mad instant, MacMahon thought of telling Tully that on the subject of defiled marriage beds, his son Vincent might be a more informed consultant than Tim Healy. But instead, he said lamely, "Dreadful news that you have there, Mr. Tully. I have heard a hint of a hint, but nothing so firm as this." And hurried off.

Within a year, when everything had begun to tumble down, MacMahon would remember that conversation, but most of all what he would remember was the blood-engorged—or so it seemed—wen, purple and pulsing. As though the wen expressed not only Tully's rage, but that of some tribal certainty, expressed a rage larger even than Tully. Or so, that night, when he found that he had things more or less in balance, it solaced him to think. And although he described the scene to Mary, he stopped short of his fanciful imaginings, which rose, he knew, from the myth of the Tullys, which for twenty years or longer it had amused him to elaborate upon. A myth of origins, like the ancient Gaelic *Book of Invasions*, which began with the first Tully, the first Kilpeder Tully at any rate, walking down, awkwardly, pack of pots and needles, awls, skillets heavy as lead, out of mountain mists—but which mountains, Boggeraghs? Derrynasaggarts?—down into what had not yet been laid out by the Ardmors as a town, but rather a meeting of roads hallowed by centuries as a meeting- and market-place, crossroads for trading, dancing. Then, when there was at last a town, laid out as afterthought by the designer of the Castle and demesne, the huckster's shop in the byroad for the packman's son. The Tullys growing and swelling generation by generation, as the wen, perhaps, in Tully's youth had grown and spread, linked by Mesmeric affinity to other family wens, the Sweeneys and the Scanlons and all the others across Munster, powers in the land, holders of some tribal energy which thrust them forward, like the stalks of potatoes upwards from the earth. What they knew they knew, and God (God!) shield anyone who stood athwart their knowledge: that the Holy Roman Catholic Church was the one true church, that usury as practised by practising Catholics was not usury but the lesson of the Good Samaritan, that defilement of the marriage bed was unforgivable.

And much more besides, MacMahon had added to himself in self-deflating conclusion, turning down the gas, and climbing upstairs to bed.

"We had other matters with which to concern ourselves than Parnell's relationship with that woman, wife to the wretched O'Shea." Always "we," Dominick Prentiss's son thought. Never an M.P., although offers of seats came to him, from Parnell and afterwards from one faction or another of the shattered party. Able defender of Land League agitators, moonlighters, consulted by Sir Charles Russell at the *Times* enquiry.

Consulted by Dillon now, O'Brien, Redmond, indifferent to their rivalries. But always "we"—gentleman, Roman Catholic, Irishman, in that order. "We had the Plan of Campaign in the first place," Prentiss's father said. He had finished his eggs, and was meticulously, evenly, buttering a piece of toast. "Oh, it looked good—first O'Brien and then Delaney and the others convicted and sentenced. Then O'Brien and Dillon fleeing the country to avoid longer sentences on other charges. The nationalist press—our press—making great play of all this. 'Remember Mitchelstown!' And O'Brien's paper leading the pack. By Jove, he was a great journalist in those days. A bit tamer now; happens to us all. Time, the larger view, call it what you will: the clock running down, I call it. But for the moment, behind the flash, the oratory of rebellion and derring-do, green bunting and bands playing 'A Nation Once Again' until you were sorry Thomas Davis had ever written the damned thing—behind all that, and for the moment only, mind you, we were stumped. Balfour held all the cards he needed, thanks to that damned Coercion Act. And"—Dominick Prentiss paused until he had chewed and swallowed his toast—"and England was behind him. His own Tories, of course, but many Liberals as well. Not all of them had Gladstone's large, statesmanly view of the Irish Question."

As always, his father's praise of Gladstone was laced with heavy sarcasm, as though largeness of mind, for example, were some kind of mental defect, or deficiency of morale. "And who could blame the English entirely, when they looked about them? Your average Englishman has a distaste for mayhem, murder, dynamite. And in particular, the maiming of cattle. The English have some sort of madness about dumb beasts, as though they possessed souls. Some notion they took away from the Hindoos, no doubt, along with their golden thrones and gem-becrusted idols."

"And mind you," his father said—but this was an hour later, as they took their "constitutional," a word that delighted his father, from Palmerston Park, and through the compact, assured suburbs to the Portobello Bridge, where Dominick Prentiss's driver waited to carry him to the Four Courts. Few cases these days. After that first stroke he had ruthlessly cut down the number of briefs which he would accept, but he savoured the smell of the Courts, the library, the dress of the law, gowns and wigs. "Mind you, nasty things were going on in the countryside; neither the League nor the Church with the best will in the world, which of course we reverently stipulate, could keep a firm control upon every band of Whiteboys in every barony—look at that ugly business at Maamtrasna. And beyond that, worse so far as the English were concerned, a new campaign of dynamiting and assassination in England itself. We all thought—the Home Secretary himself, no doubt, thought—that London Bridge had ended it all, those madmen blowing each other up. Far from it. And try arguing against a Coercion Bill when the Home Secretary has evidence of a plan to blow up the House itself, and the members along with it, Liberals and Tories alike flung upwards through shattered timber and masonry."

They had almost, by now, reached Portobello Bridge, where, taking a different walk, along the leafy banks of the canal, MacMahon and Ned Nolan had once paused, shortly before the Phoenix Park murders. When they were on the bridge itself, Dominick Prentiss paused to laugh.

"Floating upwards," he said, "towards the empyrean, colliding against each other on their heaven-bound journey—Balfour languid as ever, Bunthorne with an iris as a buttonhole, colliding against Gladstone, who, pen and copybook in hand, is using the opportunity to continue with his translations from the classical Greek." He laughed again. "Eh, Patrick?"

Now that his father had more leisure than work, now that father and son had at last reached this plateau of sorts, at once wary, testing, and trustful, reaching doubtfully towards love after years unestranged but distant, Patrick could find, with affection, the sources of his father's humour—Edward Lear and the *Bab Ballads*, Lewis Carroll and Christmas pantomimes, the pawky, deliberate eccentricities of barristers and judges.

"And the Irish members as well?" Patrick Prentiss said, "T. P. O'Connor and Healy and Justin McCarthy ascending heavenwards?"

"Ah, but that is the thing, you see," his father said. "If Government was to be credited, if the advisers to the Home Office—Anderson and Gosselin and the others—were to be credited, if the *Times* was to be credited, the Irish members—Parnell's gang, they were always called—were not only hand-in-glove with the nightwalkers in Galway and West Cork, but as well with the Fenian dynamite teams in London and Glasgow and Liverpool."

As they stood upon the short bridge, looking south, church and state—opposing icons—faced them: a Catholic church, built midcentury, flourishing post-Emancipation triumphalism, and Portobello Barracks, planted in solid strategy, guarding approaches to the city from the south.

"After all," Dominick said, as they turned and walked towards his carriage, waiting for him by Portobello House, "after all, had not the *Times* itself—the Thunderer, the Voice of England, thanks to the wonders of modern journalism and printing presses—had not the *Times* printed Ireland's fateful admission of guilt, ornamented with Parnell's own signature? Are you certain that you won't come along to the Courts with me? I haven't given up hope yet, my lad. You have the makings of a lawyer. But you ask too many questions. Sit quietly, long enough, and the other fellow will talk."

"Not today, Father. Tomorrow, perhaps."

"As you like, my boy." Luby, his coachman, was waiting for him, his hand upon the carriage door. "You used to like that," his father said, climbing in, "when you were a little chap home from Clongowes, and then a bang-up meal at the Dolphin, a pair of juicy chops, venison, a decent soup to start us out."

"The Dolphin is still there, Father. Tomorrow, the Four Courts and then a bang-up meal."

"I'll hold you to that, young fellow. All right, Luby."

And the carriage took him away, into the city's heart, past the two old cathedrals, Christ Church and Saint Patrick's—"first Christian, now Protestant," as one of the Jesuits at Clongowes said of them—Dublin Castle, the Four Courts.

"I could never feel the same about Ned," Hugh MacMahon had said to Prentiss, "not after Phoenix Park. Mind you, I could never be certain that it was Ned, never certain that it was Brady and the others that I saw him talking with in that public house off Dorset Street. But in my heart I knew, and after I had talked to Bob, the two of us knew. For a certainty. And when the bombing began, and the dynamiting, and then the waylayings and killings upon public streets, we would say, 'Ned is in that, somehow.' Oh, to be sure, there were more lots than one, competing against each other. Down in Kilpeder I wouldn't know the ins and outs of that, and Bob himself knew little more, for all that Tory M.P.'s would talk about 'men less than a half mile from where I stand whose hands are stained with the blood of Cavendish and Burke, and the women and children who died in the railway disaster.'

"No, but what I remember is that lovely spring day when we walked along the leafy canal towards the Portobello Bridge, and the bond which I could still feel between Ned and myself, for all the years and the silences. But how could Ned do the things that without doubt he was doing at the end, the terrible thing that he did as the very last act of his life, cold-blooded murder?"

"Not cold-blooded, by all that you have told me, all that I have learned about it. That night at the very end, when Ned Nolan smashed his way into Brierly Lodge and shot him as he sat there in his chair—no, as he had begun to rise up, was it not? That night, at least, was not cold-blooded. He was in a rage, a fury. Everything which for years he had been feeling beneath that Red Indian carapace broke out. He was beside himself with fury when he broke into Brierly Lodge."

For at last Prentiss had, or thought he had, the shape, the design, the patterns formed by the pieces, the beginning of the narrative, when Ned Nolan, on a day early in 1867, walked into the town of Kilpeder, case in hand, and knocked at the door of his cousin, the schoolmaster Hugh MacMahon, to the night in 1892 when he broke into Brierly Lodge, murdered a man by putting two bullets into his chest, then fled, wounded, towards Clonbrony Wood and the distant Derrynasaggarts, and the circle, one of the circles, was rounded.

"Yes," Hugh MacMahon said in the small house of his old age, facing those hills, in the room of books sagging their shelves, with its windows fronting distant purple gorse. "And when his true self burst out, it was as wild as any Comanche."

"But Delaney tried to find him, to help him, when he was wounded and on the run up there, police and soldiers pulling a net around him."

"I could never fathom either of them," MacMahon said. "My two bosom friends, themselves and Vincent Tully, and I could never fathom either of them."

"But you could fathom Vincent?" Prentiss said lightly, probingly.

But MacMahon caught the glint of the probe, laughed, and pushed it aside.

"I could not fathom Vincent either, but then that, you see, was for a different reason entirely. Vincent was a Tully, and the Tullys move by their own mysterious laws. Even Vincent. Why you bother yourself studying the ways of Fenians and priests and Land Leaguers and landlords and Parnellites when you could be studying the Tullys is a wonderment to me. Or why I should go up into the hills to take down the songs and the stories of the wild Irish speakers when I might be exploring for that lost mist out of which the first Tully emerged, pack on back. Tinkers, do you think they might be, long back, in the old, dark century? Or rapparee stock, hidden in the dark caves of Kerry cliffs, breeding and interbreeding? Or one of the Lost Tribes? I entertained once the notion that they were Firbolgs. Do you know the legend that among the ancient races of Ireland, defeated and scattered and hidden, were the Firbolgs, an unlovable people, men with sacks?"

"Vincent was lovable," Prentiss said.

"He was," MacMahon said, sobering upon the instant. "He was indeed."

"The *Times* revelations," Prentiss said, deliberately changing the subject, leaving it to rest for a bit, for later probing. "They don't seem to have worried the Irish much—neither Parnell nor any of them. Was Delaney worried?"

"Worried?" MacMahon said, flinging soaked tea leaves into the fireplace in a long-practiced arc of arm. "Indeed he was not. And why, as matters developed, need he have been?"

I remember when he was first home after the *Times* had run those pieces on "Parnellism and Crime" in the spring of 'eighty-seven, with all the facts and figures of murders and torments committed in distant places, Connemara and Donegal, and the trail leading straight to the Land League offices in London and into the House of Commons itself.

"It's a forgery, you know," Bob said, "cooked up by Houston and his Loyal and Patriotic Union, Eddy Chute's chums, and palmed off on the *Times* and then on the government. When the Chief came into the House that night, most of us had our copies of the *Times*, but it was Harrington and McCarthy and myself who reached him first, and we went into the Library, the four of us, and he sat down and read the letter. Then he looked up, smiling. 'I must be a desperate sort of fellow,' he said, 'writing letters of that sort. And the *Times* have others, do you say? "Burke got no more than his deserts." Bloodthirsty sort of fellow, bloodthirsty and desperate.' 'Of course, it's a forgery,' McCarthy said, a bit anxiously, not making it a question, but with an edge of uncertainty. Parnell smiled at him, took a cigar from that battered old case of his, clipped off the end, and lighted it. McCarthy is a decent chap, but a bit of a nervous nellie, fluttering manners, writes novels and all that. 'Do you have any doubts, Mr. McCarthy?' Parnell said. 'Oh no, none whatever,' poor McCarthy said in haste. Parnell smiled at him again, and reached over towards Campbell, who had brought in a thick pile of letters, with an opener on top of them, a melodramatic fake Morocco sort of thing. 'Why, we have proof conclusive,' Parnell said. 'Look at the signature. Chas. S. Parnell. I haven't made an S like that since the middle of 1878.' He looked from McCarthy to the rest of us, to see how we responded to this absurd sort of proof positive. 'My God,' Harrington said to me later, 'if that is the way he is going to deal with the letter in the House, there is not an Englishman who will not believe that he wrote it.' But he had been baiting us. He has an odd sense of humour—not much of one, and with a cruel claw in it. When he spoke that night—after one in the morning, it was—he lashed out. 'A villainous and bare-faced forgery,' he called it. I am with that fellow all the way, Hughie, but the more I see of him, the stranger he is."

"Strange are the ways of the gentry," I said to Bob.

"Strange are the ways of this gentleman," he said, moderate and lawyerlike.

Once he dined in our house," Patrick Prentiss said to MacMahon, "and my mother woke me up and took me downstairs to meet him. I think I remember it, but my father says that I do not."

"On the matter of your own memories," MacMahon said, "you may insist upon your point without being unfilial."

Prentiss smiled. "What I remember—if I do remember it—is black, and starched white of shirtfronts, no lady present save my mother, and Parnell in rough tweeds as though in from a day's shooting, bearded. I remember his looking at me and saying something to me about my father and the law. Then my mother took me back upstairs. I remember being three quarters asleep, so that Father may be right. 'Always remember,' my mother told me, 'that you met the Uncrowned King of Ireland!' "

"It could be a dream," MacMahon conceded, "the kind of dream an historian would have."

"But I remember what was not a dream," Prentiss said. "Mother giving me lunch at the Imperial, and Parnell trying to make a speech in Sackville Street—that final year it would have been, of course—and one mob to barrack him and another to hold his fort. He made his speech; Dublin was for him always, and the Fenians were at the end. I could see a bit of it, a wedge of movement, and when I turned away from the window, I saw that Mother was crying, and could not hide it. She had her handkerchief to her eyes, as though to clear them, but her lips told me."

"Your people were not Parnellites, surely?" MacMahon said. "After the Split? I had heard that Dominick Prentiss—"

"No," Prentiss said. "But my mother was crying that day."

"What Parnell wanted, of course," Dominick Prentiss said to his son the next day, as they sat in the Library of the Four Courts, "was a way of exposing the forgeries, and tying everything together into a neat bundle— the forger, the Loyal and Patriotic Union which had given them to the

Times, and the government itself. A conspiracy, in short. Devilish hard things to prove, conspiracies. But the government turned the things completely around—the Special Commission was instructed to look not merely into the forgeries—these became a mere detail—but into Irish violence. A scheme of rebellion, no less, with Parnell and the others instigating murders and assassinations, hand in glove with the dynamite men and the Invincibles."

"But surely that would itself be a conspiracy," Prentiss said. "And, therefore, as you say, difficult to prove."

"Much they cared," Dominick Prentiss said. "Haul all our soiled linen up into view, put Land Leaguers in the witness chair, bring land grabbers over from the back of beyond, Connemara and Dingle, to swear that they had been beaten and lashed by moonlighters, tie M.P.'s and Land Leaguers together, Land Leaguers and Fenians. That's all they wanted, and behind the scenes they would admit it—the honest ones would, not the canting hypocrites. 'We could never tie Parnell in with the Invincibles.' Balfour told me that himself. 'That gentleman has carefully burned every bridge.' 'Rubbish,' I said, 'there were no bridges.' 'Not even the letters?' Balfour said, coming all Bunthorne. 'Dear, dear, such lovely letters.' 'We will see just how lovely they are,' I said; 'by Jove, I wish I still practised at the English bar. I would love to handle those precious letters.' 'I daresay you would,' Balfour said, 'but Charlie Russell would never deny himself the treat. Greedy fellow.' "

Dominick Prentiss laughed in reminiscence. Two young barristers, gowned and wigged, paused to pay him their respects. This is what he wanted for me, Prentiss thought. Still wants. As a boy he had watched his father in court, similarly robed, but silk, not stuff, a queen's counsel, proud of his father's repertory of effects, the books carried in by Collins, his clerk, the box of throat lozenges, the spread hands pressing upon hips as he questioned. "Now, Mr. Hennessy. Under the guidance, the very proper guidance of my learned friend here, you have told his lord-ship . . ." And Hennessy or Murphy or Adam or whoever, overawed as it was intended that he should be by wigs and panoply, would gulp and nod. "Speak up, Mr. Hennessy," his father would say, "his lordship is deaf to nods. Yes is it, or no?"

"Your friend Delaney was released early in 'eighty-nine," Dominick Prentiss said. "And they were waiting for him. By George, they were waiting for him. A Land League official who was a certified Fenian rebel, an ex-convict."

"Delaney was not tied in with the Invincibles," Patrick Prentiss said. "He loathed them. I'd stake my life on that."

"Your life is not evidence, boy," his father said, in the old voice, cutting and conclusive. "What is evidence is that he was Ned Nolan's friend. What is evidence is that in the end he went out into the hills to find Nolan, help him. That is evidence, not your life."

None of it touches me, not even the forgeries." Delaney said. "I'll answer their subpoena, as a good solicitor should."

"Then why should they want you?" Sylvia Ardmor asked. It was his second night back in London; the first night he had been up until after midnight with Russell, going over his testimony. Too tired for his room in Pimlico, he had put up at the Westminster Palace Hotel. Now, in Chelsea, late at night, he stood at the bedroom window in his dressing gown, looking down into a street empty save for a strolling police constable.

Delaney shrugged. "Russell is going to call me later, as one of his witnesses. It doesn't matter, really. As I say, I have nothing to tell them. I have been very careful. We have had boycotts, very rough they were a couple of them, grabbers jostled and intimidated, cattle maimed. But the only violence against persons was when I was in Kilmainham, and now again these past months. Gaols are useful in such matters."

She lay with sheets and blankets drawn up to her naked shoulders. The fire was banked low: the room was warm.

"Was prison awful?" she asked.

"Not too bad," Delaney said. "They have a sort of tenderness for members of Parliament, and I had no wish to sit naked under prison blankets like O'Brien. A right scarecrow he must have been. I was allowed visitors once a month, and Hugh MacMahon came twice, once with a huge, prodigious history of Ireland by some eighteenth-century lunatic. God, how Irish history has come to bore me. Parnell is right."

"And your family?"

"Yes," Delaney said, edging the words with nervous sarcasm. "My family came twice. The second time she brought Conor with her."

"Pleasant for you," she said, "that 'your family' brought Conor. He was well, I trust."

"He is well," Delaney said. "Home from school. At Clongowes the boys don't know what to make of a chap with a father in gaol. I'm a hero to some of them, of course, but a fearful number of Castle Catholics send their boys there. The Jesuits tend to cater to that."

"Castle Catholics?" Sylvia said. "Catholics who have castles? Like the Kenmares?"

Delaney laughed and half turned from the window. "Catholics who are received at Dublin Castle, received by the Viceroy. The Kenmares, surely, but some of the judges as well—that sort of thing. You have really never heard the term? You know very little of my world, do you, Sylvia?"

"For me, you are your world," she said, "and my world. This room is our world."

Once, in an early spring, years before, his first year in Parliament, they had walked together along the Embankment at Chelsea. She wore a light coat, fawn-coloured, and a broad-brimmed hat with a veil that she had pinned up. Her cheeks, ivory, had been touched by spring wind, quickened. Her eyes were bright, black agates. She skipped ahead of him to the Embankment wall, and held out her arms to him. She linked his arm tightly with hers, and rested her other hand on his forearm, not lightly. Behind them, they heard occasional footsteps, unpausing.

"You see?" she said. "No one notices us here. It isn't political here, and it isn't fashionable."

"No," Delaney said, with a show of nonchalance.

"I want to go to theatres with you," she said lightly, "museums, restaurants, to ride with you in the park. But we can't. I want us to picnic in the country, along the Thames, with a white tablecloth and hampers, chicken, wine, and afterwards strawberries and cream at an inn."

"On horse," Delaney said, changing the subject, "in the park? I thought respectable women did not ride in the park."

"There is a part of it where they do not, as a rule. A part only. It is a different world out of doors, isn't it? Rules and complications. Dangers. But in any event, I am not a respectable woman."

"Because of us, do you mean?" Delaney said. "Of course you are. What a foolish thing to say, Sylvia."

"No," she said. "Not because of us."

"What then?"

"We have talked and talked and talked, but we have not talked at all. Ask Lee sometime."

"What am I to ask him?"

"Ask Lee if Sylvia Ardmor is accounted respectable."

"What then?" he said a second time.

"It is such a clear afternoon," she said. "Not a trace of fog, wind blowing the river clear. Mr. Whistler would hate it. He wants fogs as thick as barley soup, and hazy lights, a few buildings like shadows of themselves,

[594]

the Houses of Parliament like a palace in a fairy tale, almost without matter. We could ask Mr. Whistler around some night for a late dinner, but he is such a gossip—the worst kind of gossip, a witty gossip, tongue like an adder. He and Tom are marvellous together, Tom good-humoured and Whistler witty, no good humour at all."

"Is it Whistler who did that portrait of you, the marvellous one in the dining room, blacks and whites and a single stroke of red?"

"Of crimson," she said.

"Isn't that how he paints, blacks and greys and whites?"

"No," she said. "A different painter. Named Galantiere. He is very clever; he has learned from Whistler."

"It is a wonderful portrait," Delaney said.

"Yes," she said. "A bit theatrical. But Tom likes it, and he knows painting. He is going to move it over to Ardmor. Let's go back, Robert. I don't like this wind anymore."

That night, as Emily was setting dinner before the drawing-room fire, Delaney went to the painting in the dining room, which Whistler himself had designed for the Ardmors, whites and greys, as though arranged for the portrait. When he went back into the drawing room, Emily was gone. He heard the hall door close behind her.

Later, over brandy, he said, "It is a lovely picture. It is a mystery to me that so much of what a person is can be caught up with oils and put on canvas."

"He was in love with me when he painted it," she says. "That helps, some say. But others say it hinders. It all depends, I expect."

"I see," Delaney said, and then said, stiffly. "It helped that fellow."

"Was I in love with him, that is what you want to know, isn't it?" She had taken no wine at their light meal, and no brandy now, but sat facing him quietly. "I thought I was, for a bit. At first. I thought I was in love and then knew that I was not. I thought it long enough to get me through the first months of our affair, the first afternoons in bed."

He looked at her without speaking.

"I have been in love twice," she said, "twice only. First with Tom, and then with you. And for a long time, until last year, I loved you both. But now you. I have told you that."

"But not about . . . about . . ."

"About Galantiere. Because I knew how you would feel, and I was right. I broke it off, you know. He did not. I felt wretched for months, but then I was glad that I had broken it off."

"Why are you telling me this now? Because I expressed an interest in portrait painting?"

"Because it is time, Robert. More than time. Ask Lee. Lee is a good friend, and he will tell you, because he loves me and likes you. You don't get about much in London, but one or two of your members do. You could ask them."

"And you have decided to spend the evening horrifying me, is that it, Sylvia?" He poured another brandy, splashed water into it.

"Galantiere couldn't help boasting a bit, and then at the end, he was angry and vengeful. It only takes a bit. And then there was an American who was more discreet, a New Yorker named Julius Van Zandt. Americans can have splendid manners, can't they, Robert?"

"I wouldn't know," Delaney said. "Why are you telling me this, Sylvia?"

"Perhaps it will excite us," she said. "Tell me, Robert, do you still make love—no, I cannot say your family. What shall I say? Do you still make love to Mrs. Delaney?"

"For God's sake, Sylvia! Will you stop all this? You don't enjoy this. This is wretched for you. Why are you doing it?"

"Is it wretched for you, Robert? Or what is it? There is worse that I could tell you—"

"Tell me or not as you choose," Delaney said. "I don't know how I feel. I feel numb at the moment; you could tell me anything. Later I will know how I feel. Perhaps."

She had been sitting quietly, her face, for all the violence of her words, as quiet as in the portrait, the words spoken quietly. Now, his eyes intent upon her, he saw her lips begin to quiver, and in a different quiet voice, she said, "Yes, perhaps," and putting her hands to her face began to cry. Delaney reached out an arm to her, across the space between their two facing chairs, and then went to her side and, kneeling, held her in his arms.

That night, in bed, loving, they did not make love, and stroking her cheeks, in blackness, he imagined that he could feel the faint moisture of drying tears.

"You are very good to me, Robert. If only I were good for you," she said.

They fell asleep at last, long after they had ceased to talk, in each other's arms. But he was awake first, and lay quietly for a long time, not moving lest he disturb her, his free hand gentling her body, moving over small breast, firm thigh. Emily's knock on the door awakened her, and she turned her head towards him at once, eyes as bright and dark as though she had not slept at all, dark hair tangled, her lips parted.

Now, in this January, after he had come back from gaol to London, to her, they trusted each other completely, but she could not put aside her complexity of manner, her oblique bitterness. It had become the way in which she managed her life with him, her life.

"But Conor is proud of you?" she said. "Whatever the other chaps at school may say, Conor is proud of you?"

"Oh yes," Delaney said. "Conor is proud of me. He is as much Delaney as Tully, that little chap. Quite an accomplishment, my friend MacMahon would say."

"Your friend Hugh MacMahon, who is the schoolmaster in Kilpeder, and whose wife is Mary, and is very lovely but not at all like me and is musical. You see? I know about your life. What you will tell me of it."

"They will make what they can," Delaney said, as if he had not heard her, "of my having been a Fenian, served under Ned Nolan. That I worked with Hogan and Byrne. But there is nothing there for them to grab hold of. And none of it matters. Sooner or later, they will have to put Pigott on the stand, and when Russell cross-examines, he will tear him to shreds."

"Pigott?" Sylvia said.

"Pigott is the forger," Delaney said. "Do you hear nothing at those tea parties of yours that you spend your afternoons at, or is it all talk of William Morris and his bloody wallpaper?"

"It is not bloody," she said. "Merely elaborate and a bit fussy. He has a wife who— Ah! does he have a wife! There is a house where we could go together, but I am afraid of having you meet Jane. A *femme fatale,* so they all pretend, but she is a simple thing really. A bit stupid. Is it known that he is the forger?"

"By now it is. By now everyone knows that he forged those Parnell letters. But they dare not put him on the stand, and yet they know that they must. Russell will crucify him."

"Not all my friends are as frivolous as you like to think. Lee has been to the hearings several times, and one of the times took Whistler with him, and Whistler made a sketch of Parnell. Now, what do you think of that? Perhaps I can borrow it, or perhaps Jimmy will give it to me if I ask him nicely. He is much taken with me. I have told you that."

"Yes," Delaney said, turning away from the window to face her. "You have told me that." He was smiling. "You and fog and the Thames."

"And Parnell, for a few hours. He thinks that Parnell is very handsome and intense. Why should he be so intense, if Sir Charles Russell will put everything to rights?"

"Captain O'Shea was called as a witness, and he hates Parnell, of course."

"Why 'of course'?" Sylvia asked. "The miserable creature more or less sold his wife, did he not?"

"That is one way of putting it, my dear. Not perhaps the accurate one, but close enough. Perhaps that is why he hates Parnell. He hates everyone on whom he depends—Parnell, Chamberlain, Gladstone for all we know. But Parnell is the one he could hurt. Russell examined him, Healy tells me, like a man tiptoeing across a minefield. And that isn't Russell's way. That is not how Russell will deal with Pigott. And Parnell sat tense as an eagle, in his overcoat, with the collar turned up."

"Yes, yes," Sylvia said, "that is Jimmy's sketch exactly. He could really damage Parnell?"

"Oh, yes," Delaney said. "Perhaps destroy him and perhaps not, but maul him savagely, and the party along with him. Ireland along with him."

She sat up in bed, suddenly, and sheets and counterpane fell away, exposing a breast. Absently, she drew them up, and feeling along the bedside table, took cigarette and matches.

"That could happen to you, could it not, Robert?" She brushed away smoke. "Because of us?"

"Nothing quite like that," Robert said, too easily. "I am scarcely the leader of a party, of a nation. And no one is bent on my destruction. That I know of."

"Half of fashionable London has its—its romantic entanglements. At the sort of parties I go to, the ones we go to together, they are commonplace. But not in your world, are they? Not in your Irish world."

"Ach," Delaney said. "Don't sell us short. I'm forever briefing a barrister to get my brother-in-law out of one scrape or another. When I can't manage it myself with a discreet envelope of ten-pound notes."

"Vincent," Sylvia said. "The last of the rakes of Mallow."

Delaney laughed. "He is, in his way. An odd fate for the last of the Tullys."

"But it would be different, would it not," she said, "for Robert Delaney, member of Parliament, who married the prince's daughter, and their son was christened by a bishop who came to Kilpeder expressly for the purpose? Don't lie, Robert. No more lies, we agreed; do you remember?"

"Yes," he said, "it would be the same for me. Worse, perhaps. There is nothing that we can do about it."

"No," she said, and drew in smoke quickly, then stubbed out the cigarette on a small porcelain dish. "I cannot do without you."

He sat beside her, and touched her hair. "I hate those brown cigarettes of yours, whatever they are called." He kissed her.

"I know," she said, "and I thought they made me all Turkish and wanton, like an odalisque. All gauze and smoke and perfume like an odalisque."

P rentiss could, of course, have told Delaney, with history's hindsight, that Vincent was far and away from being the last of the Tullys, that Conor had inherited the kingdom, as his sons would do after him. "Yes, I remember my father well, of course," Conor had said to Prentiss on their one conversation, in his offices in Cork City, the shop long since entrusted to assistants, already a Knight of Columbanus, no sons yet but already married to Miss Irene Mary Coppinger of Montenotte. "He was a fellow of great gifts—a good lawyer, you know, and his work for those poor devils evicted in midwinter from their cabins in the Boggeraghs. That won't be forgotten. Nor Clonbrony Wood."

"You and he were great pals," Prentiss said. "So Hugh MacMahon tells me."

"Oh, yes," Conor said, "when he had time for me. When he was not—you know, this is not the most pleasant subject in the world for me." He swung black boots, mirrorlike their polish, boned, to the soft carpeting of his office. "We would do better addressing twelve of the best at the Oyster House. Shipped down from Galway on the morning train."

He called himself Conor Delaney-Tully, and it delighted MacMahon to speak of him as "Hyphen."

"A year or two ago," MacMahon said, "young Hyphen hired O'Hart, the great genealogist, to do a family history. He had done the Guinnesses to their satisfaction, and thereby proved that he had the conjoined skills of a trained scholar and a Scheherazade. The result is lovely, it is said: an elaborate, comely, balanced tree such as we imagine in the Garden of Eden. 'Are you getting on well now with the great Tully genealogy?' I asked him when he was down here searching records. 'Splendidly,' he said, 'splendidly.' A fussy, confident man. 'I have traced everything and everyone back in perfect detail, to the middle of the eighteenth century. It becomes very murky there.' I daresay it does, but nothing lies beyond O'Hart's powers of contrivance."

"Who would have thought," MacMahon said, an hour or so later, and in a different key, "that when Parnell and all of them came out of that Special Commission, triumphant, the *Times* in tatters and the government with it, Gladstone firm in Parnell's support, and Home Rule in the palm of Parnell's hand, who would have thought that it all had less than a year left before everything came tumbling down, in London, in Ireland, here in Kilpeder? How can you know that, Patrick, and believe that history has rhyme or reason or law or design? There was a fuse, I will grant you, with strands running from New York and London Bridge and Dublin and Clonbrony Wood and Muckross Abbey, far times and places, and near times, and close to that year, close to 1892, a match was set to the fuse, and it burned and flared and spluttered across an ocean and a sea, across boglands and hilly lands, until it exploded that night in Brierly Lodge, when Ned Nolan blew open a man's chest with that damned gun of his. I grant you that."

"A fuse," Prentiss said, smiling at the old survivor, eyes brown as berries, stiff as a turkeycock. "But you don't believe in history. What do you call your fuse?"

"A whim," MacMahon said, "a trope, as the poets would say. A flight of fancy."

28

[*Lionel Forrester*]

And so that year, while for once London had time for Ireland, what with the melodrama of the Parnell Special Commission and the last, lurid wave of explosions and attempted assassinations, I lived as, I suppose, most Londoners lived, relishing such high moments of tragic farce as Pigott under Charlie Russell's withering cross-examination, but with, of course, for me the special knowledge that Sylvia's happiness was bound up with Robert Delaney, and that Delaney was delicately situated, a Land League officer who might be tied, for all one knew, to people like Hogan and Byrne and the noisome Sheridan by Sir Richard Webster, who fittingly combined the two agreeable roles of attorney general and counsel for the *Times*. But Delaney sailed through the examination, not more than two hours on the stand, a bit pale after eight months in gaol, but otherwise as crisp and as sardonic as ever. I was at that day's session, by Sylvia's instruction, but Parnell was not. He was often away, to Russell's annoyance, turning up for special hours—Captain O'Shea's testimony, and, of course, the business of the forged letters.

But then much of fashionable London, so it seemed, had a habit of dropping in at Number 1 Probate Court at the Royal Courts of Justice in the Strand. Early on—he was, in fact, the third witness for the *Times*— the redoubtable Captain William O'Shea was in the witness box, as it might be called, and Parnell was present that day, depend upon it, and so, less conspicuously, so I trusted, were Jimmy Whistler and myself. O'Shea seemed to me then, as he had on the several occasions when I had encountered him on one fringe or another, a repellent little bounder—not a gentleman, but that most awful sort who gets himself described as "gentleman-like." The fellow from the *Daily Express* put it with catty accuracy: "If possible he was a greater dandy than ever. There was a fresh cluster of curls about his ears, and his well-oiled poll shone beautifully in the electric light. We all looked intently for the old eyeglasses, and, to our joy they were produced." He had little of consequence to say, although contriving to put Parnell in as bad a light as possible, and Parnell, as we now know, had given Russell orders not to press him too hard. "A ticking time bomb" is how I later heard him described.

Extraordinary that a leader almost legendary, and a nation, should shortly be brought down in ruins by such a creature. But then history does not serve us as well as do our dramatists, who would have furnished forth a roaring, swaggering bully, Jacobean in his revenges and plottings. I nudged Jimmy, and said, "There is a subject for you," but he shook his head impatiently, and nodded towards Parnell, at whom he had been staring. "Good God, what a handsome fellow to waste himself on politics," he said in his ineradicable Yankee twang with its overlay of Mayfair languor. "But he is a wild animal in his lair at the moment. Look at him!" Trust a painter to find the image. He was dead right. It was October, but the room was fairly well heated, and yet there Parnell sat in that excellently tailored but battered overcoat, its pockets bulging, and the collar pulled up, his eyes fixed upon O'Shea. Jimmy got out his sketchbook and pencils.

Later, in the Strand, on our way to my club for lunch, Jimmy said, "That's most extraordinary, is it not? All of London knows about Parnell and the O'Sheas by now. Everyone except Holy Willie Gladstone, according to the Liberal catechism. O'Shea could shatter him. Will he, do you think?"

"How would I know?" I said. "I have never met Parnell, and that little—fellow perhaps two times or three."

"Little fellow indeed!" Jimmy said. "A captain in the Hussars. How was that managed, I wonder."

"God knows," I said. "Dublin solicitor's son, went to one of their good schools over here. Good Roman Catholic schools, I mean. Oscott. But I have heard—have heard, mind you—that the family began as pawnbrokers in Limerick. Gombeen men, we call them at home."

"At home," Jimmy said. "I keep forgetting that you're Irish."

"Do you, Jimmy? I never forget that you're a Yank. No one does."

It was a Whistler day. Fog had come in during the night and had not lifted. It must be pleasant to have a bit of weather named for oneself, a bit of the soul's weather as well, autumnal and indistinct. Lucky man, Whistler, to be an artificial construction of a fellow, walking sticks and waistcoats, the celebrated witticisms, the poses, and yet to be a very fine artist, free of pose, unforgettable. Art has no notion of justice.

"Over there," Jimmy said, gesturing with his ebony stick towards the Embankment, as we came towards Trafalgar Square. "Made my reputation for me, that river did. Not my fortune, alas, but my reputation. Young Yank comes to Paris and London to seek his fortune; turns things around, doesn't it? Reverses the current of history. I had a letter from Tom the other day, by the way. Still working away with his oils upon white Italian walls, pine trees, that godsend of a sky that they have. Tom is as good as they come, you know. I've known that from our Paris days. But he never exhibits. Why, I wonder? Sylvia isn't lonely, I trust? You find time away from that dreary museum to call in at Chelsea?"

"Oh yes," I said warily. "We dine every week nearly, and there are concerts. We are both fond of music."

Horatio Lord Nelson, high upon his lion-guarded pillar, had no interest in a passing American and an Irishman of sorts. Whistler put a hand on my arm, paused to look up at him, through yellowish fog. "They have the same problem," he said, "Nelson of the Nile and Trafalgar, and the Uncrowned King of Ireland. A woman. Nelson's almost brought him low, but he weathered the storm. Will the Uncrowned King, do you think?"

"How fortunate you are to be a Yankee, Jimmy, and not have to worry about either the Empire or Ireland."

He smiled at me, almost with pleasure. "I cannot endure well-turned sentences before lunch."

At lunch, in Pall Mall—a simple lunch, clear soup, grilled sole, and a bottle of wine: a decent club, but I cannot trust their kitchen—he waited a polite interval before he said, "Sylvia is being very Irish herself these days. She has been at several receptions, rather shabby ones, with an Irish fellow, one of Parnell's men."

"Has she?" I asked.

[603]

With the delicacy of an anatomist upon some intricacy of vein and nerve, he filleted the sole, absorbed in his task, and said, almost idly, "Wouldn't know who that would be?"

"No," I said. "Nothing important, you may be certain, or she would have told me."

"She may have told you about Galantiere, but it was Galantiere who told me. Of course, that was years and years ago. There," he said, and held the fleshless, frail-boned skeleton triumphantly between fishknife and fork before setting it aside.

"There is a club rule here, I'm afraid, Jimmy. Politics and ladies are never discussed. It has worked quite well over the years."

"Has it?" Jimmy said. "Sounds like an infallible receipt for boredom. But it doesn't apply to us, surely. It is meant for gentlemen, not painters and writers."

"The great hidden sorrow of my life, Jimmy, is that I am more gentleman than writer."

He put down his glass upon the table, and sat looking at me, as though something I said had at last made an impression on him.

"Do you know, Lee, you are dead right. You are indeed. It does you credit, some would say."

And upon that basis, despite my rude evasion of his rude question, the meal went off most pleasantly. When he put aside his mannerisms, when he once in a while decided not to talk for effect, sculpting his sentences into the form if not always the substance of epigrams, he was an excellent fellow, sympathetic and, when he talked about art, simple.

But later, when we stood on the steps of the club, he had drawn on his manner; like his tight-waisted overcoat a bit too flared.

"Now then, Lee," he said, "free at last. Tell me about Sylvia's Irishman. Club rules don't apply out here on the pavement."

"Oh, there's no such rule, Jimmy. I made it up, and then we changed the subject. In fact, I don't know of any Irishman in Sylvia's life. Except me, of course. And Tom."

"And Tom," he said, raising the theatrical stick in farewell. "Poor Tom. An afterthought. But a wonderful painter. You can tell him I said so, but he knows it."

However, walking towards Saint James's Park, I was thinking not of Tom, or of Sylvia, or of Robert Delaney, but rather of myself and of the seriousness with which upon the instant Jimmy Whistler had seized upon my words—more gentleman than writer—not in malice, but as though I had given spoken shape to a truth. In the park, the great trees were half bare, but autumn leaves clung to them, brown and ochre, and fallen leaves were thick upon the path. The fog softened all objects, all perceptions, setting a key, a palette, an atmosphere, which included even a couple strolling towards me, arm-linked but so far away that I could not tell their age. And I thought once again, as I had an hour or two before, in the Strand, but more flippantly, that I was seeing the world as Jimmy Whistler had taught me to see it, as I had received visual instruction, very different in kind, from Tom's paintings and watercolours, and most of all as I had received it from those French artists whom once I had thought of simply as Tom's pals in the Café Athenée, but who now were famous. And they were all of them—tradesman's son, greengrocer's son, earl secure within his high-walled demesne—were all of them, more artist than gentleman.

Mind you, I had turned to writing to give myself an income, younger son of a younger son of the Irish gentry, so that I might be independent rather than a perpetual guest stretching house parties into weeks' invitations, the shabby-genteel, slightly raffish life that Sylvia's father had had to live, from colonel to half-pay ex-soldier. I had a knack for language, and everyone seemed to be wanting history sugarcoated: exotic locales, paragraphs scattered with adjectives, but not so many as to impede the action. That was merely a trade, respectable but no more than that. But my other books, travel sketchbooks, experiments in biography, the two little books which seemed to me and also to my friends my finest work, *From Sicily* and *Shadows on the Grand Canal*, had about them something tentative, provisional, wilful. I had allowed an intelligence and a sensibility not ill informed, not without its attractive quirks and powers of oblique discovery, to play upon what it fancied, upon landscapes which joined history to water and ancient stones. The paintings which Tom had brought back from Italy, even his paintings of that same Grand Canal—most hackneyed of subjects—came from some other, deeper part of the spirit, where passion and technique were joined.

So I thought, as I walked through Jimmy Whistler's fog, seeing a landscape through the medium of his pencil, bare branches reminding me of strokes of the pencil, rather than the other way around. It was a Wednesday, and Emily—blessed with the most complaisant of mistresses—would be joining me for tea and conversation and for the pleasures of the bed. We had come to something of a crossroads, Emily and I, for she was now, in all save the formality of the title, my mistress, rather than a maidservant whom I had years before taken between the blankets of a bed in my cousin's Irish estate. We suited each other, in ways that neither of us fully understood; but she was too loyal to leave Sylvia, and for my part, I could not afford to set her up on her own. And I would not think of setting up a household with her—not Bohemian enough, or as Jimmy would have said, too much the gentleman.

Nor should she have left Sylvia just then, as we both knew. Sylvia would be needing friends very close at hand. For we knew that in some formless way, like a heavy, shapeless shadow upon a garden wall, her love affair with Delaney would sooner or later bring disaster upon . . . upon whom, how many? Upon Delaney certainly, and upon Sylvia, and Tom perhaps. Although Tom was too remote to be affected, save that his love for Sylvia would prompt him to shield her from scandal, at whatever cost to himself.

And then, perhaps because our imaginings, forebodings, must have a shape, however unlikely or improbable, there popped up into my mind, of all things, a recollection of the Probate Court that morning, and Captain William O'Shea on the stand, dapper, too smartly dressed, his complacent finger running reflectively across his moustache to one of its waxed points, his finicking accent, a compound of his third-rate public school, the drawl of the Hussars, the grave deliberation of the man of affairs, Joe Chamberlain's friend, Irish gentleman Papist variety but not too Papist, with a third of the spectators at least knowing that Parnell slept with his wife, and O'Shea in turn knowing that that was a weapon to keep Parnell in check, to keep him furious and tense in his seat, not knowing whether to leap or to retreat, a wolf at bay, in thicket, behind beard and turned-up collar. And, of course, what is brought up to us from the well of memory has often, unrecognized, the awful majesty of prophecy. For in a sense, Captain O'Shea—the vulgarity of his clinging to that title!— did for us all, like the loose nail in the treacherous shoe of the uncertain mount who carried the messenger to the battlefield.

29

[Archibald Spencer/Ned Nolan]

Young Mr. Archibald Spencer, of the Home Office, served as an unofficial link between the Office itself and New Scotland Yard.

The Home Secretary found it distasteful to work either with Claude Carrington, who dealt with certain delicate, unseemly matters, or Robert Anderson of Scotland Yard. Carrington was decent enough, the Home Secretary conceded—Harrow, twenty-five years in the Indian civil service, and then four years in Ireland during the worst of the Land League days. He was well entitled to the knighthood he had picked up two years before. An earnest, capable chap, not terribly imaginative, and all the better for that. The Home Secretary distrusted imagination. Those years in Ireland had sullied Carrington, though; the shocking people he had to deal with— not merely the Fenians and the moonlighters, but the informers, handing them their blood money. Had to be done, of course, just as there had to be hangmen. But blood money leaves a smear on the fingers.

But Anderson, Robert Anderson! What an awful man! Irreplaceable—well perhaps not irreplaceable, but very valuable. And awful! Papist cutthroats and assassins were bad enough, but for sheer, law-abiding, day-to-day awfulness, the Papist-baiting Irish nonconformists were without parallel, and Anderson was one of them *pur sang*—Papist violence and secret conspiracy stretching in an unbroken line from Guy Fawkes to Titus Oates to the fellow who blew himself up under London Bridge. At least Fawkes and Oates were English—sodomites, which whittled away their vestigial humanity, but English sodomites. But Irish Papists! Anderson had an eye to spot them, a nose to sniff them out, like a truffle-hunting boar, and his brother Sam in Dublin and their father before them, true-blue Orangeman: now there's an Irish bull. Anderson had become a bit dotty on the subject, finding links between the Fenians and the French and Russian nihilists disporting themselves in Whitechapel amongst the Jews, safe from the laws of their own country. Anderson, the Home Secretary suspected, was not even above arranging an atrocity or two, placing an *agent provocateur*. But he was a master of his ugly craft, brought over from Dublin Castle in 1868, when the Fenians blasted open the wall of Clerkenwell Prison, reckless of lives. He knew the names, the informers, the right Dublin policemen, the right people to send reports from Cork and Boston and New York.

Rank does have its privileges, though, and young or not, Eton or not, son of "Fruity" Spencer or not, Archie Spencer could deal with Carrington and Anderson for the Home Secretary.

Spencer had spent the foggy afternoon at the task, which, however the Home Secretary felt about it, he was himself young enough to find exciting, a story to bring home to Margaret, set forth to her over a low stool by the fireplace, devils on horseback and tea laced (in his cup) with rum. There had been a time, so he had heard, when Anderson had been tucked away in a corner of the Irish Office in Queen Anne Street, and for years he had not had even that, lucky to be fobbed off with a post as secretary to the Prison Board, but still involved with Dublin Castle, with the Royal Irish Constabulary, lacking title or appropriate salary, maintaining his agents in Chicago and New York, finding money for them from obscure sources, for which he was harried by the Treasury people. But no longer. Since 1888, the year before, Anderson had been assistant commissioner of the Criminal Investigation Department at New Scotland Yard, a gentleman in command of his troops, uniformed and in plain clothes, with an office in the spanking new buildings on the Embankment, so different from the wretched warren of offices in the little street off Whitehall, and the move signalling to Anderson not only his own elevation, but the recognition by the government, by people and Parliament alike, that the Bow Street Runner mentality would no longer suffice. The old Yard had not even been able to run down that maniac the year before, the Ripper, hacking up whores in Whitechapel; much less could they deal with a far worse menace a stone's throw away—Fenians, anarchists, Jews.

"It was good of the Secretary to send you round to me so promptly," he told Archie Spencer, "but I really had been hoping for a chance to chat with the Secretary himself."

"He appreciates that," Spencer said. "The request was not ignored, I assure you, Mr. Anderson. But these are busy days, as you know. Busy days. I can give you my assurance that whatever you can lay out before us, before me, will be on his desk when he comes down to Westminster tomorrow evening."

"Evening," Anderson said. "Tomorrow evening! This empire may be governed in the evening, Mr. Spencer, but its work gets done by poor sods like myself getting here at half-eight each morning, a full hour before my own clerk."

"Yes," Spencer said. Dublin's accents were often fun, but this one had a grating edge to it.

"Do you by any chance remember the last campaigns of dynamiting?" Anderson said. "Or were you still at school? The Secretary remembers them, I am certain. He remembers them, and if he has a bit more memory than that, he remembers also that in the end, they were stopped by information which I was able to furnish."

"I am certain he does," Spencer said. "We are all most grateful to you, Mr. Anderson. Throughout the department. And the Home Secretary most especially."

"Were they all like that, do you suppose," the Home Secretary had said to Spencer earlier that day, "creepy little man catchers? Half lunatic, like the lunatic Fenians themselves, but a special spice to it for them, a special curry spice, sitting safe in their offices, and weaving their plots and their counterplots, out of thin air if nothing more substantial is available. Licensed lunatics. And yet we must depend on them, Archie. That's the devil of it, that's the sorry state to which history has brought us at the butt end of this most wonderful of centuries, telephones and electric lights and enough power in a stick of dynamite to blow up a skiff-ful of Fenian lunatics off London Bridge. But one time out of ten, a licensed lunatic like Anderson will be right—he was wrong about Davitt, wrong about Parnell, but he was right about Gallagher. Go and see him, Archie, see what he has. But don't expect a tot of whiskey. On top of everything else, he is some kind of Bible-thumping Irish nonconformist. They're the ones who think the Fenians sprang up straight from hell. They could be right, of course. Nasty lot, the Fenians. One of them took a potshot at my brother-in-law, in 'sixty-seven. Missed, of course, worse luck."

"They are bringing us tea," Anderson said, the Dublin grate modulating itself for social purposes. "I have it brought in every day at this time."

"Yes," Spencer said. "At teatime. An excellent idea."

There was a pause, which Anderson broke suddenly, almost explosively. "Oxford?"

"Sorry?" Spencer said.

"You are an Oxford man," Anderson said.

"Balliol," Spencer said, amused.

"I can always tell," Anderson said. "A trick of the craft, noting bits of accent, that sort of thing. I'm Trinity College, Dublin, you know. The silent sister. Oxford, Cambridge, Trinity, sister universities. People over here seem not to realise that. Trinity was founded by Queen Elizabeth."

And Elizabeth, Spencer thought, made use of Walsingham, the first spymaster, Guy Fawkes and Babington and the Jesuits and poor Mary of Scots herself falling into his web. Perhaps that is what the Home Secretary had meant: were they all like that? But Anderson did not seem sinister to Spencer, only awkward and vulgar and a bit pushy.

Anderson waited, drumming his fingers on his desk, until a constable had served their tea. Spencer looked beyond his shoulder to the foggy Thames. Looked a bit like a Whistler.

But Anderson had restrained himself beyond what he took to be the necessary bounds of courtesy, one gentleman to another. He handed Spencer the letter, and asked him to read it. "You can take it away with you, if you like, bring it to the Secretary. I have had it copied."

When Spencer had read it, he put it back on Anderson's desk.

"Who is this fellow?" he asked.

"Ah," Anderson said, "there I must ask your pardon, and the Secretary's as well. I have given this fellow a promise, a solemn personal promise, made years ago, that I would never, not to anyone, reveal his identity. I have other fellows to whom I made that promise. Years ago, when I was working without a budget, on a salary of fifty pounds, supporting a family on that and a few bits of land in Ireland, and managing to keep these fellows on the payroll."

"Their idea of secrecy over there," the Home Secretary had said to Spencer, "is to keep things secret from the Home Secretary. All for the best, no doubt. A dirty trade."

"No," Spencer said, "I mean the man your fellow is writing you about, the man who is on his way here."

"He is here by now," Anderson said. "You can rely on that. There are times when all of Government, and I say this without disrespect, reminds me of a chapter out of *Bleak House*. The Court of Chancery writ large."

"Dickens tends to put things in a very lurid light," Spencer said. He had spent Oxford evenings with his friends at Mr. Pater's, where Dickens was not held in high regard. "I still don't know who this man is."

"He is a gunman," Anderson said, "a dynamiter, a murderer, as the letter says. He was in the Fenian rebellion, and he paid for it. He was amnestied out in the seventies, when Mr. Gladstone and our Liberal friends were weeping for the woes of Ireland. And since then he has been in America, but with certain quiet visits over here. He helped organise the Invincibles, I am certain of it, and he organised two at least of the dynamite outrages. And now he is here again. There can be no doubt of it."

Spencer had suddenly a feeling that on a day of ordinary October dullness—fog in Whitehall, indifferent India tea—he stood teetering on the edge of a precipice, beyond which, and below, lay an unknown world, a world he did not wish to know about. Perhaps people should, after all, be deputed to such knowledge. Walsingham and Anderson.

"And that is why I want the Home Secretary to know at once that Ned Nolan is in England. Nolan isn't a boaster like Rossa, a bloodthirsty sot like Cavanagh."

"Your 'friend' doesn't tell you what this fellow has in mind," Spencer said.

"My 'friend' doesn't know. But you may depend upon it that Nolan has not come over to visit Hampton Court and the National Gallery. Unless, of course, he intends to blow them up."

"But people simply cannot organise atrocities and carry them out, and there is an end to it."

"Indeed not," Anderson said, "and that is why the Invincibles were hanged in the yard at Kilmainham, and why Clarke and Gallagher are in prison, safe and miserable for the rest of their lives. That is why Rossa stays safe at home in New York, and Patrick Ford, rattling the charity cup at Irish servant girls and bricklayers, and shipping the money over here for dynamite and the odd revolver. Some of the money. 'One pound for you and one pound for me and one pound for the organization.' Fenian bookkeeping. If ever we can find Nolan here, and if ever we can find evidence, just a bit of evidence, back to Portland he goes. He's a ticket-of-leave man, remember?"

"Good heavens," Spencer said, and standing up, walked to the tall, narrow window. Resting a hand on the brown stuff drape, he looked down upon Whistler's river, the bridge indistinct, indistinct movement upon it, the first streetlamps being lighted.

"It is not a pleasant world out there, Mr. Spencer. I discovered that in Ireland, and my father before me, and my father's father. Three centuries in Ireland, from the days of Cromwell and earlier than that, protecting the freedom, religion, and laws that you people here at home take for granted. But it need not concern you. See that the Home Secretary gets the letter from my 'friend.' "

Spencer folded the letter, and placed it in his pocket. "I will indeed, Mr. Anderson. I will indeed."

But despite the assurance as to what was not his concern, it was a good hour and a half before Spencer was able to leave Anderson's office, because Anderson was anxious that the Home Secretary, and indeed the Cabinet and the Prime Minister, should have some notion of the world which he, Anderson, dealt with daily, of which the letter from New York was but a paper boat adrift on the surface of the raging flood. Spencer listened to him half attentively, a Balliol-trained mind sifting out, like a miner's sieve, the nuggets that might be essential—a trained Irish terrorist, one of a band of five, was about to commence operations in England, in London most likely. All else was a cloud of delusion, of a piece with the folly that had persuaded the *Times* and the government—the very ministry of the day, which Spencer served—that the Irish could be brought down with a batch of letters concocted by a shabby forger, the unspeakable Pigott, whom Russell had crushed and exposed on the witness stand.

And during that hour and a half, he had the additional pleasure of watching, from the tall window, a mean drizzle commence and gradually draw itself into a steady downpour, the cold of which Spencer could already sense in his bones as he sat in the high-ceilinged, wretchedly furnished office, ill heated by a parsimonious fire of sea coals.

"Do what you can, Mr. Spencer, please do what you can," Anderson said, rising at last, and resting his fingertips on the desk, pressing them down like bridge buttresses against the floor of the river. "Do what you can to impress this upon the Home Secretary. And remind him that I stand ready to go over all this with him, at any time."

"At any time," Spencer murmured to himself as his hansom cab, rain pattering, splattering above his head, carried him to the small house in Chelsea which Margaret's father had given them three years before as a wedding gift. "At any time," he repeated, rehearsing the story as he would tell it, first to Margaret and then to the Home Secretary. He took the letter from his pocket, and by flickering match looked at a phrase, a word, leaping out from darkness, lurid, flame-wreathed—"the nature of the outrage," "a killer." He imagined Anderson's New York informer—he signed himself by a circle with a line drawn through it—bending over the task in one of their saloons, a glass of whiskey beside the paper, intent upon his task despite noises, shouts. The match came close to Spencer's fingers and he shook it out. Not an uneducated hand, though; the sentences had their flourishes upon the page, preening themselves upon some kind of education. Fumbling through overcoat, jacket, he thrust the letter carelessly into an outer pocket. And it could all be true: Pigott had concocted forgeries, but the Phoenix Park had been real enough; an informer had turned Dr. Gallagher's gang over to the Yard.

"Here we are, sir," the jarvey called out, and Spencer, peering through pelting rain, could see his lighted windows. And, as he unlatched the gate to his path, rain spattering his face, the door was flung open, sudden rectangle of yellow light, with Margaret framed, and behind her he thought he could see the housemaid, a flicker of white apron. Margaret was holding up that awkward, outsized umbrella which someone had once left behind, ribbed like a whale, unrollable; she was holding it above her head, a coat flung over her shoulders, and as she ran towards him she was laughing.

At the sound of her laughter—her laughter was the last sound that Spencer heard—two men stepped from beyond the space between two bare, sodden-branched trees, and fired their revolvers into him, crash after crash, and joined at the very end by Margaret's screams. Then there was Margaret's screaming in what would otherwise have been silence, and a shriek from the housemaid, who ran towards her. Margaret stood rooted, paralyzed. She saw, without comprehension, one of the men come forward, fall to one knee beside Archie as though in prayer, and bend over him. By the time the housemaid, as hysterical almost as herself, had reached her, the two men had gone, black shapes in the rainy night. The two women held each other, and the housemaid, an Irish girl named Kate Casey, cried in illogical fury, "It's the Ripper come back. Dear Jesus, tis the Ripper." Then Margaret pulled herself free and ran to Archie.

I made certain," Jim Morrissey said. "Eddie here and myself made certain. We emptied our guns into him at close range, as you had said, but to make certain we went to him and had a look. He was dead."

"Jim made certain," Eddie MacCurtain said. "I could not move. I bent over, and vomited over myself, over the hem of my coat, but the rain washed it all away."

"We had not counted on the rain," Nolan said. "But it did not matter."

"Tis as you said," MacCurtain said. "He came home after dark, but an hour or more later than we thought. He was delayed somewhere. And all that time it was raining. We will never be dry. Never again."

Never be clean again, Nolan thought. That is what he means. He remembered his own journey ten years ago? fifteen? to the doctor in Chicago who sent his reports to London.

They had peeled off their overcoats and were sitting around the table with Nolan and Paddy Enright, in the narrow, sooty kitchen of Enright's house. Nolan picked up the bottle, and poured stiff measures, handing one first to Morrissey. Morrissey shook his head. "Drink it," Nolan said. "Drink it straight down." He handed the other glass to MacCurtain. Perhaps they never would be dry again; their jackets were worse than damp, soaked through. Wet tweed mingled with other smells: a coal fire, cabbage.

"I was getting more and more worried that the revolvers would not fire," Morrissey said. "The bullets might have gotten wet. We kept the revolvers better shielded than we did ourselves."

"We emptied our guns into him," Eddie said, as though in wonderment.

"That might not have been the best of ideas," Nolan said mildly. "You should always have a way of defending yourselves. There is no man walking who can answer back to a heavy-calibre Colt. Not at close range."

MacCurtain gave a sudden gasp, as though he had surprised himself, and ripped the air with dry sobbing. Enright made an awkward move towards him, but Nolan said, "Leave him alone." As though speaking to all three of them, but with his eyes fixed upon MacCurtain, he said, "They will know by now. By tomorrow the country will know. No one is safe, the private secretary of the Home Secretary, son of a general who has had books written about his campaigns. The Home Secretary is not safe, Balfour is not, Salisbury is not. Not unless they put themselves on a war footing. As they should do. Because what was done tonight was an act of war. By soldiers of the Irish Republic."

"He was as good as gold," Morrissey said defensively. MacCurtain had listened to Nolan's words, and the sobs had quieted.

"It was the woman screaming," MacCurtain said. "After she ran forward laughing, with the light behind her. And an umbrella. A young woman. I could see her so plain."

"What woman?" Nolan said suddenly, fiercely. "You told me of no woman."

"His wife, I suppose," Morrissey said. "She wanted to protect him from the rain."

"You had a good clear look at her, you tell me. And did she have a good clear look at you?"

Morrissey and MacCurtain gave each other quick, frightened glances, considering the matter for the first time. Then Morrissey shook his head decisively. "It was black night and pouring rain. We saw her only because the light from the hall door fell upon her. We could even see another woman. But they could not have seen us. Never."

Nolan nodded. Morrissey would do. He was not certain about Mac-Curtain—even though he had been there when he was needed. That phrase they had always been so fond of, going back to Fenian days and earlier, perhaps.

"I bent over him and made certain," Morrissey said.

"And if the woman had seen him," Enright said, speaking for the first time since he had welcomed the two lads, a half hour before, "would you have had them shoot her, and the other woman, if there was one? Don't frighten the lads more than you must, Captain."

"No," Nolan said. "It hasn't come to that yet. Making war on women. Not yet."

"There was a paper folded over, and sticking out from his pocket," Morrissey said. "I took it along with me. I don't know why."

As evidence to himself, perhaps, Nolan thought, that he had truly done what he had done. A kind of keepsake; touchstone, perhaps.

He took the paper, unfolded it, and spread it out upon the table. Rain had smeared some of its words, and an entire patch at one side had run down the paper, a messy river of pale blue. But he could make out the better part of it, and the first words that leaped out at him were those of his own name.

He spent a good twenty minutes or more staring down at it, unmoving, one hand resting upon its damp, streaked edge.

"Well," he said at last, looking up at Enright and smiling. "The secrets of Empire unfolded." And when they looked at him in enquiry, he smiled and shook his head. "Nothing of importance, lads. And in any event, they make copies. But you were right to carry it along with you. You never know."

He walked across the small kitchen to the fireplace, and dropped the paper in it. Damp, it smoked before catching fire. For a moment, he entertained the fancy that he could see his name, illuminated.

"Pour yourselves another dram, lads. That's an order. And yourself as well, Paddy. That is why I brought the bottle. Another dram, and then we'll cork it."

In gaslight, the whiskey was dark amber, fathomless, it offered repose.

When the others had left the kitchen, Nolan lay stretched full-length on the cot beside the dying fire. By its reddish, failing light, he could make out the table scattered with mugs and greasy plates—Paddy had given the lads a fry, which they wolfed down—straight-backed chairs, no two of them matching, a narrow window, flanked by an overstuffed easy chair, and a horsehair sofa. The window was a black rectangle.

Beyond it lay London, stretched out in Nolan's imagination in blacks and grey; the river, to the north, black and serpentine, crossed by grey bridges; but the cluster of Westminster and Whitehall a baleful yellow, the great parks not green, a black and white cross-hatching, as on a map, and the city spreading endlessly, a labyrinth. All that he knew of England, save for a mission to Liverpool, one to Glasgow, save for the years in Portland Prison, work in its quarries beneath leaden skies, close to a leaden sea, all that he knew was London, safe houses like this one, meetings in ugly tenements which ran row upon row, discolored red brick, yellow brick soot-stained. And risky—no, not very risky, no warrant sworn against him, saunters through fashionable quarters, intricate fanlights, the wood fresh-painted yearly, the glass polished by platoons of lads and skivvies; theatres, gaslights, and resounding language, Othello and Lear; museums, great sprawling canvases, colours rich as velvet, a different world of ease, space, light. But now he lay alone, frightened, wide awake at two in the morning, seeing the great centreless web of black and grey, save for a sudden dab, a dab of red blood in Chelsea.

The letter no longer angered him: he should have expected treachery. Gallagher had been betrayed, and Comisskey before him; in a Kilmainham courtroom, James Carey had sworn away the lives of the Invincibles. Then why not Millen, or Circle-with-a-Line-Through-It, if he preferred that as name and signature. An affable man with expensive tastes, a woman who had an eye for clothes and ugly, costly chinaware. Why not Millen?

Before Nolan had let Morrissey and MacCurtain get their sleep, he had had them go over it again, from the beginning, a word of caution here, of praise there. And now he could almost see the scene, the moments less than a minute which had put the blob of red on imagination's map of London. He saw the woman, young, coat flung over shoulders, laughing, broad ungainly umbrella opened above her head, running towards the man with his hand upon the gate latch, saw the two fellows whom he had himself armed and sent out, stepping forward, heard the heavy, unechoing roars of exploding cartridges.

God, he thought, as in one form or another he had thought upon a hundred sleepless nights ever since that evening twelve years before when, like the two lads this night, he had stepped forward into a rutted Chicago road, more country than city out there, to carry out the orders of the Supreme Council. God, he thought, God send that I am right. A part of him knew that he was, knew that Davitt and Bob Delaney, and even Parnell, Parnell especially perhaps, were but make-weights and trimmers. And a deluded nation followed them, bought off with rent reductions, a chance to graze their cows upon wider pasturelands. There had always been but the one way: the force of arms, and the oath. If he hadn't learned that lesson in Clonbrony Wood, he had learned it in the cell in Portland Prison, and in the black hole of its solitary confinement. They respected explosions, gunfire, their own lives in danger. That was the shadow that gave Parnell his strength, the shadow of a man stepping forth, gun in hand, from between rain-sodden trees.

But he could not tear away from his mind that image of a woman whom he had never seen, young, laughing in a downpour of rain.

30

[*Patrick Prentiss/Hugh MacMahon*]

On Christmas Eve of 1889, Captain William Henry O'Shea, member of Parliament, late of the Eighteenth Hussars, filed a petition for divorce, naming as co-respondent the leader of the Irish party and his own presumed friend, Charles Stewart Parnell.

Parnell had spent the weekend before at Gladstone's estate of Hawarden. The visit was a great triumph, both in social and in political ways, and it brought him to the height of his power as a leader negotiating, almost upon equal terms with England, as the spokesman of a nation. And as more than spokesman, because the special, magical aura of the chieftain had touched him, giving him a reckless certainty of speech and action. Gladstone might have been pardoned for envying it: Gladstone was answerable to his colleagues, many of whom believed, as virtually every Tory did, that whatever findings the Special Commission might bring in, Parnell's power lay not in the House, nor on Dublin or Cork platforms, but in the houghing blade of the moonlighter and the dynamite of the Fenian. Not two weeks before, the private secretary of the Home Secretary had been murdered on his doorstep, with his young wife looking on. Neither the Home Secretary nor Arthur Balfour, the Irish Secretary, had been reluctant to draw the usual inference, but then neither had Harcourt on behalf of a strong minority among the Liberals. "The Member for Cork may not have been skulking under the trees," Balfour had pointed out with that infuriating drawl—or endearing, depending on your point of view—"indeed surely did not even anticipate this atrocity, or he would have notified Scotland Yard. Anonymously, perhaps. But he benefits from it. It helps to frighten us." Parnell was not in the House that night; he rarely was. Robert Delaney, a member for the County of Cork, answered for him. "He does not frighten an unarmed crowd by firing into them point-blank, as was done at Mitchelstown by men wearing the Queen's uniform, and answerable to the Irish Secretary." "The member for County Cork," Balfour said, sitting down and stroking the tiger-striped flower which was his buttonhole that night, "has also worn the Queen's uniform. A different sort of uniform." "I have," Delaney shouted across the table; "I have worn the only uniform in the Queen's supply house that an Irishman can wear with pride." Hansard records cries of "Withdraw!," but they were not from Balfour, who had put Delaney into that broad-arrowed prison uniform, and now sat smiling affably at him.

But none of that carried to Hawarden. Parnell arrived at teatime, and delighted the family. "He never shows emotion," Mary Gladstone noted in her journal, "has a cool, indifferent manner, in sharp contrast to the deep, piercing gaze of his eyes, which look bang through, not at, yours. He looks more ill than any other I ever saw off a deathbed, refined and gentlemanlike in looks, voice, and ways, speaks with perfect calmness on burning points and quite frankly." Her father noted with some surprise in his own diary that "he is certainly one of the very best people to deal with that I have ever known," and said as much in a memorandum dated December 23, just one day before the divorce petition was filed by William Henry O'Shea, officer and gentleman.

"Know that he would file?" O'Clery said to Patrick Prentiss. "Of course not. None of us did—none of the Irish members, at any rate. We would have been the last to know. I was home in Dublin for Christmas, saw your father at the Clandillons' Christmas party in Mountjoy Square. Most of us were home. The Times carried the story on the twenty-seventh, and very happy to carry it, thank you. Did you know that at the outset, O'Shea was using as his solicitor Joseph Soames, who was solicitor for the Times, and

the Special Commission still sitting? The *Times* was in the business up to
its neck. Someday history will sort it all out. Perhaps you will, my boy."

"I doubt that," Prentiss said, smiling. "But how did you all feel about
it, right then, at the outset?"

"How feel?" O'Clery said, smiling in return and folding small, plump
hands across his silk waistcoat, watered silk. "Odd, isn't it, barristers and
M.P.'s are rarely asked how they *feel* about things. How they think about
them, that's the ticket. I remember your father and myself and a few other
chaps standing in the dining room at the buffet, and hanging above it that
God-awful painting the Clandillons are so proud of, say it's a Maclise,
Sarsfield leading the charge at Ballyneety, the night raid on William's
artillery train, our victory. The only one. None of the ladies with us, of
course, but you may be certain that they were in the drawing room talking
of nothing else. But you see, Patrick, in that house, there was not a soul,
man or woman—I exclude the servants—who did not know about Parnell
and Katharine O'Shea. Good God, how could we not? Common gossip,
but not throughout Ireland."

Suddenly, O'Clery began to laugh, the laugh rolling across the ample
belly, rippling the silk.

"Do you know what your father said, Patrick? I remember it all word
for word almost, and the rest of us laughing, your father furious at our
laughter. 'Why the bloody hell,' he said, 'doesn't someone challenge
O'Shea to a duel, blow his awful little head off? Have to be some other
charge, but that is no difficulty. He has been mixed up in one shady
business or another. Take him over to Boulogne, put a pistol in his hand,
and blow his head off.' "

"My *father* said that?" Prentiss asked. Dominick Sarsfield Prentiss,
sternest of anti-Parnellites.

"Ah, but you see, that was then, Patrick. At the outset. We had seen
what the English had done to ruin Parnell, try to ruin him. We had seen
Pigott on the stand, as disgraceful a spectacle as Titus Oates, and strings
running from him to the *Times* and to Government. When you have a
leader, a real leader—and by God he was that!—and his enemies take out
their knives, you rally around him, you don't wait to think."

"Even if you are a barrister," Prentiss said mildly.

"Point taken," O'Clery said. "But you see, Patrick, I would not say
that those of us gathered in the dining room were men of the world,
exactly, but we lived in the world. And it is a world which does not pay
the most scrupulous regard, alas, to the Sixth Commandment. As we
would call it. Parnell, being a Protestant, would call it the seventh. Good
God, those people can't even count to ten properly. These things happen,

you know. Balfour, as you know, was Irish secretary at the time, and there is more than mere gossip about himself and a certain titled and much-married lady. Do you know what that awful little William Martin said, the chap who owns the big shop on Sackville Street? 'Don't forget,' said he, discovering some face-saving formula, 'don't forget that Parnell, after all, is a Protestant.' The rest of us stared him into silence. The innocence of some otherwise corrupt men!"

"But if you all knew about the affair—" Prentiss began.

O'Clery shook his head. "Parnell told the *Freeman*—and of course the *Freeman* printed it; in those days it was Parnell's lapdog—that the case had been concocted by the very people who had hired Pigott. And he told Davitt, who, of course, told others, that he would emerge 'without a stain on his reputation.' Those were his words, 'without a stain.' A most curious definition of the word. For years afterwards, Davitt would repeat it with fury. 'Without a stain'!"

"Surely Parnell could never have believed that," Prentiss said. "What was the point of the lie?"

O'Clery was peeling an apple with the silver blade of a small, ivory-handled penknife. He paused. "Playing for time, no doubt. A human impulse. It was in February or March, as I recall, that he said that to Davitt, and Davitt repeated the words to me—to me among others—straightaway. And the case did not come up until November. He was right in a way, you know. Parnell was right. The case was cooked up to destroy Parnell, to destroy Home Rule. He became obsessed that Gladstone was the puppet master pulling O'Shea's strings; but that's absurd, of course. I was never one of the Grand Old Man's great admirers, but he would never have stooped to that. It was Joe Chamberlain. Mark my words, Patrick. History will bear me out."

Carefully, his small plump fingers surprisingly skilful, he unwound the skin, a single, curling ribbon, red warm to the sight.

"*Cooked-up* isn't quite the word, is it, Mr. O'Clery? O'Shea had a case, after all. They were lovers, Parnell and Katharine O'Shea. Adulterous lovers."

"You sound very censorious this morning, Patrick. As your father did, after he turned against Parnell. Oh, to be sure, the captain had a case. He had had a case since 1880. She had had two daughters by Parnell. Why wait until now, why wait until every other way of destroying him had failed, after he had made an alliance for the Irish with Gladstone? Can you answer me that?"

"Was there not some matter of a will? A wealthy aunt who had died? It had been to O'Shea's interest—"

[621]

"To be sure," O'Clery said. "Aunt Ben's will. And O'Shea was in need of money, always in need of money. He had sponged off the old lady, forced Katharine to sponge off her. And there was nothing more to be gained from Parnell; Galway was the last time that Parnell could have used the party to bribe O'Shea. Oh, there were more reasons than one; there always are with little twisters like O'Shea. Your father had been speaking in the moment's heat, but there is something to be said for the notion—shoot the little bastard. Your precious friend Nolan was roaming about London in those days, armed to the teeth. There was a blow he could have struck for Ireland." The watered-silk belly heaved again with laughter. "Better than blowing up bridges, and shooting innocent young fellows."

Delicately, O'Clery cored the apple, cut it into wedges, offered one on knife's edge to Prentiss.

"For a pair of respectable public figures," Prentiss said, "my father and you did a fair job of detesting the outraged husband, as he was called. Betrayed by a friend."

"Betrayed by a friend!" O'Clery echoed. "Let us be clear about this, Patrick. Ireland was smashed by the O'Shea divorce. We are still smashed. Look at us. Dillon and Redmond and O'Brien and their factions, Davitt preaching pacifism and land reform to the world, to English factory workers. We had been a party, united, with a leader. We split for more reasons than one. Healy because he was a spiteful, vengeful little jump-up who had hated Parnell for years. And Davitt because he may be a gaolbird and a fearsome revolutionary, but he is a pious, God-fearing Catholic— typically Irish, shall we say. But from the day of divorce forward, it was clear to me, without fuss or emotion, that Parnell had to go, for a time at least. The Church had cause to speak out, could not keep its silence, and it could only speak in condemnation of the fellow. The men who stood with him only prolonged the agony. Parnell must have seen that, but he had the pride of Lucifer, that fellow. And he dragged the romantics with him, the romantics like your man, Delaney."

And my mother, Prentiss thought, remembering the shouts in Sackville Street, in the window of the Imperial, his mother pretending that she was not crying.

"Mind you, I didn't join the pack that tore him down. Remember that, Patrick. I made my position clear, and then, the gentlemen in the Party, we stood back. We were no part of the pack of wolves and wild dogs, weasels, badgers, who tore him down."

Neither, thought Prentiss, before he could suppress the thought, neither was Pilate.

"It wouldn't do," O'Clery said, mouth half full of sweet apple. He swallowed. "An ugly, messy divorce case. The facts that came out in that divorce court, that Parnell left uncontested. It wouldn't do."

For the Uncrowned King of Ireland,
Lies in Kilmainham Gaol.

"Exciting days," Prentiss said, "when he was in command of the Party. I remember at school—"

"And he *was* in command," O'Clery said. "Healy now makes his boast that towards the end, Parnell was but an effigy, half mad, wasted with illness, besotted with that woman. Never believe that. Healy was fearful to strike, until Parnell was at bay, in Committee Room Fifteen. No. Don't believe most of it. But believe that he was besotted with that woman."

"Besotted," Prentiss said.

"Love," O'Clery said. "If you prefer the word, I grant it to you readily. He was in love with her. Every disastrous move he made gave evidence of that. Not that he wasn't a skilful fighter; far from it. Fierce as a tiger and resourceful. It would have been better for him as well as the country if he had not been, if he had been battered quickly down, forced to retire. But he fought to the end, and we saw shadings of him, fierce fires and shadings that we had guessed at, but had never seen before. He could be unscrupulous when he had to be. We had always known that and had taken pride in it, called it statesmanship; but not now. He did his best to turn us against each other; he was like a man possessed. But he loved that woman."

"I remember," Prentiss said, "it is the one thing I do remember, the crowd trying to shout him down, in Sackville Street—"

"Trying to but not succeeding, I'll wager," O'Clery said, lifting another wedge of apple. "He was safe in Dublin. The Parnellites could always keep the Dublin meetings packed."

"I think that I remember, but I am not certain. I think that I remember the crowd smashing against his bodyguard, shouting out about Kitty O'Shea."

"Yes," O'Clery said. "Even in Dublin. Dublin was safe, but even in Dublin he needed a bodyguard against those ruffians. Never 'Kitty,' Patrick. Healy and his pals taught the mob to call her that. Katharine O'Shea. And Katharine Parnell for those few final months. But for as long as Parnell is remembered, she will now be Kitty O'Shea, and in Ireland, Parnell will be remembered forever."

It was the same with O'Clery as with his father, Prentiss thought: a lingering fealty to the man they had helped to destroy.

"I remember, Patrick," his father was to say to him a week later, as they sat in the study of the house in Palmerston Park, in bright Sunday morning light, home from Mass. "I remember when he was brought back to Ireland, the procession to Glasnevin Cemetery. It was a Sunday like today, October the eleventh, 1891. But not otherwise like this Sunday, a wretched day, with low skies; but a crowd larger, everyone says, than Dublin had ever seen, ever will see, and a vast concourse following the coffin, the streets lined. I walked into town from Portobello Bridge, as I often did, but why I chose to do so on that day I cannot, for the life of me, say; it was dreary weather. As I walked across the Liffey, I caught a glimpse of the draped hearse at the Carlisle Bridge. It was crossing over to go up Sackville Street towards the Rotunda. Once, years before, I had shared a platform with him in the Rotunda. I took my hat off. What I saw was but a glimpse. The crowd was immense. His followers walked behind the hearse, of course—Redmond and Kenny. Your fellow Delaney, with troubles of his own at the moment. But thousands upon thousands for whom he was a dead king, and some among them, I'll wager, had been pelting him with clods a few weeks before. It was all frightening, in a way, like some power moving down upon us from an earlier century. Ha!" his father said, ceremoniously opening his box of cigars, and holding it towards Prentiss. "I heard later that someone on Sackville Street gave a shout: 'There he is! There's Healy!' It was not, of course. He would have been torn apart limb from limb. They walked behind him, their heads uncovered, all the way to Glasnevin."

"And yet," Prentiss said, and for once he accepted a cigar. His father, selecting his own, smiled with pleasure at another of the slender bonds which, in the past year, had been drawing them closer together, towards the closeness they had known once, when the father had been at that desk, gaslight falling upon an opened brief, and Prentiss, a boy home from school, had brought him for explanation a tall bound volume opened upon an engraving of a road, soldiers, a police barracks. Why, that is the barracks in Kilpeder, his father had said, the Fenian rising, the barracks after it was over, after the battle of Clonbrony Wood. His father had been infallible, golden-bearded. "And yet," Prentiss said, "you fought him. Right down to the end, to the Kilkenny election and beyond it."

"Oh, yes," his father said. "He had to go. Absolutely. Good, aren't they, these ones? Best Havana. A few of us pool together, have them shipped over from London—Judge Goodbody, Dr. Moynahan, and myself. You can't get a decent cigar in Dublin, save, so Johnny Hungerford tells me, at the Kildare Street Club; but I'd never set foot in that place. Not that I'm likely to be asked. Little better than a Fenian in the eyes of those fellows. The devil with them. The Stephen's Green Club suits me fine."

"But you uncovered your head, that dreary Sunday," Prentiss said.

"I did. I uncovered my head."

"Why?" Prentiss asked.

"Why! Foolish damned question, Patrick. Mark of respect. We had worked together, colleagues. Death wipes out a lot, you know. Mark of respect."

"And that's all?"

"Why should it not be all?" Dominick Sarsfield asked, and suddenly he puffed furiously, noisily, at his cigar.

"I think that we buried our past with Parnell," Patrick said.

His father grunted. "A fine sort of history you have in mind, I must say." Despite his politics, he was a great admirer of Macaulay, and of Gibbon, for all of Gibbon's glib scepticism.

"It is a terrible tragedy," his mother said to him that day, as their carriage carried them home. It had not been easy. Westmoreland Street and D'Olier Street were crowded with jostling men. "Like Shakespeare. Do you remember when we went to see *Macbeth*? Mr. Parnell has done things which he ought not to have done, or so his enemies say. And say with justice, I fear. But it all came from pride, the sin from which all the others flow. You will understand all that later, Patrick."

"And we are to be against him now," Patrick said, "because of the sin of pride?" His father would not talk with him about it.

The carriage clattered across the canal bridge.

"In a way," his mother said. "In a way, yes. Oh, but Patrick," she said, "it was his pride that made him a king for us. He fought for us here, here in Ireland, and he fought in England. Ireland was his love always, only Ireland." Then, as though hearing herself, she stopped short. "And he has the look of a king, Patrick. Not many real kings can say that. But what do we care, Patrick? Think of the real heroes that we have had— Patrick Sarsfield, whose name your own father bears, and Owen Roe O'Neill, and poor Robert Emmet, who was captured close to this very spot. Lured back into Dublin because of his pure love of a fine young woman, Sarah Curran."

"Yes," Patrick said, less rattled by the Sackville Street mob than by the confusion in his mother's words. But it was indeed as Father Connell had explained *Macbeth* to them at Clongowes: a man destroyed by his own gifts turning inwards against him, turning him savage and unyielding.

We had matters of our own to attend to in Kilpeder, and they carried us through most of the year that that wretched Parnell divorce suit was hanging fire in London. We would talk of it from time to time, but it had a curious dreamlike quality, that conversation in parlour and public house, two men meeting on the thawing roads to talk. For most of us in Kilpeder—those of us who were Nationalists, of course—the whole business was a vicious plot of the English Tories and perhaps the English Liberals as well. And most of us refused to suspect that the trap might be baited with actual meat, and where would we be left, what would we do, should the charges against him be proved in the divorce court? The Church itself held back, silent; and why then should we not follow that lead, and hope that all would come right? He would emerge without a stain, so he had told our leaders; and he had come from the Special Commission clear of stain, although vicious charges had been crafted against him: murder, connivance in it, or at least approval of it.

To be sure, there were some who knew a bit more—Bob did, of course—and I did because he had told me, and Mary knew. Old Tully knew, and Vincent. Brendan Fogarty, the Catholic solicitor, had heard the rumours, and Considine, the Catholic doctor. And we all of us—almost all of us, as we shall shortly see—put the matter from our minds, like the ostrich who according to the bestiaries shoves his head in the sand when danger approaches. But that has always seemed to me most unlikely, or it would be an extinct species like the dodo, fit prey for Mr. Darwin's morbid speculations.

We had our own concerns, for Munster had still its Plan of Campaign, whatever about divorce courts, and our barony alone had three afflicted estates, of which the great central issue was Lughnavalla, outside Kilpeder on the Killarney road, the cause of Bob's arrest and gaol sentence.

It was boycotting at its most brutal. Joseph Judkins was neither Irish nor, as the new word had it, Anglo-Irish, but rather the son of an Englishman who had picked up Lughnavalla as an investment, from the Encumbered Estates Court, after the great famine. An agent, Rick Howard, managed the estate for him, sending in the rents to a London bank, and the accounts, quarterly, to Judkins, who lived in England, in Bradford. At first, Judkins had tried living a few months of each year at Lughnavalla, but he had discovered, as his father had before him, that the county families held him in low regard because of his accent and lack of breeding and other such things that matter to them. He was never a member of the hunt nor asked to any of the county balls nor even to sit upon the Board of Magistrates. Dull-witted Englishman or not, he took the hint, and came over now only in the odd year, for the shooting, as Lionel Forrester does now, ostracized, if for quite different reasons. With the difference being, of course, that Forrester is a gentleman born and a crack shot, like his cousin, the vanished earl. But Judkins was a menace to gamekeepers and gillies alike, blazing away like some street-corner ruffian and bringing down more branches than birds.

In consequence, all matters, including the response which Lugh-navalla made to the Plan of Campaign, lay in the hands of Rick Howard the agent, a solicitor by profession and an arch-crony of Eddy Chute, who headed the Property Defence Association. And with those two fighting cocks, the notion of negotiation was unthinkable. They would gladly see Joseph Judkins sink into a pauper's grave before they would treat with the Land League. All this, of course, was grist to Bob Delaney's mill, and when he was in Kilpeder, much of his time was given to gingering up the Lughnavalla tenants, who were more than happy to be thus gingered, because the Plan called upon them to offer properly reduced rents to the landlord, and if refused, the money would go into a Land League trust, pending a final settlement, a date which, so Howard and Chute had been heard to observe, would coincide with the conversion of the Jews. Between the two of them, therefore, Bob Delaney and Eddy Chute, as ingenious a machine as could be imagined had been contrived for the ruin of Lughnavalla. But not of Judkins himself, who had not only other properties in England but two small factories as well. Then Howard decided to raise the stakes by threatening the eviction of the sitting tenants.

Bob made Lughnavalla and its threatened evictions the subject of a series of articles printed first in the *Freeman's Journal*, but after that picked up by a Liberal newspaper in Manchester, so that he was able to ensure that wide attention would be given to events in Kilpeder over the months to come. This time, although he was busier than he had been on that other occasion, years before, and although London had its demanding claims upon him, he wrote the articles without any need for my literary ministrations: the platform and the House had given him a skill in language which, if anything, he employed a bit too easily.

When the League struck the Clanricarde estates at Portumna, the year before, O'Brien and the other League journalists had exhibited the

Marquis of Clanricarde as a monster of unfeeling avarice, and an easy task it was, for he was a pathological miser, loathed even by other Irish landlords. It had been a wonderfully successful strategy, and the very word *Clanricarde* promised for a time to pass into the common store of epithets. It was something of the sort which Bob had in mind for Judkins, for whom, towards the end, I felt a certain reluctant sympathy. Clanricarde, after all, was Irish, whether he himself knew it or not; but Judkins was ready to be carved by the pen of a skilful propagandist into the effigy of a particular kind of scoundrel: the English land speculator of modern times, battening upon the dreadful aftermath of the famine.

True enough in its way. Lughnavalla and its farms, its mill, and its forge had belonged time out of mind to a Gaelic family which had prudently turned Protestant in Tudor days, and had since then been bleaching the Gaelic from its veins by marriage and other devices. Major Brian O'Callaghan-Lindsay was the last of their line, a hard-drinking hard-riding squire out of the pages of Charles Lever, and if local legend be believed, a great one for taking the village belles into his bed to break them in for marriage. When the famine rolled down upon the barony, he was mortgaged to the eyeballs—*encumbered,* the official word, was, in his instance, a euphemism—and he was happy enough to sell out to Samuel Judkins on terms however poor, and carry the proud blood of the O'Callaghan-Lindsays to Boulogne, where no doubt he discovered that girls were at once more expensive and less hygienic—but more experienced, so that it may have evened out. He remained a legend in the barony: I remember once, in Conefry's, overhearing a fellow say about Vincent, after one of his escapades had become known, "Sure, O'Callaghan-Lindsay would only be limping along behind that lad."

A poor landlord but a lusty legend, he was shabbily supplanted by a Bradford land speculator, and Bob made much of this, displaying it as an instance of what had been our helplessness before we took courage and began to organize. All absolutely true, of course, and more power to Bob's pen; but he contrived, without wandering too far from fact, to make of Samuel Judkins's son Joseph a grotesque out of Dickens, somewhere between Quilp and Mr. Murdstone. And so when Howard nerved himself, or was nerved by Eddy Chute, actually to commence evictions—emergency men, battering rams, Royal Irish Constabulary, a detachment of cavalry, the whole lot—Bob and the local League were ready for them, to say nothing of *United Ireland,* which had a correspondent on the scene, one of O'Brien's protégés, a young fellow named Paschal Donnelly, with a fine line in florid prose. *Christmas in the Boggeraghs,* that early joint effort by Bob and myself, had, I flatter myself, a certain degree of restraint, a George Crabbe–like quality of austere pathos, but Bob's articles in the *Freeman* fairly tore strips of skin off Judkins and Rick Howard and Eddy Chute, and it was but muted malediction as against Paschal Donnelly's despatches, further vivified as they were by "illustration" supplied in Dublin.

Not but that the facts themselves were abundantly ugly. The evicted tenants, the most of them, were moved into cabins which the League had prepared for them, and were fed with supplies purchased in advance of the day from League funds, but it was, of course, recognized upon all sides that this was but a makeshift, pending a hoped-for victory, and after a few months, the morale of the tenants was beginning here and there to flag. "Wounded veterans of the Land War" they were grandiloquently termed upon League platforms and in the nationalist press; but the spirit cannot be fed forever upon grandiloquence, nor even true rhetoric. And if Bob had the League and Davitt and Parnell behind him, with funds direct and indirect from America, then Chute and the Property Defence Association had the none too covert support of Balfour, the Irish Secretary, which is to say, the British government.

Bob and I rode out to Lughnavalla one day, long after spring of 1890 had turned to summer, and it was as though we had ridden directly into what had been my dear mother's favorite poem, Goldsmith's "Deserted Village." The mill and the forge had been boarded up, but the emergency men, faithful to their duty, had smashed and flattened the cluster of cabins.

Once in a while, walking or riding in the hills, in an unfamiliar country, one comes upon such a scene, and nearly always the answer is that the "village," to give it a lofty name, had been swept away in the famine, in "the great hunger," as the phrase has it in the Gaelic. But four decades of work upon the tumbled stone by wind and rain, by time which itself has its secret efficacy, will have reconciled to the earth, to sky, such humble ruins. "Ach," the country people will say when later you ask them in the next village, "the poor people. They drifted away."

Lughnavalla's ruins, by contrast, were spanking new, and looked exactly as what they were, the work of a harsh stroke in an ugly, modern sort of war. There was not, of course, so much as a cur to come yelping against our wheels.

The gates of Lughnavalla House were ajar, one of them indeed half off its hinges, and with room enough, without my jumping out to give them a shove, for us to ride up the weed-choked path. It had never been one of Munster's architectural glories, a fortified house of the seventeenth century, slated, which had been added to higgledy-piggledy. By the portico, Bob reined in, and the emergency man who had been left behind, having heard our carriage wheels, opened the hall door, and came out to us.

"Good morning to you," Bob called out, and the man looked at us suspiciously.

Bob was dressed in a handsome grey suit, waistcoated, with a fine, black line in it, and a soft hat. As he jumped down, he began to pull off one of his riding gloves. "Good morning," he said again, and the man nodded. "Go ahead," Bob said, "give us a word. Exercise your voice. It must be terrible, day following night and not a soul to talk to. Do you talk to yourself at all? They say that happens."

"What are you doing here, Mr. Delaney?"

"Ah," Bob said. "And a local voice at that. But not Kilpeder by God, nor Macroom. There is no Kilpeder man signed on for emergency work."

"Millstreet, Mr. Delaney."

"Millstreet, indeed!" Bob said. "You surprise me. Millstreet is hard League country."

"'Tis only to look after the big house, like, that I was taken on. I have done no harm."

"Poor fellow," Bob said. "Such a harmless task, and there is no decent person will talk to you. Mr. MacMahon here and myself came to have a look around, and we gave ourselves dispensation to break the oath of the boycott and say good morning to you, did we not, Hugh?"

But I had no wish to bait the poor fellow, and nodded only. He was a slack, heavy-bellied man in his forties, and could have found more honourable work than he was doing.

"We have a mind to take a peek into the house, see how our betters live. Lived, I should say. You have no objection, have you, Mr. . . ."

"Dinny Trainor," the man said. "Dennis Trainor. I don't know, Mr. Delaney. The order was that none were to enter."

"And our orders were to speak to no man who was doing the landlord's bidding. We all bend orders a bit when it does no harm."

And he walked through the hall door, myself close behind him and Trainor, perplexed, following at a distance.

There was a drawing room to the left, and that is the only room we entered. It was a melancholy experience. Although Judkins came to Lughnavalla only for the shooting, there was a small staff in attendance year-round: groundsmen, a housekeeper, and several servants—all these had been ordered off by the League, no doubt with fearsome threats, and the room had gone for months unswept and undusted. O'Callaghan-Lindsay had sold off part of his furnishings to the new owner, who had added bits and pieces, as had his son, the sort of furnishings proper to a holiday house or a shooting lodge, and these comported ill with side tables and cabinets of delicate fruitwood which a century before, perhaps, had negotiated perilous hilly roads from Cork City. But if the walls had ever borne portraits of O'Callaghans, the last of the line had carried them off to Boulogne with him, and instead, over the fireplace, hung a photograph of a shooting party, hefty men in wide-checked tweeds, their legs stockinged or booted, guns held with studied negligence.

"The harp that once through Tara's halls," Bob said, half saying and half singing Tommy Moore's familiar lines:

> "The harp that once through Tara's halls,
> The soul of music shed,
> Now hangs as mute on Tara's walls
> As if that soul were fled."

"It does indeed," I said, and together we sang the next lines, laughter jarring our harmony.

> "So sleeps the pride of former days,
> So glory's thrill is o'er,
> And hearts that once beat high for praise,
> Now feel that pulse no more."

"Do him justice," Bob said. "Old Callaghan's heart oft beat high, if what is told of him is true."

"But not for praise," I said. "The old stock, Bob. The old Gaelic gentry. How will we contrive without them?"

"We must do the best we can," Bob said. "Create our own gentry. Vincent is doing his best. Well now, Dinny Trainor," he said to the fellow, who was standing in the hallway peering in. "We had best leave you to your silence. If there are books in the house, you should seek out *Robinson Crusoe*. It may have useful hints as to how to comport yourself on a desert island."

Trainor followed us gloomily outside. He did not, in fact, seem inclined to talk.

"All this will be over someday," Bob said to him as he pulled on his gloves again. "A few months, perhaps. It is a bit like *Robinson Crusoe*, yourself the ruler of Lughnavalla and all that the eye can survey."

"I would not know about that, Mr. Delaney," Trainor said. He had conducted himself as best he could, with a kind of grubby dignity.

———

But of that other part of Bob's life, he spoke seldom to me, a sentence or two broken out because he could not keep silence. And once, when he had drink taken, he told me the most of it, before I could find words to stop him, before he would listen to the words. I wanted none of it. "Tell me no more of that," I said coldly to him, "not a word." And saying that, I failed him: I know that now. In a curious way, he was himself in a kind of isolation, with the colour and warmth of his life locked into a stillness, remote. No other person in Kilpeder knew, nor would know, until everything fell apart, and that lay in the future, unthinkable to me in that warm summer, heavy with odours.

I did not want to know.

"He is coming back from Italy," Bob said, on a long summer evening, as we walked back to the town. "Back here to Kilpeder."

"Who is?" I asked, puzzled.

"Ardmor," Bob said. "Lord Ardmor. Sylvia's husband. He will be in London for a week or two, and then he is coming here. For how long I cannot say."

"Sylvia's husband." The phrase hung in the air, floating menacingly between us. I found it difficult to speak calmly. The fact, which I would not allow myself to recognise, even to consider as something possible, now was out, in the open, as evidently he wanted it to be.

"I knew that," I said at last. "I was talking a few days ago with Bat Powers." Bartholomew Powers was the head gardener of the Castle, a man of great natural dignity. "Bat told me."

"Sylvia is looking forward to his visit. They are very close, the two of them. So she tells me." He looked sideways at me, to see how I received his words. "We are very close ourselves."

"He may find that his life here is a lonely one," I said, as though I had not heard what he meant. "The smaller landlords are furious with him, and Eddy Chute has turned him into a type of Parnell, turning against his own. But then, he has kept to himself of late years."

"Sylvia will stay in London," Bob said, "but she may go for a few weeks to the place that they have in Italy. Near Florence, somewhere."

"A wise decision," I said. "London is most uncomfortable in summer, I am told, and people of fashion flee from it. Many of them, of course, are compelled by circumstances to remain in town. Several millions of them."

"You are not being a friend when you speak like that with me," Bob said quietly. "There is no one else with whom I can talk. Come off it, would you, Hughie?"

"No, you come off it, Bob." I stopped dead in the road to face him.

"What sorts of things do you expect me to say? That you are living in sin with the Countess of Ardmor is so bewildering a notion my mind cannot grapple with it. Neither can it grapple with the fact that you are betraying Agnes to do so. She and Mary are forever in and out of each other's parlours. She is lonely with you away so much of the time, and she turns to Mary. More to her family—they are close-knit, which is a blessing for her—but to Mary as well. And to me a bit. She boasts of your triumphs to me. I have said not one word to you in condemnation, but by God, don't you tell me to come off it."

Bob looked stricken, as well he might. In this life, we can do the damnedest things, provided no one chalks the words up on a wall for us to see. But there is always some helpful person, sooner or later, with a bit of chalk.

"It is not like that," he said, in a different, smaller voice.

"It never is," I said, remorselessly.

We were coming in by the Macroom road, and had reached, by chance, the rise of road from which the English soldiers first hove into the view of our lookouts, twenty years earlier. The town lay spread out before us, and a glint of the Sullane behind the indistinct wall of the Castle demesne. Where the road curved slightly, there was a bit of wall that had tumbled down, although not so badly that the farmer was as yet moved to mend it.

"Not like that," he said again, and although I felt towards him the sympathy of friendship—of love, almost—I said nothing.

"The Countess of Ardmor, you say, and it is like a fairy tale when you say it. She was Sylvia Challoner when he met her, the daughter of a half-pay colonel with a mortgaged estate in Westmeath, ten farms or so, and a battered house with a roof in need of reslating. They met in London, at a party which some artist gave. The old fellow had debts everywhere, his club, his tailor. If I had met her then . . ."

"But you did not, Bob, and that makes the difference."

Only, I thought, a bit of the difference, for I remembered Lord Ardmor bringing her home as his bride, and bonfires lit from miles away, the hillsides ablaze, and I remembered seeing, from a distance, the windows of Ardmor Castle ablaze, seeing the carriages rolling through the gates, bringing not county families alone, but guests from Dublin and Galway and London. I remembered the music floating down to us, across terraces, lake, gardens, the sounds of violins upon a summer night.

"She is a very beautiful woman," Bob said. "He is in love with her beauty."

"A common cause of marriage," I said.

From here, we could see, beyond the plantations, a bit of the Castle, a corner of white, distant stone, a terrace. Unapproachable.

"It is her beauty that he loves," Bob said. "Not Sylvia. Her beauty. But he is very kind with her, and she with him. They love each other in that way. Do you understand what I am saying, Hughie?"

And, though why this should be so I cannot say, for I am not a worldly man, I did understand, but my tongue was locked against whatever it is that Bob wanted me to say.

"Agnes?" I said, and only that. He shook his head.

"There is no end for all this, you know, Bob. Either no end or else"—I fumbled for a proper phrase or name—"or else one sunless morning your lady or yourself will find yourself feeling differently, diminished. Or else there will be some disaster."

"If she were to feel differently, Hughie, that would be the worst disaster."

"That woman," Dennis Tully said. "There is a word to describe her, but it cannot be used at any decent Christian table, and not before ladies, certainly."

"If a word is used in the Scriptures, it can be used in any Christian company," Father Meagher said. "In the New Testament at least," he amended. "A woman taken in adultery. But the New Testament also commends us to prudence. The matter has not yet been tested in the court. And Parnell has given assurances that he will emerge without a stain."

The dining room of the Tully house seemed always to me the centre of the house, and not the parlour. The house had a name now, Inchigeelagh House, and above the ornate fireplace of red-and-black marble there hung a vast painting of Inchigeelagh's lovely neighbouring site, Gougane Barra, with its hills and small perfect lake, its pilgrim island, the silvery Allua. "Did *your* Tullys come first, then, from the Inchigeelagh region?" a dinner guest, a Limerick auctioneer, once asked Dennis Tully, and I perked up my ears at the possibility of that favorite mystery of mine, the origin of the Tullys, being at last unfolded. "Not at all," Tully said, giving his chin a swipe with his immense square of damask, "not at all. Mrs. Tully and the children and I took a picnic there years ago, and it stuck in my mind, so that when I saw the oil painting for sale in Cork City, I had it bought and reframed. Do you remember, Agnes? Vincent? Or were you too small? Tis a perfect picnic site."

But on this Sunday afternoon, there was no auctioneer, but only the Tullys, even Vincent, and Bob with Agnes, and Mary and myself and

[634]

Father Meagher and Fogarty, our Catholic solicitor. Conor and our own two young fellows had had an early meal in the kitchen before setting off for a bit of shooting in Clonbrony Wood.

"It does you great credit to take that line, Father," Tully said without enthusiasm. "But there is not a person at this table who is in doubt as to what the word will be from that divorce court. And where will that leave us?"

"It does him credit as a priest," Fogarty said mildly. "It would do him credit as a lawyer as well. There has no evidence been heard."

Tully grunted, and reached towards the gravy boat and ladle which a servant girl was holding towards him. "Bend down, girl," he said, "bend down so that I can do this properly." The month was August: summer lamb, overcooked but savoursome. "There now," Tully said, drowning his meat. "I will tell you now, Father. We are a mannerly company assembled here, tidy and of neat deportment. But before we rise up from this table, there will be a stain or two upon the double damask, and down to the scullery with it—gravy or wine or candle dripping. That is the way of things. And no one leaves a divorce court without a stain. Now, I intend no blasphemy, but how does that strike you as a parable?"

"There are stains and stains," Bob cut in, to Meagher's visible relief. "If Captain O'Shea cannot prove his case, then in law there is no case, and the matter is of no concern to us."

"You can say that, can you, Bob, and yourself a member of Parliament, acquainted with the doings and goings of that fine gentleman?"

"I am not in Mr. Parnell's personal confidence," Bob said.

"Then you should talk by God to Tim Healy, for I heard what Tim Healy has been saying in Bantry and elsewhere." He jabbed fork into meat.

"Far less is Tim Healy in his confidence."

"No longer," Tully said, "but he was once his secretary, and there were certain letters which he opened by chance which he should not have opened. And from more women than one; this trollop is but the latest. You will excuse my language, ladies."

"Does your language have a word for someone who reads private letters and tittle-tattles their contents?" Bob asked. "If it does not, would *blackguard* suit?"

I cannot speak for others, but for myself, that took the savour from the lamb, and silence suddenly weighed down upon the table.

"Bob spoke too hastily, Father," Agnes said. "This has been weighing on his mind as well. How could it not? Off there in London, where it is all happening."

"I did," Bob said. "Your pardon, Dennis."

"No need," Tully said, almost in surprise, "no need." Nor was there: he was not one for the niceties of discourse. "The Church has its charitableness and the law its strange ways of thinking, but the fact is that in two months' time, the man in whom we reposed our confidence will come out of that courtroom with the stench of the divorce court clinging to him. We are a Catholic people, Father. Would you have us led by such a man?"

"By such a man?" Meagher said. He was delicately lifting the skin from a potato. "Indeed no. I cannot speak for the hierarchy, but I happen to know a bishop or two. A convicted adulterer? Indeed no. But it may not come to that. We can all of us hope, surely."

"The subject is one upon which I speak with diffidence," Vincent said, and only upon his parents and his sister, perhaps, was the irony wasted. Even Meagher had a quick, frosty smile to suppress. "But I am cursed if I can see what a man's adultery has to do with anything save his adultery. The Fenians handed out rifles, the few rifles they had, but Parnell has shaped our people into a weapon. No other man could do what he has done."

"A Catholic people, Vincent. A Catholic people," Meagher said. "It is all very difficult."

"Tim Healy does not hold that fellow in awe," Tully said, "and there are many in the party who do not. Is that not the case, Bob?"

"Parnell is the chief of that party," Bob said, "and I stand by him. The English would not have had so easy a time of it over the years if our own people had not turned against their leaders. It will not happen this time, by God."

"Well," Tully said, finishing his lamb with a sigh. "There are rights and wrongs in everything. As you say, we must wait and see. And now, good woman, what class of a sweet will you conjure up for us?"

Later, in the road, Mary and Agnes stood making their interminable good-nights to each other, after the adhesive fashion of women, and Vincent, Bob, and myself stood chatting idly together.

"The lads are home," I said, for I could see a light in Conor's window.

"Home and reading, one of them," Bob said. "The fellow is a devil for reading. More a Delaney than a Tully."

"Where is it they were?" Vincent asked.

And without reflecting, I said, "They took their guns up into Clonbrony Wood."

Then we heard my words in the warm night, all light not yet vanished, and we burst into laughter, all three of us.

"Would you not think they would make a shrine of it?" Bob said. "Put a fence all round it and set up a plaque?"

"The lads had their nerve all the same," Vincent said. "The twelfth is a full week away, and grouse are privileged creatures until then."

"Ach," I said, "I think they were in search of whatever moved, from robins on up."

"I am getting up a shooting party of my own," Vincent said, "to celebrate the twelfth, when grouse may legally be pulled down. A dozen or so of us. Could I persuade one or both of you? You might like it, Bob. The resident magistrate will be there. A good gun; I shot with him last year."

"I thank you, no, Vincent. The resident magistrate and I had sufficient conversation the day he arrested me at the Lughnavalla demonstration."

"You don't lack for healthy exercise, Vincent," I said, "what between running with the hare and hunting with the hound."

Vincent shrugged. "He is not the worst in the world. I am less political than the two of you. I take men as I find them."

"And women," I said mildly. At that moment, I heard Mary laugh, at something she had herself said, no doubt, for Agnes did not include wit among her many virtues. She was resting her hand on Agnes's forearm and laughing, her head thrown back.

"Ah well," Vincent said, "there will at least be no politics at Brierly Lodge, but only some men and some shotguns, some good food, and a few bottles of Mr. Connolly's finest malt liquor. Evans will be there, the man who replaced Chute as agent for the Ardmor lands, a decent fellow. Mixed religions—some of our lot, some of theirs. Dermot O'Connell is coming over from Kerry, a direct descendant of the Liberator."

"Good for him," Bob said frostily. "I wish him good shooting. The O'Connells have not always been partial to the sound of gunfire. Ireland is not worth the shedding of one drop of blood, your friend's noble ancestor told our parents."

"By God, but you have the rough tongue, Bob. You were a lucky man within there that your father-in-law has the skin of an elephant."

"There will be trouble enough before that matter is ended," I said. "No need to pull it down on us just yet. Father Meagher spoke very sensibly, I thought."

"That fellow," Vincent said, and he looked back reflectively towards his father's house, where Father Meagher and old Tully were still deep in conversation. "That fellow is as cute as a shit-house rat."

Bob gave an explosion of laughter.

"I have always marvelled, Vincent," I said, "at your delicacy of expression. Is it a practised art? Would you call in at the school some morning, and give a lesson to my scholars? They are a brutish lot, you know."

"How do you mean that, Vincent?" Bob asked, serious upon the instant.

"You know as well as myself, Bob. That divorce will be a mess; even I can tell that out here in the backwoods. If the party holds together, you may brazen it out, just barely. But I doubt if it will. And the Church will declare against him, against Parnell. They are waiting to see how best they can make the leap. Six months from now, Meagher in there will be pouring down fire and brimstone upon anyone who would dare say a word in Parnell's favour."

"Ten years' work," Bob said. "Ten bloody years. Smashed up. I don't accept that, Vincent. He's a fighter. He has fought for ten years, and has won every fight."

"I'd best be getting back to Brierly," Vincent said, "while there is summer light. Parnell may be a second Napoleon, able to beat off the Tories and the Property Defence Association and the Holy Roman Catholic Church and gutter sparrows like little Tim Healy. But there is a rock upon which he will smash up." Vincent pointed towards the dining-room window, where gaslight escaped towards us through a gap in the drawn drapes. "He will smash up against Dennis Tully and men like him, decent, crawthumping, money-gouging Irish Catholics spread out across the island."

"It must be wonderful not to give a damn about anything, Vincent," Bob said. "It clarifies the mind."

"There are many things I give a damn about, Bob. Friendship, for one. Decent wine, sunrise, a good morning's shooting. Not politics. I had my fill of that." Suddenly, he put his arms around us and drew us close to him, holding us in a tight embrace. Then he called, "Ladies, let your poor men get to their homes."

"A strange life Vincent leads," Mary said to me that night, as we sat in the kitchen over a cup of tea. She was still wearing the grey grosgrain, and she was lovely in it, tight-waisted after the fashion of the time, and full-bosomed in that decorous manner which is more enticing than wanton display, or so I found to be the case. "But he seems happy enough with it."

"It is a boy's life," I said, "and what man would not envy it? Money for whatever is of pleasure to him, a shooting lodge, Paris when he wants a look at the Opera House, or London. Chums scattered across Munster that he can visit when he has a mind to. And he is not anonymous. By no means. If you were to say in a hotel bar in Waterford that you came from Kilpeder, there would be someone to say, 'Vincent Tully's town. Now there is a rare bird for you.' " But they were as likely to say, "Kilpeder, is it? Turn around, let us see does Tully the gombeen man have his claws in your back."

Vincent gave once a fine long weekend treat to myself and my lads and Bob and Conor, out at Brierly Lodge. And it was, indeed, a boy's dream come true: a tackroom with the smell of leather, stables, a small gate lodge. For it was no mere shooting box, but a small estate, with a staff and a groundsman and a gatekeeper. That Friday afternoon when we arrived, there was a prodigious tea awaiting us, and a heaping breakfast the next morning, ham and devilled kidneys and whatever. And the happiest fellow there, I think, was Vincent. I had always a strange feeling about him, that for all the women and the scandals that women brought down upon him, true or false, he was happier with men than with women.

I remarked upon this now to Mary, and she smiled.

"That is like boys, is it not?" she said, looking not at me, but at the tea she was pouring. "They take delight in their own company. Later on, things change."

And later still, as we lay in bed, after love, Mary asleep, I lay awake, remembering my half joke that men in a bar in Waterford would have heard about Vincent, the wild rake, about whom legends were woven that could not be rehearsed before ladies. Ned they would surely know by name, as they knew Joe Brady's name, or the Manchester Martyrs. And Bob had by now what the newspapers were calling a "national record," a Fenian hero who was destined for a high place of some sort when we had won our independence. But the name of the schoolmaster of Kilpeder was known as far east as Macroom and as far north as Millstreet, and there was an end to it. It was known to the Gaelic-speakers of Coolea and Ballyvourney, and in the hills of the Boggeraghs and the Derrynasaggarts. A decent enough fellow they thought me, no doubt—they had no evidence to the contrary: my Gaelic stiff and bookish, taking down their tales and songs, and once in a great while, the Matterhorns of my career, my translation of some song they had given me appearing in a Dublin journal, "translated from the Gaelic by Hugh Ignatius MacMahon, County Cork." You have the best of it, Bob would tell me, or Vincent. I could hear them speaking the words in the ear's imagination, and there were times—this was one of them—when I wanted to shout, "No, I want to leave a mark of my own upon the earth."

31

[*Lionel Forrester*]

I joined Tom in Kilpeder for the shooting, and a lonely but pleasant time we had of it, the two of us, joined on occasion by Bobby Evans, the Welsh chap who had replaced the ferocious Chute as the Ardmor agent, a decent fellow and not being Irish not subject to Chute's ferocities. It was late summer drifting into autumn, dark greens of leaves turning brown, growing dry so that the wind now had its rattling rustle, and the ground dry beneath our boots. Tom was a splendid shot, always had been. The caricaturists for *Punch*—for whom all artists other than themselves are wan and listless, Bunthornes with lilies—would have been baffled by his sureness of eye and arm, the gun swinging in a graceful, seemingly casual arc.

But then that wretched book—the other and easier of the two had finished itself and was off with its publisher—drew me back to London, and smack into the Parnell divorce suit. It could not have been messier,

and the *Times* of course published full, juicy accounts. Parnell refused
even to be represented, and Frank Lockwood, Katharine O'Shea's counsel, was holding a watching brief only. So that for two days, the fifteenth
and seventeenth of November, O'Shea had a broad canvas upon which
to paint himself as the aggrieved and honourable husband, father, friend,
wise political counsellor, and Parnell as a man dead to honour, unscrupulous and mendacious, not wicked merely but contemptible as well, with
false names and lies about baggage to housemaids and the usual wretched
French-farce indignities of middle-class infidelities and frolics at seacoast
resorts. There were precious few—in London, at least—with any pretence
to worldliness who did not know a very different story, that Katharine
O'Shea had for a full decade been Parnell's mistress, and with her husband's connivance in the matter, his complaisance prompted by the most
sordid and squalid of motives—money and a chance in politics. It was not
Katharine O'Shea who had sold herself, but her husband, and not once
but twice, first to Parnell, and then, ten years later, to Joe Chamberlain,
who had been looking for a weapon with which to destroy Parnell and
Home Rule.

On November 18, the day after the divorce *nisi* was granted, a great
meeting in Dublin's Leinster Hall proclaimed its loyalty to Parnell, and
on the twenty-fifth, the eve of the parliamentary session, the members of
the Irish Parliamentary party, in Westminster, reaffirmed his leadership
by acclamation. And yet all this was but the strange overture to disaster,
for in six days, from the first to the sixth of December, in Committee
Room 15 of the House of Commons, that leadership was struck a mortal
blow; the party which he created was split down the middle, and the shock
waves, as from an earthquake, spread across the Irish Sea, embittering the
Irish and turning them against each other with a ferocity that not even
Chamberlain himself could have hoped for or dreamed of. They are
shattered yet, a civil war in the recent past, and a country dominated by
the ghost of a leader, betrayed or betraying, depending on one's point of
view.

Once, a few years ago, I was visiting a friend who is a member—for
Worcester, I think—and as we were walking down a corridor, he said, on
impulse, "Here it is, the famous battlefield, Committee Room Fifteen."
He rapped on the door and flung it open. The room was empty, a
handsome room, oak-panelled, with a horseshoe-shaped table, and tall
windows opening upon the Thames. I crossed over, and stood looking out,
then turned around, and tried to picture the scenes of those six ugly,
savage days—Parnell, Healy, Barry, Delaney, Redmond. But I could not;
the historical imagination does not come at our beck and call, any more

than imagination of any other sort. I could as well have been in Madame Tussaud's, for I saw only a meeting chamber, where much dull work had been done before and since; and yet my friend was right—it was a battlefield, and its name is still resonant in Ireland: Committee Room 15.

I had, at the time, my own privileged knowledge as to the drama of that room, for twice during that fateful week I was with Sylvia when Robert Delaney was there. But it was, of course, the talk of London. Never, I think, before or since had Ireland held centre stage: the collapse of the plot against Parnell with the smashing upon the stand of the forger Pigott, Pigott's flight to Madrid and suicide there by revolver shot as Scotland Yard men broke down the door to his hotel room, the divorce, the destruction or near-destruction of the party—all this was drama and drama which owed much of its intensity to the extraordinary, enigmatic personality of Parnell.

I remember that on the second of the Committee Room meetings, I chanced to be having dinner at our club with Frank Lockwood, Mrs. O'Shea's counsel, a sound lawyer with perhaps an unduly fashionable clientele, and of course the soul of discretion; but midway through a second bottle of claret and in the privacy of one's own club, there is a certain relaxation, unwarranted perhaps in the case of a writer as one's table companion.

"A charming lady," Frank said, "but an impossible one." I nodded to the waiter, who attended to our empty glasses. "Mind you," he said, "she made more sense than Parnell did. She wanted to fight—to make countercharges or else to prove connivance. And I could have done either of those easily enough. Easily enough. But then, you see, the case would have fallen through, and she would still have been O'Shea's wife. Parnell wouldn't hear of it."

"Chivalrous of him," I said.

"Perhaps," he said, "if you account suicide a form of chivalry. Mad, I call it."

"Ah, but you see," I said, "he loves her."

"Love," Lockwood repeated with some distaste, as though specifying a condition with no standing at law, but belying his own reputation in town.

"Mad," he said again.

"Did you have dealings with him? What do you make of him?"

"O'Shea," Lockwood said, "was given custody of all the children, and that meant two little girls who are Parnell's daughters. This has driven him into a frenzy; when I had occasion to deal with him, his manner was . . . well, grotesque. I thought he showed signs of madness. People are using that word, you know. There is more madness in that family than is good for a family."

"This means the finish of him, poor devil. He cannot survive after this. Look at Dilke. Not only a divorce, but evidence that has spattered him with mud."

"Mud!" Frank said. "Come now, Lee!"

"We are not his followers, Frank. We are not the English nonconformists either. I don't know what I would do in his case. Wicklow wouldn't be too comfortable in the circumstances. I expect I would sell out, find some nice place on the Continent, south of France perhaps, Italy. That's what Charlie Ivory did. In six months the decree will be made final, and they can marry."

"You are not, are you, Lee, a follower of the day's news? A bit of cheese and two glasses of port should round matters off nicely. Parnell isn't going anywhere. He isn't even bargaining in that room over there," he said, nodding towards the distant Thames. "He intends to remain the master of the party. And he has just strength enough to pull down the temple. At least Samson was destroying his enemies, not his own people." He raised a hand to the waiter. "If they are his own people. Seems thoroughly English to me. Excellent manners, good accent."

"He is Irish," I said. "And so am I. They are my people, you know."

"Are they indeed?" Frank asked. "I wish you joy of them. A noisy lot, some of them, eh?"

He was referring, I took it, to the dynamite attack two nights before on the Metropolitan Line at Gower Street. Mercifully, no lives were lost, but like a score of other incidents that year, the greater number of them with fatalities, we were reminded constantly that behind the words and passions on platforms and in committee rooms, there was actual violence, hatreds capable of murders. Scotland Yard had had an excellent record, running down those teams of Clan na Gael terrorists, but this one was cleverer than most, or at least more closely knit, and it left no clues. Although this time, the Yard knew the name of its leader, so we were later to discover.

It was after the meeting on the third of December that I met Delaney at Sylvia's house in Chelsea, and he should, by all rights, have been feeling crushed, for he was standing by Parnell come hell or high water, and in speaking to him, I used that phrase.

"Well, they have come," he said, "both the high water and the hell. Gladstone has let it be known that we can no longer count upon Liberal support if Parnell remains, and this very day, the Standing Committee of the bishops in Ireland have made public their denunciation of him."

"There you are then, old man," I said, spreading out my hands, "your left and right bowers shattered. You cannot stand by him now, and it is selfish of him to expect it."

"The devil we can't," he said. "I have had a day and an evening of this, and you will excuse me if I beg off from more of it. Redmond is holding at this moment a meeting of the 'Parnellites,' as they call us now, but I told him I was not needed. Everyone knows where I stand."

He crossed the room and rested his hands on the white mantelpiece, looking down into the December fire. Presently, he turned around, and it was as if he had not heard his own words. "We were not shaped as a party to do England's bidding, neither Holy William Gladstone's nor anyone else's. And the Church has no business in a matter of politics. The Irish people have not spoken yet, and it is to them alone that we are answerable."

"It has been my impression," I said, "correct me if I am wrong, that Parnell has for ten years been at infinite pains to court the English Liberals, and to secure the support of the Catholic hierarchy."

All this while Sylvia sat quietly, in a robe of red velvet, caught high at the throat, and her dark hair, lovely and fathomless, unbound.

"To be found out, Robert," she said, "that is their unforgivable sin. They will hunt him down, the hounds will rip his throat open."

"They are inside already," Delaney said, "Barry and Healy and the rest of them. 'The leader-killer,' Parnell hurled that at him this afternoon, at Barry. Barry brought down Isaac Butt in the seventies, and now he has a taller quarry."

"Parnell was not unhappy to see Butt brought down," I said.

"This could all be for the best," Delaney said. "Take a lancet to the boils, let out the pus. Fellows like Healy and Barry, O'Connor."

"Do they have a strong voice in the country?" Sylvia asked suddenly. I was surprised: I had seldom heard her speak of such matters; they seemed not to interest her.

"Not O'Connor," Bob said. "O'Connor is a useful journalist for whom Parnell found a seat in Liverpool. But Tim Healy is a great contriver of alliances; he is a priest's man and a bishop's man, and he is strong with commercial interests across Munster. It doesn't pay to underestimate him. I warned Redmond on that score, not that he needed warning."

"Across Munster," she said. "Cork is in Munster."

"So I have heard. I take your meaning. He is in close with the Condons of Millstreet and the Tullys of Kilpeder."

"But not as close as you are," Sylvia said. "Your family." She took one of her dark-tobaccoed cigarettes from an ivory box beside her chair.

"My family," he said.

"And what view of all this does your family's father take?"

It was a private language between them, of course, but one that could be read without difficulty.

"I'll sort that out later," he said. "I have a fight on my hands here in London at the moment, at Westminster."

She waved out the match, and tossed it, in an almost masculine gesture, towards the fireplace. It fell short, and lay upon the white-and-gold carpeting.

"You told me once," she said, "a long time ago, that without Tully's backing, you would never have reached Westminster."

"You are right," he said. "But that was a long time ago. I have not been idle myself when it comes to alliances: the League is at my back, and the farmers whom I fought beside from one end of the country to the other. I could take that seat on my own today and hold it, if I had to."

"And you may have to," she said. "Lee, change the subject for us."

"I'm afraid not," I said. "It is time that I found my way home."

"Of course," she said, "Emily is waiting for you. No rest for the wicked." And when she saw that I was staring at her, she shook her head and smiled. "Forgive me, Lee. I am upset. That was unkind of me. I am very pleased for you, for Emily. You know that."

"Yes," I said, "I know that. I could never stay angry with you, dearest."

But when she saw me to the door, she put a hand on my forearm. I had not yet wrestled into my greatcoat, and the touch of her fingers on my sleeve was vivid. I put my hand on hers.

"I am frightened, Lee. For him and for myself."

"Don't be," I said. "It is only politics. Politics has always bored us, you and me. It is one of the things we have together."

"Parnell is being destroyed," she said, "and not by politics."

"Shakespeare says somewhere something like, men have died and worms have eaten them, but not for love."

"Watch," she said. "Watch what will happen. You are very good for me, Lee. You ask nothing of me."

And for one of those rare times, so rare that I can remember each one, she put an arm around my neck and kissed me passionately. Taken as from a thicket, I responded; her lips were half parted. She stood back then, and said, "You should have no trouble finding a cab. No need to send out the girl."

"Like that?" Emily said to me an hour later, in bed. "Did she kiss you like that?"

"Not quite," I said. "Almost, but not quite. I felt jolly strange about it, with her lover a few feet away."

"But you didn't mind too much, did you?"

"Not too much," I said. "She aroused me, in fact, and she knew it. But she was too much a lady to say so."

"Aroused you like this?" Emily asked, and put her hand upon me. "Aren't you pleased that I am not a lady?" But she took her hand away, and rested it on my chest. "Poor Sylvia," she said. "When she is desolate or terrified or too lonely, she can only speak that way. In kisses."

"She has reason to be frightened, perhaps," I said. "Sylvia is brainy, although it amuses her to pretend that she is not. Delaney is all she cares about, and she put her finger on the spot—Kilpeder, not Committee Room Fifteen."

"Committee Room Fifteen," Emily said. "What is that?"

"Good God, woman. Everyone knows that. It is where Parnell is fighting for his life these days."

"That!" she said contemptuously. "Why in the world that man ever got himself entangled with a gang of Papishes, the slaves of their priests and bishops!"

"Oho," I said, "the bold Protestant maid."

"I am perfectly happy with Her Majesty," Emily said. "I have no need for uncrowned kings. The lily-o, the lily-o, the royal loyal lily-o."

But the second time was far different. At about eight on the sixth of December, Emily came unexpectedly around to my flat, to bring me to Chelsea. She was lucky to find me in; I had just finished dressing to go out to dinner at friends', and my hand was almost upon the knob of the hall door. "She is distraught," Emily said. "She does not know what to do with him. She does not know any of his friends. Nor, of those names he has spoken, which are now enemies or friends." She had kept the cab waiting, and as it rattled across town, I managed to make out a bit of what had happened.

The party had split all right, and had split with a vengeance. Two thirds of them or more had broken off discussion and left the room. Twenty or so—and Delaney, of course, was one of them—had stayed with Parnell. That had been in late afternoon, and since then Delaney had put in a couple of hours of solid drinking. He was uncontrollable, had broken a table at Sylvia's or something of the sort, and had struck her in the face.

"Good God," I said. That much I got from Emily in bits and pieces, dragged out of her.

"I have never seen anything like this before in my life," she said. "My brother was a bad one for the drink, but he never hit anyone. Not that I saw."

"What had she said to him?" I asked, but she shook her head.

"It would not have mattered. He did not know that it was Sylvia, nor by then did he know where he was. He has been drinking more. He is on to the brandy. The servants—the other servants—are scandalised."

"Well they might be," I said.

We found him sprawled in one of the big fireside chairs, his eyes open but glassy, a glistening river of saliva on his chin. Sylvia was on one knee, beside him, and looked up when she heard us.

There was an ugly bruise, red and angry, along one side of her face, beginning at the cheekbone. She was dressed as though she too had been intending to go out for the evening, in black, with a choker of pearls.

"He did not mean . . . this," she said, and held her fingers close to the bruise, without touching it.

"Mean it or not," I said, in a voice which carried my sense of the matter. Navvies and factory workers might hit women, their wives or their girls, but there was an end to it.

The brandy decanter, unstoppered, stood on the floor at the far side of his chair, but he had dropped a glass, and it had rolled away, staining the thick white carpet.

"He needs to be put to bed, but I can't manage it on my own," I said.

Together, Emily and I got him to his feet, and he came to a kind of consciousness, so that as we dragged him across the floor to the stairs he helped a bit, making small, stumbling steps. On the stairs, Sylvia hovered behind us, and at their head, we paused, both Emily and myself uncertain. "In there," Sylvia said, nodding to a door, and walked ahead of us to open it, and light the gas jet.

"Where are the servants?" I said to Emily.

"Ach," she said, more Westmeath than Protestant at that moment, "cowering up in their loft or else in the kitchen below with Cook, feeding each other tea. This will be the talk of these streets before morning."

"Rest him on the bed," Sylvia said. "Should we undress him?"

"I think he is indifferent on that score," I said. "Emily and I will attend to him, dear. You go back downstairs."

"No," she said fiercely. "I will stay with him. I can take care of him."

Emily and I looked at each other, then Emily left and came back a few minutes later with a basin and ewer of water, white towels on her forearm.

"You will want to tidy him up a bit," she said. "But as soon as you can, make a compress of one of these, and hold it to your cheek. At best it will look dreadful in the morning. No need to make matters worse." Sylvia nodded, but absently. She was bent down towards him. Her hair was arranged in an elaborate coiffure, pulled up high, and with a tiara. It made a grotesque contrast with the navvy's bruise.

While Emily was gone, I had a look about the room, spare and almost monastic, but with two paintings that, even in the wretched light, I knew were made of bright Mediterranean colours. Tom's room.

Later, Emily, then Emily together with Sylvia, once she was certain that he was asleep, told me what had happened. Sylvia was holding the cold compress to her cheek, and once, as we were talking, Emily got up and changed it. "In a bit," she said, "we can try witch hazel. It can't hurt."

He was drunk when he arrived, but not so drunk as to be incoherent. And so it was that in this roundabout way I learned about the sundering and the destruction of Parnell and his party. Not that it had been told to Sylvia and Emily in those terms.

"We are better off without them, so," he had said. At first, he had not asked for anything else to drink. "The bloody little shits. Excuse language, ladies. Gladstone's lickspittles, the bishops' bumboys. Know what the story is at Westminster? That Parnell was armed, meant to shoot Healy. Stupid lie. Someone should shoot him. Excuse language."

"As if," Emily said to me, "as if we had neither of us ever before heard the word *shit*. What a world you men live in!"

"Keep to the point, Emily," I said.

The group in opposition to Parnell, a group clearly in the majority, had worked out the plan in advance, that the motion calling for an end to Parnell's leadership should be made by William Abraham, one of the few non-Catholics left in the party. But when the time came, he handed the written motion to Justin McCarthy, the vice-chairman. "I have not yet been deposed," Parnell shouted, and snatched the paper. Then he made a lunge at poor McCarthy, a most inoffensive literary man of sedentary habits, and would have struck him had not Delaney and Edmund Leamy held on to Parnell's arms.

Parnell was not obeying the rules of order, Delaney freely admitted. He tore up Abraham's motion, and instead recognised John O'Connor, on whose support he could rely. "Charles Stewart Parnell is still the master of the Irish party," O'Connor said, "and he will remain the master." At this point, Tim Healy spoke. "How he contrived it, I cannot understand," Delaney said to Sylvia. "The room was a bedlam, with all of us shouting save Parnell. He stood there silent and ferocious. Then Healy spoke, and although he did not raise his voice, every man in the room heard him. 'And he will remain the master,' O'Connor had said. 'And who,' asked Healy, 'who is to be the mistress of the party?' "

Drunk though he may have been, Delaney had contrived, in that small, elegant Chelsea drawing room, to convey the shouts, passions, furies, and then the sudden, inexplicable moment's quiet, through which Healy's words had threaded, Delaney hissing them out, like a stage villain. That hits the mark almost, for when Sylvia told me, I could not believe her; it was a fiction of a drunken man's fury, expressing a truth, no doubt, but I could not believe that those words, shaped to cut like a knife down the fabric of the party, had been the actual words.

Yet they were. They were printed so, on the eighth, in the *Freeman's Journal.* Sylvia had believed the words as Bob spoke them. "And so would you, Lee. So would you. I could almost see the room, feel the air." Healy's friends had gathered around him, and one of them called out, "I appeal to my friend the chairman—" But Parnell did not lunge towards him, as Delaney had feared. Instead, he stabbed a finger towards him, with his arm extended at full length. "Better appeal to your own friends. Better appeal to that cowardly little scoundrel there who dares in an assembly of Irishmen to insult a woman."

Things went on for a few minutes after that—they always do. But it was over. Justin McCarthy made a dignified little speech, and then led the majority of the party out of the room. It was over. Barry and Healy, the leader-killers, gave the final word to McCarthy, who was after all vice-chairman, and left demurely, two men among many, departing, as Healy was to say later, "for the sake of Ireland. In sorrow cutting free from a leader who had besmirched himself and the country which he claims is his."

But all that, that side of it, was of scant interest to Sylvia, as Delaney spoke. What she saw was the destruction of a man, of a woman, of more men than one, perhaps.

"He holds the chair still," Delaney said. "We are taking this fight to Ireland. Let the Irish people decide if we have a leader yet, or if we are to be flung back to where we were ten years ago. By God, I can answer for the Irish people; I am as good an Irishman as Tim Healy or John Barry."

And that was all he would talk about, taking the fight to Ireland, until suddenly he saw her, as though for the first time that night.

"You look like a princess," he said. "No, better than a princess: a countess. The Countess of Ardmor! There is a title for you. I never saw you dressed like that before; you have never dressed like that for me."

"I was going out to dinner," she said. "Two of Tom's friends have asked me. Nice people. You would like them."

"I would like them," he said. "They are nice people. Is there a drop of brandy in the house?"

She poured two brandies, and handed him one of them.

"That glistening of diamonds and silver in your hair. Is that the thing that countesses wear—a tiara, is it?"

"Anyone can wear one," she said. "I wear it because it suits me."

"Suits you, yes. Beautiful Sylvia."

He got up unsteadily, picked up the decanter, and took it back to his chair. "Best to go," he said. "Don't want to be late. Nice people."

But she sat facing him, quietly. Alcohol had made him too excited to sleep. From time to time, his eyes would close and his head droop, and then he would sit up again and begin talking. "Bloody hell do they think they are about?" he said. "Healy, the leader-killer, the priests' bumboy. I tried to find him, tell him that to his face. He wouldn't know how to fight. Do you know who left us, passing through the door one directly behind the other? William Martin Murphy, the gombeen man, tied in with the Bantry Band, and after him Mr. Bloody J.F.X. O'Brien himself, a Fenian! A Fenian, by God, who was out with us in 'sixty-seven, last man ever sentenced to be hanged, drawn, and quartered. Too bad he wasn't. The English and their damned half measures. Do you hear, woman, do you hear?"

"Yes, Robert, I hear you."

"On Tuesday," he said. "We are going off to Dublin, Parnell and a few men that he can trust—myself and the Redmonds. The rest will follow. By God, I cannot wait to see Kingstown, Dublin hills, the Sugarloaf mountain. Dublin stands by Parnell. Dublin men are solid, not bishops' bumboys. They come out of the morning fog, those hills. You wouldn't know."

"Yes," she said. "I know. I am Irish. Sometimes you forget that."

"Irish," he said, and slopped more brandy into his glass.

"Would you like some water in that?"

"No I wouldn't like some water in that. You people, sometimes you are Irish and sometimes you are not. Green satin for the saint's day, or a spray of shamrock. Ardmor Bloody Castle, colonel in the British army, lord it over us for centuries, and call yourselves Irish when it pleases you."

"Yes," she said.

"Why don't you go off to your nice party with your nice people? Tom's friends. Dear Tom."

"I might," she said. "I might be what we fashionable people call fashionably late. I would like first to put you to bed."

"No bed," Delaney said. "This is not where I live. This is where I go to sleep with you."

"Yes, bed," she said. "You can take the brandy with you."

Once, once in a great while, twice a year perhaps, her father had been like this, but in the end, he had let her lead him quietly to his room, take off his boots, unfasten his collar.

Delaney rose unsteadily to his feet. "Go to bed," he said, "we will go to bed. Proper place for you, not with nice people, Tom's friends, nice Tom. When you are naked, by God, there is no way to know are you Irish or English, when your hair falls upon me. Do the nice people know that? That is how you are beautiful, not the way that fellow painted you, wearing black like this, that fellow you gave yourself to."

He put a hand to her gown, to tear at it, but she struck it fiercely, with the edge of her palm. He blinked, puzzled. "Keep your hands away from me, God damn you," she said. "You don't know what you are saying or doing, you are blind drunk. But keep your hands off me."

That is when he hit her. "Lady from the Castle," he said. "Beautiful lady from the Castle." He reached his hand back, and swung it forward, open-palmed, against her cheek. She screamed, and was screaming, half crying, a few moments later when Emily came in.

"He was standing like a man who has done something dreadful," Emily said, "but does not know what it is. He was blind, slobbering drunk. He made his way back to the chair on his own. I wouldn't lift a hand to help him."

"Yes," I said. "If it is any consolation to you, he will feel like hell warmed over tomorrow morning, guilty as the damned, and afraid to remember why he is feeling guilty."

"Good," Emily said. "Excellent. Whiskey was invented so that Papishes can get an early view of their purgatory."

"Stop," Sylvia said, "stop. His heart is nearly broken, and he turned to drink, as others have before him. I can remember days when there was a quarter's debt due, and nothing to pay it with. Nothing. The bills sat on a pile, and beside it, my father's list of them, in his neat, military hand. 'Not to worry, Sylvie,' he would say to me, 'not to worry.' And then, but only when the sun was well setting, he would uncork the whiskey. I have seen drunken men. But do you know, the great fear that I have had for the past years is that somewhere, somehow, I would break Robert's heart. And now, in the end, he is breaking his heart for Parnell."

"Not yet," I said. "Not by a long chalk. Parnell is a fighter, and he has fighters by his side. Not in Committee Room Fifteen, perhaps, but in Ireland." I glanced towards the stairs. "He needed to get drunk. As your father did. But not to hit you. That is inexcusable."

"He has me now for an enemy," Emily said. "Not that that counts."

"No," Sylvia said, "you must be his friend. Both of you."

At the door, she said, "Oh, dear God. It was at the Appletons' that I was to have had dinner tonight, and I didn't even send a message around. It isn't amusing, Lee. There is no need to smile."

"Why do you think I am in evening dress, Sylvia? I was going to the Appletons'. They told me they would have a surprise for me. Perhaps you were the surprise."

"No," she said. "I think not. When Tom was in London he gave them one of his new paintings. No one else has seen it. They were saving it for a small party. Tom's friends. Oh, dear God!"

"It can't be helped," I said. "Too late now. You couldn't go looking like that." I touched her cheek lightly, and she flinched.

"Feeling like this. Thank you, Lee," she said.

And I set out in the winter night, towards the King's Road, in search of a hansom.

But of course, when young Patrick Prentiss and I had lunch last week at my club, sitting at what may well have been the table where Frank Lockwood and I had been sitting, fourteen years before, I gave him a more terse account. "Oh, yes," I told him, "I chanced into Robert Delaney the very night of the party split, December the sixth. Where, I cannot remember. Perhaps at a dinner party some people named Appleton were giving, but that may have been another night. He gave me an account of what had happened. He was very highly wrought, and he had had a bit too much to drink. The Parnellites, as they were soon to be called, as you know, were rallying around Parnell, and some were going back to organize the country behind him. Delaney was, of course. It was like having a bit of history, hot from the stove."

"More than a bit of history," Prentiss said. "It tore the fabric of the century down the middle, left it in tatters. And worse was to happen, far worse, when the fight was brought over to Ireland. Did Delaney have any sense of that, any foreboding?"

"Well," I said, "he was highly wrought, but he wasn't giving much away. Not to me, at any rate. Rather taciturn, in fact."

"Of course," Prentiss said.

Of course. And that is how history, what we call history, is written, even by men as intelligent and as sceptical as young Prentiss. The stuff of the past, Delaney drunken and abusive, slobbering in the house of his mistress, murderous furies tearing at him—none of that gets itself into the books. Talleyrand or someone of that sort called history a lie agreed upon, but in fact there is little enough agreement. Sylvia's breasts pale and glowing above black velvet; Delaney's fury against the bishops, against anyone who dared to oppose Parnell; the savagery of his language: all that is history, or should be.

But for the days that followed, young Mr. Prentiss is on solid ground. Parnell, and Delaney with him, left London on the evening of the ninth, and took the night boat to Ireland. A wire had been sent ahead, and there was an immense crowd waiting to cheer him, cheers in the street, and a crowd waiting at his hotel with banners, musicians, the bobbing, glossy hats of municipal and county dignitaries lost in a sea of caps. The noise, so the *Freeman's Journal* will inform Mr. Prentiss, was deafening, but towards the end grew intelligible: "Parnell! Parnell! Parnell!" To the end, his political instincts were unerring: he had said that he could hold Dublin.

There are few Irishmen, forget their politics or creeds—Parnellite, anti-Parnellite, loyalist, Fenian, Catholic, Protestant—who can forget the ten months which followed, beginning with the Dublin crowds that met Parnell's boat and the crowds outside Morrison's Hotel, and that extraordinary scene the next day, when Parnell seized the newspaper—I forget its name—seized it by force, mind you, and thus put the country on notice that bewildering as he may have been in the past, he had a few more surprising tricks up his sleeve.

What people—especially chaps like young Prentiss—have begun to speak of as the "myth" of Parnell, as though he were some supernatural being, some doomed king out of Mesopotamian legend, began, I think, not in the decade of his achievements, when for the first time since O'Connell, he had given shape to a nation, but rather on that December morning, and built itself throughout the ten months that were left to him. I know it as a fact that some by whom he was held in execration, Irish Tories and English Tories, began now, grudgingly, to speak of him with admiration, and to remember that he was, after all, blood of their blood, a Protestant fighting man, with his back against the wall. And of course, now, at the end, their opposite numbers, the Fenians, rallied to his support, the Fenians, those connoisseurs, as they had become, of lost causes.

32

[*Patrick Prentiss/Robert Delaney/Hugh MacMahon*]

"I did not," Dominick Sarsfield Prentiss said to his son, "I did not go that night to the Rotunda for his mass meeting, and I am certain that I was not missed. I had not yet declared myself against him—why need I have? I was not an M.P., I was not a member of their political apparatus nor of any of their leagues, although God knows I had defended enough of them—hinge-jawed journalists, moonlighters, patriotic mendicants. But I was putting myself at a distance from him. No one missed me, depend upon it. The city had been all day in a turmoil, the entire day, from before the boat docked at Kingstown, and that night there was a torchlight procession from Morrison's to the Rotunda, up the entire length of Sackville Street. That poor Rotunda, one of the loveliest buildings in Dublin, the eighteenth century at its most gracious, and we have made a cockpit of it. I can imagine the scene, so can you; read it in the *Freeman's Journal*—or better yet, in *United Ireland*."

"And neither, I assume, was Mr. O'Clery in the Rotunda."

"Your assumption is well founded," Dominick Prentiss said, smiling. "Now, where would he have been? Healy was down in Cork, warming things up for Parnell. And O'Clery, I seem to recall, had gone down to Kilkenny. That was to be the great show of strength, you know. The Kilkenny by-election. If Parnell could carry it, it meant that he did indeed have the country at his back. Certainly O'Clery would not have been with Healy or Barry or Murphy or any of that lot of vulgar swine. The worst thing about the Split, on both sides, was that it flung one into the company of ruffians, jumped-up shop assistants, and shorthand writers. I would never have taken on Tim Healy as a law clerk, and look at him now, a king's counsel in silk. And he hasn't finished his rise."

"And so you were not at the great meeting at the Rotunda, when Parnell was acclaimed the King of Dublin. He must have thought himself invincible, with the cheers, and the shouting, and the music. After his speech, they thronged about him. I *have* read the *Freeman's Journal*, Father, and I have talked to old Parnellites who were there. Why was Dublin always so fierce for Parnell?" Recently, his father had developed a habit of touching upon a subject and then sheering away from it. Not rambling, quite. And his courtroom manner was as meticulous as ever.

"I know where I was that night. Good heavens, boy, you talk of these matters as though they were ancient history, the Punic Wars. It was December of 1890, mid-December; we were all preparing for Christmas. I was having dinner in the club that night, on my own. There were at most a dozen of us, and from time to time, each one of us would look up at the others, wondering. Everyone except Tisdall-O'Leary-O'Malley, as he termed himself, who was a bit cracked, said to be writing some interminable history of the Irish brigades. I doubt if the name Parnell had ever registered upon him, lucky fellow.

"I had a table overlooking the green—pitch-black outside, of course, but the lights cast a glow upon the railings, and one had a sense of winter trees, the lake iced over. Ardilaun did a smashing job for us all when he did up the green; good to have a bit of the country smack in the city; step across the road from one of the clubs, or from the Shelbourne, and there you are. Quiet enough when I was finishing dinner, but I had had to fight my way through the crowds outside Morrison's waiting for their chosen man. No, I had a sense that night that dotty old Tisdall-O'Leary-O'Malley and myself were the only two men in Dublin not up in Rutland Square cheering Parnell."

[655]

"They call it Parnell Square now," Patrick said. "Or at least they will soon. That is the plan."

"Rutland Square, boy, Rutland Square. Changing names about to suit the whim of the moment. My God, what a country! Hound a man into the grave and then name a street after him."

That night (Patrick Prentiss knew) at the Rotunda, Parnell learned that *United Ireland,* the newspaper he had founded, was in hostile hands. He was told on the platform and nodded, as though he had not quite heard. On the morning, he was to go to Cork City, where Healy and his people were gathering strength, Munster the base of their operation. But he was spending the night at Dr. Kenny's, and asked Delaney and a few others to call round for him there in the morning.

H e had had no breakfast," Bob told Hugh MacMahon three mornings later, after he had himself travelled back from Cork City to Kilpeder. "Only cup after cup of tea, black as ink. Poor Kenny was after him to take sustenance. Kenny was becoming our medical corps. But he shook his head. He had worn black at the Rotunda, a black suit, elegantly tailored; now he was in one of those battered sets of tweeds, and a woolen waistcoat of some sort. But at least he had remembered to comb his hair and beard, or the Kennys had remembered for him. The man is frail but there is some endless kind of furious energy coming out of him, like a blast furnace."

"You make him sound like Old Nick, in a pantomime," MacMahon said.

Delaney was on the point of angry protest, but stopped short. "By God, Hughie, you have hit upon it."

Leamy and Willie Redmond and John Clancy were there, but Parnell was dictating to Campbell, his secretary, who sat beside him, scribbling notes. When Delaney came into the room, he paused, and put his hand for a moment on Campbell's arm.

"We are going home, Delaney," he said. "Home for both of us."

"Cork City will stand by you, Mr. Parnell. Cork City is as solid as Dublin."

"It is a city lost in a large county," Parnell said, "the largest county in Ireland."

"I will answer for Kilpeder," Delaney said. "Kilpeder, Macroom, Millstreet."

"Kilpeder," Parnell said, his smile bleak but not unfriendly. "The Paris of the west, I have heard it called."

"Kilpeder," Delaney said, "stands at the exact geographical centre of the area which surrounds it."

After a moment, Parnell laughed. "There is a good one," he said to Campbell. "The exact geographical centre. The same is also true of Avondale, my own place. They have that in common, Delaney."

"Perhaps you will see," Delaney said. "Perhaps you will come to Kilpeder."

"Oho, I don't doubt it. Before this is over, I will have been in every town in Ireland big enough to boast a hen house and to keep the wild pigs out of the street."

"We do a bit better than that."

"You were a Fenian, were you not? In a battle. You were the leader in a battle."

"Of sorts," Delaney said, "and I was not the leader."

"You are too modest entirely. You seized a police barracks."

"With respect, we did not. We gave it a try, but we didn't make it."

"You have now your chance to redeem yourself. We are going to retake the offices of our newspaper, and if they offer us any resistance, we will smash our way in."

Bob stared at him, and then at Leamy and Redmond, and then, unbidden, pulled a chair away from the dining table and sat down.

"You cannot be serious, Mr. Parnell."

"If we have to, we will take it at gunpoint."

"If we have to," Delaney said. "But what will be our weapon of preference?"

"A mob, Delaney. A Dublin mob is by God the most frightening weapon on earth."

"I was a Fenian for a time," he said, "but I have been a solicitor for a number of years. We cannot go about seizing buildings by brute force—not in Abbey Street, certainly, in the centre of Dublin."

"You solicitors can sort the matter out later. The fact is that we have a fight on our hands, and I need that newspaper. We bought it, by God, and set William O'Brien up in it as editor, made him his reputation. Now he has gone over to the enemy, and left some little Johnny-jump-up on the premises as the acting editor. What is his name, Leamy?"

"Matty," Leamy said. "Matty Bodkin. A decent skin."

[657]

"But you will make a better editor for us, Leamy. You won't waste your time turning your coat." He shovelled the papers in front of him on the table towards Campbell. "If you would bring me an egg," he said, "an ordinary sort of egg." He drained his cup of what must by then have been lukewarm tea, and poured more from the blue-and-white pot.

"Mr. Parnell," Willie Redmond said, "what Delaney means, I think, is that you cannot smash into buildings without process of some sort. A writ of ejectment, is that what it would be? Bob?"

But Bob was becoming too bemused to answer. At last, he said, "That has been the theory for the last few centuries, Willie. Things may be changing."

"Did you have a writ of ejectment, Mr. Delaney," Parnell said, "when you set to work turfing the police out of the barracks in Kilpeder?"

He took the raw egg which Campbell had brought him on a saucer, cracked it into a tumbler, and gulped it down.

"Bit like a hunt breakfast, eh? Nothing elaborate, as things had to be done when I was MFH. But a morning's run, you know. Bleakley, my huntsman, used to crack the tops off eggs with that poacher's knife of his, and we drained them off. He'd fill the shells with brandy. I miss that, you know."

"That was an act of war," Delaney said. "The attack upon the barracks."

Parnell looked at him, calm save for the deep-sunk, burning eyes. "An act of war," he said. "Yes, good. An act of war."

"Do you know, Hughie, Vincent," Delaney said, in Kilpeder a few days later, "it is then that I knew that I was with him, come what may. It went beyond politics, or rights or wrongs. I have no need for arguments, either upon his side or upon theirs. Lads, I have no notion how the word had got about in Dublin that we, that Parnell, intended to take the building. But there was a mob in Abbey Street. The driver was uncertain what to do, but Parnell climbed out, and up into his seat, and took the reins away from him, and we went clattering at full speed down Abbey Street, with the crowd parting as best it could, like the waters of the Red Sea. At the building, he dropped the reins, as though they were of no further use to him, and leaped to the ground, walked to the door, and pounded upon it. They were ready for us, and the door was locked and bolted. 'Matty,' I heard myself shouting at the office window. 'Don't be a bloody maggot. Open the door to us.' But there was no sound within, although the first-floor window was uncurtained, and we saw movement within, and then a face, it vanished, and another face. Parnell clasped his two hands together, and smashed at the door. 'Let me in, you miserable little sparrow.' Of course there was no response. Simple fear, if nothing else, would have held them back. The crowd was roaring, a terrifying sound. He turned around to us then, in a fury. 'Give me a crowbar, someone,' he said. And begod, if there weren't workmen from a site nearby, and in three minutes he had a crowbar in his hand, and Patsy Fitzgerald a pickax. Some of us had gone down to climb in through the basement, but the most of us were with Parnell, and he working away with clumsy fury before he gave it into more practised hands, and the door came off from its hinges in a long, roaring crack. We all of us poured in then, and it was just as the fellows were thundering upstairs from the areaway. But Parnell was the first man across the sill, and I was not far behind him, the two of us chalked with dust and grime. Matty Bodkin and two of his subeditors stood facing us, and Parnell stood glaring at them, not saying a word, nor intending to. 'Now then, Matty,' John Clancy said to him, in a reasonable tone, 'will you walk out or would you like to be thrown out?' "

"And all this," Vincent Tully said, in Kilpeder, to Delaney, "all this in the respectable, law-abiding city of Dublin."

"Respectable, is it," Delaney said. "Do you know who John Clancy is? He is the high sheriff for Dublin."

J ohn Philpott Adams," Dominick Prentiss told his son, "had the ill luck to find himself in Upper Abbey Street that morning. I'm sure you remember John Philpott Adams, a decent little Protestant Q.C., slight man with a keen grasp of the law. Certain aspects of the law. He stood as though riveted, watched it all, someone knocked his hat off; and he carried an account of it to the Library of the Four Courts. They swarmed up to the second floor, and damned if they didn't take off one of the windows, ripped it out of its framing—crowbars and pickaxes get into the blood, perhaps—and the next thing Johnny knew was Parnell standing there in the aperture, and the crowd shouting. He stood perfectly quiet, without moving, his elbows cupped in his hands in that way that he had. I can remember almost Johnny Adams's words. The people, he said, were spellbound. They had been roaring, of course; the roar of Dublin when it senses passion of some sort or even simple excitement. But it fell suddenly silent. And then, Johnny Adams said—these are the words of his that I remember almost exactly: 'I felt a thrill of dread, as if I looked at a tiger in the frenzy of his rage. Then he spoke, a few words only, and his voice was more terrible than his look.' There Johnny sat, in the Library, his overcoat still upon him, and his badly dented hat. Some decent fellow in the crowd, so he told me later, had picked up the hat and brushed it off on a sleeve. The streets were dirty with December slush."

"Did Mr. Adams remember the words?" Patrick Prentiss asked his father.

"We hold Dublin," Parnell said, so Johnny Adams reported the words to Dominick Prentiss, in the ordered hubbub of the Library, but quiet now, gowned and wigged barristers, Papist and Protestant, gathered about him. "I will rely on Dublin. Dublin is our fortress. Dublin is true. What Dublin says today, Ireland will say tomorrow." All that, according to Adams, he said without so much as unfolding his arms; but then he dropped them to his side, and stepped backward into the room, and men standing around him concealed him from the crowd in Abbey Street.

"Fifteen minutes' walk from the Law Courts to Abbey Street," Dominick Prentiss said. "No, ten. But it was as though Johnny had brought us news from a battlefield of some sort, Austerlitz or Wagram, and not a street in the commercial centre of a provincial city. Extraordinary. And the thought must have crossed more minds than my own, because someone, Stephen Ronayne I believe it was, said, 'He has not come back to fight a by-election, but a war.' And with that, a most curious remark was made, curious as to its source, that is. Edward Carson—yes, Carson, 'Balfour's Hound,' as they call him, 'Bloody Carson,' the Crown prosecutor—gathered up his papers, and rose to leave, with a smile on that hard, long Orange hangman's face of his. 'A war,' he said, 'and the worst kind, a civil war. And may you go down fighting together, the two lots of you.' He was looking directly at me as he spoke. Carson and I have always got along well enough, you know; he's a fierce Tory but no bigot. 'I knew we could count on your good wishes, Ned,' I told him. 'Oh, always,' he said, walking to the door, and then added, without turning around to me, 'I know whose side I'd be on. That fellow may be a rogue, but by the Harry he can fight.' 'Protestant blood, Ned,' I called out to him, in banter. 'It counts in the end.' He was by then half through the opened door, and he turned back for a moment to smile at me without answering, and although the smile was meant to be companionable, brother barristers *et cetera*, Nature has not favoured him, and I saw, not a Dublin barrister, savage though fair in his dealings, but the smile of the whole of their damned bloody empire as it settled back to watch us tear ourselves to pieces."

And there we stand," Bob said to us, to Vincent and myself, in my kitchen. "Cork is for us, by God. Cork stands foursquare, and to the devil may the Healy clan be pitched. Why, lads, there was not a town between Dublin and Cork where there were not lads waiting to give us a shout, and a cheer for the Chief. And in Cork City, there was a vast crowd to escort us to the Victoria. Why, there was a crowd waiting at the Victoria. He made four speeches in the city in two days, and the assembly rooms were crowded. 'Cork is with us,' he said to me after one of his speeches. 'Dublin is with us and Cork. You should be proud to be a Cork man, Mr. Delaney.'"

"Cork City, that was," Vincent said, and from his massy silver flask, the flask he had carried in 'sixty-seven or its successor, he measured whiskey into our tea, with a double tot for Bob.

"Yes," Bob said, looking up on the instant from his plate of eggs. Mary had taken off our younger to visit his grandparents, leaving Brian and myself to forage as best we could. I am very good at frying eggs. "Yes, Cork City. Go on, Vincent."

"I would be less certain of the county if I were you," Vincent said. "A word of warning."

"Ach, Mallow!" Bob said. "What can be expected of Mallow? William O'Brien is a Mallow man, and look at the cut of him. A penny-a-liner swaggering about like a bold Fenian buccaneer." O'Brien had declared against Parnell, and so had Dillon; they had not yet taken up arms, so to speak, but their course was clear. Davitt had spoken out against him, almost from the first.

"Vincent," I said, "had in mind places closer to home than Mallow."

Bob's knife and fork were still held motionless above his plate, and he was looking at me intently. His jibe about Mallow had been but to gain a moment's pause.

Vincent shrugged. "The bishops have spoken out, Bob. You know that as well as I do. And since Sunday Mass, there is not a man, woman, or child in Kilpeder who does not know it, barring the Protestants."

"Meagher read it out from the pulpit?" Bob said.

"He could scarcely do that," I said. "It was not an encyclical. But Parnell has been condemned by the bishops, absolutely, no equivocal language. And Meagher told us so."

"Us," Bob repeated contemptuously, and returned to his meal. "And what did us do when us heard our leader read out from the altar?"

"There was a quiet," Vincent said, "so velvet that you could have heard a mouse fart. And I turned around in my pew, in time to see big Lanty Hanlon get up and leave, and his half dozen or so. You know the lot. A few of them, their wives are ashamed of them, tis said. The organization."

A precise statement. If the Fenians still had an existence in Kilpeder, it was Lanty Hanlon the farrier, and a few excitable young labourers and shop assistants, whom he took on pilgrimages to Clonbrony Wood, and gave them *Speeches from the Dock* to read, and the Wolfe Tone book.

"Yes," Bob said. "Lanty and the lads, God help us. And what did the rest of us do?"

"We heard Mass," I said, "and some of us received the Sacrament, and then we went to our homes."

"To meals happy or melancholy as the case may be," Vincent said.

"When Meagher came outside in his cassock, there was a crowd of men who gathered around him."

"I listen to people, Bob," Vincent said. "I keep my ears open. You will have a fight on your hands, from Macroom to the border."

"You listen to your father at Sunday dinner," Bob said, "and to every butt-sprung, decayed Catholic half-sir between here and Killarney. It is not on the likes of them that we will make our stand."

"I listen to others as well, Bob," Vincent said with, in the circumstances, a commendable mildness. "And I am telling you only that you will have a fight on your hands. That *we* will, I should say."

At the emendation, Bob smiled, a quick show of his small, even teeth. "You are with us, so, Vincent. You are, of course. The two of yez, of course you are."

"Never need to doubt that, Robert Delaney," I said.

Vincent rested his elbow on the table and pointed a forefinger at Bob, hesitated, and then said, "You know, Bob, do you not, that there is a bit of risk for Hugh in this. He is the schoolmaster, and Father Meagher is the manager. This is going to be very rough, from one end of the county to the other."

"You are right, of course," Bob said, stricken.

But I shook my head. "It has not quite come to that. No need to borrow trouble. I am a cautious fellow, you know."

"You were not cautious in 'sixty-seven," Bob said, "when you seized the row of cottages and held them to the end."

"*Young* is the word for what I was then," I said, dismissively. "There is more tea, Vincent, if there is more whiskey."

"Fogarty," Bob said. "I will need Fogarty. What do you know of him? Where does he stand?"

"He has his hands full," Vincent said, "between the poor devils that Howard and Chute evicted, and enforcing the Lughnavalla boycott and two others, keeping up the pressure. All that has not evaporated, you know, whatever trifling problems may have been caused by Mrs. O'Shea and the bishops and Mr. Gladstone."

"I still have need to know," Bob said. "And little time. I am off to Kilkenny tomorrow. I will try to see him tomorrow early, before his breakfast."

"Leave Fogarty to me, Bob," Vincent said. "We are old fishing companions. Brothers of the order of the trout."

Bob smiled again, this time more at ease, and held his hands in papal benediction. "Be thou now a fisher of men, Simon Vincent."

Vincent picked up the flask. "For our stomachs' sake," he said. "We are being very sacerdotal, the three of us, are we not?"

Later, alone, and many times since then, I have indulged my idle habit of imagination, and have seen Abbey Street, in the heart of Dublin—the crowd, which I see not as often I have seen crowds in reality, but as a painting, lithograph, whatever you will, but in motion, like those cameras they have which put flickering images upon a sheet, so that the past will never be lost to us but always available, travestied and belittled, history but a wrinkle upon the memory of a machine, and all in silence, unvivified by voice—the crowd, boisterous in silence, and that moment, upon which history hinged, when Parnell, who had held us by the bravura of his icy and collected silence, seized the crowbar of a workman to smash in a door, and stood later, dust and powder as Bob had described it to us, and ferocious, like a tiger was Bob's phrase for him. I have imagined that scene as the scene that changed our lives forever, and not scenes that held no meaning for me: Houses of Parliament and divorce courts and oak-panelled committee rooms.

"We'll smash them," Bob said. "Have no doubts on that score, lads. Bloody Pope-Hennessy below in Kilkenny. Thinks he can stand for the party and denounce its leader, all in the same breath. With a gang of crawthumpers and gombeen men at his back. And Pope-Hennessy, mind you, was our chosen man before the Split, chosen by the Chief himself, and now a wintry blast from the altar, and he turns against us."

Vincent offered the flask again, but Bob shook his head.

"Three whiskeys a day, lads, three a day, and that is the quota. And lads, I could not myself have chosen a better venue than Kilkenny to do the smashing in."

Later, once again, later, and alone—that seems to be a requisite for my thought processes—the burden of those pronouns fell upon me, as they were to fall upon all of us in the weeks to come, and the few months that were left to us, as they bear down upon us still. For we had not yet grasped what "we" and "they" were coming to mean. We meant ourselves, Parnellite and anti-Parnellite alike, for "we" were "they," and "they" were "we." It was what the English had never been able to achieve. We were rolling up our sleeves, and setting to work to destroy ourselves, "we" bashing "they," like Gog and Magog.

33

[Patrick Prentiss/Robert Delaney/Hugh MacMahon]

"I have sometimes thought," Hugh MacMahon said to Patrick Prentiss, "that only by magic or by the flickering mock-magic of the new machines could you have a knowledge of Bob Delaney as he was that evening before the Kilkenny election, and even after it. Kilkenny, Sligo, Carlow—three elections the one after the other, and each fought upon a dirty turf, Gog smashing Magog is how I put it to myself. Kilkenny, Sligo, Carlow, and each one a defeat. Kilkenny was no mortal blow, but rather a bewildering setback, but Sligo enforced a sense of apprehension, and Carlow the certainty of what was happening, so that from each one Bob came back more reckless in manner, more bitter and savage of tongue."

In later years, Delaney would repeat the names to himself, a baleful chaplet—Kilkenny, Sligo, Carlow. It was during the Kilkenny campaign that he began carrying a revolver, uncertain why—not merely the dangers which the mob were beginning to present, the Fenians an unofficial bodyguard now, and threats of death coming in Parnell's mail, waiting for him in dusty provincial towns.

Not that Kilkenny was dusty, a handsome town rather—the capital once, for all purposes, of Norman Ireland—dominated by the great Butler Castle rising above the Nore, and in the streets, sandwiched between shops and public houses, houses which had been old for centuries, the houses of the great medieval and Tudor merchant families.

Delaney walked through the streets to the Victoria Hotel, across the front of which words had been daubed in yellow paint imperfectly scrubbed out, smeared and faintly visible: "Kitty O'Shea." The reception rooms were crowded with men, the air heavy with tobacco smoke; the sounds of shouting carried from the saloon bar. Jamesey Grace stopped him on the carpeted stairs. "He is in the big room to the front," Grace said, "beyond the residents' lounge. He looks bad, Bob, tired and worn; but there is a fire burning in him. The other lot arrived before us; they have taken over the Imperial—Healy, Barry, the lot of them. Even Davitt is here. But by God, Bob, we will put them on the run—there are rough lads in North Kilkenny and Castlecomer, and the hillside men are with us; the organization has offered us its support, protection if there is trouble. Can you believe it, Bob, yourself and myself after all these years, and we are back with the organization."

Jamesey Grace had been out in 'sixty-seven, one of the Limerick men; he had drawn three years? five was it? in Dartmoor. Now he looked a political manager, Land League secretary, faint beginning of a paunch, sandy hair thinning on the crown, a face bland on most occasions, but flushed now, the eyes sharp and excited. He looks like me, Delaney thought, and put a sociable hand on his upper arm to walk past him, although Grace would have lingered.

"Two gangs of Irishmen," Delaney said, "set to carve ourselves up, one lot in a hotel called the Victoria, and the other lot in the Imperial."

"Ah well," Grace said, "what's in a name?"

"Hang on to that," Delaney said. "Fine phrases don't come to us every day."

Parnell was stretched out in a deep chair by the warmth of the turf fire, with his feet propped up on a second chair, some papers resting in his lap. Grace had the right of it: he looked tired, worn, the handsome, bearded face pale.

"It will rain tomorrow, Delaney," he said. "But we have meetings laid out for us in six towns, and we will be there, however foul the skies may be. The renegades have been to them already, Healy and Davitt— that miserable jackdaw Davitt, a jackdaw with one wing, clipped to keep him from flight."

The ugliness of the image hit Delaney like a blow. Parnell read his face.

"Oho," he said, "a vile thing to say. It is. I am losing check upon my tongue, it is running free like a riderless horse. And I don't give a damn. I can say at last what I wanted for years to say, years of being politic and demure. No longer. The lads that we will need now on our side have little need for nice manners. Davitt knows that. I have had reports of the things he has said of me on public platforms. And he is nothing, measured against that cur Healy. It is not against me alone that he has turned his tongue. He will regret it, I promise you. If needs must, I will take a whip to him, an ordinary carriage whip."

"It may not rain," Delaney said. "The evening is clear. A fine evening."

Parnell smiled. "You have become a fellow of great diplomacy and tact, Delaney. Time has worked wonders upon you. Not all for the best, perhaps. From here on in, we will not be using the nicest of weapons."

"You need not concern yourself on my account," Delaney said. "I was reared on harsh acres, and I have a good memory."

B ut we had little notion that evening, he told MacMahon, of what weapons would be of use to us. At Castlecomer, we managed to have our meeting, despite shouts and jeers, and it was there, at Castlecomer, that for the first time, there were fellows waving what they called "Kitty O'Shea's drawers" tacked to the ends of branches. At first we could not understand what they were intended to be, nor what the men were shouting, but at last we did, and I saw Parnell step backward a step or two as though staggering. But our crowd gave them as good as we got; there were blackthorns swinging and bloody heads—it was like one of the old faction fights of our grandfathers' time.

As we drove off—I chanced to be sitting in the brake with him—they were in wait for us and showered us with rocks, clods of turf, and something struck Parnell in the eye that was surely a rock, but there are those who say that it had been tipped with quicklime. Dr. Hackett was with us, thank God. Parnell sat there silently, until we were back in the safety of the town—Kilkenny town was with us almost to the end—and he spoke but twice, and each time it had to do with details of the constituencies, as though we had been riding home from the most orderly of meetings, and nothing more exciting to look forward to than salmon sandwiches. And deathly pale, hatless, his beard tangled, and now the slanting, makeshift bandage that Hackett had rigged for his injured eye.

No, there was another look as well, imposed upon that one, and Davitt was so far gone in the savagery that was descending upon us all that he spoke the very words. "Is Mr. Parnell mad?" he asked. "That there are evidences of insanity in his actions, no man can doubt." And the words, once spoken, were taken up by Healy and MacDermott, and the fellows who share with them the gutters and the drains. They deliberately misquoted Davitt. "Is there madness there? There is madness in the family, a streak of insanity running through the generations. The mad Parnells." In the streets of Irishtown, there I chanced into Billy Cummings. Well we knew each other from the old days, but he was now on Healy's side.

"Tell me, now, Billy," I said, "is this lurid history of insanity come recently into light? Yesterday in Thomastown your chum Healy told his crowd that we must not be led by a madman, certifiable. Had this been a dark secret from yourself and from Tim Healy last year, when Tim was hailing 'Charles Stewart Parnell, the man sent from on high to lead his chosen people. Our uncrowned king'? What of that, Billy?"

"We had gone too far," Billy said. "You are right, we had made a bloody anointed king out of him, and after that we could only hope for the best. But we have been running the party for the past two years, yourself and myself and Tim and the other lads. O'Brien and Dillon and yourself are managing the Plan of Campaign; without the three of yez there would have been sweet fuck-all done for the evicted poor of Galway and Tipperary and Cork. And now the time has come for blunt speaking. For two years he was away from us, sunk into his madness, dabbling in the cunt of his whore."

There was but a single appropriate response. I planted my feet firmly upon the cobbles of Irishtown, and belted him one in the mouth. Without realizing it, I had told Parnell the truth when I said that I was reared rough and had a good memory. While the shock was still upon him, I swung for the ear, but missed and hit the side of his neck, near his throat. The second one drove him to his knees, and he knelt on the cobbles, with a hand to his bloody mouth. He looked bewildered. I knelt down beside him, but with his free hand, he shoved me away from him. I moved behind him, though, got my hands under his oxters, raised him up, and he turned towards me. He made as if to swipe at me, but then dropped his arm, and I gave him my handkerchief. There we stood, two men of middle years, like two young lads in an alleyway.

"This is how it will all end, Bob," he said, and I nodded. "Do you remember the other Irishtown? In 'seventy-nine? In Mayo, when Davitt unfurled the banner."

"I remember about it," I said. "I was not there that afternoon."

"Soon enough after, though, Bob," he said. "We were in it from the first, yourself and myself. And look at the two of us."

I brushed off his coat—neither of us thought to look for his hat—and we set off in opposite directions.

Well, and that was Kilkenny, Hugh. Oh, but with one additional circumstance. I had been meeting with some of the Castlecomer men who had stayed loyal—not that there were that many of them; Castlecomer was a soft spot; they had worked that ground well, Healy and Davitt had—and I was stepping into the hotel when a young lad came up to me, in his twenties—just a fellow, you know: cloth cap and bad teeth—and said there was a man wanted to speak with me in Delarge's.

"What the hell is Delarge's?" I said.

"A public house," said he.

"Well," said I, "lead on. I will speak with any man and my throat is dry." All this being the truth.

I followed him down those laneways and through the archways that they have in Kilkenny—I swear to God you would think you had stepped back into the days of the Normans—and be damned if we were not back in Irishtown, scene of the great pugilistic encounter of Cummings versus Delaney, and so into a public house which a shebeen like Grennan's here in Kilpeder would put to shame—half shop and half boozer, but with a snug at least and a door to it, which the young fella rapped upon, and there within, sitting on one side of the table, a glass before him, and two men with him, flanking him, their backs to the wall, was Jeremiah Mulcahy, alive and well, of the Supreme Council of the Irish Republican Brotherhood, whose oath I forswore when I put my hand to the Land League.

I remember his visit to us," I said to Bob, "sitting in your office, polite and paunchy, with hair oiled down to cover a bald spot like a tonsure, the very model of a commercial traveller, and not at all the desperado that a Fenian Head Centre is supposed to resemble and be. But read us out of the organization he did, by bell, book, and candle."

"Ten years ago that was," Bob said. "He is no longer a commercial traveller, he tells me. He has retired and has a small house in Dalkey. But he has not retired from the Supreme Council. By no means."

"It is an enviable eminence, no doubt," I said, "denouncing traitors to the Republic from a cottage in Dalkey—on the hill, I have no doubt, with a view of Dublin Bay."

"He did not specify," Bob said. "He bought me a large whiskey."

"There is no such thing as a large whiskey, Vincent says."

Bob smiled.

"Had he summoned you to read you out again? Perhaps it is something that they do every ten years."

"Far from it," Bob said. "The organization has moved behind us, to back us up. There are delicacies of expression to be used. We will be calling upon the support of the 'hillside men,' the lads who never gave up, the lads who took to the hills, the mountainy men. But it will mean the organization, the IRB. 'And so, Bob,' Mulcahy says to me, 'we are back together again, as we were in 'sixty-seven.'

"But I mistook the nature of his approach to me," Bob went on. "I thought that he was sounding me out. Far from it. The IRB has instructed its members to support us, and Parnell has met with two members of the Council—unofficially, to be sure. Mulcahy was visiting me and fellows like me—Ribbon Fenians, they used call us in derision—to assure us that there were no hard feelings."

"That must have been a great relief to you," I said.

"I said as much to him, and in much the same tone of voice. All support is welcome at the present moment, I told him, but stay a safe distance away from us. That is all the Church will need, not that it hasn't plenty. That we have become a Fenian party."

"They could do you more harm than good," I said to Bob. "What are they these days, but a handful of roughnecks like Lanty—not that he isn't a decent sort when all is said and done—and those boasters in New York, and John O'Leary spouting verses from Young Ireland."

" 'We know all about keeping a safe distance, Bob; we stand in no need of your instruction on that score,' Mulcahy said to me, lifting up his glass that I had ordered to repay the round. The two fellows flanking him were a bit younger, faces on them like rocks, virtuous thick-skulled Fenians of the Joe Brady variety.

" 'That young fellow who brought you here to this house,' Mulcahy said. 'He was less than twenty feet away from you last evening, when yourself and William Cummings had your little chat. If you had encountered trouble or danger, he would have been at your side. I have put you into his safekeeping.' I looked at him, that bland little retired huckster, running a finger down the side of his glass as though to smooth it out—"

"Have a care with those lads, Bob. However bland they may look."

" 'My thanks to you,' I told him, I trust with courtesy. 'But I have been in my own safekeeping for a number of years now. I am content with that. I prefer it.' He sat quietly a moment, and then raised the finger to run it across his lip. Reflective, like. 'Have it your way, Bob,' he said; 'one way or the other, it is good to have you with us again.' 'Let us be certain about this, Jeremiah,' I said. 'I am not with you, nor you with me. We are still the Irish Parliamentary Party, which any Irishman is free to support.' 'Have it your way, Bob, have it your way,' he said. And then, for decency's sake, we gave ourselves a half hour and another round to drift into the amiable nostalgia which has become stock-in-trade for old Fenians. 'Did you know that Patsy Mangan has passed away?' 'I did not, God rest his soul.' That sort of thing."

"Parnell and the Fenians," I said, refilling our cups with innocuous tea. "Will wonders never cease?"

"He is a different man now, Hughie, a desperate man, like a swordsman making his stand in far hills. He will take any weapon, provided he can use it. He is as wily as ever. By God, Hughie, he is a man the likes of which we have not had since Sarsfield or O'Donnell."

"He has won your admiration," I said, a bit evasively, "and that is no mean victory. You are not a lad given to easy praise. You leave that to Vincent and myself."

It was as though my casual reference to us, to three of us, had touched a chord.

"There was one other thing, Hughie. It was just as I was plainly about to rise up to depart, that Mulcahy said, gently, 'Do you hear from Ned Nolan these days?' 'No,' I said, and resettled myself, with a sudden apprehensiveness, one of those an-angel-has-walked-over-your-grave sorts of thing. 'No,' I said, 'why should I? Each Christmas, Hughie MacMahon sends a letter to him from all of us, but he never knows where to send it, of course. He sends it to Tom Bonner at his brickyards on the Hudson

River, and sooner or later, a letter will find its way to us in reply.' 'Don't look for one this year,' Mulcahy said. 'Ned Nolan is in London, and he has been there for better than a year. London, Liverpool, Glasgow.' 'If he is there on organization business,' I said, 'I don't want to know about it, Jerry.' 'Well, now, Bob,' he said; 'the way things are in these latter days, that would be a difficult question to answer. He is serving the cause of the Irish Republic; we could say that, yes. But the Council takes no responsibility.' 'Have you had a chance to look about the city, Jerry?' I asked him. 'There are many fine old ruins, and a handsome round tower.' 'I must get back to Dublin early tomorrow,' he said, accepting with grace my subtle diversion, 'but I have been here often in the course of trade, in years past. A fine old Norman city, and then Owen Roe O'Neill and the Catholic Confederation, back in the old centuries. I have a great fondness for history. I will be leaving the lads here,' and he clapped one of them on a rocklike shoulder. And thus I took my leave."

"Did you take his point?" I asked. "About Ned?"

"I don't think I wanted to," Bob said. "Any more than we want either of us to remember that you may have seen him or you may not in a Dublin public house in the days of the Invincibles."

"Jesus, Mary, and Joseph," I said, but other names than their sacred ones were echoing in my head—London, Liverpool, Glasgow. In my mind, a confused, blinding, deafening moment of shattered masonry, savaged bodies.

That would have been on one of the two short visits that Bob made home from Kilkenny, where he was otherwise engaged until the very end, until the election itself on the twenty-second, close to the edge of Christmas. The papers carried his name most days; for, with most of the more celebrated names ranged upon the other side, fellows of middling importance—John Redmond and Henry Harrison and those, and Robert Delaney in particular—had become prominent. When he did come back, for our Christmas, it was in defeat. Not that you could tell it from his manner, for Kilkenny was not yet Sligo, much less Carlow, and he moved through the town, from house to office, with Fogarty to visit with the evicted tenants, as brisk as ever, more so perhaps, as though dramatising his state of being, clapping fellows on the back, as had never been his style before; and on Christmas Eve, when he was expected elsewhere, he and Vincent had the indifferent leg of winter lamb which the Kilpeder Arms served up to its victims, and sat laughing together over two bottles of red wine followed by port.

"A bottle of it," Vincent said to me, "and it might have been poured into a boot for all its effect upon him. But I was fluthered, by God. Thank God I had Sullivan to drive me back to the Lodge."

Conor is asleep," Agnes said to him when he came in. "He waited for you as long as he could, and then he went up to his room." She was standing in the darkened parlour. Behind her, the single candle had been lighted, to guide the Christ Child.

"I had business at the Arms," he said.

"With Vincent," she said.

"Family business," he said. "I like to be with my family at Christmastime. My brother-in-law, and now my wife. I am a domestic sort of fellow. Can we have no light in the house?"

"The candle has been lit," she said.

"We need more than that. A candle may do for Him." He lit the gas.

"Conor is happy that you will be home for the Christmas season," she said. "He models himself upon you, Robert. You know that, do you not?"

"Poor little chap," he said. "I found a splendid shotgun for him in Elliott's, the gunsmith in Kilkenny, shotguns for the Kilkenny gentry their specialty. An over-and-under. By George, I won't mind taking a few pulls myself. Vincent says that I could not have chosen better."

"Did Vincent tell you about Father, about how Father has come to feel about you? I was there all day, you know, until I came back here to wait for you with Conor. Mother and the cook and myself have been the livelong day making ready for the dinner—baking and roasting and broiling and basting."

"Vincent's conversation has a wide range," Delaney said, "but your father rarely turns up in it. I cannot think why." He sat down, and poured himself a small measure of brandy, and then filled the glass almost to the brim with water.

"Kilpeder is ranged with the Church, thank God. It is ranged with Father Meagher. And Father is as well. He has turned his hand against the adulterer."

"They have all turned their hands against the adulterer, have they?" Delaney said. "Kilpeder, citadel of the sinless."

"Blasphemy as well," she said. "You are adding to your repertoire."

"And you are developing a nice line in bitter sarcasm, Agnes."

"I am gaining practice," she said. "Robert." She perched on the edge of a chair to face him. "Do you realize what is happening, or has that madman so bedazzled you that you have lost your judgement in practical matters? That has always been your great strength. Leave morality aside for the moment. He cannot hold out against the entire Church and two thirds of his own party, and the great body of the people ranged up and down the country. He will go down, and he will haul down with him all those foolish enough to cleave to him."

" 'Leave morality aside for the moment,' " Delaney said. "I must ask Hughie what would be the Latin of that. It would make a grand motto for the Tully family. We could put it up on the shop front, in gilt letters on a red background. No, not red. No red ink for the Tullys."

"You were not always so contemptuous of the family," she said. "There was once a small farmer's son down from the hills, and Tully's shop seemed a palace to him."

"You have the right of matters there, Agnes," he said. "I am sorry. It was an ugly thing to say at any time, much less Christmas Eve. I am dog-tired, and had port on top of it, a treacherous drink. We will have a grand Christmas, one that Conor will remember. A good little chap, Conor."

"We can," she said. "Father has promised, as a treat to Mother and myself, that not a cross word will pass his lips."

"Nor mine, Agnes. Nor mine."

"We can have a grand season of it," she said, and relaxed into the chair, her hands folded on her lap. "All the way through to the Epiphany."

"A good season, Agnes. Yes. But not quite that long. I must get back to London for the new year."

"To London! Parliament will not be in session. What need is there for that?"

"You have said it yourself, Agnes. Our backs may be against the wall. I go where I am sent. The two lots of us are battering each other in the streets of Ireland, but there are places where we are still talking. It is like a chess game. There are funds involved, party funds, and a question of the law. We may have to meet in France, if it comes to it. There are warrants against O'Brien and Dillon. They cannot set foot either here or in England. But London is the first step."

"I can understand that," she said, a trace of the bitterness creeping back. "If there are funds, trust the Tullys to understand, eh?"

He smiled in token of conciliation. "Or the farmer's son who was clever at sums and became their bookkeeper."

"You have gone far since those days, Robert, far, and a far distance from me."

"We have gone far," he said, in a gesture that swept the room and stopped, by chance, where candlelight glowed through watered brandy.

"We had gone that far before ever you left Kilpeder. You are known now throughout the country, and a member of Parliament, your sayings and doings written up for the *Freeman's Journal* and the *Examiner* and the English papers as well. Tis small wonder that Conor is proud of you."

"And you."

"Oh, your wife. To be sure, to be sure. There will be little for either of us to be proud of when you are dragged down into the mud, through your own wilful courses."

"Let us be clear about a point or two, Agnes. I hold this constituency. I have sounded out the people. They are unhappy about events of the last few months, no question of it. But they will stand by me."

She laughed. "Now I know that you are lost for good and all, Bob. The people of Cork will tell a fellow whatever he wants to hear, and then they will do whatever they want to do. You are well liked here, Bob, and with good reason, and it is with sorrow in their hearts that they will turf you out into the ditch."

It was as though chilling air, cooled upon some Arctic of shrewd sense, had blown into the room. He noticed with surprise that he had pulled himself back slightly.

"And you, Agnes? If my folly, as you call it, turfs me out into the ditch, where will you stand?"

"I have waited these months for talk between us, and twas not I who called for it on Christmas Eve. Very well, so. You are my husband, and I went to you forsaking all others, exactly as we were prepared for marriage at convent school, leaving my father's house, roof, and protection. I will stand by you as I would had you turned to drink, or gambled away this house at race meetings or in Dublin, or wrecked your practice at law by foolishness and bad judgement. I will stand by you."

"I thank you for that," he said. "I knew it, but I am grateful to hear it spoken."

"But," she said, and she leaned forward, her hands resting now not in her lap but upon knees pressed together. "But if you were ever to bring public disgrace upon this house, upon the marriage, upon me and upon our son, then God help you."

"Because I am standing by Parnell?" he said, warily. "I do not follow you."

"You do," she said, "but you need follow me no farther, for I have nothing left to say upon that score. Never take me for a fool, Bob; you are tempted to from time to time. I have been a disappointment to you in ways that I lack even the language to say, but not such a disappointment that I did not give you a fine son. I am sorry for your disappointment, but never take me for a fool and never forget that I am a woman. We have no more to say. It lacks but two hours to midnight. Christmas blessings on you, Bob." She stood up, kissed him lightly on the lips, and left the room.

After she had gone, he stood by the window, by the lighted candle. There was another in Tully's house, across the way, and in each of the other houses in the handsome, boastful street. As a boy, on the farm, not so small a farm as he liked now to pretend, but one of moderate acres, rich grass, sleek-flanked cattle, there had been a candle in a window each Christmas Eve. Down into the valley, and up the sides of the low, fronting hills, the candles would be lit before it was full dark. One year, bundled into the warm coat from the shop in Millstreet that had been his Christmas gift, he had stood outside the farmhouse, close to the byre, the heavy scent of beasts and wet straw in his nostrils, but cut by a clear December wind, and he had watched darkness fall, a darkness without moon or stars, so that the candle flames themselves seemed stars in a fallen world, or rather, stars which had dropped down to bring promise, and the promise so immense, so prodigious, that his imagination lacked forms to contain it. It was not the promise of religion alone, although that lay at its centre, but an amorphous, boundaryless promise, stretching out into flame-pierced, unthreatening darkness. Now, there were only the lighted candles of a limited season of good cheer, a harmless ritual. As Agnes had said, he had travelled a far distance.

I count it among the not inconsiderable blessings of my life that the MacMahons, contrary to custom, did not share the Christmas dinner of the Tullys. Poor Brian had come down with the mumps, his face swollen into a travesty of itself, and that was sufficient as an excuse. The Tully dinner table seemed unlikely in this December of 1890 to be a citadel of Christmas cheer of the sort prescribed by Mr. Dickens. And indeed it was not. The account which Vincent gave me of it, two days later, when I visited him in Brierly Lodge, made the blood run cold. Not that it stands in need of rehearsing, for Christmas dinners were being ruined all over Ireland, save no doubt in loyalist households. But it might well have been a bit worse in Inchigeelagh House (oh God, the vulgarity of that name! Naming houses, indeed, as though they were Christian souls. In the city of Limerick there is a house called Sacred Heart Villa), granting Tully's position and Bob's, a merchant built into the web of county merchants and a Parnellite organiser.

"It was brutal stuff, right enough," Vincent said.

We were spending a leisurely afternoon before a good fire, a frost, bleak and cheerless, covering the ground beyond the windows, but ourselves comfortable, and putting the afternoon to good use by oiling and cleaning Vincent's shotguns and rifles. What had once been the library of Brierly Lodge, he had made into a gunroom, with cabinets, elaborate ones for guns which he had bought upon whim—an elephant gun, and two of Persian designs out of a fairy tale, but the most of them working weapons. One wall, though, did indeed serve as his library. He read far more than he pretended—novels and memoirs, Balzac and Brantôme in English, Charles Reade and Wilkie Collins.

"Brutal stuff," he repeated. "They had promised, the two of them, to be on their best behaviour, but twas no use. It was neither of them at fault; the damned thing was inevitable, like rain and frost. They cut close to the bone; things were said that are unforgivable." And Vincent, a shotgun and his tools spread out before him on the table, ramrods and cloths and oilcans, spelled out for me the unforgivable things.

"Do you know," he said, at the end of the dreadful recitation, "I felt sorry for the old man. Age must be weakening me. At the height of his anger, tears were welling up in his eyes; his eyes were brimming, and they were tears not of anger but of grief. Bob was his true son, not me. We have always known that."

"Ach now, Vincent," I began to protest.

"Save your breath to cool your porridge, Hughie. He loves me, more I sometimes think than ever he loved anyone. But Bob was the son that he wanted me to be. We know that. And now they are sundered."

"The blow is as hard for Bob, surely," I said.

"It would be, in the ordinary course of things; but events have their ways of changing shape. Bob has a bit of skirt in London, you know."

I was drawing my cloth through a barrel, and bent a bit more closely to my task. "Get along with you, Vincent! Bob Delaney? Has he told you that?"

[677]

"Indeed he has not. To the brother-in-law, is it? But I can tell, by God, I can tell. My skills are limited, Hughie, but they are acute—hunting, racing, women, whatever along those lines, I'm your man. Sure, what harm is there in it, in anyone's eyes save a priest's? And Agnes is a bit of a cold fish, if truth be told; the both of us know that. She would have been happier in the convent, but she has settled for being the world's champion mother. Bar one. If Bob were ever to turn his back to her, he would have me as his enemy, and a more formidable one than he might expect. But a bit of skirt, now. That's an entirely different matter. The institution of marriage rests upon a bit of skirt—now there is a metaphysical conundrum for you, Master MacMahon."

I drew out the rag. There is a great comfort in the performance of some tasks, and the cleaning and oiling of guns is for some reason one of them.

He was quite right when he described himself as acute, a large, sleepy cat but with a wariness always jungle-alert beneath the somnolence.

"You were saying, Hugh?"

"Nothing," I said. "My mind was wandering. I was thinking about the night we made the arms raid. And that one of our teams hit Brierly Lodge."

"Times change, Hughie. Times change."

"Not for Ned," I said.

"No," he said. "Not for Ned. But even Ned will quieten down one of these days. He has already, perhaps. Perhaps he is settling down to a career as a national shrine, like Rossa and O'Leary."

"He is in England," I said. "He has been in England for a year. He is running the dynamite team."

Vincent was holding in his hand neither rifle nor shotgun, but a revolver of American manufacture, large and deadly. I remembered the first night, Ned Nolan knocking at my door, his weapon of heavy calibre.

"Your imagination," Vincent said.

"I have heard it from Bob, who was told it by the Supreme Council."

"Do not tell me one word more about it, Hugh," he said fiercely. "Not one word. Dear Jesus. It is a wonder the Yard has not lifted him."

"They have their warrant," I said, "all made out and ready. But they need more than suspicion, such is my guess. What Bob was given was a hint and a wink."

"Hint no hints to me, Hughie. Eighteen ninety is not the year of the Rising. It is almost 'ninety-one, a few days more. The century is running down, lad, and ourselves along with it. Ned is stuck somewhere back in time, fighting invisible battles with real dynamite. The very thought of Ned frightens me. He could do for us all."

I began to speak, but he shook his head. "Not a word."

And at that word of his, Theresa Fuller, his housekeeper, came in to bring us lunch on a tray, soup and sandwiches. Housekeeper, I say, for that was the polite fiction in town, everywhere save in its public houses. She was certainly still in her young twenties; I remember her brother Eddie as my student, and he was a year or two older at most. But *housekeeper* was the word agreed upon, and I cannot speak to such matters as traffic between herself and her confessor, but certainly she received the Sacraments. You never know. "Good afternoon, Master MacMahon," she said, prim and proper. "I spoke with Mrs. MacMahon in town yesterday. A fine person, Mrs. MacMahon is, God love her."

"God loves the comely," Vincent said to her. "Mrs. MacMahon and yourself are safe in His hands."

"I would not know about that, I am sure," she said, and left.

"The two of you must have wonderful chats these long winter evenings," I said, "on the esthetic preferences of the Divine Creator."

"We do indeed," Vincent said. "We do indeed. Now, Bob and his bit of skirt. I trust that she is a girl with great consolatory capacities, for he will need them. I have been giving him a bit of help here in Kilpeder. But it is hopeless. Tis not my father and Father Meagher alone. Bob left the tenants and the Plan in Fogarty's safekeeping, and Fogarty is now Healy's man."

"Be damned to that," I said. "Fogarty is but Bob's deputy, and Bob can turf him out."

"Ah, now," Vincent said, holding the bowl of soup in his hand, and spooning it up, a rich and savoursome thick soup. "Bob is off in London saving Ireland, and in Kilkenny saving Parnell. But Fogarty has been here in Kilpeder working for the tenants, and seeing to the needs of the evicted. He is a decent fellow, Fogarty, no crawthumper. Not all the good lads are on the one side, and all the rogues on the other."

"I know that," I said.

"Parnell is smashed up," Vincent said, "like those frogs who go hopping about after the schoolboys have lopped off their heads, and then they keel over. When he sinks, he will pull men down in his wake. Not all, perhaps, but they will need a strong base at home, and Bob is losing his."

"You had best make up your mind," I said. "Is it a dying frog that Parnell is, or a sinking ship?"

"Ah now," Vincent said, "you can be the schoolmaster to the end of your days, reproving the rhetorical shortcomings of your friends, and I can hunt and wench to the end of my days, and Ned Nolan, if it comes to that, can spend the short time left to him blowing up railway platforms and innocent travellers. But Bob is the one of us who has been on the hike through life."

An hour or two after lunch, our task was finished, and guns in the racks, the walnut stocks glowing with the gratitude that fine wood seems almost capable of feeling, and the barrels clear, deadly, the opposite of wood: inhuman, cold, harder than anthracite.

Before I left, Vincent walked to the wall, stood looking a moment or two, and then took down a short-barrelled revolver and walked across the room to me, pausing as he did so to pick up a box of cartridges from the worktable.

"Give this to Bob," he said. "He can shove it in a desk drawer if he has a mind to, but it is best in these days to have one."

I shook my head. "Bob went armed to Kilkenny," I said. "He has been armed these weeks past. It is idiocy that has descended upon us all. We had an enemy before us in 'sixty-seven. Now we are armed against each other."

He would not hear of me walking back into town, but lent me one of his traps, and so I had an easy, restful journey of it for the few miles, the sun pale and the skies leaden and low. From the crest of Hoban's Hill, I saw town and castle, churches, and river, the river frozen, a tracery of ice the colour of ash.

34

[*Lionel Forrester/Hugh MacMahon/Robert Delaney*]

It was not until the end of August of that final year for us all, 1891, that I came to stay with Tom in Kilpeder, although I had crossed over a few weeks earlier to take up an invitation from Georgie Winslowe to shoot over his lands in Westmeath, outside Mullingar, a splendid Queen Anne, more or less, house, with a marvellous view of Lough Owel. It was a curious time for the island. A month before, Parnell had fought the last and most decisive of his ruinous by-elections, the one in Carlow, and his enemies were moving in for the kill. Even someone as ignorant of politics as myself—as bored by them, really—could tell that. But the remarkable thing is that I was not bored, far from it; no one in the country was. It was as though a great drama were drawing to some final curtain, with lines that could not quite be predicted. Oh, I had my special reasons, of course—my feelings for Sylvia and Tom, for Robert Delaney if it comes to that; for I had drawn closer to him. There was now, finally, the kind of affection for which Sylvia had been hoping. But the excitement was universal in Ireland, with all that was happening unprecedented, theatrical, as though upon a stage, the ending foreordained, but the chief character no actor who would get to his feet at curtain fall and dust himself off.

One of the surprising aspects for me was that Parnell, whose very name had for a decade been anathema to Irish loyalists, was spoken of now among them with an admiration and pity that was almost, but not quite, ungrudging. I got my first taste of this on my first afternoon at Hazeldene, when Georgie and his gamekeeper and Fred Keating and myself were walking the fields which we would be shooting over next morning.

"Bloody awful Carlow must have been for poor Parnell," Georgie said, giving some tall grasses a swipe with his stick. "Mobs hurling stones at him. There he was standing on a wagonette in the rain, so the papers say. And he didn't have a ghostly, you know, not a ghostly; why the hell does he do it? He had a chance in Kilkenny, you know, but not Sligo, not really, and in Carlow, not a prayer. The general election will bury him, snow him under."

"By the Harry," Fred Keating said, "he'll give them a run for their money. Brought it on himself, you know, ruling, lording it over mobs of Papists; should have known they would turn against him. They turn against their own, why not against one of ours who puts in his lot with them? But by the Harry, what a fighter, eh? What a fighter! He'll show them the sort of stuff our sort is made of, eh?"

"Good heavens," Georgie said, "what a bloody little Orangeman you are, Fred. Can't help admiring him, though. Thank God he's losing, but he's going down like a gentleman."

"Goethe," I said, introducing an exotic name upon those acres, "Goethe said that the Irish are like a pack of hounds, tearing down their own heroes."

"Did he say that?" Georgie said in mild surprise. "Wouldn't have thought he had even heard of Ireland. Can't go by me, though; never read those Germans. All beer and farts."

"The noble stag he had in mind," I said, "was the Duke of Wellington."

"Ha," Georgie said, "Wellington. Someone called him Irish once; he said, if he'd been born in a stable, would that make him a horse. In fact, you know, his wife came from near here. One of the Pakenhams, Kitty Pakenham. Not that he thought much of her."

Later, when Fred was having his late afternoon lie-down, Georgie took me to the stables, to have a look at a mare that he had acquired in a complicated bit of trading that involved ten-pound notes and access rights to some wretched bog road. He had done well: she was a fine-looking creature, fine flanks and withers, good clear eyes. He held out his hand, and the groom rooted in his jacket pocket for some lumps of sugar.

"Tom Ardmor," Georgie said, "now there's an odd sort of fellow. Smashing ball they gave, though, wasn't it? After they came home? Jean and I didn't forget that one in a hurry."

I had entirely forgotten that the Winslowes had been among that troupe of guests. "Nor I," I said. "I remember that castle in the old days, Tom's father's days. The ball was up to the old standard."

"Not so much anymore, I hear," Georgie said, as the mare nuzzled his sugary hand. "Tom away much of the year, place shut up, Sylvia in London, the county families furious with Tom. Why is that, why the fury?"

"Tom and the Land League made their peace in early days. In fact, Tom lowered his rents that first bad year, when a famine seemed likely, before the League was really in operation."

"Did that myself," Georgie said. "Any decent chap would. Only seven percent, mind you, but it saw the people through, that and a few judicious private arrangements; the hanging gale, eh? Can't let your own people lose their farms."

"Ah, but you see, you could afford it, and Tom could. The League has shoved some of the smaller landlords against the wall; some of them have had to sell out. In our barony, Tom is about as popular as Michael Davitt, and it doesn't help much that he's away most of the year. The county families in Cork are a clannish lot."

"Where are they not," he said, "where are they not? But you see Tom, of course, cousins; and you see Sylvia, you tell me. Smashing girl, she was. Grew up not twelve miles from here. Well, grew up in a manner of speaking; she was away at school a bit, and then afterwards, she and Hubert, her old fellow, Colonel Hubert, they were hard-pressed for a bit of tin. One met them, of course, at house parties, hunts, hunt balls; then they were living in London on short rations."

"Yes," I said, "that is where she and Tom met."

"I remember that!" Georgie cried, rubbing his wet hand along the mare's smooth, chestnut neck. "I remember that! Met her through someone in that artist lot he is so fond of. Rum crowd, if you ask me. Oh, a few of them are gentlemen, I daresay. But was she not a stunning bride! I hadn't seen her for two years, three. A beautiful girl, in that curious way these artists like, and that look she gives you as if to say, 'I don't give a damn what you think of me.' Challoner was so different, poor fellow: decent, unassuming fellow. A few bad patches in his life, not the most distinguished of Her Majesty's officers, but a colonel, after all. One heard stories about Sylvia, Sylvia and a young American fellow, fellow from New York, one of those Dutch-y names. Anything to that, do you suppose?"

Not looking at me, he rubbed his hand with a handkerchief drawn from his stained and frayed trousers.

"We are very close friends, Sylvia and I," I said.

"No harm intended. Not another word on the subject. But still . . ."

At dinner that night, Jean Winslowe placed me at her left, and it was certain at one point that she had the same conversation in mind. She was a dreadful gossip, and a woman much gossiped about until a few years before—custom had not staled her infinite variety, *et cetera*. "But *if* it were true, Lee—now, of course, it *isn't* true—but *if* it were true, wouldn't a teensy bit of the fault be Tom Ardmor's? Off there in—where is it, Venice?—and Sylvia alone in London. Have you seen, oh, of course you have, that painting by Galantiere? Now, you are a writer—that is a sort of artist; do you mean to tell me that that could have been painted by a man who had not seen her in bed, was not in love with her? Women don't look the same when they are making love, and he knew how Sylvia looked. That's what makes the painting so exciting. It is indecent, my dear. It should be locked up."

"It is, in a way," I said. "It is in a private house, which only friends visit."

"Ahh," she cried, in mock-agony, and touched her hand, fleetingly, to her breast, as though stabbed. "You wouldn't be a bit in love with her yourself, would you, Lee?"

But the gate lodge to the Castle was as trim as ever, and Furey, the gatekeeper, touched his forefinger to his cap, as my trap rolled through the gates. The gardens, just now feeling the touch of autumn, were still lovely, but almost too luxuriant, lacking the subtlety with which Isabel had created them, with which Tom had maintained them. Hazeldene; Carrignagort House, in Mallow, where I had spent the night before; Ardmor Castle—to leave their towns behind, Mullingar, Mallow, Kilpeder, ride through the gates, put the demesne walls safely, comfortingly behind one, was to pass into a changeless world, untouched by time. Or so, at least, things looked to the eye, seemed if one judged by sounds, odours.

But the Norrises, of Carrignagort, had been talking of moving to England, handing things over to an agent. "It isn't the same country anymore, Lee. Not our country; they don't want us to think of it as ours; we are aliens here, you see. We are, you are, the lot of us. Good God, our people have been here since long before Cromwell, before Elizabeth, even. We were Papists once ourselves, not ashamed of it."

Tom had seen me from the house, and was waiting for me on the gravelled drive. He had a short blond beard now, sun-lightened, and it became him, but he seemed otherwise unchanged, and delighted, as always, to see me.

"Delighted to see anyone here, Lee, to tell you the truth," he said, as we walked towards the Japanese garden and lake, as though we had both known, without speaking, that that was what we wanted to do. "Barring the servants," he said, "and poor Charlie Greene, the rector, I could be Robinson Crusoe. I daresay I could walk down into the town—apparently I am well liked in the town—could bend the elbow at the Kilpeder Arms, a chat with the solicitor, eh, and the resident magistrate at the far end of town. But it wouldn't quite do for an earl, a belted earl, eh? Snobbery dies hard—the most powerful of the human emotions, save perhaps for greed. I'm boycotted; that's what it is, by Jove. The only landlord in Ireland to be boycotted by the landlords."

He was talking a bit nervously, it seemed to me, although as yet I could not tell why: very faint clues, the words tripping each other a bit, his tone a bit too jokey.

I told him of my conversation the night before, with the Norrises.

"They are right, you know," he said. "It's all fading, our Ireland is, like these flowers; but everyone can see the flowers. Every fool. They are selling out, some of the smaller chaps are. No need for the Norrises to sell out, other than a wish to go home. For all the centuries that we've been here, a wish to go home. There has been a revolution here, Lee, and we are all of us too blind to see it. The winners have fallen out amongst themselves, daggers drawn, a civil war. That happens more often than not, by my reading of history. But that doesn't help us."

"But you know," I said. We had reached the edge of the delicate lake, intricately fed by underground springs, diverted at God knows what cost to satisfy the taste that Sylvia had once had for Japanese-y looks. "You know, if things had worked out a bit differently, they would have had one of our lot as their uncrowned king, one of our lot, as Georgie Winslowe would say."

"I doubt that," Tom said. He crouched down, and pulled up by its roots a waterside flower of some sort, blue-and-white-petalled, thin spear-like leaves a very dark green, the roots tender and shallow, bits of damp earth clung to them. "It was meant to happen, the destruction of Parnell. Good God, Lee, you are the novelist, not I. Could you not tell that?"

"That's the second time this week that I've been called a writer. I am not a writer, damn it, I'm a gentleman, as Congreve said to Voltaire. I wouldn't write a word if I wasn't always hard up. Meant to happen indeed!"

"I think so," he said mildly. "I think so." He wandered into Sylvia's small, graceful folly, which we had taught ourselves to call the teahouse, and sat down in one of the wicker chairs. Soon the groundsmen would be carting the furniture to the sheds, and securing the delicate structure against winter. I sat down beside him, the two of us looking out into the lake.

"Oh, yes," he said. "It was fated, the destruction of Parnell. Not everything is fated. I haven't turned mystic on you, not one of Willie Yeats's converts. It wasn't fated that Sylvia should fall in love with Robert Delaney. But it has happened."

Startled, I turned from the lake to face him. He was looking directly at me.

"Oh, yes. They are in love. You and I, we both know that. Sylvia and I have always loved each other, you see, and concealment could have wrecked everything between us. We knew that from the first. She told me about Galantiere, and then, a bit later, about Van Zandt. And then about Delaney. But with Delaney, and with time, everything changed. What she told me, first off, was that she . . . cared for him. Leave it at that. As she had cared for the other two. But not now. And not for a long while."

He was silent, as though testing words, but then what he said was simply, "I will always love her."

I sat looking at him, wanting to reach out to touch him, wanting to know what to say, to do. I remember that it was warm for the time of day that was in it, as the locals would say.

"Van Zandt had seemed to her all New World courage, cheerfulness, that sort of thing. No complexities, not a one. But Mama gave one tug of the leash from New York, and that was that."

It was a quiet day, windless. No sounds carried to us from the town, beyond the walls of the demesne: shouts, creak of wheel.

"She's had rotten luck with men, hasn't she, Lee? Rotten luck with men, and she deserves the best. At least Van Zandt was a gentleman, harmless little fellow, discreet. But Galantiere was not. After Galantiere, Sylvia's was a name one heard in London, heard at house parties. And now Delaney, a man headed for a crash, like his leader."

"I visit them, Tom," I said. "You should know that. Or rather, I visit Sylvia, and Delaney is there as often as not."

"Yes," Tom said. "Of course."

Then, for a time, we looked, without really seeing it, at the still, smooth-surfaced water, not a ripple, fringed with delicate, dying reeds.

Six cypresses, deep green, a rich, fat green, stood half concealing what might have been a ruined garden, broken statues, an overturned urn, or, then again, might not. It seemed early morning—there was a pinkish tone to the light—and the effect, despite the richness of the green, was wintry.

Tom shrugged. "Perhaps so. I painted it in February. Bloody cold in their hills in February. Sunny Italy indeed!"

I fumbled for words, as for loose change. I never knew how I felt about his paintings, what I should say about them. Oh, I do now, of course. That sort of thing is all the rage; no one can imagine having ever painted any other way. And away to the lumber room with the kind of art that we all grew up with. Now I know what Tom was doing, what many of them were, some better than Tom, some worse. But Tom is the real thing, even although to this day he never exhibits; but a dozen or more, two dozen, have managed to get loose, and Tom is a respected name. Thomas Forrester, he signs them all, the family name.

"And there it is," he said. "That one and two others are the only good things I've done in the past year. But three is enough, three is a gift. One is, come to that."

It was resting, for the moment, on an easel, in the late afternoon library light. Beyond the open window lay the terraces, gardens, lake, the teahouse where we had been sitting.

"I had lunch with Jimmy Whistler a long while ago, a long time ago," I said. "Perhaps I wrote you. During the Parnell trial. Special Commission they called it, but it was a trial, all the same. Jimmy says that you're the real thing."

"Does he indeed?" Tom asked with pleasure. "Jimmy is the really real thing, you know. Terrible liar, but never about art."

"But my trouble, you know, Tom," I said, feeling my way, "is that I can nearly always tell where I am with Jimmy's paintings. He can be as cloudy and as nocturne-y as he wants, call it *An Arrangement in Grey* or whatever, and there is a mood there that I can sink into. I can say, Yes, this is just how I sometimes feel, walking along the Embankment. Just exactly like this. But—"

"But not with mine."

"Oh, no," I said, guiltily, "that isn't at all what—"

"I know," Tom said, laughing and clapping me on the shoulder. "I know. I wish I had Jimmy's cleverness with words. But I don't. *I* know what I'm doing; I think I do. And there you are." Suddenly he laughed again, but in a different register. His hand was still on my shoulder, and he squeezed me. "Do you know who seems to know? Robert Delaney."

I thought it was a joke of some sort, but then he said, "True, dead true. He used to visit with us here; that is how the damned thing started, of course. He said to me once, 'I don't know what you see when you paint. But it is a way to see things; there is more than one way, that is what the paintings say.' And of course, he was right. That comes as close as anything. Not really close, but closer than I have words. Words don't matter to . . . to . . ." He stabbed a finger to the canvas. "Words don't matter to that thing. That thing is against words, in fact."

"Words matter to Delaney," I said.

"Oh, yes," Tom said. "For the moment."

"For the moment! He has built a life on them, on platforms, in newspapers, in Commons. Pamphlets, oratory, men straining to catch his words. A lifetime."

"For the moment," Tom said. "After a while, everything becomes as quiet as that."

And for the moment, for the moment, the room and my mind were filled with the quiet of "that thing," the cypresses, the fallen statuary, the urns, the sunken garden. For the moment, "that thing" discoursed upon silence.

It was in the last week in August that Parnell came to speak in the market square of Kilpeder. All of July, August, on into September, he was on the move from one town to the next—market towns, landlord towns, little better than hamlets, some of them. His followers, so it seemed to me now, and among these I number Bob himself, were moved by fierce impulses of savage pride, a fury at what had been lost, what was seeping away day by day, a familial hatred as furious as any that we had ever directed against the English.

Once, earlier that August, Bob and Parnell found themselves upon the same night boat out of Holyhead, standing together at the rail, the night dark and moonless, flecks of rain. The *Freeman's Journal* had days before gone over to the other side, Edmund Gray unctuously announcing that Parnell's marriage to "Mrs. O'Shea," as he pointedly called her, had made it impossible for the Irish people ever to recognise the adulterer, Parnell, as their leader. "I never liked that fellow Gray," Parnell said.

"Damned Englishman, meddling in our lives, claims to be Irish. Wait for Thurles." It was to Thurles that he was travelling. "I will have a word or two for him there, shovel a few hot coals down his breeches."

Do you know, Bob said to me with some irritability of tone, do you know that it has not once occurred to him to thank those of us who are standing with him, and at considerable risks, and fewer of us every day? Patsy Daly in Thurles has put every chip upon the board to organise the Thurles meeting. Thurles, of all the towns in Ireland, with that great ugly cathedral rising up above all and everything, the most Catholic town in Ireland, such is their boast, whatever the hell that means; but there are Parnellites in Tipperary, and Patsy will turn them out even if the Archbishop himself condemns him from that gaudy altar. And Parnell will say, at the end of it all, "Thank you, Daly," as though he had received a cup of tea.

"Tell me, Delaney," he said to me that night, as we leaned upon the railings, looking into the black night, black water beneath us. "I should like to know what you think will be the results of the general election."

Well, the problem at the moment was that I had taken aboard five large ones in the saloon bar, and so, I decided, what the hell, every Lear deserves his Kent. "I think you will come back with about five followers, Mr. Parnell. Make that four: I am no longer certain of my hold upon Kilpeder."

"Or perhaps," he said to me, "perhaps I shall come back absolutely alone, which will make one thing certain: I shall then represent an Irish party whose independence of action will not be sapped or bribed or intimidated."

Kent fell silent then, Hughie, and the two of us stood together for a good bit, facing outwards, Ireland still miles distant from us. Until at last the chill got through to me, through greatcoat and cape, and I excused myself, and left him standing there alone.

But when Bob described for me his apprehensions as to Thurles and Patsy Daly, I knew that it was Kilpeder and himself that he had in mind. The tide was running against him: the Church, Tully and all that Tully was and held and represented, the commercial interests in town and its Catholic respectability. And more menacing than that, it had been made known that Fogarty was prepared to stand against Bob in the general election, and there were farmers, strong-farmers and some less strong but in possession of the franchise nevertheless, who had good reason to stand by Fogarty. Fogarty it was who worked with them, and bore the day's burden. These things are not forgotten in Ireland, where what a man is and does is of more importance than whatever ideas he may flaunt. Bob knew that himself, and he gave Kilpeder much of his time in those final weeks, but you could sense that it was time begrudged—or at any rate, I could sense it, knowing what I did.

A full fortnight before the meeting, Bob had his bills, immense ones, posted in the town, and to the sides of friendly barns and huckster shops in the countryside: "Charles Stewart Parnell, Official Leader of the Irish People, Champion of the People's Rights, to Speak in the Market Square of Kilpeder. On the Platform with Him Will Be Robert Delaney, Kilpeder's Emissary in the Parliament of the Enemy, Defender of the Poor in the Fight Against Exterminating Landlords. Also Vincent Tully, Esquire, like Robert Delaney a Hero of Clonbrony Wood in Dark and Evil Days. God Save Ireland."

They were defaced, many of those posters, with scrawls: "Kitty O'Shea's Shift." But Lanty had his band of toughs, the organization itself, roaming the streets to protect the new set which Bob put into place. The new set had other names as well—Edmund Leamy and John Redmond, whose attendance was promised.

" 'Hero of Clonbrony Wood'!" Vincent protested. "We have never had to sink to that before, Bob."

"We'll be sunk lower than that before we are finished," Bob said. "Say your prayers, for I am fully prepared to put it up in curlicued print: 'Is Appearing on the Platform in Defiance of His Father's Strict Instructions.' "

"And another thing," Bob said to Lanty a day later. "When the Chief is in this town, I do not want his eye to rest upon any of the filth that these people are willing to scrawl upon walls."

"'Tis the filth they are likely to shout out that I can do little about ahead of the day," Lanty said. "You know yourself what happened last week in Thurles, and Ennis after Thurles. And there is a stronger organization in Ennis than there is here. What the lads and I have in mind for the day—"

"Keep it in your mind, so," Bob said. "I have no need to hear of it. And bear in mind that the constabulary and the resident magistrate will be in the square to keep order."

Lanty hawked up, and spat between his heavy, farrier's boots. "Fucking peelers."

"Fucking peelers with fucking carbines. But I want no one on our side to be armed in that square. No firearms, that is. A blackthorn stick is a different matter—it is an item of personal adornment. And for that matter, a hurling stick might well be carried by this fellow or that as a sign of devotion to our revived Gaelic athletic traditions. But not one single gun, do you understand that?"

"With respect, Mr. Delaney, I take no orders from you, but only from the organization."

"The organization and myself have come to an agreement upon that," Bob said. "If you doubt me, there is a certain person in Cork City whom you can consult, whose name is known to us both."

Extraordinary, it seems to me, and I have tried to paint for Patrick such a picture, that to the very end, until everything tumbled upon him, he was as resourceful as ever he had been on that morning in 'sixty-seven. He might, when the three of us were alone—himself and myself, and Vincent (and Mary as often as not)—he might on such occasions be naked and bleak in his estimation of Parnellite fortunes, but he moved through the town with all his old confidence.

And Agnes, it should be said for her, stood by him in all this difficult time, with communication between the two handsome houses facing each other at a standstill, by her wish as much as her father's. When foodstuffs and such things were needed in the Delaney household, she would send one of the maidservants down to the shop, where once it had been her pleasure to pick and choose for herself, and even to bargain with one of Bob's descendants as shop assistant. But she had taken seriously the words of the sacrament of marriage, as she took seriously all sacraments, and she had married Bob for better or worse, forsaking all others. Yet she would once in a while, when the coast was clear, slip across the way for a cup of tea with her mother, and once, when Mary called in upon her, the mother was in Agnes's kitchen, "the silent Tully," as Vincent called her, a heavy, bulky woman, wearing always clothes made for her by a seamstress from Cork City, but appearing shapeless upon her, and worn with a deprecating air, as though to say, "I know how I look; there is no need for this expense."

"It is terrible, Agnes," she said, "after all the thought and care and travail, the expenses of your education—not that they were begrudged, for money spent upon education is never wasted, Mr. Tully says; it has always been known to pay golden dividends—and now this."

"What is done is done," Agnes said. "Bob has thrown in his lot with those men, and there is no turning back."

"Hillside men," Mrs. Tully said, "rapparees, at the bidding of an adulterer."

"I know what they are, Mother. Will you give over? There is nothing I can do. Take your scolding to Vincent, who is by Bob's side, and on Sunday will stand beside him on the platform."

"Vincent," Mrs. Tully said, and sighed. "I do not know what have I done to deserve such a heart-scalding." And she began to cry, softly, tear streaks upon her soft, doughy face, beneath the black bonnet which she had not removed.

Later, Agnes said to Mary with a surprising flintiness, "There is far worse that Vincent has done than to stand on the platform with a convicted adulterer. Well we know it, and well she does."

Parnell arrived late on the Saturday, on the train from Cork to Macroom, and Bob brought him to Kilpeder, where he insisted upon spending the night at the Arms, although Bob had offered him a room in his house. The town was quiet, a deceptive quiet, and Parnell, with Bob beside him, and Leamy, an M.P. and one of his supporters, walked like any commercial traveller into the Arms, and registered. Bob saw his quick, familiar scrawl set onto the blue line, the signature famous since the forgery trial: "Chas. S. Parnell, M.P."

"Yes indeed," said Gilmartin, the proprietor of the Arms, "a nice quiet room in the rere of the house, Mr. Parnell, the very thing. Looking out upon the hills."

"I prefer front rooms," Parnell said. "Would you have one facing out into the square? I like the bustle of a town."

"Scant bustle on a Sunday morning," Gilmartin said, "but tomorrow evening of course—"

He halted, and Parnell said, "Yes."

The morning was as quiet as Gilmartin had promised, with the town moving quietly to Saint Jarlath's for Mass, or else the handful of Protestants to service at the other end of town. But the RIC was already out in force, augmented by men from Macroom and Millstreet, strolling two by two. From time to time, a pair of them would stand by the platform, as though soldiers surveying the fields where a battle would be fought, or else glancing up at the front windows of the Arms. Perhaps they caught a glimpse of him, as I did myself, having walked through the town for that very purpose. He was standing by the window looking down, holding a teacup and saucer. Later, he went down to the dining room, where Bob and Leamy joined him.

Parnell's meeting in Kilpeder was well reported in the newspapers, and in the books that began shortly to appear. The books, of course, knew that it was to be one of the final scenes; within weeks it would all be over. But perhaps the newspapers knew as well: their sketch artists gave him the look of a man maddened.

That evening, despite the intense, greenish summer light, the pitch torches had been lit. He came out from the Arms, with Bob and Leamy and the chaps who had been coming in all day behind him—Harrington and the two Redmonds and Harrison. His supporters had for the moment the best of it, and they gave a roar when they heard him, but he seemed not to hear it, and stood patiently—I was so close that I might have touched him—as Lanty's men cleared the way to the platform.

I had not spoken to him since that one day, early on, ten years almost, when Bob had introduced us, the most handsome man I had ever seen, I remember reporting back to Mary, and she wanted to know every word spoken, every look, how he was dressed. Later, there was a print in our kitchen, showing him as he looked then, a bit prettied-up perhaps, but not much, and beneath the engraving the famous words he had spoken at Ennis, *Keep a firm grip on your homesteads*, too handsome perhaps, looking as few men look in politics, a regal look, perhaps that Luciferian pride there as well, but we had all drawn favourable auguries from that. Now he was like an animal at bay, his eyes smoky, watchful, dangerous, almost perhaps indeed—as Davitt and Healy were infamously saying— almost mad.

The day had begun badly, with Father Meagher's sermon. "The stench of the divorce court," he said, "has been brought into Kilpeder, and is lodging in this town. The man to whom our people in their innocence and in the extremity of their need reposed their trust has dragged Ireland through the soiled sheets of an adulterer's bed. I meddle in no man's politics in this parish, but I can say without meddling that no man with decency, no man who has the best interests of Ireland at heart, would wish to wander tonight into the market square. And let us all, as we are offering up our prayers at the sacred sacrifice of the Mass, offer up a special prayer, placing our poor afflicted country under the special protection of Mary, conceived without sin, the stainless mother of our Holy Saviour."

If all those who had the best interests of Ireland at heart did indeed stay away from the square that evening, then I can only puzzle as to the identity of the mob who came to do battle, far larger in number than Parnellites and Fenians and policemen put together.

Already, that afternoon, they had managed to tear down the green bunting from the platform, with its gilt scrollwork, its harp and round tower and its motto, the words of the Manchester Martyrs, "God Save

Ireland." Lanty's men fought them for it, but lost. "The bastards," Lanty said to Bob. "'Twas their banners, their buntings, not ours—the buntings that the League has been using these ten years past."

"Never mind," Bob said. "The Chief hates the colour green. A good omen, he will call it."

But it was not.

Vincent was there with Bob and the others—as he had promised he would be, with old Tully doubtless weeping at home, as David had wept for Absalom—looking debonair as ever: a frock coat that a Tory politician would have envied, boots polished mirror-bright, a lilac tie of shot silk, a Parnellite rosette the size of a cauliflower, which all of them were wearing, John Redmond the squire from Wexford a bit embarrassed by the vulgarity of it. Vincent had also his silver flask in one tail pocket of his coat, and in the other, to balance things out, a loaded derringer with two barrels.

Throughout Bob's long speech of introduction, nothing unseemly occurred, although there was murmuring. The crowd was more against Bob than for him, and he could tell it, stumbling once or twice; but by the close he had drawn himself together, and his final words were splendid playacting, presenting Parnell to the people of Kilpeder as one might present a king or a victorious general, his very presence in the town a kind of regal condescension.

He should have changed his clothes. He was the only man of consequence on the platform not in frock coat, but rather a black short jacket of some sort, with a cardigan beneath it, and a pair of tweed trousers looking as though they had been hastily ironed. Beneath the beard, his face was deathly pale, and the eyes were burning. Does he know where he is? I asked myself, ashamed of the question. Does he know that he is in Kilpeder? Healy and the others, you see, had planted the seed in our minds. And he had been so constantly on the move, one town to the next, and all of them looking alike, the market houses of different shape, perhaps, a different statue in the square, but otherwise not different, in rain that obliterated distinctions, in dusty sunlight as today.

"Men of Kilpeder," he said, in the voice we had heard about, quiet, offhanded, "we stand today in the market square where, in the year of 'sixty-seven, the men of this town mustered their forces to do battle for our country. Here it was that Kilpeder gathered her bravest and best. There are some of them on this platform with me, but more, I daresay, stand listening to us. 'Full sixty men from Kilpeder town, to the hills above did go. Gainst troopers red and peelers black, we fought them as we could.' Isn't that how the words go? Kilpeder men, it is your song, not mine. And all Ireland honours you for it."

The square was suddenly silent, almost breathless. Dear God, I thought, he has done it again. Later, Bob told me that that morning, at breakfast, he had drilled the words of the ballad into him, at some effort, for Parnell had no taste for poetry, either doggerel or the real thing. But what matter? For that moment he held Kilpeder in the palm of his hand, and he knew it. The eyes, which had seemed furious, glowed for that moment.

Then someone shouted out, "Hey, Charley! Kitty gave you the wrong pair of trousers when you climbed out of bed this morning."

Because of the silence, the words rang out clear and appalling. Even those upon that side were for the moment mute, and that gave Parnell a deceptive chance to ignore what he had heard, and plunge on with the speech he had prepared, for which he was holding a text that he did not need: he had been making that speech for weeks.

"Now," he began, "now, when our eternal enemy across the Irish Sea has tried its worst with us and failed, they are doing what they have always done, to their eternal profit and to our everlasting disgrace. They are turning us against each other. Or let us say, rather, such is their intention. Because I know Ireland, as you know Ireland, and you and I know—"

"Mr. Fox," another voice shouted, "have you settled up your bill at the Arms?" Fox, it had come out in the divorce court, was a name that he had used; it was a name that Healy had made as common as dirt. "Did you bring Kitty along with you, or is she back spending the night with the Captain, as a good wife should?"

What next was shouted, there is no way of knowing, because the crowded market square fell into turmoil. Precisely what happened at the outset, I have no way of knowing, nor has anyone; but I think that Lanty's men moved down upon the fellow who had made the shout, and that fellow's chums grouped around him. I had seen tumultuous political meetings in my time, and had heard tales, up in the hills, of the wild, incomprehensible faction fights of the old days, the hard men of two localities meeting on an appointed day to belabour each other, and the result of their encounters skulls split open, a man or two killed. It was to such a state that the market square of Kilpeder was tumbling, and for a time I cannot measure, I stood appalled, not knowing what to do, and safe enough in the doorway of Tully's shop. But I thought then that it was the men upon the platform, Bob and Vincent among them, not to mention Parnell himself, who were most in need of protection, and so I made my cautious way, edging from shop to shop, towards the platform, a schoolteacher of middle years without so much as a pandybat to use as a weapon.

It was then I discovered what is known to every soldier, but to few others: that the scuffles that were taking place, the violence and the fists and the swinging sticks, were not the madness of a faction fight, but had a plan of a crude, primitive sort behind it. Everyone was seeking to reach the platform—the Healyite mob, if one must give it a name, however imprecise; and Lanty's mob was at the foot of the platform, determined to hold it.

At the outset of the violence, Parnell had made an attempt to continue with his speech, but there was no point to it, not even as gesture, and so he stood there, absolutely motionless. The others on the platform had risen from their chairs and were grouped around him. But Lanty's men were thinly spread, and although they held their ground in front of the platform, the other crowd had circled around, and had their hands upon the rear of the shaky floor. A minute or two before that, Major Richardson, the resident magistrate, had blown his whistle and shouted out some words, upon which the constables, with Sergeant Kelleher at their head, flung upon the crowd, their batons drawn, and set to work with reasonable impartiality, seeking to part the two mobs by a show of the Queen's uniform. Kelleher was setting them a fine example, and indeed seemed to find a certain savour in the task, but neither he nor his men seemed to be accomplishing much.

Richardson was standing on my route, if I may call it that, before Robinson's the saddler.

"My God, Major Richardson," I said, "what do you propose to do about this?"

He was a short man, stocky but with no excess flesh, in a short, checked overcoat and soft hat. He had a cigar clenched between his teeth, beneath his brisk, ex-army moustache.

"I shouted out ten minutes ago, Master MacMahon, that I intend to maintain order. Perhaps you didn't hear me. No one seems to have heard me except Sergeant Kelleher." At the moment, I was pleased to note, Kelleher was bringing his baton down on some skull, I did not care whose. "For the last ten minutes," Richardson said, "this has been an illegal assembly."

"There is comfort in that knowledge," I said, "but damned little. What else do you intend to do?"

"I have had Kelleher arm his men," Richardson said. "Do you want him to bid them fire point-blank, without discrimination, into a crowd of unarmed Irishmen? That is scarcely the spirit of Clonbrony Wood."

They were not all of them unarmed, thank God. Vincent had contrived to place himself next to Parnell, and stood as quietly, his hands folded demurely over his flat belly. He had taken out his derringer, and was holding it concealed. Vincent Tully was the most surprising person

[696]

I have ever seen, and I speak as one who in youth paid a shilling to see the half-man half-woman at Puck Fair in Tralee.

"What do you intend to do, Major?" I asked again, restraining my temper.

"I don't know, MacMahon, and that is the truth of the matter. I am having Kelleher work his way to the platform. If they can reach it, we will see what we will see. Your Parnell and your Delaney are not much to my private tastes, but they assembled lawfully, and by God, I will protect them, if I can. At that point, if it comes to using my carbines, by God I will."

The worst of it was that there seemed to me no line of retreat. I looked down the Macroom Road, and down Chapel Street, and there were crowds at each of them, whether friendly or not I could not say, and I then twisted my head, to look behind me, and I did so at exactly the moment which gave the evening its extraordinary culmination.

Out from the carriageway, past the gate lodge, past the falcon-guarded gates, a carriage came slashing, with two men in it. At the distance, short though it was, I could not make out who it was, I was that stunned. The driver had a long riding whip, and he slashed it from left to right, cutting his way to the platform. He was sitting on the edge of the seat, but the man beside him was standing, holding a gun in his hand—a revolver, as it was shortly to appear. The man with the revolver was the Earl himself, Lord Ardmor, and the driver his cousin, whom I was later to know well, but knew then only by sight and name.

"Delaney," Ardmor shouted. "Get him in here with us, and get in yourself. The rest of them will be safe enough. He's the one this rabble is after."

Neither Richardson nor I could quite see what was happening, but we could make our safe assumptions, for we could see Parnell and Bob bend down, and then vanish from the platform.

"Jesus Christ," Richardson said, whether to himself or to me or to the Person named. The square was quiet, but that could not last long. "Kelleher!" he shouted. "Group your men, and give that carriage safe conduct. If any man lays a hand upon it, use what you need, use the carbines if you must."

By this time, Forrester had swung the carriage around, and was headed back down the length of the square towards the gates. Kelleher and his men did as well as could be expected, which was little indeed. One ruffian, running alongside, reached in, and seizing Parnell by the lapels began to pull him forward. Ardmor, as cool as though putting one of his brushes to canvas, levelled his revolver against the man's shoulder, and exploded it. "No!" Richardson shouted, and then shouted again, "Jesus Christ!" He ran forward, twisting and battering his way through the crowd, and swinging himself on board the carriage.

The crowd, friend and foe alike, had come fully alive by now, and were running after the carriage, but they were no match for it. And Kelleher, with a commendable promptness, placed his men in formidable rows, three deep, across the entranceway to the Castle.

None of us knew quite what to do, what to say—none of us, that is, save for Brendan Fogarty. Violence had been drained from the square, like pus following along the line of a surgeon's lancet. I found myself standing near Bill Regan, a strong-farmer from the lands beyond Clonbrony.

"What the hell do you make of that, Hugh?" he asked, cautiously, and as cautiously I answered, "Remarkable."

"They are safe away, so, Delaney and himself."

"They are, so," I said, "and I am glad of that, although I am sorry to have missed the speech."

He smiled. "You are a Parnell man," he said.

"I am."

"I am myself," he said, and the two of us smiled in relief.

"By God," Regan said, "that was a bloody mess. There might have been red murder done. Have you ever seen the like? That carriage, and the lord himself with a great bloody gun. What sort of times are we moving into at all?"

By this time the dignitaries had all left the platform. It had been an experience far more shattering for them than for any of the rest of us, and with but a single thought—"A large one, please!"—they had repaired to the Kilpeder Arms. All, that is, save Vincent, who had spotted me, and walked towards us. He was looking pleased as Punch. "By George, lads, the old stock have their uses, God be with the gentry and their unfathomable ways. Parnell and Ardmor are both Cambridge men; do you suppose that explains matters? But the bloody swiftness of the thing! Ardmor was after all in the army in his earlier days, but Forrester has always seemed to me a bit of an old maid. Not at this moment!"

It was then that Brendan Fogarty climbed upon the empty platform, and showed us his mettle for the first time. He had been Bob's able lieutenant in the Plan of Campaign, but much in Bob's shadow. Now we had our preliminary viewing of the creature himself, an overture to a career that extends to this very day, to 1904, with Brendan Fogarty representing us at Westminster. And be damned if he hadn't told his chosen lads to move people forward to the platform, lest he be speaking to the empty air. Until that moment, I had not seen him in the crowd;

barracking speakers was not in his style, nor swinging a blackthorn like a shillelagh at Donnybrook Fair.

"There we are, lads," he said, in that voice almost preternaturally deep for one still in his twenties, a voice as smooth as golden syrup. "There it is, spelled out for us like a school lesson in arithmetic. Who is Mr. Charles Stewart Parnell, and who stands by him? We know. Kilpeder has learned the lesson that is being learned in bitterness and sorrow in every town in Ireland. There they are, together, in the one carriage. Charles Stewart Parnell, and the landlord of this town, the alien whose ancestors looted and killed and slew across these valleys and hills, and Major Bloody British Army Richardson, the resident magistrate. There is Parnellism for you, all wrapped up in a neat package, and tied with a ribbon."

The crowd gave a shout of anger and approval, and why not? Most of Lanty's handful of Fenians, Lanty himself included, had drifted away, and those of them who remained, poor baffled republican shop boys, could not find it in their hearts to stand up for landlords and British officers.

I turned in fury to Vincent and Regan, but before I could speak, Vincent said, "Brilliant. Bloody brilliant. Little Brendan Fogarty he was an hour ago, and now Cato and Cicero and Marc Antony are but trotting along behind him. For sheer, utter gall, the man has a touch worthy of a Tully. My old fellow may have lost Bob, but he may have found another son."

And prompt upon the cue, the voice of golden syrup modulated itself, took upon itself tones of compassion and sadness, perhaps a faint bewilderment at the vagaries of human nature. He was hatless, and already going a bit bald, the hair combed carefully to conceal the skin, which would have shone in the tar barrels of flame which, miraculously, had kept themselves alight.

"I was sorry to see my old friend Bob Delaney in that carriage. My old friend and commander, I should call him, for the Plan of Campaign is a war, and Bob Delaney a soldier of Ireland who has served us and served his country well for many a year. He is not the only good man to stand by the fallen Lucifer towards whom once we looked for leadership. It does Bob Delaney credit that his loyalty is so fierce that it overwhelms his common sense. And that is the most painful part of all this: that Bob Delaney must be set aside, as a rotten limb is to be hacked off that the tree may flourish. But we know, God help him, where he is at this moment, and in whose company. He has separated himself from the plain people of Ireland, by his choice, not ours. God grant he find happiness in the cause he has chosen, and thanks be to God that we have not chosen it."

"And all that he did," Vincent cried with delight, "was to leap into a carriage to avoid being murthered by a mob." He unscrewed his handsome silver flask, and handed it to Regan, who received it with pleasure, and I was not myself averse to a stiff restorative. "No, no, lads," Vincent said, "the hour brings forth the man. Such is the lesson that history teaches us. The only lesson. No, this is genius, and it does not become us to begrudge it. Brendan Fogarty stands before us as the Nelly Melba of provincial oratory. And we will not long keep him in the provinces, more's the pity. The great world beyond will soon enough be making its call upon such blackguardry."

Fogarty himself seemed to share something of that view, for after he had finished, and the crowd had moved away to Conefry's or to Grennan's or to Moore's, he still stood upon the platform, as though amazed by what he had done.

Vincent strolled towards him and stood beneath the platform, looking up.

"That was grand stuff, Brendan. Not since the days of Dan O'Connell himself—"

"All right now, Vincent. It is late at night, and your sarcasm is wearying enough in broad daylight."

"Perhaps so," Vincent said, unexpectedly. "Good night to you, Brendan. Let us leave it at that. And I look forward without malice to the supreme test of your oratorical talents."

"Indeed," Fogarty said. "And what might that be?"

"Saying what you have just said to Bob Delaney's face."

And with that, Vincent tilted his glossy silk hat to one side of his head, with its tight, silver-streaked curls, and walked away, leaving Regan and myself to follow him.

35

[*Lionel Forrester/Emily Weldon*]

Social arrangements in the carriage were somewhat strained, and especially after Richardson, the resident magistrate, joined us—awkwardly, because he had leapt aboard on the run, but with an agility which most retired military men would have envied. Not that he was not welcome; for as I could see from the corner of my eye, he had taken a short-barrelled revolver from his coat pocket, and between him, and Tom beside me, we were well protected as we dashed through the town, and through the gates.

When we were some distance down the carriageway, I turned round, and saw that the constabulary sergeant had drawn up his men in a most effective line, and accordingly, I slowed the two mares to a trot and then to a walk. I experienced the intense relief that comes from the simple knowledge of having gained safety.

"Mr. Forrester," Richardson said. We had been once or twice at the same dinner parties—not here, but we had friends in common in Mallow. "Will you oblige me? I will be leaving you here."

I drew up, and he climbed down. The weapon was back in his pocket. It was dark now, but not yet so dark that we could not see each other clearly. He stood with one hand in his pocket, and the other on the carriage. He was looking up at Tom.

"That was very effective, Ardmor," he said. "It could have been an ugly scene." But clearly, he had something more to say, and Tom, with a short nod, sat watching him. "You will bear in mind, will you not, that law in the town of Kilpeder and in this barony is maintained by myself and by the barracks of the Royal Irish Constabulary?"

"Is it indeed?" Tom asked. "Forrester and myself were having a quiet game of chess, when my gatekeeper came rushing in to tell me that a party of men, members of Parliament most of them by the looks of their silk hats, was being menaced in the market square. The R.M. and the police had lost control, so he thought. Naturally, we didn't take his word for it, so we rode down out of curiosity. Things looked out of control to me."

"And so they were. You can be damned certain that that will never happen again, not if I have to call out the army. But you will keep my words in mind?"

"Ever call in at the Kilpeder Arms? There's a handsome print of the town in the taproom. The legend reads, 'The town of Kilpeder, property of the Earl of Ardmor.' "

Richardson permitted himself a bleak, frosty smile. "In a manner of speaking. Times have moved on a bit." He leaned into the carriage. "Sorry about all this, Mr. Parnell." Parnell looked at him without seeing him, and nodded. "Good night," Richardson said, and marched off down the carriageway, a brisk, military figure.

"Decent enough fellow," Tom said.

"Better than some," Delaney said.

"I haven't played chess since Oxford," I said, as I got us moving again.

"The rest of it was all true," Tom said. "Chess added a nice touch. Perhaps I should try my hand at novels, Lee?"

Tom had one of the servants take Parnell upstairs to clean himself, and rest a bit if he wanted to, and the three of us went into the library, where we stood awkwardly.

"A whiskey," Tom said to Delaney.

"No, thank you, no," Delaney said, stiffly. "Now that I know that he is safe, I will walk back into town. But I must call around for him in the morning. There will be men come to take him to a meeting at Askeaton, in Limerick."

"For God's sake, man," Tom said. "Take a whiskey. We all need one." And he splashed heavy measures all around, gestured towards the water pitcher and the siphon, and sat down in one of the heavy chairs before the fire, above which hung the portrait of Sylvia.

"What the devil do you mean, Askeaton?" I said. "That man is not fit to travel. He is tired, and he is ill. You can see it. Look into his eyes. He is sick to death."

"I remember this room," Delaney said suddenly, blurting it out. He gestured with his glass towards the easel. "Is that a new painting?"

"Yes," Tom said. "You cannot see it in this light. Gaslight would make it look wretched. Take a look in the morning."

"I am very grateful for your help," Delaney said. "For his sake, and for my own. I had never thought that you would—that you were on our side."

"I am not," Tom said. "Far from it. I meant what I said to Richardson. Kilpeder is an Ardmor town. I am damned if I will see it smeared by a rabble."

"A rabble," Delaney said heavily, as though carrying a boundary stone, stride by heavy stride, measuring out the immense distance between them.

A diversion seemed in order. "You may not have been on the terrace, Delaney," I said. "Step out here, it might interest you. Not that we will see much in this light."

Delaney turned towards Ardmor, who smiled thinly, and nodded. "I need a rest," he said. "Your driving is nerve-racking."

Delaney and I stood together on the terrace. A few first leaves from the sycamores had fallen on the flags. "And there we are," I said, pointing, towards scattered lights. "The town of Kilpeder."

"Property of the Earls of Ardmor," Delaney said, setting down another boundary stone.

"Twenty-five years ago," I said, "when the battle was on, *your battle*, Isabel and I, Tom's mother, stood upon the terrace here. We couldn't tell what was happening, shouts and gunfire. But towards the end, we saw the long column of soldiers in their red coats, mounting the rise of the Macroom road."

"That must have been a welcome sight to you."

"It was, of course, in a way. But not as intensely so as you might imagine. It all seemed very distant from us, improbable. Like the thing tonight. It was a tableau, nothing that could ever have affected us."

"It was a rebellion," Delaney said. "We were fighting to free the country. Or so we thought. Men died, went to prison. I went to prison myself. Not for long. The man who led us was there for years; they drove him mad."

Another boundary stone.

"He knows," I said. "Did you know that?"

He turned towards me at once, but did not answer. Fearful, no doubt, that he might be misunderstanding me.

"About Sylvia and yourself. He knows that you love each other."

He stood staring at me. The air had all evening been motionless, oppressive, but now there was a breeze. There was just light enough to make out, on the horizon, the outlines of the mountains.

"How can you be certain?"

"She told him," I said. "Sylvia tells Tom everything. They also love each other. In a different way, of course. No two loves are the same."

He was thunderstruck. He was realizing, all of a heap, that there was a part of her life which she kept separate from his, which she chose not to share with him. And I was discovering it myself, so to speak. Of the fullness of her love for Delaney, I had no doubt, and I had foolishly assumed that this had meant a full opening of the gates to him. But with Sylvia, you never knew. Her heart was a collection of intricate boxes; how foolish to imagine that all of them would spring open at a touch, however deep.

"I—" he began, and then stopped, and then said again, "I—"

I put my hand on his forearm. "No need to say anything. This isn't a conversation. I thought you should know, and I was almost certain that you did. Let's not talk about it. Let's go inside; this wind is getting to me."

And it occurred to me that I might, with the best of intentions, have said exactly the wrong thing; but it did not matter at the moment. Parnell had joined Ardmor before the fire, and for an hour we sat together, all four of us, and then, after Delaney had taken his leave, the three.

It was a curious hour, because he resolutely avoided politics; even Delaney's most urgent questions, even details about the next day, he turned aside. He had changed into a loose jacket which Tom's man had given him, and sat sipping hock, a chilled bottle beside him. He talked with Tom of Cambridge for a bit, which Tom had liked but Parnell had detested, and then of fox hunting, for which he had a passion, and cubbing, shooting, and, of all things, geology and mineralogy. He had a fixed, almost obsessive belief that the legendary gold of Wicklow was not exhausted, but lay somewhere waiting for the right touch, the proper procedures. "Science is making great strides these days, you know. I have a bit of a laboratory fitted up, and make my experiments. Someday, when all this is over, when Mrs. Parnell and myself have settled into Avondale . . ." Not "my wife and I," but the more vulgar, middle-class locution, "Mrs. Parnell and I," the phrase used to emphasise the fact. He and Tom had both been MFH's in their day, and every detail of the hunt, of dogs, horses, thickets, fences, seemed of interest to him. "Why, I remember once," he would begin, two spots of red quickening in his pale face above the tangled beard.

"You still hunt, of course. Of course you must. I was looking at your countryside when I was driving here from Macroom. Splendid country, splendid."

"Not much these days," Tom said wryly, "and I am out of the country a good deal. I have a place in Italy."

"Italy," Parnell said. "Never been there. Don't care for those foreign places. Jabber, jabber, jabber."

"Good light there," Tom said. "I paint."

"Paint, do you? Paint pictures? Curious. Still, a fellow has to keep himself busy, eh? Never cared much for art, music. Too old now, leopard can't change its spots. Biggar used to haul me to operas and music halls when I was first in Parliament, in the seventies. The operas weren't much, but the music halls were grand fun—comedians, and songs that made sense, all bright colours, spangles. Yes."

And after Delaney had left, and Parnell had helped himself to a third, final tall glass of hock, I realised what was happening. For an hour, he was in his old world, the world upon which he had turned his back that evening in 1876 when he rose to his feet in Parliament to defend the Fenians, an amiable young landlord from Wicklow, soft-spoken and well mannered. He had come home, in a sense, when he came for a few hours to this landlord's castle in West Cork, in fox-hunting country, hearing accents like his own, remembering out of the ugly day that he had seen rolling fields and challenging hedges, a horizon of far mountains.

"Dear, dear, yes," he said, and laughed. "Old Biggar. You chaps down here, the saying we have in Wicklow and Wexford is that you're not hunters at all, but moss troopers, whooping savages like those Blazers above in Galway." He nodded to himself. "Ever ride with the Blazers?"

"Once," Tom said, gently, as though my own thoughts were his. "They're not so daunting, really. Our lot here could show them a trick or two."

Suddenly, Parnell turned his head towards me. "You have a good whip hand, Mr. Forrester. It *is* Forrester, the fellow upstairs told me, fellow who lent me the jacket."

"I did once," I said.

"You do. Decent of you both, helping me out of that bother. Can't be helped; the country is in a devil of a mess. We'll see things righted. Don't expect you chaps see things as I do." I began to speak, but he shook his head. "Doesn't matter. I'll make an early night of it, if you don't mind. Limerick tomorrow. Never liked Limerick, don't know why."

Tom stood up, and with his hand on the bellpull said, "None of my business, Mr. Parnell, but if I were in your place I wouldn't do that. I'd rest here a few days, and then go home, get your strength back."

"Ah, but that's it, you see," he said. "You're not in my place. No one is. Can't call off the hunt because you've got the sniffles. Not if you expect to be master of the hunt for a while."

In the morning, Delaney and the two men from Limerick called for him in a closed carriage. It was raining, and mists hid the hills from view. Delaney ran in the rain to the portico, to bring him a waterproof and a hat. He struggled into the waterproof, and held the hat to look at it.

"Where did you find this one?" he asked.

"It's something to keep the rain away," Delaney said. "We couldn't find yours."

"Call these things wideawakes, don't they? Fenian hats, some people call them. Doesn't matter. They call me a Fenian now. What do you think," he asked, pulling on the soft, wide-brimmed hat, "Forrester? Ardmor? Look like a brigand, do I?"

But he did not. He looked like a sick man harried, who will not take orders from the doctor, or his family. When he climbed into the carriage, rain pelting upon him, half turning so that he could wave to us, a sudden gust of wind caught him, and he climbed hastily, awkwardly inside, and Delaney slammed shut the door. He had then a little more than a month to live.

"Flung it into her face, poor pet," Emily said to me. " 'How can you love me as you claim to, and talk it over with him? Are you sick, are the two of you sick?' He was stone-cold sober, but passion and anger had him talking like a wild man."

"And you," I said to her, "were standing with your ear to the door, like a common servant. I never expected such a thing from you, Emily. You disappoint me."

"What do you expect from me? I am a common servant. Take one into your bed, and you will get all the gossip from the kitchen."

"Stop that," I said. "That isn't what I mean, and you bloody well know it."

"If anything or anyone is hurting my Sylvia, I will be close by to her and you bloody well know it. Or you should."

"Yes," I said, and sighed. "Good night, Emily. They made up, you said; in the end, they made up. That's the important thing, isn't it?"

"I don't know," she said. "Perhaps. I don't know what the important thing is."

In the darkness, without a change in her voice, I knew that she had begun to cry. Our thighs were touching, and she moved hers gently, slowly away from mine. Presently, we both pretended sleep, and after a bit I did in fact drop off, but in the knowledge that she lay there, remembering, with wide, tear-brimming eyes.

I told you from the first, Bob, almost from the first, that I loved him. I never lied to you about that."

"That you loved him? That you still loved him? You told me that from the first?"

"Yes, from the first."

"That first night," Delaney said, "when we first had our arms around each other in a bed, you cried out, you cried, 'I love you,' and you meant me."

"That was the truth too," she said. "That is the truth that we speak when we scream out in bed, whether a woman or a man. But it is a special kind of truth. Later, when we lay side by side, holding each other, I tried to tell you, did tell you. You remember that."

"Yes," he said. "I remember. But everything changed. We fell in love."

"We fell in love," she repeated. "I think, you know, it was not in bed, but here in this drawing room, almost unexpectedly: you were doing something ordinary, poking at the fire I think, and I knew I loved you. I know I love you."

"And that is not something to talk about with—with—"

"Why not?" she asked. "Why ever not? There is something that I have with Tom that I cannot have with anyone else, not even you."

"And is there something special remaining from the others? From the American, and from Galantiere?"

"Oh, what is the use?" she asked, sorrow and anger warring in her voice. "What is the use? Do you mean, do I remember sleeping with them? I do indeed. Did I scream into Galantiere's ear? I did indeed.

I screamed louder than— I screamed. Is that what you want to hear?"

"And did you tell Ardmor about that? About screaming in Galantiere's ear?"

For a long space there was silence, and Emily heard footsteps; she knew them as Sylvia's pacing up and down in the small, elegant parlour. Emily could almost see her: she was wearing the salmon-coloured robe.

Suddenly, the footsteps stopped. "We almost never talk about *your* family, do we, Bob? Why is that? About the old man, who is bound now to thwart you. Once you told me that Conor was ill and again that he had taken a prize in school. For rhetoric. But we never talk about your family, do we? About Agnes. Agnes Delaney. Your wife."

"That isn't—" He stopped short.

"Isn't what? Isn't any of my business? Is that what you were going to say? Then why should Tom Ardmor be any of yours?"

"Because I love you, damn it, and you love me, and I thought that I had all of your love."

"Have you told Agnes about us? Do you make love to her? If you do not, does she not think it strange? If you do, does she scream in your ear? Tell me all about it; such things are always exciting."

"Stop it," Bob said. "For God's sake, stop that talk, Sylvia."

"You bloody hypocrite," she said. "You bloody Roman Catholic hypocrite, you bloody shop-boy hypocrite."

Emily heard something smash into the fireplace. God send it is not the Meissen, she thought.

"No," Delaney said, and in a different voice, as though he wanted to bring their boat into smoother waters. "We share the same bed, but that is all. There is nothing more to tell you, nothing but one thing. She thinks that I am—am seeing someone, and she wants no scandal. I cannot blame her for that. I was disappointed with my marriage—afterwards, you understand—and she grieves over that. I cannot help myself."

But Sylvia was not accepting the difference in his tone.

"Bloody woman," she said, "bloody virgin with a son to worship. I don't know why I ever started up with you. Do you think that I care nothing about scandal, that I am taking no risks? Or do you think that with me it doesn't matter. Doesn't matter what is known about Sylvia Challoner."

"Sylvia," he said, "Sylvia, stop it. I love you. Stop it. Love me."

" 'Love me'! You have drained meaning out of the word, Bob. Take me as I am. If you cannot love what I am, that is ill fortune for us both, because I cannot change. And I would not if I could."

Then Emily heard her begin to cry, and almost reached out to put her hand on the door, but knew that that would be fatal, for herself at least. "Oh, Bob, Bob, Bob, Bob," she heard Sylvia say, four times, through sobs, and heard Delaney speaking in a voice so low that she could not make out his words. And that is why Lee Forrester had said to her, to Emily, that they had after all made up in the end, had they not, and that was the important thing after all, was it not?

Yes, Emily thought, herself no longer crying, but unhappy, feeling her eyes grow heavy, knowing that she would soon be asleep. She ran a hand along the length of her body, her throat, her two breasts, the nipples almost erect, for her unhappiness was edged with the erotic, her belly, her thighs, long, too-slender legs. Then she placed the hand against her cheek, and fell asleep, marvelling at the multiplicity of ways by which people made themselves unhappy.

36

[Hugh MacMahon/Robert Delaney]

There is a man named Jeremiah Dempsey who has a huckster's shop at the far end of town, where I will call in once every three weeks for some tobacco, or wicks for my lamps, that sort of thing, but mostly for the chance to exchange a few words with Jeremiah, who is not given to the flimsy speculation which is the ready coin of his calling, but possesses, rather, a gnomic, or at least an eccentric, wisdom, although I could never, of course, persuade Patrick Prentiss of this, and so I have never led him in for the purchase of a few pen nibs or a ball of twine. And I may well be wrong about Jeremiah, his wisdom, as I affect to think of it, an absence rather than a presence, as with his teeth.

Jeremiah, at any rate, believes that ruin came upon us with Parnell's death. He is as certain of this as might be a tribesman casting his bones before a desert hut. He reverts often to the subject, or perhaps he believes that it is of absorbing interest to me.

"Was it not pictured for us in the *Cork Examiner,* master? That great crowd following after the body up to the big graveyard that they have in Dublin? There were not so many who supported him towards the close of his day, but all who had supported him and then turned from him were affrighted, and walked in grief behind the coffin, fearful of what was to befall. And you know as well as I do myself, the stories that have been carried here that the coffin was so heavy that six men, whatever their strength, could not lift it up from the ground, let alone to their shoulders. And when at last they could lower it into the grave, on that wild day, did not a star fall from the sky in broad daylight, and was not the sky, where all had been gloom, bright with weird lights? Now these are facts, master."

Facts they are of our life as a people, whether they happened or not, and I have more than once told Patrick that he ignores them at his peril. But Patrick smiles. "John Dillon told my father a few years ago," he says, "that he was at a Wagner opera in Munich and saw Parnell there, and fellows drinking in pubs in Irishtown and Ringsend will tell you that he was off with the Boers, fighting the English in South Africa. You always have such legends when—" Then he stops.

"When kings die, Patrick. When kings die. And this one was not cut down in battle by the enemy. We slew him ourselves. Perhaps there was need that we should slay him, but slay him we did. I will admit, I grant you, that the notion of Parnell at any opera, leave alone Wagner, is grotesque, but John Dillon is an educated man, and a gentleman, far above the ruck of them. Though his conscience in this matter may not be entirely pure. I don't know."

But Jeremiah knows. "Now, master, and I say this to you in privacy, two old fellows who have had dealings for years and years past. I am a William O'Brien man myself, and when the dirty business came out in 'ninety, I kept my mouth shut—what matters the views of a huckster?— but I hardened my heart against Parnell. I say that plainly to you. He trod down his boot upon the most sacred of the commandments, by which the family itself is held together by God's ordinance, and because of what he did, the people were divided, and they are divided to this day. He may have been a bad king, but by Jesus, he was a king. And we took our knives to him."

There may be something to all that. Not all of the wisdom of the human race reposes in Oxford University, whatever Patrick Prentiss may think to the contrary. And I know myself, for reasons which need not depend upon Jeremiah Dempsey's flyspecked auguries, that when the news came to Ireland, on October seventh, that Parnell had died the midnight before, at Brighton, a silence fell upon the country that all remember, and that lasted long days after his burial in Glasnevin on the eleventh, a Sunday, the day upon which, at Cabinteely, he had promised that he would return, which added to the superstitious hysteria that lay just beneath the silence.

But I also—for reasons that may be rational or may not, how can I tell?—trace backward all that befell us in the months that followed upon the death of Parnell, as one might follow a twisting thread of yarn. It is a pattern which only later did I perceive. At first, it seemed to affect Bob only, because he had thrown in his lot with Parnell, and called himself, as he would until the week of his death, Parnell's man.

He was at Glasnevin for the burial, of course, one of the leaders of the delegation from Cork, an important delegation, to be sure, because Parnell had been member of Parliament for that vainglorious Lilliput. And so he had stood close to the grave.

"No, there were no weird lights," he told me later, "and no star dropping in the light of day. But there was a miracle, by God. Indeed there was. If all those who mourned for Parnell dead had stood by Parnell alive, he would not have wasted away his life, battering back and forth from one town to the next, enduring the insults of men that he had pulled up from the bogs. There was your miracle, by Jesus."

There seems never to have been a thought that what had come to be called Parnellism had died with Parnell, and Bob, like his other followers, flung themselves fiercely into preparations for the general election which was to come at the beginning of the summer.

"But what is it, Bob?" I asked him once. "Can you clearly and plainly—speaking, as it were, to a person rather than an audience—can you tell me what is Parnellism without Parnell?"

"We stand," Bob said, "for an Ireland without twisters, without chancers the likes of Healy or gombeen men the likes of Dennis Tully. We stand for an Ireland which does not beg favours from Holy Willie Gladstone, which is not ashamed of the fight that was made in this town in 'sixty-seven."

"Bob," I said, "I am with you, you know that. But I am damned if you have told me what Parnellism is."

Bob smiled, with a rueful honesty. "Parnellism," he said, "is telling the likes of Tim Healy and Brendan Fogarty to go fuck themselves. That may not be much of a program, but as things stand at the moment, it is all the country has to be going on with."

Well, I thought, why not? A memory rose up before me of Brendan Fogarty standing upon the platform from which Charles Stewart Parnell had been driven off, his hair neatly combed and oiled.

And Bob, despite the claims which London was making upon him through all of these months, did a remarkable task of drawing support behind himself, forcing from Fogarty a reluctant agreement that Bob was by law in control of the Plan funds for distribution to the evicted tenants; and, in countryside where such matters are not lightly forgotten, he reminded farmers that he had himself brought the Plan to the barony, with Fogarty but taken on later as deputy, by Bob's nomination. And indeed, the Land League itself, ten years or more before, had been Bob's work. He had been here when he was needed, and he had been since the year 'sixty-seven; for in this final fight, with his back to the wall, he did not burden himself with overfastidiousness, but wrapped the green flag around me, boys, and at Fogarty's meetings, Bob had his brass band— cornets, drums, and all—to parade into the market square with the march- ing version of "Clonbrony Wood," and "High upon the Gallows Tree," and "Out and Make Way for the Bold Fenian Men." Poor Fogarty could fight back with the ballads about the 1798 rebellion, "The Rising of the Moon" and "The Croppy Boy." After all, Bob could scarcely claim to have marched with Father Murphy and General Humbert and Dauntless Kelly, the Boy from Killane; but musically speaking, he held the sway.

And when it came to vilification, he displayed a talent which he had not heretofore needed, because this was nationalist territory, the loyalist vote being derisory, as the saying is; but Bob was now the choice of a minority only, unless he bettered matters, and he fought with a vitupera- tive energy which suggested that he had spent his years in the House listening attentively to Healy. The Boy Orator was his name for Fogarty, and by variations worked upon it, he turned Fogarty's debut upon the platform from triumph into farce. In all this, he had Vincent as his able seconder, for Bob had a few scruples left, but Vincent had none. "The altar boy," Vincent would say, buying a large round in Conefry's. "Have you ever noticed, lads, how wonderfully smooth his cheeks are, as though he had no need to shave? Lucky fellow. Do you never fear for him, should he ever be let loose in London, with its painted women, and boys with strange wares for purchase? Drink up, men."

So the autumn and the long winter wore themselves away, and we came towards spring. How easy it is, when speaking of the Split, of manoeuvres and strategies, of Bob contriving this and Brendan Fogarty contriving that, how easy it is to imagine that the very heart and center of Kilpeder pulsed with such concerns. When in truth, of course, we were a market town in a barony of pasturelands and hilly farms, with spring planting to look forward to in the endless winter, and dull farmers' sons who must have the elements of civilised knowledge beaten into them by rote and by caning. Even Bob himself—and Fogarty as well, of course, on his side of the divide—had the ordinary concerns of a solicitor, although more and more Bob was compelled to depute these to Jamesey Gannon, the bright young lad whom he had taken into his shop. We had our gatherings at Christmastime, and even, on the Eve itself, one stiff, formal hour all of our lot together in Inchigeelagh House, with all this done for Agnes's sake and her mother's, Bob and old Tully contriving a faint civility which Vincent did nothing to nourish, recognising it as an anomaly, a moment's deference to the season, but rather stood back and watched with cheerful, veiled malice as his father and Bob agreed upon the mildness of the weather, granted the time of year that was in it.

And on the earliest Friday in March, the fourth, before a single road had begun to thaw, I took my jaunting car up into the hills, along the road which skirted Clonbrony Wood, to visit with an old Gaelic speaker of whom I had become fond, Taedgh Morkan and his wife Bridget, toothless, small-faced, round as an apple that face was, and parchment-pale where it was not a pippin red. Two full bottles I had brought with me and a ham which Mary had baked for the occasion. She would not accompany me, although she had met the Morkans and liked them; for the sad truth of the matter was that not only did she have no Gaelic, but she was incapable of learning more than an ill-spoken sentence or two, although her French was serviceable, for she was a convent-bred girl, and had early on been instructed that the French language was a delicate and graceful one, a suitable accomplishment for a young lady of middle rank (as such matters went in Munster), but Gaelic was the tongue of herds and fisherfolk on the western seacoasts. And such feelings die hard, not to be rooted up by different ideas. She had learned by rote the words to some of the great songs of the Gaelic—"Una Bhan," for example, and the like—and she sang them well; she was a fine singer, spirited and shapely of sound, but her heart was with Balfe and Moore and Schumann. And truth to tell, she may have sung "Una Bhan" well, God rest her, but could never give it the heart-shattering utterance that I have heard in such farmhouses as that of Taedgh Morkan, where the earth itself seems to have seized upon the singer as an instrument of utterance, our particular earth, hills, horizons, which belong to us alone, and which no others can ever fully enter.

A long night we made of it, as we always did, and neighbours called in, among them John Sweeney, a noted virtuoso upon the fiddle, and also Tom Timoney, the storyteller, who was not shy before me, because I never carried with me notebook and pencil, like the gatherers who were now, in these years, the early nineties, beginning to swarm upon the Gaelic-speaking regions, and who seemed to find some bizarre partnership between poverty and what they called the "racial purity of the Gael." It is well for them that they came only in their insulated summer holidays, or else this "racial purity" notion would have taken a battering.

"Tell me now, master," Tom Timoney said to me, "is it true that Charles Parnell took away the wife of an Englishman and carried her into his own bed?"

"It is true," I said.

"Well, there was a blow well struck," he said.

"But it was not an Englishman at all, but an Irishman, an O'Shea of Limerick."

"Oh, dear, dear," Bridget Morkan said. "That is a different matter indeed. The Church is fierce to condemn such matters."

"What sort of husband was he at all who would allow such a thing?"

"I would not know that," I said, "but he carried a sword in the Queen's army, and his father was a gombeen man in the county Limerick."

Timoney spat into the fireplace. "I hold no grievance against a man who carries the Queen's sword, but gombeen men deserve whatever fate befalls their sons."

Mary and Vincent, and Bob as well in moments of vexation, used often to say that I made a cult of those mountainy Gaelic-speakers, discovering a slantwise wisdom in what was but their state of primitive deprivation, but I differed from that point of view, and I differ to this day.

I have several times since then tried to remember the next morning, the Saturday, taking my bread and tea with the Morkans, and riding home in the clear March air, spring not a presence but a vivid hope; but nothing lingers of it in particular, save a memory of the clarity of the hills at my back, the distant town coming slowly into view, the mild wonder I felt, and not for the first time, at passing along Clonbrony Wood, at a distance from me not in space only but years, the Wood reduced to the ordinary, the habitual. Clarity of air, March air, that is all that I think that I remember, and even that may be illusion, because I look back to it now as the very edge and border of our lives together in growth and possibility, Mary's and mine and even our sons' a bit, but certainly the edge for Bob and Agnes and Vincent and old Dennis Tully. And the edge, although for years he would not have reason to know it, for Bob and Agnes's son, who now styles himself Conor Tully-Delaney. And he does so in part, in good part, because of the visit which, two days later, on the Monday, Michael Patrick Murphy paid upon Bob in his office.

On the Sunday, after Mass, Bob told me that he was expected, and shrugged. There were visits back and forth between the two factions, unofficially, as soldiers will meet under a flag of truce, exchange tobacco and newspapers; but there are factions and there are factions, and Mike Murphy was not merely a Healy man, indeed, one distantly related to Healy by cousinage—not that hundreds were not so related in that spawning, sprawling clan—but a close friend and commercial associate, to speak with delicacy, of old Dennis Tully, and a man, himself a solicitor, with whom Bob had often had occasion to deal back in those days—remote now they seemed, two or three years in the past—when he had himself been Dennis's solicitor.

"A dreary way to begin the week," Bob said, "a morning's chat with Mike Murphy," and neither of us thought more of the matter. A morning's chat, because Bob was planning to take the afternoon train from Cork, being expected back in London.

Neither can I remember that morning clearly, save Kilpeder's amiable, talkative after-Mass sociability, the square clear and clean, the obelisk commemorating the coming-of-age of that now long-dead earl of Ardmor, sparkling in March sunlight, save at one edge of its base where a dog had voided upon it, the distressing sort of mild accident which one contrives not to notice if one hopes to keep alive a sense of beauty in an Irish market town.

It was the edge of spring, right enough. The day before, as I was riding home, I could see from the crown of the hill, the gardeners at work in the demesne, but Lord Ardmor had left months before, and the main gates were closed. An hour later, at home, as Mary was wetting the tea, I tried, idly, to imagine what an Italian hill town was like, with my imagination having for its straw and bricks nothing save some books of travel sketches, one of them by Lionel Forrester as it happens, and a magic-lantern performance which Mary and I had seen in Macroom a few years before—castles, hills, Renaissance squares with fountains of ornate marble, everything a sepia stained with unconvincing, contrived colouring.

What passed between Bob and Mike Murphy, Michael Patrick Murphy, to be famed in later years as the Merchant Prince of Cork City, and his son now in a highly successful partnership with Conor Tully-Delaney, I had a full report upon; but over the years, drunk or sober, Bob would add bits and pieces to it, whether remembering it with hallucinatory, unfading exactitude or else his imagination fabricating later appropriate details. Thus, long afterwards, a few years before he died, he said to me, "Do you know, before Jamesey showed him into my office"—there was no need to identify subject or scene—"I was attending to a few odds and ends of paper, and a cur was yelping outside, on the footpath, just beyond my window. I have forgotten that all these years. But I remember it clearly now, because it was distracting me, and I was about to get up and go to the hall door, and give a shout to it. Is it not strange, Hughie, that I should remember that now?"

A h, Bob, I have always envied you that desk," Murphy said, "that one and the twin to it in your front parlour. A desk gives to a man in our profession a great sense of comfort, like a quarterdeck to a ship's captain."

"You are looking well, Mike," Bob said.

"You are yourself, Bob," Murphy said, "although a bit strained, if you will pardon me for saying so. Tis an exhausting racketing life you must have to live, what with your legal responsibilities here in town, and the business of the Plan, which you took from Brendan Fogarty's shoulders and replaced upon your own, and on the top of all that, your various labours in London on our behalf." His tone was genial, with no more than the fleck of malice which Cork adds unfailingly to conversation, like a cook giving a swipe with the pepper mill.

"It suits me well enough," Bob said. "Jamesey is a skilful lad with day-to-day matters. He has the makings of a fine solicitor. He puts me in mind of myself at his age."

"And of course," Mike said mildly, "it must take a good bit of strain off your own shoulders that you are no longer managing Dennis Tully's various legal necessities, neither yourself nor Jamesey. A sad day, when the parts of a family divide."

"I am thankful for your solicitude," Bob said, who had himself been reared in the same malicious and peppery county. "I take it that you have already expressed it to Dennis."

"I have, of course," Murphy said. "He has been good enough to give me a bed last night and tonight, and then back with me to the city."

Bob said to me, in the late hallucinatory years, that he had had at times, with drink taken on his own, the fancy that it was not Murphy at all but Healy, because Murphy had taken to cultivating a neat little Healy beard and moustache, and even from time to time, as upon this occasion, a pince-nez, secured by a gilt chain, which he would take off to flourish, it catching the pale, mote-flecked sun.

"It was good of you to call in on me," Bob said, "things being as they are."

"Ach, sure Bob, are we not all good Irishmen? Underneath?"

"No doubt," Bob said. "If you dig deep enough. I have no geological skills."

Murphy gave him a complicated smile, as though to say, A nice savage touch, but it is a bit early for the blades.

"Can I be of help to you, Mike?" Bob asked.

"You can," Murphy said. "You can be of help to me, and to our poor afflicted country, and last but not least you can be of help to yourself."

"Indeed," Bob said, "and how am I to provide this benefaction?"

"You know well enough," Murphy said, shifting his small feet in their glossy elastic-sided boots, and by accident knocking over his portfolio, small, black, and shiny like the boots. "You know well enough why I asked for this conversation, Bob. I am asking you to withdraw from the election, and to give Brendan Fogarty a clear run for the seat, with naught to oppose him save the loyalists."

"I have been the member for Kilpeder for some years now," Bob said, "since the mid-eighties, and have managed matters to my own satisfaction, despite the recent strains which you have taken notice of. I intend to continue so."

"Bob, Bob," Murphy said, taking off the pince-nez, not to flourish them, but to polish them with his handkerchief. Another Healyite flourish, as Bob later informed me. "You will split the vote between yourselves, Brendan and yourself. That wretched loyalist Chute will not have so much as a look-in. But Brendan will take the sway. You know that, you are no fool."

"I do not know it at all, Mike," Bob said. "And even were I to lose this time round, it would matter sweet damn-all. I would be after Brendan with tongs and hammer. He frightens easily, Brendan does."

"Now look here," Murphy said, putting away the handkerchief, and much of his banter vanishing with it. "You chaps may pick up a few seats here and there: Johnny Redmond is safe, and a few others that we could name—twelve seats, fifteen at the outside. We will take the rest, all of it."

"We will," Bob echoed him. "And who is 'we'? At the moment 'we' is anyone who had a knife drawn when the Chief was down. But that will be a short-lived 'we.' Dillon and O'Brien are already straining against the common yoke that they are shouldering for this election, and next time around, there will be 'Dillonites' and 'O'Brienites' as well as 'Parnellites.' Not to mention your own sweet-scented champion and kinsman, Timothy Michael Healy, Esquire. So long as he is alive, there will be a 'Healyite' party. No, no, Mike. Your lot will have to deal with my lot, sooner or later. Now, there is politics dished up and served as Tim and yourself like to have it, straight and unadorned. No tiresome appeals to patriotism; we'll leave that sort of thing to Dillon and O'Brien. And to the memory of the Chief."

"No offence taken, Bob."

"Offence was given, Mike. You are not very alert this morning."

"I need no lessons in patriotism from you, Robert Delaney, and so I hear none. If you think that all this is to me but a matter of success with the voters, you misjudge me, and you misjudge Tim. The English were not uppermost in Tim's mind when he broke with the Chief, nor in Dillon's nor O'Brien's. And certainly not in Michael Davitt's, as you will yourself admit. We did not even require the voice of the bishops to remind us of our duty."

Bob sighed. "The past is the past. Let us take one morning's holiday from it."

"This is a Catholic nation, Bob, and would not be led by a confessed adulterer, a man who persisted in his adultery until the day of his death."

Bob pressed his arched, tensed fingers upon the edge of his desk.

"All right, Mike. Let us give all of this conversation a holiday. I am sick of such talk. You can carry it back with yourself to Tim, with a message that he is a sanctimonious blackguard. He will never plant his flag in this town whilst I am here to root it up."

Bob's recollection of what happened next was the same a few hours later and in the hallucinatory, alcoholic future: that Murphy looked away from him, beyond him, beyond the window with its gilt lettering. And for a moment, Bob thought, What is there to see out there, save a few old ones lounging against Conefry's door, waiting for opening time, shop fronts, perhaps a woman, shawled like a Mohammedan, hurrying along the footpath, the obelisk, a bit of demesne wall, and, in the opposite direction, Tully's shop, with the young lad who was his successor brooming dust devils through the opened doors?

"And neither will the decent Irish people of Kilpeder permit themselves to be represented in Parliament by an adulterer."

Bob looked at him for a moment, stunned. It was as though the words that had been spoken lay in a heap in his brain, and he had painfully to assemble them.

"Parnell, Bob," Murphy said in a gentle voice, as though to an invalid. "Parnell was destroyed by his adultery; and the word itself, and far more the condition of spiritual evil which it bespeaks, is a present stench in the nostrils of this country, noisome and overpowering. Parnell was given fair warning and timely warning that he should step back, that he should step aside, that he should quit politics, for a time at least. He was destroyed not only by his adultery but his pride, that he would not take the good counsel that was offered him by those who wished him well and wished Ireland well."

"We are not talking of Parnell," Bob said. "Set Parnell aside and come to your point."

"We have come to our point, Bob. You know that and I know it."

Say this for him, Bob said later. He got no pleasure from his errand, not that I could see. It seemed to pain him indeed, as if he would willingly have left it there, with the point made, and taken his leave of me if I had bid him. Tim now, Tim would have savoured every minute of it, every ugly word which he would feel himself compelled to speak, in defence of purity and Catholic Ireland. But Mike's pince-nez had fallen from his nose, and he let it dangle from its chain, as though he had not noticed. He looked directly at me as he spoke, but now the square had caught his attention again.

"No," Bob said, "I do not know it. You are going to have to spell it out for me."

"If you wish it so, Bob. If you wish it so. For a number of years, you have been conducting an illicit relationship with a lady whose name need not be mentioned, here or anywhere, unless you will have it so. A married lady, as you are yourself a married man, a father."

Bob said nothing. He was aware that his fingertips, still pressing upon the desk, had begun to hurt, the pains passing up along the nerves and muscles of his arms. He let them fall into his lap.

"I know, Bob. I know. You are wondering which would accord you the greater pleasure: to shoot me, or twist off my head. But there we are."

"And your sole concern," Bob said, "the sole concern of yourself and that little Bantry rat, is the moral purity of Kilpeder's parliamentary representation."

"This is a world, Bob," Murphy said, addressing, through glass, the market square, "in which things do not lie in neat little moral compartments. We have both been solicitors long enough to know that. We have both been in politics that long. Life is a mess."

"Fortunately for scavengers," Bob said.

"Fire away, Bob. Use what words you will. This is a shock, I know."

"I do have a mind to do you violence," Bob said. "Have you no shame, boy, to sink to such a weapon? But of course you do not. I have seen Healy at work, I have heard him. And this for the sake of a miserable seat in the London parliament."

"You are right, Bob. The seat is miserable; it is not worth the sacrifice of your good name. And it is not even at issue. Brendan will take this seat, come what may."

"Ah, but you are taking no chances, are you?" Bob shifted in his seat. "Tell me, does Brendan know about this visit of yours, and its purpose?"

"What is it that you call him, the Altar Boy? No, there is no need to shock the Altar Boy. Not for the moment."

"More to the point," Bob said. "Does Dennis Tully know?"

"He does not," Murphy said, in a quiet, level tone, "and please God he will not. You have crossed him sorely, the man who raised you up from the dirt. No, he will not hear of this from me or mine. God send you do not break his heart. If it becomes a common scandal, he will hear, of course."

"Oh? And how would that happen?"

"How would it happen indeed! We have just now seen the country split in two by the scandal leaked forth from a divorce court, and yet you ask how would it happen."

"There is a difference," Bob said, choosing his words with difficulty. "Your drama requires a local Captain O'Shea, and there is none."

"Oho!" Murphy said. "So that is the way of it. Strange indeed are the ways of the gentry. You have been moving in strange company, my lad."

Bob shrugged. He picked up his letter opener, a curved Oriental knife of razor-sharp steel that Mary and I had given him one year as a Christmas gift. He balanced it between his forefingers, drawing a faint pleasure, a relief, in the prick of the point.

"Then it would indeed become ugly. Ugly indeed, Bob. Matters would reach a stage that none of us would wish, least of all the lady in question."

He drew back his chair a few inches, in terror Bob thought at first, as though he could read through the eyes the murder in Bob's mind, but it was only so that he could bend down to bring his portfolio to his lap, open it, and take out a thick bundle, with tape wound around and around it and then tied in a knot. Red tape, the colour of blood.

"There are ways, Bob," he said, in the same gentle voice, like a surgeon taking a knife to a friend. "There are ways. The . . . the material here. There are ways in which such material can become known, in a general sort of way at least. Not in the *Cork Examiner* or the *Freeman's*

Journal, of course, nor any paper that would find its way into a Catholic parlour. But there are ways. We know them; we are both lawyers; we have handled a few messy cases in our time. Good God, come to think of it, were we not once joined together cleaning up one of Vincent's . . . what shall we call them?"

He placed the bundle of papers on the desk, and before he could draw his hand away, Bob brought the knife down, stabbing in full fury. It was by chance only that it missed Murphy's hand, instead skewering the papers and driving itself into the desktop.

As Murphy had said, they were both of them solicitors, and Bob had a sick, clear notion of what he would find if he unwrapped the tape. Years afterwards, when Bob had been found dead, it fell to Jamesey Gannon and myself, as the executors named in his will, to go through his papers, and Jamesey it was who found the bundle shoved into the back of one of the deep bottom drawers, dust-coated, dust smearing the ribbon as he drew his hand across it, the stab of the knife a deep gouge. I cut the ribbon with my own penknife, and unfolded the bundle. It took scarcely longer than a glance to see what it was—photographic reproductions of documents of diverse size and character—the reports of a private enquiry agent in London, a few hotel bills, and letters written in a vivid, jagged scrawl. I swept up the lot without reading them, and carried them to the fireplace, where Jamesey touched a match to them. They burned like dry kindling.

"I doubt if he ever read them," I said to Jamesey. "I have a feeling that we were the first to untie the knot."

"I remember them lying on the desk that morning," Jamesey said. "I was in my own room, over there, the room that Bob used as a bedroom this past year, and I heard him roar out to me. 'Jamesey,' he shouted, 'Jamesey.' I came out on the trot, and there was Mike Murphy sitting drawn as far back in his chair as he could press himself, his arm shaking, and Bob risen to his feet and looking ready to murder someone, himself by preference. The bundle was lying there on the desk between them, and the knife driven through it, no doubt, and into the desk, but mahogany is tough wood, and the knife had fallen over and lay upon the papers."

The scar was still there, on the top of the desk, which Jamesey and I had had to wipe clear of dust and grime before we could set to work.

" 'Yes, Mr. Delaney,' I said, as calmly as I could. These were early days and he was still 'Mr. Delaney' to me. 'Jamesey,' he said, 'do you know who this is?' he asked. 'I do indeed, sir,' I said; 'good morning, Mr. Murphy.' 'Good morning, James,' he said, in a voice calm but small. 'He is also a man unfit to sit in a Christian room. Fetch his coat and hat for him, and make certain that he is never again admitted to this office.' I did as I was bid, but the wits were frightened out of me. Bob was my employer, of course, and a member of Parliament and a great local hero with a reputation for controlled and murderous fury. But Michael Patrick Murphy was a most powerful man as well, no one whom a young solicitor would wish to cross. But Murphy said quietly, 'Do that like a good fellow, Jamesey. Bring me my things.' When I brought them in, he was standing, facing Bob. 'You are upset, Bob,' he said; 'most understandable. Now, do nothing rash, think matters over. No rush at all; take a week or two to think matters over.' He nodded to me before he left. Bob stood there, behind his desk, and then, on a sudden impulse so it seemed, he followed Murphy out into the square. God knows what words they spoke, but when Bob came inside, he looked worse than ever, black with rage, and no outlet for it."

God knows, and I know, what words were spoken between them. And Vincent knew, because one way or another, the two of us had the matter laid out for us by Bob.

"Say nothing," Murphy said to him. "Talk will do nothing, Bob. Take a look there, towards the far end of the square." And there, of course, at the far end, was the Protestant church, and the gates into the demesne of Ardmor Castle, the falcon-guarded gates as I always think of them, in Homeric fashion. "Think, boy," Murphy said. "Say nothing to me, but think what I am saying. Plain speaking is best. She is married to the landlord of Kilpeder. Nothing will wash that away—not Clonbrony Wood, not Fenian pikes, not the boycotting, nothing. You have fouled your nest, boy."

"Last year," Bob said, "you brought down an eagle, yourself and Healy and your gang. Was not he enough for you?"

"That is rant," Murphy said. "Listen to yourself and you will hear it. I am as good an Irishman as you are, better perhaps, as I know that Tim Healy is a better one. Since 'eighty-six, since the Galway election, Tim Healy has held that Ireland is greater than any leader. Leaders are not eagles, Bob. They are men, and if they stand in the roadway, impeding progress, they must be made to step aside."

"You sanctimonious son of a bitch," Bob said. "Get out of my town."

"Your town is it? It is the Earl of Ardmor's town, or else, although

[723]

the Earl does not know it yet, it is Dennis Tully's town. But it is not your town. You can test out what I am saying, but you will be a fool if you do."

"A while ago," Bob said, "a friend asked me what Parnellism stood for, and I told him that it was a way of telling Tim Healy and Brendan Fogarty to go fuck themselves. I overlooked you."

"If it gives you any pleasure to say that, Bob . . ." Murphy shrugged. "Let us leave it at that. My best wishes to your good wife."

And Bob watched him walk away, up the length of the square towards Inchigeelagh House. "Nemesis comes in all shapes and sizes," Bob said to me later. "Do the ancient Greeks take that into account, Nemesis with pince-nez, and little bandy legs?" But there was nothing I could say to him in response. He wanted no real response, of course, but only a friend's company—advice, perhaps. But I had no advice for him; I was out of my depth. Mary might perhaps have had a word for him, better comfort perhaps than a man could give. But he had made me promise that I would tell her nothing of this. He insisted always, from the first to the last, that he was unashamed of his love for the lady in question, but I suspect that a part of him was, a part of him was a country lad from a farm, and that lad did not want Mary to know about the entirety of it, Chelsea and Murphy's filthy bundle.

As matters stood, he let the boundary date which Murphy had given him drift dangerously close, for he spent the week following in London, in the House and with Sylvia, saying nothing to her, not knowing what to say, not knowing what he could do, and then he came back to Kilpeder. Much of that final Friday, he sat alone in his office, Jamesey told me later, behind his desk, not working. Jamesey knew, of course, that some thunderbolt had fallen, but had no notion of its nature.

He made a cup of tea, and brought it in to Bob. "If there is anything I can do to be of help to you, Mr. Delaney."

It took Bob a few moments to grasp Jamesey's words, and then he shook himself. "Oh, thank you, no, Jamesey. We won't work today, Jamesey. Not really. Take the day off. There is nothing that matters, on your desk or mine."

Nothing, Jamesey thought, save a gouge upon Bob's fine desk, the width of a knife blade. Jamesey hesitated himself for a moment, picking his words.

"What I mean, Mr. Delaney, is, if there is anything I can do, any way I can be of service to you. You have friends in this town, and you have followers. You have earned them."

"Thank you," Bob said, and smiled.

It was almost, Jamesey said, the smile that you would give a child, a small child who loved the world but was wrong about it.

[724]

And so it was that Jamesey decided that the best thing to do, the thing that would make the world appear normal and safe, was to accept his employer's offer of a half day, and take himself off. The very last thing he did, as he was walking towards the hall door, was to take from a small boy the note that Vincent had sent to Bob from Brierly Lodge.

"I cannot remember what I said precisely," Vincent told me, "but I pitched it as strong as I could: that it was urgent that I see him on the weekend, that Brierly was a better venue than Kilpeder, and I implored him, if he valued our friendship, to come there. He must have known that I had somehow gotten wind of things, and I am surprised it did not occur to him that I was luring him to Brierly that I might avenge my sister's honour in peaceful surroundings. But be that as it may, he arrived in the late afternoon, riding that bay which was his pride in those days, do you recall it, and giving it dreadful punishment. I was watching him from the window, and twice he put the whip to it. He was never an elegant horseman, but he had always behaved decently towards his mounts. In the distance, at the far end of the avenue, I saw my gatekeeper staring after him."

They sat beside the fire, holding large whiskeys, and Bob's uncut by water, as Vincent told Bob of the package of photographed papers which Michael Patrick Murphy had sent to him from Cork City.

"I took but a look at them, Bob, only so long a look as to confirm what Murphy said in his letter which accompanied them, and then in there with them." He nodded to the fireplace.

Bob sat looking at him, holding his tumbler in his two hands, saying nothing.

"Bob," Vincent said, having taken a long sigh. "Let us begin with one fact. Let us leave Agnes out of this. She is my sister, and we are a close family, however matters may stand between the old fellow and myself. But what is done is done, and my concern at the moment is for you. That gang is out to get you; you must knuckle under or go down. And they are putting pressure on you. Sending that muck to me was a way of putting pressure, although Murphy wrapped up all in loathsome expressions of concern for the family, and especially poor Agnes, but even more, a final blow upon the head of my long-suffering father. When the hell did his long-suffering begin?—but that is neither here nor there."

"Nothing is here or there," Bob said, speaking at last. "I think that I am drifting in space."

"Well, you are not, boy. You can put that notion out of your mind directly. You are sitting here in a house a few miles outside the town of Kilpeder in the county of Cork. And what you must decide is whether or not you will make it known that you do not intend to stand for reelection. There you are."

"There I am," Bob said.

"Well?"

"Those bastards," Bob said. "The same bloody bastards who brought down the Chief, and this time, they are using filthier weapons. There is a word in law for what they are doing."

"Forget that, Bob. You are the lawyer, not me, but you can forget that."

"If I could," Bob said, "I would pull down the whole damned temple, like blind Samson."

"You can," said Vincent. "That lies within your power. It is an apt parallel: you would destroy yourself and Agnes, the old fellow no doubt, and most certainly you would destroy the lady who has your affection."

"My love," Bob said.

"Whatever."

"You are telling me," Bob said, "that I must give in to them."

"Yes," Vincent said gently, adding whiskey to their two glasses. "You have no choice. But there is a bit more than that, and it is best that you should know it. You can bank down this fire by standing aside for Brendan, but you can't put it out. Consider how many people must know already about yourself and the lady in London. You can prevent a scandal, but you cannot prevent gossip from seeping out, like gas from faulty drains."

"To hell with that," Bob said.

"Perhaps so," Vincent said. "Sometimes things work themselves out. But the important thing is for you to hand in your papers, and to do it on the trot."

Delaney smiled without cheer. "I have never before known you to be so blunt."

"I have never had need to," Vincent said. "Let me show you something." He got up, and went to the door, and shouted down to the kitchen, "Bring up another bottle, like a good girl, and some fresh water. We are in for a session."

Theresa Fuller had been baking, and although she had washed her hands, her bare arms were dusted with flour.

"There is a good girl," Vincent said, "a great comfort to a man in his middle years. Are you not, pet?"

She smiled in embarrassment as she put down on the floor by the fireplace a jug and a pitcher of clear water.

"Are you not, pet?" he said again. "A great comfort to a man, snug and shapely."

"If you say so," she said, not looking at Delaney.

"I say so," Vincent said, and rested an affectionate hand lightly upon her thigh, stroking it.

When she had left, Delaney said, "What was that about?"

"A nice bit, is she not?" Vincent said. "Not the first girl here in the Lodge, but the last, perhaps. She suits me in a way. I doubt if I will ever marry now."

"Yes indeed," Delaney said. "A nice bit."

"But you have some notion, no doubt, of the words used to describe her in town. She has a father and a brother who were hopping mad for a while, but I am the 'Son' after all, of 'Tully and Son.' She has few chums in town among girls of her age. 'Housekeeper,' whereareyou. In this world of ours, ugly things happen, Bob. You recall settling a certain delicate matter for me in the town of Mallow, the wife of a certain Protestant chemist. All is well now on the domestic front, I have heard; a thousand pounds can heal a variety of wounds. But there are houses in Mallow where the good woman is no longer received. Such things can happen, in Kilpeder or in Mallow or in London. To a skivvy or a chemist's wife or the wife of a lord."

"You have made your point," Delaney said. "There is no need to keep making it, Vincent." He drained his tumbler and reached down for the jug.

"Good," Vincent said. "Enough said, then?"

"It is a messy world, so I am informed by Mike Murphy."

"The sage of Cork City," Tully said. "He is right about that one. There was a Frenchman, you know, so Hughie tells me, who said that each of us must swallow a toad each morning. Not a frog, mind you, which would be a treat in that degenerate nation, but a slimy, slithery grey toad."

"A sage named La Rochefoucauld," Delaney said, "and I am not certain it was Hughie who told you. You read more than you let on, Vincent. It is useful to have a friend like yourself, but just one will do."

"There you are, so," Vincent said. "We can put all that behind us, so, and settle in for some drinking. The nice bit will fry something up for us later, and you can stay the night if you are so inclined. And then in the morning, down to Kilpeder with you to send that letter to your party headquarters."

"Let us put it behind us by all means," Bob said. "But I am not ready for that toad, thank you very much."

Tully stretched, got up, and walked to the window. "It will be a late spring this year, I think."

"In Manchester, the prices of real property have fallen, so I have heard," Delaney said, "and there is a shortage of building timber in Glasgow. Will the French ever recover Alsace, do you think?"

The nice bit had left the door open. Tully crossed the room and closed it. Then he poured himself a drink, and swallowed it neat, in three gulps.

"Everyone, do you not see, Bob? That was the Frenchman's point. Each one of us does. I must myself gulp down my morning toad. I do it looking in the glass, as I am shaving. The toad still has a nasty taste to him, but he has shrunk a bit over the years. Let me tell you about him."

It took him a bit longer than two hours, a long, complicated narrative, with byroads and diversions, explanations of particular points, the road halting from time to time to circle back upon itself, but then, always, moving itself forward again. And Delaney would interrupt at first, crisp, particular solicitor's questions. But towards the end, he only sat and listened. Between them, they had demolished half of the bottle before he had finished, and they were drunk.

"Well, Bob," Tully said, "there is your toad for you, and a handsome little fellow he is."

But Delaney sat with his face, eyes half shut, towards the fireplace. The fire was almost out, and neither of them had thought to place more turf upon it.

"Bob?" Tully said. "Bob? Are you awake at all?" But Delaney made no response, and Tully sat looking towards him, reaching down twice to replenish their drinks.

Evening came into the room as cool, wintry light, no sign in it of spring, and fell upon gun cases, books, the masks of foxes mounted upon the wall, English sporting prints, pink-coated riders clearing walls and gates.

Presently she opened the door and came into the room, and stared at the two men.

"Will yez be wanting something to eat?" she asked.

"Not bloody likely," Tully said. "Take a look at us, would you?"

"I am," she said.

"I am going to lie down for a bit," he said. "He may want a bit when he wakes up. Make a bed for him."

"He'll not be awake for hours," she said. "Not by the looks of him."

"You cannot go by looks," he said, and rose, staggering, to his feet.

She came to his support, and he leaned his arm heavily upon her shoulder. For a young woman so slender, she possessed surprising strength, and she had the drill down pat by now, helping him to bed like this night after night, two nights at least out of every seven. Good peasant stock, Tully would say to himself at times, remembering her strength of shoulder, thigh; good peasant stock. And then he would ask himself, What other stock are we ourselves?, the origins of the Tullys being as remote and mysterious to himself as they were to Hugh MacMahon.

But by the time that Delaney had roused himself in his chair, sour-mouthed and uncertain for the moment of his whereabouts and then remembering, she was herself long asleep, in her shift, stretched with a blanket wrapped around her, in the far bedroom, beside Tully. She had wrestled off his coat and boots and he lay snoring.

Delaney was drunk, but not so drunk as to want so much as the taste of whiskey, so much as the smell of it in his nostrils. He stood up unsteadily, and then walked down the hall, and out into the moonlit night. It was a full, intense moon, and he could see clearly the stable and paddocks, the barns, low fences in the distance, the small, fanciful gatehouse. He set out to walk himself into a measure of sobriety, down the carriageway, past the gatehouse with sleeping gatekeeper and sleeping gatekeeper's wife, out into the Kilpeder road. He walked, unsteadily at first, for several hours, a good long walk, several miles towards Kilpeder, until he could almost make out a few late-burning lights, like fallen stars, and then he turned and walked back. He was still drunk, the whiskey still in his head and blood, but he could feel clarity returning, a platoon of rational, armour-clad swordsmen cutting through undergrowth, wading into bogland.

When he returned to Brierly Lodge, he was not certain enough of its plan, despite his many visits, to risk looking for a room. He had no wish to blunder in upon Tully and the nice bit, much less the two housemaids, who had a room to share between them. He hauled one of the two armchairs over towards its mate, and stretched himself, not too uncomfortably, between them.

When the nice bit came into the room in the morning, he was wide awake, standing by the window. She took him down into the kitchen, and while one of the maids made a pot of tea for him, she went to fetch Tully's shaving brush and one of his razors. He was sitting at the table, finishing his tea, when Tully came to the door to the kitchen. He stood looking at Delaney without speaking, until Delaney said, "Good morning, Vincent. The tea is first-rate. Pour yourself a cup." Then Tully smiled, nodded, and sat down.

When Delaney left, Tully walked beside him, beside the bay, down through the gates and onto the Kilpeder road.

"You have a stronger head than I do myself, by Jesus," Tully ventured.

"It seems that I have need of one, a good strong one."

Delaney pulled on his gloves, held his crop towards his bare head by way of saying good-bye, and then rode down into Kilpeder. He rode directly to his office, unlocked it, and went to his desk. At that hour, on a Saturday, the town was entirely silent. He placed paper, envelopes, and pens beside his arm, and flipped up the shining brass top of his elaborate inkstand, an acquisition from the time in the seventies when, a newly articled solicitor, he had gone down to Cork City with Agnes to furnish forth what she swore would be "the handsomest solicitor's office in all Cork, all Munster."

He wrote four letters to colleagues, telling them that personal reasons, reasons of health, would make it impossible for him to stand for Kilpeder in the general election, and urging them to find another candidate prepared to stand against Brendan Fogarty in order that the "legacy to Ireland of Charles Stewart Parnell remain intact." But he cautioned them that these same reasons of health, medical reasons, a doctor's orders, might make it difficult for him to give the candidate his active support. He would be at Westminster midweek to discuss the matter with them.

Then, without a pause, save to flex fingers which had been grasping the pen tightly, he wrote to Sylvia telling her, too, that he would be in London midweek, and that they had important matters to talk about, should have talked about before now. He closed the note, as he always did, with assurances of his love. He folded the page, then reopened it, and below his name, "Robert," he scribbled, "By the way, I am thinking of taking a bit of a holiday from politics. Does that surprise you?"

But that letter, like the others, he had delayed too long in writing. For it was sometime on that very morning that a messenger boy delivered to the house in Chelsea a bulky package, addressed to Lady Ardmor, and marked, on both back and front, "Most Urgent" and "Most Personal." Emily took it to her in the breakfast room, where she was scribbling a long, rambling letter to Tom Ardmor in Cortona. "Still no signs of a London spring," she wrote, "not a bud upon the fruit trees, but I can see them from the window, very clear in a bright, cool sunlight, lucid and shadowless, your sort of thing, Tom, not Jimmy Whistler's sort of thing at all."

37

[Emily Weldon/Lionel Forrester/Hugh MacMahon]

No, Emily told me, that last afternoon and night that they had together, before he went back to Ireland, a week and a bit before I took that wretched package from the messenger boy—not a boy really, a wizened man, a Cockney, with black crooked teeth—that last afternoon he told her nothing of what might happen, nor did he tell her that night. She would have told me, or if she had not, I would have told it from her manner.

No, far indeed was that from the case. I remember that she did indeed tell me that they had taken that special walk of theirs, along the Embankment, where they could look up along the river towards the Abbey and Houses of Parliament, and she could tease him yet again, that he was Dick Whittington, come to London to be its lord mayor. There were two small boys chasing a squirrel, and Sylvia had scolded them, but Bob said that squirrels were never caught, not by small boys. And then he told her about the wren boys that they have in his part of the world, in Kerry and across the county line in his part of Cork, traipsing about on Stephen's Day, the day after Christmas, with a poor wren imprisoned in a cage of wicker, and then butchered at the end of all. Such practices are foreign in civilised places like Westmeath. When they came back that afternoon, she looked marvellous, her cheeks flushed with the cold, but sheltered by fur, white fur with small black tippets.

I brought the package into the breakfast room to her, where she was writing, and she bade me bring her a knife, because it was bound tight with cord, and the ends of the cord sealed with wax. I was curious as to the package, needless to say, but I went off then to see to the housemaids, and left her alone with it.

She came to me an hour or two later, and said that she was going out for a few hours—to the galleries, I think she said—and had me send a girl for a hansom. When she came back, she was calm, surely, and almost offhanded in her manner, in that way she had. I remember she was going up the stairs, and paused to say something to me, one hand on the newel post, and the other perched upon her hip, with what Lord Ardmor used call her brigand's look. We bantered together a bit, as I recall.

And the next few days were ordinary sorts of days. Robert Delaney would be here on the Wednesday, she said, or the Thursday, and smiled when she told me, as she always did. Then, on the last night, she was so restless that she could not stay for twenty minutes in the chair, and would walk from room to room. Perhaps because she is expecting him, I thought, but then realised that no one has ever been that much in love. We talked, and then she would break off the talk, and look out the drawing-room window into darkness, gas-lit. And then she said that she would make an early night of it. She smiled, and made one of her pleasantries about empty beds.

And that is why I always will believe that I have the truth of the matter, that she took too much of that wretched drug, which I always hated, and which she had no need of for a year almost, but the bottle was nearly full, and she had got out of the way of using it. She must have taken a very strong dose, Dr. Cummings thinks, and then, perhaps, after a bit, woke up again, and could not face the night, and so took a very strong dose a second time, and that is what worked the evil. That is what Dr. Cummings believes, and that other fellow—the coroner, do you call him?

Yes, I told Emily, that must have been the way of it.

I was in Paris when Sylvia died, but mercifully I had sent her a note with my address on it and Emily wired me at the same time that she wired Tom in Cortona. She had not known what to do about informing Delaney, although she knew that he would be in London on the Wednesday, which was the evening I arrived, or else on the Thursday, and was to come to Sylvia's as soon as the House rose that night.

I found him there Thursday night, in the House, and he would have gone at that moment, as we stood together in the lobby, but I persuaded him to wait.

"It was her habit," I assured him, as we walked up and down, "her way of finding sleep. You must have known that, we all did. Emily did, and Tom, and myself. She had great trouble sleeping, in the past. These wretched things happen; you hear of them happening every month almost. Drugs that powerful should not be available as easily as they are, doctors scribbling out prescriptions. It isn't too long ago that not even that was necessary."

"No," Delaney said, "no." He shook his head, like a tormented bull calf. "No."

"Look here, old chap," I said. "Why don't you doss down with me tonight? You've never been to my place. I have a decent spare bed. I don't think you should be by yourself," I said, "I really don't."

"No," he said, "no." But he was not speaking to me. He did not hear me.

I arranged for her burial in her parish church, there in Chelsea, and when Tom arrived from Cortona, there was a memorial service. He sent a note to Delaney, informing him of the service. As their member of Parliament, Sylvia's and his, it would be most appropriate that he attend, and Lord Ardmor would account it an honour to the memory of his late wife.

The church was fairly full. The peerage and gentry, such of them as had known the Ardmors and found themselves in London, were in attendance, whatever they may have thought of Tom's politics and whatever they may have heard about Sylvia's adventures, as they chose to call them. And of course the artistic crowd, Tom and Sylvia's chums, or Tom's alone or Sylvia's painters and writers—Jimmy Whistler, of course, but William

Morris as well and that extraordinary wife of his who could have given Sylvia a run for her money. I have heard Oscar Wilde say that between the two of them, in their contrasting modes, they had created the new notion of beauty in women, mysterious and wild but subtle. For myself, I have never understood the fuss about Jane Morris; it is entirely the way they painted her. I found her frumpy and middle-class. Wilde himself was there, soberly dressed; he had always, I know, been fond of Sylvia.

In that company, Delaney seemed insignificant in his black coat, uncertain as to the nature of Anglican services, and looking in shocking bad form. For the first time I saw him as he would appear to any Londoner, a provincial politician, his edges still rough.

And am I in fact certain that that is how Sylvia died—"death by misadventure," as the language had it? Yes, on the whole I am: too deep a sleeping draught from a blue bottle. Emily says that when Sylvia took the package from her, she said, " 'Personal.' They mean 'Private,' of course. *Personal*, such a vulgar word!" And the package was vulgarity itself, wrapped up in paper and bound with ribbons and cord. The sort of thing that one would drive from one's mind, by sleep or alcohol or drugs. She did not read through all the papers, perhaps only the covering letter with sanctimonious threats, urging her to consider her own good name, and Robert Delaney's, which would certainly be besmirched if he continued his present course. "The tribune of the people is always subject to the scrutiny of the people." Emily remembered that phrase before she burned the bundle. It is a curious fact, as I discovered from my one, oblique conversation on the subject with MacMahon, the Kilpeder schoolmaster and Delaney's great friend, that in none of the three places to which the papers were sent—Delaney's law office, Brierly Lodge, the house in Chelsea—were they in fact read through. A whiff was enough, before burning them. That sort of thing should be carried to the fire with tongs.

No, I am almost certain that Sylvia died by misadventure, although it would not be beyond her to say, "Damn you, do you think you have me cornered? What fools you are. One always has choices." I can see her saying that in what Tom called, as I have said, her brigand's pose, fist on hip, a leg thrust forward. "Not in love with her yourself, are you?" Jean Winslowe had asked me, and I had not answered her. Yes, I know now that I was. But to look at Tom's face there in church that morning, and at Delaney's, was to know that I can only know of love when it is safe, distant, beyond my attaining. What Emily and I have together is quite different. We have Sylvia to share, for one thing.

The Parnellites put up another man to stand against Brendan Fogarty, a young Dublin journalist named Felix O'Neill, who had nothing to lose, not even his deposit, which was furnished from party funds. The campaign that July went off quietly enough; with Parnell's death there was no more need for mob action or filth or clods of mud hurled from the roadway.

Bob took little part in the campaign, although on both of the occasions when O'Neill spoke in the market square, he allowed himself to be placed upon the platform, which was towered over by an immense portrait of Parnell, draped in black and green, and bearing the legend "Our Martyred Chief." He even made the speech of introduction for O'Neill upon the first of these, speaking almost by rote: "our martyred chief," he kept calling Parnell, as though looking to the legend for inspiration. "The principles for which our party has always stood," he said. "The land of Ireland for the people of Ireland, and legislative independence for the whole of this historic nation, often conquered . . ." He paused then, as though groping for the phrase, as though his mind was somewhere else: ". . . often conquered but never crushed. Our patriot dead. The bright deeds of earlier centuries." He ended with phrases only, rather than arguments or even sentences—sketches, gestures of political sound.

But it was far different on the occasion of Brendan Fogarty's final speech, on the eve of the election, with a crowd filling the square. Lanty's men were there, a scattering, to make their boos and catcalls; but their hearts this time were not in it, without the Parnell of those final months to protect, the outlaw Parnell, near-Fenian, the hero of the "hillside men." The platform was done up proudly, with green and gilt, new banners, crepe most of them to be sure, but some of silk, with gilt images of round towers and wolfhounds, and arching overhead, on a trellis set on the rear of the platform, paintings of Owen Roe O'Neill and Daniel O'Connell and Robert Emmet—three men who would have had little to say to each other, had they met in the flesh. Michael Patrick Murphy was, of course, upon the platform, and Father Meagher, and even Dennis Tully by way of demonstrating the commercial worth and probity of the new financial order. No fewer than four members of Parliament graced the occasion, including Tim Healy himself, in frock coat, with gold-rimmed prince-nez on their chain of gold catching the late evening sun at one moment, so that the two circles of glass were perfectly opaque, and as though no eyes sheltered behind them. But at the next moment, he turned to say something to Fogarty—one of his celebrated uncharitable witticisms, no doubt, for he was smiling in a droll manner—and after he had spoken, Fogarty gave a sudden guffaw and then gulped himself into decorum.

It was when Francis Xavier Moriarty, a member of Parliament and a County Kerry man, was in full oratorical flight that Bob came out from his office. None of us noticed him at first. When I caught sight of him, he was leaning against the closed door, his arms folded across his chest. A dense crowd separated me from him, and I made no effort to weave my way through them to join him, which proved a mistake. "Flight of oratory" is almost not in the case of Francis Xavier Moriarty a figure of speech. He sends each oration up into the air, its wings kept aloft and steady by rhythmical puffs of platitudinous breath, so controlled that the wings soar, dip, glide, rise up again, and then, at the peroration, move the creature swiftly, gently, down, to perch invisible upon his shoulder.

It was at the moment of that last, descending glide that Bob shouted out, "Leader-killer Healy, and Altar Boy Fogarty, Healy's bumboy." Moriarty in literal fact broke off, startled and bewildered, wings of speech flapping distractedly. "Go on, so," Bob shouted, seizing upon that involuntary silence, "go on so, you Kerry hoor. Have you ever," he shouted to the crowd, "heard inanity such as Kerrymen are capable of bawling out?"

"I will finish my remarks now," Moriarty said, "addressed to the sober voters of Kilpeder."

"Sober now," Bob said, "but get a whiff of the breaths in the morning. Twill take a monster dram of whiskey to pour on those consciences. Healy the leader-killer. The smiler with the knife." I can swear to those words, because I was straining my ears to listen; but the crowd, before he finished, had begun to talk, one to another, each telling the other that Bob was drunk, laughing tolerantly, but also, I could sense, shocked, for they had been used, for fifteen years at the least, to see Bob as a man of authority and sobriety, drunk a few times a year, as who of us is not, but there would be the end of it.

"Get back in your office, Mr. Delaney," someone shouted, and then, the ice broken, a ruder voice shouted, "Off to Conefry's for another large one, Bob."

Healy had got up from his chair, and stood beside Moriarty, holding out one long, black-clad arm. "All right," he said, in a tenor voice with a whipcrack in it. "All right, now, lads," and they turned to look at him. I began now, belatedly, to make my way to Bob, and I could see Vincent moving towards him along the footpath.

"There you are," Healy said, "there is the heart of Parnellite power in Kilpeder, God help us. Not the scribbler sent up to us from Dublin by Redmond and the lads. There he stands, a good man in his day; many is the platform we have shared together. But that day is past. That is why tomorrow there will be another man to represent us in the den of the British lion. Brendan de Sales Fogarty. Am I right?" And he hauled Fogarty, nothing loath, to his feet.

But by the time he had finished that smooth bit of meaningless rigmarole, Vincent was at Bob's side, and I was there a minute later. Vincent put his hand on Bob's arm, but Bob pulled away from him. "Get your hands off me, you gombeen man's get," he said, and I saw Vincent pale with sudden, brief anger. "They have the world now, Hughie," Bob said to me, "they have the world, they have the world, they have the world. The gombeen men have the world. And we thought it was the landlords."

"We will get him inside," Vincent said to me, for we were providing a diversion which was as unwelcome to us as it was to Fogarty's lot, men gaping at Bob as at a natural curiosity. But Bob struck him aside, and Vincent said to me, "You may have to deal with him on your own, Hughie. I don't seem to be welcome company this evening." But I did not, because now young Jamesey Gannon was there, and between us, we half dragged and half carried him into the office. It was early July now, with its long bright evenings, and there was clear, yellowish light in the office. It fell upon the long rows of legal tomes in their bindings of buff and ebony, which Bob, like all solicitors, kept before clients as a mark of his profession, rather than because of their possible day-to-day usefulness to him.

"There they are," he said, catching sight of them himself, and waving an arm towards them. We got him into his chair, behind the desk, and Jamesey went into his room to make tea upon the contrivance that he kept there, a paraffin-fuelled menace to the safety of Kilpeder.

It must now have been the moment almost for Fogarty's speech, for the band, by way of preparation, had struck up its rousing version of "A Nation Once Again," the song which Fogarty's lot had adopted as their own.

Bob nodded his agreement with the unsung words, which all of us, everyone in our generation across the length and breadth of Ireland, knew by heart.

" 'And then I prayed I yet might see our fetters burst in twain,' " Bob said, making no attempt to sing it, " 'And Ireland long a province be, a nation once again.' There you go, Hughie. How can you resist stuff like that?"

"How long have you been here drinking?" I asked in what I trusted was a mild manner.

"Not so long, not all that long, Hughie. I was before that in the taproom of the Arms, but I was made to feel that my presence there was not welcome to that distinguished company of auctioneers and commercial travellers. Nothing was said, but I am a sensitive plant, as you know. I know when I am not wanted. I thought of strolling down to Conefry's, but I could see that it was filled with Brendan Francis de Sales Fogarty's supporters, and again I would be an intrusive presence."

When Jamesey came back, Bob took the cup from him, and took a deep swallow, and almost gagged. "Would you put a little sweetener in this, for Jesus' sake?"

Jamesey looked enquiringly at me, and by way of answer, I went behind the desk, where I found a knocked-over tumbler, and not a bottle at all, but a jug of poteen. Before I added some to his cup, I splashed a large one into the glass, knocked it back, and looked towards Jamesey. He shook his head in horror. Jamesey is still a solicitor in Kilpeder, and we on occasion have a glass in the Arms, and at times I wonder that that night did not drive him into abstinence, one of Father Matthew's lemonade-and-barley-water brigade.

"You had best come home with me," I said. "Agnes will not want to see you this night."

"Nor any night," Bob said. "Wickedness. Drunk or sober. Wickedness." The band was moving to its stirring climax, and I could imagine Brendan rising to his feet, with a helpful hand upon each elbow. Murphy. Healy.

" 'For freedom,' " Bob said, still quoting Thomas Davis's words of half a century before, " 'for freedom comes from God's right hand, / And needs a godly train.' Are they not, lads? Have you ever seen a more godly train, lads?"

"Mary will make you a decent cup," I said, "meaning no disrespect to Jamesey's concoction. And you can have one of the lads' beds. Soft as feathers."

"Mary," he said. "By the hokey, you are the fortunate man, Hugh. Soft. And strong, Hugh, strong. She is silver, silver, Hugh."

"She has a great fondness for you, Bob," I said. "For yourself and for Vincent."

"Not gold, mind," he said judiciously. "Not gold, mind you. But silver, pure, pure silver." He made a dramatic show of cocking an ear. " 'And righteous men must make our land / A nation once again.' And there they are for our instruction and edification, Hugh, in the market square of Kilpeder. The righteous men themselves. Are we not the fortunate hoors?"

But he would not go home with me, nor accept Jamesey's offer of company for the night, and so we sat with him, letting him talk in that way, becoming worse and worse, incoherent at last, his eyes bulging and watery, and a trickle of saliva which he would wipe away with the back of his hand. We stayed for another hour. We heard Brendan's words without being able to make them out, and the band concluded the occasion by playing "Let Erin Remember," one of Thomas Moore's *Irish Melodies*, which often in the old days the four of us had sung together, our three heads bent towards Mary's and hers leaning to the keyboard, no need to read the music.

Thank God, Bob was too far gone to hear that one, for its words would have been meat and drink for the drunken sarcasm which he fancied in his drunkenness to be a Swiftian irony. "Let Erin remember the days of old, / Ere her faithless sons betrayed her."

At the turning, at the end of the square, Jamesey and I said goodnight to each other.

"Have you seen much of this?" I asked him, but he shook his head. "No," he said. "Two or three times only. He has a few in the Arms each evening, on his way home, but what harm is there in that?"

What harm indeed. And indeed it was not for a long while after this that Bob would be marked as a man with what our countryside calls "a strong weakness"—there is an Irish bull for you. It takes time for such things to happen to a man, and it takes time for them to be noticed by others. It takes time for it to become a town proverb that Counsellor Delaney can always be consulted in the late afternoon at the Arms, or else, three evenings out of four, in the snug in Conefry's, and, once every few months can be seen blustering into Grennan's, when he has been refused drink elsewhere. It takes time before it is recognized by clients that work is being neglected, or dealt with negligently, on occasion with stupidity, that letters are being sent out over Bob's signature which have been composed for him by Jamesey.

"What harm is there in that?" I said that night to Jamesey, echoing his words.

"Not that he does not have the right of it, down deep at the base of things," Jamesey said.

"About Healy's crowd, do you mean?" I said. "Ach, Jamesey, there are rights and wrongs in that matter on both sides. At the end there, Parnell was wild and blind with pride, and Bob wild with some fierce kind of loyalty, beyond all reason."

"I didn't mean that," Jamesey said. "I don't give a tinker's curse for any of that. Between John Dillon and John Redmond, you would be hard-pressed to decide which shirt has the thicker stuffing. Do you recall, though, what he was bawling out to yourself and Vincent Tully, when I came to join you? We thought it was the landlords, he said, but it was the gombeen men."

"Ach," I said, "things are not well between Bob and his father-in-law. All of Kilpeder knows that."

"Judkins, that misfortunate idjeet of an Englishman, is selling out Lughnavalla," he said, and I told him I knew that.

That, too, all Kilpeder knew. It was, as events were to prove, the final victory for the Campaign in all Munster, the last of the great boycottings, and therefore, the last of Bob's victories, although Brendan Fogarty might dispute him there, for much of the final thrust had been by Brendan, with Bob off in London. But the campaign against Lughnavalla had been Bob's design, and to this day, when the memory of Kilpeder turns back to Lughnavalla, it is of Bob's Sunday meetings there, outside the gates, the banners and music, and the men whom he had brought in to embolden the tenants—O'Brien and Dillon, and the others. I remembered Bob and myself walking through the boycotted Big House, with the poor half-frightened emergency man from Millstreet trailing behind us.

"But the Big House itself," Jamesey said, "Lughnavalla House. Did you know that it has been acquired at private auction by Dennis Tully?"

I looked at him dumbfounded. It must have shown in my face, and he smiled in a manner almost patronising, although he was too courteous a fellow for that, a young solicitor bracing a middle-aged schoolmaster for the elementals of existence. "Only the demesne itself, of course, and the house will be for his use. He has settled with the tenants upon the terms stipulated by Bob at the outset of the campaign. And tis said that he is uncertain what use he will make of Lughnavalla House. Knock it down, perhaps, for the fine stones that are in it, or perhaps leave it aside for some plan which the future may unfold."

Fellows who had stopped in at Conefry's or Grennan's for a pint after the meeting were making their unsteady way home, shouting to each other, and one group of lads, too young for the vote by the looks of them, were singing "A Nation Once Again" in a variety of unlovely keys.

"Now, you are a scholarly man," Jamesey said, "our great authority upon Kilpeder back into the ancient days when there was no Kilpeder at all, but only wild O'Donovans and MacCarthys and O'Callaghans roaming the forests, and courtly Normans—Barry and Roche. You might find it of interest some wet afternoon to enquire into the ways in which real property has changed hands over the past ten years or so. Since the Land War, that is. The land of Ireland for the people of Ireland. And who could be more Irish than Dennis Tully and Michael Patrick Murphy?"

What most impressed me, I think, was young Jamesey Gannon's sudden flight of sardonic wit and wisdom. An excellent fellow he had seemed to me, if a bit callow, but at the moment, on that summer night with its bright moon, it was as though Bob's gift for savage speech had been passed on as an inheritance to his disciple.

There was a time, I thought as I walked homewards, when words such as those might have been a lighted match tossed into the powder keg of my phantasies about the Tullys, and indeed for a moment, almost halfheartedly, my imagination toyed with a vision of Dennis Tully pacing the ancestral halls which he had inherited from the Englishman who had inherited them from the last of the O'Callaghans, the photographs of shooting parties cleared away from the walls and replaced by oil paintings of the Bay of Naples, a tastefully done reproduction of the Sacred Heart, and Saint Patrick, emerald-robed, mitred. But I could not put the weight of my shoulder into the phantasy.

I was too heartsick about Bob, and I was recalling, as I neared our gate, that image of lost felicity which had drifted into my mind and out of it again an hour before, and of the parlour of our own house, and the four of us gathered, in song and friendship. No, not friendship but love. And I realised suddenly how long ago that was, because upon one of those evenings out of the scores of them, there had been not four of us but five.

Suddenly and precisely I saw Ned Nolan, the only Ned we knew, the young soldier who rapped that day upon my door, in the final days of that long-gone January, before the "battle," before the ugly disfiguring years of gaol, before taproom legends had encrusted themselves upon him, lurid and distorting. I saw him seated upon the edge of his chair, a bit apart from us, in his raven's-wing jacket, thick clumsy black boots, a smile tentative, softening into trust. And Mary, her fingers tracing elaborate, faintly sardonic frills and elaborations upon the music, and Vincent, leaning towards her slightly, the words of Moore's *Irish Melodies* shaped by his light tenor, he too faintly sardonic, like Mary gently mocking a sentiment, an effulgence of emotion which in our hearts we knew had an existence before mockery, above it. "Though lost to Mononia and cold in the grave / He returns to Kincora no more." Mononia, the fancied-up, Latinate word for Munster, our own province, and the song therefore one with its strong special claims upon us.

Ned listened, and smiled. Long before, a quarter century before.

38

[Ned Nolan]

The explosion earned itself some paragraphs in most of the metropolitan newspapers, a few on the morning after its occurrence, and a few more after the inquests upon the men who had been killed. A squalid story, edged with melodrama: an explosion in the shed behind a small house buried in the rabbit's warren of the East End, the dead man mutilated almost beyond recognition, and the other with his legs smashed, one of them ripped off above the knee. He survived in a pain-racked consciousness in Guy's Hospital for almost a day, morphia blunting the edges, drifting him into rambling speech, but never so far into garrulousness as to say who he was or where he was or why—a young fellow, in his mid-twenties, powerfully built. They could make no sense at all of what he said, and then he died. His trousers, what remained of them above the thigh, were cheap English stuff, but the jacket, although as cheap, was Yankee, with the label of a tailor on Broadway in New York City.

The inquests earned their morning in the sunlight of print. The explosion had been caused by the detonation, accidental no doubt, of gunpowder, but there was clear evidence that the shed had contained dynamite as well, which accounted for the force of the explosion—it shattered the scullery of the house and of the one to its left, the tenant of the house in question being a Patrick Enright, aged forty-two, Liverpool-born but of Irish parents, natives of Armagh. Enright was a builder by occupation, and he identified one of the dead men as Edward MacCurtain, an Irishman working with him as an apprentice, and the other as his lodger, James Morrissey, an American, occupation unknown. The coroner speculated as to Fenian terrorists being at the heart of the matter, but there was little other direct evidence, and there had been no Fenian outrages for more than a year, not since the disaster in Paddington Station.

Nolan—John Boland he called himself now, and this was the name on an American passport—waited more than a week, ten days almost, before he approached Enright, and even so, although he could tell that the police patrol had been halted from its surveillance of the house, he accosted Enright not there, but at a street corner, as Enright was walking home from a site.

"Jesus, Ned, do you want us lifted, do you want the two of us lifted?"

"We need a bit of time to talk, Paddy, ten minutes or so. We can stroll to your house, or there is a grog shop here beside us, whichever you prefer. But we cannot get along without the talk, Paddy. Neither of us."

"It is far from ended, Ned," Enright said when they were at a table in the small, grimy public house, no patrons save themselves and three navvies sitting apart from them. "I have spent three days in conversation with the Irish Branch at the Yard, and they brought two detectives over from Dublin to talk with me. They were not gentle at all, the cunts. Your own lot is always the worst. Always."

"But you stood up to them," Nolan said. "Enright, the hard man."

"I did. But they battered me, the Dublin lads did. 'Take your fucking hands off me,' I said. 'I'm a British subject,' I said. 'I'm not a fucking nigger.'"

"A telling point," Nolan said. "But they must have learned something from you, they must have learned something."

"Damned little," Enright said, and raised his glass. "Cheers. I told them that I had my suspicions about MacCurtain, a bit too much the paddy, but not Morrissey, a proper Yank. And no, there was no one called upon them, save a friend of Morrissey's named Boland. I had a drink with him once or twice, but he was a tight-mouthed fellow. 'Think now,' Anderson says to me, the canting little Protestant bastard, 'was it not Nolan, not Boland but Nolan? The names are easily confused.' 'It was not,' I said. Then he showed me the pictures they made of you in 'sixty-seven, and another taken upon a street in New York, blurred beyond recognising. This fellow had a beard, I said, but he did not look at all like this lad here. Which is the truth. My God, but you were a young lad back then. A right young holy terror, with your hair cut short into angry clumps, and you staring into the camera as though you would jump down the fellow's throat."

"You did well, Paddy," Nolan said, sipping at his tepid, oversweetened lemonade. "You did better than I expected, to tell you the honest truth."

"What is going to happen to us, Ned?"

Nolan shrugged. "Nothing. The nothing that has been happening to us for a year. Why were those two idjeets in the shed?"

"Well, I was thinking, like, Ned, that there was no point in good explosive going to waste, when I have need for it every day on the new site."

"The munitions of the Irish Republic and its army," Ned said, "at work building greater metropolitan London," and then added, seeing the quick fear in Enright's eyes, "Well, why not? It's a shame to see good material go to waste."

"What will happen to us?" Enright said again.

"Nothing," Ned said. "You will be doing your mite for the expansion of the city that rules the world. And I will be drifting away to wherever it is that I come from. Drifting in stages, I am afraid. I need money, Paddy."

"You will have it," Enright said. "There is more than a thousand pounds of organization funds that I am keeping as part of my own commercial funds, but we must wait a bit. The lads from the Yard will have their eyes on it."

"Two hundred pounds, Paddy, and a hundred American dollars. Tomorrow at your midday break. No, at teatime. I am not an urgent sort of fellow."

"God almighty, Ned," Enright began, but then he saw suddenly the bit of Nolan that he had seen from time to time: the day of Paddington Station was one such time, and the rainy day that they had waited for the lads who had done Spencer to come home. "Teatime it is," he said. "Right, Ned."

Nolan would have been the only patient in Dr. Carroll's surgery that evening, and he waited as would a patient, his arms folded across his chest, his sunken eyes half closed above long, thin curve of nose, American gunman's moustache. There was a skeleton in a corner of the room, in evidence of Carroll's knowledge of anatomy, and a chart of the human body, a male body, with blue lines for veins, red for arteries, and a minute sketchwork, fretwork of yellow for nerves, ganglia. The face glowed with the colours displayed by peeled-away epidermis, dermis.

Although still a man in his early middle years, Carroll was bald, save for a fringe of bright auburn hair, darker than his sandy eyebrows. He was short, and heavyset, and wore for his surgery a dark jacket which did not match his trousers.

"Well now, Ned," he said. "A long time. A year almost."

"And a bit," Nolan said. "A year and a bit."

"I hope you share our liking for coffee. We do it well here. Muriel and myself do. We have almost lost our taste for tea."

"Times change," Ned said, and smiled politely. Carroll was the first man Nolan had ever met who had a wife called Muriel, as in a novel.

"You understand, of course, Ned," Carroll said, looking out into his garden, "that you and I are not—"

"You long ago made that clear to me, James," Nolan said. "You take your orders directly from the Supreme Council, and I have been here on an independent mission. But before I left New York, I made certain that I had Devoy's blessing."

"His personal blessing, perhaps, Ned. You were sent out by Millen, the man whom you yourself discovered to be an informer to the English. Since then you have been on your own."

"Not so much on my own that I did not stop operations a year ago, at your orders, at the orders of the organization. I am an oath-bound man, and you know it, James."

They broke off when Muriel Carroll came in with the tray of coffee, an elaborate brass pot, and cups of some Oriental design, Persian perhaps, or Arabian.

"It is very good to see you again, Ned," she said in an English accent which Nolan could now recognise as middle-class.

"Oath-bound," Carroll said, as though holding the words in a forceps, turning it this way and that. As Muriel Carroll left, she closed the door behind her. "How have you managed for yourself this year past?"

Nolan shrugged. "This way and that. I worked with Enright for a few months. After that I found employment in Sheffield. Then back here to London." He rummaged in a pocket and drew out a folded sheet of paper. "I have made a reckoning of the funds which Enright has been holding, from which I have taken out money for my own expenses of travel and for any emergency."

"You are going back to the States, so you told me in your note. Back home."

"That is not my home," Nolan said. "Neither is England."

"No," Carroll said, pouring coffee brown but weak-looking into the exotic cups.

Nolan studied the ghostly tissue of the peeled man, corded muscles, Amazons and Mississippis of arteries and veins.

"Now then," Carroll said. "We do have one source of information at the Yard, and a good one. There is no warrant against Jack Boland, and the one against Ned Nolan lapsed almost two years ago. You can travel as you please. Enright is bloody lucky that he was in the building trades, and responsible for explosives. They gave him a hard time; they knew he had been in the organization, but he told them nothing." He shrugged. "They might put a detective on your heels, nothing worse than that. Have you booked a passage?"

"Not yet," Nolan said. "I am sailing from Queenstown. I am entitled at least to a look at Ireland after all these years, after all that has been done."

"No man deserves it more than yourself," Carroll said, sipping his unsweetened coffee. Nolan added sugar to his before tasting it, and Carroll winced faintly.

"A word of advice, Ned?" Carroll asked, and Nolan nodded. "It is all over, boy." Cork City was suddenly back in his voice. "All over. For good. That is why word was passed to you to end operations. I don't know why you lingered on here for a year. You might have gone home."

"That is not my home," Nolan said again. "I had a team here; we were in place. Orders change. It was an active team, reliable, and it got results."

"I don't want to know," Carroll cut in sharply. "Not at all. It is over. Towards the end there, teams of your sort, or Gallagher's or Lomasney's, were doing little more than giving a chance for boasting to tramway conductors in Brooklyn and housemaids in Boston. They were doing no more; they were doing harm, in fact. We want no more of it."

"We?" Nolan asked.

"As we were saying, Ned. Times change. I am on the Council now. I am not carrying messages for it."

"And what do you expect me to do? Qualify in medicine like yourself?"

"I have been qualified for more than twenty years, Ned. Surely you must have a trade of some sort."

Nolan shrugged. "I'll not starve, far from it. I have an old pal with brickyards on the Hudson River, up from the city. There is a standing offer there. He was a great lad there in the old days, one of O'Neill's crowd. A raider. Now he makes bricks."

"And I do surgery," Carroll said, "and Devoy is a journalist and MacDevitt is a captain of police in Philadelphia. It's all over, Ned. It has been over since the people swung behind Parnell and the Land League."

"Parnell is gone now," Nolan said, "dead and buried, and his lieutenants are squabbling over his bones."

"No hope for us there," Carroll said. "No hope at all."

At the hall door, Carroll said, "I expect you heard that Millen was given a Fenian funeral. In Woodlawn Cemetery in New York. A coffin draped with the flag, and a dignified speech by Rossa. It seemed best."

"A terrible accident to have befallen a man like Millen, in the prime of life, to fall into the river and no one to hear his shouts. A great soulless city New York is."

"Is it?" Carroll said. "So they say."

Carroll, holding the door open, watched him walk down the footpath, gaunt-shouldered, hands shoved into the pockets of his black weatherproof, shiny in gaslight. There was a spattering rain.

In the hall, he encountered Muriel. "He frightens me, James. He has always frightened me."

"Who has he not?" Carroll said. "We will not see him again. Ever."

"Is he going home?" she asked.

"That is a question of definition," Carroll said.

In his surgery, he looked into the darkening garden. It seemed chill and uninviting in the moonless, spattering night.

Othello's occupation's gone, he thought. Farewell the bigs wars. But at once he rebuked his own flippancy. Nolan was a hero of a sort, soldiering on, with success shrivelling up at the far end of a narrow deep perspective, the Supreme Council a ghostly body, hoping against hope, harmless almost, of no concern to the Yard these days in fact, were it not for the fanatical Anderson. French anarchists, Russian, Jewish, plotting the liberation of the entire world from what? Ireland was small potatoes. Nolan was going home, for that was his home, New York, so far as he had one, to become a straw boss in a Hudson River brickyard. He deserved a bit better.

39

[Robert Delaney/Ned Nolan/Hugh MacMahon/Vincent Tully]

Bob still spent a part of each night at home, in the same bed with Agnes. Later on, he would often go to sleep in the narrow, metal-framed bed, straw-mattressed, which he had set up in Jamesey Gannon's former office. But at first, in the first months after Sylvia's death, after Parnell's death, after Ardmor Castle had been shut down, he would sleep with Agnes in the great mahogany bed of matrimony, because no other arrangement seemed natural to either of them. But she slept turned away from him, as she had done ever since, going through the drawers and compartments of the desk in the drawing room, she had found the letters, six or eight of them, with their vivid, jagged scrawl. They would speak a curt, civil good night to each other. Lying side by side, untouching, he could sense her stiffness.

In that first year or two, he knew that he was a solicitor, still trusted, with a faithful practice, and for months on end he would drink sparingly.

He had taken to sleeping later in the mornings, a solitary breakfast in the kitchen, and then a long stretch of work, until late at night, until he knew that the public houses were closed.

It was on such a night, a Wednesday in mid-October, answering a soft tapping noise upon the glass of the office's hall door, that he opened it to Ned Nolan.

He did not recognise him, of course, could in any event not see him clearly against the night, a tall, dark shape, face occluded by a soft, floppy-brimmed hat. Light from behind Delaney fell upon the coat, not a coat really, but a shiny waterproof cape of some sort, darker than black where the light fell upon it.

"Well," he said, and the shape, darker than black, shiny as crude oil, echoed him.

"Well. Will you not ask me in, Bob?"

At once, knowledge leaping across years and bundles of nerves and switches in the mind of memory, he recognised the voice, and stood stunned.

"You might as well," Nolan said. "There is no one else in the market square to talk with. It is more silent at this hour than any tomb."

Tentatively, Delaney reached out, touched Nolan upon the shoulder, touched the waterproof, unpleasantly slippery to the touch, cold and damp. It had been raining, either here or wherever it was that Nolan had come from. But behind his shape, Delaney could see a slice of moon, clear though cloud-encircled.

"Tis yourself, Ned," Delaney said, and Nolan stood motionless, without replying.

Strengthening his grip upon the shoulder, Delaney said, "Come in, boy. Come in," and Nolan followed the welcoming hand into the hall. Delaney closed the door behind them. There was no light in the hall better than its single gas jet, but when they were in the office, with its two jets lit, and the green-globed lamp upon the desk bright, a green luminous moon, Delaney turned to face him, and what he saw drove him for the moment into silence.

"Times change, Bob," Ned said. "Time changes us," and he took off the wide-brimmed hat, damp like the waterproof. His hair was still black, although touched by grey, which was more than Delaney could say for himself, and there was a bit of grey in the downward-curving long moustaches. It was the same face, high-cheekboned. But there were now deep lines set on either side of the long, thin-lipped mouth, and lines furrowing the forehead. It was the eyes which had changed, Delaney thought, but then thought that this could have been his own imagination.

When he had helped Nolan out of the waterproof, he said, "Can I offer you a drink, Ned?"

"I would not mind a bit of whiskey," Nolan said. "It is a dirty night. I came to Macroom on the evening train, and walked here, save for a lift of a mile or two that I was given by a carter."

"Walked!" Delaney said. "Mother of God, I forgot your case."

"Did not notice it is the word," Nolan said and smiled. "I carried it in with me. Tis in the hall."

Suddenly, Delaney remembered MacMahon's description of opening the door to Ned Nolan in 1867, a fellow black as a rook, holding a heavy-looking case.

To his embarrassment, there was at most two inches of whiskey in the bottle that he took from the tall drawer of his desk, and he measured them both small ones, that he might be able to provide seconds.

"Well, Ned, well," he said, and raised his glass. "Your health."

"*Slainte,*" Nolan said, in some abominable accent, not Munster certainly. "Bob, are the drapes there for ornament, like, or can they be drawn?"

"No," Delaney said, taking the point, and not surprised, a bit amused that he was not surprised. "No, they are the real, working yoke." He reached behind him for the cords, and pulled the drapes closed, shutting out the black, invisible market square.

"Are you on the run, Ned?" he asked bluntly.

"No," Nolan said. "Not at all. But they have had a fellow fastened to the heel of my boot. He was on the night boat with me, and I saw him once in Dublin, and he was on the train with me to Cork. I waited until Cork to shake him off, give him a bit of a holiday, a sea change, and a journey across a lovely countryside. But he will have made his report to the coppers in Cork City, and it is annoying, to have such fellows tagging along. I am sailing from Queenstown on the Saturday."

"For New York," Bob said.

"Of course," Nolan said. "Where else would I go? I am going to settle down to life working in a brickyard. My chum tells me that there could be a bit of a house in it for me, with a view of the Hudson River."

"Time you settled down, Ned. We all must, sooner or later."

"You have done it in style, Bob," Nolan said, a sweep of his arm speaking for books, leather chairs, heavily framed landscapes, the rich fabric of the drawn drapes.

"I have," Delaney said. "There is no point in denying it. When last we saw each other, I was living in a room above Tully's shop."

"Not quite," Nolan said. "When last we saw each other, we were in

[750]

the lock-up in Cork City awaiting our trials, yourself and myself and Hughie and Vincent."

"Yes," Delaney said. "To be precise. And I have a grand house, standing on its own grounds. But Hughie and Mary are at the old stand. Hughie is master to this day, thumping knowledge into the lads with the help of the birch."

"I know," Nolan said. "I read all his letters, and save them and reread them. Often they come to me months late, knocked about from this place to that."

"You were later than that even in sending an answer to them," Delaney said, but with a smile to take the edge from his words.

"I was never certain what to write," Nolan said. "I would take pen and paper, every once in a while, but the words would not come to me. I remembered you, all of you, and Kilpeder and Clonbrony Wood. That is why I am here; that is why I am sailing from Queenstown and not from England."

"With a detective on your heels," Bob said. "Twill not take the peelers in Cork City long to sort matters out, and make a guess where you have gone. The sergeant here is no fool, if it comes to that, and Richardson, the R.M., is a clever bastard, ex-army fellow, India."

"What harm?" Nolan said. "There is no warrant for me, I carry an American passport. Two of them, in fact, to be on the safe side. No harm for me, that is; but you might think differently yourself, Bob, or Hughie might."

"Ned!" Delaney said. "For God's sake! But a quiet place for you to stay might be best. As we have been talking, I have had my mind on that."

"It was in the newspapers," Nolan said, "that you were quitting political life. For personal reasons, they said."

"Yes," Delaney said, and looked down at the mess of papers spread across his desk. "My expanding legal practice." He smiled, but not at Nolan.

When he looked up, he saw that Nolan was studying him. He has gained skill, no doubt, Delaney thought, at reading tones of voice, gestures, the complicated meanings of smiles. Hughie's Red Indian—or Leatherstocking, at least—reading snapped twigs, a footprint upon damp earth.

Urgent. Personal.

"I was not all that certain of my welcome, do you know," Nolan said. "A letter at Christmas is one thing. But there have been hard things said about me, nonsense much of it, like the ballad. That is why I took a chance that you would be here. Hughie wrote me years ago that you had a fine office, along the square, past the Kilpeder Arms. Does nothing ever change here?"

"Very little," Bob said.

"Save for the shop," Nolan said. "Tully and Son. Tis now a rival to the great shops on Broadway in New York."

"At the very least," Delaney said.

"Above the new front, above the lintel, there is a date," Nolan said. "Eighteen forty-six. What is the meaning of that?"

Delaney shook his head. "Ask the old man. I was still with him, in those days, when we had the builders in. 'Tully and Son,' he said, 'as with the old shop. And above all, a year. A year of founding.' But the Tullys were in Kilpeder long before that, the first lad came down from the hills or eastwards from Kerry or wherever at the turn of the old century. That much we know. Hughie is the great scholar of Tullyology. Ask Hughie."

Nolan sipped politely at his glass, but Delaney could see that it was almost empty. He gave Nolan most of the bottle's inch, wetting his own for the sake of convention. The taste was upon his tongue, a memory of sodden oblivion; once, in the past, of companionship, song.

Suddenly, his surprise past him by now, he was happy to see Nolan; suddenly he remembered, felt the special bond that had built itself up between them, back then, back a quarter century before, rousing the mild jealousy of Hughie, Vincent's wit, almost free from malice.

"Welcome home, Ned Nolan," he said, and raised his glass with its drop in it.

"It *is* my home, you know," Nolan said. "I was born here. Hughie and I are cousins. They all forget that. They call me a Yank." But his voice was now more Yank than Irish.

"Was not your own father schoolmaster in Kilpeder in the days long before Hughie? Thomas Justin Nolan. He is not forgotten here in Kilpeder, Ned. Thomas Justin Nolan."

"Ah," Nolan said. "Even in the States. When they are toasting the men of that foolish movement, they will on occasion toss in his name, the gallant patriots of Young Ireland, the men of 'forty-eight, Smith O'Brien and Thomas Francis Meagher of the Sword and Michael Doheny and this one and that one and Thomas Justin Nolan."

"Yes," Delaney said, and left it at that.

"Not that we fared better, eh Bob?" Nolan asked, lightly. "More hulks upon the strand. Not yourself, don't take me amiss. Myself I meant, and fellows like me—Rossa drinking himself to death in New York, and Lomasney blown to smithereens, and poor Tom Clarke tethered as we speak in one of their vile cells."

"It pays to be a solicitor," Bob said, with a smile that would have a different sort of meaning for Nolan to read. "Once in a great while, it pays. I have thought of exactly the place where we can put you up for your few days. You will be living in grandeur, my boy. In grandeur."

When it was light enough for Twomey to bring round to Delaney the horse and carriage and the full-packed hamper, but before the farmers would be up for their chores, they set forth on the Killarney road—the "county road," it was called by locals—past the falcon-guarded gates, the gates shut now, great iron gates like spears, and topped with spearheads, past the trim Protestant church, its grey stone demure in the brightening dawn. In the distance, themselves grey in this light, lay the Derrynasaggarts, the dawn promising a clear day, and a few pale stars fading.

"I remember this road," Nolan said. "I remember all these roads. In my case behind us there, I have a small box of maps, and I have studied them in the damnedest places, Bob. Not these lands alone, Bob, but places which I have never seen—Galway and Donegal and Mayo."

"I was but once in Donegal myself," Delaney said. "Parts of it are lovely indeed, but parts are bare and naked beyond belief. I pity the poor bastards who live there. There is now what is called the Congested Districts Board to fret over them. There you are, straight out of Lewis Carroll or *Gulliver's Travels*. The land so poor that it can support scarcely anyone, and so the government calls it 'congested.' I declare to God."

"The English government," Nolan said.

"At the moment," Bob said, "the only one we have. The time I was there, it was with another M.P. It was when we were recommencing the Land War. This fellow, Ignatius Butler is his name, a decent skin, and the band preceded him by playing, 'We'll Have the Land for the People.' A great Land War song. That gave Ignatius his cue. Ignatius comes from the rich fields of Meath, fields thick as butter. 'We'll have the land for the people,' he began, with a great show of the clenched fist, and the poor Donegals roared their approval. Then he took a good look at the field. 'But dear Jesus,' he said, 'where is the land?' It took a bit to smooth that one over. They are a touchy people, the Donegals are."

"We have had different lives, Bob, the two of us. Have we not?" Nolan said.

"All lives are different," Bob said. "When you dig down a bit."

The small farms were now astir, with the smoke of first fires rising, faint plumes, the "seed" of each fire fanned into life, and new turf shaped about it, a practical art so habitual as to be beyond art. And the mountains were in clear view now, no longer shrouded, but menacing, at a safe, far distance, but Delaney recalled them close at hand, bare save for mist-glistening rock, the heather of late spring and summer lovely but with its own harshness, tough-rooted.

At the gates of Lughnavalla House, Delaney stopped for a moment, and they grinned at each other.

"We raided it, do you recall?" Delaney said. "I forget which team it was."

"The third team," Nolan said. "The third team, under a fellow named Charlie Buckley, a short, determined, farmer's-younger-son type of fellow. Full of energy. All the houses along the Killarney road were assigned to Buckley, and that third team he ran. It was long after three, as late almost as it is now, or as early, when they reported back to us."

"An impressive feat of memory," Delaney said with a faint wryness, and gave his reins a flick.

As they stood before the door, Delaney reached into his coat pocket, and took out the heavy key, dark iron, long and surprisingly thick.

"I should not have this by rights," he said. "Lughnavalla House is now the property of my father-in-law."

"What is his is yours, almost," Nolan said. "That is the way it always was."

"Nothing is forever," Delaney said, and swung open the hall door. He reached down for the hamper of provisions and went inside. Nolan followed him.

"When I was last here," Bob said, "it was with Hughie, with the boycott under full steam. There was an emergency man, as they are called, a poor gormless creature from Millstreet. The lads there gave him a warm welcome home, you may be certain of that; but sure, everyone has to work and the times are hard."

But Nolan was walking away from him, into the drawing room, and Delaney found him there, looking from one wall to the next, at the immense vulgar photographs of shooting parties, the masks of foxes, a bell jar with a bright-plumaged pheasant in artfully contrived surroundings, grass and bits of wood, flowers pink and yellow, and a few fierce, bright hues. Air must be sealed in there as well, Delaney thought, idly, irrelevantly.

"And Dennis Tully of the town of Kilpeder is the master of this house," Nolan said. "The master of Lughnavalla."

"He is," Delaney said, "and I am no longer his solicitor. His solicitor is Brendan Fogarty, our member of Parliament. We are in trespass, we are breaking the law."

"Lawbreaking holds no novelty for me," Nolan said. "But it is different for you, for a solicitor. I daresay you have broken no law since we carted away old Judkins's weapons to serve a better purpose."

"You should have been at hand to point that out to them in 'eighty-two, when they sent me to Kilmainham, and again during the Plan of Campaign, thanks to this very house." Judkins: Ned even remembers the name.

"Umm," Nolan said noncommittally. Six months for Land League agitation would not be the sort of thing to impress Nolan, Delaney thought. But then he remembered, as Nolan walked towards the tall windows, that it was during his time in Kilmainham that Hugh MacMahon saw Ned Nolan in the snug of a public house, north of the Liffey, a few days before the butcheries in the Phoenix Park. He felt, briefly, a chill upon his spirits.

"Cold, bare mountains they are," Nolan said of the Derrynasaggarts.

"They are that," Delaney said. "But the loveliest of the world's lakes beyond them." Once, on the shore of one lake, near ruined Muckross Abbey, Hugh MacMahon had discoursed upon the poetry of a man who was buried there, who had written in the old language, in the old century. A famous poet, what was his name?

"Don't light a fire, Ned. There is no need to draw attention to the house. You will otherwise be safe as houses. The farms are all beyond the ridge, two miles or three. I will be back tonight, and Hugh with me."

"Hugh and Vincent," Nolan said. "I have a great wish to see Vincent. It was Vincent, more than once, who kept our spirits up, do you recall? A wonderful wit that man has within himself. Had, at any rate. Does he have it still?"

"He does indeed," Delaney said. "A fellow of infinite jest."

"Shakespeare," Nolan said. "*Hamlet*. He looks better than poor Yorick, I trust?"

"Better fleshed out," Delaney said, grinning. "Hughie must have written to you about him. He is a sleek fellow these days, and something of a landlord himself. The master of an elaborate class of shooting lodge called Brierly."

"Why did you not bring me there?" Nolan asked at once, and Delaney again had a sense, almost a scent, of animal quickness. "Our old chum Vincent?"

"There is a staff," Delaney said, "housemaids and a stableboy and all that. You will prefer the quiet and the solitude of Lughnavalla House, I doubt not. And in any event, the fellow of infinite jest is not in residence. He is away on a visit, to Tipperary, I think it is that Agnes told me. He will be back the morrow."

"Agnes," Nolan said. "I never knew Agnes."

"No," Delaney said.

"Brierly Lodge," Nolan said with fierce exactness, unrolling in his mind the ordnance map which he had carried there for a quarter-century. "It is not three miles from here. On the road that runs past the wood. Our wood. We tossed that place as well, Bob. Do you not recall? A bastard named Boyle. John Boyle. He was a great sportsman, which proved useful to us."

"It is better armed today than it was then," Delaney said. "Vincent has an arsenal that could be used to liberate Alsace. Or Cuba, at the least."

"But I will see him before I set forth to meet my ship in Queenstown, surely," Nolan said, seeking to bludgeon facts to fit a long-nurtured phantasy. "Hughie and Vincent and yourself."

"Hughie and myself you will see without fail, Ned. We will be back this night, the two of us, and we will make a night of it."

He walked over to the window which looked out upon an untended meadow. "Vincent might be a bit more difficult. He will be back tomorrow, so Agnes says, but that is because he has a party laid on at the Lodge. A Friday night party, gentlemen only. Judge Martin from Cork City and Richardson, our resident magistrate, and Regan, a fellow who breeds fine horses out towards Millstreet. About ten or so of them. Not our sort at all, would you say, Ned?"

"No," Nolan said. "Not our sort. Not my sort, at any rate. He is keeping strange company, Vincent is."

"We all do, Ned. In these latter days." He turned away from the window and smiled. "All save myself. I have fallen out of the ways of sociability."

"Without fail now, Bob," Nolan said, with a small anxiousness, as if a bit of certainty had crumbled beneath his boot. "Yourself and Hughie. And Vincent, if he has returned."

"There is a bottle in the hamper," Delaney said. "Vincent will not be back tonight."

Halfway down the weed-choked carriageway, he twisted around in his seat, and saw Nolan standing by the window. He lifted his hand to him.

Delaney had made an exact call of it. So Nolan discovered when he walked along a narrow boreen, untrodden for years by the look of it, and came to a pasture, with empty stables off to one side. He walked through them, smelling long-vanished oats and straw, the scent of horse piss that never leaves a stable, soaked into earth and planking. Beyond the stables, a fine, fenced pasture swept upwards towards the ridge. Along the ridge, he could almost be certain, he saw the line of a road, delicate as though drawn by pencil. He was otherwise alone, himself and not Dennis Tully, nor Judkins the Englishman; himself the master of Lughnavalla House.

Back in the house, he unpacked the hamper which Delaney's man had made for him—a ham, bread, butter, tea, some sugar, tins of American beans and tins of fish, an all-but-entire cake, one slice cut away, with currents and raisins. He found himself a bedroom, neither sheets nor blankets, but a mattress, grey-and-white ticking, two plump pillows. All had been sold, he thought, house and furnishings, as though the Englishman had wanted to go home, taking not a keepsake with him, and leaving for old Tully a kind of legacy—bell jars of pheasants, and chinaware in the dining room, no doubt, the blues and reds of China.

From his bag, black, with a double grip, he took out shirts and underwear, and then, when all else had been set neatly in a dresser drawer, his box of maps and the box of letters, the cheap, imitation-leather edition of *The Plays of William Shakespeare Complete*, a box of cartridges, and, wrapped in white flannel, his heavy, massy revolver. He unwrapped it, and placed it on the table beside the bed, and the box of cartridges with it. He would be snug enough for a day or two. He was home.

It fell to my lot, a few days later, to go through Lughnavalla House, and clear out anything which Ned Nolan might have left there, as a house is cleared after it has been visited by plague. There was nothing, of course— a few shirts, three of them clean and one soiled at collar and wrists, that sort of thing. A box of maps, and a box in which he had carried letters, years old some of them, some my own yearly letters, and some from other friends. Nothing that could tie him in with his organization. One of the two razors on the washstand might have been his; it was of American make. And on the bedside table, his copy of *The Plays of William Shakespeare Complete*.

How could you be certain that it was his? Patrick Prentiss asked me, of course.

Oh, it was his, I answered, and handed it to him. There had once no doubt been a name and perhaps a date in the upper corner of the flyleaf, but it had been cut away.

When first he was in Kilpeder, in 'sixty-seven, I told Prentiss, he had a different one, elaborate, the tops of the pages painted gilt, and the cover embossed. It had been his father's, Thomas Justin Nolan's, and the flyleaf of that one had contained an elaborate inscription from father to son. But he lost it perhaps, or perhaps it wore out. This one is his—see there where he has written in the margins, and the tops or the bottoms of some of the pages. He was a great man for the Shakespeare, was Ned.

Prentiss took the volume from me, and turned the pages with the care that comes by training to scholars.

"It can endure hard wear," I assured him, "considering the places into which Ned must have carried it."

"Curious," Prentiss said. "A passion for Shakespeare. It doesn't fit."

Patrick has a great fondness for patterns.

"There is a butcher in Macroom," I said, "with a great passion for Gilbert and Sullivan. And there was in former years a Protestant lady in Mallow whose life's ambition was to write a history of the Borgias."

And put him off in that way, as he knew that I was doing, and smiled. Patrick Prentiss and I have become great friends of a sort. In truth, I had often myself wondered about Ned Nolan and Shakespeare, and had never come close to an answer.

What I did know, and what I told Patrick, was that the evening that we had together, Ned and Bob and myself, was a great disappointment in a way, as though Ned's return was an event which should not have happened, which was out of place and time. And Patrick all to the contrary, of course, because of his great belief in pattern. A final wheel clicked into place, and the machine of history, our history, idle and rusting for years, commenced again, like those intricate devices which are on display in Exhibitions of Art and Industry to offer us glimpses into the future perfection of the machine and, by implication, of the machine maker. Bishop Paley turned inside out, and driven mad into the bargain.

But Patrick has no sense of the feel of that Thursday evening, for all my poor efforts to re-create it for him. The three of us, sitting by the light of candles placed together, before the fireplace in the drawing room. Out of delicacy, out of a sense of the great distances between us, he told us little of the life he had been leading, nor why, but rather of places where he had been, what he had seen, crossing the Mississippi, and the point in Pittsburgh, Pennsylvania, where rivers join, and the maze in Hampton Court, where he had spent a day.

"And I saw you, Bob," he said. "Three times I was in the Gallery of the House—Frank Byrne had contrived it for me—and by God, you looked splendid, standing up there against the best of them. I wanted to nudge the fellow sitting next to me, and say, 'There is my friend, Robert Delaney.' "

"And so you should have done," Bob said.

"No," Ned said. "I don't think I should."

He was curious, but in a most uninformed way, as to my great project of making a memorial of the songs and the histories and legends of the Gaelic-speakers in the hills, before all of that passed away out of memory, the last of the speakers dead, and the Gaelic beaten out of the younger ones, a despised tongue, a helot's tongue. I must have been speaking with warmth, because he said, "Good work, Hughie," and then the three of us fell silent again.

"Here I am," he would say. "A few days only. But here I am home." Or one of us would say, "By God, it is good to see you home with us for a bit, Ned." And we meant it, all three of us; all three of us wanted it to be true, and all knew that down at some bedrock or shale of actuality, it was not true, as if he had not come back at all.

But what was hardest of all for Bob and myself was to accept the way in which he would weave everything, every thought and allusion, back to those few weeks that he was with us, back to the day—back to the hours, to be precise—of the Rising.

"There is a time in youth, lads," he said, "when all is clear, an unruffled lake, a stream pellucid as crystal. Time stirs up the mud. Ourselves, the three of us, and Vincent, and the lads who were with us in Clonbrony. That is not to be wiped away, nor besmirched by a few foolish songs. Later on, we live in dirt. I lived in dirt. We do the best we can, but there are the bare bones of the matter."

"In dirt," Bob said. "Dirt and bare bones. You have a sombre view of life, Ned."

It was to be one of Bob's nights. I could tell that because I had come to know them, but Ned could as well. He was always watchful—of Bob, of me, of himself. With doors and windows shut, drapes drawn, he would have heard a footstep on the garden path. A habit which soon he would no longer have a need for.

For he would speak, in that special tone which unfailingly betrays self-delusion, of how pleasant life would be for him in the house that Tom Bonner would find for him above the brickyards, with a view of the Hudson River. A lordly river, he would call it, iced over in winter, to the north of the yards, but a channel kept open, and the rest of the year heavy with water traffic, steamboats, and vessels under sail, barges, pleasure craft.

Suddenly then, after more than two hours of avoiding it, he said, "It is all over, you know."

"It has been over for years, boy," Bob said, the whiskey but nibbling without consequence as yet at the edges of his discretion. "There is a fellow in town named Lanty Hanlon, a farrier. You would not recall him, I do not think."

Ned shook his head.

"He was with us, a gangly young fellow scarcely a year or two out of Hugh's schoolhouse. He is all the organization there is now in Kilpeder, himself and a few younger sons and the potboy at Grennan's. Towards the end, when we had need of blackthorns, Mulcahy sent down word, and they lent us a welcome hand. There is the end of it, Ned. In this country, at any rate. In New York and Boston you may still have great plans."

"And tomorrow Vincent is giving a meal to the resident magistrate of Kilpeder," Ned said. "Round is the world that goes upon wheels, as my father used to say."

"He is not the worst in the world," Bob said. "But I declined the invitation. It was on Richardson's orders that I was arrested at the time of the boycotting, and that freezes the bud of friendship. But the most of his duties involve poaching and the dynamiting of fishing streams and quarrels as to rights of way. A decent enough sort."

"If only the Rising had been general," Ned said, "as all was agreed upon, the day set and fixed. If more lads had risen up besides ourselves, and the lads in South Cork and in Limerick and in Tipperary, and in the hills above Dublin. We would have had something then, by God."

"If," Bob said, refilling our glasses. "And if Bonaparte had not had belly cramps the morning of Waterloo, and if Julius Caesar had minded the good advice of wife and soothsayer. We lacked a soothsayer of our own."

"But no lack of informers," I said. "It was informers did for the Rising, across the breadth of Ireland, Ned. You know that. Massey, Corydon, the whole lot of them. It does no good to gab away about all that. Leave it to the ballad makers."

"Bloody informers," Ned said. "At least we were clear of them in Clonbrony Wood. We will keep a clean record from that day's work, lads. Before we began to walk in dirt, move in it."

I was beginning to get a bit annoyed about this talk of dirt, which I had never noticed especially as a part of my own existence. Ned and his talk of dirt had something in common with Lady Macbeth and her distaste, belatedly, for blood. And then, at once, like a flame placing itself beside the candles, I saw the meaning of his words. It was not dirt he meant at all, not the rough soil and grime which falls upon the spirit with age, with time. He was speaking of himself, of his own life. He meant blood.

I shivered, and looked through the small, flickering light towards Bob, on the off-chance that he shared this perception, but he had thoughts of his own, and he was looking down into his glass, which he held in his two hands.

After a bit, after a long bit, after a session of four hours or more, I had had more than enough of this. Much as I had dreamed of the four of us, and Mary with us, talking together in sunlight and clear air, or the companionship of a Sunday meal, linen and what we had left of a leg of lamb, a trifle, cigar smoke and decent port, I had never held in consideration three men sitting by candlelight, in a house which time had turned into an historical travesty, rehearsing our pasts, like old fellows sitting in a pothouse, nor had I imagined Ned carrying guilt with him like a ruddy caul. No, not guilt, but simple knowledge of what he had done, how little it had accomplished.

But there was no getting Bob to leave with me, not by then, and so I left him to Lughnavalla House and to Ned, and went home along the mercifully clear, straight county road, in starshine. And that is how it happened.

When I look back upon the matter, Bob told me a few weeks later, I would place the beginning of it all with a kind of oppressiveness which was settling upon me, and the gloom of that drawing room, broken by those lurid candles, and at the centre of it the kind of pathos which Ned seemed to be carrying with him, the lack of conviction in his voice at times, so that his descriptions of life as a straw boss on the Hudson could as well have been about ferrying a sampan in the Sea of Japan. A lost man. I rose up, and with the drapes drawn, and the high ridge between us and all harm, I lit every lamp in the ill-shaped wretched room—lamps with green globes, lamps with bowls of milky white with flowers painted upon them, lamps with globes made of varicoloured panels. The entire lot. I brought two in from the dining room for good measure. And all this while, Ned looked at me with amazement, but of a mild, bemused sort. He was unused to drink, that was clear; but he had put constraint behind him.

Oh, Lordie, but that room looked awful, Hughie. Small wonder that the Englishman sold it up, contents and all. Do you recall it at all, how it looked that day when we swaggered in, the emergency man trailing behind us? It looks worse at night, in artificial light. And to think that this is the pinnacle towards which Dennis Tully has been clambering. He is welcome to it, and more.

Presently, I began talking to Ned, talking freely—there had been a special kind of bond between us, you recall that—and I told him how matters stood for me, and a good bit about what had happened. He listened—he strained to listen—but it was as if we were two fellows marooned together on the same island, but from continents with different customs, different gods.

"What matters," he said to me at one point, "is that you stood by the man to whom you were pledged. Most of those lousers left him in the ditch. But not yourself, Bob." As if any of that was mattering to me in the end, as if any of that had meaning, the whole of that bleeding away from me; and when I sat in the chapel in London with the knowledge that Sylvia was dead, and how she had died, I felt myself a shell. A shell has no meaning. And foolishly, because I could see that he could not understand, any more than if I had been talking in Welsh, I tried to talk to him about her. I must by then have been drunk, surely. And in exchange—by way of consolation, no doubt—he told me of a woman he might have married, years before, a servant girl in New York, and then other women here and there—bodies, most of them, to satisfy his needs, but two or three of them he remembered, and thought often of them. "I see, yes," I said to him, because he meant only to help, and it was clear that he had never talked of such matters before, never, to anyone.

But we could not keep away from politics; no two Irishmen can, Irishmen like ourselves at any rate, not with a bottle between us. "Devoy was able to bend," I said to him. "Devoy has your confidence, and Devoy set up the alliance between Parnell and the League." Newspaper talk. I must have sounded like the *Freeman's Journal*, and in fact I no longer gave a damn about anything; but his fierceness frightened and angered me, an iron rod. "They took it from us by the sword," he said, "and we can only take it back with the gun." Then he—he mind you, not me—poured from the bottle into our glasses.

"The gun," I said. "It was the gun that we gave a try to in 'sixty-seven. But some of us moved on. Some of us moved on to the surgical knives to hack up unarmed men, and black powder and dynamite to destroy passersby, old men and children. Women. A rare treat, to make war on women, that must be."

"I read in the papers a few years back that you were at Mitchelstown when the peelers fired into the crowd of people. Was there distinction made there between men and children? When they starved us and drove us out in the millions, in the black forties, was there a distinction made?"

"There might have been another famine in our own time," I said, "had it not been for the Land War. Sweet fucking use the organization was to us then, save to obstruct us as best it could. And we won! That war is the war we won. Look about you."

"I am," he said. "Lughnavalla House has passed from the hands of the Englishman to the hands of Dennis Tully."

In flames, I thought! Nothing will ever burn away the Lughnavalla Houses of this land but actual flames, Lughnavalla House ablaze and Ardmor Castle ablaze and Macroom Castle ablaze. If I had not been drunk before, I was now, with grand apocalyptic visions. And Ned may perhaps have been drunk, should have been drunk; but if so it was in his own way, quiet despite the violence of his language, as though all had been sorted out years before, like a proposition in Euclid. But now the geometry book had been closed shut upon him by history. He would have his nights in this wretched history-mangled island which had become his tabernacle, holy of holies, and then off to his brickyard, himself and his friend Bonner, Fenian soldier and raider turned prosperous brickmaker, the waters of the world crowded with his galleons—or at the least, his barges—taking bricks down to New York City.

There we were the two of us, ill met after a quarter century, battering away at each other, with swigs from a bottle, like a caricature in *Punch*.

Dawn, a pale grey, showed itself by a gap in the ill-drawn curtains, and rising to my feet, knocking over in my progress a tabouret of wood gaudily inlaid with mother-of-pearl or its cheap Birmingham equivalent. I pulled back the drapes, and with such force that the cord pulled one of them down entirely, and it lay athwart the windows. It was too dark to see the Derrynasaggarts.

"We have Clonbrony," Ned's voice said behind me. "This thing has happened and that thing has happened. We have Clonbrony. The four of us do. The sixty of us. Like a moment of clarity, a moment, an hour, a day of clarity." It was as though he saw that we had let a night of language wrench at us, deface something, and he was drawing me back. I knew what I should have said, some word which would be an echo of his own. This had happened and that thing had happened, and for him, the years in Portland Prison had happened, warping, bludgeoning the spirit, day after day of meaningless labour, night after night of blackness, no sound but an occasional scream of solitary anguish. Or so I imagined, and close enough to the fact. That was the price Ned paid for Clonbrony. That day that he and yourself had in Dublin, Hughie, do you recall, you asked him about it, and he shrugged. "I was in the hands of my enemies. I expected no better." And Clonbrony was the one bright, good spot of time, clear winter air it must have seemed in his recollection, bare branches pure, the distant hills, a fight well fought—foolish, no doubt, but well fought.

But the furies were at me, the furies and the drink, and I thought, Let it all come down, let nothing be left save for ruins, with truth itself as crowbar and black powder.

"Clonbrony Wood," I shouted out to him. "That drivelling ballad is not the only smear on that, Ned. We were sold by an informer. There was an informer there with us in Clonbrony Wood."

I heard nothing behind me, no sound, and I was too full of myself to turn around, and helplessly, I put my head upon the welcome cool of the window and began to cry. I went nearly mad when Sylvia—when Sylvia died, but I do not remember crying. I was crying now, tears compounded of grief and whiskey and rage, and somewhere behind all, the furtive little knowledge that I had said something which should never have been said—not by me, that day in Lughnavalla House, and surely not, surely never, to Ned. But it is right that you should know it, Hughie; let the arc bend itself into a ring, and then we will throw the bloody ring away, never speak of it again. I was aware of nothing, no sound save my own sobs, which I brought at last under control; but my eyes were wet, distasteful to my imagination, and I felt myself disordered, in disarray. Then I heard Ned say, in a voice calm and even, as though that iron bar which was his soul had been given voice, "Who, Bob? Put a name to him." And I was so disordered that I could do nothing else, so that my shout had a snarl to it, an anger with myself and with twenty-five years of our lives.

"Vincent," I said. "Vincent Tully. Vincent, the fellow of infinite jest. Vincent turned informer."

"I cannot believe you," Ned said, his voice still even, hard as iron, hard as tempered steel.

"You might as well," I said. "I have his own word for it."

"He confessed?" Ned said, and now the steel was touched by something else. "He confessed it to you?"

"You could call it a confession, I suppose," I said, and with those words I felt a measure of control coming back into my speech. "Yes, surely he himself called it a confession."

It was the day that Bob, in the intensity of his indecision, received the urgent note from Vincent to join him at Brierly Lodge, the day that Vincent told him about the small, wet, ugly toad that each of us must swallow each day, according to the cynical French contriver of maxims.

"Everyone, do you not see, Bob? That was the Frenchman's point. Each one of us does. I must myself gulp down my morning toad. I do it looking in the glass, as I am shaving. The toad still has a nasty taste to him, but he has shrunk a bit over the years. Let me tell you about him."

It was in the weeks that we were all, all four of us, Ned and Bob and Vincent and myself, and a few hundred others as well, in the gaol in Cork City, awaiting our trials. Butt had come down, upon the basis of some funds supplied by the organization, to defend Ned, against whom, as all knew, the most serious charges would be brought. But for Vincent, his beloved son, Dennis Tully had been urged by Dripsey, the solicitor he engaged, to go for the best, and the best was Emmet Bourke, the finest flower of a legal family which had been in blossom for generations. And Vincent, in his turn, had insisted that he would have no counsel at all, would settle for the first bottle-nosed, broken-veined barrister to present himself, if Bob and myself were not given legal protection and advocacy equal to that with which he was himself provided. And so it was, that a schoolmaster and a shop assistant were defended in court by the most costly barrister in Ireland, and a man worth every pound of his retainer.

I well remember my own conversation with Bourke and with Dripsey, a privileged glimpse it was into the intricacies of the law, and the delicate self-esteem of those practitioners who were its masters, dwelling in some world of language parallel to our own but distinct from it. And Bob, as he was to tell me later, had had a similar conversation. What best I remember of Bourke is a quietly opulent tie, and the patient, bored manner of a schoolmaster instructing a roomful of dullards in the mysteries of quadratic equations. "No, no," he would say, shaking his head at some comment I had ventured to make, some bit of crude fact which I had dragged into the conversation, "No, no. There is nothing to that effect in the indictment. Not that I recall. Can you, Dripsey?"

He had a sumptuous manner, and that ironical suavity which certain barristers cultivate, and which glistens the more vividly when placed against the possible disasters awaiting their clients. But he did marvellously, I thought: Vincent acquitted as one too far down in the table of command to be of concern to the law, or of no greater concern at any rate than that of the farmboys who had followed us, and four years each meted out to Bob and myself, of which we served but six months.

Bob and myself were scarcely babes in infant's frocks, and in the years that followed we often discussed, and Vincent joining in with us, the mildness of our sentences—not unparalleled, to be sure, for there were lads across the length and breadth of Munster who were being given four years or six, but none the less welcome for being common. But we always had a sense, the two of us, that Dennis Tully had contrived in some way to put his weight into the balance. In Vincent's presence, we would speak of the matter with delicacy, but he had no such scruples. "We may be damned well certain of it, lads. The old fellow knows the right word to speak into the right ear. Nothing improper, to be sure. But a friend in court, as the saying has it. And is that Emmet Bourke not a wonder, lads, a mind like a fine watch ticking away—limited, perhaps, but encased in gold."

But it had not been that way at all. A quarter century later, in Brierly Lodge, Vincent told Bob how it had been.

L et us talk plainly," the young Vincent Tully had said to Bourke. "You are suggesting that I offer myself to the Crown as an informer."

"Let us indeed speak plainly, Mr. Tully—young Mr. Tully, if I may say so. And words like *informer* are not plain talk. Anything but, not in this country. The Crown, very generously in my view of the matter, has signified its willingness to take a broad and comprehensive view of this entire matter, and if you should find some way of making yourself useful to the Crown, the Crown, in its turn, would not be unmindful of what might be construed as contrition on your part, a regret at having taken part in so farcical a calamity."

"And that," Vincent said, "would be in some way different from being a common informer? There is some fine distinction here which I seem unable to grasp."

Bourke smiled. "You have a nice irony, Mr. Tully. It must be a flower native to your barony."

"You have held such a discussion with the other Kilpeder men?" Vincent asked.

"Indeed no. There has been a rebellion in arms, shots fired, men killed. Your friend MacMahon, for example, was in a position of command. Rebellion in arms carries a stiff penalty, as of course you know."

"Position of command," Vincent said. "He was third-in-command. I would have held that post myself if—if matters had not changed."

"If Edward Nolan had not come to Kilpeder to take command. But he did. Nolan is for it. If you will pardon the legal euphemism. He will admit nothing, deny nothing, beyond saying that he was in command, and that what was done, was done on his orders. You are differently situated, yourself and Schoolmaster MacMahon. Or you could be. It is up to you, of course."

"And Robert Delaney?" Vincent asked.

"Ah," Bourke said, savouring the aspirant sound. "Now, there is a nice problem indeed for Mr. Dripsey and myself. I am defending all three of you, of course, upon Dripsey's instructions—a dreary fellow, is he not? And always with a drop on the end of his nose as though to suit the name, sort of thing you get in Dickens—and each of the three cases has its peculiarities. Delaney was not merely second-in-command, he was in command until Nolan arrived. And the Crown—foolish word, the Crown is over in Westminster Abbey or the Tower of London or someplace like that—when I say the Crown, I mean my learned friend Mr. Bodkin, the Crown prosecutor. He *is* rather learned by the way—the Crown has somehow formed the notion that Robert Delaney was the Fenian Centre for Kilpeder."

Vincent began to speak, but Bourke raised his hand. "I am representing Delaney as well as yourself. Be careful of what you say."

"And there we are," Vincent said.

A good half inch separated the bars of the small rectangular window from its grimy glass. Beyond it, as Vincent well knew, was an exercise yard, and high walls. Cork City lay beyond it, Sunday's Well and Montenotte, the theatres and the opera house, the bells of Shandon that sounded so grand on the River Lee, as the song had it, which everyone knew off by heart because of that foolish, lovable rhyme, "Shandon / grand on."

"There we are," Bourke agreed.

"Hard cheese on Robert Delaney and hard cheese, no doubt, on Hugh MacMahon, but not on Dennis Tully's son."

"Don't be absurd," Bourke said, his voice cracking like a whip in the dusty room. "If any leniency were to be shown to you, or to any of the

[767]

others, it would be upon the basis of your assistance in the restoration of tranquillity and good order to this misfortunate island. And not because your father can afford decent counsel for you. The Crown does not trade and deal. The Crown is not a gombeen man."

"The Crown," Vincent said, "is off in the Tower of London. Mr. Bodkin does trade and deal, I take it?"

"I am accustomed to all sorts and conditions of client, Mr. Tully. Snivelling, despairing, insolent, what have you. If I become sufficiently bored, I throw in my brief. In my earliest years at the bar, I could not afford such delicacy. I once defended a man who had done the most extraordinary things to a young sow, and was entirely unrepentant. I ask you! A sow! Sheep are a different matter entirely."

Suddenly, Vincent slapped his hands together and laughed. "You are a rare one, Mr. Bourke. I daresay that you have a fine dinner in view for yourself this night?"

Bourke shrugged. "Not especially. Bodkin and I are dining together at the Imperial."

"And your suggestion," Vincent said, "is that I should unburden myself to your dinner companion, after he has had his indigestible spring lamb, with that dab of green vitriol the Imperial places beside it and calls mint sauce?"

"You are perking up a bit," Bourke said. "This means that you are giving thought to what I tell you. No indeed, you will not speak to Mr. Bodkin. An inspector of constabulary and two gentlemen from Dublin Castle have signified to Mr. Dripsey a willingness, a bare willingness, to talk to yourself and to Mr. MacMahon. At the end of these conversations, they may or they may not feel inclined to place certain recommendations before Mr. Bodkin as to the best disposition of your cases."

Vincent stood up, walked to the grimy window, and looked down into the exercise yard.

"A gloomy prospect, is it not?" Bourke asked. "Perhaps one grows accustomed to it over the years, but I doubt it."

Vincent had nothing to say.

"Time is short," Bourke said. "The assizes are upon us."

"No need for haste," Vincent said. "The Crown has never lacked for informers."

"The Crown has no need for haste," Bourke said. "But you do. As you say, they are queueing up. You could lose out."

"If I were to give information," Vincent began, but Bourke cut him short. "Turn around please, Mr. Tully. Look at me." Vincent saw that Bourke had taken from his waistcoat pocket an elaborate watch, and had flipped open its cover. A theatrical gesture, Vincent knew, but it had its effect, all the same.

"This is a busy assizes for me, Mr. Tully. Barristers are not country solicitors with the long day before them to disentangle scruples of conscience. I will give you advice, short and to the point. I am not the Crown, I am not the Crown prosecutor. I am your defending counsel, I am on your side as it were, and I am being paid handsomely to give you my best advice. Let us address for a brief moment this question of informing. If, in the months before the Rising, you had gone to the constabulary barracks, or into Cork City, and told all that you knew, prompted by gain or perhaps by a nobler wish to avoid the needless and futile spilling of blood, then you would be, no doubt, an informer. But the Fenian insurrection is crushed, and whatever its hour or two of bravado in Cork and Limerick and Kerry, it has been, across the country, a fiasco. Names very high indeed in your organization are taking . . . the sensible course. I marvel, indeed, that the Crown is going out of its way to accept bargains. But then Crowns are tidy by nature. No loose ends."

"If," Vincent said, "if I were to give information, there would be certain conditions."

Bourke held up his free hand, palm outwards, and snapped his watch shut. "Should you feel inclined to make a statement and to answer questions put to you by the gentlemen who have come up from the Castle, I imagine that a word to the governor of the prison would set matters in motion."

But it took Vincent a full week to make up his mind, a full week of an hour's daily trudge about that exercise yard and then back to the cell's silence, a full week of lying sleepless on his plank, straw, a film of straw, separating him from the wood. Sometime during that week, his father visited him, and of the substance of that visit, Vincent told nothing to Bob, as though the mere fact of the visit carried its own significance. Said nothing directly, that is.

"There were no offers signified to you, were there, Bob?" Vincent asked him, in Brierly Lodge, in late afternoon light, and Bob shook his head. "No," Vincent said, "nor to Hughie. They knew their material as a stonemason knows his, tapping away with his chisel, finding the weak spot, the line of fissure."

After a week, Vincent sent out word to the governor, through the turnkey, and three days later he was in a room, spacious but meagrely furnished, with three men seated behind a long, baize-covered table who did not offer him their names. There was a plain chair, armless, facing the table, and Vincent, by a gesture, was told to sit there. The gesturer, so he learned later, was Jeremiah Callinan, an inspector from the Castle. The second man was an inspector as well, but local, a tall bald man with a large, shapeless strawberry mark; and the third one, from the Castle as well, was youngish, tall, with a yellowish moustache.

"You wish to make a statement," Yellowish said. He was English, with an accent that Vincent found it difficult to place.

"I do," Vincent said. "But on conditions."

"Conditions indeed!" Yellowish said. "There is no need for you to waste our time"—he glanced down at a sheet of names—"no need to waste our time, Tully. We are amply provided with fellows who do not require conditions."

Vincent sat, unspeaking, uncertain whether or not he was to leave.

Jeremiah Callinan leaned forward, a heavy, soft man, his paunch pressing against the table. "Out of curiosity, what sort of conditions had you had in mind?"

"I will tell you about the part which I took in the insurrection, beginning with the day that I took the oath, and going forward to the hour when I made my surrender, and leaving nothing out. I was in arms, and I fired off those arms against the Queen's troops. I helped organise the arms raid which made possible the Kilpeder uprising. But I will implicate no other man. There you are."

"Vincent," Callinan said, and he knew his Christian name without looking at the sheet. "This is no help to us, or to you. You surrendered in arms, as Nolan did, and Delaney, and MacMahon. We have as strong a case against you lads as we need. When you come cap in hand before Her Majesty, you should have something to offer her."

"This Skibbereen man," Yellowish said to Callinan, looking up with impatience from the list. "He might be worth a bit of a chat."

"Nolan never administered the oath to you, Vincent," Callinan said. "Delaney was your Centre before Nolan arrived from foreign parts, and Delaney it was, Delaney and MacMahon and yourself, who administered it to the poor idjeets who followed you. But who gave you the oath, Vincent, and who gave it to Delaney?"

This window, a tall one, had by contrast been scrubbed clear of grime, and the fellows who sat in Vincent's chair had a fine view of the city; but the three men behind the table had only a door to look at, a warder, and a succession of fellows like . . . like me, Vincent thought.

"Skibbereen," Yellowish said. "Fellow named Donovan. Might be kin to that blackguard Rossa. Real name's Donovan, isn't it?"

"You might say," Callinan said dryly.

Not that night, but the next, four days before the trials, Vincent had somehow managed to get to sleep, when he was awakened by the blinding light of a lantern, and heard a shuffling of feet. Behind the looming figures—he made them out to be two—he saw that the door of his cell was open. Far down, to the left of the corridor, there was a faint, greenish light.

"We will be grand now," Callinan said to the turnkey, who left the lantern behind with them, and closed the door. "Do you mind," Callinan said, "if I perch myself on the edge of your . . . what can it be called? Not your bed, surely. Your plank." Sleep-dazed, but coming soon afterwards aware, then alert, Vincent nodded.

"Now then, Vincent lad," Callinan said. "Tis good to have a chance to chat, away from that bloody Englishman, and that room that is like something out of the Spanish Inquisition."

Vincent studied him by deceptive lantern light. There was more there than softness, paunch. He had the look of a strong-farmer, beefy cheeks, and a broad, determined chin.

"Conditions, how are you!" Callinan said. "The Englishman was right as far as that goes, which is not far. 'I will implicate no other man.' Nobly said, by God. Nobly said. Robert Emmet could not have said it better. But let us take a look at the facts, boy."

The word *boy*, as he pronounced it, touched a bell, Shandon clear. "You are a Cork man yourself," Vincent said.

"I am, of course," Callinan said, affronted. "What else would a Callinan be? My father was a warden in the O'Connellite repeal agitation, and I used troop along behind him. Twice I saw the Liberator close enough to touch—a man of heroic build, and a voice on him like a bull, but beguiling and soft as occasion demanded."

"You have travelled far since then, Inspector," Vincent said.

"Not so far as all that, boy. Not so far. Do you know, there is a man who puts me strangely in mind of my poor father, and that is your own father, Vincent. We had a long chat together last week, Mr. Tully and myself. At his urging, I assure you. Not mine."

"Yes," Vincent said. "I can see that. My father and yourself have much in common."

"He is a coming man in the county, your father is. But all that matters not tuppence to him at the moment. He is heart-broken, Vincent. There is no need for me to tell you that."

"No," Vincent said. "No need."

"The one son," Callinan said. "You know how old fellows feel about the one son."

"I know how this one does," Vincent said, and looked away from Callinan towards the wall.

" 'I will implicate no other man,' " Callinan said. "Let us look at that a bit. There is something which I could not have told you before that damned Englishman, and should not be telling you now. Nothing can help Edward Nolan and nothing can harm him. But your chums, Delaney and MacMahon, are a bit better off than you may think. Neither the Castle nor London itself is anxious to fill up the prisons for a lifetime with foolish Fenian lads. The charge against Delaney and against MacMahon has been reduced to treason-felony, and that is a different matter. They can expect their years in durance vile, but not so long as might be imagined. Now, as to the indictment against yourself." He shrugged. "Who knows?"

"A pity," Vincent said, "that I cannot have the Liberator as my counsel. He worked wonders for those poor lads on trial in Doneraile, back in the thirties."

"You have his inheritor, boy. You have Emmet Bourke. Isaac Butt is a decent, hardworking, hard-drinking Protestant, but Emmet Bourke is the genuine object, satisfaction guaranteed and accept no substitutes. It is Emmet Bourke who bargained Bodkin, that mean Orange cunt, down to treason-felony for the three of you, and it is Emmet Bourke who put a word into Bodkin's ear that you might be of use to—to those you might be of use to, if you take my meaning. Bourke and Bodkin are old friends on the circuit. Think it over, boy. You have the whole rest of the night to ponder it. Tis just past two."

"They go to gaol," Vincent said, "my two close friends in all the world, and I go free or all but it."

"No, lad. No, no," Callinan said, in a kindly manner, as though he saw perfectly the shape and colour of Vincent's torment. "They will want everything, everything. As a token of your good intentions. But your two chums will not spend an extra day in gaol because of your testimony. You have my word on that, the word of one Cork man to another. And there will be no question of your testifying in open court. A few questions put with discretion in that room we both know, to present your credentials, like, and then a written statement, as full as you can make it."

In darkness made lurid by lantern light, Callinan was policeman, father, enemy, priest, friend.

"And what cause does your silence serve?" Callinan said. "A shattered conspiracy lying in ruins. You are a lucky young fellow to have Emmet Bourke, and myself. Not to mention, above all, your good father."

The next morning, sitting in the same chair, as clean-shaven as a curate, looking at none of the three men, at Callinan least of all, looking beyond them towards the window, beyond the window towards the city, whose river flowed into the sea past meadowlands of freedom, soft hills, the time-softened ruins of castle and abbey, Vincent said, "The Head Centre for Cork City is a man named Joseph Tumulty. He has a ships' chandlery on the quays. By rights, he should not know the names of any of the other Head Centres, but he does, and he is a talkative man with drink taken."

"You could not have made a better beginning," Callinan told him later. "Tumulty had already made his statement to us, told us everything he knew. But you were useful for confirmation. We could check what Tumulty had told us the week before, against what you were telling us now. You did yourself the best favour you could have done. I was proud of you, Vincent."

"Joe Tumulty," Bob said, at Brierly Lodge. "The little bastard. At the time of the Land League, he denounced me as a Ribbon Fenian, the little shite."

"What word have you for me?" Vincent asked, and Delaney said nothing. "They must be stacked up there in Dublin Castle, gathering dust. Statements and depositions written out by people who did what I did. Big fish and little fish."

Still Delaney said nothing.

"It was not enough," Vincent said. "They had a full statement from Tumulty, and my confirming bits and pieces of it was not enough."

A bit of turf tumbled forward into the flame, disclosing its own bright red, burning center.

"I gave them William Lomasney," Vincent said. "I sold Lomasney to them."

When Delaney did speak then, it was after his mind had been fumbling in the past, rooting among forgotten details. "You could not have done that, Vincent," he said slowly, as though placing foot by tentative foot along a treacherous ridge. "We were in Cork City Gaol when Lomasney was taken, right enough, but no one stagged him. Mackey, he was called in those days, do you recall, William Mackey. He was taken in Cork City, in a running gun battle with the police. A constable was killed." He shook his head, as though to clear it, as though to rid itself of everything that had been said.

"It was from Tumulty that he took his orders," Vincent said relentlessly, "directly from Tumulty. But he had been on the run since the attack he made on Ballyknockane. He was making raids on gun shops in the city to reoutfit his men. And he was on the loose, not reporting back to Tumulty. He suspected Tumulty, so Callinan told me. But he was using the safe house we all knew about; he was staying with the Keefes, old Francis Keefe and his son. Tumulty would not have known about it; it was in the Kilcrea command."

But Delaney shook his head again. "He was not taken there, Vincent. Haven't I told you that?"

"They tossed the Keefes the day after I told them, and the old fellow was put under arrest, and his son along with him. Lomasney was a wild fellow after that, without a safe house, distrustful of Tumulty. A gunman on the loose."

Bob sat staring at him.

"What was it they gave him," he said at last, "ten years?"

"Twelve," Vincent said. "There was some technicality. They could not make the murder charge stick, and they had him for treason-felony."

Delaney reached out towards the bottle and then, by some instinct of the nerves, his arm pulled itself back.

"Go on," Vincent said. "The whiskey is not infectious. Connolly's best."

Delaney poured a large measure, and carried his glass to the window, where he stood with his back to Vincent.

"It always seemed, later, to have been a long time," Vincent said, "weeks and weeks. And yet it was but three days and nights. In the afternoons and parts of the night, I would write away at my statement. They put a table in my cell, and I would sit on the edge of the plank. And two candles, the turnkey would light them when the light failed from the window; and in the morning I would answer their questions. Not upon what I had written; I could never tell what they would be curious about. Some questions I could answer and others I could not. After Ned came, there was little I could tell them. He was that tight-lipped, you remember? But you would go down to Cork City, with Ryan from Macroom, and come back to tell us what you had heard. You should not have done that, Bob. Ned was furious about how much Hughie and I knew."

"The mistake was mine," Delaney said to the window. "I trusted you."

"After a time," Vincent said, "I would only mark changes in my world by whether the candles were lit or not. My fingers were stiff from writing. But every day, and late at night, before I would go to sleep, Callinan would visit me. I would sit with my back against the wall of the cell, plaster filthy with the grime of other prisoners before me, and he would tell me of the two times he saw the Liberator, and his first days in the Constabulary, at the barracks in Drumshanbo, up in Leitrim. He brought mugs of cocoa with him; not the muck they served out to us, do you recall, but thick and creamy, sweetened. Are you listening, Bob?" he said to Delaney's back.

"Is that what you sold Lomasney for?" Delaney asked. "A mug of cocoa?"

"Perhaps," Vincent said. "It was for my freedom, so I thought. But perhaps it was for a mug of cocoa. 'Bits and pieces, lad,' Callinan said to me. 'Stale bread. That is what that damned Englishman calls your statement. And small wonder: this is not over yet. There were two constables killed the Tuesday at Limerick Junction, and below here, William Mackey is roaming with his men armed and equipped. But keep working away, lad. Don't give up hope. There are the three of us to make the decision, and one of us is, by God, on your side. Drink up your cocoa, lad. The cook prepares it especially for me, a decent woman from beyond the mountains, from Fenit in Kerry.' As he was getting up to go, I said, 'I can give you Mackey.' "

The gatekeeper and a young lad had rakes with them, and were smoothing the gravel of the path, taking their time about it, making the task last until sunset.

"There it is," Vincent said. "There is my toad."

When Delaney turned away from the window, he said, "Ahhh, Vincent. Vincent." He could think of nothing else to say. He could not interpret his own feelings. They were a jumble, intense but disordered.

Because there seemed nothing else to do, Delaney recrossed the room and seated himself facing Vincent. The bottle was between them.

There had been a long time when Vincent feared that their plan was to make some sort of Judas goat of him, with the signed statement to hold over his head, that they would expect reports from him. But nothing happened, and the years meted out to his friends shrivelled away to six months, and they were back in Kilpeder. Once, years and years later, in Westmoreland Street in Dublin, he had come face-to-face with Callinan, who seemed not to recognise him, a portly man now, his paunch pendulous, with thick moustaches a snowy white. He was chewing at something, a sweet perhaps, his jaws moving slowly, with a sideways motion, camellike.

"Well, Bob," Tully said again, "there is your toad for you, and a handsome little fellow he is. Bob? Bob? Are you awake at all?"

A bit of Delaney had been awake, awake enough and sober enough to hear Tully's question, but not to answer it. He remembered it, as he took his long walk to bring himself into sobriety, down the freshly raked carriageway, and out past the gatekeeper's lodge and onto the Kilpeder road. By morning, he had been ready to swallow his own toad with the cup of tea that Vincent's nice bit had made for him, and even to bid Vincent good morning when he saw him standing, silent, hesitating, by the kitchen door. And the wonder is, he had thought, as he rode down in early morning light to his office, to write out the letters which he now knew that he must write, the wonder is that it was his way of sorting out my problem for me, a gift from a friend, the confession of a young man's weakness and fatal instinct of adaptability.

I did not tell all of that to Ned, of course, Bob would later tell me, it would have been of scant interest to him; but I had said too much to unsay anything, and I told him the worst of it. I was in a terrible shape, you know, Hughie, between the drinks and the misery I felt, and there was also some muddy anger not against Vincent, but against Ned, that he thought himself so pure, that he thought Clonbrony Wood was so pure, and we were, you and I and Vincent, and all that time he was carrying blood around with him and calling it dirt. If blood is dirt, then there is dirt on all of us.

But Ned's quietness was terrifying, even though for the moment I was too drunk and angry and muddled to read his quiet properly.

He had been having a glass for every two of mine, and yet he was as sober as a judge. He was a judge, indeed, although I did not understand that—judge, and prosecutor, and jury. He had curiously few questions to put to me, though, in view of what I had told him.

"It was a long time ago," I told him.

"Oh yes," he said, "a long, long time."

"And the wretched part of it is, you know," I said, "that in the heel of the hunt, Hughie and myself served but six months of our sentences.

He would have had but six months of his life to pay out, and instead, he has had this gnawing at him."

"Life's roads are hard," Ned said, "the most of them."

"There are things I have done that I am not proud of," I said. "Yourself as well, no doubt, Ned." A chill of fear was at work on my drunkenness, like a high wind shaking a stand of aspens.

"Many things," Ned said.

"There you are, then," I said. "I have not told Hughie, of course."

"No," Ned said, in the same distant, indifferent manner. "Of course not. But you told me."

"The drink told you, Ned. Not me. I have been hitting it too hard these past months. The past year indeed."

"It is wonderful," Ned said, and his voice sounded now pure Yank, hard and metallic, "the way everything in life has an excuse. And everybody. Hell must be empty."

"Hell is here, according to some schools of thought," I said.

"And very good schools they are," he said.

That morning, home in my own kitchen, I sat at the table and drank tea, a pot of it and a bit more. Mrs. Madigan kept it hot and strong for me. A decent Macroom woman. Agnes insists that we call her "Cook." I remember once, Vincent said to Agnes, "If God had intended that she be called 'Cook' he would have organized the baptism accordingly." He was always a great deflationer of the airs and pretences of the Tullys. But not without a few of his own, mind you. Not without a few of his own. After a bit, I took a stroll through the town. I was tempted to call in on Mary and yourself—it was still early on, a bit past seven, because I had heard the tolling bell of Saint Jarlath's—but I knew that if I said a word to you, to either of you, I would say everything, and I had still that fond, foolish belief that all would come right in the end, that I would make it come right.

I walked down to the other end of the town, and stood in admiration of their church, neat and tidy, visited by God as often as our own, I daresay, but in a different form, neat and clean and well advised, and facing it, a bare ten yards away, those gates which you years ago christened for us, the falcon-guarded gates; but the gates were swung shut that day and bolted. Then up again, back into the town, and a moment's pause for reverential inspection of the obelisk. The day was now clear, windless, and the mountains were vivid in the distance. Somewhere between them and ourselves were Brierly Lodge and Lughnavalla House and Clonbrony Wood. Three commercial travellers were finishing their breakfasts in the

Arms, their table a corpse-strewn battlefield, crusts of toast and bits of brown bread lying in platters of congealed egg yolk, rinds of bacon. I sat down at a second table and told the girl—Norah Spillane, you know her, a good girl—to bring me tea and toast, and one small—small, mind you—dab of rum in the tea. A wink is as good as a word to Norah, granted the father and two brothers that she has.

I walked down then to my office, past Tully and Son, the windows catching the light, the glass almost opaque; but I could see in my mind's eye the heavy drawers of oak, within which lay oddments, razors, a row of carpenter's awls, and the tables upon which lay bolts of fabric, somber brown and flirtatious bright-coloured muslins of apple green and soft, wall-shaded peach. James had the office already open, of course, and he was surprised to see me, and beyond surprise when I sat myself behind my desk, and attended to correspondence old but not yet moribund. Without asking, he brought me tea: he knew the drill.

I saw him staring at me, and, "Well, Jamesey," I said, "what is it?"

"To tell you the God's honest truth," he said, "you look like hell."

"Hell is empty," I said. He thought that one over, and then went back into his room.

At one in the afternoon, I went into Conefry's, and had two glasses of beer in the snug. Behind the bar, beside the long, clouded mirror, where once the oleograph of Parnell had hung, bearded and pale, cheapened by the printer's art, but not without some faint sentimental value, there hung now, carried in from storeroom of banishment, a print of Daniel O'Connell, the Liberator himself, hand upraised in florid gesture, and behind him what were intended as the mountains of his native Kerry. "A fine-looking man, the Liberator must have been," I said, and Conefry smiled his agreement, measuring me with cold, Baltic eyes.

By midafternoon, I knew that Vincent would be home from Tipperary, what with his dinner laid on for that night, and indeed, the housemaid who answered my pull at the bell carried with her the fluster of anticipated hospitality. The nice bit stood behind her, in a brown skirt, and a shirt-waist of striped brown and yellow, the finest from Tully and Son.

I took Vincent by the arm, and led him into his own gun room, and before he had more than half a chance to say anything, I sat him down, and myself with him, and told him about the whole wretched business, without giving myself pause for blame or excuse. When I had finished, he sat looking into the fireplace. He had not changed, and was wearing a suit of fine, rain-coloured worsted, with a high-lapelled waistcoat. Of all of us, Vincent, I think, had changed the least in appearance; some fellows have that sort of luck.

"He was casual at the end of it all," I said, "cracking jokes about hell. But I was not fooled for a moment. There is red violence in that fellow."

"Jokes about hell," Vincent said.

"By tomorrow," I said, "he will be away to make his ship at Queenstown, but that is tomorrow, and—for God's sake, Vincent, you know why I have come to warn you."

Vincent nodded, and then waved his hand, as though there was no need for me to say anything more, nor any wish on his part that I should.

"Take a look around you," he said. "I could hold off an attack by the Zulu nation. And Richardson will be at dinner with us tonight. He travels with an RIC guard these days. There will be constables at the gatehouse. If that is your worry."

"It was yourself especially that he wanted to see, Vincent. He made a point of telling me that. Jesus, I could rip the tongue out of my head."

"Yes," Vincent said. "Would you have a short one with me, Bob? A parting glass?"

"A parting glass?" I said. "In midafternoon?"

"Unless I can persuade you to stay with us. I brought Harry Braxton with me from Tipperary. He is having a lie-down. You would enjoy Harry; he does sketches for the London sporting papers."

But I shook my head, and we had our two modest glasses, one each, Mitchell's best, ten years old, soft and languorous, then inspiriting, in small glasses of etched Waterford, very old glasses, with the dignity of vanished craftsmanship.

At the hall door, as we stood looking out into full afternoon, I said, because there was no way that I could not say it, "You understand, Vincent, do you not? There is no warrant out against him, but on the other hand . . ."

He smiled at me. "Never you fear, Bob. I have nothing to tell the resident magistrate on that score. Safe home."

When I was seated, I turned to wave good-day to him, and he walked down the stone steps towards me and then halted, his two hands deep in the pockets of his trousers, and a broad smile on his face.

But how Ned spent that day and evening, and the early night before he set out to walk the three miles to Brierly Lodge, is matter beyond conjecture, like the songs of the sirens, or the name Achilles bore when he lived among women. As I have said, he left little behind him. He took with him to Brierly Lodge the heavy, murderous metal of the American revolver and the box of cartridges for it.

But he had had a long day to think or feel about it; what he did was not done upon impulse. He left one mark at least behind him at Lughnavalla House, and I found it myself.

Beyond the house, beyond it and a bit to the west, towards the hills, there is a small, stream-fed pond, reed-fringed—a bit too pretty and purposeless, planned, no doubt, by some long-gone lady of the O'Callaghans, and left there to silt itself in time. On a flat rock, wide enough to serve as a seat, I found, in its case of cracked leatherette, the ordnance survey map, with pencil marks encircling Lughnavalla House and Brierly Lodge. As I remarked later to Bob, he had no need to carry it with him to Brierly Lodge: he had always been able, from the old days, to commit what he needed of that sort to memory, lines of blue and red for roads, cross-hatchings. One of the old half-inch maps. But there was a large-scale map of all Munster in his pocket when they had him at last, Cork and Kerry, greens and browns, fingers of headlands reaching out into a pale blue Atlantic.

40

[Ned Nolan/William Richardson/
Robert Delaney/Hugh MacMahon]

He rested before reaching another crest of the low hills, seating himself upon long grasses, his back against a rock. Rain so fine that he almost could not feel it against his cheek, a mist blown eastwards from Kerry, beyond the mountains. Pasturelands, cross-hatched by walls of loose, grey stone, stretched away from him towards those mountains. It was a lovely evening. And silent. No noises yet, although he was listening intently. Rooks wheeled above the trees, but he could not hear them crying.

He reached into the deep right-hand pocket of his coat, took out the revolver, and held it in his lap, a sudden intrusion of metal, of machinery, upon hillside, grasses, moist earth. Steel, harder and far smoother than rock; wooden butt darkened by age, sweat. Moving with care, solicitous of his injured left shoulder, he swung out the cylinder, dropped the four spent cartridges into the grasses, and fumbled out fresh ones from among those lying loose in his pocket. Then he snapped the cylinder back into place, and weighed the revolver on his open palm. Beneath the grip, his fingertips touched lettering so familiar as to have been drained of meaning: *Colt Firearm Company Hartford Conn U.S. Patent.* Words pressed upon hot metal in an American factory with tall, smoking chimneys, a landscape of greys and blacks from *Harper's Weekly.* He put the gun back into his coat. He imagined the smell of recently exploded powder.

Only then did he turn his attention to the wound, which he could just see by twisting his shoulder to the left. The bullet, fired into him from the carbine of a constabulary man as he ran from Brierly Lodge, had ploughed through flesh, sheered off from the shoulder blade, and then had spun out, leaving a gaping wound. An hour or two ago, when he had first paused to rest, winded and shaken, in the fields between Brierly and Clonbrony, on the far side of Brierly's ridge, he had undone his tie, folded it, and pressed it into the wound. Now, testing, he felt wet, soaked cloth, but could not feel a pulse of bleeding. His nerves imagined that his fingers touched splinters of bone, white, jagged.

With the coming of full night, he would sleep, if he could, and another day's walk would bring him to the foothills of the Derrynasaggarts. No roads there, save for the county road, which ran between the hills, down into Kerry, and along the Flesk. If he avoided it, if he kept to the hills, he could lose himself, they would lose him.

A faint smell of seawater clung to the misting rain, carried across Kerry, across the mountains, from the Atlantic. Far beyond him, farther than he could ever reach without help, waves broke upon steep headlands. He imagined the ocean, an image of limitless freedom. Now pasturelands held him, girdled by dry fences, strewn with rocks tumbled by glaciers.

The bullets which he had exploded with such ear-shattering noise in the dining room of Brierly Lodge were distant from him now. A few ounces of lead, but imponderable, with Vincent's life heavy upon them. When he burst into the room, Vincent chanced to be laughing. In the old days, he had laughed easily and often, and doubtless was communing now with kindred spirits, wits, humourists of infinite jest. Sounds, colours, smells of that one minute or two clung in Nolan's mind, fragrant steam rising from a tureen of soup, full-bodied and muttony. Glasses of red wine, a few tumblers of amber whiskey upon the immense spread of damask, expectant faces, roseate or bearded, but startled now by his eruption into the room. He raised the heavy weapon, recognising him at once, seeing in his eyes recognition and something different, quite different, from fear. "Hullo, what's this?" someone else asked. Upon those words, as though upon command, Nolan fired twice, taking aim upon the snowy, studded shirt, three or four inches above the looping chain of heavy gold stretched across black waistcoat.

Turned then and ran, pushing past the servant girl in the hall in her black gown and stiff white apron, eyes open with bewildered shock. Past dark shapes of cabinets and tables against the walls, yellow gaslight upon dark paintings catching streaks of gilded scrollwork. Down the gravelled carriageway, the night air promising chill, but no rain, not yet. He had made his way inside Brierly Lodge quietly and without disturbance, leaving the guards to chat together at the gatehouse, but there was no time now for that. His shots had given the alarm, and behind him, from the open door, were shouts and the sound of a woman's scream, a continuous wail. As he ran down the gravelled path, one of the two guards ran towards him, and Nolan fired at him, wildly, to ward him off. He was past the entrance gates when the bullet struck him, pushing him forward.

He ran across the road, tumbled himself over the low stone fence, and lay full-length, panting, listening to shouts, for twenty minutes, perhaps a half hour, before making his way, edging, wary, towards the byre which he had earlier marked out as his line of retreat. The empty byre was heavy with the smell of beasts; it smothered the odour of his own sweat. When it seemed safe, he struck out, doing exactly what they would not expect him to do, avoiding roads, moving across fields, on foot.

Now, shifting his position awkwardly away from the rock, he could look back, towards Kilpeder. Despite the rain, he could see scattered farmhouses, smoke from chimneys, lights pale in evening air. Across a distant field of intense green, black cattle moved homewards, their drover beside them, his switch invisible. Far to his right lay the demesne of a big house, the house itself a mass of grey, visible from this height despite its sheltering plantation, and beyond it an ornamental lake. Once, a long time before, a quarter of a century before, in the early months of 'sixty-seven, he would have known the names of those farms, that demesne. They had been names, inked upon an ordnance map beside minute squares, circles, triangles. All that had been so long ago that now, from the night of the arms raid, he best remembered that the map, as they had it spread out on the table, bore a stain of wet tea at one side, a brown Sargasso Sea.

Chill would come with the sheltering darkness. First the mist would thicken, shrouding the horizon to the west. But for this moment, the cup of pasturelands at his feet, the bit of demesne, the dark mass of Clonbrony Wood, were held in a perfect silence, dowered with noiseless rain.

Attend you gallant Irishmen, attend me as you should,
Whilst I relate the doleful tale of dark Clonbrony Wood.

A miserable business, to go through your days with a few wretched ballads fastened to you, like battered tins on a dog's tail.

Martin Egan's was the one licensed premises in the village of Graney, a cluster of shops and cabins on the ribbon of road which stretched from Kilpeder to Ballyvourney, and beyond Ballyvourney along the bleak Derrynasaggarts down into Kerry.

An hour before, in the greyness of early morning, he had answered, growling and a bit frightened, the pounding on the door, but then, courtesy and hospitality itself, he had made a turf fire to take the chill from the three men standing outside—Richardson, the resident magistrate; Neafsey, the inspector of police; and Ewing, the soldier from the army barracks. They stood together now, near a half-inch map which covered entirely one of the three small tables, holding mugs of sweetened tea.

Solicitously, Egan hovered near them. Gentry visited his tavern on occasion, a quick one on a winter evening's ride, or three or four young squireens too drunk already to give a damn where they had the next one. Or a hunt begun in sober russet morning, but by evening careless riders would have fallen away, in search of a few stiffeners. But such occasions were infrequent, to be discussed later with his regulars, farmers from the townlands of Graney and Slievemuck.

"Are you certain, now, gentlemen, you will not have a drop of something in the tea, to take the edge off the damp?"

Richardson shook his small, compact head. "Certain, Egan. Perhaps later, if we are still here." He spoke through an unlit cigar, held firmly in place by strong white teeth, bright beneath a sandy, close-cropped moustache. A short man, but solidly built. His light topcoat, the plaid a bold red against soft brown, was unbuttoned.

Neafsey was looking past the open door to the road, where ten of his men stood talking in small groups, carbines slung carelessly over shoulders. Their mounts, necks gracefully bent, cropped the long acre. All save one, which stood held high, smelling the salty air. Kelleher, their sergeant, was by himself, unbuckled helmet pushed back upon red, greying hair. His cape hung loose, and his thumbs were hooked into his broad black belt.

He stood with legs apart, and he was looking towards the hills, which mounted to an invisible Kerry.

Ewing walked idly towards the gable wall, where a poster, yellow and flyspecked, announced a race meeting which had been held in Tralee the year before. Ewing was the youngest man of the three, a captain, and he had come to Kilpeder directly upon receipt of Richardson's wire to his colonel, without wasting time changing into uniform.

"It is asking a fair amount," he said, "to set soldiers to work at the harrying of one man. That is why you people have an armed constabulary. Ten of them for a start, lounging out there in the road."

"On my responsibility, Ewing," Richardson said. "Not Neafsey's. Neafsey has his men spread out across the Millstreet road and the Macroom road. I need something more elaborate here. I need more men than Neafsey can give me. This is where we will take that fellow. Somewhere between here and those hills, or else in the hills themselves."

"Beyond the county line," Neafsey said, "he could move southwards towards Kenmare, or upwards towards Killarney. They will be on the watch for him, on that side of the mountains."

"But I want him taken here," Richardson said, patiently, as though explaining sums, "before he crosses over out of this county."

Ewing sipped at his tea, but it had grown cool, and the sweetened liquid left a poor taste upon his tongue. He put down the mug on one of the bare tables, upon which were scattered the dried circles of porter glasses. It is a squalid room, he thought.

"If I have understood you properly," he said, "this Nolan isn't a peasant; he isn't even local. He is a city criminal on a visit here from New York or London or Liverpool. He is more likely to make for Queenstown or Cork City, someplace where there are docks and ships."

Neafsey coughed suddenly, and shifted his feet. He turned his gaze back again towards his men and their mounts. Richardson smiled at him, and brought the smile to bear upon Ewing.

"The inspector is very much of your opinion, Captain. That is why he has his men in position on the Macroom road. But this is where we will take him. When your chaps arrive, we will spread out, and move towards the hills."

"To bag a murderer," Ewing said. "Fine task for Her Majesty's troops."

"None better," Richardson said. "In India they used us to catch murderers. Called it border warfare. Same thing."

"Ah," Ewing said.

Now that he had Richardson placed, he could feel at ease with him.

[785]

The very stuff of which resident magistrates were formed. Younger sons of Irish county families, respectable obscure school, and then off to India, service in one of the native regiments, bit of polo, bit of flirtation, marriage on first home leave, and then twenty more years out there, back of the neck burned brick-red, brains slowly pickled in sunset gins. Then back to Ireland and a magistracy to make ends meet and to make it all worthwhile. Small lodge with a rose garden to tend, local hunt, stiff back and a few pounds invested in consols, whist at the country club if there was one. Standing by Tipperary or Cork window at nightfall, looking past roses, fields of darkening green, remembering dusty red plains, lean cattle, a barracks.

"You and I may know a thing or two about soldiering," Richardson said, as though responding to Ewing's thought, "but the lads who know this country are Neafsey's lads. The Royal Irish Constabulary. They hold Ireland for us, not that army of ours."

Neafsey shifted uneasily. You could never be certain with Richardson, a whimsical man with a sackful of private jokes, bluff-mannered and agreeably condescending, but hard and clever beneath the manner. Like poor dead Vincent Tully, stretched flat upon the red Turkey carpet of his own dining room.

"If we bring down Ned Nolan, sir," Neafsey said, "I will be content enough. And my men as well."

"Not bring him down," Richardson said sharply. "Take him. And you must make that clear to your own people as well, Ewing. I want him taken and brought to Cork City and tried at the assizes and hanged as a common murderer. I want no legend left behind him."

"Then, by God, sir," Neafsey said, jolted out of discretion, "you have your work cut out for you."

When the snow fell fast in each mountain pass, from Cork to Aherlow,
Full sixty men from Kilpeder town to the hills above did go.
Against peelers black and troopers red, we fought them as we could,
But death was waiting with the snows of dark Clonbrony Wood.

Neafsey, youngest son of a Waterford farmer, had heard that song once, years before, in a public house in Tramore, standing with his chums on a hot summer night, the lot of them in their muddy boots and shapeless jackets, shirts unbuttoned, one hand holding a pint of porter, and the other resting on a friend's shoulder. There was one of them with a voice, Dinny Mackey, dead now God rest him, and he had run through three songs or four before lighting upon the new one about the Fenians in Cork, in a town west of Macroom, who had fought a pitched battle. In Tramore, wind-sweetened town on the eastern coast, they heard of rebels in the west who in snow had attacked a police barracks, in snow had fought through the streets of the town, in snow had made their way to a wood, where, turning, they had fought against encircling soldiers and constables.

That had been in August. In November, Neafsey had gone up to Dublin to take the examination for the Royal Irish Constabulary. Fenians belonged in a world of ballads and mountains, like Robert Emmet and the rebels of 1798, but the Constabulary existed in an actual world where the sons of small farmers looked about for respectable employment.

"This is a bad area from all I've ever heard," Ewing said. "Cork and Tipperary. Disturbed counties."

"Don't you believe it," Richardson said. "Good land, splendid people. Need a bit of understanding, kindness, firm hand. You would agree, Neafsey?"

"I am a Waterford man," Neafsey said.

"Are you now?" Richardson said. "I never knew that."

And never asked, Neafsey thought. Here we are to do their bidding, uniforms of warm, serviceable wool, capes, leather belts, tall helmets, carbines, promotions, pensions.

T he early morning air still had the cool of night upon it. Great clouds in the west, hills dark against the sky. In the bare mountain world to which Nolan walked, where he already imagined himself, he would have only memories for company, envelopes opening themselves at random, their preserved fragrances touching the mist-washed morning. In a Manhattan saloon, shadowed, cool, beyond wide doors the blazing sun of summer New York on dusty streets, Rossa leaned towards him, matted beard, eyes sunk deep, cheeks ruddy with drink. "I've given up on Devoy and his lot," he said, fellow survivor of Her Majesty's prisons, voice thickened by a decade of whiskey accepted as his due. "I collect my own funds now, and dispose of them as I see fit. Bring the war into the enemy's camp, you take my meaning. A skirmishing fund. Action delivered for every dollar paid in. Devoy is all talk now, collecting money from draymen and servant girls." Servant girl. As Margaret had been.

Stood by the window of his small, dark room, naked, a tall girl; dark hair unbound touched her shoulders. Her back was turned to him, gaslight softened flanks, long legs, curve of back. In one hand, loose, she held a shift, trailing the dusty floor. "You make too much of me," she said, "a skivvy in one of their houses, on her afternoon off." "Turn round to look at me," he said, but she did not turn. Her body, bare, a bond between them. Surrendered body. "That means nothing," he said, but saw her within the house, somewhere in Murray Hill, uniformed, white mobcap, kneeling to one of their fireplaces. "Turn round to me." She turned, faint smile, deprecating, her breasts pale. "There you are, now," she said. "You have nothing to do with that," he said; "this is how you are." "Ach, you know little of me, I am a skivvy, and all my chums are skivvies." County Cork in her voice. "From Cork," he said, "the two of us." She stood close to the bed on which he lay, her legs touching the coarse blanket. "I was two days in Queenstown, awaiting passage," she said, "and that is my travels in the world." His hand traced her belly's faint roundness, crease of thigh. She put her two hands on his. "You are a travelled man," she said, faint Cork mockery; "you have been to distant places." "To be sure," he said, parting her legs; "imaginary kingdoms."

One room only held its true colours for him, dark within the sullen fires of his imagination, burning in dreams, never to be spoken of. Straw, brown, stained. One blanket, grey, thin, stamped with broad arrows, rough to the touch. A bucket for slops, encrusted. In the morning, a ration of bread, a pint of tea measured into a tin canister held between the bars. Each man took his turn dragging the slop cart along the tier, the heavy doors memorized and the men behind them—Timmins, Corbett, Madden, Daly, the fellow who went mad, screaming in his cell, behind iron. Arctic in winter, fingers hardened from the stonecutting, turning blue; the blanket useless, shoddy. But in summer, each cell a cook oven, baking each man like pastry dough, mouth pressed to the ventilation hole, sucking warm, foetid air.

But here the sky was lightening, limitless, the coarse grasses an intense green.

That morning, Delaney stirred the fire which the skivvy had set in the front parlour. Blocks of turf, glowing red, skeletal. He straightened, and saw the room reflected in the massive oval mirror, cases of books reaching towards a scrolled ceiling white as bone china, heavy drapes the colour of old, dusty gold, papers scattered across the wide mahogany surface of the desk, twin to the knife-scarred desk in his office.

By the arm of a tall wing chair, Agnes stood watching him, slender, small-bosomed, the waist of her brown gown tight, smooth. In the mirror, his eye caught her level, remote gaze.

"By nightfall, it could be raw," he said. "I will take my heavy coat, the one with the half cape."

"Take whatever coat you will," she said. "Why should it matter to me what coat you take?"

"I was making conversation," he said, "between husband and wife. Morning conversation."

"I will wire Conor at school," she said, "to summon him. I am going back now across the road, to my father's. It is where we should all be."

"It is a terrible time for him," Delaney said, "and for you. I would help you if I could. Your father would not welcome me. I cannot blame him."

"He would not even recognise you," she said, in the dry voice that comes with uncomprehended shock. "He recognises none of us. Not me, not Dr. Considine. He will not go to his bed. He sat for hours last night, with his hands folded across his front, and his mouth open. And I sat looking at him."

"Yes," Delaney said, turning towards her. "But he knows that you are there. I am certain of that, and it is surely a comfort to him. You should be with him."

"Should I tell him that you are not in Kilpeder, that you have gone off to join that gunman, the man who murdered poor Vincent?"

"To find him," Delaney said. "Not to join him."

"Every hand in the county is turned against him. Except yours. What better could be expected from you?"

Delaney sighed. "And I will not do the finding. Richardson will, and the police. They will take him down from the hills to the gaol in Cork City, and try him, and hang him. He deserves to hang."

"But you will be there in the courtroom to defend him. The man who murdered Vincent, who came all the way here to murder Vincent. And why, in God's name, why? What harm did Vincent ever do to Ned Nolan or to any man?"

Briefly, without humour, Delaney smiled and then shook his head. "He surely did not deserve death."

"But you stand ready to help the creature who slaughtered him. Your life served you well, before you set to work, bringing it down upon your head in ruins. What with one thing or another. My father befriending you, a clever lad without prospects, taking you into the shop, sending you off to be made into a solicitor, giving you a daughter dearer to him than life itself. Twas not a life, twas a fairy tale."

Dick Whittington, Sylvia said to him, turn Dick Whittington, Lord Mayor of London. They will never make me lord mayor, he said. No Irish need apply. She laughed, and placed her two hands in the deep pocket of his overcoat, and they leaned over the Embankment, looking up the great river towards the Houses of Parliament, the great bridge, men hurrying home from work. Then turn Dick Whittington, she said, Lord President of Ireland. And heedless of passersby, she kissed him lightly, quickly, and pressed her cheek against his.

A quick glance at the clock, a wedding gift from Vincent, in its heavy, ormolu setting. He walked over to the desk.

"You have turned against us all," she said. "Our family. Against the Church itself."

"Yes," he said, forcing himself to look at her directly, into blue, youthful eyes which she had carried into their present.

"It began with her," she said. "With that whore. You may talk of politics and principles and Parnell, your other adulterer, but it began with her. We had all here, in this house, all that was ever needed." An image of lost felicity, domestic, unexacting, lingered within her final words.

Without knowing why, without a reason, he opened the knee drawer, and touched the foolish revolver that he had carried with him in the final months when mobs were rushing the platforms on which Parnell tried to speak. He lifted it up, then placed it back again.

"Take it with you," Agnes said. "You can be a gunman with him, in the hills. You keep all of your evil in there, the pistol and the letters from London in blue envelopes with silly scrawls. Things scrawled in those letters that no woman could ever bear to set on paper. So I thought."

He shut the drawer upon the revolver, upon a memory of letters.

Motionless, she stood beside the brocaded chair which she had chosen with such care in Cork City. A chair of substance, she had told him, her tone proud, affectionate.

In the small stable behind the house, Twomey had the bay saddled for him. "The weather may hold," Twomey said.

"Please God," Delaney said. "There is no need for me to be wet as well as foolish."

"Your words," Twomey said, "not mine. Let you ponder them."

The smell of the stable was acrid, comforting after the dead, dry air of the parlour. He took the reins from Twomey and led out the bay. Twomey followed him, a short man, bowlegged.

"Take a fool's advice, counsellor. He will have no need for you until they have carried him down and lodged him in the Cork Gaol. Carried him down one way or the other."

"Myself is the fool, Bill, not you. You can't advise a fool."

"Twould be the dignified way to proceed. Ride up in your carriage, yourself and your shiny top hat, present yourself to the governor of the gaol. Robert Delaney, solicitor, former member of Parliament, all the rest of it."

"Former this and former that," Delaney said.

When he was mounted, Twomey walked beside him down the short street to the square. Twomey put his hand on the bay's neck and, nervous, she pulled her head away.

"There have been peelers on the move in all directions," Twomey said, "but Major Richardson and that inspector took the county road, towards Kerry."

"Richardson knows his trade," Delaney said. "You might even have some soldiers here before the day is much older. 'Sixty-seven all over again."

"I can remember 'sixty-seven," Twomey said, "as clearly as if it was yesterday. Daddy was dead by then, but there was the mother and Paddy and myself, farming there, on the far side. She made the two of us swear on our beads that we would never take the oath. The great day came and went, and damned all did Paddy and myself know about it. We spent the day mending a fence. Ah well," Twomey said, "the mother has long gone to her rest, and Paddy as well, God be merciful to them, and the place itself long gone from us, as you well know yourself, counsellor."

"Times change," Delaney said, and set off, past a locked church and the locked gates of an estate, towards Graney.

T ime for more tea, Egan," Richardson said, a bit after noon, "and this time a stiffener in it would do no harm, no harm at all. And while you are about it, you might carry out the same to the constables. Splash in a double measure. That won't go amiss, eh, Neafsey?"

At that moment, the sergeant shouted to them, and they went outside. He pointed towards Kilpeder, where, along the ribbon of road, there seemed now to be a far-distant movement, sluggish, like a caterpillar making its way across a leaf.

"Those would be my chaps," Ewing said.

"Yes," Richardson said. He took from his topcoat pocket a pair of opera glasses, mother-of-pearl, gilt-rounded, and adjusted them. He saw Ewing looking at him. "Bit unmilitary, eh, Ewing? But better than you can manage at the moment."

He peered through them, and then handed them to Ewing. "Right you are," he said. "Your chaps."

Egan brought them out their tea, the mugs resting on a tray of chipped and stained enamel.

"Other company before them," Ewing said. "Fellow on a bay. Not a soldier. He doesn't seem to be in any special hurry. Here, take a look."

There were already low hills between himself and the townlands of Kilpeder. They would be on the hunt for him by now, but there was no point of higher vantage from which they could espy him. By nightfall, he would be so far into the mountains that he would be lost to the world. And they had no particular reason to think that he would come this way, choosing deliberately what soon would be a trackless waste, a man who they probably knew was wounded. He would more likely be lying low, favouring the wound, or trying to make his way towards Cork. But the wound was worse than he had thought at first. The shoulder and armpit of his coat were sodden with blood, and there was no way in which he could staunch it.

At a stream, pouring down the hillside along pure rock, he cupped his hands, wincing, and drank. On the far side of the hill, he found a goat's path, rising upwards, but shielded by the hill from eyes that might be watching from the east.

The tea was more than welcome. As Delaney brought it to his lips, he smelled the heavy scent of whiskey wedded to its aroma.

"Odd, isn't it?" Richardson said to him. The subaltern had had the good sense to bring field glasses, and Ewing had commandeered them at once. At the moment, Richardson was holding them to his eyes, studying the long, uneven lines of policemen and soldiers as they moved towards the foothills. Not like the ballad, Delaney thought with indifference, against peelers black and troopers red: these were military in undress, in black tunics.

"What is?"

"Why, this Edward Nolan turning up like a bad penny, of course," Richardson said, lowering the glasses, but forgetting to hand them back to Ewing. "I daresay all Kilpeder knows about it by now."

"They do indeed," Delaney said dryly. "My stableboy woke me this morning to tell me."

"They will be telling each other about it for years, eh, Mr. Delaney? We know our people, don't we, you and I?"

"What I find odd," Delaney said, "is why Neafsey and Sergeant Kelleher and yourself are certain that it is Edward Nolan. A man breaks into Brierly Lodge, commits bloody murder, and all of you are certain that it was a fellow who was last here a quarter of a century ago."

"Why should we not be certain?" Richardson asked. "You are. Who else would have brought you out here this early in the day? You have no need to drum up business among itinerant murderers, I take it?"

With an expression which mingled politeness with a mild irritation, Ewing retrieved the glasses.

"Suspected murderers, shall we say?" Delaney said. "And at the moment, there are none in view."

"How could I not be certain?" Richardson said. "I was a witness at Brierly Lodge. I was sitting at poor Tully's left, as a matter of fact. He had time to say a word or two before Nolan fired. 'Ned,' he said. 'Ned, I did not'—something of that sort, and then Nolan fired."

"We had been on the lookout for Ned Nolan, Mr. Delaney," Neafsey said. "He came over last week on the night boat, and from Dublin he was followed to Cork, where he gave our fellows the slip. There was always a chance, do you see, that he might turn up in Kilpeder. A description was sent down, and sketches; even a useless sort of photograph."

"In fact," Richardson said, "he might have been in this area for a day or two. You wouldn't know anything about that, would you?"

"Was there a warrant upon him? Was he wanted?"

Richardson sighed. "Solicitors are forever inventing difficulties. After this is all over, we'll have to do some sorting out, eh, Neafsey?"

"Ned Nolan is out there, Mr. Delaney, and he is after killing Vincent Tully. There is the long and the short of it. We all know that, you know that." Neafsey added, morosely, "Or else he is headed towards Macroom, or up into the Boggeraghs."

Richardson took out a morocco cigar case and handed it round. Ewing accepted one, but Delaney and Neafsey shook their heads.

"Damned strange business," Richardson said. "I don't expect you can shed any light on it? No. What about that schoolmaster chap?"

"Ask him," Delaney said.

"Oh, we will," Richardson said. "There will be questions enough to go around."

"Eighteen sixty-seven," Richardson said a few minutes later, to break the silence. "I was a subaltern then. You were still in infant dress, I daresay, Ewing, or in a sailor suit with a hoop to roll."

"And I was attacking the constabulary barracks in Kilpeder," Delaney said. "Under Nolan's orders."

Neafsey smiled towards the mountains, lovely at noonday, viewed in comfort, from a road outside a country pub, hands cupped about hot, whiskeyed tea.

"Yes," Richardson said. "Yourself and MacMahon the schoolmaster and Vincent Tully."

"And a few others," Delaney said.

"Damned few," Richardson said. "Thank God."

An hour's walk beyond that hill, and then another hour's, brought him into high, waste spaces, splashed with gorse. The day had turned bright, and sunlight glinted against polished rock. Here, there was not so much as a goat path, and he would find himself wading through impeding gorse. Before him, for miles, for as far as he could see, tumbled hills lay piled upon one another. At the end of all this, the hills would slope downwards, towards lands almost as harsh, but then towards valleys, farms, a river. He would have the world from which to choose. For long parts of his life—for much of it, it sometimes seemed—he had been alone; but this was solitude of a different sort. It frightened him a bit. He tried not to look backward, towards Brierly Lodge, towards what he had done. What he could not forget was Delaney telling him about Tully's treachery, there in Lughnavalla House, as though disclosing to him the ugly secret at the world's centre. But this was the world's high edge, clean-scented, the air broken only by the cries of distant, invisible birds.

Presently, so Bob told me on the night following, Richardson gave a comical sigh, and said, "Time to say good-bye to Mr. Egan. With luck, we can call in on him on our way back."

They jogged along the county road, the four of them, Neafsey and Ewing in the lead, and Richardson and Bob behind them, the four of them maintaining an evenness with the soldiers and constables stretched out in long, probing lines on either side of them. It was a road Bob had travelled a dozen times or more, on the excursions we made together to the lakes, the two of us and Mary and poor Vincent, Agnes a bit later. And Bob and myself, of course, had taken this road when we went down into Killarney on the eve of the Rising, to see what in God's name the Kerry lads were about.

Bob had no more than a thought or two to spare for Ewing, a jingly young English officer, the country meaning no more to him than the Curragh and invitations to hunt balls, no doubt. Neafsey, Bob had known all his life in one form or another, one name or another. Not the worst. But the name Callinan bobbed into his mind, poor Vincent's Iago or Machiavelli or whatever. Richardson seemed a more complicated creature entirely, which is not what he would have expected from the type, ex-India army turned resident magistrate. At first, he thought that Richardson's courtesy and helpfulness were professional, but he changed his mind as the afternoon wore on.

"He's a bad 'un, you know, your Ned Nolan," Richardson said. "Since your youthful days together, he has had his hands on some ugly engines."

"He came out of your bloody prison sane," Bob said, "which was not always the case. More than a few were driven mad by what was meted out to them. I had a taste of it, enough to last. I had a week for what they called insubordination, down in the 'pit' as they called it, deep in the bowels of the gaol."

"Sane, would you call him?" Richardson asked, and with the words, reined in, and shouted to Neafsey and Ewing. At the far edge of beaters to the left, a constable, so far off as to seem made of black splinters, was waving his arm. Ewing raised his glasses towards him.

"But one thing puzzles me," Richardson said. "I daresay we will have the answer to it." He seemed to be disregarding for the moment the waving constable, and Ewing with his field glasses. " 'Ned,' Tully said, when Nolan burst into the room. Said it twice. 'Ned,' and two or three words I could not make out. The explosions came hard upon their heels. He was terrified, oh I have no doubt that he was terrified. Who would not be? But not surprised. Almost as if he had expected it. Nolan has changed a fair bit—a wild-looking fellow, if we are to judge by the sketches—but Tully knew at once who it was. Isn't that odd?"

"Your man over there seems to have something," Bob said, and at that moment, two shots rang out, although Bob could not see the smoke. Richardson put a hand on his arm.

"That's all right," he said. "Signal shots. Yes, they have something."

He had mounted a crest of hill, laboriously, grasping with one hand the tough-branched, tough-rooted furze, and for a full minute or two risked himself against the horizon. Behind him, distant, he could see the dark, moving figures, like rooks in a cornfield, but he could hear no sound from them, unless what he had taken to be indeed the caws of rooks, of invisible gulls, had been their shouts to one another. He could not see the road, but had no doubt that they were there as well, and most probably in strength. He marvelled at space. Kilpeder could not be seen at all, unless two minute black sticks, pointing upwards, were the spires of Saint Jarlath's. But farther off to his left were bits of white that surely were scattered farmhouses, like the bits of white-painted wood in Christmas gifts for children: a bit of polished steel for a pond, glass would splinter and cut fingers, and a sheet of green felt to be unfolded and imagined into pasturelands. And in the more elaborate, costlier sets, bits of china cows, sheep, pigs.

Once, in the one room that they shared in Manhattan, before the war—a double bed, table, chairs, a wardrobe and a dresser with a drawer that refused to open—once, two days before Christmas, his father had brought him home such a set, the costly sort, in a box of blond wood, a gift too young by years for Nolan, but they had tumbled it out on the table, and for days, after their meal, would set it up afresh. Perhaps, he thought, that is how I have carried Ireland about with me all these years, a box of blond wood at the centre of my imagination, cases of maps and letters from a schoolmaster in Kilpeder, fields of green felt, and minute china beasts, paint-daubed.

At a far edge of the cornfield of rooks, he saw movement of a different sort, an arm upraised, and he turned around so that his back would be towards them, towards an Ireland suddenly vast, unboundaried, empty. As he did so, the heel of his boot caught upon a thick root, which jerked him forward, and he tumbled down the hill, in amazement and anger at first, clutching without usefulness, with his one good arm, at bushes, clawing earth, a hand sliding then along smooth, damp rock. At last, as he lay sprawled, unmoving, he felt nothing, only a dull pain, new, in his right foot and ankle. It was when he tried to rise up that he realised that he could not, and that he could not walk, although perhaps, if he could find a stick, he might be able to hobble.

That is how they found him, Bob told me, and as he and Richardson rode across the wasteland, they could see the constables and soldiers moving quickly but warily, in advance of them, to the two constables who had given the shout and fired off the two signal shots.

Do you know what I felt mostly as I rode towards Ned? Bob asked me. Shame, bloody shame is what I felt, and I did not look forward to meeting his eyes. Vincent would be alive, I thought, and Ned on his ship for America, the small house looking beyond brick kilns towards an American river. Shame for things that had nothing to do with Ned: Agnes standing by a chair that morning, which we had chosen in the first pleasures of our marriage, and Conor at that moment travelling back home from the school in Kildare to the old man who sat sleepless, without eating, dazed, in that house stuffed and crammed with furnishings. No, not shame. I don't know what it was. It was as though I felt upon myself something of that grime of which Ned had spoken there in Lughnavalla House.

But then the shots rang out, first one of them, and then a scattering in quick succession. Before we reached the men, they had run forward towards something which I knew was Ned. We made our way with difficulty, because we were now in furze, and we dismounted. When we reached them, they had gathered about him. By one of his opened hands was a bit of broken branch, and by the other, his fingers just touching it, the huge American revolver.

"It was no man's fault, sir," Kelleher said at once to Neafsey. "He was half walking, half crawling, when two of our lads heard him and gave the signal. He made a gesture of some sort with that bit of branch he had, and one of the lads was that nervous that he thought it was that bloody great cannon, and he fired at him, a warning shot, like, but it hit him. Then he did indeed draw out the revolver, and the lads opened fire."

The constable who had fired that first shot into Ned could be identified in a moment. He was standing pale and stunned.

I knelt down beside Ned. A moment before, I had been awkward about looking into his eyes, but there was no harm in them now as he looked into nothing.

"It is Nolan, I take it?" Ewing asked, his voice not unkind, but neutral, putting things in order.

"Captain Nolan," I said, "Captain Edward Nolan."

"Indeed?" Ewing said, but without enough interest to ask what I meant.

"They were friends," Richardson said to Ewing, informatively, mildest of social reproofs.

"Edward Nolan and Vincent Tully and myself," I said. "You have no idea."

T hey had no wagons with them, of course, and so they had to bring him back to Kilpeder slung across a saddle. Bob told me that. He had no need to, because I was there myself to see them ride into the market square; most of Kilpeder was. It was about eight-thirty that night. But I let Bob describe it to me, because I knew that he needed to speak out the whole of the story from beginning to end.

We were sitting in my house, Bob in the chair that usually I claimed for myself, and Mary perched upon the piano bench, quiet and motionless, her hands folded in her lap.

"And there we are," he said. Once again, I offered him a drink, and once again he refused it. Presently, I felt the need for one myself, and slipped into the kitchen, where I had a quiet, mild whiskey, sipping it, and hearing, at the short distance, the murmur of Mary's voice, but Bob saying nothing in return, nothing that I could hear. I asked her once or twice, that night and then again in the week that followed, what she had found to say to him, but she shook her head.

T here you are," Packy Lawlor said in Conefry's late that night. "In the heel of the hunt, after all the ups and downs of the past ten years and more, and here at the end of all is Ned Nolan wreaking havoc."

"A shameful business," Peter Cunningham said, and nodded, faintly, to Conefry, to signify that their glasses stood empty before them. A beefy man, solid in his black suit, the elbows and the trousers' seat shiny, but the suit well brushed, the tieless shirt collar held in place by a gold stud.

The marketplace, barely visible through the wide window behind them, was held in faint, final light. The public bar at the far end was crowded, and so too was the saloon bar, the air thick with voices and smoke, the dark scent of stout and porter, but Lawlor and Cunningham sat comfortably on their own in the snug, side by side, behind the head-high barrier of white-frosted glass, scrolled, stained gently with smoke. Behind the counter, Conefry, assisted by two curates, one of them his son and a fourth generation in the trade, commanded both bars and the snug. His eyes of intense blue patrolled his patrons, beaky, high-arched nose, down-sweeping moustaches.

He walked down along the length of the bar to the snug, measured whiskey into the two glasses, and, taking by the stem a third glass from the rack above him, he joined them. Auctioneer, strong-farmer, publican: the frosted glass separated them from the other drinkers.

Low, practiced voice not carrying beyond the snug, he said, jerking his head back towards the public bar. "By Jesus, you should hear them back there. There has not been so much excitement in their lives since Parnell tried to give that speech of his." He looked past them, to the market square, and, remembering what had happened that night, smiled grimly.

"There you have it," Lawlor said. "Farmboys and casuals. Lads like those will make a hero of every rogue and rapparee. It costs them nothing."

"Tis the old man who has all my grief and sympathy, of course," Conefry said. "Brierly Lodge laying empty and deserted. And a certain young woman cast loose upon the world without poor Vincent having had time to give her a written recommendation."

"Her talents commend themselves," Lawlor said.

"Not to Kilpeder they will not," Cunningham said. "Not while Father Meagher still has a voice."

"What will poor Dennis Tully do with Brierly Lodge?" Lawlor said to Cunningham. "After the edge of his grief has worn itself dull."

"Ah," Cunningham said, with auctioneer's discretion. "What indeed? If all that that old lad owns or controls or holds upon mortgage or note were to be stitched together, tis he would be acclaimed as the lord of Kilpeder, and not that *rara avis* off there in Italy."

"And all of that," Conefry said, "Delaney tossed away, out of too great a love for this." He sipped his whiskey, smacked his lips, and added water to his glass.

"That, and backing the wrong horse," Lawlor said, his eyes flickering towards and then quickly away from the place beside the mirror where the portrait of Parnell had hung.

"And off in search of Nolan the murderer," Cunningham said. "He is carving out for himself a new career as a failure. He does not miss a trick."

Lawlor gave a dairy farmer's deep-bellied guffaw. "Career as a failure. There you are now."

When Bill Twomey came in, he made his way to the public bar and gave his order to the white-aproned curate, but Conefry saw him, and motioned him into the snug.

"You were observed making your farewells to your man this morning, Bill. Before he set out."

"Twas no secret departure," Twomey said.

"Mr. Lawlor here and Mr. Cunningham and myself were just speculating upon the great topic and riddle of the hour," Conefry said. "Ned Nolan and the killing of poor Vincent Tully. I daresay Bob Delaney might be able to drop a crumb of light upon that?"

"Do you think so?" Twomey answered helpfully.

The curate set the tall shell of porter before him, and he began to shove forward his two coppers, but Lawlor shook his head; the pint was to be on his round.

"But you did have your bit of a chat with Bob this morning," Lawlor said, "and the subject must surely have come up."

"Not that I recall it," Twomey said. He touched the cool pint with short, work-weathered fingers, but did not draw it towards himself.

"A clever man, Bob Delaney," Cunningham said. "We were also just now remarking upon that. But he has seen better days. He's not at the top of his form any longer, would you say, Bill?"

Now Twomey picked up the pint, and took a long swallow from it.

There was a vacant stool beside Lawlor and Cunningham, but he remained standing.

"When I was turfed out from my place during the Land War," Twomey said, "twas Bob Delaney who took me in and offered me work. Farm work is what I know best, but there were no farmers came forward to me." He looked up quickly towards Lawlor and then back, demurely, into the thick, creamy head of porter. "To be sure, times were hard for one and all, in those days."

"Ach, sure the Land War," Conefry said. "Ancient history."

"I have a good memory, thanks be to God," Twomey said. He took three long swallows, and then held the shell a bit away from himself, to study his progress. He should not be here at all, but in the public bar. He worked away at the pint, getting no enjoyment. The three wise men of Kilpeder, senators and deliberators, were losing interest in him. In the public bar, he could be at ease with his own kind, perhaps two or three of the Lughnavalla lads. The sounds from the bar were a confused babble, someone laughing and then the sound of someone far gone in drink, shouting incoherently.

Conefry, annoyed, peered down the counter, cold pale eyes. "The curse of a nation," he said. "The wealth of a nation drunk down and then pissed away."

"Go ahead, so, Dan," a voice in the bar shouted. "Give out with it." The level of voices dropped, wavering, a receding tide.

Twomey placed his empty shell, foam-coated, and Cunningham, halfheartedly, offered him a second, but Twomey smiled his thanks, and made his way down to the public bar. In trousers' pocket, he rubbed two heavy coppers against each other. He arrived at a pause. A few were still talking. Someone—the bellowing drunk, no doubt—sat with his arms and head resting on the counter, plain deal here, not mahogany, porter-smeared. "Go ahead," the voice shouted again. The room was quiet now, expectant. Another voice rose, tenor, clear within smoke, the darkening space of night:

> Attend you gallant Irishmen, attend me as you should,
>   Whilst I relate the doleful tale of dark Clonbrony Wood.

Twomey signalled the curate, and then found a chair not beside a Lughnavalla man, but a decent skin named Spring, who had once been a gamekeeper at Ardmor Castle, but was now a handyman of sorts, with a bit of poaching thrown in.

Familiar as a travelled road, as the look of the marketplace in morning light, melody wed the easy pattering words to their own lives, bound them within history, legend.

In the snug, Lawlor said in a low, growling voice, "Is there not a rule of the house about singing?" But Conefry, frowning, shook his head. He had taken a step back from the counter, and was standing with folded arms, an impassive listener.

There were so many verses that no one ever sang them all. The singer, Phil Hennessy's next-to-youngest, who helped out with the gardening at Colonel Saunderson's, gave them good value, six or eight verses, and then, as tradition specified, spoke rather than sang the last line quickly, returning his listeners from song to speech, settling them back on the uneven, spittle-flecked floorboards.

"A lovely voice," Spring said. "He does a lovely *Stabat Mater.* If the professors in Cork City could hear him, his fortune would be made."

And may God show mercy to the men who held Clonbrony Wood.

"Jesus wept," Lawlor said wrathfully. "They will be good now until closing time, and then streeling up the streets of a quiet town. 'The Smashing of the Van' and 'The Rising of the Moon,' and the rest of them. God be with the days when patriotic ballads were banned by the cruel oppressor, and a ball of malt might be enjoyed in quiet in a respectable licensed premises."

" 'May God show mercy to the men who held Clonbrony Wood,' " Cunningham quoted. "A queer sort of mercy he showed to Vincent Tully and Ned Nolan."

"Not to mention Delaney," Lawlor said.

"Have you ever noticed," Conefry said, "how careful they are in recent years to avoid the other ballad, the one about Nolan?"

But he had spoken too soon. At someone's urging, prompting him at one side, *sotto voce,* Hennessy sang a verse of it.

Beneath the oaks brave Nolan turned and faced his grim-faced men.
"Take heart, my boys, tis joy to know we face the foes again.
Like great Tyrone and Sarsfield bold, and all who've understood,
That freedom's won 'neath blood-red sun or in dark Clonbrony Wood."

"Next thing we know," Cunningham said, "there will be a ballad for Lynchehaun, the mad murderer of Achill, or Brennan, the bandit of Cashel."

"Ach, sure it does no harm," Conefry said, and with the diplomacy of an hereditary publican, he walked down to the public bar, pulled a fresh pint for young Hennessy, and persuaded him to sing "Eilin Arun," one of the old Gaelic love songs, to which English words had been fitted. The pure voice, threading its way through the complex melody, cleared the crowded room of the whiff of gunpowder, the echoes of distant dynamite.

Twomey slipped away early, and made his way through the quiet town to his room above the stable. There were no lights in the Delaney house, he saw, but the first floor of Inchigeelagh House blazed with light, and, although the heavy drapes were drawn, he could see that the front parlour was lit. A crack of light, no more.

41

[Hugh MacMahon/Lionel Forrester]

One of Patrick Prentiss's last visits to me was on a weekend of splendid summer in 1908, four years after he had come to me for the first time. He had given up the formality of booking a room at the Kilpeder Arms, but instead would send a wire, telling me when I might expect him. And I would set to work, bringing the trundle bed into the front room, making it up before the fireplace, planning a meal for us, perhaps planning an excursion for the next day.

But on that first, far-off day he had travelled to me from the town in a horse and trap rented from Trainor's livery stable, which Bob and I had once commandeered, for a few hours, as our supplier of cavalry. And Trainor's still enjoyed his patronage, I observed, as I stood by my gate and watched him rising a hill in the distance; but he was this time equipped not with wood, harness, and obedient beast, but rather was mounted on a bicycle. And why not?

Trainor's, in addition to its ordinary livery custom, was making a handsome profit from the hire of bicycles every clement weekend of the weeks of late spring through early autumn. They are wonderful contrivances, bringing the clear air and beauty of the countryside to young people from Cork City and Dublin. Singly, or more often in pairs or small groups, they will take the train to Macroom, and there or in Kilpeder rent their bicycles, and set forth for as long a time as pleases them—a fortnight it may be. Most will take the county road, over the Derrynasaggarts and on into Killarney country, on southwards towards Tralee. There will always be a farmer's wife to give them water for their tea, or to find beds for them. And there is ample time for them to rest their machines against a stone fence, and, clambering over, walk across the grasses to the roofless, ruined abbeys and friaries, the shattered Norman keeps. They are splendid young people for the most part, high-spirited, intelligent, and ill informed.

Many of them are students of Gaelic—Irish, they insist it should be called, and why not?—and for them the great attraction is my own long-standing love, the Gaelic-speaking stretches about Ballyvourney and Coolea. Some of them have become friends of my own old friends there, the storytellers and singers and fiddlers; and these fellows, it seems to me, have grown a bit puffed-up of late, what with their being assured by well-dressed young gentlemen and ladies from Dublin that they are the last, precious repositories of the noble traditions of the Gael. Ah well, it does no harm.

The cyclists will all have their side journeys and excursions as well, and occasionally they will pass my cottage. I will wave my greeting, and when I reply in kind to their shouts in Irish, they will conclude that they have come upon the first outpost of the noble aborigines, and will wheel over for a chat. They will be fierce with enthusiasm and downcast a bit to discover that I am a retired schoolmaster, born and reared in an English-speaking area; but I will put our time to good use, making them tea, and telling them of beauty spots which they must be certain not to miss, such as Gougane Barra. Most of them are stern patriots. "Kilpeder was great during the Fenian war," one of them said to me, fumbling for the words in his slender hoard. "As such things went," I said politely, yet respectful of truth. "Of course it was," he said, "and the Irish-speakers must have been the heart and soul of it." I had a mouthful of scalding tea, and I damned near choked upon it. If Hugh O'Neill himself had returned with a ghostly armada of Spanish men-of-war riding at anchor in Bantry Bay, those lads might just possibly have got off their backsides; but more likely historical memories of the disaster at Kinsale, buried deep in their noble racial souls, would have held them back. "Are you taken sick, master?" the lad asked me, and I shook my head without speaking, not trusting myself to speak. A decent Dublin lad, and like many of these young people, a member of Sinn Fein. After he had gone, I washed the sounds of his Dublin Gaelic from my ears by reading a few pages of my beloved Montaigne, in John Florio's wonderful, sinuous English, and recited to myself a few verses from Brian Merriman's *Cúirt an Mheán Oíche,* an eighteenth-century Clare poet whose views on various subjects will in due time surprise the lad from Dublin.

They all of them, so I am told, want to be shown Clonbrony Wood, which is little enough to be asking about in these days, for the estate agent, Robert Evans, has been selling off sections for timber. And, of course, they will want to be shown from the county road the stretch of barren hillside where Ned Nolan was killed. And yet by cycling on, they could drop down at last towards lakes so lovely that no tourists can spoil them, and picnic outside the ruins of Muckross Abbey, in mild air savoursome as apples. I was the same at their age.

Patrick always brought with him a hamper, packed half with the expected, and half with surprises. On this occasion, there was, as always, a bottle of Jameson, and two bottles of fine Châteauneuf, some copies of Paris newspapers, Mr. Kipling's *Puck of Pook's Hill,* and an elegant small four-volume set, discovered on the quays for a mere two quid, so he claimed, of Motley's *Rise of the Dutch Republic.*

When he had settled himself in, for he is a man of rituals, the disposition of the toothbrush and that sort of nonsense, we took our chairs outside into the front garden, and sat with our tall glasses of the wine of France. The bottle rested between us on the grass.

Patrick himself remarked to me upon the number of fellow cyclists whom he had encountered on the road before veering off to the road which leads to this cottage.

"Indeed yes," I said. "Ireland on the move. There is a tannery will be built next year, out along the Macroom road. The Sullane may not be so soft to the senses in the future. But sure, leather has to be cured somewhere, and it will bring employment. The young people may be able to live their lives here, and not in Boston or Liverpool. And the clothing manufactory that was begun at the time of your last visit has become a vast triumph."

"I don't remember it at all, Hugh, to be honest," he said. "Should I have? Is it a Tully enterprise?"

"Not exactly," I said, looking off into the distance. "'Tis a man from Bantry who is related by cousinage both to Michael Patrick Murphy and to Tim Healy. But I have been told that his grandmother, on his own mother's side, was a Tully, the same stock but a different branch."

"A rare avenue of possibility," Patrick said. "That must have whetted your scholarly curiosity."

"Ach, Patrick. I have given up on the Tullys. Life is too short. This fellow's name is Moran, and he's related to the Tullys and the Michael Patrick Murphys. They're all related. Incest will creep in sooner or later and do for the lot of them; they will start producing infants with rudimentary tails. Mr. Moran's speciality is piety. As an earthly down payment, he has a contract to supply undergarments to the holy sisters in half of the convents in Ireland. There were shocking rumours last year, last March, that the stuff supplied was so lacking in weight and substance that the poor ladies nearly had their backsides frozen, even when wearing two pair at a time. But how could knowledge of such a thing pass beyond convent walls? At any event, Moran is to be made a papal count, and His Holiness would never ennoble a petrifier of nuns. Count Moran, he will be."

Patrick sat with his legs stretched out, holding his glass to catch the sunlight. "You don't deceive, Hugh. A small itch of curiosity as to the Tullys is still there, and at the bottom of it is a superstitious dread."

"I have done wonders with the roses this year, and not a word of congratulations from you."

"A young lady of good family told me in London, last year, and in a conservatory, mark you, that roses were becoming vulgar."

"Avoid her," I said. "Yours is a higher destiny."

"Is it? We will have time to talk about that. But I have been a diligent scholar, at odd moments. I have worked out why the year 1846 stands forth above the pediment of Tully and Son. Not everyone starved in the year of the great hunger. A few did well, a few did very well indeed. Houses were founded upon their good fortune."

"But few of those had the neck to celebrate their luck by incising the date upon stone, and this where there is a mass famine grave but three miles outside the town. Superstitious, how are you!"

"You have great skill at reading history from stones," Patrick said. "Perhaps archaeology was your true bent."

"Perhaps," I said. "Let us take Brierly Lodge. Brierly Lodge, as you know, lay empty from the day of Vincent's death, not even a caretaker. I doubt was the key even turned in the door. Tinkers broke in, and lads pelted the windows with stones. At last, old Dennis sold off the furnishings and let the place stand derelict. But when he died last year and his will was read, it was revealed that Brierly Lodge is to go to the Ursulines, together with an annual income for its upkeep and appearance. And the

Ursulines are bidden to accept as paying guests widows and elderly spinsters of family, who wish to spend their final years in prayer and in a conventual atmosphere."

"A pleasant thought," Patrick said, a bit surprised. "I would not have expected it of the old ruffian."

"He intends it as a memorial to Vincent. There will be a chapel for Vincent there. And most appropriate, when you reflect upon how many young widows Vincent was able to bring comfort to in this present life of ours, and more than a few before they had even attained that melancholy state."

Patrick had his glass to his lips, but he began to laugh and put it down hastily.

"In all fairness, Hugh. A sardonic turn of phrase was once a part of your makeup, an agreeable part. But you have turned into a Timon of Athens."

I was remorseless. "The Ursulines have begun accepting applicants, and at the head of the list is Agnes Delaney. The house is too large for her, and the shop manages nicely with its monthly inspections by Conor Tully Hyphen Delaney. And it was the great love of her life, the conventual life, before she met Bob and they fell in love."

"The Vincent Tully Chapel," Patrick said, almost bemused. "Do you know, Hugh, aside from yourself, of all those involved in this matter, I think it is Vincent whom I would have most enjoyed knowing."

"And there you are, I have no further matter upon which to pour the vials of my bad humour. But if you think of Agnes, you know, you can grow inclined to reflect upon how often life closes upon itself, fulfills its original designs, whatever the years in between."

Presently, we set out for a saunter, but not before I had given careful attention to my stew, which had now been two days in the making, and gave promise of being one of my triumphs. And to think that poor Mary lived and died without my doing more in the kitchen than making tea and boiling eggs and once in a great while frying up some bread. But the pleasures of the old are simple: rich boneless stews, a glass of wine, regular bowel movements, sleep undisturbed by the bladder. Poor innocent Patrick Prentiss—thinking me Timon of Athens. Thank God that he has not looked down into the furies and rages of the old, the great secret that we try to keep from them, for the health of the race.

We took the long, winding boreen that runs along a bog, and then pasturelands of a sort, and then to a hill gentle enough to climb, but with a good view, eastwards and northwards towards the Derrynasaggarts and the Boggeraghs, and southwards towards the town itself. Patrick had for several years now had his own blackthorn, which he would leave in my stand, a powerful creature made by the same craftsman who fashions my own, a publican who must have a touch of a faction fighter's blood.

"What about yourself, Hugh?" Patrick said. "Can you stand away from your own life and see the shape of it?"

"Don't be absurd," I said. "Why is it, Patrick?—I am curious—why would you have most liked to know Vincent?"

"For the simple pleasure of him, to tell you the truth. He must have been able to charm the birds from the trees. Men who knew him in Dublin and Cork City say that they knew no one with such a love of life, such a delight in freedom."

"He set great value upon his freedom," I said. "He moved with a wonderful grace, the way he held his head, the way he would congratulate a friend, the swaggering sort of walk he had, like one of the squireens of the old century, half jockey and half gentleman. Once—I don't think I have told you this—when our little fellow was in hospital in Cork City for that operation on his hip, there arrived one morning at our door an envelope without a single word on it, and inside it, three hundred pounds in twenty-pound notes. 'Me!' Vincent said when I went to him. 'Me, a Tully and proud of it, to let out money without interest. What sort of fellow do you take me for? For God's sake, Hugh, don't spread that kind of wild story about Kilpeder.' I laughed. Everyone loved Vincent."

"Ned Nolan did not."

"Don't be too certain of that. All we know is that he killed him. Ned loved him too, I think, in that way of love that he had."

"Then why in God's name did he kill him? I began with that question and I am no closer to an answer."

I said nothing. I had long ago known that this was with the deep, buried matter of our lives, mine and Bob's and Vincent's and Ned's. There it would rest.

"That time when you sent me out to talk with Bill Twomey, in the workhouse. He said that no sooner had he brought the news to Bob Delaney than Bob scribbled a note for him to carry around to you. But you stood there at the hall door, reading the scribble and rereading it, and then you shook your head, and said there was no reply."

It was strange to be talking of such matters in this leafy lane, untended hedges heavy on either side of us, tall and straggling. Beyond, on the left, lay Lucey's bog. The air was heavy with the scent of foliage and dung.

"He wanted me to set out with him, to look for Ned, up towards the Derrynasaggarts. But it was as though Ned had at last passed some line which he had been walking towards for twenty years. I would love him, and grieve for him, but I would not lift my hand to help him. Nations, it may be, need their Ned Nolans, but I do not."

"He has become a hero of sorts to the patriotic young bicyclists," Patrick said.

"And well he might," I said. "My military career, as you might call it, was brief and inglorious, but by God, when you encounter a hero-commander, you know it, and that Ned was. The battle inside Kilpeder, the retreat towards Clonbrony, the Arms Raid before any of that . . . He was a fine soldier, fierce and gallant, cool-tempered. Nations need such men in their memories. A few months later, he was a shape in a shapeless prison uniform, ill treated, disfigured in his mind. May the earth rest lightly on him, and on the others. Enough of that now, Patrick; tis no talk for such a day."

"More than enough," Patrick said, with a sharpness I had not expected. "More than enough, Hugh."

When we reached the crest of the hill, with, it must be confessed, two pauses which I bargained for, once by alleging a call of nature, and once to admire a kind of wild flower which Patrick had never seen before, both of the ranges of hills seemed to rest in pellucid air, and the town to be stretched before us like an artful contrivance for children, and Ardmor Castle a child's fairy-tale palace, with its tall, sun-fronting windows, broad terraces, gardens, the little Japanese lake catching the sun at that moment, as was the Sullane.

With my stick, I pointed a few miles down along the Sullane towards Macroom.

"There is the site for the wonderful new tannery."

But Patrick was staring at the demesne. "My God," he said, "it is going back into nature, unweeded; the flower gardens are moving almost past redemption; an entire terrace looks to be falling in upon itself—that one there, look!"

"What can be expected?" I said. "The fellow that the agent has put in, together with his two helpers, they are good lads, but groundsmen, really, not proper gardeners, and the caretaker is no help at all. Ledger books alone are of concern to Robert Evans, and willow trees and small useless lakes are beyond such calculations. Twas different before Lionel Forrester gave up coming here each year for the shooting. For a month or two at least each year, there would be a firm hand at Ardmor Castle."

"We still see a fair bit of each other," Patrick said. "Become good friends, in fact. We dine together every few weeks, go to galleries, that sort of thing. He sends you his best wishes."

"And return mine to him, Patrick, by all means return mine." I have had always the notion that there might not have been two faster friends in the world than Lionel Forrester and myself, but too much held us apart, the world of the town and the world of the Castle.

"Over there," Patrick said, swinging his outstretched arm towards it, "which house is that?" It was at a distance so far that it was but chimneys, turrets, a glint of sunlight on window glass. "I should remember, should I not, from back in the days when you were encouraging me with my foolish project."

"Not foolish at all," I said. "Why do you say that? But, yes. That is one of the big houses that we raided. Mount Harmony is its name, and the family is called Rhys. But they have sold out under the provisions of the Act, and have moved to England."

He shook his head. "It is a world vanishing," he said. "Vanishing before our eyes, almost literally."

"The Act put the cap upon all," I said.

The Act was the famous Wyndham Act, by which landlords are encouraged to sell not this bit and then that, but their entire estates, up to their hall doors and past the doors if need be. But many, like the Otways and the Childresses and the O'Mahony-Robertses, sold only up to their demesne walls and now are holding on for dear life.

But Patrick had the right of it. It is a world vanishing, and almost without knowledge of what is happening to it. They see their neighbours selling up, and heading out for London, or perhaps the British colonies in Rome and Florence, but it does not register upon their imaginations. And they have their hunt balls, and their hunts, magnificent spectacles, scarlet coats crashing across landscapes of green and brown; their sons still go off to serve the army—*their* army—in India and Africa and wherever else their empire may have need of them. Their fading battle standards hang in their churches, and plaques to brave young fellows killed at Ladysmith or Spion Kop. But many of them stay on, deliberately and at financial peril to themselves, because they account themselves Irishmen, not English, even though loyal to the Crown. But the fierce republicans would claim that they are not Irish at all. Foolishness! Of course they are Irish. On the other hand, I am an old Fenian, when all is said and done, and—ah well!

"I've met Wyndham," Patrick said. "Witty and quite bookish. I liked him. He speaks of himself as being Irish himself, in his way. Apparently, Lord Edward Fitzgerald was his great-grandfather."

I made some unenthusiastic response.

"Wasn't Mount Harmony boycotted during the Land War as well?" Patrick said, suddenly remembering.

"Ho ho, was it ever boycotted!" I said, "Bob waged one of the most ferocious of his campaigns against Mount Harmony. Only poor Judkins at Lughnavalla outcapped it. He shaped Neville Rhys into a kind of blending of the worst qualities of King Herod and Merlin the magician. The Rhyses are of Welsh ancestry."

Patrick walked to the far edge of the hill, facing himself northwards, looking towards the Boggeraghs.

"That day, Hugh, on our first walk together, you said that that was the real revolution, not the guns and drums and drums and guns of the Fenians but the Land League and Parnell."

"Something like that," I said. "In the heel of the hunt, there may be more guns and drums, but that will be to make matters official, like."

Patrick turned back towards me. "Delaney was a remarkable man," he said. "He commanded the Fenians here, and he was in command during the Land War, and after that the Plan of Campaign. Parnell is back in fashion, you know, now that he's safely dead, and the factions back in alliance, his statue by Saint Gaudens dominating Sackville Street."

"But not Bob," I said, answering his unspoken question. "Fellows like Bob should slip quietly away to some exotic clime when their hour is past. It does not do to let yourself be seen in town, a town character, unshaven, drinking in public houses and turning the drunken savagery of your tongue wherever you will. For all of the last years, he was never seen once at Mass, and he died without the last rites. He was found dead lying atop that bed in his office."

"Yes," Patrick said. "Yourself and Jamesey. You have described it to me. Horrible."

"Well you may say. Is that why you decided against writing your book—our book, I had come to think of it?"

"Oh no," he said, "not at all. Well, yes, perhaps, in an odd way. We will talk about it. I promise you."

And talk we did, at our meal, the table spread with the one of Mary's damask cloths that I had held out for myself. The others, of course, I had given to our lads and their brides. I had a bowl of roses at the centre in reproof of that foolish girl who had said in a conservatory (of all places!) that roses were going out of fashion. We had the second bottle of

Châteauneuf, and the stew, I must admit, was perfection itself, the lamb, the carrots, the potatoes blended perfectly together as a consequence of my special methods. But he moved at matters crabwise, by indirection; year by year, Patrick was becoming more Irish, some inheritance of the blood moving in upon him like a nearing tide.

He had first to tell me of his last visit with Lionel Forrester, in the flat where Forrester and Emily based themselves in London. "He has no real money, of course, poor fellow," Patrick said, "but he manages. Years and years ago, he actually persuaded Whistler—James Whistler!—to design the paints and decorations for the rooms, in exchange for one of Ardmor's paintings. Ardmor had agreed, of course. And one doesn't notice the tables and that sort of thing, nor how indifferent the food is, because Ardmor's paintings are there, four or five of them in each room. And Hugh, they are magnificent! There are only a few places where Ardmors can be seen, and Lee's flat is one of them. 'He's the real thing,' Lee said to me. 'Jimmy Whistler told me that long ago, and he didn't praise easily, a spiteful chap really.' "

But I knew that. Even schoolmasters in Munster were hearing Lord Ardmor's name linked with those Frenchmen who had once seemed so odd, *Punch* making jokes about them. Bob had known! He came back from that first visit to the demesne, and said that there were pictures there that made you see the world differently. What does that mean? I thought, and still do. How could Bob have known?

"He has the Galantiere portrait," Patrick said. "He is taking care of it for Ardmor. Ardmor doesn't like it left in the Castle, things being as they are."

"What portrait is that?" I asked, and Patrick looked at me with something close to astonishment, but then realizing, as I did, and as happened often in our talks, that he was holding in his head the story of two worlds, my world and the world of the Forresters, and that there was much from my world that I had never told him, and Lionel Forrester had also, no doubt, his numerous reticences. Bits and pieces of worlds. Fragments.

"A portrait," he said, with deliberate, strategic bluntness, "of Sylvia Challoner, the woman whom Bob Delaney loved. His mistress."

"Ah," I said, refusing the strategy, "Bob and I talked of that no more than three times or four, and briefly. I know little of all that. That sort of thing makes little sense to me."

"Of course," he said. "I had forgotten, Hugh." And he refilled our glasses, the red of the Châteauneuf catching and holding the hot glow of the turf fire.

T ell me, Lee," Patrick Prentiss said to me one afternoon, when Emily was off visiting friends—not that she has that many of them, poor thing, not in her circumstances. She is more than welcome, of course, among my Bohemian friends, but she can't abide them. She is a most proper lady of the Irish Protestant persuasion, deep down, but a dear good creature. It was her ill fortune to fall in love with two such reprobates as Sylvia and myself. "Tell me, Lee," Patrick said, "is she never jealous that the portrait of another woman has the place of honour above the mantel in the drawing room?"

"Dear me, no," I said. "She has the greatest respect for the memory of Lady Ardmor. They were almost friends." Patrick is coming along splendidly in life; scarcely a trace of the young New College pedant who first called on me at Ardmor Castle in 1904. But there seemed no point in unsettling whatever may be his view of the relationships that life creates among men and women. Life itself will do that for him, no doubt.

But as I say, he is coming along splendidly, and I was not at all surprised to hear him tell me that he was setting aside that book of his, and probably not returning to it.

"Got too messy, did it?" I asked, setting biscuits and a bit of Madeira between us, and thinking, with a pang, of Sylvia. She loved Madeira. "Good!" she would say, and draw her tongue along her lips.

"You wanted only the Fenian rising, a few hours in 1867, and the thing began spinning itself out, decade after decade. That sort of thing can happen. Nearly happened to me when I did that little book on the Fronde."

"No," he said, "it isn't that. I have exactly the shape I need, from the Rising through the Plan of Campaign and the fall of Parnell. It is a story that needs to be told by someone, God knows who. There are no Irish historians. A fine bit of recent history-making it would be, make my reputation as a coming man. Those papers I've been publishing have gone well. There were a few hints when I was back in Oxford last month."

"Well?" I asked.

"It isn't the actual story," he said at once. "Robert Delaney's love for Sylvia Ardmor is part of the story, and Tom Ardmor's love for her, and I can never tell that. And of course, I know next to nothing about it, in any event. You have been most discreet."

"Have I?" I said. "And yet I'm always priding myself upon my manly, indeed boyish, candour."

He has learned to overlook my affectations of speech, which my generation, having learned to think of them as wit, lack now the strength to shed. Wilde has more to answer for than a few ruined telegraph boys.

"Do you know what is at the heart, the very heart of Clonbrony Wood? The hour, long afterwards, when Ned Nolan broke into Brierly Lodge, and murdered Vincent Tully, or executed him, or assassinated him, or whatever idea it was that Nolan had in his mind. And that is an impenetrable mystery and will remain so forever."

"It may have had nothing to do with Clonbrony Wood at all," I said, "nothing to do with 1867. Nolan had become a madman with an idea, a killer on the prowl, like those nihilists in Russia."

"No, no," Patrick said, shaking his head. "But did he come to Kilpeder to kill Tully, or was it something that he learned while he was there? And Hugh MacMahon knows, you see. I could never ask him about it. He would tell me about it if he could; we are friends and he is an honest man, with a schoolmaster's respect for history. More respect than the two of us have, I suspect. But he is bound to silence by loyalty or by love or by both. I have one guess, by the way, and I trust to God that I am wrong."

"Oh?" I asked, and he smiled and shook his head, and with that smile, several centuries of Irish peasants shook their heads at British magistrates.

"But the answer could not be a part of the book, any more than Sylvia Challoner, or the ways in which my own feelings have changed in the course of these years, talking to improbable men—retired gunmen, ruined landlords, tavern boasters. The book would not be history in the eyes of our ancient universities, or those less ancient, for that matter. And there you are."

But his last words seemed addressed to Sylvia: he could not take his eyes from her, slim, black-gowned, the portrait an almost flamboyant arrangement of blacks and whites, and the woman asserting against the formality the shy courage of her individuality, the black ball gown dangerously décolleté, small-waisted, the breasts small and certain of themselves. It was as though, so Prentiss had thought when he first saw the portrait, as though she looked beyond the canvas, not to the viewer but to the painter, with eyes instinct with intelligence and wit, and said to him, "I am late for another engagement. I cannot wait to be arranged into whites, blacks, grey shadows."

"That tutor of yours, at New College, have you told him of this?"

"Oh yes," Prentiss said. "He was devastated, and then he made fresh toast. He suspects that I have fallen in with some people at the German universities who claim that the past can never be known, history never be written, the histories we have mere pleasant narratives, or rousing narratives, pathetic, whatever. 'Yes indeed,' he said in that feline, oily voice of his. 'I can hear the very *umlauts* in your voice. You have been with them. They will do you no good.' "

"They may be right," I said, "these ferocious Huns. Nothing wrong with narratives. A history is a kind of narrative, a fiction. I've always thought so myself, to tell you the truth."

"A taste for fiction," he said, so promptly that he must have rehearsed the line, "has always seemed to me the unfailing mark of an imaginative deficiency." He smiled.

Damn! I thought. I've taught him only too well. And I helped him, and myself, to a second glass of Sylvia's Madeira, as I always think of it.

"That has her to the life," I said, nodding towards the painting.

"Yes," he said, and at that moment the hall door opened, and then Emily came into the room, her stride, as always, long-legged and easy.

"Patrick!" she said, with pleasure and affectionate malice. "The historian of our meagre lives. There is a fierce spring wind," she said, unfastening her bonnet. "I've had a long walk, all along the Embankment."

I take that walk myself, often, and of course I know why I take it. I haven't seen Tom in two years now, although we are as close as ever. I visited him in Cortona, and we had a wonderful week of it, the air cool but bracing, and magnificent after the fog and slush of a London winter, the interminable rain. It was warm enough for us to sit on the terrace, looking out towards his neighbour's groves. "I know him a bit," Tom said of the neighbour; "comes from some prehistoric family, and has a title of some sort. They all do down here. 'My English friend, the great French painter,' he tells his friends, and then roars with laughter. I've given up painting, by the way. I'd done about what I set out to do, emptied out my bag of tricks. I'm doing a bit of sculpting now, but only to keep myself busy." "Odd," he said a bit later; "we would go for months without seeing each other, almost half a year once. And yet her absence is an aching gap that nothing seems to dull. Miserable, miserable luck that poor girl had. If only I—" But I put my hand on his forearm and shook my head. We sat in companionable silence, looking beyond the groves towards hills as different as hills can be from those at home, brown, terraced.

And the Thames is not the Sullane. To say the least. We have our regulars along the Embankment, and a few of us are on nodding terms—a retired army officer, a tea planter's widow home from Ceylon, even another Irishman, a doctor who spent more than half his life in the Straits Settlements, beet-red whiskey face and neck, a sackful of cheerful platitudes. Even Tom, I sometimes think on these walks—especially Tom, perhaps—became involved in the mess of life, got himself battered by it, found out cruel things about himself, loved Sylvia without having her, painted those wonderful landscapes. But I managed to preserve myself, keep myself fit for that future when I would stroll along the Embankment, beside a retired doctor, a retired army officer, a tea planter's widow.

A nd so Lionel Forrester and yourself have decided that history is little better than a novel," said I. "And what the hell am I supposed to do with all my books, my Gibbon and my Lingard and the handsome set of Motley that you have brought to me this day? Am I to suspect that the Dutch Republic never did rise? A sorrowful time it will be for schoolmasters, if this sort of nonsense is allowed to walk abroad."

"There is more to life than history," he said. "I've decided to read for the bar. After all, I'm living in Pump Court. I couldn't be better situated."

"Ah," I said, "so you are to become a lawyer, are you?" I ladled out full helpings of the stew onto our empty plates. It was really an excellent lamb stew, I must say: it's all in the small secret touches, the small onions and the cut-up bits of leek.

"My father will be leaving the bar soon. He's looking forward to it in a way, and it will give him great pleasure to think of his son using his rooms."

"Not to mention his gown," I said.

"Not straight off, I'm afraid," Patrick said. "Dominick Sarsfield Prentiss is a king's counsel, he has a gown of silk. Mine will be of stuff. But I can use his wig and bands, I expect."

"You have no fear, I take it, that the law will prove itself to be a fiction, like history."

"Ah, but I know that already," he said. "Most lawyers do, it seems. My father is most eloquent on that subject. We have grown close together in recent years. He is quite a brilliant fellow, I discover."

"My own sons have made the same discovery," I said. "There must be some strange new wind blowing out of the Arctic, and improving beyond measure the intelligence of elderly men."

Patrick went to the hamper, and took from it his final treat, a bottle of Monsieur Courvoisier's cognac, for which I discovered two glasses of appropriate shape.

"For a few years there," Patrick said, "I had two other fathers, quite different ones. Yourself and Lee Forrester."

"I know that, Patrick, I know that. I love you because of it. But it is time to be moving on, time to be moving back to Dominick Sarsfield Prentiss." Lamb stew and the red wine of France and the best of brandies: that is the top of everything. "You will practise in Ireland, then?"

"Where else would I practise?" he asked. "I'm an Irishman. This is my country. I'll need to test the waters a bit first, of course, but I've been thinking, in time, of politics. A seat in Parliament. Our own parliament, of course. Home Rule is coming, Hugh. It's only a matter of time."

"Home Rule," I said, slamming down my spoon, "a few ladlesful of self-government doled out by Mother Britannia, and John Redmond bobbing his head, and saying, 'Thank you, ma'am.' There is the one cause, and the one cause only, Patrick Prentiss, and don't you forget it—a free people in a free land, the Republic of Ireland, and don't you ever forget it."

"Oh, and who's to get that for us, the patriotic young bicyclists?"

"Perhaps," I said. "Stranger things have happened." I bent towards my brandy, and saw him smiling at me.

And nothing would suit him other than to be off at dawn for Kilpeder, to hire a horse and trap and bring it back for me, that we might have a day's outing to the lakes and to the "abbey" at Muckross, as it is always called, although it is in truth a friary, founded by the great Donal Mac-Carthy in the fifteenth century for the Observant Franciscans. Few care about such matters. We had first to call in at the Kilpeder Arms, in the town, and I sat in the trap until Patrick came out, weighted down by the picnic hamper which he had organised.

Gilmartin came with him, and stood in the morning sun, stretching himself like a great cat.

"Off to the lakes, are you, master?" he asked, resting a hand upon the trap.

"A lovely day for it, thank God," I said.

"Like the days of old," he said, "when I was myself one of your scholars and of a Saturday or a Sunday, I would see Mrs. MacMahon and yourself setting forth with . . . well, with one or another of your many friends."

"With Vincent Tully, most likely," I said, "and certainly with Robert Delaney. They were our great friends." Never back away from fellows like Gilmartin: easy malice is the worst kind there is.

"To be sure," Gilmartin said.

"There," Patrick said. He placed the hamper in the trap, and putting his foot upon the iron step, swung himself aboard with a young man's thoughtless grace.

The town sparkled: what a summer that was! The gilt lettering and crimson background of Tully's sign glistened like a great Russian ornament, and the spires of Saint Jarlath's behind us, and of the Protestant church facing us, caught the sun and held it. The obelisk to the long-dead young earl of Ardmor, most familiar, absurd of objects, had in this light the purity of novelty. And the market house, successor to the one where, in an earlier century, Ellen O'Connell, young and passionate gentlewoman from Kerry, had seen, lounging against the gable end, Art O'Leary, handsome and reckless, in his coat and surcoat of French cut, hand, long-accustomed to sword hilt, resting negligently upon hip. A few lines from the Gaelic of her great lament for him came to my mind, welcome and unbidden. No history indeed! It is in song, in poetry, beyond challenge.

At the locked gates to Ardmor Castle, Patrick paused again, got out, and walked over to one of the falcons, stone bird clawing its stone globe, wings outstretched. He ran his hand across the creature, from wing-tip to wing-tip, brushed his fingers across the bill of cruel stone. He caught me smiling at him.

"For luck," he said.

"You might have waited too long," I said. "Mischievous lads will be playing their pranks upon those one of these days." And having heard my casual words, it was as though I had passed a sentence upon the world of the Ardmors.

We had great luck at Muckross, after the long journey across the mountains, and then along the green, lovely valley of the Flesk. The town of Killarney, which must have Port Said as its only rival in charm and virtue, was relatively quiet, few trippers abroad yet, but the jarveys lurking for them outside the hotels of the town, with their jaunting cars and outside cars, and their sacks full of fables about the Colleen Bawn and the rest of it. Vincent said to us once, "If the tablets of the law are ever discovered, with the commandments written upon them in bolts of lightning, they will be taken to Killarney and exhibited at two bob a peep." "Or Veronica's Veil," Bob said, "with shamrocks edged about the hem, and a round tower in the corner." "You are shocking blasphemers, the pair of you," Mary said laughing; "I tremble to think what life will have in store for you."

"Bob Delaney and yourself were here on the eve of the Rising, were you not?" Patrick asked.

"We were," I said, "we were. And scared out of our wits to discover the town crowded with soldiers rushed down from Limerick City. The fine hotels—the great railway hotel and the others—were filled to overflowing with the gentry of Kerry, who had poured helter-skelter into Killarney with as much silver plate and gold plate as they could fit into their carriages. Great excitement, and Bob grinning like a lynx despite his fear, to think that we were the cause of it all. A few weeks later it was all over. It was as though it had never happened."

"It happened," Patrick said.

But at the quiet friary, which we had to ourselves, my memory began to echo with their voices, Bob's and Vincent's and Mary's. And Ned's! But Ned had never been here with us, cool ancient stonework, tall grasses, the water's edge. Patrick and I walked through nave and chancel, stood in the elegant small cloister.

"A world of ruins," Patrick said.

"Ruins can be put to work," I said. "Sometime towards the end of the Elizabethan world, the beautiful young heiress of the great Mac-Carthy Mor escaped from her father's castle with her beloved, and they fled in the night, and were married here. Right where we are standing, so tradition has it. It was a ruin even then."

"Good," Patrick said. "Like a fairy tale, with a happy ending."

"Perhaps," I said. "Her beloved was slapped into the Tower of London, and spent there the years of a long, bitter honeymoon. They are all buried here, the great chieftains of Kerry, the MacCarthy Mors and the O'Donoghues of the Glens. Not to mention the finest of our poets— O'Rahilly and Owen Ruagh O'Sullivan." Unroofed, like all the old friaries and abbeys. Above us, a sky of clear, cloudless blue. Rooks circled above the shattered belfry.

We walked then towards the lake's edge, and presently the echoing voices died away in my ears, and I heard only our boots moving through the tall, wet grasses, the cawing of the rooks. Behind us, the lost, lovely church in which lay buried chieftains and poets, and a host of lesser folk, names washed from their tombstones by centuries of rain, mists carried upon winds from the invisible Atlantic.

The Characters

ARDMOR, ISABEL FORRESTER, DOWAGER COUNTESS OF. Mother of Tom.

ARDMOR, SYLVIA FORRESTER, COUNTESS OF. *Née* Challoner.

ARDMOR, THOMAS FORRESTER, EARL OF.

BELTON, PAUDGE. Constable of Irish Constabulary, Kilpeder barracks (1867).

BONNER, THOMAS. Fenian soldier; exile in America; brickmaker on the Hudson River.

BOURKE, EMMET. Queen's Counsel; briefed for the defence of Robert Delaney, Hugh MacMahon, and Vincent Tully (1867).

BOYCOTT, CAPTAIN CHARLES CUNNINGHAM. Land agent in Mayo; unwilling contributor of his surname to the lexicons of many languages.

BOYLE, JOHNNY. Master of Brierly Lodge, outside Kilpeder (1867).

BRADY, JOE. Member of the Invincibles; hanged in Kilmainham Gaol, May 14, 1883.

BRENNAN, MATTY. Fenian soldier, battle of Kilpeder and Clonbrony Wood.

BRICK, JEREMIAH. Fenian; livery-stable keeper in Killarney.

BURKE, THOMAS. Undersecretary for Ireland; murdered in Phoenix Park, Dublin, May 6, 1882.

BUTT, ISAAC. Queen's Counsel; briefed for the defence of Edward Nolan (1867); organiser and first leader of the Irish Home Rule party in Parliament.

BYRNE, FRANK. A secretary of the Land League organization in Great Britain; suspected of complicity with the Invincibles (1882).

[821]

CALLINAN, JEREMIAH. Inspector of Irish Constabulary; based in Dublin Castle (1867).

CAREY, JAMES. Head of the Dublin "Circle" of the Invincible organization.

CARROLL, JAMES. Fenian conspirator; medical doctor in London.

CASEY, BRENDAN. Fenian soldier, battle of Kilpeder and Clonbrony Wood.

CAVENDISH, LORD FREDERICK. Newly appointed Chief Secretary for Ireland; murdered in Phoenix Park, Dublin, on the evening of his arrival, May 6, 1882.

CHALLONER, COLONEL HUBERT. British Army, retired; small landlord in Westmeath; father of Sylvia Ardmor.

CHAMBERLAIN, JOSEPH. British politician. First a cautious supporter, then an opponent of Home Rule for Ireland.

CHUTE, EDWARD. Successor to his father, Everard, as agent of the Ardmor estates; later, organiser of the Property Defence Association.

COLTHURST, BARTHOLOMEW. Landlord of the mountain hamlet of Aghabullogue.

CONEFRY, BART. Proprietor, in succession to his father, of Kilpeder's leading public house (late 1880s to early 1900s).

CONSIDINE, DONALD. Medical doctor, Kilpeder.

CREMIN, FATHER GABRIEL. Parish priest in Kilpeder (1860s to mid-1870s).

CUMMINGS, BILLY. Anti-Parnell nationalist.

CUNNINGHAM, PETER. Auctioneer in Kilpeder (1892).

DAVITT, MICHAEL. Fenian; prisoner in Dartmoor; organiser of Land League.

DELANEY, AGNES. Wife of Robert; daughter of Dennis Tully.

DELANEY, ROBERT. Fenian; later, solicitor, Land League agent in Kilpeder, secretary in London of Irish national Land League, Home Rule member of Parliament.

DEVOY, JOHN. Veteran Fenian conspirator; exile in New York.

DILLON, JOHN. Nationalist politician; organiser, with William O'Brien, of Plan of Campaign; colleague, later opponent, of Charles Stewart Parnell.

DINEEN, DANIEL. Sergeant of Royal Irish Constabulary, Kilpeder barracks (1870s).

DRIPSEY, PETER. Cork City solicitor (1867).

DUIGNAN, CHARLIE. American Fenian; Nolan's colleague on Chicago assignment.

DUNPHY, PAT. Fenian sergeant, battle of Kilpeder and Clonbrony Wood.

ENRIGHT, PADDY. Member of Nolan's London-based Delta team.

EVANS, ROBERT. Agent of the Ardmor estates, replacing Edward Chute (1880–1904).

EWING, CAPTAIN LESLIE. Commander of military detachment sent to Kilpeder region (1892).

FOGARTY, BRENDAN. Kilpeder solicitor and Land League agent; later, anti-Parnellite candidate for Parliament.

FORRESTER, LIONEL. Essayist and novelist; cousin and friend of Thomas Ardmor.

FORSTER, WILLIAM EDWARD. British statesman; Chief Secretary for Ireland (1880–1882); nicknamed "Buckshot" by Irish nationalists.

FULLER, THERESA. Vincent Tully's companion in later years.

GALANTIERE, PAUL. Painter of fashionable portraits.

GANNON, JAMESEY. Robert Delaney's law clerk (from late 1880s on).

GILMARTIN, PAUL. Proprietor, in succession to his father, of the Kilpeder Arms (1904).

GRACE, JAMESEY. Home Rule politician; Parnellite.

HAGGERTY, JOSEPH. Tenant evicted from Aghabullogue (1879).

HANLON, LANTY. Fenian leader in Kilpeder (1890–1892).

HEALY, TIMOTHY MICHAEL. Nationalist politician; supporter, later opponent, of Charles Stewart Parnell.

HOGAN, PATRICK. A treasurer of Land League; suspected of complicity with the Invincibles (1882).

HONAN, CORNELIUS. Sergeant of Irish Constabulary, Kilpeder barracks (1867).

JUDKINS, JOSEPH. English-born master of Lughnavalla House, outside Kilpeder (1887).

KELLEHER, EDWARD. Sergeant of Royal Irish Constabulary, Kilpeder barracks (1880s–1890s).

LAFFAN, PAT. Small farmer and distiller of illegal spirits, Kilpeder.

LAWLOR, PACKY. Kilpeder strong-farmer.

LEAMY, EDMUND. Home Rule member of parliament; Parnellite.

LEESE, DICK. Rector of a parish in Devon; friend of Patrick Prentiss.

LEESE, ELEANOR. Wife of Dick.

LOMASNEY, WILLIAM MACKEY. Veteran Fenian; killed in London dynamite explosion, December 13, 1884.

MCCARTHY, JUSTIN. Home Rule member of Parliament; supporter, later opponent, of Charles Stewart Parnell.

MACCURTAIN, EDDIE. Member of Nolan's Delta team.

MACMAHON, HUGH. Fenian; schoolmaster; antiquarian.

MACMAHON, MARY. Wife of Hugh.

MAGUIRE, FATHER STEPHEN. Parish priest of Macroom, County Cork (early 1880s).

MEAGHER, FATHER IGNATIUS. Parish priest of Kilpeder (late 1870s–1890s).

MILLEN, GERALD ARTHUR. Member, Supreme Council of Delta organization.

MORRISSEY, JIM. Member of Nolan's Delta team.

MULCAHY, JEREMIAH. Member of Supreme Council of Irish Republican Brotherhood (1870s to early 1890s).

MULLANE, FATHER DENNIS. Curate in Kilpeder (1880s–1890s).

MURPHY, JOHN STEPHEN. Solicitor and Land League agent in Macroom (1880s).

MURPHY, MICHAEL PATRICK. Solicitor; nationalist politician; anti-Parnellite (1892).

NEAFSEY, PHILLIP. Inspector of Royal Irish Constabulary (1892).

NOLAN, EDWARD. Fenian commander in Kilpeder (1867); prisoner in Portland Gaol; conspirator in America and England.

NOLAN, THOMAS JUSTIN. Veteran of abortive 1848 Rising; exile in America; father of Edward.

O'BRIEN, WILLIAM. Nationalist journalist, politician, agitator.

O'CLERY, MYLES. Queen's Counsel; Home Rule member of Parliament.

O'DONOVAN, MAJOR OLIVER. British Army, retired; Kilpeder landlord; chairman, Property Defence Association.

O'GORMAN, MAJOR PURCELL. Home Rule member of Parliament.

O'MAHONY, JOHN. Veteran of 1848 Rising; exile in America; founder in 1850s, with James Stephens, of the Fenian movement; later, deposed from military command.

O'SHEA, KATHARINE. Mistress of Charles Stewart Parnell.

O'SHEA, CAPTAIN WILLIAM. Late of the Eighteenth Hussars; member of Parliament for Galway; husband of Katharine.

PARNELL, CHARLES STEWART.

PATCH, MERTON. London journalist; correspondent in Kilpeder during Land War.

PIGOTT, RICHARD. Nationalist journalist; forger of the notorious "Parnellism and Crime" letters.

PRENTISS, DOMINICK SARSFIELD. Queen's Counsel; father of Patrick.

PRENTISS, PATRICK. A.M., Oxon.; amateur of history.

QUINN, MARGARET. Servant girl in New York's Murray Hill.

REILLY, CAPTAIN EUGENE. Fenian commander in Killarney (1867).

RICHARDSON, MAJOR WILLIAM. Late of the Punjabi Lancers; resident magistrate in Kilpeder (1880s to 1892).

ROSSA, JEREMIAH O'DONOVAN. Fenian conspirator; exiled in America after long years in English prisons.

SHEEHAN, KEVIN TIMOTHY. Fenian conspirator; medical doctor in Chicago.

SPELLACY, JAMESEY. Fenian soldier, battle of Kilpeder and Clonbrony Wood.

SPENCER, ARCHIBALD. Private secretary to the Home Secretary, Westminister (1889).

STEPHENS, JAMES. Veteran of the 1848 Rising; founder in America, with John O'Mahony, of Fenian movement; later, forcibly deposed.

TIERNEY, MICHAEL. President of the New Hibernia Asphalt Company in New York; supporter of Irish revolutionary causes.

TIMONEY, MARTIN. Fenian Centre in Killarney (1867).

TULLY, DENNIS. Merchant in Kilpeder.

TULLY, MALACHI ("The Founder"). Huckster; father of Dennis.

TULLY, MARY ELLEN. Wife of Dennis.

TULLY, VINCENT. Son of Dennis; local officer of Fenians (1867); later, squire.

TUMULTY, JOSEPH. Fenian Centre in Cork City; ship's chandler.

TWOMEY, BILL. Tenant evicted from Lughnavalla land (1887); later, retainer to Robert Delaney.

TYNAN, PATRICK. Self-styled "Number One" of the Irish National Invincibles.

WELDON, EMILY. Personal maid to Sylvia Ardmor; later, mistress to Lionel Forrester.

WHISTLER, JAMES ABBOTT MACNEILL. American artist and expatriate.